FIV

ADV
NOVELS

FIVE CLASSIC

ADVENTURE NOVELS

Introduction by

GEORGE MACDONALD FRASER

HarperCollins*Publishers*

HarperCollins*Publishers*
P.O. Box, Glasgow G4 0NB

King Solomon's Mines first published 1885
The Prisoner of Zenda first published 1894
Under the Red Robe first published 1894
The Lost World first published 1912
Beau Geste first published 1924

This collection first published 1995

ISBN 0 00 470808 3
Reprint 10 9 8 7 6 5 4 3 2 1 0

A catalogue record for this book is available from the British Library.

Typeset in Ehrhardt by
Rowland Phototypesetting Ltd
Bury St Edmunds, Suffolk

Printed in Great Britain by
HarperCollins Manufacturing, Glasgow

Contents

Introduction
by
George MacDonald Fraser

THE adventure story is the oldest, and over the centuries has proved the most popular, of all literary forms. The Iliad and the Odyssey, the Old Testament, the classical myths, the Norse sagas, the legends of Arthur and Ogier, the Thousand Nights and a Night, the first fairy-tales we learn as children, are all adventures, full of action and danger, pursuit and escape, heroism and villainy, romance and violence and, above all, suspense. Theseus in the gloom of the labyrinth, Beowulf at grips with Grendel and his ghastly mother, Christian fearful but standing firm before Apollyon, Red Riding Hood nervously noting the length of grandma's teeth, James Bond crawling through tarantula-infested pipes, Gulliver staked out by the Lilliputians, Jack labouring his reckless way up the beanstalk or stuffing his shirt with porridge to fool the giant, the hobbits in flight through the booming caves of Moria, Crusoe staring at a footprint in the sand – they all belong to the same immortal company of gallant, terrified, all-too-human proxies through whom we indulge our atavistic delight in pure excitement. 'Get him out of this', 'One dam' thing after another', 'Make 'em laugh, make 'em cry, make 'em wait!' are the action writer's watchwords, and have been from David and Goliath to Indiana Jones.

It may be said, fairly enough, that many of these stories were told or written with loftier aims than merely to thrill the reader. Dean Swift, at the end of one of the most spellbinding books in our language, tells us primly that it was written to instruct, not to amuse. No doubt, but he took good care to pack it with freaks, monsters, pirates, eccentrics, and a fine succession of fantastic incidents, knowing perfectly well that for every reader who appreciated it as a satire, a thousand would devour it simply to find out what was going to happen next. Despite his disclaimer, *Gulliver's Travels* carries that tell-tale stamp of the writer who, however sublime his purpose, has adventure in his blood: he plainly had great fun doing it.

John Bunyan, characteristically, was more forthright. 'I did it my own self to gratify', he tells us in his Apology to *The Pilgrim's Progress*, and having confessed how, writing of the race of saints, he 'fell suddenly into an allegory', goes on to describe precisely the adventure writer's impulse at work

> . . . in more than twenty things which I set down.
> This done, I twenty more had in my crown;
> And they again began to multiply,
> Like sparks that from the coals of fire do fly.

This is an author in the grip of the story-teller's dæmon, not certain where he is going with his 'scribble', admitting that he has no intent 'but to divert myself', trusting his imagination and delighting in his inventions: the Valley of the Shadow, Doubting Castle, Giant Despair, the allurements of Vanity Fair, the dreadful death of Faithful, the fight with Apollyon (which is a model of close combat description), and all the snares and horrors and temptations before the Celestial City is reached at last. The result was the greatest of all allegories, a spiritual masterpiece which touched the hearts and uplifted the minds of countless millions – and an adventure story which for action, colour, and sheer vitality has never been surpassed. He did it again with a sequel, and yet again with *The Holy War*, in which he employed blood and thunder on an even more spectacular scale.

In singling out these two immortals of English literature as adventurers under the skin, I am not trying to confer stature by association on that great host of humbler writers whose chief aim is simply to excite and entertain, who place narrative and action above what Hugh Walpole called the modern 'passion for psycho-analysis in the novel', and who are consequently disdained by those who prefer more supposedly cerebral diversions. It is a sad fact that the adventurers' very popularity tends to diminish their standing, for it is a truth universally acknowledged that books which appeal to the exclusive few must be better than books which are enjoyed by the common many – until time proves otherwise, at any rate.

No, I am not comparing Gulliver to *Tarzan of the Apes*, or suggesting that Bulldog Drummond belongs in the same literary firmament as Mr Worldly Wiseman, but only pointing out that whatever an author's purpose, whether he be satirist or swashbuckler, allegorist or thriller-writer, chronicler or cliff-hanger, if he uses the tools of action and excitement he is inevitably bound by a particular set of rules, exercises the same technique, and makes the same direct appeal to the human (primitive, if you like) emotions – in short, he is practising a craft as different from that of the purely intellectual writer as chalk from cheese. (I suspect that if Sapper and Edgar Rice Burroughs were cast in the company of Proust and E. M. Forster they would probably find little common ground for professional discussion beyond royalities and publishers; put them next to Walter Scott and Homer, on the other hand, and one could reasonably expect a more congenial understanding and mutual appreciation.)

Some day, perhaps, scholarship will be applied to the 'adventure theme', tracing in analytical detail those bright threads which wind their way through literature – but we may hope not. Adventure as such is fortunate in being generally held to be beneath critical attention; when its best practitioners, the Homers and Defoes and Bunyans and Scotts and other giants, come under the microscope, it is for their illumination of the human condition, their delineation of character, their moral and instructive content, or their mastery of style, rather than for their gift of enthralling and exciting. It is best so; adventure is to be enjoyed, not analysed, and its readers, heaven knows, stand in no need of academic guidance.

No one is likely ever to undertake a word-by-word dissection of the five novels in this volume, and for this we may be thankful. Sufficient that each one is a well-loved masterpiece. None would be included in a list of the greatest literary works of the past century, but three of their titles have passed into the language, another may be said to have inspired a whole school of writing, and the fifth is simply the best adventure story I have ever read.

All five, incidentally, were written by professional men – three barristers, a doctor, and an ex-headmaster. This is not as strange as it may seem; the higher professions have always been a great breeding ground of adventure writing, as far back as the third century A.D., when Heliodorus of Emesa, who may have been a bishop, no less, and was certainly a scholar, produced the first European novel, the *Aethiopica*, a stirring tale of love, battle, piracy, torture, kidnapping, and kindred excitements. Since then the link has been maintained by a host of authors who were (or trained to be) lawyers, doctors, clergymen, teachers, and service officers – Smollet, Scott, Marryat, Charles Reade, Stevenson, Lew Wallace, Fenimore Cooper, Mayne Reid, Buchan, Forester, Tolkien, and many more, including the five represented here. One might be tempted to seek deep psychological reasons for this apparent lust for action in the higher callings, if a simple explanation did not suggest itself: it is not the profession that makes the adventure writer, but the born adventure writer who, being a man of imagination, gravitates to the profession, not from any strong sense of vocation, but so that he can mark time in reasonable comfort while practising his real trade of telling stories, waiting for the great day when he discovers, to his joy and wonder, that people will actually pay to read them.

This happened to our five, in various curious ways, and since the men themselves are as interesting as their works, and also because the most heinous sin a writer of introductions can commit is to give away more than a brief and vague outline of plot, I shall concentrate on the authors rather than on their books – those who have read them before need no recapitulation, and those who haven't are not going to have their enjoyment spoiled by me.

First, in chronological order of publication, comes Henry Rider Haggard. The son of a Norfolk barrister, and himself called by Lincoln's Inn, he went to Africa in his 'teens, served in government during a vital period which included the Zulu War of 1879, and in the process got the Dark Continent into his blood. He published *Cetewayo and His White Neighbours* (1882), followed by two novels, and then, in 1884, his fate was decided by *Treasure Island*, which had recently appeared. Haggard is said to have bet his brother that he could write an adventure every bit as good as Stevenson's; whether he succeeded or not is arguable, but certainly in

King Solomon's Mines he created a classic, an 'outposts of Empire' romance that was an instant best-seller, made his name overnight, and has never been out of print.

Like *Treasure Island*, it describes a quest, the search for fabulous mines in the unexplored heart of Africa by Quatermain the white hunter, Curtis the muscular baronet, Good the comic naval officer, and Umbopa their mysterious black servant. Following an ancient map (shades of Stevenson again) they survive a perilous trek before reaching a strange and savage land where Good awes the natives by predicting an eclipse,[1] Umbopa's identity is revealed, and there is witch-hunting by a fearsome crone, Gagool, tribal warfare, and tingling suspense before the goal is reached.

Haggard's imaginative and narrative gifts apart, two things make *King Solomon's Mines* an outstanding work. First, he was steeped in Africa, and could bring it to life as no writer had done before; the reader is gripped by the evident authenticity of his detail, and impressed by the respect with which he treats his subject; this, you feel, is the real thing. His Victorian public had been to Africa before, with R. M. Ballantyne's *Gorilla Hunters*, to say nothing of the factual accounts of Livingstone, Burton, and V. L. Cameron, but Haggard marched them across it, thrust them into its wonders and terrors, and showed them the land and people in all their barbaric splendour. Secondly, he did it through the eyes of his best creation, the grizzled old hunter, Allan Quatermain, with his gentle, naive philosophy, modest cunning, and sterling quality. Even Haggard's Africans, to whom he gave immense strength and dignity, are not more convincing than old Allan; the character was based on Fred Selous, the famous scout who founded the Legion of Frontiersmen in the Great War, and was killed in the march on Tanga, aged 65. My father served with him, which is why I have a special affection for Hunter Quatermain.

Nine years after Haggard's success the public was enthralled by two adventures of a very different kind. *Under the Red Robe*, by Stanley J. Weyman, is probably the least well-known of our five choices, but its author can fairly be said to have revived the cloak-and-sword tradition of Dumas, and inspired a whole school of imitators, most notably Sabatini, who rang the changes on *Under the Red Robe* more than once. It was not Weyman's first venture into costume fiction; having failed to set the Oxford Circuit on fire as a barrister, he was moved by the chance reading of an account of the Massacre of St Bartholomew to try his hand at swashbucklers, and had a popular success in 1893 with *A Gentleman of France*. He followed it with *Under the Red Robe*, which for me is his best work.

It is a curious, rather dark book, whose hero (or anti-hero), Gil de Berault, is a callous, truculent professional swordsman and gambler,

[1] Whether Haggard knew it or not, this had actually happened, though not in Africa. John Carey Cremony (1815–79), an American frontiersman, astonished the Apaches by predicting an eclipse in 1850. (See J. C. Cremony, *Life Among the Apaches*, 1868.)

known as the Black Death. Given the choice by Cardinal Richelieu between the gallows and dishonourable service, he does not hesitate, and in a sense the story is one long crisis of conscience as he finds himself involved in espionage, deceit, and betrayal of a beauteous rebel noble-woman with whom he has, inevitably, fallen in love. There is also sword-play, passion, constant danger, intrigue in a longely chateau, and rather more brutality than one would expect from 1894, before all is resolved and, in an excellent closing twist, de Berault is able to repay the scheming Cardinal.

Conventional stuff, perhaps, but written in a sparse, direct style unusual in historical novels, admirably researched, and with characters quite out of the common run. Really, de Berault was ahead of his time; his worldly realism is closer to twentieth century fiction than to that of the nineteenth. But the strength of the book lies in Weyman's atmospheric gift; he made a point of travelling to the scenes of his novels – once he was even arrested in France on suspicion of spying – and no writer ever had a better sense of period. His books had an enthusiastic admirer in Oscar Wilde, who wanted them for the library of Reading Gaol.

While Weyman was writing *Under the Red Robe*, a considerably more successful barrister and occasional author, Anthony Hope Hawkins (he wrote under his two first names), was walking back to his Temple chambers after winning a court case. The story goes that on the way he noticed a strikingly handsome red-haired man, and wondered idly if such a distinctive person could possibly have a double; in a few minutes a plot had fallen into place, he started writing it next day, and within a month had finished *The Prisoner of Zenda*.

There is nothing like it in literature. It is one of those thunderbolts that hits a lucky author once in a lifetime, and if he has the wit and skill to seize the moment and drive through to the finish, he has a masterpiece. *Zenda* is nothing less; Hope's Ruritanian fantasy of royal impersonation has all the zest and swing and irrepressible charm of a Strauss waltz, its characters move and fight and love and intrigue as though they were choreographed, action, humour, suspense, and twists of plot swirl over each other in heady succession to a bitter-sweet ending (it is about half the length of an ordinary novel), and envious authors can only exclaim: 'I wish I'd thought of that!' They delude themselves; the idea is genius, but only Anthony Hope could have exploited it.

It brought him enduring fame, and the ultimate accolade – a letter of admiration from Robert Louis Stevenson in distant Samoa. And *Zenda* has never dated; it is as fresh and lively today as when it entranced readers a century ago, and gave them something new: the villain-hero. There have been likeable rogues as long as there have been stories, but none quite like Rupert of Hentzau, the debonair, handsome youth who is the personification of wickedness – and quite irresistible. Generations of readers have secretly willed him on in his contest with the upright paladin, Rudolf

Rassendyll, and hoped that he would at least survive to conspire and seduce and betray another day. He is Anthony Hope's finest creation, and altogether worthy of an author who, on first seeing Barrie's *Peter Pan*, was heard to sigh: 'Oh, for an hour of Herod!'

Character, drawn with a master's touch, is at the heart of *The Lost World*, which is my own first choice among all adventure stories, because it is the only book, I think, that has actually kept me up all night. The character is that of Professor Challenger, the domineering, roaring, intolerable scientific genius who, for my money, towers over all the rest of Conan Doyle's inventions like a colossus. I said so, in a centenary article on Doyle many years ago, and was delighted beyond telling to receive a letter from his daughter saying that her father had been of the same opinion. This is the more remarkable when one considers the sheer range of his character studies: Holmes, Watson, Sir Nigel, the swaggering bantam Gerard, Captain Sharkey, and all the rest of those beautifully observed figures who people his books. (There are those, incredibly, who dismiss Doyle as not being in the first literary flight; he has even been called a bad writer, whatever that means. Well, if it takes bad writing to create the most famous character in the whole of the world's fiction, let us all stop trying to improve.)

Like Holmes, Challenger was based on one of Doyle's professors at Edinburgh – and on Doyle himself, the gentle giant who would plainly have loved to play the ebullient hectoring genius; indeed, there is a photograph of Doyle *as* Challenger, beard and all, but whether for theatricals or some other purpose, I don't recall. The other curiosity of 'casting' in *The Lost World* is the adventurer Roxton, said to have been inspired by Roger Casement, the anti-slavery crusader and Irish nationalist who was hanged for treason only four years after *The Lost World* was published.

Of the book itself I shall say only that it is an enthralling and often very funny account of an expedition seeking prehistoric monsters, and that its early chapters are an object lesson in suspense building. It is the old fairy-tale situation of the safe haven and the distant menace which inevitably must be faced, and Doyle exploits it brilliantly in his reassuringly domestic scenes of peaceful London, with the eccentric professor fulminating in his study, the sceptics scoffing, the band of half-convinced adventurers drawing together, their characters established in vivid cameos – and all the while, the reader knows, the Lost World is out there, unknown, terrible . . . and waiting. 'Make 'em wait', indeed. In *The Lost World* it is well worth it.

Finally, to *Beau Geste* and P. C. Wren, the most recent and yet the most mysterious of our five writers. Hard facts about him are scarce, and he himself seems to have been as reserved as his more laconic heroes. His *Who's Who* entry simply describes him as a J.P. and M.A., and lists his books; his BBC obituary in 1941 referred to him as 'Major Wren', noted his authorship, and added that 'he served in the British and Indian armies and in the French Foreign Legion.' This echoed the biographical material put out with his books, and the vividness and detail of the novels themselves left his public in no doubt that here was an author writing from personal experience in the Legion and elsewhere. How far this was true, readers may care to judge after considering the biographical note given later in this volume.

For a moment it is enough to say that Wren the writer had an easy, confident style, and a gift of stretching credibility to the limit. *Beau Geste* is actually one of his less extravagant adventures, with the three Geste brothers joining the Legion after the theft of their aunt's priceless diamond (by whom? Wren changed his mind about that in his sequels), and there is battle, mutiny, crucifixion with bayonets, a splendidly sadistic villain (who is also, the brothers agree, 'a topping soldier . . . let's forgive him', a typically Geste-ish view), and an action-packed denouement in a besieged desert outpost. Of course the scene which everyone remembers, thanks to Hollywood, is the book's opening sequence: the discovery of the lonely fort with its garrison of dead legionnaires propped up on the walls.

Strangely enough, this most modern of our five novels is in some ways the most dated. Wren was a true reactionary, if a wry and witty one, and his sublime snobbery and unabashed chauvinism may jar some sensibilities in 1994. There is also a strong tragic vein running through his writing, at odds with his equally strong sense of humour. His books rarely have happy or optimistic endings (*Beau Geste* is no exception), and his heroes, usually true-blue paragons with the highest ideals, have little luck; he seems to take a grim satisfaction in making them suffer, often in vain. For example, in *Beggars' Horses*, characters have their dearest wishes granted, with some unexpectedly bitter results; in *The Wages of Virtue*, his first Legion novel, the wages is ultimately death. One feels that P. C. Wren was a writer with few illusions.

Never mind, he was a sure hand with narrative, and *Beau Geste* is compulsively readable not only as a full-blooded adventure but as a vivid picture of life in the Foreign Legion a century ago – or Wren's version of it, anyway.

So there they are, five gentlemen-adventurers, old-style Ancient Mariners with the God-given gift of holding us with a glittering eye – each, it is worth noting, writes here in the first person. Some of their attitudes and values will seem strange, even deplorable, to modern readers, for they belong to a different world which began to pass away in 1914 and had vanished almost completely by 1945. They are not, most emphatically, 'politically correct' – and if the phrase could be explained to them they would react with amused disbelief, contempt, and finally sorrow for human folly. They were men of their time, men of common sense, believing in outmoded things like honour and loyalty and fair play and good manners (there is no steamy sex or filthy language in their books), and whatever faults they may seem to have in modern eyes, their quality is summed up in the inscription of Conan Doyle's tombstone: Steel true, blade straight. Whether today's world is better than the one which shaped them and their writing, is a matter of opinion; it prides itself on being more civilised and enlightened – which is interesting, when one compares, for example, Rider Haggard's despised colonial Africa with modern Rwanda.

But that is another matter. Take them as they are, story-tellers of their time, and fit to rank with the best of any time. They would be delighted to know that they have been assembled here for a new readership, and take pride each in the others' company. Enjoy them, for they have fine tales to tell, and don't be surprised if they not only amuse you but (as Dean Swift would have to admit) instruct you, too.

GEORGE MACDONALD FRASER was born in 1925, educated at Carlisle Grammar School and Glasgow Academy, served as an infantryman in Burma, and was commissioned in the Gordon Highlanders. After the war he worked on newspapers in England, Canada, and Scotland before beginning his series of Flashman novels, the latest of which, *Flashman and the Angel of the Lord*, was published in 1994. His other books include the McAuslan series, based on his time in the Gordons; *Quartered Safe Out Here*, a military autobiography; and *The Steel Bonnets*, a history of the Border reivers. His screenplays include *The Three Musketeers* and the James Bond film, *Octopussy*.

King Solomon's Mines

Introduction

NOW that this book is printed, and about to be given to the world, the sense of its shortcomings, both in style and contents, weighs very heavily upon me. As regards the latter, I can only say that it does not pretend to be a full account of everything we did and saw. There are many things connected with our journey into Kukuanaland which I should have liked to dwell upon at length, and which have, as it is, been scarcely alluded to. Amongst these are the curious legends which I collected about the chain armour that saved us from destruction in the great battle of Loo, and also about the 'silent ones' or colossi at the mouth of the stalactite cave. Again, if I had given way to my own impulses, I should have liked to go into the differences, some of which are to my mind very suggestive, between the Zulu and Kukuana dialects. Also a few pages might profitably have been given up to the consideration of the indigenous flora and fauna of Kukuanaland.[1] Then there remains the most interesting subject – that, as it is, has only been incidentally alluded to – of the magnificent system of military organization in force in that country, which is, in my opinion, much superior to that inaugurated by Chaka in Zululand, inasmuch as it permits of even more rapid mobilization, and does not necessitate the employment of the pernicious system of forced celibacy. And, lastly, I have scarcely touched on the domestic and family customs of the Kukuanas, many of which are exceedingly quaint, or on their proficiency in the art of smelting and welding metals. This last they carry to considerable perfection, of which a good example is to be seen in their 'tollas', or heavy throwing knives, the backs of these knives being made of hammered iron, and the edges of beautiful steel welded with great skill on to the iron backs. The fact of the matter is, that I thought (and so did Henry Curtis and Captain Good) that the best plan would be to tell the story in a plain, straightforward manner, and leave these matters to be dealt with subsequently in whatever way may ultimately appear to be desirable. In the meanwhile I shall, of course, be delighted to give any information in my power to anybody interested in such things.

And now it only remains for me to offer my apologies for my blunt way of writing. I can only say in excuse for it that I am more accustomed to handle a rifle than a pen, and cannot make any pretence to the grand literary flights and flourishes which I see in novels – for I sometimes like to read a novel. I suppose they – the flights and flourishes – are desirable, and I regret not being able to supply them; but at the same time I cannot help thinking that simple things are always the most impressive, and books

---

[1] I discovered eight varieties of antelope, with which I was previously totally unacquainted, and many new species of plants, for the most part of the bulbous tribe. – A.Q.

are easier to understand when they are written in plain language, though I have perhaps no right to set up an opinion on such a matter. 'A sharp spear,' runs the Kukuana saying, 'needs no polish'; and on the same principle I venture to hope that a true story, however strange it may be, does not require to be decked out in fine words.

ALLAN QUATERMAIN

1

I Meet Sir Henry Curtis

IT is a curious thing that at my age – fifty-five last birthday – I should find myself taking up a pen to try and write a history. I wonder what sort of a history it will be when I have done it, if I ever come to the end of the trip! I have done a good many things in my life, which seems a long one to me, owing to my having begun so young, perhaps. At an age when other boys are at school, I was earning my living as a trader in the old Colony. I have been trading, hunting, fighting, or mining ever since. And yet it is only eight months ago that I made my pile. It is a big pile now I have got it – I don't yet know how big – but I don't think I would go through the last fifteen or sixteen months again for it; no, not if I knew that I should come out safe at the end, pile and all. But then I am a timid man, and don't like violence, and am pretty sick of adventure. I wonder why I am going to write this book: it is not in my line. I am not a literary man, though very devoted to the Old Testament and also to the *Ingoldsby Legends*. Let me try and set down my reasons, just to see if I have any.

First reason: Because Sir Henry Curtis and Captain John Good asked me to.

Second reason: Because I am laid up here at Durban with the pain and trouble in my left leg. Ever since that confounded lion got hold of me I have been liable to it, and its being rather bad just now makes me limp more than ever. There must be some poison in a lion's teeth, otherwise how is it that when your wounds are healed they break out again, generally, mark you, at the same time of year that you got your mauling? It is a hard thing that when one has shot sixty-five lions as I have in the course of my life, that the sixty-sixth should chew your leg like a quid of tobacco. It breaks the routine of the thing, and putting other considerations aside, I am an orderly man and don't like that. This is by the way.

Third reason: Because I want my boy Harry, who is over there at the hospital in London studying to become a doctor, to have something to amuse him and keep him out of mischief for a week or so. Hospital work must sometimes pall and get rather dull, for even of cutting up dead bodies there must come satiety, and as this history won't be dull, whatever else it may be, it may put a little life into things for a day or two while he is reading it.

Fourth reason and last: Because I am going to tell the strangest story that I know of. It may seem a queer thing to say that, especially considering that there is no woman in it – except Foulata. Stop, though! there is Gagoola, if she was a woman and not a fiend. But she was a hundred at least, and therefore not marriageable, so I don't count her. At any rate, I can safely say that there is not a *petticoat* in the whole history. Well I had better come to the yoke. It's a stiff place, and I feel as though I were bogged up to the axle. But 'sutjes, sutjes,' as the Boers say (I'm sure I don't know how they spell it), softly does it. A strong team will come through at last, that is if they ain't too poor. You will never do anything with poor oxen. Now to begin.

I, Allan Quatermain, of Durban, Natal, Gentleman, make oath and say – That's how I began my deposition before the magistrate, about poor Khiva's and Ventvögel's sad deaths; but somehow it doesn't seem quite the right way to begin a book. And, besides, am I a gentleman? What is a gentleman? I don't quite know, and yet I have had to do with niggers – no, I'll scratch that word 'niggers' out, for I don't like it. I've known natives who *are*, and so you'll say, Harry, my boy, before you're done with this tale, and I have known mean whites with lots of money and fresh out from home, too, who *ain't*. Well, at any rate, I was born a gentleman, though I've been nothing but a poor travelling trader and hunter all my life. Whether I have remained so I know not, you must judge of that. Heaven knows I've tried. I've killed many men in my time, but I have never slain wantonly or stained my hand in innocent blood, only in self-defence. The Almighty gave us our lives, and I suppose he meant us to defend them, at least I have always acted on that, and I hope it won't be brought up against me when my clock strikes. There, there, it is a cruel and a wicked world, and for a timid man I have been mixed up in a deal of slaughter. I can't tell the rights of it, but at any rate I have never stolen, though I once cheated a Kafir out of a herd of cattle. But then he had done me a dirty turn, and it has troubled me ever since into the bargain.

Well it's eighteen months or so ago since I first met Sir Henry Curtis and Captain Good, and it was in this way. I had been up elephant hunting beyond Bamangwato and had had bad luck. Everything went wrong that trip, and to top up with I got the fever badly. So soon as I was well enough I trekked down to the Diamond Fields, sold such ivory as I had, and also my wagon and oxen, discharged my hunters, and took the post-cart to the Cape. After spending a week in Cape Town, finding that they overcharged me at the hotel, and having seen everything there was to see, including the botanical gardens, which seem to me likely to confer a great benefit on the country, and the new Houses of Parliament, which I expect will do nothing of the sort, I determined to go on back to Natal by the *Dunkeld*, then lying in the docks waiting for the *Edinburgh Castle* due in from England. I took my berth and went aboard, and that afternoon the Natal passengers from the *Edinburgh Castle* transhipped, and we weighed and put out to sea.

Among the passengers who came on board there were two who excited my curiosity. One, a man of about thirty, was one of the biggest-chested and longest-armed men I ever saw. He had yellow hair, a big yellow beard, clear-cut features, and large grey eyes set deep into his head. I never saw a finer-looking man, and somehow he reminded me of an ancient Dane. Not that I know much of ancient Danes, though I remember a modern Dane who did me out of ten pounds; but I remember once seeing a picture of some of those gentry, who, I take it, were a kind of white Zulus. They were drinking out of big horns, and their long hair hung down their backs, and as I looked at my friend standing there by the companion-ladder, I thought that if one only let his hair grow a bit, put one of those chain shirts on to those great shoulders of his, and gave him a big battle-axe and a horn mug, he might have sat as a model for that picture. And by the way it is a curious thing, and just shows how the blood will show out, I found out afterwards that Sir Henry Curtis, for that was the big man's name, was of Danish blood.[1] He also reminded me strongly of somebody else, but at the time I could not remember who it was.

The other man who stood talking to Sir Henry was short, stout, and dark, and of quite a different cut. I suspected at once that he was a naval officer. I don't know why, but it is difficult to mistake a navy man. I have gone shooting trips with several of them in the course of my life, and they have always been just the best and bravest and nicest fellows I ever met, though given to the use of profane language.

I asked a page or two back, what is a gentleman? I'll answer it now: a Royal Naval officer is, in a general sort of a way, though, of course, there may be black sheep among them here and there. I fancy it is just the wide sea and the breath of God's winds that washes their hearts and blows the bitterness out of their minds and makes them what men ought to be. Well, to return, I was right again; I found out that he *was* a naval officer, a lieutenant of thirty-one, who, after seventeen years' service, had been turned out of her Majesty's employ with the barren honour of a commander's rank, because it was impossible that he should be promoted. That is what people who serve the Queen have to expect: to be shot out into the cold world to find a living just when they are beginning to really understand their work, and to get to the prime of life. Well, I suppose they don't mind it, but for my part I had rather earn my bread as a hunter. One's halfpence are as scarce perhaps, but you don't get so many kicks. His name I found out – by referring to the passenger list – was Good – Captain John Good. He was broad, of medium height, dark, stout, and rather a curious man to look at. He was so very neat and so very clean shaved, and he always wore an eye-glass in his right eye. It seemed to grow there, for it had no string, and he never took it out except to wipe it. At first I thought he used to sleep in it, but I afterwards found that

[1] Mr. Quatermain's ideas about ancient Danes seem to be rather confused; we have always understood that they were dark-haired people. Probably he was thinking of Saxons. – *Editor.*

this was a mistake. He put it in his trousers pocket when he went to bed, together with his false teeth, of which he had two beautiful sets that have often, my own being none of the best, caused me to break the tenth commandment. But I am anticipating.

Soon after we had got under way evening closed in, and brought with it very dirty weather. A keen breeze sprang up off land, and a kind of aggravated Scotch mist soon drove everybody from the deck. And as for that *Dunkeld*, she is a flat-bottomed punt, and going up light as she was, she rolled very heavily. It almost seemed as though she would go right over, but she never did. It was quite impossible to walk about, so I stood near the engines where it was warm, and amused myself with watching the pendulum, which was fixed opposite to me, swinging slowly backwards and forwards as the vessel rolled, and marking the angle she touched at each lurch.

'That pendulum's wrong; it is not properly weighted,' suddenly said a voice at my shoulder, somewhat testily. Looking round I saw the naval officer I had noticed when the passengers came aboard.

'Indeed, now what makes you think so?' I asked.

'Think so. I don't think at all. Why there' – as she righted herself after a roll – 'if the ship had really rolled to the degree that thing pointed to then she would never have rolled again, that's all. But it is just like these merchant skippers, they always are so confoundedly careless.'

Just then the dinner-bell rang, and I was not sorry, for it is a dreadful thing to have to listen to an officer of the Royal Navy when he gets on to that subject. I only know one worse thing, and that is to hear a merchant skipper express his candid opinion of officers of the Royal Navy.

Captain Good and I went down to dinner together, and there we found Sir Henry Curtis already seated. He and Captain Good sat together, and I sat opposite to them. The captain and I soon got into talk about shooting and what not; he asking me many questions, and I answering as well as I could. Presently he got on to elephants.

'Ah, sir,' called out somebody who was sitting near me, 'you've got to the right man for that; Hunter Quatermain should be able to tell you about elephants if anybody can.'

Sir Henry, who had been sitting quite quiet listening to our talk, started visibly.

'Excuse me, sir,' he said, leaning forward across the table, and speaking in a low, deep voice, a very suitable voice it seemed to me, to come out of those great lungs. 'Excuse me sir, but is your name Allan Quatermain?'

I said it was.

The big man made no further remark, but I heard him mutter 'fortunate' into his beard.

Presently dinner came to an end, and as we were leaving the saloon Sir Henry came up and asked me if I would come into his cabin and smoke a pipe. I accepted, and he led the way to the *Dunkeld* deck cabin, and a very good cabin it was. It had been two cabins, but when Sir Garnet or one of those big swells went down the coast in the *Dunkeld*, they had knocked away the partition and never put it up again. There was a sofa in the cabin, and a little table in front of it. Sir Henry sent the steward for a bottle of whisky, and the three of us sat down and lit our pipes.

'Mr. Quatermain,' said Sir Henry Curtis, when the steward had brought the whisky and lit the lamp, 'the year before last about this time you were, I believe, at a place called Bamangwato, to the north of the Transvaal.'

'I was,' I answered, rather surprised that this gentleman should be so well acquainted with my movements, which were not, so far as I was aware, considered of general interest.

'You were trading there, were you not?' put in Captain Good, in his quick way.

'I was. I took up a wagon-load of goods, and made a camp outside the settlement, and stopped till I had sold them.'

Sir Henry was sitting opposite to me in a Madeira chair, his arms leaning on the table. He now looked up, fixing his large grey eyes full upon my face. There was a curious anxiety in them I thought.

'Did you happen to meet a man called Neville there?'

'Oh, yes; he outspanned alongside of me for a fortnight to rest his oxen before going on to the interior. I had a letter from a lawyer a few months back asking me if I knew what had become of him, which I answered to the best of my ability at the time.'

'Yes,' said Sir Henry, 'your letter was forwarded to me. You said in it that the gentleman called Neville left Bamangwato in the beginning of May in a wagon with a driver, a voorlooper, and a Kafir hunter called Jim, announcing his intention of trekking if possible as far as Inyati, the extreme trading post in the Matabele country, where he would sell his wagon and proceed on foot. You also said that he did sell his wagon, for six months afterwards you saw the wagon in the possession of a Portuguese trader, who told you that he had bought it at Inyati from a white man whose name he had forgotten, and that the white man with a native servant had started off for the interior on a shooting trip, he believed.'

'Yes.'

Then came a pause.

'Mr. Quatermain,' said Sir Henry, suddenly, 'I suppose you know or can guess nothing more of the reasons of my – of Mr. Neville's journey to the northward, or as to what point that journey was directed?'

'I heard something,' I answered, and stopped. The subject was one which I did not care to discuss.

Sir Henry and Captain Good looked at each other, and Captain Good nodded.

'Mr. Quatermain,' said the former, 'I am going to tell you a story, and ask your advice, and perhaps your assistance. The agent who forwarded me your letter told me that I might implicitly rely upon it, as you were,' he said, 'well known and universally respected in Natal, and especially noted for your discretion.'

I bowed and drank some whisky and water to hide my confusion, for I am a modest man – and Sir Henry went on.

'Mr. Neville was my brother.'

'Oh,' I said, starting, for now I knew who Sir Henry had reminded me of when I first saw him. His brother was a much smaller man and had a dark beard, but now I thought of it, he possessed eyes of the same shade of grey and with the same keen look in them, and the features too were not unlike.

'He was,' went on Sir Henry, 'my only and younger brother, and till five years ago I do not suppose we were ever a month away from each other. But just about five years ago a misfortune befell us, as sometimes does happen in families. We quarrelled bitterly, and I behaved very unjustly to my brother in my anger.' Here Captain Good nodded his head vigorously to himself. The ship gave a big roll just then, so that the looking-glass, which was fixed opposite us to starboard, was for a moment nearly over our heads, and as I was sitting with my hands in my pockets and staring upwards, I could see him nodding like anything.

'As I daresay you know,' went on Sir Henry, 'if a man dies intestate, and has no property but land, real property it is called in England, it all descends to his eldest son. It so happened that just at the time when we quarrelled our father died intestate. He had put off making his will until it was too late. The result was that my brother, who had not been brought up to any profession, was left without a penny. Of course it would have been my duty to provide for him, but at the time the quarrel between us was so bitter that I did not – to my shame I say it' (and he sighed deeply) 'offer to do anything. It was not that I grudged him anything, but I waited for him to make advances, and he made none. I am sorry to trouble you with all this, Mr. Quatermain, but I must to make things clear, eh, Good?'

'Quite so, quite so,' said the captain. 'Mr. Quatermain will, I am sure, keep this history to himself.'

'Of course,' said I, for I rather pride myself on my discretion.

'Well,' went on Sir Henry, 'my brother had a few hundred pounds to his account at the time, and without saying anything to me he drew out this paltry sum, and, having adopted the name of Neville, started off for South Africa in the wild hope of making a fortune. This I heard afterwards. Some three years passed, and I heard nothing of my brother, though I wrote several times. Doubtless the letters never reached him. But as time went on I grew more and more troubled about him. I found out, Mr. Quatermain, that blood is thicker than water.'

'That's true,' said I, thinking of my boy Harry.

'I found out, Mr. Quatermain, that I would have given half my fortune to know that my brother George, the only relation I have, was safe and well, and that I should see him again.'

'But you never did, Curtis,' jerked out Captain Good, glancing at the big man's face.

'Well, Mr. Quatermain, as time went on, I became more and more anxious to find out if my brother was alive or dead, and if alive to get him home again. I set inquiries on foot, and your letter was one of the results. So far as it went it was satisfactory, for it showed that till lately George was alive, but it did not go far enough. So, to cut a long story short, I made up my mind to come out and look for him myself, and Captain Good was so kind as to come with me.'

'Yes,' said the captain; 'nothing else to do, you see. Turned out by my Lords of the Admiralty to starve on half-pay. And now perhaps, sir, you will tell us what you know or have heard of the gentleman called Neville.'

2

The Legend of Solomon's Mines

'WHAT was it that you heard about my brother's journey at Bamangwato?' said Sir Henry, as I paused to fill my pipe before answering Captain Good.

'I heard this,' I answered, 'and I have never mentioned it to a soul till today. I heard that he was starting for Solomon's Mines.'

'Solomon's Mines!' ejaculated both my hearers at once. 'Where are they?'

'I don't know,' I said; 'I know where they are said to be. I once saw the peaks of the mountains that border them, but there was a hundred and thirty miles of desert between me and them, and I am not aware that any white man ever got across it save one. But perhaps the best thing I can do is to tell you the legend of Solomon's Mines as I know it, you passing your word not to reveal anything I tell you without my permission. Do you agree to that? I have my reasons for asking it.'

Sir Henry nodded, and Captain Good replied, 'Certainly, certainly.'

'Well,' I began, 'as you may guess, in a general way, elephant hunters are a rough set of men, and don't trouble themselves with much beyond the facts of life and the way of Kafirs. But here and there you meet a man who takes the trouble to collect traditions from the natives, and tries to make out a little piece of the history of this dark land. It was such a man as this who first told me the legend of Solomon's Mines, now a matter of nearly thirty years ago. It was when I was on my first elephant hunt in the Matabele country. His name was Evans, and he was killed next year, poor fellow, by a wounded buffalo, and lies buried near the Zambesi Falls. I was telling Evans one night, I remember, of some wonderful workings I had found whilst hunting koodoo and eland in what is now the Lydenburg district of the Transvaal. I see they have come across these workings again lately in prospecting for gold, but I knew of them years ago. There is a great wide wagon road cut out of the solid rock, and leading to the mouth of the working or gallery. Inside the mouth of this gallery are stacks of gold quartz piled up ready for crushing, which shows that the workers, whoever they were, must have left in a hurry, and about twenty paces in the gallery is built across, and a beautiful bit of masonry it is.

'"Ay," said Evans, "but I will tell you a queerer thing than that"; and he went on to tell me how he had found in the far interior a ruined city, which he believed to be the Ophir of the Bible, and, by the way, other more learned men have said the same long since poor Evans' time. I was, I remember, listening open-eared to all these wonders, for I was young at the time, and this story of an ancient civilization and of the treasure which those old Jewish or Phoenician adventurers used to extract from a country long since lapsed into the darkest barbarism took a great hold upon my imagination, when suddenly he said to me, "Lad, did you ever hear of the Suliman Mountains up to the north-west of the Mashukulumbwe country?" I told him I never had. "Ah, well," he said, "that was where Solomon really had his mines, his diamond mines, I mean."

'"How do you know that?" I asked.

'"Know it; why what is 'Suliman' but a corruption of Solomon![1] and, besides, an old Isanusi (witch doctor) up in the Manica country told me all about it. She said that the people who lived across those mountains were a branch of the Zulus, speaking a dialect of Zulu, but finer and bigger men even; that there lived among them great wizards, who had learnt their art from white men when 'all the world was dark,' and who had the secret of a wonderful mine of 'bright stones.'"

'Well, I laughed at this story at the time, though it interested me, for the diamond fields were not discovered then, and poor Evans went off and got killed, and for twenty years I never thought any more of the matter. But just twenty years afterwards – and that is a long time, gentlemen, an elephant hunter does not often live for twenty years at his business – I heard something more definite about Suliman's Mountains and the country which lies beyond it. I was up beyond the Manica country at a place called Sitanda's Kraal, and a miserable place it was, for one could get nothing to eat there, and there was but little game about. I had an attack of fever, and was in a bad way generally, when one day a Portugee arrived with a single companion – a half-breed. Now I know your Delagoa Portugee well. There is no greater devil unhung in a general way, battening

[1] Suliman is the Arabic form of Solomon. – *Editor.*

as he does upon human agony and flesh in the shape of slaves. But this was quite a different type of man to the low fellows I had been accustomed to meet; he reminded me more of the polite dons I have read about. He was tall and thin, with large dark eyes and curling grey moustachios. We talked together a little, for he could speak broken English, and I understood a little Portugee, and he told me that his name was José Silvestre, and that he had a place near Delagoa Bay; and when he went on next day with his half-breed companion, he said "Good-bye," taking off his hat quite in the old style. "Good-bye, senhor," he said; "if ever we meet again I shall be the richest man in the world, and I will remember you." I laughed a little – I was too weak to laugh much – and watched him strike out for the great desert to the west, wondering if he was mad, or what he thought he was going to find there.

'A week passed, and I got the better of my fever. One evening I was sitting on the ground in front of the little tent I had with me, chewing the last leg of a miserable fowl I had bought from a native for a bit of cloth worth twenty fowls, and staring at the hot red sun sinking down into the desert, when suddenly I saw a figure, apparently that of a European, for it wore a coat, on the slope of the rising ground opposite to me, about three hundred yards away. The figure crept along on its hands and knees, then it got up and staggered along a few yards on its legs, only to fall and crawl along again. Seeing that it must be somebody in distress, I sent one of my hunters to help him, and presently he arrived, and who do you suppose it turned out to be?'

'José Silvestre, of course,' said Captain Good.

'Yes, José Silvestre, or rather his skeleton and a little skin. His face was bright yellow with bilious fever, and his large, dark eyes stood nearly out of his head, for all his flesh had gone. There was nothing but yellow parchment-like skin, white hair, and the gaunt bones sticking up beneath.

'"Water! for the sake of Christ, water!" he moaned. I saw that his lips were cracked, and his tongue, which protruded between them, swollen and blackish.

'I gave him water with a little milk in it, and he drank it in great gulps, two quarts or more, without stopping. I would not let him have any more. Then the fever took him again, and he fell down and began to rave about Suliman's Mountains, and the diamonds, and the desert. I took him into the tent and did what I could for him, which was little enough; but I saw how it must end. About eleven o'clock he got quieter, and I lay down for a little rest and went to sleep. At dawn I woke again, and saw him in the half-light sitting up, a strange, gaunt form, and gazing out towards the desert. Presently the first ray of the sun shot right across the wide plain before us till it reached the far-away crest of one of the tallest of the Suliman Mountains more than a hundred miles away.

'"There it is!" cried the dying man in Portuguese, stretching out his long, thin arm, "but I shall never reach it, never. No one will ever reach it!"

'Suddenly he paused, and seemed to take a resolution. "Friend," he said, turning towards me, "are you there? My eyes grow dark."

'"Yes," I said; "yes, lie down now, and rest."

'"Ay," he answered, "I shall rest soon, I have time to rest – all eternity. Listen, I am dying! You have been good to me. I will give you the paper. Perhaps you will get there if you can live through the desert, which has killed my poor servant and me."

'Then he groped in his shirt and brought out what I thought was a Boer tobacco pouch of the skin of the Swart-vet-pens (sable antelope). It was fastened with a little strip of hide, what we call a rimpi, and this he tried to untie, but could not. He handed it to me. "Untie it," he said. I did so, and extracted a bit of torn yellow linen, on which something was written in rusty letters. Inside was a paper.

'Then he went on feebly, for he was growing weak: "The paper has it all, that is on the rag. It took me years to read. Listen: my ancestor, a political refugee from Lisbon, and one of the first Portuguese who landed on these shores, wrote that when he was dying on those mountains which no white foot ever pressed before or since. His name was José da Silvestra, and he lived three hundred years ago. His slave, who waited for him on this side the mountains, found him dead, and brought the writing home to Delagoa. It has been in the family ever since, but none have cared to read it till at last I did. And I have lost my life over it, but another may succeed, and become the richest man in the world – the richest man in the world. Only give it to no one; go yourself!" Then he began to wander again, and in an hour it was all over.

'God rest him! he died very quietly, and I buried him deep, with big boulders on his breast; so I do not think that the jackals can have dug him up. And then I came away.'

'Ay, but the document,' said Sir Henry, in a tone of deep interest.

'Yes, the document; what was in it?' added the captain.

'Well, gentlemen, if you like I will tell you. I have never showed it to anybody yet except my dear wife, who is dead, and she thought it was all nonsense, and a drunken old Portuguese trader who translated it for me, and had forgotten all about it next morning. The original rag is at my home in Durban, together with poor Dom José's translation, but I have the English rendering in my pocket-book, and a facsimile of the map, if it can be called a map. Here it is.'

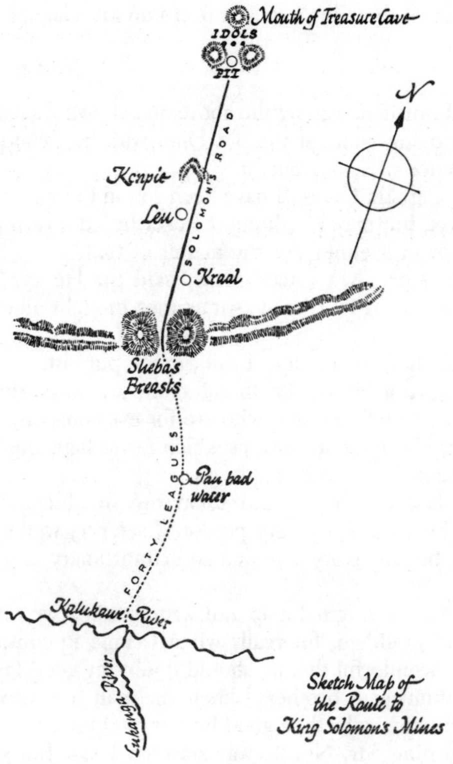

I, José da Silvestra, who am now dying of hunger in the little cave where no snow is on the north side of the nipple of the southernmost of the two mountains I have named Sheba's Breasts, write this in the year 1590 with a cleft bone upon a remnant of my raiment, my blood being the ink. If my slave should find it when he comes, and should bring it to Delagoa, let my friend (name illegible) bring the matter to the knowledge of the king, that he may send an army which, if they live through the desert and the mountains, and can overcome the brave Kukuanes and their devilish arts, to which end many priests should be brought, will make him the richest king since Solomon. With my own eyes have I seen the countless diamonds stored in Solomon's treasure chamber behind the white Death; but through the treachery of Gagool the witch-finder I might bring nought away, scarcely my life. Let him who comes follow the map, and climb the snow of Sheba's left breast till he comes to the nipple, on the north side of which is the great road Solomon made, from whence three days' journey to the King's Palace. Let him kill Gagool. Pray for my soul. Farewell.

JOSÉ DA SILVESTRA[1]

When I had finished reading the above and shown the copy of the map, drawn by the dying hand of the old Dom with his blood for ink, there followed a silence of astonishment.

'Well,' said Captain Good, 'I have been round the world twice, and put in at most ports, but may I be hung if I ever heard a yarn like that out of a story book, or in it either, for the matter of that.'

'It's a queer story, Mr. Quatermain,' said Sir Henry. 'I suppose you are not hoaxing us? It is, I know, sometimes thought allowable to take a greenhorn in.'

'If you think that, Sir Henry,' I said, much put out, and pocketing my paper, for I do not like to be thought one of those silly fellows who consider it witty to tell lies, and who are for ever boasting to new comers of extraordinary hunting adventures which never happened, 'why there is an end of the matter,' and I rose to go.

Sir Henry laid his large hand upon my shoulder. 'Sit down, Mr. Quatermain,' he said, 'I beg your pardon; I see very well you do not wish to deceive us, but the story sounded so extraordinary that I could hardly believe it.'

'You shall see the original map and writing when we reach Durban,' I said, somewhat mollified, for really when I came to consider the matter it was scarcely wonderful that he should doubt my good faith. 'But I have not told you about your brother. I knew the man Jim who was with him. He was a Bechuana by birth, a good hunter, and for a native a very clever man. The morning Mr. Neville was starting, I saw Jim standing by my wagon and cutting up tobacco on the disselboom.

'"Jim," said I, "where are you off to this trip? Is it elephants?"

---

[1] En José da Silvestra que estou morrendo de fame na pequena cova onde não ha neve ao lado norte do bico mais ao sul das duas montanhas que chamei seio de Sheba; escrevo isto no anno 1590; escrevo isto com um pedaço d'ôsso n'um farrapo de minha roupa e com sangue meu por tinta; se o meu escravo dér com isto quando venha ao levar para Lourenzo Marquez, que o meu amigo (——) leve a cousa ao conhecimento d' El Rei, para que possa mandar um exercito que, se desfiler pelo deserto e pelas montanhas e mesmo sobrepujar os bravos Kukuanes e suas artes diabolicas, pelo que se deviam trazer muitos padres Faro o Rei mais rico depois de Salomão. Com meus proprios olhos vé os diamantes sem conto guardados nas camaras do thesouro de Salomão a traz da morte branca, mas pela traição de Gagoal a feiticeira achadora, nada poderia evar, e apenas a minha vida. Quem vier siga o mappa e trepe pela neve de Sheba peito à esquerda até chegar ao bico, do lado norte do qual está a grande estrada do Salomão por elle feita, donde ha tres dias de jornada até ao Palacio do Rei. Mate Gagoal. Reze por minha alma. Adeus.

JOSÉ DA SILVESTRA

'"No, Baas," he answered, "we are after something worth more than ivory."

'"And what might that be?" I said, for I was curious. "Is it gold?"

'"No, Baas, something worth more than gold," and he grinned.

'I did not ask any more questions, for I did not like to lower my dignity by seeming curious, but I was puzzled. Presently Jim finished cutting his tobacco.

'"Baas," said he.

'I took no notice.

'"Baas," said he again.

'"Eh, boy, what is it?" said I.

'"Baas, we are going after diamonds."

'"Diamonds! why, then, you are going in the wrong direction; you should head for the Fields."

'"Baas, have you ever heard of Suliman's Berg?" (Solomon's Mountains).

'"Ay!"

'"Have you ever heard of the diamonds there?"

'"I have heard a foolish story, Jim."

'"It is no story, Baas. I once knew a woman who came from there, and got to Natal with her child, she told me: – she is dead now."

'"Your master will feed the aasvogels (vultures), Jim, if he tries to reach Suliman's country, and so will you if they can get any pickings off your worthless old carcass," said I.

'He grinned. "Mayhap, Baas. Man must die; I'd rather like to try a new country myself; the elephants are getting worked out about here."

'"Ah! my boy," I said, "you wait till the 'pale old man' (death) gets a grip of your yellow throat, and then we'll hear what sort of a tune you sing."

'Half an hour after that I saw Neville's wagon move off. Presently Jim came running back. "Good-bye, Baas," he said. "I didn't like to start without bidding you good-bye, for I daresay you are right, and we shall never come back again."

'"Is your master really going to Suliman's Berg, Jim, or are you lying?"

'"No," says he; "he is going. He told me he was bound to make his fortune somehow, or try to; so he might as well try the diamonds."

'"Oh!" said I; "wait a bit, Jim; will you take a note to your master, Jim, and promise not to give it to him till you reach Inyati?" (which was some hundred miles off).

'"Yes," said he.

'So I took a scrap of paper, and wrote on it, "Let him who comes . . . climb the snow of Sheba's left breast, till he comes to the nipple, on the north side of which is Solomon's great road.'

'"Now, Jim," I said, "when you give this to your master, tell him he had better follow the advice implicitly. You are not to give it to him now, because I don't want him back asking me questions which I won't answer. Now be off, you idle fellow, the wagon is nearly out of sight."

'Jim took the note and went, and that is all I know about your brother, Sir Henry; but I am much afraid –'

'Mr. Quatermain,' said Sir Henry, 'I am going to look for my brother; I am going to trace him to Suliman's Mountains, and over them if necessary, till I find him, or till I know that he is dead. Will you come with me?'

I am, as I think I have said, a cautious man, indeed a timid one, and I shrank from such an idea. It seemed to me that to start on such a journey would be to go to certain death, and putting others things aside, as I had a son to support, I could not afford to die just then.

'No, thank you, Sir Henry, I think I had rather not,' I answered. 'I am too old for wild-goose chases of that sort, and we should only end up like my poor friend Silvestre. I have a son dependent on me, so cannot afford to risk my life.'

Both Sir Henry and Captain Good looked very disappointed.

'Mr. Quatermain,' said the former, 'I am well of, and I am bent upon this business. You may put the remuneration for your services at whatever figure you like in reason, and it shall be paid over to you before we start. Moreover, I will, before we start, arrange that in the event of anything happening to us or to you, that your son shall be suitably provided for. You will see from this how necessary I think your presence. Also if by any chance we should reach this place, and find diamonds, they shall belong to you and Good equally. I do not want them. But of course the chance is as good as nothing, though the same thing would apply to any ivory we might get. You may pretty well make your own terms with me, Mr. Quatermain; and of course I shall pay all expenses.'

'Sir Henry,' said I, 'this is the most liberal offer I ever had, and one not to be sneezed at by a poor hunter and trader. But the job is the biggest I ever came across, and I must take time to think it over. I will give you my answer before we get to Durban.'

'Very good,' answered Sir Henry, and then I said goodnight and turned in, and dreamt about poor long-dead Silvestre and the diamonds.

3

Umbopa Enters Our Service

IT takes from four to five days, according to the vessel and the state of the weather, to run up from the Cape to Durban. Sometimes, if the landing is bad at East London, where they have not yet got that wonderful harbour they talk so much of, and sink such a mint of money in, one is delayed for twenty-four hours before the cargo boats can get out to take the goods off. But on this occasion we had not to wait at all, for there were no breakers on the Bar to speak of, and the tugs came out at once with their long strings of ugly flat-bottomed boats, into which the goods were bundled with a crash. It did not matter what they were, over they went slap bang; whether they were china or woollen goods they met with the same treatment. I saw one case containing four dozen of champagne smashed all to bits, and there was the champagne fizzing and boiling about in the bottom of the dirty cargo boat. It was a wicked waste, and so evidently the Kafirs in the boat thought, for they found a couple of unbroken bottles, and knocking the tops off drank the contents. But they had not allowed for the expansion caused by the fizz in the wine, and feeling themselves swelling, rolled about in the bottom of the boat, calling out that the good liquor was 'tagati' (bewitched). I spoke to them from the vessel, and told them that it was the white man's strongest medicine, and that they were as good as dead men. They went on to the shore in a very great fright, and I do not think that they will touch champagne again.

Well, all the time we were running up to Natal I was thinking over Sir Henry Curtis' offer. We did not speak any more on the subject for a day or two, though I told them many hunting yarns, all true ones. There is no need to tell lies about hunting, for so many curious things happen within the knowledge of a man whose business it is to hunt; but this is by the way.

At last, one beautiful evening in January, which is our hottest month, we steamed along the coast of Natal, expecting to make Durban Point by sunset. It is a lovely coast all along from East London, with its red sandhills and wide sweeps of vivid green, dotted here and there with Kafir kraals, and bordered by a ribbon of white surf, which spouts up in pillars of foam where it hits the rocks. But just before you get to Durban there is a peculiar richness about it. There are the deep kloofs cut in the hills by the rushing rains of centuries, down which the rivers sparkle; there is the deepest green of the bush, growing as God planted it, and the other greens of the mealie gardens and the sugar patches, while here and there a white house, smiling out at the placid sea, puts a finish and gives an air of homeliness to the scene. For to my mind, however beautiful a view may be, it requires the presence of man to make it complete, but perhaps that is because I have lived so much in the wilderness, and therefore know the value of civilization, though to be sure it drives away the game. The Garden of Eden, no doubt, was fair before man was, but I always think it must have been fairer when Eve was walking about it. But we had miscalculated a little, and the sun was well down before we dropped anchor off the Point, and heard the gun which told the good folk that the English Mail was in. It was too late to think of getting over the Bar that night, so we went down comfortably to dinner, after seeing the Mails carried off in the lifeboat.

When we came up again the moon was up, and shining so brightly over sea and shore that she almost paled the quick large flashes from the lighthouse. From the shore floated sweet spicy odours that always remind me of hymns and missionaries, and in the windows of the houses on the Berea sparkled a hundred lights. From a large brig lying near came the music of the sailors as they worked at getting the anchor up to be ready for the wind. Altogether it was a perfect night, such a night as you only get in Southern Africa, and it threw a garment of peace over everybody as the moon threw a garment of silver over everything. Even the great bulldog, belonging to a sporting passenger, seemed to yield to the gentle influences, and giving up yearning to come to close quarters with the baboon in a cage on the foc'sle, snored happily in the door of the cabin, dreaming no doubt that he had finished him, and happy in his dream.

We all – that is, Sir Henry Curtis, Captain Good, and myself – went and sat by the wheel, and were quiet for a while.

'Well, Mr. Quatermain,' said Sir Henry presently, 'have you been thinking about my proposals?'

'Ay,' echoed Captain Good, 'what do you think of them, Mr. Quatermain? I hope you are going to give us the pleasure of your company as far as Solomon's Mines, or wherever the gentleman you knew as Neville may have got to.'

I rose and knocked out my pipe before I answered. I had not made up my mind, and wanted the additional moment to complete it. Before the burning tobacco had fallen into the sea it was completed; just that little extra second did the trick. It is often the way when you have been bothering a long time over a thing.

'Yes, gentlemen,' I said, sitting down again, 'I will go, and by your leave I will tell you why and on what terms. First for the terms which I ask.

'1. You are to pay all expenses, and any ivory or other valuables we may get is to be divided between Captain Good and myself.

'2. That you pay me £500 for my services on the trip before we start, I undertaking to serve you faithfully till you choose to abandon the enterprise, or till we succeed, or disaster overtakes us.

'3. That before we start you execute a deed agreeing, in the event of my death or disablement, to pay my boy Harry, who is studying medicine over there in London at Guy's Hospital, a sum of £200 a year for five years, by which time he ought to be able to earn a living for himself. That is all, I think, and I daresay you will say quite enough too.'

'No,' answered Sir Henry, 'I accept them gladly. I am bent upon this project, and would pay more than that for your help, especially considering the peculiar knowledge you possess.'

'Very well. And now that I have made my terms I will tell you my reasons for making up my mind to go. First of all, gentlemen, I have been observing you both for the last few days, and if you will not think me impertinent I will say that I like you, and think that we shall come up well to the yoke together. That is something, let me tell you, when one has a long journey like this before one.

'And now as to the journey itself, I tell you flatly, Sir Henry and Captain Good, that I do not think it probable that we can come out of it alive, that is, if we attempt to cross the Suliman Mountains. What was the fate of the old Dom da Silvestra three hundred years ago? What was the fate of his descendant twenty years ago? What has been your brother's fate? I tell you frankly, gentlemen, that as their fate was so I believe ours will be.'

I paused to watch the effect of my words. Captain Good looked a little uncomfortable; but Sir Henry's face did not change. 'We must take our chance,' he said.

'You may perhaps wonder,' I went on, 'why, if I think this, I, who am, as I told you, a timid man, should undertake such a journey. It is for two reasons. First I am a fatalist, and believe that my time is appointed to come quite independently of my own movements, and that if I am to go to Suliman's Mountains to be killed, I shall go there and shall be killed there. God Almighty, no doubt, knows His mind about me, so I need not trouble on that point. Secondly, I am a poor man. For nearly forty years I have hunted and traded, but I have never made more than a living. Well, gentlemen, I don't know if you are aware that the average life of an elephant hunter from the time he takes to the trade is from four to five years. So you see I have lived through about seven generations of my class, and I should think that my time cannot be far off anyway. Now, if anything were to happen to me in the ordinary course of business, by the time my debts were paid there would be nothing left to support my son Harry whilst he was getting in the way of earning a living, whereas now he would be provided for for five years. There is the whole affair in a nutshell.'

'Mr. Quatermain,' said Sir Henry, who had been giving me the most serious attention; 'your motives for undertaking an enterprise which you believe can only end in disaster reflect a great deal of credit on you. Whether or not you are right, time and the event of course alone can show. But whether you are right or wrong, I may as well tell you at once that I am going through with it to the end, sweet or bitter. If we are going to be knocked on the head, all I have to say is that I hope we shall get a little shooting first, eh, Good?'

'Yes, yes,' put in the captain. 'We have all three of us been accustomed to face danger, and hold our lives in our hands in various ways, so it is no good turning back now.'

'And now I vote we go down to the saloon and take an observation, just for luck, you know.' And we did – through the bottom of a tumbler.

Next day we went ashore, and I put Sir Henry and Captain Good up at the little shanty I have on the Berea, and which I call my home. There are only three rooms and a kitchen in it and it is built of green brick with a galvanized iron roof, but there is a good garden with the best loquot trees in it that I know, and some nice young mangoes, of which I hope great things. The curator of the botanical gardens gave them to me. It is looked after by an old hunter of mine, named Jack, whose thigh was so badly broken by a buffalo cow in Sikukunïs country, that he will never hunt again. But he can potter about and garden, being a Griqua by birth. You can never get your Zulu to take much interest in gardening. It is a peaceful art, and peaceful arts are not in his line.

Sir Henry and Good slept in a tent pitched in my little grove of orange trees at the end of the garden (for there was no room for them in the house), and what with the smell of the bloom and the sight of the green and golden fruit – for in Durban you will see all three on the tree together – I daresay it is a pleasant place enough (for we have few mosquitoes here unless there happens to come an unusually heavy rain).

Well, to get on – for unless I do you will be tired of my story before ever we fetch up at Suliman's Mountains – having once made up my mind to go I set about making the necessary preparations. First I got the deed from Sir Henry, providing for my boy in case of accidents. There was some little difficulty about getting this legally executed, as Sir Henry was a stranger here, and the property to be charged was over the water, but it was ultimately got over with the help of a lawyer, who charged £20 for the job – a price that I thought outrageous. Then I got my cheque for £500. Having paid this tribute to my bump of caution, I bought a wagon and a span of oxen on Sir Henry's behalf, and beauties they were. It was a twenty-two-foot wagon with iron axles, very strong, very light, and built throughout of stink wood. It was not quite a new one, having been to the Diamond Fields and back, but in my opinion it was all the better for that, for one could see that the wood was well seasoned. If anything is going to give in a wagon, or if there is green wood in it, it will show out on the first trip. It was what we call a 'half-tented' wagon, that is to say, it was only covered in over the after twelve feet, leaving all the front part free for the necessaries we had to carry with us. In this after part was a hide 'cartle', or bed, on which two people could sleep, also racks for rifles, and many other little conveniences. I gave £125 for it, and think it was cheap at the price. Then I bought a beautiful team of twenty salted Zulu oxen, which I had had my eye on for a year or two. Sixteen oxen are the usual number for a team, but I had four extra to allow for casualties. These Zulu oxen are small and light, not more than half the size of the Africander oxen, which are generally used for transport purposes; but they will live where the Africanders will starve, and with a light load will make five miles a day better going, being quicker and not so liable to get footsore. What is more, this lot were thoroughly 'salted', that is, they had worked all over South Africa, and so had become proof (comparatively speaking) against red water, which so frequently destroys whole teams of oxen when they get on to strange 'veldt' (grass country). As for 'lung sick', which is a dreadful form of pneumonia, very prevalent in this country, they had all been inoculated against it. This is done by cutting a slit in the tail of an ox, and binding in a piece of the diseased lung of an animal which has died of the sickness. The result is that the ox sickens, takes the disease in a mild form, which causes its tail to drop off, as a rule about a foot from the root, and becomes proof against future attacks. It seems cruel to rob the animal of his tail, especially in a country where there are so many flies, but it is better to sacrifice the tail and keep the ox than to lose both tail and ox, for a tail without an ox is not much good except to dust with. Still it does look odd to trek along behind twenty stumps, where there ought to be tails. It seems as though nature had made a trifling mistake, and stuck the stern ornaments of a lot of prize bulldogs on to the rumps of the oxen.

Next came the question of provisioning and medicines, one which required the most careful consideration, for what one had to do was to avoid lumbering the wagon up, and yet take everything absolutely necessary. Fortunately, it turned out that Good was a bit of a doctor, having at some period in his previous career managed to pass through a course of medical and surgical instruction, which he had more or less kept up. He was not, of course, qualified, but he knew more about it than many a man who could write M.D. after his name, as we found out afterwards, and he had a splendid travelling medicine chest and a set of instruments. Whilst we were at Durban he cut off a Kafir's big toe in a way which it was a pleasure to see. But he was quite flabbergasted when the Kafir, who had sat stolidly watching the operation, asked him to put on another, saying that a 'white one' would do at a pinch.

There remained, when these questions were satisfactorily settled, two further important points for consideration, namely, that of arms and that of servants. As to the arms I cannot do better than put down a list of those we finally decided on from among the ample store that Sir Henry had brought with him from England, and those which I had. I copy it from my pocket-book, where I made the entry at the time.

'Three heavy breechloading double-eight elephant guns, weighing about fifteen pounds each, with a charge of eleven drachms of black powder.' Two of these were by a well-known London firm, most excellent makers, but I do not know by whom mine, which was not so highly finished, was made. I had used it on several trips, and shot a good many elephants with it, and it had always proved a most superior weapon, thoroughly to be relied on.

'Three double .500 expresses, constructed to carry a charge of six drachms,' sweet weapons, and admirable for medium-sized game, such as eland or sable antelope, or for men, especially in an open country and with the semi-hollow bullet.

'One double No. 12 central-fire Keeper's shot-gun, full choke both barrels.' This gun proved of the greatest service to us afterwards in shooting game for the pot.

'Three Winchester repeating rifles (not carbines), spare guns.

'Three single-action Colt's revolvers, with the heavier pattern of cartridge.'

This was our total armament, and the reader will doubtless observe that the weapons of each class were of the same make and calibre, so that the cartridges were interchangeable, a very important point. I make no apology for detailing it at length, for every experienced hunter will know how vital a proper supply of guns and ammunition is to the success of an expedition.

Now as to the men who were to go with us. After much consultation we decided that their number should be limited to five, namely, a driver, a leader, and three servants.

The driver and leader I got without much difficulty, two Zulus, named respectively Goza and Tom; but the servants were a more difficult matter. It was necessary that they should be thoroughly trustworthy and brave men, as in a business of this sort our lives might depend upon their conduct. At last I secured two, one a Hottentot called Ventvögel (windbird), and one a little Zulu named Khiva, who had the merit of speaking English perfectly. Ventvögel I had known before; he was one of the most perfect 'spoorers' (game trackers) I ever had to do with, and tough as whipcord. He never seemed to tire. But he had one failing, so common with his race, drink. Put him within reach of a bottle of grog and you could not trust him. But as we were going beyond the region of grog-shops this little weakness of his did not so much matter.

Having got these two men I looked in vain for a third to suit my purpose, so we determined to start without one, trusting to luck to find a suitable man on our way up country. But on the evening before the day we had fixed for our departure the Zulu Khiva informed me that a man was waiting to see me. Accordingly when we had done dinner, for we were at table at the time, I told him to bring him in. Presently a very tall, handsome-looking man, somewhere about thirty years of age, and very light-coloured for a Zulu, entered, and, lifting his knob-stick by way of salute, squatted himself down in the corner on his haunches, and sat silent. I did not take any notice of him for a while, for it is a great mistake to do so. If you rush into conversation at once, a Zulu is apt to think you a person of little dignity or consideration. I observed, however, that he was a 'Keshla' (ringed man), that is, that he wore on his head the black ring, made of a species of gum polished with fat and worked in with the hair, usually assumed by Zulus on attaining a certain age or dignity. Also it struck me that his face was familiar to me.

'Well,' I said at last, 'what is your name?'

'Umbopa,' answered the man in a slow, deep voice.

'I have seen your face before.'

'Yes; the Inkosi (chief) saw my face at the place of the Little Hand (Isandhlwana) the day before the battle.'

Then I remembered. I had been one of Lord Chelmsford's guides in that unlucky Zulu War, and had had the good fortune to leave the camp in charge of some wagons the day before the battle. While I had been waiting for the cattle to be inspanned I had fallen into conversation with this man, who held some small command among the native auxiliaries, and he had expressed to me his doubts of the safety of the camp. At the time I had told him to hold his tongue, and leave such matters to wiser heads; but afterwards I thought of his words.

'I remember,' I said; 'what is it you want?'

'It is this, "Macumazahn"' – that is my Kafir name, and means the man who gets up in the middle of the night, or, in vulgar English, he who keeps his eyes open – 'I hear that you go on a great expedition far into the North with the white chiefs from over the water. Is it a true word?'

'It is.'

'I hear that you go even to the Lukanga River, a moon's journey beyond the Manica country. Is this so also, "Macumazahn"?'

'Why do you ask whither we go? What is it to thee?' I answered, suspiciously, for the objects of our journey had been kept a dead secret.

'It is this, O white men, that if indeed you travel so far I would travel with you.'

There was a certain assumption of dignity in the man's mode of speech, and especially in his use of the words 'O white men,' instead of 'O Inkosis' (chiefs), which struck me.

'You forget yourself a little,' I said. 'Your words come out unawares. That is not the way to speak. What is your name, and where is your kraal? Tell us, that we may know with whom we have to deal.'

'My name is Umbopa. I am of the Zulu people, yet not of them. The house of my tribe is in the far North; it was left behind when the Zulus came down here a "thousand years ago," long before Chaka reigned in Zululand. I have no kraal. I have wandered for many years. I came from the North as a child to Zululand. I was Cetywayo's man in the Nkomabakosi Regiment. I ran away from Zululand and came to Natal because I wanted to see the white man's ways. Then I served against Cetywayo in the war. Since then I have been working in Natal. Now I am tired, and would go North again. Here is not my place. I want no money, but I am a brave man, and am worth my place and meat. I have spoken.'

I was rather puzzled at this man and his way of speech. It was evident to me from his manner that he was in the main telling the truth, but he was somehow different from the ordinary run of Zulus, and I rather mistrusted his offer to come without pay. Being in a difficulty, I translated his words to Sir Henry and Good, and asked them their opinion. Sir Henry told me to ask him to stand up. Umbopa did so, at the same time slipping off the long military great coat he wore, and revealing himself naked except for the moocha round his centre and a necklace of lions' claws. He certainly was a magnificent-looking man; I never saw a finer native. Standing about six foot three high, he was broad in proportion, and very shapely. In that light, too, his skin looked scarcely more than dark, except here and there where deep black scars marked old assegai wounds. Sir Henry walked up to him and looked into his proud, handsome face.

'They make a good pair, don't they?' said Good; 'one as big as the other.'

'I like your looks, Mr. Umbopa, and I will take you as my servant,' said Sir Henry in English.

Umbopa evidently understood him, for he answered in Zulu, 'It is well'; and then with a glance at the white man's great stature and breadth, 'we are men, you and I.'

4

An Elephant Hunt

NOW I do not propose to narrate at full length all the incidents of our long journey up to Sitanda's Kraal, near the junction of the Lukanga and Kalukwe Rivers, a journey of more than a thousand miles from Durban, the last three hundred or so of which, owing to the frequent presence of the dreadful 'tsetse' fly, whose bite is fatal to all animals except donkeys and men, we had to make on foot.

We left Durban at the end of January, and it was in the second week of May that we camped near Sitanda's Kraal. Our adventures on the way were many and various, but as they were of the sort which befall every African hunter, I shall not – with one exception to be presently detailed – set them down here, lest I should render this history too wearisome.

At Inyati, the outlying trading station in the Matabele country, of which Lobengula (a great scoundrel) is king, we with many regrets parted from our comfortable wagon. Only twelve oxen remained to us out of the beautiful span of twenty which I had bought at Durban. One we had lost from the bite of a cobra, three had perished from poverty and the want of water, one had been lost, and the other three had died from eating the poisonous herb called 'tulip'. Five more sickened from this cause, but we managed to cure them with doses of an infusion made by boiling down the tulip leaves. If administered in time this is a very effective antidote. The wagon and oxen we left in the immediate charge of Goza and Tom, the driver and leader, both of them trustworthy boys, requesting a worthy Scotch missionary who lived in this wild place to keep an eye to it. Then, accompanied by Umbopa, Khiva, Ventvögel, and half a dozen bearers whom we hired on the spot, we started off on foot upon our wild quest. I remember we were all a little silent on the occasion of that departure, and I think that each of us was wondering if we should ever see that wagon again;

for my part I never expected to. For a while we tramped on in silence, till Umbopa, who was marching in front, broke into a Zulu chant about how some brave men, tired of life and the tameness of things, started off into a great wilderness to find new things or die, and how, lo, and behold! when they had got far into the wilderness, they found it was not a wilderness at all, but a beautiful place full of young wives and fat cattle, of game to hunt and enemies to kill.

Then we all laughed and took it for a good omen. He was a cheerful savage was Umbopa, in a dignified sort of a way, when he had not got one of his fits of brooding, and had a wonderful knack of keeping one's spirits up. We all got very fond of him.

And now for the one adventure I am going to treat myself to, for I do dearly love a hunting yarn.

About a fortnight's march from Inyati, we came across a peculiarly beautiful bit of fairly-watered wooded country. The kloofs in the hills were covered with dense bush, 'idoro' bush as the natives call it, and in some places, with the 'wachteen-beche' (wait-a-little) thorn, and there were great quantities of the beautiful 'machabell' tree, laden with refreshing yellow fruit with enormous stones. This tree is the elephant's favourite food, and there were not wanting signs that the great brutes were about, for not only was their spoor frequent, but in many places the trees were broken down and even up-rooted. The elephant is a destructive feeder.

One evening, after a long day's march, we came to a spot of peculiar loveliness. At the foot of a bush-clad hill was a dry river-bed, in which, however, were to be found pools of crystal water all trodden round with the hoof-prints of game. Facing this hill was a park-like plain, where grew clumps of flat-topped mimosa, varied with occasional glossy-leaved machabells, and all round was the great sea of pathless, silent bush.

As we emerged into this river-bed path we suddenly started a troop of tall giraffes, who galloped, or rather sailed off, with their strange gait, their tails screwed up over their backs, and their hoofs rattling like castanets. They were about three hundred yards from us, and therefore practically out of shot, but Good, who was walking ahead, and had an express loaded with solid ball in his hand, could not resist, but upped gun and let drive at the last, a young cow. By some extraordinary chance the ball struck it full on the back of the neck, shattering the spinal column, and that giraffe went rolling head over heels just like a rabbit. I never saw a more curious thing.

'Curse it!' said Good – for I am sorry to say he had a habit of using strong language when excited – contracted, no doubt, in the course of his nautical career; 'curse it! I've killed him.'

'Ou, Bougwan,' ejaculated the Kafirs; 'ou! ou!'

They called Good 'Bougwan' (glass eye) because of his eyeglass.

'Ou, "Bougwan"!' re-echoed Sir Henry and I, and from that day Good's reputation as a marvellous shot was established, at any rate among the

Kafirs. Really he was a bad one, but whenever he missed we overlooked it for the sake of that giraffe.

Having set some of the 'boys' to cut off the best of the giraffe meat, we went to work to build a 'scherm' near one of the pools about a hundred yards to the right of it. This is done by cutting a quantity of thorn bushes and laying them in the shape of a circular hedge. Then the space enclosed is smoothed, and dry tambouki grass, if obtainable, is made into a bed in the centre, and a fire or fires lighted.

By the time the 'scherm' was finished the moon was coming up, and our dinner of giraffe steaks and roasted marrow bones was ready. How we enjoyed those marrow-bones, though it was rather a job to crack them! I know no greater luxury than giraffe marrow, unless it is elephant's heart, and we had that on the morrow. We ate our simple meal, pausing at times to thank Good for his wonderful shot, by the light of the full moon, and then we began to smoke and yarn, and a curious picture we must have made squatted there round the fire. I, with my short, grizzled hair sticking up straight, and Sir Henry with his yellow locks, which were getting rather long, were rather a contrast, especially as I am thin, and short, and dark, weighing only nine stone and a half, and Sir Henry is tall, and broad, and fair, and weighs fifteen. But perhaps the most curious looking of the three, taking all the circumstances of the case into consideration, was Captain John Good, R.N. There he sat upon a leather bag, looking just as though he had come in from a comfortable day's shooting in a civilized country, absolutely clean, tidy, and well dressed. He had on a shooting suit of brown tweed, with a hat to match, and neat gaiters. He was, as usual, beautifully shaved, his eyeglass and his false teeth appeared to be in perfect order, and altogether he was the neatest man I ever had to do with in the wilderness. He even had on a collar, of which he had a supply, made of white guttapercha.

'You see, they weigh so little,' he said to me, innocently, when I expressed my astonishment at the fact; 'I always like to look like a gentleman.'

Well, there we all sat yarning away in the beautiful moonlight, and watching the Kafirs a few yards off sucking their intoxicating 'daccha' in a pipe of which the mouthpiece was made of the horn of an eland, till they one by one rolled themselves up in their blankets and went to sleep by the fire, that is, all except Umbopa, who sat a little apart (I noticed he never mixed much with the other Kafirs), his chin resting on his hand, apparently thinking deeply.

Presently, from the depths of the bush behind us, came a loud 'woof, woof!' 'That's a lion,' said I, and we all started up to listen. Hardly had we done so, when from the pool, about a hundred yards off, came the strident trumpeting of an elephant. 'Unkungunklovo! Unkungunklovo!' (elephant! elephant!) whispered the Kafirs; and a few minutes afterwards we saw a succession of vast shadowy forms moving slowly from the direction of the water towards the bush. Up jumped Good, burning for slaughter, and thinking, perhaps, that it was as easy to kill elephant as he had found it to shoot giraffe, but I caught him by the arm and pulled him down.

'It's no good,' I said, 'let them go.'

'It seems that we are in a paradise of game. I vote we stop here a day or two, and have a go at them,' said Sir Henry presently.

I was rather surprised, for hitherto Sir Henry had always been for pushing on as fast as possible, more especially since we had ascertained at Inyati that about two years ago an Englishman of the name of Neville *had* sold his wagon there, and gone on up country; but I suppose his hunter instincts had got the better of him.

Good jumped at the idea, for he was longing to have a go at those elephants; and so, to speak the truth, did I, for it went against my conscience to let such a herd as that escape without having a pull at them.

'All right, my hearties,' said I. 'I think we want a little recreation. And now let's turn in, for we ought to be off by dawn, and then perhaps we may catch them feeding before they move on.'

The others agreed, and we proceeded to make preparations. Good took off his clothes, shook them, put his eyeglass and his false teeth into his trousers pocket, and folding them all up neatly, placed them out of the dew under a corner of his mackintosh sheet. Sir Henry and I contented ourselves with rougher arrangements, and were soon curled up in our blankets, and dropping off into the dreamless sleep that rewards the traveller.

Going, going, go – What was that?

Suddenly from the direction of the water came a sound of violent scuffling, and next instant there broke upon our ears a succession of the most awful roars. There was no mistaking what they came from; only a lion could make such a noise as that. We all jumped up and looked towards the water, in the direction of which we saw a confused mass, yellow and black in colour, staggering and struggling towards us. We seized our rifles, and slipping on our veldtschoons (shoes made of untanned hide), ran out of the scherm towards it. By this time it had fallen, and was rolling over and over on the ground, and by the time we reached it it struggled no longer, but was quite still.

And this was what it was. On the grass there lay a sable antelope bull – the most beautiful of all the African antelopes – quite dead, and transfixed by its great curved horns was a magnificent black-maned lion, also dead. What had happened evidently was this. The sable antelope had come down to drink at the pool where the lion – no doubt the same we had heard – had been lying in wait. While the antelope was drinking the lion had sprung upon him, but was received upon the sharp curved horns and transfixed. I once saw the same thing happen before. The lion, unable to free himself, had torn and bitten at the back and neck of the bull, which, maddened with fear and pain, had rushed on till it dropped dead.

As soon as we had sufficiently examined the dead beasts we called the Kafirs, and between us managed to drag their carcasses up to the scherm. Then we went in and lay down, to wake no more till dawn.

With the first light we were up and making ready for the fray. We took with us the three eight-bore rifles, a good supply of ammunition, and our large water-bottles, filled with weak, cold tea, which I have always found the best stuff to shoot on. After swallowing a little breakfast we started, Umbopa, Khiva, and Ventvögel accompanying us. The other Kafirs we left with instructions to skin the lion and the sable antelope, and cut up the latter.

We had no difficulty in finding the broad elephant trail, which Ventvögel, after examination, pronounced to have been made by between twenty and thirty elephants, most of them full-grown bulls. But the herd had moved on some way during the night, and it was nine o'clock, and already very hot, before, from the broken trees, bruised leaves and bark, and smoking dung, we knew we could not be far off them.

Presently we caught sight of the herd, numbering, as Ventvögel had said, between twenty and thirty, standing in a hollow, having finished their morning meal, and flapping their great ears. It was a splendid sight.

They were about two hundred yards from us. Taking a handful of dry grass I threw it into the air to see how the wind was; for if once they winded us I knew they would be off before we could get a shot. Finding that, if anything, it blew from the elephants to us, we crept stealthily on, and thanks to the cover managed to get within forty yards or so of the great brutes. Just in front of us and broadside on stood three splendid bulls, one of them with enormous tusks. I whispered to the others that I would take the middle one; Sir Henry covered the one to the left, and Good the bull with the big tusks.

'Now,' I whispered.

Boom! boom! boom! went the three heavy rifles, and down went Sir Henry's elephant dead as a hammer, shot right through the heart. Mine fell on to its knees, and I thought he was going to die, but in another moment he was up and off, tearing along straight past me. As he went I gave him the second barrel in the ribs, and this brought him down in good earnest. Hastily slipping in two fresh cartridges, I ran close up to him, and a ball through the brain put an end to the poor brute's struggles. Then I turned to see how Good had fared with the big bull, which I had heard screaming with rage and pain as I gave mine its quietus. On reaching the captain I found him in a great state of excitement. It appeared that on receiving the bullet the bull had turned and come straight for his assailant, who had barely time to get out of his way, and then charged blindly on past him, in the direction of our encampment. Meanwhile the herd had crashed off in wild alarm in the other direction.

For a while we debated whether to go after the wounded bull or follow the herd, and finally decided for the latter alternative, and departed thinking that we had seen the last of those big tusks. I have often wished since that we had. It was easy work to follow the elephants, for they had left a trail like a carriage road behind them, crushing down the thick bush in their furious flight as though it were tambouki grass.

But to come up with them was another matter, and we had struggled on under a broiling sun for over two hours before we found them. They were, with the exception of one bull, standing together, and I could see, from their unquiet way and the manner in which they kept lifting their trunks to test the air, that they were on the look out for mischief. The solitary bull stood fifty yards or so this side of the herd, over which he was evidently keeping sentry, and about sixty yards from us. Thinking that he would see or wind us, and that it would probably start them all off again if we tried to get nearer, especially as the ground was rather open, we all aimed at this bull, and at my whispered word fired. All three shots took effect, and down he went, dead. Again the herd started on, but unfortunately for them about a hundred yards farther on was a nullah, or dried water track, with steep banks, a place very much resembling the one the Prince Imperial was killed in in Zululand. Into this the elephants plunged, and when we reached the edge we found them struggling in wild confusion to get up the other bank, and filling the air with their screams, and trumpeting as they pushed one another aside in their selfish panic, just like so many human beings. Now was our opportunity, and firing away as quick as we could load we killed five of the poor beasts, and no doubt should have bagged the whole herd had they not suddenly given up their attempts to climb the bank and rushed headlong down the nullah. We were too tired to follow them, and perhaps also a little sick of slaughter, eight elephants being a pretty good bag for one day.

So after we had rested a little, and the Kafirs had cut out the hearts of two of the dead elephants for supper, we started homewards, very well pleased with ourselves, having made up our minds to send the bearers on the morrow to chop out the tusks.

Shortly after we had passed the spot where Good had wounded the patriarchal bull we came across a herd of eland, but did not shoot at them, as we had already plenty of meat. They trotted past us, and then stopped behind a little patch of bush about a hundred yards away and wheeled round to look at us. As Good was anxious to get a near view of them, never having seen an eland close, he handed his rifle to Umbopa, and, followed by Khiva, strolled up to the patch of bush. We sat down and waited for him, not sorry of the excuse for a little rest.

The sun was just going down in its reddest glory, and Sir Henry and I were admiring the lovely scene, when suddenly we heard an elephant scream, and saw its huge and charging form with uplifted trunk and tail silhouetted against the great red globe of the sun. Next second we saw something else, and that was Good and Khiva tearing back towards us with the wounded bull (for it was he) charging after them. For a moment we did not dare to fire – though it would have been little use if we had at that distance – for fear of hitting one of them, and the next a dreadful thing happened – Good fell a victim to his passion for civilized dress. Had he consented to discard his trousers and gaiters as we had, and hunt in a flannel shirt and a pair of veldtschoons, it would have been all right, but as it was his trousers cumbered him in that desperate race, and presently, when he was about sixty yards from us, his boot, polished by the dry grass, slipped, and down he went on his face right in front of the elephant.

We gave a gasp, for we knew he must die, and ran as hard as we could towards him. In three seconds it had ended, but not as we thought. Khiva, the Zulu boy, had seen his master fall, and brave lad that he was, had turned and flung his assegai straight into the elephant's face. It stuck in his trunk.

With a scream of pain the brute seized the poor Zulu, hurled him to the earth, and placing his huge foot on to his body about the middle, twined his trunk round his upper part and tore him in two.

We rushed up mad with horror, and fired again, and again, and presently the elephant fell upon the fragments of the Zulu.

As for Good, he got up and wrung his hands over the brave man who had given his life to save him, and myself, though an old hand, I felt a lump in my throat. Umbopa stood and contemplated the huge dead elephant and the mangled remains of poor Khiva.

'Ah well,' he said presently, 'he is dead, but he died like a man.'

5

Our March into the Desert

WE had killed nine elephants, and it took us two days to cut out the tusks and get them home and bury them carefully in the sand under a large tree, which made a conspicuous mark for miles round. It was a wonderfully fine lot of ivory. I never saw a better, averaging as it did between forty and fifty pounds a tusk. The tusks of the great bull that kiled poor Khiva scaled one hundred and seventy pounds the pair, as nearly as we could judge.

As for Khiva himself, we buried what remained of him in an ant-bear hole, together with an assegai to protect himself with on his journey to a better world. On the third day we started on, hoping that we might one day return to dig up our buried ivory, and in due course, after a long and wearisome tramp, and many adventures which I have no space to detail, reached Sitanda's Kraal, near the Lukanga River, the real starting-point of our expedition. Very well do I recollect our arrival at that place. To the right was a scattered native settlement with a few stone cattle kraals and some cultivated lands down by the water, where these savages grew their scanty supply of grain, and beyond it great tracts of waving 'veldt' covered with tall grass, over which herds of the smaller game were wandering. To the left was the vast desert. This spot appeared to be the outpost of the fertile country, and it would be difficult to say to what natural causes such an abrupt change in the character of the soil was due. But so it was. Just below our encampment flowed a little stream, on the father side of which was a stony slope, the same down which I had twenty years before seen poor Silvestre creeping back after his attempt to reach Solomon's Mines, and beyond that slope began the waterless desert covered with a species of karoo shrub. It was evening when we pitched our camp, and the great fiery ball of the sun was sinking into the desert, sending glorious rays of many-coloured light flying over all the vast expanse. Leaving Good to superintend the arrangement of our little camp, I took Sir Henry with me, and we walked to the top of the slope opposite and gazed out across the desert. The air was very clear, and far, far away I could distinguish the faint blue outlines here and there capped with white of the great Suliman Berg.

'There,' I said, 'there is the wall of Solomon's Mines, but God knows if we shall ever climb it.'

'My brother should be there, and if he is, I shall reach him somehow,' said Sir Henry, in that tone of quiet confidence which marked the man.

'I hope so,' I answered, and turned to go back to the camp, when I saw that we were not alone. Behind us, also gazing earnestly towards the far-off mountains, stood the great Zulu Umbopa.

The Zulu spoke when he saw that I had observed him, but addressed himself to Sir Henry, to whom he had attached himself.

'Is it to that land that thou wouldst journey, Incubu?' (a native word meaning, I believe, an elephant, and the name given to Sir Henry by the Kafirs) he said, pointing towards the mountains with his broad assegai.

I asked him sharply what he meant by addressing his master in that familiar way. It is very well for natives to have a name for one among themselves, but it is not decent that they should call one by their heathenish appellations to one's face. The man laughed a quiet little laugh which angered me.

'How dost thou know that I am not the equal of the Inkosi I serve?' he said. 'He is of a royal house, no doubt; one can see it in his size and in his eye; so, mayhap, am I. At least I am as great a man. Be my mouth, oh Macumazahn, and say my words to the Inkoos Incubu, my master, for I would speak to him and to thee.'

I was angry with the man, for I am not accustomed to be talked to in that way by Kafirs, but somehow he impressed me, and besides I was curious to know what he had to say, so I translated, expressing my opinion at the same time that he was an impudent fellow, and that his swagger was outrageous.

'Yes, Umbopa,' answered Sir Henry, 'I would journey there.'

'The desert is wide and there is no water, the mountains are high and covered with snow, and man cannot say what is beyond them behind the place where the sun sets; how shalt thou come thither, Incubu, and wherefore dost thou go?'

I translated again.

'Tell him,' answered Sir Henry, 'that I go because I believe that a man of my blood, my brother, has gone there before me, and I go to seek him.'

'That is so, Incubu; a man I met on the road told me that a white man went out into the desert two years ago towards those mountains with one servant, a hunter. They never came back.'

'How do you know it was my brother?' asked Sir Henry.

'Nay, I know not. But the man, when I asked what the white man was like, said that he had thine eyes and a black beard. He said, too, that the name of the hunter with him was Jim, that he was a Bechuana hunter and wore clothes.'

'There is no doubt about it,' said I; 'I knew Jim well.'

Sir Henry nodded. 'I was sure of it,' he said. 'If George set his mind upon a thing he generally did it. It was always so from his boyhood. If he meant to cross the Suliman Berg he has crossed it, unless some accident has overtaken him, and we must look for him on the other side.'

Umbopa understood English, though he rarely spoke it.

'It is a far journey, Incubu,' he put in, and I translated his remark.

'Yes,' answered Sir Henry, 'it is far. But there is no journey upon this earth that a man may not make if he sets his heart to it. There is nothing, Umbopa, that he cannot do, there are no mountains he may not climb, there are no deserts he cannot cross, save a mountain and a desert of which you are spared the knowledge, if love leads him and he holds his life in his hand counting it as nothing, ready to keep it or to lose it as Providence may order.'

I translated.

'Great words, my father,' answered the Zulu (I always called him a Zulu, though he was not really one), 'great swelling words fit to fill the mouth of a man. Thou art right, my father Incubu. Listen! what is Life? It is a feather, it is the seed of the grass, blown hither and thither, sometimes multiplying itself and dying in the act, sometimes carried away into the heavens. But if the seed be good and heavy it may perchance travel a little way on the road it wills. It is well to try and journey one's road and to fight with the air. Man must die. At the worst he can but die a little sooner. I will go with thee across the desert and over the mountains, unless perchance I fall to the ground on the way, my father.'

He paused awhile, and then went on with one of those strange bursts of rhetorical eloquence which Zulus sometimes indulge in, and which to my mind, full as they are of vain repetitions, show that the race is by no means devoid of poetic instinct and of intellectual power.

'What is life? Tell me, O white men, who are wise, who know the secrets of the world, and the world of stars, and the world that lies above and around the stars; who flash their words from afar without a voice; tell me, white men, the secret of our life – whither it goes and whence it comes!

'Ye cannot answer; ye know not. Listen, I will answer. Out of the dark we came, into the dark we go. Like a storm-driven bird at night we fly out of the Nowhere; for a moment our wings are seen in the light of the fire, and, lo! we are gone again into the Nowhere. Life is nothing. Life is all. It is the hand with which we hold off Death. It is the glow-worm that shines in the night-time and is black in the morning; it is the white breath of the oxen in winter; it is the little shadow that runs across the grass and loses itself at sunset.'

'You are a strange man,' said Sir Henry, when he ceased.

Umbopa laughed. 'It seems to me that we are much alike, Incubu. Perhaps *I* seek a brother over the mountains.'

I looked at him suspiciously. 'What dost thou meant?' I asked; 'what dost thou know of the mountains:'

'A little; a very little. There is a strange land there, a land of witchcraft and beautiful things; a land of brave people, and of trees, and streams, and white mountains, and of a great white road. I have heard of it. But what is the good of talking: it grows dark. Those who live to see will see.'

Again I looked at him doubtfully. The man knew too much.

'Ye need not fear me, Macumazahn,' he said interpreting my look. 'I dig no holes for ye to fall in. I make no plots. If ever we cross those mountains behind the sun, I will tell what I know. But Death sits upon them. Be wise and turn back. Go and hunt elephant. I have spoken.'

And without another word he lifted his spear in salutation, and returned towards the camp, where shortly afterwards we found him cleaning a gun like any other Kafir.

'That is an odd man,' said Sir Henry.

'Yes,' answered I, 'too odd by half. I don't like his little ways. He knows something, and won't speak out. But I suppose it is no use quarrelling with him. We are in for a curious trip, and a mysterious Zulu won't make much difference one way or another.'

Next day we made our arrangements for starting. Of course it was impossible to drag our heavy elephant rifles and other kit with us across the desert, so dismissing our bearers we made an arrangement with an old native who had a kraal close by to take care of them till we returned. It went to my heart to leave such things as those sweet tools to the tender mercies of an old thief, of a savage whose greedy eyes I could see gloating over them. But I took some precautions.

First of all I loaded all the rifles, and informed him that if he touched them they would go off. He instantly tried the experiment with my eight bore, and it did go off, and blew a hole right through one of his oxen, which were just then being driven up to the kraal, to say nothing of knocking him head over heels with the recoil. He got up considerably startled, and not at all pleased at the loss of the ox, which he had the impudence to ask me to pay for, and nothing would induce him to touch them again.

'Put the live devils up there in the thatch,' he said, 'out of the way, or they will kill us all.'

Then I told him that if, when we came back, one of those things was missing I would kill him and all his people by witchcraft; and if we died and he tried to steal the things I would come and haunt him and turn his cattle mad and his milk sour till life was a weariness, and make the devils in the guns come out and talk to him in a way he would not like, and generally gave him a good idea of judgement to come. After that he swore he would look after them as though they were his father's spirit. He was a very superstitious old Kafir and a great villain.

Having thus disposed of our superfluous gear we arranged the kit we five – Sir Henry, Good, myself, Umbopa, and the Hottentot, Ventvögel – were to take with us on our journey. It was small enough, but do what we would we could not get it down under about forty pounds a man. This is what it consisted of:

The three express rifles and two hundred rounds of ammunition.

The two Winchester repeating rifles (for Umbopa and Ventvögel), with two hundred rounds of cartridge.

Three 'Colt' revolvers and sixty rounds of cartridge.

Five Cochrane's water-bottles, each holding four pints.

Five blankets.

Twenty-five pounds' weight of biltong (sun-dried game flesh).

Ten pounds' weight of best mixed beads for gifts.

A selection of medicine, including an ounce of quinine, and one or two small surgical instruments.

Our knives, a few sundries, such as a compass, matches, a pocket filter, tobacco, a trowel, a bottle of brandy, and the clothes we stood in.

This was our total equipment, a small one indeed for such a venture, but we dared not attempt to carry more. As it was that load was a heavy one per man to travel across the burning desert with, for in such places every additional ounce tells upon one. But try as we would we could not see our way to reducing it. There was nothing but what was absolutely necessary.

With great difficulty, and by the promise of a present of a good hunting knife each, I succeeded in persuading three wretched natives from the village to come with us for the first stage, twenty miles, and to carry each a large gourd holding a gallon of water. My object was to enable us to refill our water-bottles after the first night's march, for we determined to start in the cool of the night. I gave out to these natives that we were going to shoot ostriches, with which the desert abounded. They jabbered and shrugged their shoulders, and said we were mad and should perish of thirst, which I must say seemed very probable; but being desirous of obtaining the knives, which were almost unknown treasures up there, they consented to come, having probably reflected that, after all, our subsequent extinction would be no affair of theirs.

All next day we rested and slept, and at sunset ate a hearty meal of fresh beef washed down with tea, the last, as Good sadly remarked, we were likely to drink for many a long day. Then, having made our final preparations, we lay down and waited for the moon to rise. At last about nine o'clock up she came in all her chastened glory, flooding the wild country with silver light, and throwing a weird sheen on the vast expanse of rolling desert before us, which looked as solemn and quiet and as alien to man as the star-studded firmament above. We rose up, and in a few minutes were ready, and yet we hesitated a little, as human nature is prone to hesitate on the threshold of an irrevocable step. We three white men stood there by ourselves. Umbopa, assegai in hand and the rifle across his shoulders, a few paces ahead of us, looked out fixedly across the desert; the three hired natives, with the gourds of water, and Ventvögel, were gathered in a little knot behind.

'Gentlemen,' said Sir Henry, presently, in his low, deep voice, 'we are going on about as strange a journey as men can make in this world. It is very doubtful if we can succeed in it. But we are three men who will stand together for good or for evil to the last. And now before we start let us for a moment pray to the Power who shapes the destinies of men, and who ages since has marked out our paths, that it may please Him to direct our steps in accordance with His will.'

Taking off his hat he, for the space of a minute or so, covered his face with his hands, and Good and I did likewise.

I do not say that I am a first-rate praying man, few hunters are, and as for Sir Henry I never heard him speak like that before, and only once since, though deep down in his heart I believe he is very religious. Good, too, is pious, though very apt to swear. Anyhow I do not think I ever, excepting on one single occasion, put in a better prayer in my life than I did during that minute, and somehow I felt the happier for it. Our future was so completely unknown, and I think the unknown and the awful always bring a man nearer to his Maker.

'And now,' said Sir Henry, '*trek*.'

So we started.

We had nothing to guide ourselves by except the distant mountains and old José da Silvestra's chart, which, considering that it was drawn by a dying and half-distraught man on a fragment of linen three centuries ago, was not a very satisfactory sort of thing to work on. Still, such as it was, our sole hope of success depended on it. If we failed in finding that pool of bad water which the old Dom marked as being situated in the middle of the desert, about sixty miles from our starting-point, and as far from the mountains, we must in all probability perish miserably of thirst. And to my mind the chances of our finding it in that great sea of sand and karoo scrub seemed almost infinitesimal. Even supposing da Silvestra had marked it right, what was there to prevent its having been generations ago dried up by the sun, or trampled in by game, or filled with the drifting sand?

On we tramped silently as shades through the night and in the heavy sand. The karoo bushes caught our shins and retarded us, and the sand got into our veldtschoons and Good's shooting boots, so that every few miles we had to stop and empty them; but still the night was fairly cool, though the atmosphere was thick and heavy, giving a sort of creamy feel to the air, and we made fair progress. It was very still and lonely there in the desert, oppressively so indeed. Good felt this, and once began to whistle the 'Girl I left behind me', but the notes sounded lugubrious in that vast place, and he gave it up. Shortly afterwards a little incident occurred which, though it made us jump at the time, gave rise to a laugh. Good, as the holder of the compass, which, being a sailor, of course he thoroughly understood, was leading, and we were toiling along in single file behind him, when suddenly we heard the sound of an exclamation, and he vanished. Next second there arose all round us a most extraordinary hubbub, snorts, groans, wild sounds of rushing feet. In the faint light too we could descry dim galloping forms half hidden by wreaths of sand. The natives threw down their loads and prepared to bolt, but remembering that there was nowhere to run to, cast themselves upon the ground and howled out that it was the devil. As for Sir Henry and myself we stood amazed; nor was our amazement lessened when we perceived the form of Good careering off in the direction of the mountains, apparently mounted on the back of a horse and halloaing like mad. In another second he threw up his arms, and we heard him come to the earth with a thud. Then I saw what had happened; we had stumbled right on to a herd of sleeping quagga, on to the back of one of which Good had actually fallen, and the brute had naturally enough got up and made off with him. Singing out to the others that it was all right I ran towards Good, much afraid lest he should be hurt, but to my great relief found him sitting in the sand, his eye-glass still fixed firmly in his eye, rather shaken and very much startled, but not in any way injured.

After this we travelled on without any further misadventure till after one o'clock, when we called a halt, and having drunk a little water, not much, for water was precious, and rested for half an hour, started on again.

On, on we went, till at last the east began to blush like the cheek of a girl. Then there came faint rays of primrose light, that changed presently to golden bars, through which the dawn glided out across the desert. The stars grew pale and paler still till at last they vanished; the golden moon waxed wan, and her mountain ridges stood out clear against her sickly face like the bones on the face of a dying man; then came spear upon spear of glorious light flashing far away across the boundless wilderness, piercing and firing the veils of mist, till the desert was draped in a tremulous golden glow, and it was day.

Still we did not halt, though by this time we should have been glad enough to do so, for we knew that when once the sun was fully up it would be almost impossible for us to travel in it. At length, about an hour later, we spied a little pile of rocks rising out of the plain, and to this we dragged ourselves. As luck would have it here we found an overhanging slab of rock carpeted beneath with smooth sand, which afforded a most grateful shelter from the heat. Underneath this we crept, and having drunk some water each and eaten a bit of biltong, we laid down and were soon sound asleep.

It was three o'clock in the afternoon before we woke, to find our three bearers preparing to return. They had already had enough of the desert, and no number of knives would have tempted them to come a step farther. So we had a hearty drink, and having emptied our water bottles filled them up again from the gourds they had brought with them, and then watched them depart on their twenty miles' tramp home.

At half past four we also started on. It was lonely and desolate work, for with the exception of a few ostriches there was not a single living creature to be seen on all the vast expanse of sandy plain. It was evidently too dry for game, and with the exception of a deadly-looking cobra or two we saw no reptiles. One insect, however, was abundant, and that was the common or house fly. There they came, 'not as single spies, but in battalions,' as I think the Old Testament says somewhere. He is an extraordinary animal is the house fly. Go where you will you find him, and so it must always have been. I have seen him enclosed in amber, which must, I was told, have been half a million years old, looking exactly like his descendant of today, and I have little doubt but that when the last man lies dying on the earth he will be buzzing round – if that event should happen to occur in summer – watching for an opportunity to settle on his nose.

At sunset we halted, waiting for the moon to rise. At ten she came up beautiful and serene as ever, and with one halt about two o'clock in the morning, we trudged wearily on through the night, till at last the welcome sun put a period to our labours. We drank a little and flung ourselves down, thoroughly tired out, on the sand, and were soon all asleep. There was no need to set a watch, for we had nothing to fear from anybody or anything in that vast untenanted plain. Our only enemies were heat, thirst, and flies, but far rather would I have faced any danger from man or beast than that awful trinity. This time we were not so lucky as to find a sheltering rock to guard us from the glare of the sun, with the result that about seven o'clock we woke up experiencing the exact sensations one would attribute to a beefsteak on a gridiron. We were literally being baked through and through. The burning sun seemed to be sucking our very blood out of us. We sat up and gasped.

'Phew,' said I, grabbing at the halo of flies, which buzzed cheerfully round my head. The heat did not affect them.

'My word,' said Sir Henry.

'It *is* hot!' said Good.

It was hot, indeed, and there was not a bit of shelter to be had. Look where we would there was no rock or tree, nothing but an unending glare, rendered dazzling by the hot air which danced over the surface of the desert as it does over a red-hot stove.

'What is to be done?' asked Sir Henry; 'we can't stand this for long.'

We looked at each other blankly.

'I have it,' said Good, 'we must dig a hole and get in it, and cover ourselves with the karoo bushes.'

It did not seem a very promising suggestion, but at least it was better than nothing, so we set to work, and with the trowel we had brought with us and our hands succeeded in about an hour in delving out a patch of ground about ten feet long by twelve wide to the depth of two feet. Then we cut a quantity of low scrub with our hunting knives, and creeping into the hole pulled it over us all, with the exception of Ventvögel, on whom, being a Hottentot, the sun had no particular effect. This gave us some slight shelter from the burning rays of the sun, but the heat in that amateur grave can be better imagined than described. The Black Hole of Calcutta must have been a fool to it; indeed, to this moment I do not know how we lived through the day. There we lay panting, and every now and again moistening our lips from our scanty supply of water. Had we followed our inclinations we should have finished all we had off in the first two hours, but we had to exercise the most rigid care, for if our water failed us we knew that we must quickly perish miserably.

But everything has an end, if only you live long enough to see it, and somehow that miserable day wore on towards evening. About three o'clock in the afternoon we determined that we could stand it no longer. It would be better to die walking than to be slowly killed by heat and thirst in that dreadful hole. So taking each of us a little drink from our fast diminishing supply of water, now heated to about the same temperature as a man's blood, we staggered on.

We had now covered some fifty miles of desert. If my reader will refer to the rough copy and translation of old da Silvestra's map, he will see that the desert is marked as being forty leagues across, and the 'pan bad water' is set down as being about in the middle of it. Now forty leagues is one hundred and twenty miles, consequently we ought at the most to be within twelve or fifteen miles of the water if any should really exist.

Through the afternoon we crept slowly and painfully along, scarcely doing more than a mile and a half an hour. At sunset we again rested, waiting for the moon, and after drinking a little managed to get some sleep.

Before we lay down, Umbopa pointed out to us a slight and indistinct hillock on the flat surface of the desert about eight miles away. At the distance it looked like an ant-hill, and as I was dropping off to sleep I fell to wondering what it could be.

With the moon we started on again, feeling dreadfully exhausted, and suffering tortures from thirst and prickly heat. Nobody who has not felt it can know what we went through. We no longer walked, we staggered, now and again falling from exhaustion, and being obliged to call a halt every hour or so. We had scarcely energy left in us to speak. Up to now Good had chatted and joked, for he was a merry fellow; but now he had not a joke left in him.

At last, about two o'clock, utterly worn out in body and mind, we came to the foot of this queer hill, or sand koppie, which did at first sight resemble a gigantic ant-heap about a hundred feet high, and covering at the base nearly a morgen (two acres) of ground.

Here we halted, and driven by our desperate thirst sucked down our last drops of water. We had but half a pint a head, and we could each have drunk a gallon.

Then we lay down. Just as I was dropping off to sleep I heard Umbopa remark to himself in Zulu:

'If we cannot find water we shall all be dead before the moon rises tomorrow.'

I shuddered, hot as it was. The near prospect of such an awful death is not pleasant, but even the thought of it could not keep me from sleeping.

6

Water! Water!

IN two hours time, about four o'clock, I woke up. As soon as the first heavy demand of bodily fatigue had been satisfied, the torturing thirst from which I was suffering asserted itself. I could sleep no more. I had been dreaming that I was bathing in a running stream, with green banks and trees upon them, and I awoke to find myself in that arid wilderness, and to remember that, as Umbopa had said, if we did not find water that day we must certainly perish miserably. No human creature could live long without water in that heat. I sat up and rubbed my grimy face with my dry and horny hands. My lips and eyelids were stuck together, and it was only after some rubbing and with an effort that I was able to open them. It was not far off the dawn, but there was none of the bright feel of dawn in the air, which was thick with a hot murkiness I cannot describe.

The others were still sleeping. Presently it began to grow light enough to read, so I drew out a little pocket copy of the *Ingoldsby Legends* I had brought with me, and read the 'Jackdaw of Rheims'. When I got to where

> A nice little boy held a golden ewer,
> Embossed, and filled with water as pure
> As any that flows between Rheims and Namur,

I literally smacked my cracked lips, or rather tried to smack them. The mere thought of that pure water made me mad. If the Cardinal had been there with his bell, book, and candle, I would have whipped in and drunk his water up, yes, even if he had already filled it with the suds of soap worthy of washing the hands of the Pope, and I knew that the whole concentrated curse of the Catholic Church should fall upon me for so doing. I almost think I must have been a little light-headed with thirst and weariness and want of food; for I fell to thinking how astonished the Cardinal and his nice little boy and the jackdaw would have looked to see a burnt up, brown-eyed, grizzled-haired little elephant hunter suddenly bound in and put his dirty face into the basin, and swallow every drop of the precious water. The idea amused me so that I laughed or rather cackled aloud, which woke the others up, and they began to rub *their* dirty faces and get *their* gummed-up lips and eyelids apart.

As soon as we were all well awake, we fell to discussing the situation, which was serious enough. Not a drop of water was left. We turned the water-bottles upside down, and licked the tops, but it was a failure, they were as dry as a bone. Good, who had charge of the bottle of brandy, got it out and looked at it longingly; but Sir Henry promptly took it away from him, for to drink raw spirit would only have been to precipitate the end.

'If we do not find water we shall die,' he said.

'If we can trust to the old Dom's map there should be some about,' I said; but nobody seemed to derive much satisfaction from that remark. It was so evident that no great faith could be put in the map. It was now gradually growing light, and as we sat blankly staring at each other, I observed the Hottentot Ventvögel rise and begin to walk about with his eyes on the ground. Presently he stopped short, and uttering a guttural exclamation, pointed to the earth.

'What is it?' we exclaimed; and simultaneously rose and went to where he was standing pointing at the ground.

'Well,' I said, 'it is pretty fresh Springbok spoor; what of it?'

'Springboks do not go far from water,' he answered in Dutch.

'No,' I answered, 'I forgot; and thank God for it.'

This little discovery put new life into us; it is wonderful how, when one is in a desperate position, one catches at the slightest hope, and feels almost happy in it. On a dark night a single star is better than nothing.

Meanwhile Ventvögel was lifting his snub nose, and sniffing the hot air for all the world like an old Impala ram who scents danger. Presently he spoke again.

'I *smell* water,' he said.

Then we felt quite jubilant, for we knew what a wonderful instinct these wild-bred men possess.

Just at that moment the sun came up gloriously, and revealed so grand a sight to our astonished eyes that for a moment or two we even forgot our thirst.

For there, not more than forty or fifty miles from us, glittering like silver in the early rays of the morning sun, were Sheba's breasts; and stretching away for hundreds of miles on each side of them was the great Suliman Berg. Now that I, sitting here, attempt to describe the extraordinary grandeur and beauty of that sight language seems to fail me. I am impotent even before its memory. There, straight before us, were two enormous mountains, the like of which are not, I believe, to be seen in Africa, if, indeed, there are any other such in the world, measuring each at least fifteen thousand feet in height, standing not more than a dozen miles apart, connected by a precipitous cliff of rock, and towering up in awful white solemnity straight into the sky. These mountains standing thus, like the pillars of a gigantic gateway, are shaped exactly like a woman's breasts. Their bases swelled gently up from the plain, looking, at that distance, perfectly round and smooth; and on the top of each was a vast round hillock covered with snow, exactly corresponding to the nipple on the female breast. The stretch of cliff which connected them appeared to be some thousand feet in height, and perfectly precipitous, and on each side of them, as far as the eye could reach, extended similar lines of cliff, broken only here and there by flat table-topped mountains, something like the world-famed one at Cape Town; a formation, by the way, very common in Africa.

To describe the grandeur of the whole view is beyond my powers. There was something so inexpressibly solemn and overpowering about those huge volcanoes – for doubtless they are extinct volcanoes – that it fairly took our breath away. For a while the morning lights played upon the snow and the brown and swelling masses beneath, and then, as though to veil the majestic sight from our curious eyes, strange mists and clouds gathered and increased around them, till presently we could only trace their pure and gigantic outline swelling ghostlike through the fleecy envelope. Indeed, as we afterwards discovered, they were normally wrapped in this curious gauzy mist, which doubtless accounted for one not having made them out more clearly before.

The mountains had scarcely vanished into cloud-clad privacy before our thirst – literally a burning question – reasserted itself.

It was all very well for Ventvögel to say he smelt water, but look which way we would we could see no signs of it. So far as the eye could reach there was nothing but arid sweltering sand and karoo scrub. We walked round the hillock and gazed about anxiously on the other side, but it was the same story, not a drop of water was to be seen; there was no indication of a pan, a pool, or a spring.

'You are a fool,' I said, angrily, to Ventvögel; 'there is no water.'

But still he lifted his ugly snub nose and sniffed.

'I smell it, Baas,' (master), he answered; 'it is somewhere in the air.'

'Yes,' I said, 'no doubt it is in the clouds, and about two months hence it will fall and wash our bones.'

Sir Henry stroked his yellow beard thoughtfully. 'Perhaps it is on the top of the hill,' he suggested.

'Rot,' said Good; 'whoever heard of water being found on the top of a hill!'

'Let us go and look,' I put in, and hopelessly enough we scrambled up the sandy sides of the hillock, Umbopa leading. Presently he stopped as though he was petrified.

'Nanzia manzie!' (here is water), he cried with a loud voice.

We rushed up to him, and there, sure enough, in a deep cup or indentation on the very top of the sand koppie was an undoubted pool of water. How it came to be in such a strange place we did not stop to inquire, nor did we hesitate at its black and uninviting appearance. It was water, or a good imitation of it, and that was enough for us. We gave a bound and a rush, and in another second were all down on our stomachs sucking up the uninviting fluid as though it were nectar fit for the gods. Heavens, how we did drink! Then when we had done drinking we tore off our clothes and sat down in it, absorbing the moisture through our parched skins. You, my reader, who have only to turn on a couple of taps and summon 'hot' and 'cold' from an unseen vasty boiler, can have little idea of the luxury of that muddy wallow in brackish, tepid water.

After a while we arose from it, refreshed indeed, and fell to on our 'biltong', of which we had scarcely been able to touch a mouthful for twenty-four hours, and ate our fill. Then we smoked a pipe, and lay down by the side of that blessed pool under the overhanging shadow of the bank, and slept till midday.

All that day we rested there by the water, thanking our stars that we had been lucky enough to find it, bad as it was, and not forgetting to render a due share of gratitude to the shade of the long-departed da Silvestra, who had corked it down so accurately on the tail of his shirt. The wonderful thing to us was that it should have lasted so long, and the only way that I can account for it is by the supposition that it is fed by some spring deep down in the sand.

Having filled both ourselves and our water-bottles as full as possible, in far better spirits we started off again with the moon. That night we covered nearly five-and-twenty miles, but, needless to say, found no more water, though we were lucky enough on the following day to get a little shade behind some ant-heaps. When the sun rose and, for a while, cleared away the mysterious mists, Suliman's Berg and the two majestic breasts, now only about twenty miles off, seemed to be towering right above us, and looked grander than ever. At the approach of evening we started on again, and, to cut a long story short, by daylight next morning found ourselves upon the lowest slopes of Sheba's left breast, for which we had been steadily steering. By this time our water was again exhausted and we were suffering severely from thirst, nor indeed could we see any chance of relieving it till we reached the snow line far far above us. After resting an hour or two, driven to it by our torturing thirst, we went on again, toiling painfully in the burning heat up the lava slopes, for we found that the huge base of the mountain was composed entirely of lava beds belched out in some far past age.

By eleven o'clock we were utterly exhausted, and were, generally speaking, in a very bad way indeed. The lava clinker, over which we had to make our way, though comparatively smooth compared with some clinker I have heard of, such as that on the Island of Ascension for instance, was yet rough enough to make our feet very sore, and this, together with our other misteries, had pretty well finished us. A few hundred yards above us were some large lumps of lava, and towards these we made with the intention of lying down beneath their shade. We reached them, and to our surprise, so far as we had a capacity for surprise left in us, on a little plateau or ridge close by we saw that the lava was covered with a dense green growth. Evidently soil formed from decomposed lava had rested there, and in due course had become the receptacle of seeds deposited by birds. But we did not take much further interest in the green growth, for one cannot live on grass like Nebuchadnezzar. That requires a special dispensation of Providence and peculiar digestive organs. So we sat down under the rocks and groaned, and I for one heartily wished that we had never started on this fool's errand. As we were sitting there I saw Umbopa get up and hobble off towards the patch of green, and a few minutes afterwards, to my great astonishment, I perceived that usually uncommonly dignified individual dancing and shouting like a maniac, and waving something green. Off we all scrambled towards him as fast as our wearied limbs would carry us, hoping that he had found water.

'What is it, Umbopa, son of a fool?' I shouted in Zulu.

'It is food and water, Macumazahn,' and again he waved the green thing.

Then I saw what he had got. It was a melon. We had hit upon a patch of wild melons, thousands of them, and dead ripe.

'Melons!' I yelled to Good, who was next me; and in another second he had his false teeth fixed in one.

I think we ate about six each before we had done, and, poor fruit as they were, I doubt if I ever thought anything nicer.

But melons are not very satisfying, and when we had satisfied our thirst with their pulpy substance, and set a stock to cool by the simple process of cutting them in two and setting them end on in the hot sun to get cold by evaporation, we began to feel exceedingly hungry. We had still some biltong left, but our stomachs turned from biltong, and besides we had to be very sparing of it, for we could not say when we should get more food. Just at this moment a lucky thing happened. Looking towards the desert I saw a flock of about ten large birds flying straight towards us.

'Skit, Baas, skit!' (shoot, master, shoot), whispered the Hottentot, throwing himself on his face, an example which we all followed.

Then I saw that the birds were a flock of pauw (bustards), and that they would pass within fifty yards of my head. Taking one of the repeating Winchesters I waited till they were nearly over us, and then jumped on to my feet. On seeing me the pauw bunched up together, as I expected they would, and I fired two shots straight into the thick of them, and, as luck would have it, brought one down, a fine fellow, that weighed about twenty pounds. In half an hour we had a fire made of dry melon stalks, and he was toasting over it, and we had such a feed as we had not had for a week. We ate that pauw; nothing was left of him but his bones and his beak, and felt not a little the better afterwards.

That night we again went on with the moon, carrying as many melons as we could with us. As we got higher up we found the air get cooler and cooler, which was a great relief to us, and at dawn, so far as we could judge, were not more than about a dozen miles from the snow line. Here we found more melons, so had no longer any anxiety about water, for we knew that we should soon get plenty of snow. But the ascent had now become very precipitous, and we made but slow progress, not more than a mile an hour. Also that night we ate our last morsel of biltong. As yet, with the exception of the pauw, we had seen no living thing on the mountain, nor had we come across a single spring or stream of water, which struck us as very odd, considering all the snow above us, which must, we thought, melt sometimes. But as we afterwards discovered, owing to some cause, which it is quite beyond my power to explain, all the streams flowed down upon the north side of the mountains.

We now began to grow very anxious about food. We had escaped death by thirst, but it seemed probable that it was only to die of hunger. The events of the next three miserable days are best described by copying the entries made at the time in my note-book.

21st May. – Started 11 a.m., finding the atmosphere quite cold enough to travel by day, carrying some water-melons with us. Struggled on all day, but saw no more melons, having, evidently, passed out of their district. Saw no game of any sort. Halted for the night at sundown, having had no food for many hours. Suffered much during the night from cold.

22nd. – Started at sunrise again, feeling very faint and weak. Only made five miles all day; found some patches of snow, of which we ate, but nothing else. Camped at night under the edge of a great plateau. Cold bitter. Drank a little brandy each, and huddled ourselves together, each wrapped up in our blanket to keep ourselves alive. Are now suffering frightfully from starvation and weariness. Thought that Ventvögel would have died during the night.

23rd. – Struggled forward once more as soon as the sun was well up, and had thawed our limbs a little. We are now in a dreadful plight, and I fear that unless we get food this will be our last day's journey. But little brandy left. Good, Sir Henry, and Umbopa bear up wonderfully, but Ventvögel is in a very bad way. Like most Hottentots, he cannot stand cold. Pangs of hunger not so bad, but have a sort of numb feeling about the stomach. Others say the same. We are now on a level with the precipitous chain, or wall of lava, connecting the two breasts, and the view is glorious. Behind us the great glowing desert rolls away to the horizon, and before us lies mile upon mile of smooth, hard snow almost level, but swelling gently upwards, out of the centre of which the nipple of the mountain, which appears to be some miles in circumference, rises about four thousand feet into the sky. Not a living thing is to be seen. God help us, I fear our time has come.

And now I will drop the journal, partly because it is not very interesting reading, and partly because what follows requires perhaps rather more accurate telling.

All that day (the 23rd May) we struggled slowly on up the incline of snow, lying down from time to time to rest. A strange, gaunt crew we must have looked, as, laden as we were, we dragged our weary feet over the dazzling plain, glaring round us with hungry eyes. Not that there was much use in glaring, for there was nothing to eat. We did not do more than seven miles that day. Just before sunset we found ourselves right under the nipple of Sheba's left breast, which towered up thousands of feet into the air above us, a vast, smooth hillock of frozen snow. Bad as we felt we could not but appreciate the wonderful scene, made even more wonderful by the flying rays of light from the setting sun, which here and there stained the snow blood-red, and crowned the towering mass above us with a diadem of glory.

'I say,' gasped Good, presently, 'we ought to be somewhere near the cave the old gentleman wrote about.'

'Yes,' said I, 'if there is a cave.'

'Come, Quatermain,' groaned Sir Henry, 'don't talk like that; I have every faith in the Dom; remember the water. We shall find the place soon.'

'If we don't find it before dark we are dead men, that is all about it,' was my consolatory reply.

For the next ten minutes we trudged on in silence, when suddenly, Umbopa, who was marching along beside me, wrapped up in his blanket, and with a leather belt strapped so tight round his stomach to 'make his hunger small,' as he said, that his waist looked like a girl's, caught me by the arm.

'Look!' he said, pointing towards the springing slope of the nipple.

I followed his glance, and perceived some two hundred yards from us what appeared to be a hole in the snow.

'It is the cave,' said Umbopa.

We made the best of our way to the spot, and found sure enough that the hole was the mouth of a cave, no doubt the same as that of which da Silvestra wrote. We were none too soon, for just as we reached shelter the sun went down with startling rapidity, leaving the whole place nearly dark. In these latitudes there is but little twilight. We crept into the cave, which did not appear to be very big, and huddling ourselves together for warmth, swallowed what remained of our brandy – barely a mouthful each – and tried to forget our miseries in sleep. But this the cold was too intense to allow us to do. I am convinced that at that great altitude the thermometer cannot have been less than fourteen or fifteen degrees below freezing point. What this meant to us, enervated as we were by hardship, want of food, and the great heat of the desert, my reader can imagine better than I can describe. Suffice it to say that it was something as near death from exposure as I have ever felt. There we sat hour after hour through the bitter night, feeling the frost wander round and nip us now in the finger, now in the foot, and now in the face. In vain did we huddle up closer and closer; there was no warmth in our miserable starved carcasses. Sometimes one of us would drop into an uneasy slumber for a few minutes, but we could not sleep long, and perhaps it was fortunate, for I doubt if we should ever have woken again. I believe it was only by force of will that we kept ourselves alive at all.

Not very long before dawn I heard the Hottentot, Ventvögel, whose teeth had been chattering all night like castanets, give a deep sigh, and then his teeth stopped chattering. I did not think anything of it at the time, concluding that he had gone to sleep. His back was resting against mine, and it seemed to grow colder and colder, till at last it was like ice.

At length the air began to grow grey with light, then swift, golden arrows came flashing across the snow, and at last the glorious sun peeped up above the lava wall and looked in upon our half-frozen forms and upon Ventvögel, sitting there amongst us *stone dead*. No wonder his back had felt cold, poor fellow. He had died when I heard him sigh, and was now almost frozen stiff. Shocked beyond measure we dragged ourselves from the corpse (strange the horror we all have of the companionship of a dead body), and left it still sitting there, with its arms clasped round its knees.

By this time the sunlight was pouring its cold rays (for here they were cold) straight in at the mouth of the cave. Suddenly I heard an exclamation of fear from someone, and turned my head down the cave.

And this was what I saw. Sitting at the end of it, for it was not more than twenty feet long, was another form, of which the head rested on the chest and the long arms hung down. I stared at it, and saw that it too was a *dead man*, and what was more, a white man.

The others saw it too, and the sight proved too much for our shattered nerves. One and all we scrambled out of the cave as fast as our half-frozen limbs would allow.

7

Solomon's Road

OUTSIDE the cave we halted, feeling rather foolish.

'I am going back,' said Sir Henry.

'Why?' asked Good.

'Because it has struck me that – what we saw – may be my brother.'

This was a new idea, and we re-entered the cave to put it to the proof. After the bright light outside, our eyes, weak as they were with staring at the snow, could not for a while pierce the gloom of the cave. Presently however we grew accustomed to the semi-darkness, and advanced on the dead form.

Sir Henry knelt down and peered into its face.

'Thank God,' he said, with a sigh of relief, 'it is not my brother.'

Then I went and looked. The corpse was that of a tall man in middle life with aquiline features, grizzled hair, and a long black moustache. The skin was perfectly yellow, and stretched tightly over the bones. Its clothing, with the exception of what seemed to be the remains of a woollen pair of hose, had been removed, leaving the skeleton-like frame naked. Round the neck hung a yellow ivory crucifix. The corpse was frozen perfectly stiff.

'Who on earth can it be?' said I.

'Can't you guess?' asked Good.

I shook my head.

'Why, the old Dom, José da Silvestra, of course – who else?'

'Impossible,' I gasped, 'he died three hundred years ago.'

'And what is there to prevent his lasting for three thousand years in this atmosphere I should like to know?' asked Good. 'If only the air is cold enough, flesh and blood will keep as fresh as New Zealand mutton for ever, and Heaven knows it is cold enough here. The sun never gets in here; no animal comes here to tear or destroy. No doubt his slave, of whom he speaks on the map, took off his clothes and left him. He could not have buried him alone. Look here,' he went on, stooping down and picking up a queer shaped bone scraped at the end into a sharp point, 'here is the "cleft-bone" that he used to draw the map with.'

We gazed astonished for a moment forgetting our own miseries in this extraordinary and, as it seemed to us, semi-miraculous sight.

'Ay,' said Sir Henry, 'and here is where he got his ink from,' and he pointed to a small wound on the dead man's left arm. 'Did ever man see such a thing before?'

There was no longer any doubt about the matter, which I confess for my own part perfectly appalled me. There he sat, the dead man, whose directions, written some ten generations ago, had led us to this spot. There in my own hand was the rude pen with which he had written them, and there round his neck was the crucifix his dying lips had kissed. Gazing at him my imagination could reconstruct the whole scene, the traveller dying of cold and starvation, and yet striving to convey the great secret he had discovered to the world: – the awful loneliness of his death, of which the evidence sat before us. It even seemed to me that I could trace in his strongly marked features a likeness to those of my poor friend Silvestre his descendant, who had died twenty years ago in my arms, but perhaps that was fancy. At any rate, there he sat, a sad memento of the fate that so often overtakes those who would penetrate into the unknown; and there probably he will still sit, crowned with the dread majesty of death, for centuries yet unborn, to startle the eyes of wanderers like ourselves, if any such should ever come again to invade his loneliness. The thing overpowered us, already nearly done to death as we were with cold and hunger.

'Let us go,' said Sir Henry, in a low voice; 'stay, we will give him a companion,' and lifting up the dead body of the Hottentot Ventvögel, he placed it near that of the old Dom. Then he stooped down, and with a jerk broke the rotten string of the crucifix round his neck, for his fingers were too cold to attempt to unfasten it. I believe that he still has it. I took the pen, and it is before me as I write – sometimes I sign my name with it.

Then leaving those two, the proud white man of a past age, and the poor Hottentot, to keep their eternal vigil in the midst of the eternal snows, we crept out of the cave into the welcome sunshine and resumed our path, wondering in our hearts how many hours it would be before we were even as they are.

When we had gone about half a mile we came to the edge of the plateau, for the nipple of the mountain did not rise out of its exact centre, though from the desert side it seemed to do so. What lay below us we could not see, for the landscape was wreathed in billows of morning mist. Presently, however, the higher layers of mist cleared a little, and revealed some five hundred yards beneath us, at the end of a long slope of snow, a patch of green grass, through which a stream was running. Nor was this all. By the stream, basking in the morning sun, stood and lay a group of from ten to fifteen *large antelopes* – at that distance we could not see what they were.

The sight filled us with an unreasoning joy. There was food in plenty if only we could get it. But the question was how to get it. The beasts were fully six hundred yards off, a very long shot, and one not to be depended on when one's life hung on the results.

Rapidly we discussed the advisability of trying to stalk the game, but finally reluctantly dismissed it. To begin with the wind was not favourable, and further, we should be certain to be perceived, however careful we were, against the blinding background of snow, which we should be obliged to traverse.

'Well, we must have a try from where we are,' said Sir Henry. 'Which shall it be, Quatermain, the repeating rifles of the expresses?'

Here again was a question. The Winchester repeaters – of which we had two, Umbopa carrying poor Ventvögel's as well as his own – were sighted up to a thousand yards, whereas the expresses were only sighted to three hundred and fifty, beyond which distance shooting with them was more or less guess work. On the other hand, if they did hit, the express bullets being expanding, were much more likely to bring the game down. It was a knotty point, but I made up my mind that we must risk it and use the expresses.

'Let each of us take the buck opposite to him. Aim well at the point of the shoulder, and high up,' said I; 'and Umbopa do you give the word, so that we may all fire together.'

Then came a pause, each man aiming his level best, as indeed one is likely to do when one knows that life itself depends upon the shot.

'Fire!' said Umbopa, in Zulu, and at almost the same instant the three rifles rang out loudly; three clouds of smoke hung for a moment before us, and a hundred echoes went flying away over the silent snow. Presently the smoke cleared, and revealed – oh, joy! – a great buck lying on its back and kicking furiously in its death agony. We gave a yell of triumph – we were saved, we should not starve. Weak as we were, we rushed down the intervening slope of snow, and in ten minutes from the time of firing, the animal's heart and liver were lying smoking before us. But now a new difficulty arose, we had no fuel, and therefore could make no fire to cook them at. We gazed at each other in dismay.

'Starving men must not be fanciful,' said Good; 'we must eat raw meat.'

There was no other way out of the dilemma, and our gnawing hunger made the proposition less distasteful than it would otherwise have been. So we took the heart and liver and buried them for a few minutes in a patch of snow to cool them. Then we washed them in the ice-cold water of the stream, and lastly ate them greedily. It sounds horrible enough, but honestly, I never tasted anything so good as that raw meat. In a quarter of an hour we were changed men. Our life and our vigour came back to us, our feeble pulses grew strong again, and the blood went coursing through our veins. But mindful of the results of over-feeding on starving stomachs, we were careful not to eat too much, stopping whilst we were still hungry.

'Thank God!' said Sir Henry; 'that brute has saved our lives. What is it, Quatermain?'

I rose and went to look at the antelope, for I was not certain. It was about the size of a donkey, with large curved horns. I had never seen one like it before, the species was new to me. It was brown, with faint red stripes, and a thick coat. I afterwards discovered that the natives of that wonderful country called the species 'Inco'. It was very rare, and only found at great altitude where no other game would live. The animal was fairly shot high up in the shoulder, though whose bullet it was that brought it down we could not, of course, discover. I believe that Good, mindful of his marvellous shot at the giraffe, secretly set it down to his own prowess, and we did not contradict him.

We had been so busy satisfying our starving stomachs that we had hitherto not found time to look about us. But now, having set Umbopa to cut off as much of the best meat as we were likely to be able to carry, we began to inspect our surroundings. The mist had now cleared away, for it was eight o'clock, and the sun had sucked it up, so we were able to take in all the country before us at a glance. I know not how to describe the glorious panorama which unfolded itself to our enraptured gaze. I have never seen anything like it before, nor shall, I suppose, again.

Behind and over us towered Sheba's snowy breasts, and below, some five thousand feet beneath where we stood, lay league on league of the most lovely champaign country. Here were dense patches of lofty forest, there a great river wound its silvery way. To the left stretched a vast expanse of rich, undulating veldt or grass land, on which we could just make out countless herds of game or cattle, at that distance we could not tell which. This expanse appeared to be ringed in by a wall of distant mountains. To the right the country was more or less mountainous, that is, solitary hills stood up from its level, with stretches of cultivated lands between, amongst which we could distinctly see groups of dome-shaped huts. The landscape lay before us like a map, in which rivers flashed like silver snakes, and Alp-like peaks crowned with wildly twisted snow wreaths rose in solemn grandeur, whilst over all was the glad sunlight and the wide breath of Nature's happy life.

Two curious things struck us as we gazed. First, that the country before us must lie at least five thousand feet higher than the desert we had crossed, and secondly, that all the rivers flowed from south to north. As we had painful reason to know, there was no water at all on the southern side of the vast range on which we stood, but on the northern side were many streams, most of which appeared to unite with the great river we could trace winding away farther than we could follow it.

We sat down for a while and gazed in silence at this wonderful view. Presently Sir Henry spoke.

'Isn't there something on the map about Solomon's Great Road?' he said.

I nodded, my eyes still looking out over the far country.

'Well, look; there it is!' and he pointed a little to our right.

Good and I looked accordingly, and there, winding away towards the plain, was what appeared to be a wide turnpike road. We had not seen it at first because it, on reaching the plain, turned behind some broken country. We did not say anything, at least not much; we were beginning to lose the sense of wonder. Somehow it did not seem particularly unnatural that we should find a sort of Roman road in this strange land. We accepted the fact, that was all.

'Well,' said Good, 'it must be quite near us if we cut off to the right. Hadn't we better be making a start?'

This was sound advice, and so soon as we had washed our faces and hands in the stream, we acted on it. For a mile or so we made our way over boulders and across patches of snow, till suddenly, on reaching the top of the little rise, there lay the road at our feet. It was a splendid road cut out of the solid rock, at least fifty feet wide, and apparently well kept; but the odd thing about it was that it seemed to begin there. We walked down and stood on it, but one single hundred paces behind us, in the direction of Sheba's breasts, it vanished, the whole surface of the mountain being strewn with boulders interspersed with patches of snow.

'What do you make of that, Quatermain?' asked Sir Henry.

I shook my head, I could make nothing of it.

'I have it!' said Good; 'the road no doubt ran right over the range and across the desert the other side, but the sand of the desert has covered it up, and above us it has been obliterated by some volcanic eruption of molten lava.'

This seemed a good suggestion; at any rate, we accepted it, and proceeded down the mountain. It was a very different business travelling along downhill on that magnificent pathway with full stomachs from what it had been travelling uphill over the snow quite starved and almost frozen. Indeed, had it not been for melancholy recollections of poor Ventvögel's sad fate, and of that grim cave where he kept company with the old Dom, we should have been positively cheerful, notwithstanding the sense of unknown dangers before us. Every mile we walked the atmosphere grew softer and balmier, and the country before us shone with a yet more luminous beauty. As for the road itself, I never saw such an engineering work, though Sir Henry said that the great road over the St Gotthard in Switzerland was very like it. No difficulty had been too great for the Old World engineer who designed it. At one place we came to a great ravine three hundred feet broad and at least a hundred deep. This vast gulf was actually filled in, apparently with huge blocks of dressed stone, with arches pierced at the bottom for a water-way, over which the road went sublimely on. At another place it was cut in zigzags out of the side of a precipice five hundred feet deep, and in a third it tunnelled right through the base of an intervening ridge a space of thirty yards or more.

Here we noticed that the sides of the tunnel were covered with quaint sculptures mostly of mailed figures driving in chariots. One, which was exceedingly beautiful, represented a whole battle scene with a convoy of captives being marched off in the distance.

'Well,' said Sir Henry, after inspecting this ancient work of art, 'it is very well to call this Solomon's Road, but my humble opinion is that the Egyptians have been here before Solomon's people ever set a foot on it. If that isn't Egyptian handiwork, all I have to say is it is very like it.'

By midday we had advanced sufficiently far down the mountain to reach the region where wood was to be met with. First we came to scattered bushes which grew more and more frequent, till at last we found the road winding through a vast grove of silver trees similar to those which are to be seen on the slopes of Table Mountain at Cape Town. I had never before met with them in all my wanderings, except at the Cape, and their appearance here astonished me greatly.

'Ah!' said Good, surveying these shining-leaved trees with evident enthusiasm, 'here is lots of wood, let us stop and cook some dinner; I have about digested that raw meat.'

Nobody objected to this, so leaving the road we made our way to a stream which was babbling away not far off, and soon had a goodly fire of dry boughs blazing. Cutting off some substantial hunks from the flesh of the inco which we had brought with us, we proceeded to toast them on the end of sharp sticks, as one sees the Kafirs do, and ate them with relish. After filling ourselves, we lit our pipes and gave ourselves up to enjoyment, which, compared to the hardships we had recently undergone, seemed almost heavenly.

The brook, of which the banks were clothed with dense masses of a gigantic species of maidenhair fern interspersed with feathery tufts of wild asparagus, babbled away merrily at our side, the soft air murmured through the leaves of the silver trees, doves cooed around, and bright-winged birds flashed like living gems from bough to bough. It was like Paradise.

The magic of the place, combined with the overwhelming sense of dangers left behind, and of the promised land reached at last, seemed to charm us into silence. Sir Henry and Umbopa sat conversing in a mixture of broken English and Kitchin Zulu in a low voice, but earnestly enough, and I lay, with my eyes half shut, upon that fragrant bed of fern and watched them. Presently I missed Good, and looked to see what had become of him. As I did so I observed him sitting by the bank of the stream, in which he had been bathing. He had nothing on but his flannel shirt and, his natural habits of extreme neatness having reasserted themselves, was actively employed in making a most elaborate toilet. He had washed his guttapercha collar, thoroughly shaken out his trousers, coat, and waistcoat, and was now folding them up neatly till he was ready to put them on, shaking his head sadly as he did so over the numerous rents and tears in them, which had naturally resulted from our frightful journey.

Then he took his boots, scrubbed them with a handful of fern, and finally rubbed them over with a piece of fat, which he had carefully saved from the inco meat, till they looked, comparatively speaking, respectable. Having inspected them judiciously through his eye-glass, he put them on and began a fresh operation. From a little bag he carried he produced a pocket comb in which was fixed a tiny looking-glass, and in this he surveyed himself. Apparently he was not satisfied, for he proceeded to do his hair with great care. Then came a pause whilst he again contemplated the effect; still it was not satisfactory. He felt his chin, on which was now the accumulated scrub of a ten days' beard. 'Surely,' thought I, 'he is not going to try and shave.' But so it was. Taking the piece of fat with which he had greased his boots he washed it carefully in the stream. Then diving again into the bag he brought out a little pocket razor with a guard to it, such as are sold to people afraid of cutting themselves, or to those about to undertake a sea voyage. Then he vigorously scrubbed his face and chin with the fat and began. But it was evidently a painful process for he groaned very much over it, and I was convulsed with inward laughter as I watched him struggling with that stubbly beard. It seemed so very odd that a man should take the trouble to shave himself with a piece of fat in such a place and under such circumstances. At last he succeeded in getting the worst of the scrub off the right side of his face and chin, when suddenly I, who was watching, became aware of a flash of light that passed just by his head.

Good sprang up with a profane exclamation (if it had not been a safety razor he would certainly have cut his throat), and so did I, without the exclamation, and this was what I saw. Standing there, not more than twenty paces from where I was, and ten from Good, were a group of men. They were very tall and copper-coloured, and some of them wore great plumes of black feathers and short cloaks of leopard skins; this was all I noticed at the moment. In front of them stood a youth of about seventeen, his hand still raised and his body bent forward in the attitude of a Grecian statue of a spear thrower. Evidently the flash of light had been a weapon, and he had thrown it.

As I looked, an old soldier-like looking man stepped forward out of the group, and catching the youth by the arm said something to him. Then they advanced upon us.

Sir Henry, Good, and Umbopa had by this time seized their rifles and lifted them threateningly. The party of natives still came on. It struck me that they could not know what rifles were, or they would not have treated them with such contempt.

'Put down your guns!' I halloed to the others, seeing that our only chance of safety lay in conciliation. They obeyed, and walking to the front I addressed the elderly man who had checked the youth.

'Greeting,' I said, in Zulu, not knowing what language to use. To my surprise I was understood.

'Greeting,' answered the man, not, indeed, in the same tongue, but in a dialect so closely allied to it, that neither Umbopa nor myself had any difficulty in understanding it. Indeed, as we afterwards found out, the language spoken by this people was an old-fashioned form of the Zulu tongue, bearing about the same relationship to it that the English of Chaucer does to the English of the nineteenth century.

'Whence come ye?' he went on, 'what are ye? and why are the faces of three of ye white, and the face of the fourth as the face of our mother's sons?' and he pointed to Umbopa. I looked at Umbopa as he said it, and it flashed across me that he was right. Umbopa was like the faces of the men before me, so was his great form. But I had not time to reflect on this coincidence.

'We are strangers, and come in peace,' I answered, speaking very slow, so that he might understand me, 'and this man is our servant.'

'Ye lie,' he answered, 'no strangers can cross the mountains where all things die. But what do your lies matter, if ye are strangers then ye must die, for no strangers may live in the land of the Kukuanas. It is the king's law. Prepare then to die, O strangers!'

I was slightly staggered at this, more especially as I saw the hands of some of the party of men steal down to their sides, where hung on each what looked to me like a large and heavy knife.

'What does that beggar say?' asked Good.

'He says we are going to be scragged,' I answered grimly.

'Oh, Lord,' groaned Good; and, as was his way when perplexed, put his hand to his false teeth, dragging the top set down and allowing them to fly back to his jaw with a snap. It was a most fortunate move, for next second the dignified crowd of Kukuanas gave a simultaneous yell of horror, and bolted back some yards.

'What's up?' said I.

'It's his teeth,' whispered Sir Henry, excitedly. 'He moved them. Take them out, Good, take them out!'

He obeyed, slipping the set into the sleeve of his flannel shirt.

In another second curiosity had overcome fear, and the men advanced slowly. Apparently they had now forgotten their amiable intentions of doing for us.

'How is it, O strangers,' asked the old man solemnly, 'that the teeth of the man' (pointing to Good, who had nothing on but a flannel shirt, and had only half finished his shaving) 'whose body is clothed, and whose legs are bare, who grows hair on one side of his sickly face and not on the other, and who has one shining and transparent eye, and teeth that move of themselves, coming away from the jaws and returning of their own will?'

'Open your mouth,' I said to Good, who promptly curled up his lips and grinned at the old gentleman like an angry dog, revealing to their astonished gaze two thin red lines of gum as utterly innocent of ivories as a new-born elephant. His audience gasped.

'Where are his teeth?' they shouted; 'with our eyes we saw them.'

Turning his head slowly and with a gesture of ineffable contempt, Good swept his hand across his mouth. Then he grinned again, and lo, there were two rows of lovely teeth.

The young man who had flung the knife threw himself down on the grass and gave went to a prolonged howl of terror; and as for the old gentleman his knees knocked together with fear.

'I see that ye are spirits,' he said falteringly; 'did ever man born of woman have hair on one side of his face and not on the other, or a round and transparent eye, or teeth which moved and melted away and grew again? Pardon us, O my lords.'

Here was luck indeed, and, needless to say, I jumped at the chance.

'It is granted,' I said, with an imperial smile. 'Nay, ye shall know the truth. We come from another world, though we are men such as ye; we come,' I went on, 'from the biggest star that shines at night.'

'Oh! oh!' groaned the chorus of astonished aborigines.

'Yes,' I went on, 'we do, indeed'; and I again smiled benignly as I uttered that amazing lie. 'We come to stay with you a little while, and bless you by our sojourn. Ye will see, O friends, that I have prepared myself by learning your language.'

'It is so, it is so,' said the chorus.

'Only, my lord,' put in the old gentleman, 'thou hast learnt it very badly.'

I cast an indignant glance at him, and he quailed.

'Now, friends,' I continued, 'ye might think that after so long a journey we should find it in our hearts to avenge such a reception, mayhap to strike cold in death the impious hand that – that, in short – threw a knife at the head of him whose teeth come and go.'

'Spare him, my lords,' said the old man in supplication; 'he is the king's son, and I am his uncle. If anything befalls him his blood will be required at my hands.'

'Yes, that is certainly so,' put in the young man with great emphasis.

'You may perhaps doubt our power to avenge,' I went on, heedless of this by-play. 'Stay, I will show you. Here, you dog and slave' (addressing Umbopa in a savage tone), 'give me the magic tube that speaks'; and I tipped a wink towards my express rifle.

Umbopa rose to the occasion, and with something as nearly resembling a grin as I have ever seen on his dignified face, handed me the rifle.

'It is here, O lord of lords,' he said, with a deep obeisance.

Now, just before I asked for the rifle I had perceived a little klipspringer antelope standing on a mass of rock about seventy yards away, and determined to risk a shot at it.

'Ye see that buck,' I said, pointing the animal out to the party before me. 'Tell me, is it possible for man, born of woman, to kill it from here with a noise?'

'It is not possible, my lord,' answered the old man.

'Yet shall I kill it,' said I, quietly.

The old man smiled. 'That my lord cannot do,' he said.

I raised the rifle, and covered the buck. It was a small animal, and one which one might well be excused for missing, but I knew that it would not do to miss.

I drew a deep breath, and slowly pressed on the trigger. The buck stood still as stone.

'Bang! thud!' The buck sprang into the air and fell on the rock dead as a door nail.

A groan of terror burst from the group before us.

'If ye want meat,' I remarked coolly, 'go fetch that buck.'

The old man made a sign, and one of his followers departed, and presently returned bearing the klipspringer. I noticed, with satisfaction, that I had hit it fairly behind the shoulder. They gathered round the poor creature's body, gazing at the bullet hole in consternation.

'Ye see,' I said, 'I do not speak empty words.'

There was no answer.

'If ye yet doubt our power,' I went on, 'let one of ye go stand upon that rock that I may make him as this buck.'

None of them seemed at all inclined to take the hint, till at last the king's son spoke.

'It is well said. Do thou, my uncle, go stand upon the rock. It is but a buck that the magic has killed. Surely it cannot kill a man.'

The old gentleman did not take the suggestion in good part. Indeed, he seemed hurt.

'No! no!' he ejaculated, hastily, 'my old eyes have seen enough. These are wizards, indeed. Let us bring them to the king. Yet if any should wish a further proof, let *him* stand upon the rock, that the magic tube may speak with him.'

There was a most general and hasty expression of dissent.

'Let not good magic be wasted on our poor bodies,' said one, 'we are satisfied. All the witchcraft of our people cannot show the like of this.'

'It is so,' remarked the old gentleman, in a tone of intense relief; 'without any doubt it is so. Listen, children of the stars, children of the shining eye and the movable teeth, who roar out in thunder and slay from afar. I am Infadoos, son of Kafa, once King of the Kukuana people. This youth is Scragga.'

'He nearly scragged me,' murmured Good.

'Scragga, son of Twala, the great king – Twala, husband of a thousand wives, chief and lord paramount of the Kukuanas, keeper of the great road, terror of his enemies, student of the Black Arts, leader of an hundred thousand warriors, Twala the One-eyed, the Black, the Terrible.'

'So,' said I, superciliously, 'lead us then to Twala. We do not talk with low people and underlings.'

'It is well, my lords, we will lead you, but the way is long. We are hunting three days' journey from the place of the king. But let my lords have patience, and we will lead them.'

'It is well,' I said, carelessly, 'all time is before us, for we do not die. We are ready, lead on. But Infadoos, and thou, Scragga, beware! Play us no tricks, make for us no snares, for before your brains of mud have thought of them, we shall know them and avenge them. The light from the transparent eye of him with the bare legs and the half-haired face (Good) shall destroy you, and go through your land: his vanishing teeth shall fix themselves fast in you and eat you up, you and your wives and children; the magic tubes shall talk with you loudly, and make you as sieves. Beware!'

This magnificent address did not fail of its effect; indeed, it was hardly needed, so deeply were our friends already impressed with our powers.

The old man made a deep obeisance, and murmured the word 'Koom, Koom,' which I afterwards discovered was their royal salute, corresponding to the Bayéte of the Zulus, and turning, addressed his followers. These at once proceeded to lay hold of all our goods and chattels, in order to bear them for us, excepting only the guns, which they would on no account touch. They even seized Good's clothes, which were, as the reader may remember, neatly folded up beside him.

He at once made a dive for them, and a loud altercation ensued.

'Let not my lord of the transparent eye and the melting teeth touch them,' said the old man. 'Surely his slaves shall carry the things.'

'But I want to put 'em on!' roared Good, in nervous English.

Umbopa translated.

'Nay, my lord,' put in Infadoos, 'would my lord cover up his beautiful white legs' (although he was so dark, Good had a singularly white skin) 'from the eyes of his servants? Have we offended my lord that he should do such a thing?'

Here I nearly exploded with laughing; and meanwhile, one of the men started on with the garments.

'Damn it!' roared Good, 'that black villain has got my trousers.'

'Look here, Good,' said Sir Henry, 'you have appeared in this country in a certain character, and you must live up to it. It will never do for you to put on trousers again. Henceforth you must live in a flannel shirt, a pair of boots and an eyeglass.'

'Yes,' I said, 'and with whiskers on one side of your face and not on the other. If you change any of these things they will think that we are impostors. I am very sorry for you, but, seriously, you must do it. If once they begin to suspect us, our lives will not be worth a brass farthing.'

'Do you really think so?' said Good, gloomily.

'I do, indeed. Your "beautiful white legs" and your eye glass are now *the* feature of our party, and as Sir Henry says, you must live up to them. Be thankful that you have got your boots on, and that the air is warm.'

Good sighed, and said no more, but it took him a fortnight to get accustomed to his attire.

8

We Enter Kukuanaland

ALL that afternoon we travelled on along the magnificent roadway, which headed steadily in a north-westerly direction. Infadoos and Scragga walked with us, but their followers marched about one hundred paces ahead.

'Infadoos,' I said at length, 'who made this road?'

'It was made, my lord, of old time, none know how or when, not even the wise woman Gagool, who has lived for generations. We are not old enough to remember its making. None can make such roads now, but the king lets no grass grow upon it.'

'And whose are the writings on the walls of the caves through which we have passed on the road?' I asked, referring to the Egyptian-like sculptures we had seen.

'My lord, the hands that made the road wrote the wonderful writings. We know not who wrote them.'

'When did the Kukuana race come into this country?'

'My lord, the race came down here like the breath of a storm ten thousand moons ago, from the great lands which lie there beyond,' and he pointed to the north. 'They could travel no farther, so say the old voices of our fathers that have come down to us, the children, and so says Gagool, the wise woman, the smeller out of witches, because of the great mountains which ring in the land,' and he pointed to the snow-clad peaks. 'The country, too, was good, so they settled here and grew strong and powerful, and now our numbers are like the sea sand, and when Twala the king calls up his regiments their plumes cover the plain as far as the eye of man can reach.'

'And if the land is walled in with mountains, who is there for the regiments to fight with?'

'Nay, my lord, the country is open there,' and again he pointed towards the north, 'and now and again warriors sweep down upon us in clouds from a land we know not, and we slay them. It is the third part of the life of a man since there was a war. Many thousands died in it, but we destroyed those who came to eat us up. So since then there has been no war.'

'Your warriors must grow weary of resting on their spears.'

'My lord, there was one war, just after we destroyed the people that came down upon us, but it was a civil war, dog eat dog.'

'How was that?'

'My lord, the king, my half-brother, had a brother born at the same birth, and of the same woman. It is not our custom, my lord, to let twins live, the weakest must always die. But the mother of the king hid away the weakest child, which was born the last, for her heart yearned over it, and the child is Twala the king. I am his younger brother born of another wife.'

'Well?'

'My lord, Kafa, our father, died when we came to manhood, and my brother Imotu was made king in his place, and for a space reigned and had a son by his favourite wife. When the babe was three years old, just after the great war, during which no man could sow or reap, a famine came upon the land, and the people murmured because of the famine, and looked round like a starved lion for something to rend. Then it was that Gagool, the wise and terrible woman, who does not die, proclaimed to the people, saying, "The king Imotu is no king." And at the time Imotu was sick with a wound, and lay in his hut not able to move.

'Then Gagool went into a hut and led out Twala, my half-brother, and the twin brother of the king, whom she had hidden since he was born among the caves and rocks, and stripping the "moocha" (waist-cloth) off his loins, showed the people of the Kukuanas the mark of the sacred snake coiled round his waist, wherewith the eldest son of the king is marked at birth, and cried out loud, "Behold, your king whom I have saved for you even to this day!" And the people being mad with hunger, and altogether bereft of reason and the knowledge of truth, cried out, "The king! The king!" but I knew that it was not so, for Imotu, my brother, was the elder of the twins, and was the lawful king. And just as the tumult was at its height Imotu the king, though he was very sick, came crawling from his hut holding his wife by the hand, and followed by his little son Ignosi (the lightning).

'"What is this noise?" he asked; "Why cry ye *The king! The king?*"

'Then Twala, his own brother, born of the same woman and in the same hour, ran to him, and taking him by the hair stabbed him through the heart with his knife. And the people being fickle, and ever ready to worship the rising sun, clapped their hands and cried, "*Twala is king!* Now we know that Twala is king!"

'And what became of his wife and her son Ignosi? Did Twala kill them too?'

'Nay, my lord. When she saw that her lord was dead, she seized the child with a cry, and ran away. Two days afterwards she came to a kraal very hungry, and none would give her milk or food, now that her lord the king was dead, for all men hate the unfortunate. But at nightfall a little child, a girl, crept out and brought her to eat, and she blessed the child, and went on towards the mountains with her boy before the sun rose again, where she must have perished, for none have seen her since, nor the child Ignosi.'

'Then if this child Ignosi had lived, he would be the true king of the Kukuana people?'

'That is so, my lord; the sacred snake is round his middle. If he lives he is the king; but alas! he is long dead.'

'See, my lord,' and he pointed to a vast collection of huts surrounded with a fence, which was in its turn surrounded by a great ditch, that lay on the plain beneath us. 'That is the kraal where the wife of Imotu was last seen with the child Ignosi. It is there that we shall sleep tonight, if, indeed,' he added doubtfully, 'my lords sleep at all upon this earth.'

'When we are among the Kukuanas, my good friend Infadoos, we do as the Kukuanas do,' I said, majestically, and I turned round suddenly to address Good, who was tramping along sullenly behind, his mind fully occupied with unsatisfactory attempts to keep his flannel shirt from flapping up in the evening breeze, and to my astonishment butted into Umbopa, who was walking along immediately behind me, and had very evidently been listening with the greatest interest to my conversation with Infadoos. The expression on his face was most curious, and gave the idea of a man who was struggling with partial success to bring something long ago forgotten back into his mind.

All this while we had been pressing on at a good rate down towards the undulating plain beneath. The mountains we had crossed now loomed high above us, and Sheba's breasts were modestly veiled in diaphanous wreaths of mist. As we went on the country grew more and more lovely. The vegetation was luxuriant; without being tropical, the sun was bright and warm, but not burning, and a gracious breeze blew softly along the odorous slopes of the mountains. And, indeed, this new land was little less than an earthly paradise; in beauty, in natural wealth, and in climate I have never seen its like. The Transvaal is a fine country, but it is nothing to Kukuanaland.

So soon as we started, Infadoos had dispatched a runner on to warn the people of the kraal, which, by the way, was in his military command, of our arrival. This man had departed at an extraordinary speed, which Infadoos had informed me he would keep up all the way, as running was an exercise much practised among his people.

The result of this message now became apparent. When we got within two miles of the kraal we could see that company after company of men was issuing from its gates and marching towards us.

Sir Henry laid his hand upon my arm, and remarked that it looked as though we were going to meet with a warm reception. Something in his tone attracted Infadoos' attention.

'Let not my lords be afraid,' he said hastily, 'for in my breast there dwells no guile. This regiment is one under my command, and comes out by my orders to greet you.'

I nodded easily, though I was not quite easy in my mind.

About half a mile from the gates of the kraal was a long stretch of rising ground sloping gently upwards from the road, and on this the companies formed up. It was a splendid sight to see them, each company about three hundred strong, charging swiftly up the slope, with flashing spears and waving plumes, and taking their appointed place. By the time we came to the slope, twelve such companies, or in all three thousand six hundred men, had passed out and taken up their positions along the road.

Presently we came to the first company, and were able to gaze in astonishment on the most magnificent set of men I have ever seen. They were all men of mature age, mostly veterans of about forty, and not one of them was under six feet in height, whilst many were six feet three or four. They wore upon their heads heavy black plumes of Sakaboola feathers, like those which adorned our guides. Round their waists, and also beneath the right knee were bound circlets of white ox tails, and in their left hands were round shields about twenty inches across. These shields were very curious. The framework consisted of an iron plate beaten out thin, over which was stretched milk-white ox hide. The weapons that each man bore were simple, but most effective, consisting of a short and very heavy two-edged spear with a wooden shaft, the blade being about six inches across at the widest part. These spears were not used for throwing, but like the Zulu 'bangwan', or stabbing assegai, were for close quarters only, when the wound inflicted by them was terrible. In addition to these bangwans each man also carried three large and heavy knives, each knife weighing about two pounds. One knife was fixed in the ox tail girdle, and the other two at the back of the round shield. These knives, which are called 'tollas' by the Kukuanas, take the place of the throwing assegai of the Zulus. A Kukuana warrior can throw them with great accuracy at a distance of fifty yards, and it is their custom on charging to hurl a volley of them at the enemy as they come to close quarters.

Each company stood like a collection of bronze statues till we were opposite to it, when at a signal given by its commanding officer who, distinguished by a leopard skin cloak, stood some paces in front, every spear was raised into the air, and from three hundred throats sprang forth with a sudden roar the royal salute of '*Koom*'. Then when we had passed the company formed up behind us, and followed us towards the kraal, till at last the whole regiment of the 'Greys' (so called from their white shields), the crack corps of the Kukuana people, was marching behind us with a tread that shook the ground.

At length, branching off from Solomon's Great Road, we came to the wide fosse surrounding the kraal, which was at least a mile round, and fenced with a strong palisade of piles formed of the trunks of trees. At the gateway this fosse was spanned by a primitive drawbridge which was let down by the guard to allow us to pass in. The kraal was exceedingly well laid out. Through the centre ran a wide pathway intersected at right angles by other pathways so arranged as to cut the huts into square blocks, each block being the quarters of a company. The huts were dome-shaped, and built, like those of the Zulus, of a framework of wattle, beautifully thatched with grass; but, unlike the Zulu huts, they had doorways through which one could walk. Also they were much larger and surrounded with a verandah about six feet wide, beautifully paved with powdered lime trodden hard. All along each side of the wide pathway that pierced the kraal were ranged hundreds of women, brought out by curiosity to look at us. These women are, for a native race, exceedingly handsome. They are tall and graceful, and their figures are wonderfully fine. The hair, though short, is rather curly than woolly, the features are frequently aquiline, and the lips are not unpleasantly thick as is the case in most African races. But what struck us most was their exceedingly quiet, dignified air. They were as well-bred in their way as the habituées of a fashionable drawing-room, and in this respect differ from Zulu women, and their cousins the Masai who inhabit the district behind Zanzibar. Their curiosity had brought them out to see us, but they allowed no rude expressions of wonder or savage criticism to pass their lips as we trudged wearily in front of them. Not even when old Infadoos with a surreptitious motion of the hand pointed out the crowning wonder of poor Good's 'beautiful white legs', did they allow the feeling of intense admiration which evidently mastered their minds to find expression. They fixed their dark eyes upon their snowy loveliness (Good's skin is exceedingly white), and that was all. But this was quite enough for Good, who is modest by nature.

When we got to the centre of the kraal, Infadoos halted at the door of a large hut, which was surrounded at a distance by a circle of smaller ones.

'Enter, sons of the stars,' he said, in a magniloquent voice, 'and deign to rest awhile in our humble habitations. A little food shall be brought to you, so that ye shall have no need to draw your belts tight from hunger; some honey and some milk, and an ox or two, and a few sheep; not much, my lords, but still a little food.'

'It is good,' said I, 'Infadoos, we are weary with travelling through realms of air; now let us rest.'

Accordingly we entered into the hut, which we found amply prepared for our comfort. Couches of tanned skins were spread for us to rest on, and water was placed for us to wash in.

Presently we heard a shouting outside, and stepping to the door, saw a line of damsels bearing milk and roasted mealies, and honey in a pot. Behind these were some youths driving a fat young ox. We received the gifts, and then one of the young men took the knife from his girdle and dexterously cut the ox's throat. In ten minutes it was dead, skinned, and cut up. The best of the meat was then cut off for us, and the rest I, in the name of our party, presented to the warriors round us, who took it off and distributed the 'white men's gift'.

Umbopa set to work, with the assistance of an extremely prepossessing young woman, to boil our portion in a large earthenware pot over a fire which was built outside the hut, and when it was nearly ready we sent a message to Infadoos, and asked him, and Scragga the king's son, to join us.

Presently they came, and sitting down upon little stools, of which there were several about the hut (for the Kukuana do not in general squat upon their haunches like the Zulus), helped us to get through our dinner. The old gentleman was most affable and polite, but it struck us that the young one regarded us with suspicion. He had, together with the rest of the party, been overawed by our white appearance and by our magic properties; but it seemed to me that on discovering that we ate, drank, and slept like other mortals, his awe was beginning to wear off and be replaced by a sullen suspicion – which made us feel rather uncomfortable.

In the course of our meal Sir Henry suggested to me that it might be well to try and discover if our hosts knew anything of his brother's fate, or if they had ever seen or heard of him; but, on the whole, I thought that it would be wiser to say nothing of the matter at that time.

After supper we filled our pipes and lit them: a proceeding which filled Infadoos and Scragga with astonishment. The Kukuanas were evidently unacquainted with the divine uses of tobacco-smoke. The herb was grown among them extensively; but, like the Zulus, they only used it for snuff, and quite failed to identify it in its new form.

Presently I asked Infadoos when we were to proceed on our journey, and was delighted to learn that preparations had been made for us to leave on the following morning, messengers having already left to inform Twala the king of our coming. It appeared that Twala was at his principal place, known as Loo, making ready for the great annual feast which was held in the first week of June. At this gathering, all the regiments with the exception of certain detachments left behind for garrison purposes, were brought up and paraded before the king; and the great annual witch-hunt, of which more by-and-by, was held.

We were to start at dawn; and Infadoos, who was to accompany us, expected that we should, unless we were detained by accident or by swollen rivers, reach Loo on the night of the second day.

When they had given us this information our visitors bade us good night; and, having arranged to watch turn and turn about, three of us flung ourselves down and slept the sweet sleep of the weary, whilst the fourth sat up on the look-out for possible treachery.

9

Twala the King

IT will not be necessary for me to detail at length the incidents of our journey to Loo. It took two good days' travelling along Solomon's Great Road, which pursued its even course right into the heart of Kukuanaland. Suffice it to say that as we went, the country seemed to grow richer and richer, and the kraals, with their wide surrounding belts of cultivation, more and more numerous. They were all built upon the same principles as the first one we had reached, and were guarded by ample garrisons of troops. Indeed, in Kukuanaland, as among the Germans, the Zulus, and the Masai, every able-bodied man is a soldier, so that the whole force of the nation is available for its wars, offensive or defensive. As we travelled along we were overtaken by thousands of warriors hurrying up to Loo to be present at the great annual review and festival, and a grander series of troops I never saw. At sunset on the second day we stopped to rest awhile upon the summit of some heights over which the road ran, and there on a beautiful and fertile plain before us was Loo itself. For a native town it was an enormous place, quite five miles round I should say, with outlying kraals jutting out from it, which served on grand occasions as cantonments for the regiments, and a curious horse-shoe-shaped hill, with which we were destined to become better acquainted, about two miles to the north. It was beautifully situated, and through the centre of the kraal, dividing it into two portions, ran a river, which appeared to be bridged at several places, the same perhaps that we had seen from the slopes of Sheba's Breasts. Sixty or seventy miles away three great snow-capped mountains, placed like the points of a triangle, started up out of the level plain. The conformation of these mountains was unlike that of Sheba's Breasts, being sheer and precipitous, instead of smooth and rounded.

Infadoos saw us looking at them and volunteered a remark:

'The road ends there,' he said, pointing to the mountains known among the Kukuanas as the 'Three Witches'.

'Why does it end?' I asked.

'Who knows?' he answered, with a shrug; 'the mountains are full of caves, and there is a great pit between them. It is there that the wise men of old time used to go to get whatever it was they came to this country for, and it is there now that our kings are buried in the Place of Death.'

'What was it they came for?' I asked eagerly.

'Nay, I know not. My lords who come from the stars should know,' he answered with a quick look. Evidently he knew more than he chose to say.

'Yes,' I went on, 'you are right, in the stars we know many things. I have heard, for instance, that the wise men of old came to those mountains to get bright stones, pretty play-things, and yellow iron.'

'My lord is wise,' he answered coldly, 'I am but a child and cannot talk with my lord on such things. My lord must speak with Gagool the old, at the king's place, who is wise even as my lord,' and he turned away.

As soon as he was gone, I turned to the others and pointed out the mountains. 'There are Solomon's diamond mines,' I said.

Umbopa was standing with them, apparently plunged in one of the fits of abstraction which were common to him, and caught my words.

'Yes, Macumazahn,' he put in, in Zulu, 'the diamonds are surely there, and you shall have them since you white men are so fond of toys and money.'

'How dost thou know that, Umbopa?' I asked sharply, for I did not like his mysterious ways.

He laughed; 'I dreamed it in the night, white men,' and then he too turned upon his heel and went.

'Now what,' said Sir Henry, 'is our black friend at? He knows more than he chooses to say, that is clear. By the way, Quatermain, has he heard anything of – of my brother?'

'Nothing; he has asked everyone he has got friendly with, but they all declare no white man has ever been seen in the country before.'

'Do you suppose he ever got here at all?' suggested Good; 'we have only reached the place by a miracle; is it likely he could have reached it at all without the map?'

'I don't know,' said Sir Henry, gloomily, 'but somehow I think that I shall find him.'

Slowly the sun sank, and then suddenly darkness rushed down on the land like a tangible thing. There was no breathing-space between the day and the night, no soft transformation scene, for in these latitudes twilight does not exist. The change from day to night is as quick and as absolute as the change from life to death. The sun sank and the world was wreathed in shadows. But not for long, for see in the east there is a glow, then a bent edge of silver light, and at last the full and glorious moon peeps above the plain and shoots its gleaming arrows far and wide, filling the earth with a faint refulgence, as the glow of a good man's deeds shines for a while upon his little world after his sun has set, lighting the fainthearted travellers who follow on towards a fuller dawn.

We stood and watched the lovely sight, whilst the stars grew pale before this chastened majesty, and felt our hearts lifted up in the presence of a beauty we could not realize, much less describe. Mine has been a rough life, my reader, but there are a few things I am thankful to have lived for, and one of them is to have seen that moon rise over Kukuanaland. Presently our meditations were broken in upon by our polite friend Infadoos.

'If my lords are rested we will journey on to Loo, where a hut is made ready for my lords tonight. The moon is now bright, so that we shall not fall on the way.'

We assented, and in an hour's time were at the outskirts of the town, of which the extent, mapped out as it was by thousands of camp fires, appeared absolutely endless. Indeed, Good, who was always fond of a bad joke, christened it 'Unlimited Loo'. Presently we came to a moat with a draw-bridge, where we were met by the rattling of arms and the hoarse challenge of a sentry. Infadoos gave some password that I could not catch, which was met with a salute, and we passed on through the central street of the great grass city. After nearly half an hour's tramp, past endless lines of huts, Infadoos at last halted at the gate of a little group of huts which surrounded a small courtyard of powdered limestone, and informed us that these were to be our 'poor' quarters.

We entered, and found that a hut had been assigned to each of us. These huts were superior to any which we had yet seen, and in each was a most comfortable bed made of tanned skins spread upon mattresses of aromatic grass. Food, too, was ready for us, and as soon as we had washed ourselves with water, which stood ready in earthenware jars, some young women of handsome appearance brought us roasted meat and mealie cobs daintily served on wooden platters, and presented it to us with deep obeisances.

We ate and drank, and then the beds having by our request been all moved into one hut, a precaution at which the amiable young ladies smiled, we flung ourselves down to sleep, thoroughly wearied out with our long journey.

When we woke, it was to find that the sun was high in the heavens, and that the female attendants, who did not seem to be troubled by any false shame, were already standing inside the hut, having been ordered to attend and help us to 'make ready'.

'Make ready, indeed,' growled Good, 'when one has only a flannel shirt and a pair of boots, that does not take long. I wish you would ask them for my trousers.'

I asked accordingly, but was informed that these sacred relics had already been taken to the king, who would see us in the forenoon.

Having, somewhat to their astonishment and disappointment, requested the young ladies to step outside, we proceeded to make the best toilet that the circumstances admitted of Good even went the length of again shaving the right side of his face; the left, on which now appeared a very fair crop of whiskers, we impressed upon him he must on no account touch. As for ourselves, we were contented with a good wash and combing our hair. Sir Henry's yellow locks were now almost down to his shoulders, and he looked more like an ancient Dane than ever, while my grizzled scrub was fully an inch long, instead of half an inch, which in a general way I considered my maximum length.

By the time that we had eaten our breakfasts, and smoked a pipe, a message was brought to us by no less a personage than Infadoos himself that Twala, the king, was ready to see us, if we would be pleased to come.

We remarked in reply that we should prefer to wait till the sun was a little higher, we were yet weary with our journey, etc., etc. It is always well, when dealing with uncivilized people, not to be in too great a hurry. They are apt to mistake politeness for awe or servility. So, although we were quite as anxious to see Twala as Twala could be to see us, we sat down and waited for an hour, employing the interval in preparing such presents as our slender stock of goods permitted – namely the Winchester rifle which had been used by poor Ventvögel, and some beads. The rifle and ammunition we determined to present to his Royal Highness, and the beads were for his wives and courtiers. We had already given a few to Infadoos and Scragga, and found that they were delighted with them, never having seen anything like them before. At length we declared that we were ready, and guided by Infadoos, started off to the levée, Umbopa carrying the rifle and beads.

After walking a few hundred yards, we came to an enclosure, something like that which surrounded the huts that had been allotted to us, only fifty times as big. It could not have been less than six or seven acres in extent. All round the outside fence was a row of huts, which were the habitations of the king's wives. Exactly opposite the gateway, on the farther side of the open space, was a very large hut, which stood by itself, in which his Majesty resided. All the rest was open ground; that is to say, it would have been open had it not been filled by company after company of warriors, who were mustered there to the number of seven or eight thousand. These men stood still as statues as we advanced through them, and it would be impossible to give an idea of the grandeur of the spectacle which they presented, in their waving plumes, their glancing spears, and iron-backed ox-hide shields.

The space in front of the large hut was empty, but before it were placed several stools. On three of these, at a sign from Infadoos, we seated ourselves, Umbopa standing behind us. As for Infadoos, he took up a position by the door of the hut. So we waited for ten minutes or more in the midst of a dead silence, but conscious that we were the object of the concentrated gaze of some eight thousand pairs of eyes. It was a somewhat trying ordeal, but we carried it off as best we could. At length the door of the hut opened, and a gigantic figure, with a splendid tiger-skin karross flung over its shoulders, stepped out, followed by the boy Scragga, and what appeared to us to be a withered-up monkey, wrapped in a fur cloak. The figure seated itself upon a stool, Scragga took his stand behind it, and the withered-up monkey crept on all fours into the shade of the hut and squatted down.

Still there was silence.

Then the gigantic figure slipped off the karross and stood up before us, a truly alarming spectacle. It was that of an enormous man with the most entirely repulsive countenance we had ever beheld. The lips were as thick as a Negro's, the nose was flat, it had but one gleaming black eye (for the other was represented by a hollow in the face), and its whole expression was cruel and sensual to a degree. From the large head rose a magnificent plume of white ostrich feathers, the body was clad in a shirt of shining chain armour, whilst round the waist and right knee was the usual garnish of white ox-tails. In the right hand was a huge spear. Round the neck was a thick torque of gold, and bound on to the forehead was a single and enormous uncut diamond.

Still there was silence; but not for long. Presently the figure, whom we rightly guessed to be the king, raised the great spear in its hand. Instantly eight thousand spears were raised in answer, and from eight thousand throats rang out the royal salute of '*Koom*'. Three times this was repeated, and each time the earth shook with the noise, that can only be compared to the deepest notes of thunder.

'Be humble, O people,' piped out a thin voice which seemed to come from the monkey in the shade, 'it is the king.'

'*It is the king*,' boomed out eight thousand throats, in answer. '*Be humble, O people, it is the king.*'

Then there was silence again – dead silence. Presently, however, it was broken. A soldier on our left dropped his shield, which fell with a clatter on the limestone flooring.

Twala turned his one cold eye in the direction of the noise.

'Come hither, thou,' he said, in a voice of thunder.

A fine young man stepped out of the ranks, and stood before him.

'It was thy shield that fell, thou awkward dog. Wilt thou make me a reproach in the eyes of strangers from the stars? What hast thou to say?'

And then we saw the poor fellow turn pale under his dusky skin.

'It was by chance, O calf of the black cow,' he murmured.

'Then it is a chance for which thou must pay. Thou hast made me foolish; prepare for death.'

'I am the king's ox,' was the low answer.

'Scragga,' roared the king, 'let me see how thou canst use thy spear. Kill me this awkward dog.'

Scragga stepped forward with an ill-favoured grin, and lifted his spear. The poor victim covered his eyes with his hand and stood still. As for us, we were petrified with horror.

'Once, twice,' he waved the spear and then struck, ah, God! right home – the spear stood out a foot behind the soldier's back. He flung up his hands and dropped dead. From the multitude around rose something like a murmur, it rolled round and round, and died away. The tragedy was finished; there lay the corpse, and we had not yet realized that it had been enacted. Sir Henry sprang up and swore a great oath, then, overpowered by the sense of silence, sat down again.

'The thrust was a good one,' said the king; 'take him away.'

Four men stepped out of the ranks, and lifting the body of the murdered man, carried it away.

'Cover up the blood-stains, cover them up,' piped out the thin voice from the monkey-like figure; 'the king's word is spoken, the king's doom is done.'

Thereupon a girl came forward from behind the hut, bearing a jar filled with powdered lime, which she scattered over the red mark, blotting it from sight.

Sir Henry meanwhile was boiling with rage at what had happened; indeed, it was with difficulty that we could keep him still.

'Sit down, for heaven's sake,' I whispered; 'our lives depend on it.'

He yielded and remained quiet.

Twala sat still until the traces of the tragedy had been removed, then he addressed us.

'White people,' he said, 'who come hither, whence I know not, and why I know not, greeting.'

'Greeting Twala, King of the Kukuanas,' I answered.

'White people, whence come ye, and what seek ye?'

'We come from the stars, ask us not how. We come to see this land.'

'Ye come from far to see a little thing. And that man with ye,' pointing to Umbopa, 'does he too come from the stars?'

'Even so; there are people of thy colour in the heavens above; but ask not of matters too high for thee, Twala, the king.'

'Ye speak with a loud voice, people of the stars,' Twala answered, in a tone which I scarcely liked. 'Remember that the stars are far off, and ye are here. How if I make ye as him whom they bear away?'

I laughed out loud, though there was little laughter in my heart.

'O king,' I said, 'be careful, walk warily over hot stones, lest thou shouldst burn thy feet; hold the spear by the handle, lest thou shouldst cut thy hands. Touch but one hair of our heads, and destruction shall come upon thee. What, have not these,' pointing to Infadoos and Scragga (who, young villain that he was, was employed in cleaning the blood of the soldier off his spear), 'told thee what manner of men we are? Hast thou ever seen the like of us?' and I pointed to Good, feeling quite sure that he had never seen anybody before who looked in the least like *him* as he then appeared.

'It is true, I have not,' said the king.

'Have they not told thee how we strike with death from afar?' I went on.

'They have told me, but I believe them not. Let me see you kill. Kill me a man among those who stand yonder' – and he pointed to the opposite side of the kraal – 'and I will believe.'

'Nay,' I answered; 'we shed no blood of man except in just punishment; but if thou wilt see, bid thy servants drive in an ox through the kraal gates, and before he has run twenty paces I will strike him dead.'

'Nay,' laughed the king, 'kill me a man, and I will believe.'

'Good, O king, so be it,' I answered coolly; 'do thou walk across the open space, and before thy feet reach the gate thou shalt be dead; or if thou wilt not, send thy son Scragga' (whom at that moment it would have given me much pleasure to shoot).

On hearing this suggestion, Scragga gave a sort of howl, and bolted into the hut.

Twala frowned majestically; the suggestion did not please him.

'Let a young ox be driven in,' he said.

Two men at once departed, running swiftly.

'Now, Sir Henry,' said I, 'do you shoot. I want to show this ruffian that I am not the only magician of the party.'

Sir Henry accordingly took the 'express', and made ready.

'I hope I shall make a good shot,' he groaned.

'You must,' I answered. 'If you miss with the first barrel, let him have the second. Sight for 150 yards, and wait till the beast turns broadside on.'

Then came a pause, till presently we caught sight of an ox running straight for the kraal gate. It came on through the gate, and then, catching sight of the vast concourse of people, stopped stupidly, turned round, and bellowed.

'Now's your time,' I whispered.

Up went the rifle.

Bang! thud! and the ox was kicking on his back, shot in the ribs. The semi-hollow bullet had done its work well, and a sigh of astonishment went up from the assembled thousands.

I turned coolly round:

'Have I lied, O king?'

'Nay, white man, it is a truth,' was the somewhat awed answer.

'Listen, Twala,' I went on. 'Thou hast seen. Now know we come in peace, not in war. See here' (and I held up the Winchester repeater); 'here is a hollow staff that shall enable you to kill even as we kill, only this charm I lay upon it, thou shalt kill no man with it. If thou liftest it against a man, it shall kill thee. Stay, I will show thee. Bid a man step forty paces and place the shaft of a spear in the ground so that the flat blade looks towards us.'

In a few seconds it was done.

'Now, see, I will break the spear.'

Taking a careful sight I fired. The bullet struck the flat of the spear, and broke the blade into fragments

Again the sigh of astonishment went up.

'Now, Twala' (handing him the rifle), 'this magic tube we give to thee, and by-and-by I will show thee how to use it; but beware how thou usest the magic of the stars against a man of earth,' and I handed him the rifle. He took it very gingerly, and laid it down at his feet. As he did so I observed the wizened monkey-like figure creeping up from the shadow of the hut. It crept on all fours, but when it reached the place where the king sat, it rose upon its feet, and throwing the furry covering off its face, revealed a most extraordinary and weird countenance. It was (apparently) that of a woman of great age, so shrunken that in size it was no larger than that of a year-old child, and was made up of a collection of deep yellow wrinkles. Set in the wrinkles was a sunken slit, that represented the mouth, beneath which the chin curved outwards to a point. There was no nose to speak of; indeed, the whole countenance might have been taken for that of a sun-dried corpse had it not been for a pair of large black eyes, still full of fire and intelligence, which gleamed and played under the snow-white eyebrows, and the projecting parchment-coloured skull, like jewels in a charnel-house. As for the skull itself, it was perfectly bare, and yellow in hue, while its wrinkled scalp moved and contracted like the hood of a cobra.

The figure to whom this fearful countenance, which caused a shiver of fear to pass through us as we gazed on it, belonged, stood still for a moment, and then suddenly projected a skinny claw armed with nails nearly an inch long, and laid it on the shoulder of Twala, the king, and began to speak in a thin, piercing voice:

'Listen, O king! Listen, O people! Listen, O mountains and plains and rivers, home of the Kukuana race! Listen, O skies and sun, O rain and storm and mist! Listen, all things that live and must die! Listen, all dead things that must live again – again to die! Listen, the spirit of life is in me, and I prophesy. I prophesy! I prophesy!'

The words died away in a faint wail and terror seemed to seize upon the hearts of all who heard them, including ourselves. The old woman was very terrible.

'*Blood! blood! blood!* rivers of blood; blood everywhere. I see it, I smell it, I taste it – it is salt; it runs red upon the ground, it rains down from the skies.

'*Footsteps! footsteps! footsteps!* the tread of the white man coming from afar. It shakes the earth; the earth trembles before her master.

'Blood is good, the red blood is bright; there is no smell like the smell of new-shed blood. The lions shall lap it and roar, the vultures shall wash their wings in it, and shriek in joy.

'I am old! I am old! I have seen much blood; ha, ha! but I shall see more ere I die, and be merry. How old am I, think ye? Your fathers knew me, and *their* fathers knew me, and *their* fathers' fathers. I have seen the white man, and know his desires. I am old, but the mountains are older than I. Who made the great road, tell me? Who wrote in pictures on the rocks, tell me? Who reared up the three silent ones yonder, who gaze across the pit, tell me?' (And she pointed towards the three precipitous mountains we had noticed on the previous night.)

'Ye know not, but I know. It was a white people who were before ye are, who shall be when ye are not, who shall eat ye up, and destroy ye. *Yea! yea! yea*!

'And what came they for, the white ones, the terrible ones, the skilled in magic and all learning, the strong, the unswerving? What is that bright stone upon thy forehead, O king? Whose hands made the iron garments upon thy breast, O king? Ye know not, but I know. I the old one, I the wise one, I the Isanusi!' (witch doctress.)

Then she turned her bald vulture-head towards us.

'What seek ye, white men of the stars – ah, yes, of the stars? Do ye seek a lost one? Ye shall not find him here. He is not here. Never for ages upon ages has a white foot pressed this land; never but once, and he left it but to die. Ye come for bright stones; I know it – I know it; ye shall find them when the blood is dry; but shall ye return whence ye came, or shall ye stop with me? Ha! ha! ha!

'And thou, thou with the dark skin and the proud bearing' (pointing her skinny finger at Umbopa), 'who art *thou*, and what seekest *thou*? Not stones that shine, not yellow metal that gleams, that thou leavest to "white men from the stars". Methinks I know thee; methinks I can smell the smell of the blood in thy veins. Strip off the girdle –'

Here the features of this extraordinary creature became convulsed, and she fell to the ground foaming in an epileptic fit, and was carried off into the hut.

The king rose up trembling, and waved his hand. Instantly the regiments began to file off, and in ten minutes, save for ourselves, the king, and a few attendants, the great space was left clear.

'White people,' he said, 'it passes in my mind to kill ye. Gagool has spoken strange words. What say ye?'

I laughed. 'Be careful, O king, we are not easy to slay. Thou hast seen the fate of the ox; wouldst thou be as the ox?'

The king frowned. 'It is not well to threaten a king.'

'We threaten not, we speak what is true. Try to kill us, O king, and learn.'

The great man put his hand to his forehead.

'Go in peace,' he said, at length. 'Tonight is the great dance. Ye shall see it. Fear not that I shall set a snare for ye. Tomorrow I shall think.'

'It is well, O king,' I answered, unconcernedly, and then, accompanied by Infadoos, we rose, and went back to our kraal.

10

The Witch Hunt

ON reaching our hut, I motioned to Infadoos to enter with us.

'Now, Infadoos,' I said, 'we would speak with thee.'

'Let my lords say on.'

'It seems to us, Infadoos, that Twala, the king, is a cruel man.'

'It is so, my lords. Alas! the land cries out with his cruelties. Tonight ye will see. It is the great witch-hunt, and many will be smelt out as wizards and slain. No man's life is safe. If the king covets a man's cattle, or a man's life, or if he fears a man that he should excite a rebellion against him, then Gagool, whom ye saw, or some of the witch-finding women whom she has taught, will smell that man out as a wizard, and he will be killed. Many will die before the moon grows pale tonight. It is ever so. Perhaps I, too, shall be killed. As yet I have been spared, because I am skilled in war, and beloved by the soldiers; but I know not how long I shall live. The land groans at the cruelties of Twala, the king; it is wearied of him and his red ways.'

'Then why is it, Infadoos, that the people do not cast him down?'

'Nay, my lords, he is the king, and if he were killed Scragga would reign in his place, and the heart of Scragga is blacker than the heart of Twala, his father. If Scragga were king, the yoke upon our neck would be heavier than the yoke of Twala. If Imotu had never been slain, or if Ignosi, his son, had lived, it had been otherwise; but they are both dead.'

'How know you that Ignosi is dead?' said a voice behind us. We looked round with astonishment to see who spoke. It was Umbopa.

'What meanest thou, boy?' asked Infadoos; 'who told thee to speak?'

'Listen, Infadoos,' was the answer, 'and I will tell thee a story. Years ago the King Imotu was killed in this country, and his wife fled with the boy Ignosi. Is it not so?'

'It is so.'

'It was said that the woman and the boy died upon the mountains. Is it not so?'

'It is even so.'

'Well, it came to pass that the mother and the boy Ignosi did not die. They crossed the mountains, and were led by a tribe of wandering desert men across the sands beyond, till at last they came to water and grass and trees again.'

'How knowest thou that?'

'Listen. They travelled on and on, many months' journey, till they reached a land where a people called the Amazulu, who too are of the Kukuana stock, live by war, and with them they tarried many years, till at length the mother died. Then the son, Ignosi, again became a wanderer, and went on into a land of wonders, where white people live, and for many more years learned the wisdom of the white people.'

'It is a pretty story,' said Infadoos, incredulously.

'For many years he lived there working as a servant and a soldier, but holding in his heart all that his mother had told him of his own place, and casting about in his mind to find how he might get back there to see his own people and his father's house before he died. For many years he lived and waited, and at last the time came, as it ever comes to him who can wait for it, and he met some white men who would seek this unknown land, and joined himself to them. The white men started and journeyed on and on, seeking for one who is lost. They crossed the burning desert, they crossed the snowclad mountains, and reached the land of the Kukuanas, and there they met thee, O Infadoos.'

'Surely thou art mad to talk thus,' said the astonished old soldier.

'Thou thinkest so; see, I will show thee, oh my uncle.

'*I am Ignosi, rightful king of the Kukuanas!*'

Then with a single movement he slipped off the 'moocha' or girdle round his middle, and stood naked before us.

'Look,' he said, 'what is this?' and he pointed to the mark of a great snake tattooed in blue round his middle, its tail disappearing in its open mouth just above where the thighs are set into the body.

Infadoos looked, his eyes starting nearly out of his head, and then fell upon his knees.

'*Koom! Koom!*' he ejaculated; 'it is my brother's son; it is the king.'

'Did I not tell thee so, my uncle? Rise; I am not yet the king, but with thy help, and with the help of these brave white men, who are my friends, I shall be. But the old woman Gagool was right, the land shall run with blood first, and hers shall run with it, for she killed my father with her words, and drove my mother forth. And now, Infadoos, choose thou. Wilt thou put thy hands between my hands and be my man? Wilt thou share the dangers that lie before me, and help me to overthrow this tyrant and murderer, or wilt thou not? Choose thou.'

The old man put his hand to his head and thought. Then he rose, and advancing to where Umbopa, or rather Ignosi, stood, knelt before him and took his hand.

'Ignosi, rightful king of the Kukuanas, I put my hand between thy hands, and am thy man till death. When thou wast a babe I dandled thee upon my knee, now shall my old arm strike for thee and freedom.'

'It is well, Infadoos; if I conquer, thou shalt be the greatest man in the kingdom after the king. If I fail, thou canst only die, and death is not far off for thee. Rise, my uncle.'

'And ye, white men, will ye help me? What have I to offer ye! The white stones, if I conquer and can find them, ye shall have as many as ye can carry hence. Will that suffice ye?'

I translated this remark.

'Tell him,' answered Sir Henry, 'that he mistakes an Englishman. Wealth is good, and if it comes in our way we will take it; but a gentleman does not sell himself for wealth. But, speaking for myself, I say this. I have always liked Umbopa, and so far as lies in me will stand by him in this business. It will be very pleasant to me to try and square matters with that cruel devil, Twala. What do you say, Good, and you, Quatermain?'

'Well,' said Good, 'to adopt the language of hyperbole, in which all these people seem to indulge, you can tell him that a row is surely good, and warms the cockles of the heart, and that so far as I am concerned I'm his boy. My only stipulation is, that he allows me to wear trousers.'

I translated these answers.

'It is well, my friends,' said Ignosi, late Umbopa; 'and what say you, Macumazahn, art thou too with me, old hunter, cleverer than a wounded buffalo?'

I thought a while and scratched my head.

'Umbopa, or Ignosi,' I said, 'I don't like revolutions. I am a man of peace, and a bit of a coward,' (here Umbopa smiled), 'but, on the other hand, I stick to my friends, Ignosi. You have stuck to us and played the part of a man, and I will stick to you. But mind you I am a trader, and have to make my living, so I accept your offer about those diamonds in case we should ever be in a position to avail ourselves of it. Another thing: we came, as you know, to look for Incubu's (Sir Henry's) lost brother. You must help us to find him.'

'That will I do,' answered Ignosi. 'Stay, Infadoos, by the sign of the snake round my middle, tell me the truth. Has any white man to thy knowledge set his foot within the land?'

'None, O Ignosi.'

'If any white man had been seen or heard of, wouldst thou have known it?'

'I should certainly have known.'

'Thou hearest, Incubu,' said Ignosi to Sir Henry, 'he has not been here.'

'Well, well,' said Sir Henry, with a sigh; 'there it is; I suppose he never got here. Poor fellow, poor fellow! So it has all been for nothing. God's will be done.'

'Now for business,' I put in, anxious to escape from a painful subject. 'It is very well to be a king by right divine, Ignosi, but how dost thou purpose to become a king indeed?'

'Nay, I know not. Infadoos, hast thou a plan?'

'Ignosi, son of the lightning,' answered his uncle, 'tonight is the great dance and witch-hunt. Many will be smelt out and perish, and in the hearts of many others there will be grief and anguish and anger against the King Twala. When the dance is over, then will I speak to some of the great chiefs, who in turn, if I can win them over, shall speak to their regiments. I shall speak to the chiefs softly at first, and bring them to see that thou art indeed the king, and I think that by tomorrow's light thou shalt have twenty thousand spears at thy command. And now must I go and think, and hear, and make ready. After the dance is done I will, if I am yet alive, and we are all alive, meet thee here, and we will talk. At the best there will be war.'

At this moment our conference was interrupted by the cry that messengers had come from the king. Advancing to the door of the hut we ordered that they should be admitted, and presently three men entered, each bearing a shining shirt of chain armour, and a magnificent battle-axe.

'The gifts of my lord the king to the white men from the stars!' exclaimed a herald who came with them.

'We thank the king,' I answered; 'withdraw.'

The men went, and we examined the armour with great interest. It was the most beautiful chain work we had ever seen. A whole coat fell together so closely that it formed a mass of links scarcely too big to be covered with both hands.

'Do you make these things in this country, Infadoos?' I asked; 'they are very beautiful.'

'Nay, my lord, they come down to us from our forefathers. We know not who made them, and there are but few left. None but those of royal blood may wear them. They are magic coats through which no spear can pass. He who wears them is well-nigh safe in the battle. The king is well pleased or much afraid, or he would not have sent them. Wear them tonight, my lords.'

The rest of the day we spent quietly resting and talking over the situation, which was sufficiently exciting. At last the sun went down, the thousand watchfires glowed out, and through the darkness we heard the tramp of many feet and the clashing of hundreds of spears, as the regiments passed to their appointed places to be ready for the great dance. About eight the full moon came up in splendour, and as we stood watching her ascent Infadoos arrived, clad in full war toggery, and accompanied by a guard of twenty men to escort us to the dance. We had already, as he recommended, donned the shirts of chain armour which the king had sent us, putting them on under our ordinary clothing, and finding to our surprise that they were neither very heavy nor uncomfortable. These steel shirts, which had evidently been made for men of a very large stature, hung somewhat loosely upon Good and myself, but Sir Henry's fitted his magnificent frame like a glove. Then strapping our revolvers round our waists, and taking the battle-axes which the king had sent with the armour in our hands, we started.

On arriving at the great kraal, where we had that morning been interviewed by the king, we found that it was closely packed with some twenty thousand men arranged in regiments round it. The regiments were in turn divided into companies, and between each company was a little path to allow free passage to the witch-finders to pass up and down. Anything more imposing than the sight that was presented by this vast and orderly concourse of armed men it is impossible for one to conceive. There they stood perfectly silent, and the moon poured her light upon the forest of their raised spears, upon their majestic forms, waving plumes, and the harmonious shading of their various-coloured shields. Wherever we looked was line upon line of dim faces surmounted by range upon range of shimmering spears.

'Surely,' I said to Infadoos, 'the whole army is here?'

'Nay, Macumazahn,' he answered, 'but a third part of it. One third part is present at this dance each year, another third part is mustered outside in case there should be trouble when the killing begins, ten thousand more garrison the outposts round Loo, and the rest watch at the kraals in the country. Thou seest it is a very great people.'

'They are very silent,' said Good; and indeed the intense stillness among such a vast concourse of living men was almost overpowering.

'What says Bougwan?' asked Infadoos.

I translated.

'Those over whom the shadow of Death is hovering are silent,' he answered, grimly.

'Will many be killed?'

'Very many.'

'It seems,' I said to the others, 'that we are going to assist at a gladiatorial show arranged regardless of expense.'

Sir Henry shivered, and Good said that he wished that we could get out of it.

'Tell me,' I asked Infadoos, 'are we in danger?'

'I know not, my lords, I trust not; but do not seem afraid. If ye live through the night all may go well. The soldiers murmur against the king.'

All this while we had been advancing steadily towards the centre of the open space, in the midst of which were placed some stools. As we proceeded we perceived another small party coming from the direction of the royal hut.

'It is the king, Twala, and Scragga his son, and Gagool the old, and see, with them are those who slay,' and he pointed to a little group of about a dozen gigantic and savage-looking men, armed with spears in one hand and heavy kerries in the other.

The king seated himself upon the centre stool, Gagool crouched at his feet, and the others stood behind.

'Greeting, white lords,' he cried, as we came up; 'be seated, waste not the precious time – the night is all too short for the deeds that must be done. Ye come in a good hour, and shall see a glorious show. Look round, white lords; look round,' and he rolled his one wicked eye from regiment to regiment. 'Can the stars show ye such a sight as this? See how they shake in their wickedness, all those who have evil in their hearts and fear the judgement of "heaven above".'

'*Begin! begin*!' cried out Gagool in her thin, piercing voice; 'the hyaenas are hungry, they howl for food. *Begin! begin*!' Then for a moment there was intense stillness, made horrible by a presage of what was to come.

The king lifted his spear, and suddenly twenty thousand feet were raised, as though they belonged to one man, and brought down with a stamp upon the earth. This was repeated three times, causing the solid ground to shake and tremble. Then from a far point of the circle a solitary voice began a wailing song, of which the refrain ran something as follows:

'*What is the lot of man born of woman*?'

Back came the answer rolling out from every throat in that vast company:

'*Death*!'

Gradually, however, the song was taken up by company after company, till the whole armed multitude were singing it, and I could no longer follow the words, except in so far as they appeared to represent various phases of human passions, fears, and joys. Now it seemed to be a love song, now a majestic swelling war chant, and last of all a death-dirge ending suddenly in one heartbreaking wail that went echoing and rolling away in a volume of blood-curdling sound. Again the silence fell upon the place, and again it was broken by the king lifting up his hand. Instantly there was a pattering of feet, and from out of the masses of the warriors strange and awful figures came running towards us. As they drew near we saw that they were those of women, most of them aged, for their white hair, ornamented with small bladders taken from fish, streamed out behind them. Their faces were painted in stripes of white and yellow; down their backs hung snake-skins, and round their waists rattled circlets of human bones, while each held in her shrivelled hand a small forked wand. In all there were ten of them. When they arrived in front of us they halted, and one of them pointing with her wand towards the crouching figure of Gagool, cried out:

'Mother, old mother, we are here.'

'*Good! good! good*!' piped out that aged iniquity. 'Are your eyes keen, Isanusis (witch doctresses), ye seers in dark places?'

'Mother, they are keen.'

'*Good! good! good*! Are your ears open, Isanusis, ye who hear words that come not from the tongue?'

'Mother, they are open.'

'*Good! good! good*! Are your senses awake, Isanusis – can ye smell blood, can ye purge the land of the wicked ones who compass evil against the king and against their neighbours? Are ye ready to do the justice of "Heaven above", ye whom I have taught, who have eaten of the bread of my wisdom and drunk of the water of my magic?

'Mother, we can.'

'Then go! Tarry not, ye vultures; see the slayers,' pointing to the ominous group of executioners behind; 'make sharp their spears; the white men from afar are hungry to see. *Go*.'

With a wild yell the weird party broke away in every direction, like fragments from a shell, and the dry bones round their waists rattling as they ran, made direct for various points of the dense human circle. We could not watch them all, so fixed our eyes upon the Isanusi nearest us. When she came within a few paces of the warriors, she halted and began to dance wildly, turning round and round with an almost incredible rapidity, and shrieking out sentences such as 'I smell him, the evil-doer!' 'He is near, he who poisoned his mother!' 'I hear the thoughts of him who thought evil of the king!'

Quicker and quicker she danced, till she lashed herself into such a frenzy of excitement that the foam flew in flecks from her gnashing jaws, her eyes seemed to start from her head, and her flesh to quiver visibly. Suddenly she stopped dead, and stiffened all over, like a pointer dog when he scents game, and then with outstretched wand began to creep stealthily towards the soldiers before her. It seemed to us that as she came their stoicism gave way, and that they shrank from her. As for ourselves, we followed her movements with a horrible fascination. Presently, still creeping and crouching like a dog, she was before them. Then she stopped and pointed, and then again crept on a pace or two.

Suddenly the end came. With a shriek she sprang in and touched a tall warrior with the forked wand. Instantly two of his comrades, those standing immediately next to him, seized the doomed man, each by one arm, and advanced with him towards the king.

He did not resist, but we saw that he dragged his limbs as though they were paralysed, and his fingers, from which the spear had fallen, were limp as those of a man newly dead.

As he came, two of the villainous executioners stepped forward to meet him. Presently they met, and the executioners turned round towards the king as though for orders.

'*Kill*!' said the king.

'*Kill*!' squeaked Gagool.

'*Kill*!' re-echoed Scragga, with a hollow chuckle.

Almost before the words were uttered, the horrible deed was done. One man had driven his spear into the victim's heart, and to make assurance doubly sure, the other had dashed out his brains with his great club.

'*One*,' counted Twala the king, just like a black Madame Defarge, as Good said, and the body was dragged a few paces away and stretched out.

Hardly was this done, before another poor wretch was brought up, like an ox to the slaughter. This time we could see, from the leopard-skin cloak, that the man was a person of rank. Again the awful syllables were spoken, and the victim fell dead.

'*Two*,' counted the king.

And so the deadly game went on, till some hundred bodies were stretched in rows behind us. I have heard of the gladiatorial shows of the Caesars, and of the Spanish bull-fights, but I take the liberty of doubting if they were either of them half as horrible as this Kukuana witch hunt. Gladiatorial shows and Spanish bull-fights, at any rate, contributed to the public amusement, which certainly was not the case here. The most confirmed sensation-monger would fight shy of sensation if he knew that it was well on the cards that he would, in his own proper person, be the subject of the next 'event'.

Once we rose and tried to remonstrate, but were sternly repressed by Twala.

'Let the law take its course, white men. These dogs are magicians and evil-doers; it is well that they should die,' was the only answer vouchsafed to us.

About half past ten there was a pause. The witch-finders gathered themselves together, apparently exhausted with their bloody work, and we thought that the whole performance was done with. But it was not so, for presently, to our surprise, the old woman, Gagool, rose from her crouching position, and supporting herself with a stick, staggered off into the open space. It was an extraordinary sight to see this frightful vulture-headed old creature, bent nearly double with extreme age, gather strength by degrees till at last she rushed about almost as actively as her ill-omened pupils. To and fro she ran, chanting to herself, till suddenly she made a dash at a tall man standing in front of one of the regiments, and touched him. As she did so, a sort of groan went up from the regiment, which he evidently commanded. But all the same, two of its members seized him and brought him up for execution. We afterwards leaned that he was a man of great wealth and importance, being, indeed, a cousin of the king's.

He was slain, and the king counted one hundred and three. Then Gagool again sprang to and fro, gradually drawing nearer and nearer to ourselves.

'Hang me if I don't believe she is going to try her games on us,' ejaculated Good in horror.

'Nonsense!' said Sir Henry.

As for myself, as I saw that old fiend dancing nearer and nearer, my heart positively sank into my boots. I glanced behind us at the long rows of corpses, and shivered.

Nearer and nearer waltzed Gagool, looking for all the world like an animated crooked stick, her horrid eyes gleaming and glowing with a most unholy lustre.

Nearer she came, and nearer yet, every pair of eyes in that vast assemblage watching her movements with intense anxiety. At last she stood still and pointed.

'Which is it to be?' asked Sir Henry to himself.

In a moment all doubts were set at rest, for the old woman had rushed in and touched Umbopa, alias Ignosi, on the shoulder.

'I smell him out,' she shrieked. 'Kill him, kill him, he is full of evil; kill him, the stranger, before blood flows for him. Slay him, O king.'

There was a pause, which I instantly took advantage of.

'O King,' I called out, rising from my seat, 'this man is the servant of thy guests, he is their dog; whosoever sheds the blood of our dog sheds our blood. By the sacred law of hospitality I claim protection for him.'

'Gagool, mother of the witch doctors, has smelt him out; he must die, white men,' was the sullen answer.

'Nay, he shall not die,' I replied; 'he who tries to touch him shall die indeed.'

'Seize him!' roared Twala to the executioners, who stood around red to the eyes with the blood of their victims.

They advanced towards us, and then hesitated. As for Ignosi, he raised his spear, and raised it as though determined to sell his life dearly.

'Stand back, ye dogs,' I shouted, 'if ye would see tomorrow's light. Touch one hair of his head and your king dies,' and I covered Twala with my revolver. Sir Henry and Good also drew their pistols, Sir Henry pointing his at the leading executioner, who was advancing to carry out the sentence, and Good taking a deliberate aim at Gagool.

Twala winced perceptibly, as my barrel came in a line with his broad chest.

'Well,' I said, 'what is it to be, Twala?'

Then he spoke.

'Put away your magic tubes,' he said; 'ye have adjured me in the name of hospitality, and for that reason, but not from fear of what ye can do, I spare him. Go in peace.'

'It is well,' I answered, unconcernedly; 'we are weary of slaughter, and would sleep. Is the dance ended?'

'It is ended,' Twala answered, sulkily. 'Let these dogs,' pointing to the long rows of corpses, 'be flung out to the hyaenas and the vultures,' and he lifted his spear.

Instantly the regiments began in perfect silence to defile off through the kraal gateway, a fatigue party only remaining behind to drag away the corpses of those who had been sacrificed.

Then we, too, rose, and making our salaam to his majesty, which he hardly deigned to acknowledge, departed to our kraal.

'Well,' said Sir Henry, as we sat down, having first lit a lamp of the sort used by the Kukuanas, of which the wick is made of the fibre of a species of palm leaf, and the oil of clarified hippopotamus fat, 'well, I feel uncommonly inclined to be sick.'

'If I had any doubts about helping Umbopa to rebel against that infernal blackguard,' put in Good, 'they are gone now. It was as much as I could do to sit still while that slaughter was going on. I tried to keep my eyes shut, but they would open just at the wrong time. I wonder where Infadoos is. Umbopa, my friend, you ought to be grateful to us; your skin came near to having an air-hole made in it.'

'I am grateful, Bougwan,' was Umbopa's answer, when I had translated, 'and I shall not forget. As for Infadoos, he will be here by-and-by. We must wait.'

So we lit our pipes and waited.

11

We Give a Sign

FOR a long while – two hours, I should think – we sat there in silence, for we were too overwhelmed by the recollection of the horrors we had seen to talk. At last, just as we were thinking of turning in – for the night was drawing nigh to dawn – we heard the sound of steps. Then came the challenge of the sentry, who was posted at the kraal gate, which was apparently answered, though not in an audible tone, for the steps came on; and in another second Infadoos had entered the hut followed by some half-dozen stately looking chiefs.

'My lords,' he said, 'I have come according to my word. My lords and Ignosi, rightful King of the Kukuanas, I have brought with me these men,' pointing to the row of chiefs, 'who are great men among us, having each one of them the command of three thousand soldiers, who live but to do their bidding, under the king's. I have told them of what I have seen, and what my ears have heard. Now let them also see the sacred snake around thee, and hear thy story, Ignosi, that they may say whether or no they will make cause with thee against Twala, the king.'

For answer, Ignosi again stripped off his girdle, and exhibited the snake tattooed around him. Each chief in turn drew near and examined it by the dim light of the lamp, and without saying a word passed on to the other side.

Then Ignosi resumed his moocha, and addressing them, repeated the history he had detailed in the morning.

'Now ye have heard, chiefs,' said Infadoos, when he had done, 'what say ye; will ye stand by this man and help him to his father's throne, or will ye not? The land cries out against Twala, and the blood of the people flows like the waters in spring. Ye have seen tonight. Two other chiefs there were with whom I had it in my mind to speak, and where are they now? The hyenas howl over their corpses. Soon will ye be as they are if ye strike not. Choose then, my brothers.'

The eldest of the six men, a short, thick-set warrior with white hair, stepped forward a pace and answered:

'Thy words are true, Infadoos; the land cries out. My own brother is among those who died tonight; but this is a great matter, and the thing is hard to believe. How know we that if we lift our spears it may not be for an impostor? It is a great matter, I say, and none may see the end of it. For of this be sure, blood will flow in rivers before the deed is done; many will still cleave to the king, for men worship the sun that still shines bright in the heavens, and not that which has not risen. These white men from the stars, their magic is great, and Ignosi is under the cover of their wing. If he be indeed the rightful king, let them give us a sign, and let the people have a sign, that all may see. So shall men cleave to us, knowing that the white man's magic is with them.'

'Ye have the sign of the snake,' I answered.

'My lord, it is not enough. The snake may have been placed there since the man's birth. Show us a sign. We will not move without a sign.'

The others gave a decided assent, and I turned in perplexity to Sir Henry and Good, and explained the situation.

'I think I have it,' said Good, exultingly; 'ask them to give us a moment to think.'

I did so, and the chiefs withdrew. As soon as they were gone, Good went to the little box in which his medicines were, unlocked it, and took out a note-book, in the front of which was an almanack. 'Now, look here, you fellows, isn't tomorrow the fourth of June?'

We had kept a careful note of the days, so were able to answer that it was.

'Very good; then here we have it – "4 June, total eclipse of the moon commences at 8.15 Greenwich time, visible in Teneriffe – *Africa*, etc." There's a sign for you. Tell them that you will darken the moon tomorrow night.'

The idea was a splendid one; indeed, the only fear about it was a fear lest Good's almanack might be incorrect. If we made a false prophecy on such a subject, our prestige would be gone for ever, and so would Ignosi's chance of the throne of the Kukuanas.

'Suppose the almanack is wrong,' suggested Sir Henry to Good, who was busily employed in working out something on the fly-leaf of the book.

'I don't see any reason to suppose anything of the sort,' was his answer. 'Eclipses always come up to time; at least, that is my experience of them, and it especially states that it will be visible in Africa. I have worked out the reckonings as well as I can, without knowing our exact position; and I make out that the eclipse should begin here about ten o'clock tomorrow night, and last till half past twelve. For an hour and a half or more there should be almost total darkness.'

'Well,' said Sir Henry, 'I suppose we had better risk it.'

I acquiesced, though doubtfully, for eclipses are queer cattle to deal with, and sent Umbopa to summon the chiefs back. Presently they came, and I addressed them thus:

'Great men of the Kukuanas, and thou, Infadoos, listen. We love not to show our powers, since to do so is to interfere with the course of nature, and plunge the world into fear and confusion; but as this matter is a great one, and as we are angered against the king because of the slaughter we have seen, and because of the act of the Isanusi Gagool, who would have put our friend Ignosi to death, we have determined to break a rule, and to give such a sign as all men may see. Come hither'; and I led them to the door of the hut and pointed to the red ball of the westering moon. 'What see ye there?'

'We see the sinking moon,' answered the spokesman of the party.

'It is so. Now tell me, can any mortal man put out that moon before her hour of setting, and bring the curtain of black night down on to the land?'

The chief laughed a little. 'No, my lord, that no man can do. The moon is stronger than man who looks on her, nor can she vary in her courses.'

'Ye say so. Yet I tell you that tomorrow night, two hours before midnight, will we cause that moon to be eaten up for a space of an hour and half an hour, and deep darkness shall cover the earth, and it shall be for a sign that Ignosi is indeed King of the Kukuanas. If we do this thing, will ye be satisfied?'

'Yea, my lords,' answered the old chief with a smile, which was reflected on the faces of his companions; '*if* ye do this thing we will be satisfied indeed.'

'It shall be done; we three, Incubu, Bougwan, and Macumazahn, have said it, and it shall be done. Dost thou hear, Infadoos?'

'I hear, my lord, but it is a wonderful thing that ye promise, to put out the moon, the mother of the world, when she is at her full.'

'Yet shall we do it, Infadoos.'

'It is well, my lords. Today, two hours after sunset, will Twala send for my lords to witness the girls dance, and one hour after the dance begins shall the girl whom Twala thinks the fairest be killed by Scragga, the king's son, as a sacrifice to the silent stone ones, who sit and keep watch by the mountains yonder,' and he pointed to the three strange-looking peaks where Solomon's road was supposed to end. 'Then let my lords darken the moon, and save the maiden's life, and the people will indeed believe.'

'Ay,' said the old chief, still smiling a little, 'the people will believe indeed.'

'Two miles from Loo,' went on Infadoos, 'there is a hill curved like the new moon, a stronghold, where my regiment, and three other regiments which these men command, are stationed. This morning we will make a plan whereby other regiments, two or three, may be moved there also. Then if my lords can indeed darken the moon, in the darkness I will take my lords by the hand and lead them out of Loo to this place, where they shall be safe, and thence can we make war upon Twala, the king.'

'It is good,' said I. 'Now leave us to sleep awhile and make ready our magic.'

Infadoos rose, and, having saluted us, departed with the chiefs.

'My friends,' said Ignosi, as soon as they were gone, 'can ye indeed do this wonderful thing, or were ye speaking empty words to the men?'

'We believe that we can do it, Umbopa – Ignosi, I mean.'

'It is strange,' he answered, 'and had ye not been Englishmen I would not have believed it; but English "gentlemen" tell no lies. If we live through the matter, be sure I will repay ye!'

'Ignosi,' said Sir Henry, 'promise me one thing.'

'I will promise, Incubu, my friend, even before I hear it,' answered the big man with a smile. 'What is it?'

'This: that if you ever come to be king of this people you will do away with the smelling out of witches such as we have seen last night; and that the killing of men without trial shall not take place in the land.'

Ignosi thought for a moment, after I had translated this, and then answered:

'The ways of black people are not as the ways of white men, Incubu, nor do we hold life so high as ye. Yet will I promise it. If it be in my power to hold them back, the witch-finders shall hunt no more, nor shall any man die the death without judgement.'

'That's a bargain, then,' said Sir Henry; 'and now let us get a little rest.'

Thoroughly wearied out, we were soon sound asleep, and slept till Ignosi woke us about eleven o'clock. Then we got up, washed, and ate a hearty breakfast. After that we went outside the hut and walked about, amusing ourselves with examining the structure of the Kukuana huts and observing the customs of the women.

'I hope that eclipse will come off,' said Sir Henry, presently.

'If it does not, it will soon be up with us,' I answered, mournfully; 'for so sure as we are living men, some of those chiefs will tell the whole story to the king, and then there will be another sort of eclipse, and one that we shall not like.'

Returning to the hut we had some dinner, and passed the rest of the day in receiving visits of ceremony and curiosity. At length the sun set, and we had a couple of hours of such quiet as our melancholy forebodings would allow us. Finally, about half past eight, a messenger came from Twala to bid us to the great annual 'dance of girls' which was about to be celebrated.

We hastily put on the chain shirts that the king had sent us, and taking our rifles and ammunition with us, so as to have them handy in case we had to fly, as suggested by Infadoos, started boldly enough, though with inward fear and trembling. The great space in front of the king's kraal bore a very different appearance from that which it had presented on the previous evening. In the place of the grim ranks of serried warriors were company after company of Kukuana girls, not overdressed, so far as clothing went, but each crowned with a wreath of flowers, and holding a palm leaf in one hand and a tall white lily (the arum) in the other. In the centre of the open moonlit space sat Twala, the king, with old Gagool at his feet, attended by Infadoos, the boy Scragga, and twelve guards. There were also present about a score of chiefs, amongst whom I recognized most of our friends of the night before.

Twala greeted us with much apparent cordiality, though I saw him fix his one eye viciously on Umbopa.

'Welcome, white men from the stars,' he said; 'this is a different sight from what your eyes gazed on by the light of last night's moon, but it is not so good a sight. Girls are pleasant, and were it not for such as these' (and he pointed round him) 'we should none of us be here this night; but men are better. Kisses and the tender words of women are sweet, but the sound of the clashing of men's spears, and the smell of men's blood, are sweeter far! Would ye have wives from among our people, white men? If so, choose the fairest here, and ye shall have them, as many as ye will,' and he paused for an answer.

As the prospect did not seem to be without attractions to Good, who was, like most sailors, of a susceptible nature, I, being elderly and wise, and foreseeing the endless complications that anything of the sort would involve (for women bring trouble as surely as the night follows the day), put in a hasty answer:

'Thanks, O king, but we white men wed only with white women like ourselves. Your maidens are fair, but they are not for us!'

The king laughed. 'It is well. In our land there is a proverb which says, "Woman's eyes are always bright, whatever the colour," and another which says, "Love her who is present, for be sure she who is absent is false to thee"; but perhaps these things are not so in the stars. In a land where men are white all things are possible. So be it, white men; the girls will not go begging! Welcome again; and welcome, too, thou black one; if Gagool here had had her way thou wouldst have been stiff and cold by now. It is lucky that thou, too, camest from the stars; ha! ha!'

'I can kill thee before thou killest me, O king,' was Ignosi's calm answer, 'and thou shalt be stiff before my limbs cease to bend.'

Twala started. 'Thou speakest boldly, boy,' he replied, angrily; 'presume not too far.'

'He may well be bold in whose lips are truth. The truth is a sharp spear which flies home and fails not. It is a message from "the stars", O king!'

Twala scowled, and his one eye gleamed fiercely, but he said nothing more.

'Let the dance begin,' he cried, and next second the flower-crowned girls sprang forward in companies, singing a sweet song and waving the delicate palms and white flowers. On they danced, looking weird and spiritual in the delicate sad light of the risen moon; now whirling round and round, now meeting in mimic warfare, swaying, eddying here and there, coming forward, falling back in an ordered confusion delightful to witness. At last they paused, and a beautiful young woman sprang out of the ranks and began to pirouette in front of us with a grace and vigour which would have put most ballet girls to shame. At length she retired exhausted, and another took her place, then another and another, but none of them, either in grace, skill, or personal attractions, came up to the first.

When the chosen girls had all danced, the king lifted his hand.

'Which think ye the fairest, white men?' he asked.

'The first,' said I, unthinkingly. Next second I regretted it, for I remembered that Infadoos had said that the fairest woman was offered as a sacrifice.

'Then is my mind as your minds, and my eyes as your eyes. She is the fairest; and a sorry thing it is for her, for she must die!'

'*Ay, must die*!' piped out Gagool, casting a glance from her quick eyes in the direction of the poor girl, who, as yet ignorant of the awful fate in store for her, was standing some ten yards off in front of a company of girls, engaged in nervously picking a flower from her wreath to pieces, petal by petal.

'Why, O king?' said I, restraining my indignation with difficulty, 'the girl has danced well and pleased us; she is fair, too; it would be hard to reward her with death.'

Twala laughed as he answered:

'It is our custom, and the figures who sit in stone yonder' (and he pointed towards the three distant peaks) 'must have their due. Did I fail to put the fairest girl to death today misfortune would fall upon me and my house. Thus runs the prophecy of my people: "If the king offer not a sacrifice of a fair girl on the day of the dance of maidens to the old ones who sit and watch on the mountains, then shall he fall and his house." Look ye, white men, my brother who reigned before me offered not the sacrifice, because of the tears of the woman, and he fell, and his house, and I reign in his stead. It is finished; she must die!' Then turning to the guards: 'Bring her hither; Scragga, make sharp thy spear.'

Two of the men stepped forward, and as they did so, the girl, for the first time realizing her impending fate, screamed aloud and turned to fly. But the strong hands caught her fast, and brought her, struggling and weeping, up before us.

'What is thy name, girl?' piped Gagool. 'What! wilt thou not answer; shall the king's son do his work at once?'

At this hint, Scragga, looking more evil than ever, advanced a step and lifted his great spear, and as he did so I saw Good's hand creep to his revolver. The poor girl caught the faint glint of the steel through her tears, and it sobered her anguish. She ceased struggling, but merely clasped her hands convulsively, and stood shuddering from head to foot.

'See,' cried Scragga in high glee, 'she shrinks from the sight of my little plaything even before she has tasted it,' and he tapped the broad blade of the spear.

'If ever I get the chance, you shall pay for that, you young hound!' I heard Good mutter beneath his breath.

'Now that thou art quiet, give us thy name, my dear. Come speak up, and fear not,' said Gagool in mockery.

'O mother,' answered the girl in trembling accents, 'my name is Foulata, of the house of Suko. O mother, why must I die? I have done no wrong!'

'Be comforted,' went on the old woman in her hateful tone of mockery. 'Thou must die indeed, as a sacrifice to the old ones who sit yonder' (and she pointed to the peaks): 'but it is better to sleep in the night than to toil in the day-time; it is better to die than to live, and thou shalt die by the royal hand of the king's own son.'

The girl Foulata wrung her hands in anguish, and cried out aloud: 'Oh, cruel; and I so young! What have I done that I should never again see the sun rise out of the night, or the stars come following on his track in the evening: that I should no more gather the flowers when the dew is heavy, or listen to the laughing of the waters! Woe is me, that I shall never see my father's hut again, nor feel my mother's kiss, nor tend the kid that is sick! Woe is me, that no lover shall put his arm around me and look into my eyes, nor shall men children be born of me! Oh, cruel, cruel!' and again she wrung her hands and turned her tear-stained, flower-crowned face to Heaven, looking so lovely in her despair – for she was indeed a beautiful woman – that it would assuredly have melted the hearts of anyone less cruel than the three fiends before us. Prince Arthur's appeal to the ruffians who came to blind him was not more touching than this savage girl's.

But it did not move Gagool or Gagool's master, though I saw signs of pity among the guard behind, and on the faces of the chiefs; and as for Good, he gave a sort of snort of indignation, and made a motion as though to go to her. With all a woman's quickness, the doomed girl interpreted what was passing in his mind, and with a sudden movement flung herself before him, and clasped his 'beautiful white legs' with her hands.

'O white father from the stars!' she cried, 'throw over me the mantle of thy protection; let me creep into the shadow of thy strength, that I may be saved. Oh, keep me from these cruel men and from the mercies of Gagool!'

'All right, my hearty, I'll look after you,' sang out Good, in nervous Saxon. 'Come, get up, there's a good girl,' and he stooped and caught her hand.

Twala turned and motioned to his son, who advanced with his spear lifted.

'Now's your time,' whispered Sir Henry to me; 'what are you waiting for?'

'I am waiting for the eclipse,' I answered; 'I have had my eye on the moon for the last half-hour, and I never saw it look healthier.'

'Well, you must risk it now, or the girl will be killed. Twala is losing patience.'

Recognizing the force of the argument, having cast one more despairing look at the bright face of the moon, for never did the most ardent astronomer with a theory to prove await a celestial event with such anxiety, I stepped with all the dignity I could command between the prostrate girl and the advancing spear of Scragga.

'King,' I said, 'this shall not be; we will not tolerate such a thing; let the girl go in safety.'

Twala rose from his seat in his wrath and astonishment, and from the chiefs and serried ranks of girls, who had slowly closed up upon us in anticipation of the tragedy, came a murmur of amazement.

'*Shall not be*, thou white dog, who yaps at the lion in his cave, *shall not be*! art thou mad? Be careful lest this chicken's fate overtakes thee, and those with thee. How canst thou prevent it? Who art thou that thou standest between me and my will? Withdraw, I say; Scragga, kill her. Ho, guards! seize these men.'

At his cry armed men came running swiftly from behind the hut, where they had evidently been placed beforehand.

Sir Henry, Good, and Umbopa ranged themselves alongside of me, and lifted their rifles.

'Stop!' I shouted boldly, though at the moment my heart was in my boots. 'Stop! we, the white men from the stars, say that it shall not be. Come but one pace nearer, and we will put out the moon and plunge the land in darkness. Ye shall taste of our magic.'

My threat produced an effect; the men halted, and Scragga stood still before us, his spear lifted.

'Hear him! hear him!' piped Gagool; 'hear the liar who says he will put out the moon like a lamp. Let him do it, and the girl shall be spared. Yes, let him do it, or die with the girl, he and those with him.'

I glanced up at the moon, and to my intense joy and relief saw that we had made no mistake. On the edge of the great orb was a faint rim of shadow, while a smoky hue grew and gathered on its bright surface.

I lifted my hand solemnly towards the sky, an example which Sir Henry and Good followed, and quoted a line or two of the *Ingoldsby Legends* at it in the most impressive tones I could command. Sir Henry followed suit with a verse out of the Old Testament, whilst Good addressed the Queen of Night in a volume of the most classical bad language that he could think of.

Slowly the penumbra, the shadow of a shadow, crept on over the bright surface, and as it did so I heard a deep gasp of fear rise from the multitude around.

'Look, O king!' I cried; 'look, Gagool! Look, chiefs and people and women, and see if the white men from the stars keep their word, or if they be but empty liars!

'The moon grows dark before your eyes; soon there will be darkness – ay, darkness in the hour of the full moon. Ye have asked for a sign; it is given to you. Grow dark, O moon! withdraw thy light, thou pure and holy one; bring the proud heart to the dust, and eat up the world with shadows.'

A groan of terror rose from the onlookers. Some stood petrified with fear, others threw themselves upon their knees, and cried out. As for the king, he sat still and turned pale beneath his dusky skin. Only Gagool kept her courage.

'It will pass,' she cried; 'I have seen the like before; no man can put out the moon; lose not heart; sit still – the shadow will pass.'

'Wait, and ye shall see,' I replied, hopping with excitement.

'Keep it up, Good, I can't remember any more poetry. Curse away, there's a good fellow.'

Good responded nobly to the tax upon his inventive faculties. Never before had I the faintest conception of the breadth and depth and height of a naval officer's objurgatory powers. For ten minutes he went on without stopping, and he scarcely ever repeated himself.

Meanwhile the dark ring crept on, and that whole great assembly fixed their eyes upon the sky and stared and stared in fascinated silence. Strange and unholy shadows encroached upon the moonlight, an ominous quiet filled the place, everything grew still as death. Slowly and in the midst of this most solemn silence the minutes sped away, and while they sped the full moon passed deeper and deeper into the shadow of the earth, as the inky segment of its circle crept in awful majesty across the lunar craters. The great pale orb seemed to draw near and grow in size. She turned a coppery hue, then that portion of her surface which was unobscured as yet grew grey and ashen, and finally, as totality approached, her mountains and her plains were to be seen glowing luridly through a crimson gloom.

On, yet on, crept the ring of darkness; it was now more than half across the blood-red orb. The air grew thick, and still more deeply tinged with dusky crimson. On, yet on, till we could scarcely see the fierce faces of the group before us. No sound rose now from the spectators, and Good stopped swearing.

'The moon is dying – the wizards have killed the moon,' yelled out the boy Scragga at last. 'We shall all perish in the dark,' and animated by fear or fury, or both, he lifted his spear, and drove it with all his force at Sir Henry's broad chest. But he had forgotten the mail shirts that the king had given us, and which we wore beneath our clothing. The steel rebounded harmless, and before he could repeat the blow Sir Henry had snatched the spear from his hand, and sent it straight through him. He dropped dead.

At the sight, and driven mad with fear of the gathering darkness, and of the unholy shadow which, as they believed, was swallowing up the moon, the companies of girls broke up in wild confusion, and ran screeching for the gateways. Nor did the panic stop there. The king himself, followed by the guards, some of the chiefs, and Gagool, who hobbled away after them with marvellous alacrity, fled for the huts, so that in another minute or so ourselves, the would-be victim, Foulata, Infadoos, and most of the chiefs who had interviewed us on the previous night, were left alone upon the scene together with the dead body of Scragga.

'Now, chiefs,' I said, 'we have given you the sign. If ye are satisfied, let us fly swiftly to the place ye spoke of. The charm cannot now be stopped. It will work for an hour and half an hour. Let us take advantage of the darkness.'

'Come,' said Infadoos, turning to go, an example which was followed by the awed chiefs, ourselves, and the girl Foulata, whom Good took by the hand.

Before we reached the gate of the kraal the moon went out utterly, and from every quarter of the firmament the stars rushed forth into the inky sky.

Holding each other by the hand we stumbled on through the darkness.

12

Before the Battle

LUCKILY for us, Infadoos and the chiefs knew all the pathways of the great town perfectly, so that notwithstanding the gloom we made fair progress.

For an hour and more we journeyed on, till at length the eclipse began to pass, and that edge of the moon which had disappeared the first became again visible. Suddenly, as we watched, there burst from it a silver streak of light, accompanied by a wondrous ruddy glow, which hung upon the blackness of the sky like a celestial lamp, and a wild and lovely sight it was. In another five minutes the stars began to fade, and there was sufficient light to see our whereabouts. We then discovered that we were clear of the town of Loo, and approaching a large, flat-topped hill, measuring some two miles in circumference. This hill, which was of a formation common in Southern Africa, was not very high; indeed, its greatest elevation was not more than 200 feet, but it was shaped like a horseshoe, and its sides were rather precipitous, and strewn with boulders. On the grass table-land at the top was ample camping ground, which had been utilized as a military cantonment of no mean strength. Its ordinary garrison was one regiment of three thousand men, but as we toiled up the steep side of the hill in the returning moonlight, we perceived that here were many more warriors than that upon it.

Reaching the table-land at last, we found crowds of men roused from their sleep, and huddled up together, shivering with fear and in the utmost consternation at the natural phenomenon which they were witnessing. Passing through these without a word, we gained a hut in the centre of the ground, where we were astonished to find two men waiting, laden with our few goods and chattels, which we had, of course, been obliged to leave behind in our hasty flight.

'I sent for them,' explained Infadoos; 'also for these,' and he lifted up Good's long-lost trousers.

With an exclamation of rapturous delight, Good sprang at them, and instantly proceeded to put them on.

'Surely, my lord will not hide his beautiful white legs!' exclaimed Infadoos, regretfully.

But Good persisted, and once only did the Kukuana people get the chance of seeing his beautiful legs again. Good is a very modest man. Henceforward they had to satisfy their aesthetic longings with his one whisker, his transparent eye, and his movable teeth.

Still gazing with fond remembrance at Good's trousers, Infadoos next informed us that he had commanded the regiments to muster as soon as the day broke, in order to explain to them fully the circumstances of the rebellion which was decided on by the chiefs, and to introduce to them the rightful heir to the throne, Ignosi.

Accordingly, so soon as the sun was up, the troops – in all nearly twenty thousand men, constituting the flower of the Kukuana army – were mustered on a large open space, to which we proceeded. The men were drawn up in three sides of a dense square, and presented a magnificent spectacle. We took our station on the open side of the square, and were speedily surrounded by all the principal chiefs and officers.

These, after silence had been proclaimed, Infadoos proceeded to address. He narrated to them in vigorous and graceful language – for like most Kukuanas of high rank, he was a born orator – the history of Ignosi's father, how he had been basely murdered by Twala, the king, and his wife and child driven out to starve. Then he pointed out how the land suffered and groaned under Twala's cruel rule, instancing the proceedings of the previous night, when under pretence of their being evildoers, many of the noblest in the land had been hauled forth and cruelly done to death. Next he went on to say that the white lords from the stars, looking down on the land, had perceived its trouble, and determined, at great personal inconvenience, to alleviate its lot; how they had accordingly taken the real king of the country, Ignosi, who was languishing in exile, by the hand, and led him over the mountains; how they had seen the wickedness of Twala's doings, and for a sign to the wavering, and to save the life of the girl Foulata, had actually, by the exercise of their high magic, put out the moon, and slain the young fiend, Scragga; and how they were prepared to stand by them, and assist them to overthrow Twala, and set up the rightful king, Ignosi, in his place.

He finished his discourse amidst a murmur of approbation, and then Ignosi stepped forward, and began to speak. Having reiterated all that Infadoos his uncle had said, he concluded a powerful speech in these words:

'O chiefs, captains, soldiers, and people, ye have heard my words. Now must ye make choice between me and him who sits upon my throne, the uncle who killed his brother, and hunted his brother's child forth to die in the cold and the night. That I am indeed the king these' – pointing to the chiefs – 'can tell ye, for they have seen the snake about my middle. If I were not the king, would these white men be on my side, with all their magic? Tremble, chiefs, captains, soldiers, and people! Is not the darkness they have brought upon the land to confound Twala, and cover our flight, darkness even in the hour of the full moon, yet before your eyes?'

'It is,' answered the soldiers.

'I am the king; I say to ye, I am the king,' went on Ignosi, drawing up his great stature to its full, and lifting his broadbladed battle-axe above his head. 'If there be any man among you who says that it is not so, let him stand forth, and I will fight him now, and his blood shall be a red token that I tell ye true. Let him stand forth, I say;' and he shook the great axe till it flashed in the sunlight.

As nobody seemed inclined to respond to this heroic version of 'Dilly, Dilly, come and be killed,' our late henchman proceeded with his address.

'I am indeed the king, and if ye do stand by my side in the battle, if I win the day, ye shall go with me to victory and honour. I will give ye oxen and wives, and ye shall take place of all the regiments; and if ye fall I will fall with ye.

'And, behold, this promise do I give ye, that when I sit upon the seat of my fathers, bloodshed shall cease in the land. No longer shall ye cry for justice to find slaughter, no longer shall the witch-finder hunt ye out so that ye be slain without a cause. No man shall die save he who offendeth against the laws. The "eating up" of your kraals shall cease; each shall sleep secure in his own hut and fear not, and justice shall walk blind throughout the land. Have ye chosen, chiefs, captains, soldiers, and people?'

'We have chosen, O king,' came back the answer.

'It is well. Turn your heads and see how Twala's messengers go forth from the great town, east and west, and north and south, to gather a mighty army to slay me and ye, and these my friends and my protectors. Tomorrow, or perchance the next day, will he come with all who are faithful to him. Then shall I see the man who is indeed my man, the man who fears not to die for his cause; and I tell ye he shall not be forgotten in the time of spoil. I have spoken, O chiefs, captains, soldiers, and people. Now go to your huts and make you ready for war.'

There was a pause, and then one of the chiefs lifted his hand, and out rolled the royal salute, 'Koom'. It was a sign that the regiments accepted Ignosi as their king. Then they marched off in battalions.

Half an hour afterwards we held a council of war, at which all the commanders of regiments were present. It was evident to us that before very long we should be attacked in overwhelming force. Indeed, from our point of vantage on the hill we could see troops mustering, and messengers going forth from Loo in every direction, doubtless to summon regiments to the king's assistance. We had on our side about twenty thousand men, composed of seven of the best regiments in the country. Twala had, so Infadoos and the chiefs calculated, at least thirty to thirty-five thousand on whom he could rely at present assembled in Loo, and they thought that by midday on the morrow he would be able to gather another five thousand or more to his aid. It was, of course, possible that some of his troops would desert and come over to us, but it was not a contingency that could be reckoned on. Meanwhile, it was clear that active preparations were being made to subdue us. Already strong bodies of armed men were patrolling round and round the foot of the hill, and there were other signs of a coming attack.

Infadoos and the chiefs, however, were of opinion that no attack would take place that day, which would be devoted to preparation and to the removal by every possible means of the moral effect produced upon the minds of the soldiery by the supposed magical darkening of the moon. The attack would be on the morrow, they said, and they proved to be right.

Meanwhile, we set to work to strengthen the position as much as possible. Nearly the entire force was turned out, and in the course of the day, which seemed all too short, much was done. The paths up the hill, which was rather a sanitarium than a fortress, being used generally as the camping place of regiments suffering from recent service in unhealthy portions of the country, were carefully blocked with masses of stones, and every other possible approach was made as impregnable as time would allow. Piles of boulders were collected at various spots to be rolled down upon an advancing enemy, stations were appointed to the different regiments, and every other preparation which our joint ingenuity could suggest was taken.

Just before sundown, as we rested after our toil, we perceived a small company of men advancing towards us from the direction of Loo, one of whom bore a palm leaf in his hand as a sign that he came as a herald.

As he came, Ignosi, Infadoos, one or two chiefs, and ourselves, went down to the foot of the mountain to meet him. He was a gallant-looking fellow, with the regulation leopard-skin cloak.

'Greeting!' he cried, as he came near; 'the king's greeting to those who make unholy war against the king; the lion's greeting to the jackals who snarl around his heels.'

'Speak,' I said.

'These are the king's words. Surrender to the king's mercy ere a worse thing befall ye. Already the shoulder has been torn from the black bull, and the king drives him bleeding about the camp.'[1]

'What are Twala's terms?' I asked for curiosity.

'His terms are merciful, worthy of a great king. These are the words of Twala, the one-eyed, the mighty, the husband of a thousand wives, lord of the Kukuanas, keeper of the great road (Solomon's Road), beloved of the strange ones who sit in silence at the mountains yonder (the three Witches), calf of the black cow, elephant whose tread shakes the earth, terror of the evildoer, ostrich whose feet devour the desert, huge one, black one, wise one, king from generation to generation! These are the words of Twala: "I will have mercy and be satisfied with a little blood. One in every ten shall die, the rest shall go free; but the white man Incubu, who slew Scragga, my son, and the black man, his servant, who pretends to my throne, and Infadoos, my brother, who brews rebellion against me, these shall die by torture as an offering to the silent ones." Such are the merciful words of Twala.'

After consulting with the others a little, I answered him in a loud voice, so that the soldiers might hear, thus:

'Go back, thou dog, to Twala, who sent thee, and say that we, Ignosi, veritable king of the Kukuanas, Incubu, Bougwan, and Macumazahn, the wise white ones from the stars, who make dark the moon, Infadoos, of the royal house, and the chiefs, captains, and people here gathered, make answer and say, "That we will not surrender; that before the sun has twice gone down Twala's corpse shall stiffen at Twala's gate, and Ignosi, whose father Twala slew, shall reign in his stead." Now go, ere we whip thee away, and beware how ye lift a hand against such as we.'

The herald laughed loud. 'Ye frighten not men with such swelling words,' he cried out. 'Show yourselves as bold tomorrow, O ye who darken the moon. Be bold, fight, and be merry, before the crows pick your bones till they are whiter than your faces. Farewell; perhaps we may meet in the fight; wait for me, I pray, white men.' And with this shaft of sarcasm he retired, and almost immediately the sun sank.

That night was a busy one, for weary as we were, as far as was possible by the moonlight all preparations for the morrow's fight were continued, and messengers were constantly coming and going from the place where we sat in council. At last, about an hour after midnight, everything that could be done was done, and the camp, save for the occasional challenge of a sentry, sank into sleep. Sir Henry and I, accompanied by Ignosi and one of the chiefs, descended the hill and made the round of the outposts. As we went, suddenly, from all sorts of unexpected places, spears gleamed out in the moonlight, only to vanish again as we uttered the password. It

[1] This cruel custom is not confined to the Kukuanas, but is by no means uncommon amongst African tribes on the occasion of the outbreak of war or any other important public event.

was clear to us that none were sleeping at their posts. Then we returned, picking our way through thousands of sleeping warriors, many of whom were taking their last earthly rest.

The moonlight flickered along their spears, and played upon their features and made them ghastly; the chilly night wind tossed their tall and hearse-like plumes. There they lay in wild confusion, with arms outstretched and twisted limbs; their stern, stalwart forms looking weird and un-human in the moonlight.

'How many of these do you suppose will be alive at this time tomorrow?' asked Sir Henry.

I shook my head and looked again at the sleeping men, and to my tired and yet excited imagination it seemed as though death had already touched them. My mind's eye singled out those who were sealed to slaughter, and there rushed in upon my heart a great sense of the mystery of human life, and an overwhelming sorrow at its futility and sadness. Tonight these thousands slept their healthy sleep, tomorrow they, and many others with them, ourselves perhaps among them, would be stiffening in the cold; their wives would be widows, their children fatherless, and their place know them no more for ever. Only the old moon would shine serenely on, the night wind would stir the grasses, and the wide earth would take its happy rest, even as it did aeons before these were, and will do aeons after they have been forgotten.

All sorts of reflections of this sort passed through my mind – for as I get older I regret to say that a detestable habit of thinking seems to be getting a hold of me – while I stood and stared at those grim yet fantastic lines of warriors sleeping, as their saying goes, 'upon their spears'.

'Curtis,' I said to Sir Henry, 'I am in a condition of pitiable funk.'

Sir Henry stroked his yellow beard and laughed, as he answered:

'I've heard you make that sort of remark before, Quatermain.'

'Well, I mean it now. Do you know, I very much doubt if one of us will be alive tomorrow night. We shall be attacked in overwhelming force, and it is exceedingly doubtful if we can hold this place.'

'We'll give a good account of some of them, at any rate. Look here, Quatermain, the business is a nasty one, and one with which, properly speaking, we ought not to be mixed up, but we are in for it, so we must make the best of it. Speaking personally, I had rather be killed fighting than any other way, and now that there seems little chance of my finding my poor brother, it makes the idea easier to me. But fortune favours the brave, and we may succeed. Anyway, the slaughter will be awful, and as we have a reputation to keep up, we shall have to be in the thick of it.'

Sir Henry made this last remark in a mournful voice, but there was a gleam in his eye which belied it. I have a sort of idea that Sir Henry Curtis actually likes fighting.

After this we went and slept for a couple of hours.

Just about dawn we were awakened by Infadoos, who came to say that great activity was to be observed in Loo, and that parties of the king's skirmishers were driving in our outposts.

We got up and dressed ourselves for the fray, each putting on our chain-armour shirt, for which at the present juncture we felt exceedingly thankful. Sir Henry went the whole length about the matter, and dressed himself like a native warrior. 'When you are in Kukuanaland, do as the Kukuanas do,' he remarked, as he drew the shining steel over his broad shoulders which it fitted like a glove. Nor did he stop there. At his request, Infadoos had provided him with a complete set of war uniform. Round his throat he fastened the leopard skin cloak of a commanding officer, on his brows he bound the plume of black ostrich feathers, worn only by generals of high rank, and round his centre a magnificent moocha of white ox-tails. A pair of sandals, a leglet of goats' hair, a heavy battle-axe, with a rhinoceros-horn handle, a round iron shield, covered with white ox-hide, and the regulation number of tollas, or throwing knives, made up his equipment, to which, however, he added his revolver. The dress was, no doubt, a savage one, but I am bound to say I never saw a finer sight than Sir Henry Curtis presented in this guise. It showed off his magnificent physique to the greatest advantage, and when Ignosi arrived presently, arrayed in similar costume, I thought to myself that I never before saw two such splendid men. As for Good and myself, the chain armour did not suit us nearly so well. To begin with, Good insisted upon keeping on his trousers, and a stout, short gentleman with an eye-glass, and one half of his face shaved, arrayed in a mail shirt carefully tucked into a very seedy pair of corduroys, looks more striking than imposing. As for myself, my chain shirt being too big for me, I put it on over all my clothes, which caused it to bulge out in a somewhat ungainly fashion. I discarded my trousers, however, determined to go into battle with bare legs, in order to be the lighter, in case it became necessary to retire quickly, retaining only my veldtschoons. This, a spear, a shield, which I did not know how to use, a couple of tollas, a revolver, and a huge plume, which I pinned into the top of my shooting hat, in order to give a bloodthirsty finish to my appearance, completed my modest equipment. In addition to all these articles, of course we had our rifles, but as ammunition was scarce, and they would be useless in case of a charge, we had arranged to have them carried behind us by bearers.

As soon as we had equipped ourselves, we hastily swallowed some food, and then started out to see how things were progressing. At one point in the table-land of the mountain there was a little koppie of brown stone, which served for the double purpose of headquarters and a conning tower. Here we found Infadoos surrounded by his own regiment, the Greys, which was undoubtedly the finest in the Kukuana army, and the same which we had first seen at the outlying kraal. This regiment, now three thousand five hundred strong, was being held in reserve, and the men were lying down on the grass in companies, and watching the king's forces creep out of Loo in long ant-like columns. There seemed to be no end to these columns – three in all, and each numbering at least eleven or twelve thousand men.

As soon as they were clear of the town, they formed up. Then one body marched off to the right, one to the left, and the third came slowly on towards us.

'Ah,' said Infadoos, 'they are going to attack us on three sides at once.'

This was rather serious news, for as our position on the top of the mountain, which was at least a mile and a half in circumference, was an extended one, it was important to us to concentrate our comparatively small defending force as much as possible. But as it was impossible for us to dictate in what way we should be attacked, we had to make the best of it, and accordingly sent orders to the various regiments to prepare to receive the separate onslaughts.

13

The Attack

SLOWLY, and without the slightest appearance of haste or excitement, the three columns crept on. When within about five hundred yards of us, the main or centre column halted at the root of a tongue of open plain which ran up into the hill, to enable the other two to circumvent our position, which was shaped more or less in the form of a horse-shoe, the two points being towards the town of Loo, their object being, no doubt, that the threefold assault should be delivered simultaneously.

'Oh, for a Gatling!' groaned Good, as he contemplated the serried phalanxes beneath us. 'I would clear the plain in twenty minutes.'

'We have not got one, so it is no use yearning for it; but suppose you try a shot, Quatermain. See how near you can go to that tall fellow who appears to be in command. Two to one you miss him, and an even sovereign, to be honestly paid if ever we get out of this, that you don't drop the ball within ten yards.'

This piqued me, so, loading the express with solid ball, I waited till my friend walked some ten yards out from his force, in order to get a better view of our position, accompanied only by an orderly, and then, lying down and resting the express upon a rock, I covered him. The rifle, like all expresses, was only sighted to three hundred and fifty yards, so to allow for the drop in trajectory I took him half-way down the neck, which ought, I calculated, to find him in the chest. He stood quite still and gave me every opportunity, but whether it was the excitement or the wind, or the fact of the man being a long shot, I don't know, but this was what happened. Getting dead on, as I thought, a fine sight, I pressed, and when the puff of smoke had cleared away, I, to my disgust, saw my man standing unharmed, whilst his orderly, who was at least three paces to the left, was stretched upon the ground, apparently dead. Turning swiftly, the officer I had aimed at began to run towards his force, in evident alarm.

'Bravo, Quatermain!' sang out Good; 'you've frightened him.'

This made me very angry, for if possible to avoid it, I hate to miss in public. When one can only do one thing well, one likes to keep up one's reputation in that thing. Moved quite out of myself at my failure, I did a rash thing. Rapidly covering the general as he ran, I let drive with the second barrel. The poor man threw up his arms, and fell forward on to his face. This time I had made no mistake; and – I say it as proof of how little we think of others when our own pride or reputation are in question – I was brute enough to feel delighted at the sight.

The regiments who had seen the feat cheered wildly at this exhibition of the white man's magic, which they took as an omen of success, while the force to which the general had belonged – which, indeed, as we afterwards ascertained, he had commanded – began to fall back in confusion. Sir Henry and Good now took up their rifles, and began to fire, the latter industriously 'browning' the dense mass before him with a Winchester repeater, and I also had another shot or two, with the result that so far as we could judge we put some eight or ten men *hors de combat* before they got out of range.

Just as we stopped firing there came an ominous roar from our far right, then a similar roar from our left. The two other divisions were engaging us.

At the sound, the mass of men before us opened out a little, and came on towards the hill up the spit of bare grassland at a slow trot, singing a deep-throated song as they advanced. We kept up a steady fire from our rifles as they came, Ignosi joining in occasionally, and accounted for several men, but of course produced no more effect upon that mighty rush of armed humanity than he who throws pebbles does on the advancing wave.

On they came, with a shout and the clashing of spears; now they were driving in the outposts we had placed among the rocks at the foot of the hill. After that the advance was a little slower, for though as yet we had offered no serious opposition, the attacking force had to come uphill, and came slowly to save their breath. Our first line of defence was about half-way up the side, our second fifty yards farther back, while our third occupied the edge of the plain.

On they came, shouting their war-cry, '*Twala! Twala! Chielé! Chielé!*' (Twala! Twala! Smite! Smite!). '*Ignosi! Ignosi! Chielé! Chielé!*' answered our people. They were quite close now, and the tollas, or throwing knives, began to flash backwards and forwards, and now with an awful yell the battle closed in.

To and fro swayed the mass of struggling warriors, men falling thick as leaves in an autumn wind; but before long the superior weight of the attacking force began to tell, and our first line of defence was slowly pressed back, till it merged into the second. Here the struggle was very fierce, but again our people were driven back and up, till at length, within twenty minutes of the commencement of the fight, our third line came into action.

But by this time the assailants were much exhausted, and had besides lost many men killed and wounded, and to break through that third impenetrable hedge of spears proved beyond their powers. For a while the dense mass of struggling warriors swung backwards and forwards in the fierce ebb and flow of battle, and the issue was doubtful. Sir Henry watched the desperate struggle with a kindling eye, and then without a word he rushed off, followed by Good, and flung himself into the hottest of the fray. As for myself, I stopped where I was.

The soldiers caught sight of his tall form as he plunged into the battle, and there rose a cry of:

'*Nanzia Incubu! Nanzia Unkungunklovo*!' (Here is the Elephant!) '*Chielé! Chielé*!

From that moment the issue was no longer in doubt. Inch by inch, fighting with desperate gallantry, the attacking force was pressed back down the hillside, till at last it retreated upon its reserves in something like confusion. At that moment, too, a messenger arrived to say that the left attack had been repulsed; and I was just beginning to congratulate myself that the affair was over for the present, when, to our horror, we perceived our men who had been engaged in the right defence being driven towards us across the plain, followed by swarms of the enemy, who had evidently succeeded at this point.

Ignosi, who was standing by me, took in the situation at a glance, and issued a rapid order. Instantly the reserve regiment round us (the Greys) extended itself.

Again Ignosi gave a word of command, which was taken up and repeated by the captains, and in another second, to my intense disgust, I found myself involved in a furious onslaught upon the advancing foe. Getting as much as I could behind Ignosi's huge frame, I made the best of a bad job, and toddled along to be killed, as though I liked it. In a minute or two – the time seemed all too short to me – we were plunging through the flying groups of our men, who at once began to re-form behind us, and then I am sure I do not know what happened. All I can remember is a dreadful rolling noise of the meeting of shields, and the sudden apparition of a huge ruffian, whose eyes seemed literally to be starting out of his head, making straight at me with a bloody spear. But – I say it with pride – I rose to the occasion. It was an occasion before which most people would have collapsed once and for all. Seeing that if I stood where I was I must be done for, I, as the horrid apparition came, flung myself down in front of him so cleverly, that, being unable to stop himself, he took a header right over my prostrate form. Before he could rise again, I had risen and settled the matter from behind with my revolver.

Shortly after this, somebody knocked me down, and I remember no more of the charge.

When I came to, I found myself back at the koppie, with Good bending over me with some water in a gourd.

'How do you feel, old fellow?' he asked, anxiously.

I got up and shook myself before answering.

'Pretty well, thank you,' I answered.

'Thank Heaven! When I saw them carry you in I felt quite sick; I thought you were done for.'

'Not this time, my boy. I fancy I only got a rap on the head, which knocked me out of time. How has it ended?'

'They are repulsed at every point for the time. The loss is dreadfully heavy; we have lost quite two thousand killed and wounded, and they must have lost three. Look, there's a sight!' and he pointed to long lines of men advancing by fours. In the centre of, and being borne by each group of four, was a kind of hide tray, of which a Kukuana force always carried a quantity, with a loop for a handle at each corner. On these trays – and their number seemed endless – lay wounded men, who as they arrived were hastily examined by the medicine men, of whom ten were attached to each regiment. If the wound was not of a fatal character, the sufferer was taken away and attended to as carefully as circumstances would allow. But if, on the other hand, the wounded man's condition was hopeless, what followed was very dreadful, though doubtless it was the truest mercy. One of the doctors, under pretence of carrying out an examination, swiftly opened an artery with a sharp knife, and in a minute or two the sufferer expired painlessly. There were many cases that day in which this was done. In fact, it was done in most cases when the wound was in the body, for the gash made by the entry of the enormously broad spears used by the Kukuanas generally rendered recovery hopeless. In most cases the poor sufferers were already unconscious, and in others the fatal 'nick' of the artery was done so swiftly and painlessly that they did not seem to notice it. Still it was a ghastly sight, and one from which we were glad to escape; indeed, I never remember one which affected me more than seeing those gallant soldiers thus put out of pain by the red-handed medicine men, except, indeed, on an occasion when, after an attack, I saw a force of Swazis burying their hopelessly wounded *alive*.

Hurrying from this dreadful scene to the farther side of the koppie, we found Sir Henry (who still held a bloody battle-axe in his hand), Ignosi, Infadoos, and one or two of the chiefs in deep consultation.

'Thank heavens, here you are, Quatermain! I can't quite make out what Ignosi wants to do. It seems that, though we have beaten off the attack, Twala is now receiving large reinforcements, and is showing a disposition to invest us, with a view of starving us out.'

'That's awkward.'

'Yes; especially as Infadoos says that the water supply has given out.'

'My lord, that is so,' said Infadoos; 'the spring cannot supply the wants of so great a multitude, and is failing rapidly. Before night we shall all be thirsty. Listen, Macumazahn. Thou art wise, and hast doubtless seen many wars in the lands from whence thou camest – that is, if, indeed, they make wars in the stars. Now tell us, what shall we do? Twala has brought up many fresh men to take the place of those who have fallen. But Twala has learnt a lesson; the hawk did not think to find the heron ready; but our beak has pierced his breast; he will not strike at us again. We too are wounded, and he will wait for us to die; he will wind himself round us like a snakeround a buck, and fight the fight of "sit down".'

'I hear you,' I said.

'So, Macumazahn, thou seest we have no water here, and but a little food, and we must choose between these three things – to languish like a starving lion in his den, or to strive to break away towards the north, or' – and here he rose and pointed towards the dense mass of our foes – 'to launch ourselves straight at Twala's throat. Incubu, the great warrior – for today he fought like a buffalo in a net, and Twala's soldiers went down before his axe like corn before the hail; with these eyes I saw it – Incubu says "Charge"; but the Elephant is ever prone to charge. Now what says Macumazahn, the wily old fox, who has seen much, and loves to bite his enemy from behind? The last word is in Ignosi the king, for it is a king's right to speak of war; but let us hear thy voice, O Macumazahn, who watchest by night, and the voice, too, of him of the transparent eye.'

'What sayest thou, Ignosi?' I asked.

'Nay, my father,' answered our quondam servant, who now, clad as he was in the full panoply of savage war, looked every inch a warrior king, 'do thou speak, and let me, who am but a child in wisdom beside thee, hearken to thy words.'

Thus abjured, I, after taking hasty counsel with Good and Sir Henry, delivered my opinion briefly to the effect that, being trapped, our best chance, especially in view of the failure of our water supply, was to initiate an attack upon Twala's forces, and then I recommended that the attack should be delivered at once, 'before our wounds grew stiff', and also before the sight of Twala's overpowering force caused the hearts of our soldiers 'to wax small like fat before a fire'. Otherwise, I pointed out, some of the captains might change their minds, and, making peace with Twala, desert to him, or even betray us into his hands.

This expression of opinion seemed, on the whole, to be favourably received; indeed, among the Kukuanas my utterances met with a respect which has never been accorded to them before or since. But the real decision as to our course lay with Ignosi, who, since he had been recognized as rightful king, could exercise the almost unbounded rights of sovereignty, including, of course, the final decision on matters of generalship, and it was to him that all eyes were now turned.

At length, after a pause, during which he appeared to be thinking deeply, he spoke:

'Incubu, Macumazahn, and Bougwan, brave white men, and my friends; Infadoos, my uncle, and chiefs; my heart is fixed. I will strike at Twala this day, and set my fortunes on the blow, ay, and my life; my life and your lives also. Listen: thus will I strike. Ye see how the hill curves round like the half-moon, and how the plain runs like a green tongue towards us within the curve?'

'We see,' I answered.

'Good; it is now midday, and the men eat and rest after the toil of battle. When the sun has turned and travelled a little way towards the dark, let thy regiment, my uncle, advance with one other down to the green tongue. And it shall be that when Twala sees it he shall hurl his force at it to crush it. But the spot is narrow, and the regiments can come against thee one at a time only; so shall they be destroyed one by one, and the eyes of all Twala's army shall be fixed upon a struggle the like of which has not been seen by living man. And with thee my uncle shall go Incubu my friend, that when Twala sees his battle-axe flashing in the first rank of the "Greys" his heart may grow faint. And I will come with the second regiment, that which follows thee, so that if ye are destroyed, as it may happen, there may yet be a king left to fight for; and with me shall come Macumazahn the wise.'

'It is well, O king,' said Infadoos, apparently contemplating the certainty of the complete annihilation of his regiment with perfect calmness. Truly these Kukuanas are a wonderful people. Death has no terrors for them when it is incurred in the course of duty.

'And whilst the eyes of the multitude of Twala's regiments are thus fixed upon the fight,' went on Ignosi, 'behold, one-third of the men who are left alive to us (i.e., about 6,000) shall creep along the right horn of the hill and fall upon the left flank of Twala's force, and one-third shall creep along the left horn and fall upon Twala's right flank. And when I see that the horns are ready to toss Twala, then will I, with the men who are left to me, charge home in Twala's face, and if fortune goes with us the day will be ours, and before Night drives her horses from the mountains to the mountains we shall sit in peace at Loo. And now let us eat and make ready; and, Infadoos, do thou prepare, that the plan be carried out; and stay, let my white father Bougwan go with the right horn, that his shining eye may give courage to the men.'

The arrangements for attack thus briefly indicated were set in motion with a rapidity that spoke well for the perfection of the Kukuana military system. Within little more than an hour rations had been served out to the men and devoured, the three divisions were formed, the plan of attack explained to the leaders, and the whole force, with the exception of a guard left with the wounded, now numbering about 18,000 men in all, was ready to be put in motion.

Presently Good came up and shook hands with Sir Henry and myself.

'Good-bye, you fellows,' he said, 'I am off with the right wing according to orders; and so I have come to shake hands in case we should not meet again, you know,' he added significantly.

We shook hands in silence, and not without the exhibition of as much emotion as Englishmen are wont to show.

'It is a queer business,' said Sir Henry, his deep voice shaking a little, 'and I confess I never expect to see tomorrow's sun. As far as I can make out, the Greys, with whom I am to go, are to fight until they are wiped out in order to enable the wings to slip round unawares and outflank Twala. Well, so be it; at any rate, it will be a man's death! Good-bye, old fellow. God bless you! I hope you will pull through and live to collar the diamonds; but if you do, take my advice and don't have anything more to do with pretenders!'

In another second, Good had wrung us both by the hand and gone; and then Infadoos came up and led off Sir Henry to his place in the forefront of the Greys, whilst, with many misgivings, I departed with Ignosi to my station in the second attacking regiment.

14

The Last Stand of the Greys

IN a few more minutes the regiments destined to carry out the flanking movements had tramped off in silence, keeping carefully under the lee of the rising ground in order to conceal the movement from the keen eyes of Twala's scouts.

Half an hour or more was allowed to elapse between the setting out of the horns or wings of the army before any movement was made by the Greys and the supporting regiment, known as the Buffaloes, which formed its chest, and which were destined to bear the brunt of the battle.

Both of these regiments were almost perfectly fresh, and of full strength, the Greys having been in reserve in the morning, and having lost but a small number of men in sweeping back that part of the attack which had proved successful in breaking the line of defence, on the occasion when I charged with them and got knocked silly for my pains. As for the Buffaloes, they had formed the third line of defence on the left, and as the attacking force at that point had not succeeded in breaking through the second, had scarcely come into action at all.

Infadoos, who was a wary old general, and knew the absolute importance of keeping up the spirits of his men on the eve of such a desperate encounter, employed the pause in addressing his own regiment, the Greys, in poetical language: in explaining to them the honour that they were receiving in being put thus in the forefront of the battle, and in having the great white warrior from the stars to fight with them in their ranks, and in promising large rewards of cattle and promotion to all who survived in the event of Ignosi's arms being successful.

I looked down the long lines of waving black plumes and stern faces beneath them, and sighed to think that within one short hour most, if not all, of those magnificent veteran warriors, not a man of whom was under forty years of age, would be laid dead or dying in the dust. It could not be otherwise; they were being condemned, with that wise recklessness of human life that marks the great general, and often saves his forces and attains his ends, to certain slaughter, in order to give the cause and the remainder of the army a chance of success. They were foredoomed to die, and they knew it. It was to be their task to engage regiment after regiment of Twala's army on the narrow strip of green beneath us, till they were exterminated, or till the wings found a favourable opportunity for their onslaught. And yet they never hesitated, nor could I detect a sign of fear upon the face of a single warrior. There they were – going to certain death, about to quit the blessed light of day for ever, and yet able to contemplate their doom without a tremor. I could not even at that moment help contrasting their state of mind with my own, which was far from comfortable, and breathing a sigh of envy and admiration. Never before had I seen such an absolute devotion to the idea of duty, and such a complete indifference to its bitter fruits.

'Behold your king!' ended old Infadoos, pointing to Ignosi; 'go fight and fall for him, as is the duty of brave men, and cursed and shameful for ever be the name of him who shrinks from death for his king, or who turns his back to his enemy. Behold your king! chiefs, captains, and soldiers; now do your homage to the sacred snake, and then follow on, that Incubu and I may show ye the road to the heart of Twala's forces.'

There was a moment's pause, then suddenly there rose from the serried phalanxes before us a murmur, like the distant whisper of the sea, caused by the gentle tapping of the handles of six thousand spears against their holders' shields. Slowly it swelled, till its growing volume deepened and widened into a roar of rolling noise, that echoed like thunder against the mountains, and filled the air with heavy waves of sound. Then it decreased and slowly died away into nothing, and suddenly out crashed the royal salute.

Ignosi, I thought to myself, might well be a proud man that day, for no Roman emperor ever had such a salutation from gladiators 'about to die'.

Ignosi acknowledged this magnificent act of homage by lifting his battle-axe, and then the Greys filed off in a triple-line formation, each line containing about one thousand fighting men, exclusive of officers. When the last line had gone some five hundred yards, Ignosi put himself at the head of the Buffaloes, which regiment was drawn up in a similar three-line formation, and gave the word to march, and off we went, I, needless to say, uttering the most heartfelt prayers that I might come out of that job with a whole skin. Many a queer position have I found myself in, but never before in one quite so unpleasant as the present, or one in which my chance of coming off safe was so small.

By the time that we reached the edge of the plateau the Greys were already half-way down the slope ending in the tongue of grassland that ran up into the bend of the mountain, something as the frog of a horse's foot runs up into the shoe. The excitement in Twala's camp on the plain beyond was very great, and regiment after regiment were starting forward at a long swinging trot in order to reach the root of the tongue of land before the attacking force could emerge into the plain of Loo.

This tongue of land, which was some three hundred yards in depth, was even at its root or widest part not more than four hundred and fifty paces across, while at its tip it scarcely measured ninety. The Greys, who, in passing down the side of the hill and on to the tip of the tongue, had formed in column, on reaching the spot where it broadened out again reassumed their triple-line formation, and halted dead.

Then we – that is, the Buffaloes – moved down the tip of the tongue and took our stand in reserve, about one hundred yards behind the last line of the Greys, and on slightly higher ground. Meanwhile we had leisure to observe Twala's entire force, which had evidently been reinforced since the morning attack, and could not now, notwithstanding their losses, number less than forty thousand, moving swiftly up towards us. But as they drew near the root of the tongue they hesitated, having discovered that only one regiment could advance into the gorge at a time, and that there, some seventy yards from the mouth of it, unassailable except in front, on account of the high walls of boulder-strewn ground on either side, stood the famous regiment of Greys, the pride and glory of the Kukuana army, ready to hold the way against their forces as the three Romans once held the bridge against thousands. They hesitated, and finally stopped their advance; there was no eagerness to cross spears with those three lines of grim warriors who stood so firm and ready. Presently, however, a tall general, with the customary head-dress of nodding ostrich plumes, came running up, attended by a group of chiefs and orderlies, being, I thought, none other than Twala himself, and gave an order, and the first regiment raised a shout, and charged up towards the Greys, who remained perfectly still and silent till the attacking troops were within forty yards, and a volley of tollas, or throwing knives, came rattling among their ranks.

Then suddenly, with a bound and a roar, they sprang forward with uplifted spears, and the two regiments met in deadly strife. Next second, the roll of the meeting shields came to our ears like the sound of thunder, and the whole plain seemed to be alive with flashes of light reflected from the stabbing spears. To and fro swung the heaving mass of struggling, stabbing humanity, but not for long. Suddenly the attacking lines seemed to grow thinner, and then with a slow, long heave the Greys passed over them, just as a great wave heaves up and passes over a sunken ridge. It was done; that regiment was completely destroyed, but the Greys had but two lines left now; a third of their number were dead.

Closing up shoulder to shoulder once more, they halted in silence and awaited attack; and I was rejoiced to catch sight of Sir Henry's yellow beard as he moved to and fro, arranging the ranks. So he was yet alive!

Meanwhile we moved up on to the ground of the encounter, which was cumbered by about four thousand prostrate human beings, dead, dying, and wounded, and literally stained red with blood. Ignosi issued an order, which was rapidly passed down the ranks, to the effect that none of the enemies' wounded were to be killed, and so far as we could see this order was scrupulously carried out. It would have been a shocking sight, if we had had time to think of it.

But now a second regiment, distinguished by white plumes, kilts, and shields, was moving up to the attack of the two thousand remaining Greys, who stood waiting in the same ominous silence as before, till the foe was within forty yards or so, when they hurled themselves with irresistible force upon them. Again there came the awful roll of the meeting shields, and as we watched the grim tragedy repeated itself. But this time the issue was left longer in doubt; indeed, it seemed for awhile almost impossible that the Greys should again prevail. The attacking regiment, which was one formed of young men, fought with the utmost fury, and at first seemed by sheer weight to be driving the veterans back. The slaughter was something awful, hundreds falling every minute; and from among the shouts of the warriors and the groans of the dying, set to the clashing music of meeting spears, came a continuous hissing undertone of *'S'gee, s'gee'*, the note of triumph of each victor as he passed his spear through and through the body of his fallen foe.

But perfect discipline and steady and unchanging valour can do wonders, and one veteran soldier is worth two young ones, as soon became apparent in the present case. For just as we thought that it was all up with the Greys, and were preparing to take their place so soon as they made room by being destroyed, I heard Sir Henry's deep voice ringing out above the din, and caught a glimpse of his circling battle-axe as he waved it high above his plumes. Then came a change; the Greys ceased to give; they stood still as a rock, against which the furious waves of spearmen broke again and again, only to recoil. Presently they began to move again – forward this time; as they had no firearms, there was no smoke, so we could see it all. Another minute and the onslaught grew fainter.

'Ah, they are *men* indeed; they will conquer again,' called out Ignosi, who was grinding his teeth with excitement at my side. 'See, it is done!'

Suddenly, like puffs of smoke from the mouth of a cannon, the attacking regiment broke away in flying groups, their white head-dresses streaming behind them in the wind, and left their opponents victors, indeed, but, alas! no more a regiment. Of the gallant triple line, which, forty minutes before, had gone into action three thousand strong, there remained at most some six hundred blood-bespattered men; the rest were under foot. And yet they cheered and waved their spears in triumph, and then, instead of falling back upon us as we expected, they ran forward, for a hundred yards or so, after the flying groups of foemen, took possession of a gently rising knoll of ground, and, resuming the old triple formation, formed a threefold ring around it. And then, thanks be to God, standing on the top of the mound for a minute, I saw Sir Henry, apparently unharmed, and with him our old friend Infadoos. Then Twala's regiments rolled down upon the doomed band, and once more the battle closed in.

As those who read this history will probably long ago have gathered, I am, to be honest, a bit of a coward, and certainly in no way given to fighting, though, somehow, it has often been my lot to get into unpleasant positions, and to be obliged to shed man's blood. But I have always hated it, and kept my own blood as undiminished in quantity as possible, sometimes by a judicious use of my heels. At this moment, however, for the first time in my life, I felt my bosom burn with martial ardour. Warlike fragments from the *Ingoldsby Legends*, together with numbers of sanguinary verses from the Old Testament, sprang up in my brain like mushrooms in the dark; my blood, which hitherto had been half-frozen with horror, went beating through my veins, and there came upon me a savage desire to kill and spare not. I glanced round at the serried ranks of warriors behind us, and somehow, all in an instant, began to wonder if my face looked like theirs. There they stood, their heads craned forward over their shields, the hands twitching, the lips apart, the fierce features instinct with the hungry lust of battle, and in the eyes a look like the glare of a bloodhound when he sights his quarry.

Only Ignosi's heart seemed, to judge from his comparative self-possession, to all appearance, to beat as calmly as ever beneath his leopard-skin cloak, though even *he* still kept on grinding his teeth. I could stand it no longer.

'Are we to stand here till we put out roots, Umbopa – Ignosi, I mean – while Twala swallows our brothers yonder?' I asked.

'Nay, Macumazahn,' was the answer, 'see, now is the ripe moment: let us pluck it.'

As he spoke, a fresh regiment rushed past the ring upon the little mound, and wheeling round, attacked it from the hither side.

Then, lifting his battle-axe, Ignosi gave the signal to advance, and, raising the Kukuana battle-cry, the Buffaloes charged home with a rush like the rush of the sea.

What followed immediately on this it is out of my power to tell. All I can remember is a wild, yet ordered rushing, that seemed to shake the ground; a sudden change of front and forming up on the part of the regiment against which the charge was directed; then an awful shock, a dull roar of voices, and a continuous flashing of spears, seen through a red mist of blood.

When my mind cleared I found myself standing inside the remnant of the Greys near the top of the mound, and just behind no less a person than Sir Henry himself. How I got there I had, at the moment, no idea, but Sir Henry afterwards told me that I was borne up by the first furious charge of the Buffaloes almost to his feet, and then left, as they in turn were pressed back. Thereon he dashed out of the circle and dragged me into it.

As for the fight that followed, who can describe it? Again and again the multitudes surged up against our momentarily lessening circle, and again and again we beat them back.

> The stubborn spearmen still made good
> The dark impenetrable wood;
> Each stepping where his comrade stood
> The instant that he fell,

as some one or other beautifully puts it.

It was a splendid thing to see those brave battalions come on time after time over the barriers of their dead, sometimes holding corpses before them to receive our spear thrusts, only to leave their own corpses to swell the rising piles. It was a gallant sight to see that sturdy old warrior, Infadoos, as cool as though he were on parade, shouting out orders, taunts, and even jests, to keep up the spirit of his few remaining men, and then, as each charge rolled up, stepping forward to wherever the fighting was thickest, to bear his share in repelling it. And yet more gallant was the vision of Sir Henry, whose ostrich plumes had been shorn off by a spear stroke, so that his long yellow hair streamed out in the breeze behind him. There he stood, the great Dane, for he was nothing else, his hands, his axe, and his armour, all red with blood, and none could live before his stroke. Time after time I saw it come sweeping down, as some great warrior ventured to give him battle, and as he struck he shouted, '*O-hoy! O-hoy!*' like his Bersekir forefathers, and the blow went crashing through shield and spear, through head-dress, hair, and skull, till at last none would of their own will come near the great white 'tagati' (wizard), who killed and failed not.

But suddenly there rose a cry of '*Twala, y' Twala*,' and out of the press sprang forward none other than the gigantic one-eyed king himself, also armed with battle-axe and shield, and clad in chain armour.

'Where art thou, Incubu, thou white man, who slew Scragga, my son – see if thou canst kill me !' he shouted, and at the same time hurled a tolla straight at Sir Henry, who, fortunately, saw it coming, and caught it on his shield, which it transfixed, remaining wedged in the iron plate behind the hide.

Then, with a cry, Twala sprang forward straight at him, and with his battle-axe struck him such a blow upon the shield, that the mere force and shock of it brought Sir Henry, strong man as he was, down upon his knees.

But at the time the matter went no further, for at that instant there rose from the regiments pressing round us something like a shout of dismay, and on looking up I saw the cause.

To the right and to the left the plain was alive with the plumes of charging warriors. The outflanking squadrons had come to our relief. The time could not have been better chosen. All Twala's army had, as Ignosi had predicted would be the case, fixed their attention on the bloody struggle which was raging round the remmant of the Greys and the Buffaloes, who were now carrying on a battle of their own at a little distance, which two regiments had formed the chest of our army. It was not until the horns were about to close upon them that they had dreamed of their approach. And now, before they could even assume a proper formation for defence, the outflanking Impis had leapt, like greyhounds, on their flanks.

In five minutes the fate of the battle was decided. Taken on both flanks, and dismayed by the awful slaughter inflicted upon them by the Greys and Buffaloes, Twala's regiments broke into flight, and soon the whole plain between us and Loo was scattered with groups of flying soldiers, making good their retreat. As for the forces that had so recently surrounded us and the Buffaloes, they melted away as though by magic, and presently we were left standing there like a rock from which the sea has retreated. But what a sight it was! Around us the dead and dying lay in heaped-up masses, and of the gallant Greys there remained alive but ninety-five men. More than 2,900 had fallen in this one regiment, most of them never to rise again.

'Men,' said Infadoos, calmly, as between the intervals of binding up a wound in his arm he surveyed what remained to him of his corps, 'ye have kept up the reputation of your regiment, and this day's fighting will be spoken of by your children's children.' Then he turned round and shook Sir Henry Curtis by the hand. 'Thou art a great man, Incubu,' he said, simply; 'I have lived a long life among warriors, and known many a brave one, yet have I never seen a man like thee.'

At this moment the Buffaloes began to march past our position on the road to Loo, and as they did so a message was brought to us from Ignosi requesting Infadoos, Sir Henry, and myself to join him. Accordingly, orders having been issued to the remaining ninety men of the Greys to employ themselves in collecting the wounded, we joined Ignosi, who informed us that he was pressing on to Loo to complete the victory by capturing Twala, if that should be possible. Before we had gone far we suddenly discovered the figure of Good sitting on an ant-heap about one hundred paces from us. Close beside him was the body of a Kukuana.

'He must be wounded,' said Sir Henry, anxiously. As he made the remark, an untoward thing happened. The dead body of the Kukuana soldier, or rather what had appeared to be his dead body, suddenly sprang up, knocked Good head over heels off the ant-heap, and began to spear him. We rushed forward in terror, and as we drew near we saw the brawny warrior making dig after dig at the prostrate Good, who at each prod jerked all his limbs into the air. Seeing us coming, the Kukuana gave one final most vicious dig, and with a shout of 'Take that, wizard,' bolted off. Good did not move, and we concluded that our poor comrade was done for. Sadly we came towards him, and were indeed astonished to find him pale and faint indeed, but with a serene smile upon his face, and his eye-glass still fixed in his eye.

'Capital armour this,' he murmured, on catching sight of our faces bending over him. 'How sold he must have been,' and then he fainted. On examination we discovered that he had been seriously wounded in the leg by a tolla in the course of the pursuit, but that the chain armour had prevented his last assailant's spear from doing anything more than bruise him badly. It was a merciful escape. As nothing could be done for him at the moment, he was placed on one of the wicker shields used for the wounded, and carried along with us.

On arriving before the nearest gate of Loo, we found one of our regiments watching it in obedience to orders received from Ignosi. The remaining regiments were in the same way watching the other exits to the town. The officer in command of this regiment coming up, saluted Ignosi as king, and informed him that Twala's army had taken refuge in the town, whither Twala himself had also escaped, but that he thought that they were thoroughly demoralized, and would surrender. Thereupon Ignosi, after taking counsel with us, sent forward heralds to each gate ordering the defenders to open, and promising on his royal word life and forgiveness to every soldier who laid down his arms. The message was not without its effect. Presently, amid the shouts and cheers of the Buffaloes, the bridge was dropped across the fosse, and the gates upon the further side flung open.

Taking due precautions against treachery, we marched on into the town. All along the roadways stood dejected warriors, their heads drooping, and their shields and spears at their feet, who, as Ignosi passed, saluted him as king. On we marched, straight to Twala's kraal. When we reached the great space, where a day or two previously we had seen the review and the witch hunt, we found it deserted. No, not quite deserted, for there, on the further side, in front of his hut, sat Twala himself, with but one attendant – Gagool.

It was a melancholy sight to see him seated there, his battle-axe and shield by his side, his chin upon his mailed breast, with but one old crone for companion, and notwithstanding his cruelties and misdeeds, a pang of compassion shot through me as I saw him thus 'fallen from his high estate'. Not a soldier of all his armies, not a courtier out of the hundreds who had cringed round him, not even a solitary wife, remained to share his fate or halve the bitterness of his fall. Poor savage! he was learning the lesson that Fate teaches to most who live long enough, that the eyes of mankind are blind to the discredited, and that he who is defenceless and fallen finds few friends and little mercy. Nor, indeed, in this case did he deserve any.

Filing through the kraal gate, we marched straight across the open space to where the ex-king sat. When within about fifty yards the regiment was halted, and accompanied only by a small guard we advanced towards him, Gagool reviling us bitterly as we came. As we drew near, Twala, for the first time, lifted up his plumed head, and fixed his one eye, which seemed to flash with suppressed fury almost as brightly as the great diamond bound round his forehead, upon his successful rival – Ignosi.

'Hail, O king!' he said, with bitter mockery; 'thou who hast eaten of my bread, and now by the aid of the white man's magic has seduced my regiments and defeated mine army, hail! what fate hast thou for me, O king?'

'The fate thou gavest to my father, whose throne thou hast sat on these many years!' was the stern answer.

'It is well. I will show thee how to die, that thou mayest remember it against thine own time. See, the sun sinks in blood,' and he pointed with his red battle-axe towards the fiery orb now going down; 'it is well that my sun should sink with it. And now, O king! I am ready to die, but I crave the boon of the Kukuana royal house[1] to die fighting. Thou canst not refuse it, or even those cowards who fled today will hold thee shamed.'

'It is granted. Choose – with whom wilt thou fight? Myself I cannot fight with thee, for the king fights not except in war.'

Twala's sombre eye ran up and down our ranks, and I felt, as for a moment it rested on myself, that the position had developed a new horror. What if he chose to begin by fighting *me*? What chance should I have against a desperate savage six feet five high, and broad in proportion? I might as well commit suicide at once. Hastily I made up my mind to decline the combat, even if I were hooted out of Kukuanaland as a consequence. It is, I think, better to be hooted than to be quartered with a battle-axe.

Presently he spoke.

---

[1] It is a law amongst the Kukuanas that no man of the royal blood can be put to death unless by his own consent, which is, however, never refused. He is allowed to choose a succession of antagonists, to be approved by the king, with whom he fights, till one of them kills him.

'Incubu, what sayest thou, shall we end what we began today, or shall I call thee coward, white – even to the liver?'

'Nay,' interposed Ignosi, hastily; 'thou shalt not fight with Incubu.'

'Not if he is afraid,' said Twala.

Unfortunately Sir Henry understood this remark, and the blood flamed up into his cheeks.

'I will fight him,' he said; 'he shall see if I am afraid.'

'For God's sake,' I entreated, 'don't risk your life against that of a desperate man. Anybody who saw you today will know that you are not a coward.'

'I will fight him,' was the sullen answer. 'No living man shall call me a coward. I am ready now!' and he stepped forward and lifted his axe.

I wrung my hands over this absurd piece of Quixotism; but if he was determined on fighting, of course I could not stop him.

'Fight not, my white brother,' said Ignosi, laying his hand affectionately on Sir Henry's arm; 'thou hast fought enough, and if aught befell thee at his hands it would cut my heart in twain.'

'I will fight, Ignosi,' was Sir Henry's answer.

'It is well, Incubu; thou art a brave man. It will be a good fight. Behold, Twala, the elephant is ready for thee.'

The ex-king laughed savagely, and stepped forward and faced Curtis. For a moment they stood thus, and the setting sun caught their stalwart frames and clothed them both in fire. They were a well-matched pair.

Then they began to circle round each other, their battle-axes raised.

Suddenly Sir Henry sprang forward and struck a fearful blow at Twala, who stepped to one side. So heavy was the stroke that the striker half overbalanced himself, a circumstance of which his antagonist took a prompt advantage. Circling his heavy battle-axe round his head, he brought it down with tremendous force. My heart jumped into my mouth; I thought that the affair was already finished. But no; with a quick upward movement of the left arm Sir Henry interposed his shield between himself and the axe, with the result that its outer edge was shorn clean off, the axe falling on his left shoulder, but not heavily enough to do any serious damage. In another second, Sir Henry got in another blow, which was also received by Twala upon his shield. Then followed blow upon blow, which were, in turn, either received upon the shield or avoided. The excitement grew intense; the regiment which was watching the encounter forgot its discipline, and, drawing near, shouted and groaned at every stroke. Just at this time, too, Good, who had been laid upon the ground by me, recovered from his faint, and, sitting up, perceived what was going on. In an instant he was up, and, catching hold of my arm, hopped about from place to place on one leg, dragging me after him, yelling out encouragements to Sir Henry:

'Go it, old fellow!' he halloed. 'That was a good one! Give it him amidships,' and so on.

Presently Sir Henry, having caught a fresh stroke upon his shield, hit out with all his force. The stroke cut through Twala's shield and through the tough chain armour behind it, gashing him in the shoulder. With a yell of pain and fury Twala returned the stroke with interest, and, such was his strength, shore right through the rhinoceros' horn handle of his antagonist's battle-axe, strengthened as it was with bands of steel, wounding Curtis in the face.

A cry of dismay rose from the Buffaloes as our hero's broad axe-head fell to the ground; and Twala, again raising his weapon, flew at him with a shout. I shut my eyes. When I opened them again, it was to see Sir Henry's shield lying on the ground, and Sir Henry himself with his great arms twined round Twala's middle. To and fro they swung, hugging each other like bears, straining with all their mighty muscles for dear life and dearer honour. With a supreme effort Twala swung the Englishman clean off his feet, and down they came together, rolling over and over on the lime paving, Twala striking out at Curtis' head with the battle-axe, and Sir Henry trying to drive the tolla he had drawn from his belt through Twala's armour.

It was a mighty struggle, and an awful thing to see.

'Get his axe!' yelled Good; and perhaps our champion heard him.

At any rate, dropping the tolla, he made a grab at the axe, which was fastened to Twala's wrist by a strip of buffalo hide, and still rolling over and over, they fought for it like wild cats, drawing their breath in heavy gasps. Suddenly the hide string burst, and then, with a great effort, Sir Henry freed himself, the weapon remaining in his grasp. Another second, and he was up upon his feet, the red blood streaming from the wound in his face, and so was Twala. Drawing the heavy tolla from his belt, he staggered straight at Curtis and struck him upon the breast. The blow came home true and strong, but whoever it was made that chain armour understood his art, for it withstood the steel. Again Twala struck out with a savage yell, and again the heavy knife rebounded, and Sir Henry went staggering back. Once more Twala came on, and as he came our great Englishman gathered himself together, and, swinging the heavy axe round his head, hit at him with all his force. There was a shriek of excitement from a thousand throats, and, behold! Twala's head seemed to spring from his shoulders and then fell and came rolling and bounding along the ground towards Ignosi, stopping just at his feet. For a second the corpse stood upright, the blood spouting in fountains from the severed arteries; then with a dull crash it fell to the earth, and the gold torque from the neck went rolling away across the pavement. As it did so, Sir Henry, overpowered by faintness and loss of blood, fell heavily across it.

In a second he was lifted up, and eager hands were pouring water on his face. Another minute, and the great grey eyes opened wide.

He was not dead.

Then I, just as the sun sank, stepping to where Twala's head lay in the dust, unloosed the diamond from the dead brows, and handed it to Ignosi.

'Take it,' I said, 'lawful King of the Kukuanas.'

Ignosi bound the diadem upon his brows, and then advancing, placed his foot upon the broad chest of his headless foe and broke out into a chant, or rather a paean of victory, so beautiful, and yet so utterly savage, that I despair of being able to give an adequate idea of it. I once heard a scholar with a fine voice read aloud from the Greek poet Homer, and I remember that the sound of the rolling lines seemed to make my blood stand still. Ignosi's chant, uttered as it was in a language as beautiful and sonorous as the old Greek, produced excactly the same effect on me, although I was exhausted with toil and many emotions.

'*Now*,' he began, '*now is our rebellion swallowed up in victory, and our evil-doing justified by strength.*

'*In the morning the oppressors rose up and shook themselves; they bound on their plumes and made them ready for war.*

'*They rose up and grasped their spears: the soldiers called to the captains, "Come, lead us" – and the captains cried to the king, "Direct thou the battle."*

'*They rose up in their pride, twenty thousand men, and yet a twenty thousand.*

'*Their plumes covered the earth as the plumes of a bird cover her nest; they shook their spears and shouted, yea they hurled their spears into the sunlight; they lusted for the battle and were glad.*

'*They came up against me; their strong ones came running swiftly to crush me; they cried, "Ha! ha! he is as one already dead."*

'*Then breathed I on them, and my breath was as the breath of a storm, and lo! they were not.*

'*My lightnings pierced them; I licked up their strength with the lightning of my spears; I shook them to the earth with the thunder of my shouting.*

'*They broke – they scattered – they were gone as the mists of the morning.*

'*They are food for the crows and the foxes, and the place of battle is fat with their blood.*

'*Where are the mighty ones who rose up in the morning?*

'*Where are the proud ones who tossed their plumes and cried, "He is as one already dead?"*

'*They bow their heads, but not in sleep; they are stretched out, but not in sleep.*

'*They are forgotten; they have gone into the blackness, and shall not return; yea, others shall lead away their wives, and their children shall remember them no more.*

'*And I – I! the king – like an eagle have I found my eyrie.*

'*Behold! far have I wandered in the night-time, yet have I returned to my little ones at the daybreak.*

'*Creep ye under the shadow of my wings, O people, and I will comfort ye, and ye shall not be dismayed.*

'*Now is the good time, the time of spoil.*

'*Mine are the cattle in the valleys, the virgins in the kraals are mine also.*

'The winter is overpast, the summer is at hand.

'Now shall Evil cover up her face, and Prosperity shall bloom in the land like a lily.

'Rejoice, rejoice, my people! let all the land rejoice in that the tyranny is trodden down, in that I am the king.'

He paused, and out of the gathering gloom there came back the deep reply:

'Thou art the king.'

Thus it was that my prophecy to the herald came true, and within the forty-eight hours, Twala's headless corpse was stiffening at Twala's gate.

15

Good Falls Sick

AFTER the fight was ended, Sir Henry and Good were carried into Twala's hut, where I joined them. They were both utterly exhausted by exertion and loss of blood, and, indeed, my own condition was little better. I am very wiry, and can stand more fatigue than most men, probably on account of my light weight and long training; but that night I was fairly done up, and, as is always the case with me when exhausted, that old wound the lion gave me began to pain me. Also my head was aching violently from the blow I had received in the morning when I was knocked senseless. Altogether, a more miserable trio than we were that evening it would have been difficult to discover; and our only comfort lay in the reflection that we were exceedingly fortunate to be there to feel miserable, instead of being stretched dead upon the plain, as so many thousands of brave men were that night, who had risen well and strong in the morning. Somehow, with the assistance of the beautiful Foulata, who, since we had been the means of saving her life, had constituted herself our handmaiden, and especially Good's, we managed to get off the chain shirts, which had certainly saved the lives of two of us that day, when we found that the flesh underneath was terribly bruised, for though the steel links had prevented the weapons from entering, they had not prevented them from bruising. Both Sir Henry and Good were a mass of bruises, and I was by no means free. As a remedy, Foulata brought us some pounded green leaves, with an aromatic odour, which, when applied as a plaster, gave us considerable relief. But though the bruises were painful, they did not give us such anxiety as Sir Henry's and Good's wounds. Good had a hole right through the fleshy part of his 'beautiful white leg', from which he had lost a great deal of blood; and Sir Henry had a deep cut over the jaw, inflicted by Twala's battle-axe. Luckily Good was a very decent surgeon, and as soon as his small box of medicines was forthcoming, he, having thoroughly cleansed the wounds, managed to stitch up first Sir

Henry's and then his own pretty satisfactorily, considering the imperfect light given by the primitive Kukuana lamp in the hut. Afterwards he plentifully smeared the wounds with some antiseptic ointment of which there was a pot in the little box, and we covered them with the remains of a pocket-handkerchief which we possessed.

Meanwhile Foulata had prepared us some strong broth, for we were too weary to eat. This we swallowed, and then threw ourselves down on the piles of magnificent karosses, or fur rugs, which were scattered about the dead king's great hut. By a very strange instance of the irony of fate, it was on Twala's own couch, and wrapped in Twala's own particular kaross, that Sir Henry, the man who had slain him, slept that night.

I say slept; but after that day's work sleep was indeed difficult. To begin with, in very truth the air was full

Of farewells to the dying
And mournings for the dead.

From every direction came the sound of the wailing of women whose husbands, sons, and brothers had perished in the fight. No wonder that they wailed, for over twenty thousand men, or nearly a third of the Kukuana army, had been destroyed in that awful struggle. It was heart-rending to lie and listen to their cries for those who would never return; and it made one realize the full horror of the work done that day to further man's ambition. Towards midnight, however, the ceaseless crying of the women grew less frequent, till at length the silence was only broken at intervals of a few minutes by a long, piercing howl that came from a hut in our immediate rear, and which I afterwards discovered proceeded from Gagool wailing for the dead king Twala.

After that I got a little fitful sleep, only to wake from time to time with a start, thinking that I was once more an actor in the terrible events of the last twenty-four hours. Now I seemed to see that warrior, whom my hand had sent to his last account, charging at me on the mountain-top; now I was once more in that glorious ring of Greys, which made its immortal stand against all Twala's regiments, upon the little mound; and now again I saw Twala's plumed and gory head roll past my feet with gnashing teeth and glaring eye. At last, somehow or other, the night passed away; but when dawn broke I found that my companions had slept no better than myself. Good, indeed, was in a high fever, and very soon afterwards began to grow light-headed, and also, to my alarm, to spit blood, the result, no doubt, of some internal injury inflicted by the desperate efforts made by the Kukuana warrior on the previous day to get his big spear through the chain armour. Sir Henry, however, seemed pretty fresh, notwithstanding his wound on the face, which made eating difficult and laughter an impossibility, though he was so sore and stiff that he could scarcely stir.

About eight o'clock we had a visit from Infadoos, who seemed but little the worse – tough old warrior that he was – for his exertions on the previous day, though he informed us he had been up all night. He was delighted to see us, though much grieved at Good's condition, and shook hands cordially; but I noticed that he addressed Sir Henry with a kind of reverence, as though he were something more than man; and indeed, as we afterwards found out, the great Englishman was looked on throughout Kukuanaland as a supernatural being. No man, the soldiers said, could have fought as he fought, or could, at the end of a day of such toil and bloodshed, have slain Twala, who, in addition to being the king, was supposed to be the strongest warrior in Kukuanaland, in single combat, sheering through his bull-neck at a stroke. Indeed, that stroke became proverbial in Kukuanaland, and any extraordinary blow or feat of strength was thenceforth known as 'Incubu's blow'.

Infadoos told us also that all Twala's regiments had submitted to Ignosi, and that like submissions were beginning to arrive from chiefs in the country. Twala's death at the hands of Sir Henry had put an end to all further chance of disturbance; for Scragga had been his only son, and there was no rival claimant left alive.

I remarked that Ignosi had swum to the throne through blood. The old chief shrugged his shoulders. 'Yes,' he answered; 'but the Kukuana people can only be kept cool by letting the blood flow sometimes. Many were killed indeed, but the women were left, and others would soon grow up to take the places of the fallen. After this the land would be quiet for a while.'

Afterwards, in the course of the morning, we had a short visit from Ignosi, on whose brows the royal diadem was now bound. As I contemplated him advancing with kingly dignity, an obsequious guard following his steps, I could not help recalling to my mind the tall Zulu who had presented himself to us at Durban some few months back, asking to be taken into our service, and reflecting on the strange revolutions of the wheel of fortune.

'Hail, O king!' I said, rising.

'Yes, Macumazahn. King at last, by the grace of your three right hands,' was the ready answer.

All was, he said, going on well; and he hoped to arrange a great feast in two weeks' time in order to show himself to the people.

I asked him what he had settled to do with Gagool.

'She is the evil genius of the land,' he answered, 'and I shall kill her, and all the witch doctors with her! She has lived so long that none can remember when she was not old, and always she it is who has trained the witch-hunters, and made the land evil in the sight of the heavens above.'

'Yet she knows much,' I replied; 'it is easier to destroy knowledge, Ignosi, than to gather it.'

'It is so,' he said, thoughtfully. 'She, and she only, knows the secret of the "Three Witches" yonder, whither the great road runs, where the kings are buried, and the silent ones sit.'

'Yes, and the diamonds are. Forget not thy promise, Ignosi; thou must lead us to the mines, even if thou hast to spare Gagool alive to show the way.'

'I will not forget, Macumazahn, and I will think on what thou sayest.'

After Ignosi's visit I went to see Good, and found him quite delirious. The fever from his wound seemed to have taken a firm hold of his system, and to be complicated by an internal injury. For four or five days his condition was most critical; indeed, I firmly believe that had it not been for Foulata's indefatigable nursing he must have died.

Women are women, all the world over, whatever their colour. Yet somehow it seemed curious to watch this dusky beauty bending night and day over the fevered man's couch, and performing all the merciful errands of the sick-room as swiftly, gently, and with as fine an instinct as a trained hospital nurse. For the first night or two I tried to help her, and so did Sir Henry so soon as his stiffness allowed him to move, but she bore our interference with impatience, and finally insisted upon our leaving him to her, saying that our movements made him restless, which I think was true. Day and night she watched and tended him, giving him his only medicine, a native cooling drink made of milk, in which was infused the juice of the bulb of a species of tulip, and keeping the flies from settling on him. I can see the whole picture now as it appeared night after night by the light of our primitive lamp, Good tossing to and fro, his features emaciated, his eyes shining large and luminous, and jabbering nonsense by the yard; and seated on the ground by his side, her back resting against the wall of the hut, the soft-eyed, shapely Kukuana beauty, her whole face weary as it was, animated by a look of infinite compassion – or was it something more than compassion?

For two days we thought that he must die, and crept about with heavy hearts. Only Foulata would not believe it.

'He will live,' she said.

For three hundred yards or more around Twala's chief hut, where the sufferer lay, there was silence; for by the king's order all who lived in the habitations behind it had, except Sir Henry and myself, been removed, lest any noise should come to the sick man's ears. One night, it was the fifth night of his illness, as was my habit, I went across to see how he was getting on before turning in for a few hours.

I entered the hut carefully. The lamp placed upon the floor showed the figure of Good, tossing no more, but lying quite still.

So it had come at last! and in the bitterness of my heart I gave something like a sob.

'Hush-h-h!' came from the patch of dark shadow behind Good's head.

Then, creeping closer, I saw that he was not dead, but sleeping soundly, with Foulata's taper fingers clasped tightly in his poor white hand. The crisis had passed, and he would live. He slept like that for eighteen hours; and I scarcely like to say it, for fear I should not be believed, but during the entire period did that devoted girl sit by him, fearing that if she moved and drew away her hand it would wake him. What she must have suffered from cramp, stiffness, and weariness, to say nothing of want of food, nobody will ever know; but it is a fact that, when at last he woke, she had to be carried away – her limbs were so stiff that she could not move them.

After the turn had once been taken, Good's recovery was rapid and complete. It was not till he was nearly well that Sir Henry told him of all he owed to Foulata; and when he came to the story of how she sat by his side for eighteen hours, fearing lest by moving she should wake him, the honest sailor's eyes filled with tears. He turned and went straight to the hut where Foulata was preparing the midday meal (we were back in our old quarters now), taking me with him to interpret in case he could not make his meaning clear to her, though I am bound to say she understood him marvellously as a rule, considering how extremely limited was his foreign vocabulary.

'Tell her,' said Good, 'that I owe her my life, and that I will never forget her kindness.'

I interpreted, and under her dark skin she actually seemed to blush.

Turning to him with one of those swift and graceful motions that in her always reminded me of the flight of a wild bird, she answered softly, glancing at him with her large brown eyes:

'Nay, my lord; my lord forgets! Did he not save *my* life, and am I not my lord's handmaiden?'

It will be observed that the young lady appeared to have entirely forgotten the share which Sir Henry and myself had had in her preservation from Twala's clutches. But that is the way of women! I remember my dear wife was just the same. I retired from that little interview sad at heart. I did not like Miss Foulata's soft glances, for I knew the fatal amorous propensities of sailors in general, and Good in particular.

There are two things in the world, as I have found it, which cannot be prevented: you cannot keep a Zulu from fighting, or a sailor from falling in love upon the slightest provocation!

It was a few days after this last occurrence that Ignosi held his great 'indaba' (council), and was formally recognized as king by the 'indunas' (head men) of Kukuanaland. The spectacle was a most imposing one, including, as it did, a great review of troops. On this day the remaining fragment of the Greys were formally paraded, and in the face of the army thanked for their splendid conduct in the great battle. To each man the king made a large present of cattle, promoting them one and all to the rank of officers in the new corps of Greys, which was in process of formation. An order was also promulgated throughout the length and breadth of Kukuanaland that, whilst we honoured the country with our presence, we three were to be greeted with the royal salute, to be treated with the same ceremony and respect that was by custom accorded to the king, and the power of life and death was publicly conferred upon us. Ignosi, too, in the presence of his people, reaffirmed the promises that he had made, to the effect that no man's blood should be shed without trial, and that witch-hunting should cease in the land.

When the ceremony was over, we waited upon Ignosi, and informed him that we were now anxious to investigate the mystery of the mines to which Solomon's Road ran, asking him if he had discovered anything about them.

'My friends,' he answered, 'this have I discovered. It is there that the three great figures sit, who here are called the "Silent Ones", and to whom Twala would have offered the girl, Foulata, as a sacrifice. It is there, too, in a great cave deep in the mountain, that the kings of the land are buried; there shall ye find Twala's body, sitting with those who went before him. There, too, is a great pit, which, at some time, long-dead men dug out, mayhap for the stones ye speak of, such as I have heard men in Natal speak of at Kimberley. There, too, in the Place of Death is a secret chamber, known to none but the king and Gagool. But Twala, who knew it, is dead, and I know it not, nor know I what is in it. But there is a legend in the land that once, many generations gone, a white man crossed the mountains, and was led by a woman to the secret chamber and shown the wealth, but before he could take it she betrayed him, and he was driven by the king of the day back to the mountains, and since then no man has entered the chamber.'

'The story is surely true, Ignosi, for on the mountains we found the white man,' I said.

'Yes, we found him. And now I have promised ye that if ye can find that chamber, and the stones are there – '

'The stone upon thy forehead proves that they are there,' I put in, pointing to the great diamond I had taken from Twala's dead brows.

'Mayhap; if they are there,' he said, 'ye shall have as many as ye can take hence – if, indeed, ye would leave me, my brothers.'

'First we must find the chamber,' said I.

'There is but one who can show it to thee – Gagool.'

'And if she will not?'

'Then shall she die,' said Ignosi, sternly. 'I have saved her alive but for this. Stay, she shall choose,' and calling to a messenger he ordered Gagool to be brought.

In a few minutes she came, hurried along by two guards, whom she was cursing as she walked.

'Leave her,' said the king to the guards.

As soon as their support was withdrawn, the withered old bundle, for she looked more like a bundle than anything else, sank into a heap on to the floor, out of which her two bright wicked eyes gleamed like a snake's.

'What will ye with me, Ignosi?' she piped. 'Ye dare not touch me. If ye touch me I will blast ye as ye sit. Beware of my magic.'

'Thy magic could not save Twala, old she-wolf, and it cannot hurt me,' was the answer. 'Listen: I will this of thee, that thou reveal where is the chamber where are the shining stones.'

'Ha! ha!' she piped, 'none know but I, and I will never tell thee. The white devils shall go hence empty-handed.'

'Thou wilt tell me. I will make thee tell me.'

'How, O king? Thou art great, but can thy power wring the truth from a woman?'

'It is difficult, yet will I do it.'

'How, O king?'

'Nay, thus; if thou tellest not thou shalt slowly die.'

'Die!' she shrieked, in terror and fury; 'ye dare not touch me – man, ye know not who I am. How old think ye am I? I knew your fathers, and your fathers' fathers' fathers. When the country was young I was here, when the country grows old I shall still be here. I cannot die unless I be killed by chance, for none dare slay me.'

'Yet will I slay thee. See, Gagool, mother of evil, thou art so old thou canst no longer love thy life. What can life be to such a hag as thee, who hast no shape, nor form, nor hair, nor teeth – hast naught, save wickedness and evil eyes? It will be mercy to slay thee, Gagool.'

'Thou fool,' shrieked the old fiend, 'thou accursed fool, thinkest thou that life is sweet only to the young? It is not so, and naught thou knowest of the heart of man to think it. To the young, indeed, death is sometimes welcome, for the young can feel. They love and suffer, and it wrings them to see their beloved pass to the land of shadows. But the old feel not, they love not, and, *ha*! *ha*! they laugh to see another go out into the dark; *ha*! *ha*! they laugh to see the evil that is done under the sun. All they love is life, the warm, warm sun, and the sweet, sweet air. They are afraid of the cold, afraid of the cold and the dark, *ha*! *ha*! *ha*!' and the old hag writhed in ghastly merriment on the ground.

'Cease thine evil talk and answer me,' said Ignosi, angrily. 'Wilt thou show the place where the stones are, or wilt thou not? If thou wilt not thou diest, even now,' and he seized a spear and held it over her.

'I will not show it; thou darest not kill me, darest not. He who slays me will be accursed for ever.'

Slowly Ignosi brought down the spear till it pricked the prostrate heap of rags.

With a wild yell she sprang to her feet, and then again fell and rolled upon the floor.

'Nay, I will show it. Only let me live, let me sit in the sun and have a bit of meat to suck, and I will show thee.'

'It is well. I thought I should find a way to reason with thee. Tomorrow shalt thou go with Infadoos and my white brothers to the place, and beware how thou failest, for if thou showest it not, then shalt thou slowly die. I have spoken.'

'I will not fail, Ignosi. I always keep my word: *ha*! *ha*! *ha*! Once a woman showed the place to a white man before, and behold evil befell him,' and here her wicked eyes glinted. 'Her name was Gagool too. Perchance I was that woman.'

'Thou liest,' I said, 'that was ten generations gone.'

'Mayhap, mayhap; when one lives long one forgets. Perhaps it was my mother's mother who told me, surely her name was Gagool also. But mark, ye will find in the place where the bright playthings are, a bag of hide full of stones. The man filled that bag, but he never took it away. Evil befell him, I say, evil befell him! Perhaps it was my mother's mother who told me. It will be a merry journey – we can see the bodies of those who died in the battle as we go. Their eyes will be gone by now, and their ribs will be hollow. *Ha*! *ha*! *ha*!'

16

The Place of Death

IT was already dark on the third day after the scene described in the previous chapter, when we camped in some huts at the foot of the 'Three Witches', as the triangle of mountains were called to which Solomon's great road ran. Our party consisted of our three selves and Foulata, who waited on us – especially on Good – Infadoos, Gagool, who was borne along in a litter, inside which she could be heard muttering and cursing all day long, and a party of guards and attendants. The mountains, or rather the three peaks of the mountains, for the whole mass evidently consisted of a solitary upheaval, were, as I have said, in the form of a triangle, of which the base was towards us, one peak being on our right, one on our left, and one straight in front of us. Never shall I forget the sight afforded by those three towering peaks in the early sunlight of the following morning. High, high above us, up into the blue air, soared their twisted snow-wreaths. Beneath the snow the peaks were purple with heaths, and so were the wild moors that ran up the slopes towards them. Straight before us the white ribbon of Solomon's great road stretched away uphill to the foot of the centre peak, about five miles from us, and there stopped. It was its terminus.

I had better leave the feelings of intense excitement with which we set out on our march that morning to the imagination of those who read this history. At last we were drawing near to the wonderful mines that had been the cause of the miserable death of the old Portuguese Dom, three centuries ago, of my poor friend, his ill-starred descendant, and also, as we feared, of George Curtis, Sir Henry's brother. Were we destined, after all that we had gone through, to fare any better? Evil befell them, as that old fiend Gagool said, would it also befall us? Somehow, as we were marching up that last stretch of beautiful road, I could not help feeling a little superstitious about the matter, and so I think did Good and Sir Henry.

For an hour and a half or more we tramped on up the heather-fringed road, going so fast in our excitement that the bearers with Gagool's hammock could scarcely keep pace with us, and its occupant piped out to us to stop.

'Go more slowly, white men,' she said, projecting her hideous shrivelled countenance between the curtains, and fixing her gleaming eyes upon us; 'why will ye run to meet the evil that shall befall ye, ye seekers after treasure?' and she laughed that horrible laugh which always sent a cold shiver down my back, and which for a while quite took the enthusiasm out of us.

However, on we went, till we saw before us, and between ourselves and the peak, a vast circular hole with sloping sides, three hundred feet or more in depth, and quite half a mile round.

'Can't you guess what this is?' I said to Sir Henry and Good, who were staring in astonishment down into the awful pit before us.

They shook their heads.

'Then it is clear that you have never seen the diamond mines at Kimberley. You may depend on it that this is Solomon's Diamond Mine; look there,' I said, pointing to the stiff blue clay which was yet to be seen among the grass and bushes which clothed the sides of the pit, 'the formation is the same. I'll be bound that if we went down there we should find "pipes" of soapy brecciated rock. Look, too,' and I pointed to a series of worn flat slabs of rock which were placed on a gentle slope below the level of a watercourse which had in some past age been cut out of the solid rock; 'if those are not tables once used to wash the "stuff", I'm a Dutchman.'

At the edge of this vast hole, which was the pit marked on the old Dom's map, the great road branched into two and circumvented it. In many places this circumventing road was built entirely of vast blocks of stone, apparently with the object of supporting the edges of the pit and preventing falls of reef. Along this road we pressed, driven by curiosity to see what the three towering objects were which we could discern from the hither side of the great hole. As we got nearer we perceived that they were colossi of some sort or another, and rightly conjectured that these were the three 'Silent Ones' that were held in such awe by the Kukuana people. But it was not until we got quite close that we recognized the full majesty of these 'Silent Ones'.

There upon huge pedestals of dark rock, sculptured in unknown characters, twenty paces between each, and looking down the road which crossed some sixty miles of plain to Loo, were three colossal seated forms – two males and one female – each measuring about twenty feet from the crown of the head to the pedestal.

The female form, which was nude, was of great though severe beauty, but unfortunately the features were injured by centuries of exposure to the weather. Rising from each side of her head were the points of a crescent. The two male colossi were, on the contrary, draped, and presented a terrifying cast of features, especially the one to our right, which had the face of a devil. That to our left was serene in countenance, but the calm upon it was dreadful. It was the calm of inhuman cruelty, the cruelty, Sir Henry remarked, that the ancients attributed to beings potent for good, who could yet watch the sufferings of humanity, if not with rejoicing, at least without suffering themselves. The three formed a most awe-inspiring trinity, as they sat there in their solitude and gazed out across the plain for ever. Contemplating these 'Silent Ones', as the Kukuanas called them, an intense curiosity again seized us to know whose were the hands that had shaped them, who was it that had dug the pit and made the road. Whilst I was gazing and wondering, it suddenly occurred to me (being familiar with the Old Testament) that Solomon went astray after strange gods, the names of three of whom I remembered – 'Ashtoreth the goddess of the Zidonians, Chemosh the god of the Moabites, and Milcom the god of the children of Ammon' – and I suggested to my companions that the three figures before us might represent these false divinities.

'Hum,' said Sir Henry, who was a scholar, having taken a high degree in classics at college, 'there may be something in that; Ashtoreth of the Hebrews was the Astarte of the Phoenicians, who were the great traders of Solomon's time. Astarte, who afterwards was the Aphrodite of the Greeks, was represented with horns like the half-moon, and there on the brow of the female figure are distinct horns. Perhaps these colossi were designed by some Phoenician official who managed the mines. Who can say?'

Before we had finished examining these extraordinary relics of remote antiquity, Infadoos came up, and, having saluted the 'Silent Ones' by lifting his spear, asked us if we intended entering the 'Place of Death' at once, or if we would wait till after we had taken food at midday. If we were ready to go at once, Gagool had announced her willingness to guide us. As it was not more than eleven o'clock, we – driven to it by a burning curiosity – announced our intention of proceeding instantly, and I suggested that, in case we should be detained in the cave, we should take some food with us. Accordingly Gagool's litter was brought up, and that lady herself assisted out of it; and meanwhile Foulata, at my request, stored some 'biltong', or dried game-flesh, together with a couple of gourds of water in a reed basket. Straight in front of us, at a distance of some fifty paces from the backs of the colossi, rose a sheer wall of rock, eighty feet or more in height, that gradually sloped up till it formed the base of the lofty snow-wreathed peak, which soared up into the air three thousand feet above us. As soon as she was clear of her hammock, Gagool cast one evil grin upon us, and then, leaning on a stick, hobbled off towards the sheer face of the rock. We followed her till we came to a narrow portal solidly arched, that looked like the opening of a gallery of a mine.

Here Gagool was waiting for us, still with that evil grin upon her horrid face.

'Now, white men from the stars,' she piped; 'great warriors, Incubu, Bougwan, and Macumazahn the wise, are ye ready? Behold, I am here to do the bidding of my lord the king, and to show ye the store of bright stones.'

'We are ready,' I said.

'Good! good! Make strong your hearts to bear what ye shall see. Comest thou too, Infadoos, who didst betray thy master?'

Infadoos frowned as he answered:

'Nay, I come not, it is not for me to enter there. But thou, Gagool, curb thy tongue, and beware how thou dealest with my lords. At thy hands will I require them, and if a hair of them be hurt, Gagool, be'st thou fifty times a witch, thou shalt die. Hearest thou?'

'I hear, Infadoos; I know thee, thou didst ever love big words; when thou wast a babe I remember thou didst threaten thine own mother. That was but the other day. But fear not, fear not, I live but to do the bidding of the king. I have done the bidding of many kings, Infadoos, till in the end they did mine. Ha! ha! I go to look upon their faces once more, and Twala's too! Come on, come on, here is the lamp,' and she drew a great gourd full of oil, and fitted with a rush wick, from under her fur cloak.

'Art thou coming, Foulata?' asked Good in his villainous kitchen Kukuana, in which he had been improving himself under that young lady's tuition.

'I fear, my lord,' the girl answered, timidly.

'Then give me the basket.'

'Nay, my lord, whither thou goest, there will I go also.'

'The deuce you will!' thought I to myself; 'that will be rather awkward if ever we get out of this.'

Without further ado, Gagool plunged into the passage, which was wide enough to admit of two walking abreast, and quite dark, we following her voice as she piped to us to come on, in some fear and trembling, which was not allayed by the sound of a sudden rush of wings.

'Hullo! what's that?' halloed Good; 'somebody hit me in the face.'

'Bats,' said I; 'on you go.'

When we had, so far as we could judge, gone some fifty paces, we perceived that the passage was growing faintly light. Another minute, and we stood in the most wonderful place that the eyes of living man ever lit on.

Let the reader picture to himself the hall of the vastest cathedral he ever stood in, windowless indeed, but dimly lighted from above (presumably by shafts connected with the outer air and driven in the roof, which arched away a hundred feet above our head), and he will get some idea of the size of the enormous cave in which we stood, with the difference that this cathedral designed of nature was loftier and wider than any built by man. But its stupendous size was the least of the wonders of the place, for running in rows adown its length were gigantic pillars of what looked like ice, but were, in reality, huge stalactites. It is impossible for me to convey any idea of the overpowering beauty and grandeur of these pillars of white spar, some of which were not less than twenty feet in diameter at the base, and sprang up in lofty and yet delicate beauty sheer to the distant roof. Others again were in process of formation. On the rock floor there was in these cases what looked, Sir Henry said, exactly like a broken column in an old Grecian temple, whilst high above, depending from the roof, the point of a huge icicle could be dimly seen. And even as we gazed we could hear the process going on, for presently with a tiny splash a drop of water would fall from the far-off icicle on to the column below. On some columns the drops only fell once in two or three minutes, and in these cases it would form an interesting calculation to discover how long, at that rate of dripping, it would take to form a pillar, say eighty feet high by ten in diameter. That the process was, in at least one instance, incalculably slow, the following instance will suffice to show. Cut on one of these pillars we discovered a rude likeness of a mummy, by the head of which sat what appeared to be one of the Egyptian gods, doubtless the handiwork of some old-world labourer in the mine. This work of art was executed at about the natural height at which an idle fellow, be he Phoenician workman or British cad, is in the habit of trying to immortalize himself at the expense of nature's masterpieces, namely, about five feet from the ground; yet at the time that we saw it, which *must* have been nearly three thousand years after the date of the execution of the drawing, the column was only eight feet high, and was still in process of formation, which gives a rate of growth of a foot to a thousand years, or an inch and a fraction to a century. This we knew because, as we were standing by it, we heard a drop of water fall.

Sometimes the stalactites took strange forms, presumably where the dropping of the water had not always been on the same spot. Thus, one huge mass, which must have weighed a hundred tons or so, was in the form of a pulpit, beautifully fretted over outside with what looked like lace. Others resembled strange beasts, and on the sides of the cave were fan-like ivory tracings, such as the frost leaves upon a pane.

Out of the vast main aisle, there opened here and there smaller caves, exactly, Sir Henry said, as chapels open out of great cathedrals. Some were large, but one or two – and this is a wonderful instance of how nature carries out her handiwork by the same unvarying laws, utterly irrespective of size – were tiny. One little nook, for instance, was no larger than an unusually big doll's house, and yet it might have been the model of the whole place, for the water dropped, the tiny icicles hung, and the spar columns were forming in just the same way.

We had not, however, as much time to examine this beautiful place as thoroughly as we should have liked to do, for unfortunately Gagool seemed to be indifferent to stalactites, and only anxious to get her business over. This annoyed me the more, as I was particularly anxious to discover, if possible, by what system the light was admitted into the place, and whether it was by the hand of man or of nature that this was done, also if it had been used in any way in ancient times, as seemed probable. However, we consoled ourselves with the idea that we would examine it thoroughly on our return, and followed on after our uncanny guide.

On she led us, straight to the top of the vast and silent cave, where we found another doorway, not arched as the first was, but square at the top, something like the doorways of Egyptian temples.

'Are ye prepared to enter the Place of Death?' asked Gagool, evidently with a view to making us feel uncomfortable.

'Lead on, Macduff,' said Good, solemnly, trying to look as though he was not at all alarmed, as indeed did we all except Foulata, who caught Good by the arm for protection.

'This is getting rather ghastly,' said Sir Henry, peeping into the dark doorway. 'Come on, Quatermain – *seniores priores*. Don't keep the old lady waiting!' and he politely made way for me to lead the van, for which I inwardly did not bless him.

Tap, tap, went old Gagool's stick down the passage, as she trotted along, chuckling hideously; and still overcome by some unaccountable presentiment of evil, I hung back.

'Come, get on, old fellow,' said Good, 'or we shall lose our fair guide.'

Thus adjured, I started down the passage, and after about twenty paces found myself in a gloomy apartment some forty feet long, by thirty broad, and thirty high, which in some past age had evidently been hollowed, by hand-labour, out of the mountain. This apartment was not nearly so well lighted as the vast stalactite ante-cave, and at the first glance all I could make out was a massive stone table running its length, with a colossal white figure at its head, and life-sized white figures all round it. Next I made out a brown thing, seated on the table in the centre, and in another moment my eyes grew accustomed to the light, and I saw what all these things were, and I was tailing out of it as hard as my legs would carry me. I am not a nervous man, in a general way, and very little troubled with superstitions, of which I have lived to see the folly; but I am free to own that that sight quite upset me, and had it not been that Sir Henry caught me by the collar and held me, I do honestly believe that in another five minutes I should have been outside that stalactite cave, and that the promise of all the diamonds in Kimberley would not have induced me to enter it again. But he held me tight, so I stopped because I could not help myself. But next second his eyes got accustomed to the light, too, and he let go of me, and began to mop the perspiration off his forehead. As for Good he swore feebly, and Foulata threw her arms round his neck and shrieked.

Only Gagool chuckled loud and long.

It *was* a ghastly sight. There at the end of the long stone table, holding in his skeleton fingers a great white spear, sat *Death* himself, shaped in the form of a colossal human skeleton, fifteen feet or more in height. High above his head he held the spear, as though in the act to strike; one bony hand rested on the stone table before him, in the position a man assumes on rising from his seat, whilst his frame was bent forward so that the vertebrae of the neck and the grinning, gleaming skull projected towards us, and fixed its hollow eyeplaces upon us, the jaws a little open, as though it were about to speak.

'Great heavens!' said I, faintly, at last, 'what can it be?'

'And what are *those things*?' said Good, pointing to the white company round the table.

'And what on earth is *that thing*?' said Sir Henry, pointing to the brown creature seated on the table.

'Hee! hee! hee!' laughed Gagool. 'To those who enter the Hall of the Dead, evil comes. Hee! hee! hee! ha! ha!'

'Come, Incubu, brave in battle, come and see him thou slewest'; and the old creature caught his coat in her skinny fingers, and led him away towards the table. We followed.

Presently she stopped and pointed at the brown object seated on the table. Sir Henry looked, and started back with an exclamation; and no wonder, for there seated, quite naked, on the table, the head which Sir Henry's battle-axe had shorn from the body resting on its knees, was the gaunt corpse of Twala, last king of the Kukuanas. Yes, there, the head perched upon the knees, it sat in all its ugliness, the vertebrae projecting a full inch above the level of the shrunken flesh of the neck, for all the world like a black double of Hamilton Tighe.[1] Over the whole surface of the corpse there was gathered a thin, glassy film, which made its appearance yet more appalling, and for which we were, at the moment, quite unable to account, till we presently observed that from the roof of the chamber the water fell steadily, *drip! drop! drip!* on to the neck of the corpse, from whence it ran down over the entire surface, and finally escaped into the rock through a tiny hole in the table. Then I guessed what it was – *Twala's body was being transformed into a stalactite.*

A look at the white forms seated on the stone bench that ran around that ghastly board confirmed this view. They were human forms indeed,

[1] 'Now haste ye, my handmaidens, haste and see
How he sits there and glowers with his head on his knee.'

or rather had been human forms; now they were *stalactites*. This was the way in which the Kukuana people had from time immemorial preserved their Royal dead. They petrified them. What the exact system was, if there was any, beyond placing them for a long period of years under the drip, I never discovered, but there they sat, iced over and preserved for ever by the silicious fluid. Anything more awe-inspiring than the spectacle of this long line of departed royalties, wrapped in a shroud of ice-like spar, through which the features could be dimly made out (there were twenty-seven of them, the last being Ignosi's father), and seated round that inhospitable board, with Death himself for a host, it is impossible to imagine. That the practice of thus preserving their kings must have been an ancient one is evident from the number, which, allowing for an average reign of fifteen years, would, supposing that every king who reigned was placed here – an improbable thing, as some are sure to have perished in battle far from home – fix the date of its commencement at four and a quarter centuries back. But the colossal Death, who sits at the head of the board, is far older than that, and unless I am much mistaken, owes his origin to the same artist who designed the three colossi. He was hewn out of a single stalactite, and, looked at as a work of art, was most admirably conceived and executed. Good, who understood anatomy, declared that so far as he could see the anatomical design of the skeleton was perfect down to the smallest bones.

My own idea is, that this terrific object was a freak of fancy on the part of some old-world sculptor, and that its presence had suggested to the Kukuanas the idea of placing their royal dead under its awful presidency. Or perhaps it was placed there to frighten away any marauders who might have designs upon the treasure chamber beyond. I cannot say. All I can do is to describe it as it is, and the reader must form his own conclusion.

Such at any rate was the White Death and such were the White Dead!

17

Solomon's Treasure Chamber

WHILE we had been engaged in getting over our fright, and in examining the grisly wonders of the place, Gagool had been differently occupied. Somehow or other – for she was marvellously active when she chose – she had scrambled on to the great table, and made her way to where our departed friend Twala was placed, under the drip, to see, suggested Good, how he was 'pickling', or for some dark purpose of her own. Then she came hobbling back, stopping now and again to address a remark (the tenor of which I could not catch) to one or other of the shrouded forms, just as you or I might greet an old acquaintance. Having gone through this mysterious and horrible ceremony, she squatted herself down on the table immediately under the White Death, and began, so far as I could make out, to offer up prayers to it. The spectacle of this wicked old creature pouring out supplications (evil ones, no doubt) to the arch enemy of mankind, was so uncanny that it caused us to hasten our inspection.

'Now, Gagool,' said I, in a low voice – somehow one did not dare to speak above a whisper in that place – 'lead us to the chamber.'

The old creature promptly scrambled down off the table.

'My lords are not afraid?' she said, leering up into my face.

'Lead on.'

'Good, my lords,' and she hobbled round to the back of the great Death. 'Here is the chamber; let my lords light the lamp, and enter,' and she placed the gourd full of oil upon the floor, and leaned herself against the side of the cave. I took out a match, of which we still had a few in a box, and lit the rush wick, and then looked for the doorway, but there was nothing before us but the solid rock. Gagool grinned. 'The way is there, my lords.'

'Do not jest with us,' I said, sternly.

'I jest not, my lords. See!' and she pointed at the rock.

As she did so, on holding up the lamp we perceived that a mass of stone was slowly rising from the floor and vanishing into the rock above, where doubtless there was a cavity prepared to receive it. The mass was of the width of a good-sized door, about ten feet high and not less than five feet thick. It must have weighed at least twenty or thirty tons, and was clearly moved upon some simple balance principle, probably the same as that upon which the opening and shutting of an ordinary modern window is arranged. How the principle was set in motion, of course none of us saw; Gagool was careful to avoid that; but I have little doubt that there was some very simple lever, which was moved ever so little by pressure on a secret spot, thereby throwing additional weight on to the hidden counterbalances, and causing the whole huge mass to be lifted from the ground. Very slowly and gently the great stone raised itself, till at last it had vanished altogether, and a dark hole presented itself to us in the place which it had filled.

Our excitement was so intense, as we saw the way to Solomon's treasure chamber at last thrown open, that I for one began to tremble and shake. Would it prove a hoax after all, I wondered, or was old da Silvestra right? and were there vast hoards of wealth stored in that dark place, hoards which would make us the richest men in the whole world? We should know in a minute or two.

'Enter, white men from the stars,' said Gagool, advancing into the doorway; 'but first hear your servant, Gagaoola the old. The bright stones that ye will see were dug out of the pit over which the Silent Ones are set, and stored here, I know not by whom. But once has this place been entered since the time that those who stored the stones departed in haste, leaving them behind. The report of the treasure went down among the people who lived in the country from age to age, but none knew where the chamber was, nor the secret of the door. But it happened that a white man reached this country from over the mountains, perchance he, too, came "from the stars", and was well received of the king of the day. He it is who sits yonder,' and she pointed to the fifth king at the table of the dead. 'And it came to pass that he and a woman of the country who was with him came to this place, and that by chance the woman learnt the secret of the door – a thousand years might ye search, but ye should never find it. Then the white man entered with the woman, and found the stones, and filled with stones the skin of a small goat, which the woman had with her to hold food. And as he was going from the chamber he took up one more stone, a large one, and held it in his hand.' Here she paused.

'Well,' I asked, breathless with interest as we all were, 'what happened to da Silvestra?'

The old hag started at the mention of the name.

'How knowest thou the dead man's name?' she asked, sharply; and then, without waiting for an answer, went on:

'None know what happened; but it came about that the white man was frightened, for he flung down the goat-skin, with the stones, and fled out with only the one stone in his hand, and that the king took, and it is the stone that thou, Macumazahn, didst take from Twala's brows.'

'Have none entered here since?' I asked, peering again down the dark passage.

'None, my lords. Only the secret of the door hath been kept, and every king hath opened it, though he hath not entered. There is a saying, that those who enter there will die within a moon, even as the white man died in the cave upon the mountain, where ye found him, Macumazahn. *Ha! ha!* mine are true words.'

Our eyes met as she said it, and I turned sick and cold. How did the old hag know all these things?

'Enter, my lords. If I speak truth the goat-skin with the stones will lie upon the floor; and if there is truth as to whether it is death to enter here, that will ye learn afterwards. Ha! ha! ha!' And she hobbled through the doorway, bearing the light with her; but I confess that once more I hesitated about following.

'Oh, confound it all!' said Good, 'here goes. I am not going to be frightened by that old devil'; and followed by Foulata, who, however, evidently did not at all like the job, for she was shivering with fear, he plunged into the passage after Gagool – an example which we quickly followed.

A few yards down the passage, in the narrow way hewn out of the living rock, Gagool had paused, and was waiting for us.

'See, my lords,' she said, holding the light before her, 'those who stored the treasure here fled in haste, and bethought them to guard against any who should find the secret of the door, but had not the time,' and she pointed to large square blocks of stone, which had, to the height of two courses (about two feet three), been placed across the passage with a view to walling it up. Along the side of the passage were similar blocks ready for use, and, most curious of all, a heap of mortar and a couple of trowels, which, so far as we had time to examine them, appeared to be of a similar shape and make to those used by workmen to this day.

Here, Foulata, who had throughout been in a state of great fear and agitation, said that she felt faint and could go no farther, but would wait there. Accordingly we set her down on the unfinished wall, placing the basket of provisions by her side, and left her to recover.

Following the passage for about fifteen paces farther, we suddenly came to an elaborately painted wooden door. It was standing wide open. Whoever was last there had either not had the time, or had forgotten, to shut it.

Across the threshold lay a skin bag, formed of a goat-skin, that appeared to be full of pebbles.

'Hee! hee! white men,' sniggered Gagool, as the light from the lamp fell upon it. 'What did I tell ye, that the white man who came here fled in haste, and dropped the woman's bag – behold it!'

Good stooped down and lifted it. It was heavy and jingled.

'By Jove! I believe it's full of diamonds,' he said, in an awed whisper; and, indeed, the idea of a small goat-skin full of diamonds is enough to awe anybody.

'Go on,' said Sir Henry, impatiently. 'Here, old lady, give me the lamp,' and taking it from Gagool's hand, he stepped through the doorway and held it high above his head.

We pressed in after him, forgetful, for the moment, of the bag of diamonds, and found ourselves in Solomon's treasure chamber.

At first, all that the somewhat faint light given by the lamp revealed was a room hewn out of the living rock, and apparently not more than ten feet square. Next there came into sight, stored one on the other as high as the roof, a splendid collection of elephant-tusks. How many of them there were we did not know, for of course we could not see how far they went back, but there could not have been less than the ends of four or five hundred tusks of the first quality visible to our eyes. There, alone, was enough ivory before us to make a man wealthy for life. Perhaps, I thought, it was from this very store that Solomon drew his material for his 'great throne of ivory', of which there was not the like made in any kingdom.

On the opposite side of the chamber were about a score of wooden boxes, something like Martini-Henry ammunition boxes, only rather larger, and painted red.

'There are the diamonds,' cried I; 'bring the light.'

Sir Henry did so, holding it close to the top box, of which the lid, rendered rotten by time even in that dry place, appeared to have been smashed in, probably by da Silvestra himself. Pushing my hand through the hole in the lid I drew it out full, not of diamonds, but of gold pieces, of a shape that none of us had seen before, and with what looked like Hebrew characters stamped upon them.

'Ah!' I said, replacing the coin, 'we shan't go back empty-handed, anyhow. There must be a couple of thousand pieces in each box, and there are eighteen boxes. I suppose it was the money to pay the workmen and merchants.'

'Well,' put in Good, 'I think that is the lot; I don't see any diamonds, unless the old Portuguese put them all into this bag.'

'Let my lords look yonder where it is darkest, if they would find the stones,' said Gagool, interpreting our looks. 'There my lords will find a nook, and three stone chests in the nook, two sealed and one open.'

Before interpreting this to Sir Henry, who had the light, I could not resist asking how she knew these things, if no one had entered the place since the white man, generations ago.

'Ah, Macumazahn, who watchest by night,' was the mocking answer, 'ye who live in the stars, do ye not know that some have eyes that can see through rock?'

'Look in that corner, Curtis,' I said, indicating the spot Gagool had pointed out.

'Hullo, you fellows,' he said, 'here's a recess. Great heavens! look here.'

We hurried up to where he was standing in a nook, something like a small bow window. Against the wall of this recess were placed three stone chests, each about two feet square. Two were fitted with stone lids, the lid of the third rested against the side of the chest, which was open.

'*Look!*' he repeated, hoarsely, holding the lamp over the open chest. We looked, and for a moment could make nothing out, on account of a silvery sheen that dazzled us. When our eyes got used to it, we saw that the chest was three-parts full of uncut diamonds, most of them of considerable size. Stooping, I picked some up. Yes, there was no mistake about it, there was the unmistakable soapy feel about them.

I fairly gasped as I dropped them.

'We are the richest men in the whole world,' I said. 'Monte Cristo is a fool to us.'

'We shall flood the market with diamonds,' said Good.

'Got to get them there first,' suggested Sir Henry.

And we stood with pale faces and stared at each other, with the lantern in the middle, and the glimmering gems below, as though we were conspirators about to commit a crime, instead of being, as we thought, the three most fortunate men on earth.

'Hee! hee! hee!' went old Gagool behind us, as she flitted about like a vampire bat. 'There are the bright stones that ye love, white men, as many as ye will; take them, run them through your fingers, *eat* of them, hee! hee! *drink* of them, ha! ha!'

There was something so ridiculous at that moment to my mind in the idea of eating and drinking diamonds, that I began to laugh outrageously, an example which the others followed, without knowing why. There we stood and shrieked with laughter over the gems which were ours, which had been found for *us* thousands of years ago by the patient delvers in the great hole yonder, and stored for *us* by Solomon's long-dead overseer, whose name, perchance, was written in the characters stamped on the faded wax that yet adhered to the lids of the chest. Solomon never got them, nor David, nor da Silvestra, nor anybody else. *We* had got them; there before us were millions of pounds' worth of diamonds, and thousands of pounds worth of gold and ivory, only waiting to be taken away.

Suddenly the fit passed off, and we stopped laughing.

'Open the other chests, white men,' croaked Gagool, 'there are surely more therein. Take your fill, white lords!'

Thus adjured, we set to work to pull up the stone lids on the other too, first – not without a feeling of sacrilege – breaking the seals that fastened them.

Hoorah! they were full too, full to the brim; at least, the second one was; no wretched da Silvestra had been filling goat-skins out of that. As for the third chest, it was only about a fourth full, but the stones were all picked ones; none less than twenty carats, and some of them as large as pigeon-eggs. Some of these biggest ones, however, we could see by holding them up to the light, were a little yellow, 'off coloured', as they call it at Kimberley.

What we did not *see*, however, was the look of fearful malevolence that old Gagool favoured us with as she crept, crept like a snake, out of the treasure chamber and down the passage towards the massive door of solid rock.

Hark! Cry upon cry comes ringing up the vaulted path. It is Foulata's voice!

'*Oh, Bougwan! help! help! the rock falls!*'

'Leave go, girl! Then –'

'*Help, help! she has stabbed me!*'

By now we are running down the passage, and this is what the light from the lamp falls on. The door of rock is slowly closing down; it is not three feet from the floor. Near it struggle Foulata and Gagool. The red blood of the former runs to her knee, but still the brave girl holds the old witch, who fights like a wild cat. Ah! she is free! Foulata falls, and Gagool throws herself on the ground, to twist herself like a snake through the crack of the closing stone. She is under – ah, God! too late! too late. The stone nips her, and she yells in agony. Down, down it comes, all the thirty tons of it, slowly pressing her old body against the rock below. Shriek upon shriek, such as we never heard, then a long sickening *crunch*, and the door was shut just as we, rushing down the passage, hurled ourselves against it.

It was all done in four seconds.

Then we turned to Foulata. The poor girl was stabbed in the body, and could not, I saw, live long.

'Ah! Bougwan, I die!' gasped the beautiful creature. 'She crept out – Gagool; I did not see her, I was faint – and the door began to fall; then she came back, and was looking up the path – and I saw her come in through the slowly falling door, and caught her and held her, and she stabbed me, and *I die*, Bougwan.'

'Poor girl! poor girl!' Good cried; and then, as he could do nothing else, he fell to kissing her.

'Bougwan,' she said, after a pause, 'is Macumazahn there? it grows so dark, I cannot see.'

'Here I am, Foulata.'

'Macumazahn, be my tongue for a moment, I pray thee, for Bougwan cannot understand me, and before I go into the darkness – I would speak a word.'

'Say on, Foulata, I will render it.'

'Say to my lord, Bougwan, that – I love him, and that I am glad to die because I know that he cannot cumber his life with such as me, for the sun cannot mate with the darkness, nor the white with the black.

'Say that at times I have felt as though there were a bird in my bosom, which would one day fly hence and sing elsewhere. Even now, though I cannot lift my hand, and my brain grows cold, I do not feel as though my heart were dying; it is so full of love that it could live a thousand years, and yet be young. Say that if I live again, mayhap I shall see him in the stars, and that – I will search them all, though perchance I should there still be black and he would – still be white. Say – nay, Macumazahn, say no more, save that I love – Oh, hold me closer, Bougwan, I cannot feel thine arms – *oh*! *oh*!'

'She is dead – she is dead!' said Good, rising in grief, the tears running down his honest face.

'You need not let that trouble you, old fellow,' said Sir Henry.

'Eh!' said Good; 'what do you mean?'

'I mean that you will soon be in a position to join her. *Man, don't you see that we are buried alive*?'

Until Sir Henry uttered these words, I do not think the full horror of what had happened had come home to us, preoccupied as we were with the sight of poor Foulata's end. But now we understood. The ponderous mass of rock had closed, probably for ever, for the only brain which knew its secret was crushed to powder beneath it. This was a door that none could hope to force with anything short of dynamite in large quantities. And we were the wrong side of it!

For a few minutes we stood horrified there over the corpse of Foulata. All the manhood seemed to have gone out of us. The first shock of this idea of the slow and miserable end that awaited us was overpowering. We saw it all now; that fiend Gagool had planned this snare for us from the first. It would have been just the jest that her evil mind would have rejoiced in, the idea of the three white men, whom, for some reason of her own, she had always hated, slowly perishing of thirst and hunger in the company of the treasure they had coveted. I saw the point of that sneer of hers about eating and drinking the diamonds now. Perhaps somebody had tried to serve the poor old Dom in the same way, when he abandoned the skin full of jewels.

'This will never do,' said Sir Henry hoarsely; 'the lamp will soon go out. Let us see if we can't find the spring that works the rock.'

We sprang forward with desperate energy, and standing in a bloody ooze, began to feel up and down the door and the sides of the passage. But no knob or spring could we discover.

'Depend on it,' I said, 'it does not work from the inside; if it did, Gagool would not have risked trying to crawl underneath the stone. It was the knowledge of this that made her try to escape at all hazards, curse her.'

'At all events,' said Sir Henry, with a hard little laugh, 'retribution was swift; hers was almost as awful an end as ours is likely to be. We can do nothing with the door; let us go back to the treasure room.' We turned and went, and as we did so I perceived by the unfinished wall across the passage the basket of food which poor Foulata had carried. I took it up, and brought it with me back to that accursed treasure chamber that was to be our grave. Then we went back and reverently bore in Foulata's corpse, laying it on the floor by the boxes of coin.

Next we seated ourselves, leaning our backs against the three stone chests of priceless treasures.

'Let us divide the food,' said Sir Henry, 'so as to make it last as long as possible.' Accordingly we did so. It would, we reckoned, make four infinitesimally small meals for each of us, enough, say, to support life for a couple of days. Besides the 'biltong', or dried game-flesh, there were two gourds of water each holding about a quart.

'Now,' said Sir Henry, 'let us eat and drink, for tomorrow we die.'

We each ate a small portion of the 'biltong', and drank a sip of water. We had, needless to say, but little appetite, though we were sadly in need of food, and felt better after swallowing it. Then we got up and made a systematic examination of the walls of our prison-house, in the faint hope of finding some means of exit, sounding them and the floor carefully.

There was none. It was not probable that there would be one to a treasure chamber.

The lamp began to burn dim. The fat was nearly exhausted.

'Quatermain,' said Sir Henry, 'what is the time – your watch goes?'

I drew it out, and looked at it. It was six o'clock; we had entered the cave at eleven.

'Infadoos will miss us,' I suggested. 'If we do not return tonight, he will search for us in the morning, Curtis.'

'He may search in vain. He does not know the secret of the door, not even where it is. No living person knew it yesterday except Gagool. Today no one knows it. Even if he found the door he could not break it down. All the Kukuana army could not break through five feet of living rock. My friends, I see nothing for it but to bow ourselves to the will of the Almighty. The search for treasure has brought many to a bad end; we shall go to swell their number.'

The lamp grew dimmer yet.

Presently it flared up and showed the whole scene in strong relief, the great mass of white tusks, the boxes full of gold, the corpse of poor Foulata stretched before them, the goat-skin full of treasure, the dim glimmer of the diamonds, and the wild, wan faces of us three white men seated there awaiting death by starvation.

Suddenly it sank, and expired.

18

We Abandon Hope

I CAN give no adequate description of the horrors of the night which followed. Mercifully they were to some extent mitigated by sleep, for even in such a position as ours, wearied nature will sometimes assert itself. But I, at any rate, found it impossible to sleep much. Putting aside the terrifying thought of our impending doom – for the bravest man on earth might well quail from such a fate as awaited us, and I never had any great pretensions to be brave – the *silence* itself was too great to allow of it. Reader, you may have lain awake at night and thought the silence oppressive, but I say with confidence that you can have no idea what a vivid tangible thing perfect silence really is. On the surface of the earth there is always some sound or motion, and though it may in itself be imperceptible, yet does it deaden the sharp edge of absolute silence. But here there was none. We were buried in the bowels of a huge snow-clad peak. Thousands of feet above us the fresh air rushed over the white snow, but no sound of it reached us. We were separated by a long tunnel and five feet of rock even from the awful chamber of the dead; and the dead make no noise. The crashing of all the artillery of earth and heaven could not have come to our ears in our living tomb. We were cut off from all echoes of the world – we were as already dead.

And then the irony of the situation forced itself upon me. There around us lay treasures enough to pay off a moderate national debt, or to build a fleet of ironclads, and yet we would gladly have bartered them all for the faintest chance of escape. Soon, doubtless, we should be glad to exchange them for a bit of food or a cup of water, and, after that, even for the privilege of a speedy close to our sufferings. Truly wealth, which men spend all their lives in acquiring, is a valueless thing at the last.

And so the night wore on.

'Good,' said Sir Henry's voice at last, and it sounded awfull in the intense stillness, 'how many matches have you in the box?'

'Eight, Curtis.'

'Strike one, and let us see the time.'

He did so, and in contrast to the dense darkness the flame nearly blinded us. It was five o'clock by my watch. The beautiful dawn was now blushing on the snow-wreaths far over our heads, and the breeze would be stirring the night mists in the hollows.

'We had better eat something and keep up our strength,' said I.

'What is the good of eating?' answered Good; 'the sooner we die and get it over the better.'

'While there is life there is hope,' said Sir Henry.

Accordingly we ate and sipped some water, and another period of time passed, when somebody suggested that it might be as well to get as near to the door as possible, and halloa, on the faint chance of somebody catching a sound outside. Accordingly Good, who, from long practice at sea, has a fine piercing note, groped his way down the passage and began, and I must say he made a most diabolical noise. I never heard such yells; but it might have been a mosquito buzzing for all the effect it produced.

After a while he gave it up, and came back very thirsty, and had to have some water. After that we gave up yelling, as it encroached on the supply of water.

So we all sat down once more against our chests of useless diamonds in that dreadful inaction, which was one of the hardest circumstances of our fate; and I am bound to say that, for my part, I gave way in despair. Laying my head against Sir Henry's broad shoulder I burst into tears; and I think I heard Good gulping away on the other side, and swearing hoarsely at himself for doing so.

Ah, how good and brave that great man was! Had we been two frightened children, and he our nurse, he could not have treated us more tenderly. Forgetting his own share of miseries, he did all he could to soothe our broken nerves, telling stories of men who had been in somewhat similar circumstances, and miraculously escaped; and when these failed to cheer us, pointing out how, after all, it was only anticipating an end that must come to us all, that it would soon be over, and that death from exhaustion was a merciful one (which is not true). Then, in a diffident sort of a way, as I had once before heard him do, he suggested that we should throw ourselves on the mercy of a higher Power, which for my part I did with great vigour.

His is a beautiful character, very quiet, but very strong.

And so somehow the day went as the night had gone (if, indeed, one can use the terms where all was densest night), and when I lit a match to see the time it was seven o'clock.

Once more we ate and drank, and as we did so an idea occurred to me.

'How is it,' said I, 'that the air in this place keeps fresh? It is thick and heavy, but it is perfectly fresh.'

'Great heavens!' said Good, starting up, 'I never thought of that. It can't come through the stone door, for it is air-tight, if ever a door was. It must come from somewhere. If there were no current of air in the place we should have been stifled when we first came in. Let us have a look.'

It was wonderful what a change this mere spark of hope wrought in us. In a moment we were all three groping about the place on our hands and knees, feeling for the slightest indication of a draught. Presently my ardour received a check. I put my hand on something cold. It was poor Foulata's dead face.

For an hour or more we went on feeling about, till at last Sir Henry and I gave it up in despair, having got considerably hurt by constantly knocking our heads against tusks, chests, and the sides of the chamber. But Good still persevered, saying, with an approach to cheerfulness, that it was better than doing nothing.

'I say, you fellows,' he said, presently, in a constrained sort of voice, 'come here.'

Needless to say we scrambled over towards him quick enough.

'Quatermain, put your hand here where mine is. Now, do you feel anything?'

'I *think* I feel air coming up.'

'Now, listen.' He rose and stamped upon the place, and a flame of hope shot up in our hearts. *It rang hollow.*

With trembling hands I lit a match. I had only three left, and we saw that we were in the angle of the far corner of the chamber, a fact that accounted for our not having noticed the hollow ring of the place during our former exhaustive examination. As the match burnt we scrutinized the spot. There was a join in the solid rock floor, and, great heavens! there, let in level with the rock, was a stone ring. We said no word, we were too excited, and our hearts beat too wildly with hope to allow us to speak. Good had a knife, at the back of which was one of those hooks that are made to extract stones from horses' hoofs. He opened it, and scratched away at the ring with it. Finally he got it under, and levered away gently for fear of breaking the hook. The ring began to move. Being of stone, it had not got set fast in all the centuries it had lain there, as would have been the case had it been of iron. Presently it was upright. Then he got his hands into it and tugged with all his force, but nothing budged.

'Let me try,' I said, impatiently, for the situation of the stone, right in the angle of the corner, was such that it was impossible for two to pull at once. I got hold and strained away, but with no results.

Then Sir Henry tried and failed.

Taking the hook again, Good scratched all round the crack where we felt the air coming up.

'Now, Curtis,' he said, 'tackle on, and put your back into it; you are as strong as two. Stop,' and he took off a stout black silk handkerchief, which, true to his habits of neatness, he still wore, and ran it through the ring. 'Quatermain, get Curtis round the middle and pull for dear life when I give the word. *Now*.'

Sir Henry put out all his enormous strength, and Good and I did the same, with such power as nature had given us.

'Heave! heave! it's giving,' gasped Sir Henry; and I heard the muscles of his great back cracking. Suddenly there came a parting sound, then a rush of air, and we were all on our backs on the floor with a great flag-stone on the top of us. Sir Henry's strength had done it, and never did muscular power stand a man in better stead.

'Light a match, Quatermain,' he said, as soon as we had picked ourselves up and got our breath; 'carefully, now.'

I did so, and there before us was, God be praised! the *first step of a stone stair*.

'Now what is to be done?' asked Good.

'Follow the stair, of course, and trust to Providence.'

'Stop!' said Sir Henry. 'Quatermain, get the bit of biltong and the water that is left; we may want them.'

I went creeping back to our place by the chests for that purpose, and as I was coming away an idea struck me. We had not thought much of the diamonds for the last twenty-four hours or so; indeed, the idea of diamonds was nauseous, seeing what they had entailed upon us; but, thought I, I may as well pocket a few in case we ever should get out of this ghastly hole. So I just stuck my fist into the first chest and filled all the available pockets of my old shooting coat, topping up – this was a happy thought – with a couple of handfuls of big ones out of the third chest.

'I say, you fellows,' I sang out, 'won't you take some diamonds with you? I've filled my pockets.'

'Oh! hang the diamonds!' said Sir Henry. 'I hope that I may never see another.'

As for Good, he made no answer. He was, I think, taking a last farewell of all that was left of the poor girl who loved him so well. And, curious as it may seem to you, my reader, sitting at home at ease and reflecting on the vast, indeed the immeasurable, wealth which we were thus abandoning, I can assure you that if you had passed some twenty-eight hours with next to nothing to eat and drink in that place, you would not have cared to cumber yourself with diamonds whilst plunging down into the unknown bowels of the earth, in the wild hope of escape from an agonizing death. If it had not, from the habits of a lifetime, become a sort of second nature with me never to leave anything worth having behind, if there was the slightest chance of my being able to carry it away, I am sure I should not have bothered to fill my pockets.

'Come on, Quatermain,' said Sir Henry, who was already standing on the first step of the stone stair. 'Steady, I will go first.'

'Mind where you put your feet; there may be some awful hole underneath,' said I.

'Much more likely to be another room,' said Sir Henry, as he slowly descended, counting the steps as he went.

When he got to 'fifteen' he stopped. 'Here's the bottom,' he stopped. 'Here's the bottom,' he said. 'Thank goodness! I think it's a passage. Come on down.'

Good descended next, and I followed last, and on reaching the bottom lit one of the two remaining matches. By its light we could just see that we were standing in a narrow tunnel, which ran right and left at right angles to the staircase we had descended. Before we could make out any more, the match burnt my fingers and went out. Then arose the delicate question of which way to turn. Of course, it was impossible to know what the tunnel was or where it ran to, and yet to turn one way might lead us to safety, and the other to destruction. We were utterly perplexed, till suddenly it struck Good that when I had lit the match the draught of the passage blew the flame to the left.

'Let us go against the draught,' he said; 'air draws inwards, not outwards.'

We took this suggestion, and feeling along the wall with the hand, whilst trying the ground before us at every step, we departed from that accursed treasure chamber on our terrible quest. If ever it should be entered again by living man, which I do not think it will be, he will find a token of our presence in the open chests of jewels, the empty lamp, and the white bones of poor Foulata.

When we had groped our way for about a quarter of an hour along the passage, it suddenly took a sharp turn, or else was bisected by another, which we followed, only in course of time to be led into a third. And so it went on for some hours. We seemed to be in a stone labyrinth which led nowhere. What all these passages are, of course I cannot say, but we thought that they must be the ancient workings of a mine, of which the various shafts travelled hither and thither as the ore led them. This is the only way in which we could account for such a multitude of passages.

At length we halted, thoroughly worn out with fatigue, and with that hope deferred which maketh the heart sick, and ate up our poor remaining piece of biltong, and drank our last sup of water, for our throats were like lime-kilns. It seemed to us that we had escaped Death in the darkness of the chamber only to meet him in the darkness of the tunnels.

As we stood, once more utterly depressed, I thought I caught a sound, to which I called the attention of the others. It was very faint and very far off, but it *was* a sound, a faint, murmuring sound, for the others heard it too, and no words can describe the blessedness of it after all those hours of utter, awful stillness.

'By heaven! it's running water,' said Good. 'Come on.'

Off we started again in the direction from which the faint murmur seemed to come, groping our way as before along the rocky walls. As we went it got more and more audible, till at last it seemed quite loud in the quiet. On, yet on; now we could distinctly make out the unmistakable swirl of rushing water. And yet how could there be running water in the bowels of the earth? Now we were quite near to it, and Good, who was leading, swore that he could smell it.

'Go gently, Good,' said Sir Henry, 'we must be close.' *Splash*! and a cry from Good.

He had fallen in.

'Good! Good! where are you?' we shouted, in terrified distress. To our intense relief, an answer came back in a choky voice.

'All right; I've got hold of a rock. Strike a light to show me where you are.'

Hastily I lit the last remaining match. Its faint gleam discovered to us a dark mass of water running at our feet. How wide it was we could not see, but there, some way out, was the dark form of our companion hanging on to a projecting rock.

'Stand clear to catch me,' sung out Good. 'I must swim for it.'

Then we heard a splash, and a great struggle. Another minute and he had grabbed at and caught Sir Henry's outstretched hand, and we had pulled him up high and dry into the tunnel.

'My word!' he said, between his gasps, 'that was touch and go. If I hadn't caught that rock, and known how to swim, I should have been done. It runs like a mill-race, and I could feel no bottom.'

It was clear that this would not do; so after Good had rested a little, and we had drunk our fill from the water of the subterranean river, which was sweet and fresh, and washed our faces, which sadly needed it, as well as we could, we started from the banks of this African Styx, and began to retrace our steps along the tunnel, Good dripping unpleasantly in front of us. At length we came to another tunnel leading to our right.

'We may as well take it,' said Sir Henry, wearily; 'all roads are alike here; we can only go on till we drop.'

Slowly, for a long, long while, we stumbled, utterly weary, along this new tunnel, Sir Henry leading now.

Suddenly he stopped, and we bumped up against him.

'Look!' he whispered, 'is my brain going, or is that light?'

We stared with all our eyes, and there, yes, there, far ahead of us, was a faint, glimmering spot, no larger than a cottage window pane. It was so faint that I doubt if any eyes, except those which, like ours, had for days seen nothing but blackness, could have perceived it at all.

With a sort of gasp of hope we pushed on. In five minutes there was no longer any doubt: it *was* a patch of faint light. A minute more and a breath of real live air was fanning us. On we struggled. All at once the tunnel narrowed. Sir Henry went on his knees. Smaller yet it grew, till it was only the size of a large fox's earth – it was *earth* now, mind you; the rock had ceased.

A squeeze, a struggle, and Sir Henry was out, and so was Good, and so was I, and there above us were the blessed stars, and in our nostrils was the sweet air; then suddenly something gave, and we were all rolling over and over and over through grass and bushes, and soft, wet soil.

I caught at something and stopped. Sitting up I halloed lustily. An answering shout came from just below, where Sir Henry's wild career had been stopped by some level ground. I scrambled to him, and found him unhurt, though breathless. Then we looked for Good. A little way off we found him too, jammed in a forked root. He was a good deal knocked about, but soon came to.

We sat down together there on the grass, and the revulsion of feeling was so great, that I really think we cried for joy. We had escaped from that awful dungeon, that was so near to becoming our grave. Surely some merciful Power must have guided our footsteps to the jackal hole at the termination of the tunnel (for that is what it must have been). And see, there on the mountains, the dawn we had never thought to look upon again was blushing rosy red.

Presently the grey light stole down the slopes, and we saw that we were at the bottom, or rather, nearly at the bottom, of the vast pit in front of the entrance to the cave. Now we could make out the dim forms of the three colossi who sat upon its verge. Doubtless those awful passages, along which we had wandered the livelong night, had originally been, in some way, connected with the great diamond mine. As for the subterranean river in the bowels of the mountain, Heaven only knows what it was, or whence it flows, or whither it goes. I for one have no anxiety to trace its course.

Lighter it grew, and lighter yet. We could see each other now, and such a spectacle as we presented I have never set eyes on before or since. Gaunt-cheeked, hollow-eyed wretches, smeared all over with dust and mud, bruised, bleeding, the long fear of imminent death yet written on our countenances, we were, indeed, a sight to frighten the daylight. And yet it is a solemn fact that Good's eye-glass was still fixed in Good's eye. I doubt whether he had ever taken it out at all. Neither the darkness, nor the plunge in the subterranean river, nor the roll down the slope, had been able to separate Good and his eye-glass.

Presently we rose, fearing that our limbs would stiffen if we stopped there longer, and commenced with slow and painful steps to struggle up the sloping sides of the great pit. For an hour or more we toiled steadfastly up the blue clay, dragging ourselves on by the help of the roots and grasses with which it was clothed.

At last it was done, and we stood on the great road, on the side of the pit opposite to the colossi.

By the side of the road, a hundred yards off, a fire was burning in front of some huts, and round the fire were figures. We made towards them, supporting one another, and halting every few paces. Presently, one of the figures rose, saw us, and fell on to the ground, crying out for fear.

'Infadoos, Infadoos! it is us, thy friends.'

He rose; he ran to us, staring wildly, and still shaking with fear.

'Oh, my lords, my lords, it is indeed you come back from the dead! – come back from the dead!'

And the old warrior flung himself down before us, and clasped Sir Henry's knees, and wept aloud for joy.

19

Ignosi's Farewell

TEN days from that eventful morning found us once more in our old quarters at Loo; and, strange to say, but little the worse for our terrible experience, except that my stubbly hair came out of that cave about three shades greyer than it went in, and that Good never was quite the same after Foulata's death, which seemed to move him very greatly. I am bound to say that, looking at the thing from the point of view of an oldish man of the world, I consider her removal was a fortunate occurrence, since, otherwise, complications would have been sure to ensue. The poor creature was no ordinary native girl, but a person of great, I had almost said stately, beauty, and of considerable refinement of mind. But no amount of beauty or refinement could have made an entanglement between Good and herself a desirable occurrence; for, as she herself put it, 'Can the sun mate with the darkness, or the white with the black?'

I need hardly state that we never again penetrated into Solomon's treasure chamber. After we had recovered from our fatigues, a process which took us forty-eight hours, we descended into the great pit in the hope of finding the hole by which we had crept out of the mountain, but with no success. To begin with, rain had fallen, and obliterated our spoor; and what is more, the sides of the vast pit were full of ant-bear and other holes. It was impossible to say to which of these we owed our salvation. We also, on the day before we started back to Loo, made a further examination of the wonders of the stalactite cave, and, drawn by a kind of restless feeling, even penetrated once more into the Chamber of the Dead; and, passing beneath the spear of the white Death, gazed with sensations which it would be quite impossible for me to describe, at the mass of rock which had shut us off from escape, thinking, the while, of the priceless treasures beyond, of the mysterious old hag whose flattened fragments lay crushed beneath it, and of the fair girl of whose tomb it was the portal. I say gazed at the 'rock', for examine as we would, we could find no traces of the join of the sliding door; nor, indeed, could we hit upon the secret, now utterly lost, that worked it, though we tried for an hour or more. It was certainly a marvellous bit of mechanism, characteristic, in its massive and yet inscrutable simplicity, of the age which produced it; and I doubt if the world has such another to show.

At last we gave it up in disgust; though, if the mass had suddenly risen before our eyes, I doubt if we should have screwed up courage to step over Gagool's mangled remains, and once more enter the treasure chamber, even in the sure and certain hope of unlimited diamonds. And yet I could have cried at the idea of leaving all that treasure, the biggest treasure probably that has ever in the world's history been accumulated in one spot. But there was no help for it. Only dynamite could force its way through five feet of solid rock. And so we left it. Perhaps, in some remote, unborn century, a more fortunate explorer may hit upon the 'Open Sesame', and flood the world with gems. But, myself, I doubt it. Somehow, I seem to feel that the millions of pounds' worth of gems that lie in the three stone coffers will never shine round the neck of an earthly beauty. They and Foulata's bones will keep cold company till the end of all things.

With a sigh of disappointment we made our way back, and next day started for Loo. And yet it was really very ungrateful of us to be disappointed; for, as the reader will remember, I had, by a lucky thought, taken the precaution to fill the pockets of my old shooting coat with gems before we left our prison-house. A good many of these fell out in the course of our roll down the side of the pit, including most of the big ones, which I had crammed in on the top. But, comparatively speaking, an enormous quantity still remained, including eighteen large stones ranging from about one hundred to thirty carats in weight. My old shooting coat still held enough treasure to make us all, if not millionaires, at least exceedingly wealthy men, and yet to keep enough stones each to make the three finest sets of gems in Europe. So we had not done so badly.

On arriving at Loo, we were most cordially received by Ignosi, whom we found well, and busily engaged in consolidating his power, and reorganizing the regiments which had suffered most in the great struggle with Twala.

He listened with breathless interest to our wonderful story; but when we told him of old Gagool's frightful end, he grew thoughtful.

'Come hither,' he called, to a very old Induna (councillor), who was sitting with others in a circle round the king, but out of ear-shot. The old man rose, approached, saluted, and seated himself.

'Thou art old,' said Ignosi.

'Ay, my lord the king!'

'Tell me, when thou wast little, didst thou know Gagoola the witch doctress?'

'Ay, my lord, the king!'

'How was she then – young, like thee?'

'Not so, my lord the king! She was even as now; old and dried, very ugly, and full of wickedness.'

'She is no more; she is dead.'

'So, O king! then is a curse taken from the land.'

'Go!'

'*Koom*! I go, black puppy, who tore out the old dog's throat. *Koom*!'

'Ye see, my brothers,' said Ignosi, 'this was a strange woman, and I rejoice that she is dead. She would have let ye die in the dark place, and mayhap afterwards she had found a way to slay me as she found a way to slay my father, and set up Twala, whom her heart loved, in his place. Now go on with the tale; surely there never was the like!'

After I had narrated all the story of our escape, I, as we had agreed between ourselves that I should, took the opportunity to address Ignosi as to our departure from Kukuanaland.

'And now, Ignosi, the time has come for us to bid thee farewell, and start to seek once more our own land. Behold, Ignosi, with us thou camest a servant, and now we leave thee a mighty king. If thou art grateful to us, remember to do even as thou didst promise: to rule justly, to respect the law, and to put none to death without a cause. So shalt thou prosper. Tomorrow, at break of day, Ignosi, wilt thou give us an escort who shall lead us across the mountains: Is it not so, O king?'

Ignosi covered his face with his hands for a while before answering.

'My heart is sore,' he said at last; 'your words split my heart in twain. What have I done to ye, Incubu, Macumazahn, and Bougwan, that ye should leave me desolate? Ye who stood by me in rebellion and in battle, will ye leave me in the day of peace and victory? What will ye – wives? Choose from out the land! A place to live in? Behold, the land is yours as far as ye can see. The white man's houses? Ye shall teach my people how to build them. Cattle for beef and milk? Every married man shall bring ye an ox or a cow. Wild game to hunt? Does not the elephant walk through my forests, and the river-horse sleep in the reeds? Would ye make war? My Impis (regiments) wait your word. If there is anything more that I can give, that will I give ye.'

'Nay, Ignosi, we want not these things,' I answered; 'we would seek our own place.'

'Now do I perceive,' said Ignosi, bitterly, and with flashing eyes, 'that it is the bright stones that ye love more than me, your friend. Ye have the stones; now would ye go to Natal and across the moving black water and sell them, and be rich, as it is the desire of a white man's heart to be. Cursed for your sake be the stones, and cursed he who seeks them. Death shall it be to him who sets foot in the place of Death to seek them. I have spoken, white men; ye can go.'

I laid my hand upon his arm. 'Ignosi,' I said, 'tell us, when thou didst wander in Zululand, and among the white men in Natal, did not thine heart turn to the land thy mother told thee of, thy native land, where thou didst see the light, and play when thou wast little, the land where thy place was?'

'It was even so, Macumazahn.'

'Then thus does our heart turn to our land and to our own place.'

Then came a pause. When Ignosi broke it, it was in a different voice.

'I do perceive that thy words are, now as ever, wise and full of reason, Macumazahn; that which flies in the air loves not to run along the ground; the white man loves not to live on the level of the black. Well, ye must go, and leave my heart sore, because ye will be as dead to me, since from where ye will be no tidings can come to me.

'But listen, and let all the white men know my words. No other white man shall cross the mountains, even if any may live to come so far. I will see no traders with their guns and rum. My people shall fight with the spear, and drink water, like their forefathers before them. I will have no praying-men to put fear of death into men's hearts, to stir them up against the king, and make a path for the white men who follow to run on. If a white man comes to my gates I will send him back; if a hundred come, I will push them back; if an army comes, I will make war on them with all my strength, and they shall not prevail against me. None shall ever come for the shining stones; no, not an army, for if they come I will send a regiment and fill up the pit and break down the white columns in the caves and fill them with rocks, so that none can come even to that door of which ye speak, and whereof the way to move it is lost. But for ye three, Incubu, Macumazahn, and Bougwan, the path is always open; for behold, ye are dearer to me than aught that breathes.

'And ye would go. Infadoos, my uncle, and my Induna, shall take thee by the hand and guide thee, with a regiment. There is, as I have learnt, another way across the mountains that he shall show ye. Farewell, my brothers, brave white men. See me no more, for I have no heart to bear it. Behold, I make a decree, and it shall be published from the mountains to the mountains, your names, Incubu, Macumazahn, and Bougwan, shall be as the names of dead kings, and he who speaks them shall die.[1] So shall your memory be preserved in the land for ever.

---

[1] This extraordinary and negative way of showing intense respect is by no means unknown among African people, and the result is that if, as is usual, the name in question has a significance, the meaning has to be expressed by an idiom or another word. In this way a memory is preserved for generations, or until the new word supplants the old one.

'Go now, ere my eyes rain tears like a woman's. At times when ye look back down the path of life, or when ye are old and gather yourselves together to crouch before the fire, because the sun has no more heat, ye will think of how we stood shoulder to shoulder in that great battle that thy wise words planned, Macumazahn, of how thou wast the point of that horn that galled Twala's flank, Bougwan; whilst thou stoodst in the ring of the Greys, Incubu, and men went down before thine axe like corn before a sickle; ay, and of how thou didst break the wild bull's (Twala's) strength, and bring his pride to dust. Fare ye well for ever, Incubu, Macumazahn, and Bougwan, my lords and my friends.'

He rose, looked earnestly at us for a few seconds, and then threw the corner of his kaross over his head, so as to cover his face from us.

We went in silence.

Next day at dawn we left Loo, escorted by our old friend Infadoos, who was heart-broken at our departure, and the regiment of Buffaloes. Early as the hour was, all the main street of the town was lined with multitudes of people, who gave us the royal salute as we passed at the head of the regiment, while the women blessed us as having rid the land of Twala, throwing flowers before us as we went. It really was very affecting, and not the sort of thing one is accustomed to meet with from natives.

One very ludicrous incident occurred, however, which I rather welcomed, as it gave us something to laugh at.

Just before we got to the confines of the town, a pretty young girl, with some beautiful lilies in her hand, came running forward and presented them to Good (somehow they all seemed to like Good; I think his eyeglass and solitary whisker gave him a fictitious value), and then said she had a boon to ask.

'Speak on.'

'Let my lord show his servant his beautiful white legs, that his servant may look on them, and remember them all her days, and tell of them to her children; his servant has travelled four days' journey to see them, for the fame of them has gone throughout the land.'

'I'll be hanged if I do!' said Good, excitedly.

'Come, come, my dear fellow,' said Sir Henry, 'you can't refuse to oblige a lady.'

'I won't,' said Good, obstinately; 'it is positively indecent.'

However, in the end he consented to draw up his trousers to the knee, amidst notes of rapturous admiration from all the women present, especially the gratified young lady, and in this guise he had to walk till we got clear of the town.

Good's legs will, I fear, never be so greatly admired again. Of his melting teeth, and even of his 'transparent eye', they wearied more or less, but of his legs, never.

As we travelled, Infadoos told us that there was another pass over the mountains to the north of the one followed by Solomon's great road, or rather that there was a place where it was possible to climb down the wall of cliff that separated Kukuanaland from the desert, and was broken by the towering shapes of Sheba's Breasts. It appeared, too, that rather more than two years previously a party of Kukuana hunters had descended this path into the desert in search of ostriches, whose plumes were much prized among them for war head-dresses, and that in the course of their hunt they had been led far from the mountains, and were much troubled by thirst. Seeing, however, trees on the horizon, they made towards them, and discovered a large and fertile oasis of some miles in extent, and plentifully watered. It was by way of this oasis that he suggested that we should return, and the idea seemed to us a good one, as it appeared that we should escape the rigours of the mountain pass, and as some of the hunters were in attendance to guide us to the oasis, from which, they stated, they could perceive more fertile spots far away in the desert.[1]

Travelling easily, on the night of the fourth day's journey we found ourselves once more on the crest of the mountains that separate Kukuanaland from the desert, which rolled away in sandy billows at our feet, and about twenty-five miles to the north of Sheba's Breasts.

At dawn on the following day, we were led to the commencement of a precipitous descent, by which we were to descend the precipice and gain the desert two thousand and more feet below.

Here we bade farewell to that true friend and sturdy old warrior, Infadoos, who solemnly wished all good upon us, and neatly wept with grief. 'Never, my lords,' he said, 'shall mine old eyes see the like of ye again. Ah! the way that Incubu cut his men down in the battle! Ah! for the sight of that stroke with which he swept off my brother Twala's head! It was beautiful – beautiful! I may never hope to see such another, except perchance in happy dreams.'

We were very sorry to part from him; indeed, Good was so moved that he gave him as a souvenir – what do you think? – an *eye-glass*. (Afterwards we discovered that it was a spare one.) Infadoos was delighted, foreseeing that the possession of such an article would enormously increase his prestige, and after several vain attempts actually succeeded in screwing it into his own eye. Anything more incongruous than the old warrior looked with an eye-glass I never saw. Eye-glasses don't go well with leopard-skin cloaks and black ostrich plumes.

[1] It often puzzled all of us to understand how it was possible that Ignosi's mother, bearing the child with her, should have survived the dangers of the journey across the mountains and the desert, dangers which so nearly proved fatal to ourselves. It has since occurred to me, and I give the idea to the reader for what it is worth, that she must have taken this second route, and wandered out like Hagar into the desert. If she did so, there is no longer anything inexplicable about the story, since she may well, as Ignosi himself related, have been picked up by some ostrich hunters before she or the child were exhausted, and led by them to the oasis, and thence by stages to the fertile country, and so on by slow degrees southwards to Zululand. – A. Q.

Then, having seen that our guides were well laden with water and provisions, and having received a thundering farewell salute from the Buffaloes, we wrung the old warrior's hand, and began our downward climb. A very arduous business it proved to be, but somehow that evening we found ourselves at the bottom without accident.

'Do you know,' said Sir Henry that night, as we sat by our fire and gazed up at the beetling cliffs above us, 'I think that there are worse places than Kukuanaland in the world, and that I have spent unhappier times than the last month or two, though I have never spent such queer ones. Eh! you fellows?'

'I almost wish I were back,' said Good, with a sigh.

As for myself, I reflected that all's well that ends well; but in the course of a long life of shaves, I never had such shaves as those I had recently experienced. The thought of that battle still makes me feel cold all over, and as for our experience in the treasure chamber . . . !

Next morning we started on a toilsome march across the desert, having with us a good supply of water carried by our five guides, and camped that night in the open, starting again at dawn on the morrow.

By midday of the third day's journey we could see the trees of the oasis of which the guides spoke, and by an hour before sundown we were once more walking upon grass and listening to the sound of running water.

20

Found

AND now I come to perhaps the strangest thing that happened to us in all that strange business, and one which shows how wonderfully things are brought about.

I was walking quietly along, some way in front of the other two, down the banks of the stream, which ran from the oasis till it was swallowed up in the hungry desert sands, when suddenly I stopped and rubbed my eyes, as well I might. There, not twenty yards in front, placed in a charming situation, under the shade of a species of fig tree, and facing to the stream, was a cosy hut, built more or less on the Kafir principle of grass and withes, only with a full-length door instead of a bee-hole.

'What the dickens,' said I to myself, 'can a hut be doing here!' Even as I said it, the door of the hut opened, and there limped out of it *a white man* clothed in skins, and with an enormous black beard. I thought that I must have got a touch of the sun. It was impossible. No hunter ever came to such a place as this. Certainly no hunter would ever settle in it. I stared and stared, and so did the other man, and just at that juncture Sir Henry and Good came up.

'Look here, you fellows,' I said, 'is that a white man, or am I mad?'

Sir Henry looked, and Good looked, and then all of a sudden the lame white man with the black beard gave a great cry, and came hobbling towards us. When he got close, he fell down in a sort of faint.

With a spring Sir Henry was by his side.

'Great Powers!' he cried, *'it is my brother George!'*

At the sound of the disturbance, another figure, also clad in skins, emerged from the hut, with a gun in his hand, and came running towards us. On seeing me he, too, gave a cry.

'Macumazahn,' he halloed, 'don't you know me. Baas? I'm Jim the hunter. I lost the note you gave me to give to the Baas, and we have been here nearly two years.' And the fellow fell at my feet, and rolled over and over, weeping for joy.

'You careless scoundrel!' I said; 'you ought to be well hided.'

Meanwhile the man with the black beard had recovered and got up, and he and Sir Henry were pump-handling away at each other, apparently without a word to say. But whatever they had quarrelled about in the past (I suspect it was a lady, though I never asked), it was evidently forgotten now.

'My dear old fellow,' burst out Sir Henry at last, 'I thought that you were dead. I have been over Solomon's Mountains to find you, and now I come across you perched in the desert, like an old Aasvögel (vulture).'

'I tried to go over Solomon's Mountains nearly two years ago,' was the answer, spoken in the hesitating voice of a man who has had little recent opportunity of using his tongue, 'but when I got here, a boulder fell on my leg and crushed it, and I have been able to go neither forward nor back.'

Then I came up. 'How do you do, Mr. Neville?' I said, 'do you remember me?'

'Why,' he said, 'isn't it Quatermain, eh, and Good too? Hold on a minute, you fellows, I am getting dizzy again. It is all so very strange, and, when a man has ceased to hope, so very happy.'

That evening, over the camp fire, George Curtis told us his story, which, in its way, was almost as eventful as our own, and amounted shortly to this. A little short of two years before, he had started from Sitanda's Kraal, to try and reach the mountains. As for the note I had sent him by Jim, that worthy had lost it, and he had never heard of it till today. But, acting upon information he had received from the natives, he made, not for Sheba's Breasts, but for the ladder-like descent of the mountains down which we had just come, which was clearly a better route than that marked out in old Dom Silvestra's plan. In the desert he and Jim suffered great hardships, but finally they reached this oasis, where a terrible accident befell George Curtis. On the day of their arrival, he was sitting by the stream, and Jim was extracting the honey from the nest of a stingless bee, which is to be found in the desert, on the top of the bank immediately above him. In so doing he loosed a great boulder of rock, which fell upon

George Curtis' right leg, crushing it frightfully. From that day he had been so dreadfully lame, that he had found it impossible to go either forward or back, and had preferred to take the chances of dying in the oasis to the certainty of perishing in the desert.

As for food, however, they had got on pretty well, for they had a good supply of ammunition, and the oasis was frequented, especially at night, by large quantities of game, which came thither for water. These they shot, or trapped in pitfalls, using their flesh for food, and, after their clothes wore out, their hides for covering.

'And so,' he ended, 'we have lived for nearly two years, like a second Robinson Crusoe and his man Friday, hoping against hope that some natives might come here and help us away, but none have come. Only last night we settled that Jim should leave me, and try to reach Sitanda's Kraal and get assistance. He was to go tomorrow, but I had little hope of ever seeing him back again. And now *you*, of all people in the world, *you*, who I fancied had long ago forgotten all about me, and were living comfortably in old England, turn up in a promiscuous way and find me where you least expected. It is the most wonderful thing I ever heard of, and the most merciful, too.'

Then Sir Henry set to work and told him the main facts of our adventures, sitting till late into the night to do it.

'By Jove!' he said, when I showed him some of the diamonds; 'well, at least you have got something for your pains, besides my worthless self'

Sir Henry laughed. 'They belong to Quatermain and Good. It was part of the bargain that they should share any spoils there might be.'

This remark set me thinking, and having spoken to Good, I told Sir Henry that it was our unanimous wish that he should take a third share of the diamonds, or if he would not, that his share should be handed to his brother, who had suffered even more than ourselves on the chance of getting them. Finally, we prevailed upon him to consent to this arrangement, but George Curtis did not know of it till some time afterwards.

And here, at this point, I think I shall end this history. Our journey across the desert back to Sitanda's Kraal was most arduous, especially as we had to support George Curtis; whose right leg was very weak indeed, and continually threw out splinters of bone; but we did accomplish it somehow, and to give its details would only be to reproduce much of what happened to us on the former occasion.

Six months from the date of our re-arrival at Sitanda's, where we found our guns and other goods quite safe, though the old scoundrel in charge was much disgusted at our surviving to claim them, saw us all once more safe and sound at my little place on the Berea, near Durban, where I am now writing, and whence I bid farewell to all who have accompanied me throughout the strangest trip I ever made in the course of a long and varied experience.

Just as I had written the last word, a Kafir came up my avenue of orange trees, with a letter in a cleft stick, which he had brought from the post. It turned out to be from Sir Henry, and as it speaks for itself I give it in full.

Brayley Hall, Yorkshire

My dear Quatermain,

I sent you a line a few mails back to say that the three of us, George, Good, and myself, fetched up all right in England. We got off the boat at Southampton, and went up to town. You should have seen what a swell Good turned out the very next day, beautifully shaved, frock coat fitting like a glove, brand new eye-glass, &c. &c. I went and walked in the park with him, where I met some people I know, and at once told them the story of his 'beautiful white legs'.

He is furious, especially as some ill-natured person has printed it in a society paper.

To come to business, Good and I took the diamonds to Streeter's to be valued, as we arranged, and I am really afraid to tell you what they put them at, it seems so enormous. They say that of course it is more or less guess-work, as such stones have never to their knowledge been put on the market in anything like such quantities. It appears that they are (with the exception of one or two of the largest) of the finest water, and equal in every way to the best Brazilian stones. I asked them if they would buy them, but they said that it was beyond their power to do so, and recommended us to sell by degrees, for fear we should flood the market. They offer, however, a hundred and eighty thousand for a small portion of them.

You must come home, Quatermain, and see about these things, especially if you insist upon making the magnificent present of the third share, which does *not* belong to me, to my brother George. As for Good, he is *no good*. His time is too much occupied in shaving, and other matters connected with the vain adorning of the body. But I think he is still down on his luck about Foulata. He told me that since he had been home he hadn't seen a woman to touch her, either as regards her figure or the sweetness of her expression.

I want you to come home, my dear old comrade, and buy a place near here. You have done your day's work, and have lots of money now, and there is a place for sale quite close which would suit you admirably. Do come; the sooner the better; you can finish writing the story of your adventures on board ship. We have refused to tell the story till it is written by you, for fear that we shall not be believed. If you start on receipt of this, you will reach here by Christmas, and I book you to stay with me for that. Good is coming, and George, and so, by the way, is your boy Harry (there's a bribe for you). I have had him down for a week's shooting, and like him. He is a cool young hand; he shot me in the leg, cut out the pellets, and then remarked upon the advantage of having a medical student in every shooting party.

Good-bye, old boy; I can't say any more, but I know that you will come, if only to oblige

Your sincere friend,
HENRY CURTIS

P. S. – The tusks of the great bull that killed poor Khiva have now been put up in the hall here, over the pair of buffalo horns you gave me, and look magnificent; and the axe with which I chopped off Twala's head is stuck up over my writing table. I wish we could have managed to bring away the coats of chain armour.

H. C.

Today is Tuesday. There is a steamer going on Friday, and I really think I must take Curtis at his word, and sail by her for England, if it is only to see my boy Harry and look after the printing of this history, which is a task I do not like to trust to anybody else.

Under the Red Robe

1

At Zaton's

'MARKED cards!'

There were a score round us when the fool, little knowing the man with whom he had to deal, and as little how to lose like a gentleman, flung the words in my teeth. He thought, I'll be sworn, that I should storm and swear and ruffle it like any common cock of the hackle. But that was never Gil de Berault's way. For a few seconds after he had spoken I did not even look at him. I passed my eye instead – smiling, *bien entendu* – round the ring of waiting faces, saw that there was no one except De Pombal I had cause to fear; and then at last I rose and looked at the fool with the grim face I have known impose on older and wiser men.

'Marked cards, M. l'Anglais?' I said, with a chilling sneer. 'They are used, I am told, to trap players – not unbirched schoolboys.'

'Yet I say that they are marked!' he replied hotly, in his queer foreign jargon. 'In my last hand I had nothing. You doubled the stakes. Bah, sir, you knew! You have swindled me!'

'Monsieur is easy to swindle – when he plays with a mirror behind him,' I answered tartly.

At that there was a great roar of laughter, which might have been heard in the street, and which brought to the table everyone in the eating-house whom his voice had not already attracted. But I did not relax my face. I waited until all was quiet again, and then waving aside two or three who stood between us and the entrance, I pointed gravely to the door.

'There is a little space behind the church of St. Jacques, M. l'Etranger,' I said, putting on my hat and taking my cloak on my arm. 'Doubtless you will accompany me thither?'

He snatched up his hat, his face burning with shame and rage.

'With pleasure!' he blurted out. 'To the devil, if you like!'

I thought the matter arranged, when the Marquis laid his hand on the young fellow's arm and checked him.

'This must not be,' he said, turning from him to me with his grand, fine-gentleman's air.

'You know me, M. de Berault. This matter has gone far enough.'

'Too far! M. de Pombal,' I answered bitterly. 'Still, if you wish to take your friend's place, I shall raise no objection.'

'Chut, man!' he retorted, shrugging his shoulders negligently. 'I know you, and I do not fight with men of your stamp. Nor need this gentleman.'

'Undoubtedly,' I replied, bowing low, 'if he prefers to be caned in the streets.'

That stung the Marquis.

'Have a care! have a care!' he cried hotly. 'You go too far, M. Berault.'

'De Berault, if you please,' I objected, eyeing him sternly. 'My family has borne the *de* as long as yours, M. de Pombal.'

He could not deny that, and he answered, 'As you please'; at the same time restraining his friend by a gesture. 'But none the less,' he continued, 'take my advice. The Cardinal has forbidden duelling, and this time he means it! You have been in trouble once and gone free. A second time it may fare worse with you. Let this gentleman go, therefore, M. de Berault. Besides – why, shame upon you, man!' he exclaimed hotly; 'he is but a lad!'

Two or three who stood behind me applauded that. But I turned and they met my eye; and they were as mum as mice.

'His age is his own concern,' I said grimly. 'He was old enough a while ago to insult me.'

'And I will prove my words!' the lad cried, exploding at last. He had spirit enough, and the Marquis had had hard work to restrain him so long. 'You do me no service, M. de Pombal,' he continued, pettishly shaking off his friend's hand. 'By your leave, this gentleman and I will settle this matter.'

'That is better,' I said, nodding drily, while the Marquis stood aside, frowning and baffled. 'Permit me to lead the way.'

Zaton's eating-house stands scarcely a hundred paces from St. Jacques la Boucherie, and half the company went thither with us. The evening was wet, the light in the streets was waning, the streets themselves were dirty and slippery. There were few passers in the Rue St. Antoine; and our party, which earlier in the day must have attracted notice and a crowd, crossed unmarked, and entered without interruption the paved triangle which lies immediately behind the church. I saw in the distance one of the Cardinal's guard loitering in front of the scaffolding round the new Hôtel Richelieu; and the sight of the uniform gave me pause for a moment. But it was too late to repent.

The Englishman began at once to strip off his clothes. I closed mine to the throat, for the air was chilly. At that moment, while we stood preparing, and most of the company seemed a little inclined to stand off from me, I felt a hand on my arm, and turning, saw the dwarfish tailor at whose house, in the Rue Savonnerie, I lodged at the time. The fellow's presence was unwelcome, to say the least of it; and though for want of better company I had sometimes encouraged him to be free with me at home, I took that to be no reason why I should be plagued with him before gentlemen. I shook him off, therefore, hoping by a frown to silence him.

He was not to be so easily put down, however, and perforce I had to speak to him.

'Afterwards, afterwards,' I said hurriedly. 'I am engaged now.'

'For God's sake, don't, sir!' the poor fool cried, clinging to my sleeve. 'Don't do it! You will bring a curse on the house. He is but a lad, and –'

'You, too!' I exclaimed, losing patience.

'Be silent, you scum! What do you know about gentlemen's quarrels? Leave me; do you hear?'

'But the Cardinal!' he cried in a quavering voice. 'The Cardinal, M. de Berault! The last man you killed is not forgotten yet. This time he will be sure to – '

'Leave me, do you hear?' I hissed. The fellow's impudence passed all bounds. It was as bad as his croaking. 'Begone!' I added. 'I suppose you are afraid that he will kill me, and you will lose your money.'

Frison fell back at that almost as if I had struck him, and I turned to my adversary, who had been awaiting my motions with impatience. God knows he did look young as he stood with his head bare and his fair hair drooping over his smooth woman's forehead – a mere lad fresh from the college of Burgundy, if they have such a thing in England. I felt a sudden chill as I looked at him: a qualm, a tremor, a presentiment. What was it the little tailor had said? That I should – but there, he did not know. What did he know of such things? If I let this pass I must kill a man a day, or leave Paris and the eating-house, and starve.

'A thousand pardons,' I said gravely, as I drew and took my place. 'A dun. I am sorry that the poor devil caught me so inopportunely. Now, however, I am at your service.'

He saluted and we crossed swords and began. But from the first I had no doubt what the result would be. The slippery stones and fading light gave him, it is true, some chance, some advantage, more than he deserved; but I had no sooner felt his blade than I knew that he was no swordsman. Possibly he had taken half a dozen lessons in rapier art, and practised what he learned with an Englishman as heavy and awkward as himself. But that was all. He made a few wild clumsy rushes, parrying widely. When I had foiled these, the danger was over, and I held him at my mercy.

I played with him a little while, watching the sweat gather on his brow, and the shadow of the church tower fall deeper and darker, like the shadow of doom, on his face. Not out of cruelty – God knows I have never erred in that direction! – but because, for the first time in my life, I felt a strange reluctance to strike the blow. The curls clung to his forehead; his breath came and went in gasps; I heard the men behind me murmur, and one or two of them drop an oath; and then I slipped – slipped, and was down in a moment on my right side, my elbow striking the pavement so sharply that the arm grew numb to the wrist.

He held off. I heard a dozen voices cry, 'Now! now you have him!' But he held off. He stood back and waited with his breast heaving and his point lowered until I had risen and stood again on my guard.

'Enough! enough!' a rough voice behind me cried. 'Don't hurt the man after that.'

'On guard, sir!' I answered coldly – for he seemed to waver, and be in doubt. 'It was an accident. It shall not avail you again.'

Several voices cried 'Shame!' and one, 'You coward!' But the Englishman stepped forward, a fixed look in his blue eyes. He took his place without a word. I read in his drawn white face that he had made up his mind to the worst, and his courage so won my admiration that I would gladly and thankfully have set one of the lookers-on – any of the lookers-on – in his place; but that could not be. So I thought of Zaton's closed to me, of Pombal's insult, of the sneers and slights I had long kept at the sword's point; and, pressing him suddenly in a heat of affected anger, I thrust strongly over his guard, which had grown feeble, and ran him through the chest.

When I saw him lying, laid out on the stones with his eyes half shut, and his face glimmering white in the dusk – not that I saw him thus long, for there were a dozen kneeling round him in a twinkling – I felt an unwonted pang. It passed, however, in a moment. For I found myself confronted by a ring of angry faces – of men who, keeping at a distance, hissed and cursed and threatened me, calling me Black Death and the like.

They were mostly canaille, who had gathered during the fight, and had viewed all that passed from the farther side of the railings. While some snarled and raged at me like wolves, calling me 'Butcher!' and 'Cutthroat!' or cried out that Berault was at his trade again, others threatened me with the vengeance of the Cardinal, flung the edict in my teeth, and said with glee that the guard were coming – they would see me hanged yet.

'His blood is on your head!' one cried furiously. 'He will dead in an hour. And you will swing for him! Hurrah!'

'Begone,' I said.

'Ay, to Montfaucon,' he answered, mocking me.

'No; to your kennel!' I replied, with a look which sent him a yard backwards, though the railings were between us. And I wiped my blade carefully, standing a little apart. For – well, I could understand it – it was one of those moments when a man is not popular. Those who had come with me from the eating-house eyed me askance, and turned their backs when I drew nearer; and those who had joined us and obtained admission were scarcely more polite.

But I was not to be outdone in sang-froid. I cocked my hat, and drawing my cloak over my shoulders, went out with a swagger which drove the curs from the gate before I came within a dozen paces of it. The rascals outside fell back as quickly, and in a moment I was in the street. Another moment and I should have been clear of the place and free to lie by for a while – when, without warning, a scurry took place round me. The crowd fled every way into the gloom, and in a hand-turn a dozen of the Cardinal's guards closed round me.

I had some acquaintance with the officer in command, and he saluted me civilly.

'This is a bad business, M. de Berault,' he said. 'The man is dead they tell me.'

'Neither dying nor dead,' I answered lightly. 'If that be all you may go home again.'

'With you,' he replied, with a grin, 'certainly. And as it rains, the sooner the better. I must ask you for your sword, I am afraid.'

'Take it,' I said, with the philosophy which never deserts me. 'But the man will not die.'

'I hope that may avail you,' he answered in a tone I did not like. 'Left wheel, my friends! To the Châtelet! March!'

'There are worse places,' I said, and resigned myself to fate. After all, I had been in a prison before, and learned that only one jail lets no prisoner escape.

But when I found that my friend's orders were to hand me over to the watch, and that I was to be confined like any common jail-bird caught cutting a purse or slitting a throat, I confess my heart sank. If I could get speech with the Cardinal, all would probably be well; but if I failed in this, or if the case came before him in strange guise, or if he were in a hard mood himself, then it might go ill with me. The edict said, death!

And the lieutenant at the Châtelet did not put himself to much trouble to hearten me. 'What! again, M. de Berault?' he said, raising his eyebrows as he received me at the gate, and recognised me by the light of the brazier which his men were just kindling outside. 'You are a very bold man, or a very foolhardy one, to come here again. The old business, I suppose?'

'Yes, but he is not dead,' I answered coolly. 'He has a trifle – a mere scratch. It was behind the church of St. Jacques.'

'He looked dead enough, my friend,' the guardsman interposed. He had not yet left us.

'Bah!' I answered scornfully. 'Have you ever known me make a mistake? When I kill a man I kill him. I put myself to pains, I tell you, not to kill this Englishman. Therefore he will live.'

'I hope so,' the lieutenant said, with a dry smile. 'And you had better hope so, too, M. de Berault. For if not –'

'Well?' I said, somewhat troubled. 'If not, what, my friend?'

'I fear he will be the last man you will fight,' he answered. 'And even if he lives, I would not be too sure, my friend. This time the Cardinal is determined to put it down.'

'He and I are old friends,' I said confidently.

'So I have heard,' he answered, with a short laugh. 'I think that the same was said of Chalais. I do not remember that it saved his head.'

This was not reassuring. But worse was to come. Early in the morning orders were received that I should be treated with especial strictness, and

I was given the choice between irons and one of the cells below the level. Choosing the latter, I was left to reflect upon many things; among others, on the queer and uncertain nature of the Cardinal, who loved, I knew, to play with a man as a cat with a mouse; and on the ill effects which sometimes attend a high chest-thrust however carefully delivered. I only rescued myself at last from these and other unpleasant reflections by obtaining the loan of a pair of dice; and the light being just enough to enable me to reckon the throws, I amused myself for hours by casting them on certain principles of my own. But a long run again and again upset my calculations; and at last brought me to the conclusion that a run of bad luck may be so persistent as to see out the most sagacious player. This was not a reflection very welcome to me at the moment.

Nevertheless, for three days it was all the company I had. At the end of that time, the knave of a jailor who attended me, and who had never grown tired of telling me, after the fashion of his kind, that I should be hanged, came to me with a less assured air.

'Perhaps you would like a little water?' he said civilly.

'Why, rascal?' I asked.

'To wash with,' he answered.

'I asked for some yesterday, and you would not bring it,' I grumbled. 'However, better late than never. Bring it now. If I must hang, I will hang like a gentleman. But, depend upon it, the Cardinal will not serve an old friend so scurvy a trick.'

'You are to go to him,' he announced, when he came back with the water.

'What? To the Cardinal?' I cried.

'Yes,' he answered.

'Good!' I exclaimed; and in my joy and relief I sprang up at once, and began to refresh my dress. 'So all this time I have been doing him an injustice,' I continued. '*Vive Monseigneur!* Long live the little Bishop of Luchon! I might have known it, too.'

'Don't make too sure!' the man answered spitefully. Then he went on, 'I have something else for you. A friend of yours left it at the gate,' and he handed me a packet.

'Quite so!' I said, reading his rascally face aright. 'And you kept it as long as you dared – as long as you thought I should hang, you knave! Was not that so? But there, do not lie to me. Tell me instead which of my friends left it.' For, to confess the truth, I had not so many friends at this time; and ten good crowns – the packet contained no less sum – argued a pretty staunch friend, and one of whom a man might reasonably be proud.

The knave sniggered maliciously. 'A crooked dwarfish man left it,' he said. 'I doubt I might call him a tailor and not be far out.'

'Chut!' I answered – but I was a little out of countenance, nevertheless.

'I understand. An honest fellow enough, and in debt to me! I am glad he remembered. But when am I to go, friend?'

'In an hour,' he answered sullenly. Doubtless he had looked to get one of the crowns; but I was too old a hand for that. If I came back I could buy his services; and if I did not I should have wasted my money.

Nevertheless, a little later, when I found myself on my way to the Hôtel Richelieu under so close a guard that I could see nothing in the street except the figures that immediately surrounded me, I wished that I had given him the money. At such times, when all hangs in the balance and the sky is overcast, the mind runs on luck and old superstitions, and is prone to think a crown given here may avail there – though *there* be a hundred leagues away.

The Palais Richelieu was at this time in building, and we were required to wait in a long, bare gallery, where the masons were at work. I was kept a full hour here, pondering uncomfortably on the strange whims and fancies of the great man who then ruled France as the King's Lieutenant-General, with all the King's powers, and whose life I had once been the means of saving by a little timely information. On occasion he had done something to wipe out the debt; and at other times he had permitted me to be free with him, and so far we were not unknown to one another.

Nevertheless, when the doors were at last thrown open, and I was led into his presence, my confidence underwent a shock. His cold glance, that, roving over me, regarded me not as a man but an item, the steely glitter of his southern eyes, chilled me to the bone. The room was bare, the floor without carpet or covering. Some of the woodwork lay about, unfinished and in pieces. But the man – this man – needed no surroundings. His keen pale face, his brilliant eyes, even his presence – though he was of no great height, and began already to stoop at the shoulders – were enough to awe the boldest. I recalled, as I looked at him, a hundred tales of his iron will, his cold heart, his unerring craft. He had humbled the King's brother, the splendid Duke of Orléans, in the dust. He had curbed the Queen-mother. A dozen heads, the noblest in France, had come to the block through him. Only two years before he had quelled Rochelle; only a few months before he had crushed the great insurrection in Languedoc: and though the south, stripped of its old privileges, still seethed with discontent, no one in this year 1630 dared lift a hand against him – openly, at any rate. Under the surface a hundred plots, a thousand intrigues, sought his life or his power; but these, I suppose, are the hap of every great man.

No wonder, then, that the courage on which I plumed myself sank low at sight of him; or that it was as much as I could do to mingle with the humility of my salute some touch of the sang-froid of old acquaintanceship.

And perhaps that had been better left out. For it seemed that this man was without bowels. For a moment, while he stood looking at me, and before he spoke to me, I gave myself up for lost. There was a glint of cruel satisfaction in his eyes that warned me, before he opened his mouth, what he was going to say to me.

'I could not have made a better catch, M. de Berault,' he said, smiling villainously, while he gently smoothed the fur of a cat that had sprung on the table beside him. 'An old offender, and an excellent example. I doubt it will not stop with you. But later, we will make you the warrant for flying at higher game.'

'Monseigneur has handled a sword himself,' I blurted out. The very room seemed to be growing darker, the air colder. I was never nearer fear in my life.

'Yes?' he said, smiling delicately. 'And so – ?'

'Will not be too hard on the failings of a poor gentleman.'

'He shall suffer no more than a rich one,' he replied suavely as he stroked the cat. 'Enjoy that satisfaction, M. de Berault. Is that all?'

'Once I was of service to your Eminence,' I said desperately.

'Payment has been made,' he answered, 'more than once. But for that I should not have seen you.'

'The King's face!' I cried, snatching at the straw he seemed to hold out.

He laughed cynically, smoothly. His thin face, his dark moustache, and whitening hair, gave him an air of indescribable keeness.

'I am not the King,' he said. 'Besides, I am told that you have killed as many as six men in duels. You owe the King, therefore, one life at least. You must pay it. There is no more to be said, M. de Berault,' he continued coldly, turning away and beginning to collect some papers. 'The law must take its course.'

I thought that he was about to nod to the lieutenant to withdraw me, and a chilling sweat broke out down my back. I saw the scaffold, I felt the cords. A moment, and it would be too late.

'I have a favour to ask,' I stammered desperately, 'if your Eminence will give me a moment alone.'

'To what end?' he answered, turning and eyeing me with cold disfavour. 'I know you – your past – all. It can do no good, my friend.'

'No harm!' I cried. 'And I am a dying man, Monseigneur!'

'That is true,' he said thoughtfully. Still he seemed to hesitate; and my heart beat fast. At last he looked at the lieutenant. 'You may leave us,' he said shortly. 'Now,' he continued, when the officer had withdrawn and left us alone, 'what is it? Say what you have to say quickly, and, above all, do not try to fool me, M. de Berault.'

But his piercing eyes so disconcerted me now that I had my chance, and was alone with him, that I could not find a word to say, and stood before him mute. I think this pleased him, for his face relaxed.

'Well?' he said at last. 'Is that all?'

'The man is not dead,' I muttered.

He shrugged his shoulders contemptuously.

'What of that?' he said. 'That was not what you wanted to say to me!'

'Once I saved your Eminence's life,' I faltered miserably.

'Admitted,' he answered in his thin, incisive voice. 'You mentioned the fact before. On the other hand, you have taken six to my knowledge, M. de Berault. You have lived the life of a bully, a common bravo, a gamester. You, a man of family! For shame! Do you wonder that it has brought you to this? Yet on that one point I am willing to hear more,' he added abruptly.

'I might save your Eminence's life again,' I cried. It was a sudden inspiration.

'You know something?' he said quickly, fixing me with his eyes. 'But no,' he continued, shaking his head gently. 'Pshaw! The trick is old. I have better spies than you, M. de Berault.'

'But no better sword,' I cried hoarsely. 'No, not in all your guard!'

'That is true,' he said slowly. 'That is true.' To my surprise, he spoke in a tone of consideration; and he looked down at the floor. 'Let me think, my friend,' he continued.

He walked two or three times up and down the room, while I stood trembling. I confess it, trembling. The man whose pulses danger has no power to quicken is seldom proof against suspense; and the sudden hope his words awakened in me so shook me that his figure, as he trod lightly to and fro with the cat rubbing against his robe and turning time for time with him, wavered before my eyes. I grasped the table to steady myself. I had not admitted even in my own mind how darkly the shadow of Montfaucon and the gallows had fallen across me.

I had leisure to recover myself, for it was some time before he spoke. When he did, it was in a voice harsh, changed, imperative. 'You have the reputation of a man faithful, at least, to his employer,' he said. 'Do not answer me. I say it is so. Well, I will trust you. I will give you one more chance – though it is a desperate one. Woe to you if you fail me! Do you know Cocheforêt in Béarn? It is not far from Auch.'

'No, your Eminence.'

'Nor M. de Cocheforêt?'

'No, your Eminence.'

'So much the better,' he replied. 'But you have heard of him. He has been engaged in every Gascon plot since the late King's death, and gave more trouble last year in the Vivarais than any man twice his years. At present he is at Bosost in Spain, with other refugees, but I have learned that at frequent intervals he visits his wife at Cocheforêt, which is six leagues within the border. On one of these visits he must be arrested.'

'That should be easy,' I said.

The Cardinal looked at me. 'Chut, man! what do you know about it?' he answered bluntly. 'It is whispered at Cocheforêt if a soldier crosses the street at Auch. In the house are only two or three servants, but they have the countryside with them to a man, and they are a dangerous breed.

A spark might kindle a fresh rising. The arrest, therefore, must be made secretly.'

I bowed.

'One resolute man inside the house,' the Cardinal continued, thoughtfully glancing at a paper which lay on the table, 'with the help of two or three servants whom he could summon to his aid at will, might effect it. The question is, Will you be the man, my friend?'

I hesitated; then I bowed. What choice had I?

'Nay, nay, speak out!' he said sharply. 'Yes or no, M. de Berault?'

'Yes, your Eminence,' I said reluctantly. Again, I say, what choice had I?

'You will bring him to Paris, and alive. He knows things, and that is why I want him. You understand?'

'I understand, Monseigneur,' I answered.

'You will get into the house as you can,' he continued with energy. 'For that you will need strategy, and good strategy. They suspect everybody. You must deceive them. If you fail to deceive them, or, deceiving them, are found out later, I do not think that you will trouble me again, or break the edict a second time. On the other hand, should you deceive *me*' – he smiled still more subtly, but his voice sank to a purring note – 'I will break you on the wheel like the ruined gamester you are!'

I met his look without quailing. 'So be it!' I said recklessly. 'If I do not bring M. de Cocheforêt to Paris, you may do that to me, and more also!'

'It is a bargain!' he answered slowly. 'I think that you will be faithful. For money, here are a hundred crowns. That sum should suffice; but if you succeed you shall have twice as much more. That is all, I think. You understand?'

'Yes, Monseigneur.'

'Then why do you wait?'

'The lieutenant?' I said modestly.

The Cardinal laughed to himself, and sitting down wrote a word or two on a slip of paper. 'Give him that,' he said in high good-humour. 'I fear, M. de Berault, you will never get your deserts – in this world!'

2

At the Green Pillar

COCHEFORÊT lies in a billowy land of oak and beech and chestnuts – a land of deep, leafy bottoms and hills clothed with forest. Ridge and valley, glen and knoll, the woodland, sparsely peopled and more sparsely tilled, stretches away to the great snow mountains that here limit France. It swarms with game – with wolves and bears, deer and boars. To the end of his life I have heard that the great king loved this district, and would sigh, when years and State fell heavily on him, for the beech groves and box-covered hills of South Béarn. From the terraced steps of Auch you can see the forest roll away in light and shadow, vale and upland, to the base of the snow peaks; and though I come from Brittany and love the smell of the salt wind, I have seen few sights that outdo this.

It was the second week of October when I came to Cocheforêt, and, dropping down from the last wooded brow, rode quietly into the place at evening. I was alone, and had ridden all day in a glory of ruddy beech leaves, through the silence of forest roads, across clear brooks and glades still green. I had seen more of the quiet and peace of the country than had been my share since boyhood, and for that reason, or because I had no great taste for the task before me – the task now so imminent – I felt a little hipped. In good faith, it was not a gentleman's work that I was come to do, look at it how you might.

But beggars must not be choosers, and I knew that this feeling would not last. At the inn, in the presence of others, under the spur of necessity, or in the excitement of the chase were that once begun, I should lose the feeling. When a man is young he seeks solitude, when he is middle-aged he flies it and his thoughts. I made therefore for the 'Green Pillar,' a little inn in the village street, to which I had been directed at Auch, and, thundering on the door with the knob of my riding-switch, railed at the man for keeping me waiting.

Here and there at hovel doors in the street – which was a mean, poor place, not worthy of the name – men and women looked out at me suspiciously. But I affected to ignore them; and at last the host came. He was a fair-haired man, half Basque, half Frenchman, and had scanned me well, I was sure, through some window or peep-hole; for when he came out he betrayed no surprise at the sight of a well-dressed stranger – a portent in that out-of-the-way village – but eyed me with a kind of sullen reserve.

'I can lie here to-night, I suppose?' I said, dropping the reins on the sorrel's neck. The horse hung its head.

'I don't know,' he answered stupidly.

I pointed to the green bough which topped a post that stood opposite the door.

'This is an inn, is it not?' I said.

'Yes,' he answered slowly. 'It is an inn. But –'

'But you are full, or you are out of food, or your wife is ill, or something else is amiss,' I answered peevishly. 'All the same, I am going to lie here. So you must make the best of it, and your wife, too – if you have one.'

He scratched his head, looking at me with an ugly glitter in his eyes. But he said nothing, and I dismounted.

'Where can I stable my horse?' I asked.

'I'll put it up,' he answered sullenly, stepping forward and taking the reins in his hand.

'Very well,' I said. 'But I go with you. A merciful man is merciful to his beast, and wherever I go I see my horse fed.'

'It will be fed,' he said shortly. And then he waited for me to go into the house. 'The wife is in there,' he continued, looking at me stubbornly.

'*Imprimis* – if you understand Latin, my friend,' I answered; 'the horse in the stall.'

He saw that it was no good, turned the sorrel slowly round, and began to lead it across the village street. There was a shed behind the inn, which I had already marked, and taken for the stable. I was surprised when I found that he was not going there, but I made no remark, and in a few minutes saw the horse made comfortable in a hovel which seemed to belong to a neighbour.

This done, the man led the way back to the inn, carrying my valise.

'You have no other guests?' I said, with a casual air. I knew that he was watching me closely.

'No,' he answered.

'This is not much in the way to anywhere, I suppose?'

'No.'

That was so evident, that I never saw a more retired place. The hanging woods, rising steeply to a great height, so shut the valley in that I was puzzled to think how a man could leave it save by the road I had come. The cottages, which were no more than mean, small huts, ran in a straggling double line, with many gaps – through fallen trees and ill-cleared meadows. Among them a noisy brook ran in and out. And the inhabitants – charcoal-burners, or swine-herds, or poor devils of the like class – were no better than their dwellings. I looked in vain for the Château. It was not to be seen, and I dared not ask for it.

The man led me into the common room of the tavern – a low-roofed, poor place, lacking a chimney or glazed windows, and grimy with smoke and use. The fire – a great half-burned tree – smouldered on a stone hearth, raised a foot from the floor. A huge black pot simmered over it, and beside one window lounged a country fellow talking with the goodwife. In the dusk I could not see his face, but I gave the woman a word, and sat down to wait for my supper.

She seemed more silent than the common run of her kind; but this might be because her husband was present. While she moved about, getting my meal, he took his place against the door-post and fell to staring at me so persistently that I felt by no means at my ease. He was a tall, strong fellow, with a shaggy moustache and brown beard, cut in the mode Henri Quatre; and on the subject of that king – a safe one, I knew, with a Béarnais – and on that alone, I found it possible to make him talk. Even then there was a suspicious gleam in his eyes that bade me abstain from questions; so that as the darkness deepened behind him, and the firelight played more and more strongly on his features, and I thought of the leagues of woodland that lay between this remote valley and Auch, I recalled the Cardinal's warning that if I failed in my attempt I should be little likely to trouble Paris again.

The lout by the window paid no attention to me; nor I to him, when I had once satisfied myself that he was really what he seemed to be. But by and by two or three men – rough, uncouth fellows – dropped in to reinforce the landlord, and they, too, seemed to have no other business than to sit in silence looking at me, or now and again to exchange a word in a patois of their own. By the time my supper was ready, the knaves numbered six in all; and, as they were armed to a man with huge Spanish knives, and made it clear that they resented my presence in their dull rustic fashion – every rustic is suspicious – I began to think that, unwittingly, I had put my head into a wasps' nest.

Nevertheless, I ate and drank with apparent appetite; but little that passed within the circle of light cast by the smoky lamp escaped me. I watched the men's looks and gestures at least as sharply as they watched mine; and all the time I was racking my wits for some mode of disarming their suspicions, or failing that, of learning something more of the position, which far exceeded in difficulty and danger anything that I had expected. The whole valley, it would seem, was on the look-out to protect my man!

I had purposely brought with me from Auch a couple of bottles of choice Armagnac; and these had been carried into the house with my saddle-bags. I took one out now and opened it and carelessly offered a dram of the spirit to the landlord. He took it. As he drank it, I saw his face flush; he handed back the cup reluctantly, and on that hint I offered him another. The strong spirit was already beginning to work, and he accepted, and in a few minutes began to talk more freely and with less of the constraint which had before marked us all. Still, his tongue ran chiefly on questions – he would know this, he would learn that; but even this was a welcome change. I told him openly whence I had come, by what road, how long I had stayed in Auch, and where; and so far I satisfied his curiosity. Only when I came to the subject of my visit to Cocheforêt I kept a mysterious silence, hinting darkly at business in Spain and friends across the border, and this and that; in this way giving the peasants to understand, if they pleased, that I was in the same interest as their exiled master.

They took the bait, winked at one another, and began to look at me in a more friendly way – the landlord foremost. But when I had led them so far, I dared go no farther, lest I should commit myself and be found out. I stopped, therefore, and, harking back to general subjects, chanced to compare my province with theirs. The landlord, now become almost talkative, was not slow to take up this challenge; and it presently led to my acquiring a curious piece of knowledge. He was boasting of his great snow mountains, the forests that propped them, the bears that roamed in them, the izards that loved the ice, and the boars that fed on the oak mast.

'Well,' I said, quite by chance, 'we have not these things, it is true. But we have things in the north you have not. We have tens of thousands of good horses – not such ponies as you breed here. At the horse fair at Fécamp my sorrel would be lost in a crowd. Here in the south you will not meet his match in a long day's journey.'

'Do not make too sure of that,' the man replied, his eyes bright with triumph and the dram. 'What would you say if I showed you a better – in my own stable?'

I saw that his words sent a kind of thrill through his other hearers, and that such of them as understood – for two or three of them talked their patois only – looked at him angrily; and in a twinkling I began to comprehend. But I affected dullness, and laughed in scorn.

'Seeing is believing,' I said. 'I doubt if you know a good horse when you see one, my friend.'

'Oh, don't I?' he said, winking. 'Indeed!'

'I doubt it,' I answered stubbornly.

'Then come with me, and I will show you one,' he retorted, discretion giving way to vainglory. His wife and the others, I saw, looked at him dumbfounded; but, without paying any heed to them, he rose, took up a lanthorn, and, assuming an air of peculiar wisdom, opened the door. 'Come with me,' he continued. 'I don't know a good horse when I see one, don't I? I know a better than yours, at any rate!'

I should not have been surprised if the other men had interfered; but I suppose as he was a leader among then they did not, and in a moment we were outside. Three paces through the darkness took us to the stable, an offset at the back of the inn. My man twirled the pin, and, leading the way in, raised his lanthorn. A horse whinnied softly, and turned its bright, mild eyes on us – a bald-faced chestnut, with white hairs in its tail and one white stocking.

'There!' my guide exclaimed, waving the lanthorn to and fro boastfully, that I might see its points. 'What do you say to that? Is that an undersized pony?'

'No,' I answered, purposely stinting my praise. 'It is pretty fair – for this country.'

'Or any country,' he answered wrathfully. 'Or any country, I say – I don't care where it is! And I have reason to know! Why, man, that horse is – But there, that is good horse, if ever you saw one!' And with that he ended – abruptly and lamely, lowered the lanthorn with a sudden gesture, and turned to the door. He was on the instant in such hurry to leave that he almost shouldered me out.

But I understood. I knew that he had nearly betrayed all – that he had been on the point of blurting out that that was M. de Cocheforêt's horse! M. Cocheforêt *comprenez bien*! And while I turned away my face in the darkness that he might not see me smile, I was not surprised to find the man in a moment changed, and become, in the closing of the door, as sober and suspicious as before, ashamed of himself and enraged with me, and in a mood to cut my throat for a trifle.

It was not my cue to quarrel, however. I made, therefore, as if I had seen nothing, and when we were back in the inn praised the horse grudgingly, and like a man but half convinced. The ugly looks and ugly weapons I saw round me were fine incentives to caution; and no Italian, I flatter myself, could have played his part more nicely than I did. But I was heartily glad when it was over, and I found myself, at last, left alone for the night in a little garret – a mere fowl-house – upstairs, formed by the roof and gable walls, and hung with strings of apples and chestnuts. It was a poor sleeping-place – rough, chilly, and unclean. I ascended to it by a ladder; my cloak and a little fern formed my only bed. But I was glad to accept it, for it enabled me to be alone and to think out the position unwatched.

Of course M. de Cocheforêt was at the Château. He had left his horse here, and gone up on foot; probably that was his usual plan. He was therefore within my reach, in one sense – I could not have come at a better time – but in another he was as much beyond it as if I were still in Paris. For so far was I from being able to seize him that I dared not ask a question, or let fall a rash word, or even look about me freely. I saw I dared not. The slightest hint of my mission, the faintest breath of distrust, would lead to throat-cutting – and the throat would be mine; while the longer I lay in the village, the greater suspicion I should incur, and the closer would be the watch kept upon me.

In such a position some men might have given up the attempt in despair, and saved themselves across the border. But I have always valued myself on my fidelity, and I did not shrink. If not to-day, to-morrow; if not this time, next time. The dice do not always turn up aces. Bracing myself, therefore, to the occasion, I crept, as soon as the house was quiet, to the window, a small, square, open lattice, much cobwebbed, and partly stuffed with hay. I looked out. The village seemed to be asleep. The dark branches of trees hung a few feet away, and almost obscured a grey, cloudy sky, through which a wet moon sailed drearily. Looking downwards, I could at first see nothing; but as my eyes grew used to the darkness – I had only just put out my rushlight – I made out the stable door and the shadowy outlines of the lean-to roof.

I had hoped for this, for I could now keep watch, and learn at least whether Cocheforêt left before morning. If he did not, I should know he was still here. If he did, I should be the better for seeing his features, and learning, perhaps, other things that might be of use to me in the future.

Making up my mind to the uncomfortable, I sat down on the floor by the lattice, and began a vigil that might last, I knew, until morning. It did last about an hour, at the end of which time I heard whispering below, then footsteps; then, as some persons turned a corner, a voice speaking aloud and carelessly. I could not catch the words or meaning, but the voice was a gentleman's, and its bold accents and masterful tone left me in no doubt that the speaker was M. de Cocheforêt himself. Hoping to learn more, I pressed my face nearer to the opening, and had just made out through the gloom two figures – one that of a tall, slight man, wearing a cloak; the other, I fancied, a woman's, in a sheeny white dress – when a thundering rap on the door of my garret made me spring back a yard from the lattice, and lie down hurriedly on my couch. The summons was repeated.

'Well?' I cried, rising on my elbow, and cursing the untimely interruption. I was burning with anxiety to see more. 'What is it? What is the matter?'

The trap-door was lifted a foot or more. The landlord thrust up his head.

'You called, did you not?' he said.

He held up a rushlight, which illumined half the room and lit up his grinning face.

'Called – at this hour of the night, you fool?' I answered angrily. 'No! I did not call. Go to bed, man!'

But he remained on the ladder, gaping stupidly. 'I heard you,' he said.

'Go to bed! You are drunk,' I answered, sitting up. 'I tell you I did not call.'

'Oh, very well,' he answered slowly. 'And you do not want anything?'

'Nothing – except to be left alone,' I replied sourly.

'Umph!' he said. 'Good night!'

'Good night! Good night!' I answered with what patience I might. The tramp of the horse's hoofs as it was led out of the stable was in my ears at the moment. 'Good night!' I continued feverishly, hoping that he would still retire in time, and I have a chance to look out. 'I want to sleep.'

'Good,' he said, with a broad grin. 'But it is early yet, and you have plenty of time.'

And then, at last, he slowly let down the trap-door, and I heard him chuckle as he went down the ladder.

Before he reached the bottom I was at the window. The woman, whom I had seen, still stood below in the same place, and beside her was a man in a peasant's dress, holding a lanthorn. But the man, the man I wanted to see, was no longer there. He was gone, and it was evident that the others no longer feared me; for while I gazed the landlord came out to them with another lanthorn swinging in his hand, and said something to the lady, and she looked up at my window and laughed.

It was a warm night, and she wore nothing over her white dress. I could see her tall, shapely figure and shining eyes, and the firm contour of her beautiful face, which, if any fault might be found with it, erred in being too regular. She looked like a woman formed by nature to meet dangers and difficulties, and to play a great part; even here, at midnight, in the midst of these desperate men, she did not seem out of place. I could fancy – I did not find it impossible to fancy – that under her queenly exterior, and behind the contemptuous laugh with which she heard the landlord's story, there lurked a woman's soul, a soul capable of folly and tenderness. But no outward sign betrayed its presence – as I saw her then.

I scanned her very carefully; and secretly, if the truth be told, I was glad to find that Madame de Cocheforêt was such a woman. I was glad that she had laughed as she had – with a ring of disdain and defiance; glad that she was not a little, tender, child-like woman, to be crushed by the first pinch of trouble. For if I succeeded in my task, if I contrived to – but, pish! Women, I told myself, were all alike. She would find consolation quickly enough.

I watched until the group broke up, and Madame, with one of the men, went her way round the corner of the inn, and out of my sight. Then I retired to bed again, feeling more than ever perplexed what course I should adopt. It was clear that to succeed I must obtain admission to the house, which was garrisoned, according to my instructions, by two or three old men-servants only, and as many women; since Madame, to disguise her husband's visits the more easily, lived, and gave out that she lived, in great retirement. To seize her husband at home, therefore, might be no impossible task; though here, in the heart of the village, a troop of horse might make the attempt and fail.

But how was I to gain admission to the house – a house guarded by quick-witted women, and fenced with all the precautions love could devise? That was the question; and dawn found me still debating it, still as far as ever from an answer. Anxious and feverish, I was glad when the light came, and I could get up. I thought that the fresh air might inspire me, and I was tired of my stuffy closet. I crept stealthily down the ladder, and managed to pass unseen through the lower room, in which several persons were snoring heavily. The outer door was not fastened, and in a hand-turn I was in the street.

It was still so early that the trees stood up black against the reddening sky, but the bough upon the post before the door was growing green, and in a few minutes the grey light would be everywhere. Already, even in the roadway, there was a glimmering of it; and as I stood at the corner of the house – where I could command both the front and the side on which the stable opened – sniffing the fresh air, and looking for any trace of the midnight departure, my eyes detected something light-coloured lying on the ground. It was not more than two or three paces from me, and I stepped to it and picked it up curiously, hoping that it might be a note. It was not a note, however, but a tiny orange-coloured sachet such as women carry in the bosom. It was full of some faintly scented powder, and bore on one side the initial 'E,' worked in white silk; and was altogether a dainty little toy, such as women love.

Doubtless Madame de Cocheforêt had dropped it in the night. I turned it over and over; and then I put it in my pouch with a smile, thinking that it might be useful some time, and in some way. I had scarcely done this, and turned with the intention of exploring the street, when the door behind me creaked on its leather hinges, and in a moment the host stood at my elbow, and gave me a surly greeting.

Evidently his suspicions were again aroused, for from this time he managed to be with me on one pretence or another until noon. Moreover, his manner grew each moment more churlish, his hints plainer; until I could scarcely avoid noticing the one or the other. About midday, having followed me for the twentieth time into the street, he came to the point by asking me rudely if I did not need my horse.

'No,' I said. 'Why do you ask?'

'Because,' he answered, with an ugly smile, 'this is not a very healthy place for strangers.'

'Ah!' I retorted. 'But the border air suits me you see.'

It was a lucky answer, for, taken with my talk the night before, it puzzled him, by suggesting that I was on the losing side, and had my reasons for lying near Spain. Before he had done scratching his head over it, the clatter of hoofs broke the sleepy quiet of the village street, and the lady I had seen the night before rode quickly round the corner, and drew her horse on to its haunches. Without looking at me, she called to the innkeeper to come to her stirrup.

He went. The moment his back was turned, I slipped away, and in a twinkling was hidden by a house. Two or three glum-looking fellows stared at me as I passed down the street, but no one moved: and in two minutes I was clear of the village, and in a half-worn track which ran through the wood, and led – if my ideas were right – to the Château. To discover the house and learn all that was to be learned about its situation were my most pressing needs; and these, even at the risk of a knife thrust, I was determined to satisfy.

I had not gone two hundred paces along the path, however, before I heard the tread of a horse behind me, and I had just time to hide myself before Madame came up and rode by me, sitting her horse gracefully, and with all the courage of a northern woman. I watched her pass, and then, assured by her presence that I was in the right road, I hurried after her. Two minutes' walking at speed brought me to a light wooden bridge spanning a stream. I crossed this, and, as the wood opened, saw before me first a wide, pleasant meadow, and beyond this a terrace. On the terrace, pressed upon on three sides by thick woods, stood a grey mansion, with the corner *tourelles*, steep, high roofs and round balconies that men loved and built in the days of the first Francis.

It was of good size, but wore a gloomy aspect. A great yew hedge, which seemed to enclose a walk or bowling-green, hid the ground floor of the east wing from view, while a formal rosegarden, stiff even in neglect, lay in front of the main building. The west wing, of which the lower roofs fell gradually away to the woods, probably contained the stables and granaries.

I stood a moment only, but I marked all, and noted how the road reached the house, and which windows were open to attack; then I turned and hastened back. Fortunately, I met no one between the house and the village, and was able to enter my host's with an air of the most complete innocence.

Short as had been my absence, however, I found things altered there. Round the door lounged three strangers – stout, well-armed fellows, whose bearing, as they loitered and chattered, suggested a curious mixture of smugness and independence. Half a dozen pack-horses stood tethered to the post in front of the house: and the landlord's manner, from being rude and churlish only, had grown perplexed and almost timid. One of the strangers, I soon found, supplied him with wine; the others were travelling merchants, who rode in the first one's company for the sake of safety. All were substantial men from Tarbes – solid burgesses; and I was not long in guessing that my host, fearing what might leak out before them, and, particularly, that I might refer to the previous night's disturbance, was on tenterhooks while they remained.

For a time this did not suggest anything to me. But when we had all taken our seats for supper, there came an addition to the party. The door opened and the fellow whom I had seen the night before with Madame de Cocheforêt entered and took a stool by the fire. I felt sure that he was one of the servants at the Château; and in a flash his presence inspired me with the most feasible plan for obtaining admission which I had yet hit upon. I felt myself grow hot at the thought – it seemed so full of promise, yet so doubtful – and, on the instant, without giving myself time to think too much, I began to carry it into effect.

I called for two or three bottles of better wine, and, assuming a jovial air, passed it round the table. When we had drunk a few glasses I fell to talking, and, choosing politics, took the side of the Languedoc party and the malcontents in so reckless a fashion that the innkeeper was beside himself at my imprudence. The merchants, who belonged to the class with whom the Cardinal was always most popular, looked first astonished and then enraged. But I was not to be checked; hints and sour looks were lost upon me. I grew more outspoken with every glass, I drank to the Rochellois, I swore it would not be long before they raised their heads again; and, at last, while the innkeeper and his wife were engaged lighting the lamp, I passed round the bottle and called on all for a toast.

'I'll give you one to begin,' I bragged noisily. 'A gentleman's toast! A southern toast! Here is confusion to the Cardinal, and a health to all who hate him!'

'*Mon Dieu!*' one of the strangers cried, springing from his seat in a rage. 'I am not going to stomach that! Is your house a common treason-hole,' he continued, turning furiously on the landlord, 'that you suffer this?'

'Hoity-toity!' I answered, coolly keeping my seat. 'What is all this? Don't you relish my toast, little man?'

'No – nor you!' he retorted hotly; 'Whoever you may be!'

'Then I will give you another,' I answered, with a hiccough. 'Perhaps it will be more to your taste. Here is the Duke of Orléans, and may he soon he King!'

3

The House in the Wood

WORDS so reckless fairly shook the three men out of their anger. For a moment they glared at me as if they had seen a ghost. Then the wine merchant clapped his hand on the table.

'That is enough,' he said, with a look at his companions. 'I think that there can be no mistake about that. As damnable treason as ever I heard whispered! I congratulate you, sir, on your boldness. As for you,' he continued, tuning with an ugly sneer to the landlord, 'I shall know now the company you keep! I was not aware that my wine wet whistles to such a tune!'

But if he was startled, the innkeeper was furious, seeing his character thus taken away; and, being at no time a man of many words, he vented his rage exactly in the way I wished, raising in a twinking such an uproar as can scarcely be conceived. With a roar like a bull's, he ran headlong at the table, and overturned it on the top of me. Fortunately the woman saved the lamp, and fled with it into a corner, whence she and the man from the Château watched the skirmish in silence; but the pewter cups and platters flew spinning across the floor, while the table pinned me to the ground among the ruins of my stool. Having me at this disadvantage – for at first I made no resistance – the landlord began to belabour me with the first thing he snatched up, and when I tried to defend myself, cursed me with each blow for a treacherous rogue and a vagrant. Meanwhile the three merchants, delighted with the turn things had taken, skipped round us laughing, and now hounded him on, now bantered me with 'How is that for the Duke or Orléans?' and 'How now, traitor?'

When I thought that this had lasted long enough – or, to speak more plainly, when I could stand the innkeeper's drubbing no longer – I threw him off, and struggled to my feet; but still, though the blood was trickling down my face, I refrained from drawing my sword. I caught up instead a leg of the stool which lay handy, and, watching my opportunity, dealt the landlord a shrewd blow under the ear, which laid him out in a moment on the wreck of his own table.

'Now,' I cried, brandishing my new weapon, which fitted the hand to a nicety, 'come on! Come on! if you dare to strike a blow, you peddling, truckling, huckstering knaves! A fig for you and your shaveling Cardinal!'

The red-faced wine merchant drew his sword in a one-two.

'Why, you drunken fool,' he said wrathfully, 'put that stick down, or I will spit you like a lark!'

'Lark in your teeth!' I cried, staggering as if the wine were in my head. 'And cuckoo, too! Another word, and I –'

He made a couple of savage passes at me, but in a twinkling his sword flew across the room.

'*Voilà!*' I shouted, lurching forward, as if I had luck and not skill to thank for my victory. 'Now, the next! Come on, come on – you white-livered knaves!' And, pretending a drunken frenzy, I flung my weapon bodily amongst them, and seizing the nearest, began to wrestle with him.

In a moment they all threw themselves upon me, and swearing copiously, bore me back to the door. The wine merchant cried breathlessly to the woman to open it, and in a twinkling they had me through it, and halfway across the road. The one thing I feared was a knife-thrust in the *mêlée*, but I had to run that risk, and the men were honest, and, thinking me drunk, indulgent. In a trice I found myself on my back in the dirt, with my head humming; and heard the bars of the door fall noisily into their places.

I got up and went to the door, and, to play out my part, hammered on it frantically; crying out to them to let me in. But the three travellers only jeered at me, and the landlord, coming to the window, with his head bleeding, shook his fist at me, and cursed me for a mischief-maker.

Baffled in this, I retired to a log which lay in the road a few paces from the house, and sat down on it to await events. With torn clothes and bleeding face, hatless and covered with dirt, I was in little better case than my opponent. It was raining, too, and the dripping branches swayed over my head. The wind was in the south – the coldest quarter. I began to feel chilled and dispirited. If my scheme failed, I had forfeited roof and bed to no purpose, and placed future progress out of the question. It was a critical moment.

But at last that happened for which I had been looking. The door swung open a few inches, and a man came noiselessly out; it was quickly barred behind him. He stood a moment waiting on the threshold and peering into the gloom; and seemed to expect to be attacked. Finding himself unmolested, however, and all quiet, he went off steadily down the street – towards the Château.

I let a couple of minutes go by, and then followed. I had no difficulty in hitting on the track at the end of the street, but when I had once plunged into the wood, I found myself in darkness so intense that I soon strayed from the path, and fell over roots, and tore my clothes with thorns, and lost my temper twenty times before I found the path again. However, I gained the bridge at last, and thence caught sight of a light twinkling before me. To make for it across the meadow and terrace was an easy task; yet, when I had reached the door and had hammered upon it, I was so worn out and in so sorry a plight that I sank down, and had little need to play a part, or pretend to be worse than I was.

For a long time no one answered. The dark house towering above me remained silent. I could hear, mingled with the throbbings of my heart, the steady croaking of the frogs in a pond near the stables; but no other sound. In a frenzy of impatience and disgust, I stood up again and hammered, kicking with my heels on the nail-studded door, and crying out desperately:

'*A moi! A moi!*'

Then, or a moment later, I heard a remote door opened; footsteps as of more than one person drew near. I raised my voice and cried again:

'*A moi!*'

'Who is there?' a voice asked.

'A gentleman in distress,' I answered piteously, moving my hand across the doors. 'For God's sake open and let me in. I am hurt, and dying of cold.'

'What brings you here?' the voice asked sharply. Despite its tartness, I fancied that it was a woman's.

'Heaven knows!' I answered desperately. 'I cannot tell. They maltreated me at the inn, and threw me into the street. I crawled away, and have been wandering in the woods for hours. Then I saw a light here.'

On that some muttering took place on the other side of the door – to which I had my ear. It ended in the bars being lowered. The door swung partly open, and a light shone out, dazzling me. I tried to shade my eyes with my fingers, and, as I did so, fancied I heard a murmur of pity. But when I looked in, under screen of my hand, I saw only one person – the man who held the light, and his aspect was so strange, so terrifying, that, shaken as I was by fatigue, I recoiled a step.

He was a tall and very thin man, meanly dressed in a short, scanty jacket and well-darned hose. Unable, for some reason, to bend his neck, he carried his head with a strange stiffness.

And that head – never did living man show a face so like death. His forehead was bald and yellow, his cheek-bones stood out under the strained skin, all the lower part of his face fell in, his jaws receded, his cheeks were hollow, his lips and chin were thin and fleshless. He seemed to have only one expression – a fixed grin.

While I stood looking at this formidable creature, he made a quick movement to shut the door again, smiling more widely. I had the presence of mind to thrust in my foot, and, before he could resent the act, a voice in the background cried:

'For shame, Clon! Stand back, stand back! do you hear? I am afraid, Monsieur, that you are hurt.'

Those words were my welcome to that house; and, spoken at an hour and in circumstances so gloomy, they made a lasting impression. Round the hall ran a gallery, and this, the height of the apartment, and the dark panelling seemed to swallow up the light. I stood within the entrance (as it seemed to me) of a huge cave; the skull-headed porter had the air of an ogre. Only the voice which greeted me dispelled the illusion. I turned trembling towards the quarter whence it came, and, shading my eyes, made out a woman's form standing in a doorway under the gallery. A second figure, which I took to be that of the servant I had seen at the inn, loomed uncertainly beside her.

I bowed in silence. My teeth were chattering. I was faint without feigning, and felt a kind of terror, hard to explain, at the sound of this woman's voice.

'One of our people has told me about you,' she continued, speaking out of the darkness. 'I am sorry that this has happened to you here, but I am afraid that you were indiscreet.'

'I take all the blame, Madame,' I answered humbly. 'I ask only shelter for the night.'

'The time has not yet come when we cannot give our friends that!' she answered with noble courtesy. 'When it does, Monsieur, we shall be homeless ourselves.'

I shivered, looking anywhere but at her; for, if the truth be told, I had not sufficiently pictured this scene of my arrival – I had not foredrawn its details; and now I took part in it I felt a miserable meanness weigh me down. I had never from the first liked the work, but I had had no choice, and I had no choice now. Luckily, the guise in which I came, my fatigue and wound were a sufficient mask, or I should have incurred suspicion at once. For I am sure that if ever in this world a brave man wore a hang-dog air, or Gil de Berault fell below himself, it was then and there – on Madame de Cocheforêt's threshold, with her welcome sounding in my ears.

One, I think, did suspect me. Clon, the porter, continued to hold the door obstinately ajar and to eye me with grinning spite, until his mistress, with some sharpness, bade him drop the bars and conduct me to a room.

'Do you go also, Louis,' she continued, speaking to the man beside her, 'and see this gentleman comfortably disposed. I am sorry,' she added, addressing me in the graceful tone she had before used, and I thought that I could see her head bend in the darkness, 'that our present circumstances do not permit us to welcome you more fitly, Monsieur. But the troubles of the times – however, you will excuse what is lacking. Until to-morrow, I have the honour to bid you good night.'

'Good night, Madame,' I stammered, trembling. I had not been able to distinguish her face in the gloom of the doorway, but her voice, her greeting, her presence unmanned me. I was troubled and perplexed; I had not spirit to kick a dog. I followed the two servants from the hall without heeding how we went; nor was it until we came to a full stop at a door in a whitewashed corridor, and it was forced upon me that something was in question between my two conductors, that I began to take notice.

Then I saw that one of them, Louis, wished to lodge me here where we stood. The porter, on the other hand, who held the keys, would not. He did not speak a word, nor did the other – and this gave a queer ominous character to the debate; but he continued to jerk his head towards the farther end of the corridor; and, at last, he carried his point. Louis shrugged his shoulders and moved on, glancing askance at me; and I, not understanding the matter in debate, followed the pair in silence.

We reached the end of the corridor, and there for an instant the monster with the keys paused and grinned at me. Then he turned into a narrow passage on the left, and after following it for some paces, halted before a small, strong door. His key jarred in the lock, but he forced it shrieking around, and with a savage flourish threw the door open.

I walked in and saw a mean, bare chamber with barred windows. The floor was indifferently clean, there was no furniture. The yellow light of the lanthorn falling on the stained walls gave the place the look of a dungeon. I turned to the two men. 'This is not a very good room,' I said. 'And it feels damp. Have you no other?'

Louis looked doubtfully at his companion. But the porter shook his head stubbornly.

'Why does he not speak?' I asked with impatience.

'He is dumb,' Louis answered.

'Dumb!' I exclaimed. 'But he hears.'

'He has ears,' the servant answered drily. 'But he has no tongue, Monsieur.'

I shuddered. 'How did he lose it?' I asked.

'At Rochelle. He was a spy, and the king's people took him the day the town surrendered. They spared his life, but cut out his tongue.'

'Ah!' I said. I wished to say more, to be natural, to show myself at my ease. But the porter's eyes seemed to burn into me, and my own tongue clave to the roof of my mouth. He opened his lips and pointed to his throat with a horrid gesture, and I shook my head and turned from him. 'You can let me have some bedding?' I murmured hastily, for the sake of saying something, and to escape.

'Of course, Monsieur,' Louis answered. 'I will fetch some.'

He went away, thinking doubtless that Clon would stay with me. But after waiting a minute the porter strode off also with the lanthorn, leaving me to stand in the middle of the damp, dark room and reflect on the position. It was plain that Clon suspected me. This prison-like room, with its barred window, at the back of the house, and in the wing farthest from the stables, proved so much. Clearly, he was a dangerous fellow, of whom I must beware. I had just begun to wonder how Madame could keep such a monster in her house, when I heard his step returning. He came in, lighting Louis, who carried a small pallet and a bundle of coverings.

The dumb man had, besides the lanthorn, a bowl of water and a piece of rag in his hand. He set them down, and going out again, fetched in a stool. Then he hung up the lanthorn on a nail, took the bowl and rag, and invited me to sit down.

I was loth to let him touch me; but he continued to stand over me, pointing and grinning with dark persistence, and rather than stand on a trifle I sat down at last and gave him his way. He bathed my head carefully enough, and I dare say did it good; but I understood. I knew that his only desire was to learn whether the cut was real or a pretence, and I began to fear him more and more; until he was gone from the room, I dared scarcely lift my face lest he should read too much in it.

Alone, even, I felt uncomfortable, this seemed so sinister a business, and so ill begun. I was in the house. But Madame's frank voice haunted me, and the dumb man's eyes, full of suspicion and menace. When I presently got up and tried my door, I found it locked. The room smelt dank and close – like a vault. I could not see through the barred window, but I could hear the boughs sweep it in ghostly fashion; and I guessed that it looked out where the wood grew close to the walls of the house, and that even in the day the sun never peeped through it.

Nevertheless, tired and worn out, I slept at last. When I awoke the room was full of grey light, the door stood open, and Louis, looking ashamed of himself, waited by my pallet with a cup of wine in his hand, and some bread and fruit on a platter.

'Will Monsieur be good enough to rise?' he said. 'It is eight o'clock.'

'Willingly,' I answered tartly. 'Now that the door is unlocked.'

He turned red. 'It was an oversight,' he stammered. 'Clon is accustomed to lock the door, and he did it inadvertently, forgetting that there was anyone –'

'Inside,' I said drily.

'Precisely, Monsieur.'

'Ah!' I replied. 'Well, I do not think the oversight would please Madame de Cocheforêt if she heard of it?'

'If Monsieur would have the kindness not to –'

'Mention it, my good fellow?' I answered, looking at him with meaning as I rose. 'No. But it must not occur again.'

I saw that this man was not like Clon. He had the instincts of the family servant, and freed from the influences of fear and darkness felt ashamed of his conduct. While he arranged my clothes, he looked round the room with an air of distaste, and muttered once or twice that the furniture of the principal chambers was packed away.

'M. de Cocheforêt is abroad, I think?' I said as I dressed.

'And likely to remain there,' the man answered carelessly, shrugging his shoulders. 'Monsieur will doubtless have heard that he is in trouble. In the meantime, the house is *triste*, and Monsieur must overlook much, if he stays. Madame lives retired and the roads are ill-made and visitors few.'

'When the lion was ill the jackals left him,' I said.

Louis nodded. 'It is true,' he answered simply. He made no boast or brag on his own account, I noticed; and it came home to me that he was a faithful fellow, such as I love. I questioned him discreetly, and learned that he and Clon and an older man who lived over the stables were the only male servants left of a great household. Madame, her sister-in-law, and three women completed the family.

It took me some time to repair my wardrobe, so that I dare say it was nearly ten when I left my dismal little room. I found Louis waiting in the corridor, and he told me that Madame de Cocheforêt and Mademoiselle were in the rose garden, and would be pleased to receive me. I nodded, and he guided me through several dim passages to a parlour with an open door, through which the sun shone gaily on the floor. Cheered by the morning air and this sudden change to pleasantness and life, I stepped lightly out.

The two ladies were walking up and down a wide path which bisected the garden. The weeds grew rankly in the gravel under foot, the rose bushes which bordered the walk thrust their branches here and there in untrained freedom, a dark yew hedge which formed the background bristled with rough shoots and sadly needed trimming. But I did not see any of these things. The grace, the noble air, the distinction of the two women who paced slowly to meet me – and who shared all these qualities, greatly as they differed in others – left me no power to notice trifles.

Mademoiselle was a head shorter than her *belle sœur* – a slender woman and petite, with a beautiful face and a fair complexion; a woman wholly womanly. She walked with dignity, but beside Madame's stately figure she had an air almost childish. And it was characteristic of the two that Mademoiselle as they drew near to me regarded me with sorrowful attention, Madame with a grave smile.

I bowed low. They returned the salute. 'This is my sister,' Madame de Cocheforêt said, with a very slight air of condescension. 'Will you please to tell me your name, Monsieur?'

'I am M. de Barthe, a gentleman of Normandy,' I said, taking on impulse the name of my mother. My own, by a possibility, might be known.

Madame's face wore a puzzled look. 'I do not know that name I think,' she said thoughtfully. Doubtless she was going over in her mind all the names with which conspiracy had made her familiar.

'That is my misfortune, Madame,' I said humbly.

'Nevertheless I am going to scold you,' she rejoined, still eyeing me with some keenness. 'I am glad to see that you are none the worse for your adventure – but others may be. And you should have borne that in mind, sir.'

'I do not think that I hurt the man seriously,' I stammered.

'I do not refer to that,' she answered coldly. 'You know, or should know, that we are in disgrace here; that the Government regards us already with an evil eye, and that a very small thing would lead them to garrison the village, and perhaps oust us from the little the wars have left us. You should have known this, and considered it,' she continued. 'Whereas – I do not say that you are a braggart, M. de Barthe. But on this one occasion you seem to have played the part of one.'

'Madame, I did not think,' I stammered.

'Want of thought causes much evil,' she answered, smiling. 'However, I have spoken, and we trust that while you stay with us you will be more careful. For the rest, Monsieur,' she continued graciously, raising her hand to prevent me speaking, 'we do not know why you are here, or what plans you are pursuing. And we do not wish to know. It is enough that you are of our side. This house is at your service as long as you please to use it. And if we can aid you in any other way we will do so.'

'Madame!' I exclaimed; and there I stopped. I could say no more. The rose garden, with its air of neglect, the shadow of the quiet house that fell across it, the great yew hedge which backed it, and was the pattern of one under which I had played in childhood – all had points that pricked me. But the women's kindness, their unquestioning confidence, the noble air of hospitality which moved them! Against these and their placid beauty in its peaceful frame I had no shield, no defence. I turned away, and feigned to be overcome by gratitude.

'I have no words – to thank you!' I muttered presently. 'I am a little shaken this morning. I – pardon me.'

'We will leave you for a while,' Mademoiselle de Cocheforêt said in gentle pitying tones. 'The air will revive you. Louis shall call you when we go to dinner, M. de Barthe. Come, Elise.'

I bowed low to hide my face, and they nodded pleasantly – not looking closely at me – as they walked by me to the house. I watched the two gracious, pale-robed figures until the doorway swallowed them, and then I walked away to a quiet corner where the shrubs grew highest and the yew hedge threw its deepest shadow, and I stood to think.

And, *mon Dieu!* strange thoughts. If the oak can think at the moment the wind uproots it, or the gnarled thorn-bush when the landslip tears it from the slope, they may have such thoughts. I stared at the leaves, at the rotting blossoms, into the dark cavities of the hedge; I stared mechanically, dazed and wondering. What was the purpose for which I was here? What was the work I had come to do? Above all, how – my God! how was I to do it in the face of these helpless women, who trusted me, who believed in me, who opened their house to me? Clon had not frightened me, nor the loneliness of the leagued village, nor the remoteness of this corner where the dread Cardinal seemed a name, and the King's writ ran slowly, and the rebellion, long quenched elsewhere, still smouldered. But Madame's pure faith, the younger woman's tenderness – how I was to face these?

I cursed the Cardinal – would he had stayed at Luchon. I cursed the English fool who had brought me to this, I cursed the years of plenty and scarceness, and the Quartier Marais, and Zaton's, where I had lived like a pig, and –

A touch fell on my arm. I turned. It was Clon. How he had stolen up so quietly, how long he had been at my elbow, I could not tell. But his eyes gleamed spitefully in their deep sockets, and he laughed with his fleshless lips; and I hated him. In the daylight the man looked more like a death's-head than ever. I fancied that I read in his face that he knew my secret, and I flashed into rage at sight of him.

'What is it?' I cried, with another oath. 'Don't lay your corpse-claws on me!'

He mowed at me, and, bowing with ironical politeness, pointed to the house.

'Is Madame served?' I said impatiently, crushing down my anger. 'Is that what you mean, fool?'

He nodded.

'Very well,' I retorted. 'I can find my way then. You may go!'

He fell behind, and I strode back through the sunshine and flowers, and along the grass-grown paths, to the door by which I had come. I walked fast but his shadow kept pace with me, driving out the unaccustomed thoughts in which I had been indulging. Slowly but surely it darkened my mood. After all, this was a little, little place; the people who lived here – I shrugged my shoulders. France, power, pleasure, life, everything worth winning, worth having, lay yonder in the great city. A boy might wreck himself here for a fancy; a man of the world, never. When I entered the room, where the two ladies stood waiting for me by the table, I was nearly my old self again. And a chance word presently completed the work.

'Clon made you understand, then?' the young woman said kindly, as I took my seat.

'Yes, Mademoiselle,' I answered. On that I saw the two smile at one another, and I added: 'He is a strange creature. I wonder that you can bear to have him near you.'

'Poor man! You do not know his story?' Madame said.

'I have heard something of it,' I answered. 'Louis told me.'

'Well, I do shudder at him sometimes,' she replied, in a low voice. 'He has suffered – and horribly, and for us. But I wish that it had been on any other service. Spies are necessary things, but one does not wish to have to do with them. Anything in the nature of treachery is so horrible.'

'Quick, Louis!' Mademoiselle exclaimed, 'the cognac, if you have any there! I am sure that you are – still feeling ill, Monsieur.'

'No, I thank you,' I muttered hoarsely, making an effort to recover myself. 'I am quite well. It was – an old wound that sometimes touches me.'

4

Madame and Mademoiselle

TO be frank, however, it was not the old would that touched me so nearly, but Madame's words; which, finishing what Clon's sudden appearance in the garden had begun, went a long way towards hardening me and throwing me back into myself. I saw with bitterness – what I had perhaps forgotten for a moment – how great was the chasm that separated me from these women; how impossible it was that we could long think alike; how far apart in views, in experience, in aims we were. And while I made a mock in my heart of their high-flown sentiments – or thought I did – I laughed no less at the folly which had led me to dream, even for a moment, that I could, at my age, go back – go back and risk all for a whim, a scruple, the fancy of a lonely hour.

I dare say something of this showed in my face; for Madame's eyes mirrored a dim reflection of trouble as she looked at me, and Mademoiselle talked nervously and at random. At any rate, I fancied so, and I hastened to compose myself; and the two, in pressing upon me the simple dianties of the table soon forgot, or appeared to forget, the incident.

Yet in spite of this *contretemps*, that first meal had a strange charm for me. The round table wherat we dined was spread inside the open door which led to the garden, so that the October sunshine fell full on the spotless linen and quaint old plate, and the fresh balmy air filled the room with the scent of sweet herbs. Louis served us with the mien of a major-domo, and set on each dish as though it had been a peacock or a mess of ortolans. The woods provided the larger portion of our meal; the garden did its part; the confections Mademoiselle had cooked with her own hand.

By and by, as the meal went on, as Louis trod to and fro across the polished floor, and the last insects of summer hummed sleepily outside, and the two gracious faces continued to smile at me out of the gloom – for the ladies sat with their backs to the door – I began to dream again. I began to sink again into folly, that was half-pleasure, half-pain. The fury of the gaming-house and the riot of Zaton's seemed far away. The triumphs of the fencing-room – even they grew cheap and tawdry. I thought of existence as one outside it. I balanced this against that, and wondered whether, after all, the red soutane were so much better than the homely jerkin, or the fame of a day than ease and safety.

And life at Cocheforêt was all after the pattern of this dinner. Each day, I might almost say each meal, gave rise to the same sequence of thoughts. In Clon's presence, or when some word of Madame's, unconsciously harsh, reminded me of the distance between us, I was myself. At other times, in face of this peaceful and intimate life, which was only rendered possible by the remoteness of the place and the peculiar circumstances in which the ladies stood, I felt a strange weakness. The loneliness of the woods that encircled the house, and only here and there afforded a distant glimpse of snow-clad peaks; the absence of any link to blind me to the old life, so that at intervals it seemed unreal; the remoteness of the great world, all tended to sap my will and weaken the purpose which had brought me to this place.

On the fourth day after my coming, however, something happened to break the spell. It chanced that I came late to dinner, and entered the room hastily and without ceremony, expecting to find Madame and her sister already seated. Instead, I found them talking in a low tone by the open door, with every mark of disorder in their appearance; while Clon and Louis stood at a little distance with downcast faces and perplexed looks.

I had time to see all this, and then my entrance wrought a sudden change. Clon and Louis sprang to attention; Madame and her sister came to the table and sat down; and all made a shallow pretence of being at their ease. But Mademoiselle's face was pale, her hand trembled; and thought Madame's greater self-command enabled her to carry off the matter better, I saw that she was not herself. Once or twice she spoke harshly to Louis; she fell at other times into a brown study; and when she thought that I was not watching her face wore a look of deep anxiety.

I wondered what all this meant; and I wondered more when, after the meal, the two walked in the garden for an hour with Clon. Mademoiselle came from this interview alone, and I was sure that she had been weeping. Madame and the dark porter stayed outside some time longer; then she, too, came in, and disappeared.

Clon did not return with her, and when I went into the garden five minutes later, Louis also had vanished. Save for two women who sat sewing at an upper window, the house seemed to be deserted. Not a sound broke the afternoon stillness of room or garden, and yet I felt that more was happening in this silence than appeared on the surface. I began to grow curious – suspicious, and presently slipped out myself by way of the stables, and skirting the wood at the back of the house, gained with a little trouble the bridge which crossed the stream and led to the village.

Turning round at this point I could see the house, and I moved a little aside into the underwood, and stood gazing at the windows, trying to unriddle the matter. It was not likely that M. de Cocheforêt would repeat his visit so soon; and, besides, the women's emotions had been those of pure dismay and grief, unmixed with any of the satisfaction to which such a meeting, though snatched by stealth, must give rise. I discarded my first thought therefore – that he had returned unexpectedly – and I sought for another solution.

But no other was on the instant forthcoming. The windows remained obstinately blind, no figures appeared on the terrace, the garden lay deserted, and without life. My departure had not, as I half expected it would, drawn the secret into light.

I watched awhile, at times cursing my own meanness; but the excitement of the moment and the quest tided me over that. Then I determined to go down into the village and see whether anything was moving there. I had been down to the inn once, and had been received half sulkily, half courteously, as a person privileged at the great house, and therefore to be accepted. It would not be thought odd if I went again, and after a moment's thought I started down the track.

This, where it ran through the wood, was so densely shaded that the sun penetrated to it little, and in patches only. A squirrel stirred at times, sliding round a trunk or scampering across the dry leaves. Occasionally a pig grunted and moved farther into the wood. But the place was very quiet, and I do not know how it was that I surprised Clon instead of being surprised by him.

He was walking along the path before me with his eyes on the ground – walking so slowly, and with his lean frame so bent that I might have supposed him ill if I had not remarked the steady movement of his head from right to left, and the alert touch with which he now and again displaced a clod of earth or a cluster of leaves. By and by the rose stiffly, and looked round him suspiciously; but by that time I had slipped behind a trunk, and was not to be seen; and after a brief interval he went back to his task, stooping over it more closely, if possible, than before, and applying himself with even greater care.

By that time I had made up my mind that he was tracking someone. But whom? I could not make a guess at that. I only knew that the plot was thickening, and began to feel the eagerness of the chase. Of course, if the matter had not to do with Cocheforêt, it was no affair of mine; but though it seemed unlikely that anything could bring him back so soon, he might still be at the bottom of this. And, besides, I felt a natural curiosity. When Clon at last improved his pace, and went on to the village, I took up his task. I called to mind all the wood-lore I had ever learned, and scanned trodden mould and crushed leaves with eager eyes. But in vain. I could make nothing of it all, and rose at last with an aching back and no advantage.

I did not go on to the village after that, but returned to the house, where I found Madame pacing the garden. She looked up eagerly on hearing my step; and I was mistaken if she was not disappointed – if she had not been expecting someone else. She hid the feeling bravely, however, and met me with a careless word; but she turned to the house more than once while we talked, and she seemed to be all the while on the watch, and uneasy. I was not surprised when Clon's figure presently appeared in the doorway, and she left me abruptly, and went to him. I only felt more certain than before that there was something strange on foot. What it was, and whether it had to do with M. de Cocheforêt, I could not tell. But there is was, and I grew more curious the longer I remained alone.

She came back to me presently, looking thoughtful and a trifle downcast.

'That was Clon, was is not?' I said, studying her face.

'Yes,' she answered. She spoke absently, and did not look at me.

'How does he talk to you?' I asked, speaking a trifle curtly.

As I intended, my tone roused her.

'By signs,' she said

'Is he – is he not a little mad?' I ventured. I wanted to make her talk and forget herself.

She looked at me with sudden keenness, then dropped her eyes.

'You do not like him?' she said, a note of challenge in her voice. 'I have noticed that, Monsieur.'

'I think he does not like me,' I replied.

'He is less trustful than we are,' she answered naïvely. 'It is natural that he should be. He has seen more of the world.'

That silenced me for a moment, but she did not seem to notice it.

'I was looking for him a little while ago, and I could not find him,' I said, after a pause.

'He has been into the village,' she answered.

I longed to pursue the matter further; but though she seemed to entertain no suspicion of me, I dared not run the risk. I tried her, instead, on another tack.

'Mademoiselle de Cocheforêt does not seem very well to-day?' I said.

'No?' she answered carelessly. 'Well, now you speak of it, I do not think that she is. She is often anxious about – one we love.'

She uttered the last words with a little hesitation, and looked at me quickly when she had spoken them. We were sitting at the moment on a stone seat which had the wall of the house for a back; and, fortunately, I was toying with the branch of a creeping plant that hung over it, so that she could not see more than the side of my face. For I knew that it altered. Over my voice, however, I had more control, and I hastened to answer, 'Yes, I suppose so,' as innocently as possible.

'He is at Bosost, in Spain. You knew that, I conclude?' she said, with a certain sharpness. And she looked me in the face again very directly.

'Yes,' I answered, beginning to tremble.

'I suppose you have heard, too, that he – that he sometimes crosses the border?' she continued in a low voice, but with a certain ring of insistence in her tone. 'Or, if you have not heard it, you guess it?'

I was in a quandary, and grew, in one second, hot all over. Uncertain what amount of knowledge I ought to admit, I took refuge in gallantry.

'I should be surprised if he did not,' I answered , with a bow, 'being, as he is, so close, and having such an inducement to return, Madame.'

She drew a long, shivering sigh, at the thought of his peril, I fancied, and she sat back against the wall. Nor did she say any more, though I heard her sigh again. In a moment she rose.

'The afternoons are growing chilly,' she said; 'I will go in and see how Mademoiselle is. Sometimes she does not come to supper. If she cannot descend this evening, I am afraid that you must excuse me too, Monsieur.'

I said what was right, and watched her go in; and as I did so, I loathed my errand, and the mean contemptible curiosity which it had planted in my mind, more than at any former time. These women – I could find it in my heart to hate them for their frankness, for their foolish confidence, and the silly trustfulness that made them so easy a prey!

Nom de Dieu! What did the woman mean by telling me all this? To meet me in such a way, to disarm one by such methods, was to take an unfair advantage. It put a vile – ay, the vilest – aspect on the work I had to do.

Yet it was very odd! What could M. de Chocheforêt mean by returning so soon, if M. de Cocheforêt was here? And, on the other hand, if it was not his unexpected presence that had so upset the house, what was the secret? Whom had Clon been tracking? And what was the cause of Madame's anxiety? In a few minutes I began to grow curious again; and, as the ladies did not appear at supper, I had leisure to give my brain full licence, and, in the course of an hour, thought of a hundred keys to the mystery. But none exactly fitted the lock, or laid open the secret.

A false alarm that evening helped to puzzle me still more. I was sitting about an hour after supper on the same seat in the garden – I had my cloak and was smoking – when Madame came out like a ghost, and, without seeing me, flitted away through the darkness towards the stables. For a moment I hesitated, and then I followed her. She went down the path and round the stables, and, so far, I saw nothing strange in her actions; but when she had in his way gained the rear of the west wing, she took a track through the thicket to the east of the house again, and so came back to the garden. This gained, she came up the path and went in through the parlour door, and disappeared – after making a clear circuit of the house, and not once pausing or looking to right or left! I confess I was fairly baffled. I sank back on the seat I had left, and said to myself that this was the lamest of all conclusions. I was sure that she had exchanged no word with anyone. I was equally sure that she had not detected my presence behind her. Why, then, had she made this strange promenade, alone, unprotected, an hour after nightfall? No dog had bayed, no one had moved, she had not once paused, or listened, like a person expecting a rencontre. I could not make it out. And I came no nearer to solving it, though I lay awake an hour beyond my usual time.

In the morning, neither of the ladies descended to dinner, and I heard that Mademoiselle was not so well. After a lonely meal, therefore – I missed them more than I should have supposed – I retired to my favourite seat and fell to meditating.

The day was fine, and the garden pleasant. Sitting there with my eyes on the old-fashioned herb-beds, with the old-fashioned scents in the air, and the dark belt of trees bounding the view on either side, I could believe that I had been out of Paris not three weeks, but three months. The quiet lapped me round. I could fancy that I had never loved anything else. The wood-doves cooed in the stillness; occasionally the harsh cry of a jay jarred the silence. It was an hour after noon, and hot. I think I nodded.

On a sudden, as if in a dream, I saw Clon's face peering at me round the angle of the parlour door. He looked, and in a moment withdrew, and I heard whispering. The door was gently closed. Then all was still again.

But I was wide awake now, and thinking. Clearly the people of the house wished to assure themselves that I was asleep and safely out of the way. As clearly, it was to my interest to be in the way. Giving place to the temptation, I rose quietly, and stooping below the level of the windows, slipped round the east end of the house, passing between it and the great yew hedge. Here I found all still and no one stirring; so, keeping a wary eye about me, I went on round the house – reversing the route which Madame had taken the night before – until I gained the rear of the stables. Here I had scarcely paused a second to scan the ground before two persons came out of the stable-court. They were Madame and the porter.

They stood a brief while outside and looked up and down. Then Madame said something to the man, and he nodded. Leaving him standing where he was, she crossed the grass with a quick, light step, and vanished among the trees.

In a moment my mind was made up to follow and, as Clon turned at once and went in, I was able to do so before it was too late. Bending low among the shrubs, I ran hot-foot to the point where Madame had entered the wood. Here I found a narrow path, and ran nimbly along it, and presently saw her grey robe fluttering among the trees before me. It only remained to keep out of her sight and give her no chance of discovering that she was followed; and this I set myself to do. Once or twice she glanced round, but the wood was of beech, the light which passed between the leaves was mere twilight, and my clothes were dark-coloured. I had every advantage, therefore, and little to fear as long as I could keep her in view and still remain myself at such a distance that the rustle of my tread would not disturb her.

Assured that she was on her way to meet her husband, whom my presence kept from the house, I felt that the crisis had come at last, and I grew more excited with each step I took. I detested the task of watching her; it filled me with peevish disgust. But in proportion as I hated it I was eager to have it done and be done with it, and succeed, and stuff my ears and begone from the scene. When she presently came to the verge of the beech wood, and, entering a little open clearing, seemed to loiter, I went cautiously. This, I thought, must be the rendezvous; and I held back warily, looking to see him step out of the thicket.

But he did not, and by and by she quickened her pace. She crossed the open and entered a wide ride cut through a low, dense wood of alder and dwarf oak – a wood so closely planted and so interwined with hazel and elder and box that the branches rose like a solid wall, twelve feet high, on either side of the track.

Down this she passed, and I stood and watched her go, for I dared not follow. The ride stretched away as straight as a line for four or five hundred yards, a green path between green walls. To enter it was to be immediately detected, if she turned; while the thicket itself permitted no passage. I stood, baffled and raging, and watched her pass along. It seemed an age before she at last reached the end, and, turning sharply to the right, was in an instant gone from sight.

I waited then no longer. I started off, and, running as lightly and quietly as I could, I sped down the green alley. The sun shone into it, the trees kept off the wind, and between heat and haste I sweated finely. But the turf was soft, and the ground fell slightly, and in little more than a minute I gained the end. Fifty yards short of the turning I stopped, and, stealing on, looked cautiously the way she had gone.

I saw before me a second ride, the twin of the other, and a hundred and fifty paces down it her grey figure tripping on between the green hedges. I stood and took breath, and cursed the wood and the heat and Madame's wariness. We must have come a league, or two-thirds of a league, at least. How far did the man expect her to plod to meet him? I began to grow angry. There is moderation even in the cooking of eggs, and this wood might stretch into Spain, for all I knew!

Presently she turned the corner and was gone again, and I had to repeat my manœuvre. This time, surely, I should find a change. But no! Another green ride stretched away into the depths of the forest, with hedges of varying shades – here light and there dark, as hazel and elder, or thorn, and yew and box prevailed – but always high and stiff and impervious. Half-way down the ride Madame's figure tripped steadily on, the only moving thing in sight. I wondered, stood, and, when she vanished, followed – only to find that she had entered another track, a little narrower but in every other respect alike.

And so it went on for quite half an hour. Sometimes Madame turned to the right, sometimes to the left. The maze seemed to be endless. Once or twice I wondered whether she had lost her way, and was merely seeking to return. But her steady, purposeful gait, her measured pace, forbade the idea. I noticed, too, that she seldom looked behind her – rarely to right or left. Once the ride down which she passed was carpeted, not with green, but with the silvery, sheeny leaves of some creeping plant that in the distance had a shimmer like that of water at evening. As she trod this, with her face to the low sun, her tall grey figure had a pure air that for the moment startled me – she looked unearthly. Then I swore in scorn of myself, and at the next corner I had my reward. She was no longer walking on. She had stopped, I found, and seated herself on a fallen tree that lay in the ride.

For some time I stood in ambush watching her, and with each minute I grew more impatient. At last I began to doubt – to have strange thoughts. The green walls were growing dark. The sun was sinking; a sharp, white peak, miles and miles away, which closed the vista of the ride, began to flush and colour rosily. Finally, but not before I had had leisure to grow uneasy, she stood up and walked on more slowly. I waited, as usual, until the next turning hid her. Then I hastened after her and, warily passing round the corner – came face to face with her!

I knew all in a moment – saw all in a flash: that she had fooled me, tricked me, lured me away. Her face was white with scorn; her eyes blazed; her figure as she confronted me, trembled with anger and infinite contempt.

'You spy!' she cried. 'You hound! You – gentleman! Oh, *mon Dieu!* if you are one of us – if you are really not of the canaille – we shall pay for this some day! We shall pay a heavy reckoning in the time to come! I did not think,' she continued, and her every syllable was like the lash of a whip, 'that there was anything so vile as you in this world!'

I stammered something – I do not know what. Her words burned into me – into my heart! Had she been a man, I would have struck her dead!

'You thought that you deceived me yesterday,' she continued, lowering her tone, but with no lessening of the passion, the contempt, the indignation, which curled her lip and gave fullness to her voice. 'You plotter! You surface trickster! You thought it an easy task to delude a woman – you find yourself deluded. God give you shame that you may suffer!' she continued mercilessly. 'You talked of Clon, but Clon before you is the most spotless, the most honourable of men!'

'Madame,' I said hoarsely – and I know that my face was grey as ashes – 'let us understand one another.'

'God forbid!' She cried on the instant. 'I would not soil myself!'

'Fie! Madame,' I said, trembling. 'But then you are a woman. That should cost a man his life.'

She laughed bitterly.

'You say well,' she retorted. 'I am not a man – and if you are one, thank God for it. Neither am I Madame. Madame de Cocheforêt has spent this afternoon – thanks to your absence and your imbecility – with her husband. Yes, I hope that hurts you!' she went on, savagely snapping her little white teeth together. 'I hope that stings you; to spy and to vile work, and do it ill, Monsieur Mouchard – Monsieur de Mouchard, I should say – I congratulate you!'

'You are not Madame de Cocheforêt?' I cried, stunned, even in the midst of my shame and rage, by this blow.

'No, Monsieur!' she answered grimly. 'I am not! I am not. And permit me to point out – for we do not all lie easily – that I never said I was. You deceived yourself, so skilfully that we had no need to trick you.'

'Mademoiselle, then?' I muttered.

'Is Madame!' she cried. 'Yes, and I am Mademoiselle de Cocheforêt. And in that character, and in all other, I beg from this moment to close our acquaintance, sir. When we meet again – if we ever do meet, which God forbid!' she went on, her eyes sparkling – 'do not presume to speak to me, or I will have you flogged by the grooms. And do not stain our roof by sleeping under it again. You may lie to-night in the inn. It shall not be said that Cocheforêt,' she continued proudly, 'returned even treachery with inhospitality; and I will give orders to that end. But to-morrow begone back to your master, like the whipped cur you are! Spy and coward!'

With those last words she moved away. I would have said something, I could almost have found it in my heart to stop her and make her hear. Nay, I had dreadful thoughts; for I was the stronger, and I might have done with her as I pleased. But she swept by me so fearlessly, as I might pass some loathsome cripple on the road, that I stood turned to stone. Without looking at me, without turning her head to see whether I followed or remained, or what I did, she went steadily down the track until the trees and the shadow and the growing darkness hid her grey figure from me; and I found myself alone.

5

Revenge

AND full of black rage! Had she only reproached me, or, turning on me in the hour of *my* victory, said all that she had now said in the moment of her own, I could have borne it.

She might have shamed me then, and I might have taken the shame to myself and forgiven her. But, as it was, I stood there in the gathering dusk, between the darkening hedges, baffled, tricked, defeated! And by a woman! She had pitted her wits against mine, her woman's will against my experience, and she had come off the victor. And then she had reviled me! As I took it all in, and began to comprehend also the more remote results, and how completely her move had made further progress on my part impossible, I hated her. She had tricked me with her gracious ways and her slow-coming smile. And, after all – for what she had said – it was this man's life or mine. What had I done that another man would not do? *Mon Dieu!* in the future there was nothing I would not do. I would make her smart for those words of hers! I would bring her to her knees!

Still, hot as I was, an hour might have restored me to coolness. But when I started to return, I fell into a fresh rage, for I remembered that I did not know my way out of the maze of rides and paths into which she had drawn me; and this, and the mishaps which followed, kept my rage hot. For a full hour I wandered in the wood, unable, though I knew where the village lay, to find any track which led continuously in one direction. Whenever, at the end of each attempt, the thicket brought me up short, I fancied that I heard her laughing on the farther side of the brake; and the ignominy of this chance punishment, and the check which the confinement placed on my rage, almost maddened me. In the darkness I fell, and rose cursing; I tore my hands with thorns; I stained my suit, which had suffered sadly once before. At length, when I had almost resigned myself to lie in the wood, I caught sight of the lights of the village, and, trembling between haste and anger, pressed towards them. In a few minutes I stood in the little street.

The lights of the inn shone only fifty yards away; but before I could show myself even there pride suggested that I should do something to repair my clothes. I stopped, and scraped and brushed them; and, at the same time, did what I could to compose my features. Then I advanced to the door and knocked. Almost on the instant the landlord's voice cried from the inside, 'Enter, Monsieur!'

I raised the latch and went in. The man was alone, squatting over the fire warming his hands. A black pot simmered on the ashes. As I entered he raised the lid and peeped inside. Then he glanced over his shoulder.

'You expected me?' I said defiantly, walking to the hearth and setting one of my damp boots on the logs.

'Yes,' he answered, nodding curtly. 'Your supper is just ready. I thought that you would be in about this time.'

He grinned as he spoke, and it was with difficulty I suppressed my wrath.

'Mademoiselle de Cocheforêt told you,' I said, affecting indifference, 'where I was?'

'Ay, Mademoiselle – or Madame,' he replied, grinning afresh.

So she had told him: where she had left me, and how she had tricked me! She had made me the village laughing-stock! My rage flashed out afresh at the thought, and, at the sight of his mocking face, I raised my fist.

But he read the threat in my eyes, and was up in a moment, snarling, with his hand on his knife.

'Not again, Monsieur!' he cried in his vile patois. 'My head is sore still. Raise your hand and I will rip you up as I would a pig!'

'Sit down, fool,' I said. 'I am not going to harm you. Where is your wife?'

'About her business.'

'Which should be getting my supper,' I retorted.

He rose sullenly, and, fetching a platter, poured the mess of broth and vegetables into it. Then he went to a cupboard and brought out a loaf of black bread and a measure of wine, and set them also on the table.

'You see it,' he said laconically.

'And a poor welcome!' I replied.

He flamed into sudden passion at that. Leaning with both his hands on the table he thrust his rugged face and blood-shot eyes close to mine. His moustachios bristled, his beard trembled.

'Hark ye, sirrah!' he muttered, with sullen emphasis, 'be content! I have my suspicions. And if it were not for my lady's orders I would put a knife into you, fair or foul, this very night. You would lie snug outside, instead of inside, and I do not think anyone would be the worse. But as it is, be content. Keep a still tongue; and when you turn your back on Cocheforêt to-morrow keep it turned.'

'Tut! tut!' I said – but I confess that I was a little out of countenance. 'Threatened men live long, you rascal!'

'In Paris!' he answered significantly. 'Not here, Monsieur.'

He straightened himself with that, nodded once, and went back to the fire; and I shrugged my shoulders and began to eat, affecting to forget his presence. The logs on the hearth burned sullenly, and gave no light. The poor oil-lamp, casting weird shadows from wall to wall, served only to discover the darkness. The room, with its low roof and earthen floor, and foul clothes flung here and there, reeked of stale meals and garlic and vile cooking. I thought of the parlour at Coche-forêt, and the dainty table, and the stillness, and the scented pot-herbs; and though I was too old a soldier to eat the worse because my spoon lacked washing, I felt the change, and laid it savagely at Mademoiselle's door.

The landlord, watching me stealthily from his place by the hearth, read my thoughts and chuckled aloud.

'Palace fare, palace manners!' he muttered scornfully. 'Set a beggar on horse-back, and he will ride – back to the inn.'

'Keep a civil tongue, will you!' I answered, scowling at him.

'Have you finished?' he retorted.

I rose, without deigning to reply, and, going to the fire, drew off my boots, which were wet through. He, on the instant, swept off the wine and loaf to the cupboard, and then, coming back for the platter I had used, took it, opened the back door, and went out, leaving the door ajar. The draught which came in beat the flame of the lamp this way and that, and gave the dingy, gloomy room an air still more miserable. I rose angrily from the fire, and went to the door intending to close it with a bang.

But when I reached it, I saw something, between door and jamb, which stayed my hand. The door led to a shed in which the housewife washed pots and the like. I felt some surprise, therefore, when I found a light there at this time of night; still more surprise when I saw what she was doing.

She was seated on the mud floor, with a rushlight before her, and on either side of her a high-piled heap of refuse and rubbish. From one of these, at the moment I caught sight of her, she was sorting things –

horrible filthy sweepings of road or floor – to the other; shaking and sifting each article as she passed it across, and then taking up another and repeating the action with it, and so on – all minutely, warily, with an air of so much patience and persistence that I stood wondering. Some things – rags – she held up between her eyes and the light, some she passed through her fingers, some she fairly tore in pieces. And all the time her husband stood watching her greedily, my platter still in his hand, as if her strange occupation fascinated him.

I stood looking, also, for half a minute, perhaps; then the man's eye, raised for a single second to the doorway, met mine. He started, muttered something to his wife, and, quick as thought, he kicked the light out, leaving the shed in darkness. Cursing him for an illconditioned fellow, I walked back to the fire, laughing. In a twinkling he followed me, his face dark with rage.

'*Ventre-saint-Gris!*' he exclaimed, thrusting himself close to me. 'Is not a man's house his own?'

'It is, for me,' I answered coolly, shrugging my shoulders. 'And his wife: if she likes to pick dirty rags at this hour, that is your affair.'

'Pig of a spy!' he cried, foaming with rage. I was angry enough at bottom, but I had nothing to gain by quarrelling with the fellow, and I curtly bade him remember himself.

'Your mistress gave you orders,' I said contemptuously. 'Obey them.'

He spat on the floor, but at the same time he grew calmer.

'You are right there,' he answered spitefully. 'What matter, after all, since you leave to-morrow at six? Your horse has been sent down, and your baggage is above.'

'I will go to it,' I retorted. 'I want none of your company. Give me a light, fellow!'

He obeyed reluctantly, and, glad to turn my back on him, I went up the ladder, still wondering faintly, in the midst of my annoyance, what his wife was about that my chance detection of her had so enraged him. Even now he was not quite himself. He followed me with abuse, and deprived by my departure of any other means of showing his spite, fell to shouting through the floor, bidding me remember six o'clock, and be stirring; with other taunts, which did not cease until he had tired himself out.

The sight of my belongings – which I had left a few hours before at the Château – strewn about the floor of this garret, went some way towards firing me again. But I was worn out. The indignities and mishaps of the evening had, for once, crushed my spirit, and after swearing an oath or two I began to pack my bags. Vengeance I would have; but the time and manner I left for daylight thought. Beyond six o'clock in the morning I did not look forward; and if I longed for anything it was for a little of the good Armagnac I had wasted on those louts of merchants in the kitchen below. It might have done me good now.

I had wearily strapped up one bag, and nearly filled the other, when I came upon something which did, for the moment, rouse the devil in me. This was the tiny orange-coloured sachet which Mademoiselle had dropped the night I first saw her at the inn, and which, it will be remembered, I picked up. Since that night I had not seen it, and had as good as forgotten it. Now, as I folded up my other doublet, the one I had then been wearing, it dropped from my pocket.

The sight of it recalled all – that night, and Mademoiselle's face in the lantern light, and my fine plans, and the end of them; and, in a fit of childish fury, the outcome of long-suppressed passion, I snatched up the sachet from the floor and tore it across and across, and flung the pieces down. As they fell, a cloud of fine pungent dust burst from them, and with the dust, something more solid, which tinkled sharply on the boards as it fell. I looked down to see what this was – perhaps I already repented of my act; but for a moment I could see nothing. The floor was grimy and uninviting, the light bad.

In certain moods, however, a man is obstinate about small things, and I moved the taper nearer. As I did so a point of light, a flashing sparkle that shone for a second among the dirt and refuse on the floor, caught my eye. It was gone in a moment, but I had seen it. I stared, and moved the light again, and the spark flashed out afresh, this time in a different place. Much puzzled, I knelt, and, in a twinkling, found a tiny crystal. Hard by it lay another – and another; each as large as a fair-sized pea. I took up the three, and rose to my feet again, the light in one hand, the crystals in the palm of the other.

They were diamonds! Diamonds of price! I knew it in a moment. As I moved the taper to and fro above them, and watched the fire glow and tremble in their depths, I knew that I held in my hand that which would buy the crazy inn and all its contents a dozen times over! They were diamonds! Gems so fine, and of so rare a water – or I had never seen gems – that my hand trembled as I held them, and my head grew hot and my heart beat furiously. For a moment I thought that I dreamed, that my fancy played me some trick; and I closed my eyes and did not open them again for a minute. But when I did, there they were, hard, real, and angular. Convinced at last, in a maze of joy and fear, I closed my hand upon them and, stealing on tiptoe to the trap-door, laid first my saddle on it and then my bags, and over all my cloak, breathing fast the while.

Then I stole back, and, taking up the light again, began to search the floor, patiently, inch by inch, with naked feet, every sound making me tremble as I crept hither and thither over the creaking boards. And never was search more successful or better paid. In the fragments of the sachet I found six smaller diamonds and a pair of rubies. Eight large diamonds I found on the floor. One, the largest and last found, had bounded away, and lay against the wall in the farthest corner. It took me an hour to run that one to earth; but afterwards I spent another hour on my hands and knees before I gave up the search, and, satisfied at last that I had collected all, sat down on my saddle on the trap-door, and, by the last flickering light of a candle which I had taken from my bag, gloated over my treasure – a treasure worthy of fabled Golconda.

Hardly could I believe in its reality, even now. Recalling the jewels which the English Duke of Buckingham wore on the occasion of his visit to Paris in 1625, and whereof there was so much talk, I took these to be as fine, though less in number. They should be worth fifteen thousand crowns, more or less. Fifteen thousand crowns! And I held them in the hollow of my hand – I, who was scarcely worth ten thousand sous.

The candle going out cut short my admiration. Left in the dark with these precious atoms, my first thought was how I might dispose of them safely; which I did, for the time, by secreting them in the lining of my boot. My second thought turned on the question how they had come where I had found them, among the powdered spice and perfumes in Mademoiselle de Cocheforêt's sachet.

A minute's reflections enabled me to come very near the secret, and at the same time shed a flood of light on several dark places. What Clon had been seeking on the path between the house and the village, what the goodwife of the inn had sought among the sweepings of yard and floor, I knew now – the sachet. I knew, too, what had caused the marked and sudden anxiety I had noticed at the Château – the loss of this sachet.

And there for a while I came to a check. But one step more up the ladder of thought brought all in view. In a flash I guessed how the jewels had come to be in the sachet; and that it was not Mademoiselle but M. de Cocheforêt who had mislaid them. I thought this last discovery so important that I began to pace the room softly, unable, in my excitement, to remain still.

Doubtless he had dropped the jewels in the hurry of his start from the inn that night! Doubtless, too, he had carried them in that bizarre hiding-place for the sake of safety, considering it unlikely that robbers, if he fell into their hands, would take the sachet from him; as still less likely that they would suspect it to contain anything of value. Everywhere it would pass for a love-gift, the work of his mistress.

Nor did my penetration stop there. I guessed that the gems were family property, the last treasure of the house; and that M. de Cocheforêt, when I saw him at the inn, was on his way to convey them out of the country; either to secure them from seizure by the Government or to raise money by selling them – money to be spent in some last desperate enterprise. For a day or two, perhaps, after leaving Cocheforêt, while the mountain road and its chances occupied his thoughts, he had not discovered his loss. Then he had searched for the precious sachet, missed it, and returned hot-foot on his tracks.

The longer I considered the circumstances the more certain I was that I had hit on the true solution; and all that night I sat wakeful in the darkness, pondering what I should do. The stones, unset as they were, could never be identified, never be claimed. The channel by which they had come to my hands could never be traced. To all intents they were mine; mine, to do with as I pleased! Fifteen thousand crowns, perhaps twenty thousand crowns, and I to leave at six in the morning, whether I would or no! I might leave for Spain with the jewels in my pocket. Why not?

I confess I was tempted. And indeed the gems were so fine that I doubt not some indifferently honest men would have sold salvation for them. But – a Berault his honour? No. I was tempted, I say; but not for long. Thank God, a man may be reduced to living by the fortunes of the dice, and may even be called by a woman 'spy' and 'coward', without becoming a thief! The temptation soon left me – I take credit for it – and I fell to thinking of this and that plan for making use of them. Once it occurred to me to take the jewels to the Cardinal and buy my pardon with them; again, to use them as a trap to capture Cocheforêt; again, to – and then, about five in the morning, as I sat up on my wretched pallet, while the first light stole slowly in through the cobwebbed, hay-stuffed lattice, there came to me the real plan, the plan of plans, on which I acted.

It charmed me. I smacked my lips over it, and hugged myself, and felt my eyes dilate in the darkness, as I conned it. It seemed cruel, it seemed mean; I cared nothing. Mademoiselle had boasted of her victory over me, of her woman's wits and her acuteness; and of my dullness. She had said that her grooms should flog me. She had rated me as if I had been a dog. Very well; we would see now whose brains were the better, whose was the master mind, whose should be the whipping.

The one thing required by my plan was that I should get speech with her; that done, I could trust myself and my new-found weapon for the rest. But that was absolutely necessary, and, seeing that there might be some difficulty about it, I determined to descend as if my mind were made up to go; then, on pretence of saddling my horse, I would slip away on foot, and lie in wait near the Château until I saw her come out. Or if I could not effect my purpose in that way – either by reason of the landlord's vigilance, or for any other cause – my course was still easy. I would ride away, and when I had proceeded a mile or so, tie up my horse in the forest and return to the wooden bridge. Thence I could watch the garden and front of the Château until time and chance gave me the opportunity I sought.

So I saw my way quite clearly; and when the fellow below called me, reminding me rudely that I must be going, and that it was six o'clock, I was ready with my answer. I shouted sulkily that I was coming, and, after a decent delay, I took up my saddle and bags and went down.

Viewed by the light of a cold morning, the inn room looked more smoky, more grimy, more wretched than when I had last seen it. The goodwife was not visible. The fire was not lighted. No provision, not so much as a stirrup-cup or bowl of porridge, cheered the heart.

I looked round, sniffing the stale smell of last night's lamp, and grunted.

'Are you going to send me out fasting?' I said, affecting a worse humour than I felt.

The landlord was standing by the window, stooping over a great pair of frayed and furrowed thigh-boots which he was labouring to soften with copious grease.

'Mademoiselle ordered no breakfast,' he answered, with a malicious grin.

'Well, it does not much matter,' I replied grandly. 'I shall be at Auch by noon.'

'That is as may be,' he answered with another grin.

I did not understand him, but I had something else to think about, and I opened the door and stepped out, intending to go to the stable. Then in a second I comprehended. The cold air laden with woodland moisture met me and went to my bones; but it was not that which made me shiver. Outside the door, in the road, sitting on horseback in silence, were two men. One was Clon. The other, who held a spare horse by the rein – my horse – was a man I had seen at the inn, a rough, shock-headed, hard-bitten fellow. Both were armed, and Clon was booted. His mate rode barefoot, with a rusty spur strapped to one heel.

The moment I saw them a sure and certain fear crept into my mind; it was that which made me shiver. But I did not speak to them. I went in again and closed the door behind me. The landlord was putting on his boots.

'What does this mean?' I said hoarsely – though I had a clear prescience of what was coming. 'Why are these men here?'

'Orders,' he answered laconically.

'Whose orders?' I retorted.

'Whose?' he answered bluntly. 'Well, Monsieur, that is my business. Enough that we mean to see you out of the country, and out of harm's way.'

'But if I will not go?' I cried.

'Monsieur will go,' he answered coolly. 'There are no strangers in the village to-day,' he added, with a significant smile.

'Do you mean to kidnap me?' I replied in a rage.

But behind the rage was something else – I will not call it terror, for the brave feel no terror – but it was near akin to it. I had had to do with rough men all my life, but there was a grimness and truculence in the aspect of these three that shook me. When I thought of the dark path and narrow lanes and cliff sides we must traverse, whichever road we took, I trembled.

'Kidnap you, Monsieur?' he answered, with an everyday air. 'That is as you please to call it. One thing is certain, however,' he continued, maliciously touching an arquebuss which he had brought out and set upright against a chair while I was at the door; 'if you attempt the slightest resistance, we shall know how to put an end to it, either here or on the road.'

I drew a deep breath, the very imminence of the danger restoring me to the use of my faculties. I changed my tone and laughed aloud.

'So that is your plan, is it?' I said. 'The sooner we start the better, then. And the sooner I see Auch and your back turned, the more I shall be pleased.'

He rose. 'After you, Monsieur,' he said.

I could not restrain a slight shiver. His new-born politeness alarmed me more than his threats. I knew the man and his ways, and I was sure that it boded ill to me.

But I had no pistols, and only my sword and knife, and I knew that resistance at this point must be worse than vain. I went out jauntily, therefore, the landlord coming after me with my saddle and bags.

The street was empty, save for the two waiting horsemen who sat in their saddles looking doggedly before them. The sun had not yet risen, the air was raw. The sky was grey, cloudly, and cold. My thoughts flew back to the morning on which I had found the sachet – at that very spot, almost at that very hour; and for a moment I grew warm again at the thought of the little packet I carried in my boot. But the landlord's dry manner, the sullen silence of his two companions, whose eyes steadily refused to meet mine, chilled me again. For an instant the impulse to refuse to mount, to refuse to go, was almost irresistible; then, knowing the madness of such a course, which might, and probably would, give the men the chance they desired, I crushed it down and went slowly to my stirrup.

'I wonder you do not want my sword,' I said by way of sarcasm, as I swung myself up.

'We are not afraid of it,' the innkeeper answered gravely. 'You may keep it – for the present.'

I made no answer – what answer had I to make? – and we rode at a foot-pace down the street; he and I leading, Clon and the shock headed man bringing up the rear. The leisurely mode of our departure, the absence of hurry or even haste, the men's indifference whether they were seen, or what was thought, all served to sink my spirits and deepen my sense of peril. I felt that they suspected me, that they more than half-guessed the nature of my errand at Cocheforêt, and that they were not minded to be bound by Mademoiselle's orders. In particular, I augured the worst from Clon's appearance. His lean malevolent face and sunken eyes, his very dumbness chilled me. Mercy had no place there.

We rode soberly, so that nearly half an hour elapsed before we gained the brow from which I had taken my first look at Cocheforêt. Among the dwarf oaks whence I had viewed the valley we paused to breathe our horses, and the strange feelings with which I looked back on the scene may be imagined. But I had short time for indulging in sentiment or recollections. A curt word, and we were moving again.

A quarter of a mile farther on, the road to Auch dipped into the valley. When we were already half-way down this descent the innkeeper suddenly stretched out his hand and caught my rein.

'This way!' he said.

I saw that he would have me turn into a by-path leading south-westwards – a mere track, faint and little trodden and encroached on by trees, which led I knew not whither. I checked my horse.

'Why?' I said rebelliously. 'Do you think I do not know the road? The road we are in is the way to Auch.'

'To Auch – yes,' he answered bluntly. 'But we are not going to Auch.'

'Whither then?' I said angrily.

'You will see presently,' he replied with an ugly smile.

'Yes, but I will know now!' I retorted, passion getting the better of me. 'I have come so far with you. You will find it more easy to take me farther if you tell me your plans.'

'You are a fool!' he cried with a snarl.

'Not so,' I answered. 'I ask only to know whither I am going.'

'Into Spain,' he said. 'Will that satisfy you?'

'And what will you do with me there?' I asked, my heart giving a greater bound.

'Hand you over to some friends of ours,' he answered curtly, 'if you behave yourself. If not, there is a shorter way, and one that will save us some travelling. Make up your mind, Monsieur. Which shall it be?'

6

Under the Pic du Midi

SO that was their plan. Two or three hours to the southward, the long, white, glittering wall stretched east and west above the brown woods. Beyond that lay Spain. Once across the border, I might be detained, if no worse happened to me, as a prisoner of war; for we were then at war with Spain on the Italian side. Or I might be handed over to one of the savage bands, half smugglers, half brigands, that held the passes; or be delivered, worse fate of all, into the power of the French Exiles, of whom some would be likely to recognise me and cut my throat.

'It is a long way into Spain,' I muttered, watching in a kind of fascination Clon handling his pistols.

'I think you will find the other road longer still,' the landlord answered grimly. 'But choose, and be quick about it.'

They were three to one, and they had firearms. In effect I had no choice.

'Well, if I must I must!' I cried, making up my mind with seeming recklessness. '*Vogue la galère!* Spain be it. It will not be the first time I have heard the dons talk.'

The men nodded as much as to say that they had known what the end would be; the landlord released my rein; and in a trice we were riding down the narrow track, with our faces set towards the mountains.

On one point my mind was now more easy. The men meant fairly by me, and I had no longer to fear, as I had feared, a pistol-shot in the back at the first convenient ravine. As far as that went, I might ride in peace. On the other hand, if I let them carry me across the border my fate was sealed. A man set down without credentials or guards among the wild desperadoes who swarmed in war-time in the Asturian passes might consider himself fortunate if an easy death fell to his lot. In my case I could make a shrewd guess what would happen. A single nod of meaning, one muttered word, dropped among the savage men with whom I should be left, and the diamonds hidden in my boot would go neither to the Cardinal nor back to Mademoiselle – nor would it matter to me whither they went.

So while the others talked in their taciturn fashion, or sometimes grinned at my gloomy face, I looked out over the brown woods with eyes that saw, yet did not see. The red squirrel swarming up the trunk, the startled pigs that rushed away grunting from their feast of mast, the solitary rider who met us, armed to the teeth, and passed northwards after whispering with the landlord – all these I saw. But my mind was not with them. It was groping and feeling about like a hunted mole for some way of escape. For time pressed. The slope we were on was growing steeper. By and by we fell into a southward valley, and began to follow it steadily upwards, crossing and recrossing a swiftly rushing stream. The snow peaks began to be hidden behind the rising bulk of hills that overhung us, and sometimes we could see nothing before or behind but the wooded walls of our valley rising sheer and green a thousand paces high on either hand; with grey rocks half masked by fern and ivy jutting here and there through the firs and alders.

It was a wild and sombre scene even at that hour, with the midday sun shining on the rushing water and drawing the scent out of the pines; but I knew that there was worse to come, and sought desperately for some ruse by which I might at least separate the men. Three were too many; with one I might deal. At last, when I had cudgelled my brain for an hour, and almost resigned myself to a sudden charge on the men single-handed – a last desperate resort – I thought of a plan: dangerous, too, and almost desperate, but which still seemed to promise something. It came of my fingers resting, as they lay in my pocket, on the fragments of the orange sachet; which, without having any particular design in my mind, I had taken care to bring with me. I had torn the sachet into four pieces – four corners. As I played mechanically with them, one of my fingers fitted into one, as into a glove; a second finger into another. And the plan came.

Before I could move in it, however, I had to wait until we stopped to bait the flagging horses, which we did about noon at the head of the valley. Then, pretending to drink from the stream, I managed to secure unseen a handful of pebbles, slipping them into the same pocket with the morsels of stuff. On getting to horse again, I carefully fitted a pebble, not too tightly, into the largest scrap, and made ready for the attempt.

The landlord rode on my left, abreast of me; the other two knaves behind. The road at this stage favoured me, for the valley, which drained the bare uplands that lay between the lower hills and the base of the real mountains, had become wide and shallow. Here were no trees, and the path was a mere sheep-track covered with short, crisp grass, and running sometimes on this bank of the stream and sometimes on that.

I waited until the ruffian beside me turned to speak to the men behind. The moment he did so, and his eyes were averted, I slipped out the scrap of satin in which I had placed the pebble, and balancing it carefully on my right thigh as I rode, I flipped it forward with all the strength of my thumb and finger. I meant it to fall a few paces before us in the path, where it could be seen. But alas for my hopes! At the critical moment my horse started, my finger struck the scrap aslant, the pebble flew out, and the bit of stuff fluttered into a whin-bush close to my stirrup – and was lost!

I was bitterly disappointed, for the same thing might happen again, and I had now only three scraps left. But fortune favoured me, by putting it into my neighbour's head to plunge into a hot debate with the shock-headed man on the nature of some animals seen on a distant brow; which he said were izards, while the other maintained that they were common goats. He continued, on this account, to ride with his face turned from me, and I had time to fit another pebble into the second piece of stuff. Sliding it on to my thigh, I poised it, and flipped it.

This time my finger struck the tiny missile fairly in the middle, and shot it so far and so truly that it dropped exactly in the path ten paces in front of us. The moment I saw it fall I kicked my neighbour's nag in the ribs; it started, and he, turning in a rage, hit it. The next instant he pulled it almost on to its haunches.

'*Saint Gris!*' he cried; and sat glaring at the bit of yellow satin, with his face turned purple and his jaw fallen.

'What is it?' I said, staring at him in turn. 'What is the matter, fool?'

'Matter?' he blurted out. '*Mon Dieu!*'

But Clon's excitement surpassed even his. The dumb man no sooner saw what had attracted his comrade's attention than he uttered an inarticulate and horrible noise, and tumbling off his horse, more like a beast than a man threw himself bodily on the precious morsel.

The innkeeper was not far behind him. An instant and he was down, too, peering at the thing; and for an instant I thought that they would fight over it. However, though their jealousy was evident, their excitement cooled a little when they discovered that the scrap of stuff was empty; for, fortunately, the pebble had fallen out of it. Still, it threw them into such a fever of eagerness as it was wonderful to witness. They nosed the ground where it had lain, they plucked up the grass and turf, and passed it through their fingers, they ran to and fro like dogs on a trail; and, glancing askance at one another, came back always together to the point of departure. Neither in his jealousy would suffer the other to be there alone.

The shock-headed man and I sat our horses and looked on; he marvelling, and I pretending to marvel. As the two searched up and down the path, we moved a little out of it to give them space; and presently, when all their heads were turned from me, I let a second morsel drop under a gorse-bush. The shock-headed man, by and by, found this, and gave it to Clon; and as from the circumstances of the first discovery no suspicion attached to me, I ventured to find the third and last scrap myself. I did not pick it up, but I called the innkeeper, and he pounced upon it as I have seen a hawk pounce on a chicken.

They hunted for the fourth morsel, but, of course, in vain, and in the end they desisted, and fitted the three they had together; neither would let his own portion out of his hands, and each looked at the other across the spoil with eyes of suspicion. It was strange to see them in that wide-stretching valley, whence grey boar-backs of hills swelled up into the silence of the snow – it was strange, I say, in that vast solitude, to see these two, mere dots on its bosom, circling round one another in fierce forgetfulness of the outside world, glaring and shifting their ground like cocks about to engage, and wholly engrossed – by three scraps of orange-colour, invisible at fifty paces!

At last the innkeeper cried with an oath, 'I am going back. This must be known down yonder. Give me your pieces, man, and do you go on with Antoine. It will be all right.'

But Clon, waving a scrap of the stuff in either hand, and thrusting his ghastly mask into the other's face, shook his head in passionate denial. He could not speak, but he made it as clear as daylight that if anyone went back with the news, he was the man to go.

'Nonsense!' the landlord rejoined fiercely. 'We cannot leave Antoine to go on alone with him. 'Give me the stuff.'

But Clon would not. He had no though of resigning the credit of the discovery; and I began to think that the two would really come to blows. But there was an alternative – an alternative in which I was concerned; and first one and then the other looked at me. It was a moment of peril, and I knew it. My stratagement might react on myself, and the two, to put an end to their difficulty, agree to put an end to me. But I faced them so coolly, and showed so bold a front and the ground where we stood was so open, that the idea took no root. They fell to wrangling again more viciously than before. One tapped his gun and the other his pistols. The landlord scolded, the dumb man gurgled. At last their difference ended as I had hoped it would.

'Very well then, we will both go back!' the innkeeper cried in a rage. 'And Antoine must see him on. But the blame be on your head. Do your give the lad your pistols.'

Clon took one pistol, and gave it to the shock-headed man.

'The other!' the innkeeper said impatiently.

But Clon shook his head with a grim smile, and pointed to the arquebuss.

By a sudden movement, the landlord snatched the pistol, and averted Clon's vengeance by placing both it and the gun in the shock-headed man's hands.

'There!' he said, addressing the later, 'now can you do? If Monsieur tries to escape or turn back, shoot him! But four hours' riding should bring you to the Roca Blanca. You will find the men there, and will have no more to do with it.'

Antoine did not see things quite in that light, however. He looked at me, and then at the wild track in front of us: and he muttered an oath and said he would die if he would.

But the landlord, who was in a frenzy of impatience, drew him aside and talked to him, and in the end seemed to persuade him; for in a few minutes the matter was settled.

Antoine came back, and said sullenly, 'Forward, Monsieur,' the two others stood on one side, I shrugged my shoulders and kicked up my horse, and in a twinkling we two were riding on together – man to man. I turned once or twice to see what those we had left behind were doing, and always found them standing in apparent debate; but my guard showed so much jealousy of these movements that I presently shrugged my shoulders again and desisted.

I had racked my brains to bring about this state of things. Strange to say, now I had succeeded, I found it less satisfactory than I had hoped. I had reduced the odds and got rid of my most dangerous antagonists; but Antoine, left to himself, proved to be as full of suspicion as an egg of meat. He rode a little behind me, with his gun across his saddle-bow, and a pistol near his hand; and at the slightest pause on my part, or if I turned to look at him, he muttered his constant 'Forward, Monsieur!' in a tone which warned me that his finger was on the trigger. At such a distance he could not miss; and I saw nothing for it but to go on meekly before him to the Roca Blanca – and my fate.

What was to be done? The road presently reached the end of the valley and entered a narrow pine-clad defile, strewn with rocks and boulders, over which the torrent plunged and eddied with a deafening roar. In front the white gleam of waterfalls broke the sombre ranks of climbing trunks. The snow line lay less than half a mile away on either hand; and crowning all – at the end of the pass, as it seemed to the eye – rose the pure white pillar of the Pic du Midi shooting up six thousand feet into the blue of heaven. Such a scene so suddenly disclosed was enough to drive the sense of danger from my mind; and for a moment I reined in my horse. But 'Forward, Monsieur!' came the grating order. I fell to earth again, and went on. What was to be done?

I was at my wits' end to know. The man refused to talk, refused to ride abreast of me, would have no dismounting, no halting, no communication at all. He would have nothing but this silent, lonely procession of two, with the muzzle of his gun at my back. And meanwhile we were fast climbing the pass. We had left the others an hour – nearly two. The sun was declining; the time, I supposed, about half-past three.

If he would only let me come within reach of him! Or if anything would fall out to take his attention! When the pass presently widened into a bare and dreary valley, strewn with huge boulders and with snow lying here and there in the hollows, I looked desperately before me, and scanned even the vast snow-fields that overhung us and stretched away to the base of the ice-peak. But I saw nothing. No bear swung across the path, no izard showed itself on the cliffs. The keen, sharp air cut our cheeks and warned me that we were approaching the summit of the ridge. On all sides were silence and desolation.

Mon Dieu! And the ruffians on whose tender mercies I was to be thrown might come to meet us! They might appear at any moment. In my despair I loosened my hat on my head, and let the first gust carry it to the ground, and then with an oath of annoyance tossed my feet from the stirrups to go after it. But the rascal roared to me to keep my seat.

'Forward, Monsieur!' he shouted brutally. 'Go on –'

'But my hat!' I cried. '*Mille tonnerres*, man! I must –'

'Forward, Monsieur, or I shoot!' he replied, inexorably raising his gun. 'One – two –'

And I went on. But, ah, I was wrathful! That I, Gil de Berault, should be outwitted, and led by the nose like a ringed bull, by this Gascon lout! That I, whom all Paris knew and feared – if it did not love – the terror of Zaton's, should come to my end in this dismal waste of snow and rock, done to death by some pitiful smuggler or thief! It must not be. Surely in the last resort I could give an account of one man, though his belt were stuffed with pistols.

But how? Only, it seemed, by open force. My heart began to flutter as I planned it; and then grew steady again. A hundred paces before us a gully or ravine on the left ran up into the snow-field. Opposite its mouth a jumble of stones and broken rocks covered the path. I marked this for the place. The knave would need both his hands to hold up his nag over the stones, and, if I turned on him suddenly enough, he might either drop his gun or fire it harmlessly.

But in the meantime something happened; as, at the last moment, things do happen. While we were still fifty yards short of the place, I found his horse's nose creeping forward on a level with my crupper; and, still advancing, still advancing, until I could see it out of the tail of my eye, and my heart gave a great bound. He was coming abreast of me; he was going to deliver himself into my hands! To cover my excitement, I began to whistle.

'Hush!' he muttered fiercely, his voice sounding so strange and unnatural, that my first thought was that he was ill; and I turned to him. But he only said again:

'Hush! Pass by here quietly, Monsieur.'

'Why?' I asked mutinously, curiosity getting the better of me. For had I been wise I had taken no notice; every second his horse was coming up with mine. Its nose was level with my stirrup already.

'Hush, man!' he said again. This time there was no mistake about the panic in his voice. 'They call this the Devil's Chapel. God send us safe by it! It is late to be here. Look at those!' he continued, pointing with a finger which visibly shook.

I looked. At the mouth of the gully, in a small space partly cleared of stones, stood three broken shafts, raised on rude pedestals.

'Well?' I said in a low voice. The sun, which was near setting, flushed the great peak above to the colour of blood; but the valley was growing grey and each moment more dreary. 'Well, what of those?' I said.

In spite of my peril and the excitement of the coming struggle I felt the chill of his fear. Never had I seen so grim, so desolate, so God-forsaken a place! Involuntarily, I shivered.

'They were crosses,' he muttered in a voice little above a whisper, while his eyes roved this way and that in terror. 'The Curé of Gabas blessed the place, and set them up. But next morning they were as you see them now. Come on, Monsieur; come on!' he continued, plucking at my arm. 'It is not safe here after sunset. Pray God, Satan be not at home!'

He had completely forgotten in his panic that he had anything to fear from me. His gun dropped loosely across his saddle, his leg rubbed mine. I saw this, and I changed my plan of action. As our horses reached the stones I stooped, as if to encourage mine, and, with a sudden clutch, snatched the gun bodily from his hand, at the same time that I backed my horse with all my strength. It was done in a moment! A second and I had him at the end of the gun, and my finger was on the trigger. Never was victory more easily gained.

He looked at me between rage and terror, his jaw fallen.

'Are you mad?' he cried, his teeth chattering as he spoke. Even in this strait his eyes left me and wandered round in alarm.

'No, sane!' I retorted fiercely. 'But I do not like this place any better than you do.' Which was true enough, if not quite true. 'So, by your right, quick march!' I continued imperatively. 'Turn your horse, my friend, or take the consequences.'

He turned like a lamb, and headed down the valley again, without giving a thought to his pistols. I kept close to him, and in less than a minute we had left the Devil's Chapel well behind us, and were moving down again as we had come up. Only now I held the gun.

When we had gone half a mile or so – until then I did not feel comfortable myself, and though I thanked heaven that the place existed, I thanked heaven also that I was out of it – I bade him halt.

'Take off your belt,' I said curtly, 'and throw it down. But mark me, if you turn I fire.'

The spirit was quite gone out of him, and he obeyed mechanically. I jumped down, still covering him with the gun, and picked up the belt, pistols and all. Then I remounted, and we went on. By and by he asked me sullenly what I was going to do.

'Go back,' I said, 'and take the road to Auch when I come to it.'

'It will be dark in an hour,' he answered sulkily.

'I know that,' I retorted. 'We must camp and do the best we can.'

And as I said, we did. The daylight held until we gained the skirts of the pine-wood at the head of the pass. Here I chose a corner a little off the track and well sheltered from the wind, and bade him light a fire. I tethered the horses near this and within sight. Then it remained only to sup. I had a piece of bread; he had another and an onion. We ate in silence, sitting on opposite sides of the fire.

But after supper I found myself in a dilemma; I did not see how I was to sleep. The ruddy light which gleamed on the knave's swart face and sinewy hands showed also his eyes, black, sullen, and watchful. I knew that the man was plotting revenge; that he would not hesitate to plant his knife between my ribs should I give him the chance; and I could find only one alternative to remaining awake. Had I been bloody-minded, I should have chosen it and solved the question at once and in my favour by shooting him as he sat.

But I have never been a cruel man, and I could not find it in my heart to do this. The silence of the mountain and the sky – which seemed a thing apart from the roar of the torrent and not to be broken by it – awed me. The vastness of the solitude in which we sat, the dark void above, through which the stars kept shooting, the black gulf below in which the unseen waters boiled and surged, the absence of other human company or other signs of human existence, put such a face upon the deed that I gave up the thought of it with a shudder, and resigned myself, instead, to watch through the night – the long, cold, Pyrenean night. Presently he curled himself up like a dog and slept in the blaze, and then for a couple of hours I sat opposite him, thinking. It seemed years since I had seen Zaton's or thrown the dice. The old life, the old employments – should I ever go back to them? – seemed dim and distant. Would Cocheforêt, the forest and the mountain, the grey Château and its mistresses, seem one day as dim? And if one bit of life could fade so quickly at the unrolling of another, and seem in a moment pale and colourless, would all life some day and somewhere, and all the things we – But enough! I was growing foolish. I sprang up and kicked the wood together, and, taking up the gun, began to pace to and fro under the cliff. Strange that a little moonlight, a few stars, a breath of solitude should carry a man back to childhood and childish things.

It was three in the afternoon of the next day, and the sun lay hot on the oak groves, and the air was full of warmth as we began to climb the slope midway up which the road to Auch shoots out of the track. The yellow bracken and the fallen leaves underfoot seemed to throw up light of themselves; and here and there a patch of ruddy beech lay like a bloodstain on the hillside. In front a herd of pigs routed among the mast, and grunted lazily; and high above us a boy lay watching them.

'We part here,' I said to my companion.

It was my plan to ride a little way along the road to Auch so as to blind his eyes; then, leaving my horse in the forest, I would go on foot to the Château.

'The sooner the better!' he answered with a snarl. 'And I hope I may never see your face again, Monsieur.'

But when we came to the wooden cross at the fork of the roads, and were about to part, the boy we had seen leapt out of the fern and came to meet us.

'Hello!' he cried in a sing-song tone.

'Well,' my companion answered, drawing rein impatiently. 'What is it?'

'There are soldiers in the village.'

'Soldiers?' Antoine cried incredulously.

'Ay, devils on horseback,' the lad answered, spitting on the ground. 'Three score of them. From Auch.'

Antoine turned to me, his face transformed with fury.

'Curse you!' he cried. 'This is some of your work. Now we are all undone. And my mistresses? *Sacré!* if I had that gun I would shoot you like a rat.'

'Steady, fool,' I answered roughly. 'I know no more of this than you do.'

Which was so true that my surprise was at least as great as his, and better grounded. The Cardinal, who rarely made a change of front, had sent me hither that he might not be forced to send soldiers, and run the risk of all that might arise from such a movement. What of this invasion, then, than which nothing could be less consistent with his plans? I wondered. It was possible that the travelling merchants, before whom I had played at treason, had reported the facts; and that on this the Commandant at Auch had acted. But it seemed unlikely since he had had his orders, too, and under the Cardinal's rule there was small place for individual enterprise. Frankly I could not understand it, and found only one thing clear; I might now enter the village as I pleased.

'I am going on to look into this,' I said to Antoine. 'Come, my man.'

He shrugged his shoulders, and stood still.

'Not I!' he answered, with an oath. 'No soldiers for me! I have lain out one night and I can lie out another.'

I nodded indifferently, for I no longer wanted him; and we parted. After this, twenty minutes' riding brought me to the entrance of the village, and here the change was great indeed. Not one of the ordinary dwellers in the place was to be seen: either they had shut themselves up in their hovels, or, like Antoine, they had fled to the woods. Their doors were closed, their windows shuttered. But lounging about the street were a score of dragoons, in boots and breastplates, whose short-barrelled muskets, with pouches and bandoliers attached, were piled near the inn door. In an open space, where there was a gap in the street, a long row of horses, linked head to head, stood bending their muzzles over bundles of rough forage; and on all sides the cheerful jingle of chains and bridles and the sound of coarse jokes and laughter filled the air.

As I rode up to the inn door an old sergeant, with squinting eyes and his tongue in his cheek, scanned me inquisitively, and started to cross the street to challenge me. Fortunately, at that moment the two knaves whom I had brought from Paris with me, and whom I had left at Auch to await my orders, came up. I made them a sign not to speak to me, and they passed on; but I suppose that they told the sergeant that I was not the man he wanted, for I saw no more of him.

After picketing my horse behind the inn – I could find no better stable, every place being full – I pushed my way through the group at the door, and entered. The old room, with the low, grimy roof and the reeking floor, was half full of strange figures, and for a few minutes I stood unseen in the smoke and confusion. Then the landlord came my way, and as he passed me I caught his eye. He uttered a low curse, dropped the pitcher he was carrying, and stood glaring at me like a man possessed.

The soldier whose wine he was carrying flung a crust in his face with: 'Now, greasy fingers! What are you staring at?'

'The devil!' the landlord muttered, beginning to tremble.

'Then let me look at him!' the man retorted, and he turned on his stool.

He started, finding me standing over him.

'At your service!' I said grimly. 'A little time and it will be the other way, my friend.'

7

A Master Stroke

I HAVE a way with me which commonly commands respect; and when the landlord's first terror was over and he would serve me, I managed to get my supper – the first good meal I had had in two days – pretty comfortably in spite of the soldiers' presence. The crowd, too, which filled the room, soon began to melt. The men strayed off in groups to water their horses, or went to hunt up their quarters, until only two or three were left. Dusk had fallen outside; the noise in the street grew less. The firelight began to glow and flicker on the walls, and the wretched room to look as homely as it was in its nature to look. I was pondering for the twentieth time what step I should take next, and questioning why the soldiers were here, and whether I should let the night pass before I moved, when the door, which had been turning on its hinges almost without pause for an hour, opened again, and a woman came in.

She paused a moment on the threshold looking round, and I saw that she had a shawl on her head and a milk-pitcher in her hand, and that her feet and ankles were bare. There was a great rent in her coarse stuff petticoat, and the hand which held the shawl together was brown and dirty. More I did not see: for, supposing her to be a neighbour stolen in, now that the house was quiet, to get some milk for her child or the like, I took no further heed of her. I turned to the fire again and plunged into my thoughts.

But to get to the hearth where the goodwife was fidgeting the woman had to pass in front of me; and as she passed I suppose that she stole a look at me from under her shawl. For just when she came between me and the blaze she uttered a low cry and shrank aside – so quickly that she almost stepped on the hearth. The next moment she turned her back to me, and was stooping whispering in the housewife's ear. A stranger might have thought that she had trodden on a hot ember.

But another idea, and a very strange one, came into my mind; and I stood up silently. The woman's back was towards me, but something in her height, her shape, the pose of her head, hidden as it was by her shawl, seemed familiar. I waited while she hung over the fire whispering, and while the goodwife slowly filled her pitcher out of the great black pot. But when she turned to go, I took a step forward so as to bar her way. And our eyes met.

I could not see her features; they were lost in the shadow of the hood. But I saw a shiver run through her from head to foot. And I knew then that I had made no mistake.

'That is too heavy for you, my girl,' I said familiarly, as I might have spoken to a village wench. 'I will carry it for you.'

One of the men, who remained lolling at the table, laughed, and the other began to sing a low song. The woman trembled in rage or fear, but she kept silence and let me take the jug from her hands; and when I went to the door and opened it, she followed mechanically. An instant, and the door fell to behind us, shutting off the light and glow, and we two stood together in the growing dusk.

'It is late for you to be out, Mademoiselle,' I said politely. 'You might meet with some rudeness, dressed as you are. Permit me to see you home.'

She shuddered, and I thought that I heard her sob, but she did not answer. Instead, she turned and walked quickly through the village in the direction of the Château, keeping in the shadow of the houses. I carried the pitcher and walked close to her, beside her; and in the dark I smiled. I knew how shame and impotent rage were working in her. This was something like revenge!

Presently I spoke.

'Well, Mademoiselle,' I said, 'where are your grooms?'

She gave me one look, her eyes blazing with anger, her face like hate itself; and after that I said no more, but left her in peace, and contented myself with walking at her shoulder until we came to the end of the village, where the track to the great house plunged into the wood. There she stopped, and turned on me like a wild creature at bay.

'What do you want?' she cried hoarsely, breathing as if she had been running.

'To see you safe to the house,' I answered coolly. 'Alone you might be insulted.'

'And if I will not?' she retorted.

'The choice does not lie with you, Mademoiselle,' I answered sternly. 'You will go to the house with me, and on the way you will give me an interview – late as it is; but not here. Here we are not private enough. We may be interrupted at any moment, and I wish to speak to you at length.'

'At length?' she muttered.

'Yes, Mademoiselle.'

I saw her shiver. 'What if I will not?' she said again.

'I might call to the nearest soldiers and tell them who you are,' I answered coolly. 'I might do that, but I should not. That were a clumsy way of punishing you, and I know a better way. I should go to the Captain, Mademoiselle, and tell him whose horse is locked up in the inn stable. A trooper told me – as someone had told him – that it belonged to one of his officers; but I looked through the crack, and I knew the horse again.'

She could not repress a groan. I waited; still she did not speak.

'Shall I go to the Captain?' I said ruthlessly.

She shook the hood back from her face and looked at me.

'Oh, you coward! you coward!' she hissed through her teeth. 'If I had a knife!'

'But you have not, Mademoiselle,' I answered, unmoved. 'Be good enough, therefore, to make up your mind which it is to be. Am I to go with my news to the Captain, or am I to come with you?'

'Give me the pitcher,' she said harshly.

I did so, wondering. In a moment she flung it with a savage gesture far into the bushes.

'Come!' she said, 'if you will. But some day God will punish you!'

Without another word she turned and entered the path through the trees, and I followed her. I suppose that every one of its windings, every hollow and broken place in it had been known to her from childhood, for she followed it swiftly and unerringly, barefoot as she was. I had to walk fast through the darkness to keep up with her. The wood was quiet, but the frogs were beginning to croak in the pool, and their persistent chorus reminded me of the night when I had come to the house-door, hurt and worn out, and Clon had admitted me, and she had stood under the gallery in the hall. Things had looked dark then. I had seen but a very little way ahead then. Now all was plain. The commandant might be here with all his soldiers, but it was I who held the strings.

We came to the little wooden bridge and saw beyond the dark meadows the lights of the house. All the windows were bright. Doubtless the troopers were making merry.

'Now, Mademoiselle,' I said quietly, 'I must trouble you to stop here, and give me your attention for a few minutes. Afterwards you may go your way.'

'Speak!' she said defiantly. 'And be quick! I cannot breathe the air where you are! It poisons me!'

'Ah!' I said slowly. 'Do you think that you make things better by such speeches as those?'

'Oh!' she cried – and I heard her teeth click together. 'Would you have me fawn on you?'

'Perhaps not,' I answered. 'Still you make one mistake.'

'What is it?' she panted.

'You forget that I am to be feared as well as – loathed, Mademoiselle! Ay, Mademoiselle, to be feared!' I continued grimly. 'Do you think that I do not know why you are here in this guise? Do you think that I do not know for whom that pitcher of broth was intended? Or who will now have to fast to-night? I tell you I know all these things. Your house was full of soldiers; your servants were watched and could not leave. You had to come yourself and get food for him?'

She clutched at the handrail of the bridge, and for an instant clung to it for support. Her face, from which the shawl had fallen, glimmered white in the shadow of the trees. At last I had shaken her pride. At last!

'What is your price?' she murmured faintly.

'I am going to tell you,' I replied, speaking so that every word might fall distinctly on her ears, and sating my eyes the while on her proud face.

I had never dreamed of such revenge as this! 'About a fortnight ago, M. de Cocheforêt left here at night with a little orange-coloured sachet in his possession.'

She uttered a stifled cry, and drew herself stiffly erect.

'It contained – but there, Mademoiselle, you know its contents,' I went on. 'Whatever they were, M. de Cocheforêt lost it and them at starting. A week ago he came back – unfotunately for himself – to seek them.'

She was looking full in my face now. She seemed scarcely to breathe in the intensity of her surprise and expectation.

'You had a search made, Mademoiselle,' I continued quietly. 'Your servants left no place unexplored. The paths, the roads, the very woods were ransacked. But in vain, because all the while the orange sachet lay whole and unopened in my pocket.'

'No!' she cried impetuously. 'There, you lie, sir, as usual! The sachet was found, torn open, many leagues from this place!'

'Where I threw it, Mademoiselle,' I replied, 'that I might mislead your rascals and be free to return to you. Oh! believe me,' I continued, letting something of my true self, something of my triumph, appear at last in my voice. 'You have made a mistake! You would have done better had you trusted me. I am no bundle of sawdust, Mademoiselle, though once you got the better of me, but a man; a man with an arm to shield and a brain to serve, and – as I am going to teach you – a heart also!'

She shivered.

'In the orange-coloured sachet that you lost I believe that there were eighteen stones of great value?'

She made no answer, but she looked at me as if I fascinated her. Her very breath seemed to pause and wait on my words. She was so little conscious of anything else, of anything outside ourselves, that a score of men might have come up behind her, unseen and unnoticed.

8

A Master Stroke (continued)

I TOOK from my breast a little packet wrapped in soft leather, and I held it towards her.

'Will you open this?' I said. 'I believe that it contains what your brother lost. That it contains all I will not answer, Mademoiselle, because I spilled the stones on the floor of my room, and I may have failed to find some. But the others can be recovered; I know where they are.'

She took the packet slowly and began to unroll it, her fingers shaking. A few turns and the mild lustre of the stones shone out, making a kind of moonlight in her hands – such a shimmering glory of imprisoned light as has ruined many a woman and robbed many a man of his honour.

Morbleu! as I looked at them – and as she stood looking at them in dull, entranced perplexity – I wondered how I had come to resist the temptation.

While I gazed her hands began to waver.

'I cannot count,' she muttered helplessly. 'How many are there?'

'In all, eighteen.'

'There should be eighteen,' she said.

She closed her hand on them with that and opened it again, and did so twice, as if to reassure herself that the stones were real and that she was not dreaming. Then she turned to me with sudden fierceness, and I saw that her beautiful face, sharpened by the greed of possession, was grown as keen and vicious as before.

'Well?' she muttered between her teeth. 'Your price, man? Your price?'

'I am coming to it now, Mademoiselle,' I said gravely. 'It is a simple matter. You remember the afternoon when I followed you – clumsily and thoughtlessly perhaps – through the wood to restore these things? In seeming that happened about a month ago. I believe that it happened the day before yesterday. You called me then some very harsh name which I will not hurt you by repeating. The only price I ask for the restoration of your jewels is that you on your part recall those names.'

'How?' she muttered. 'I do not understand.'

I repeated my words very slowly. 'The only price or reward I ask, Mademoiselle, is that you take back those names and say that they are not deserved.'

'And the jewels?' she exclaimed hoarsely.

'They are yours. They are not mine. They are nothing to me. Take them, and say that you do not think of me – Nay, I cannot say the words, Mademoiselle.'

'But there is something – else! What else?' she cried, her head thrown back, her eyes, bright as any wild animal's, searching mine. 'Ha! my brother? What of him? What of him, sir?'

'For him, Mademoiselle – I would prefer that you should tell me no more than I know already,' I answered in a low voice. 'I do not wish to be in that affair. But yes; there is one thing I have not mentioned. You are right.'

She sighed so deeply that I caught the sound.

'It is,' I continued slowly, 'that you will permit me to remain at Cocheforêt for a few days while the soldiers are here. I am told that there are twenty men and two officers quartered in your house. Your brother is away. I ask to be permitted, Mademoiselle, to take his place for the time, and to be priviledged to protect your sister and yourself from insult. That is all.'

She raised her hand to her head. After a long pause:

'The frogs!' she muttered, 'they croack! I cannot hear.'

Then, to my surprise, she turned quickly and suddenly on her heel, and walked over the bridge, leaving me standing there. For a moment I stood aghast, peering after her shadowy figure, and wondering what had taken her. Then, in a minute or less, she came quickly back to me, I understood. She was crying.

'M. de Barthe,' she said, in a trembling voice, which told me that victory was won, 'is there nothing else? Have you no other penance for me?'

'None, Mademoiselle.'

She had drawn the shawl over her head, and I no longer saw her face.

'That is all you ask?' she murmured.

'That is all I ask now,' I answered.

'It is granted,' she said slowly and firmly.

'Forgive me if I seem to speak lightly – if I seem to make little of your generosity or my shame but I can say no more now. I am so deep in trouble and so gnawed by terror that – I cannot feel anything keenly to-night, either shame or gratitude. I am in a dream; God grant that it may pass as a dream! We are sunk in trouble. But for you and what you have done, M. de Barthe – I –' She paused and I heard her fighting with the sobs which choked her. 'Forgive me . . . I am overwrought. And my – my feet are cold,' she added, suddenly and irrelevantly. 'Will you take me home?'

'Ah, Mademoiselle.' I cried remorsefully, 'I have been a beast! You are barefoot, and I have kept you here.'

'It is nothing,' she said in a voice which thrilled me. 'My heart is warm, Monsieur – thanks to you. It is many hours since it has been as warm.'

She stepped out of the shadow as she spoke – and there, the thing was done. As I had planned, so it had come about. Once more I was crossing the meadow in the dark to be received at Cocheforet, a welcome guest. The frogs croaked in the pond and a bat swooped round us in circles; and surely never – never, I thought, with a kind of exaltation in my breast – had man been placed in a stranger position.

Somewhere in the black wood behind us – probably in the outskirts of the village – lurked M. de Cocheforêt. In the great house before us, outlined by a score of lighted windows, were the soldiers come from Auch to take him. Between the two, moving side by side in the darkness, in a silence which each found to be eloquent, were Mademoiselle and I: she who knew so much, I who know all – all but one little thing!

We reached the house, and I suggested that she should steal in first by the way she had come out, and that I should wait a little and knock at the door when she had had time to explain matters to Clon.

'They do not let me see Clon,' she answered slowly.

'Then your woman must tell him,' I rejoined, 'or he may do something and betray me.'

'They will not let our women come to us.'

'What?' I cried, astonished. 'But this is infamous. You are not prisoners!'

Mademoiselle laughed harshly.

'Are we not? Well, I suppose not; for if we wanted company, Captain Larolle said that he would be delighted to see us – in the parlour.'

'He has taken your parlour?' I said.

'He and his lieutenant sit there. But I suppose that we rebels should be thankful,' she added bitterly; 'we have still our bedrooms left to us.'

'Very well,' I said. 'Then I must deal with Clon as I can. But I have still a favour to ask, Mademoiselle. It is only that you and your sister will descend to-morrow at your usual time. I shall be in the parlour.'

'I would rather not,' she said, pausing and speaking in a troubled voice.

'Are you afraid?'

'No, Monsieur, I am not afraid,' she answered proudly, 'but –'

'You will come?' I said.

She sighed before she spoke. At length –

'Yes, I will come – if you wish it,' she answered. And the next moment she was gone round the corner of the house, while I laughed to think of the excellent watch these gallant gentlemen were keeping. M. de Cocheforêt might have been with her in the garden, might have talked with her as I had talked, might have entered the house even, and passed under their noses scot-free. But that is the way of soldiers. They are always ready for the enemy, with drums beating and flags flying – at ten o'clock in the morning. But he does not always come at that hour.

I waited a little, and then I groped my way to the door and knocked on it with the hilt of my sword. The dogs began to bark at the back, and the chorus of a drinking-song, which came fitfully from the east wing, ceased altogether. An inner door opened, and an angry voice, apparently an officer's, began to rate someone for not coming. Another moment, and a clamour of voices and footsteps seemed to pour into the hall, and fill it. I heard the bar jerked away, the door was flung open, and in a twinkling a lanthorn, behind which a dozen flushed visages were dimly seen, was thrust into my face.

'Why, who the fiend is this?' one cried, glaring at me in astonishment.

'*Morbleu!* It is the man!' another shrieked. 'Seize him!'

In a moment half a dozen hands were laid on my shoulders, but I only bowed politely.

'The officer, my friends,' I said, 'M. le Capitaine Larolle. Where is he?'

'*Diable!* but who are you, first?' the lanthorn-bearer retorted bluntly. He was a tall, lanky sergeant, with a sinister face.

'Well, I am not M. de Cocheforêt,' I replied; 'and that must satisfy you, my man. For the rest, if you do not fetch Captain Larolle at once and admit me, you will find the consequences inconvenient.'

'Ho! ho!' he said with a sneer. 'You can crow, it seems. Well, come in.'

They made way, and I walked into the hall, keeping my hat on. On the great hearth a fire had been kindled, but it had gone out. Three or four carbines stood against one wall, and beside them lay a heap of haversacks and some straw. A shattered stool, broken in a frolic, and half a dozen empty wine-skins strewed the floor, and helped to give the place an air of untidiness and disorder. I looked round with eyes of disgust and my gorge rose. They had spilled oil, and the place reeked foully.

'*Ventre bleu!*' I said. 'Is this conduct in a gentleman's house, you rascals? *Ma vie!* If I had you I would send half of you to the wooden horse!'

They gazed at me open-mouthed; my arrogance startled them. The sergeant alone scowled. When he could find his voice for rage:

'This way!' he said. 'We did not know that a general officer was coming, or we would have been better prepared!' And muttering oaths under his breath, he led me down the well-known passage. At the door of the parlour he stopped. 'Introduce yourself!' he said rudely. 'And if you find the air warm, don't blame me!'

I raised the latch and went in. At a table in front of the hearth, half covered with glasses and bottles, sat two men playing hazard. The dice rang sharply as I entered, and he who had just thrown kept the box over them while he turned, scowling, to see who came in. He was a fair-haired, blonde man, large-framed and florid. He had put off his cuirass and boots, and his doublet showed frayed and stained where the armour had pressed on it. Otherwise he was in the extreme of last year's fashion. His deep cravat, folded over so that the laced ends dropped a little in front, was of the finest; his great sash of blue and silver was a foot wide. He had a little jewel in one ear, and his tiny beard was peaked *à l'Espagnole.* Probably when he turned he expected to see the sergeant, for at sight of me he rose slowly, leaving the dice still covered.

'What folly is this?' he cried wrathfully. 'Here, sergeant! Sergeant! – without there! What the –! Who are you, sir?'

'Captain Larolle,' I said, uncovering politely, 'I believe?'

'Yes, I am Captain Larolle,' he retorted.

'But who, in the fiend's name, are you? You are not the man we are after!'

'I am not M. de Cocheforêt,' I said coolly. 'I am merely a guest in the house, M. le Capitaine. I have been enjoying Madame de Cocheforêt's hospitality for some time, but by an evil chance I was away when you arrived.' And with that I walked to the hearth, and, gently pushing aside his great boots which stood there drying, I kicked the logs into a blaze.

'*Mille diables!*' he whispered. And never did I see a man more confounded. But I affected to be taken up with his companion, a sturdy, white-moustachioed old veteran, who sat back in his chair, eyeing me with swollen cheeks and eyes surcharged with surprise.

'Good evening, M. le Lieutenant,' I said, bowing gravely. 'It is a fine night.'

Then the storm burst.

'Fine night!' the Captain shrieked, finding his voice at last. '*Mille diables!*

Are you aware, sir, that I am in possession of this house, and that no one harbours here without my permission? Guest? Hospitality? Bundle of fiddle-faddle! Lieutenant, call the guard! Call the guard!' he continued passionately. 'Where is that ape of a sergeant?'

The Lieutenant rose to obey, but I lifted my hand.

'Gently, gently, Captain,' I said. 'Not so fast. You seem surprised to see me here. Believe me, I am much more surprised to see you.'

'*Sacré!*' he cried, recoiling at this fresh impertinence, while the Lieutenant's eyes almost jumped out of his head.

But nothing moved me.

'Is the door closed?' I said sweetly. 'Thank you; it is, I see. Then permit me to say again, gentlemen, that I am much more surprised to see you than you can be to see me. For when Monseigneur the Cardinal honoured me by sending me from Paris to conduct this matter, he gave me the fullest – the fullest powers, M. le Capitaine – to see the affair to an end. I was not led to expect that my plans would be spoiled on the eve of success by the intrusion of half the garrison from Auch.'

'Oh, ho!' the Captain said softly – in a very different tone, and with a very different face. 'So you are the gentleman I heard of at Auch?'

'Very likely,' I said drily. 'But I am from Paris, not from Auch.'

'To be sure,' he answered thoughtfully. 'Eh, Lieutenant?'

'Yes, M. le Capitaine, no doubt,' the inferior replied. And they both looked at one another, and then at me, in a way I did not understand.

'I think,' said I, to clinch the matter, 'that you have made a mistake, Captain; or that the Commandant has. And it occurs to me that the Cardinal will not be best pleased.'

'I hold the King's commission,' he answered rather stiffly.

'To be sure,' I replied. 'But you see, the Cardinal –'

'Ay, but the Cardinal –' he rejoined quickly; and then he stopped and shrugged his shoulders. And they both looked at me.

'Well?' I said.

'The King,' he answered slowly.

'Tut-tut!' I exclaimed, spreading out my hands. 'The Cardinal. Let us stick to him. You were saying?'

'Well, the Cardinal, you see –' And then again, after the same words, he stopped – stopped abruptly, and shrugged his shoulders.

I began to suspect something.

'If you have anything to say against Monseigneur,' I answered, watching him narrowly, 'say it. But take a word of advice. Don't let it go beyond the door of this room, my friend, and it will do you no harm.'

'Neither here nor outside,' he retorted, looking for a moment at his comrade. 'Only I hold the King's commission. That is all, and, I think, enough.'

'Well?' I said.

'Well – for the rest, will you throw a main?' he answered evasively.

'Good! Lieutenant, find a glass, and the gentleman a seat. And here, for my part, I will give you a toast. The Cardinal – whatever betide!'

I drank it, and sat down to play with him; I had not heard the music of the dice for a month, and the temptation was irresistible. But I was not satisfied. I called the mains and won his crowns – he was a mere baby at the game – but half my mind was elsewhere. There was something here that I did not understand; some influence at work on which I had not counted; something moving under the surface as unintelligible to me as the soldiers' presence. Had the Captain repudiated my commission altogether, and put me to the door or sent me to the guard-house, I could have followed that. But these dubious hints, this passive resistance, puzzled me. Had they news from Paris, I wondered? Was the King dead? Or the Cardinal ill? I asked them, but they said no, no, no to all, and gave me guarded answers. And midnight found us still playing; and still fencing.

9

The Question

'SWEEP the room, Monsieur? And remove this medley? But M. le Capitaine –'

'The Captain is in the village,' I replied sternly. 'And do you move. Move, man, and the thing will be done while you are talking about it. Set the door into the garden open – so.'

'Certainly, it is a fine morning. And the tobacco of M. le Lieutenant. But M. le Capitaine did not –'

'Give orders? Well, I give them,' I answered. 'First of all, remove these beds. And bustle, man, bustle, or I will find something to quicken you!'

In a moment: 'And M. le Capitaine's riding-boots?'

'Place them in the passage,' I replied.

'*Ohé!* in the passage?' He paused, looking at them in doubt.

'Yes, booby; in the passage.'

'And the cloaks, Monsieur?'

'There is a bush handy outside the window. Let them air.'

'*Ohé*, the bush? Well, to be sure they are damp. But – yes, yes, Monsieur, it is done. And the holsters?'

'There also,' I said harshly. 'Throw them out. Faugh! The place reeks of leather. Now, a clean hearth. And set the table before the open door, so that we may see the garden – so. And tell the cook that we dine at eleven, and that Madame and Mademoiselle will descend.'

'*Ohé!* But M. le Capitaine ordered the dinner for half-past eleven.'

'It must be advanced, then; and, mark you, my friend, if it is not ready when Madame comes down, you will suffer, and the cook too.'

When he was gone on his errand, I looked round. What else was lacking?

The sun shone cheerily on the polished floor; the air, freshened by the rain which had fallen in the night, entered freely through the open doorway. A few bees lingering with the summer hummed outside. The fire crackled bravely; an old hound, blind and past work, lay warming its hide on the hearth. I could think of nothing more, and I stood and stood and watched the man set out the table and spread the cloth.

'For how many, Monsieur?' he asked in a scared tone.

'For five,' I answered; and I could not help smiling at myself.

For what would Zaton's say could it see Berault turned housewife? There was a white glanzed cup, an old-fashioned piece of the second Henry's time, standing on a shelf. I took it down and put some late flowers in it, and set it in the middle of the table, and stood off myself to look at it. But a moment later, thinking I heard them coming, I hurried it away in a kind of panic, feeling on a sudden ashamed of the thing. The alarm proved to be false, however; and then again, taking another turn, I set the piece back. I had done nothing so foolish for – for more years than I like to count.

But when Madame and Mademoiselle came down, they had eyes neither for the flowers nor the room. They had heard that the Captain was out beating the village and the woods for the fugitive, and where I had looked for a comedy I found a tragedy. Madame's face was so red with weeping that all her beauty was gone. She started and shook at the slightest sound, and, unable to find any words to answer my greeting, could only sink into a chair and sit crying silently.

Mademoiselle was in a mood scarcely more cheerful. She did not weep, but her manner was hard and fierce. She spoke absently, and answered fretfully. Her eyes glittered, and she had the air of straining her ears continually to catch some dreaded sound.

'There is no news, Monsieur?' she said as she took her seat. And she shot a swift look at me.

'None, Mademoiselle.'

'They are searching the village?'

'I believe so.'

'Where is Clon?' This is a lower voice, and with a kind of shrinking in her face.

I shook my head. 'I believe that they have him confined somewhere. And Louis, too,' I said. 'But I have not seen either of them.'

'And where are – I thought these people would be here,' she muttered. And she glanced askance at the two vacant places. The servant had brought in the meal.

'They will be here presently,' I said coolly. 'Let us make the most of the time. A little wine and food will do Madame good.'

She smiled rather sadly.

'I think that we have changed places,' she said. 'And that you have turned host and we guests.'

'Let it be so,' I said cheerfully. 'I recommend some of this ragoût.

Come, Mademoiselle, fasting can aid no one. A full meal has saved many a man's life.'

It was clumsily said, perhaps; for she shuddered and looked at me with a ghastly smile. But she persuaded her sister to take something; and she took something on her own plate and raised her fork to her lips. But in a moment she laid it down again.

'I cannot,' she murmured. 'I cannot swallow. Oh, my God, at this moment they may be taking him.'

I thought that she was about to burst into a passion of tears, and I repented that I had induced her to descend. But her self-control was not yet exhausted. By an effort, painful to see, she recovered her composure. She took up her fork and ate a few mouthfuls. Then she looked at me with a fierce under-look.

'I want to see Clon,' she whispered feverishly. The man who waited on us had left the room.

'He knows?' I said.

She nodded, her beautiful face strangely disfigured. Her closed teeth showed between her lips. Two red spots burned in her white cheeks, and she breathed quickly. I felt, as I looked at her, a sudden pain at my heart, and a shuddering fear, such as a man, awaking to find himself falling over a precipice, might feel. How these women loved the man!

For a moment I could not speak. When I found my voice it sounded dry and husky.

'He is a safe confidant,' I muttered. 'He can neither read nor write, Mademoiselle.'

'No, but –' and then her face became fixed. 'They are coming,' she whispered. 'Hush!' She rose stiffly, and stood supporting herself by the table. 'Have they – have they – found him?' she muttered. The woman by her side wept on, unconscious of what was impending.

I heard the Captain stumble far down the passage, and swear loudly; and I touched Mademoiselle's hand.

'They have not!' I whispered. 'All is well, Mademoiselle. Pray, pray calm yourself. Sit down and meet them as if nothing were the matter. And your sister! Madame, Madame,' I cried, almost harshly, 'compose yourself. Remember that you have a part to play.'

My appeal did something. Madame stifled her sobs. Mademoiselle drew a deep breath and sat down; and though she was still pale and still trembled, the worst was past.

And only just in time. The door flew open with a crash. The Captain stumbled into the room, swearing afresh.

'*Sacré nom du diable!*' he cried, his face crimson with rage. 'What fool placed these things here? My boots? My –'

His jaw fell. He stopped on the word, stricken silent by the new aspect of the room, by the sight of the little party at the table, by all the changes I had worked.

'*Saint Siège!*' he muttered. 'What is this?'

The Lieutenant's grizzled face peering over his shoulder completed the picture.

'You are rather late, M. le Capitaine,' I said cheerfully. 'Madame's hour is eleven. But, come, here are your seats for you.'

'*Mille tonnerres!*' he muttered, advancing into the room, and glaring at us.

'I am afraid that the ragoût is cold,' I continued, peering into the dish and affecting to see nothing. 'The soup, however, has been kept hot by the fire. But I think that you do not see Madame.'

He opened his mouth to swear, but for the moment he thought better of it.

'Who – who put my boots in the passage?' he asked, his voice thick with rage. He did not bow to the ladies, or take any notice of their presence.

'One of the men, I suppose,' I said indifferently. 'Is anything missing?'

He glared at me. Then his cloak, spread outside, caught his eye. He strode through the door, saw his holsters lying on the grass, and other things strewn about. He came back.

'Whose monkey game is this?' he snarled, and his face was very ugly. 'Who is at the bottom of this? Speak, Sir, or I –'

'Tut-tut – the ladies.' I said. 'You forget yourself, Monsieur.'

'Forget myself?' he hissed, and this time he did not check his oath 'Don't talk to me of the ladies! Madame? Bah! Do you think, fool, that we are put into rebels' houses to bow and smile and take dancing lessons?'

'In this case a lesson in politeness were more to the point, Monsieur,' I said sternly. And I rose.

'Was it by your orders that this was done?' he retorted his brow black with passion.

'Answer, will you?'

'It was!' I replied outright.

'Then take that!' he cried, dashing his hat violently in my face, 'and come outside.'

'With pleasure, Monsieur,' I answered, bowing; 'in one moment. Permit me to find my sword. I think that it is in the passage.'

I went thither to get it.

When I returned, I found that the two men were waiting for me in the garden, while the ladies had risen from the table, and were standing near it with blanched faces.

'You had better take your sister upstairs, Mademoiselle,' I said gently, pausing a moment beside them. 'Have no fear. All will be well.'

'But what is it?' she answered, looking troubled. 'It was so sudden. I am – I did not understand. You quarrelled so quickly.'

'It is very simple,' I answered, smiling. 'M. le Capitaine insulted you yesterday; he will pay for it to-day. That is all. Or, not quite all,' I continued, dropping my voice and speaking in a different tone. 'His removal may help you, Mademoiselle. Do you understand? I think that there will be no more searching to-day.'

She uttered an exclamation, grasping my arm and peering into my face. 'You will kill him?' she muttered.

I nodded.

'Why not?' I said.

She caught her breath, and stood with one hand clasped to her bosom, gazing at me with parted lips, the blood mounting to her cheeks. Gradually the flush melted into a fierce smile.

'Yes, yes, why not?' she repeated between her teeth. 'Why not?' She had her hand on my arm, and I felt her fingers tighten until I could have winced. 'Why not? So you planned this – for us, Monsieur?'

I nodded.

'But can you?'

'Safely,' I said; then, muttering to her to take her sister upstairs, I turned towards the garden. My foot was already on the threshold, and I was composing my face to meet the enemy, when I heard a movement behind me. The next moment her hand was on my arm.

'Wait! Wait a moment! Come back!' she panted. I turned. The smile and flush had vanished; her face was pale. 'No!' she said abruptly. 'I was wrong! I will not have it. I will have no part in it! You planned it last night, M. de Barthe. It is murder.'

'Mademoiselle!' I exclaimed, wondering. 'Murder? Why? It is a duel.'

'It is murder,' she answered persistently. 'You planned it last night. You said so.'

'But I risk my own life,' I replied sharply.

'Nevertheless – I will have no part in it,' she answered more faintly. She was trembling with agitation. Her eyes avoided mine.

'On my shoulders be it then!' I replied stoutly. 'It is too late, Mademoiselle, to go back. They are waiting for me. Only, before I go, let me beg of you to retire.'

And I turned from her and went out, wondering and thinking. First, that women were strange things. Secondly – *murder*? Merely because I had planned the duel and provoked the quarrel! Never had I heard anything so preposterous. Grant it, and dub every man who kept his honour with his hands a Cain – and a good many branded faces would be seen in some streets. I laughed at the fancy as I strode down the garden walk.

And yet, perhaps, I was going to do a foolish thing. The Lieutenant would still be here; a hard-bitten man, of stiffer stuff than his Captain. And the troopers. What if when I had killed their leader, they made the place too hot for me, Monseigneur's commission notwithstanding? I should look silly, indeed, if on the eve of success I were driven from the place by a parcel of jack-boots.

I liked the thought so little that I hesitated. Yet it seemed too late to retreat. The Captain and the Lieutenant were waiting for me in a little open space fifty yards from the house, where a narrower path crossed the broad walk, down which I had first seen Mademoiselle and her sister pacing. The Captain had removed his doublet, and stood in his shirt leaning against the sundial, his head bare and his sinewy throat uncovered. He had drawn his rapier and stood pricking the ground impatiently. I marked his strong and nervous frame and his sanguine air: and twenty years earlier the sight might have damped me. But no thought of the kind entered my head now, and though I felt with each moment greater reluctance to engage, doubt of the issue had no place in my calculations.

I made ready slowly, and would gladly, to gain time, have found some fault with the place. But the sun was sufficiently high to give no advantage to either. The ground was good, the spot well chosen. I could find no excuse to put off the man, and I was about to salute him and fall to work when a thought crossed my mind.

'One moment!' I said. 'Supposing I kill you, M. le Capitaine, what becomes of your errand here?'

'Don't trouble yourself,' he answered with a sneer – he had misread my slowness and hesitation. 'It will not happen, Monsieur. And in any case the thought need not harass you. I have a lieutenant.'

'Yes, but what of my mission?' I replied bluntly. 'I have no lieutenant.'

'You should have thought of that before you interfered with my boots,' he retorted with contempt.

'True,' I said, overlooking his manner. 'But better late than never. I am not sure, now I think of it, that my duty to Monseigneur will let me fight.'

'You will swallow the blow?' he cried, spitting on the ground offensively. '*Diable!*' And the Lieutenant, standing on one side with his hands behind him and his shoulders squared, laughed grimly.

'I have not made up my mind,' I answered irresolutely.

'Well, *nom de Dieu!* make it up,' the Captain replied, with an ugly sneer. He took a swaggering step this way and that, playing his weapon. 'I am afraid, Lieutenant, that there will be no sport to-day,' he continued in a loud aside. 'Our cock has but a chicken heart.'

'Well,' I said coolly, 'I do not know what to do. Certainly it is a fine day, and a fair piece of ground. And the sun stands well. But I have not much to gain by killing you, M. le Capitaine, and it might get me into an awkward fix. On the other hand, it would not hurt me to let you go.'

'Indeed!' he said contemptuously, looking at me as I should look at a lackey.

'No!' I replied. 'For if you were to say that you had struck Gil de Berault and left the ground with a whole skin, no one would believe you.'

'Gil de Berault!' he exclaimed, frowning.

'Yes, Monsieur,' I replied suavely. 'At your service. You did not know my name?'

'I thought that your name was De Barthe,' he said. His voice sounded queerly; and he waited for the answer with parted lips, and a shadow in his eyes which I had seen in men's eyes before.

'No,' I said; 'that was my mother's name. I took it for this occasion only.'

His florid cheek lost a shade of its colour, and he bit his lips as he glanced at the Lieutenant, trouble in his eyes. I had seen these signs before, and knew them, and I might have cried 'Chickenheart!' in my turn; but I had not made a way of escape for him – before I declared myself – for nothing, and I held to my purpose.

'I think you will allow now,' I said grimly, 'that it will not harm me even if I put up with a blow!'

'M. de Berault's courage is known,' he muttered.

'And with reason,' I said. 'That being so, suppose that we say this day three months, M. le Capitaine? The postponement to be for my convenience.'

He caught the Lieutenant's eye and looked down sullenly, the conflict in his mind as plain as daylight. He had only to insist that I must fight; and if by luck or skill he could master me his fame as a duellist would run, like a ripple over water, through every garrison town in France and make him a name even in Paris. On the other side were the imminent peril of death, the gleam of cold steel already in fancy at his breast, the loss of life and sunshine, and the possibility of a retreat with honour, if without glory. I read his face, and knew before he spoke what he would do.

'It appears to me that the burden is with you,' he said huskily; 'but for my part I am satisfied.'

'Very well,' I said, 'I take the burden. Permit me to apologise for having caused you to strip unnecessarily. Fortunately the sun is shining.'

'Yes,' he said gloomily. And he took his clothes from the sundial and began to put them on. He had expressed himself satisfied, but I knew that he was feeling very ill-satisfied indeed with himself; and I was not surprised when he presently said abruptly and almost rudely, 'There is one thing that I think we must settle here.'

'Yes?' I said. 'What is that?'

'Our positions,' he blurted out. 'Or we shall cross one another again within the hour.'

'Umph! I am not quite sure that I understand,' I said.

'That is precisely what I don't do – understand!' he retorted, in a tone of surly triumph. 'Before I came on this duty, I was told that there was a gentleman here, bearing sealed orders from the Cardinal to arrest M. de Cocheforêt; and I was instructed to avoid collision with him so far as might be possible. At first I took you for the gentleman. But the plague take me if I understand the matter now.'

'Why not?' I said coldly.

'Because – well, the question is in a nut-shell!' he answered impetuously. 'Are you here on behalf of Madame de Cocheforêt, to shield her husband? Or are you here to arrest him? That is what I do not understand, M. de Berault.'

'If you mean, am I the Cardinal's agent – I am!' I answered sternly.

'To arrest M. de Cocheforêt?'

'To arrest M. de Cocheforêt.'

'Well – you surprise me,' he said.

Only that; but he spoke so drily that I felt the blood rush to my face.

'Take care, Monsieur,' I said severely. 'Do not presume too far on the inconvenience to which your death might put me.'

He shrugged his shoulders.

'No offence,' he said. 'But you do not seem, M. de Berault, to comprehend the difficulty. If we do not settle things now, we shall be bickering twenty times a day.'

'Well, what do you want?' I asked impatiently.

'Simply to know how you are going to proceed. So that our plans may not clash.'

'But surely, M. le Capitaine, that is my affair,' I said.

'The clashing?' he answered bitterly. Then he waived aside my wrath. 'Pardon,' he said, 'the point is simply this. How do you propose to find him if he is here?'

'That again is my affair,' I answered.

He threw up his hands in despair; but in a moment his place was taken by an unexpected disputant.

The Lieutenant, who had stood by all the time, listening and tugging at his grey moustache, suddenly spoke.

'Look here, M. de Berault,' he said, confronting me roughly, 'I do not fight duels. I am from the ranks. I proved my courage at Montauban in '21, and my honour is good enough to take care of itself. So I say what I like, and I ask you plainly what M. le Capitaine doubtless has in his mind, but does not ask: Are you running with the hare and hunting with the hounds in this matter? In other words, have you thrown up Monseigneur's commission in all but name, and become Madame's ally; or – it is the only other alternative – are you getting at the man through the women?'

'You villain!' I cried, glaring at him in such a rage and fury that I could scarcely get the words out. This was plain speaking with a vengeance! 'How dare you? How dare you say that I am false to the hand that pays me?'

I thought that he would blench, but he did not. He stood up stiff as a poker.

'I do not say; I ask!' he replied, facing me squarely, and slapping his fist into his open hand to drive home his words the better. 'I ask you whether you are playing the traitor to the Cardinal, or to these two women? It is a simple question.'

I fairly chocked. 'You impudent scoundrel!' I said.

'Steady, steady!' he replied. 'Pitch sticks where it belongs, and nowhere else. But that is enough. I see which it is, M. le Capitaine; this way a moment, by your leave.'

And in a very cavalier fashion he took his officer by the arm, and drew him into a side-walk, leaving me to stand in the sun, bursting with anger and spleen. The gutter-bred rascal! That such a man should insult me, and with impunity! In Paris, I might have made him fight, but here it was impossible.

I was still foaming with rage when they returned.

'We have come to a determination,' the Lieutenant said, tugging his grey moustachios, and standing like a ramrod. 'We shall leave you the house and Madame, and you can take your own line to find the man. For ourselves, we shall draw off our men to the village, and we shall take our line. That is all, M. le Capitaine, is it not?'

'I think so,' the Captain muttered, looking anywhere but at me.

'Then we bid you good day, Monsieur,' the Lieutenant added, and in a moment he turned his companion round, and the two retired up the walk to the house, leaving me to look after them in a black fit of rage and incredulity.

At the first flush, there was something so offensive in the manner of their going that anger had the upper hand. I thought of the Lieutenant's words, and I cursed him to hell with a sickening consciousness that I should not forget them in a hurry.

'Was I playing the traitor to the Cardinal or to these women – which?' *Mon Dieu!* if ever question – but there, some day I would punish him. And the Captain? I could put an end to his amusement, at any rate; and I would. Doubtless among the country bucks of Auch he lorded it as a chief provincial bully, but I would cut his comb for him some fine morning behind the barracks.

And then as I grew cooler I began to wonder why they were going, and what they were going to do. They might be already on the track, or have the information they required under hand; in that case I could understand the movement. But if they were still searching vaguely, uncertain whether their quarry were in the neighbourhood or not, and uncertain how long they might have to stay, it seemed incredible that soldiers should move from good quarters to bad without motive.

I wandered down the garden, thinking sullenly of this, and pettishly cutting off the heads of the flowers with my sheathed sword. After all, if they found and arrested the man, what then? I should have to make my peace with the Cardinal as I best might. He would have gained his point, but not through me, and I should have to look to myself. On the other hand, if I anticipated them – and, as a fact, I believed that I could lay my hand on the fugitive within a few hours – there would come a time when I must face Mademoiselle.

A little while back that had not seemed so difficult a thing. From the day of our first meeting – and in a higher degree since that afternoon when she had lashed me with her scorn – my views of her, and my feelings towards her, had been strangely made up of antagonism and sympathy; of repulsion, because in her past and present she was so different from me; of yearning, because she was a woman and friendless. Later I had duped her and bought her confidence by returning the jewels, and so in a measure I had sated my vengeance; then, as a consequence, sympathy had again got the better of me, until now I hardly knew my own mind, or what I felt, or what I intended. I *did not know*, in fact, what I intended. I stood there in the garden with that conviction suddenly newborn in my mind; and then, in a moment, I heard her step, and I turned to find her behind me.

Her face was like April, smiles breaking through her tears. As she stood with a tall hedge of sunflowers behind her, I started to see how beautiful she was.

'I am here in search of you, M. de Barthe,' she said, colouring slightly, perhaps because my eyes betrayed my thought; 'to thank you. You have not fought, and yet you have conquered. My woman has just been with me, and she tells me that they are going.'

'Going?' I said. 'Yes, Mademoiselle, they are leaving the house.'

She did not understand my reservation.

'What magic have you used?' she said almost gaily; it was wonderful how hope had changed her. 'Besides, I am curious to learn how you managed to avoid fighting.'

'After taking a blow?' I said bitterly.

'Monsieur, I did not mean that,' she said reproachfully.

But her face clouded. I saw that, viewed in this light – in which, I suppose, she had not hitherto – the matter perplexed her more than before.

I took a sudden resolution.

'Have you ever heard, Mademoiselle,' I said gravely, plucking off while I spoke the dead leaves from a plant beside me, 'of a gentleman by name De Berault? Known in Paris, I have heard, by the sobriquet of the Black Death?'

'The duellist?' she answered, looking at me in wonder. 'Yes, I have heard of him. He killed a young gentleman of this province at Nancy two years back. It was a sad story,' she continued, shuddering slightly, 'of a dreadful man. God keep our friends from such!'

'Amen!' I said quietly. But, in spite of myself, I could not meet her eyes.

'Why?' she answered, quickly taking alarm at my silence. 'What of him, M. de Barthe? Why have you mentioned him?'

'Because he is here, Mademoiselle.'

'Here?' she exclaimed. 'At Cocheforêt?'

'Yes, Mademoiselle,' I answered soberly. 'I am he.'

10

Clon

'YOU!' she cried, in a voice which pierced my heart. 'You are M. de Berault? It is impossible!' But, glancing askance at her – I could not face her – I saw that the blood had left her cheeks.

'Yes, Mademoiselle,' I answered in a low tone. 'De Barthe was my mother's name. When I came here, a stranger, I took it that I might not be known; that I might again speak to a good woman, and not see her shrink. That, and – but why trouble you with all this?' I continued, rebelling against her silence, her turned shoulder, her averted face. 'You asked me, Mademoiselle, how I could take a blow and let the striker go. I have answered. It is the one privile M. de Berault possesses.'

'Then,' she replied almost in a whisper, 'if I were M. de Berault, I would avail myself of it, and never fight again.'

'In that event, Mademoiselle,' I answered coldly, 'I should lose my men friends as well as my women friends. Like Monseigneur the Cardinal, I rule by fear.'

She shuddered, either at the name or at the idea my words called up; and, for a moment, we stood awkwardly silent. The shadow of the sundial fell between us; the garden was still; here and there a leaf fluttered slowly down. With each instant of that silence, of that aversion, I felt the gulf between us growing wider, I felt myself growing harder; I mocked at her past which was so unlike mine; I mocked at mine, and called it fate. I was on the point of turning from her with a bow – and with a furnace in my breast – when she spoke.

'There is a last rose lingering there,' she said, a slight tremor in her voice. 'I cannot reach it. Will you pluck it for me, M. de Berault?'

I obeyed her, my hand trembling, my face on fire. She took the rose from me, and placed it in the bosom of her dress. And I saw that her hand trembled too, and that her cheek was dark with blushes.

She turned without more ado and began to walk towards the house. 'Heaven forbid that I should misjudge you a second time!' she said in a low voice. 'And, after all, who am I that I should judge you at all? An hour ago I would have killed that man had I possessed the power.'

'You repented, Mademoiselle,' I said huskily. I could scarcely speak.

'Do you never repent?' she said.

'Yes. But too late, Mademoiselle.'

'Perhaps it is never too late,' she answered softly.

'Alas, when a man is dead –'

'You may rob a man of worse than life!' she replied with energy, stopping me by a gesture. 'If you have never robbed a man – or a woman – of honour! If you have never ruined boy or girl, M. de Berault! If you have never pushed another into the pit and gone by it yourself! If – but, for murder? Listen. You are a Romanist, but I am a Huguenot, and have read. "Thou shall not kill!" it is written; and the penalty, "By man shall thy blood be shed!" But, "if you cause one of these little ones to offend, it were *better* for you that a mill-stone were hanged about your neck, and that you were cast into the depths of the sea." '

'Mademoiselle, you are merciful,' I muttered.

'I need mercy myself,' she answered, sighing. 'And I have had few temptations. How do I know what you have suffered?'

'Or done!' I said, almost rudely.

'Where a man has not lied, nor betrayed, nor sold himself or others,' she answered in a low tone, 'I think I can forgive all else. I can better put up with force,' she added, smiling sadly, 'than with fraud.'

Ah, *Dieu*! I turned away my face that she might not see how pale it grew; that she might not guess how her words, meant in mercy, stabbed me to the heart. And yet, then, for the first time, while viewing in all its depth and width the gulf which separated us, I was not hardened; I was not cast back upon myself. Her gentleness, her pity, her humility softened me, after this, could I do that which I had come to do? How could I stab her in the tenderest part, how could I inflict on her that rending pang, how could I meet her eyes, and stand before her, a Caliban, a Judas, the vilest, lowest thing she could conceive?

I stood a moment, speechless and disordered; overcome by her words, by my thoughts. I have seen a man so stand when he has lost all at the tables. Then I turned to her; and for an instant I thought that my tale was told already, I thought that she had pierced my disguise. For her face was changed – stricken as with fear. The next moment, I saw that she was not looking at me, but beyond me; and I turned quickly and saw a servant hurrying from the house to us. It was Louis. His eyes were staring, his hair waved, his cheeks were flabby with dismay. He breathed as if he had been running.

'What is it?' Mademoiselle cried, while he was still some way off. 'Speak, man. My sister? Is she –'

'Clon,' he gasped.

The name changed her to stone.

'Clon? What of him?' she muttered.

'In the village!' Louis panted, his tongue stuttering with terror. 'They are flogging him. They are killing him! To make him tell!'

Mademoiselle grasped the sundial and leant against it, her face colourless; and, for an instant, I thought that she was fainting.

'Tell?' I said mechanically. 'But he cannot tell. He is dumb, man.'

'They will make him guide them,' Louis groaned, covering his ears with his shaking hands, his face the colour of paper, 'And his cries! Oh, Monsieur, go, go!' he continued in a thrilling tone. 'Save him. All through the wood I heard his cries. It was horrible! horrible!'

Mademoiselle uttered a moan of pain; and I turned to support her, thinking each second to see her fall. But with a sudden movement she straightened herself, and, quickly slipping by me, with eyes that seemed to see nothing, she set off swiftly down the walk towards the meadow gate.

I ran after her; but, taken by surprise as I was, it was only by a great effort I reached the gate before her, and thrusting myself in the road, barred the way.

'Let me pass!' she panted, striving to thrust me on one side. 'Out of my way, sir! I am going to the village.'

'You are not going to the village,' I said sternly. 'Go back to the house, Mademoiselle, and at once.'

'My servant!' she wailed. 'Let me go! Let me go! Do you think I can rest here while they torture him? He cannot speak, and they – they –'

'Go back, Mademoiselle,' I said, with decision. 'Your presence would only make matters worse! I will go myself, and what one man can do against many, I will! Louis, give your mistress your arm and take her to the house. Take her to Madame.'

'But you will go?' she cried. And before I could stay her – I swear I would have stopped her if I could – she raised my hand and carried it to her trembling lips. 'You will go! Go and stop them! Stop them, and Heaven reward you, Monsieur!'

I did not answer; nay, I did not once look back as I crossed the meadow; but I did not look forward either. Doubtless it was grass I trod, and the wood was before me with the sun shining aslant on it; doubtless the house rose behind me with a flame here and there in the windows. But I went in a dream, among shadows; with a racing pulse, in a glow from head to heel; conscious of nothing but the touch of Mademoiselle's warm lips on my hand, seeing neither meadow nor house, nor even the dark fringe of wood before me, but only Mademoiselle's passionate face. For the moment I was drunk: drunk with that to which I had been so long a stranger, with that which a man may scorn for years, to find it at last beyond his reach – drunk with the touch of a good woman's lips.

I passed the bridge in this state; and my feet were among the brushwood before the heat and fervour in which I moved found on a sudden their direction. Something began to penetrate to my veiled senses – a hoarse inarticulate cry, now deep, now shrilling horribly, that of itself seemed to fill the wood. It came at intervals of half a minute or so, and made the flesh creep, it rang so full of dumb pain, of impotent wrestling, of unspeakable agony. I am a man and have seen things. I saw the Concini beheaded, and Chalais ten years later – they gave him thirty-four blows; and when

I was a boy I escaped from the college and viewed from a great distance Ravaillac torn by horses – that was in the year ten. But the horrible cries I now heard filled me, perhaps because I was alone and fresh from the sight of Mademoiselle, with loathing inexpressible. The very wood, though the sun had not yet set, seemed to grow dark. I ran on through it, cursing, until the hovels of the village came in sight. Again the shriek rose, a pulsing horror; and this time I could hear the lash fall on the sodden flesh, I could see in fancy the dumb man, trembling, quivering, straining against his bonds. And then, in a moment, I was in the street, and, as the scream once more tore the air, I dashed round the corner by the inn, and came upon them.

I did not look at *him*, but I saw Captain Larolle and the Lieutenant, and a ring of troopers, and one man, bare-armed, teasing out with his fingers the thongs of a whip. The thongs dripped blood, and the sight fired mine. The rage I had suppressed when the Lieutenant bearded me earlier in the afternoon, the passion with which Mademoiselle's distress had filled my breast, on the instant found vent. I sprang through the line of soldiers, and striking the man with the whip a buffet between the shoulders, which hurled him breathless to the ground, I turned on the leaders.

'You fiends!' I cried. 'Shame on you! The man is dumb! Dumb; and if I had ten men with me, I would sweep you and your scum out of the village with broomsticks. Lay on another lash,' I continued recklessly, 'and I will see whether you or the Cardinal be the stronger.'

The Lieutenant glared at me, his grey moustache bristling, his eyes almost starting from his head. Some of the troopers laid their hands on their swords, but no one moved, and only the Captain spoke.

'*Mille diables!*' he swore. 'What is all this about? Are you mad, sir?'

'Mad or sane!' I cried furiously. 'Lay on another lash, and you shall repent it.'

For an instant there was a pause of astonishment. Then, to my surprise, the Captain laughed – laughed loudly.

'Very heroic,' he said. 'Quite magnificent, M. Chevalier-errant. But you see, unfortunately, you come too late.'

'Too late,' I said incredulously.

'Yes, too late,' he replied, with a mocking smile. And the Lieutenant grinned too. 'Unfortunately, you see, the man has just confessed. We have only been giving him an extra touch or two to impress his memory, and save us the trouble of lashing him up again.'

'I don't believe it,' I said bluntly – but I felt the check, and fell to earth. 'The man cannot speak.'

'No, but he has managed to tell us what we want; that he will guide us to the place we are seeking,' the Captain answered drily. 'The whip, if it cannot find a man a tongue, can find him wits. What is more, I think that he will keep his word,' he continued, with a hideous scowl. 'For I warn him that if he does not, all your heroics shall not save him. He is a rebel dog, and known to us of old; and I will flay his back to the bones, ay, until we can see his heart beating through his ribs, but I will have what I want – in your teeth, too, you d – d meddler.'

'Steady, steady!' I said, sobered. I saw that he was telling the truth. 'Is he going to take you to M. de Cocheforêt's hiding-place?'

'Yes, he is!' the Captain retorted. 'Have you any objection to that, Master Spy?'

'None,' I replied. 'Only I shall go with you. And if you live three months, I shall kill you for that name – behind the barracks at Auch, M. le Capitaine.'

He changed colour, but he answered me boldly enough.

'I don't know that you will go with us,' he said, with a snarl. 'That is as we please.'

'I have the Cardinal's orders,' I said sternly.

'The Cardinal?' he exclaimed, stung to fury by this repetition of the name. 'The Cardinal be –'

But the Lieutenant laid his hand on his lips and stopped him.

'Hush!' he said. Then more quietly, 'Your pardon, M. le Capitaine; but the least said the soonest mended. Shall I give orders to the men to fall in?'

The Captain nodded sullenly.

The Lieutenant turned to his prisoner.

'Take him down!' he commanded in his harsh, monotonous voice. 'Throw his blouse over him, and tie his hands. And do you two, Paul and Lebrun, guard him. Michel, bring the whip, or he may forget how it tastes. Sergeant, choose four good men, and dismiss the rest to their quarters.'

'Shall we need the horses?' the sergeant asked.

'I don't know,' the Captain answered peevishly. 'What does the rogue say?'

The Lieutenant stepped up to him.

'Listen!' he said grimly. 'Nod if you mean yes, and shake your head if you mean no. And have a care you answer truly. Is it more than a mile to this place?'

They had loosened the poor wretch's fastenings and covered his back. He stood leaning his shoulder against the wall, his mouth still panting, the sweat running down his hollow cheeks. His sunken eyes were closed, but a quiver now and again ran through his frame. The Lieutenant repeated his question, and, getting no answer, looked round for orders. The Captain met the look, and crying savagely, 'Answer, will you, you mule!' struck the half-swooning miserable across the back with his switch. The effect was magical. Covered, as his shoulders were, the man sprang erect with a shriek of pain, raising his chin and hollowing his back; and in that attitude stood an instant with starting eyes, gasping for breath. Then he sank back against the wall, moving his mouth spasmodically. His face was the colour of lead.

'*Diable!* I think that we have gone too far with him!' the Captain muttered.

'Bring some wine!' the Lieutenant replied. 'Quick with it!'

I looked on, burning with indignation, and in some excitement besides. For if the man took them to the place, and they succeeded in seizing Cocheforêt, there was an end of the matter as far as I was concerned. It was off my shoulders, and I might leave the village when I pleased; nor was it likely – since he would have his man, though not through me – that the Cardinal would refuse to grant me an amnesty. On the whole, I thought that he would prefer that things should take this course; and assuming the issue, I began to wonder whether it would be necessary in that event that Madame should know the truth. I had a kind of vision of a reformed Berault, dead to play and purging himself at a distance from Zaton's; winning, perhaps, a name in the Italian war, and finally – but, pshaw! I was a fool.

However, be these things as they might, it was essential that I should see the arrest made; and I waited patiently while they revived the tortured man and made their dispositions. These took some time; so that the sun was down, and it was growing dusk when we marched out, Clon going first, supported by his two guards, the Captain and I following – abreast, and eyeing one another suspiciously; the Lieutenant, with the sergeant and five troopers, bringing up the rear. Clon moved slowly, moaning from time to time; and but for the aid given him by the two men with him, must have sunk down again and again.

He led the way out between two houses close to the inn, and struck a narrow track, scarcely discernible, which ran behind other houses, and then plunged into the thickest part of the wood. A single person, traversing the covert, might have made such a track; or pigs, or children. But it was the first idea that occurred to us, and put us all on the alert. The Captain carried a cocked pistol, I held my sword drawn, and kept a watchful eye on *him*; and the deeper the dusk fell in the wood, the more cautiously we went, until at last we came out with a sort of jump into a wider and lighter path.

I looked up and down, and saw behind me a vista of tree-trunks, before me a wooden bridge and an open meadow, lying cold and grey in the twilight; and I stood in astonishment. We were in the old path to the Château! I shivered at the thought that he was going to take us there, to the house, to Mademoiselle!

The Captain also recognised the place, and swore aloud. But the dumb man went on unheeding until he reached the wooden bridge. There he stopped short, and looked towards the dark outline of the house, which was just visible, one faint light twinkling sadly in the west wing. As the Captain and I pressed up behind him, he raised his hands and seemed to wring them towards the house.

'Have a care!' the Captain growled. 'Play me no tricks, or –'

He did not finish the sentence, for Clon, as if he well understood his impatience, turned back from the bridge, and, entering the wood to the left, began to ascend the bank of the stream. We had not gone a hundred yards before the ground grew rough, and the undergrowth thick; and yet through all ran a kind of path which enabled us to advance, dark as it was now growing. Very soon the bank on which we moved began to rise above the water, and grew steep and rugged. We turned a shoulder, where the stream swept round a curve, and saw we were in the mouth of a small ravine, dark and sheer-sided. The water brawled along the bottom, over boulders and through chasms. In front, the slope on which we stood shaped itself into a low cliff; but half-way between its summit and the water a ledge, or narrow terrace, running along the face, was dimly visible.

'Ten to one, a cave!' the Captain muttered. 'It is a likely place.'

'And an ugly one!' I replied with a sneer. 'Which one against ten might hold for hours!'

'If the ten had no pistols – yes!' he answered viciously. 'But you see we have. Is he going that way?'

He was. As soon as this was clear, Larolle turned to his comrade.

'Lieutenant,' he said, speaking in a low voice, though the chafing of the stream below us covered ordinary sounds, 'what say you? Shall we light the lanthorns, or press on while there is still a glimmering of day?'

'On, I should say, M. le Capitaine,' the Lieutenant answered. 'Prick him in the back if he falters. I will warrant,' the brute added with a chuckle, 'he has a tender place or two.'

The Captaine gave the word and we moved forward. It was evident now that the cliffpath was our destination. It was possible for the eye to follow the track all the way to it, through rough stones and brushwood; and though Clon climbed feebly, and with many groans, two minutes saw us step on to it. It did not prove to be, in fact, the perilous place it looked at a distance. The ledge, grassy and terrace-like, sloped slightly downwards and outwards, and in parts was slippery; but it was as wide as a highway, and the fall to the water did not exceed thirty feet. Even in such a dim light as now displayed it to us, and by increasing the depth and unseen dangers of the gorge gave a kind of impressiveness to our movements, a nervous woman need not have feared to tread it. I wondered how often Mademoiselle had passed along it with her milk-pitcher.

'I think that we have him now,' Captain Larolle muttered, twisting his moustachios, and looking about to make his last dispositions. 'Paul and Lebrun, see that your man makes no noise. Sergeant, come forward with your carbine, but do not fire without orders. Now, silence all, and close up, Lieutenant. Forward!'

We advanced about a hundred paces, keeping the cliff on our left, turned a shoulder, and saw, a few paces in front of us, a slight hollow, a black blotch in the grey darkness of the cliffside. The prisoner stopped, and, raising his bound hands, pointed to it.

'There?' the Captain whispered, pressing forward. 'Is it the place?'

Clon nodded. The Captain's voice shook with excitement.

'Paul and Lebrun, remain here with the prisoner,' he said in a low tone. 'Sergeant, come forward with me. Now, are you ready? Forward!'

At the word he and the sergeant passed quickly, one on either side of Clon and his guards. The path grew narrow here, and the Captain passed outside. The eyes of all but one were on the black blotch, the hollow in the cliff-side, expecting we knew not what – a sudden shot or the rush of a desperate man; and no one saw exactly what happened. But somehow, as the Captain passed abreast of him, the prisoner thrust back his guards, and leaping sideways, flung his unbound arms round Larolle's body, and in an instant swept him, shouting, to the verge of the precipice.

It was done in a moment. By the time our startled wits and eyes were back with them, the two were already tottering on the edge, looking in the gloom like one dark form. The sergeant, who was the first to find his head, levelled his carbine, but, as the wrestlers twirled and twisted, the Captain, shrieking out oaths and threats, the mute silent as death, it was impossible to see which was which and the sergeant lowered his gun again, while the men held back nervously. The ledge sloped steeply there, the edge was vague, already the two seemed to be wrestling in mid air; and the mute was desperate.

That moment of hesitation was fatal. Clon's long arms were round the other's arms, crushing them into his ribs; Clon's skull-like face grinned hate into the other's eyes; his bony limbs curled round him like the folds of a snake. Larolle's strength gave way.

'Damn you all! Why don't you come up?' he cried. And then, 'Ah! Mercy! mercy!' came in one last scream from his lips. As the Lieutenant, taken aback before, sprang forward to his aid, the two toppled over the edge, and in a second hurtled out of sight.

'*Mon Dieu!*' the Lieutenant cried; the answer was a dull splash in the depths below. He flung up his arms. 'Water!' he said. 'Quick, men, get down. We may save him yet.'

But there was no path, and night was come, and the men's nerves were shaken. The lanthorns had to be lit, and the way to be retraced; by the time we reached the dark pool which lay below, the last bubbles were gone from the surface, the last ripples had beaten themselves out against the banks. The pool still rocked sullenly, and the yellow light showed a man's hat floating, and near it a glove three parts submerged. But that was all. The mute's dying grip had known no loosening, nor his hate any fear. I heard afterwards that when they dragged the two out next day, his fingers were in the other's eye-sockets, his teeth in his throat. If ever man found death sweet, it was he!

As we turned slowly from the black water, some shuddering, some crossing themselves, the Lieutenant looked at me.

'Curse you!' he said passionately. 'I believe that you are glad.'

'He deserved his fate,' I answered coldly. 'Why should I pretend to be sorry? It was now or in three months. And for the other poor devil's sake I am glad.'

He glared at me for a moment in speechless anger.

At last, 'I should like to have you tied up!' he said between his teeth.

'I should think that you had had enough of tying up for one day!' I retorted. 'But there,' I went on contemptuously, 'it comes of making officers out of the canaille. Dogs love blood. The teamster must lash something if he can no longer lash his horses.'

We were back, a sombre little procession, at the wooden bridge when I said this. He stopped.

'Very well,' he replied, nodding viciously. 'That decides me. Sergeant, light me this way with a lanthorn. The rest of you to the village. Now, Master Spy,' he continued, glancing at me with gloomy spite. 'Your road is my road. I think I know how to spoil your game.'

I shrugged my shoulders in disdain, and together, the sergeant leading the way with the light, we crossed the dim meadow, and passed through the gate where Mademoiselle had kissed my hand, and up the ghostly walk between the rose-bushes. I wondered uneasily what the Lieutenant would be at, and what he intended; but the lanthorn-light which now fell on the ground at our feet, and now showed one of us to the other, high-lit in a frame of blackness, discovered nothing in his grizzled face but settled hostility. He wheeled at the end of the walk to go to the main door, but as he did so I saw the flutter of a white skirt by the stone seat against the house, and I stepped that way.

'Mademoiselle?' I said softly. 'Is it you?'

'Clon?' she muttered, her voice quivering. 'What of him?'

'He is past pain,' I answered gently. 'He is dead – yes, dead, Mademoiselle, but in his own way. Take comfort.'

She stifled a sob; then before I could say more, the Lieutenant, with his sergeant and light, were at my elbow. He saluted Mademoiselle roughly. She looked at him with shuddering abhorrence.

'Are you come to flog me too, sir?' she said passionately. 'Is it not enough that you have murdered my servant?'

'On the contrary, it was he who killed my Captain,' the Lieutenant answered, in another tone than I had expected. 'If your servant is dead, so is my comrade.'

'Captain Larolle?' she murmured, gazing with startled eyes, not at him but at me.

I nodded.

'How?' she asked.

'Clon flung the Captain and himself – into the river pool above the bridge,' I said.

She uttered a low cry of awe and stood silent; but her lips moved and I think that she prayed for Clon, though she was a Huguenot. Meanwhile,

I had a fright. The lanthorn, swinging in the sergeant's hand, and throwing its smoky light now on the stone seat, now on the rough wall above it, showed me something else. On the seat, doubtless where Mademoiselle's hand had lain as she sat in the dark, listening and watching and shivering, stood a pitcher of food. Beside her, in that place, it was damning evidence, and I trembled lest the Lieutenant's eye should fall upon it, lest the sergeant should see it; and then, in a moment, I forgot all about it. The Lieutenant was speaking and his voice was doom. My throat grew dry as I listened; my tongue stuck to my mouth. I tried to look at Mademoiselle, but I could not.

'It is true that the Captain is gone,' he said stiffly, 'but others are alive, and about one of them a word with you, by your leave, Mademoiselle. I have listened to a good deal of talk from this fine gentleman friend of yours. He has spent the last twenty-four hours saying "You shall!" and "You shall not!" He came from you and took a very high tone because we laid a little whip-lash about that dumb devil of yours. He called us brutes and beasts, and but for him I am not sure that my friend would not now be alive. But when he said a few minutes ago that he was glad – glad of it, d – him! – then I fixed it in my mind that I would be even with him. And I am going to be!'

'What do you mean?' Mademoiselle asked, wearily interrupting him. 'If you think that you can prejudice me against this gentleman –'

'That is precisely what I am going to do! And a little more than that!' he answered.

'You will be only wasting your breath!' she retorted.

'Wait! Wait, Mademoiselle – until you have heard,' he said. 'For I swear to you that if ever a black-hearted scoundrel, a dastardly sneaking spy trod the earth, it is this fellow! And I am going to expose him. Your own eyes and your own ears shall persuade you. I am not particular, but I would not eat, I would not drink, I would not sit down with him! I would rather be beholden to the meanest trooper in my squadron than to him! Ay, I would, so help me Heaven!'

And the Lieutenant, turning squarely on his heel, spat on the ground.

11

The Arrest

IT had come, and I saw no way of escape. The sergeant was between us and I could not strike him. And I found no words. A score of times I had thought with shrinking how I should reveal my secret to Mademoiselle – what I should say, and how she would take it; but in my mind it had been always a voluntary act, this disclosure; it had been always I who unmasked myself and she who listened – alone; and in this voluntariness and this privacy there had been something which took from the shame of anticipation. But here – here was no voluntary act on my part, no privacy, nothing but shame. And I stood mute, convicted, speechless, under her eyes – like the thing I was.

Yet if anything could have braced me it was Mademoiselle's voice when she answered him.

'Go on, Monsieur,' she said calmly. 'You will have done the sooner.'

'You do not believe me?' he replied.

'Then, I say, look at him! Look at him! If ever shame – '

'Monsieur,' she said abruptly – she did not look at me, 'I am ashamed of myself.'

'But you don't hear me,' the Lieutenant rejoined hotly. 'His very name is not his own! He is not Barthe at all. He is Berault, the gambler, the duellist, the bully; whom if you – '

Again she interrupted him.

'I know it,' she said coldly. 'I know it all; and if you have nothing more to tell me, go, Monsieur. Go!' she continued in a tone of infinite scorn. 'Be satisfied that you have earned my contempt as well as my abhorrence.'

He looked for a moment taken aback. Then:

'Ay, but I *have* more,' he cried, his voice stubbornly triumphant. 'I forgot that you would think little of that. I forgot that a swordsman has always the ladies' hearts – but I have more. Do you know, too, that he is in the Cardinal's pay? Do you know that he is here on the same errand which brings us here – to arrest M. de Cocheforêt? Do you know that while we go about the business openly and in soldier fashion, it is his part to worm himself into your confidence, to sneak into Madame's intimacy, to listen at your door, to follow your footsteps, to hang on your lips, to track you – track you until you betray yourselves and the man? Do you know this, and that all his sympathy is a lie, Mademoiselle? His help, so much bait to catch the secret? His aim, blood money – blood money? Why, *morbleu*!' the Lieutenant continued, pointing his finger at me, and so carried away by passion, so lifted out of himself by wrath and indignation that I shrank before him – 'you talk, lady, of contempt and abhorrence in the same breath with me, but what have you for him – what have you for him – the spy, the informer, the hired traitor? And if you doubt me, if you want evidence, look at him. Only look at him, I say.'

And he might say it; for I stood silent still, cowering and despairing, white with rage and hate. But Mademoiselle did not look. She gazed straight at the Lieutenant.

'Have you done?' she said.

'Done?' he stammered; her words, her air, bringing him to earth again. 'Done? Yes, if you believe me.'

'I do not,' she answered proudly. 'If that be all, be satisfied, Monsieur. I do not believe you.'

'Then tell me this,' he retorted, after a moment of stunned surprise.

'Answer me this! Why, if he was not on our side, do you think that we let him remain here? Why did we suffer him to stay in a suspected house, bullying us, annoying us, thwarting us, taking your part from hour to hour?'

'He has a sword, Monsieur,' she answered with fine contempt.

'*Mille diables!*' he cried, snapping his fingers in a rage. 'That for his sword! It was because he held the Cardinal's commission, I tell you, because he had equal authority with us. Because we had no choice.'

'And that being so, Monsieur, why are you now betraying him?' she asked.

He swore at that, feeling the stroke go home.

'You must be mad!' he said, glaring at her. 'Cannot you see that the man is what I tell you? Look at him! Look at him, I say! Listen to him! Has he a word to say for himself?'

Still she did not look.

'It is late,' she replied coldly. 'And I am not very well. If you have done, quite done – perhaps you will leave me, Monsieur.'

'*Mon Dieu!*' he exclaimed, shrugging his shoulders, and grinding his teeth in impotent rage. 'You *are* mad! I have told you the truth, and you will not believe it. Well – on your head be it then, Mademoiselle. I have no more to say! You will see.'

And with that, without more, fairly conquered by her staunchness, he saluted her, gave the word to the sergeant, turned and went down the path.

The sergeant went after him, the lanthorn swaying in his hand. And we two were left alone. The frogs were croaking in the pool; a bat flew round in circles; the house, the garden, all lay quiet under the darkness, as on the night when I first came to it.

And would to Heaven I had never come – that was the cry in my heart. Would to Heaven I had never seen this woman, whose nobleness and faith were a continual shame to me; a reproach branding me every hour I stood in her presence with all vile and hateful names. The man just gone, coarse, low-bred, brutal soldier as he was, man-flogger and drilling-block, had yet found heart to feel my baseness, and words in which to denounce it. What, then, would she say, when the truth came home to her? What shape should I take in her eyes then? How should I be remembered through all the years then?

Then? But now? What was she thinking now, at this moment, as she stood silent and absorbed near the stone seat, a shadowy figure with face turned from me? Was she recalling the man's words, fitting them to the facts and the past, adding this and that circumstance? Was she, though she had rebuffed him in the body, collating, now he was gone, all that he had said, and out of these scraps piercing together the damning truth? Was she, for all that she had said, beginning to see me as I was? The thought tortured me. I could brook uncertainty no longer. I went nearer to her and touched her sleeve.

'Mademoiselle,' I said in a voice which sounded hoarse and unnatural even in my own ears, 'do you believe this of me?'

She started violently, and turned.

'Pardon, Monsieur!' she murmured, passing her hand over her brow; 'I had forgotten that you were here. Do I believe – what?'

'What that man said of me,' I muttered.

'That!' she exclaimed. And then she stood a moment gazing at me in a strange fashion. 'Do I believe that, Monsieur? But come, come!' she continued impetuosly. 'Come, and I will show you if I believe it. But not here.'

She turned as she spoke, and led the way on the instant into the house through the parlour door, which stood half open. The room inside was pitch dark, but she took me fearlessly by the hand and led me quickly through it, and along the passage, until we came to the cheerful lighted hall, where a great fire burned on the hearth. All traces of the soldiers' occupation had been swept away. But the room was empty.

She led me to the fire, and there in the full light, no longer a shadowy creature, but red-lipped, brilliant, throbbing with life and beauty, she stood opposite me – her eyes shining, her colour high, her breast heaving.

'Do I believe it?' she said in a thrilling voice. 'I will tell you. M. de Cocheforêt's hiding-place is in the hut behind the fern-stack, two furlongs beyond the village on the road to Auch. You know now what no one else knows, he and I and Madame excepted. You hold in your hands his life and my honour; and you know also, M. de Berault, whether I believe that tale.'

'My God!' I cried. And I stood looking at her until something of the horror in my eyes crept into hers, and she shuddered and stepped back from me.

'What is it? What is it?' she whispered, clasping her hands. And with all the colour gone suddenly from her cheeks she peered trembling into the corners and towards the door. 'There is no one here.'

I forced myself to speak, though I was trembling all over like a man in an ague. 'No, Mademoiselle, there is no one here,' I muttered. 'There is no one here.' And then I let my head fall on my breast, and I stood before her, the statue of despair. Had she felt a grain of suspicion, a grain of doubt, my bearing must have opened her eyes; but her mind was cast in so noble a mould that, having once thought ill of me and been converted, she could feel no doubt again. She must trust all in all. A little recovered from her fright, she stood looking at me in great wonder; and at last she had a thought:

'You are not well?' she said suddenly. 'It is your old wound, Monsieur. Now I have it?'

'Yes, Mademoiselle,' I muttered faintly, 'it is.'

'I will call Clon!' she cried impetuously. And then, with a sob: 'Ah!

poor Clon! He is gone. But there is still Louis. I will call him and he will get you something.'

She was gone from the room before I could stop her, and I stood leaning against the table, possessor at last of the secret which I had come so far to win; able in a moment to open the door and go out into the night, and make use of it – and yet the most unhappy of men. The sweat stood on my brow; my eyes wandered round the room; I turned towards the door, with some mad thought of flight – of flight from her, from the house, from everything; and I had actually taken a step towards this, when on the door, the outer door, there came a sudden hurried knocking which jarred every nerve in my body. I started, and stopped. I stood a moment in the middle of the floor gazing at the door, as at a ghost. Then, glad of action, glad of anything that might relieve the tension of my feelings, I strode to it and pulled it sharply open.

On the threshold, his flushed face lit up by the light behind me, stood one of the knaves whom I had brought with me to Auch. He had been running, and panted heavily; but he had kept his wits, and the instant I appeared he grasped my sleeve.

'Ah! Monsieur, the very man!' he cried. 'Quick! come this instant, lose not a moment, and you may yet be first. They have the secret! The soldiers have found Monsieur!'

'Found him?' I echoed. 'M. de Cocheforêt?'

'No; but they know the place where he lies. It was found by accident. The Lieutenant was gathering his men when I came away. If we are quick, we may yet be first.'

'But the place?' I said.

'I could not hear,' he answered bluntly. 'We must hang on their skirts, and at the last moment strike in. It is the only way, Monsieur.'

The pair of pistols I had taken from the shock-headed man lay on a chest by the door. Without waiting for more I snatched them up and my hat, and joined him, and in a moment we were running down the garden. I looked back once before we passed the gate, and I saw the light streaming out through the door which I had left open; and I fancied that for an instant a figure darkened the gap. But the fancy only strengthened the one single purpose, the iron resolve, which had taken possession of me and all my thoughts. I must be first; I must anticipate the Lieutenant; I must make the arrest myself. I must be first. And I ran on only the faster.

We were across the meadow and in the wood in a moment. There, instead of keeping along the common path, I boldly singled out – my senses seemed to be preternaturally keen – the smaller trail by which Clon had brought us. Along this I ran unfalteringly, avoiding logs and pitfalls as by instinct, and following all its turns and twists, until we came to the back of the inn, and could hear the murmur of subdued voices in the village street, the sharp low word of command, and the clink of weapons;

and could see over and between the houses the dull glare of lanthorns and torches.

I grasped my man's arm, and crouched down listening. When I had heard enough, 'Where is your mate?' I said in his ear.

'With them,' he muttered.

'Then, come,' I whispered, rising. 'I have seen what I want. Let us go.' But he caught me by the arm and detained me.

'You don't know the way,' he said. 'Steady, steady, Monsieur. You go too fast. They are just moving. Let us join them, and strike in when the time comes. We must let them guide us.'

'Fool!' I said, shaking off his hand. 'I tell you, I know where he is! I know where they are going. Come, and we will pluck the fruit while they are on the road to it.'

His only answer was an exclamation of surprise. At that moment the lights began to move. The Lieutenant was starting. The moon was not yet up, the sky was grey and cloudy; to advance where we were was to step into a wall of blackness. But we had lost too much already, and I did not hesitate. Bidding my companion follow me and use his legs, I sprang through a low fence which rose before us; then stumbling blindly over some broken ground in the rear of the houses, I came with a fall or two to a little watercourse with steep sides. Through this I plunged recklessly and up the further side, and, breathless and panting, gained the road, beyond the village, and fifty yards in advance of the Lieutenant's troop.

They had only two lanthorns burning, and we were beyond the circle of light cast by these; while the steady tramp of so many footsteps covered the noise we made. We were in no danger of being noticed, and in a twinkling we turned our backs, and as fast as we could we ran down the road. Fortunately, they were thinking more of secrecy than speed, and in a minute we had doubled the distance between them and us. In two minutes their lights were mere sparks shining in the gloom behind us. We lost even the tramp of their feet. Then I began to look out and go more slowly, peering into the shadows on either side for the fernstack.

On one hand the hill rose steeply, on the other it fell away to the stream. On either side was close wood, or my difficulties had been immensely increased; but scattered oak trees stood here and there among the bracken. This helped me, and presently, on the upper side, I came upon the dense substance of the stack looming black against the lighter hill.

My heart beat fast, but it was no time for thought. Bidding the man in a whisper to follow me and be ready to back me up, I climbed the bank softly, and, with a pistol in my hand, felt my way to the rear of the stack, thinking to find a hut there, set against the fern, and M. de Cocheforêt in it. But I found no hut. There was none; and, moreover, it was so dark now we were off the road, that it came upon me suddenly, as I stood between the hill and the stack, that I had undertaken a very difficult thing.

The hut behind the fernstack. But how far behind? how far from it? The dark slope stretched above us, infinite, immesurable, shrouded in night. To begin to climb it in search of a tiny hut, possibly well hidden and hard to find in day-light, seemed an endeavour as hopeless as to meet with the needle in the hay! And now while I stood, chilled and doubting, almost despairing, the steps of the troop in the road began to grow audible, began to come nearer.

'Well, Monsieur le Capitaine?' the man beside me muttered – in wonder why I stood. 'Which way? or they will be before us yet.'

I tried to think, to reason it out; to consider where the hut should be; while the wind sighed through the oaks, and here and there I could hear an acorn fall. But the thing pressed too close on me; my thoughts would not be hurried, and at last I said at a venture:

'Up the hill. Straight up from the stack.'

He did not demur, and we plunged at the ascent, knee-deep in bracken and furze, sweating at every pore with our exertions, and hearing the troop come every moment nearer on the road below. Doubtless they knew exactly whither to go! Forced to stop and take breath when we had scrambled up fifty yards or so, I saw their lanthorns shining like moving glow-worms; I could even hear the clink of steel. For all I could tell, the hut might be down there, and we be moving from it. But it was too late to go back now – they were close to the fernstack; and in despair I turned to the hill again. A dozen steps and I stumbled. I rose and plunged on again; again stumbled. Then I found that I was treading level earth. And – was it water I saw before me, below me? or some mirage of the sky?

Neither; and I gripped my fellow's arm, as he came abreast of me, and stopped him sharply. Below us in the middle of a steep hollow, a pit in the hillside, a light shone out through some aperture and quivered on the mist, like the pale lamp of a moorland hobgoblin. It made itself visible, displaying nothing else; a wisp of light in the bottom of a black bowl. Yet my spirits rose with a great bound at sight of it; for I knew that I had stumbled on the place I sought.

In the common run of things I should have weighed my next step carefully, and gone about it slowly. But here was no place for thought, nor room for delay; and I slid down the side of the hollow on the instant, and the moment my feet touched the bottom sprang to the door of the little hut, whence the light issued. A stone turned under my feet in my rush, and I fell on my knees on the threshold; but the fall only brought my face to a level with the face of the man who lay inside on a bed of fern. He had been reading. Startled by the sound I made, he dropped his book, and in a flash stretched out his hand for a weapon. But the muzzle of my pistol covered him, he was not in a posture from which he could spring, and at a sharp word from me he dropped his hand; the tigerish glare which flickered for an instant in his eyes gave place to a languid smile, and he shrugged his shoulders.

'*Eh bien!*' he said with marvellous composure. 'Taken at last! Well, I was tired of it.'

'You are my prisoner, M. de Cocheforêt,' I answered. 'Move a hand and I kill you. But you have still a choice.'

'Truly?' he said, raising his eyebrows.

'Yes. My orders are to take you to Paris alive or dead. Give me your parole that you will make no attempt to escape, and you shall go thither at your ease and as a gentleman. Refuse, and I shall disarm and bind you, and you go as a prisoner.'

'What force have you?' he asked curtly. He still lay on his elbow, his cloak covering him, the little Marot in which he had been reading close to his hand. But his quick black eyes, which looked the keener for the pallor and thinness of his face, roved ceaselessly over me, probed the darkness behind me, took note of everything.

'Enough to compel you, Monsieur,' I replied sternly; 'but that is not all. There are thirty dragoons coming up the hill to secure you, and they will make you no such offer. Surrender to me before they come, and give me your parole, and I will do all I can for your comfort. Delay, and you must fall into their hands. There can be no escape.'

'You will take my word?' he said slowly.

'Give it, and you may keep your pistols, M. de Cocheforêt.'

'Tell me at least that you are not alone.'

'I am not alone.'

'Then I give it,' he said with a sigh. 'And for Heaven's sake get me something to eat and a bed. I am tired of this pig-sty. *Mon Dieu!* it is a fortnight since I slept between sheets.'

'You shall sleep to-night in your own house, if you please,' I answered hurriedly. 'But here they come. Be good enough to stay where you are for a moment and I will meet them.'

I stepped out into the darkness, just as the Lieutenant, after posting his men round the hollow, slid down with a couple of sergeants to make the arrest. The place round the open door was pitch dark. He had not espied my man, who had lodged himself in the deepest shadow of the hut, and when he saw me come out across the light he took me for Cocheforêt. In a twinkling he thrust a pistol into my face, and cried triumphantly: 'You are my prisoner!' while one of the sergeants raised a lanthorn and threw its light into my eyes.

'What folly is this?' I said savagely.

The Lieutenant's jaw fell, and he stood for a moment paralysed with astonishment. Less than an hour before he had left me at the Château. Thence he had come hither with the briefest delay; yet he found me here before him. He swore fearfully, his face black, his moustachios stiff with rage.

'What is this? What is it?' he cried. 'Where is the man?'

'What man?' I said.

'This Cochefôret!' he roared, carried away by his passion. 'Don't lie to me! He is here, and I will have him!'

'You are too late,' I said, watching him heedfully. 'M. de Cochefôret is here, but he has already surrendered to me, and is my prisoner.'

'Your prisoner?'

'Certainly!' I answered, facing the man with all the harshness I could muster. 'I have arrested him by virtue of the Cardinal's commission granted to me. And by virtue of the same I shall keep him.'

'You will keep him?'

'I shall!'

He stared at me for a moment, utterly aghast; the picture of defeat. Then on a sudden I saw his face lighten with a new idea.

'It is a d – d ruse!' he shouted, brandishing his pistol like a madman. 'It is a cheat and a fraud! By God! You have no commision! I see through it! I see through it all! You have come here, and you have hocussed us! You are of their side, and this is your last shift to save him!'

'What folly is this?' I said contemptuously.

'No folly at all,' he answered, perfect conviction in his tone. 'You have played upon us. You have fooled us. But I see through it now. An hour ago I exposed you to that fine Madame at the house there, and I thought it a marvel that she did not believe me. I thought it a marvel that she did not see through you, when you stood there before her, confounded, tongue-tied, a rogue convicted. But I understand now. She knew you. She was in the plot, and you were in the plot, and I, who thought that I was opening her eyes, was the only one fooled. But it is my turn now. You have played a bold part and a clever one,' he continued, a sinister light in his little eyes, 'and I congratulate you. But it is at an end now, Monsieur. You took us in finely with your talk of Monseigneur, and his commission and your commission, and the rest. But I am not to be blinded any longer – or bullied. You have arrested him, have you? *You* have arrested him. Well, by G –, I shall arrest him, and I shall arrest you too.'

'You are mad!' I said, staggered as much by this new view of the matter as by his perfect certainty. 'Mad, Lieutenant.'

'I was,' he snarled. 'But I am same now. I was mad when you imposed upon us, when you persuaded me to think that you were fooling the women to get the secret out of them, while all the time you were sheltering them, protecting them, aiding them, and hiding him – then I was mad. But not now. However, I ask your pardon. I thought you the cleverest sneak and the dirtiest hound Heaven ever made. I find you are cleverer than I thought, and an honest traitor. Your pardon.'

One of the men, who stood about the rim of the bowl above us, laughed. I looked at the Lieutenant and could willingly have killed him.

'*Mon Dieu!*' I said – and I was so furious in my turn that I could scarcely speak. 'Do you say that I am an impostor – that I do not hold the Cardinal's commission?'

'I do say that,' he answered coolly.

'And that I belong to the rebel party?'

'I do,' he replied in the same tone. 'In fact,' with a grin, 'I say that you are an honest man on the wrong side, M. de Berault. And you say that you are a scoundrel on the right.

The advantage, however, is with me, and I shall back my opinion by arresting you.' A ripple of coarse laughter ran round the hollow.

The sergeant who held the lanthorn grinned, and a trooper at a distance called out of the darkness '*A bon chat bon rat!*' This brought a fresh burst of laughter, while I stood speechless, confounded by the stubbornness, the crassness, the insolence of the man. 'You fool!' I cried at last, 'you fool!' And then M. de Cocheforêt, who had come out of the hut and taken his stand at my elbow, interrupted me.

'Pardon me one moment,' he said airily, looking at the Lieutenant with raised eyebrows and pointing to me with his thumb, 'but I am puzzled between you. This gentleman's name? Is it De Berault or De Barthe?'

'I am M. de Berault,' I said brusquely, answering for myself.

'Of Paris?'

'Yes, Monsieur, of Paris.'

'You are not, then, the gentleman who has been honouring my poor house with his presence?'

'Oh, yes!' the Lieutenant struck in, grinning. 'He is that gentleman, too.'

'But I thought – I understood that that was M. de Barthe!'

'I am M. de Barthe, also,' I retorted impatiently. 'What of that, Monsieur? It was my mother's name. I took it when I came down here.'

'To – er – to arrest me, may I ask?'

'Yes,' I said doggedly; 'to arrest you. What of that?'

'Nothing,' he replied slowly and with a steady look at me – a look I could not meet. 'Except that, had I known this before, M. de Berault, I should have thought longer before I surrendered to you.'

The Lieutenant laughed, and I felt my cheek burn; but I affected to see nothing, and turned to him again. 'Now, Monsieur,' I said, 'are you satisfied?'

'No,' he answered, 'I am not! You two may have rehearsed this pretty scene a dozen times. The word, it seems to me, is – Quick march, back to quarters.'

At length I found myself driven to play my last card; much against my will.

'Not so,' I said. 'I have my commission.'

'Produce it!' he replied incredulously.

'Do you think that I carry it with me?' I cried in scorn. 'Do you think that when I came here, alone, and not with fifty dragoons at my back, I carried the Cardinal's seal in my pocket for the first lackey to find? But you shall have it. Where is that knave of mine?'

The words were scarcely out of my mouth before a ready hand thrust a paper into my fingers. I opened it slowly, glanced at it, and amid a pause of surprise gave it to the Lieutenant. He looked for a moment confounded. Then, with a last instinct of suspicion, he bade the sergeant hold up the lanthorn; and by its light he proceeded to spell through the document.

'Umph!' he ejaculated with an ugly look when he had come to the end, 'I see.' And he read it aloud:

'By these presents, I command and empower Gilles de Berault, sieur de Berault, to seek for, hold, arrest, and deliver to the Governor of the Bastille the body of Henri de Cocheforêt, and to do all such acts and things as shall be necessary to effect such arrest and delivery, for which these shall be his warrant.

(*Signed*) THE CARDINAL DE RICHELIEU.'

When he had done – he read the signature with a peculiar intonation – someone said softly, '*Vive le Roi!*' and there was a moment's silence. The sergeant lowered his lanthorn. 'Is it enough?' I said hoarsely, glaring from face to face.

The Lieutenant bowed stiffly.

'For me?' he said. 'Quite, Monsieur. I beg your pardon again. I find that my first impressions were the correct ones. Sergeant I give the gentleman his papers!' and, turning his shoulder rudely, he tossed the commission to the sergeant, who gave it to me, grinning.

I knew that the clown would not fight, and he had his men round him; and I had no choice but to swallow the insult. I put the paper in my breast, with as much indifference as I could assume; and as I did so, he gave a sharp order. The troopers began to form on the edge above; the men who had descended to climb the bank again.

As the group behind him began to open and melt away, I caught sight of a white robe in the middle of it. The next moment, appearing with a suddenness which was like a blow on the cheek to me, Mademoiselle de Cocheforêt glided forward towards me. She had a hood on her head, drawn low; and for a moment I could not see her face. I forgot her brother's presence at my elbow, I forgot other things, and, from habit and impulse rather than calculation, I took a step forward to meet her; though my tongue cleaved to the roof of my mouth, and I was dumb and trembling.

But she recoiled – with such a look of white hate, of staring, frozen-eyed abhorrence, that I stepped back as if she had indeed struck me. It did not need the words which accompanied the look – the '*Do not touch me!*' which she hissed at me as she drew her skirts together – to drive me to the further edge of the hollow; where I stood with clenched teeth, and nails driven into the flesh, while she hung, sobbing tearless sobs, on her brother's neck.

12

The Road to Paris

I REMEMBER hearing Marshal Bassompierre, who, of all the men within my knowledge, had the widest experience, say that not dangers but discomforts prove a man and show what he is; and that the worst sores in life are caused by crumpled rose-leaves and not by thorns.

I am inclined to think him right, for I remember that when I came from my room on the morning after the arrest, and found hall and parlour and passage empty, and all the common rooms of the house deserted, and no meal laid; and when I divined anew from this discovery the feeling of the house towards me – however natural and to be expected – I remember that I felt as sharp a pang as when, the night before, I had had to face discovery and open rage and scorn. I stood in the silent empty parlour, and looked on the familiar things with a sense of desolation, of something lost and gone, which I could not understand. The morning was grey and cloudy, the air sharp, a shower was falling. The rose-bushes outside swayed in the wind, and inside, where I could remember the hot sunshine lying on floor and table, the rain beat in and stained the boards. The inner door flapped and creaked on its hinges. I thought of other days and of meals I had taken there, and of the scent of flowers; and I fled to the hall in despair.

But here, too, were no signs of life or company, no comfort, no attendance. The ashes of the logs, by whose blaze Mademoiselle had told me the secret, lay on the hearth white and cold – fit emblem of the change that had taken place; and now and then a drop of moisture, sliding down the great chimney, pattered among them. The main door stood open, as if the house had no longer anything to guard. The only living thing to be seen was a hound which roamed about restlessy, now gazing at the empty hearth, now lying down with pricked ears and watchful eyes. Some leaves, which had been blown in by the wind, rustled in a corner.

I went out moodily into the garden and wandered down one path and up another, looking at the dripping woods, and remembering things, until I came to the stone seat. On it, against the wall, trickling with raindrops, and with a dead leaf half filling its narrow neck, stood the pitcher of food. I thought how much had happened since Mademoiselle took her hand from it and the sergeant's lanthorn disclosed it to me; and, sighing grimly, I went in again through the parlour door.

A woman was on her knees on the hearth, kindling the belated fire. She had her back to me, and I stood for a moment looking at her doubtfully, wondering how she would bear herself and what she would say to me. Then she turned, and I started back, crying out her name in horror – for it was Madame! Madame de Cocheforêt!

She was plainly dressed, and her childish face was wan and piteous with weeping; but either the night had worn out her passion and drained her tears, or some great exigency had given her temporary calmness, for she was perfectly composed. She shivered as her eyes met mine, and she blinked as if a bright light had been suddenly thrust before her; but that was all, and she turned again to her task without speaking.

'Madame! Madame!' I cried in a frenzy of distress. 'What is this?'

'The servants would not do it,' she answered in a low but steady voice. 'You are still our guest, Monsieur.'

'But I cannot suffer it!' I cried. 'Madame de Cocheforêt, I will not – '

She raised her hand with a strange patient expression in her face.

'Hush! please,' she said. 'Hush! you trouble me.'

The fire blazed up as she spoke, and she rose slowly from it, and with a lingering look at it went out, leaving me to stand and stare and listen in the middle of the floor. Presently I heard her coming back along the passage, and she entered bearing a tray with wine and meat and bread. She set it down on the table, and with the same wan face, trembling always on the verge of tears, she began to lay out the things. The glasses clinked fitfully against the plates as she handled them; the knives jarred with one another. And I stood by, trembling myself, and endured this strange kind of penance.

She signed to me at last to sit down; and she went herself, and stood in the garden doorway with her back to me. I obeyed. I sat down. But though I had eaten nothing since the afternoon of the day before, I could not swallow. I fumbled with my knife, and drank; and grew hot and angry at this farce; and then looked through the window at the dripping bushes, and the rain and the distant sundial – and grew cold again.

Suddenly she turned round and came to my side.

'You do not eat,' she said.

I threw down my knife, and sprang up in a frenzy of passion. '*Mon Dieu!* Madame,' I cried, 'do you think that I have *no* heart?'

And then in a moment I knew what I had done, what a folly I had committed. For in a moment she was on her knees on the floor, clasping my knees, pressing her wet cheeks to my rough clothes, crying to me for mercy – for life! life! his life! Oh, it was horrible! It was horrible to hear her gasping voice, to see her fair hair falling over my mud-stained boots, to mark her slender little form convulsed with sobs, to feel that it was a woman, a gentlewoman, who thus abased herself at my feet!

'Oh, Madame! Madame!' I cried in my pain, 'I beg you to rise. Rise, or I must go!'

'His life! Only his life!' she moaned passionately. 'What had he done to you – that you should hunt him down? What have we done to you that you should slay us? Oh! have mercy! Have mercy! Let him go, and we will pray for you, I and my sister will pray for you, every morning and night of our lives.'

I was in terror lest lest someone should come and see her lying there, and I stooped and tried to raise her. But she only sank the lower, until her tender little hands touched the rowels of my spurs. I dared not move. At last I took a sudden resolution.

'Listen, then, Madame!' I said almost sternly, 'if you will not rise. You forget everything, both how I stand, and how small my power is! You forget that if I were to release your husband to-day he would be seized within the hour by those who are still in the village and who are watching every road – who have not ceased to suspect my movements and my intentions. You forget, I say, my circumstances –'

She cut me short on that word. She sprang to her feet and faced me. One moment more and I should have said something to the purpose. But at that word she stood before me, white, breathless, dishevelled, struggling for speech.

'Oh, yes, yes!' she panted eagerly. I know – I know!' And she thrust her hand into her bosom and plucked something out and gave it to me – forced it upon me. 'I know – I know!' she said again. 'Take it, and God reward you, Monsieur! God reward you! We give it freely – freely and thankfully!'

I stood and looked at her and it; and slowly I froze. She had given me the packet – the packet I had restored to Mademoiselle – the parcel of jewels. I weighted it in my hands, and my heart grew hard again, for I knew that this was Mademoiselle's doing; that it was she who, mistrusting the effect of Madame's tears and prayers, had armed her with this last weapon – this dirty bribe. I flung it down on the table among the plates.

'Madame!' I cried ruthlessly, all my pity changed to anger, 'you mistake me altogether! I have heard hard words enough in the last twenty-four hours, and I know what you think of me! But you have yet to learn that I have never done one thing. I have never turned traitor to the hand that employed me, nor sold my own side! When I do so for a treasure ten times the worth of that, may my hand rot off!'

She sank on a seat with a moan of despair; and precisely at that moment M. de Cocheforêt opened the door and came in. Over his shoulder I had a glimpse of Mademoiselle's proud face, a little whiter than of yore, with dark marks under the eyes, but like Satan's for coldness.

'What is this?' he said, frowning, as his eyes lighted on Madame.

'It is – that we start at eleven o'clock, Monsieur,' I answered, bowing curtly. And I went out by the other door.

That I might not be present at their parting I remained in the garden until the hour I had appointed was well past; and then, without entering the house, I went to the stable entrance. Here I found all in readiness, the two troopers whose company I had requisitioned as far as Auch, already in the saddle, my own two knaves waiting with my sorrel and M. de Cocheforêt's chestnut. Another horse was being led up and down by

Louis, and, alas! my heart moved at the sight, for it bore a lady's saddle. We were to have company then. Was it Madame who meant to come with us, or Mademoiselle? And how far? To Auch?

I suppose that they had set some kind of a watch on me, for as I walked up M. de Cocheforêt and his sister came out of the house; he with a pale face and bright eyes, and a twitching visible in his cheek – though he still affected a jaunty bearing; she wearing a black mask.

'Mademoiselle accompanies us?' I said formally.

'With your permission, Monsieur,' he answered with bitter politeness. But I saw that he was choking with emotion; he had just parted from his wife, and I turned away.

When we were all mounted he looked at me.

'Perhaps – as you have my parole, you will permit me to ride alone?' he said with a little hesitation. 'And –'

'Without me!' I rejoined keenly. 'Assuredly, so far as is possible.'

Accordingly I directed the troopers to ride before him, keeping out of earshot, while my two men followed him at a little distance with their carbines on their knees. Last of all, I rode myself with my eyes open and a pistol loose in my holster. M. de Cocheforêt muttered a sneer at so many precautions and the mountain made of his request; but I had not done so much and come so far, I had not faced scorn and insults to be cheated of my prize at last; and aware that until we were beyond Auch there must be hourly and pressing danger of a rescue, I was determined that he who should wrest my prisoner from me should pay dearly for it. Only pride, and, perhaps in a degree also, appetite for a fight, had prevented me borrowing ten troopers instead of two.

As was wont I looked with a lingering eye and many memories at the little bridge, the narrow woodland path, the first roofs of the village, all now familiar, all seen for the last time. Up the brook a party of soldiers were dragging for the Captain's body. A furlong farther on, a cottage, burned by some carelessness in the night, lay a heap of black ashes. Louis ran beside us weeping; the last brown leaves fluttered down in showers. And between my eyes and all, the slow steady rain fell and fell. And so I left Cocheforêt.

Louis went with us to a point a mile beyond the village, and there stood and saw us go, cursing me furiously as I passed. Looking back when we had ridden on, I still saw him standing, and after a moment's hesitation I rode back to him.

'Listen, fool!' I said, cutting him short in the midst of his moving and snarling, 'and give this message to your mistress. Tell her from me that it will be with her husband as it was with M. de Regnier, when he fell into the hands of his enemy – no better and no worse.'

'You want to kill her, too, I suppose?' he answered, glowering at me.

'No, fool, I want to save her,' I retorted wrathfully. 'Tell her that, just that and no more, and you will see the result.'

'I shall not,' he said sullenly. 'A message from you indeed!' And he spat on the ground.

'Then on your head be it,' I answered solemnly. And I turned my horse's head and galloped fast after the others. But I felt sure that he would report what I had said, if it were only out of curiosity; and it would be strange if Madame, a gentlewoman of the south, bred among old family traditions, did not understand the reference.

And so we began our journey, sadly, under dripping trees and a leaden sky. The country we had to traverse was the same I had trodden on the last day of my march southwards, but the passage of a month had changed the face of everything. Green dells, where springs welling out of the chalk had once made of the leafy bottom a fairies' home, strewn with delicate ferns and hung with mosses, were now swamps into which our horses sank to the fetlock. Sunny brows, whence I had viewed the campaign and traced my forward path, had become bare, wind-swept ridges. The beech woods that had glowed with ruddy light were naked now; mere black trunks and rigid arms pointing to heaven. An earthy smell filled the air; a hundred paces away a wall of mist closed the view. We plodded on sadly uphill and downhill, now fording brooks, already stained with flood-water, now crossing barren heaths. But uphill or downhill, whatever the outlook, I was never permitted to forget that I was the jailer, the ogre, the villain; that I, riding behind in my loneliness, was the blight on all – the death-spot. True, I was behind the others – I escaped their eyes. But there was not a line of Mademoiselle's figure that did not speak scorn to me; not a turn of head that did not seem to say, 'Oh, God, that such a thing should breathe.'

I had only speech with her once during the day, and that was on the last ridge before we went down into the valley to climb up again to Auch. The rain had ceased; the sun, near its setting, shone faintly; for a few moments we stood on the brow and looked southwards while we breathed the horses. The mist lay like a pall on the country we had traversed; but beyond and above it, gleaming pearl-like in the level rays, the line of the mountains stood up like a land of enchantment, soft, radiant, wonderful! – or like one of those castles on the Hill of Glass of which the old romances tell us. I forgot for an instant how we were placed, and I cried to my neighbour that it was the fairest pageant I had ever seen.

She – it was Mademoiselle, and she had taken off her mask – cast one look at me in answer; only one, but it conveyed disgust and loathing so unspeakable that scorn beside them would have been a gift. I reined in my horse as if she had struck me, and felt myself go first hot and then cold under her eyes. Then she looked another way.

But I did not forget the lesson; and after that I avoided her more sedulously than before. We lay that night at Auch, and I gave M. de Cocheforêt the utmost liberty, even permitting him to go out and return at his will. In the morning, believing that on the further side of Auch we ran little risk of attack, I dismissed the two dragoons, and an hour after sunrise we set out again. The day was dry and cold, the weather more promising. I proposed to go by way of Lectoure, crossing the Garonne at Agen; and I thought that, with roads continually improving as we moved northwards, we should be able to make good progress before night. My two men rode first, I came last by myself.

Our way lay down the valley of the Gers, under poplars and by long rows of willows, and presently the sun came out and warmed us. Unfortunately the rain of the day before had swollen the brooks which crossed our path, and we more than once had a difficulty in fording them. Noon found us little more than half-way to Lectoure, and I was growing each minute more impatient when our road, which had for a little while left the river bank, dropped down to it again, and I saw before us another crossing, half-ford half-slough. My men tried it gingerly and gave back and tried it again in another place; and finally, just as Mademoiselle and her brother came up to them, floundered through and sprang slantwise up the further bank.

The delay had been long enough to bring me, with no good will of my own, close upon the Cocheforêts. Mademoiselle's horse made a little business of the place, and in the result we entered the water almost together; and I crossed close on her heels. The bank on either side was steep; while crossing we could see neither before nor behind. But at the moment I thought nothing of this nor of her delay; and I was following her quite at my leisure and picking my way, when the sudden report of a carbine, a second report, and a yell of alarm in front thrilled me through.

On the instant, while the sound was still in my ears, I saw it all. Like a hot iron piercing my brain the truth flashed into my mind. We were attacked! We were attacked, and I was here helpless in this pit, this trap! The loss of a second while I fumbled here, Mademoiselle's horse barring the way, might be fatal.

There was but one way. I turned my horse straight at the steep bank, and he breasted it. One moment he hung as if he must fall back. Then, with a snort of terror and a desperate bound, he topped it and gained the level, trembling and snorting.

Seventy paces away on the road lay one of my men. He had fallen, horse and man, and lay still. Near him, with his back against a bank, stood his fellow, on foot, pressed by four horsemen, and shouting. As my eyes lighted on the scence he let fly with a carbine, and dropped one.

I clutched a pistol from my holster and seized my horse by the head. I might save the man yet, I shouted to him to encourage him, and was driving in my spurs to second my voice, when a sudden vicious blow, swift and unexpected, struck the pistol from my hands.

I made a snatch at it as it fell, but missed, it, and before I could recover myself, mademoiselle thrust her horse furiously against mine and with her riding-whip lashed the sorrel across the ears. As the horse reared up madly, I had a glimpse of her eyes flashing hate through her mask; of her hand again uplifted; the next moment, I was down in the road, ingloriously unhorsed, the sorrel was galloping away, and her horse, scared in its turn, was plunging unmanageably a score of paces from me.

But for that I think that she would have trampled on me. As it was, I was free to rise, and draw, and in a twinkling was running towards the fighters. All had happened in a few seconds. My man was still defending himself, the smoke of the carbine had scarcely risen. I sprang across a fallen tree that intervened, and at the same moment two of the men detached themselves and rode to meet me. One, whom I took to be a leader, was masked. He came furiously at me to ride me down, but I leaped aside nimbly, and, evading him, rushed at the other, and scaring his horse, so that he dropped his point, cut him across the shoulder before he could guard himself. He plunged away, cursing and trying to hold in his horse, and I turned to meet the masked man.

'You villain!' he cried, riding at me again. This time he manœuvred his horse so skillfully that I was hard put to it to prevent him knocking me down; while I could not with all my efforts reach him to hurt him. 'Surrender, will you?' he cried, 'you bloodhound!'

I wounded him slightly in the knee for answer; before I could do more his companion came back, and the two set upon me, slashing at my head so furiously and towering above me with so great an advantage that it was all I could do to guard it. I was soon glad to fall back against the bank. In this sort of conflict my rapier would have been of little use, but fortunately I had armed myself before I left Paris with a cut-and-thrust sword for the road; and though my mastery of the weapon was not on a par with my rapier play, I was able to fend off their cuts, and by an occasional prick keep the horses at a distance. Still, they swore and cut at me; and it was trying work. A little delay might enable the other man to come to their help, or Mademoiselle, for all I knew, might shoot me with my own pistol. I was unfeignedly glad when a lucky parade sent the masked man's sword flying across the road. On that he pushed his horse recklessly at me, spurring it without mercy; but the animal, which I had several times touched, reared up instead and threw him at the very moment that I wounded his companion a second time in the arm, and made him give back.

The scene was now changed. The man in the mask staggered to his feet, and felt stupidly for a pistol. But he could not find one, and he was in no state to use it if he had. He reeled helplessly to the bank and leaned against it. The man I had wounded was in scarcely better condition. He retreated before me, but in a moment, losing courage, let drop his sword, and, wheeling round, cantered off, clinging to his pommel. There remained only the fellow engaged with my man, and I turned to see how they were getting on. They were standing to take breath, so I ran towards them; but on seeing me coming, this rascal, too, whipped round his horse and disappeared in the wood, and left us victors.

The first thing I did – and I remember it to this day with pleasure – was to plunge my hand into my pocket, take out half of all the money I had in the world, and press it on the man who had fought for me so stoutly. In my joy I could have kissed him! It was not only that I had escaped defeat by the skin of my teeth – and his good sword; but I knew, and felt, and thrilled with the knowledge that the fight had, in a sense, redeemed my character. He was wounded in two places, and I had a scratch or two, and had lost my horse; and my other poor fellow was dead as a herring. But, speaking for myself, I would have spent half the blood in my body to purchase the feeling with which I turned back to speak to M. de Cocheforêt and his sister. Mademoiselle had dismounted, and with her face averted and her mask pushed on one side, was openly weeping. Her brother, who had faithfully kept his place by the ford from the beginning of the fight to the end, met me with raised eyebrows and a peculiar smile.

'Acknowledge my virtue,' he said airily. 'I am here, M. de Berault; which is more than can be said of the two gentlemen who have just ridden off.'

'Yes,' I answered with a touch of bitterness. 'I wish that they had not shot my poor man before they went.'

He shrugged his shoulders.

'They were my friends,' he said. 'You must not expect me to blame them. But that is not all, M. de Berault.'

'No,' I said, wiping my sword. 'There is this gentleman in the mask.' And I turned to go towards him.

'M. de Berault!' Cocheforêt called after me, his tone strained and abrupt.

I stood. 'Pardon?' I said, turning.

'That gentleman?' he said, hesitating and looking at me doubtfully. 'Have you considered what will happen to him if you give him up to the authorities?'

'Who is he?' I asked sharply.

'That is rather a delicate question,' he answered, frowning.

'Not for me,' I replied brutally, 'since he is in my power. If he will take off his mask I shall know better what I intend to do with him.'

The stranger had lost his hat in his fall, and his fair hair, stained with dust, hung in curls on his shoulders. He was a tall man, of a slender, handsome presence, and, though his dress was plain and almost rough, I espied a splendid jewel on his hand, and fancied that I detected other signs of high quality. He still lay against the bank in a half-swooning condition, and seemed unconscious of my scrutiny.

'Should I know him if he unmasked?' I said suddenly, a new idea in my head.

'You would,' M. de Cocheforêt answered.

'And?'

'It would be bad for everyone.'

'Ho! ho!' I replied softly, looking hard first at my old prisoner, and then at my new one. 'Then – what do you wish me to do?'

'Leave him here!' M. de Cocheforêt answered, his face flushed, the pulse in his cheek beating.

I had known him for a man of perfect honour before, and trusted him. But this evident earnest anxiety on behalf of his friend touched me not a little. Besides, I knew that I was treading on slippery ground; that it behoved me to be careful.

'I will do it,' I said after a moment's reflection. 'He will play me no tricks, I suppose? A letter of –'

'*Mon Dieu*, no! He will understand,' Cocheforêt answered eagerly. 'You will not repent it. Let us be going.'

'Well, but my horse?' I said, somewhat taken aback by this extreme haste. 'How am I to –'

'We shall overtake it,' he assured me. 'It will have kept the road. Lectoure is no more than a league from here, and we can give orders there to have these two fetched and buried.'

I had nothing to gain by demurring, and so, after another word or two, it was arranged. We picked up what we had dropped, M. de Cocheforêt helped his sister to mount and within five minutes we were gone. Casting a glance back from the skirts of the wood I fancied that I saw the masked man straighten himself and turn to look after us, but the leaves were beginning to intervene, the distance may have cheated me. And yet I was not indisposed to think the unknown a trifle more observant, and a little less seriously hurt, than he seemed.

13

At the Finger-post

THROUGH all, it will have been noticed, Mademoiselle had not spoken to me, nor said one word, good or bad. She had played her part grimly, had taken defeat in silence if with tears, had tried neither prayer nor defence nor apology. And the fact that the fight was now over, and the scene left behind, made no difference in her conduct. She kept her face studiously turned from me and affected to ignore my presence. I caught my horse feeding by the roadside, a furlong forward, and mounted and fell into place behind the two, as in the morning. And just as we had plodded on then in silence we plodded on now; almost as if nothing had happened; while I wondered at the unfathomable ways of women, and marvelled that she could take part in such an incident and remain unchanged.

Yet, though she strove to hide it, it had made a change in her. Though her mask served her well it could not entirely hide her emotions; and by and by I marked that her head drooped, that she rode listlessly, that the lines of her figure were altered. I noticed that she had flung away, or furtively dropped, her riding-whip; and I began to understand that, far from the fight having set me in my former place, to the old hatred of me were now added shame and vexation on her own account; shame that she had so lowered herself, even to save her brother, vexation that defeat had been her only reward.

Of this I saw a sign at Lectourne, where the inn had but one common room and we must all dine in company. I secured for them a table by the fire, and leaving them standing by it, retired myself to a smaller one near the door. There were no other guests; which made the separation between us more marked. M. de Cocheforêt seemed to feel this. He shrugged his shoulders and looked across the room at me with a smile half-sad, half-comical. But Mademoiselle was implacable. She had taken off her mask, and her face was like stone. Once, only once during the meal, I saw a change come over her. She coloured, I suppose at her thoughts, until her face flamed from brow to chin. I watched the blush spread and spread; and then she slowly and proudly turned her shoulder to me and looked through the window at the shabby street.

I suppose that she and her brother had both built on this attempt, which must have been arranged at Auch. For when we went on in the afternoon, I marked a change in them. They rode like people resigned to the worst. The grey realities of the position, the dreary future began to hang like a mist before their eyes, began to tinge the landscape with sadness, robbed even the sunset of its colours. With each hour Monsieur's spirits flagged and his speech became less frequent; until presently when the light was nearly gone and the dusk was round us the brother and sister rode hand in hand, silent, gloomy, one at least of them weeping. The cold shadow of the Cardinal, of Paris, of the scaffold, fell on them, and chilled them. As the mountains which they had known all their lives sank and faded behind us, and we entered on the wide, low valley of the Garonne, their hopes sank and faded also – sank to the dead level of despair. Surrounded by guards, a mark for curious glances, with pride for a companion, M. de Cocheforêt could have borne himself bravely; doubtless would bear himself bravely still when the end came. But almost alone, moving forward through the grey evening to a prison with so many measured days before him, and nothing to exhilarate or anger – in this condition it was little wonder if he felt, and betrayed that he felt, the blood run slow in his veins; if he thought more of the weeping wife and ruined home which he had left behind him than of the cause in which he had spent himself.

But God knows, they had no monopoly of gloom. I felt almost as sad myself. Long before sunset the flush of triumph, the heat of battle which had warmed my heart at noon, were gone, giving place to a chill dissatisfaction, a nausea, a despondency such as I have known follow a long night at the tables. Hitherto there had been difficulties to be overcome, risks to be run, doubts about the end. Now the end was certain and very near; so near that it filled all the prospect. One hour of triumph I might have, and would have, and I hugged the thought of it as a gambler hugs his last stake, planning the place and time and mode, and trying to occupy myself wholly with it. But the price? Alas! that too would intrude itself, and more frequently as the evening waned; so that as I marked this or that thing by the road, which I could recall passing on my journey south with thoughts so different, with plans that now seemed so very, very old, I asked myself grimly if this were really I; if this were Gil de Berault, known at Zaton's, *premier joueur*, or some Don Quichotte from Castille, tilting at windmills and taking barbers' bowls for gold.

We reached Agen very late that evening, after groping our way through a by-road near the river, set with holes and willow-stools and frog-spawn – a place no better than a slough; so that after it the great fires and lights of the Blue Maid seemed like a glimpse of a new world, and in a twinkling put something of life and spirits into two at least of us. There was queer talk round the hearth here, of doings in Paris, of a stir against the Cardinal with the Queen-mother at bottom, and of grounded expectations that something might this time come of it. But the landlord pooh-poohed the idea; and I more than agreed with him. Even M. de Cocheforêt, who was at first inclined to build on it, gave up hope when he heard that it came only by way of Montauban; whence – since its reduction the year before – all sort of canards against the Cardinal were always on the wing.

'They kill him about once a month,' our host said with a grin. 'Sometimes it is *Monsieur* is to prove a match for him, sometimes *César Monsieur* – the Duke of Vendôme, you understand – and sometimes the Queen-mother. But since M. de Chalais and the Marshal made a mess of it and paid forfeit, I pin my faith to his Eminence – that is his new title, they tell me.'

'Things are quiet round here?' I asked.

'Perfectly. Since the Languedoc business came to an end, all goes well,' he answered.

Mademoiselle had retired on our arrival, so that her brother and I were for an hour or two this evening thrown together. I left him at liberty to separate himself from me if he pleased, but he did not use the opportunity. A kind of comradeship, rendered piquant by our peculiar relations, had begun to spring up between us. He seemed to take an odd pleasure in my company, more than once rallied me on my post of jailor, would ask humorously if he might do this or that; and once even enquired what I should do if he broke his parole.

'Or take it this way,' he continued flippantly. 'Suppose I had struck you in the back this evening in that cursed swamp by the river, M. de Berault? What then! *Pardieu*, I am astonished at myself that I did not do it. I could have been in Montauban within twenty-four hours, and found fifty hiding-places and no one the wiser.'

'Except your sister,' I said quietly.

He made a wry face. 'Yes,' he said, 'I am afraid that I must have stabbed her too, to preserve my self-respect. You are right.' And he fell into a reverie which held him for a few minutes. Then I found him looking at me with a kind of frank perplexity that invited question.

'What is it?' I said.

'You have fought a great many duels?'

'Yes,' I said.

'Did you ever strike a foul blow in one?'

'Never,' I answered. 'Why do you ask?'

'Well, because I – wanted to confirm an impression. To be frank, M. de Berault, I seem to see in you two men.'

'Two men?'

'Yes, two men. One, the man who captured me; the other, the man who let my friend go free to-day.'

'It surprised you that I let him go? That was prudence, M. de Cocheforêt,' I replied. 'I am an old gambler. I know when the stakes are too high for me. The man who caught a lion in his wolf-pit had no great catch.'

'No, that is true,' he answered, smiling. 'And yet – I find two men in your skin.'

'I daresay that there are two in most men's skins,' I answered with a sigh. 'But not always together. Sometimes one is there, and sometimes the other.'

'How does the one like taking up the other's work?' he asked keenly.

I shrugged my shoulders. 'That is as may be,' I said. 'You do not take an estate without the debts.'

He did not answer for a moment, and I fancied that his thoughts had reverted to his own case. But on a sudden he looked at me again. 'Will you answer a question, M. de Berault?' he said winningly.

'Perhaps,' I replied.

'Then tell me – it is a tale I am sure worth the telling. What was it that, in a very evil hour for me, sent you in search of me?'

'My Lord Cardinal,' I answered.

'I did not ask who,' he replied drily. 'I asked, what. You had no grudge against me?'

'No.'

'No knowlege of me?'

'No.'

'Then what on earth induced you to do it? Heavens! man,' he continued bluntly, and speaking with greater freedom than he had before used, 'Nature never intended you for a tipstaff. What was it then?'

I rose. It was very late, and the room was empty, the fire low.

'I will tell you – to-morrow,' I said. 'I shall have something to say to you then, of which that will be part.'

He looked at me in great astonishment, and with a little suspicion. But I called for a light, and by going at once to bed, cut short his questions. In the morning we did not meet until it was time to start.

Those who know the south road to Agen, and how the vineyards rise in terraces north of the town, one level of red earth above another, green in summer, but in late autumn bare and stony, may remember a particular place where the road, two leagues from the town, runs up a steep hill. At the top of the hill four roads meet; and there, plain to be seen against the sky, is a finger-post indicating which way leads to Bordeaux, and which to old tiled Montauban, and which to Perigueux.

This hill had impressed me greatly on my journey south; perhaps because I had enjoyed from it my first extended view of the Garonne Valley, and had there felt myself on the verge of the south country where my mission lay. It had taken root in my memory, so that I had come to look upon its bare rounded head, with the guide-post, and the four roads, as the first outpost of Paris, as the first sign of return to the old life.

Now for two days I had been looking forward to seeing it again. That long stretch of road would do admirably for something I had in my mind. That sign-post, with the roads pointing north, south, east and west – could there be a better place for meetings and partings?

We came to the bottom of the ascent about an hour before noon, M. de Cocheforêt, Mademoiselle and I. We had reversed the order of yesterday, and I rode ahead; they came after at their leisure. Now, at the foot of the hill I stopped, and letting Mademoiselle pass on, detained M. de Cocheforêt by a gesture.

'Pardon me one moment,' I said. 'I want to ask a favour.'

He looked at me somewhat fretfully; with a gleam of wildness in his eyes that betrayed how the iron was, little by little, eating into his heart. He had started after breakfast as gaily as a bridegroom, but gradually he had sunk below himself; and now he had much ado to curb to impatience.

'Of me?' he said bitterly. 'What is it?'

'I wish to have a few words with Mademoiselle – alone,' I said.

'Alone?' he exclaimed in astonishment.

'Yes,' I replied, without blenching, though his face grew dark. 'For the matter of that, you can be within call all the time, if you please. But I have a reason for wishing to ride a little way with her.'

'To tell her something?'

'Yes.'

'Then you can tell it to me,' he retorted suspiciously. 'Mademoiselle, I will answer for it, has no desire to –'

'See me or speak to me? No,' I said. 'I can understand that. Yet I want to speak to her.'

'Very well, you can speak in my presence,' he answered rudely. 'If that be all, let us ride on and join her.' And he made a movement as if to do so.

'That will not do, M. de Cocheforêt,' I said firmly, stopping him with my hand. 'Let me beg you to be more complaisant. It is a small thing I ask, a very small thing; but I swear to you to you that if Mademoiselle does not grant it, she will repent it all her life.'

He looked at me, his face growing darker and darker.

'Fine words,' he said, with a sneer. 'Yet I fancy I understand them.' And then with a passionate oath he broke out: 'But I will not have it! I have not been blind, M. de Berault, and I understand. But I will not have it. I will have no such Judas bargain made. *Pardieu!* do you think I could suffer it and show my face again?'

'I don't know what you mean,' I said, restraining myself with difficulty. I could have struck the fool.

'But I know what *you* mean,' he replied in a tone of suppressed rage. 'You would have her sell herself; sell herself to you to save me. And you would have me stand by and see the thing done. No, sir, never; never, though I go to the wheel. I will die a gentleman, if I have lived a fool.'

'I think that you will do the one as certainly as you have done the other,' I retorted in my exasperation. And yet I admired him.

'Oh, I am not quite a fool!' he cried, scowling at me. 'I have used my eyes.'

'Then be good enough to favour me with your ears!' I answered drily. 'For just a moment. And listen when I say that no such bargain has ever crossed my mind. You were kind enough to think well of me last night, M. de Cocheforêt. Why should the mention of Mademoiselle in a moment change your opinion? I wish simply to speak to her. I have nothing to ask from her, nothing to expect from her, either favour or anything else. What I say she will doubtless tell you. *Ciel*, man! what harm can I do to her in the road in your sight?'

He looked at me sullenly, his face still flushed, his eyes suspicious.

'What do you want to say to her?' he asked jealously. He was quite unlike himself. His airy nonchalance, his careless gaiety were gone.

'You know what I do not want to say to her, M. de Cocheforêt,' I answered. 'That should be enough.'

He glowered at me in a moment, still ill content. Then, without a word, he made me a gesture to go to her.

She had halted a score of paces away; wondering, doubtless, what was on foot. I rode towards her. She wore her mask, so that I missed the expression of her face as I approached; but the manner in which she turned her horse's head uncompromisingly towards her brother and looked past me was full of meaning. I felt the ground suddenly cut from under me. I saluted her, trembling.

'Mademoiselle,' I said, 'will you grant me the privilege of your company for a few minutes as we ride?'

'To what purpose?' she answered; surely in the coldest voice in which a woman ever spoke to a man.

'That I may explain to you a great many things you do not understand,' I murmured.

'I prefer to be in the dark,' she replied. And her manner was more cruel than her words.

'But, Mademoiselle,' I pleaded – I would not be discouraged – 'you told me one day, not so long ago, that you would never judge me hastily again.'

'Facts judge you, not I,' she answered icily. 'I am not sufficiently on a level with you to be able to judge you – I thank God.'

I shivered, though the sun was on me and the hollow where we stood was warm.

'Still, once before you thought the same,' I exclaimed after a pause, 'and afterwards you found that you had been wrong. It may be so again, Mademoiselle.'

'Impossible,' she said.

That stung me.

'No,' I cried. 'It is not impossible. It is you who are impossible. It is you who are heartless, Mademoiselle. I have done much in the last three days to make things lighter for you, much to make things more easy; now I ask you to do something in return which can cost you nothing.'

'Nothing?' she answered slowly – and she looked at me; and her eyes and her voice cut me as if they had been knives. 'Nothing? Do you think, Monsieur, it costs me nothing to lose my self-respect, as I do with every word I speak to you? Do you think it costs me nothing to be here when I feel every look you cast upon me an insult, every breath I take in your presence a contamination? Nothing, Monsieur?' she continued with bitter irony. 'Nay, something! But something which I could not hope to make clear to you.'

I sat for a moment confounded, quivering with pain. It had been one thing to feel that she hated and scorned me, to know that the trust and confidence which she had begun to place in me were transformed to loathing. It was another to listen to her hard, pitiless words, to change colour under the lash of her gibing tongue. For a moment I could not find voice to answer her. Then I pointed to M. de Cocheforêt.

'Do you love him?' I said hoarsely, roughly. The gibing tone had passed from her voice to mine.

She did not answer.

'Because if you do you will let me tell my tale. Say no, but once more, Mademoiselle – I am only human – and I go. And you will repent it all your life.'

I had done better had I taken that tone from the beginning. She winced, her head dropped, she seemed to grow smaller. All in a moment, as it were, her pride collapsed.

'I will hear you,' she murmured.

'Then we will ride on, if you please,' I said, keeping the advantage I had gained. 'You need not fear. Your brother will follow.'

I caught hold of her rein and turned her horse, and she suffered it without demur; and in a moment we were pacing side by side, with the long straight road before us. At the end where it topped the hill, I could see the fingerpost, two faint black lines against the sky. When we reached that – involuntarily I checked my horse and made it move more slowly.

'Well, sir?' she said impatiently. And her figure shook as with cold.

'It is a tale I desire to tell you, Mademoiselle,' I answered. 'Perhaps I may seem to begin a long way off, but before I end I promise to interest you. Two months ago there was living in Paris a man – perhaps a bad man – at any rate, by common report a hard man; a man with a peculiar reputation.'

She turned on me suddenly, her eyes gleaming through her mask.

'Oh, Monsieur, spare me this!' she said, quietly scornful. 'I will take it for granted.'

'Very well,' I replied steadfastly. 'Good or bad, he one day, in defiance of the Cardinal's edict against duelling, fought with a young Englishman behind St. Jacques' Church. The Englishman had influence, the person of whom I speak had none, and an indifferent name; he was arrested, thrown into the Châtelet, cast for death, left for days to face death. At last an offer was made to him. If he would seek out and deliver up another man, an outlaw with a price upon his head, he should himself go free.'

I paused and drew a deep breath. Then I continued, looking not at her, but into the distance, and speaking slowly.

'Mademoiselle, it seems easy now to say what course he should have chosen. It seems hard now to find excuses for him. But there was one thing which I plead for him. The task he was asked to undertake was a dangerous one. He risked, he knew that he must risk, and the event proved him to be right, his life against the life of this unknown man. And one thing more; time was before him. The outlaw might be taken by another, might be killed, might die, might – But there, Mademoiselle, we know what answer this person made. He took the baser course, and on his honour, on his parole, with money supplied to him, he went free; free on the condition that he delivered up this other man.'

I paused again, but I did not dare to look at her; and after a moment of silence I resumed.

'Some portion of the second half of the story you know, Mademoiselle; but not all. Suffice it that this man came down to a remote village, and there, at risk, but, Heaven knows, basely enough, found his way to his victim's home. Once there, however, his heart began to fail him. Had he found the house garrisoned by men, he might have pressed to his end with little remorse. But he found there only two helpless loyal women; and I say again that from the first hour of his entrance he sickened at the work which he had in hand, the work which ill-fortune had laid upon him. Still he pursued it. He had given his word; and if there was one tradition of his race which this man had never broken, it was that of fidelity to his side – to the man who paid him. But he pursued it with only half his mind, in great misery, if you will believe me; sometimes in agonies of shame. Gradually, however, almost against his will, the drama worked itself out before him, until he needed only one thing.'

I looked at Mademoiselle, trembling. But her head was averted: I could gather nothing from the outlines of her form; and I went on.

'Do not misunderstand me,' I said in a lower voice. 'Do not misunderstand what I am going to say next. This is no love-story, and can have no ending such as romancers love to set to their tales. But I am bound to mention, Mademoiselle, that this man who had lived almost all his life about inns and eating-houses and at the gaming-tables, met here for the first time for years a good woman, and learned by the light of her loyalty and devotion to see what his life had been, and what was the real nature of the work he was doing. I think – nay, I know,' I continued, 'that it added a hundredfold to his misery that when he learned at last the secret he had come to surprise, he learned it from her lips, and in such a way that had he felt no shame, hell could have been no place for him. But in one thing I hope she misjudged him. She thought, and had reason to think, that the moment he knew her secret he went out, not even closing the door, and used it. But the truth was that while her words were still in his ears news came to him that others had the secret; and had he not gone out on the instant and done what he did, and forestalled them, M. de Cocheforêt would have been taken, but by others.'

Mademoiselle broke her long silence so suddenly that her horse sprang forward.

'Would to Heaven he had!' she wailed.

'Been taken by others?' I exclaimed, startled out of my false composure.

'Oh, yes, yes!' she answered with a passionate gesture. 'Why did you not tell me? Why did you not confess to me, sir, even at the last moment? I – But, no more! No more!' she continued in a piteous voice; and she tried to urge her horse forward. 'I have heard enough. You are racking my heart, M. de Berault. Some day I will ask God to give me strength to forgive you.'

'But you have not heard me out,' I said.

'I will hear no more,' she answered in a voice she vainly strove to render steady. 'To what end? Can I say more than I have said? Or did you think that I could forgive you now – with him behind us going to his death? Oh, no, no!' she continued. 'Leave me! I implore you to leave me, sir. I am not well.'

She drooped over her horse's neck as she spoke, and began to weep so passionately that the tears ran down her cheeks under her mask, and fell and sparkled like dew on the mane; while her sobs shook her so that I thought she must fall. I stretched out my hand instinctively to give her help, but she shrank from me. 'No!' she gasped, between her sobs. 'Do not touch me. There is too much between us.'

'Yet there must be one thing more between us,' I answered firmly. 'You must listen to me a little longer whether you will or no, Mademoiselle; for the love you bear to your brother. There is one course still open to me by which I may redeem my honour; and it has been in my mind for some time back to take that course. To-day, I am thankful to say, I can take it cheerfully, if not without regret; with a steadfast heart, if no light one, Mademoiselle,' I continued earnestly, feeling none of the triumph, none of the vanity, none of the elation I had foreseen, but only simple joy in the joy I could give her, 'I thank God that it *is* still in my power to undo what I have done; that it is still in my power to go back to him who sent me, and telling him that I have changed my mind, and will bear my own burdens, to pay the penalty.'

We were within a hundred paces of the top and the finger-post. She cried out wildly that she did not understand. 'What is it you – you – have just said?' she murmured. 'I cannot hear.' And she began to fumble with the ribbon of her mask.

'Only this, Mademoiselle,' I answered gently. 'I give your brother back his word, his parole. From this moment he is free to go whither he pleases. Here, where we stand, four roads meet. That to the right goes to Montauban, where you have doubtless friends, and can lie hid for a time. Or that to the left leads to Bordeaux, where you can take ship if you please. And in a word, Mademoiselle,' I continued, ending a little feebly, 'I hope that your troubles are now over.'

She turned her face to me – we had both come to a standstill – and plucked at the fastenings of her mask. But her trembling fingers had knotted the string, and in a moment she dropped her hand, with a cry of despair.

'But you? You?' she wailed in a voice so changed that I should not have known it for hers. 'What will you do? I do not understand, Monsieur.'

'There is a third road,' I answered. 'It leads to Paris. That is my road, Mademoiselle. We part here.'

'But why?' she cried wildly.

'Because from to-day I would fain begin to be honourable,' I answered in a low voice.

'Because I dare not be generous at another's cost. I must go back whence I came.'

'To the Châtelet?' she muttered.

'Yes, Mademoiselle, to the Châtelet.'

She tried feverishly to raise her mask with her hand.

'I am not well,' she stammered. 'I cannot breathe.'

And she began to sway so violently in her sadle that I sprang down, and, running round her horse's head, was just in time to catch her as she fell. She was not quite unconscious then, for, as I supported her, she cried out:

'Do not touch me! Do not touch me! You kill me with shame!'

But as she spoke she clung to me; and I made no mistake. Those words made me happy. I carried her to the bank, my heart on fire, and laid her against it just as M. de Cocheforêt rode up. He sprang from his horse, his eyes blazing. 'What is this?' he cried. 'What have you been saying to her, man?'

'She will tell you,' I answered drily, my composure returning under his eye. 'Amongst other things, that you are free. From his moment, M. de Cochforêt, I give you back your parole, and I take my own honour. Farewell.'

He cried out something as I mounted, but I did not stay to heed or answer. I dashed the spurs into my horse, and rode away past the cross-roads, past the finger-post; away with the level upland stretching before me, dry, bare, almost treeless; and behind me, all I loved. Once, when I had gone a hundred yards, I looked back and saw him standing upright against the sky, staring after me across her body. And again a minute later I looked back. This time saw only the slender wooden cross, and below it a dark blurred mass.

14

St. Martin's Eve

IT was late evening on the twenty-ninth of November when I rode into Paris through the Orleans gate. The wind was in the north-east, and a great cloud of vapour hung in the eye of an angry sunset. The air seemed to be heavy with smoke, the kennels reeked, my gorge rose at the city's smell; and with all my heart I envied the man who had gone out of it by the same gate nearly two months before, with his face to the south and the prospect of riding day after day and league after league across heath and moor and pasture. At least he had had some weeks of life before him, and freedom and the open air, and hope and uncertainty; while I came back under doom, and in the pall of smoke that hung over the huddle of innumerable roofs saw a gloomy shadowing of my own fate.

For make no mistake. A man in middle life does not strip himself of the wordly habit with which experience has clothed him, does not run counter to all the hard saws and instances by which he has governed his course so long, without shiverings and doubts and horrible misgivings, and struggles of heart. At least a dozen times between the Loire and Paris

I asked myself what honour was, and what good it could do me when I lay rotting and forgotten; if I were not a fool following a Jack o' Lanthorn; and whether, of all the men in the world, the relentless man to whom I was returning would not be the first to gibe at my folly?

However, shame kept me straight; shame and the memory of Mademoiselle's looks and words. I dared not be false to her again; I could not, after speaking so loftily, fall so low. And therefore – though not without many a secret struggle and quaking – I came, on the last evening but one of November, to the Orleans gate, and rode slowly and sadly through the streets by the Luxembourg on my way to the Pont au Change.

The struggle had sapped my last strength, however; and with the first whiff of the gutters, the first rush of barefooted gamins under my horse's hoofs, the first babel of street cries – the first breath, in a word, of Paris – there came a new temptation; to go for one last night to Zaton's, to see the tables again and the faces of surprise, to be for an hour or two the old Berault. That would be no breach of honour, for in any case I could not reach the Cardinal before to-morrow. And it could do no harm. It could make no change in anything. It would not have been a thing worth struggling about, indeed; only – only I had in my inmost heart a suspicion that the stoutest resolutions might lose their force in that atmosphere; and that there even such a talisman as the memory of a woman's looks and words might lose its virtue.

Still, I think that I should have succumbed in the end if I had not received at the corner of the Luxembourg a shock which sobered me effectually. As I passed the gates, a coach, followed by two outriders, swept out of the Palace courtyard; it was going at a great pace, and I reined my jaded horse on one side to give it room. By chance as it whirled by me, one of the leather curtains flapped back, and I saw for a second by the waning light – the nearer wheels were no more than two feet from my boot – a face inside.

A face and no more, and that only for a second. But it froze me. It was Richelieu's, the Cardinal's; but not as I had been wont to see it – keen, cold, acute, with intellect and indomitable will in every feature. This face was contorted with the rage of impatience, was grim with the fever of haste, and the fear of death. The eyes burned under the pale brow, the moustache bristled, the teeth showed through the beard; I could fancy the man crying 'Faster! Faster!' and gnawing his nails in the impotence of passion; and I shrank back as if I had been struck. The next moment the outriders splashed me, the coach was a hundred paces ahead, and I was left chilled and wondering, foreseeing the worst, and no longer in any mood for Zaton's.

Such a revelation of such a man was enough to appal me; for a moment conscience cried out that he must have heard that Cocheforêt had escaped him, and through me. But I dismissed the idea as soon as formed. In the vast meshes of the Cardinal's schemes Cocheforêt could be only a small fish; and to account for the face in the coach I needed a cataclysm, a catastrophe, a misfortune as far above ordinary mishaps as this man's intellect rose above the common run of minds.

It was almost dark when I crossed the bridges, and crept despondently to the Rue Savonnerie. After stabling my horse I took my bag and holsters, and climbing the stairs to my old landlord's – I remember that the place had grown, as it seemed to me, strangely mean and small and ill-smelling in my absence – I knocked at the door. It was promptly opened by the litle tailor himself, who threw up his arms and opened his eyes at sight of me.

'By Saint Geneviève!' he said, 'if it is not M. de Berault?'

'It is,' I said. It touched me a little, after my lonely journey, to find him so glad to see me; though I had never done him a greater benefit than sometimes to unbend with him and borrow his money. 'You look surprised, little man!' I continued, as he made way for me to enter. 'I'll be sworn that you have been pawning my goods and letting my room, you knave!'

'Never, your Excellency!' he answered. 'On the contrary, I have been expecting you.'

'How?' I said. 'To-day?'

'To-day or to-morrow,' he answered, following me in and closing the door. 'The first thing I said when I heard the news this morning was – now we shall have M. de Berault back again. Your Excellency will pardon the children,' he continued, bobbing round me, as I took the old seat on the three-legged stool before the hearth. 'The night is cold and there is no fire in your room.'

While he ran to and fro with my cloak and bags, little Gil, to whom I had stood at St. Sulpice's, borrowing ten crowns the same day I remember, came shyly to play with my sword-hilt.

'So you expected me back when you heard the news, Frison, did you?' I said, taking the lad on my knee.

'To be sure, your Excellency,' he answered, peeping into the black pot before he lifted it to the hook.

'Very good. Then now let us hear what the news is,' I said drily.

'Of the Cardinal, M. de Berault.'

'Ah! And what?'

He looked at me, holding the heavy pot suspended in his hands.

'You have not heard?' he exclaimed in astonishment.

'Not a title. Tell it me, my good fellow.'

'You have not heard that his Eminence is disgraced?'

I stared at him. 'Not a word,' I said.

He set down the pot.

'Then your Excellency must have made a very long journey indeed,' he said with conviction. 'For it has been in the air a week or more, and I thought that it had brought you back. A week? A month, I daresay. They whisper that it is the Old Queen's doing. At any rate it is certain that they have cancelled his commissions and displaced his officers. There are rumours of immediate peace with Spain. Everywhere his enemies are lifting up their heads; and I hear that he has relays of horses set all the way to the coast that he might fly at any moment. For what I know he may be gone already.'

'But, man –' I said, surprised out of my composure. 'The King! You forget the King. Let the Cardinal once pipe to him and he will dance. And they will dance too!' I added grimly.

'Yes,' Frison answered eagerly. 'True, your Excellency, but the King will not see him. Three times to-day, as I am told, the Cardinal has driven to the Luxembourg and stood like any common man in the ante-chamber, so that I hear it was pitiful to see him. But his Majesty would not admit him. And when he went away the last time I am told that his face was like death! Well, he was a great man, and we may be worse ruled, M. de Berault, saving your presence. If the nobles did not like him, he was good to the traders and the bourgeoisie, and equal to all.'

'Silence, man! Silence, and let me think,' I said, much excited. And while he bustled to and fro, getting my supper, and the firelight played about the snug, sorry little room, and the child toyed with his plaything, I fell to digesting this great news, and pondering how I stood now and what I ought to do. At first sight, I know, it seemed to me that I had nothing to do but to sit still. In a few hours the man who had taken my bond would be powerless, and I should be free; in a few hours I might smile at him. To all appearance the dice had fallen well for me. I had done a great thing, run a great risk, won a woman's love; and, after all, I was not to pay the penalty.

But a word which fell from Frison as he fluttered round me, pouring out the broth and cutting the bread, dropped into my mind and spoiled my satisfaction.

'Yes, your Excellency,' he said, confirming something he had stated before and which I had missed, 'and I am told that the last time he came into the gallery there was not a man of all the scores who had been at his levée last Monday would speak to him. They fell off like rats – just like rats – until he was left standing alone. And I have seen him!' – Frison lifted up his eyes and his hands and drew in his breath – 'Ah! I have seen the King look shabby beside him! And his eye! I would not like to meet it now.'

'Pish!' I growled. 'Someone has fooled you. Men are wiser than that.'

'So? Well, your Excellency understands,' he answered meekly. 'But – there are no cats on a cold hearth.'

I told him again that he was a fool. But for all that, and my reasoning, I felt uncomfortable. This was a great man, if ever a great man lived, and they were all leaving him; and I – well, I had no cause to love him. But I had taken his money, I had accepted his commission, and I had betrayed him. These three things being so, if he fell before I could – with the best will in the world – set myself right with him, so much the better for me. That was my gain – the fortune of war, the turn of the dice. But if I lay hid, and took time for my ally, and being here while he still stood, though tottering, waited until he fell, what of my honour then? What of the grand words I had said to Mademoiselle at Agen? I should be like the recreant in the old romance, who, lying in the ditch while the battle raged, came out afterwards and boasted of his courage.

And yet the flesh was weak. A day, twenty-four hours, two days, might make a difference between life and death, love and death; and I wavered. But at last I settled what I would do. At noon the next day, the time at which I should have presented myself if I had not heard this news, at that time I would still present myself. Not earlier; I owed myself the chance; Not later; that was due to him.

Having so settled it, I thought to rest in peace. But with the first light I was awake, and it was all I could do to keep myself quiet until I heard Frison stirring. I called to him then to know if there was any news, and lay waiting and listening while he went down to the street to learn. It seemed an endless time before he came back; an age, when he came back, before he spoke.

'Well, he has not set off?' I asked at last, unable to control my eagerness.

Of course he had not; and at nine o'clock I sent Frison out again; and at ten and eleven – always with the same result. I was like a man waiting and looking and, above all, listening for a reprieve; and as sick as any craven. But when he came back, at eleven, I gave up hope and dressed myself carefully. I suppose I had an odd look then, however, for Frison stopped me at the door, and asked me, with evident alarm, where I was going.

I put the little man aside gently.

'To the tables,' I said, 'to make a big throw, my friend.'

It was a fine morning, sunny, keen, pleasant, when I went out into the street; but I scarcely noticed it. All my thoughts were where I was going, so that it seemed but a step from my threshold to the Hôtel Richelieu; I was no sooner gone from the one than I found myself at the other. Now, as on a memorable evening when I had crossed the street in a drizzling rain, and looked that way with foreboding, there were two or three guards, in the Cardinal's livery, loitering in front of the great gates. Coming nearer, I found the opposite pavement under the Louvre thronged with people, not moving about their business, but standing all silent, all looking across furtively, all with the air of persons who wished to be thought passing by. Their silence and their keen looks had in some way an air of menace. Looking back after I had turned in towards the gates, I found them devouring me with their eyes.

And certainly they had little else to look at. In the courtyard, where, some mornings, when the Court was in Paris, I had seen a score of coaches waiting and thrice as many servants, were now emptiness and sunshine and stillness. The officer on guard, twirling his moustachios, looked at me in wonder as I passed him; the lackeys lounging in the portico, and all too much taken up with whispering to make a pretence of being of service, grinned at my appearance. But that which happened when I had mounted the stairs and came to the door of the ante-chamber outdid all. The man on guard would have opened the door, but when I went to enter, a major-domo who was standing by, muttering with two or three of his kind, hastened forward and stopped me.

'Your business, Monsieur, if you please?' he said inquisitively; while I wondered why he and the others looked at me so strangely.

'I am M. de Berault,' I answered sharply. 'I have the entrée.'

He bowed politely enough.

'Yes, M. de Berault, I have the honour to know your face,' he said. 'But – pardon me. Have you business with his Eminence?'

'I have the common business,' I answered sharply. 'By which many of us live, sirrah! To wait on him.'

'But – by appointment, Monsieur?'

'No,' I said, astonished. 'It is the usual hour. For the matter of that, however, I have business with him.'

The man still looked at me for a moment in seeming embarrassment. Then he stood aside and signed to the door-keeper to open the door. I passed in, uncovering, with an assured face and steadfast mien, ready to meet all eyes. In a moment, on the threshold, the mystery was explained.

The room was empty.

15

St. Martin's Summer

YES, at the great Cardinal's levée, I was the only client! I stared round the room, a long, narrow gallery, through which it was his custom to walk every morning, after receiving his more important visitors. I stared, I say, from side to side, in a state of stupefaction. The seats against either wall were empty, the recesses of the windows empty too. The hat sculptured and painted here and there, the staring R, the blazoned arms looked down on a vacant floor. Only on a little stool by the furthest door, sat a quiet-faced man in black, who read, or pretended to read, in a little book, and never looked up: one of those men, blind, deaf, secretive, who fatten in the shadow of the great.

Suddenly, while I stood confounded and full of shamed thought – for I had seen the antechamber of Richelieu's old hotel so crowded that he could not walk through it – this man closed his book, rose, and came noiselessly towards me.

'M. de Berault?' he said.

'Yes,' I answered.

'His Eminence awaits you. Be good enough to follow me.'

I did so, in a deeper stupor than before. For how could the Cardinal know that I was here? How could he have known when he gave the order? But I had short time to think of these things, or others. We passed through two rooms, in one of which some secretaries were writing, we stopped at a third door. Over all brooded a silence which could be felt. The usher knocked, opened, and, with his finger on his lip, pushed aside a curtain and signed to me to enter. I did so and found myself behind a screen.

'Is that M. de Berault?' asked a thin, high-pitched voice.

'Yes, Monseigneur,' I answered, trembling.

'Then come, my friend, and talk to me.'

I went round the screen, and I know not how it was, the watching crowd outside, the vacant ante-chamber in which I had stood, the stillness and silence all seemed to be concentrated here, and to give to the man I saw before me a dignity which he had never possessed for me when the world passed through his doors, and the proudest fawned on him for a smile. He sat in a great chair on the further side if the hearth, a little red skull-cap on his head, his fine hands lying still in his lap. The collar of lawn which fell over his cape was quite plain, but the skirts of his red robe were covered with rich lace, and the order of the Holy Ghost, a white dove on a gold cross, shone on his breast. Among the multitudinous papers on the great table near him I saw a sword and pistols; and some tapestry that covered a little table behind him failed to hide a pair of spurred riding-boots. But as I advanced he looked towards me with the utmost composure; with a face mild and almost benign, in which I strove in vain to read the traces of last night's passion. So that it flashed across me that if this man really stood (and afterwards I knew that he did) on the thin razor-edge between life and death, between the supreme of earthly power, lord of France and arbiter of Europe, and the nothingness of the clod, he justified his fame. He gave weaker natures no room for triumph.

The thought was no sooner entertained than it was gone.

'And so you are back at last, M. de Berault,' he said gently. 'I have been expecting to see you since nine this morning.'

'Your Eminence knew, then – ' I muttered.

'That you returned to Paris by the Orleans gate last evening alone?' he answered, fitting together the ends of his fingers, and looking at me over them with inscrutable eyes. 'Yes, I knew all that last night. And now, of your business. You have been faithful and diligent, I am sure. Where is he?'

I stared at him and was dumb. In some way the strange things I had seen since I had left my lodgings, the surprises I had found awaiting me here, had driven my own fortunes, my own peril, out of my head – until this moment. Now, at this question, all returned with a rush, and I remembered where I stood. My heart heaved suddenly in my breast. I strove for a savour of the old hardihood, but for the moment I could not find a word.

'Well,' he said lightly, a faint smile lifting his moustache. 'You do not speak. You left Auch with him on the twenty-fourth, M. de Berault. So much I know. And you reached Paris without him last night. He has not given you the slip?'

'No, Monseigneur,' I muttered.

'Ha! that is good,' he answered, sinking back again in his chair. 'For the moment – but I knew that I could depend on you. And now where is he? What have you done with him? He knows much, and the sooner I know it the better. Are your people bringing him, M. de Berault?'

'No, Monseigneur,' I stammered, with dry lips. His very good-humour, his benignity, appalled me. I knew how terrible would be the change, how fearful his rage, when I should tell him the truth. And yet that I, Gil de Berault, should tremble before any man! With that thought I spurred myself, as it were, to the task. 'No, your Eminence,' I said, with the energy of despair. 'I have not brought him, because I have set him free.'

'Because you have – *what*?' he exclaimed. He leaned forward as he spoke, his hands on the arm of the chair; and his eyes growing each instant smaller, seemed to read my soul.

'Because I have let him go,' I repeated.

'And why?' he said, in a voice like the rasping of a file.

'Because I took him unfairly,' I answered. 'Because, Monseigneur, I am a gentleman, and this task should have been given to one who was not. I took him, if you must know,' I continued impatiently – the fence once crossed I was growing bolder – 'by dogging a woman's steps and winning her confidence and betraying it. And whatever I have done ill in my life – of which you were good enough to throw something in my teeth when I was last here – I have never done that, and I will not!'

'And so you set him free?'

'Yes.'

'After you had brought him to Auch?'

'Yes.'

'And, in point of fact, saved him from falling into the hands of the Commandant at Auch?'

'Yes,' I answered desperately to all.

'Then, what of the trust I placed in you, sirrah?' he rejoined, in a terrible voice; and stopping still farther forward he probed me with his eyes. 'You who prate of trust and confidence, who received your life on parole, and but for your promise to me would have been carrion this month past, answer me that? What of the trust I placed in you?'

'The answer is simple,' I said, shrugging my shoulders with a touch of my old self. 'I am here to pay the penalty.'

'And do you think that I do not know why?' he retorted, striking one hand on the arm of his chair with a force that startled me. 'Because you have heard, sir, that my power is gone! Because you have heard that I, who was yesterday the King's right hand, am to-day dried up, withered and paralysed! Because you have heard – but have a care! have a care!' he continued with extraordinary vehemence, and in a voice like a dog's snarl. 'You and those others! Have a care, I say, or you may find yourselves mistaken yet.'

'As Heaven shall judge me,' I answered solemnly, 'that is not true. Until I reached Paris last night I knew nothing of this report. I came here with a single mind, to redeem my honour by placing again in your Eminence's hands that which you gave me on trust, and here I do place it.'

For a moment he remained in the same attitude, staring at me fixedly. Then his face relaxed somewhat.

'Be good enough to ring that bell,' he said.

It stood on the table near me. I rang it, and a velvet-footed man in black came in, and gliding up to the Cardinal, placed a paper in his hand. The Cardinal looked at it; while the man stood with his head obsequiously bent, and my heart beat furiously.

'Very good,' his Eminence said, after a pause which seemed to me to be endless. 'Let the doors be thrown open.'

The man bowed low, and retired behind the screen. I heard a little bell ring somewhere in the silence, and in a moment the Cardinal stood up.

'Follow me!' he said, with a strange flash of his keen eyes.

Astonished, I stood aside while he passed to the screen; then I followed him. Outside the first door, which stood open, we found eight or nine persons – pages, a monk, the major-domo, and several guards waiting like mutes. These signed to me to precede them and fell in behind us, and in that order we passed through the first room and the second, where the clerks stood with bent heads to receive us. The last door, the door of the ante-chamber, flew open as we approached; voices cried, 'Room! Room for his Eminence!' We passed through two lines of bowing lackeys, and entered – an empty chamber.

The ushers did not know how to look at one another; the lackeys trembled in their shoes. But the Cardinal walked on apparently unmoved, until he had passed slowly half the length of the chamber. Then he turned himself about, looking first to one and then to the other, with a low laugh of derision.

'Father,' he said in his thin voice, 'what does the Psalmist say? "I am become like a pelican in the wilderness and like an owl that is in the desert!"'

The monk mumbled assent.

'And later in the same psalm, is it not written, "They shall perish, but thou shalt endure"?'

'It is so,' the father answered. 'Amen.'

'Doubtless though, that refers to another life,' the Cardinal said, with his slow wintry smile. 'In the meantime we will go back to our books, and serve God and the King in small things if not in great. Come, father, this is no longer a place for us. *Vanitas vanitatum omnia vanitas*! We will retire.'

And as solemnly as we had come we marched back through the first and second and third doors until we stood again in the silence of the Cardinal's chamber – he and I and the velvet-footed man in black. For a while Richelieu seemed to forget me. He stood brooding on the hearth, his eyes on a small fire, which burned there though the weather was warm. Once I heard him laugh, and twice he uttered in a tone of bitter mockery the words:

'Fools! Fools! Fools!'

At last he looked up, saw me, and started.

'Ah!' he said, 'I had forgotten you. Well, you are fortunate, M. de Berault. Yesterday I had a hundred clients; to-day I have only one, and I cannot afford to hang him. But for your liberty – that is another matter.'

I would have said something, pleaded something; but he turned abruptly to the table and sitting down wrote a few lines on a piece of paper. Then he rang his bell, while I stood waiting and confounded.

The man in black came from behind the screen.

'Take this letter and that gentleman to the upper guard-room,' the Cardinal said sharply. 'I can hear no more,' he continued, frowning and raising his hand to forbid interruption. 'The matter is ended, M. de Berault. Be thankful.'

In a moment I was outside the door, my head in a whirl, my heart divided between gratitude and resentment. I would fain have stood to consider my position; but I had no time. Obeying a gesture, I followed my guide along several passages, and everywhere found the same silence, the same monastic stillness. At length, while I was dolefully considering whether the Bastille or the Châtelet would be my fate, he stopped at a door, thrust the letter into my hands, and lifting the latch, signed to me to enter.

I went in in amazement, and stopped in confusion. Before me, alone, just risen from a chair, with her face one moment pale, the next crimson with blushes, stood Mademoiselle de Cocheforêt. I cried out her name.

'M. de Berault,' she said, trembling. 'You did not expect to see me?'

'I expected to see no one so little, Mademoiselle,' I answered, striving to recover my composure.

'Yet you might have thought that we should not utterly desert you,' she replied, with a reproachful humility which went to my heart. 'We should have been base indeed, if we had not made some attempt to save you. I thank Heaven, M. de Berault, that it has so far succeeded that that strange man has promised me your life. You have seen him?' she continued eagerly and in another tone, while her eyes grew on a sudden large with fear.

'Yes, Mademoiselle,' I said. 'I have seen him, and it is true. He has given me my life.'

'And –?'

'And sent me into imprisonment.'

'For how long?' she whispered.

'I do not know,' I answered. 'I fear during the King's pleasure.'

She shuddered.

'I may have done more harm than good,' she murmured, looking at me piteously. 'But I did it for the best. I told him all, and perhaps I did harm.'

But to hear her accuse herself thus when she had made this long and lonely journey to save me, when she had forced herself into her enemy's presence, and had, as I was sure she had, abased herself for me, was more than I could bear.

'Hush, Mademoiselle, hush!' I said, almost roughly. 'You hurt me. You have made me happy; and yet I wish that you were not here, where, I fear, you have few friends, but back at Cocheforêt. You have done more for me than I expected, and a hundred times more than I deserved. But it must end here. I was a ruined man before this happened, before I ever saw you. I am no worse now, but I am still that; and I would not have your name pinned to mine on Paris lips. Therefore, good-bye. God forbid I should say more to you, or let you stay where foul tongues would soon malign you.'

She looked at me in a kind of wonder; then with a growing smile –

'It is too late,' she said gently.

'Too late?' I exclaimed. 'How, Mademoiselle?'

'Because – do you remember, M. de Berault, what you told me of your love-story under the guide-post by Agen? That it could have no happy ending? For the same reason I was not ashamed to tell mine to the Cardinal. By this time it is common property.'

I looked at her as she stood facing me. Her eyes shone under the lashes that almost hid them. Her figure drooped, and yet a smile trembled on her lips.

'*What* did you tell him, Mademoiselle?' I whispered, my breath coming quickly.

'That I loved,' she answered boldly, raising her clear eyes to mine. 'And therefore that I was not ashamed to beg – even on my knees.'

I fell on mine, and caught her hand before the last word passed her lips. For the moment I forgot King and Cardinal, prison and the future, all; all except that this woman, so pure and so beautiful, so far above me in all things, loved me. For the moment, I say. Then I remembered myself. I stood up, and stood back from her in a sudden revulsion of feeling.

'You do not know me!' I cried. 'You do not know what I have done!'

'That is what I do know,' she answered, looking at me with a wondrous smile.

'Ah! but you do not!' I cried. 'And besides there is this – this between us.' And I picked up the Cardinal's letter. It had fallen on the floor.

She turned a shade paler. Then she cried quickly:

'Open it! open it! It is not sealed nor closed.'

I obeyed mechanically, dreading with a horrible dread what I might see. Even when I had it open I looked at the finely scrawled characters with eyes askance. But at last I made it out. And it ran thus:

> '*The King's pleasure is that M. Gil de Berault, having mixed himself up with affairs of state, retire forthwith to the demesne of Cocheforêt, and confine himself within its limits until the King's pleasure be further known.*
>
> 'THE CARDINAL DE RICHELIEU.'

We were married next day, and a fortnight later were at Cocheforêt, in the brown woods under the southern mountains; while the great Cardinal, once more triumphant over his enemies, saw with cold, smiling eyes the world pass through his chamber. The flood-tide of his prosperity lasted thirteen years from that time, and ceased only with his death. For the world had learned its lesson; to his hour they call that day, which saw me stand alone for all his friends, 'The Day of Dupes.'

THE PRISONER OF ZENDA

1

The Rassendylls – with a Word on the Elphbergs

'I WONDER when in the world you're going to do anything, Rudolf?' said my brother's wife.

'My dear Rose,' I answered, laying down my egg-spoon, 'why in the world should I do anything? My position is a comfortable one. I have an income nearly sufficient for my wants (no one's income is ever quite sufficient, you know), I enjoy an enviable social position: I am brother to Lord Burlesdon, and brother-in-law to that most charming lady, his countess. Behold, it is enough!'

'You are nine-and-twenty,' she observed, 'and you've done nothing but –'

'Knock about? It is true. Our family doesn't need to do things.'

This remark of mine rather annoyed Rose, for everybody knows (and therefore there can be no harm in referring to the fact) that, pretty and accomplished as she herself is, her family is hardly of the same standing as the Rassendylls. Besides her attractions, she possessed a large fortune, and my brother Robert was wise enough not to mind about her ancestry. Ancestry is, in fact, a matter concerning which the next observation of Rose's has some truth.

'Good families are generally worse than any others,' she said.

Upon this I stroked my hair: I knew quite well what she meant.

'I'm so glad Robert's is black!' she cried.

At this moment Robert (who rises at seven and works before breakfast) came in. He glanced at his wife: her cheek was slightly flushed; he patted it caressingly.

'What's the matter, my dear?' he asked.

'She objects to my doing nothing and having red hair,' said I, in an injured tone.

'Oh! of course he can't help his hair,' admitted Rose.

'It generally crops out once in a generation,' said my brother. 'So does the nose. Rudolf has got them both.'

'I wish they didn't crop out,' said Rose, still flushed.

'I rather like them myself,' said I, and, rising, I bowed to the portrait of Countess Amelia.

My brother's wife uttered an exclamation of impatience.

'I wish you'd take that picture away, Robert,' said she.

'My dear!' he cried.

'Good heavens!' I added.

'Then it might be forgotten,' she continued.

'Hardly – with Rudolf about,' said Robert, shaking his head.

'Why should it be forgotten?' I asked.

'Rudolf!' exclaimed my brother's wife, blushing very prettily.

I laughed, and went on with my egg. At least I had shelved the question of what (if anything) I ought to do. And, by way of closing the discussion – and also, I must admit, of exasperating my strict little sister-in-law a trifle more – I observed:

'I rather like being an Elphberg myself.'

When I read a story, I skip the explanations; yet the moment I begin to write one, I find that I must have an explanation. For it is manifest that I must explain why my sister-in-law was vexed with my nose and hair, and why I ventured to call myself an Elphberg. For eminent as, I must protest, the Rassendylls have been for many generations, yet participation in their blood of course does not, at first sight, justify the boast of a connection with the grander stock of the Elphbergs or a claim to be one of that Royal House. For what relationship is there between Ruritania and Burlesdon, between the Palace at Strelsau or the Castle of Zenda and Number 305 Park Lane, W.?

Well then – and I must premise that I am going, perforce, to rake up the very scandal which my dear Lady Burlesdon wishes forgotten – in the year 1733, George II sitting then on the throne, peace reigning for the moment, and the King and the Prince of Wales being not yet at loggerheads, there came on a visit to the English Court a certain prince, who was afterwards known to history as Rudolf the Third of Ruritania. The prince was a tall, handsome young fellow, marked (maybe marred, it is not for me to say) by a somewhat unusually long, sharp and straight nose, and a mass of dark-red hair – in fact, the nose and the hair which have stamped the Elphbergs time out of mind. He stayed some months in England, where he was most courteously received; yet, in the end, he left rather under a cloud. For he fought a duel (it was considered highly well-bred of him to waive all question of his rank) with a nobleman, well known in the society of the day, not only for his own merits, but as the husband of a very beautiful wife. In that duel Prince Rudolf received a severe wound, and, recovering therefrom, was adroitly smuggled off by the Ruritanian ambassador, who had found him a pretty handful. The nobleman was not wounded in the duel; but the morning being raw and damp on the occasion of the meeting, he contracted a severe chill, and, failing to throw it off, he died some six months after the departture of Prince Rudolf, without having found leisure to adjust his relations with his wife – who, after another two months, bore an heir to the title and estates of the family of Burlesdon. This lady was the Countess Amelia, whose picture my sister-in-law wished to remove from the drawing-room in Park Lane; and her husband was James, fifth Earl of Burlesdon and twenty-second Baron Rassendyll, both in the peerage of England, and a Knight of the Garter. As for Rudolf, he went back to Ruritania, married a wife, and ascended the throne, whereon his progeny in the direct line have sat from then till this very hour – with one short interval. And, finally, if you walk through the picture-galleries at Burlesdon, among the fifty portraits or so of the last century-and-a-half, you will find five or six, including that of the sixth earl, distinguished by long, sharp, straight noses and a quantity of dark-red hair; these five or six have also blue eyes, whereas among the Rassendylls dark eyes are the commoner.

That is the explanation, and I am glad to have finished it: the blemishes on honourable lineage are a delicate subject, and certainly this heredity we hear so much about is the finest scandalmonger in the world; it laughs at discretion, and writes strange entries between the lines of the 'Peerages.'

It will be observed that my sister-in-law, with a want of logic that must have been peculiar to herself (since we are no longer allowed to lay it to the charge of her sex), treated my complexion almost as an offence for which I was responsible, hastening to assume from that external sign inward qualities of which I protest my entire innocence; and this unjust inference she sought to buttress by pointing to the uselessness of the life I had led. Well, be that as it may, I had picked up a good deal of pleasure and a good deal of knowledge. I had been to a German school and a German University, and spoke German as readily and perfectly as English; I was thoroughly at home in French; I had a smattering of Italian and enough Spanish to swear by. I was, I believe, a strong, though hardly a fine swordsman and a good shot. I could ride anything that had a back to sit on; and my head was as cool a one as you could find, for all its flaming cover. If you say that I ought to have spent my time in useful labour, I am out of Court and have nothing to say, save that my parents had no business to leave me two thousand pounds a year and a roving disposition.

'The difference between you and Robert,' said my sister-in-law, who often (bless her!) speaks on a platform, and oftener still as if she were on one, 'is that he recognises the duties of his position, and you only see the opportunities of yours.'

'To a man of spirit, my dear Rose,' I answered, 'opportunities are duties.'

'Nonsense!' said she, tossing her head; and after a moment she went on: 'Now, here's Sir Jacob Borrodaile offering you exactly what you might be equal to.'

'A thousand thanks!' I murmured.

'He's to have an Embassy in six months, and Robert says he is sure that he'll take you as an *attaché*. Do take it, Rudolf – to please me.'

Now, when my sister-in-law puts the matter in that way, wrinkling her pretty brows, twisting her little hands, and growing wistful in the eyes, all on account of an idle scamp like myself, for whom she has no natural responsibility, I am visited with compunction. Moreover, I thought it possible that I could pass the time in the position suggested with some tolerable amusement. Therefore I said:

'My dear sister, if in six months' time no unforeseen obstacle has arisen, and Sir Jacob invites me, hang me if I don't go with Sir Jacob!'

'Oh, Rudolf, how good of you! I am glad!'

'Where's he going to?'

'He doesn't know yet; but it's sure to be a good Embassy.'

'Madame,' said I, 'for your sake I'll go, if it's no more than a beggarly Legation. When I do a thing, I don't do it by halves.'

My promise, then, was given; but six months are six months, and seem an eternity, and, inasmuch as they stretched between me and my prospective industry (I suppose *attachés* are industrious; but I know not, for I never became *attaché* to Sir Jacob or anybody else), I cast about for some desirable mode of spending them. And it occurred to me suddenly that I would visit Ruritania. It may seem strange that I had never visited that country yet; but my father (in spite of a sneaking fondness for the Elphbergs, which led him to give me, his second son, the famous Elphberg name of Rudolf) had always been averse from my going, and, since his death, my brother, prompted by Rose, had accepted the family tradition which taught that a wide berth was to be given to that country. But the moment Ruritania had come into my head I was eaten up with a curiosity to see it. After all, red hair and long noses are not confined to the House of Elphberg, and the old story seemed a preposterously insufficient reason for debarring myself from acquaintance with an highly interesting and important kingdom, one which had played no small part in European history, and might do the like again under the sway of a young and vigorous ruler, such as the new King was rumoured to be. My determination was clinched by reading in *The Times* that Rudolf the Fifth was to be crowned at Strelsau in the course of the next three weeks, and that great magnificence was to mark the occasion. At once I made up my mind to be present, and began my preparations. But, inasmuch as it has never been my practice to furnish my relatives with an itinerary of my journeys and in this case I anticipated opposition to my wishes, I gave out that I was going for a ramble in the Tyrol – an old haunt of mine – and propitiated Rose's wrath by declaring that I intended to study the political and social problems of the interesting community which dwells in that neighbourhood.

'Perhaps,' I hinted darkly, 'there may be an outcome of the expedition.'

'What do you mean?' she asked.

'Well,' said I carelessly, 'there seems a gap that might be filled by an exhaustive work on – '

'Oh! will you write a book?' she cried, clapping her hands. 'That would be splendid, wouldn't it, Robert?'

'It's the best of introductions to political life nowadays,' observed my brother, who has, by the way, introduced himself in this manner several times over. *Burlesdon on Ancient Theories and Modern Facts* and *The Ultimate Outcome, by a Political Student*, are both works of recognised eminence.

'I believe you are right, Bob, my boy,' said I.

'Now promise you'll do it,' said Rose earnestly.

'No, I won't promise; but if I find enough material, I will.'

'That's fair enough,' said Robert.

'Oh, material doesn't matter! she said, pouting.

But this time she could get no more than a qualified promise out of me. To tell the truth, I would have wagered a handsome sum that the story of my expedition that summer would stain no paper and spoil not a single pen. And that shows how little we know what the future holds; for here I am, fulfilling my qualified promise, and writing, as I never thought to write, a book – though it will hardly serve as an introduction to political life, and has not a jot to do with the Tyrol.

Neither would it, I fear, please Lady Burlesdon, if I were to submit it to her critical eye – a step which I have no intention of taking.

2

Concerning the Colour of Men's Hair

IT was a maxim of my Uncle William's that no man should pass through Paris without spending four-and-twenty hours there. My uncle spoke out of a ripe experience of the world, and I honoured his advice by putting up for a day and a night at 'The Continental' on my way to – the Tyrol. I called on George Featherly at the Embassy, and we had a bit of dinner together at Durand's, and afterwards dropped in to the Opera; and after that we had a little supper, and after that we called on Bertram Bertrand, a versifier of some repute and Paris correspondent to *The Critic.* He had a very comfortable suite of rooms, and we found some pleasant fellows smoking and talking. It struck me, however, that Bertram himself was absent and in low spirits, and when everybody except ourselves had gone, I rallied him on his moping preoccupation. He fenced with me for a while, but at last, flinging himself on a sofa, he exclaimed:

'Very well; have it your own way. I am in love – infernally in love!'

'Oh, you'll write the better poetry,' said I, by way of consolation.

He ruffled his hair with his hand and smoked furiously. George Featherly, standing with his back to the mantelpiece, smiled unkindly.

'If it's the old affair,' said he, 'you may as well throw it, up, Bert. She's leaving Paris to-morrow.'

'I know that,' snapped Bertram.

'Not that it would make any difference if she stayed,' pursued the relentless George. 'She flies higher than the paper-trade, my boy!'

'Hang her!' said Bertram.

'It would make it more interesting for me,' I ventured to observe, 'if I knew who you were talking about.'

'Antoinette Mauban,' said George.

'De Mauban,' growled Bertram.

'Oho!' said I, passing by the question of the 'de.' 'You don't mean to say, Bert – ?'

'Can't you let me alone?'

'Where's she going to?' I asked, for the lady was something of a celebrity.

George jingled his money, smiled cruelly at poor Bertram, and answered pleasantly:

'Nobody knows. By the way, Bert, I met a great man at her house the other night – at least, about a month ago. Did you ever meet him – the Duke of Strelsau?'

'Yes, I did,' growled Bertram.

'An extremely accomplished man, I thought him.'

It was not hard to see that George's references to the duke were intended to aggravate poor Bertram's sufferings, so that I drew the inference that the duke had distinguished Madame de Mauban by his attentions. She was a widow, rich, handsome, and, according to repute, ambitious. It was quite possible that she, as George put it, was flying as high as a personage who was everything he could be, short of enjoying strictly royal rank: for the duke was the son of the late King of Ruritania by a second and morganatic marriage, and half-brother to the new King. He had been his father's favourite, and it had occasioned some unfavourable comment when he had been created a duke, with a title derived from no less a city than the capital itself. His mother had been of good, but not exalted, birth.

'He's not in Paris now, is he?' I asked.

'Oh no! He's gone back to be present at the King's coronation; a ceremony which, I should say, he'll not enjoy much. But, Bert, old man, don't despair! He won't marry the fair Antoinette – at least, not unless another plan comes to nothing. Still, perhaps, she – ' He paused and added, with a laugh: 'Royal attentions are hard to resist – you know that, don't you, Rudolf?'

'Confound you!' said I; and rising, I left the hapless Bertram in George's hands and went home to bed.

The next day George Featherly went with me to the station, where I took a ticket for Dresden.

'Going to see the pictures?' asked George, with a grin.

George is an inveterate gossip, and had I told him that I was off to Ruritania, the news would have been in London in three days and in Park Lane in a week. I was, therefore, about to return an evasive answer, when he saved my conscience by leaving me suddenly and darting across the platform. Following him with my eyes, I saw him lift his hat and accost a graceful, fashionably-dressed woman who had just appeared from the booking-office. She was, perhaps, a year or two over thirty, tall, dark, and of rather full figure. As George talked, I saw her glance at me, and my vanity was hurt by the thought that, muffled in a fur-coat and a neck-wrapper (for it was a chilly April day) and wearing a soft travelling hat pulled down to my ears, I must be looking very far from my best. A moment later, George rejoined me.

'You've got a charming travelling companion,' he said. 'That's poor Bert Bertrand's goddess, Antoinette de Mauban, and, like you, she's going to Dresden – also, no doubt, to see the pictures. It's very queer, though, that she doesn't at present desire the honour of your acquaintance.'

'I didn't ask to be introduced,' I observed, a little annoyed.

'Well, I offered to bring you to her; but she said, "Another time." Never mind, old fellow, perhaps there'll be a smash, and you'll have a chance of rescuing her and cutting out the Duke of Strelsau!'

No smash, however, happened, either to me or to Madame de Mauban. I can speak for her as confidently as for myself; for when, after a night's rest in Dresden, I continued my journey, she got into the same train. Understanding that she wished to be let alone, I avoided her carefully, but I saw that she went the same way as I did to the very end of my journey, and I took opportunities of having a good look at her, when I could do so unobserved.

As soon as we reached the Ruritanian frontier (where the old officer who presided over the Custom House favoured me with such a stare that I felt surer than before of my Elphberg physiognomy), I bought the papers, and found in them news which affected my movements. For some reason, which was not clearly explained, and seemed to be something of a mystery, the date of the coronation had been suddenly advanced, and the ceremony was to take place on the next day but one. The whole country seemed in a stir about it, and it was evident that Strelsau was thronged. Rooms were all let and hotels overflowing; there would be very little chance of my obtaining a lodging, and I should certainly have to pay an exorbitant charge for it. I made up my mind to stop at Zenda, a small town fifty miles short of the capital, and about ten from the frontier. My train reached there in the evening; I would spend the next day, Tuesday, in a wander over the hills, which were said to be very fine, and in taking a glance at the famous Castle, and go over by train to Strelsau on the Wednesday morning, returning at night to sleep at Zenda.

Accordingly at Zenda I got out, and as the train passed where I stood on the platform, I saw my friend Madame de Mauban in her place; clearly she was going through to Strelsau, having, with more providence than I could boast, secured apartments there. I smiled to think how surprised George Featherly would have been to know that she and I had been fellow-travellers for so long.

I was very kindly received at the hotel – it was really no more than an inn – kept by a fat old lady and her two daughters. They were good, quiet people, and seemed very little interested in the great doings at Strelsau. The old lady's hero was the duke, for he was now, under the late King's will, master of the Zenda estates and of the Castle, which rose grandly on its steep hill at the end of the valley a mile or so from the inn. The old lady, indeed, did not hesitate to express regret that the duke was not on the throne, instead of his brother.

'We know Duke Michael,' said she. 'He has always lived among us; every Ruritanian knows Duke Michael. But the King is almost a stranger; he has been so much abroad, not one in ten knows him even by sight.'

'And now,' chimed in one of the young women, 'they say he has shaved off his beard, so that no one at all knows him.'

'Shaved his beard!' exclaimed her mother. 'Who says so?'

'Johann, the duke's keeper. He has seen the King.'

'Ah, yes. The King, sir, is now at the duke's hunting-lodge in the forest here; from here he goes to Strelsau to be crowned on Wednesday morning.'

I was interested to hear this, and made up my mind to walk next day in the direction of the lodge, on the chance of coming across the King. The old lady ran on garrulously:

'Ah, and I wish he would stay at his hunting – that and wine (and one thing more) are all he loves, they say – and suffer our duke to be crowned on Wednesday. That I wish, and I don't care who knows it.'

'Hush, mother!' urged the daughters.

'Oh, there's many to think as I do!' cried the old woman stubbornly.

I threw myself back in my deep armchair, and laughed at her zeal.

'For my part,' said the younger and prettier of the two daughters, a fair, buxom, smiling wench, 'I hate Black Michael! A red Elphberg for me, mother! The King, they say, is as red as a fox or as –'

And she laughed mischievously as she cast a glance at me, and tossed her head at her sister's reproving face.

'Many a man has cursed their red hair before now,' muttered the old lady – and I remembered James, fifth Earl of Burlesdon.

'But never a woman!' cried the girl.

'Ay, and women, when it was too late,' was the stern answer, reducing the girl to silence and blushes.

'How comes the King here?' I asked, to break an embarrassed silence. 'It is the duke's land here, you say.'

'The duke invited him, sir, to rest here till Wednesday. The duke is at Strelsau, preparing the King's reception.'

'Then they're friends?'

'None better,' said the old lady.

But my rosy damsel tossed her head again; she was not to be repressed for long, and she broke out again:

'Ay, they love one another as men do who want the same place and the same wife!'

The old woman glowered; but the last words pricked my curiosity, and I interposed before she could begin scolding:

'What, the same wife, too! How's that, young lady?'

'All the world knows that Black Michael – well then, mother, the duke

– would give his soul to marry his cousin, the Princess Flavia, and that she is to be the queen.'

'Upon my word,' said I, 'I begin to be sorry for your duke. But if a man will be a younger son, why he must take what the elder leaves, and be as thankful to God as he can'; and, thinking of myself, I shrugged my shoulders and laughed. And then I thought also of Antoinette de Mauban and her journey to Strelsau.

'It's little dealing Black Michael has with –' began the girl, braving her mother's anger; but as she spoke a heavy step sounded on the floor, and a gruff voice asked in a threatening tone:

'Who talks of "Black Michael" in his Highness's own burgh?'

The girl gave a little shriek, half of fright – half, I think, of amusement.

'You'll not tell of me, Johann?' she said.

'See where your chatter leads,' said the old lady.

The man who had spoken came forward.

'We have company, Johann,' said my hostess, and the fellow plucked off his cap. A moment later he saw me, and, to my amazement, he started back a step, as though he had seen something wonderful.

'What ails you, Johann?' asked the elder girl. 'This is a gentleman on his travels, come to see the coronation.'

The man had recovered himself, but he was staring at me with an intense, searching, almost fierce glance.

'Good evening to you,' said I.

'Good evening, sir,' he muttered, still scrutinising me, and the merry girl began to laugh as she called –

'See, Johann, it is the colour you love! He started to see your hair, sir. It's not the colour we see most of here in Zenda.'

'I crave your pardon, sir,' stammered the fellow, with puzzled eyes. 'I expected to see no one.'

'Give him a glass to drink my health in; and I'll bid you good night, and thanks to you, ladies, for your courtesy and pleasant conversation.'

So speaking, I rose to my feet, and with a slight bow turned to the door. The young girl ran to light me on the way, and the man fell back to let me pass, his eyes still fixed on me. The moment I was by, he started a step forward, asking:

'Pray, sir, do you know our King?'

'I never saw him,' said I. 'I hope to do so on Wednesday.'

He said no more, but I felt his eyes following me till the door closed behind me. My saucy conductor, looking over her shoulder at me as she preceded me upstairs, said:

'There's no pleasing Master Johann for one of your colour, sir.'

'He prefers yours, may be?' I suggested.

'I meant, sir, in a man,' she answered, with a coquettish glance.

'What,' asked I, taking hold of the other side of the candlestick, 'does colour matter in a man?'

'Nay, but I love yours – it's the Elphberg red.'

'Colour in a man,' said I, 'is a matter of no more moment than that!' – and I gave her something of no value.

'God send the kitchen-door be shut!' said she.

'Amen!' said I, and left her.

In fact, however, as I now know, colour is sometimes of considerable moment to a man.

3

A Merry Evening with a Distant Relative

I WAS not so unreasonable as to be prejudiced against the duke's keeper because he disliked my complexion; and if I had been, his most civil and obliging conduct (as it seemed to me to be) next morning would have disarmed me. Hearing that I was bound for Strelsau, he came to see me while I was breakfasting, and told me that a sister of his who had married a well-to-do tradesman and lived in the capital, had invited him to occupy a room in her house. He had gladly accepted, but now found that his duties would not permit of his absence. He begged therefore that, if such humble (though, as he added, clean and comfortable) lodgings would satisfy me, I would take his place. He pledged his sister's acquiescence, and urged the inconvenience and crowding to which I should be subject in my journeys to and from Strelsau the next day. I accepted his offer without a moment's hesitation, and he went off to telegraph to his sister, while I packed up and prepared to take the next train. But I still hankered after the forest and the hunting-lodge, and when my little maid told me that I could, by walking ten miles or so through the forest, hit the railway at a roadside station, I decided to send my luggage direct to the address which Johann had given, take my walk, and follow to Strelsau myself. Johann had gone off and was not aware of the change in my plans; but, as its only effect was to delay my arrival at his sister's for a few hours, there was no reason for troubling to inform him of it. Doubtless the good lady would waste no anxiety on my account.

I took an early luncheon, and, having bidden my kind entertainers farewell, promising to return to them on my way home, I set out to climb the hill that led to the Castle, and thence to the forest of Zenda. Half-an-hour's leisurely walking brought me to the Castle. It had been a fortress in old days, and the ancient keep was still in good preservation and very imposing. Behind it stood another portion of the original castle, and behind that again, and separated from it by a deep and broad moat, which ran all round the old buildings, was a handsome modern *château*, erected by the last king, and now forming the country residence of the Duke of Strelsau. The old and the new portions were connected by a drawbridge, and this indirect mode of access formed the only passage between the old building and the outer world; but leading to the modern *château* there was a broad and handsome avenue. It was an ideal residence: when 'Black Michael' desired company, he could dwell in his *château*; if a fit of misanthropy seized him, he had merely to cross the bridge and draw it up after him (it ran on rollers), and nothing short of a regiment and a train of artillery could fetch him out. I went on my way, glad that poor Black Michael, though he could not have the throne or the princess, had, at least, as fine a residence as any prince in Europe.

Soon I entered the forest, and walked on for an hour or more in its cool sombre shade. The great trees enlaced with one another over my head, and the sunshine stole through in patches as bright as diamonds, and hardly bigger. I was enchanted with the place, and, finding a felled tree-trunk, propped my back against it, and stretching my legs out gave myself up to undisturbed contemplation of the solemn beauty of the woods and to the comfort of a good cigar. And when the cigar was finished and I had (I suppose) inhaled as much beauty as I could, I went off into the most delightful sleep, regardless of my train to Strelsau and of the fast-waning afternoon. To remember a train in such a spot would have been rank sacrilege. Instead of that, I fell to dreaming that I was married to the Princess Flavia and dwelt in the Castle of Zenda, and beguiled whole days with my love in the glades of the forest – which made a very pleasant dream. In fact, I was just impressing a fervent kiss on the charming lips of the princess, when I heard (and the voice seemed at first a part of the dream) someone exclaim, in rough strident tones.

'Why, the devil's in it! Shave him, and he'd be the King!'

The idea seemed whimsical enough for a dream: by the sacrifice of my heavy moustache and carefully pointed imperial, I was to be transformed into a monarch! I was about to kiss the princess again, when I arrived (very reluctantly) at the conclusion that I was awake.

I opened my eyes, and found two men regarding me with much curiosity. Both wore shooting costumes and carried guns. One was rather short and very stoutly built, with a big bullet-shaped head, a bristly grey moustache, and small pale-blue eyes, a trifle bloodshot. The other was a slender young fellow, of middle height, dark in complexion, and bearing himself with grace and distinction. I set the one down as an old soldier: the other for a gentleman accustomed to move in good society, but not unused to military life either. It turned out afterwards that my guess was a good one.

The elder man approached me, beckoning the younger to follow. He did so, courteously raising his hat. I rose slowly to my feet.

'He's the height, too!' I heard the elder murmur, as he surveyed my six feet two inches of stature. Then, with a cavalier touch of the cap, he addressed me:

'May I ask your name?'

'As you have taken the first step in the acquaintance, gentlemen,' said I, with a smile, 'suppose you give me a lead in the matter of names.'

The young man stepped forward with a pleasant smile.

'This,' said he, 'is Colonel Sapt, and I am called Fritz von Tarlenheim: we are both in the service of the King of Ruritania.'

I bowed and, baring my head, answered:

'I am Rudolf Rassendyll. I am a traveller from England; and once for a year or two I held a commission from Her Majesty the Queen.'

'Then we are all brethren of the sword,' answered Tarlenheim, holding out his hand, which I took readily.

'Rassendyll, Rassendyll!' muttered Colonel Sapt; then a gleam of intelligence flitted across his face.

'By Heaven!' he cried, 'you're of the Burlesdons?'

'My brother is now Lord Burlesdon,' said I.

'Thy head bewrayeth thee,' he chuckled, pointing to my uncovered poll. – 'Why, Fritz, you know the story?'

The young man glanced apologetically at me. He felt a delicacy which my sister-in-law would have admired. To put him at his ease, I remarked with a smile:

'Ah! the story is known here as well as among us, it seems.'

'Known!' cried Sapt. 'If you stay here, the deuce a man in all Ruritania will doubt of it – or a woman either.'

I began to feel uncomfortable. Had I realised what a very plainly-written pedigree I carried about with me, I should have thought long before I visited Ruritania. However, I was in for it now.

At this moment a ringing voice sounded from the wood behind us:

'Fritz, Fritz! where are you, man?'

Tarlenheim started, and said hastily:

'It's the King!'

Old Sapt chuckled again.

Then a young man jumped out from behind the trunk of a tree and stood beside us. As I looked on him, I uttered an astonished cry; and he, seeing me, drew back in sudden wonder. Saving the hair on my face and a manner of conscious dignity which his position gave him, saving also that he lacked perhaps half-an-inch – nay, less than that, but still something – of my height, the King of Ruritania might have been Rudolf Rassendyll, and I, Rudolf, the King.

For an instant we stood motionless, looking at one another. Then I bared my head again and bowed respectfully. The King found his voice, and asked in bewilderment:

'Colonel – Fritz – who is this gentleman?'

I was about to answer, when Colonel Sapt stepped between the King and me, and began to talk to his Majesty in a low growl. The King towered over Sapt, and, as he listened, his eyes now and again sought mine. I looked at him long and carefully. The likeness was certainly astonishing, though I saw the points of difference also. The King's face was slightly more fleshy than mine, the oval of its contour the least trifle more pronounced, and, as I fancied, his mouth lacking something of the firmness (or obstinacy) which was to be gathered from my close-shutting lips. But, for all that, and above all minor distinctions, the likeness rose striking, salient, wonderful.

Sapt ceased speaking, and the King still frowned. Then, gradually, the corners of his mouth began to twitch, his nose came down (as mine does when I laugh), his eyes twinkled, and, behold! he burst into the merriest fit of irrepressible laughter, which rang through the woods and proclaimed him a jovial soul.

'Well met, cousin!' he cried, stepping up to me, clapping me on the back, and laughing still. 'You must forgive me if I was taken aback. A man doesn't expect to see double at this time of day, eh, Fritz?'

'I must pray pardon, sire, for my presumption,' said I. 'I trust it will not forfeit your Majesty's favour.'

'By Heaven! you'll always enjoy the King's countenance,' he laughed, 'whether I like it or not; and, sir, I shall very gladly add to it what services I can. Where are you travelling to?'

'To Strelsau, sire – to the coronation.

The King looked at his friends: he still smiled, though his expression hinted some uneasiness. But the humorous side of the matter caught him again.

'Fritz, Fritz!' he cried, 'a thousand crowns for a sight of brother Michael's face when he sees a pair of us!' and the merry laugh rang out again.

'Seriously,' observed Fritz von Tarlenheim, 'I question Mr. Rassendyll's wisdom in visiting Strelsau just now.'

The King lit a cigarette.

'Well, Sapt?' said he, questioningly.

'He mustn't go,' growled the old fellow.

'Come, colonel, you mean that I should be in Mr. Rassendyll's debt, if –'

'Oh, ay! wrap it up in the right way,' said Sapt, hauling a great pipe out of his pocket.

'Enough, sire,' said I. 'I'll leave Ruritania to-day.'

'Now, by thunder, you shan't – and that's *sans phrase*, as Sapt likes it. For you shall dine with me to-night, happen what will afterwards. Come man, you don't meet a new relation every day!'

'We dine sparingly to-night,' said Fritz von Tarlenheim.

'Not we – with our new cousin for a guest!' cried the King; and, as Fritz shrugged his shoulders, he added: 'Oh! I'll remember our early start, Fritz.'

'So will I – to-morrow morning,' said old Sapt, pulling at his pipe.

'O wise old Sapt!' cried the King. 'Come, Mr. Rassendyll – by the way, what name did they give you?'

'Your Majesty's,' I answered, bowing.

'Well, that shows they weren't ashamed of us,' he laughed. 'Come, then, cousin Rudolf; I've got no house of my own here, but my dear brother Michael lends us a place of his, and we'll make shift to entertain you there'; and he put his arm through mine and, signing to the others to accompany us, walked me off, westerly, through the forest.

We walked for more than half an hour, and the King smoked cigarettes and chattered incessantly. He was full of interest in my family, laughed heartily when I told him of the portraits with Elphberg hair in our galleries, and yet more heartily when he heard that my expedition to Ruritania was a secret one.

'You have to visit your disreputable cousin on the sly, have you?' said he.

Suddenly emerging from the wood, we came on a small and rude hunting-lodge. It was a one-story building, a sort of bungalow, built entirely of wood. As we approached it, a little man in a plain livery came out to meet us. The only other person I saw about the place was a fat elderly woman, whom I afterwards discovered to be the mother of Johann, the duke's keeper.

'Well, is dinner ready, Josef?' asked the King.

The little servant informed us that it was, and we soon sat down to a plentiful meal. The fare was plain enough: the King ate heartily, Fritz von Tarlenheim delicately, old Sapt voraciously. I played a good knife and fork, as my custom is; the King noticed my performance with approval.

'We're all good trenchermen, we Elphbergs,' said he. 'But what? – we're eating dry! Wine, Josef! wine, man! Are we beasts, to eat without drinking? Are we cattle, Josef?'

At this reproof Josef hastened to load the table with bottles.

'Remember to-morrow!' said Fritz.

'Ay – to-morrow!' said old Sapt.

The King drained a bumper to his 'Cousin Rudolf,' as he was gracious – or merry – enough to call me; and I drank its fellow to the 'Elphberg Red,' whereat he laughed loudly.

Now, be the meat what it might, the wine we drank was beyond all price or praise, and we did it justice. Fritz ventured once to stay the King's hand.

'What?' cried the King. 'Remember you start before I do, Master Fritz – you must be more sparing by two hours than I.'

Fritz saw that I did not understand.

'The colonel and I,' he explained, 'leave here at six: we ride down to Zenda and return with the guard of honour to fetch the King at eight, and then we all ride together to the station.'

'Hang that same guard!' growled Sapt.

'Oh! it's very civil of my brother to ask the honour for his regiment,' said the King. 'Come, cousin, you need not start early. Another bottle, man!'

I had another bottle – or, rather, a part of one, for the larger half travelled quickly down his Majesty's throat. Fritz gave up his attempts at persuasion: from persuading, he fell to being persuaded, and soon we were all of us as full of wine as we had any right to be. The King began talking of what he would do in the future, old Sapt of what he had done in the past, Fritz of some beautiful girl or other, and I of the wonderful merits of the Elphberg dynasty. We all talked at once, and followed to the letter Sapt's exhortation to let the morrow take care of itself.

At last the King set down his glass and leant back in his chair.

'I have drunk enough,' said he.

'Far be it from me to contradict the King,' said I.

Indeed, his remark was most absolutely true – so far as it went.

While I yet spoke, Josef came and set before the King a marvellous old wicker-covered flagon. It had lain so long in some darkened cellar that it seemed to blink in the candlelight.

'His Highness the Duke of Strelsau bade me set this wine before the King, when the King was weary of all other wines, and pray the King to drink, for the love that he bears his brother.'

'Well done, Black Michael!' said the King. 'Out with the cork, Josef. Hang him! Did he think I'd flinch from his bottle?'

The bottle was opened, and Josef filled the King's glass. The King tasted it. Then, with a solemnity born of the hour and his own condition, he looked round on us:

'Gentlemen, my friends – Rudolf, my cousin ('tis a scandalous story, Rudolf, on my honour!), everything is yours to the half of Ruritania. But ask me not for a single drop of this divine bottle, which I will drink to the health of that – that sly knave, my brother, Black Michael.'

And the King seized the bottle and turned it over his mouth, and drained it and flung it from him, and laid his head on his arms on the table.

And we drank pleasant dreams to his Majesty – and that is all I remember of the evening. Perhaps it is enough.

4

The King keeps his Appointment

WHETHER I had slept a minute or a year I knew not. I awoke with a start and a shiver; my face, hair and clothes dripped water, and opposite me stood old Sapt, a sneering smile on his face and an empty bucket in his hand. On the table by him sat Fritz von Tarlenheim, pale as a ghost and black as a crow under the eyes.

I leapt to my feet in anger.

'Your joke goes too far, sir!' I cried.

'Tut, man, we've no time for quarrelling. Nothing else would rouse you. It's five o'clock.'

'I'll thank you, Colonel Sapt – ' I began again, hot in spirit, though I was uncommonly cold in body.

'Rassendyll,' interrupted Fritz, getting down from the table and taking my arm, 'look here.'

The King lay full length on the floor. His face was red as his hair, and he breathed heavily. Sapt, the disrespectful old dog, kicked him sharply. He did not stir, nor was there any break in his breathing. I saw that his face and head were wet with water, as were mine.

'We've spent half an hour on him,' said Fritz.

'He drank three times what either of you did,' growled Sapt.

I knelt down and felt his pulse. It was alarmingly languid and slow. We three looked at one another.

'Was it drugged – that last bottle?' I asked in a whisper.

'I don't know,' said Sapt.

'We must get a doctor.'

'There's none within ten miles, and a thousand doctors wouldn't take him to Strelsau to-day. I know the look of it. He'll not move for six or seven hours yet.'

'But the coronation!' I cried in horror.

Fritz shrugged his shoulders, as I began to see was his habit on most occasions.

'We must send word that he's ill,' he said.

'I suppose so,' said I.

Old Sapt, who seemed as fresh as a daisy, had lit his pipe and was puffing hard at it.

'If he's not crowned to-day,' said he, 'I'll lay a crown he's never crowned.'

'But heavens, why?'

'The whole nation's there to meet him; half the army – ay, and Black Michael at the head. Shall we send word that the King's drunk?'

'That he's ill,' said I, in correction.

'Ill!' echoed Sapt, with a scornful laugh. 'They know his illnesses too well. He's been "ill" before!'

'Well, we must chance what they think,' said Fritz helplessly. 'I'll carry the news and make the best of it.'

Sapt raised his hand.

'Tell me,' said he. 'Do you think the King was drugged?'

'I do,' said I.

'And who drugged him?'

'That damned hound, Black Michael,' said Fritz between his teeth.

'Ay,' said Sapt, 'that he might not come to be crowned. Rassendyll here doesn't know our pretty Michael. What think you, Fritz, has Michael no king ready? Has half Strelsau no other candidate? As God's alive, man, the throne's lost if the King show himself not in Strelsau to-day. I know Black Michael.'

'We could carry him there,' said I.

'And a very pretty picture he makes,' sneered Sapt.

Fritz von Tarlenheim buried his face in his hands. The King breathed loudly and heavily. Sapt stirred him again with his foot.

'The drunken dog!' he said; 'but he's an Elphberg and the son of his father, and may I rot in hell before Black Michael sits in his place!'

For a moment or two we were all silent; then Sapt, knitting his bushy grey brows, took his pipe from his mouth and said to me:

'As a man grows old he believes in Fate. Fate sent you here. Fate sends you now to Strelsau.'

I staggered back, murmuring 'Good God!'

Fritz looked up with an eager, bewildered gaze.

'Impossible!' I muttered. 'I should be known.'

'It's a risk – against a certainty,' said Sapt. 'If you shave, I'll wager you'll not be known. Are you afraid?'

'Sir!'

'Come, lad, there, there; but it's your life, you know, if you're known – and mine – and Fritz's here. But, if you don't go, I swear to you Black Michael will sit to-night on the throne, and the King lie in prison or his grave.'

'The King would never forgive it,' I stammered.

'Are we women? Who cares for his forgiveness?'

The clock ticked fifty times, and sixty and seventy times, as I stood in thought. Then I suppose a look came over my face, for old Sapt caught me by the hand, crying:

'You'll go?'

'Yes, I'll go,' said I, and I turned my eyes on the prostrate figure of the King on the floor.

'To-night,' Sapt went on in a hasty whisper, 'we are to lodge in the Palace. The moment they leave us you and I will mount our horses – Fritz must stay there and guard the King's room – and ride here at a gallop. The King will be ready – Josef will tell him – and he must ride back with me to Strelsau, and you ride as if the devil were behind you to the frontier.'

I took it all in in a second, and nodded my head.

'There's a chance,' said Fritz, with his first sign of hopefulness.

'If I escape detection,' said I.

'If we're detected,' said Sapt. 'I'll send Black Michael down below before I go myself, so help me heaven! Sit in that chair, man.'

I obeyed him.

He darted from the room, calling 'Josef! Josef!' In three minutes he was back, and Josef with him. The latter carried a jug of hot water, soap, and razors. He was trembling as Sapt told him how the land lay, and bade him shave me.

Suddenly Fritz smote on his thigh:

'But the guard! They'll know! they'll know!'

'Pooh! We shan't wait for the guard. We'll ride to Hofbau and catch a train there. When they come, the bird'll be flown.'

'But the King?'

'The King will be in the wine-cellar. I'm going to carry him there now.'

'If they find him?'

'They won't. How should they? Josef will put them off.'

'But –'

Sapt stamped his foot.

'We're not playing,' he roared. 'My God! don't I know the risk? If they do find him, he's no worse off than if he isn't crowned to-day in Strelsau.'

So speaking, he flung the door open and, stooping, put forth a strength I did not dream he had, and lifted the King in his hands. And as he did so, the old woman, Johann the keeper's mother, stood in the doorway. For a moment she stood, then she turned on her heel, without a sign of surprise, and clattered down the passage.

'Has she heard?' cried Fritz.

'I'll shut her mouth!' said Sapt grimly, and he bore off the King in his arms.

For me, I sat down in an arm-chair, and as I sat there, half-dazed, Josef clipped and scraped me till my moustache and imperial were things of the past and my face was as bare as the King's. And when Fritz saw me thus he drew a long breath and exclaimed:

'By Jove, we shall do it!'

It was six o'clock now, and we had no time to lose. Sapt hurried me into the King's room, and I dressed myself in the uniform of a colonel of the Guard, finding time as I slipped on the King's boots to ask Sapt what he had done with the old woman.

'She swore she'd heard nothing,' said he; 'but to make sure I tied her legs together and put a handkerchief in her mouth and bound her hands, and locked her up in the coal-cellar, next door to the King. Josef will look after them both later on.'

Then I burst out laughing, and even old Sapt grimly smiled.

'I fancy,' said he, 'that when Josef tells them the King is gone they'll think it is because we smelt a rat. For you may swear Black Michael doesn't expect to see him in Strelsau to-day.'

I put the King's helmet on my head. Old Sapt handed me the King's sword, looking at me long and carefully.

'Thank God, he shaved his beard!' he exclaimed.

'Why did he?' I asked.

'Because Princess Flavia said he grazed her cheek when he was graciously pleased to give her a cousinly kiss. Come though, we must ride.'

'Is all safe here?'

'Nothing's safe anywhere,' said Sapt, 'but we can make it no safer.'

Fritz now rejoined us in the uniform of a captain in the same regiment as that to which my dress belonged. In four minutes Sapt had arrayed himself in his uniform. Josef called that the horses were ready. We jumped on their backs and started at a rapid trot. The game had begun. What would the issue of it be?

The cool morning air cleared my head, and I was able to take in all Sapt said to me. He was wonderful. Fritz hardly spoke, riding like a man asleep, but Sapt, without another word for the King, began at once to instruct me most minutely in the history of my past life, of my family, of my tastes, pursuits, weaknesses, friends, companions, and servants. He told me the etiquette of the Ruritanian Court, promising to be constantly at my elbow to point out everybody whom I ought to know, and give me hints with what degree of favour to greet them.

'By the way,' he said, 'you're a Catholic, I suppose?'

'Not I,' I answered.

'Lord, he's a heretic!' groaned Sapt, and forthwith he fell to a rudimentary lesson in the practices and observances of the Romish faith.

'Luckily,' said he, 'you won't be expected to know much, for the King's notoriously lax and careless about such matters. But you must be as civil as butter to the Cardinal. We hope to win him over, because he and Michael have a standing quarrel about their precedence.'

We were by now at the station. Fritz had recovered nerve enough to explain to the astonished station master that the King had changed his plans. The train steamed up. We got into a first-class carriage, and Sapt, leaning back on the cushions, went on with his lesson. I looked at my watch – the King's watch it was, of course. It was just eight.

'I wonder if they've gone to look for us,' I said.

'I hope they won't find the King,' said Fritz nervously, and this time it was Sapt who shrugged his shoulders.

The train travelled well, and at half-past nine, looking out of the window, I saw the towers and spires of a great city.

'Your capital, my liege,' grinned old Sapt, with a wave of his hand, and, leaning forward, he laid his finger on my pulse. 'A little too quick,' said he, in his grumbling tone.

'I'm not made of stone!' I exclaimed.

'You'll do,' said he, with a nod. 'We must say Fritz here has caught the ague. Drain your flask, Fritz, for heaven's sake, boy!'

Fritz did as he was bid.

'We're an hour early,' said Sapt. 'We'll send word forward of your Majesty's arrival, for there'll be no one here to meet us yet. And meanwhile – '

'Meanwhile,' said I, 'the King 'll be hanged if he doesn't have some breakfast.'

Old Sapt chuckled, and held out his hand.

'You're an Elphberg, every inch of you,' said he. Then he paused, and looking at us, said quietly, 'God send we may be alive to-night!'

'Amen!' said Fritz von Tarlenheim.

The train stopped. Fritz and Sapt leapt out, uncovered, and held the door for me. I choked down a lump that rose in my throat, settled my helmet firmly on my head, and (I'm not ashamed to say it) breathed a short prayer to God. Then I stepped on the platform of the station at Strelsau.

A moment later, all was bustle and confusion: men hurrying up, hats in hand, and hurrying off again; men conducting me to the *buffet*; men mounting and riding in hot haste to the quarters of the troops, to the Cathedral, to the residence of Duke Michael. Even as I swallowed the last drop of my cup of coffee, the bells throughout all the city broke out into a joyful peal, and the sound of a military band and of men cheering smote upon my ear.

King Rudolf the Fifth was in his good city of Strelsau! And they shouted outside –

'God save the King!'

Old Sapt's mouth wrinkled into a smile.

'God save 'em both!' he whispered. 'Courage, lad!' and I felt his hand press my knee.

5

The Adventures of an Understudy

WITH Fritz von Tarlenheim and Colonel Sapt close behind me, I stepped out of the *buffet* on to the platform. The last thing I did was to feel if my revolver were handy and my sword loose in the scabbard. A gay group of officers and high dignitaries stood waiting me, at their head a tall old man, covered with medals, and of military bearing. He wore the yellow-and-red ribbon of the Red Rose of Ruritania – which, by the way, decorated my unworthy breast also.

'Marshal Strakencz,' whispered Sapt, and I knew that I was in the presence of the most famous veteran of the Ruritanian army.

Just behind the Marshal stood a short spare man, in flowing robes of black and crimson.

'The Chancellor of the Kingdom,' whispered Sapt.

The Marshal greeted me in a few loyal words, and proceeded to deliver an apology from the Duke of Strelsau. The duke, it seemed, had been afflicted with a sudden indisposition which made it impossible for him to come to the station, but he craved leave to await his Majesty at the Cathedral. I expressed my concern, accepted the Marshal's excuses very suavely, and received the compliments of a large number of distinguished personages. No one betrayed the least suspicion, and I felt my nerve returning and the agitated beating of my heart subsiding. But Fritz was still pale, and his hand shook like a leaf as he extended it to the Marshal.

Presently we formed procession and took our way to the door of the station. Here I mounted my horse, the Marshal holding my stirrup. The civil dignitaries went off to their carriages, and I started to ride through the streets with the Marshal on my right and Sapt (who, as my chief *aide-de-camp*, was entitled to the place) on my left. The city of Strelsau is partly old and partly new. Spacious modern boulevards and residential quarters surround and embrace the narrow, tortuous and picturesque streets of the original town. In the outer circles the upper classes live; in the inner the shops are situated; and, behind their prosperous fronts, lie hidden populous but wretched lanes and alleys, filled with a poverty-stricken, turbulent, and (in large measure) criminal class. These social and local divisions corresponded, as I knew from Sapt's information, to another division more important to me. The New Town was for the King; but to the Old Town Michael of Strelsau was a hope, a hero, and a darling.

The scene was very brilliant as we passed along the Grand Boulevard and on to the great square where the Royal Palace stood. Here I was in the midst of my devoted adherents. Every house was hung with red and bedecked with flags and mottoes. The streets were lined with raised seats on each side, and I passed along, bowing this way and that, under a shower of cheers, blessings, and waving handkerchiefs. The balconies were full of gaily-dressed ladies, who clapped their hands and curtsied and threw their brightest glances at me. A torrent of red roses fell on me; one bloom lodged in my horse's mane, and I took it and stuck it in my coat. The Marshal smiled grimly. I had stolen some glances at his face, but he was too impassive to show me whether his sympathies were with me or not.

'The red rose for the Elphbergs, Marshal,' said I gaily, and he nodded.

I have written 'gaily,' and a strange word it must seem. But the truth is, that I was drunk with excitement. At that moment I believed – I almost believed – that I was in very truth the King; and, with a look of laughing triumph, I raised my eyes to the beautyladen balconies again . . . and then I started. For, looking down on me, with her handsome face and proud smile, was the lady who had been my fellow-traveller – Antoinette de Mauban; and I saw her also start, and her lips moved, and she leant forward and gazed at me. And I, collecting myself, met her eyes full and square, while again I felt my revolver. Suppose she had cried aloud, 'That's not the King!'

Well, we went by; and then the Marshal, turning round in his saddle, waved his hand, and the Cuiracsiers closed round us, so that the crowd could not come near me. We were leaving my quarter and entering Duke Michael's, and this action of the Marshal's showed me more clearly than words what the state of feeling in the town must be. But if Fate made me a King, the least I could do was to play the part handsomely.

'Why this change in our order, Marshal?' said I.

The Marshal bit his white moustache.

'It is more prudent, sire,' he murmured.

I drew rein.

'Let those in front ride on,' said I, 'till they are fifty yards ahead. But do you, Marshal, and Colonel Sapt and my friends, wait here till I have ridden fifty yards. And see that no one is nearer to me. I will have my people see that their King trusts them.'

Sapt laid his hand on my arm. I shook him off. The Marshal hesitated.

'Am I not understood?' said I; and, biting his moustache again, he gave the orders. I saw old Sapt smiling into his beard, but he shook his head at me. If I had been killed in open day in the streets of Strelsau, Sapt's position would have been a difficult one.

Perhaps I ought to say that I was dressed all in white, except my boots. I wore a silver helmet with gilt ornaments, and the broad ribbon of the Rose looked well across my chest. I should be paying a poor compliment to the King if I did not set modesty aside and admit that I made a very fine figure. So the people thought; for when I, riding alone, entered the dingy, sparsely-decorated, sombre streets of the Old Town, there was first a murmur, then a cheer, and a woman, from a window above a cookshop, cried the old local saying:

'If he's red, he's right!' whereat I laughed and took off my helmet that she might see that I was of the right colour and they cheered me again at that.

It was more interesting riding thus alone, for I heard the comments of the crowd.

'He looks paler than his wont,' said one.

'You'd look pale if you lived as he does,' was the highly disrespectful retort.

'He's a bigger man than I thought,' said another.

'So he had a good jaw under that beard after all,' commented a third.

'The pictures of him aren't handsome enough,' declared a pretty girl, taking great care that I should hear. No doubt it was mere flattery.

But, in spite of these signs of approval and interest, the mass of the people received me in silence and with sullen looks, and my dear brother's portrait ornamented most of the windows – which was an ironical sort of greeting to the King. I was quite glad that he had been spared the unpleasant sight. He was a man of quick temper, and perhaps he would not have taken it so placidly as I did.

At last we were at the Cathedral. Its great grey front, embellished with hundreds of statues and boasting a pair of the finest oak doors in Europe, rose for the first time before me, and the sudden sense of my audacity almost overcame me. Everything was in a mist as I dismounted. I saw the

Marshal and Sapt dimly, and dimly the throng of gorgeously-robed priests who awaited me. And my eyes were still dim as I walked up the great nave, with the pealing of the organ in my ears. I saw nothing of the brilliant throng that filled it, I hardly distinguished the stately figure of the Cardinal as he rose from the archiepiscopal throne to greet me. Two faces only stood out side by side clearly before my eyes – the face of a girl, pale and lovely, surmounted by a crown of the glorious Elphberg hair (for in a woman it is glorious), and the face of a man, whose full-blooded red cheeks, black hair, and dark deep eyes told me that at last I was in presence of my brother, Black Michael. And when he saw me his red cheeks went pale all in a moment, and his helmet fell with a clatter on the floor. Till that moment I believe that he had not realised that the King was in very truth come to Strelsau.

Of what followed next I remember nothing. I knelt before the altar and the Cardinal anointed my head. Then I rose to my feet, and stretched out my hand and took from him the crown of Ruritania and set it on my head, and I swore the old oath of the King; and (if it were a sin, may it be forgiven me) I received the Holy Sacrament there before them all. Then the great organ pealed out again, the Marshal bade the heralds proclaim me, and Rudolf the Fifth was crowned King; of which imposing ceremony an excellent picture hangs now in my dining-room. The portrait of the King is very good.

Then the lady with the pale face and the glorious hair, her train held by two pages, stepped from her place and came to where I stood. And a herald cried:

'Her Royal Highness the Princess Flavia!'

She curtsied low, and put her hand under mine and raised my hand and kissed it. And for an instant I thought what I had best do. Then I drew her to me and kissed her twice on the cheek, and she blushed red, and – then his Eminence the Cardinal Archbishop slipped in front of Black Michael, and kissed my hand and presented me with a letter from the Pope – the first and last which I have ever received from that exalted quarter!

And then came the Duke of Strelsau. His step trembled, I swear, and he looked to the right and to the left, as a man looks who thinks on flight; and his face was patched with red and white, and his hand shook so that it jumped under mine, and I felt his lips dry and parched. And I glanced at Sapt, who was smiling again into his beard, and, resolutely doing my duty in that station of life to which I had been marvellously called, I took my dear Michael by both hands and kissed him on the cheek. I think we were both glad when that was over!

But neither in the face of the princess nor in that of any other did I see the least doubt or questioning. Yet, had I and the King stood side by side, she could have told us in an instant, or, at least, on a little consideration. But neither she nor anyone else dreamed or imagined that I could be other than the King. So the likeness served, and for an hour I stood there, feeling as weary and *blasé* as though I had been a king all my life; and everybody kissed my hand, and the ambassadors paid me their respects, among them old Lord Topham, at whose house in Grosvenor Square I had danced a score of times. Thank heaven, the old man was as blind as a bat, and did not claim my acquaintance.

Then back we went through the streets to the Palace, and I heard them cheering Black Michael; but he, Fritz told me, sat biting his nails like a man in a reverie, and even his own friends said that he should have made a braver show. I was in a carriage now, side by side with the Princess Flavia, and a rough fellow cried out:

'And when's the wedding?' and as he spoke another struck him in the face, crying 'Long live Duke Michael!' and the princess coloured – it was an admirable tint – and looked straight in front of her.

Now I felt in a difficulty, because I had forgotten to ask Sapt the state of my affections, or how far matters had gone between the princess and myself. Frankly, had I been the King, the further they had gone the better should I have been pleased. For I am not a slow-blooded man, and I had not kissed Princess Flavia's cheek for nothing. These thoughts passed through my head, but, not being sure of my ground, I said nothing; and in a moment or two the princess, recovering her equanimity, turned to me.

'Do you know, Rudolf,' said she, 'you look somehow different to-day?'

The fact was not surprising, but the remark was disquieting.

'You look,' she went on, 'more sober, more sedate; you're almost care-worn, and I declare you're thinner. Surely it's not possible that you've begun to take anything seriously?'

The princess seemed to hold of the King much the same opinion that Lady Burlesdon held of me.

I braced myself up to the conversation.

'Would that please you?' I asked softly.

'Oh, you know my views,' said she, turning her eyes away.

'Whatever pleases you I try to do,' I said; and, as I saw her smile and blush, I thought that I was playing the King's hand very well for him. So I continued and what I said was perfectly true:

'I assure you, my dear cousin, that nothing in my life has affected me more than the reception I've been greeted with to-day.'

She smiled brightly, but in an instant grew grave again, and whispered: 'Did you notice Michael?'

'Yes,' said I, adding, 'he wasn't enjoying himself.'

'Do be careful!' she went on. 'You don't – indeed you don't – keep enough watch on him. You know – '

'I know,' said I, 'that he wants what I've got.'

'Yes. Hush!'

Then – and I can't justify it, for I committed the King far beyond what

I had a right to do – I suppose she carried me off my feet – I went on:

'And perhaps also something which I haven't got yet, but hope to win some day.'

This was my answer. Had I been the King, I should have thought it encouraging:

'Haven't you enough responsibilities on you for one day, cousin?'

Bang, bang! Blare, blare! We were at the Palace. Guns were firing and trumpets blowing. Rows of lackeys stood waiting, and, handing the princess up the broad marble staircase, I took formal possession, as a crowned King, of the House of my ancestors, and sat down at my own table, with my cousin on my right hand, on her other side Black Michael, and on my left his Eminence the Cardinal. Behind my chair stood Sapt; and at the end of the table, I saw Fritz von Tarlenheim drain to the bottom his glass of champagne rather sooner than he decently should.

I wondered what the King of Ruritania was doing.

6

The Secret of a Cellar

WE were in the King's dressing-room – Fritz von Tarlenheim, Sapt, and I. I flung myself exhausted into an arm-chair. Sapt lit his pipe. He uttered no congratulations on the marvellous success of our wild risk, but his whole bearing was eloquent of satisfaction. The triumph, aided perhaps by good wine, had made a new man of Fritz.

'What a day for you to remember!' he cried. 'Gad, I'd like to be a King for twelve hours myself! But, Rassendyll, you mustn't throw your heart too much into the part. I don't wonder Black Michael looked blacker than ever – you and the princess had so much to say to one another.'

'How beautiful she is!' I exclaimed.

'Never mind the woman,' growled Sapt. 'Are you ready to start?'

'Yes,' said I, with a sigh.

It was five o'clock, and at twelve I should be no more than Rudolf Rassendyll. I remarked on it in a joking tone.

'You'll be lucky,' observed Sapt grimly, 'if you're not the late Rudolf Rassendyll. By Heaven! I feel my head wobbling on my shoulders every minute you're in the city. Do you know, friend, that Michael has had news from Zenda? He went into a room alone to read it – and he came out looking like a man dazed.'

'I'm ready,' said I, this news making me none the more eager to linger.

Sapt sat down.

'I must write us an order to leave the city. Michael's Governor, you know, and we must be prepared for hindrances. You must sign the order.'

'My dear colonel, I've not been bred a forger!'

Out of his pocket Sapt produced a piece of paper.

'There's the King's signature,' he said, 'and here,' he went on, after another search in his pocket, 'is some tracing paper. If you can't manage a "Rudolf" in ten minutes, why – I can.'

'Your education has been more comprehensive than mine,' said I. 'You write it.'

And a very tolerable forgery did this versatile hero produce.

'Now, Fritz,' said he, 'the King goes to bed. He is upset. No one is to see him till nine o'clock to-morrow. You understand – no one?'

'I understand,' answered Fritz.

'Michael may come, and claim immediate audience. You'll answer that only princes of the blood are entitled to it.'

'That'll annoy Michael,' laughed Fritz.

'You quite understand?' asked Sapt again. 'If the door of this room is opened while we're away, you're not to be alive to tell us about it.'

'I need no schooling, colonel,' said Fritz, a trifle haughtily.

'Here, wrap yourself in this big cloak,' Sapt continued to me, 'and put on this flat cap. My orderly rides with me to the hunting-lodge to-night.'

'There's an obstacle,' I observed. 'The horse doesn't live that can carry me forty miles.'

'Oh, yes, he does – two of him: one here – one at the lodge. Now are you ready?'

'I'm ready,' said I.

Fritz held out his hand.

'In case,' said he; and we shook hands heartily.

'Damn your sentiment!' growled Sapt. 'Come along.'

He went, not to the door, but to a panel in the wall.

'In the old King's time,' said he, 'I knew this way well.'

I followed him, and we walked, as I should estimate, near two hundred yards along a narrow passage. Then we came to a stout oak door. Sapt unlocked it. We passed through, and found ourselves in a quiet street that ran along the back of the Palace gardens. A man was waiting for us with two horses. One was a magnificent bay, up to any weight; the other a sturdy brown. Sapt signed to me to mount the bay. Without a word to the man, we mounted and rode away. The town was full of noise and merriment, but we took secluded ways. My cloak was wrapped over half my face; the capacious flat cap hid every lock of my tell-tale hair. By Sapt's directions, I crouched on my saddle, and rode with such a round back as I hope never to exhibit on a horse again. Down a long narrow lane we went, meeting some wanderers and some roisterers; and, as we rode, we heard the Cathedral bells still clanging out their welcome to the King. It was half-past six, and still light. At last we came to the city wall and to a gate.

'Have your weapon ready,' whispered Sapt. 'We must stop his mouth, if he talks.'

I put my hand on my revolver. Sapt hailed the doorkeeper. The stars fought for us! A little girl of fourteen tripped out.

'Please, sir, father's gone to see the King.'

'He'd better have stayed here,' said Sapt to me, grinning.

'But he said I wasn't to open the gate, sir.'

'Did he, my dear?' said Sapt, dismounting. 'Then give me the key.'

The key was in the child's hand. Sapt gave her a crown.

'Here's an order from the King. Show it to your father. Orderly, open the gate!'

I leapt down. Between us we rolled back the great gate, led our horses out, and closed it again.

'I shall be sorry for the doorkeeper if Michael finds out that he wasn't there. Now then, lad, for a canter. We mustn't go too fast while we're near the town.'

Once, however, outside the city, we ran little danger, for everybody else was inside, merry-making; and as the evening fell we quickened our pace, my splendid horse bounding along under me as though I had been a feather. It was a fine night, and presently the moon appeared. We talked little on the way, and chiefly about the progress we were making.

'I wonder what the duke's despatches told him,' said I, once.

'Ay, I wonder!' responded Sapt.

We stopped for a draught of wine and to bait our horses, losing half an hour thus. I dared not go into the inn, and stayed with the horses in the stable. Then we went ahead again, and had covered some five-and-twenty miles, when Sapt abruptly stopped.

'Hark!' he cried.

I listened. Away, far behind us, in the still of the evening – it was just half-past nine – we heard the beat of horses' hoofs. The wind blowing strong behind us, carried the sound. I glanced at Sapt.

'Come on!' he cried, and spurred his horse into a gallop. When we next paused to listen, the hoof-beats were not audible, and we relaxed our pace. Then we heard them again. Sapt jumped down and laid his ear to the ground.

'There are two,' he said. 'They're only a mile behind. Thank God the road curves in and out, and the wind's our way.'

We galloped on. We seemed to be holding our own. We had entered the outskirts of the forest of Zenda, and the trees, closing in behind us as the track zigged and zagged, prevented us seeing our pursuers, and them from seeing us.

Another half-hour brought us to a divide of the road. Sapt drew rein.

'To the right is our road,' he said. 'To the left, to the Castle. Each about eight miles. Get down.'

'But they'll be on us!' I cried.

'Get down!' he repeated brusquely; and I obeyed. The wood was dense up to the very edge of the road. We led our horses into the covert, bound handkerchiefs over their eyes, and stood beside them.

'You want to see who they are?' I whispered.

'Ay, and where they're going,' he answered.

I saw that his revolver was in his hand.

Nearer and nearer came the hoofs. The moon shone out now clear and full, so that the road was white with it. The ground was hard, and we had left no traces.

'Here they come!' whispered Sapt.

'It's the Duke!'

'I thought so,' he answered.

It was the Duke; and with him a burly fellow whom I knew well, and who had cause to know me afterwards – Max Holf, brother to Johann the keeper, and bodyservant to his Highness. They were up to us: the duke reined up. I saw Sapt's finger curl lovingly towards the trigger. I believe he would have given ten years of his life for a shot; and he could have picked off Black Michael as easily as I could a barn-door fowl in a farmyard. I laid my hand on his arm. He nodded reassuringly: he was always ready to sacrifice inclination to duty.

'Which way?' asked Black Michael.

'To the Castle, your Highness,' urged his companion. 'There we shall learn the truth.'

For an instant the duke hesitated.

'I thought I heard hoofs,' said he.

'I think not, your Highness.'

'Why shouldn't we go to the lodge?'

'I fear a trap. If all is well, why go to the lodge? If not, it's a snare to trap us.'

Suddenly the duke's horse neighed. In an instant we folded our cloaks close round our horses' heads, and, holding them thus, covered the duke and his attendant with our revolvers. If they had found us, they had been dead men, or our prisoners.

Michael waited a moment longer. Then he cried:

'To Zenda, then!' and setting spurs to his horse, galloped on.

Sapt raised his weapon after him, and there was such an expression of wistful regret on his face that I had much ado not to burst out laughing.

For ten minutes we stayed where we were.

'You see,' said Sapt, 'they've sent him news that all is well.'

'What does that mean?' I asked.

'God knows,' said Sapt, frowning heavily. 'But it's brought him from Strelsau in a rare puzzle.'

Then we mounted, and rode as fast as our weary horses could lay their feet to the ground. For those last eight miles we spoke no more. Our minds were full of apprehension. 'All is well.' What did it mean? Was all well with the King?

At last the lodge came in sight. Spurring our horses to a last gallop, we rode up to the gate. All was still and quiet. Not a soul came to meet us. We dismounted in haste. Suddenly Sapt caught me by the arm.

'Look there!' he said, pointing to the ground.

I looked down. At my feet lay five or six silk handkerchiefs, torn and slashed and rent. I turned to him questioningly.

'They're what I tied the old woman up with,' said he. 'Fasten the horses, and come along.'

The handle of the door turned without resistance. We passed into the room which had been the scene of last night's bout. It was still strewn with the remnants of our meal and with empty bottles.

'Come on,' cried Sapt, whose marvellous composure had at last almost given way.

We rushed down the passage towards the cellars. The door of the coal-cellar stood wide open.

'They found the old woman,' said I.

'You might have known that from the handkerchiefs,' he said.

Then we came opposite the door of the wine cellar. It was shut. It looked in all respects as it had looked when we left it that morning.

'Come, it's all right,' said I.

A loud oath from Sapt rang out. His face turned pale, and he pointed again at the floor. From under the door a red stain had spread over the floor of the passage and dried there. Sapt sank against the opposite wall. I tried the door. It was locked.

'Where's Josef?' muttered Sapt.

'Where's the King?' I responded.

Sapt took out a flask and put it to his lips. I ran back to the dining-room, and seized a heavy poker from the fireplace. In my terror and excitement I rained blows on the lock of the door, and I fired a cartridge into it. It gave way, and the door swung open.

'Give me a light,' said I; but Sapt still leant against the wall.

He was, of course, more moved than I, for he loved his master. Afraid for himself he was not – no man ever saw him that; but to think what might lie in that dark cellar was enough to turn any man's face pale. I went myself, and took a silver candlestick from the dining-table and struck a light, and, as I returned, I felt the hot wax drip on my naked hand as the candle swayed to and fro; so that I cannot afford to despise Colonel Sapt for his agitation.

I came to the door of the cellar. The red stain turning more and more to a dull brown, stretched inside. I walked two yards into the cellar, and held the candle high above my head. I saw the full bins of wine; I saw spiders crawling on the walls; I saw, too, a couple of empty bottles lying on the floor; and then, away in the corner, I saw the body of a man, lying flat on his back, with his arms stretched wide, and a crimson gash across his throat. I walked to him and knelt down beside him, and commended to God the soul of a faithful man. For it was the body of Josef, the little servant, slain in guarding the King.

I felt a hand on my shoulders, and, turning, saw Sapt, eyes glaring and terror-struck, beside me.

'The King? My God! the King?' he whispered hoarsely.

I threw the candle's gleam over every inch of the cellar.

'The King is not here,' said I.

7

His Majesty sleeps in Strelsau

I PUT my arm round Sapt's waist and supported him out of the cellar, drawing the battered door close after me. For ten minutes or more we sat silent in the dining-room. Then old Sapt rubbed his knuckles into his eyes, gave one great gasp, and was himself again. As the clock on the mantelpiece struck one he stamped his foot on the floor, saying:

'They've got the King!'

'Yes,' said I, '"all's well!" as Black Michael's despatch said. What a moment it must have been for him when the royal salutes fired at Strelsau this morning! I wonder when he got the message?'

'It must have been sent in the morning' said Sapt. 'They must have sent it before news of your arrival at Strelsau reached Zenda – I suppose it came from Zenda.'

'And he's carried it about all day!' I exclaimed. 'Upon my honour, I'm not the only man who's had a trying day! What did he think, Sapt?'

'What does that matter? What does he think, lad, now?'

I rose to my feet.

'We must get back,' I said, 'and rouse every soldier in Strelsau. We ought to be in pursuit of Michael before mid-day.'

Old Sapt pulled out his pipe and carefully lit it from the candle which guttered on the table.

'The King may be murdered while we sit here!' I urged.

Sapt smoked on for a moment in silence.

'That cursed old woman!' he broke out. 'She must have attracted their attention somehow. I see the game. They came up to kidnap the King, and – as I say – somehow they found him. If you hadn't gone to Strelsau, you and I and Fritz had been in heaven by now!'

'And the King?'

'Who knows where the King is now?' he asked.

'Come, let's be off!' said I; but he sat still. And suddenly he burst into one of his grating chuckles:

'By Jove, we've shaken up Black Michael!'

'Come, come!' I repeated impatiently.

'And we'll shake him up a bit more,' he added, a cunning smile broadening on his wrinkled, weather-beaten face, and his teeth working on an end of his grizzled moustache. 'Ay, lad, we'll go back to Strelsau. The King shall be in his capital again to-morrow.'

'The King?'

'The crowned King!'

'You're mad!' I cried.

'If we go back and tell the trick we played, what would you give for our lives?'

'Just what they're worth,' said I.

'And for the King's throne? Do you think that the nobles and the people will enjoy being fooled as you've fooled them? Do you think they'll love a King who was too drunk to be crowned, and sent a servant to personate him?'

'He was drugged – and I'm no servant.'

'Mine will be Black Michael's version.'

He rose, came to me, and laid his hand on my shoulder.

'Lad,' he said, 'if you play the man, you may save the King yet. Go back and keep his throne warm for him.'

'But the duke knows – the villains he has employed know –'

'Ay, but they can't speak!' roared Sapt in grim triumph. 'We've got 'em! How can they denounce you without denouncing themselves? "This is not the King, because we kidnapped the King and murdered his servant." Can they say that?'

The position flashed on me. Whether Michael knew me or not, he could not speak. Unless he produced the King, what could he do? And if he produced the King, where was he? For a moment I was carried away headlong; but in an instant the difficulties came strong upon me.

'I must be found out,' I urged.

'Perhaps; but every hour's something. Above all, we must have a King in Strelsau, or the city will be Michael's in four-and-twenty hours, and what would the King's life be worth then – or his throne? Lad, you must do it!'

'Suppose they kill the King?'

'They'll kill him, if you don't.'

'Sapt, suppose they have killed the King?'

'Then, by heaven, you're as good an Elphberg as Black Michael, and you shall reign in Ruritania! But I don't believe they have; nor will they kill him if you're on the throne. Will they kill him, to put you in?'

It was a wild plan – wilder even and more hopeless than the trick we had already carried through; but as I listened to Sapt I saw the strong points in our game. And then I was a young man and I loved action, and I was offered such a hand in such a game as perhaps never man played yet.

'I shall be found out,' I said.

'Perhaps,' said Sapt. 'Come! to Strelsau! We shall be caught like rats in a trap if we stay here.'

'Sapt,' I cried, 'I'll try it!'

'Well played!' said he. 'I hope they've left us the horses. I'll go and see.'

'We must bury that poor fellow,' said I.

'No time,' said Sapt.

'I'll do it.'

'Hang you!' he grinned. 'I make you a King, and – Well, do it. Go and fetch him, while I look to the horses. He can't lie very deep, but I doubt if he'll care about that. Poor little Josef! He was an honest bit of a man.'

He went out, and I went to the cellar. I raised poor Josef in my arms and bore him into the passage and thence towards the door of the house. Just inside I laid him down, remembering that I must find spades for our task. At this instant Sapt came up.

'The horses are all right; there's the own brother to the one that brought you here. But you may save yourself that job.'

'I'll not go before he's buried.'

'Yes, you will.'

'Not I, Colonel Sapt; not for all Ruritania.'

'You fool!' said he. 'Come here.'

He drew me to the door. The moon was sinking, but about three hundred yards away, coming along the road from Zenda, I made out a party of men. There were seven or eight of them; four were on horseback and the rest were walking, and I saw that they carried long implements, which I guessed to be spades and mattocks, on their shoulders.

'They'll save you the trouble,' said Sapt. 'Come along.'

He was right. The approaching party must, beyond doubt, be Duke Michael's men, come to remove the traces of their evil work. I hesitated no longer, but an irresistible desire seized me. Pointing to the corpse of poor little Josef, I said to Sapt:

'Colonel, we ought to strike a blow for him!'

'You'd like to give him some company, eh? But it's too risky work, your Majesty.'

'I must have a slap at 'em,' said I.

Sapt wavered.

'Well,' said he, 'it's not business, you know; but you've been a good boy – and if we come to grief, why, hang me, it'll save us a lot of thinking! I'll show you how to touch them.'

He cautiously closed the open chink of the door.

Then we retreated through the house and made our our way to the back entrance. Here our horses were standing. A carriage-drive swept all round the lodge.

'Revolver ready?' asked Sapt.

'No; steel for me,' said I.

'Gad, you're thirsty to-night,' chuckled Sapt. 'So be it.'

We mounted, drawing our swords, and waited silently for a minute or two. Then we heard the tramp of men on the drive the other side of the house. They came to a stand, and one cried:

'Now then, fetch him out!'

'Now!' whispered Sapt.

Driving the spurs into our horses, we rushed at a gallop round the house, and in a moment we were among the ruffians. Sapt told me afterwards that he killed a man, and I believe him; but I saw no more of him. With a cut, I split the head of a fellow on a brown horse, and he fell to the ground. Then I found myself opposite a big man, and I was half conscious of another to my right. It was too warm to stay, and with a simultaneous action I drove my spurs into my horse again and my sword full into the big man's breast. His bullet whizzed past my ear – I could almost swear it touched it. I wrenched at the sword, but it would not come, and I dropped it and galloped after Sapt, whom I now saw about twenty yards ahead. I waved my hand in farewell, and dropped it a second later with a yell, for a bullet had grazed my finger and I felt the blood. Old Sapt turned round in the saddle. Someone fired again, but they had no rifles, and we were out of range. Sapt fell to laughing.

'That's one to me and two to you, with decent luck,' said he. 'Little Josef will have company.'

'Ay, they'll be a *partie carrée*,' said I. My blood was up, and I rejoiced to have killed them.

'Well, a pleasant night's work to the rest!' said he. 'I wonder if they noticed you?'

'The big fellow did; as I stuck him I heard him cry, "The King!"'

'Good! good! Oh, we'll give Black Michael some work before we've done!'

Pausing an instant, we made a bandage for my wounded finger, which was bleeding freely and ached severely, the bone being much bruised. Then we rode on, asking of our good horses all that was in them. The excitement of the fight and of our great resolve died away, and we rode in gloomy silence. Day broke clear and cold. We found a farmer just up, and made him give us sustenance for ourselves and our horses. I, feigning a toothache, muffled my face closely. Then ahead again, till Strelsau lay before us. It was eight o'clock or nearing nine, and the gates were all open, as they always were save when the duke's caprice or intrigues shut them. We rode in by the same way as we had come out the evening before, all four of us – the men and the horses – wearied and jaded. The streets were even quieter than when we had gone: everyone was sleeping off last night's revelry, and we met hardly a soul till we reached the little gate of the Palace. There Sapt's old groom was waiting for us.

'Is all well, sir!' he asked.

'All's well,' said Sapt, and the man, coming to me, took my hand to kiss.

'The King's hurt!' he cried.

'It's nothing,' said I, as I dismounted; 'I caught my finger in the door.'

'Remember – silence!' said Sapt. 'Ah! but, my good Freyler, I do not need to tell you that!'

The old fellow shrugged his shoulders.

'All young men like to ride abroad now and again, why not the King?' said he; and Sapt's laugh left his opinion of my motives undisturbed.

'You should always trust a man,' observed Sapt, fitting the key in the lock – 'just as far as you must.'

We went in and reached the dressing-room. Flinging open the door, we saw Fritz von Tarlenheim stretched, fully dressed, on the sofa. He seemed to have been sleeping, but our entry woke him. He leapt to his feet, gave one glance at me, and with a joyful cry, threw himself on his knees before me.

'Thank God, sire! thank God, you're safe!' he cried, stretching his hand up to catch hold of mine.

I confess that I was moved. This King, whatever his faults, made people love him. For a moment I could not bear to speak or break the poor fellow's illusion. But tough old Sapt had no such feeling. He slapped his hand on his thigh delightedly.

'Bravo, lad!' cried he. 'We shall do!'

Fritz looked up in bewilderment. I held out my hand.

'You're wounded, sire!' he exclaimed.

'It's only a scratch,' said I, 'but –' I paused.

He rose to his feet with a bewildered air. Holding my hand, he looked me up and down, and down and up. Then suddenly he dropped my hand and reeled back.

'Where's the King? Where's the King?' he cried.

'Hush, you fool!' hissed Sapt. 'Not so loud! Here's the King!'

A knock sounded on the door. Sapt seized me by the hand.

'Here, quick, to the bedroom! Off with your cap and boots. Get into bed. Cover everything up.'

I did as I was bid. A moment later Sapt looked in, nodded, grinned, and introduced an extremely smart and deferential young gentleman, who came up to my bedside, bowing again and again, and informed me that he was of the household of the Princess Flavia, and that her Royal Highness had sent him especially to inquire how the King's health was after the fatigues which his Majesty had undergone yesterday.

'My best thanks, sir, to my cousin,' said I; 'and tell her Royal Highness that I was never better in my life.'

'The King,' added old Sapt (who, I began to find, loved a good lie for its own sake), 'has slept without a break all night.'

The young gentleman (he reminded me of 'Osric' in *Hamlet*) bowed himself out again. The farce was over, and Fritz von Tarlenheim's pale face recalled us to reality – though, in faith, the farce had to be reality for us now.

'Is the King dead?' he whispered.

'Please God, no,' said I. 'But he's in the hands of Black Michael!'

8

A Fair Cousin and a Dark Brother

A REAL king's life is perhaps a hard one; but a pretended king's is, I warrant, much harder. On the next day, Sapt instructed me in my duties – what I ought to do and what I ought to know – for three hours; then I snatched breakfast, with Sapt still opposite me, telling me that the King always took white wine in the morning and was known to detest all highly-seasoned dishes. Then came the Chancellor, for another three hours; and to him I had to explain that the hurt to my finger (we turned that bullet to happy account) prevented me from writing – whence arose great to-do, hunting of precedents and so forth, ending in my 'making my mark,' and the Chancellor attesting it with a superfluity of solemn oaths. Then the French ambassador was introduced, to present his credentials; here my ignorance was of no importance, as the King would have been equally raw to the business (we worked through the whole *corps diplomatique* in the next few days, a demise of the Crown necessitating all this pother).

Then, at last, I was left alone. I called my new servant (we had chosen, to succeed poor Josef, a young man who had never known the King), had a brandy-and-soda brought to me, and observed to Sapt that I trusted that I might now have a rest.

Fritz von Tarlenheim was standing by.

'By heaven!' he cried, 'we waste time. Aren't we going to throw Black Michael by the heels?'

'Gently, my son, gently,' said Sapt, knitting his brows. 'It would be a pleasure, but it might cost us dear. Would Michael fall and leave the King alive?'

'And,' I suggested, 'while the King is here in Strelsau, on his throne, what grievance has he against his dear brother Michael?'

'Are we to do nothing, then?'

'We're to do nothing stupid,' growled Sapt.

'In fact, Fritz,' said I, 'I am reminded of a situation in one of our English plays – *The Critic* – have you heard of it? Or, if you like, of two men, each covering the other with a revolver. For I can't expose Michael without exposing myself –'

'And the King,' put in Sapt.

'And, hang me if Michael won't expose himself, if he tries to expose me!'

'It's very pretty,' said old Sapt.

'If I'm found out,' I pursued, 'I will make a clean breast of it, and fight it out with the duke; but at present I'm waiting for a move from him.'

'He'll kill the King,' said Fritz.

'Not he,' said Sapt.

'Half of the Six are in Strelsau,' said Fritz.

'Only half? You're sure?' asked Sapt eagerly.

'Yes – only half.'

'Then the King's alive, for the other three are guarding him!' cried Sapt.

'Yes – you're right!' exclaimed Fritz, his face brightening. 'If the King were dead and buried, they'd all be here with Michael. You know Michael's back, colonel?'

'I know, curse him!'

'Gentlemen, gentlemen,' said I, 'who are the Six?'

'I think you'll make their acquaintance soon,' said Sapt. 'They are six gentlemen whom Michael maintains in his household: they belong to him body and soul. There are three Ruritanians; then there's a Frenchman, a Belgian, and one of your countrymen.'

'They'd all cut a throat if Michael told them,' said Fritz.

'Perhaps they'll cut mine,' I suggested.

'Nothing more likely,' agreed Sapt. 'Who are here, Fritz?'

'De Gautet, Bersonin, and Detchard.'

'The foreigners! It's as plain as a pikestaff. He's brought them, and left the Ruritanians with the King: that's because he wants to commit the Ruritanians as deep as he can.'

'They were none of them among our friends at the lodge, then?' I asked.

'I wish they had been,' said Sapt wistfully. 'They had been, not six, but four, by now.'

I had already developed one attribute of royalty – a feeling that I need not reveal all my mind or my secret designs even to my intimate friends. I had fully resolved on my course of action. I meant to make myself as popular as I could, and at the same time to show no disfavour to Michael. By these means I hoped to allay the hostility of his adherents, and make it appear, if an open conflict came about, that he was ungrateful and not oppressed.

Yet an open conflict was not what I hoped for.

The King's interest demanded secrecy; and while secrecy lasted, I had a fine game to play in Strelsau, Michael should not grow stronger for delay!

I ordered my horse, and, attended by Fritz von Tarlenheim, rode in the grand new avenue of the Royal Park, returning all the salutes which I received with punctilious politeness. Then I rode through a few of the streets, stopped and bought flowers of a pretty girl, paying her with a piece of gold; and then, having attracted the desired amount of attention (for I had a trail of half-a-thousand people after me), I rode to the residence of the Princess Flavia, and asked if she would receive me. This step created much interest, and was met with shouts of approval. The princess was very popular, and the Chancellor himself had not scrupled to hint to me that the more I pressed my suit, and the more rapidly I brought it to a prosperous conclusion, the stronger should I be in the affection of my subjects. The Chancellor, of course, did not understand the difficulties which lay in the way of following his loyal and excellent advice. However, I thought I could do no harm by calling; and in this view Fritz supported me with a cordiality that surprised me, until he confessed that he also had his motives for liking a visit to the princess's house, which motive was no other than a great desire to see the princess's lady-in-waiting and bosom friend, the Countess Helga von Strofzin.

Etiquette seconded Fritz's hopes. While I was ushered into the princess's room, he remained with the countess in the ante-chamber: in spite of the people and servants who were hanging about, I doubt not that they managed a *tête-à-tête*; but I had no leisure to think of them, for I was playing the most delicate move in all my difficult game. I had to keep the princess devoted to me – and yet indifferent to me: I had to show affection for her – and not feel it. I had to make love for another, and that to a girl who – princess or no princess – was the most beautiful I had ever seen. Well, I braced myself to the task, made no easier by the charming embarrassment with which I was received. How I succeeded in carrying out my programme will appear hereafter.

'You are gaining golden laurels,' she said. 'You are like the prince in Shakespeare who was transformed by becoming king. But I'm forgetting you are King, sire.'

'I ask you to speak nothing but what your heart tells you – and to call me nothing but my name.'

She looked at me for a moment.

'Then I'm glad and proud, Rudolf,' said she. 'Why, as I told you, your very face is changed.'

I acknowledged the compliment, but I disliked the topic; so I said:

'My brother is back, I hear. He made an excursion, didn't he?'

'Yes, he is here,' she said, frowning a little.

'He can't stay long from Strelsau, it seems,' I observed, smiling. 'Well, we are all glad to see him. The nearer he is, the better.'

The princess glanced at me with a gleam of amusement in her eyes.

'Why, cousin? Is it that you can –?'

'See better what he's doing? Perhaps,' said I. 'And why are you glad?'

'I didn't say I was glad,' she answered.

'Some people say so for you.'

'There are many insolent people,' she said, with delightful haughtiness.

'Possibly you mean that I am one?'

'Your Majesty could not be,' she said, curtseying in feigned deference, but adding, mischievously, after a pause: 'Unless, that is – '

'Well, unless what?'

'Unless you tell me that I mind a snap of my fingers where the Duke of Strelsau is.'

Really, I wished that I had been the King.

'You don't care where cousin Michael – '

'Ah, cousin Michael! I call him the Duke of Strelsau.'

'You call him Michael when you meet him?'

'Yes – by the orders of your father.'

'I see. And now by mine?'

'If those are your orders.'

'Oh, decidedly! We must all be pleasant to our dear Michael.'

'You order me to receive his friends, too, I suppose?'

'The Six?'

'You call them that, too?'

'To be in the fashion, I do. But I order you to receive no one unless you like.'

'Except yourself?'

'I pray for myself. I could not order.'

As I spoke, there came a cheer from the street. The princess ran to the window.

'It is he!' she cried. 'It is – the Duke of Strelsau!'

I smiled, but said nothing. She returned to her seat. For a few moments we sat in silence. The noise outside subsided, but I heard the tread of feet in the ante-room. I began to talk on general subjects. This went on for some minutes. I wondered what had become of Michael, but it did not seem to be for me to interfere. All at once, to my great surprise, Flavia, clasping her hands asked in an agitated voice:

'Are you wise to make him angry?'

'What? Who? How am I making him angry?'

'Why, by keeping him waiting.'

'My dear cousin, I don't want to keep him – '

'Well, then, is he to come in?'

'Of course, if you wish it.'

She looked at me curiously.

'How funny you are,' she said. 'Of course no one could be announced while I was with you.'

Here was a charming attribute of royalty!

'An excellent etiquette!' I cried. 'But I had clean forgotten it; and if I were alone with someone else, couldn't you be announced?'

'You know as well as I do. I could be, because I am of the Blood'; and she still looked puzzled.

'I never could remember all these silly rules,' said I, rather feebly, as I inwardly cursed Fritz for not posting me up. 'But I'll repair my fault.'

I jumped up, flung open the door, and advanced into the ante-room. Michael was sitting at a table, a heavy frown on his face. Everyone else was standing, save that impudent young dog Fritz, who was lounging easily in an arm-chair, and flirting with the Countess Helga. He leapt up as I entered, with a deferential alacrity that lent point to his former nonchalance. I had no difficulty in understanding that the duke might not like young Fritz.

I held out my hand, Michael took it, and I embraced him. Then I drew him with me into the inner room.

'Brother,' I said, 'if I had known you were here, you should not have waited a moment before I asked the princess to permit me to bring you to her.'

He thanked me, but coldly. The man had many qualities, but he could not hide his feelings. A mere stranger could have seen that he hated me, and hated worse to see me with Princess Flavia; yet I am persuaded that he tried to conceal both feelings, and, further, that he tried to persuade me that he believed I was verily the King. I did not know, of course; but, unless the King were an imposter, at once cleverer and more audacious than I (and I began to think something of myself in that *rôle*), Michael could not believe that. And, if he didn't, how he must have loathed paying me deference, and hearing my 'Michael' and my 'Flavia'!

'Your hand is hurt, sire,' he observed, with concern.

'Yes, I was playing a game with a mongrel dog' (I meant to stir him), 'and you know, brother, such have uncertain tempers.'

He smiled sourly, and his dark eyes rested on me for a moment.

'But is there no danger from the bite?' cried Flavia anxiously.

'None from this,' said I. 'If I gave him a chance to bite deeper, it would be different, cousin.'

'But surely he has been destroyed?' said she.

'Not yet. We're waiting to see if his bite is harmful.'

'And if it is?' asked Michael, with his sour smile.

'He'll be knocked on the head, brother,' said I.

'You won't play with him any more?' urged Flavia.

'Perhaps I shall.'

'He might bite again.'

'Doubtless he'll try,' said I, smiling.

Then, fearing Michael would say something which I must appear to resent (for, though I might show him my hate, I must seem to be full of favour), I began to compliment him on the magnificent condition of his regiment, and of their loyal greeting to me on the day of my coronation. Thence I passed to a rapturous description of the hunting-lodge which he had lent me. But he rose suddenly to his feet. His temper was failing him, and, with an excuse, he said farewell. However, as he reached the door he stopped, saying:

'Three friends of mine are very anxious to have the honour of being presented to you, sire. They are here in the ante-chamber.'

I joined him directly, passing my arm through his. The look on his face was honey to me. We entered the ante-chamber in fraternal fashion. Michael beckoned, and three men came forward.

'These gentlemen,' said Michael, with a stately courtesy which, to do him justice, he could assume with perfect grace and ease, 'are the loyalest and most devoted of your Majesty's servants, and are my very faithful and attached friends.'

'On the last ground as much as the first,' said I, 'I am very pleased to see them.'

They came one by one and kissed my hand – De Gautet, a tall lean fellow, with hair standing straight up and waxed moustache; Bersonin, the Belgian, a portly man of middle height with a bald head (though he was not far past thirty); and last, the Englishman, Detchard, a narrow-faced fellow, with close-cut fair hair and a bronzed complexion. He was a finely-made man, broad in the shoulders and slender in the hips. A good fighter, but a crooked customer, I put him down for. I spoke to him in English, with a slight foreign accent, and I swear the fellow smiled, though he hid the smile in an instant.

'So Mr. Detchard is in the secret,' thought I.

Having got rid of my dear brother and his friends, I returned to make my adieu to my cousin. She was standing at the door. I bade her farewell, taking her hand in mine.

'Rudolf,' she said, very low, 'be careful, won't you?'

'Of what?'

'You know – I can't say. But think what your life is to –'

'Well, to –?'

'To Ruritania.'

Was I right to play the part, or wrong to play the part? I know not: evil lay both ways, and I dared not tell her the truth.

'Only to Ruritania?' I asked softly.

A sudden flush spread over her incomparable face.

'To your friends, too,' she said.

'Friends?'

'And to your cousin,' she whispered, 'and loving servant.'

I could not speak. I kissed her hand, and went out cursing myself.

Outside I found Master Fritz, quite reckless of the footmen, playing at cat's-cradle with the Countess Helga.

'Hang it!' said he, 'we can't always be plotting. Love claims his share.'

'I'm inclined to think he does,' said I; and Fritz, who had been by my side, dropped respectfully behind.

9

A New use for a Tea Table

IF I were to detail the ordinary events of my daily life at this time, they might prove instructive to people who are not familiar with the inside of palaces; if I revealed some of the secrets I learnt, they might prove of interest to the statesmen of Europe. I intend to do neither of these things. I should be between the Scylla of dullness and the Charybdis of indiscretion, and I feel that I had far better confine myself strictly to the underground drama which was being played beneath the surface of Ruritarian politics. I need only say that the secret of my imposture defied detection. I made mistakes. I had bad minutes: it needed all the tact and graciousness whereof I was master to smooth over some apparent lapses of memory and unmindfulness of old acquaintances of which I was guilty. But I escaped, and I attribute my escape, as I have said before, most of all, to the very audacity of the enterprise. It is my belief that, given the necessary physical likeness, it was far easier to pretend to be King of Ruritania than it would have been to personate my next-door neighbour.

One day Sapt came into my room. He threw me a letter, saying:

'That's for you – a woman's hand, I think. But I've some news for you first.'

'What's that?'

'The King's at the Castle of Zenda,' said he.

'How do you know?'

'Because the other half of Michael's Six are there. I had enquiries made, and they're all there – Lauengram, Krafstein, and young Rupert Hentzau: three rogues, too, on my honour, as fine as live in Ruritania.'

'Well?'

'Well, Fritz wants you to march to the Castle with horse, foot, and artillery.'

'And drag the moat?' I asked.

'That would be about it,' grinned Sapt, 'and we shouldn't find the King's body then.'

'You think it's certain he's there?'

'Very probable. Besides the fact of those three being there, the drawbridge is kept up, and no one goes in without an order from young Hentzau or Black Michael himself. We must tie Fritz up.'

'I'll go to Zenda,' said I.

'You're mad.'

'Some day.'

'Oh, perhaps. You'll very likely stay there though, if you do.'

'That may be, my friend,' said I carelessly.

'His Majesty looks sulky,' observed Sapt. 'How's the love affair?'

'Damn you, hold your tongue!' I said.

He looked at me for a moment, then he lit his pipe. It was quite true that I was in a bad temper, and I went on perversely:

'Wherever I go, I'm dodged by half-a-dozen fellows.'

'I know you are; I send 'em,' he replied composedly.

'What for?'

'Well,' said Sapt, puffing away, 'it wouldn't be exactly inconvenient for Black Michael if you disappeared. With you gone, the old game that we stopped would be played – or he'd have a shot at it.'

'I can take care of myself.'

'De Gautet, Bersonin, and Detchard are in Strelsau; and any one of them, lad, would cut your throat as readily – as readily as I would Black Michael's, and a deal more treacherously. What's the letter?'

I opened it and read it aloud:

> 'If the King desires to know what it deeply concerns the King to know, let him do as this letter bids him. At the end of the New Avenue there stands a house in large grounds. The house has a portico, with a statue of a nymph on it. A wall encloses the garden; there is a gate in the wall at the back. At twelve o'clock to-night, if the King enters alone by that gate, turns to the right, and walks twenty yards, he will find a summer-house, approached by a flight of six steps. If he mounts and enters, he will find someone who will tell him what touches most dearly his life and his throne. This is written by a faithful friend. He must be alone. If he neglects the invitation his life will be in danger. Let him show this to no one, or he will ruin a woman who loves him: Black Michael does not pardon.'

'No,' observed Sapt, as I ended, 'but he can dictate a very pretty letter.'

I had arrived at the same conclusion, and was about to throw the letter away, when I saw there was more writing on the other side.

'Hallo! there's some more.'

'*If you hestitate*,' the writer continued, '*consult Colonel Sapt* –'

'Eh,' exclaimed that gentleman, genuinely astonished. 'Does she take me for a greater fool than you?'

I waved to him to be silent.

'*Ask him what woman would do most to prevent the duke from marrying his cousin, and therefore most to prevent him becoming king? And ask if her name begins with – A?*'

I sprang to my feet. Sapt laid down his pipe.

'Antoinette de Mauban, by heaven!' I cried.

'How do you know?' asked Sapt.

I told him what I knew of the lady, and how I knew it. He nodded.

'It's so far true that she's had a great row with Michael,' said he, thoughtfully.

'If she would, she could be useful,' I said.

'I believe, though, that Michael wrote that letter.'

'So do I, but I mean to know for certain. I shall go, Sapt.'

'No, I shall go,' said he.

'You may go as far as the gate.'

'I shall go to the summer-house.'

'I'm hanged if you shall!'

I rose and leant my back against the mantelpiece.

'Sapt, I believe in that woman, and I shall go.'

'I don't believe in any woman,' said Sapt, 'and you shan't go.'

'I either go to the summer-house or back to England,' said I.

Sapt began to know exactly how far he could lead or drive, and when he must follow.

'We're playing against time,' I added. 'Every day we leave the King where he is there is fresh risk. Every day I masquerade like this, there is fresh risk. Sapt, we must play high; we must force the game.'

'So be it,' he said, with a sigh.

To cut the story short, at half-past eleven that night Sapt and I mounted our horses. Fritz was again left on guard, our destination not being revealed to him. It was a very dark night. I wore no sword, but I carried a revolver, a long knife, and a bull's-eye lantern. We arrived outside the gate. I dismounted. Sapt held out his hand.

'I shall wait here,' he said. 'If I hear a shot, I'll – '

'Stay where you are; it's the King's only chance. You mustn't come to grief too.'

'You're right, lad. Good luck!'

I pressed the little gate. It yielded, and I found myself in a wild sort of shrubbery. There was a grass-grown path and, turning to the right as I had been bidden, I followed it cautiously. My lantern was closed, the revolver was in my hand. I heard not a sound. Presently a large dark object loomed out of the gloom ahead of me. It was the summer-house. Reaching the steps, I mounted them and found myself confronted by a weak, rickety wooden door, which hung upon the latch. I pushed it open and walked in. A woman flew to me and seized my hand.

'Shut the door,' she whispered.

I obeyed and turned the light of my lantern on her. She was in evening dress, arrayed very sumptuously, and her dark striking beauty was marvellously displayed in the glare of the bull's-eye. The summer-house was a bare little room, furnished only with a couple of chairs and a small iron table, such as one sees in a tea-garden or an open-air café.

'Don't talk,' she said. 'We've no time. Listen! I know you, Mr. Rassendyll. I wrote that letter at the duke's orders.'

'So I thought,' said I.

'In twenty minutes three men will be here to kill you.'

'Three – *the* three?'

'Yes. You must be gone by then. If not, to-night you'll be killed –'

'Or they will.'

'Listen, listen! When you're killed, your body will be taken to a low quarter of the town. It will be found there. Michael will at once arrest all your friends – Colonel Sapt and Captain von Tarlenheim first, – proclaim a state of siege in Strelsau, and send a messenger to Zenda. The other three will murder the King in the Castle, and the duke will proclaim either himself or the princess – himself, if he is strong enough. Anyhow, he'll marry her, and become king in fact, and soon in name. Do you see?'

'It's a pretty plot. But why, madame, do you –?'

'Say I'm a Christian – or say I'm jealous. My God! shall I see him marry her? Now go; but remember – this is what I have to tell you – that never, by night or by day, are you safe. Three men follow you as a guard. Is it not so ? Well, three follow them; Michael's three are never two hundred yards from you. Your life is not worth a moment if ever they find you alone. Now go. Stay, the gate will be guarded by now. Go down softly, go past the summer-house, on for a hundred yards, and you'll find a ladder against the wall. Get over it, and fly for your life.'

'And you?' I asked.

'I have my game to play too. If he finds out what I have done, we shall not meet again. If not, I may yet – But never mind. Go at once.'

'But what will you tell him?'

'That you never came – that you saw through the trick.'

I took her hand and kissed it.

'Madame,' said I, 'you have served the King well to-night.' Where is he in the Castle?'

She sank her voice to a fearful whisper. I listened eagerly.

'Across the drawbridge you come to a heavy door; behind that lies – Hark! What's that?'

There were steps outside.

'They're coming! They're too soon! Heavens! they're too soon!' and she turned pale as death.

'They seem to me,' said I, 'to be in the nick of time.'

'Close your lantern. See, there's a chink in the door. Can you see them?'

I put my eye to the chink. On the lowest step I saw three dim figures. I cocked my revolver. Antoinette hastily laid her hand on mine.

'You may kill one,' said she. 'But what then?'

A voice came from outside – a voice that spoke perfect English.

'Mr. Rassendyll,' it said.

I made no answer.

'We want to talk to you. Will you promise not to shoot till we've done?'

'Have I the pleasure of addressing Mr. Detchard?' I said.

'Never mind names.'

'Then let mine alone.'

'All right, *sire*. I've an offer for you.'

I still had my eye to the chink. The three had mounted two steps more; three revolvers pointed full at the door.

'Will you let us in? We pledge our honour to observe the truce.'

'Don't trust them,' whispered Antoinette.

'We can speak through the door,' said I.

'But you might open it and fire,' objected Detchard; 'and though we should finish you, you might finish one of us. Will you give your honour not to fire while we talk?'

'Don't trust them,' whispered Antoinette again.

A sudden idea struck me. I considered it for a moment. It seemed feasible.

'I give my honour not to fire before you do,' said I; 'but I won't let you in. Stand outside and talk.'

'That's sensible,' he said.

The three mounted the last step, and stood just outside the door. I laid my ear to the chink. I could hear no words, but Detchard's head was close to that of the taller of his companions (De Gautet, I guessed).

'H'm! Private communications,' thought I. Then I said aloud:

'Well, gentlemen, what's the offer?'

'A safe-conduct to the frontier, and fifty thousand pounds English.'

'No, no,' whispered Antoinette in the lowest of whispers. 'They are treacherous.'

'That seems handsome,' said I, reconnoitring through the chink. They were all close together, just outside the door now.

I had probed the hearts of the ruffians, and I did not need Antoinette's warning. They meant to 'rush' me as soon as I was engaged in talk.

'Give me a minute to consider,' said I; and I thought I heard a laugh outside.

I turned to Antoinette.

'Stand up close to the wall, out of the line of fire from the door,' I whispered.

'What are you going to do?' she asked in fright.

'You'll see,' said I.

I took up the little iron table. It was not very heavy for a man of my strength, and I held it by the legs. The top, protruding in front of me, made a complete screen for my head and body. I fastened my closed lantern to my belt and put my revolver in a handy pocket. Suddenly I saw the door move ever so slightly – perhaps it was the wind, perhaps it was a hand trying it outside.

I drew back as far as I could from the door, holding the table in the position that I have described. Then I called out:

'Gentlemen, I accept your offer, relying on your honour. If you will open the door –'

'Open it yourself,' said Detchard.

'It opens outwards,' said I. 'Stand back a little, gentlemen, or I shall hit you when I open it.'

I went and fumbled with the latch. Then I stole back to my place on tiptoe.

'I can't open it!' I cried. 'The latch has caught.'

'Tut! I'll open it!' cried Detchard. 'Nonsense, Bersonin, why not? Are you afraid of one man?'

I smiled to myself. An instant later the door was flung back. The gleam of a lantern showed me the three close together outside, their revolvers levelled. With a shout, I charged at my utmost pace across the summer-house and through the doorway. Three shots rang out and battered into my shield. Another moment, and I leapt out and the table caught them full and square, and in a tumbling, swearing, struggling mass they and I and that brave table, rolled down the steps of the summer-house to the ground below. Antoinette de Mauban shrieked, but I rose to my feet, laughing aloud.

De Gautet and Bersonin lay like men stunned. Detchard was under the table, but, as I rose, he pushed it from him and fired again. I raised my revolver and took a snap shot; I heard him curse, and then I ran like a hare, laughing as I went, past the summer-house and along by the wall. I heard steps behind me, and turning round I fired again for luck. The steps ceased.

'Please God,' said I, 'she told me the truth about the ladder!' for the wall was high and topped with iron spikes.

Yes, there it was. I was up and over in a minute. Doubling back, I saw the horses; then I heard a shot. It was Sapt. He had heard us, and was battling and raging with the locked gate, hammering it and firing into the keyhole like a man possessed. He had quite forgotten that he was not to take part in the fight. Whereat I laughed again, and said, as I clapped him on the shoulder:

'Come home to bed, old chap. I've got the finest tea-table story that ever you heard!'

He started and cried: 'You're safe!' and wrung my hand. But a moment later he added:

'And what the devil are you laughing at?'

'Four gentlemen round a tea-table,' said I, laughing still, for it had been uncommonly ludicrous to see the formidable three altogether routed and scattered with no more deadly weapon than an ordinary tea-table.

Moreover, you will observe that I had honourably kept my word, and not fired till they did.

10

A Great Chance for a Villain

IT was the custom that the Prefect of Police should send every afternoon a report to me on the condition of the capital and the feeling of the people: the document included also an account of the movements of any persons whom the police had received instructions to watch. Since I had been in Strelsau, Sapt had been in the habit of reading the report and telling me any items of interest which it might contain. On the day after my adventure in the summer-house, he came in as I was playing a hand of *écarté* with Fritz von Tarlenheim.

'The report is rather full of interest this afternoon,' he observed, sitting down.

'Do you find,' I asked, 'any mention of a certain *fracas*?'

He shook his head with a smile.

'I find this first,' he said: '"His Highness the Duke of Strelsau left the city (so far as it appears, suddenly), accompanied by several of his household. His destination is believed to be the Castle of Zenda, but the party travelled by road and not by train. MM. De Gautet, Bersonin and Detchard followed an hour later, the last-named carrying his arm in a sling. The cause of his wound is not known, but it is suspected that he has fought a duel, probably incidental to a love affair."'

'That is remotely true,' I observed, very well pleased to find that I had left my mark on the fellow.

'Then we come to this,' pursued Sapt: '"Madame de Mauban, whose movements have been watched according to instructions, left by train at midday. She took a ticket for Dresden –"'

'It's an old habit of hers,' said I.

'"The Dresden train stops at Zenda." An acute fellow, this. And finally listen to this: "The state of feeling in the city is not satisfactory. The King is much criticised" (you know, he's told to be quite frank), "for taking no steps about his marriage. From enquiries among the *entourage* of the Princess Flavia her Royal Highness is believed to be deeply offended by the remissness of his Majesty. The common people are coupling her name with that of the Duke of Strelsau, and the Duke gains much popularity from the suggestion. I have caused the announcement that the King gives a ball to-night in honour of the princess to be widely diffused, and the effect is good".'

'That is news to me,' said I.

'Oh, the preparations are all made!' laughed Fritz. 'I've seen to that.'

Sapt turned to me and said, in a sharp, decisive voice:

'You must make love to her to-night, you know.'

'I think it is very likely I shall, if I see her alone,' said I. 'Hang it, Sapt, you don't suppose I find it difficult?'

Fritz whistled a bar or two; then he said: 'You'll find it only too easy. Look here, I hate telling you this, but I must. The Countess Helga told me that the princess had become most attached to the King. Since the coronation, her feelings have undergone a marked development. It's quite true that she is deeply wounded by the King's apparent neglect.'

'Here's a kettle of fish!' I groaned.

'Tut, tut!' said Sapt. 'I suppose you've made pretty speeches to a girl before now? That's all she wants.'

Fritz, himself a lover, understood better my distress. He laid his hand on my shoulder, but said nothing.

'I think, though,' pursued that cold-blooded old Sapt, 'that you'd better make your offer to-night.'

'Good heavens!'

'Or, any rate, go near it: and I shall send a "semi-official" to the papers.'

'I'll do nothing of the sort – no more will you!' said I. 'I utterly refuse to take part in making a fool of the princess.'

Sapt looked at me with his small keen eyes. A slow cunning smile passed over his face.

'All right, lad, all right,' said he. 'We mustn't press you too hard. Soothe her down a bit, if you can, you know. Now for Michael!'

'Oh, damn Michael!' said I. 'He'll do to-morrow. Here, Fritz, come for a stroll in the garden.'

Sapt at once yielded. His rough manner covered a wonderful tact – and, as I came to recognise more and more, a remarkable knowledge of human nature. Why did he urge me so little about the princess? Because he knew that her beauty and my ardour would carry me further than all his arguments – and that the less I thought about the thing, the more likely was I to do it. He must have seen the unhappiness he might bring on the princess; but that went for nothing with him. Can I say, confidently, that he was wrong? If the King were restored, the princess must turn to him, either knowing or not knowing the change. And if the King were not restored to us? It was a subject that we had never yet spoken of. But I had an idea that, in such a case, Sapt meant to seat me on the throne of Ruritania for the term of my life. He would have set Satan himself there sooner than that pupil of his, Black Michael.

The ball was a sumptuous affair. I opened it by dancing a quadrille with Flavia: then I waltzed with her. Curious eyes and eager whispers attended us. We went in to supper; and, half-way through, I, half-mad by then, for her glance had answered mine, and her quick breathing met my stammered sentences – I rose in my place before all the brilliant crowd, and taking the Red Rose that I wore, flung the ribbon with its jewelled badge round her neck. In a tumult of applause I sat down: I saw Sapt smiling over his wine, and Fritz frowning. The rest of the meal passed in silence; neither Flavia nor I could speak. Fritz touched me on the shoulder, and I rose, gave her my arm, and walked down the hall into a little room, where coffee was served to us. The gentlemen and ladies in attendance withdrew, and we were alone.

The little room had French windows opening on the gardens. The night was fine, cool, and fragrant. Flavia sat down, and I stood opposite her. I was struggling with myself: if she had not looked at me, I believe that even then I should have won my fight. But suddenly, involuntarily, she gave me one brief glance – a glance of question, hurriedly turned aside; a blush that the question had ever come spread over her cheek, and she caught her breath. Ah, if you had seen her! I forgot the King in Zenda. I forgot the King in Strelsau. She was a princess – and I an impostor. Do you think I remembered that? I threw myself on my knee and seized her hands in mine. I said nothing. Why should I? The soft sounds of the night set my wooing to a wordless melody, as I pressed my kisses on her lips.

She pushed me from her, crying suddenly:

'Ah! is it true? or is it only because you must?'

'It's true!' I said, in low smothered tones – 'true that I love you more than life – or truth – or honour!'

She set no meaning to my words, treating them as one of love's sweet extravagances. She came close to me, and whispered:

'Oh, if you were not the King! Then I could show you how I love you! How is it that I love you now, Rudolf?'

'Now?'

'Yes – just lately. I – I never did before.'

Pure triumph filled me. It was I – Rudolf Rassendyll – who had won her! I caught her round the waist.

'You didn't love me before?' I asked.

She looked up into my face, smiling, as she whispered:

'It must have been your Crown. I felt it first on the Coronation Day.'

'Never before?' I asked eagerly.

She laughed low.

'You speak as if you would be pleased to hear me say "Yes" to that,' she said.

'Would "Yes" be true?'

'Yes,' I just heard her breathe, and she went on in an instant: 'Be careful, Rudolf; be careful, dear. He will be mad now.'

'What, Michael? If Michael were the worst –'

'What worse is there?'

There was yet a chance for me. Controlling myself with a mighty effort, I took my hands off her and stood a yard or two away. I remember now the note of the wind in the elm-trees outside.

'If I were not the King,' I began, 'if I were only a private gentleman –'

Before I could finish, her hand was in mine.

'If you were a convict in the prison of Strelsau, you would be my King,' she said.

And under my breath I groaned, 'God forgive me!' and, holding her hand in mine, I said again:

'If I were not the King –'

'Hush, hush!' she whispered. 'I don't deserve it – I don't deserve to be doubted. Ah, Rudolf! does a woman who marries without love look on the man as I look on you?'

And she hid her face from me.

For more than a minute we stood there together; and I, even with my arm about her, summoned up what honour and conscience her beauty and the toils that I was in had left me.

'Flavia,' I said, in a strange dry voice that seemed not my own, 'I am not –'

As I spoke – as she raised her eyes to me – there was a heavy step on the gravel outside, and a man appeared at the window. A little cry burst from Flavia, as she sprang back from me. My half-finished sentence died on my lips. Sapt stood there, bowing low, but with a stern frown on his face.

'A thousand pardons, sire,' said he, 'but his Eminence the Cardinal has waited this quarter of an hour to offer his respectful adieu to your Majesty.'

I met his eye full and square; and I read in it an angry warning. How long he had been a listener I knew not, but he had come in upon us in the nick of time.

'We must not keep his Eminence waiting,' said I.

But Flavia, in whose love there lay no shame, with radiant eyes and blushing face, held out her hand to Sapt. She said nothing, but no man could have missed her meaning who had ever seen a woman in the exultation of love. A sour, yet sad, smile passed over the old soldier's face, and there was tenderness in his voice, as bending to kiss her hand, he said:

'In joy and sorrow, in good times and bad, God save your Royal Highness!'

He paused and added, glancing at me and drawing himself up to military erectness:

'But, before all comes the King – God save the King!'

And Flavia caught at my hand and kissed it, murmuring:

'Amen! Good God, Amen!'

We went into the ball-room again. Forced to receive adieus, I was separated from Flavia: everyone, when they left me, went to her. Sapt was out and in of the throng, and where he had been, glances, smiles, and whispers were rife. I doubted not that, true to his relentless purpose, he was spreading the news that he had learnt. To uphold the Crown and beat Black Michael – that was his one resolve. Flavia, myself – ay, and the real King in Zenda, were pieces in his game; and pawns have no business with passions. Not even at the walls of the Palace did he stop; for when at last I handed Flavia down the broad marble steps and into her carriage, there was a great crowd awaiting us, and we were welcomed with deafening cheers. What could I do? Had I spoken then, they would have refused to believe that I was not the King; they might have believed that the King had run mad. By Sapt's devices and my own ungoverned passion I had been forced on, and the way back had closed behind me; and the passion still drove me in the same direction as the devices seduced me. I faced all Strelsau that night as the King and the accepted suitor of the Princess Flavia.

At last, at three in the morning, when the cold light of dawning day began to steal in, I was in my dressing-room, and Sapt alone was with me. I sat like a man dazed, staring into the fire; he puffed at his pipe; Fritz was gone to bed, having almost refused to speak to me. On the table by me lay a rose; it had been in Flavia's dress, and, as we parted, she had kissed it and given it to me.

Sapt advanced his hand towards the rose, but, with a quick movement, I shut mine down upon it.

'That's mine,' I said, 'not yours – nor the King's either.'

'We struck a good blow for the King to-night,' said he.

I turned on him fiercely.

'What's to prevent me striking a blow for myself?' I said.

He nodded his head.

'I know what's in your mind,' he said. 'Yes, lad; but you're bound in honour.'

'Have you left me any honour?'

'Oh, come, to play a little trick on a girl –'

'You can spare me that. Colonel Sapt, if you would not have me utterly a villain – if you would not have your King rot in Zenda, while Michael and I play for the great stake outside – You follow me?'

'Ay, I follow you.'

'We must act, and quickly! You saw to-night – you heard to-night –'

'I did,' said he.

'Your cursed acuteness told you what I should do. Well, leave me here a week and there's another problem for you. Do you find the answer?'

'Yes, I find it,' he answered, frowning heavily. 'But if you did that, you'd have to fight me first – and kill me.'

'Well, and if I had – or a score of men? I tell you, I could raise all Strelsau on you in an hour, and choke you with your lies – yes, your mad lies – in your mouth.'

'It's gospel truth,' he said – 'thanks to my advice you could.'

'I could marry the princess, and send Michael and his brother together to –'

'I'm not denying it, lad,' said he.

'Then, in God's name,' I cried, stretching out my hands to him, 'let us go to Zenda and crush this Michael, and bring the King back to his own again.'

The old fellow stood and looked at me for full a minute.

'And the princess?' he said.

I bowed my head to meet my hands, and crushed the rose between my fingers and my lips.

I felt his hand on my shoulder, and his voice sounded husky as he whispered low in my ear:

'Before God, you're the finest Elphberg of them all. But I have eaten of the King's bread, and I am the King's servant. Come we will go to Zenda!'

And I looked up and caught him by the hand. And the eyes of both of us were wet.

11

Hunting a very Big Boar

THE terrible temptation which was assailing me will now be understood. I could so force Michael's hand that he must kill the King. I was in a position to bid him defiance and tighten my grasp on the crown – not for its own sake, but because the King of Ruritania was to wed the Princess Flavia. What of Sapt and Fritz? Ah! but a man cannot be held to write down in cold blood the wild and black thoughts that storm his brain when an uncontrolled passion has battered a breach for them. Yet, unless he sets up as a saint, he need not hate himself for them. He is better employed, as it humbly seems to me, in giving thanks that power to resist was vouchsafed to him, than in fretting over wicked impulses which come unsought and extort an unwilling hospitality from the weakness of our nature.

It was a fine bright morning when I walked, unattended, to the princess's house, carrying a nosegay in my hand. Policy made excuses for love, and every attention that I paid her, while it riveted my own chains, bound closer to me the people of the great city, who worshipped her. I found Fritz's *inamorata*, the Countess Helga, gathering blooms in the garden for her mistress's wear, and prevailed on her to take mine in their place. The girl was rosy with happiness, for Fritz, in his turn, had not wasted his evening, and no dark shadow hung over his wooing, save the hatred which the Duke of Strelsau was known to bear him.

'And that,' she said, with a mischievous smile, 'your Majesty has made of no moment. Yes, I will take the flowers; shall I tell you, sire, what is the first thing the princess does with them?'

We were talking on a broad terrace that ran along the back of the house, and a window above our heads stood open.

'Madame!' cried the countess merrily, and Flavia herself looked out. I bared my head and bowed. She wore a white gown, and her hair was loosely gathered in a knot. She kissed her hand to me, crying:

'Bring the King up, Helga; I'll give him some coffee.'

The countess, with a gay glance, led the way, and took me into Flavia's morning-room. And, left alone, we greeted one another as lovers are wont. Then the princess laid two letters before me. One was from Black Michael – a most courteous request that she would honour him by spending a day at his Castle of Zenda, as had been her custom once a year in the summer, when the place and its gardens were in the height of their great beauty. I threw the letter down in disgust, and Flavia laughed at me. Then, growing grave again, she pointed to the other sheet.

'I don't know who that comes from,' she said. 'Read it.'

I knew in a moment. There was no signature at all this time, but the handwriting was the same as that which had told me of the snare in the summer-house: it was Antoinette de Mauban's.

'*I have no cause to love you*,' it ran, '*but God forbid that you should fall into the power of the duke. Accept no invitations of his. Go nowhere without a large guard – a regiment is not too much to make you safe. Show this if you can, to him who reigns in Strelsau.*'

'Why doesn't it say "the King"?' asked Flavia, leaning over my shoulder, so that the ripple of her hair played on my cheek. 'Is it a hoax?'

'As you value life, and more than life, my queen,' I said, 'obey it to the very letter. A regiment shall camp round your house to-day. See that you do not go out unless well guarded.'

'An order, sire?' she asked, a little rebellious.

'Yes, an order, madame – if you love me.'

'Ah!' she cried; and I could not but kiss her.

'You know who sent it?' she asked.

'I guess,' said I. 'It is from a good friend – and I fear, an unhappy woman. You must be ill, Flavia and unable to go to Zenda. Make your excuses as cold and formal as you like.'

'So you feel strong enough to anger Michael?' she said, with a proud smile.

'I'm strong enough for anything, while you are safe,' said I.

Soon I tore myself away from her, and then, without consulting Sapt, I took my way to the house of Marshal Strakencz. I had seen something of the old general, and I liked and trusted him. Sapt was less enthusiastic, but I had learnt by now that Sapt was best pleased when he could do everything, and jealousy played some part in his views. As things were now, I had more work than Sapt and Fritz could manage, for they must come with me to Zenda, and I wanted a man to guard what I loved most in all the world, and suffer me to set about my task of releasing the King with a quiet mind.

The Marshal received me with most loyal kindness. To some extent, I took him into my confidence. I charged him with the care of the princess, looking him full and significantly in the face as I bade him let no one from her cousin the duke approach her, unless he himself were there and a dozen of his men with him.

'You may be right, sire,' said he, shaking his grey head sadly. 'I have known better men than the duke do worse things than that for love.'

I could quite appreciate the remark, but I said:

'There's something beside love, Marshal. Love's for the heart; is there nothing my brother might like for his head?'

'I pray that you wrong him, sire.'

'Marshal, I'm leaving Strelsau for a few days. Every evening I will send a courier to you. If for three days none comes, you will publish an order which I will give you, depriving Duke Michael of the governorship of Strelsau and appointing you in his place. You will declare a state of siege. Then you will send word to Michael that you demand an audience of the King – You follow me?'

'Ay, sire.'

'– In twenty-four hours. If he does not produce the King' (I laid my hand on his knee), 'then the King is dead, and you will proclaim the next heir. You know who that is?'

'The Princess Flavia.'

'And swear to me, on your faith and honour and by the fear of the living God, that you will stand by her to the death, and kill that reptile, and seat her where I sit now.'

'On my faith and honour, and by the fear of God, I swear it! And may Almighty God preserve your Majesty, for I think that you go on an errand of danger.'

'I hope that no life more precious than mine may be demanded,' said I, rising. Then I held out my hand to him.

'Marshal,' I said, 'in days to come, it may be – I know not – that you will hear strange things of the man who speaks to you now. Let him be what he may, and who he may, what say you of the manner in which he has borne himself as King in Strelsau?'

The old man, holding my hand, spoke to me, man to man.

'I have known many of the Elphbergs,' said he, 'and I have seen you. And, happen what may, you have borne yourself as a wise King and a brave man; ay, and you have proved as courteous a gentleman and as gallant a lover as any that have been of the House.'

'Be that my epitaph,' said I, 'when the time comes that another sits on the throne of Ruritania.'

'God send a far day, and may I not see it!' said he.

I was much moved, and the Marshal's worn face twitched. I sat down and wrote my order.

'I can hardly yet write,' said I; 'my finger is stiff still.'

It was, in fact, the first time that I had ventured to write more than a signature; and in spite of the pains I had taken to learn the King's hand, I was not yet perfect in it.

'Indeed, sire,' he said, 'it differs a little from your ordinary handwriting. It is unfortunate, for it may lead to a suspicion of forgery.'

'Marshal,' said I, with a laugh, 'what use are the guns of Strelsau, if they can't assuage a little suspicion?'

He smiled grimly, and took the paper.

'Colonel Sapt and Fritz von Tarlenheim go with me,' I continued.

'You go to seek the duke?' he asked in a low tone.

'Yes, the Duke, and someone else of whom I have need, and who is at Zenda,' I replied.

'I wish I could go with you,' he cried, tugging at his white moustache. 'I'd like to strike a blow for you and your crown.'

'I leave you what is more than my life and more than my crown,' said I, 'because you are the man I trust more than all others in Ruritania.'

'I will deliver her to you safe and sound,' said he, 'and, failing that, I will make her queen.'

We parted, and I returned to the Palace and told Sapt and Fritz what I had done. Sapt had a few faults to find and a few grumbles to utter. This was merely what I expected, for Sapt liked to be consulted beforehand, not informed afterwards; but on the whole he approved of my plans, and his spirits rose high as the hour of action drew nearer and nearer. Fritz, too, was ready; though he, poor fellow, risked more than Sapt did, for he was a lover, and his happiness hung in the scale. Yet how I envied him! For the triumphant issue which would crown him with happiness and unite him to his mistress, the success for which we were bound to hope and strive and struggle, meant to me sorrow more certain and greater than if I were doomed to fail. He understood something of this, for when we were alone (save for old Sapt, who was smoking at the other end of the room) he passed his arm through mine, saying:

'It's hard for you. Don't think I don't trust you; I know you have nothing but true thoughts in your heart.'

But I turned away from him, thankful that he could not see what my heart held, but only be witness to the deeds that my hands were to do.

Yet even he did not understand, for he had not dared to lift his eyes to the Princess Flavia, as I had lifted mine.

Our plans were now all made, even as we proceeded to carry them out, and as they will hereafter appear. The next morning we were to start on the hunting excursion. I had made all arrangements for being absent, and now there was only one thing left to do – the hardest, the most heartbreaking. As evening fell, I drove through the busy streets to Flavia's residence. I was recognised as I went and heartily cheered. I played my part, and made shift to look the happy lover. In spite of my depression, I was almost amused at the coolness and delicate *hauteur* with which my sweet lover received me. She had heard that the King was leaving Strelsau on a hunting expedition.

'I regret that we cannot amuse your Majesty here in Strelsau,' she said, tapping her foot lightly on the floor. 'I would have offered you more entertainment, but I was foolish enough to think –'

'Well, what?' I asked, leaning over her.

'That just for a day or two after, – after last night – you might be happy without much gaiety'; and she turned pettishly from me, as she added, 'I hope the boars will be more engrossing.'

'I'm going after a very big boar,' said I; and, because I could not help it, I began to play with her hair, but she moved her head away.

'Are you offended with me?' I asked, in feigned surprise, for I could not resist tormenting her a little. I had never seen her angry, and every fresh aspect of her was a delight to me.

'What right have I to be offended? True, you said last night that every hour away from me was wasted. But a very big boar! that's a different thing.'

'Perhaps the boar will hunt me,' I suggested. 'Perhaps, Flavia, he'll catch me.'

She made no answer.

'You are not touched even by that danger?'

Still she said nothing; and I, stealing round, found her eyes full of tears.

'You weep for my danger?'

Then she spoke very low:

'This is like what you used to be; but not like the King – the King I – I have come to love!'

With a sudden great groan, I caught her to my heart.

'My darling!' I cried, forgetting everything but her, 'did you dream that I left you to go hunting?'

'What then, Rudolf? Ah! you're not going –?'

'Well, it is hunting. I go to seek Michael in his lair.'

She had turned very pale.

'So, you see, sweet, I was not so poor a lover as you thought me. I shall not be long gone.'

'You will write to me, Rudolf?'

I was weak, but I could not say a word to stir suspicion in her.

'I'll send you all my heart every day,' said I.

'And you'll run no danger?'

'None that I need not.'

'And when will you be back? Ah, how long will it be!'

'When shall I be back?' I repeated.

'Yes, yes! Don't be long, dear, don't be long. I shan't sleep while you're away.'

'I don't know when I shall be back,' said I.

'Soon, Rudolf, soon?'

'God knows, my darling. But, if never –'

'Hush, hush!' and she pressed her lips to mine.

'If never,' I whispered, 'you must take my place; you'll be the only one of the House then. You must reign, and not weep for me.'

For a moment she drew herself up like a very queen.

'Yes, I will!' she said. 'I will reign. I will do my part, though all my life will be empty and my heart dead; yet I'll do it!'

She paused, and sinking against me again, wailed softly.

'Come soon! come soon!'

Carried away, I cried loudly:

'As God lives, I – yes, I myself – will see you once more before I die!'

'What do you mean?' she exclaimed, with wondering eyes; but I had no answer for her, and she gazed at me with her wondering eyes.

I dared not ask her to forget, she would have found it an insult. I could not tell her then who and what I was. She was weeping, and I had but to dry her tears.

'Shall a man not come back to the loveliest lady in all the wide world?' said I. 'A thousand Michaels should not keep me from you!'

She clung to me, a little comforted.

'You won't let Michael hurt you?'

'No, sweetheart.'

'Or keep you from me?'

'No, sweetheart.'

'Nor anyone else?'

And again I answered:

'No, sweetheart.'

Yet there was one – not Michael – who, if he lived, must keep me from her; and for whose life I was going forth to stake my own. And his figure – the lithe, buoyant figure I had met in the woods of Zenda – the dull, inert mass I had left in the cellar of the hunting-lodge – seemed to rise, double-shaped, before me, and to come between us, thrusting itself in even where she lay, pale, exhausted, fainting, in my arms, and yet looking up at me with those eyes that bore such love as I have never seen, and haunt me now, and will till the ground closes over me – and (who knows?) perhaps beyond.

12

I Receive a Visitor and Bait a Hook

ABOUT five miles from Zenda – on the opposite side from that on which the Castle is situated, there lies a large tract of wood. It is rising ground, and in the centre of the demesne, on the top of the hill, stands a fine modern *château*, the property of a distant kinsman of Fritz's, the Count

Stanislas von Tarlenheim. Count Stanislas himself was a student and a recluse. He seldom visited the house, and had, on Fritz's request, very readily and courteously offered me its hospitality for myself and my party. This, then, was our destination; chosen ostensibly for the sake of the boar-hunting (for the wood was carefully preserved, and boars, once common all over Ruritania, were still to be found there in considerable numbers), really because it brought us within striking distance of the Duke of Strelsau's more magnificent dwelling on the other side of the town. A large party of servants, with horses and luggage, started early in the morning; we followed at midday, travelling by train for thirty miles, and then mounting our horses to ride the remaining distance to the *château*.

We were a gallant party. Besides Sapt and Fritz, I was accompanied by ten gentlemen: every one of them had been carefully chosen, and no less carefully sounded, by my two friends, and all were devotedly attached to the person of the King. They were told a part of the truth: the attempt on my life in the summer-house was revealed to them, as a spur to their loyalty and an incitement against Michael. They were also informed that a friend of the King's was suspected to be forcibly confined within the Castle of Zenda. His rescue was one of the objects of the expedition; but, it was added, the King's main desire was to carry into effect certain steps against his treacherous brother, as to the precise nature of which they could not at present be further enlightened. Enough that the King commanded their services, and would rely on their devotion when occasion arose to call for it. Young, well-bred, brave, and loyal, they asked no more: they were ready to prove their dutiful obedience, and prayed for a fight as the best and most exhilarating mode of showing it.

Thus the scene was shifted from Strelsau to the *château* of Tarlenheim and Castle of Zenda, which frowned at us across the valley. I tried to shift my thoughts also, to forget my love, and to bend all my energies to the task before me. It was to get the King out of the Castle alive. Force was useless: in some trick lay the chance; and I had already an inkling of what we must do. But I was terribly hampered by the publicity which attended my movements. Michael must know by now of my expedition; and I knew Michael too well to suppose that his eyes would be blinded by the feint of the boar-hunt. He would understand very well what the real quarry was. That, however, must be risked – that and all it might mean; for Sapt, no less than myself, recognised that the present state of things had become unendurable. And there was one thing that I dared to calculate on – not, as I now know, without warrant. It was this – that Black Michael would not believe that I meant well by the King. He could not appreciate – I will not say an honest man, for the thoughts of my own heart have been revealed – but a man acting honestly. He saw my opportunity as I had seen it, as Sapt had seen it; he knew the princess – nay (and I declare that a sneaking sort of pity for him invaded me), in his way he loved her; he would think that Sapt and Fritz could be bribed, so the bribe was large enough. Thinking thus, would he kill the King, my rival and my danger? Ay, verily, that he would, with as little compunction as he would kill a rat. But he would kill Rudolf Rassendyll first, if he could; and nothing but the certainty of being utterly damned by the release of the King alive and his restoration to the throne would drive him to throw away the trump card which he held in reserve to baulk the supposed game of the impudent impostor Rassendyll. Musing on all this as I rode along, I took courage.

Michael knew of my coming, sure enough. I had not been in the house an hour, when an imposing Embassy arrived from him. He did not quite reach the impudence of sending my would-be assassins, but he sent the other three of his famous Six – the three Ruritanian gentlemen – Lauengram, Krafstein, and Rupert Hentzau. A fine, strapping trio they were, splendidly horsed and admirably equipped. Young Rupert, who looked a dare-devil, and could not have been more than twenty-two or twenty-three, took the lead, and made us the neatest speech, wherein my devoted subject and loving brother Michael of Strelsau, prayed me to pardon him for not paying his addresses in person, and, further, for not putting his Castle at my disposal; the reason for both of these apparent derelictions being that he and several of his servants lay sick of scarlet fever, and were in a very sad, and also a very infectious, state. So declared young Rupert with an insolent smile on his curling upper-lip and a toss of his thick hair – he was a handsome villain, and the gossip ran that many a lady had troubled her heart for him already.

'If my brother has scarlet fever,' said I, 'he is nearer my complexion than he is wont to be, my lord. I trust he does not suffer?'

'He is able to attend to his affairs, sire.'

'I hope all beneath your roof are not sick. What of my good friends, De Gautet, Bersonin, and Detchard? I heard the last had suffered a hurt.'

Lauengram and Krafstein looked glum and uneasy, but young Rupert's smile grew broader.

'He hopes soon to find a medicine for it, sire,' he answered.

And I burst out laughing, for I knew what medicine Detchard longed for – it is called Revenge.

'You will dine with us, gentlemen?' I asked.

Young Rupert was profuse in apologies. They had urgent duties at the Castle.

'Then,' said I, with a wave of my hand, 'to our next meeting, gentlemen. May it make us better acquainted.'

'We will pray your Majesty for an early opportunity,' quoth Rupert airily; and he strode past Sapt with such jeering scorn on his face that I saw the old fellow clench his fist and scowl black as night.

For my part, if a man must needs be a knave, I would have him a debonair knave, and I liked Rupert Hentzau better than his long-faced, close-eyed companions. It makes your sin no worse, as I conceive, to do it *à la mode* and stylishly.

Now it was a curious thing that on this first night, instead of eating the excellent dinner my cooks had prepared for me, I must needs leave my gentlemen to eat it alone, under Sapt's presiding care, and ride myself with Fritz to the town of Zenda and a certain little inn that I knew of. There was little danger in the excursion; the evenings were long and light, and the road this side of Zenda well frequented. So off we rode, with a groom behind us. I muffled myself up in a big cloak.

'Fritz,' said I, as we entered the town, 'there's an uncommonly pretty girl at this inn.'

'How do you know?' he asked.

'Because I've been there,' said I.

'Since – ?' he began.

'No. Before,' said I.

'But they'll recognise you?'

'Well, of course they will. Now, don't argue, my good fellow, but listen to me. We're two gentlemen of the King's household, and one of us has a toothache. The other will order a private room and dinner, and, further, a bottle of the best wine for the sufferer. And if he be as clever a fellow as I take him for, the pretty girl and no other will wait on us.'

'What if she won't?' objected Fritz.

'My dear Fritz,' said I, 'if she won't for you, she will for me.'

We were at the inn. Nothing of me but my eyes was visible as I walked in. The landlady received us; two minutes later, my little friend (ever, I fear me, on the look out for such guests as might prove amusing) made her appearance. Dinner and the wine were ordered. I sat down in the private room. A minute later Fritz came in.

'She's coming,' he said.

'If she were not, I should have to doubt the Countess Helga's taste.'

She came in. I gave her time to set the wine down – I didn't want it dropped. Fritz poured out a glass and gave it to me.

'Is the gentleman in great pain?' the girl asked, sympathetically.

'The gentleman is no worse than when he saw you last,' said I, throwing away my cloak.

She started, with a little shriek. Then she cried:

'It was the King, then! I told mother so the moment I saw his picture. Oh, sir, forgive me!'

'Faith, you gave me nothing that hurt much,' said I.

'But the things we said!'

'I forgive them for the thing you did.'

'I must go and tell mother.'

'Stop,' said I, assuming a graver air. 'We are not here for sport to-night. Go and bring dinner, and not a word of the King being here.'

She came back in a few minutes, looking grave, yet very curious.

'Well, how is Johann?' I asked, beginning my dinner.

'Oh, that fellow, sir – my lord King, I mean!'

'"Sir" will do, please. How is he?'

'We hardly see him now, sir.'

'And why not?'

'I told him he came too often, sir,' said she, tossing her head.

'So he sulks and stays away?'

'Yes, sir.'

'But you could bring him back?' I suggested with a smile.

'Perhaps I could,' said she.

'I know your powers, you see,' said I, and she blushed with pleasure.

'It's not only that, sir, that keeps him away. He's very busy at the Castle.'

'But there's no shooting on now.'

'No, sir; but he's in charge of the house.'

'Johann turned housemaid?'

The little girl was brimming over with gossip.

'Well, there are no others,' said she. 'There's not a woman there – not as a servant, I mean. They do say – but perhaps it's false, sir.'

'Let's have it for what it's worth,' said I.

'Indeed, I'm ashamed to tell you, sir.'

'Oh, see, I'm looking at the ceiling.'

'They do say there is a lady there, sir; but, except for her, there's not a woman in the place. And Johann has to wait on the gentlemen.'

'Poor Johann! He must be overworked. Yet I'm sure he could find half an hour to come and see you.'

'It would depend on the time, sir, perhaps.'

'Do you love him?' I asked.

'Not I, sir.'

'And you wish to serve the King?'

'Yes, sir.'

'Then tell him to meet you at the second milestone out of Zenda to-morrow evening at ten o'clock. Say you'll be there and will walk home with him.'

'Do you mean him harm, sir?'

'Not if he will do as I bid him. But I think I've told you enough, my pretty maid. See that you do as I bid you. And, mind, no one is to know that the King has been here.'

I spoke a little sternly, for there is seldom harm in infusing a little fear into a woman's liking for you, and I softened the effect by giving her a handsome present. Then we dined, and, wrapping my cloak about my face, with Fritz leading the way, we went downstairs to our horses again.

It was but half-past eight, and hardly yet dark; the streets were full for such a quiet little place, and I could see that gossip was all agog. With the King on one side and the duke on the other, Zenda felt itself the centre of all Ruritania. We jogged gently through the town, but set our horses to a sharper pace when we reached the open country.

'You want to catch this fellow Johann?' asked Fritz.

'Ay, and I fancy I've baited the hook right. Our little Delilah will bring our Samson. It is not enough, Fritz, to have no women in a house, though brother Michael shows some wisdom there. If you want safety, you must have none within fifty miles.'

'None nearer than Strelsau, for instance,' said poor Fritz, with a lovelorn sigh.

We reached the avenue of the *château*, and were soon at the house. As the hoofs of our horses sounded on the gravel, Sapt rushed out to meet us.

'Thank God, you're safe!' he cried. 'Have you seen anything of them?'

'Of whom?' I asked, dismounting.

He drew us aside, that the grooms might not hear.

'Lad,' he said to me, 'you must not ride about here, unless with half a dozen of us. You know among our men a tall young fellow, Bernenstein by name?'

I knew him. He was a fine strapping young man, almost of my height, and of light complexion.

'He lies in his room upstairs, with a bullet through his arm.'

'The deuce he does!'

'After dinner he strolled out alone, and went a mile or so into the wood; and as he walked, he thought he saw three men among the trees; and one levelled a gun at him. He had no weapon, and he started at a run back towards the house. But one of them fired, and he was hit, and had much ado to reach here before he fainted. By good luck, they feared to pursue him nearer the house.'

He paused and added:

'Lad, the bullet was meant for you.'

'It is very likely,' said I, 'and it's first blood to brother Michael.'

'I wonder which three it was,' said Fritz.

'Well, Sapt,' I said, 'I went out to-night for no idle purpose, as you shall hear. But there's one thing in my mind.'

'What's that?' he asked.

'Why this,' I answered. 'That I shall ill requite the very great honours Ruritania has done me if I depart from it leaving one of those Six alive – neither, with the help of God, will I.'

And Sapt shook my hand on that.

13

An Improvement on Jacob's Ladder

IN the morning of the day after that on which I swore my oath against the Six, I gave certain orders, and then rested in greater contentment than I had known for some time. I was at work; and work, though it cannot cure love, is yet a narcotic to it; so that Sapt, who grew feverish, marvelled to see me sprawling in an arm-chair in the sunshine, listening to one of my friends who sang me amorous songs in a mellow voice and induced in me a pleasing melancholy. Thus was I engaged when young Rupert Hentzau, who feared neither man nor devil, and rode through the demesne – where every tree might hide a marksman, for all he knew – as though it had been the park at Strelsau, cantered up to where I lay, bowing with burlesque deference, and craving private speech with me in order to deliver a message from the Duke of Strelsau. I made all withdraw, and then he said, seating himself by me:

'The King is in love, it seems?'

'Not with life, my lord,' said I, smiling.

'It is well,' he rejoined. 'Come, we are alone. Rassendyll –'

I rose to a sitting posture.

'What's the matter?' he asked.

'I was about to call one of my gentlemen to bring your horse, my lord. If you do not know how to address the King, my brother must find another messenger.'

'Why keep up the farce?' he asked, negligently dusting his boot with his glove.

'Because it is not finished yet; and meanwhile I'll choose my own name.'

'Oh, so be it! Yet I spoke in love for you; for indeed you are a man after my own heart.'

'Saving my poor honesty,' said I, 'maybe I am. But that I keep faith with men, and honour with women, maybe I am, my lord.'

He darted a glance at me – a glance of anger.

'Is your mother dead?' said I.

'Ay, she's dead.'

'She may thank God,' said I, and I heard him curse me softly. 'Well, what's the message?' I continued.

I had touched him on the raw, for all the world knew he had broken his mother's heart and flaunted his mistresses in her house; and his airy manner was gone for the moment.

'The duke offers you more than I would,' he growled. 'A halter for you, *sire*, was my suggestion. But he offers you safe-conduct across the frontier and a million crowns.'

'I prefer your offer, my lord, if I am bound to one.'

'You refuse?'

'Of course.'

'I told Michael you would'; and the villain, his temper restored, gave me the sunniest of smiles. 'The fact is, between ourselves,' he continued, 'Michael doesn't understand a gentleman.'

I began to laugh.

'And you?' I asked.

'I do,' he said. 'Well, well, the halter be it.'

'I'm sorry you won't live to see it,' I observed.

'Has his Majesty done me the honour to fasten a particular quarrel on me?'

'I would you were a few years older, though.'

'Oh, God gives years, but the devil gives increase,' laughed he. 'I can hold my own.'

'How is your prisoner?' I asked.

'The K – ?'

'Your prisoner.'

'I forgot your wishes, sire. Well, he is alive.'

He rose to his feet; I imitated him. Then, with a smile, he said:

'And the pretty princess? Faith, I'll wager the next Elphberg will be red enough, for all that Black Michael will be called his father.'

I sprang a step towards him, clenching my hand. He did not move an inch, and his lip curled in insolent amusement.

'Go, while your skin's whole!' I muttered. He had repaid me with interest my hit about his mother.

Then came the most audacious thing I have known in my life. My friends were some thirty yards away. Rupert called to a groom to bring him his horse, and dismissed the fellow with a crown. The horse stood near. I stood still, suspecting nothing. Rupert made as though to mount; then he suddenly turned to me: his left hand resting in his belt, his right outstretched:

'Shake hands,' he said.

I bowed, and did as he had foreseen – I put my hands behind me. Quicker than thought, his left hand darted out at me, and a small dagger flashed in the air; he struck me in the left shoulder – had I not swerved, it had been my heart. With a cry, I staggered back. Without touching the stirrup, he leapt upon his horse and was off like an arrow, pursued by cries and revolver-shots – the last as useless as the first – and I sank into my chair, bleeding profusely, as I watched the devil's brat disappear down the long avenue. My friends surrounded me, and then I fainted.

I suppose that I was put to bed, and there lay, unconscious, or half-conscious, for many hours; for it was night when I awoke to my full mind, and found Fritz beside me. I was weak and weary, but he bade me be of good cheer, saying that my wound would soon heal, and that meanwhile all had gone well, for Johann, the keeper, had fallen into the snare we had laid for him, and was even now in the house.

'And the queer thing is,' pursued Fritz, 'that I fancy he's not altogether sorry to find himself here. He seems to think that when Black Michael has brought off his *coup*, witnesses of how it was effected – saving, of course, the Six themselves – will not be at a premium.'

This idea argued a shrewdness in our captive which led me to build hopes on his assistance. I ordered him to be brought in at once. Sapt conducted him, and set him in a chair by my bedside. He was sullen and afraid; but, to say truth, after young Rupert's exploit, we also had our fears, and, if he got as far as possible from Sapt's formidable six-shooter, Sapt kept him as far as he could from me. Moreover, when he came in his hands were bound, but that I would not suffer.

I need not stay to recount the safeguards and rewards we promised the fellow – all of which were honourably observed and paid, so that he lives now in prosperity (though where I may not mention); and we were the more free inasmuch as we soon learnt that he was rather a weak man than a wicked, and had acted throughout this matter more from fear of the duke and of his own brother Max than for any love of what was done. But he had persuaded all of his loyalty; and though not in their secret counsels, was yet, by his knowledge of their dispositions within the Castle, able to lay bare before us the very heart of their devices. And here, in brief, is his story:

Below the level of the ground in the Castle, approached by a flight of stone steps which abutted on the end of the drawbridge, were situate two small rooms, cut out of the rock itself. The outer of the two had no windows, but was always lighted with candles; the inner had one square window, which gave upon the moat. In the outer room there lay always, day and night, three of the Six; and the instructions of Duke Michael were, that on any attack being made on the outer room, the three were to defend the door of it so long as they could without risk to themselves. But, so soon as the door should be in danger of being forced, then Rupert Hentzau or Detchard (for one of these two was always there) should leave the others to hold it as long as they could, and himself pass into the inner room, and, without more ado, kill the King who lay there, well-treated indeed, but without weapons, and with his arms confined in fine steel chains, which did not allow him to move his elbow more than three inches from his side. Thus, before the outer door were stormed, the King would be dead. And his body? For his body would be evidence as damning as himself.

'Nay, sir,' said Johann, 'his Highness has thought of that. While the two hold the outer room, the one who has killed the King unlocks the bars in the square window (they turn on a hinge). The window now gives no light, for its mouth is choked by a great pipe of earthenware; and this pipe, which is large enough to let pass through it the body of a man, passes into the moat, coming to an end immediately above the surface of the water, so that there is no perceptible interval between water and pipe. The King being dead, his murderer swiftly ties a weight to the body, and, dragging it to the window, raises it by a pulley (for, lest the weight should prove too great, Detchard has provided one) till it is level with the mouth of the pipe. He inserts the feet in the pipe, and pushes the body down. Silently, without splash or sound, it falls into the water and thence to the bottom of the moat, which is twenty feet deep thereabouts. This done, the murderer cries loudly, 'All's well!' and himself slides down the pipe; and the others, if they can and the attack is not too hot, run to the inner room and, seeking a moment's delay, bar the door, and in their turn slide down. And though the King rises not from the bottom, they rise and swim round to the other side, where the orders are for men to wait them with ropes, to haul them out, and horses. And here, if things go ill, the duke will join them and seek safety by riding; but if all goes well, they will return to the Castle, and have their enemies in a trap. That, sir, is the plan of his Highness for the disposal of the King in case of need. But it is not to be used till the last; for, as we all know, he is not minded to kill the King unless he can, before or soon after, kill you also, sir. Now, sir, I have spoken the truth, as God is my witness, and I pray you to shield me from the vengeance of Duke Michael; for if, after he knows what I have done, I fall into his hands, I shall pray for one thing out of all the world – a speedy death, and that I shall not obtain from him!'

The fellow's story was rudely told, but our questions supplemented his narrative. What he had told us applied to an armed attack; but if suspicions were aroused, and there came overwhelming force – such, for instance, as I, the King, could bring – the idea of resistance would be abandoned; the King would be quietly murdered and slid down the pipe. And – here comes an ingenious touch – one of the Six would take his place in the cell, and, on the entrance of the searchers, loudly demand release and redress; and Michael, being summoned, would confess to hasty action, but he would say the man had angered him by seeking the favour of a lady in the Castle (this was Antoinette de Mauban) and he had confined him there, as he conceived he, as Lord of Zenda, had right to do. But he was now, on receiving his apology, content to let him go, and so end the gossip which, to his Highness's annoyance, had arisen concerning a prisoner in Zenda, and had given his visitors the trouble of this inquiry. The visitors, baffled, would retire, and Michael could, at his leisure, dispose of the body of the King.

Sapt, Fritz, and I in my bed, looked round on one another in horror and bewilderment at the cruelty and cunning of the plan. Whether I went in peace or in war, openly at the head of a *corps*, or secretly by a stealthy assault, the King would be dead before I could come near him. If Michael were stronger and overcame my party, there would be an end. But if I were stronger, I should have no way to punish him, no means of proving any guilt in him without proving my own guilt also. On the other hand, I should be left as King (ah! for a moment my pulse quickened) and it would be for the future to witness the final struggle between him and me. He seemed to have made triumph possible and ruin impossible. At the worst, he would stand as well as he had stood before I crossed his path – with but one man between him and the throne, and that man an impostor; at best, there would be none left to stand against him. I had begun to think that Black Michael was over fond of leaving the fighting to his friends; but now I acknowledged that the brains, if not the arms, of the conspiracy were his.

'Does the King know this?' I asked.

'I and my brother,' answered Johann, 'put up the pipe, under the orders of my Lord of Hentzau. He was on guard that day, and the King asked my lord what it meant. "Faith," he answered, with his airy laugh, "it's a new improvement on the ladder of Jacob, whereby, as you have read, sire, men pass from earth to heaven. We thought it not meet that your Majesty should go, in case, sire, you must go, by the common route. So we have made you a pretty private passage where the vulgar cannot stare at you or incommode your passage. That, sire, is the meaning of that pipe." And he laughed and bowed, and prayed the King's leave to replenish the King's glass – for the King was at supper. And the King, though he is a brave man, as are all of his House, grew red and then white as he looked on the pipe and at the merry devil who mocked him. Ah, sir' (and the fellow shuddered), 'it is not easy to sleep quiet in the Castle of Zenda, for all of them would as soon cut a man's throat as play a game at cards; and my Lord Rupert would choose it sooner for a pastime than any other – ay, sooner than he would ruin a woman, though that he loves also.'

The man ceased, and I bade Fritz take him away and have him carefully guarded; and, turning to him, I added:

'If anyone asks you if there is a prisoner in Zenda, you may answer "Yes." But if any asks who the prisoner is, do not answer. For all my promises will not save you if any man here learns from you the truth as to the prisoner in Zenda. I'll kill you like a dog if the thing be so much as breathed within the house!'

Then, when he was gone, I looked at Sapt.

'It's a hard nut!' said I.

'So hard,' said he, shaking his grizzled head, 'that, as I think, this time next year is like to find you still King of Ruritania!' and he broke out into curses on Michael's cunning.

I lay back on my pillows.

'There seem to me,' I observed, 'to be two ways by which the King can come out of Zenda alive. One is by treachery in the duke's followers.'

'You can leave that out,' said Sapt.

'I hope not,' I rejoined, 'because the other I was about to mention is – by a miracle from heaven!'

14

A Night outside the Castle

IT would have surprised the good people of Ruritania to know of the foregoing talk; for, according to the official reports, I had suffered a grievous and dangerous hurt from an accidental spear-thrust, received in the course of my sport. I caused the bulletins to be of a very serious character, and created great public excitement, whereby three things occurred: first, I gravely offended the medical faculty of Strelsau by refusing to summon to my bedside any of them, save a young man, a friend of Fritz's, whom we could trust; secondly, I received word from Marshal Strakencz that my orders seemed to have no more weight than his, and that the Princess Flavia was leaving for Tarlenheim under his unwilling escort (news whereat I strove not to be glad and proud); and thirdly, my brother, the Duke of Strelsau, although too well informed to believe the account of the origin of my sickness, was yet persuaded by the reports and by my seeming inactivity that I was in truth incapable of action, and that my life was in some danger. This I learnt from the man Johann, whom I was compelled to trust and send back to Zenda, where, by the way, Rupert Hentzau had him soundly flogged for daring to smirch the morals of Zenda by staying out all night in the pursuits of love. This, from Rupert, Johann deeply resented, and the duke's approval of it did more to bind the keeper to my side than all my promises.

On Flavia's arrival I cannot dwell. Her joy at finding me up and well, instead of on my back and fighting with death, makes a picture that even now dances before my eyes till they grow too dim to see it; and her reproaches that I had not trusted even her must excuse the means I took to quiet them. In truth, to have her with me once more was like a taste of heaven to a damned soul, the sweeter for the inevitable doom that was to follow; and I rejoiced in being able to waste two whole days with her. And when I had wasted two days, the Duke of Strelsau arranged a hunting-party.

The stroke was near now. For Sapt and I, after anxious consultations, had resolved that we must risk a blow, our resolution being clinched by Johann's news that the King grew peaked, pale, and ill, and that his health was breaking down under his rigorous confinement. Now a man – be he king or no king – may as well die swiftly and as becomes a gentleman, from bullet or thrust, as rot his life out in a cellar! That thought made prompt action advisable in the interests of the King; from my own point of view, it grew more and more necessary. For Strakencz urged on me the need of a speedy marriage, and my own inclinations seconded him with such terrible insistence that I feared for my resolution. I do not believe that I should have done the deed I dreamt of; but I might have come to flight, and my flight would have ruined the cause. And – yes, I am no saint (ask my little sister-in-law), and worse still might have happened.

It is perhaps as strange a thing as has ever been in the history of a country that the King's brother and the King's personator, in a time of profound outward peace, near a placid undisturbed country town, under semblance of amity, should wage a desperate war for the person and life of the King. Yet such was the struggle that began now between Zenda and Tarlenheim. When I look back on the time, I seem to myself to have been half-mad. Sapt has told me that I suffered no interference and listened to no remonstrances; and if ever a King of Ruritania ruled like a despot, I was, in those days, the man. Look where I would, I saw nothing that made life sweet to me, and I took my life in my hand and carried it carelessly as a man dangles an old glove. At first they strove to guard me, to keep me safe, to persuade me not to expose myself; but when they saw how I was set, there grew up among them – whether they knew the truth or not – a feeling that Fate ruled the issue, and that I must be left to play my game with Michael my own way.

Late next night I rose from table, where Flavia had sat by me, and conducted her to the door of her apartment. There I kissed her hand, and bade her sleep sound and wake to happy days. Then I changed my clothes and went out. Sapt and Fritz were waiting for me with six men and the horses. Over his saddle Sapt carried a long coil of rope, and both were heavily armed. I had with me a short stout cudgel and a long knife. Making a circuit, we avoided the town, and in an hour found ourselves slowly mounting the hill that led to the Castle of Zenda. The night was dark and very stormy; gusts of wind and spits of rain caught us as we breasted the incline, and the great trees moaned and sighed. When we came to a thick clump, about a quarter of a mile from the Castle, we bade our six friends hide there with the horses. Sapt had a whistle, and they could rejoin us in a few moments if danger came: but, up to now, we had met no one. I hoped that Michael was still off his guard, believing me to be safe in bed. However that might be, we gained the top of the hill without accident, and found ourselves on the edge of the moat where it sweeps under the road, separating the Old Castle from it. A tree stood on the edge of the bank, and Sapt, silently and diligently, set to make fast the rope. I stripped off my boots, took a pull at a flask of brandy, loosened the knife in its sheath, and took the cudgel between my teeth. Then I shook hands with my friends, not heeding a last look of entreaty from Fritz, and laid hold of the rope. I was going to have a look at 'Jacob's Ladder.'

Gently I lowered myself into the water. Though the night was wild, the day had been warm and bright, and the water was not cold. I struck out, and began to swim round the great walls which frowned above me. I could see only three yards ahead; I had then good hopes of not being seen, as I crept along close under the damp, moss-grown masonry. There were lights from the new part of the Castle on the other side, and now and again I heard laughter and merry shouts. I fancied I recognised young Rupert Hentzau's ringing tones, and pictured him flushed with wine. Recalling my thoughts to the business in hand, I rested a moment. If Johann's description were right, I must be near the window now. Very slowly I moved; and out of the darkness ahead loomed a shape. It was the pipe, curving from the window to the water: about four feet of its surface were displayed; it was as big round as two men. I was about to approach it, when I saw something else, and my heart stood still. The nose of a boat protruded beyond the pipe on the other side; and listening intently, I heard a slight shuffle – as of a man shifting his position. Who was the man who guarded Michael's invention? Was he awake or was he asleep? I felt if my knife were ready, and trod water; as I did so, I found bottom under my feet. The foundations of the Castle extended some fifteen inches, making a ledge; and I stood on it, out of water from my armpits upwards. Then I crouched and peered through the darkness under the pipe, where, curving, it left a space.

There was a man in the boat. A rifle lay by him – I saw the gleam of the barrel. Here was the sentinel! He sat very still. I listened: he breathed heavily, regularly, monotonously. By heaven, he slept! Kneeling on the shelf, I drew forward under the pipe till my face was within two feet of his. He was a big man, I saw. It was Max Holf, the brother of Johann. My hand stole to my belt, and I drew out my knife. Of all the deeds of my life, I love the least to think of this, and whether it were the act of a man or a traitor I will not ask. I said to myself: 'It is war – and the King's life is the stake.' And I raised myself from beneath the pipe and stood up by the boat, which lay moored by the ledge. Holding my breath, I marked the spot and raised my arm. The great fellow stirred. He opened his eyes – wide, wider. He gasped in terror at my face and clutched at his rifle. I struck home. And I heard the chorus of a love-song from the opposite bank.

Leaving him where he lay, a huddled mass, I turned to 'Jacob's Ladder.' My time was short. This fellow's turn of watching might be over directly, and relief would come. Leaning over the pipe, I examined it, from the end near the water to the topmost extremity where it passed, or seemed to pass, through the masonry of the wall. There was no break in it, no chink. Dropping on my knees, I tested the under side. And my breath went quick and fast, for on this lower side, where the pipe should have clung close to the masonry, there was a gleam of light! That light must come from the cell of the King! I set my shoulder against the pipe and exerted my strength. The chink widened a very, very little, and hastily I desisted; I had done enough to show that the pipe was not fixed in the masonry at the lower side.

Then I heard a voice – a harsh, grating voice:

'Well, sire, if you have had enough of my society, I will leave you to repose; but I must fasten the little ornaments first.'

It was Detchard! I caught the English accent in a moment.

'Have you anything to ask, sire, before we part?'

The King's voice followed. It was his, though it was faint and hollow – different from the merry tones I had heard in the glades of the forest.

'Pray my brother,' said the King, 'to kill me. I am dying by inches here.'

'The duke does not desire your death, sire – yet,' sneered Detchard; 'when he does, behold your path to heaven!'

The King answered:

'So be it! And now, if your orders allow it, pray leave me.'

'May you dream of paradise!' said the ruffian.

The light disappeared. I heard the bolts of the door run home. And then I heard the sobs of the King. He was alone, as he thought. Who dares mock at him?

I did not venture to speak to him. The risk of some exclamation escaping him in surprise was too great. I dared do nothing that night; and my task now was to get myself away in safety, and to carry off the carcase of the dead man. To leave him there would tell too much. Casting loose the boat, I got in. The wind was blowing a gale now, and there was little danger of oars being heard. I rowed swiftly round to where my friends waited. I had just reached the spot, when a loud whistle sounded over the moat behind me.

'Hullo, Max!' I heard shouted.

I hailed Sapt in a low tone. The rope came down. I tied it round the corpse, and then went up it myself.

'Whistle you too,' I whispered, 'for our men, and haul in the line. No talk now.'

They hauled up the body. Just as it reached the road, three men on horseback swept round from the front of the Castle. We saw them; but, being on foot ourselves, we escaped their notice. But we heard our men coming up with a shout.

'The devil, but it's dark!' cried a ringing voice.

It was young Rupert. A moment later, shots rang out. Our people had met them. I started forward at a run, Sapt and Fritz following me.

'Thrust, thrust!' cried Rupert again, and a loud groan following told that he himself was not behind-hand.

'I'm done, Rupert!' cried a voice. 'They're three to one. Save yourself!'

I ran on, holding my cudgel in my hand. Suddenly a horse came towards me. A man was on it, leaning over his shoulder.

'Are you cooked too, Krafstein?' he cried.

There was no answer.

I sprang to the horse's head. It was Rupert Hentzau.

'At last!' I cried.

For we seemed to have him. He had only his sword in his hand. My men were hot upon him; Sapt and Fritz were running up. I had outstripped them; but if they got close enough to fire, he must die or surrender.

'At last!' I cried.

'It's the play-actor!' cried he, slashing at my cudgel. He cut it clean in two; and, judging discretion better than death, I ducked my head and (I blush to tell it) scampered for my life. The devil was in Rupert Hentzau; for he put spurs to his horse, and I, turning to look, saw him ride, full gallop, to the edge of the moat and leap in, while the shots of our party fell thick round him like hail. With one gleam of moonlight we should have riddled him with balls; but, in the darkness, he won to the corner of the Castle, and vanished from our sight.

'The deuce take him!' grinned Sapt.

'It's a pity,' said I, 'that he's a villain. Whom have we got?'

We had Lauengram and Krafstein: they lay dead; and, concealment being no longer possible, we flung them, with Max, into the moat; and, drawing together in a compact body, rode off down the hill. And, in our midst, went the bodies of three gallant gentlemen. Thus we travelled home, heavy at heart for the death of our friends, sore uneasy concerning the King, and cut to the quick that young Rupert had played yet another winning hand with us.

For my own part, I was vexed and angry that I had killed no man in open fight, but only stabbed a knave in his sleep. And I did not love to hear Rupert call me a play-actor.

15

I Talk with a Tempter

RURITANIA is not England, or the quarrel between Duke Michael and myself could not have gone on, with the extraordinary incidents which marked it, without more public notice being directed to it. Duels were frequent among all the upper classes, and private quarrels between great men kept the old habit of spreading to their friends and dependents. Nevertheless, after the affray which I have just related, such reports began to circulate that I felt it necessary to be on my guard. The death of the gentlemen involved could not be hidden from their relatives. I issued a stern order, declaring that duelling had attained unprecedented license (the Chancellor drew up the document for me, and very well he did it), and forbidding it save in the gravest cases. I sent a public and stately apology to Michael, and he returned a deferential and courteous reply to me; for our one point of union was – and it underlay all our differences and induced an unwilling harmony between our actions – that we could neither of us afford to throw our cards on the table. He, as well as I, was a 'play-actor', and, hating one another, we combined to dupe public opinion. Unfortunately, however, the necessity for concealment involved the necessity of delay: the King might die in his prison, or even be spirited off somewhere else; it could not be helped. For a little while I was compelled to observe a truce, and my only consolation was that Flavia most warmly approved of my edict against duelling, and, when I expressed delight at having won her favour, prayed me, if her favour were any motive to me, to prohibit the practice altogether.

'Wait till we are married,' said I, smiling.

Not the least peculiar result of the truce and of the secrecy which dictated it was that the town of Zenda became in the daytime . . . I would not have trusted far to its protection by night – a sort of neutral zone, where both parties could safely go; and I, riding down one day with Flavia and Sapt, had an encounter with an acquaintance, which presented a ludicrous side, but was at the same time embarrassing. As I rode along, I met a dignified-looking person driving in a two-horsed carriage. He stopped his horses, got out, and approached me, bowing low, I recognised the Head of the Strelsau Police.

'Your Majesty's ordinance as to duelling is receiving our best attention,' he assured me.

If the best attention involved his presence in Zenda, I determined at once to dispense with it.

'Is that what brings you to Zenda, Prefect?' I asked.

'Why no, sire; I am here because I desired to oblige the British Ambassador.'

'What's the British Ambassador doing *dans cette galère*?' said I, carelessly.

'A young countryman of his, sire – a man of some position, – is missing. His friends have not heard from him for two months, and there is reason to believe that he was last seen in Zenda.'

Flavia was paying little attention. I dared not look at Sapt.

'What reason?'

'A friend of his in Paris – a certain M. Featherly – has given us information which makes it possible that he came here, and the officials of the railway recollect his name on some luggage.'

'What was his name?'

'Rassendyll, sire,' he answered; and I saw that the name meant nothing to him. But, glancing at Flavia he lowered his voice, as he went on: 'It is thought that he may have followed a lady here. Has your Majesty heard of a certain Madame de Mauban?'

'Why, yes,' said I, my eye involuntarily travelling towards the Castle.

'She arrived in Ruritania about the same time as this Rassendyll.'

I caught the Prefect's glance; he was regarding me with inquiry writ large on his face.

'Sapt,' said I, 'I must speak a word to the Prefect. Will you ride on a few paces with the princess?' And I added to the Prefect: 'Come, sir, what do you mean?'

He drew close to me, and I bent in the saddle.

'If he were in love with the lady?' he whispered. 'Nothing has been heard of him for two months'; and this time it was the eye of the Prefect which travelled towards the Castle.

'Yes, the lady is there,' I said quietly. 'But I don't suppose Mr. Rassendyll – is that the name? – is.'

'The duke,' he whispered, 'does not like rivals, sire.'

'You're right there,' said I, with all sincerity. 'But surely you hint at a very grave charge?'

He spread his hands out in apology. I whispered in his ear:

'This is a grave matter. Go back to Strelsau – '

'But, sire, if I have a clue here?'

'Go back to Strelsau,' I repeated. 'Tell the Ambassador that you have a clue, but that you must be left alone for a week or two. Meanwhile, I'll charge myself with looking into the matter.'

'The Ambassador is very pressing, sire.'

'You must quiet him. Come, sir; you see that if your suspicions are correct, it is an affair in which we must move with caution. We can have no scandal. Mind you return to-night.'

He promised to obey me, and I rode on to rejoin my companions, a little easier in my mind. Inquiries after me must be stopped at all hazards for a week or two; and this clever official had come surprisingly near the truth. His impression might be useful some day, but if he acted on it now it might mean the worse to the King. Heartily did I curse George Featherly for not holding his tongue.

'Well,' asked Flavia, 'have you finished your business?'

'Most satisfactorily,' said I. 'Come, shall we turn round? We are almost trenching on my brother's territory.'

We were, in fact, at the extreme end of the town, just where the hill begins to mount towards the Castle. We cast our eyes up, admiring the massive beauty of the old walls, and we saw a *cortège* winding slowly down the hill. On it came.

'Let us go back,' said Sapt.

'I should like to stay,' said Flavia; and I reined my horse beside hers.

We could distinguish the approaching party now. There came first two mounted servants in black uniforms, relieved only by a silver badge. These were followed by a car drawn by four horses: on it, under a heavy pall, lay a coffin; behind it rode a man in plain black clothes, carrying his hat in his hand. Sapt uncovered, and we stood waiting, Flavia keeping by me and laying her hand on my arm.

'It is one of the gentlemen killed in the quarrel, I expect,' she said.

I beckoned to a groom.

'Ride and ask whom they escort,' I ordered.

He rode up to the servants, and I saw him pass on to the gentleman who rode behind.

'Its Rupert of Hentzau,' whispered Sapt.

Rupert it was, and directly afterwards, waving to the procession to stand still, Rupert trotted up to me. He was in a frock-coat, tightly buttoned, and trousers. He wore an aspect of sadness, and he bowed with profound respect. Yet suddenly he smiled, and I smiled too, for old Sapt's hand lay in his left breastpocket, and Rupert and I both guessed what lay in the hand inside the pocket.

'Your Majesty asks whom we escort,' said Rupert 'It is my dear friend, Albert of Lauengram.'

'Sir,' said I, 'no one regrets the unfortunate affair more than I. My ordinance, which I mean to have obeyed, is witness to it.'

'Poor fellow!' said Flavia softly, and I saw Rupert's eyes flash at her. Whereat I grew red; for, if I had my way, Rupert Hentzau should not have defiled her by so much as a glance. Yet he did it and dared to let admiration be seen in his look.

'Your Majesty's, words are gracious,' he said. 'I grieve for my friend. Yet, sire, others must soon lie as he lies now.'

'It is a thing we all do well to remember, my lord,' I rejoined.

'Even kings, sire,' said Rupert, in a moralising tone and old Sapt swore softly by my side.

'It is true,' said I. 'How fares my brother, my lord?'

'He is better, sire.'

'I am rejoiced.'

'He hopes soon to leave for Strelsau, when his health is secured.'

'He is only convalescent then?'

'There remain one or two small troubles,' answered the insolent fellow, in the mildest tone in the world.

'Express my earnest hope,' said Flavia, 'that they may soon cease to trouble him.'

'Your Royal Highness's wish is, humbly, my own,' said Rupert, with a bold glance that brought a blush to Flavia's cheek.

I bowed; and Rupert, bowing lower, backed his horse and signed to his party to proceed. With a sudden impulse, I rode after him. He turned swiftly, fearing that, even in the presence of the dead and before a lady's eyes, I meant him mischief.

'You fought as a brave man the other night,' I said. 'Come, you are young, sir. If you will deliver your prisoner alive to me, you shall come to no hurt.'

He looked at me with a mocking smile; but suddenly he rode nearer to me.

'I'm unarmed,' he said; 'and our old Sapt there could pick me off in a minute.'

'I'm not afraid,' said I.

'No, curse you!' he answered. 'Look here, I made you a proposal from the duke once.'

'I'll hear nothing from Black Michael,' said I.

'Then hear one from me.' He lowered his voice to a whisper. 'Attack the Castle boldly. Let Sapt and Tarlenheim lead.'

'Go on,' said I.

'Arrange the time with me.'

'I have such confidence in you, my lord!'

'Tut! I'm talking business now. Sapt there and Fritz will fall; Black Michael will fall – '

'What!'

'– Black Michael will fall, like the dog he is; the prisoner, as you call him, will go by 'Jacob's Ladder' – ah, you know that! – to hell! Two men will be left – I, Rupert Hentzau, and you, the King of Ruritania.'

He paused, and then, in a voice that quivered with eagerness, added:

'Isn't that a hand to play? – a throne and your princess! And for me, say a competence and your Majesty's gratitude.'

'Surely,' I exclaimed, 'while you're above ground, hell wants its master!'

'Well, think it over,' he said. 'And, look you, it would take more than a scruple or two to keep me from yonder girl,' and his evil eye flashed again at her I loved.

'Get out of my reach!' said I; and yet in a moment I began to laugh for the very audacity of it.

'Would you turn against your master?' I asked.

He swored at Michael for being what the offspring of a legal, though morganatic, union should not be called, and said to me, in an almost confidential and apparently friendly tone:

'He gets in my way, you know. He's a jealous brute! Faith, I nearly stuck a knife into him last night; he came most cursedly *mal à propos*!'

My temper was well under control now; I was learning something.

'A lady?' I asked negligently.

'Ay, and a beauty,' he nodded. 'But you've seen her.'

'Ah! was it at a tea-party, when some of your friends got on the wrong side of the table?'

'What can you expect of fools like Detchard and De Gautet? I wish I'd been there.'

'And the duke interferes?'

'Well,' said Rupert meditatively, 'that's hardly a fair way of putting it, perhaps. I want to interfere.'

'And she prefers the duke?'

'Ay, the silly creature! Ah, well, you think about my plan,' and, with a bow, he pricked his horse and trotted after the body of his friend.

I went back to Flavia and Sapt, pondering on the strangeness of the man. Wicked men I have known in plenty, but Rupert Hentzau remains unique in my experience. And if there be another anywhere, let him be caught and hanged out of hand. So say I!

'He's very handsome, isn't he?' said Flavia.

Well, of course, she didn't know him as I did; yet I was put out, for I thought his bold glances would have made her angry. But my dear Flavia was a woman, and so – she was not put out. On the contrary, she thought young Rupert very handsome – as, beyond question, the ruffian was.

'And how sad he looked at his friend's death!' said she.

'He'll have better reason to be sad at his own,' observed Sapt, with a grim smile.

As for me, I grew sulky; unreasonable it was perhaps, for what better business had I to look at her with love than had even Rupert's lustful eyes? And sulky I remained till, as evening fell and we rode up to Tarlenheim, Sapt having fallen behind in case anyone should be following us, Flavia, riding close beside me, said softly, with a little half-ashamed laugh:

'Unless you smile, Rudolf, I cry. Why are you angry?'

'It was something that fellow said to me,' said I but I was smiling as we reached the door and dismounted.

There a servant handed me a note: it was unaddressed.

'Is it for me?' I asked.

'Yes, sire; a boy brought it.'

I tore it open:

> 'Johann carries this for me. I warned you once. In the name of God, and if you are a man, rescue me from this den of murderers! – A. de M.'

I handed it to Sapt; but all that the tough old soul said in reply to this piteous appeal was:

'Whose fault brought her there?'

Nevertheless, not being faultless myself, I took leave to pity Antoinette de Mauban.

16

A Desperate Plan

AS I had ridden publicly in Zenda, and had talked there with Rupert Hentzau, of course all pretence of illness was at an end. I marked the effect on the garrison of Zenda: they ceased to be seen abroad; and any of my men who went near the Castle reported that the utmost vigilance prevailed there. Touched as I was by Madame de Mauban's appeal, I seemed as powerless to befriend her as I had proved to help the King. Michael bade me defiance; and although he too had been seen outside the walls, with more disregard for appearances than he had hitherto shown, he did not take the trouble to send any excuse for his failure to wait on the King. Time ran on in inactivity, when every moment was pressing; for not only was I faced with the new danger which the stir about my disappearance brought on me, but great murmurs had arisen in Strelsau at my continued absence from the city. They had been greater, but for the knowledge that Flavia was with me; and for this reason I suffered her to stay, though I hated to have her where danger was, and though every day of our present sweet intercourse strained my endurance almost to breaking. As a final blow, nothing would content my advisers, Strakencz and the Chancellor (who came out from Strelsau to make an urgent representation to me) save that I should appoint a day for the public solemnisation of my betrothal, a ceremony which in Ruritania is well-nigh as binding and great a thing as the marriage itself. And this – with Flavia sitting by me – I was forced to do, setting a date a fortnight ahead, and appointing the Cathedral in Strelsau as the place. And this formal act being published far and wide, caused great joy throughout the kingdom, and was the talk of all tongues; so that I reckoned there were but two men who chafed at it – I mean Black Michael and myself; and but one who did not know of it – that one the man whose name I bore, the King of Ruritania.

In truth, I heard something of the way the news was received in the Castle; for after an interval of three days, the man Johann, greedy for more money, though fearful for his life, again found means to visit us. He had been waiting on the duke when the tidings came. Black Michael's face had grown blacker still, and he had sworn savagely; nor was he better pleased when young Rupert took oath that I meant to do as I said, and turning to Madame de Mauban, wished her joy on a rival gone. Michael's hand stole towards his sword (said Johann), but not a bit did Rupert care; for he rallied the duke on having made a better King than had reigned for years past in Ruritania. 'And,' said he, with a meaning bow to his exasperated master, 'the devil sends the princess a finer man than heaven had marked out for her, by my soul, it does!' Then Michael harshly bade him hold his tongue, and leave them; but Rupert must needs first kiss madame's hand, which he did as though he loved her, while Michael glared at him.

This was the lighter side of the fellow's news; but more serious came behind, and it was plain that if time pressed at Tarlenheim, it pressed none the less fiercely at Zenda. For the King was very sick: Johann had seen him, and he was wasted and hardly able to move. 'There could be no thought of taking another for him now.' So alarmed were they, that they had sent for a physician from Strelsau; and the physician having been introduced into the King's cell, had come forth pale and trembling, and urgently prayed the duke to let him go back and meddle no more in the affair; but the duke would not, and held him there a prisoner, telling him his life was safe if the King lived while the duke desired and died when the duke desired – not otherwise. And, persuaded by the physician, they had allowed Madame de Mauban to visit the King and give him such attendance as his state needed, and as only a woman can give. Yet his life hung in the balance; and I was still strong and whole and free. Wherefore great gloom reigned at Zenda; and save when they quarrelled, to which they were very prone, they hardly spoke. But the deeper the depression of the rest, young Rupert went about Satan's work with a smile in his eye and a song on his lip; and laughed 'fit to burst' (said Johann) because the duke always set Detchard to guard the King when Madame de Mauban was in the cell – which precaution was, indeed, not unwise in my careful brother. Thus Johann told his tale and seized his crowns. Yet he besought us to allow him to stay with us in Tarlenheim, and not venture his head again in the lion's den; but we had need of him there, and, although I refused to constrain him, I prevailed on him by increased rewards to go back and carry tidings to Madame de Mauban that I was working for her, and that, if she could, she should speak one word of comfort to the King. For while suspense is bad for the sick, yet despair is worse still, and it might be that the King lay dying of mere hopelessness, for I could learn of no definite disease that afflicted him.

'And how do they guard the King now?' I asked, remembering that two of the Six were dead, and Max Holf also.

'Detchard and Bersonin watch by night, Rupert Hentzau and De Gautet by day, sir,' he answered.

'Only two at a time?'

'Ay, sir; but the others rest in a room just above, and are within sound of a cry or a whistle.'

'A room just above? I didn't know of that. Is there any communication between it and the room where they watch?'

'No, sir. You must go down a few stairs and through the door by the drawbridge, and so to where the King is lodged.'

'And that door is locked?'

'Only the four lords have keys, sir.'

I drew nearer to him.

'And have they keys of the grating?' I asked in a low whisper.

'I think, sir, only Detchard and Rupert.'

'Where does the duke lodge?'

'In the *château*, on the first floor. His apartments are on the right as you go towards the drawbridge.'

'And Madame de Mauban?'

'Just opposite, on the left. But her door is locked after she has entered.'

'To keep her in?'

'Doubtless, sir.'

'Perhaps for another reason?'

'It is possible.'

'And the duke, I suppose, has the key?'

'Yes. And the drawbridge is drawn back at night, and of that, too, the duke holds the key, so that it cannot be run across the moat without application to him.'

'And where do you sleep?'

'In the entrance hall of the *château*, with five servants.'

'Armed?'

'They have pikes, sir, but no firearms. The duke will not trust them with firearms.'

Then at last I took the matter boldly in my hands. I had failed once at 'Jacob's Ladder'; I should fail again there. I must make the attack from the other side.

'I have promised you twenty thousand crowns,' said I. 'You shall have fifty thousand if you will do what I ask of you to-morrow night. But, first, do those servants know who your prisoner is?'

'No, sir. They believe him to be some private enemy of the duke's.'

'And they would not doubt that I am the King?'

'How should they?' he asked.

'Look to this, then. To-morrow, at two in the morning exactly, fling open the front door of the *château*. Don't fail by an instant.'

'Shall you be there, sir?'

'Ask no questions. Do what I tell you. Say the hall is close, or what you will. That is all I ask of you.'

'And may I escape by the door, sir, when I have opened it?'

'Yes, as quick as your legs will carry you. One thing more. Carry this note to madame – oh, it's in French, you can't read it – and charge her, for the sake of all our lives, not to fail in what it orders.'

The man was trembling but I had to trust to what he had of courage and to what he had of honesty. I dared not wait, for I feared that the King would die.

When the fellow was gone, I called Sapt and Fritz to me, and unfolded the plan that I had formed. Sapt shook his head over it.

'Why can't you wait?' he asked.

'The King may die.'

'Michael will be forced to act before that.'

'Then,' said I, 'the King may live.'

'Well, and if he does?'

'For a fortnight?' I asked simply.

And Sapt bit his moustache.

Suddenly Fritz von Tarlenheim laid his hand on my shoulder.

'Let us go and make the attempt,' said he.

'I mean you to go – don't be afraid,' said I.

'Ay, but do you stay here, and take care of the princess.'

A gleam came into old Sapt's eye.

'We should have Michael one way or the other then,' he chuckled; 'whereas if you go and are killed with the King, what will become of those of us who are left?'

'They will serve Queen Flavia,' said I, 'and I would to God I could be one of them.'

A pause followed. Old Sapt broke it by saying sadly, yet with an unmeant drollery that set Fritz and me laughing:

'Why didn't old Rudolf the Third marry your – great-grandmother, was it?'

'Come,' said I, 'it is the King we are thinking about.'

'It is true,' said Fritz.

'Moreover,' I went on, 'I have been an impostor for the profit of another, but I will not be one for my own; and if the King is not alive and on his throne before the day of betrothal comes, I will tell the truth, come what may.'

'You shall go, lad,' said Sapt.

Here is the plan I had made. A strong party under Sapt's command was to steal up to the door of the *château*. If discovered prematurely, they were to kill anyone who found them – with their swords, for I wanted no noise of firing. If all went well, they would be at the door when Johann opened it. They were to rush in and secure the servants if their mere presence and the use of the King's name were not enough. At the same moment – and on this hinged the plan – a woman's cry was to ring out loud and shrill from Antoinette de Mauban's chamber. Again and again she was to cry: 'Help, help! Michael, help!' and then to utter the name of young Rupert Hentzau. Then, as we hoped, Michael, in fury, would rush out of his apartments opposite, and fall alive into the hands of Sapt. Still the cries would go on; and my men would let down the drawbridge; and it would be strange if Rupert, hearing his name thus taken in vain, did not descend from where he slept and seek to cross. De Gautet might or might not come with him: that must be left to chance.

And when Rupert set his foot on the drawbridge? There was my part: for I was minded for another swim in the moat; and, lest I should grow weary, I had resolved to take with me a small wooden ladder, on which I could rest my arms in the water – and my feet when I left it. I would rear it against the wall just by the bridge; and when the bridge was across, I would stealthily creep on to it – and then if Rupert or De Gautet crossed in safety, it would be my misfortune, not my fault. They dead, two men only would remain; and for them we must trust to the confusion we had created and to a sudden rush. We should have the keys of the door that led to the all-important rooms. Perhaps they would rush out. If they stood by their orders, then the King's life hung on the swiftness with which we could force the outer door; and I thanked God that not Rupert Hentzau watched, but Detchard. For though Detchard was a cool man, relentless, and no coward, he had neither the dash nor the recklessness of Rupert. Moreover, he, if any one of them, really loved Black Michael, and it might be that he would leave Bersonin to guard the King, and rush across the bridge to take part in the affray on the other side.

So I planned – desperately. And, that our enemy might be the better lulled to security, I gave orders that our residence should be brilliantly lighted from top to bottom, as though we were engaged in revelry; and should so be kept all night, with music playing and people moving to and fro. Strakencz would be there, and he was to conceal our departure, if he could, from Flavia. And if we came not again by the morning, he was to march, openly and in force to the Castle, and demand the person of the King; if Black Michael were not there, as I did not think he would be, the marshal would take Flavia with him, as swiftly as he could, to Strelsau, and there proclaim Black Michael's treachery and the probable death of the King, and rally all that there was honest and true round the banner of the princess. And, to say truth, this was what I thought most likely to happen. For I had great doubts whether either the King or Black Michael or I had more than a day to live. Well, if Black Michael died, and if I, the play-actor, slew Rupert Hentzau with my own hand, and then died myself, it might be that Fate would deal as lightly with Ruritania as could be hoped, notwithstanding that she demanded the life of the King – and to her dealing thus with me, I was in no temper to make objection.

It was late when we rose from conference, and I betook me to the princess's apartments. She was pensive that evening; yet, when I left her, she flung her arms about me and grew, for an instant, bashfully radiant as she slipped a ring on my finger. I was wearing the King's ring; but I had also on my little finger a plain band of gold engraved with the motto of our family: '*Nil Quae Feci.*' This I took off and put on her, and signed to her to let me go. And she, understanding, stood away and watched me with dimmed eyes.

'Wear that ring, even though you wear another when you are queen,' I said.

'Whatever else I wear, this I will wear till I die and after,' said she, as she kissed the ring.

17

Young Rupert's Midnight Diversions

THE night came fine and clear. I had prayed for dirty weather, such as had favoured my previous voyage in the moat, but Fortune was this time against me. Still I reckoned that by keeping close under the wall and in the shadow I could escape detection from the windows of the *château* that looked out on the scene of my efforts. If they searched the moat, indeed, my scheme must fail; but I did not think they would. They had made 'Jacob's Ladder' secure against attack. Johann had himself helped to fix it closely to the masonry on the under side, so that it could not now be moved from below any more than from above. An assault with explosives or a long battering with picks alone could displace it, and the noise involved in either of these operations put them out of the question. What harm, then, could a man do in the moat? I trusted that Black Michael, putting this query to himself, would answer confidently, 'None'; while, even if Johann meant treachery, he did not know my scheme, and would doubtless expect to see me, at the head of my friends, before the front entrance to the *château*. There, I said to Sapt, was the real danger.

'And there,' I added, 'you shall be. Doesn't that content you?'

But it did not. Dearly would he have liked to come with me, had I not utterly refused to take him. One man might escape notice, to double the party more than doubled the risk; and when he ventured to hint once again that my life was too valuable, I, knowing the secret thought he clung to, sternly bade him be silent, assuring him that unless the King lived through the night, I would not live through it either.

At twelve o'clock, Sapt's command left the *château* of Tarlenheim and struck off to the right, riding by unfrequented roads, and avoiding the town of Zenda. If all went well, they would be in front of the Castle by about a quarter to two. Leaving their horses half a mile off, they were to steal up to the entrance and hold themselves in readiness for the opening of the door. If the door were not opened by two, they were to send Fritz von Tarlenheim round to the other side of the Castle. I would meet him there if I were alive, and we would consult whether to storm the Castle or not. If I were not there, they were to return with all speed to Tarlenheim, rouse the Marshal, and march in force to Zenda. For if not there, I should be dead; and I knew that the King would not be alive five minutes after I had ceased to breathe.

I must now leave Sapt and his friends, and relate how I myself proceeded on this eventful night. I went out on the good horse which had carried me, on the night of the coronation, back from the hunting-lodge to Strelsau. I carried a revolver in the saddle and my sword. I was covered with a large cloak, and under this I wore a warm, tight-fitting woollen jersey, a pair of knickerbockers, thick stockings, and light canvas shoes. I had rubbed myself thoroughly with oil, and I carried a large flask of whisky. The night was warm, but I might probably be immersed a long while, and it was necessary to take every precaution against cold: for cold not only saps a man's courage if he has to die, but impairs his energy if others have to die, and, finally, gives him rheumatics, if it be God's will that he lives. Also I tied round my body a length of thin but stout cord, and I did not forget my ladder. I, starting after Sapt, took a shorter route, skirting the town to the left, and found myself in the outskirts of the forest at about half past twelve. I tied my horse up in a thick clump of trees, leaving the revolver in its pocket in the saddle – it would be no use to me, – and, ladder in hand, made my way to the edge of the moat. Here I unwound my rope from about my waist, bound it securely round the trunk of a tree on the bank, and let myself down. The Castle clock struck a quarter to one as I felt the water under me and began to swim round the keep, pushing the ladder before me, and hugging the Castle wall. Thus voyaging, I came to my old friend, 'Jacob's Ladder,' and felt the ledge of the masonry under me. I crouched down in the shadow of the great pipe – I tried to stir it, but it was quite immovable – and waited. I remember that my predominant feeling was, neither anxiety for the King nor longing for Flavia, but an intense desire to smoke; and this craving, of course, I could not gratify.

The drawbridge was still in its place. I saw its airy, slight framework above me, some ten yards to my right, as I crouched with my back against the wall of the King's cell. I made out a window two yards my side of it and nearly on the same level. That, if Johann spoke true, must belong to the duke's apartments; and on the other side, in about the same relative position, must be Madame de Mauban's window. Women are careless, forgetful creatures. I prayed that she might not forget that she was to be the victim of a brutal attempt at two o'clock precisely. I was rather amused at the part I had assigned to my young friend Rupert Hentzau; but I owed him a stroke, – for, even as I sat, my shoulder ached where he had, with an audacity that seemed half to hide his treachery, struck at me, in the sight of all my friends, on the terrace at Tarlenheim.

Suddenly the duke's window grew bright. The shutters were not closed, and the interior became partially visible to me as I cautiously raised myself till I stood on tiptoe. Thus placed, my range of sight embraced a yard or more inside the window, while the radius of light did not reach me. The window was flung open and someone looked out. I marked Antoinette de Mauban's graceful figure, and, though her face was in shadow, the fine outline of her head was revealed against the light behind. I longed to cry softly, 'Remember!' but I dared not – and happily, for a moment later a man came up and stood by her. He tried to put his arm round her waist, but with a swift motion she sprang away and leant against the shutter, her profile towards me. I made out who the new-comer was: it was young Rupert. A low laugh from him made me sure, as he leant forward, stretching out his hand towards her.

'Gently, gently!' I murmured. 'You're too soon, my boy!'

His head was close to hers. I suppose he whispered to her, for I saw her point to the moat, and I heard her say, in slow and distinct tones:

'I had rather throw myself out of this window!'

He came close up to the window and looked out.

'It looks cold,' said he. 'Come, Antoinette, are you serious?'

She made no answer so far as I heard; and he smiting his hand petulantly on the window-sill, went on, in the voice of some spoilt child:

'Hang Black Michael! Isn't the princess enough for him? Is he to have everything? What the devil do you see in Black Michael?'

'If I told him what you say –' she began.

'Well, tell him,' said Rupert, carelessly; and, catching her off her guard, he sprang forward and kissed her, laughing, and crying, 'There's something to tell him!'

If I had kept my revolver with me, I should have been very sorely tempted. Being spared the temptation, I merely added this new score to his account.

'Though, faith,' said Rupert, 'it's little he cares. He's mad about the princess, you know. He talks of nothing but cutting the play-actor's throat.'

Didn't he, indeed?

'And if I do it for him, what do you think he's promised me?'

The unhappy woman raised her hands above her head, in prayer or in despair.

'But I detest waiting,' said Rupert; and I saw that he was about to lay his hand on her again, when there was a noise of a door in the room opening, and a harsh voice cried:

'What are you doing here, sir?'

Rupert turned his back to the window, bowed low, and said, in his loud, merry tones:

'Apologising for your absence, sir. Could I leave the lady alone?'

The new-comer must be Black Michael. I saw him directly, as he advanced towards the window. He caught young Rupert by the arm.

'The moat would hold more than the King!' said he, with a significant gesture.

'Does your Highness threaten me?' asked Rupert.

'A threat is more warning than most men get from me.'

'Yet,' observed Rupert, 'Rudolf Rassendyll has been much threatened, and yet lives!'

'Am I in fault because my servants bungle?' asked Michael scornfully.

'Your Highness has run no risk of bungling!' sneered Rupert.

It was telling the duke that he shirked danger as plain as ever I have heard a man told. Black Michael had self-control. I daresay he scowled – it was a great regret to me that I could not see their faces better, – but his voice was even and calm, as he answered:

'Enough, enough! We mustn't quarrel, Rupert. Are Detchard and Bersonin at their posts?'

'They are, sir.'

'I need you no more.'

'Nay, I'm not oppressed with fatigue,' said Rupert.

'Pray, sir, leave us,' said Michael, more impatiently. 'In ten minutes the drawbridge will be drawn back, and I presume you have no wish to swim to your bed.'

Rupert's figure disappeared. I heard the door open and shut again. Michael and Antoinette de Mauban were left together. To my chagrin, the duke laid his hand on the window and closed it. He stood talking to Antoinette for a moment or two. She shook her head, and he turned impatiently away. She left the window. The door sounded again, and Black Michael closed the shutters.

'De Gautet, De Gautet, man!' sounded from the drawbridge. 'Unless you want a bath before your bed, come along!'

It was Rupert's voice, coming from the end of the drawbridge. A moment later he and De Gautet stepped out on the bridge. Rupert's arm was through De Gautet's, and in the middle of the bridge he detained his companion and leant over. I dropped behind the shelter of 'Jacob's Ladder.'

Then Master Rupert had a little sport. He took from De Gautet a bottle which he carried, and put it to his lips.

'Hardly a drop!' he cried discontentedly, and flung it in the moat.

It fell, as I judged from the sound and the circles on the water, within a yard of the pipe. And Rupert, taking out his revolver, began to shoot at it. The first two shots missed the bottle, but hit the pipe. The third shattered the bottle. I hoped that the young ruffian would be content; but he emptied the other barrels at the pipe, and one, skimming over the pipe, whistled through my hair as I crouched on the other side.

''Ware bridge!' a voice cried, to my relief.

Rupert and De Gautet cried, 'A moment!' and ran across. The bridge was drawn back, and all became still. The clock struck a quarter-past one. I rose and stretched myself and yawned.

I think some ten minutes had passed when I heard a slight noise to my right. I peered over the pipe, and saw a dark figure standing in the gateway that led to the bridge. It was a man. By the careless, graceful poise, I guessed it to be Rupert again. He held a sword in his hand, and he stood motionless for a minute or two. Wild thoughts ran through me. On what mischief was the young fiend bent now? Then he laughed low to himself; then he turned his face to the wall, took a step in my direction, and, to my surprise, began to climb down the wall. In an instant I saw that there must be steps in the wall; it was plain. They were cut into or affixed to the wall, at intervals of about eighteen inches. Rupert set his foot on the lower one. Then he placed his sword between his teeth, turned round, and noiselessly let himself down into the water. Had it been a matter of my life only, I would have swum to meet him. Dearly would I have loved to fight it out with him then and there – with steel, on a fine night, and none to come between us. But there was the King! I restrained myself, but I could not bridle my swift breathing, and I watched him with the intensest eagerness.

He swam leisurely and quietly across. There were more steps up on the other side, and he climbed them. When he set foot in the gateway, standing on the drawn-back bridge, he felt in his pocket and took something out. I heard him unlock the door. I could hear no noise of its closing behind him. He vanished from my sight.

Abandoning my ladder – I saw I did not need it now, – I swam to the side of the bridge and climbed halfway up the steps. There I hung with my sword in my hand, listening eagerly. The duke's room was shuttered and dark. There was a light in the window on the opposite side of the bridge. Not a sound broke the silence, till half-past one chimed from the great clock in the tower of the *château*.

There were other plots than mine afoot in the Castle that night.

18

The Forcing of the Trap

THE position wherein I stood does not appear very favourable to thought; yet for the next moment or two I thought profoundly. I had, I told myself, scored one point. Be Rupert Hentzau's errand what it might, and the villainy he was engaged on what it would, I had scored one point. He was on the other side of the moat from the King, and it would be by no fault of mine if ever he set foot on the same side again. I had three left to deal with: two on guard and De Gautet in his bed. Ah, if I had the keys! I would have risked everything and attacked Detchard and Bersonin before their friends could join them. But I was powerless. I must wait till the coming of my friends enticed someone to cross the bridge – someone with the keys. And I waited, as it seemed, for half an hour, really for about five minutes, before the next act in the rapid drama began.

All was still on the other side. The duke's room remained inscrutable behind its shutters. The light burnt steadily in Madame de Mauban's window. Then I heard the faintest, faintest sound: it came from behind the door which led to the drawbridge on the other side of the moat. It but just reached my ear, yet I could not be mistaken as to what it was. It was made by a key being turned very carefully and slowly. Who was turning it? And of what room was it the key? There leapt before my eyes the picture of young Rupert, with the key in one hand, his sword in the other, and an evil smile on his face. But I did not know what door it was, nor on which of his favourite pursuits young Rupert was spending the hours of that night.

I was soon to be enlightened, for the next moment – before my friends could be near the *château* door – before Johann the keeper would have thought to nerve himself for his task – there was a sudden crash from the room with the lighted window. It sounded as though someone had flung down a lamp; and the window went dark and black. At the same instant a cry rang out, shrill in the night: 'Help, help! Michael, help!' and was followed by a shriek of utter terror.

I was tingling in every nerve. I stood on the top most step, clinging to the threshold of the gate with my right hand and holding my sword in my left. Suddenly I perceived that the gateway was broader than the bridge; there was a dark corner on the opposite side where a man could stand. I darted across and stood there. Thus placed, I commanded the path, and no man could pass between the *château* and the old Castle till he had tried conclusions with me.

There was another shriek. Then a door was flung open and clanged against the wall, and I heard the handle of a door savagely twisted.

'Open the door! In God's name, what's the matter?' cried a voice – the voice of Black Michael himself.

He was answered by the very words I had written in my letter.

'Help, Michael – Hentzau!'

A fierce oath rang out from the duke, and with a loud thud he threw himself against the door. At the same moment I heard a window above my head open, and a voice cried: 'What's the matter?' and I heard a man's hasty footsteps. I grasped my sword. If De Gautet came my way, the Six would be less by one more.

Then I heard the clash of crossed swords and a tramp of feet, and – I cannot tell the thing so quickly as it happened, for all seemed to come at once. There was an angry cry from madame's room, the cry of a wounded man; the window was flung open; young Rupert stood there sword in hand. He turned his back, and I saw his body go forward to the lunge.

'Ah, Johann, there's one for you! Come on, Michael!'

Johann was there, then – come to the rescue of the duke! How would he open the door for me? For I feared that Rupert had slain him.

'Help!' cried the duke's voice, faint and husky.

I heard a step on the stairs above me; and I heard a stir down to my left, in the direction of the King's cell. But, before anything happened on my side of the moat, I saw five or six men round young Rupert in the embrasure of madame's window. Three or four times he lunged with incomparable dash and dexterity. For an instant they fell back, leaving a ring round him. He leapt on the parapet of the window, laughing as he leapt, and waving his sword in his hand. He was drunk with blood, and he laughed again wildly as he flung himself headlong into the moat.

What became of him then? I did not see: for as he leapt, De Gautet's lean face looked out through the door by me, and, without a second's hesitation, I struck at him with all the strength God had given me, and he fell dead in the doorway without a word or a groan. I dropped on my knees by him. Where were the keys? I found myself muttering: 'The keys, man, the keys?' as though he had been yet alive and could listen; and when I could not find them, I – God forgive me! – I believe I struck a dead man's face.

At last I had them. There were but three. Seizing the largest, I felt the lock of the door that led to the cell. I fitted in the key. It was right. The lock turned. I drew the door close behind me and locked it as noiselessly as I could, putting the key in my pocket.

I found myself at the top of a flight of steep stone stairs. An oil-lamp burnt dimly in the bracket. I took it down and held it in my hand; and I stood and listened.

'What in the devil can it be?' I heard a voices say.

It came from behind a door that faced me at the bottom of the stairs.

And another answered:

'Shall we kill him?'

I strained to hear the answer, and could have sobbed with relief when Detchard's voice came grating and cold:

'Wait a bit. There'll be trouble if we strike too soon.'

There was a moment's silence. Then I heard the bolt of the door cautiously drawn back. Instantly I put out the light I held, replacing the lamp in the bracket.

'It's dark – the lamp's out. Have you a light?' said the other voice – Bersonin's.

No doubt they had a light, but they should not use it. It was come to the crisis now, and I rushed down the steps and flung myself against the door. Bersonin had unbolted it and it gave way before me. The Belgian stood there sword in hand, and Detchard was sitting on a couch at the side of the room. In astonishment at seeing me, Bersonin recoiled; Detchard jumped to his sword. I rushed madly at the Belgian: he gave way before me, and I drove him up against the wall. He was no swords man, though he fought bravely, and in a moment he lay on the floor before me. I turned – Detchard was not there. Faithful to his orders, he had not risked a fight with me, but had rushed straight to the door of the King's room, opened it and slammed it behind him. Even now he was at his work inside.

And surely he would have killed the King, and perhaps me also, had it not been for one devoted man who gave his life for the King. For when I forced the door, the sight I saw was this: the King stood in the corner of the room: broken by his sickness, he could do nothing; his fettered hands moved uselessly up and down, and he was laughing horribly in half-mad delirium. Detchard and the doctor were together in the middle of the room; and the doctor had flung himself on the murderer, pinning his hands to his sides for an instant. Then Detchard wrenched himself free from the feeble grip, and, as I entered, drove his sword through the hapless man.

Then he turned on me, crying:

'At last!'

We were sword to sword. By blessed chance, neither he nor Bersonin had been wearing their revolvers. I found them afterwards, ready loaded, on the mantelpiece of the outer room: it was hard by the door, ready to their hands, but my sudden rush in had cut off access to them. Yes, we were man to man: and we began to fight, silently, sternly, and hard. Yet I remember little of it, save that the man was my match with the sword – nay, and more, for he knew more tricks than I; and that he forced me back against the bars that guarded the entrance to 'Jacob's Ladder.' And I saw a smile on his face, and he wounded me in the left arm.

No glory do I take for that contest. I believe that the man would have mastered me and slain me, and then done his butcher's work, for he was the most skilful swordsman I have ever met; but even as he pressed me hard, the half-mad, wasted, wan creature in the corner leapt high in lunatic mirth, shrieking:

'It's cousin Rudolf! Cousin Rudolf! I'll help you, cousin Rudolf!' and catching up a chair in his hands (he could but just lift it from the ground and hold it uselessly before him) he came towards us. Hope came to me.

'Come on!' I cried. 'Come on! Drive it against his legs.'

Detchard replied with a savage thrust. He all but had me.

'Come on! Come on, man!' I cried. 'Come and share the fun!'

And the King laughed gleefully, and came on, pushing his chair before him.

With an oath Detchard skipped back, and, before I knew what he was doing, had turned his sword against the King. He made one fierce cut at the King, and the King, with a piteous cry, dropped where he stood. The stout ruffian turned to face me again. But his own hand had prepared his destruction: for in turning he trod in the pool of blood that flowed from the dead physician. He slipped; he fell. Like a dart I was upon him. I caught him by the throat, and before he could recover himself I drove my point though his neck, and with a stifled curse he fell across the body of his victim.

Was the King dead? It was my first thought. I rushed to where he lay. Ay, it seemed as if he were dead, for he had a great gash across his forehead, and he lay still in a huddled heap on the floor. I dropped on my knees beside him, and leant my ear down to hear if he breathed. But before I could there was a loud rattle from the outside. I knew the sound: the drawbridge was being pushed out. A moment later it rang home against the wall on my side of the moat. I should be caught in a trap and the King with me, if he yet lived. He must take his chance, to live or to die. I took my sword, and passed into the outer room. Who were pushing the drawbridge out – my men? If so, all was well. My eye fell on the revolvers, and I seized one; and paused to listen in the doorway of the outer room. To listen, say I? Yes, and to get my breath: and I tore my shirt and twisted a strip of it round my bleeding arm; and stood listening again. I would have given the world to hear Sapt's voice. For I was faint, spent, and weary. And that wild-cat Rupert Hentzau was yet at large in the Castle. Yet, because I could better defend the narrow door at the top of the stairs than the wider entrance to the room, I dragged myself up the steps, and stood behind it listening.

What was the sound? Again a strange one for the place and the time. An easy, scornful, merry laugh – the laugh of young Rupert Hentzau! I could scarcely believe that a sane man would laugh. Yet the laugh told me that my men had not come; for they must have shot Rupert ere now, if they had come. And the clock struck half-past two! My God! The door had not been opened! They had gone to the bank! They had not found me! They had gone by now back to Tarlenheim, with the news of the King's death – and mine. Well, it would be true before they got there. Was not Rupert laughing in triumph?

For a moment I sank, unnerved, against the door. Then I started up alert again, for Rupert cried scornfully:

'Well, the bridge is there! Come over it! And in God's name, let's see Black Michael. Keep back, you curs! Michael, come and fight for her!'

If it were a three-cornered fight, I might yet bear my part. I turned the key in the door and looked out.

19

Face to Face in the Forest

FOR a moment I could see nothing, for the glare of lanterns and torches caught me full in the eyes from the other side of the bridge. But soon the scene grew clear: and it was a strange scene. The bridge was in its place. At the far end of it stood a group of the duke's servants; two or three carried the lights which had dazzled me, three or four held pikes in rest. They were huddled together: their weapons were protruded before them; their faces were pale and agitated. To put it plainly, they looked in as arrant a fright as I have seen men look, and they gazed apprehensively at a man who stood in the middle of the bridge, sword in hand. Rupert Hentzau was in his trousers and shirt; the white linen was stained with blood, but his easy, buoyant pose told me that he was himself either not touched at all or merely scratched. There he stood, holding the bridge against them, and daring them to come on; or, rather, bidding them send Black Michael to him; and they, having no firearms, cowered before the desperate man and dared not attack him. They whispered to one another; and in the backmost rank, I saw my friend Johann, leaning against the portal of the door and stanching with a handkerchief the blood which flowed from a wound in his cheek.

By marvellous chance, I was master. The cravens would oppose me no more than they dared attack Rupert. I had but to raise my revolver, and I sent him to his account with his sins on his head. He did not so much as know that I was there. I did nothing – why, I hardly know to this day. I had killed one man stealthily that night, and another by luck rather than skill – perhaps it was that. Again, villain as the man was, I did not relish being one of a crowd against him – perhaps it was that. But stronger than either of these restrained feelings came a curiosity and a fascination which held me spellbound, watching for the outcome of the scene.

'Michael, you dog! Michael! If you can stand, come on!' cried Rupert; and he advanced a step, the group shrinking back a little before him. 'Michael, you bastard! Come on!'

The answer to his taunts came in the wild cry of a woman:

'He's dead! My God, he's dead!'

'Dead!' shouted Rupert. 'I struck better than I knew!' and he laughed triumphantly. Then he went on: 'Down with your weapons there! I'm your master now! Down with them, I say!'

I believe they would have obeyed, but as he spoke came new things. First, there arose a distant sound, as of shouts and knockings from the other side of the *château*. My heart leapt. It must be my men, come by a happy disobedience to seek me. The noise continued, but none of the rest seemed to heed it. Their attention was chained by what now happened before their eyes. The group of servants parted and a woman staggered on to the bridge. Antoinette de Mauban was in a loose white robe, her dark hair streamed over her shoulders, her face was ghastly pale, and her eyes gleamed wildly in the light of the torches. In her shaking hand she held a revolver, and, as she tottered forward, she fired it at Rupert Hentzau. The ball missed him, and struck the woodwork over my head.

'Faith, madame,' laughed Rupert, 'had your eyes been no more deadly than your shooting, I had not been in this scrape – nor Black Michael in hell – to-night!'

She took no notice of his words. With a wonderful effort, she calmed herself till she stood still and rigid. Then very slowly and deliberately she began to raise her arm again, taking most careful aim.

He would be mad to risk it. He must rush on her, chancing the bullet, or retreat towards me. I covered him with my weapon.

He did neither. Before she had got her aim, he bowed in his most graceful fashion, cried 'I can't kill where I've kissed,' and before she or I could stop him, laid his hand on the parapet of the bridge, and lightly leapt into the moat.

At that very moment I heard a rush of feet, and a voice I knew – Sapt's – cry: 'God! it's the duke – dead!' Then I knew that the King needed me no more, and, throwing down my revolver, I sprang out on the bridge. There was a cry of wild wonder, 'The King!' and then I, like Rupert Hentzau, sword in hand, vaulted over the parapet, intent on finishing my quarrel with him where I saw his curly head fifteen yards off in the water of the moat.

He swam swiftly and easily. I was weary and half-crippled with my wounded arm. I could not gain on him. For a time I made no sound, but as we rounded the corner of the old keep I cried:

'Stop, Rupert, stop!'

I saw him look over his shoulder, but he swam on. He was under the bank now, searching, as I guessed, for a spot that he could climb. I knew there to be none – but there was my rope, which would still be hanging where I had left it. He would come to where it was before I could. Perhaps he would miss it – perhaps he would find it; and if he drew it up after him, he would get a good start of me. I put forth all my remaining strength and pressed on. At last I began to gain on him; for he, occupied with his search, unconsciously slackened his pace.

Ah, he had found it! A low shout of triumph came from him. He laid hold of it and began to haul himself up. I was near enough to hear him mutter: 'How the devil comes this here?' I was at the rope, and he, hanging in mid-air, saw me, but I could not reach him.

'Hullo! who's here?' he cried in startled tones.

For a moment, I believe, he took me for the King – I daresay I was pale enough to lend colour to the thought; but an instant later he cried:

'Why it's the play-actor! How came you here, man?'

And so saying he gained the bank.

I laid hold of the rope, but I paused. He stood on the bank, sword in hand, and he could cut my head open or spit me through the heart as I came up. I let go the rope.

'Never mind,' said I; 'but as I am here, I think I'll stay.'

He smiled down on me.

'These women are the deuce – ' he began; when suddenly the great bell of the Castle started to ring furiously, and a loud shout reached us from the moat.

Rupert smiled again, and waved his hand to me.

'I should like a turn with you, but it's a little too hot!' said he, and he disappeared from above me.

In an instant, without thinking of danger, I laid my hand to the rope. I was up. I saw him thirty yards off, running like a deer towards the shelter of the forest. For once Rupert Hentzau had chosen discretion for his part. I laid my feet to the ground and rushed after him, calling to him to stand. He would not. Unwounded and vigorous, he gained on me at every step; but, forgetting everything in the world except him and my thirst for his blood, I pressed on, and soon the deep shades of the forest of Zenda engulfed us both, pursued and pursuer.

It was three o'clock now, and day was dawning. I was on a long straight grass avenue, and a hundred yards ahead ran young Rupert, his curls waving in the fresh breeze. I was weary and panting, he looked over his shoulder and waved his hand again to me. He was mocking me, for he saw he had the pace of me. I was forced to pause for breath. A moment later, Rupert turned sharply to the right and was lost from my sight.

I thought all was over, and in deep vexation sank on the ground. But I was up again directly, for a scream rang through the forest – a woman's scream. Putting forth the last of my strength, I ran on to the place where he had turned out of my sight, and, turning also, I saw him again. But alas! I could not touch him. He was in the act of lifting a girl down from her horse; doubtless it was her scream that I heard. She looked like a small farmer's or a peasant's daughter, and she carried a basket on her arm. Probably she was on her way to the early market at Zenda. Her horse was a stout, well shaped animal. Master Rupert lifted her down amid her shrieks – the sight of him frightened her; but he treated her gently, laughed, kissed her, and gave her money. Then he jumped on the horse, sitting sideways like a woman; and then he waited for me. I, on my part, waited for him.

Presently he rode towards me, keeping his distance, however. He lifted up his hand, saying:

'What did you in the Castle?'

'I killed three of your friends,' said I.

'What! You got to the cells?'

'Yes.'

'And the King?'

'He was hurt by Detchard before I killed Detchard, but I pray that he lives.'

'You fool!' said Rupert, pleasantly.

'One thing more I did.'

'And what's that?'

'I spared your life. I was behind you on the bridge, with a revolver in my hand.'

'No? Faith, I was between two fires!'

'Get off your horse,' I cried, 'and fight like a man.'

'Before a lady!' said he, pointing to the girl. 'Fie, your Majesty!'

Then in my rage, hardly knowing what I did, I rushed at him. For a moment he seemed to waver. Then he reined his horse in and stood waiting for me. On I went in my folly. I seized the bridle and I struck at him. He parried and thrust at me. I fell back a pace and rushed in at him again; and this time I reached his face and laid his cheek open, and darted back almost before he could strike me. He seemed almost mazed at the fierceness of my attack; otherwise I think he must have killed me. I sank on my knee panting, expecting him to ride at me. And so he would have done, and then and there, I doubt not, one or both of us would have died; but at the moment there came a shout from behind us, and, looking round, I saw, just at the turn of the avenue, a man on a horse. He was riding hard, and he carried a revolver in his hand. It was Fritz von Tarlenheim, my faithful friend. Rupert saw him, and knew that the game was up. He checked his rush at me and flung his leg over the saddle, but yet for just a moment he waited. Leaning forward, he tossed his hair off his forehead and smiled, and said:

'*Au revoir*, Rudolf Rassendyll!'

Then, with his cheek, streaming blood, but his lips laughing and his body swaying with ease and grace, he bowed to me; and he bowed to the farm-girl, who had drawn near in trembling fascination, and he waved his hand to Fritz, who was just within range and let fly a shot at him. The ball came nigh doing its work, for it struck the sword he held, and he dropped the sword with an oath, wringing his fingers and clapped his heels hard on his horse's belly, and rode away at a gallop.

And I watched him go down the long avenue, riding as though he rode for his pleasure and singing as he went, for all there was that gash in his cheek.

Once again he turned to wave his hand, and then the gloom of the thickets swallowed him and he was lost from our sight. Thus he vanished – reckless and wary, graceful and graceless, handsome, debonair, vile, and unconquered. And I flung my sword passionately on the ground and cried to Fritz to ride after him. But Fritz stopped his horse, and leapt down and ran to me, and knelt, putting his arm about me. And indeed it was time for the wound that Detchard had given me was broken forth afresh, and my blood was staining the ground.

'Then give me the horse!' I cried, staggering to my feet and throwing his arms off me. And the strength of my rage carried me so far as where the horse stood, and then I fell prone beside it. And Fritz knelt by me again.

'Fritz!' I said.

'Ay, friend – dear friend!' he said, tender as a woman.

'Is the King alive?'

He took his handkerchief and wiped my lips, and bent and kissed me on the forehead.

'Thanks to the most gallant gentleman that lives,' said he softly, 'the King is alive!'

The little farm-girl stood by us, weeping for fright and wide-eyed for wonder; for she had seen me at Zenda: and was not I, pallid, dripping, foul, and bloody as I was – yet was not I the King?

And when I heard that the King was alive, I strove to cry 'Hurrah!' But I could not speak, and I laid my head back in Fritz's arms and closed my eyes, and I groaned; and then, lest Fritz should do me wrong in his thoughts, I opened my eyes and tried to say 'Hurrah!' again. But I could not. And being very tired, and now very cold, I huddled myself close up to Fritz, to get the warmth of him, and shut my eyes again and went to sleep.

20

The Prisoner and the King

IN order to a full understanding of what had occurred in the Castle of Zenda, it is necessary to supplement my account of what I myself saw and did on that night by relating briefly what I afterwards learnt from Fritz and Madame de Mauban. The story told by the latter explained clearly how it happened that the cry which I had arranged as a stratagem and a sham had come, in dreadful reality, before its time, and had thus, as it seemed at the moment, ruined our hopes, while in the end it had favoured them. The unhappy woman, fired, I believe by a genuine attachment to the Duke of Strelsau, no less than by the dazzling prospects which a dominion over him opened before her eyes, had followed him at his request from Paris to Ruritania. He was a man of strong passions, but of stronger will, and his cool head ruled both. He was content to take all and give nothing. When she arrived, she was not long in finding that she had a rival in the Princess Flavia; rendered desperate, she stood at nothing which might give, or keep for her, her power over the duke. As I say, he took and gave not. Simultaneously, Antionette found herself entangled in his audacious schemes. Unwilling to abandon him, bound to him by the chains of shame and hope, yet she would not be a decoy, nor, at his bidding, lure me to death. Hence the letters of warning she had written. Whether the lines she sent to Flavia were inspired by good or bad feeling, by jealousy or by pity, I do not know; but here also she served us well. When the duke went to Zenda, she accompanied him; and here for the first time she learnt the full measure of his cruelty, and was touched with compassion for the unfortunate King. From this time she was with us; yet, from what she told me, I know that she still (as women will) loved Michael, and trusted to gain his life, if not his pardon, from the King, as the reward for her assistance. His triumph she did not desire, for she loathed his crime, and loathed yet more fiercely what would be the prize of it – his marriage with his cousin, Princess Flavia.

At Zenda new forces came into play – the lust and daring of young Rupert. He was caught by her beauty, perhaps; perhaps it was enough for him that she belonged to another man, and that she hated him. For many days there had been quarrels and ill-will between him and the duke, and the scene which I had witnessed in the duke's room was but one of many. Rupert's proposals to me, of which she had, of course, been ignorant, in no way surprised her when I related them; she had herself warned Michael against Rupert, even when she was calling on me to deliver her from both of them. On this night, then, Rupert had determined to have his will. When she had gone to her room, he, having furnished himself with a key to it, had made his entrance. Her cries had brought the duke, and there in the dark room, while she screamed, the men had fought; and Rupert, having wounded his master with a mortal blow, had, on the servants rushing in, escaped through the window as I have described. The duke's blood, spurting out, had stained his opponent's shirt; but Rupert, not knowing that he had dealt Michael his death, was eager to finish the encounter. How he meant to deal with the other three of the band, I know not. I daresay he did not think, for the killing of Michael was not premeditated. Antoinette, left along with the duke, had tried to stanch his wound, and thus was she busied till he died; and then, hearing Rupert's taunts, she had come forth to avenge him. Me she had not seen, nor did she till I darted out of my ambush, and leapt after Rupert into the moat.

The same moment found my friends on the scene. They had reached the *château* in due time, and waited ready by the door. But Johann, swept with the rest to the rescue of the duke, did not open it; nay, he took a part against Rupert, putting himself forward more bravely than any in his anxiety to avert suspicion; and he had received a wound, in the embrasure of the window. Till nearly half-past two Sapt waited; then, following my orders, he had sent Fritz to search the banks of the moat. I was not there. Hastening back, Fritz told Sapt; and Sapt was for following orders still, and riding at full speed back to Tarlenheim; while Fritz would not hear of abandoning me, let me have ordered what I would. On this they disputed some few minutes; then Sapt, persuaded by Fritz, detached a party under Bernenstein to gallop back to Tarlenheim and bring up the marshal, while the rest fell to on the great door of the *châtaeu*. For several minutes it resisted them; then, just as Antoinette de Mauban fired at Rupert Hentzau on the bridge, they broke in, eight of them in all: and the first door they came to was the door of Michael's room; and Michael lay dead across the threshold, with a sword-thrust through his breast. Sapt cried out at his death, as I had heard, and they rushed on the servants; but these, in fear, dropped their weapons, and Antoinette flung herself weeping at Sapt's feet. And all she cried was, that I had been at the end of the bridge and had leapt off. 'What of the prisoner?' asked Sapt; but she shook her head. Then Sapt and Fritz, with the gentlemen behind them, crossed the bridge, slowly, warily, and without noise; and Fritz stumbled over the body of De Gautet in the way of the door. The felt him and found him dead.

Then they consulted, listening eagerly for any sound from the cells below; but there came none, and they were greatly afraid that the King's guards had killed him, and having pushed his body through the great pipe, had escaped the same way themselves. Yet, because I had been seen here, they had still some hope (thus indeed Fritz, in his friendship, told me); and going back to Michael's body, pushing aside Antoinette, who prayed by it, they found a key to the door which I had locked, and opened the door. The staircase was dark, and they would not use a torch at first, lest they should be the more exposed to fire. But soon Fritz cried: 'The door down there is open! See, there is light! So they went on boldly, and found none to oppose them. And when they came to the outer room and saw the Belgian, Bersonin, lying dead, they thanked God, Sapt saying: 'Ay, he has been here.' Then rushing into the King's cell, they found Detchard lying dead across the dead physician, and the King on his back with his chair by him. And Fritz cried: 'He's dead!' and Sapt drove all out of the room except Fritz, and knelt down by the King; and, having learnt more of wounds and the sign of death than I, he soon knew that the King was not dead, nor, if properly attended, would die. And they covered his face and carried him to Duke Michael's room, and laid him there; and Antoinette rose from praying by the body of the duke and went to bathe the King's head and dress his wounds, till a doctor came. And Sapt, seeing

I had been there, and having heard Antoinette's story, sent Fritz to search the moat and then the forest. He dared send no one else. And Fritz found my horse, and feared the worst. Then, as I have told, he found me, guided by the shout with which I had called on Rupert to stop and face me. And I think a man has never been more glad to find his own brother alive than was Fritz to come on me; so that, in love and anxiety for me, he thought nothing of a thing so great as would have been the death of Rupert Hentzau. Yet, had Fritz killed him, I should have grudged it.

The enterprise of the King's rescue being thus prosperously concluded, it lay on Colonel Sapt to secure secrecy as to the King ever having been in need of rescue. Antoinette de Mauban and Johann the keeper (who, indeed, was too much hurt to be wagging his tongue just now) were sworn to reveal nothing; and Fritz went forth to find – not the King, but the unnamed friend of the King, who had lain in Zenda and flashed for a moment before the dazed eyes of Duke Michael's servants on the drawbridge. The metamorphosis had happened; and the King, wounded almost to death by the attacks of the gaolers who guarded his friend, had at last overcome them, and rested now, wounded but alive, in Black Michael's own room in the Castle. There he had been carried, his face covered with a cloak, from the cell; and thence orders issued, that if his friend were found, he should be brought directly and privately to the King, and that meanwhile messengers should ride at full speed to Tarlenheim, to tell Marshal Strakencz to assure the princess of the King's safety, and to come himself with all speed to greet the King. The princess was enjoined to remain at Tarlenheim, and there await her cousin's coming or his further injunctions. Thus the King would come to his own again, having wrought brave deeds, and escaped, almost by a miracle, the treacherous assault of his unnatural brother.

This ingenious arrangement of my long-headed old friend prospered in every way, save where it encountered a force that often defeats the most cunning schemes. I mean nothing else than the pleasure of a woman. For, let her cousin and sovereign send what command he chose (or Colonel Sapt chose for him), and let Marshal Strakencz insist as he would, the Princess Flavia was in no way minded to rest at Tarlenheim while her lover lay wounded at Zenda; and when the marshal, with a small *suite*, rode forth from Tarlenheim on the way to Zenda, the princess's carriage followed immediately behind, and in this order they passed through the town, where the report was already rife that the King, going the night before to remonstrate with his brother, in all friendliness, for that he held one of the King's friends in confinement in the Castle, had been most traitorously set upon; that there had been a desperate conflict; that the duke was slain with several of his gentlemen; and that the King, wounded as he was, had seized and held the Castle of Zenda. All of which talk made, as may be supposed, a mighty excitement: and the wires were set in motion, and the tidings came to Strelsau only just after orders had been sent thither to parade the troops and overawe the dissatisfied quarters of the town with a display of force.

Thus the Princess Flavia came to Zenda. And as she drove up the hill, with the marshal riding by the wheel and still imploring her to return in obedience to the King's orders, Fritz von Tarlenheim, with the prisoner of Zenda, came to the edge of the forest. I had revived from my swoon, and walked, resting on Fritz's arm; and looking out from the cover of the trees, I saw the princess. Suddenly understanding from a glance at my companion's face that we must not meet her, I sank on my knees behind a clump of bushes. But there was one whom we had forgotten, but who followed us, and was not disposed to let slip the chance of earning a smile and maybe a crown or two; and, while we lay hidden, the little farm-girl came by us and ran to the princess, curtseying and crying:

'Madame, the King is here – in the bushes! May I guide you to him, madame?'

'Nonsense, child!' said old Strakencz; 'the King lies wounded in the Castle.'

'Yes, sir, he's wounded, I know; but he's there – with Count Fritz – and not at the Castle,' she persisted.

'Is he in two places, or are there two Kings?' asked Flavia, bewildered. 'And how should he be here?'

'He pursued a gentleman, madame, and they fought till Count Fritz came; and the other gentleman took my father's horse from me and rode away; but the King is here with Count Fritz. Why, madame, is there another man in Ruritania like the King?'

'No, my child,' said Flavia softly (I was told it afterwards), and she smiled and gave the girl money. 'I will go and see this gentleman,' and she rose to alight from the carriage.

But at this moment Sapt came riding from the Castle, and, seeing the princess, made the best of a bad job, and cried to her that the King was well tended and in no danger.

'In the Castle?' she asked.

'Where else, madame?' said he, bowing.

'But this girl says he is yonder – with Count Fritz.'

Sapt turned his eyes on the child with an incredulous smile.

'Every fine gentleman is a King to such,' said he.

'Why, he's as like the King as one pea to another, madame!' cried the girl, a little shaken but still obstinate.

Sapt started round. The old marshal's face asked unspoken questions. Flavia's glance was no less eloquent. Suspicion spreads quick.

'I'll ride myself and see this man,' said Sapt, hastily.

'Nay, I'll come myself,' said the princess.

'Then come alone,' he whispered.

And she, obedient to the strange hinting in his face, prayed the marshal and the rest to wait; and she and Sapt came on foot towards where we lay, Sapt waving to the farm-girl to keep at a distance. And when I saw them coming, I sat in a sad heap on the ground, and buried my face in my hands. I could not look at her. Fritz knelt by me, laying his hand on my shoulder.

'Speak low, whatever you say,' I heard Sapt whisper as they came up; and the next thing I heard was a low cry – half of joy, half of fear – from the princess:

'It is he! Are you hurt?'

And she fell on the ground by me, and gently pulled my hands away; but I kept my eyes to the ground.

'It is the King!' she said. 'Pray, Colonel Sapt, tell me where lay the wit of the joke you played on me?'

We answered none of us: we three were silent before her. Regardless of them, she threw her arms round my neck and kissed me. Then Sapt spoke in a low hoarse whisper:

'It is not the King. Don't kiss him; he's not the King.'

She drew back for a moment; then, with an arm still round my neck, she asked, in superb indignation:

'Do I not know my love? Rudolf, my love!'

'It is not the King,' said old Sapt again; and a sudden sob broke from tender-hearted Fritz.

It was the sob that told her no comedy was afoot.

'He is the King!' she cried. 'It is the King's face – the King's ring – my ring! It is my love!'

'Your love, madame,' said old Sapt, 'but not the King. The King is there in the Castle. This gentleman – '

'Look at me, Rudolf! look at me!' she cried, taking my face between her hands. 'Why do you let them torment me? Tell me what it means!'

Then I spoke, gazing into her eyes.

'God forgive me, madame!' I said. 'I am not the King!'

I felt her hands clutch my cheeks. She gazed at me as never man's face was scanned yet. And I, silent again, saw wonder born, and doubt grow, and terror spring to life as she looked. And very gradually the grasp of her hands slackened: she turned to Sapt, to Fritz, and back to me: then suddenly she reeled forward and fell in my arms; and with a great cry of pain I gathered her to me and kissed her lips. Sapt laid his hand on my arm. I looked up in his face. And I laid her softly on the ground, and stood up, looking on her, cursing heaven that young Rupert's sword had spared me for this sharper pang.

21

If Love were All!

IT was night, and I was in the cell wherein the King had lain in the Castle of Zenda. The great pipe that Rupert of Hentzau had nicknamed 'Jacob's Ladder' was gone, and the lights in the room across the moat twinkled in the darkness. All was still; the din and clash of strife were gone. I had spent the day hidden in the forest, from the time when Fritz had led me off, leaving Sapt with the princess. Under cover of dusk, muffled up, I had been brought to the Castle and lodged where I now lay. Though three men had died there – two of them by my hand – I was not troubled by ghosts. I had thrown myself on a pallet by the window, and was looking out on the black water; Johann, the keeper, still pale from his wound, but not much hurt besides, had brought me supper. He told me that the King was doing well, that he had seen the princess; that she and he, Sapt and Fritz, had been long together. Marshal Strakencz was gone to Strelsau; Black Michael lay in his coffin, and Antoinette de Mauban watched by him; had I not heard, from the chapel, priests singing mass for him?

Outside there were strange rumours afloat. Some said that the prisoner of Zenda was dead; some, that he had vanished yet alive; some, that he was a friend who had served the King well in some adventure in England; others, that he had discovered the duke's plots, and had therefore been kidnapped by him. One or two shrewd fellows shook their heads and said only that they would say nothing, but they had suspicions that more was to be known than was known, if Colonel Sapt would tell all he knew.

Thus Johann chattered till I sent him away and lay there alone, thinking, not of the future, but – as a man is wont to do when stirring things have happened to him – rehearsing the events of the past weeks, and wondering how strangely they had fallen out. And above me, in the stillness of the night, I heard the standards flapping against their poles, for Black Michael's banner hung there half-mast high, and above it the royal flag of Ruritania, floating for one night more over my head. Habit grows so quick, that only by an effort did I recollect that it floated no longer for me.

Presently Fritz von Tarlenheim came into the room. I was standing then by the window; the glass was opened, and I was idly fingering the cement which clung to the masonry where 'Jacob's Ladder' had been. He told me briefly that the King wanted me, and together we crossed the drawbridge and entered the room that had been Black Michael's.

The King was lying there in bed; our doctor from Tarlenheim was in attendance on him, and whispered to me that my visit must be brief. The King held out his hand and shook mine. Fritz and the doctor withdrew to the window.

I took the King's ring from my finger and placed it on his.

'I have tried not to dishonour it, sire,' said I.

'I can't talk much to you,' he said, in a weak voice. 'I have had a great fight with Sapt and the marshal – for we have told the marshal everything. I wanted to take you to Strelsau and keep you with me, and tell everyone of what you had done; and you would have been my best and nearest friend, Cousin Rudolf. But they tell me I must not, and that the secret must be kept – if kept it can be.'

'They are right, sire. Let me go. My work here is done.'

'Yes, it is done, as no man but you could have done it. When they see me again, I shall have my beard on; I shall – yes, faith, I shall be wasted with sickness. They will not wonder that the King looks changed in face. Cousin, I shall try to let them find him changed in nothing else. You have shown me how to play the King.'

'Sire,' said I, 'I can take no praise from you. It is by the narrowest grace of God that I was not a worse traitor than your brother.'

He turned inquiring eyes on me; but a sick man shrinks from puzzles, and he had no strength to question me. His glance fell on Flavia's ring, which I wore. I thought he would question me about it; but, after fingering it idly, he let his head fall on his pillow.

'I don't know when I shall see you again,' he said faintly, almost listlessly.

'If I can ever serve you again, sire,' I answered.

His eyelids closed. Fritz came with the doctor. I kissed the King's hand, and let Fritz lead me away. I have never seen the King since.

Outside, Fritz turned, not to the right, back towards the drawbridge, but to the left, and without speaking led me upstairs, through a handsome corridor in the *château*.

'Where are we going?' I asked.

Looking away from me, Fritz answered:

'She has sent for you. When it is over, come back to the bridge. I'll wait for you there.'

'What does she want?' said I, breathing quickly.

He shook his head.

'Does she know everything?'

'Yes, everything.

He opened a door, and gently pushing me in, closed it behind me. I found myself in a drawing-room, small and richly furnished. At first I thought that I was alone, for the light that came from a pair of shaded candles on the mantelpiece was very dim. But presently I discerned a woman's figure standing by the window. I knew it was the princess, and I walked up to her, fell on one knee, and carried the hand that hung by her side to my lips. She neither moved nor spoke. I rose to my feet, and, piercing the gloom with my eager eyes, saw her pale face and the gleam of her hair, and before I knew, I spoke softly:

'Flavia!'

She trembled a little, and looked round. Then she darted to me, taking hold of me.

'Don't stand, don't stand! No, you mustn't! You're hurt! Sit down – here, here!'

She made me sit on a sofa, and put her hand on my forehead.

'How hot your head is,' she said, sinking on her knees by me. Then she laid her head against me, and I heard her murmur: 'My darling, how hot your head is!'

Somehow love gives even to a dull man the knowledge of his lover's heart. I had come to humble myself and pray pardon for my presumption; but what I said now was:

'I love you with all my heart and soul!'

For what troubled and shamed her? Not her love for me, but the fear that I had counterfeited the lover as I had acted the King, and taken her kisses with a smothered smile.

'With all my life and heart,' said I, as she clung to me. 'Always, from the first moment I saw you in the Cathedral! There has been but one woman in the world to me – and there will be no other. But God forgive me the wrong I've done you!'

'They made you do it!' she said quickly; and she added, raising her head and looking in my eyes; 'It might have made no difference if I'd known it. It was always you, never the King!'

'I meant to tell you,' said I. 'I was going to on the night of the ball in Strelsau, when Sapt interrupted me. After that, I couldn't – I couldn't risk losing you before – before – I must! My darling, for you I nearly left the King to die!'

'I know, I know! What are we to do now, Rudolf?'

I put my arm round her and held her up while I said:

'I am going away to-night.'

'Ah, no, no!' she cried. 'Not to-night!'

'I must go to-night, before more people have seen me. And how would you have me stay, sweetheart, except –?'

'If I could come with you!' she whispered very low.

'My God!' said I roughly, 'don't talk about that!' and I thrust her a little back from me.

'Why not? I love you. You are as good a gentleman as the King!'

Then I was false to all that I should have held by. For I caught her in my arms and prayed her, in words that I will not write, to come with me, daring all Ruritania to take her from me. And for a while she listened, with wondering, dazzled eyes. But as her eyes looked on me, I grew ashamed, and my voice died away in broken murmurs and stammerings, and at last I was silent.

She drew herself away from me and stood against the wall, while I sat on the edge of the sofa, trembling in every limb, knowing what I had done – loathing it, obstinate not to undo it. So we rested a long time.

'I am mad!' I said sullenly.

'I love your madness, dear,' she answered.

Her face was away from me, but I caught the sparkle of a tear on her cheek. I clutched the sofa with my hand and held myself there.

'Is love the only thing?' she asked, in low, sweet tones that seemed to bring a calm even to my wrung heart. 'If love were the only thing, I would follow you – in rags, if need be – to the world's end; for you hold my heart in the hollow of your hand! But is love the only thing?'

I made no answer. It gives me shame now to think that I would not help her.

She came near me and laid her hand on my shoulder. I put my hand up and held hers.

'I know people write and talk as if it were. Perhaps, for some, Fate lets it be. Ah, if I were one of them! But if love had been the only thing, you would have let the King die in his cell.'

I kissed her hand.

'Honour binds a woman too, Rudolf. My honour lies in being true to my country and my House. I don't know why God has let me love you; but I know that I must stay.'

Still I said nothing; and she, pausing a while, then went on:

'Your ring will always be on my finger, your heart in my heart, the touch of your lips on mine. But you must go and I must stay. Perhaps I must do what it kills me to think of doing.'

I knew what she meant, and a shiver ran through me. But I could not utterly fail beside her. I rose and took her hand.

'Do what you will, or what you must,' I said. 'I think God shows His purposes to such as you. My part is lighter; for your ring shall be on my finger and your heart in mine, and no touch save of your lips will ever be on mine. So, may God comfort you, my darling!'

There struck on our ears the sound of singing. The priests in the chapel were singing masses for the souls of those who lay dead. They seemed to chant a requiem over our buried joy, to pray forgiveness for our love that would not die. The soft, sweet, pitiful music rose and fell as we stood opposite one another, her hands in mine.

'My queen and my beauty!' said I.

'My lover and true knight!' she said. 'Perhaps we shall never see one another again. Kiss me, my dear, and go!'

I kissed her as she bade me; but at the last she clung to me, whispering nothing but my name, and that over and over again – and again – and again; and then I left her.

Rapidly I walked down to the bridge. Sapt and Fritz were waiting for me. Under their directions I changed my dress, and muffling my face, as I had done more than once before, I mounted with them at the door of the Castle, and we three rode through the night and on to the breaking day, and found ourselves at a little roadside station just over the border of Ruritania. The train was not quite due, and I walked with them in a meadow by a little brook while we waited for it. They promised to send me all news; they overwhelmed me with kindness – even old Sapt was touched to gentleness, while Fritz was half-unmanned. I listened in a kind of dream to all they said. 'Rudolf! Rudolf! Rudolf!' still rang in my ears – a burden of sorrow and of love. At last they saw that I could not heed them, and we walked up and down in silence, till Fritz touched me on the arm, and I saw, a mile or more away, the blue smoke of the train. Then I held out a hand to each of them.

'We are all but half-men this morning,' said I, smiling. 'But we have been men, eh, Sapt and Fritz, old friends? We have run a good course between us.'

'We have defeated traitors and set the King firm on his throne,' said Sapt.

Then Fritz von Tarlenheim suddenly, before I could discern his purpose or stay him, uncovered his head and bent as he used to do, and kissed my hand; and, as I snatched it away, he said, trying to laugh:

'Heaven doesn't always make the right men kings!'

Old Sapt twisted his mouth as he wrung my hand.

'The devil has his share in most things,' said he.

The people at the station looked curiously at the tall man with the muffled face, but we took no notice of their glances. I stood with my two friends and waited till the train came up to us. Then we shook hands again, saying nothing; and both this time – and, indeed, from old Sapt it seemed strange – bared their heads, and so stood still till the train bore me away from their sight. So that it was thought some great man travelled privately for his pleasure from the little station that morning; whereas, in truth, it was only I, Rudolf Rassendyll, an English gentleman, a cadet of a good house, but a man of no wealth nor position, nor of much rank. They would have been disappointed to know that. Yet had they known all they would have looked more curiously still. For, be I what I might now, I had been for three months a King, which, if not a thing to be proud of, is at least an experience to have undergone. Doubtless I should have thought more of it, had there not echoed through the air, from the towers of Zenda that we were leaving far away, into my ears and into my heart the cry of a woman's love – 'Rudolf! Rudolf! Rudolf!'

Hark! I hear it now!

22

Present, Past – and Future?

THE details of my return home can have but little interest. I went straight to the Tyrol and spent a quiet fortnight – mostly on my back, for a severe chill developed itself; and I was also the victim of a nervous reaction, which made me weak as a baby. As soon as I had reached my quarters, I sent an apparently careless postcard to my brother, announcing my good health and prospective return. That would serve to satisfy the inquiries as to my whereabouts, which were probably still vexing the Prefect of the Police of Strelsau. I let my moustache and imperial grow again; and as hair comes quickly on my face, they were respectable, though not luxuriant, by the time that I landed myself in Paris and called on my friend George Featherly. My interview with him was chiefly remarkable for the number of unwilling but necessary falsehoods that I told; and I rallied him unmercifully when he told me that he had made up his mind that I had gone in the track of Madame de Mauban to Strelsau. The lady, it appeared, was back in Paris, but was living in great seclusion – a fact for which gossip found no difficulty in accounting. Did not all the world know of the treachery and death of Duke Michael? Nevertheless, George bade Bertram Bertrand be of good cheer, 'for,' said he flippantly, 'a live poet is better than a dead duke.' Then he turned on me and asked:

'What have you been doing to your moustache?'

'To tell the truth,' I answered, assuming a sly air, 'a man now and then has reasons for wishing to alter his appearance. But it's coming on very well again.'

'What? Then I wasn't so far out! If not the fair Antoinette, there was a charmer?'

'There is always a charmer,' said I, sententiously.

But George would not be satisfied till he had wormed out of me (he took much pride in his ingenuity) an absolutely imaginary love-affair, attended with the proper *soupçon* of scandal, which had kept me all this time in the peaceful regions of the Tyrol. In return for this narrative, George regaled me with a great deal of what he called 'inside information' (known only to diplomatists), as to the true course of events in Ruritania, the plots and counter-plots. In his opinion, he told me, with a significant nod, there was more to be said for Black Michael than the public supposed; and he hinted at a well-founded suspicion that the mysterious prisoner of Zenda, concerning whom a good many paragraphs had appeared, was not a man at all, but (here I had much ado not to smile) a woman disguised as a man; and that strife between the King and his brother for this imaginary lady's favour was at the bottom of their quarrel.

'Perhaps it was Madame de Mauban herself,' I suggested.

'No!' said George decisively. 'Antoinette de Mauban was jealous of her, and betrayed the duke to the King for that reason. And, to confirm what I say, it's well known that the Princess Flavia is now extremely cold to the King, after having been most affectionate.'

At this point I changed the subject, and escaped from George's 'inspired' delusions. But if diplomatists never know anything more than they had succeeded in finding out in this instance, they appear to me to be somewhat expensive luxuries.

While in Paris I wrote to Antoinette, though I did not venture to call upon her. I received in return a very affecting letter, in which she assured me that the King's generosity and kindness, no less than her regard for me, bound her conscience to absolute secrecy. She expressed the intention of settling in the country, and withdrawing herself entirely from society. Whether she carried out her designs, I have never heard; but as I have not met her, or heard news of her up to this time, it is probable that she did. There is no doubt that she was deeply attached to the Duke of Strelsau; and her conduct at the time of his death proved that no knowledge of the man's real character was enough to root her regard for him out of her heart.

I had one more battle left to fight – a battle that would, I knew, be severe, and was bound to end in my complete defeat. Was I not back from the Tyrol, without having made any study of its inhabitants, institutions, scenery, fauna, flora, or other features? Had I not simply wasted my time in my usual frivolous good-for-nothing way? That was the aspect of the matter which, I was obliged to admit, would present itself to my sister-in-law; and against a verdict based on such evidence, I had really no defence to offer. It may be supposed, then, that I presented myself in Park Lane in a shamefaced, sheepish fashion. On the whole, my reception was not so alarming as I had feared. It turned out that I had done, not what Rose wished, but – the next best thing – what she prophesied. She had declared that I should make no notes, record no observations, gather no materials. My brother, on the other hand, had been weak enough to maintain that a really serious resolve had at length animated me.

When I returned empty-handed, Rose was so occupied in triumphing over Burlesdon that she let me down quite easily, devoting the greater part of her reproaches to my failure to advertise my friends of my whereabouts.

'We've wasted a lot of time trying to find you,' she said.

'I know you have,' said I. 'Half our ambassadors have led weary lives on my account. George Featherly told me so. But why should you have been anxious? I can take care of myself.'

'Oh, it wasn't that,' she cried scornfully, 'but I wanted to tell you about Sir Jacob Borodaile. You know, he's got an Embassy – at least, he will have in a month – and he wrote to say he hoped you would go with him.'

'Where's he going to?'

'He's going to succeed Lord Topham at Strelsau,' said she. 'You couldn't have a nicer place, short of Paris.'

'Strelsau! H'm!' said I, glancing at my brother.

'Oh, *that* doesn't matter!' exclaimed Rose impatiently. 'Now, you will go, won't you?'

'I don't know that I care about it!'

'Oh, you're too exasperating!'

'And I don't think I can go to Strelsau. My dear Rose, would it be – suitable?'

'Oh, nobody remembers that horrid old story now.'

Upon this, I took out of my pocket a portrait of the King of Ruritania. It had been taken a month or two before he ascended the throne. She could not miss my point when I said, putting it into her hands:

'In case you've not seen, or not noticed, a picture of Rudolf V, there he is. Don't you think they might recall the story, if I appeared at the Court of Ruritania?'

My sister-in-law looked at the portrait, and then at me.

'Good gracious!' she said, and flung the photograph down on the table.

'What do you say, Bob?' I asked.

Burlesdon got up, went to a corner of the room, and searched in a heap of newspapers. Presently he came back with a copy of the *Illustrated London News*. Opening the paper, he displayed a double-page engraving of the Coronation of Rudolf V at Strelsau. The photograph and the picture he laid side by side. I sat at the table fronting them; and, as I looked, I grew absorbed. My eye travelled from my own portrait to Sapt, to Strakencz, to the rich robes of the Cardinal, to Black Michael's face, to the stately figure of the princess by his side. Long I looked and eagerly. I was roused by my brother's hand on my shoulder. He was gazing down at me with a puzzled expression.

'It's a remarkable likeness, you see,' said I, 'I really think I had better not go to Ruritania.'

Rose, though half convinced, would not abandon her position.

'It's just an excuse,' she said pettishly. 'You don't want to do anything. Why, you might become an ambassador!'

'I don't think I want to be an ambassador,' said I.

'It's more than you ever will be,' she retorted.

That is very likely true, but it is not more than I have been. The idea of being an ambassador could scarcely dazzle me. I had been a king!

So pretty Rose left us in dudgeon; and Burlesdon, lighting a cigarette, looked at me still with that curious gaze.

'That picture in the paper –' he said.

'Well, what of it? It shows that the King of Ruritania and your humble servant are as like as two peas.'

My brother shook his head.

'I suppose so,' he said. 'But I should know you from the man in the photograph.'

'And not from the picture in the paper?'

'I should know the photograph from the picture: the picture's very like the photograph, but – '

'Well?'

'It's more like you!' said my brother.

My brother is a good man and true – so that, for all that he is a married man and mighty fond of his wife, he should know any secret of mine. But this secret was not mine, and I could not tell it to him.

'I don't think it's so much like me as the photograph,' said I boldly. 'But, anyhow, Bob, I won't go to Strelsau.'

'No, don't go to Strelsau, Rudolf,' said he.

And whether he suspects anything, or has a glimmer of the truth, I do not know. If he has, he keeps it to himself, and he and I never refer to it. And we let Sir Jacob Borrodaile find another *attaché*.

Since all these events whose history I have set down happened I have lived a very quiet life at a small house which I have taken in the country. The ordinary ambitions and aims of men in my position seem to me dull and unattractive. I have little fancy for the whirl of society, and none for the jostle of politics. Lady Burlesdon utterly despairs of me; my neighbours think me an indolent, dreamy, unsociable fellow. Yet I am a young man; and sometimes I have a fancy – the superstitious would call it a presentiment – that my part in life is not yet altogether played; that, somehow and some day, I shall mix again in great affairs, I shall again spin policies in a busy brain, match my wits against my enemies', brace my muscles to fight a good fight and strike stout blows. Such is the tissue of my thoughts as, with gun or rod in hand, I wander through the woods or by the side of the stream. Whether the fancy will be fulfilled, I cannot tell – still less whether the scene that, led by memory, I lay for my new exploits will be the true one – for I love to see myself once again in the crowded streets of Strelsau, or beneath the frowning keep of the Castle of Zenda.

Thus led, my broodings leave the future, and turn back on the past. Shapes rise before me in long array – the wild first revel with the King, the rush with my brave tea-table, the night in the moat, the pursuit in the forest: my friends and my foes, the people who learnt to love and honour me, the desperate men who tried to kill me. And, from amidst these last, comes one who alone of all of them yet moves on earth, though where I know not, yet plans (as I do not doubt) wickedness, yet turns women's hearts to softness and men's to fear and hate. Where is young Rupert of Hentzau – the boy who came so nigh to beating me? When his name comes into my head, I feel my hand grip and the blood move quicker through my veins: and the hint of Fate – the presentiment – seems to grow stronger and more definite, and to whisper insistently in my ear that I have yet a hand to play with young Rupert; therefore I exercise myself in arms, and seek to put off the day when the vigour of youth must leave me.

One break comes every year in my quiet life. Then I go to Dresden, and there I am met by my dear friend and companion, Fritz von Tarlenheim. Last time, his pretty wife Helga came, and a lusty crowing baby with her. And for a week Fritz and I are together, and I hear all of what falls out in Strelsau; and in the evenings, as we walk and smoke together, we talk of Sapt, and of the King, and often of young Rupert; and, as the hours grow small, at last we speak of Flavia. For every year Fritz carried with him to Dresden a little box; in it lies a red rose, and round the stalk of the rose is a slip of paper with the words written: 'Rudolf – Flavia – always.' And the like I send back by him. That message, and the wearing of the rings, are all that now bind me and the Queen of Ruritania. For – nobler, as I hold her, for the act – she has followed where her duty to her country and her House led her, and is the wife of the King, uniting his subjects to him by the love they bear to her, giving peace and quiet days to thousands by her self-sacrifice. There are moments when I dare not think of it, but there are others when I rise in spirit to where she ever dwells; then I can thank God that I love the noblest lady in the world, the most gracious and beautiful, and that there was nothing in my love that made her fall short in her high duty.

Shall I see her face again – the pale face and the glorious hair? Of that I know nothing; Fate has no hint, my heart no presentiment. I do not know. In this world, perhaps – nay, it is likely – never. And can it be that somewhere, in a manner whereof our flesh-bound minds have no apprehension, she and I will be together again, with nothing to come between us, nothing to forbid our love? That I know not, nor wiser heads than mine. But if it be never – if I can never hold sweet converse again with her, or look upon her face, or know from her her love; why, then, this side the grave, I will live as becomes the man whom she loves; and, for the other side, I must pray a dreamless sleep.

The Lost World

1

There Are Heroisms All Round Us

MR. HUNGERTON, her father, really was the most tactless person upon earth – a fluffy, feathery, untidy cockatoo of a man, perfectly good-natured, but absolutely centred upon his own silly self. If anything could have driven me from Gladys, it would have been the thought of such a father-in-law. I am convinced that he really believed in his heart that I came round to the Chestnuts three days a week for the pleasure of his company, and very especially to hear his views upon bimetallism – a subject upon which he was by way of being an authority.

For an hour or more that evening I listened to his monotonous chirrup about bad money driving out good, the token value of silver, the depreciation of the rupee, and the true standards of exchange.

'Suppose,' he cried, with feeble violence, 'that all the debts in the world were called up simultaneously and immediate payment insisted upon. What, under our present conditions, would happen then?'

I gave the self-evident answer that I should be a ruined man, upon which he jumped from his chair, reproved me for my habitual levity, which made it impossible for him to discuss any reasonable subject in my presence, and bounced off out of the room to dress for a Masonic meeting.

At last I was alone with Gladys, and the moment of fate had come! All that evening I had felt like the soldier who awaits the signal which will send him on a forlorn hope, hope of victory and fear of repulse alternating in his mind.

She sat with that proud, delicate profile of hers outlined against the red curtain. How beautiful she was! And yet how aloof! We had been friends, quite good friends; but never could I get beyond the same comradeship which I might have established with one of my fellow-reporters upon the *Gazette* – perfectly frank, perfectly kindly, and perfectly unsexual. My instincts are all against a woman being too frank and at her ease with me. It is no compliment to a man. Where the real sex feeling begins, timidity and distrust are its companions, heritage from old wicked days when love and violence went often hand in hand. The bent head, the averted eye, the faltering voice, the wincing figure – these, and not the unshrinking gaze and frank reply, are the true signals of passion. Even in my short life I had learned as much as that – or had inherited it in that race-memory which we call instinct.

Gladys was full of every womanly quality. Some judged her to be cold and hard, but such a thought was treason. That delicately-bronzed skin, almost Oriental in its colouring, that raven hair, the large liquid eyes, the full but exquisite lips – all the stigmata of passion were there. But I was sadly conscious that up to now I had never found the secret of drawing it forth. However, come what might, I should have done with suspense and bring matters to a head tonight. She could but refuse me, and better be a repulsed lover than an accepted brother.

So far my thoughts had carried me, and I was about to break the long and uneasy silence when two critical dark eyes looked round at me, and the proud head was shaken in smiling reproof.

'I have a presentiment that you are going to propose, Ned. I do wish you wouldn't, for things are so much nicer as they are.'

I drew my chair a little nearer.

'Now, how did you know that I was going to propose?' I asked, in genuine wonder.

'Don't women always know? Do you suppose any woman in the world was ever taken unawares? But, oh, Ned, our friendship has been so good and so pleasant! What a pity to spoil it! Don't you feel how splendid it is that a young man and a young woman should be able to talk face to face as we have talked?'

'I don't know, Gladys. You see, I can talk face to face with – with the station-master.' I can't imagine how that official came into the matter, but in he trotted and set us both laughing. 'That does not satisfy me in the least. I want my arms around you and your head on my breast, and, oh, Gladys, I want – '

She had sprung from her chair as she saw signs that I proposed to demonstrate some of my wants.

'You've spoiled everything, Ned,' she said. 'It's all so beautiful and natural until this kind of thing comes in. It is such a pity. Why can't you control yourself?'

'I didn't invent it,' I pleaded. 'It's nature. It's love!'

'Well, perhaps if both love it may be different. I have never felt it.'

'But you must – you, with your beauty, with your soul! Oh, Gladys, you were made for love! You must love!'

'One must wait till it comes.'

'But why can't you love me, Gladys? Is it my appearance, or what?'

She did unbend a little. She put forward a hand – such a gracious, stooping attitude it was – and she pressed back my head. Then she looked into my upturned face with a very wistful smile.

'No, it isn't that,' she said at last. 'You're not a conceited boy by nature, and so I can safely tell you that it is not that. It's deeper.'

'My character?'

She nodded severely.

'What can I do to mend it? Do sit down and talk it over. No, really I won't, if you'll only sit down!'

She was looking at me with a wondering distrust which was much more to my mind than her whole-hearted confidence. How primitive and bestial it looks when you put it down in black and white! And perhaps after all it is only a feeling peculiar to myself. Anyhow, she sat down.

'Now tell me what's amiss with me.'

'I'm in love with somebody else,' she said.

It was my turn to jump out of my chair.

'It's nobody in particular,' she explained, laughing at the expression of my face, 'only an ideal. I've never met the kind of man I mean.'

'Tell me about him. What does he look like?'

'Oh, he might look very much like you.'

'How dear of you to say that! Well, what is it that he does that I don't do? Just say the word – teetotal, vegetarian, aeronaut, Theosophist, Superman – I'll have a try at it, Gladys, if you will only give me an idea what would please you.'

She laughed at the elasticity of my character. 'Well, in the first place, I don't think my ideal would speak like that,' she said. 'He would be a harder, sterner man, not so ready to adapt himself to a silly girl's whim. But above all he must be a man who could do, who could act, who would look death in the face and have no fear of him – a man of great deeds and strange experiences. It is never a man that I should love, but always the glories he had won, for they would be reflected upon me. Think of Richard Burton! When I read his wife's life of him I could so understand her love. And Lady Stanley! Did you ever read the wonderful last chapter of that book about her husband? These are the sort of men that a woman could worship with all her soul and yet be the greater, not the less, on account of her love, honoured by all the world as the inspirer of noble deeds.'

She looked so beautiful in her enthusiasm that I nearly brought down the whole level of the interview. I gripped myself hard, and went on with the argument.

'We can't all be Stanleys and Burtons,' said I. 'Besides, we don't get the chance – at least, I never had the chance. If I did I should try to take it.'

'But chances are all around you. It is the mark of the kind of man I mean that he makes his own chances. You can't hold him back. I've never met him, and yet I seem to know him so well. There are heroisms all round us waiting to be done. It's for men to do them, and for women to reserve their love as a reward for such men. Look at that young Frenchman who went up last week in a balloon. It was blowing a gale of wind, but because he was announced to go he insisted on starting. The wind blew him one thousand five hundred miles in twenty-four hours, and he fell in the middle of Russia. That was the kind of man I mean. Think of the woman he loved, and how other women must have envied her! That's what I should like – to be envied for my man.'

'I'd have done it to please you.'

'But you shouldn't do it merely to please me. You should do it because you can't help it, because it's natural to you – because the man in you is crying out for heroic expression. Now, when you described the Wigan coal explosion last month, could you not have gone down and helped those people, in spite of the choke-damp?'

'I did.'

'You never said so.'

'There was nothing worth bucking about.'

'I didn't know.' She looked at me with rather more interest. 'That was brave of you.'

'I had to. If you want to write good copy you must be where the things are.'

'What a prosaic motive! It seems to take all the romance out of it. But still, whatever your motive, I am glad that you went down that mine.' She gave me her hand, but with such sweetness and dignity that I could only stoop and kiss it. 'I dare say I am merely a foolish woman with a young girl's fancies. And yet it is so real with me, so entirely part of my very self, that I cannot help acting upon it. If I marry, I do want to marry a famous man.'

'Why should you not?' I cried. 'It is women like you who brace men up. Give me a chance and see if I will take it! Besides, as you say, men ought to *make* their own chances, and not wait until they are given. Look at Clive – just a clerk, and he conquered India. By George! I'll do something in the world yet!'

She laughed at my sudden Irish effervescence.

'Why not?' she said. 'You have everything a man could have – youth, health, strength, education, energy. I was sorry you spoke. And now I am glad – so glad – if it wakens these thoughts in you.'

'And if I do –?'

Her hand rested like warm velvet upon my lips.

'Not another word, sir. You should have been at the office for evening duty half an hour ago, only I hadn't the heart to remind you. Some day, perhaps, when you have won your place in the world, we shall talk it over again.'

And so it was that I found myself that foggy November evening pursuing the Camberwell tram with my heart glowing within me, and with the eager determination that not another day should elapse before I should find some deed which was worthy of my lady. But who in all this wide world could ever have imagined the incredible shape which that deed was to take, or the strange steps by which I was led to the doing of it?

And, after all, this opening chapter will seem to the reader to have nothing to do with my narrative; and yet there would have been no narrative without it, for it is only when a man goes out into the world with the thought that there are heroisms all round him, and with the desire all alive in his heart to follow any which may come within sight of him, that he breaks away as I did from the life he knows, and ventures forth into the wonderful mystic twilight land where lie the great adventures and the great rewards. Behold me, then, at the office of the *Daily Gazette*, on the staff of which I was a most insignificant unit, with the settled determination that very night, if possible, to find the quest which should be worthy of my Gladys! Was it hardness, was it selfishness, that she should ask me to risk my life for her own glorification? Such thoughts may come to middle age, but never to ardent three-and-twenty in the fever of his first love.

2

Try Your Luck with Professor Challenger

I ALWAYS liked McArdle, the crabbed old, round-backed, red-headed news editor, and I rather hoped that he liked me. Of course, Beaumont was the real boss, but he lived in the rarified atmosphere of some Olympian height from which he could distinguish nothing smaller than an international crisis or a split in the Cabinet. Sometimes we saw him passing in lonely majesty to his inner sanctum with his eyes staring vaguely and his mind hovering over the Balkans or the Persian Gulf. He was above and beyond us. But McArdle was his first lieutenant, and it was he that we knew. The old man nodded as I entered the room, and he pushed his spectacles far up on his bald forehead.

'Well, Mr. Malone, from all I hear, you seem to be doing very well,' said he, in his kindly Scotch accent.

I thanked him.

'The colliery explosion was excellent. So was the Southwark fire. You have the true descreeptive touch. What did you want to see me about?'

'To ask a favour.'

He looked alarmed and his eyes shunned mine.

'Tut! tut! What is it?'

'Do you think, sir, that you could possibly send me on some mission for the paper? I would do my best to put it through and get you some good copy.'

'What sort of a meesion had you in your mind, Mr. Malone?'

'Well, sir, anything that had adventure and danger in it. I would really do my very best. The more difficult it was the better it would suit me.'

'You seem very anxious to lose your life.'

'To justify my life, sir.'

'Dear me, Mr. Malone, this is very – very exalted. I'm afraid the day for this sort of thing is rather past. The expense of the "special meesion" business hardly justifies the result, and, of course, in any case it would only be an experienced man with a name that would command public confidence who would get such an order. The big blank spaces in the map are all being filled in, and there's no room for romance anywhere. Wait a bit, though!' he added, with a sudden smile upon his face. 'Talking of the blank spaces of the map gives me an idea. What about exposing a fraud – a modern Munchausen – and making him rideeculous? You could show him up as the liar that he is! Eh, man, it would be fine. How does it appeal to you?'

'Anything – anywhere – I care nothing.'

McArdle was plunged in thought for some minutes.

'I wonder whether you could get on friendly – or at least on talking terms with the fellow,' he said, at last. 'You seem to have a sort of genius for establishing relations with people – seempathy, I suppose, or animal magnetism, or youthful vitality, or something. I am conscious of it myself.'

'You are very good, sir.'

'So why should you not try your luck with Professor Challenger, of Enmore Park?'

I dare say I looked a little startled.

'Challenger!' I cried. 'Professor Challenger, the famous zoologist! Wasn't he the man who broke the skull of Blundell, of the *Telegraph*?'

The news editor smiled grimly.

'Do you mind? Didn't you say it was adventures you were after?'

'It is all in the way of business, sir,' I answered.

'Exactly. I don't suppose he can always be so violent as that. I'm thinking that Blundell got him at the wrong moment, maybe, or in the wrong fashion. You may have better luck, or more tact in handling him. There's something in your line there, I am sure, and the *Gazette* should work it.'

'I really know nothing about him,' said I. 'I only remember his name in connection with the police-court proceedings, for striking Blundell.'

'I have a few notes for your guidance, Mr. Malone. I've had my eye on the Professor for some little time.' He took a paper from a drawer. 'Here is a summary of his record. I give it you briefly: –

'"Challenger, George Edward. *Born*: Largs, N. B., 1863. *Educ.*: Largs Academy; Edinburgh University. British Museum Assistant, 1892. Assistant-Keeper of Comparative Anthropology Department, 1893. Resigned after acrimonious Correspondence same year. Winner of Crayston Medal for Zoological Research. Foreign Member of" – well, quite a lot of things, about two inches of small type – "Société Belge, American Academy of Sciences, La Plata, etc., etc. Ex-President Palæontological Society. Section H, British Association" – so on, so on! – "*Publications*: 'Some Observations Upon a Series of Kalmuck Skulls'; 'Outlines of Vertebrate Evolution'; and numerous papers, including 'The Underlying Fallacy of Weissmannism', which caused heated discussion at the Zoological Congress of Vienna. *Recreations*: Walking, Alpine climbing. *Address*: Enmore Park, Kensington, W."

'There, take it with you. I've nothing more for you to-night.'

I pocketed the slip of paper.

'One moment, sir,' I said, as I realized that it was a pink bald head, and not a red face, which was fronting me. 'I am not very clear yet why I am to interview this gentleman. What has he done?'

The face flashed back again.

'Went to South America on a solitary expedition two years ago. Came back last year. Had undoubtedly been to South America, but refused to say exactly where. Began to tell his adventures in a vague way, but somebody started to pick holes, and he just shut up like an oyster. Something wonderful happened – or the man's a champion liar, which is the more probable supposeetion. Had some damaged photographs, said to be fakes. Got so touchy that he assaults anyone who asks questions, and heaves reporters doun the stairs. In my opinion he's just a homicidal megalomaniac with a turn for science. That's your man, Mr. Malone. Now, off you run, and see what you can make of him. You're big enough to look after yourself. Anyway, you are all safe. Employers' Liability Act, you know.'

A grinning red face turned once more into a pink oval, fringed with gingery fluff: the interview was at an end.

I walked across to the Savage Club, but instead of turning into it I leaned upon the railings of Adelphi Terrace and gazed thoughtfully for a long time at the brown, oily river. I can always think most sanely and clearly in the open air. I took out the list of Professor Challenger's exploits, and I read it over under the electric lamp. Then I had what I can only regard as an inspiration. As a Pressman, I felt sure from what I had been told that I could never hope to get into touch with this cantankerous Professor. But these recriminations, twice mentioned in his skeleton biography, could only mean that he was a fanatic in science. Was there not an exposed margin there upon which he might be accessible? I would try.

I entered the club. It was just after eleven, and the big room was fairly full, though the rush had not yet set in. I noticed a tall, thin, angular man seated in an arm-chair by the fire. He turned as I drew my chair up to him. It was the man of all others whom I should have chosen – Tarp Henry of the staff of *Nature*, a thin, dry, leathery creature, who was full, to those who knew him, of kindly humanity. I plunged instantly into my subject.

'What do you know of Professor Challenger?'

'Challenger?' He gathered his brows in scientific disapproval. 'Challenger was the man who came with some cock-and-bull story from South America.'

'What story?'

'Oh, it was rank nonsense about some queer animals he had discovered. I believe he has retracted since. Anyhow, he has suppressed it all. He gave an interview to Reuter's, and there was such a howl that he saw it wouldn't do. It was a discreditable business. There were one or two folk who were inclined to take him seriously, but he soon choked them off.'

'How?'

'Well, by his insufferable rudeness and impossible behaviour. There was poor old Wadley, of the Zoological Institute. Wadley sent a message: "The President of the Zoological Institute presents his compliments to Professor Challenger, and would take it as a personal favour if he would do them the honour to come to their next meeting." The answer was unprintable.'

'You don't say?'

'Well, a bowdlerized version of it would run: "Professor Challenger presents his compliments to the President of the Zoological Institute, and would take it as a personal favour if he would go to the devil."'

'Good Lord!'

'Yes, I expect that's what old Wadley said. I remember his wail at the meeting, which began: "In fifty years' experience of scientific intercourse –" It quite broke the old man up.'

'Anything more about Challenger?'

'Well, I'm a bacteriologist, you know. I live in a nine-hundred-diameter microscope. I can hardly claim to take serious notice of anything that I can see with my naked eye. I'm a frontiersman from the extreme edge of the Knowable, and I feel quite out of place when I leave my study and come into touch with all you great, rough, hulking creatures. I'm too detached to talk scandal, and yet at scientific conversaziones I *have* heard something of Challenger, for he is one of those men whom nobody can ignore. He's as clever as they make 'em – a full-charged battery of force and vitality, but a quarrelsome, ill-conditioned faddist, and unscrupulous at that. He had gone the length of faking some photographs over the South American business.'

'You say he is a faddist. What is his particular fad?'

'He has a thousand, but the latest is something about Weissmann and Evolution. He had a fearful row about it in Vienna, I believe.'

'Can't you tell me the point?'

'Not at the moment, but a translation of the proceedings exists. We have it filed at the office. Would you care to come?'

'It's just what I want. I have to interview the fellow, and I need some lead up to him. It's really awfully good of you to give me a lift. I'll go with you now, if it is not too late.'

Half an hour later I was seated in the newspaper office with a huge tome in front of me, which had been opened at the article 'Weissmann *versus* Darwin', with the sub-heading, 'Spirited Protest at Vienna. Lively Proceedings'. My scientific education having been somewhat neglected I was unable to follow the whole argument, but it was evident that the English Professor had handled his subject in a very aggressive fashion, and had thoroughly annoyed his Continental colleagues. 'Protests', 'Uproar', and 'General appeal to the Chairman' were three of the first brackets which caught my eye. Most of the matter might have been written in Chinese for any definite meaning that it conveyed to my brain.

'I wish you could translate it into English for me,' I said, pathetically, to my helpmate.

'Well, it is a translation.'

'Then I'd better try my luck with the original.'

'It is certainly rather deep for a layman.'

'If I could only get a single good, meaty sentence which seemed to convey some sort of definite human idea, it would serve my turn. Ah, yes, this one will do. I seem in a vague way almost to understand it. I'll copy it out. This shall be my link with the terrible Professor.'

'Nothing else I can do?'

'Well, yes; I propose to write to him. If I could frame the letter here, and use your address, it would give atmosphere.'

'We'll have the fellow round here making a row and breaking the furniture.'

'No, no; you'll see the letter – nothing contentious, I assure you.'

'Well, that's my chair and desk. You'll find paper there. I'd like to censor it before it goes.'

It took some doing, but I flatter myself that it wasn't such a bad job when it was finished. I read it aloud to the critical bacteriologist with some pride in my handiwork.

> 'DEAR PROFESSOR CHALLENGER,' it said. 'As a humble student of Nature, I have always taken the most profound interest in your speculations as to the differences between Darwin and Weissmann. I have recently had occasion to refresh my memory by re-reading –'
>
> 'You infernal liar!' murmured Tarp Henry.
>
> – 'by re-reading your masterly address at Vienna. That lucid and admirable statement seems to be the last word in the matter. There is one sentence in it, however – namely: "I protest strongly against the insufferable and entirely dogmatic assertion that each separate *id* is a microcosm possessed of an historical architecture elaborated slowly through the series of generations." Have you no desire, in view of later research, to modify this statement? Do you not think that it is over-accentuated? With your permission, I would ask the favour of an interview, as I feel strongly upon the subject, and have certain suggestions which I could only elaborate in a personal conversation. With your consent, I trust to have the honour of calling at eleven o'clock the day after to-morrow (Wednesday) morning.
>
> 'I remain, Sir, with assurances of profound respect, yours very truly,
>
> EDWARD D. MALONE.'

'How's that?' I asked, triumphantly.

'Well, if your conscience can stand it –'

'It has never failed me yet.'

'But what do you mean to do?'

'To get there. Once I am in his room I may see some opening. I may even go the length of open confession. If he is a sportsman he will be tickled.'

'Tickled, indeed! He's much more likely to do the tickling. Chain mail, or an American football suit – that's what you'll want. Well, good-bye. I'll have the answer for you here on Wednesday morning – if he ever deigns to answer you. He is a violent, dangerous, cantankerous character, hated by everyone who comes across him, and the butt of the students, so far as they dare take a liberty with him. Perhaps it would be best for you if you never heard from the fellow at all.'

3

He is a Perfectly Impossible Person

MY friend's fear or hope was not destined to be realized. When I called on Wednesday there was a letter with the West Kensington postmark upon it, and my name scrawled across the envelope in a hand-writing which looked like a barbed-wire railing. The contents were as follows: –

'Enmore Park, W.

'SIR, – I have duly received your note, in which you claim to endorse my views, although I am not aware that they are dependent upon endorsement either from you or anyone else. You have ventured to use the word "speculation" with regard to my statement upon the subject of Darwinism, and I would call your attention to the fact that such a word in such a connection is offensive to a degree. The context convinces me, however, that you have sinned rather through ignorance and tactlessness than through malice, so I am content to pass the matter by. You quote an isolated sentence from my lecture, and appear to have some difficulty in understanding it. I should have thought that only a sub-human intelligence could have failed to grasp the point, but if it really needs amplification I shall consent to see you at the hour named, though visits and visitors of every sort are exceedingly distasteful to me. As to your suggestion that I may modify my opinion, I would have you know that it is not my habit to do so after a deliberate expression of my mature views. You will kindly show the envelope of this letter to my man, Austin, when you call, as he has to take every precaution to shield me from the intrusive rascals who call themselves "journalists".

'Yours faithfully,
GEORGE EDWARD CHALLENGER.'

This was the letter that I read aloud to Tarp Henry, who had come down early to hear the result of my venture. His only remark was, 'There's some new stuff, cuticura or something, which is better than arnica.' Some people have such extraordinary notions of humour.

It was nearly half-past ten before I had received my message, but a taxicab took me round in good time for my appointment. It was an imposing porticoed house at which we stopped, and the heavily-curtained windows gave every indication of wealth upon the part of this formidable Professor. The door was opened by an odd, swarthy, dried-up person of uncertain age, with a dark pilot jacket and brown leather gaiters. I found afterwards that he was the chauffeur, who filled the gaps left by a succession of fugitive butlers. He looked me up and down with a searching light blue eye.

'Expected?' he asked.

'An appointment.'

'Got your letter?'

I produced the envelope.

'Right!' He seemed to be a person of few words. Following him down the passage I was suddenly interrupted by a small woman, who stepped out from what proved to be the dining-room door. She was a bright, vivacious, dark-eyed lady, more French than English in her type.

'One moment,' she said. 'You can wait, Austin. Step in here, sir. May I ask if you have met my husband before?'

'No, madam, I have not had the honour.'

'Then I apologize to you in advance. I must tell you that he is a perfectly impossible person – absolutely impossible. If you are forewarned you will be the more ready to make allowances.'

'It is most considerate of you, madam.'

'Get quickly out of the room if he seems inclined to be violent. Don't wait to argue with him. Several people have been injured through doing that. Afterwards there is a public scandal, and it reflects upon me and all of us. I suppose it wasn't about South America you wanted to see him?'

I could not lie to a lady.

'Dear me! That is his most dangerous subject. You won't believe a word he says – I'm sure I don't wonder. But don't tell him so, for it makes him very violent. Pretend to believe him, and you may get through all right. Remember he believes it himself. Of that you may be assured. A more honest man never lived. Don't wait any longer or he may suspect. If you find him dangerous – really dangerous – ring the bell and hold him off until I come. Even at his worst I can usually control him.'

With these encouraging words the lady handed me over to the taciturn Austin, who had waited like a bronze statue of discretion during our short interview, and I was conducted to the end of the passage. There was a tap at a door, a bull's bellow from within, and I was face to face with the Professor.

He sat in a rotating chair behind a broad table, which was covered with books, maps, and diagrams. As I entered, his seat spun round to face me.

His appearance made me gasp. I was prepared for something strange, but not for so overpowering a personality as this. It was his size which took one's breath away – his size and his imposing presence. His head was enormous, the largest I have ever seen upon a human being. I am sure that his top-hat, had I ventured to don it, would have slipped over me entirely and rested on my shoulders. He had the face and beard which I associate with an Assyrian bull; the former florid, the latter so black as almost to have a suspicion of blue, spade-shaped and rippling down over his chest. The hair was peculiar, plastered down in front in a long, curving wisp over his massive forehead. The eyes were blue-grey under great black tufts, very clear, very critical, and very masterful. A huge spread of shoulders and a chest like a barrel were the other parts of him which appeared above the table, save for two enormous hands covered with long black hair. This and a bellowing, roaring, rumbling voice made up my first impression of the notorious Professor Challenger.

'Well?' said he, with a most insolent stare. 'What now?'

I must keep up my deception for at least a little time longer, otherwise here was evidently an end of the interview.

'You were good enough to give me an appointment, sir,' said I, humbly, producing his envelope.

He took my letter from his desk and laid it out before him.

'Oh, you are the young person who cannot understand plain English, are you? My general conclusions you are good enough to approve, as I understand?'

'Entirely, sir – entirely!' I was very emphatic.

'Dear me! That strengthens my position very much, does it not? Your age and appearance make your support doubly valuable. Well, at least you are better than that herd of swine in Vienna, whose gregarious grunt is, however, not more offensive than the isolated effort of the British hog.' He glared at me as the present representative of the beast.

'They seem to have behaved abominably,' said I.

'I assure you that I can fight my own battles, and that I have no possible need of your sympathy. Put me alone, sir, and with my back to the wall. G.E.C. is happiest then. Well, sir, let us do what we can to curtail this visit, which can hardly be agreeable to you, and is inexpressibly irksome to me. You had, as I have been led to believe, some comments to make upon the proposition which I advanced in my thesis.'

There was a brutal directness about his methods which made evasion difficult. I must still make play and wait for a better opening. It had seemed simple enough at a distance. Oh, my Irish wits, could they not help me now, when I needed help so sorely? He transfixed me with two sharp, steely eyes. 'Come, come!' he rumbled.

'I am, of course, a mere student,' said I, with a fatuous smile, 'hardly more, I might say, than an earnest inquirer. At the same time, it seemed to me that you were a little severe upon Weissmann in this matter. Has not the general evidence since that date tended to – well, to strengthen his position?'

'What evidence?' He spoke with a menacing calm.

'Well, of course, I am aware that there is not any what you might call *definite* evidence. I alluded merely to the trend of modern thought and the general scientific point of view, if I might so express it.'

He leaned forward with great earnestness.

'I suppose you are aware,' said he, checking off points upon his fingers, 'that the cranial index is a constant factor?'

'Naturally,' said I.

'And that telegony is still *sub judice*?'

'Undoubtedly.'

'And that the germ plasm is different from the parthenogenetic egg?'

'Why, surely!' I cried, and gloried in my own audacity.

'But what does that prove?' he asked, in a gentle, persuasive voice.

'Ah, what indeed?' I murmured. 'What does it prove?'

'Shall I tell you?' he cooed.

'Pray do.'

'It proves,' he roared, with a sudden blast of fury, 'that you are the rankest impostor in London – a vile, crawling journalist, who has no more science than he has decency in his composition!'

He had sprung to his feet with a mad rage in his eyes. Even at that moment of tension I found time for amazement at the discovery that he was quite a short man, his head not higher than my shoulder – a stunted Hercules whose tremendous vitality had all run to depth, breadth, and brain.

'Gibberish!' he cried, leaning forward, with his fingers on the table and his face projecting. 'That's what I have been talking to you, sir – scientific gibberish! Did you think you could match cunning with me – you with your walnut of a brain? You think you are omnipotent, you infernal scribblers, don't you? That your praise can make a man and your blame can break him? We must all bow to you, and try to get a favourable word, must we? This man shall have a leg up, and this man shall have a dressing down! Creeping vermin, I know you! You've got out of your station. Time was when your ears were clipped. You've lost your sense of proportion. Swollen gas-bags! I'll keep you in your proper place. Yes, sir, you haven't got over G.E.C. There's one man who is still your master. He warned you off, but if you *will* come, by the Lord you do it at your own risk. Forfeit, my good Mr. Malone, I claim forfeit! You have played a rather dangerous game, and it strikes me that you have lost it.'

'Look here, sir,' said I, backing to the door and opening it; 'you can be as abusive as you like. But there is a limit. You shall not assault me.'

'Shall I not?' He was slowly advancing in a peculiarly menacing way, but he stopped now and put his big hands into the side pockets of a rather boyish short jacket which he wore. 'I have thrown several of you out of the house. You will be the fourth or fifth. Three pound fifteen each – that is how it averaged. Expensive, but very necessary. Now, sir, why should you not follow your brethren? I rather think you must.' He resumed his unpleasant and stealthy advance, pointing his toes as he walked, like a dancing master.

I could have bolted for the hall door, but it would have been too ignominious. Besides, a little glow of righteous anger was springing up within me. I had been hopelessly in the wrong before, but this man's menaces were putting me in the right.

'I'll trouble you to keep your hands off, sir. I'll not stand it.'

'Dear me!' His black moustache lifted and a white fang twinkled in a sneer. 'You won't stand it, eh?'

'Don't be such a fool, Professor!' I cried, 'what can you hope for? I'm fifteen stone, as hard as nails, and play centre three-quarter every Saturday for the London Irish. I'm not the man –

It was at that moment that he rushed me. It was lucky that I had opened the door, or we should have gone through it. We did a Catherine-wheel together down the passage. Somehow we gathered up a chair upon our way, and bounded on with it towards the street. My mouth was full of his beard, our arms were locked, our bodies intertwined, and that infernal chair radiated its legs all round us. The watchful Austin had thrown open the hall door. We went with a back somersault down the front steps. I have seen the two Macs attempt something of the kind at the halls, but it appears to take some practice to do it without hurting oneself. The chair went to matchwood at the bottom, and we rolled apart into the gutter. He sprang to his feet, waving his fists and wheezing like an asthmatic.

'Had enough?' he panted.

'You infernal bully!' I cried, as I gathered myself together.

Then and there we should have tried the thing out, for he was effervescing with fight, but fortunately I was rescued from an odious situation. A policeman was beside us, his notebook in his hand.

'What's all this? You ought to be ashamed,' said the policeman. It was the most rational remark which I had heard in Enmore Park. 'Well,' he insisted, turning to me, 'what is it, then?'

'This man attacked me,' said I.

'Did you attack him?' asked the policeman.

The Professor breathed hard and said nothing.

'It's not the first time, either,' said the policeman, severely, shaking his head. 'You were in trouble last month for the same thing. You've blackened this young man's eye. Do you give him in charge, sir?'

I relented.

'No,' said I, 'I do not.'

'What's that?' said the policeman.

'I was to blame myself. I intruded upon him. He gave me fair warning.'

The policeman snapped up his notebook.

'Don't let us have any more such goings-on,' said he. 'Now, then! Move on, there, move on!' This to a butcher's boy, a maid, and one or two loafers who had collected. He clumped heavily down the street, driving this little flock before him. The Professor looked at me, and there was something humorous at the back of his eyes.

'Come in!' said he. 'I've not done with you yet.'

The speech had a sinister sound, but I followed him none the less into the house. The man-servant, Austin, like a wooden image, closed the door behind us.

4

It's Just the Very Biggest Thing in the World

HARDLY was it shut than Mrs. Challenger darted out from the dining-room. The small woman was in a furious temper. She barred her husband's way like an enraged chicken in front of a bulldog. It was evident that she had seen my exit, but had not observed my return.

'You brute, George!' she screamed. 'You've hurt that nice young man.'

He jerked backwards with his thumb.

'Here he is, safe and sound behind me.'

She was confused, but not unduly so.

'I am sorry, I didn't see you.'

'I assure you, madam, that it is all right.'

'He has marked your poor face! Oh, George, what a brute you are! Nothing but scandals from one end of the week to the other. Everyone hating and making fun of you. You've finished my patience. This ends it.'

'Dirty linen,' he rumbled.

'It's not a secret,' she cried. 'Do you suppose that the whole street – the whole of London, for that matter –

Get away, Austin, we don't want you here. Do you suppose they don't all talk about you? Where is your dignity? You, a man who should have been Regius Professor at a great University with a thousand students all revering you. Where is your dignity, George?'

'How about yours, my dear?'

'You try me too much. A ruffian – a common brawling ruffian – that's what you have become.'

'Be good, Jessie.'

'A roaring, raging bully!'

'That's done it! Stool of penance!' said he.

To my amazement he stooped, picked her up, and placed her sitting upon a high pedestal of black marble in the angle of the hall. It was at least seven feet high, and so thin that she could hardly balance upon it.

A more absurd object than she presented cocked up there with her face convulsed with anger, her feet dangling, and her body rigid for fear of an upset, I could not imagine.

'Let me down!' she wailed.

'Say "please".'

'You brute, George! Let me down this instant!'

'Come into the study, Mr. Malone.'

'Really, sir –!' said I, looking at the lady.

'Here's Mr. Malone pleading for you, Jessie. Say "please", and down you come.'

'Oh, you brute! Please! please!'

He took her down as if she had been a canary.

'You must behave yourself, dear. Mr. Malone is a Pressman. He will have it all in his rag to-morrow, and sell an extra dozen among our neighbours. "Strange story of high life!" – you felt fairly high on that pedestal, did you not? Then a subtitle, "Glimpse of a singular menage". He's a foul feeder, is Mr. Malone, a carrion eater, like all of his kind – porcus ex grege – diaboli – a swine from the devil's herd. That's it, Malone – what?'

'You are really intolerable!' said I, hotly.

He bellowed with laughter.

'We shall have a coalition presently,' he boomed, looking from his wife to me and puffing out his enormous chest. Then, suddenly altering his tone, 'Excuse this frivolous family badinage, Mr. Malone. I called you back for some more serious purpose than to mix you up with our little domestic pleasantries. Run away, little woman, and don't fret.' He placed a huge hand upon each of her shoulders. All that you say is perfectly true. I should be a better man if I did what you advise, but I shouldn't be quite George Edward Challenger. There are plenty of better men, my dear, but only one G. E. C. So make the best of him.' He suddenly gave her a resounding kiss, which embarrassed me even more than his violence had done. 'Now Mr. Malone,' he continued, with a great accession of dignity; this way if you please.'

We re-entered the room which we had left so tumultuously ten minutes before. The Professor closed the door carefully behind us, motioned me into an arm-chair, and pushed a cigar-box under my nose.

'Real San Juan Colorado,' he said. 'Excitable people like you are the better for narcotics. Heavens! don't bite it! Cut – and cut with reverence! Now lean back, and listen attentively to whatever I may care to say to you. If any remark should occur to you, you can reserve it for some more opportune time.

'First of all, as to your return to my house after your most justifiable expulsion –' he protruded his beard, and stared at me as one who challenges and invites contradiction – 'after, as I say, your well-merited expulsion. The reason lay in your answer to that most officious policeman, in which I seemed to discern some glimmering of good feeling upon your part – more, at any rate, than I am accustomed to associate with your profession. In admitting that the fault of the incident lay with you, you gave some evidence of a certain mental detachment and breadth of view which attracted my favourable notice. The sub-species of the human race to which you unfortunately belong has always been below my mental horizon. Your words brought you suddenly above it. You swam up into my serious notice. For this reason I asked you to return with me, as I was minded to make your further acquaintance. You will kindly deposit your ash in the small Japanese tray on the bamboo table which stands at your left elbow.'

All this he boomed forth like a professor addressing his class. He had swung round his revolving-chair so as to face me, and he sat all puffed out like an enormous bull-frog, his head laid back, and his eyes half-covered by supercilious lids. Now he suddenly turned himself sideways, and all I could see of him was tangled hair with a red, protruding ear. He was scratching about among the litter of papers upon his desk. He faced me presently with what looked like a very tattered sketch-book in his hand.

'I am going to talk to you about South America,' said he. 'No comments if you please. First of all, I wish you to understand that nothing I tell you now is to be repeated in any public way unless you have my express permission. That permission will, in all human probability, never be given. Is that clear?'

'It is very hard,' said I. 'Surely a judicious account – '

He replaced the notebook upon the table.

'That ends it,' said he. 'I wish you a very good morning.'

'No, no!' I cried. 'I submit to any conditions. So far as I can see, I have no choice.'

'None in the world,' said he.

'Well, then, I promise.'

'Word of honour?'

'Word of honour.'

He looked at me with doubt in his insolent eyes.

'After all, what do I know about your honour?' said he.

'Upon my word, sir,' I cried, angrily, 'you take very great liberties! I have never been so insulted in my life.'

He seemed more interested than annoyed at my outbreak.

'Round-headed,' he muttered. 'Brachycephalic, grey-eyed, black-haired, with suggestion of the negroid. Celtic, I presume?'

'I am an Irishman, sir.'

'Irish Irish?'

'Yes, sir.'

'That, of course, explains it. Let me see; you have given me your promise that my confidence will be respected? That confidence, I may say, will be far from complete. But I am prepared to give you a few indications which will be of interest. In the first place, you are probably aware that two years ago I made a journey to South America – one which will be classical in the scientific history of the world? The object of my journey was to verify some conclusions of Wallace and of Bates, which could only be done by observing their reported facts under the same conditions in which they had themselves noted them. If my expedition had no other results it would still have been noteworthy, but a curious incident occurred to me while there which opened up an entirely fresh line of inquiry.

'You are aware – or probably, in this half-educated age, you are not aware – that the country round some parts of the Amazon is still only partially explored, and that a great number of tributaries, some of them entirely uncharted, run into the main river. It was my business to visit this little-known back-country and to examine its fauna, which furnished me with the materials for several chapters for that great and monumental work upon zoology which will be my life's justification. I was returning, my work accomplished, when I had occasion to spend a night at a small Indian village at a point where a certain tributary – the name and position of which I withhold – opens into the main river. The natives were Cucama Indians, an amiable but degraded race, with mental powers hardly superior to the average Londoner. I had effected some cures among them upon my way up the river, and had impressed them considerably with my personality, so that I was not surprised to find myself eagerly awaited upon my return. I gathered from their signs that someone had urgent need of my medical services, and I followed the chief to one of his huts. When I entered I found that the sufferer to whose aid I had been summoned had that instant expired. He was, to my surprise, no Indian, but a white man; indeed, I may say a very white man, for he was flaxen-haired and had some characteristics of an albino. He was clad in rags, was very emaciated, and bore every trace of prolonged hardship. So far as I could understand the account of the natives, he was a complete stranger to them, and had come upon their village through the woods alone and in the last stage of exhaustion.

'The man's knapsack lay beside the couch, and I examined the contents. His name was written upon a tab within it – Maple White, Lake Avenue, Detroit, Michigan. It is a name to which I am prepared always to lift my hat. It is not too much to say that it will rank level with my own when the final credit of this business comes to be apportioned.

'From the contents of the knapsack it was evident that this man had been an artist and poet in search of effects. There were scraps of verse. I do not profess to be a judge of such things, but they appeared to me to be singularly wanting in merit. There were also some rather commonplace pictures of river scenery, a paint-box, a box of coloured chalks, some brushes, that curved bone which lies upon my inkstand, a volume of Baxter's "Moths and Butterflies", a cheap revolver, and a few cartridges.

Of personal equipment he either had none or he had lost it in his journey. Such were the total effects of this strange American Bohemian.

'I was turning away from him when I observed that something projected from the front of his ragged jacket. It was this sketch-book, which was as dilapidated then as you see it now. Indeed, I can assure you that a first folio of Shakespeare could not be treated with greater reverence than this relic has been since it came into my possession. I hand it to you now, and I ask you to take it page by page and to examine the contents.'

He helped himself to a cigar and leaned back with a fiercely critical pair of eyes, taking note of the effect which this document would produce.

I had opened the volume with some expectation of a revelation, though of what nature I could not imagine. The first page was disappointing, however, as it contained nothing but the picture of a very fat man in a pea-jacket, with the legend, 'Jimmy Colver on the Mail-boat', written beneath it. There followed several pages which were filled with small sketches of Indians and their ways. Then came a picture of a cheerful and corpulent ecclesiastic in a shovel hat, sitting opposite a very thin European, and the inscription: 'Lunch with Fra Cristofero at Rosario'. Studies of women and babies accounted for several more pages, and then there was an unbroken series of animal drawings with such explanations as 'Manatee upon Sandbank', 'Turtles and their Eggs', 'Black Ajouti under a Miriti Palm' – the latter disclosing some sort of pig-like animal; and finally came a double page of studies of long-snouted and very unpleasant saurians. I could make nothing of it, and said so to the Professor.

'Surely these are only crocodiles?'

'Alligators! Alligators! There is hardly such a thing as a true crocodile in South America. The distinction between them –'

'I meant that I could see nothing unusual – nothing to justify what you have said.'

He smiled serenely.

'Try the next page,' said he.

I was still unable to sympathize. It was a full-page sketch of a landscape roughly tinted in colour – the kind of painting which an open-air artist takes as a guide to a future more elaborate effort. There was a pale-green foreground of feathery vegetation, which sloped upwards and ended in a line of cliffs dark red in colour, and curiously ribbed like some basaltic formations which I have seen. They extended in an unbroken wall right across the background. At one point was an isolated pyramidal rock, crowned by a great tree, which appeared to be separated by a cleft from the main crag. Behind it all, a blue tropical sky. A thin green line of vegetation fringed the summit of the ruddy cliff. On the next page was another water-colour wash of the same place, but much nearer, so that one could clearly see the details.

'Well?' he asked.

'It is no doubt a curious formation,' said I, 'but I am not geologist enough to say that it is wonderful.'

'Wonderful!' he repeated. 'It is unique. It is incredible. No one on earth has ever dreamed of such a possibility. Now the next.'

I turned it over, and gave an exclamation of surprise. There was a full-page picture of the most extraordinary creature that I had ever seen. It was the wild dream of an opium smoker, a vision of delirium. The head was like that of a fowl, the body that of a bloated lizard, the trailing tail was furnished with upward-turned spikes, and the curved back was edged with a high serrated fringe, which looked like a dozen cocks' wattles placed behind each other. In front of this creature was an absurd mannikin, or dwarf in the human form, who stood staring at it.

'Well, what do you think of that?' cried the Professor, rubbing his hands with an air of triumph.

'It is monstrous – grotesque.'

'But what made him draw such an animal?'

'Trade gin, I should think.'

'Oh, that's the best explanation you can give, is it?'

'Well, sir, what is yours?'

'The obvious one that the creature exists. That it is actually sketched from the life.'

I should have laughed only that I had a vision of our doing another Catherine-wheel down the passage.

'No doubt,' said I, 'no doubt,' as one humours an imbecile. 'I confess, however,' I added, 'that this tiny human figure puzzles me. If it were an Indian we could set it down as evidence of some pigmy race in America, but it appears to be a European in a sun-hat.'

The Professor snorted like an angry buffalo. 'You really touch the limit,' said he. 'You enlarge my view of the possible. Cerebral paresis! Mental inertia! Wonderful!'

He was too absurd to make me angry. Indeed, it was a waste of energy, for if you were going to be angry with this man you would be angry all the time. I contented myself with smiling wearily. 'It struck me that the man was small,' said I.

'Look here!' he cried, leaning forward and dabbing a great hairy sausage of a finger on to the picture. 'You see that plant behind the animal; I suppose you thought it was a dandelion or a brussels sprout – what? Well, it is a vegetable ivory palm, and they run to about fifty or sixty feet. Don't you see that the man is put in for a purpose? He couldn't really have stood in front of that brute and lived to draw it. He sketched himself in to give a scale of heights. He was, we will say, over five feet high. The tree is ten times bigger, which is what one would expect.'

'Good heavens!' I cried. 'Then you think the beast was – Why, Charing Cross Station would hardly make a kennel for such a brute!'

'Apart from exaggeration, he is certainly a well-grown specimen,' said the Professor, complacently.

'But,' I cried, 'surely the whole experience of the human race is not to be set aside on account of a single sketch –' I had turned over the leaves and ascertained that there was nothing more in the book – 'a single sketch by a wandering American artist who may have done it under hashish, or in the delirium of fever, or simply in order to gratify a freakish imagination. You can't, as a man of science, defend such a position as that.'

For answer the Professor took a book down from a shelf.

'This is an excellent monograph by my gifted friend, Ray Lankester!' said he. 'There is an illustration here which would interest you. Ah, yes, here it is! The inscription beneath it runs: "Probable appearance in life of the Jurassic Dinosaur Stegosaurus. The hind leg alone is twice as tall as a full-grown man." Well, what do you make of that?'

He handed me the open book. I started as I looked at the picture. In this reconstructed animal of a dead world there was certainly a very great resemblance to the sketch of the unknown artist.

'That is certainly remarkable,' said I.

'But you won't admit that it is final?'

'Surely it might be a coincidence, or this American may have seen a picture of the kind and carried it in his memory. It would be likely to recur to a man in a delirium.'

'Very good,' said the Professor, indulgently; 'we leave it at that. I will now ask you to look at this bone.' He handed over the bone which he had already described as part of the dead man's possessions. It was about six inches long, and thicker than my thumb, with some indications of dried cartilage at one end of it.

'To what known creature does that bone belong?' asked the Professor.

I examined it with care, and tried to recall some half-forgotten knowledge.

'It might be a very thick human collar-bone,' I said.

My companion waved his hand in contemptuous deprecation.

'The human collar-bone is curved. This is straight. There is a groove upon its surface showing that a great tendon played across it, which could not be the case with a clavicle.'

'Then I must confess that I don't know what it is.'

'You need not be ashamed to expose your ignorance, for I don't suppose the whole South Kensington staff could give a name to it.' He took a little bone the size of a bean out of a pill-box. 'So far as I am a judge this human bone is the analogue of the one which you hold in your hand. That will give you some idea of the size of the creature. You will observe from the cartilage that this is no fossil specimen, but recent. What do you say to that?'

'Surely in an elephant –'

He winced as if in pain.

'Don't! Don't talk of elephants in South America. Even in these days of Board Schools – '

'Well,' I interrupted, 'any large South American animal – a tapir, for example.'

'You may take it, young man, that I am versed in the elements of my business. This is not a conceivable bone either of a tapir or of any other creature known to zoology. It belongs to a very large, a very strong, and, by all analogy, a very fierce animal which exists upon the face of the earth, but has not yet come under the notice of science. You are unconvinced?'

'I am at least deeply interested.'

'Then your case is not hopeless. I feel that there is reason lurking in you somewhere, so we will patiently grope round for it. We will now leave the dead American and proceed with my narrative. You can imagine that I could hardly come away from the Amazon without probing deeper into the matter. There were indications as to the direction from which the dead traveller had come. Indian legends would alone have been my guide, for I found that rumours of a strange land were common among all the riverine tribes. You have heard, no doubt, of Curupuri?'

'Never.'

'Curupuri is the spirit of the woods, something terrible, something malevolent, something to be avoided. None can describe its shape or nature, but it is a word of terror along the Amazon. Now all tribes agree as to the direction in which Curupuri lives. It was the same direction from which the American had come. Something terrible lay that way. It was my business to find out what it was.'

'What did you do?' My flippancy was all gone. This massive man compelled one's attention and respect.

'I overcame the extreme reluctance of the natives – a reluctance which extends even to talk upon the subject – and by judicious persuasion and gifts, aided, I will admit, by some threats of coercion, I got two of them to act as guides. After many adventures which I need not describe, and after travelling a distance which I will not mention, in a direction which I withhold, we came at last to a tract of country which has never been described, nor, indeed, visited save by my unfortunate predecessor. Would you kindly look at this?'

He handed me a photograph – half-plate size.

'The unsatisfactory appearance of it is due to the fact,' said he, 'that on descending the river the boat was upset and the case which contained the undeveloped films was broken, with disastrous results. Nearly all of them were totally ruined – an irreparable loss. This is one of the few which partially escaped. This explanation of deficiencies or abnormalities you will kindly accept. There was talk of faking. I am not in a mood to argue such a point.'

The photograph was certainly very off-coloured. An unkind critic might easily have misinterpreted that dim surface. It was a dull grey landscape, and as I gradually deciphered the details of it I realized that it represented a long and enormously high line of cliffs exactly like an immense cataract seen in the distance, with a sloping, tree-clad plain in the foreground.

'I believe it is the same place as the painted picture,' said I.

'It *is* the same place,' the Professor answered. 'I found traces of the fellow's camp. Now look at this.'

It was a nearer view of the same scene, though the photograph was extremely defective. I could distinctly see the isolated, tree-crowned pinnacle of rock which was detached from the crag.

'I have no doubt of it at all,' said I.

'Well, that is something gained,' said he. 'We progress, do we not? Now, will you please look at the top of that rocky pinnacle? Do you observe something there?'

'An enormous tree.'

'But on the tree?'

'A large bird,' said I.

He handed me a lens.

'Yes,' I said, peering through it, 'a large bird stands on the tree. It appears to have a considerable beak. I should say it was a pelican.'

'I cannot congratulate you upon your eyesight,' said the Professor. 'It is not a pelican, nor, indeed, is it a bird. It may interest you to know that I succeeded in shooting that particular specimen. It was the only absolute proof of my experiences which I was able to bring away with me.'

'You have it, then?' Here at last was tangible corroboration.

'I had it. It was unfortunately lost with so much else in the same boat accident which ruined my photographs. I clutched at it as it disappeared in the swirl of the rapids, and part of its wing was left in my hand. I was insensible when washed ashore, but the miserable remnant of my superb specimen was still intact; I now lay it before you.'

From a drawer he produced what seemed to me to be the upper portion of the wing of a large bat. It was at least two feet in length, a curved bone, with a membranous veil beneath it.

'A monstrous bat!' I suggested.

'Nothing of the sort,' said the Professor, severely. 'Living, as I do, in an educated and scientific atmosphere, I could not have conceived that the first principles of zoology were so little known. Is it possible that you do not know the elementary fact in comparative anatomy, that the wing of a bird is really the forearm, while the wing of a bat consists of three elongated fingers with membranes between? Now, in this case, the bone is certainly not the forearm, and you can see for yourself that this is a single membrane hanging upon a single bone, and therefore that it cannot belong to a bat. But if it is neither bird not bat, what is it?'

My small stock of knowledge was exhausted.

'I really do not know,' said I.

He opened the standard work to which he had already referred me.

'Here,' said he, pointing to the picture of an extraordinary flying monster, 'is an excellent reproduction of the dimorphodon, or pterodactyl, a flying reptile of the Jurassic period. On the next page is a diagram of the mechanism of its wing. Kindly compare it with the specimen in your hand.'

A wave of amazement passed over me as I looked. I was convinced. There could be no getting away from it. The cumulative proof was overwhelming. The sketch, the photographs, the narrative, and now the actual specimen – the evidence was complete. I said so – I said so warmly, for I felt that the Professor was an ill-used man. He leaned back in his chair with drooping eyelids and a tolerant smile, basking in this sudden gleam of sunshine.

'It's just the very biggest thing that I ever heard of!' said I, though it was my journalistic rather than my scientific enthusiasm that was roused. 'It is colossal. You are a Columbus of science who has discovered a lost world. I'm really awfully sorry if I seemed to doubt you. It was all so unthinkable. But I understand evidence when I see it, and this should be good enough for anyone.'

The Professor purred with satisfaction.

'And then, sir, what did you do next?'

'It was the wet season, Mr. Malone, and my stores were exhausted. I explored some portion of this huge cliff, but I was unable to find any way to scale it. The pyramidal rock upon which I saw and shot the pterodactyl was more accessible. Being something of a cragsman, I did manage to get half-way to the top of that. From that height I had a better idea of the plateau upon the top of the crags. It appeared to be very large; neither to east nor to west could I see any end to the vista of green-capped cliffs. Below, it is a swampy, jungly region, full of snakes, insects, and fever. It is a natural protection to this singular country.'

'Did you see any other trace of life?'

'No, sir, I did not; but during the week that we lay encamped at the base of the cliff we heard some very strange noises from above.'

'But the creature that the American drew? How do you account for that?'

'We can only suppose that he must have made his way to the summit and seen it there. We know, therefore, that there *is* a way up. We know equally that it must be a very difficult one, otherwise the creatures would have come down and overrun the surrounding country. Surely that is clear?'

'But how do they come to be there?'

'I do not think that the problem is a very obscure one,' said the Professor; 'there can only be one explanation. South America is, as you may have heard, a granite continent. At this single point in the interior there has been, in some far distant age, a great, sudden volcanic upheaval. These cliffs, I may remark, are basaltic, and therefore plutonic. An area, as large perhaps as Sussex, has been lifted up *en bloc* with all its living contents, and cut off by perpendicular precipices of a hardness which defies erosion from all the rest of the continent. What is the result? Why, the ordinary laws of nature are suspended. The various checks which influence the struggle for existence in the world at large are all neutralized or altered. Creatures survive which would otherwise disappear. You will observe that both the pterodactyl and the stegosaurus are Jurassic, and therefore of a great age in the order of life. They have been artificically conserved by those strange accidental conditions.'

'But surely your evidence is conclusive. You have only to lay it before the proper authorities.'

'So, in my simplicity, I had imagined,' said the Professor, bitterly. 'I can only tell you that it was not so, that I was met at every turn by incredulity, born partly of stupidity and partly of jealousy. It is not my nature, sir, to cringe to any man, or to seek to prove a fact if my word has been doubted. After the first I have not condescended to show such corroborative proofs as I possess. The subject became hateful to me – I would not speak of it. When men like yourself, who represent the foolish curiosity of the public, came to disturb my privacy I was unable to meet them with dignified reserve. By nature I am, I admit, somewhat fiery, and under provocation I am inclined to be violent. I fear you may have remarked it.'

I nursed my eye and was silent.

'My wife has frequently remonstrated with me upon the subject, and yet I fancy that any man of honour would feel the same. To-night, however, I propose to give an extreme example of the control of the will over the emotions. I invite you to be present at the exhibition.' He handed me a card from his desk. 'You will perceive that Mr. Percival Waldron, a naturalist of some popular repute, is announced to lecture at eight-thirty at the Zoological Institute's Hall upon "The Record of the Ages". I have been specially invited to be present upon the platform, and to move a vote of thanks to the lecturer. While doing so, I shall make it my business, with infinite tact and delicacy, to throw out a few remarks which may arouse the interest of the audience and cause some of them to desire to go more deeply into the matter. Nothing contentious, you understand, but only an indication that there are greater deeps beyond. I shall hold myself strongly in leash, and see whether by this selfrestraint I attain a more favourable result.'

'And I may come?' I asked eagerly.

'Why, surely,' he answered, cordially. He had an enormously massive genial manner, which was almost as over-powering as his violence. His smile of benevolence was a wonderful thing, when his cheeks would suddenly bunch into two red apples, between his half-closed eyes and his great black beard. 'By all means, come. It will be a comfort to me to know that I have one ally in the hall, however inefficient and ignorant of the subject he may be. I fancy there will be a large audience, for Waldron, though an absolute charlatan, has a considerable popular following. Now, Mr. Malone, I have given you rather more of my time than I had intended. The individual must not monopolize what is meant for the world. I shall be pleased to see you at the lecture to-night. In the meantime, you will understand that no public use is to be made of any of the material that I have given you.'

'But Mr. McArdle – my news editor, you know – will want to know what I have done.'

'Tell him what you like. You can say, among other things, that if he sends anyone else to intrude upon me I shall call upon him with a riding whip. But I leave it to you that nothing of all this appears in print. Very good. Then the Zoological Institute's Hall at eight-thirty tonight.' I had a last impression of red cheeks, blue rippling beard, and tolerant eyes, as he waved me out of the room.

5

Question!

WHAT with the physical shocks incidental to my first interview with Professor Challenger and the mental ones which accompanied the second, I was a somewhat demoralized journalist by the time I found myself in Enmore Park once more. In my aching head the one thought was throbbing that there really *was* truth in this man's story, that it was of tremendous consequence, and that it would work up into inconceivable copy for the *Gazette* when I could obtain permission to use it. A taxicab was waiting at the end of the road, so I sprang into it and drove down to the office. McArdle was at his post as usual.

'Well,' he cried, expectantly, 'what may it run to? I'm thinking, young man, you have been in the wars. Don't tell me that he assaulted you.'

'We had a little difference at first.'

'What a man it is! What did you do?'

'Well, he became more reasonable and we had a chat. But I got nothing out of him – nothing for publication.'

'I'm not so sure about that. You got a black eye out of him, and that's for publication. We can't have this reign of terror, Mr. Malone. We must bring the man to his bearings. I'll have a leaderette on him to-morrow that will raise a blister. Just give me the material and I will engage to brand the fellow for ever. Professor Munchausen – how's that for an inset headline? Sir John Mandeville redivivus – Cagliostro – all the impostors and bullies in history. I'll show him up for the fraud he is.'

'I wouldn't do that, sir.'

'Why not?'

'Because he is not a fraud at all.'

'What!' roared McArdle. 'You don't mean to say you really believe this stuff of his about mammoths and mastodons and great sea sairpents?'

'Well, I don't know about that. I don't think he makes any claims of that kind. But I do believe that he has got something new.'

'Then for Heaven's sake, man, write it up!'

'I'm longing to, but all I know he gave me in confidence and on condition that I didn't.' I condensed into a few sentences the Professor's narrative. 'That's how it stands.'

McArdle looked deeply incredulous.

'Well, Mr. Malone,' he said at last, 'about this scientific meeting to-night; there can be no privacy about that, anyhow. I don't suppose any paper will want to report it, for Waldron has been reported already a dozen times, and no one is aware that Challenger will speak. We may get a scoop, if we are lucky. You'll be there in any case, so you'll just give us a pretty full report. I'll keep space up to midnight.'

My day was a busy one, and I had an early dinner at the Savage Club with Tarp Henry, to whom I gave some account of my adventures. He listened with a sceptical smile on his gaunt face, and roared with laughter on hearing that the Professor had convinced me.

'My dear chap, things don't happen like that in real life. People don't stumble upon enormous discoveries and then lose their evidence. Leave that to the novelists. The fellow is as full of tricks as the monkey-house at the Zoo. It's all absolute bosh.'

'But the American poet?'

'He never existed.'

'I saw his sketch-book.'

'Challenger's sketch-book.'

'You think he drew that animal?'

'Of course he did. Who else?'

'Well, then, the photographs?'

'There was nothing in the photographs. By your own admission you only saw a bird.'

'A pterodactyl.'

'That's what *he* says. He put the pterodactyl into your head.'

'Well, then, the bones?'

'First one out of an Irish stew. Second one vamped up for the occasion. If you are clever and you know your business you can fake a bone as easily as you can a photograph.'

I began to feel uneasy. Perhaps, after all, I had been premature in my acquiescence. Then I had a sudden happy thought.

'Will you come to the meeting?' I asked.

Tarp Henry looked thoughtful.

'He is not a popular person, the genial Challenger,' said he. 'A lot of people have accounts to settle with him. I should say he is about the best-hated man in London. If the medical students turn out there will be no end of a rag. I don't want to get into a bear-garden.'

'You might at least do him the justice to hear him state his own case.'

'Well, perhaps it's only fair. All right. I'm your man for the evening.'

When we arrived at the hall we found a much greater concourse than I had expected. A line of electric broughams discharged their little cargoes of white-bearded professors, while the dark stream of humbler pedestrians, who crowded through the arched doorway, showed that the audience would be popular as well as scientific. Indeed, it became evident to us as soon as we had taken our seats that a youthful and even boyish spirit was abroad in the gallery and the back portions of the hall. Looking behind me, I could see rows of faces of the familiar medical student type. Apparently the great hospitals had each sent down their contingent. The behaviour of the audience at present was good-humoured, but mischievous. Scraps of popular songs were chorused with an enthusiasm which was a strange prelude to a scientific lecture, and there was already a tendency to personal chaff which promised a jovial evening to others, however embarrassing it might be to the recipients of these dubious honours.

Thus, when old Doctor Meldrum, with his well-known curly-brimmed opera-hat, appeared upon the platform, there was such a universal query of 'Where *did* you get that tile?' that he hurriedly removed it, and concealed it furtively under his chair. When gouty Professor Wadley limped down to his seat there were general affectionate inquiries from all parts of the hall as to the exact state of his poor toe, which caused him obvious embarrassment. The greatest demonstration of all, however, was at the entrance of my new acquaintance, Professor Challenger, when he passed down to take his place at the extreme end of the front row of the platform. Such a yell of welcome broke forth when his black beard first protruded round the corner that I began to suspect Tarp Henry was right in his surmise, and that this assemblage was there not merely for the sake of the lecture, but because it had got rumoured abroad that the famous Professor would take part in the proceedings.

There was some sympathetic laughter on his entrance among the front benches of well-dressed spectators, as though the demonstration of the students in this instance was not unwelcome to them. That greeting was, indeed, a frightful outburst of sound, the uproar of the carnivora cage when the step of the bucket-bearing keeper is heard in the distance. There was an offensive tone in it, perhaps, and yet in the main it struck me as mere riotous outcry, the noisy reception of one who amused and interested them, rather than of one they disliked or despised. Challenger smiled with weary and tolerant contempt, as a kindly man would meet the yapping of a litter of puppies. He sat slowly down, blew out his chest, passed his hand caressingly down his beard, and looked with drooping eyelids and supercilious eyes at the crowded hall before him. The uproar of his advent had not yet died away when Professor Ronald Murray, the Chairman, and Mr. Waldron, the lecturer, threaded their way to the front, and the proceedings began.

Professor Murray will, I am sure, excuse me if I say that he has the common fault of most Englishmen of being inaudible. Why on earth people who have something to say which is worth hearing should not take the slight trouble to learn how to make it heard is one of the strange mysteries of modern life. Their methods are as reasonable as to try to pour some precious stuff from the spring to the reservoir through a non-conducting pipe, which could by the least effort be opened. Professor Murray made several profound remarks to his white tie and to the water-carafe upon the table, with a humorous, twinkling aside to the silver candlestick upon his right. Then he sat down, and Mr. Waldron, the famous lecturer, rose amid a general murmur of applause. He was a stern, gaunt man, with a harsh voice and an aggressive manner, but he had the merit of knowing how to assimilate the ideas of other men, and to pass them on in a way which was intelligible and even interesting to the lay public, with a happy knack of being funny about the most unlikely objects, so that the precession of the Equinox or the formation of a vertebrate became a highly humorous process as treated by him.

It was a bird's-eye view of creation, as interpreted by science, which, in language always clear and sometimes picturesque, he unfolded before us. He told us of the globe, a huge mass of flaming gas, flaring through the heavens. Then he pictured the solidification, the cooling, the wrinkling which formed the mountains, the steam which turned to water, the slow preparation of the stage upon which was to be played the inexplicable drama of life. On the origin of life itself he was discreetly vague. That the germs of it could hardly have survived the original roasting was, he declared, fairly certain. Therefore it had come later. Had it built itself out of the cooling, inorganic elements of the globe? Very likely. Had the germs of it arrived from outside upon a meteor? It was hardly conceivable. On the whole, the wisest man was the least dogmatic upon the point. We could not – or at least we had not succeeded up to date in making organic life in our laboratories out of inorganic materials. The gulf between the dead and the living was something which our chemistry could not as yet bridge. But there was a higher and subtler chemistry of Nature, which, working with great forces over long epochs, might well produce results which were impossible for us. There the matter must be left.

This brought the lecturer to the great ladder of animal life, beginning low down in molluscs and feeble sea creatures, then up rung by rung through reptiles and fishes, till at last we came to a kangaroo-rat, a creature which brought forth its young alive, the direct ancestor of all mammals, and presumably, therefore, of everyone in the audience. ('No, no,' from a sceptical student in the back row.) If the young gentleman in the red tie who cried 'No, no', and who presumably claimed to have been hatched out of an egg, would wait upon him after the lecture, he would be glad to see such a curiosity. (Laughter.) It was strange to think that the climax of all the age-long processes of Nature had been the creation of that gentleman in the red tie. But had the process stopped? Was this gentleman to be taken as the final type – the be-all and end-all of development? He hoped that he would not hurt the feelings of the gentleman in the red tie if he maintained that, whatever virtues that gentleman might possess in private life, still the vast processes of the universe were not fully justified if they were to end entirely in his production. Evolution was not a spent force, but one still working, and even greater achievements were in store.

Having thus, amid a general titter, played very prettily with his interrupter, the lecturer went back to his picture of the past, the drying of the seas, the emergence of the sand-bank, the sluggish, viscous life which lay upon their margins, the overcrowded lagoons, the tendency of the sea creatures to take refuge upon the mud-flats, the abundance of food awaiting them, their consequent enormous growth. 'Hence, ladies and gentleman,' he added, 'that frightful brood of saurians which still affright our eyes when seen in the Wealden or in the Solenhofen slates, but which were fortunately extinct long before the first appearance of mankind upon this planet.'

'Question!' boomed a voice from the platform.

Mr. Waldron was a strict disciplinarian with a gift of acid humour, as exemplified upon the gentleman with the red tie, which made it perilous to interrupt him. But this interjection appeared to him so absurd that he was at a loss how to deal with it. So looks the Shakespearean who is confronted by a rancid Baconian, or the astronomer who is assailed by a flat-earth fanatic. He paused for a moment, and then, raising his voice, repeated slowly the words: Which were extinct before the coming of man.'

'Question!' boomed the voice once more.

Waldron looked with amazement along the line of professors upon the platform until his eyes fell upon the figure of Challenger, who leaned back in his chair with closed eyes and an amused expression, as if he were smiling in his sleep.

'I see!' said Waldron, with a shrug. 'It is my friend Professor Challenger,' and amid laughter he renewed his lecture as if this was a final explanation and no more need be said.

But the incident was far from being closed. Whatever path the lecturer took amid the wilds of the past seemed invariably to lead him to some assertion as to extinct or prehistoric life which instantly brought the same bull's bellow from the Professor. The audience began to anticipate it and to roar with delight when it came. The packed benches of students joined in, and every time Challenger's beard opened, before any sound could come forth, there was a yell of 'Question!' from a hundred voices, and an answering counter-cry of 'Order!' and 'Shame!' from as many more. Waldron, though a hardened lecturer and a strong man, became rattled.

He hesitated, stammered, repeated himself, got snarled in a long sentence, and finally turned furiously upon the cause of his troubles.

'This is really intolerable!' he cried, glaring across the platform. 'I must ask you, Professor Challenger, to cease these ignorant and unmannerly interruptions.'

There was a hush over the hall, the students rigid with delight at seeing the high gods on Olympus quarrelling among themselves. Challenger levered his bulky figure slowly out of his chair.

'I must in turn ask you, Mr. Waldron,' he said, 'to cease to make assertions which are not in strict accordance with scientific fact.'

The words unloosed a tempest. 'Shame! Shame!' 'Give him a hearing!' 'Put him out!' 'Shove him off the platform!' 'Fair play!' emerged from a general roar of amusement or execration. The chairman was on his feet flapping both his hands and bleating excitedly. 'Professor Challenger – personal – views – later,' were the solid peaks above his clouds of inaudible mutter. The interrupter bowed, smiled, stroked his beard, and relapsed into his chair. Waldron, very flushed and warlike, continued his observations. Now and then, as he made an assertion, he shot a venemous glance at his opponent, who seemed to be slumbering deeply, with the same broad, happy smile upon his face.

At last the lecture came to an end – I am inclined to think that it was a premature one, as the peroration was hurried and disconnected. The thread of the argument had been rudely broken, and the audience was restless and expectant. Waldron sat down, and after a chirrup from the chairman, Professor Challenger rose and advanced to the edge of the platform. In the interests of my paper I took down his speech verbatim.

'Ladies and Gentlemen, ' he began, amid a sustained interruption from the back. 'I beg pardon – Ladies, Gentlemen, and Children – I must apologize, I had inadvertently omitted a considerable section of this audience' (tumult, during which the Professor stood with one hand raised and his enormous head nodding sympathetically, as if he were bestowing a pontifical blessing upon the crowd), 'I have been selected to move a vote of thanks to Mr. Waldron for the very picturesque and imaginative address to which we have just listened. There are points in it with which I disagree, and it has been my duty to indicate them as they aro:se, but, none the less, Mr. Waldron has accomplished his object well, that object being to give a simple and interesting account of what he conceives to have been the history of our planet. Popular lectures are the easiest to listen to, but Mr. Waldron' (here he beamed and blinked at the lecturer) 'will excuse me when I say that they are necessarily both superficial and misleading, since they have to be graded to the comprehension of an ignorant audience.' (Ironical cheering.) 'Popular lecturers are in their nature parasitic.' (Angry gesture of protest from Mr. Waldron.) 'They exploit for fame or cash the work which has been done by the indigent and unknown brethren. One smallest new fact obtained in the laboratory, one brick built into the temple of science, far outweighs any second-hand exposition which passes an idle hour, but can leave no useful result behind it. I put forward this obvious reflection, not out of any desire to disparage Mr. Waldron in particular, but that you may not lose your sense of proportion and mistake the acolyte for the high priest.' (At this point Mr. Waldron whispered to the chairman, who half rose and said something severely to his water-carafe.) 'But enough of this!' (Loud and prolonged cheers.) 'Let me pass to some subject of wider interest. What is the particular point upon which I, as an original investigator, have challenged our lecturer's accuracy? It is upon the permanence of certain types of animal life upon the earth. I do not speak upon this subject as an amateur, nor, I may add, as a popular lecturer, but I speak as one whose scientific conscience compels him to adhere closely to facts, when I say that Mr. Waldron is very wrong in supposing that because he has never himself seen a so-called prehistoric animal, therefore these creatures no longer exist. They are indeed, as he has said, our ancestors, but they are, if I may use the expression, our contemporary ancestors, who can still be found with all their hideous and formidable characteristics if one has but the energy and hardihood to seek their haunts. Creatures which were supposed to be Jurassic, monsters who would hunt down and devour our largest and fiercest mammals, still exist.' (Cries of 'Bosh!' 'Prove it!' 'How do *you* know?' 'Question!') 'How do I know? you ask me. I know because I have visited their secret haunts. I know because I have seen some of them.' (Applause, uproar, and a voice, 'Liar!') 'Am I a liar?' (General hearty and noisy assent.) 'Did I hear someone say that I was a liar? Will the person who called me a liar kindly stand up that I may know him?' (A voice, 'Here he is, sir!' and an inoffensive little person in spectacles, struggling violently, was held up among a group of students.) 'Did you venture to call me a liar?' ('No, sir, no!' shouted the accused, and disappeared like a Jack-in-the-box.) 'If any person in this hall dares to doubt my veracity, I shall be glad to have a few words with him after the lecture.' ('Liar!') 'Who said that?' (Again the inoffensive one, plunging desperately was elevated high in the air.) 'If I come down among you – ' (General chorus of 'Come, love, come!' which interrupted the proceedings for some moments, while the chairman, standing up and waving both his arms, seemed to be conducting the music. The Professor, with his face flushed, his nostrils dilated, and his beard bristling, was now in a proper Berserk mood.) 'Every great discoverer has been met with the same incredulity – the sure brand of a generation of fools. When great facts are laid before you, you have not the intuition, the imagination which would help you to understand them. You can only throw mud at the men who have risked their lives to open new fields to science. You persecute the prophets! Galileo, Darwin, and I – ' (Prolonged cheering and complete interruption.)

All this is from my hurried notes taken at the time, which give little notion of the absolute chaos to which the assembly had by this time been reduced. So terrific was the uproar that several ladies had already beaten a hurried retreat. Grave and reverend seniors seemed to have caught the prevailing spirit as badly as the students, and I saw white-bearded men rising and shaking their fists at the obdurate Professor. The whole great audience seethed and simmered like a boiling pot. The Professor took a step forward and raised both his hands. There was something so big and arresting and virile in the man that the clatter and shouting died gradually away before his commanding gesture and his masterful eyes. He seemed to have a definite message. They hushed to hear it.

'I will not detain you,' he said. 'It is not worth it. Truth is truth, and the noise of a number of foolish young men – and, I fear I must add, of their equally foolish seniors – cannot affect the matter. I claim that I have opened a new field of science. You dispute it.' (Cheers.) 'Then I put you to the test. Will you accredit one or more of your own number to go out as your representatives and test my statement in your name?'

Mr. Summerlee, the veteran Professor of Comparative Anatomy, rose among the audience, a tall, thin, bitter man, with the withered aspect of a theologian. He wished, he said, to ask Professor Challenger whether the results to which he had alluded in his remarks had been obtained during a journey to the headwaters of the Amazon made by him two years before.

Professor Challenger answered that they had.

Mr. Summerlee desired to know how it was that Professor Challenger claimed to have made discoveries in those regions which had been overlooked by Wallace, Bates, and other previous explorers of established scientific repute.

Professor Challenger answered that Mr. Summerlee appeared to be confusing the Amazon with the Thames; that it was in reality a somewhat larger river; that Mr. Summerlee might be interested to know that with the Orinoco, which communicated with it, some fifty thousand miles of country were opened up, and that in so vast a space it was not impossible for one person to find what another had missed.

Mr. Summerlee declared, with an acid smile, that he fully appreciated the difference between the Thames and the Amazon, which lay in the fact that any assertion about the former could be tested, while about the latter it could not. He would be obliged if Professor Challenger would give the latitude and the longitude of the country in which prehistoric animals were to be found.

Professor Challenger replied that he reserved such information for good reasons of his own, but would be prepared to give it with proper precautions to a committee chosen from the audience. Would Mr. Summerlee serve on such a committee and test his story in person?

Mr. Summerlee: 'Yes, I will.' (Great cheering.)

Professor Challenger: 'Then I guarantee that I will place in your hands such material as will enable you to find your way. It is only right, however, since Mr. Summerlee goes to check my statement that I should have one or more with him who may check his. I will not disguise from you that there are difficulties and dangers. Mr. Summerlee will need a younger colleague. May I ask for volunteers?'

It is thus that the great crisis of a man's life springs out at him. Could I have imagined when I entered that hall that I was about to pledge myself to a wilder adventure than had ever come to me in my dreams? But Gladys – was it not the very opportunity of which she spoke? Gladys would have told me to go. I had sprung to my feet. I was speaking, and yet I had prepared no words. Tarp Henry, my companion, was plucking at my skirts and I heard him whispering, 'Sit down, Malone! Don't make a public ass of yourself.' At the same time I was aware that a tall, thin man, with dark gingery hair, a few seats in front of me, was also upon his feet. He glared back at me with hard angry eyes, but I refused to give way.

'I will go, Mr. Chairman,' I kept repeating over and over again.

'Name! Name!' cried the audience.

'My name is Edward Dunn Malone. I am the reporter of the *Daily Gazette*. I claim to be an absolutely unprejudiced witness.'

'What is *your* name, sir?' the chairman asked of my tall rival.

'I am Lord John Roxton. I have already been up the Amazon, I know all the ground, and have special qualifications for this investigation.'

'Lord John Roxton's reputation as a sportsman and a traveller is, of course, world-famous,' said the chairman; 'at the same time it would certainly be as well to have a member of the Press upon such an expedition.'

'Then I move,' said Professor Challenger, 'that both these gentlemen be elected, as representatives of this meeting, to accompany Professor Summerlee upon his journey to investigate and to report upon the truth of my statements.'

And so, amid shouting and cheering, our fate was decided, and I found myself borne away in the human current which swirled towards the door, with my mind half stunned by the vast new project which had risen so suddenly before it. As I emerged from the hall I was conscious for a moment of a rush of laughing students down the pavement, and of an arm wielding a heavy umbrella, which rose and fell in the midst of them. Then, amid a mixture of groans and cheers, Professor Challenger's electric brougham slid from the kerb, and I found myself walking under the silvery lights of Regent Street, full of thoughts of Gladys and of wonder as to my future.

Suddenly there was a touch at my elbow. I turned, and found myself looking into the humorous, masterful eyes of the tall, thin man who had volunteered to be my companion on this strange quest.

'Mr. Malone, I understand,' said he. 'We are to be companions – what? My rooms are just over the road, in the Albany. Perhaps you would have the kindness to spare me half an hour, for there are one or two things that I badly want to say to you.'

6

I Was the Flail of the Lord

LORD JOHN ROXTON and I turned down Vigo Street together and through the dingy portals of the famous aristocratic rookery. At the end of a long drab passage my new acquaintance pushed open a door and turned on an electric switch. A number of lamps shining through tinted shades bathed the whole great room before us in a ruddy radiance. Standing in the doorway and glancing round me, I had a general impression of extraordinary comfort and elegance compared with an atmosphere of masculine virility. Everywhere there were mingled the luxury of the wealthy man of taste and the careless untidiness of the bachelor. Rich furs and strange iridescent mats from some Oriental bazaar were scattered upon the floor. Pictures and prints which even my unpractised eyes could recognize as being of great price and rarity hung thick upon the walls. Sketches of boxers, of ballet-girls, and of race-horses alternated with a sensuous Fragonard, a martial Girardet, and a dreamy Turner. But amid these varied ornaments there were scattered the trophies which brought back strongly to my recollection the fact that Lord John Roxton was one of the great all-round sportsmen and athletes of his day. A dark-blue oar crossed with a cherry-pink one above his mantel-piece spoke of the old Oxonian and Leander man, while the foils and boxing-gloves above and below them were the tools of a man who had won supremacy with each. Like a dado round the room was the jutting line of splendid heavy game-heads, the best of their sort from every quarter of the world, with the rare white rhinoceros of the Lado Enclave drooping its supercilious lip above them all.

In the centre of the rich red carpet was a black and gold Louis Quinze table, a lovely antique, now sacrilegiously desecrated with marks of glasses and the scars of cigarstumps. On it stood a silver tray of smokables and a burnished spirit-stand, from which and an adjacent siphon my silent host proceeded to charge two high glasses. Having indicated an arm-chair to me and placed my refreshment near it, he handed me a long, smooth Havana. Then, seating himself opposite to me, he looked at me long and fixedly with his strange, twinkling, reckless eyes – eyes of a cold light blue, the colour of a glacier lake.

Through the thin haze of my cigar smoke I noted the details of a face which was already familiar to me from many photographs – the strongly-curved nose, the hollow, worn cheeks, the dark, ruddy hair, thin at the top, the crisp, virile moustaches, the small, aggressive tuft upon his projecting chin. Something there was of Napoleon III, something of Don Quixote, and yet again something which was the essence of the English country gentleman, the keen alert, open-air lover of dogs and of horses. His skin was of a rich flower-pot red from sun and wind. His eyebrows were tufted and overhanging, which gave those naturally cold eyes an almost ferocious aspect, an impression which was increased by his strong and furrowed brow. In figure he was spare, but very strongly built – indeed, he had often proved that there were few men in England capable of such sustained exertions. His height was a little over six feet, but he seemed shorter on account of a peculiar rounding of the shoulders. Such was the famous Lord John Roxton as he sat opposite to me, biting hard upon his cigar and watching me steadily in a long and embarrassing silence.

'Well,' said he, at last, 'we've gone and done it, young fellah-my-lad.' (This curious phrase he pronounced as if it were all one word – 'young fellah-my-lad'.) 'Yes, we've taken a jump, you an' me. I suppose, now, when you went into that room there was no such notion in your head – what?'

'No thought of it.'

'The same here. No thought of it. And here we are, up to our necks in the tureen. Why, I've only been back three weeks from Uganda, and taken a place in Scotland, and signed the lease and all. Pretty goin's on – what? How does it hit you?'

'Well, it is all in the main line of my business. I am a journalist on the *Gazette*.'

'Of course – you said so when you took it on. By the way, I've got a small job for you, if you'll help me.'

'With pleasure.'

'Don't mind takin' a risk, do you?'

'What is the risk?'

'Well, it's Ballinger – he's the risk. You've heard of him?'

'No.'

'Why, young fellah, where *have* you lived? Sir John Ballinger is the best gentleman jock in the north country. I could hold him on the flat at my best, but over jumps he's my master. Well, it's an open secret that when he's out of trainin' he drinks hard – strikin' an average, he calls it. He got delirium on Toosday, and has been ragin' like a devil ever since. His room is above this. The doctors say that it is all up with the old dear unless some food is got into him, but as he lies in bed with a revolver on his coverlet, and swears he will put six of the best through anyone that comes near him, there's been a bit of a strike among the serving-men. He's a hard nail, is Jack, and a dead shot, too, but you can't leave a Grand National winner to die like that – what?'

'What do you mean to do, then?' I asked.

'Well, my idea was that you and I could rush him. He may be dozin', and at the worst he can only wing one of us, and the other should have him. If we can get his bolster-cover round his arms and then 'phone up a stomach-pump, we'll give the old dear the supper of his life.'

It was rather a desperate business to come suddenly into one's day's work. I don't think that I am a particularly brave man. I have an Irish imagination which makes the unknown and the untried more terrible than they are. On the other hand, I was brought up with a horror of cowardice and with a terror of such a stigma. I dare say that I could throw myself over a precipice, like the Hun in the history books, if my courage to do it were questioned, and yet it would surely be pride and fear, rather than courage, which would be my inspiration. Therefore, although every nerve in my body shrank from the whisky-maddened figure which I pictured in the room above, I still answered, in as careless a voice as I could command, that I was ready to go. Some further remark of Lord Roxton's about the danger only made me irritable.

'Talking won't make it any better,' said I. 'Come on.'

I rose from my chair and he from his. Then, with a little confidential chuckle of laughter, he patted me two or three times on the chest, finally pushing me back into my chair.

'All right, sonny my lad – you'll do,' said he.

I looked up in surprise.

'I saw after Jack Ballinger myself this mornin'. He blew a hole in the skirt of my kimono, bless his shaky old hand but we got a jacket on him, and he's to be all right in a week. I say, young fellah, I hope you don't mind – what? You see, between you an' me close-tiled, I look on this South American business as a mighty serious thing, and if I have a pal with me I want a man I can bank on. So I sized you down, and I'm bound to say that you came well out of it. You see, it's all up to you and me, for this old Summerlee man will want dry-nursin' from the first. By the way, are you by any chance the Malone who is expected to get his Rugby cap for Ireland?'

'A reserve, perhaps.'

'I thought I remembered your face. Why, I was there when you got that try against Richmond – as fine a swervin' run as I saw the whole season. I never miss a Rugby match if I can help it, for it is the manliest game we have left. Well, I didn't ask you in here just to talk sport. We've got to fix our business. Here are the sailin's, on the first page of *The Times*. There's a Booth boat for Para next Wednesday week, and if the Professor and you can work it, I think we should take it – what? Very good, I'll fix it with him. What about your outfit?'

'My paper will see to that.'

'Can you shoot?'

'About average Territorial standard.'

'Good Lord! as bad as that? It's the last thing you young fellahs think of learnin'. You're all bees without stings, so far as lookin' after the hive goes. You'll look silly, some o' these days, when someone comes along an' sneaks the honey. But you'll need to hold your gun straight in South America, for unless our friend the Professor is a madman or a liar, we may see some queer things before we get back. What gun have you?'

He crossed to an oaken cupboard, and as he threw it open I caught a glimpse of glistening rows of parallel barrels, like the pipes of an organ.

'I'll see what I can spare you out of my own battery,' said he.

One by one he took out a succession of beautiful rifles, opening and shutting them with a snap and a clang, and then patting them as he put them back into the rack as tenderly as a mother would fondle her children.

'This is a Bland's .577 axite express,' said he. 'I got that big fellow with it.' He glanced up at the white rhinoceros. 'Ten more yards, and he'd have added me to *his* collection.

"On that conical bullet his one chance hangs,
'Tis the weak one's advantage fair."

Hope you know your Gordon, for he's the poet of the horse and the gun and the man that handles both. Now, here's a useful tool – .470, telescopic sight, double ejector, point-blank up to three-fifty. That's the rifle I used against the Peruvian slave-drivers three years ago. I was the flail of the Lord up in those parts, I may tell you, though you won't find it in any Blue-book. There are times, young fellah, when every one of us must make a stand for human right and justice, or you never feel clean again. That's why I made a little war on my own. Declared it myself, waged it myself, ended it myself. Each of those nicks is for a slave murderer – a good row of them – what? That big one is for Pedro Lopez, the king of them all, that I killed in a back-water of the Putomayo River. Now, here's something that would do for you.' He took out a beautiful brown-and-silver rifle. 'Well rubbered at the stock, sharply sighted, five cartridges to the clip. You can trust your life to that.' He handed it to me and closed the door of his oak cabinet. 'By the way,' he continued, coming back to his chair, 'what do you know of this Professor Challenger?'

'I never saw him till to-day.'

'Well, neither did I. It's funny we should both sail under sealed orders from a man we don't know. He seemed an uppish old bird. His brothers of science don't seem too fond of him either. How came you to take an interest in the affair?'

I told him shortly my experiences of the morning, and he listened intently. Then he drew out a map of South America and laid it on the table.

'I believe every single word he said to you was the truth,' said he, earnestly, 'and, mind you, I have something to go on when I speak like that. South America is a place I love, and I think, if you take it right through from Darien to Fuego, it's the grandest, richest, most wonderful bit of earth upon this planet. People don't know it yet, and don't realize what it may become. I've been up an' down it from end to end, and had two dry seasons in those very parts, as I told you when I spoke of the war I made on the slave-dealers. Well, when I was up there I heard some yarns of the same kind – traditions of Indians and the like, but with somethin' behind them, no doubt. The more you knew of that country, young fellah, the more you would understand that anythin' was possible – *anythin'*. There are just some narrow water-lanes along which folk travel, and outside that it is all darkness. Now, down here in the Matto Grosso' – he swept his cigar over a part of the map – 'or up in this corner where three countries meet, nothin' would surprise me. As that chap said to-night, there are fifty thousand miles of water-way runnin' through a forest that is very near the size of Europe. You and I could be as far away from each other as Scotland is from Constantinople, and yet each of us be in the same great Brazilian forest. Man has just made a track here and a scrape there in the maze. Why, the river rises and falls the best part of forty feet, and half the country is a morass that you can't pass over. Why shouldn't somethin' new and wonderful lie in such a country? And why shouldn't we be the men to find it out? Besides,' he added, his queer, gaunt face shining with delight, 'there's a sportin' risk in every mile of it. I'm like an old golfball – I've had all the white paint knocked off me long ago. Life can whack me about now and it can't leave a mark. But a sportin' risk, young fellah, that's the salt of existence. Then it's worth livin' again. We're all gettin' a deal too soft and dull and comfy. Give me the great waste lands and the wide spaces, with a gun in my fist and somethin' to look for that's worth findin'. I've tried war and steeplechasin' and aeroplanes, but this huntin' of beasts that look like a lobster-supper dream is a brand-new sensation.' He chuckled with glee at the prospect.

Perhaps I have dwelt too long upon this new acquaintance, but he is to be my comrade for many a day, and so I have tried to set him down as I first saw him, with his quaint personality and his queer little tricks of speech and of thought. It was only the need of getting in the account of my meeting which drew me at last from his company. I left him seated amid his pink radiance, oiling the lock of his favourite rifle, while he still chuckled to himself at the thought of the adventures which awaited us. It was very clear to me that if dangers lay before us I could not in all England have found a cooler head or a braver spirit with which to share them.

That night, wearied as I was after the wonderful happenings of the day, I sat with McArdle, the news editor, explaining to him the whole situation, which he thought important enough to bring next morning before the notice of Sir George Beaumont, the chief. It was agreed that I should write home full accounts of my adventures in the shape of successive letters to McArdle, and that these should either be edited for the *Gazette* as they arrived, or held back to be published later, according to the wishes of Professor Challenger, since we could not yet know what conditions he might attach to those directions which should guide us to the unknown land. In response to a telephone inquiry, we received nothing more definite than a fulmination against the Press, ending up with the remark that if we would notify our boat he would hand us any directions which he might think it proper to give us at the moment of starting. A second question from us failed to elicit any answer at all, save a plaintive bleat from his wife to the effect that her husband was in a very violent temper already, and that she hoped we would do nothing to make it worse. A third attempt, later in the day, provoked a terrific crash, and a subsequent message from the Central Exchange that Professor Challenger's receiver had been shattered. After that we abandoned all attempt at communication.

And now, my patient readers, I can address you directly no longer. From now onwards (if, indeed, any continuation of this narrative should ever reach you) it can only be through the paper which I represent. In the hands of the editor I leave this account of the events which have led up to one of the most remarkable expeditions of all time, so that if I never return to England there shall be some record as to how the affair came about. I am writing these last lines in the saloon of the Booth liner *Francisca*, and they will go back by the pilot to the keeping of Mr. McArdle. Let me draw one last picture before I close the notebook – a picture which is the last memory of the old country which I bear away with me. It is a wet, foggy morning in the late spring; a thin, cold rain is falling. Three shining mackintoshed figures are walking down the quay, making for the gang-plank of the great liner from which the blue-peter is flying. In front of them a porter pushes a trolley piled high with trunks, wraps, and gun-cases. Professor Summerlee, a long, melancholy figure, walks with dragging steps and drooping head, as one who is already profoundly sorry for himself. Lord John Roxton steps briskly, and his thin, eager face beams forth between his hunting-cap and his muffler. As for myself, I am glad to have got the bustling days of preparation and the pangs of leave-taking behind me, and I have no doubt that I show it in my bearing. Suddenly, just as we reach the vessel, there is a shout behind us. It is Professor Challenger, who had promised to see us off. He runs after us, a puffing, red-faced irascible figure.

'No, thank you,' says he; 'I should much prefer not to go aboard. I have only a few words to say to you, and they can very well be said where we are. I beg you not to imagine that I am in any way indebted to you for making this journey. I would have you to understand that it is a matter of perfect indifference to me, and I refuse to entertain the most remote sense of personal obligation. Truth is truth, and nothing which you can report can affect it in any way, though it may excite the emotions and allay the curiosity of a number of very ineffectual people. My directions for your instruction and guidance are in this sealed envelope. You will open it when you reach a town upon the Amazon which is called Manaos, but not until the date and hour which is marked upon the outside. Have I made myself clear? I leave the strict observance of my conditions entirely to your honour. No, Mr. Malone, I will place no restriction upon your correspondence, since the ventilation of the facts is the object of your journey; but I demand that you shall give no particulars as to your exact destination, and that nothing be actually published until your return. Good-bye, sir. You have done something to mitigate my feelings for the loathsome profession to which you unhappily belong. Good-bye, Lord John. Science is, as I understand, a sealed book to you; but you may congratulate yourself upon the hunting-field which awaits you. You will, no doubt, have the opportunity of describing in the *Field* how you brought down the rocketing dimorphodon. And good-bye to you also, Professor Summerlee. If you are still capable of self-improvement, of which I am frankly unconvinced, you will surely return to London a wiser man.'

So he turned upon his heel, and a minute later from the deck I could see his short, squat figure bobbing about in the distance as he made his way back to his train. Well, we are well down Channel now. There's the last bell for letters and it's good-bye to the pilot. We'll be 'down, hull-down, on the old trail' from now on. God bless all we leave behind us, and send us safely back.

7

To-morrow We Disappear Into the Unknown

I WILL not bore those whom this narrative may reach by an account of our luxurious voyage upon the Booth liner, nor will I tell of our week's stay at Para (save that I should wish to acknowledge the great kindness of the Pereira da Pinta Company in helping us to get together our equipment). I will also allude very briefly to our river journey, up a wide, slow-moving, clay-tinted stream, in a steamer which was little smaller than that which had carried us across the Atlantic. Eventually we found ourselves through the narrows of Obidos and reached the town of Manaos. Here we were rescued from the limited attractions of the local inn by Mr. Shortman, the representative of the British and Brazilian Trading Company. In his hospitable fazenda we spent our time until the day when we were empowered to open the letter of instructions given to us by Professor Challenger. Before I reach the surprising events of that date I would desire to give a clearer sketch of my comrades in this enterprise, and of the associates whom we had already gathered together in South America. I speak freely, and I leave the use of my material to your own discretion, Mr. McArdle, since it is through your hands that this report must pass before it reaches the world.

The scientific attainments of Professor Summerlee are too well known for me to trouble to recapitulate them. He is better equipped for a rough expedition of this sort than one would imagine at first sight. His tall, gaunt, stringy figure is insensible to fatigue, and his dry, half-sarcastic and often wholly unsympathetic manner is uninfluenced by any change in his surroundings. Though in his sixty-sixth year, I have never heard him express any dissatisfaction at the occasional hardships which we have had to encounter. I had regarded his presence as an encumbrance to the expedition, but, as a matter of fact, I am now well convinced that his power of endurance is as great as my own. In temper he is naturally acid and sceptical. From the beginning he has never concealed his belief that Professor Challenger is an absolute fraud, that we are all embarked upon an absurd wild-goose chase and that we are likely to reap nothing but disappointment and danger in South America, and corresponding ridicule in England. Such are the views which, with much passionate distortion of his thin features and wagging of his thin, goat-like beard, he poured into our ears all the way from Southampton to Manaos. Since landing from the boat he has obtained some consolation from the beauty and variety of the insect and bird life around him, for he is absolutely whole-hearted in his devotion to science. He spends his days flitting through the woods with his shot-gun and his butterfly-net, and his evenings in mounting the many specimens he has acquired. Among his minor peculiarities are that he is careless as to his attire, unclean in his person, exceedingly absent-minded in his habits, and addicted to smoking a short briar pipe, which is seldom out of his mouth. He has been upon several scientific expeditions in his youth (he was with Robertson in Papua), and the life of the camp and the canoe is nothing fresh to him.

Lord John Roxton has some points in common with Professor Summerlee and others in which they are the very antithesis to each other. He is twenty years younger, but has something of the same spare, scraggy physique. As to his appearance, I have, as I recollect, described it in that portion of my narrative which I have left behind me in London. He is exceedingly neat and prim in his ways, dresses always with great care in white drill suits and high brown mosquito-boots, and shaves at least once a day. Like most men of action, he is laconic in speech, and sinks readily into his own thoughts, but he is always quick to answer a question or join in a conversation, talking in a queer, half-humorous fashion. His knowledge of the world, and very especially of South America, is surprising, and he has a whole-hearted belief in the possibilities of our journey which is not to be dashed by the sneers of Professor Summerlee. He has a gentle voice and a quiet manner, but behind his twinkling blue eyes there lurks a capacity for furious wrath and implacable resolution, the more dangerous because they are held in leash. He spoke little of his own exploits in Brazil and Peru, but it was a revelation to me to find the excitement which was caused by his presence among the riverine natives, who looked upon him as their champion and protector. The exploits of the Red Chief, as they called him, had become legends among them, but the real facts, as far as I could learn them, were amazing enough.

These were that Lord John had found himself some years before in that no-man's land which is formed by the half-defined frontiers between Peru, Brazil, and Colombia. In this great district the wild rubber tree flourishes, and has become, as in the Congo, a curse to the natives which can only be compared to their forced labour under the Spaniards upon the old silver mines of Darien. A handful of villainous half-breeds dominated the country, armed such Indians as would support them, and turned the rest into slaves, terrorizing them with the most inhuman tortures in order to force them to gather the india-rubber, which was then floated down the river to Para. Lord John Roxton expostulated on behalf of the wretched victims and received nothing but threats and insults for his pains. He then formally declared war against Pedro Lopez, the leader of the slave-drivers, enrolled a band of runaway slaves in his service, armed them, and conducted a campaign, which ended by his killing with his own hands the notorious half-breed and breaking down the system which he represented.

No wonder that the ginger-headed man with the silky voice and the free and easy manners was now looked upon with deep interest upon the banks of the great South American river, though the feelings he inspired were naturally mixed, since the gratitude of the natives was equalled by the resentment of those who desired to exploit them. One useful result of his former experiences was that he could talk fluently in the Lingoa Geral, which is the peculiar talk, one-third Portuguese and two-thirds Indian, which is current all over Brazil.

I have said before that Lord John Roxton was a South Americomaniac. He could not speak of that great country without ardour, and this ardour was infectious, for, ignorant as I was, he fixed my attention and stimulated my curiosity. How I wish I could reproduce the glamour of his discourses, the peculiar mixture of accurate knowledge and of racy imagination which gave them their fascination, until even the Professor's cynical and sceptical smile would gradually vanish from his thin face as he listened. He would tell the history of the mighty river so rapidly explored (for some of the first conquerors of Peru actually crossed the entire continent upon its waters), and yet so unknown in regard to all that lay behind its ever-changing banks.

'What is there?' he would cry, pointing to the north. 'Wood and marsh and unpenetrated jungle. Who knows what it may shelter? And there to the south? A wilderness of swampy forests, where no white man has ever been. The unknown is up against us on every side. Outside the narrow lines of the rivers what does anyone know? Who will say what is possible in such a country? Why should old man Challenger not be right?' At which direct defiance the stubborn sneer would reappear upon Professor Summerlee's face, and he would sit, shaking his sardonic head in unsympathetic silence, behind the cloud of his briar-root pipe.

So much, for the moment, for my two white companions, whose

characters and limitations will be further exposed, as surely as my own, as this narrative proceeds. But already we have enrolled certain retainers who may play no small part in what is to come. The first is a gigantic negro named Zambo, who is a black Hercules, as willing as any horse, and about as intelligent. Him we enlisted at Para, on the recommendation of the steamship company, on whose vessels he had learned to speak a halting English.

It was at Para also that we engaged Gomez and Manuel, two half-breeds from up the river, just come down with a cargo of redwood. They were swarthy fellows, bearded and fierce, as active and wiry as panthers. Both of them had spent their lives in those upper waters of the Amazon which we were to explore, and it was this recommendation which had caused Lord John to engage them. One of them, Gomez, had the further advantage that he could speak excellent English. These men were willing to act as our personal servants, to cook, to row, or to make themselves useful in any way at a payment of fifteen dollars a month. Besides these, we had engaged three Mojo Indians from Bolivia, who are the most skilful at fishing and boat work of all the river tribes. The chief of these we called Mojo, after his tribe, and the others are known as José and Fernando. Three white men, then, two half-breeds, one negro, and three Indians made up the personnel of the little expedition which lay waiting for its instructions at Manaos, before starting upon its singular quest.

At last after a weary week, the day had come and the hour. I ask you to picture the shaded sitting-room of the Fazenda Santa Ignacio, two miles inland from the town of Manaos. Outside lay the yellow, brassy glare of the sunshine, with the shadows of the palm trees as black and definite as the trees themselves. The air was calm, full of the eternal hum of insects, a tropical chorus of many octaves, from the deep drone of the bee to the high, keen pipe of the mosquito. Beyond the veranda was a small cleared garden, bounded with cactus hedges and adorned with clumps of flowering shrubs, round which the great blue butterflies and the tiny humming-birds fluttered and darted in crescents of sparkling light. Within we were seated round the cane table, on which lay a sealed envelope. Inscribed upon it, in the jagged handwriting of Professor Challenger, were the words:

> 'Instructions to Lord John Roxton and party. To be opened at Manaos upon July 15th, at 12 o'clock precisely.'

Lord John had placed his watch upon the table beside him.

'We have seven more minutes,' said he. 'The old dear is very precise.'

Professor Summerlee gave an acid smile as he picked up the envelope in his gaunt hand.

'What can it possibly matter whether we open it now or in seven minutes?' said he. 'It is all part and parcel of the same system of quackery and nonsense for which I regret to say that the writer is notorious.'

'Oh, come, we must play the game accordin' to rules,' said Lord John. 'It's old man Challenger's show and we are here by his good will, so it would be rotten bad form if we didn't follow his instructions to the letter.'

'A pretty business it is!' cried the Professor, bitterly. 'It struck me as preposterous in London, but I'm bound to say that it seems even more so upon closer acquaintance. I don't know what is inside this envelope, but, unless it is something pretty definite, I shall be much tempted to take the next down-river boat and catch the *Bolivia* at Para. After all, I have some more responsible work in the world than to run about disproving the assertions of a lunatic. Now, Roxton, surely it is time.'

'Time it is,' said Lord John. 'You can blow the whistle.' He took up the envelope and cut it with his penknife. From it he drew a folded sheet of paper. This he carefully opened out and flattened on the table. It was a blank sheet. He turned it over. Again it was blank. We looked at each other in a bewildered silence, which was broken by a discordant burst of derisive laughter from Professor Summerlee.

'It is an open admission,' he cried. 'What more do you want? The fellow is a self-confessed humbug. We have only to return home and report him as the brazen impostor that he is.'

'Invisible ink!' I suggested.

'I don't think!' said Lord Roxton, holding the paper to the light. 'No, young fellah-my-lad, there is no use deceiving yourself. I'll go bail for it that nothing has ever been written upon this paper.'

'May I come in?' boomed a voice from the veranda.

The shadow of a squat figure had stolen across the patch of sunlight. That voice! That monstrous breadth of shoulder! We sprang to our feet with a gasp of astonishment as Challenger, in a round, boyish straw-hat with a coloured ribbon – Challenger, with his hands in his jacket-pockets and his canvas shoes daintily pointing as he walked – appeared in the open space before us. He threw back his head, and there he stood in the golden glow with all his old Assyrian luxuriance of beard, all his native insolence of drooping eyelids and intolerant eyes.

'I fear,' said he, taking out his watch, 'that I am a few minutes too late. When I gave you this envelope I must confess that I had never intended that you should open it, for it had been my fixed intention to be with you before the hour. The unfortunate delay can be apportioned between a blundering pilot and an intrusive sandbank. I fear that it has given my colleague, Professor Summerlee, occasion to blaspheme.'

'I am bound to say, sir,' said Lord John, with some sternness of voice, 'that your turning up is a considerable relief to us, for our mission seemed to have come to a premature end. Even now I can't for the life of me understand why you should have worked it in so extraordinary a manner.'

Instead of answering, Professor Challenger entered, shook hands with myself and Lord John, bowed with ponderous insolence to Professor

Summerlee, and sank back into a basket-chair, which creaked and swayed beneath his weight.

'Is all ready for your journey?' he asked.

'We can start to-morrow.'

'Then so you shall. You need no chart of directions now, since you will have the inestimable advantage of my own guidance. From the first I had determined that I would myself preside over your investigation. The most elaborate charts would, as you will readily admit, be a poor substitute for my own intelligence and advice. As to the small ruse which I played upon you in the matter of the envelope, it is clear that, had I told you all my intentions, I should have been forced to resist unwelcome pressure to travel out with you.'

'Not from me, sir!' exclaimed Professor Summerlee, heartily. 'So long as there was another ship upon the Atlantic.'

Challenger waved him away with his great hairy hand.

'Your common sense will, I am sure, sustain my objection and realize that it was better that I should direct my own movements and appear only at the exact moment when my presence was needed. That moment has now arrived. You are in safe hands. You will not now fail to reach your destination. From henceforth I take command of this expedition, and I must ask you to complete your preparations to-night, so that we may be able to make an early start in the morning. My time is of value, and the same thing may be said, no doubt; in a lesser degree of your own. I propose, therefore, that we push on as rapidly as possible, until I have demonstrated what you have come to see.'

Lord John Roxton had chartered a large steam-launch, the *Esmeralda*, which was to carry us up the river. So far as climate goes, it was immaterial what time we chose for our expedition, as the temperature ranges from seventy-five to ninety degrees both summer and winter, with no appreciable difference in heat. In moisture, however, it is otherwise; from December to May is the period of the rains, and during this time the river slowly rises until it attains a height of nearly forty feet above its low-water mark. It floods the banks, extends in great lagoons over a monstrous waste of country, and forms a huge district, called locally the Gapo, which is for the most part too marshy for foot-travel and too shallow for boating. About June the waters begin to fall, and are at their lowest at October or November. Thus our expedition was at the time of the dry season, when the great river and its tributaries were more or less in a normal condition.

The current of the river is a slight one, the drop being not greater than eight inches in a mile. No stream could be more convenient for navigation, since the prevailing wind is south-east, and sailing boats may make a continuous progress to the Peruvian frontier, dropping down again with the current. In our own case the excellent engines of the *Esmeralda* could disregard the sluggish flow of the stream, and we made as rapid progress as if we were navigating a stagnant lake. For three days we steamed north-westwards up a stream which even here, a thousand miles from its mouth, was still so enormous that from its centre the two banks were mere shadows upon the distant skyline. On the fourth day after leaving Manaos we turned into a tributary which at its mouth was little smaller than the main stream. It narrowed rapidly, however, and after two more days' steaming we reached an Indian village, where the Professor insisted that we should land, and that the *Esmeralda* should be sent back to Manaos. We should soon come upon rapids, he explained, which would make its further use impossible. He added privately that we were now approaching the door of the unknown country, and that the fewer whom we took into our confidence the better it would be. To this end also he made each of us give our word of honour that we would publish or say nothing which would give any exact clue as to the whereabouts of our travels, while the servants were all solemnly sworn to the same effect. It is for this reason that I am compelled to be vague in my narrative, and I would warn my readers that in any map or diagram which I may give the relation of places to each other may be correct, but the points of the compass are carefully confused, so that in no way can it be taken as an actual guide to the country. Professor Challenger's reasons for secrecy may be valid or not, but we had no choice but to adopt them, for he was prepared to abandon the whole expedition rather than modify the conditions upon which he would guide us.

It was August 2nd when we snapped our last link with the outer world by bidding farewell to the *Esmeralda*. Since then four days have passed, during which we have engaged two large canoes from the Indians, made of so light a material (skins over a bamboo framework) that we should be able to carry them round any obstacle. These we have loaded with all our effects, and have engaged two additional Indians to help us in the navigation. I understand that they are the very two – Ataca and Ipetu by name – who accompanied Professor Challenger upon his previous journey. They appeared to be terrified at the prospect of repeating it, but the chief has patriarchal powers in these countries, and if the bargain is good in his eyes the clansman has little choice in the matter.

So to-morrow we disappear into the unknown. This account I am transmitting down the river by canoe, and it may be our last word to those who are interested in our fate. I have, according to our arrangement, addressed it to you, my dear Mr. McArdle, and I leave it to your discretion to delete, alter, or do what you like with it. From the assurance of Professor Challenger's manner – and in spite of the continued scepticism of Professor Summerlee – I have no doubt that our leader will make good his statement, and that we are really on the eve of some most remarkable experiences.

8

The Outlying Pickets of the New World

OUR friends at home may well rejoice with us, for we are at our goal, and up to a point, at least, we have shown that the statement of Professor Challenger can be verified. We have not, it is true, ascended the plateau, but it lies before us, and even Professor Summerlee is in a more chastened mood. Not that he will for an instant admit that his rival could be right, but he is less persistent in his incessant objections, and has sunk for the most part into an observant silence. I must hark back, however, and continue my narrative from where I dropped it. We are sending home one of our local Indians who is injured, and I am committing this letter to his charge, with considerable doubts in my mind as to whether it will ever come to hand.

When I wrote last we were about to leave the Indian village where we had been deposited by the *Esmeralda*. I have to begin my report by bad news, for the first serious personal trouble (I pass over the incessant bickerings between the Professors) occurred this evening, and might have had a tragic ending. I have spoken of our English-speaking half-breed, Gomez – a fine worker and a willing fellow, but afflicted, I fancy, with the vice of curiosity, which is common enough among such men. On the last evening he seems to have hid himself near the hut in which we were discussing our plans, and, being observed by our huge negro Zambo, who is as faithful as a dog and has the hatred which all his race bear to the half-breeds, he was dragged out and carried into our presence. Gomez whipped out his knife, however, and but for the huge strength of his captor, which enabled him to disarm him with one hand, he would certainly have stabbed him. The matter has ended in reprimands, the opponents have been compelled to shake hands, and there is every hope that all will be well. As to the feuds of the two learned men, they are continuous and bitter. It must be admitted that Challenger is provocative in the last degree, but Summerlee has an acid tongue, which makes matters worse. Last night Challenger said that he never cared to walk on the Thames Embankment and look up the river, as it was always sad to see one's own eventual goal. He is convinced, of course, that he is destined for Westminster Abbey. Summerlee retorted, however, with a sour smile, by saying that he understood that Millbank Prison had been pulled down. Challenger's conceit is too colossal to allow him to be really annoyed. He only smiled in his beard and repeated 'Really! really!' in the pitying tone one would use to a child. Indeed, they are children both – the one wizened and cantankerous, the other formidable and overbearing, yet each with a brain which has put him in the front rank of his scientific age. Brain, character, soul – only as one sees more of life does one understand how distinct is each.

The very next day we did actually make our start upon this remarkable expedition. We found that all our possessions fitted very easily into the two canoes, and we divided our personnel, six in each, taking the obvious precaution in the interests of peace of putting one Professor into each canoe. Personally, I was with Challenger, who was in a beatific humour, moving about as one in a silent ecstasy and beaming benevolence from every feature. I have had some experience of him in other moods, however, and shall be the less surprised when the thunderstorms suddenly come up amidst the sunshine. If it is impossible to be at your ease, it is equally impossible to be dull in his company, for one is always in a state of half-tremulous doubt as to what sudden turn his formidable temper may take.

For two days we made our way up a good-sized river, some hundreds of yards broad, and dark in colour, but transparent, so that one could usually see the bottom. The affluents of the Amazon are, half of them, of this nature, while the other half are whitish and opaque, the difference depending upon the class of country through which they have flowed. The dark indicate vegetable decay, while the others point to clayey soil. Twice we came across rapids, and in each case made a portage of half a mile or so to avoid them. The woods on either side were primeval, which are more easily penetrated than woods of the second growth, and we had no great difficulty in carrying our canoes through them. How shall I ever forget the solemn mystery of it? The height of the trees and the thickness of the boles exceeding anything which I in my town-bred life could have imagined, shooting upwards in magnificent columns until, at an enormous distance above our heads, we could dimly discern the spot where they threw out their side-branches into Gothic upward curves which coalesced to form one great matted roof of verdure, through which only an occasional golden ray of sunshine shot downwards to trace a thin dazzling line of light amidst the majestic obscurity. As we walked noiselessly amid the thick, soft carpet of decaying vegetation the hush fell upon our souls which comes upon us in the twilight of the Abbey, and even Professor Challenger's full-chested notes sank into a whisper. Alone, I should have been ignorant of the names of these giant growths, but our men of science pointed out the cedars, the great silk cotton trees, and the redwood trees, with all that profusion of various plants which has made this continent the chief supplier to the human race of those gifts of nature which depend upon the vegetable world, while it is the most backward in those products which come from animal life. Vivid orchids and wonderful coloured lichens smouldered upon the swarthy tree-trunks, and where a wandering shaft of light fell full upon the golden allamanda, the scarlet star-clusters of the tacsonia, or the rich deep blue of ipomea the effect was as a dream of fairyland. In these great wastes of forest, life, which abhors darkness, struggles ever upwards to the light. Every plant, even the smaller ones, curls and writhes to the green surface, twining itself round its stronger and taller brethren in the effort. Climbing plants are monstrous and luxuriant, but others which have never been known to climb elsewhere learn the art as an escape from that sombre shadow, so that the common nettle, the jasmine, and even the jacitara palm tree can be seen circling the stems of the cedars and striving to reach their crowns. Of animal life there was no movement amid the majestic vaulted aisles which stretched from us as we walked, but a constant movement far above our heads told of that multitudinous world of snake and monkey, bird and sloth, which lived in the sunshine, and looked down in wonder at our tiny, dark, stumbling figures in the obscure depths immeasurably below them. At dawn and at sunset the howler monkeys screamed together and the parakeets broke into shrill chatter, but during the hot hours of the day, only the full drone of insects, like the beat of a distant surf, filled the ear, while nothing moved amid the solemn vistas of stupendous trunks, fading away into the darkness which held us in. Once some bandy-legged, lurching creature, an ant-eater or a bear, scuttled clumsily amid the shadows. It was the only sign of earth life which I saw in this great Amazonian forest.

And yet there were indications that even human life itself was not far from us in those mysterious recesses. On the third day out we were aware of a singular deep throbbing in the air, rhythmic and solemn, coming and going fitfully throughout the morning. The two boats were paddling within a few yards of each other when we first heard it, and our Indians remained motionless, as if they had been turned to bronze, listening intently with expressions of terror upon their faces.

'What is it, then?' I asked.

'Drums,' said Lord John, carelessly; 'war drums. I have heard them before.'

'Yes, sir, war drums,' said Gomez, the half-breed. 'Wild Indians, bravos, not mansos; they watch us every mile of the way; kill us if they can.'

'How can they watch us?' I asked, gazing into the dark, motionless void.

The half-breed shrugged his broad shoulders.

'The Indians know. They have their own way. They watch us. They talk the drum talk to each other. Kill us if they can.'

By the afternoon of that day – my pocket diary shows me that it was Tuesday, August 18th – at least six or seven drums were throbbing from various points. Sometimes they beat quickly, sometimes slowly, sometimes in obvious question and answer, one far to the east breaking out in a high staccato rattle, and being followed after a pause by a deep roll from the north. There was something indescribably nerve-shaking and menacing in that constant mutter, which seemed to shape itself into the very syllables of the half-breed, endlessly repeated, 'We will kill you if we can. We will kill you if we can.' No one ever moved in the silent woods. All the peace and soothing of quiet Nature lay in that dark curtain of vegetation, but away from behind there came ever the one message from our fellow-man. 'We will kill you if we can,' said the men in the east. 'We will kill you if we can,' said the men in the north.

All day the drums rumbled and whispered, while their menace reflected itself in the faces of our coloured companions. Even the hardy, swaggering half-breed seemed cowed. I learned, however, that day once for all that both Summerlee and Challenger possessed that highest type of bravery, the bravery of the scientific mind. Theirs was the spirit which upheld Darwin among the gauchos of the Argentine or Wallace among the head-hunters of Malaya. It is decreed by a merciful Nature that the human brain cannot think of two things simultaneously, so that if it be steeped in curiosity as to science it has no room for merely personal considerations. All day amid that incessant and mysterious menace our two Professors watched every bird upon the wing, and every shrub upon the bank, with many a sharp wordy contention, when the snarl of Summerlee came quick upon the deep growl of Challenger, but with no more sense of danger and no more reference to drumbeating Indians than if they were seated together in the smoking-room of the Royal Society's Club in St. James's Street. Once only did they condescend to discuss them.

'Miranha or Amajuaca cannibals,' said Challenger, jerking his thumb towards the reverberating wood.

'No doubt, sir,' Summerlee answered. 'Like all such tribes, I shall expect to find them of polysynthetic speech and of Mongolian type.'

'Polysynthetic certainly,' said Challenger, indulgently. 'I am not aware that any other type of language exists in this continent, and I have notes of more than a hundred. The Mongolian theory I regard with deep suspicion.'

'I should have thought that even a limited knowledge of comparative anatomy would have helped to verify it,' said Summerlee, bitterly.

Challenger thrust out his aggressive chin until he was all beard and hat-rim. 'No doubt, sir, a limited knowledge would have that effect. When one's knowledge is exhaustive, one comes to other conclusions.' They glared at each other in mutual defiance, while all round rose the distant whisper, 'We will kill you – we will kill you if we can.'

That night we moored our canoes with heavy stones for anchors in the centre of the stream, and made every preparation for a possible attack. Nothing came, however, and with the dawn we pushed upon our way, the drum-beating dying out behind us. About three o'clock in the afternoon we came to a very steep rapid, more than a mile long – the very one in which Professor Challenger had suffered disaster upon his first journey. I confess that the sight of it consoled me, for it was really the first direct corroboration, slight as it was, of the truth of his story. The Indians carried first our canoes and then our stores through the brushwood, which is very thick at this point, while we four whites, our rifles on our shoulders, walked between them and any danger coming from the woods. Before evening we had successfully passed the rapids, and made our way some ten miles above them, where we anchored for the night. At this point I reckoned that we had come not less than a hundred miles up the tributary from the main stream.

It was in the early forenoon of the next day that we made the great departure. Since dawn Professor Challenger had been acutely uneasy, continually scanning each bank of the river. Suddenly he gave an exclamation of satisfaction and pointed to a single tree, which projected at a peculiar angle over the side of the stream.

'What do you make of that?' he asked.

'It is surely an Assai palm,' said Summerlee.

'Exactly. It was an Assai palm which I took for my landmark. The secret opening is half a mile onwards upon the other side of the river. There is no break in the trees. That is the wonder and the mystery of it. There where you see light-green rushes instead of dark-green undergrowth, there between the great cotton woods, that is my private gate into the unknown. Push through, and you will understand.'

It was indeed a wonderful place. Having reached the spot marked by a line of light-green rushes, we poled our two canoes through them for some hundreds of yards, and eventually emerged into a placid and shallow stream, running clear and transparent over a sandy bottom. It may have been twenty yards across, and was banked in on each side by most luxuriant vegetation. No one who had not observed that for a short distance reeds had taken the place of shrubs could possibly have guessed the existence of such a stream or dreamed of the fairyland beyond.

For a fairyland it was – the most wonderful that the imagination of man could conceive. The thick vegetation met overhead, interlacing into a natural pergola, and through this tunnel of verdure in a golden twilight flowed the green, pellucid river, beautiful in itself, but marvellous from the strange tints thrown by the vivid light from above filtered and tempered in its fall. Clear as crystal, motionless as a sheet of glass, green as the edge of an iceberg, it stretched in front of us under its leafy archway, every stroke of our paddles sending a thousand ripples across its shining surface. It was a fitting avenue to a land of wonders. All sign of the Indians had passed away, but animal life was more frequent, and the tameness of the creatures showed that they knew nothing of the hunter. Fuzzy little black-velvet monkeys, with snow-white teeth and gleaming mocking eyes, chattered at us as we passed. With a dull, heavy splash an occasional cayman plunged in from the bank. Once a dark, clumsy tapir stared at us from a gap in the bushes, and then lumbered away through the forest; once, too, the yellow, sinuous form of a great puma whisked amid the brushwood, and its green, baleful eyes glared hatred at us over its tawny shoulder. Bird life was abundant, especially the wading birds, stork, heron, and ibis gathering in little groups, blue, scarlet, and white, upon every log which jutted from the bank, while beneath us the crystal water was alive with fish of every shape and colour.

For three days we made our way up this tunnel of hazy green sunshine. On the longer stretches one could hardly tell as one looked ahead where the distant green water ended and the distant green archway began. The deep peace of this strange waterway was unbroken by any sign of man.

'No Indian here. Too much afraid. Curupuri,' said Gomez.

'Curupuri is the spirit of the woods,' Lord John explained. 'It's the name for any kind of devil. The poor beggars think that there is something fearsome in this direction, and therefore they avoid it.'

On the third day it became evident that our journey in the canoes could not last much longer, for the stream was rapidly growing more shallow. Twice in as many hours we stuck upon the bottom. Finally we pulled the boats up among the brushwood and spent the night on the bank of the river. In the morning Lord John and I made our way for a couple of miles through the forest, keeping parallel with the stream; but as it grew ever shallower we returned and reported, what Professor Challenger had already suspected, that we had reached the highest point to which the canoes could be brought. We drew them up, therefore, and concealed them among the bushes, blazing a tree with our axes, so that we should find them again. Then we distributed the various burdens among us – guns, ammunition, food, a tent, blankets, and the rest – and, shouldering our packages, we set forth upon the more laborious stage of our journey.

An unfortunate quarrel between our pepperpots marked the outset of our new stage. Challenger had from the moment of joining us issued directions to the whole party, much to the evident discontent of Summerlee. Now, upon his assigning some duty to his fellow-Professor (it was only the carrying of an aneroid barometer), the matter suddenly came to a head.

'May I ask, sir,' said Summerlee, with vicious calm, 'in what capacity you take it upon yourself to issue these orders?'

Challenger glared and bristled.

'I do it, Professor Summerlee, as leader of this expedition.'

'I am compelled to tell you, sir, that I do not recognize you in that capacity.'

'Indeed!' Challenger bowed with unwieldy sarcasm. 'Perhaps you would define my exact position.'

'Yes, sir. You are a man whose veracity is upon trial, and this committee is here to try it. You walk, sir, with your judges.'

'Dear me!' said Challenger, seating himself on the side of one of the canoes. 'In that case you will, of course, go on your way, and I will follow at my leisure. If I am not the leader you cannot expect me to lead.'

Thank heaven that there were two sane men – Lord John Roxton and myself – to prevent the petulance and folly of our learned Professors from sending us back empty-handed to London. Such arguing and pleading and explaining before we could get them mollified! Then at last Summerlee, with his sneer and his pipe, would move forwards, and Challenger would come rolling and grumbling after. By some good fortune we discovered about this time that both our savants had the very poorest opinion of Dr. Illingworth of Edinburgh. Thenceforward that was our one safety, and every strained situation was relieved by our introducing the name of the Scotch zoologist, when both our Professors would form a temporary alliance and friendship in their detestation and abuse of this common rival.

Advancing in single file along the bank of the stream, we soon found that it narrowed down to a mere brook, and finally that it lost itself in a great green morass of sponge-like mosses, into which we sank up to our knees. The place was horribly haunted by clouds of mosquitoes and every form of flying pest, so we were glad to find solid ground again and to make a circuit among the trees, which enabled us to outflank this pestilent morass, which droned like an organ in the distance, so loud was it with insect life.

On the second day after leaving our canoes we found that the whole character of the country changed. Our road was persistently upwards, and as we ascended the woods became thinner and lost their tropical luxuriance. The huge trees of the alluvial Amazonian plain gave place to the Phœnix and coco palms, growing in scattered clumps, with thick brushwood between. In the damper hollows the Mauritia palms threw out their graceful drooping fronds. We travelled entirely by compass, and once or twice there were differences of opinion between Challenger and the two Indians, when, to quote the Professor's indignant words, the whole party agreed to 'trust the fallacious instincts of undeveloped savages rather than the highest product of modern European culture'. That we were justified in doing so was shown upon the third day, when Challenger admitted that he recognized several landmarks of his former journey, and in one spot we actually came upon four fire-blackened stones, which must have marked a camping-place.

The road still ascended, and we crossed a rock-studded slope which took two days to traverse. The vegetation had again changed, and only the vegetable ivory tree remained, with a great profusion of wonderful orchids, among which I learned to recognize the rare *Nuttonia Vexillaria* and the glorious pink and scarlet blossoms of Cattleya and odontoglossum. Occasional brooks with pebbly bottoms and fern-draped banks gurgled down the shallow gorges in the hill, and offered good camping-grounds every evening on the banks of some rock-studded pool, where swarms of little blue-backed fish, about the size and shape of English trout, gave us a delicious supper.

On the ninth day after leaving the canoes, having done, as I reckon, about a hundred and twenty miles, we began to emerge from the trees, which had grown smaller until they were mere shrubs. Their place was taken by an immense wilderness of bamboo, which grew so thickly that we could only penetrate it by cutting a pathway with the machetes and bill-hooks of the Indians. It took us a long day, travelling from seven in the morning till eight at night, with only two breaks of one hour each, to get through this obstacle. Anything more monotonous and wearying could not be imagined, for, even at the most open places, I could not see more than ten or twelve yards, while usually my vision was limited to the back of Lord John's cotton jacket in front of me, and to the yellow wall within a foot of me on either side. From above came one thin knife-edge of sunshine, and fifteen feet over our heads one saw the tops of the reeds swaying against the deep blue sky. I do not know what kind of creatures inhabit such a thicket, but several times we heard the plunging of large, heavy animals quite close to us. From their sounds Lord John judged them to be some form of wild cattle. Just as night fell we cleared the belt of bamboos, and at once formed our camp, exhausted by the interminable day.

Early next morning we were again afoot, and found that the character of the country had changed once again. Behind us was the wall of bamboo, as definite as if it marked the course of a river. In front was an open plain, sloping slightly upwards and dotted with clumps of tree-ferns, the whole curving before us until it ended in a long, whale-backed ridge. This we reached about midday, only to find a shallow valley beyond, rising once again into a gentle incline which led to a low, rounded sky-line. It was here, while we crossed the first of these hills, that an incident occurred which may or may not have been important.

Professor Challenger, who, with the two local Indians, was in the van of the party, stopped suddenly and pointed excitedly to the right. As he did so we saw, at the distance of a mile or so, something which appeared to be a huge grey bird flap slowly up from the ground and skim smoothly off, flying very low and straight, until it was lost among the tree-ferns.

'Did you see it?' cried Challenger, in exultation. 'Summerlee, did you see it?'

His colleague was staring at the spot where the creature had disappeared.

'What do you claim that it was?' he asked.

'To the best of my belief, a pterodactyl.'

Summerlee burst into derisive laughter. 'A ptero-fiddlestick!' said he. 'It was a stork, if ever I saw one.'

Challenger was too furious to speak. He simply swung his pack upon his back and continued upon his march. Lord John came abreast of me, however, and his face was more grave than was his wont. He had his Zeiss glasses in his hand.

'I focused it before it got over the trees,' said he. 'I won't undertake to say what it was, but I'll risk my reputation as a sportsman that it wasn't any bird that ever I clapped eyes on in my life.'

So there the matter stands. Are we really just at the edge of the unknown, encountering the outlying pickets of this lost world of which our leader speaks? I give you the incident as it occurred and you will know as much as I do. It stands alone, for we saw nothing more which could be called remarkable.

And now, my readers, if ever I have any, I have brought you up the broad river, and through the screen of rushes, and down the green tunnel, and up the long slope of palm trees, and through the bamboo brake, and across the plain of tree-ferns. At last our destination lay in full sight of us. When we had crossed the second ridge we saw before us an irregular, palm-studded plain, and then the line of high red cliffs which I have seen in the picture. There it lies, even as I write, and there can be no question that it is the same. At the nearest point it is about seven miles from our present camp, and it curves away, stretching as far as I can see. Challenger struts about like a prize peacock, and Summerlee is silent, but still sceptical. Another day should bring some of our doubts to an end. Meanwhile, as José, whose arm was pierced by a broken bamboo, insists upon returning, I send this letter back in his charge, and only hope that it may eventually come to hand. I will write again as the occasion serves. I have enclosed with this a rough chart of our journey, which may have the effect of making the account rather easier to understand.

9

Who Could Have Foreseen It

A DREADFUL thing has happened to us. Who could have foreseen it? I cannot foresee any end to our troubles. It may be that we are condemned to spend our whole lives in this strange, inaccessible place. I am still so confused that I can hardly think clearly of the facts of the present or of the chances of the future. To my astounded senses the one seems most terrible and the other as black as night.

No men have ever found themselves in a worse position; nor is there any use in disclosing to you our exact geographical situation and asking our friends for a relief party. Even if they could send one, our fate will in all human probability be decided long before it could arrive in South America.

We are, in truth, as far from any human aid as if we were in the moon. If we are to win through, it is only our own qualities which can save us. I have as companions three remarkable men, men of great brain-power and of unshaken courage. There lies our one and only hope. It is only when I look upon the untroubled faces of my comrades that I see some glimmer through the darkness. Outwardly I trust that I appear as unconcerned as they. Inwardly I am filled with apprehension.

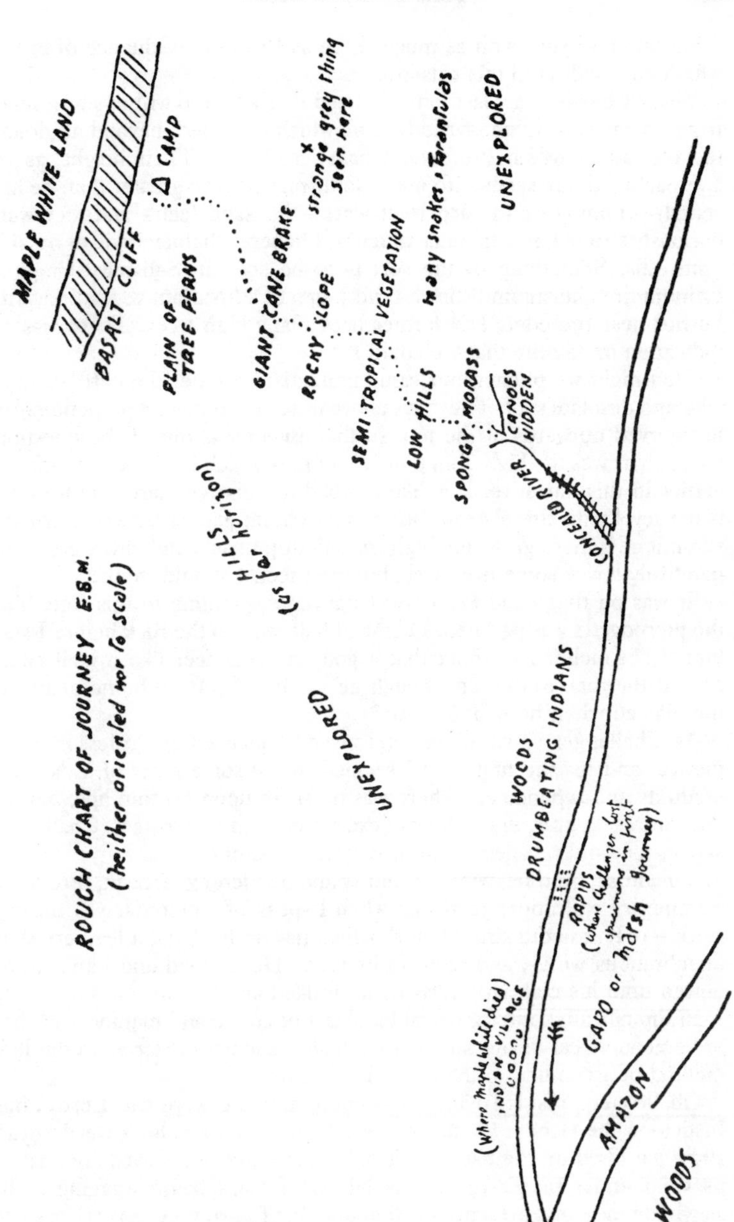
ROUGH CHART OF JOURNEY E.D.M.
(neither oriented nor to scale)
MAPLE WHITE LAND
BASALT CLIFF
Δ CAMP
PLAIN OF TREE FERNS
GIANT CANE BRAKE
x strange grey thing seen here
ROCKY SLOPE
SEMI-TROPICAL VEGETATION
many snakes & Tarantulas
UNEXPLORED
LOW HILLS
SPONGY MORASS
CANOES HIDDEN
CONCEALED RIVER
HILLS
(as far horizon)
UNEXPLORED
WOODS
DRUMBEATING INDIANS
RAPIDS
(where Challenger lost specimens in first journey)
GAPO or marsh
(where Maple White died)
INDIAN VILLAGE
AMAZON
WOODS

Let me give you, with as much detail as I can, the sequence of events which have led us to this catastrophe.

When I finished my last letter I stated that we were within seven miles from an enormous line of ruddy cliffs which encircled, beyond all doubt, the plateau of which Professor Challenger spoke. Their height, as we approached them, seemed to me in some places to be greater than he had stated – running up in parts to at least a thousand feet – and they were curiously striated, in a manner which is, I believe, characteristic of basaltic upheavals. Something of the sort is to be seen in Salisbury Crags at Edinburgh. The summit showed every sign of a luxuriant vegetation, with bushes near the edge, and farther back many high trees. There was no indication of any life that we could see.

That night we pitched our camp immediately under the cliff – a most wild and desolate spot. The crags above us were not merely perpendicular, but curved outwards at the top, so that ascent was out of the question. Close to us was the high, thin pinnacle of rock which I believe I mentioned earlier in this narrative. It is like a broad red church spire, the top of it being level with the plateau, but a great chasm gaping between. On the summit of it there grew one high tree. Both pinnacle and cliff were comparatively low – some five or six hundred feet, I should think.

'It was on that,' said Professor Challenger, pointing to this tree, 'that the pterodactyl was perched. I climbed half-way up the rock before I shot him. I am inclined to think that a good mountaineer like myself could ascend the rock to the top, though he would, of course, be no nearer to the plateau when he had done so.'

As Challenger spoke of his pterodactyl I glanced at Professor Summerlee, and for the first time I seemed to see some signs of a dawning credulity and repentance. There was no sneer upon his thin lips, but, on the contrary, a grey, drawn look of excitement and amazement. Challenger saw it, too, and revelled in the first taste of victory.

'Of course,' said he, with his clumsy and ponderous sarcasm, 'Professor Summerlee will understand that when I speak of a pterodactyl I mean a stork – only it is the kind of stork which has no feathers, a leathery skin, membranous wings, and teeth in its jaws.' He grinned and blinked and bowed until his colleague turned and walked away.

In the morning, after a frugal breakfast of coffee and manioc – we had to be economical of our stores – we held a council of war as to the best method of ascending to the plateau above us.

Challenger presided with a solemnity as if he were the Lord Chief Justice on the Bench. Picture him seated upon a rock, his absurd boyish straw hat tilted on the back of his head, his supercilious eyes dominating us from under his drooping lids, his great black beard wagging as he slowly defined our present situation and our future movements.

Beneath him you might have seen the three of us – myself, sunburnt, young, and vigorous after our open-air tramp; Summerlee, solemn, but still critical, behind his eternal pipe; Lord John, as keen as a razor-edge, with his supple, alert figure leaning upon his rifle, and his eagle eyes fixed eagerly upon the speaker. Behind us were grouped the two swarthy half-breeds and the little knot of Indians, while in front and above us towered those huge, ruddy ribs of rocks which kept us from our goal.

'I need not say,' said our leader, 'that on the occasion of my last visit I exhausted every means of climbing the cliff, and where I failed I do not think that anyone else is likely to succeed, for I am something of a mountaineer. I had none of the appliances of a rock-climber with me, but I have taken the precaution to bring them now. With their aid I am positive I could climb that detached pinnacle to the summit; but so long as the main cliff overhangs, it is vain to attempt ascending that. I was hurried upon my last visit by the approach of the rainy season and by the exhaustion of my supplies. These considerations limited my time, and I can only claim that I have surveyed about six miles of the cliff to the east of us, finding no possible way up. What, then, shall we now do?'

'There seems to be only one reasonable course,' said Professor Summerlee. 'If you have explored the east, we should travel along the base of the cliff to the west, and seek for a practicable point for our ascent.'

'That's it,' said Lord John. 'The odds are that this plateau is of no great size, and we shall travel round it until we either find an easy way up it, or come back to the point from which we started.'

'I have already explained to our young friend here,' said Challenger (he has a way of alluding to me as if I were a school child ten years old), 'that it is quite impossible that there should be an easy way up anywhere, for the simple reason that if there were the summit would not be isolated, and those conditions would not obtain which have effected so singular an interference with the general laws of survival. Yet I admit that there may very well be places where an expert human climber may reach the summit, and yet a cumbrous and heavy animal be unable to descend. It is certain that there *is* a point where ascent is possible.'

'How do you know that, sir?' asked Summerlee, sharply.

'Because my predecessor, the American Maple White, actually made such an ascent. How otherwise could he have seen the monster which he sketched in his notebook?'

'There you reason somewhat ahead of the proved facts,' said the stubborn Summerlee. 'I admit your plateau, because I have seen it; but I have not as yet satisfied myself that it contains any form of life whatever.'

'What you admit, sir, or what you do not admit, is really of inconceivably small importance. I am glad to perceive that the plateau itself has actually obtruded itself upon your intelligence.' He glanced up at it, and then, to our amazement, he sprang from his rock, and, seizing Summerlee by the neck, he tilted his face into the air. 'Now, sir!' he shouted, hoarse with excitement. 'Do I help you to realize that the plateau contains some animal life?'

I have said that a thick fringe of green overhung the edge of the cliff. Out of this there had emerged a black, glistening object. As it came slowly forth and overhung the chasm, we saw that it was a very large snake with a peculiar flat spade-like head. It wavered and quivered above us for a minute, the morning sun gleaming upon its sleek, sinuous coils. Then it slowly drew inwards and disappeared.

Summerlee had been so interested that he had stood unresisting while Challenger tilted his head into the air. Now he shook his colleague off and came back to his dignity.

'I should be glad, Professor Challenger,' said he, 'if you could see your way to make any remarks which may occur to you without seizing me by the chin. Even the appearance of a very ordinary rock python does not appear to justify such a liberty.'

'But there is life upon the plateau all the same,' his colleague replied in triumph. 'And now, having demonstrated this important conclusion so that it is clear to anyone however prejudiced or obtuse, I am of opinion that we cannot do better than break up our camp and travel westward until we find some means of ascent.'

The ground at the foot of the cliff was rocky and broken, so that the going was slow and difficult. Suddenly we came, however, upon something which cheered our hearts. It was the site of an old encampment, with several empty Chicago meat tins, a bottle labelled 'Brandy,' a broken tin-opener, and a quantity of other travellers' debris. A crumpled, disintegrated newspaper revealed itself as the *Chicago Democrat*, though the date had been obliterated.

'Not mine,' said Challenger. 'It must be Maple White's.'

Lord John had been gazing curiously at a great tree-fern which overshadowed the encampment. 'I say, look at this,' said he. 'I believe it is meant for a sign-post.'

A slip of hard wood had been nailed to the tree in such a way as to point to the westward.

'Most certainly a sign-post,' said Challenger. 'What else? Finding himself upon a dangerous errand, our pioneer has left this so that any party which follows him may know the way he has taken. Perhaps we shall come upon some other indications as we proceed.'

We did indeed, but they were of a terrible and most unexpected nature. Immediately beneath the cliff there grew a considerable patch of high bamboo, like that which we had traversed in our journey. Many of these stems were twenty feet high, with sharp, strong tops, so that even as they stood they made formidable spears. We were passing along the edge of this cover when my eye was caught by the gleam of something white within it. Thrusting in my head between the stems, I found myself gazing at a fleshless skull. The whole skeleton was there, but the skull had detatched itself and lay some feet nearer to the open.

With a few blows from the machetes of our Indians we cleared the spot and were able to study the details of this old tragedy. Only a few shreds of clothes could still be distinguished, but there were the remains of boots upon the bony feet, and it was very clear that the dead man was a European. A gold watch by Hudson, of New York, and a chain which held a stylographic pen, lay among the bones. There was also a silver cigarette-case, with 'J. G., from A. E. S.,' upon the lid. The state of the metal seemed to show that the catastrophe had occurred no great time before.

'Who can he be?' asked Lord John. 'Poor devil! every bone in his body seems to be broken.'

'And the bamboo grows through his smashed ribs,' said Summerlee. 'It is a fast-growing plant, but it is surely inconceivable that this body could have been here while the canes grew to be twenty feet in length.'

'As to the man's identity,' said Professor Challenger, 'I have no doubt whatever upon that point. As I made my way up the river before I reached you at the fazenda I instituted very particular inquiries about Maple White. At Para they knew nothing. Fortunately, I had a definite clue, for there was a particular picture in his sketch-book which showed him taking lunch with a certain ecclesiastic at Rosario. This priest I was able to find, and though he proved a very argumentative fellow, who took it absurdly amiss that I should point out to him the corrosive effect which modern science must have upon his beliefs, he none the less gave me some positive information. Maple White passed Rosario four years ago, or two years before I saw his dead body. He was not alone at the time, but there was a friend, an American named James Colver, who remained in the boat and did not meet this ecclesiastic. I think, therefore, that there can be no doubt that we are now looking upon the remains of this James Colver.'

'Nor,' said Lord John, 'is there much doubt as to how he met his death. He has fallen or been chucked from the top, and so been impaled. How else could he come by his broken bones, and how could he have been stuck through by these canes with their points so high above our heads?'

A hush came over us as we stood round these shattered remains and realized the truth of Lord John Roxton's words. The beetling head of the cliff projected over the cane-brake. Undoubtedly he had fallen from above. But *had* he fallen? Had it been an accident? Or – Already ominous and terrible possibilities began to form round that unknown land.

We moved off in silence, and continued to coast round the line of cliffs, which were as even and unbroken as some of those monstrous Antarctic ice-fields which I have seen depicted as stretching from horizon to horizon and towering high above the mast-heads of the exploring vessel. In five miles we saw no rift or break. And then suddenly we perceived something which filled us with new hope. In a hollow of the rock, protected from rain, there was drawn a rough arrow in chalk, pointing still to the westward.

'Maple White again,' said Professor Challenger. 'He had some presentiment that worthy footsteps would follow close behind him.'

'He had chalk, then?'

'A box of coloured chalks was among the effects I found in his knapsack. I remember that the white one was worn to a stump.'

'That is certainly good evidence,' said Summerlee. 'We can only accept his guidance and follow on to the westward.'

We had proceeded some five more miles when again we saw a white arrow upon the rocks. It was at a point where the face of the cliff was for the first time split into a narrow cleft. Inside the cleft was a second guidance mark, which pointed right up it with the tip somewhat elevated, as if the spot indicated were above the level of the ground.

It was a solemn place, for the walls were so gigantic and the slit of blue sky so narrow and so obscured by a double fringe of verdure that only a dim and shadowy light penetrated to the bottom. We had had no food for many hours, and we were very weary with the stony and irregular journey, but our nerves were too strung to allow us to halt. We ordered the camp to be pitched, however, and leaving the Indians to arrange it, we four, with the two half-breeds, proceeded up the narrow gorge.

It was not more than forty feet across at the mouth, but it rapidly closed until it ended in an acute angle, too straight and smooth for an ascent. Certainly it was not this which our pioneer had attempted to indicate. We made our way back – the whole gorge was not more than a quarter of a mile deep – and then suddenly the quick eyes of Lord John fell upon what we were seeking. High up above our heads, amid the dark shadows, there was one circle of deeper gloom. Surely it could only be the opening of a cave.

The base of the cliff was heaped with loose stones at the spot, and it was not difficult to clamber up. When we reached it, all doubt was removed. Not only was it an opening into the rock, but on the side of it was marked once again the sign of the arrow. Here was the point, and this the means by which Maple White and his ill-fated comrade had made their ascent.

We were too excited to return to the camp, but must make our first exploration at once. Lord John had an electric torch in his knapsack, and this had to serve us as light. He advanced, throwing his little clear circlet of yellow radiance before him, while in single file we followed at his heels.

The cave had evidently been water-worn, the sides being smooth and the floor covered with rounded stones. It was of such a size that a single man could just fit through by stooping. For fifty yards it ran almost straight into the rock, and then it ascended at an angle of forty-five. Presently this incline became even steeper, and we found ourselves climbing upon hands and knees among loose rubble which slid from beneath us. Suddenly an exclamation broke from Lord Roxton.

'It's blocked!' said he.

Clustering behind him we saw in the yellow field of light a wall of broken basalt which extended to the ceiling.

'The roof has fallen in!'

In vain we dragged out some of the pieces. The only effect was that the larger ones became detached and threatened to roll down the gradient and crush us. It was evident that the obstacle was far beyond any efforts which we could make to remove it. The road by which Maple White had ascended was no longer available.

Too much cast down to speak, we stumbled down the dark tunnel and made our way back to the camp.

One incident occurred, however, before we left the gorge, which is of importance in view of what came afterwards.

We had gathered in a little group at the bottom of the chasm, some forty feet beneath the mouth of the cave, when a huge rock rolled suddenly downwards and shot past us with tremendous force. It was the narrowest escape for one or all of us. We could not ourselves see whence the rock had come, but our half-breed servants, who were still at the opening of the cave, said that it had flown past them, and must therefore have fallen from the summit. Looking upwards, we could see no sign of movement above us amidst the green jungle which topped the cliff. There could be little doubt, however, that the stone was aimed at us, so the incident surely pointed to humanity – and malevolent humanity – upon the plateau!

We withdrew hurriedly from the chasm, our minds full of this new development and its bearing upon our plans. The situation was difficult enough before, but if the obstructions of Nature were increased by the deliberate opposition of man, then our case was indeed a hopeless one. And yet, as we looked up at that beautiful fringe of verdure only a few hundreds of feet above our heads, there was not one of us who could conceive the idea of returning to London until we had explored it to its depths.

On discussing the situation, we determined that our best course was to continue to coast round the plateau in the hope of finding some other means of reaching the top. The line of cliffs, which had decreased considerably in height had already begun to trend from west to north, and if we could take this as representing the arc of a circle, the whole circumference could not be very great. At the worst, then, we should be back in a few days at our starting-point.

We made a march that day which totalled some two-and-twenty miles, without any change in our prospects. I may mention that our aneroid shows us that in the continual incline which we have ascended since we abandoned our canoes we have risen to no less than three thousand feet above sea-level. Hence there is a considerable change both in the temperature and in the vegetation. We have shaken off some of that horrible insect life which is the bane of tropical travel. A few palms still survive, and many tree-ferns, but the Amazonian trees have been all left behind. It was pleasant to see the convolvulus, the passion-flower, and the begonia, all reminding me of home, here among these inhospitable rocks. There was a red begonia just the same colour as one that is kept in a pot in the window of a certain villa in Streatham – but I am drifting into private reminiscence.

That night – I am still speaking of the first day of our circumnavigation of the plateau – a great experience awaited us, and one which for ever set at rest any doubt which we could have had as to the wonders so near us.

You will realize as you read it, my dear Mr. McArdle, and possibly for the first time, that the paper has not sent me on a wild-goose chase, and that there is inconceivably fine copy waiting for the world whenever we have the Professor's leave to make use of it. I shall not dare to publish these articles unless I can bring back my proofs to England, or I shall be hailed as the journalistic Munchausen of all time. I have no doubt that you feel the same way yourself, and that you would not care to stake the whole credit of the *Gazette* upon this adventure until we can meet the chorus of criticism and scepticism which such articles must of necessity elicit. So this wonderful incident, which would make such a headline for the old paper, must still wait its turn in the editorial drawer.

And yet it was all over in a flash, and there was no sequel to it, save in our own convictions.

What occurred was this. Lord John had shot an ajouti – which is a small, pig-like animal – and, half of it having been given to the Indians, we were cooking the other half upon our fire. There is a chill in the air after dark, and we had all drawn close to the blaze. The night was moonless, but there were some stars, and one could see for a little distance across the plain. Well, suddenly out of the darkness, out of the night, there swooped something with a swish like an aeroplane. The whole group of us were covered for an instant by a canopy of leathery wings, and I had a momentary vision of a long, snake-like neck, a fierce, red, greedy eye, and a great snapping beak, filled, to my amazement, with little, gleaming teeth. The next instant it was gone – and so was our dinner. A huge black shadow, twenty feet across, skimmed up into the air; for an instant the monster wings blotted out the stars, and then it vanished over the brow of the cliff above us. We all sat in amazed silence round the fire, like the heroes of Virgil when the Harpies came down upon them. It was Summerlee who was the first to speak.

'Professor Challenger,' said he, in a solemn voice, which quavered with emotion, 'I owe you an apology. Sir, I am very much in the wrong, and I beg that you will forget what is past.'

It was handsomely said, and the two men for the first time shook hands. So much we have gained by this clear vision of our first pterodactyl. It was worth a stolen supper to bring two such men together.

But if prehistoric life existed upon the plateau, it was not superabundant, for we had no further glimpse of it during the next three days. During this time we traversed a barren and forbidding country, which alternated between stony desert and desolate marshes full of many wild-fowl, upon the north and east of the cliffs. From this direction the place is really inaccessible, and, were it not for a hardish ledge which runs at the very base of the precipice, we should have had to turn back. Many times we were up to our waists in the slime and blubber of an old, semi-tropical swamp. To make matters worse, the place seemed to be a favourite breeding-place of the Jaracaca snake, the most venomous and aggressive in South America. Again and again these horrible creatures came writhing and springing towards us across the surface of this putrid bog, and it was only by keeping our shot-guns for ever ready that we could feel safe from them. One funnel-shaped depression in the morass, of a livid green in colour from some lichen which festered in it, will always remain as a nightmare memory in my mind. It seems to have been a special nest of these vermin, and the slopes were alive with them, all writhing in our direction, for it is a peculiarity of the Jaracaca that it will always attack man at first sight. There were too many for us to shoot, so we fairly took to our heels and ran until we were exhausted. I shall always remember as we looked back how far behind we could see the heads and necks of our horrible pursuers rising and falling amid the reeds. Jaracaca Swamp we named it in the map which we are constructing.

The cliffs upon the farther side had lost their ruddy tint, being chocolate-brown in colour; the vegetation was more scattered along the top of them, and they had sunk to three or four hundred feet in height, but in no place did we find any point where they could be ascended. If anything, they were more impossible than at the first point where we had met them. Their absolute steepness is indicated in the photograph which I took over the stony desert.

'Surely,' said I, as we discussed the situation, 'the rain must find its way down somehow. There are bound to be water-channels in the rocks.'

'Our young friend has glimpses of lucidity,' said Professor Challenger, patting me upon the shoulder.

'The rain must go somewhere,' I repeated.

'He keeps a firm grip upon actuality. The only drawback is that we have conclusively proved by ocular demonstration that there are *no* water channels down the rocks.'

'Where, then, does it go?' I persisted.

'I think it may be fairly assumed that if it does not come outwards it must run inwards.'

'Then there is a lake in the centre.'

'So I should suppose.'

'It is more than likely that the lake may be an old crater,' said Summerlee. 'The whole formation is, of course, highly volcanic. But however that may be, I should expect to find the surface of the plateau slope inwards with a considerable sheet of water in the centre, which may drain off, by some subterranean channel, into the marshes of the Jaracaca Swamp.'

'Or evaporation might preserve an equilibrium,' remarked Challenger, and the two learned men wandered off into one of their usual scientific arguments, which were as comprehensible as Chinese to the layman.

On the sixth day we completed our circuit of the cliffs, and found ourselves back at the first camp, beside the isolated pinnacle of rock. We were a disconsolate party, for nothing could have been more minute than our investigation, and it was absolutely certain that there was no single point where the most active human being could possibly hope to scale the cliff. The place which Maple White's chalk-marks had indicated as his own means of access was now entirely impassable.

What were we to do now? Our stores of provisions, supplemented by our guns, were holding out well, but the day must come when they would need replenishment. In a couple of months the rains might be expected, and we should be washed out of our camp. The rock was harder than marble, and any attempt at cutting a path for so great a height was more than our time or resources would admit. No wonder that we looked gloomily at each other that night, and sought our blankets without hardly a word exchanged. I remember that as I dropped off to sleep my last recollection was that Challenger was squatting, like a monstrous bull-frog, by the fire, his huge head in his hands, sunk apparently in the deepest thought, and entirely oblivious to the good-night which I wished him.

But it was a very different Challenger who greeted us in the morning – a Challenger with contentment and self-congratulation shining from his whole person. He faced us as we assembled for breakfast with a deprecating false modesty in his eyes, as who should say, 'I know that I deserve all that you can say, but I pray you to spare my blushes by not saying it.' His beard bristled exultantly, his chest was thrown out, and his hand was thrust into the front of his jacket. So, in his fancy, may he see himself sometimes, gracing the vacant pedestal in Trafalgar-Square, and adding one more to the horrors of the London streets.

'Eureka!' he cried, his teeth shining through his beard. 'Gentlemen, you may congratulate me and we may congratulate each other. The problem is solved.'

'You have found a way up?'

'I venture to think so.'

'And where?'

For answer he pointed to the spire-like pinnacle upon our right.

Our faces – or mine, at least – fell as we surveyed it. That it could be climbed we had our companion's assurance. But a horrible abyss lay between it and the plateau.

'We can never get across,' I gasped.

'We can at least all reach the summit,' said he. 'When we are up I may be able to show you that the resources of an inventive mind are not yet exhausted.'

After breakfast we unpacked the bundle in which our leader had brought his climbing accessories. From it he took a coil of the strongest and lightest rope, a hundred and fifty feet in length, and climbing irons, clamps, and other devices. Lord John was an experienced mountaineer, and Summerlee had done some rough climbing at various times, so that I was really the novice at rock-work of the party; but my strength and activity may have made up for my want of experience.

It was not in reality a very stiff task, though there were moments which made my hair bristle upon my head. The first half was perfectly easy, but from there upwards it became continually steeper, until, for the last fifty feet, we were literally clinging with our fingers and toes to tiny ledges and crevices in the rock. I could not have accomplished it, nor could Summerlee, if Challenger had not gained the summit (it was extraordinary to see such activity in so unwieldy a creature) and there fixed the rope round the trunk of the considerable tree which grew there. With this as our support, we were soon able to scramble up the jagged wall until we found ourselves upon the small grassy platform, some twenty-five feet each way, which formed the summit.

The first impression which I received when I had recovered my breath was the extraordinary view over the country which we traversed. The whole Brazilian plain seemed to lie beneath us, extending away and away until it ended in dim blue mists upon the farthest sky-line. In the foreground was the long slope, strewn with rocks and dotted with tree-ferns; farther off in the middle distance, looking over the saddle-back hill, I could just see the yellow and green mass of bamboos through which we had passed; and then gradually, the vegetation increased until it formed the huge forest which extended as far as the eyes could reach, and for a good two thousand miles beyond.

I was still drinking in this wonderful panorama when the heavy hand of the Professor fell upon my shoulder.

'This way, my young friend,' said he; '*vestigia nulla restrorsum*. Never look rearwards, but always to our glorious goal.'

The level of the plateau, when I turned, was, exactly that on which we stood, and the green bank of bushes, with occasional trees, was so near that it was difficult to realize how inaccessible it remained. At a rough guess the gulf was forty feet across, but, so far as I could see, it might as well have been forty miles. I placed one arm round the trunk of the tree and leaned over the abyss. Far down were the small dark figures of our servants, looking up at us. The wall was absolutely precipitous, as was that which faced me.

'This is indeed curious,' said the creaking voice of Professor Summerlee.

I turned, and found that he was examining with great interest the tree to which I clung. That smooth bark and those small, ribbed leaves seemed familiar to my eyes. 'Why,' I cried, 'it's a beech!'

'Exactly,' said Summerlee. 'A fellow-countryman in a far land.'

'Not only a fellow-countryman, my good sir,' said Challenger, 'but also, if I may be allowed to enlarge your smile, an ally of the first value. This beech tree will be our saviour.'

'By George!' cried Lord John, 'a bridge!'

'Exactly, my friends, a bridge! It is not for nothing that I expended an hour last night in focusing my mind upon the situation. I have some recollection of once remarking to our young friend here that G. E. C. is at his best when his back is to the wall. Last night you will admit that all our backs were to the wall. But where will-power and intellect go together, there is always a way out. A drawbridge had to be found which could be dropped across the abyss. Behold it!'

It was certainly a brilliant idea. The tree was a good sixty feet in height, and if it only fell the right way it would easily cross the chasm. Challenger had slung the camp axe over his shoulder when he ascended. Now he handed it to me.

'Our young friend has the thews and sinews,' said he. 'I think he will be the most useful at this task. I must beg, however, that you will kindly refrain from thinking for yourself, and that you will do exactly what you are told.'

Under his direction I cut such gashes in the sides of the tree as would ensure that it should fall as we desired. It had already a strong, natural tilt in the direction of the plateau, so that the matter was not difficult. Finally I set to work in earnest upon the trunk, taking turn and turn with Lord John. In a little over an hour there was a loud crack, the tree swayed forward, and then crashed over, burying its branches among the bushes on the farther side. The severed trunk rolled to the very edge of our platform, and for one terrible second we all thought that it was over. It balanced itself, however, a few inches from the edge, and there was our bridge to the unknown.

All of us, without a word, shook hands with Professor Challenger, who raised his straw hat and bowed deeply to each in turn.

'I claim the honour,' said he, 'to be the first to cross to the unknown land – a fitting subject, no doubt, for some future historical painting.'

He had approached the bridge when Lord John laid his hand upon his coat.

'My dear chap,' said he, 'I really cannot allow it.'

'Cannot allow it, sir!' The head went back and the beard forward.

'When it is a matter of science, don't you know, I follow your lead because you are by way of bein' a man of science. But it's up to you to follow me when you come into my department.'

'Your department, sir?'

'We all have our professions, and soldierin' is mine. We are, accordin' to my ideas, invadin' a new country, which may or may not be chock-full of enemies of sorts. To barge blindly into it for want of a little common sense and patience isn't my notion of management.'

The remonstrance was too reasonable to be disregarded. Challenger tossed his head and shrugged his heavy shoulders.

'Well, sir, what do you propose?'

'For all I know there may be a tribe of cannibals waitin' for lunch-time among those very bushes,' said Lord John, looking across the bridge. 'It's better to learn wisdom before you get into a cookin'-pot; so we will content ourselves with hopin' that there is no trouble waitin' for us, and at the same time we will act as if there were. Malone and I will go down again, therefore, and we will fetch up the four rifles, together with Gomez and the others. One man can then go across and the rest will cover him with guns, until he sees that it is safe for the whole crowd to come along.'

Challenger sat down upon the cut stump and groaned his impatience; but Summerlee and I were of one mind that Lord John was our leader when such practical details were in question. The climb was a more simple thing now that the rope dangled down the face of the worst part of the ascent. Within an hour we had brought up the rifles and a shot-gun. The half-breeds had ascended also, and under Lord John's orders they had carried up a bale of provisions in case our first exploration should be a long one. We had each bandoliers of cartridges.

'Now, Challenger, if you really insist upon being the first man in,' said Lord John, when every preparation was complete.

'I am much indebted to you for your gracious permission,' said the angry Professor; for never was a man so intolerant of every form of authority. 'Since you are good enough to allow it, I shall most certainly take it upon myself to act as pioneer upon this occasion.'

Seating himself with a leg overhanging the abyss on each side, and his hatchet slung upon his back, Challenger hopped his way across the trunk and was soon at the other side. He clambered up and waved his arms in the air.

'At last!' he cried; 'at last!'

I gazed anxiously at him, with a vague expectation that some terrible fate would dart at him from the curtain of green behind him. But all was quiet, save that a strange, many-coloured bird flew up from under his feet and vanished among the trees.

Summerlee was the second. His wiry energy is wonderful in so frail a frame. He insisted upon having two rifles slung upon his back, so that both Professors were armed when he had made his transit. I came next, and tried not to look down into the horrible gulf over which I was passing. Summerlee held out the butt-end of his rifle, and an instant later I was able to grasp his hand. As to Lord John, he walked across – actually walked, without support! He must have nerves of iron.

And there we were, the four of us, upon the dreamland, the lost world, of Maple White. To all of us it seemed the moment of our supreme triumph. Who could have guessed that it was the prelude to our supreme disaster? Let me say in a few words how the crushing blow fell upon us.

We had turned away from the edge, and had penetrated about fifty yards of close brushwood, when there came a frightful rending crash from behind us. With one impulse we rushed back the way we had come. The bridge was gone!

Far down at the base of the cliff I saw, as I looked over, a tangled mass of branches and splintered trunk. It was our beech tree. Had the edge of the platform crumbled and let it through? For a moment this explanation was in all our minds. The next, from the farther side of the rocky pinnacle before us a swarthy face, the face of Gomez the half-breed, was slowly protruded. Yes, it was Gomez, but no longer the Gomez of the demure smile and the mask-like expression. Here was a face with flashing eyes and distorted features, a face convulsed with hatred and with the mad joy of gratified revenge.

'Lord Roxton!' he shouted. 'Lord John Roxton!'

'Well,' said our companion, 'here I am.'

A shriek of laughter came across the abyss.

'Yes, there you are, you English dog, and there you will remain! I have waited and waited, and now has come my chance. You found it hard to get up; you will find it harder to get down. You cursed fools, you are trapped, every one of you!'

We were too astounded to speak. We could only stand there staring in amazement. A great broken bough upon the grass showed whence he had gained his leverage to tilt over our bridge. The face had vanished, but presently it was up again, more frantic than before.

'We nearly killed you with a stone at the cave,' he cried, 'but this is better. It is slower and more terrible. Your bones will whiten up there, and none will know where you lie or come to cover them. As you lie dying, think of Lopez, whom you shot five years ago on the Putomayo River. I am his brother, and, come what will, I die happy now, for his memory has been avenged.' A furious hand was shaken at us, and then all was quiet.

Had the half-breed simply wrought his vengeance and then escaped, all might have been well with him. It was that foolish, irresistible Latin impulse to be dramatic which brought his own downfall. Roxton, the man who had earned himself the name of the Flail of the Lord through three countries, was not one who could be safely taunted. The half-breed was descending on the farther side of the pinnacle; but before he could reach the ground Lord John had run along the edge of the plateau and gained a point from which he could see his man. There was a single crack of his rifle, and, though we saw nothing, we heard the scream and then the distant thud of the falling body. Roxton came back to us with a face of granite.

'I have been a blind simpleton,' said he, bitterly. 'It's my folly that has brought you all into this trouble. I should have remembered that these people have long memories for blood-feuds, and have been more upon my guard.'

'What about the other one? It took two of them to lever that tree over the edge.'

'I could have shot him, but I let him go. He may have had no part in it. Perhaps it would have been better if I had killed him, for he must, as you say, have lent a hand.'

Now that we had the clue to his action, each of us could cast back and remember some sinister act upon the part of the half-breed – his constant desire to know our plans, his arrest outside our tent when he was overhearing them, the furtive looks of hatred which from time to time one or other of us had surprised. We were still discussing it, endeavouring to adjust our minds to these new conditions, when a singular scene in the plain below arrested our attention.

A man in white clothes, who could only be the surviving half-breed, was running as one does run when Death is the pacemaker. Behind him, only a few yards in his rear, bounded the huge ebony figure of Zambo, our devoted negro. Even as we looked, he sprang upon the back of the fugitive and flung his arms round his neck. They rolled on the ground together. An instant afterwards Zambo rose, looked at the prostrate man, and then, waving his hand joyously to us, came running in our direction. The white figure lay motionless in the middle of the great plain.

Our two traitors had been destroyed, but the mischief that they had done lived after them. By no possible means could we get back to the pinnacle. We had been natives of the world; now we were natives of the plateau. The two things were separate and apart. There was the plain which led to the canoes. Yonder, beyond the violet, hazy horizon, was the stream which led back to civilization. But the link between was missing. No human ingenuity could suggest a means of bridging the chasm which yawned between ourselves and our past lives. One instant had altered the whole conditions of our existence.

It was at such a moment that I learned the stuff of which my three comrades were composed. They were grave, it is true, and thoughtful, but of an invincible serenity. For the moment we could only sit among the bushes in patience and wait the coming of Zambo. Presently his honest black face topped the rocks and his Herculean figure emerged upon the top of the pinnacle.

'What I do now?' he cried. 'You tell me and I do it.'

It was a question which it was easier to ask than to answer. One thing only was clear. He was our one trusty link with the outside world. On no account must he leave us.

'No, no!' he cried. 'I not leave you. Whatever come, you always find me here. But no able to keep Indians. Already they say too much, Curupuri live on this place, and they go home. Now you leave them me no able to keep them.'

'Make them wait till to-morrow, Zambo,' I shouted; 'then I can send letter back by them.'

'Very good, sarr! I promise they wait till to-morrow,' said the negro. 'But what I do for you now?'

There was plenty for him to do, and admirably the faithful fellow did it. First of all, under our directions, he undid the rope from the tree-stump and threw one end of it across to us. It was not thicker than a clothes-line, but it was of great strength, and though we could not make a bridge of it, we might well find it invaluable if we had any climbing to do. He then fastened his end of the rope to the package of supplies which had been carried up, and we were able to drag it across. This gave us the means of life for at least a week, even if we found nothing else. Finally he descended and carried up two other packets of mixed goods – a box of ammunition and a number of other things, all of which we got across by throwing our rope to him and hauling it back. It was evening when he at last climbed down, with a final assurance that he would keep the Indians till next morning.

And so it is that I have spent nearly the whole of this our first night upon the plateau writing up our experiences by the light of a single candle-lantern.

We supped and camped at the very edge of the cliff, quenching our thirst with two bottles of Apollinaris which were in one of the cases. It is vital to us to find water, but I think even Lord John himself had had adventures enough for one day, and none of us felt inclined to make the first push into the unknown. We forbore to light a fire or to make any unnecessary sound.

To-morrow (or to-day, rather, for it is already dawn as I write) we shall make our first venture into this strange land. When I shall be able to write again – or if I ever shall write again – I know not. Meanwhile, I can see that the Indians are still in their place, and I am sure that the faithful Zambo will be here presently to get my letter. I only trust that it will come to hand.

P.S. – The more I think the more desperate does our position seem. I see no possible hope of our return. If there were a high tree near the edge of the plateau we might drop a return bridge across, but there is none within fifty yards. Our united strength could not carry a trunk which would serve our purpose. The rope, of course, is far too short that we could descend by it. No, our position is hopeless – hopeless!

10

The Most Wonderful Things Have Happened

THE most wonderful things have happened and are continually happening to us. All the paper that I possess consists of five old notebooks and a lot of scraps, and I have only the one stylographic pencil; but so long as I can move my hand I will continue to set down our experiences and impressions, for, since we are the only men of the whole human race to see such things, it is of enormous importance that I should record them whilst they are fresh in my memory and before that fate which seems to be constantly impending does actually overtake us. Whether Zambo can at last take these letters to the river, or whether I shall myself in some miraculous way carry them back with me, or, finally, whether some daring explorer, coming upon our tracks, with the advantage, perhaps, of a perfected monoplane, should find this bundle of manuscript, in any case I can see that what I am writing is destined to immortality as a classic of true adventure.

On the morning after our being trapped upon the plateau by the villainous Gomez we began a new stage in our experiences. The first incident in it was not such as to give me a very favourable opinion of the place to which we had wandered. As I roused myself from a short nap after day had dawned, my eyes fell upon a most singular appearance upon my own leg. My trouser had slipped up, exposing a few inches of my skin above my sock. On this there rested a large, purplish grape. Astonished at the sight, I leaned forward to pick it off, when, to my horror, it burst between my finger and thumb, squirting blood in every direction. My cry of disgust had brought the two Professors to my side.

'Most interesting,' said Summerlee, bending over my shin. 'An enormous blood-tick, as yet, I believe, unclassified.'

'The first fruits of our labours,' said Challenger in his booming pedantic fashion. 'We cannot do less than call it *Ixodes Maloni*. The very small inconvenience of being bitten, my young friend, cannot, I am sure, weigh with you as against the glorious privilege of having your name inscribed in the deathless roll of zoology. Unhappily you have crushed this fine specimen at the moment of satiation.'

'Filthy vermin!' I cried.

Professor Challenger raised his great eyebrows in protest, and placed a soothing paw upon my shoulder.

'You should cultivate the scientific eye and the detached scientific mind,' said he. 'To a man of philosophic temperament like myself the blood-tick, with its lancet-like proboscis and its distending stomach, is as beautiful a work of Nature as the peacock, or for that matter, the aurora borealis. It pains me to hear you speak of it in so unappreciative a fashion. No doubt, with due diligence, we can secure some other specimen.'

'There can be no doubt of that,' said Summerlee, grimly, 'for one has just disappeared behind your shirt-collar.'

Challenger sprang into the air bellowing like a bull and tore frantically at his coat and shirt to get them off. Summerlee and I laughed so that we could hardly help him. At last we exposed that monstrous torso (fifty-four inches, by the tailor's tape). His body was all matted with black hair, out of which jungle we picked the wandering tick before it had bitten him. But the bushes round were full of the horrible pests, and it was clear that we must shift our camp.

But first of all it was necessary to make our arrangements with the faithful negro, who appeared presently on the pinnacle with a number of tins of cocoa and biscuits, which he tossed over to us. Of the stores which remained below he was ordered to retain as much as would keep him for two months. The Indians were to have the remainder as a reward for their services and as payment for taking our letters back to the Amazon. Some hours later we saw them in single file far out upon the plain, each with a bundle on his head, making their way back along the path we had come. Zambo occupied our little tent at the base of the pinnacle, and there he remained, our one link with the world below.

And now we had to decide upon our immediate movements. We shifted our position from among the tick-laden bushes until we came to a small clearing thickly surrounded by trees upon all sides. There were some flat slabs of rock in the centre, with an excellent well close by, and there we sat in cleanly comfort while we made our first plans for the invasion of this new country. Birds were calling among the foliage – especially one with a peculiar whooping cry which was new to us – but beyond these sounds there were no signs of life.

Our first care was to make some sort of list of our own stores, so that we might know what we had to rely upon. What with the things we had ourselves brought up and those which Zambo had sent across on the rope, we were fairly well supplied. Most important of all, in view of the dangers which might surround us, we had our four rifles and one thousand three hundred rounds, also a shot-gun, but not more than a hundred and fifty medium pellet cartridges. In the matter of provisions we had enough to last for several weeks, with a sufficiency of tobacco and a few scientific implements, including a large telescope and a good field-glass. All these things we collected together in the clearing, and as a first precaution, we cut down with our hatchet and knives a number of thorny bushes, which we piled round in a circle some fifteen yards in diameter. This was to be our headquarters for the time – our place of refuge against sudden danger and the guard-house for our stores. Fort Challenger, we called it.

It was midday before we had made ourselves secure, but the heat was not oppressive, and the general character of the plateau, both in its temperature and in its vegetation, was almost temperate. The beech, the oak, and even the birch were to be found among the tangle of trees which girt us in. One huge gingko tree, topping all the others, shot its great limbs and maidenhair foliage over the fort which we had constructed. In its shade we continued our discussion, while Lord John, who had quickly taken command in the hour of action, gave us his views.

'So long as neither man nor beast has seen or heard us, we are safe,' said he. 'From the time they know we are here our troubles begin. There are no signs that they have found us out as yet. So our game surely is to lie low for a time and spy out the land. We want to have a good look at our neighbours before we get on visitin' terms.'

'But we must advance,' I ventured to remark.

'By all means, sonny my boy! we will advance. But with common sense. We must never go so far that we can't get back to our base. Above all, we must never, unless it is life or death, fire off our guns.'

'But *you* fired yesterday,' said Summerlee.

'Well, it couldn't be helped. However, the wind was strong and blew outwards. It is not likely that the sound could have travelled far into the plateau. By the way, what shall we call this place? I suppose it is up to us to give it a name?'

There were several suggestions, more or less happy, but Challenger's was final.

'It can only have one name,' said he. 'It is called after the pioneer who discovered it. It is Maple White Land.'

Maple White Land it became, and so it is named in that chart which has become my special task. So it will, I trust, appear in the atlas of the future.

The peaceful penetration of Maple White Land was the pressing subject before us. We had the evidence of our own eyes that the place was inhabited by some unknown creatures, and there was that of Maple White's sketch-book to show that more dreadful and more dangerous monsters might still appear. That there might also prove to be human occupants and that they were of a malevolent character was suggested by the skeleton impaled upon the bamboos, which could not have got there had it not been dropped from above. Our situation, stranded without possibility of escape in such a land, was clearly full of danger, and our reason endorsed every measure of caution which Lord John's experience could suggest. Yet it was surely impossible that we should halt on the edge of this world of mystery when our very souls were tingling with impatience to push forward and to pluck the heart from it.

We therefore blocked the entrance to our zareba by filling it up with several thorny bushes, and left our camp with the stores entirely surrounded by this protecting hedge. We then slowly and cautiously set forth into the unknown, following the course of the little stream which flowed from our spring, as it should always serve us as a guide on our return.

Hardly had we started when we came across signs that there were indeed wonders awaiting us. After a few hundred yards of thick forest, containing many trees which were quite unknown to me, but which Summerlee, who was the botanist of the party, recognized as forms of conifera and of cycadaceous plants which have long passed away in the world below, we entered a region where the stream widened out and formed a considerable bog. High reeds of a peculiar type grew thickly before us, which were pronounced to be equisetacea, or mare's-tails, with tree-ferns scattered amongst them, all of them swaying in a brisk wind. Suddenly Lord John, who was walking first, halted with uplifted hand.

'Look at this!' said he. 'By George, this must be the trail of the father of all birds!'

An enormous three-toed track was imprinted in the soft mud before us. The creature, whatever it was, had crossed the swamp and had passed on into the forest. We all stopped to examine that monstrous spoor. If it were indeed a bird – and what animal could leave such a mark? – its foot was so much larger than an ostrich's that its height upon the same scale must be enormous. Lord John looked eagerly round him and slipped two cartridges into his elephant-gun.

'I'll stake my good name as a shikaree,' said he, 'that the track is a fresh one. The creature has not passed ten minutes. Look how the water is still oozing into that deeper print! By Jove! See, here is the mark of a little one!'

Sure enough, smaller tracks of the same general form were running parallel to the large one!'

'But what do you make of this?' cried Professor Summerlee, triumphantly, pointing to what looked like the huge print of a five-fingered human hand appearing among the three-toed marks.

'Wealden!' cried Challenger, in an ecstasy. 'I've seen them in the Wealden clay. It is a creature walking erect upon three-toed feet, and occasionally putting one of its five-fingered fore-paws upon the ground. Not a bird, my dear Roxton – not a bird.'

'A beast?'

'No; a reptile – a dinosaur. Nothing else could have left such a track. They puzzled a worthy Sussex doctor some ninety years ago; but who in the world could have hoped – hoped – to have seen a sight like that?'

His words died away into a whisper and we all stood in motionless amazement. Following the tracks, we had left the morass and passed through a screen of brushwood and trees. Beyond was an open glade, and in this were five of the most extraordinary creatures that I have ever seen. Crouching down among the bushes, we observed them at our leisure.

There were, as I say, five of them, two being adults and three young ones. In size they were enormous. Even the babies were as big as elephants, while the two large ones were far beyond all creatures I have ever seen. They had slate-coloured skin, which was scaled like a lizard's and shimmered where the sun shone upon it. All five were sitting up, balancing themselves upon their broad, powerful tails and their huge three-toed hind-feet, while with their small five-fingered front-feet they pulled down the branches upon which they browsed. I do not know that I can bring their appearance home to you better than by saying that they looked like monstrous kangaroos, twenty feet in length, and with skins like black crocodiles.

I do not know how long we stayed motionless gazing at this marvellous spectacle. A strong wind blew towards us and we were well concealed, so there was no chance of discovery. From time to time the little ones played round their parents in unwieldy gambols, the great beasts bounding into the air and falling with dull thuds upon the earth. The strength of the parents seemed to be limitless, for one of them, having some difficulty in reaching a bunch of foliage which grew upon a considerable-sized tree, put his fore-legs round the trunk and tore it down as if it had been a sapling. The action seemed, as I thought, to show not only the great development of its muscles, but also the small one of its brain, for the whole weight came crashing down upon the top of it, and it uttered a series of shrill yelps to show that, big as it was, there was a limit to what it could endure. The incident made it think, apparently, that the neighbourhood was dangerous, for it slowly lurched off through the wood, followed by its mate and its three enormous infants. We saw the shimmering slatey gleam of their skins between the tree-trunks, and their heads undulating high above the brushwood. Then they vanished from our sight.

I looked at my comrades. Lord John was standing at gaze with his finger on the trigger of his elephant-gun, his eager hunter's soul shining from his fierce eyes. What would he not give for one such head to place between the two crossed oars above the mantelpiece in his snuggery at the Albany! And yet his reason held him in, for all our exploration of the wonders of this unknown land depended upon our presence being concealed from its inhabitants. The two professors were in silent ecstasy. In their excitement they had unconsciously seized each other by the hand, and stood like two little children in the presence of a marvel, Challenger's cheeks bunched up into a seraphic smile, and Summerlee's sardonic face softening for the moment into wonder and reverence.

'*Nunc dimittis!*' he cried at last. 'What will they say in England of this?'

'My dear Summerlee, I will tell you with great confidence exactly what they will say in England,' said Challenger. 'They will say that you are an infernal liar and a scientific charlatan, exactly as you and others said of me.'

'In the face of photographs?'

'Faked, Summerlee! Clumsily faked!'

'In the face of specimens?'

'Ah, there we may have them! Malone and his filthy Fleet Street crew may be all yelping our praises yet. August the twenty-eighth – the day we saw five live iguanodons in a glade of Maple White Land. Put it down in your diary, my young friend, and send it to your rag.'

'And be ready to get the toe-end of the editorial boot in return,' said Lord John. 'Things look a bit different from the latitude of London, young fellah-my-lad. There's many a man who never tells his adventures, for he can't hope to be believed. Who's to blame them? For this will seem a bit of a dream to ourselves in a month or two. *What* did you say they were?'

'Iguanodons,' said Summerlee. 'You'll find their footmarks all over the Hastings sands, in Kent, and in Sussex. The South of England was alive with them when there was plenty of good lush green-stuff to keep them going. Conditions have changed, and the beasts died. Here it seems that the conditions have not changed, and the beasts have lived.'

'If ever we get out of this alive, I must have a head with me,' said Lord John. 'Lord, how some of that Somaliland-Uganda crowd would turn a beautiful pea-green if they saw it! I don't know what you chaps think, but it strikes me that we are on mighty thin ice all this time.'

I had the same feeling of mystery and danger around us. In the gloom of the trees there seemed a constant menace, and as we looked up into their shadowy foliage vague terrors crept into one's heart. It is true that these monstrous creatures which we had seen were lumbering, inoffensive brutes which were unlikely to hurt anyone, but in this world of wonders what other survivals might there not be – what fierce, active horrors ready to pounce upon us from their lair among the rocks or brushwood? I knew little of prehistoric life, but I had a clear remembrance of one book which I had read in which it spoke of creatures who would live upon our lions and tigers as a cat lives upon mice. What if these also were to be found in the woods of Maple White Land!

It was destined that on this very morning – our first in the new country – we were to find out what strange hazards lay around us. It was a loathsome adventure, and one of which I hate to think. If, as Lord John said, the glade of the iguanodons will remain with us as a dream, then surely the swamp of the pterodactyls will for ever be our nightmare. Let me set down exactly what occurred.

We passed very slowly through the woods, partly because Lord John acted as scout before he would let us advance, and partly because at every second step one or other of our professors would fall, with a cry of wonder, before some flower or insect which presented him with a new type. We may have travelled two or three miles in all, keeping to the right of the line of the stream, when we came upon a considerable opening in the trees. A belt of brushwood led up to a tangle of rocks – the whole plateau was strewn with boulders. We were walking slowly towards these rocks, among bushes which reached over our waists, when we became aware of a strange low gabbling and whistling sound, which filled the air with a constant clamour and appeared to come from some spot immediately before us. Lord John held up his hand as a signal for us to stop, and he made his way swiftly, stooping and running, to the line of rocks. We saw him peep over them and give a gesture of amazement. Then he stood staring as if forgetting us, so utterly entranced was he by what he saw. Finally he waved us to come on, holding up his hand as a signal for caution. His whole bearing made me feel that something wonderful but dangerous lay before us.

Creeping to his side, we looked over the rocks. The place into which we gazed was a pit, and may, in the early days, have been one of the smaller volcanic blow-holes of the plateau. It was bowl-shaped, and at the bottom, some hundreds of yards from where we lay, were pools of green-scummed, stagnant water, fringed with bulrushes. It was a weird place in itself, but its occupants made it seem like a scene from the Seven Circles of Dante. The place was a rookery of pterodactyls. There were hundreds of them congregated within view. All the bottom area round the wateredge was alive with their young ones, and with hideous mothers brooding upon their leathery, yellowish eggs. From this crawling flapping mass of obscene reptilian life came the shocking clamour which filled the air and the mephitic, horrible, musty odour which turned us sick. But above, perched each upon its own stone, tall, grey, and withered, more like dead and dried specimens than actual living creatures, sat the horrible males, absolutely motionless save for the rolling of their red eyes or an occasional snap of their rat-trap beaks as a dragon-fly went past them. Their huge, membranous wings were closed by folding their forearms, so that they sat like gigantic old women, wrapped in hideous web-coloured shawls, and with their ferocious heads protruding above them. Large and small, not less than a thousand of these filthy creatures lay in the hollow before us.

Our professors would gladly have stayed there all day, so entranced were they by this opportunity of studying the life of a prehistoric age. They pointed out the fish and dead birds lying about among the rocks as proving the nature of the food of these creatures, and I heard them congratulating each other on having cleared up the point why the bones of this flying dragon are found in such great numbers in certain well-defined areas, as in the Cambridge Green-sand, since it was now seen that, like penguins, they lived in gregarious fashion.

Finally, however, Challenger, bent upon proving some point which Summerlee had contested, thrust his head over the rock and nearly brought destruction upon us all. In an instant the nearest male gave a shrill, whistling cry, and flapped its twenty-foot span of leathery wings as it soared up into the air. The females and young ones huddled together beside the water, while the whole circle of sentinels rose one after the other and sailed off into the sky. It was a wonderful sight to see at least a hundred creatures of such enormous size and hideous appearance all swooping like swallows with swift, shearing wing-strokes above us; but soon we realized that it was not one on which we could afford to linger. At first the great brutes flew round in a huge ring, as if to make sure what the exact extent of the danger might be. Then, the flight grew lower and the circle narrower, until they were whizzing round and round us, the dry, rustling flap of their huge slate-coloured wings filling the air with a volume of sound that made me think of Hendon aerodrome upon a race day.

'Make for the wood and keep together,' cried Lord John, clubbing his rifle. 'The brutes mean mischief.'

The moment we attempted to retreat the circle closed in upon us, until the tips of the wings of those nearest to us nearly touched our faces. We beat at them with the stocks of our guns, but there was nothing solid or vulnerable to strike. Then suddenly out of the whizzing, slate-coloured circle a long neck shot out, and a fierce beak made a thrust at us. Another and another followed. Summerlee gave a cry and put his hand to his face, from which the blood was streaming. I felt a prod at the back of my neck, and turned dizzy with the shock. Challenger fell, and as I stooped to pick him up I was again struck from behind and dropped on top of him. At the same instant I heard the crash of Lord John's elephant-gun, and, looking up, saw one of the creatures with a broken wing struggling upon the ground, spitting and gurgling at us with a wide-opened beak and blood-shot, goggled eyes, like some devil in a mediåval picture. Its comrades had flown higher at the sudden sound, and were circling above our heads.

'Now,' cried Lord John, 'now for our lives!'

We staggered through the brushwood, and even as we reached the trees the harpies were on us again. Summerlee was knocked down, but we bore him up and rushed among the trunks. Once there we were safe, for those huge wings had no space for their sweep beneath the branches. As we limped homewards, sadly mauled and discomfited, we saw them for a long time flying at a great height against the deep blue sky above our heads, soaring round and round, no bigger than wood-pigeons, with their eyes no doubt still following our progress. At last, however, as we reached the thicker woods they gave up the chase, and we saw them no more.

'A most interesting and convincing experience,' said Challenger, as we halted beside the brook and he bathed a swollen knee. 'We are exceptionally well informed, Summerlee, as to the habits of the enraged pterodactyl.'

Summerlee was wiping the blood from a cut in his forehead, while I was tying up a nasty stab in the muscle of the neck. Lord John had the shoulder of his coat torn away, but the creature's teeth had only grazed the flesh.

'It is worth noting,' Challenger continued, 'that our young friend has received an undoubted stab, while Lord John's coat could only have been torn by a bite. In my own case, I was beaten about the head by their wings, so we have had a remarkable exhibition of their various methods of offence.'

'It has been touch and go for our lives,' said Lord John, gravely, 'and

I could not think of a more rotten sort of death than to be outed by such filthy vermin. I was sorry to fire my rifle, but, by Jove! there was no great choice.'

'We should not be here if you hadn't,' said I, with conviction.

'It may do no harm,' said he. 'Among these woods there must be many loud cracks from splitting or falling trees which would be just like the sound of a gun. But now, if you are of my opinion, we have had thrills enough for one day, and had best get back to the surgical box at the camp for some carbolic. Who knows what venom these beasts may have in their hideous jaws?'

But surely no men ever had just such a day since the world began. Some fresh surprise was ever in store for us. When, following the course of our brook, we at last reached our glade and saw the thorny barricade of our camp, we thought that our adventures were at an end. But we had something more to think of before we could rest. The gate of Fort Challenger had been untouched, the walls were unbroken, and yet it had been visited by some strange and powerful creature in our absence. No foot-mark showed a trace of its nature, and only the overhanging branch of the enormous gingko tree suggested how it might have come and gone; but of its malevolent strength there was ample evidence in the condition of our stores. They were strewn at random all over the ground, and one tin of meat had been crushed into pieces so as to extract the contents. A case of cartridges had been shattered into matchwood, and one of the brass shells lay shredded into pieces beside it. Again the feeling of vague horror came upon our souls, and we gazed round with frightened eyes at the dark shadows which lay round us, in all of which some fearsome shape might be lurking. How good it was when we were hailed by the voice of Zambo, and going to the edge of the plateau, saw him sitting grinning at us upon the top of the opposite pinnacle.

'All well, Massa Challenger, all well!' he cried. 'Me stay here. No fear. You always find me when you want.'

His honest black face and the immense view before us, which carried us half-way back to the affluent of the Amazon, helped us to remember that we really were upon this earth in the twentieth century, and had not by some magic been conveyed to some raw planet in its earliest and wildest state. How difflcult it was to realize that the violet line upon the far horizon was well advanced to that great river upon which huge steamers ran, and folk talked of the small affairs of life, while we, marooned among the creatures of a bygone age, could but gaze towards it and yearn for all that it meant!

One other memory remains with me of this wonderful day, and with it I will close this letter. The two professors, their tempers aggravated no doubt by their injuries, had fallen out as to whether our assailants were of the genus pterodactylus or dimorphodon, and high words had ensued. To avoid their wrangling I moved some little way apart, and was seated smoking upon the trunk of a fallen tree, when Lord John strolled over in my direction.

'I say, Malone,' said he, 'do you remember that place where those beasts were?'

'Very clearly.'

'A sort of volcanic pit, was it not?'

'Exactly,' said I.

'Did you notice the soil?'

'Rocks.'

'But round the water – where the reeds were?'

'It was a bluish soil. It looked like clay.'

'Exactly. A volcanic tube full of blue clay.'

'What of that?' I asked.

'Oh, nothing, nothing,' said he, and strolled back to where the voices of the contending men of science rose in a prolonged duet, the high, strident note of Summerlee rising and falling to the sonorous bass of Challenger. I should have thought no more of Lord John's remark were it not that once again that night I heard him mutter to himself: 'Blue clay – clay in a volcanic tube!' They were the last words I heard before I dropped into an exhausted sleep.

11

For Once I Was the Hero

LORD JOHN ROXTON was right when he thought that some specially toxic quality might lie in the bite of the horrible creatures which had attacked us. On the morning after our first adventure upon the plateau, both Summerlee and I were in great pain and fever, while Challenger's knee was so bruised that he could hardly limp. We kept to our camp all day, therefore, Lord John busying himself, with such help as we could give him, in raising the height and thickness of the thorny walls which were our only defence. I remember that during the whole long day I was haunted by the feeling that we were closely observed, though by whom or whence I could give no guess.

So strong was the impression that I told Professor Challenger of it, who put it down to the cerebral excitement caused by my fever. Again and again I glanced round swiftly, with the conviction that I was about to see something, but only to meet the dark tangle of our hedge or the solemn and cavernous gloom of the great trees which arched above our heads. And yet the feeling grew ever stronger in my own mind that something observant and something malevolent was at our very elbow. I thought of the Indian superstition of the Curupuri – the dreadful lurking spirit of the woods – and I could have imagined that his terrible presence haunted those who have invaded his most remote and sacred retreat.

That night (our third in Maple White Land) we had an experience which left a fearful impression upon our minds, and made us thankful that Lord John had worked so hard in making our retreat impregnable. We were all sleeping round our dying fire when we were aroused – or, rather, I should say, shot out of our slumbers – by a succession of the most frightful cries and screams to which I have ever listened. I know no sound to which I could compare this amazing tumult, which seemed to come from some spot within a few hundred yards of our camp. It was as ear-splitting as any whistle of a railway-engine; but whereas the whistle is a clear, mechanical, sharp-edged sound, this was far deeper in volume and vibrant with the uttermost strain of agony and horror. We clapped our hands to our ears to shut out that nerve-shaking appeal. A cold sweat broke out over my body, and my heart turned sick at the misery of it. All the woes of tortured life, all its stupendous indictment of high heaven, its innumerable sorrows, seemed to be centred and condensed into that one dreadful, agonized cry. And then, under this high-pitched, ringing sound there was another, more intermittent, a low, deep-chested laugh, a growling, throaty gurgle of merriment which formed a grotesque accompaniment to the shriek with which it was blended. For three or four minutes on end the fearsome duet continued, while all the foliage rustled with the rising of startled birds. Then it shut off as suddenly as it began. For a long time we sat in horrified silence. Then Lord John threw a bundle of twigs upon the fire, and their red glare lit up the intent faces of my companions and flickered over the great boughs above our heads.

'What was it?' I whispered.

'We shall know in the morning,' said Lord John. 'It was close to us – not farther than the glade.'

'We have been privileged to overhear a prehistoric tragedy, the sort of drama which occurred among the reeds upon the border of some Jurassic lagoon, when the greater dragon pinned the lesser among the slime,' said Challenger, with more solemnity than I had ever heard in his voice. 'It was surely well for man that he came late in the order of creation. There were powers abroad in earlier days which no courage and no mechanism of his could have met. What could his sling, his throwing-stick, or his arrow avail him against such forces as have been loose to-night? Even with a modern rifle it would be all odds on the monster.'

'I think I should back my little friend,' said Lord John, caressing his Express. 'But the beast would certainly have a good sporting chance.'

Summerlee raised his hand.

'Hush!' he cried. 'Surely I hear something?'

From the utter silence there emerged a deep, regular pat-pat. It was the tread of some animal – the rhythm of soft but heavy pads placed cautiously upon the ground. It stole slowly round the camp, and then halted near our gateway. There was a low, sibilant rise and fall – the breathing of the creature. Only our feeble hedge separated us from this horror of the night. Each of us had seized his rifle, and Lord John had pulled out a small bush to make an embrasure in the hedge.

'By George!' he whispered. 'I think I can see it!'

I stooped and peered over his shoulder through the gap. Yes, I could see it, too. In the deep shadow of the tree there was a deeper shadow yet, black, inchoate, vague – a crouching form full of savage vigour and menace. It was no higher than a horse, but the dim outline suggested vast bulk and strength. That hissing pant, as regular and fullvolumed as the exhaust of an engine, spoke of a monstrous organism. Once, as it moved, I thought I saw the glint of two terrible, greenish eyes. There was an uneasy rustling, as if it were crawling slowly forward.

'I believe it is going to spring!' said I, cocking my rifle.

'Don't fire! Don't fire!' whispered Lord John. 'The crash of a gun in this silent night would be heard for miles. Keep it as a last card.'

'If it gets over the hedge we're done,' said Summerlee, and his voice crackled into a nervous laugh as he spoke.

'No, it must not get over,' cried Lord John; 'but hold your fire to the last. Perhaps I can make something of the fellow. I'll chance it, anyhow.'

It was as brave an act as ever I saw a man do. He stooped to the fire, picked up a blazing branch, and slipped in an instant through a sallyport which he had made in our gateway. The thing moved forward with a dreadful snarl. Lord John never hesitated, but, running towards it with a quick, light step, he dashed the flaming wood into the brute's face. For one moment I had a vision of a horrible mask like a giant toad's, of a warty, leprous skin, and of a loose mouth all beslobbered with fresh blood. The next, there was a crash in the underwood and our dreadful visitor was gone.

'I thought he wouldn't face the fire,' said Lord John, laughing, as he came back and threw his branch among the faggots.

'You should not have taken such a risk!' we all cried.

'There was nothing else to be done. If he had got among us we should have shot each other in tryin' to down him. On the other hand, if we had fired through the hedge and wounded him he would soon have been on the top of us – to say nothin' of giving ourselves away. On the whole, I think that we are jolly well out of it. What was he, then?'

Our learned men looked at each other with some hesitation.

'Personally, I am unable to classify the creature with any certainty,' said Summerlee, lighting his pipe from the fire.

'In refusing to commit yourself you are but showing a proper scientific reserve,' said Challenger with massive condescension. 'I am not myself prepared to go farther than to say in general terms that we have almost certainly been in contact to-night with some form of carnivorous dinosaur.

I have already expressed my anticipation that something of the sort might exist upon this plateau.'

'We have to bear in mind,' remarked Summerlee, 'that there are many prehistoric forms which have never come down to us. It would be rash to suppose that we can give a name to all that we are likely to meet.'

'Exactly. A rough classification may be the best that we can attempt. To-morrow some further evidence may help us to an identification. Meantime we can only renew our interrupted slumbers.'

'But not without a sentinel,' said Lord John, with decision. 'We can't afford to take chances in a country like this. Two-hour spells in the future for each of us.'

'Then I'll just finish my pipe in starting the first one,' said Professor Summerlee; and from that time onwards we never trusted ourselves again without a watchman.

In the morning it was not long before we discovered the source of the hideous uproar which had aroused us in the night. The iguanodon glade was the scene of a horrible butchery. From the pools of blood and the enormous lumps of flesh scattered in every direction over the green sward we imagined at first that a number of animals had been killed, but on examining the remains more closely we discovered that all this carnage came from one of these unwieldy monsters, which had been literally torn to pieces by some creature not larger, perhaps, but far more ferocious, than itself.

Our two professors sat in absorbed argument, examining piece after piece, which showed the marks of savage teeth and of enormous claws.

'Our judgment must still be in abeyance,' said Professor Challenger, with a huge slab of whitish-coloured flesh across his knee. 'The indications would be consistent with the presence of a sabre-toothed tiger, such as are still found among the breccia of our caverns; but the creature actually seen was undoubtedly of a larger and more reptilian character. Personally, I should pronounce for allosaurus.'

'Or megalosaurus,' said Summerlee.

'Exactly. Any one of the larger carnivorous dinosaurs would meet the case. Among them are to be found all the most terrible types of animal-life that have ever cursed the earth or blessed a museum.' He laughed sonorously at his own conceit, for, though he had little sense of humour, the crudest pleasantry from his own lips moved him always to roars of appreciation.

'The less noise the better,' said Lord John, curtly. 'We don't know who or what may be near us. If this fellah comes back for his breakfast and catches us here we won't have so much to laugh at. By the way, what is this mark upon the iguanodon's hide?'

On the dull, scaly, slate-coloured skin, somewhere above the shoulder, there was a singular black circle of some substance which looked like asphalt. None of us could suggest what it meant, though Summerlee was of opinion that he had seen something similar upon one of the young ones two days before. Challenger said nothing, but looked pompous and puffy, as if he could if he would, so that finally Lord John asked his opinion direct.

'If your lordship will graciously permit me to open my mouth, I shall be happy to express my sentiments,' said he, with elaborate sarcasm. 'I am not in the habit of being taken to task in the fashion which seems to be customary with your lordship. I was not aware that it was necessary to ask your permission before smiling at a harmless pleasantry.'

It was not until he had received his apology that our touchy friend would suffer himself to be appeased. When at last his ruffled feelings were at ease, he addressed us at some length from his seat upon a fallen tree, speaking, as his habit was, as if he were imparting most precious information to a class of a thousand.

'With regard to the marking,' said he, 'I am inclined to agree with my friend and colleague, Professor Summerlee, that the stains are from asphalt. As this plateau is, in its very nature, highly volcanic, and as asphalt is a substance which one associates with Plutonic forces, I cannot doubt that it exists in the free liquid state, and that the creatures may have come in contact with it. A much more important problem is the question as to the existence of the carnivorous monster which has left its traces in this glade. We know roughly that this plateau is not larger than an average English county. Within this confined space a certain number of creatures, mostly types which have passed away in the world below, have lived together for innumerable years. Now, it is very clear to me that in so long a period one would have expected that the carnivorous creatures, multiplying unchecked, would have exhausted their food supply and have been compelled to either modify their flesh-eating habits or die of hunger. This we see has not been so. We can only imagine therefore, that the balance of Nature is preserved by some check which limits the numbers of these ferocious creatures. One of the many interesting problems, therefore, which await our solution is to discover what that check may be and how it operates. I venture to trust that we may have some future opportunity for the closer study of the carnivorous dinosaurs.'

'And I venture to trust that we may not,' I observed.

The Professor only raised his great eyebrows, as the schoolmaster meets the irrelevant observation of the naughty boy.

'Perhaps Professor Summerlee may have an observation to make,' he said, and the two *savants* ascended together into some rarified scientific atmosphere, where the possibilities of a modification of the birth-rate were weighed against the decline of the food supply as a check in the struggle for existence.

That morning we mapped out a small portion of the plateau, avoiding the swamp of the pterodactyls, and keeping to the east of our brook instead of to the west. In that direction the country was still thickly wooded, with so much undergrowth that our progress was very slow.

I have dwelt up to now upon the terrors of Maple White Land; but there was another side to the subject, for all that morning we wandered among lovely flowers – mostly, as I observed, white or yellow in colour, these being, as our professors explained, the primitive flower-shades. In many places the ground was absolutely covered with them, and as we walked ankle-deep on that wonderful yielding carpet the scent was almost intoxicating in its sweetness and intensity. The homely English bee buzzed everywhere around us. Many of the trees under which we passed had their branches bowed down with fruit, some of which were of familiar sorts, while other varieties were new. By observing which of them were pecked by the birds we avoided all danger of poison and added a delicious variety to our food reserve. In the jungle which we traversed were numerous hard-trodden paths made by the wild-beasts, and in the more marshy places we saw a profusion of strange footmarks, including many of the iguanodon. Once in a grove we observed several of these great creatures grazing and Lord John, with his glass, was able to report that they also were spotted with asphalt, though in a different place to the one which we had examined in the morning. What this phenomenon meant we could not imagine.

We saw many small animals, such as porcupines, a scaly ant-eater, and a wild pig, piebald in colour and with long curved tusks. Once, through a break in the trees, we saw a clear shoulder of green hill some distance away, and across this a large dun-coloured animal was travelling at a considerable pace. It passed so swiftly that we were unable to say what it was; but if it were a deer, as was claimed by Lord John, it must have been as large as those monstrous Irish elk which are still dug up from time to time in the bogs of my native land.

Ever since the mysterious visit which had been paid to our camp we always returned to it with some misgivings. However, on this occasion we found everything in order. That evening we had a grand discussion upon our present situation and future plans, which I must describe at some length, as it led to a new departure by which we were enabled to gain a more complete knowledge of Maple White Land than might have come in many weeks of exploring. It was Summerlee who opened the debate. All day he had been querulous in manner, and now some remark of Lord John's as to what we should do on the morrow brought all his bitterness to a head.

'What we ought to be doing to-day, to-morrow, and all the time,' said he, 'is finding some way out of the trap into which we have fallen. You are all turning your brains towards getting into this country. I say that we should be scheming how to get out of it.'

'I am surprised, sir,' boomed Challenger, stroking his majestic beard, 'that any man of science should commit himself to so ignoble a sentiment.

You are in a land which offers such an inducement to the ambitious naturalist as none ever has since the world began, and you suggest leaving it before we have acquired more than the most superficial knowledge of it or of its contents. I expected better things of you, Professor Summerlee.'

'You must remember,' said Summerlee, sourly, 'that I have a large class in London who are at present at the mercy of an extremely inefficient *locum tenens*. This makes my situation different from yours, Professor Challenger, since so far as I know, you have never been entrusted with any responsible educational work.'

'Quite so,' said Challenger. 'I have felt it to be a sacrilege to divert a brain which is capable of the highest original research to any lesser object. That is why I have sternly set my face against any proffered scholastic appointment.'

'For example?' asked Summerlee, with a sneer; but Lord John hastened to change the conversation.

'I must say,' said he, 'that I think it would be a mighty poor thing to go back to London before I know a great deal more of this place than I do at present.'

'I could never dare to walk into the back office of my paper and face old McArdle,' said I. (You will excuse the frankness of this report, will you not, sir?) 'He'd never forgive me for leaving such unexhausted copy behind me. Besides, so far as I can see, it is not worth discussing, since we can't get down, even if we wanted.'

'Our young friend makes up for many obvious mental lacunæ by some measure of primitive common sense,' remarked Challenger. 'The interests of his deplorable profession are immaterial to us; but as he observes, we cannot get down in any case, so it is a waste of energy to discuss it.'

'It is a waste of energy to do anything else,' growled Summerlee from behind his pipe. 'Let me remind you that we came here upon a perfectly definite mission, entrusted to us at the meeting of the Zoological Institute in London. That mission was to test the truth of Professor Challenger's statements. Those statements, as I am bound to admit, we are now in a position to endorse. Our ostensible work is therefore done. As to the detail which remains to be worked out upon this plateau, it is so enormous that only a large expedition, with a very special equipment, could hope to cope with it. Should we attempt to do so ourselves, the only possible result must be that we shall never return with the important contribution to science which we have already gained. Professor Challenger has devised means for getting us on to this plateau when it appeared to be inaccessible; I think that we should now call upon him to use the same ingenuity in getting us back to the world from which we came.'

I confess that as Summerlee stated his view it struck me as altogether reasonable. Even Challenger was affected by the consideration that his enemies would never stand confuted if the confirmation of his statements should never reach those who had doubted them.

'The problem of the descent is at first sight a formidable one,' said he, 'and yet I cannot doubt that the intellect can solve it. I am prepared to agree with our colleague that a protracted stay in Maple White Land is at present inadvisable, and that the question of our return will soon have to be faced. I absolutely refuse to leave, however, until we have made at least a superficial examination of this country, and are able to take back with us something in the nature of a chart.'

Professor Summerlee gave a snort of impatience.

'We have spent two long days in exploration,' said he, 'and we are no wiser as to the actual geography of the place than when we started. It is clear that it is all thickly wooded, and it would take months to penetrate it and to learn the relations of one part to another. If there were some central peak it would be different, but it all slopes downwards, so far as we can see. The farther we go the less likely it is that we will get any general view.'

It was at that moment that I had my inspiration. My eyes chanced to light upon the enormous gnarled trunk of the gingko tree which cast its huge branches over us. Surely, if its bole exceeded that of all the others, its height must do the same. If the rim of the plateau was indeed the highest point, then why should this mighty tree not prove to be a watch-tower which commanded the whole country? Now, ever since I ran wild as a lad in Ireland I have been a bold and skilled tree-climber. My comrades might be my masters on the rocks, but I knew that I would be supreme among those branches. Could I only get my legs on to the lowest of the giant off-shoots, then it would be strange indeed if I could not make my way to the top. My comrades were delighted at my idea.

'Our young friend,' said Challenger, bunching up the red apples of his cheeks, 'is capable of acrobatic exertions which would be impossible to a man of a more solid, though possibly of a more commanding, appearance. I applaud his resolution.'

'By George, young fellah, you've put your hand on it!' said Lord John, clapping me on the back. 'How we never came to think of it before I can't imagine! There's not more than an hour of daylight left, but if you take your notebook you may be able to get some rough sketch of the place. If we put these three ammunition cases under the branch, I will soon hoist you on to it.'

He stood on the boxes while I faced the trunk, and was gently raising me when Challenger sprang forward and gave me such a thrust with his huge hand that he fairly shot me into the tree. With both arms clasping the branch, I scrambled hard with my feet until I had worked, first my body, and then my knees, on to it. There were three excellent off-shoots, like huge rungs of a ladder, above my head, and a tangle of convenient branches beyond, so that I clambered onwards with such speed that I soon lost sight of the ground and had nothing but foliage beneath me. Now and then I encountered a check, and once I had to shin up a creeper for eight or ten feet, but I made excellent progress, and the booming of Challenger's voice seemed to be a great distance beneath me. The tree was, however, enormous, and, looking upwards, I could see no thinning of the leaves above my head. There was some thick, bush-like clump which seemed to be a parasite upon a branch up which I was swarming. I leaned my head round it in order to see what was beyond, and I nearly fell out of the tree in my surprise and horror at what I saw.

A face was gazing into mine – at the distance of only a foot or two. The creature that owned it had been crouching behind the parasite, and had looked round it at the same instant that I did. It was a human face – or at least it was far more human than any monkey's that I have ever seen. It was long, whitish, and blotched with pimples, the nose flattened, and the lower jaw projecting, with a bristle of coarse whiskers round the chin. The eyes, which were under thick and heavy brows, were bestial and ferocious, and as it opened its mouth to snarl what sounded like a curse at me I observed that it had curved, sharp canine teeth. For an instant I read hatred and menace in the evil eyes. Then, as quick as a flash, came an expression of overpowering fear. There was a crash of broken boughs as it dived wildly down into the tangle of green. I caught a glimpse of a hairy body like that of a reddish pig, and then it was gone amid a swirl of leaves and branches.

'What's the matter?' shouted Roxton from below. 'Anything wrong with you?'

'Did you see it?' I cried with my arms round the branch and all my nerves tingling.

'We heard a row, as if your foot had slipped. What was it?'

I was so shocked at the sudden and strange appearance of this ape-man that I hesitated whether I should not climb down again and tell my experience to my companions. But I was already so far up the great tree that it seemed a humiliation to return without having carried out my mission.

After a long pause therefore, to recover my breath and my courage, I continued my ascent. Once I put my weight upon a rotten branch and swung for a few seconds by my hands, but in the main it was all easy climbing. Gradually the leaves thinned around me, and I was aware, from the wind upon my face, that I had topped all the trees of the forest. I was determined, however, not to look about me before I had reached the very highest point, so I scrambled on until I had got so far that the topmost branch was bending beneath my weight. There I settled into a convenient fork, and, balancing myself securely, I found myself looking down at a most wonderful panorama of this strange country in which we found ourselves.

The sun was just above the western sky-line, and the evening was a particularly bright and clear one, so that the whole extent of the plateau was visible beneath me. It was, as seen from this height, of an oval contour, with a breadth of about thirty miles and a width of twenty. Its general shape was that of a shallow funnel, all the sides sloping down to a considerable lake in the centre. This lake may have been ten miles in circumference, and lay very green and beautiful in the evening light, with a thick fringe of reeds at its edges, and with its surface broken by several yellow sandbanks, which gleamed golden in the mellow sunshine. A number of long dark objects, which were too large for alligators and too long for canoes, lay upon the edges of these patches of sand. With my glass I could clearly see that they were alive, but what their nature might be I could not imagine.

From the side of the plateau on which we were, slopes of woodland, with occasional glades, stretched down for five or six miles to the central lake. I could see at my very feet the glade of the iguanodons, and farther off was a round opening in the trees which marked the swamp of the pterodactyls. On the side facing me, however, the plateau presented a very different aspect. There the basalt cliffs of the outside were reproduced upon the inside, forming an escarpment about two hundred feet high, with a woody slope beneath it. Along the base of these red cliffs, some distance above the ground, I could see a number of dark holes through the glass, which I conjectured to be the mouths of caves. At the opening of one of these something white was shimmering, but I was unable to make out what it was. I sat charting the country until the sun had set and it was so dark that I could no longer distinguish details. Then I climbed down to my companions waiting for me so eagerly at the bottom of the great tree. For once I was the hero of the expedition. Alone I had thought of it, and alone I had done it; and here was the chart which would save us a month's blind groping among unknown dangers. Each of them shook me solemnly by the hand. But before they discussed the details of my map I had to tell them of my encounter with the ape-man among the branches.

'He has been there all the time,' said I.

'How do you know that?' asked Lord John.

'Because I have never been without that feeling that something malevolent was watching us. I mentioned it to you, Professor Challenger.'

'Our young friend certainly said something of the kind. He is also the one among us who is endowed with that Celtic temperament which would make him sensitive to such impressions.'

'The whole theory of telepathy –' began Summerlee, filling his pipe.

'Is too vast to be now discussed,' said Challenger, with decision. 'Tell me, now,' he added, with the air of a bishop addressing a Sunday-school, 'did you happen to observe whether the creature could cross its thumb over its palm?'

'No, indeed.'

'Had it a tail?'

'No.'

'Was the foot prehensile?'

'I do not think it could have made off so fast among the branches if it could not get a grip with its feet.'

'In South America there are, if my memory serves me – you will check the observation, Professor Summerlee – some thirty-six species of monkeys, but the anthropoid ape is unknown. It is clear, however, that he exists in this country, and that he is not the hairy, gorilla-like variety, which is never seen out of Africa or the East.' (I was inclined to interpolate, as I looked at him, that I had seen his first cousin in Kensington.) 'This is a whiskered and colourless type, the latter characteristic pointing to the fact that he spends his days in arboreal seclusion. The question which we have to face is whether he approaches more closely to the ape or the man. In the latter case, he may well approximate to what the vulgar have called the "missing link". The solution of this problem is our immediate duty.'

'It is nothing of the sort,' said Summerlee, abruptly. 'Now that, through the intelligence and activity of Mr. Malone' (I cannot help quoting the words), 'we have got our chart, our one and only immediate duty is to get ourselves safe and sound out of this awful place.'

'The flesh-pots of civilization,' groaned Challenger.

'The ink-pots of civilization, sir. It is our task to put on record what we have seen, and to leave the further exploration to others. You all agreed as much before Mr. Malone got us the chart.'

'Well,' said Challenger, 'I admit that my mind will be more at ease when I am assured that the result of our expedition has been conveyed to our friends. How we are to get down from this place I have not as yet an idea. I have never yet encountered any problem, however, which my inventive brain was unable to solve, and I promise you that to-morrow I will turn my attention to the question of our descent.'

And so the matter was allowed to rest. But that evening, by the light of the fire and of a single candle, the first map of the lost world was elaborated. Every detail which I had roughly noted from my watch-tower was drawn out in its relative place. Challenger's pencil hovered over the great blank which marked the lake.

'What shall we call it?' he asked.

'Why should you not take the chance of perpetuating your own name?' said Summerlee, with his usual touch of acidity.

'I trust, sir, that my name will have other and more personal claims upon posterity,' said Challenger, severely. 'Any ignoramus can hand down his worthless memory by imposing a mountain or a river. I need no such monument.'

Summerlee, with a twisted smile, was about to make some fresh assault when Lord John hastened to intervene.

'It is up to you, young fellah, to name the lake,' said he. 'You saw it

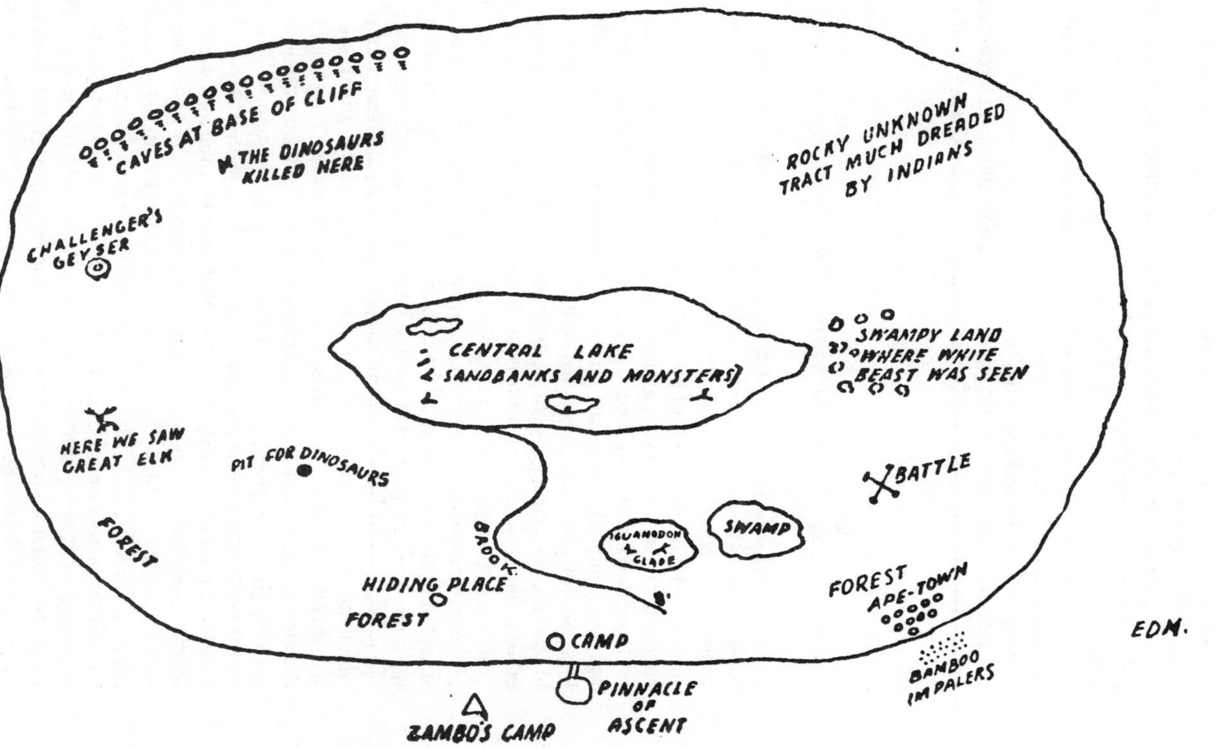
ROUGH CHART OF MAPLE-WHITE LAND
CAVES AT BASE OF CLIFF
THE DINOSAURS KILLED HERE
ROCKY UNKNOWN TRACT MUCH DREADED BY INDIANS
CHALLENGER'S GEYSER
CENTRAL LAKE
SANDBANKS AND MONSTERS
SWAMPY LAND WHERE WHITE BEAST WAS SEEN
HERE WE SAW GREAT ELK
PIT FOR DINOSAURS
BATTLE
FOREST
BROOK
IGUANODON GLADE
SWAMP
HIDING PLACE
FOREST
FOREST
APE-TOWN
EDM.
CAMP
BAMBOO IMPALERS
PINNACLE OF ASCENT
ZAMBO'S CAMP

first, and, by George, if you choose to put "Lake Malone" on it, no one has a better right.'

'By all means. Let our young friend give it a name,' said Challenger.

'Then,' said I, blushing, I dare say, as I said it, 'let it be named Lake Gladys.'

'Don't you think the Central Lake would be more descriptive?' remarked Summerlee.

'I should prefer Lake Gladys.'

Challenger looked at me sympathetically, and shook his great head in mock disapproval. 'Boys will be boys,' said he. 'Lake Gladys let it be.'

12

It Was Dreadful in the Forest

I HAVE said – or perhaps I have not said, for my memory plays me sad tricks these days – that I glowed with pride when three such men as my comrades thanked me for having saved, or at least greatly helped, the situation. As the youngster of the party, not merely in years, but in experience, character, knowledge, and all that goes to make a man, I had been overshadowed from the first. And now I was coming into my own. I warmed at the thought. Alas! for the pride which goes before a fall! That little glow of self-satisfaction, that added measure of self-confidence, were to lead me on that very night to the most dreadful experience of my life, ending with a shock which turns my heart sick when I think of it.

It came about in this way. I had been unduly excited by the adventure of the tree, and sleep seemed to be impossible. Summerlee was on guard, sitting hunched over our small fire, a quaint, angular figure, his rifle across his knees and his pointed, goat-like beard wagging with each weary nod of his head. Lord John lay silent, wrapped in the South American poncho which he wore, while Challenger snored with a roll and rattle which reverberated through the woods. The full moon was shining brightly, and the air was crisply cold. What a night for a walk! And then suddenly came the thought, 'Why not?' Suppose I stole softly away, suppose I made my way down to the central lake, suppose I was back at breakfast with some record of the place – would I not in that case be thought an even more worthy associate? Then, if Summerlee carried the day and some means of escape were found, we should return to London with first-hand knowledge of the central mystery of the plateau, to which I alone, of all men, would have penetrated. I thought of Gladys, with her 'There are heroisms all round us'. I seemed to hear her voice as she said it. I thought also of McArdle. What a three-column article for the paper! What a foundation for a career! A correspondentship in the next great war might be within my reach. I clutched at a gun – my pockets were full of cartridges – and, parting the thorn bushes at the gate of our zareba, I quickly slipped out. My last glance showed me the unconscious Summerlee, most futile of sentinels, still nodding away like a queer mechanical toy in front of the smouldering fire.

I had not gone a hundred yards before I deeply repented my rashness. I may have said somewhere in this chronicle that I am too imaginative to be a really courageous man, but that I have an overpowering fear of seeming afraid. This was the power which now carried me onwards. I simply could not slink back with nothing done. Even if my comrades should not have missed me, and should never know of my weakness, there would still remain some intolerable self-shame in my own soul. And yet I shuddered at the position in which I found myself, and would have given all I possessed at that moment to have been honourably free of the whole business.

It was dreadful in the forest. The trees grew so thickly and their foliage spread so widely that I could see nothing of the moonlight save that here and there the high branches made a tangled filigree against the starry sky. As the eyes became more used to the obscurity one learned that there were different degrees of darkness among the trees – that some were dimly visible, while between and among them there were coal-black shadowed patches, like the mouths of caves, from which I shrank in horror as I passed. I thought of the despairing yell of the tortured iguanodon – that dreadful cry which had echoed through the woods. I thought, too, of the glimpse I had in the light of Lord John's torch of that bloated, warty, blood-slavering muzzle. Even now I was on its hunting-ground. At any instant it might spring upon me from the shadows – this nameless and horrible monster. I stopped, and, picking a cartridge from my pocket, I opened the breech of my gun. As I touched the lever my heart leaped within me. It was the shot-gun, not the rifle, which I had taken!

Again the impulse to return swept over me. Here, surely, was a most excellent reason for my failure – one for which no one would think the less of me. And again the foolish pride fought against that very word. I could not – must not – fail. After all, my rifle would probably have been as useless as a shot-gun against such dangers as I might meet. If I were to go back to camp to change my weapon I could hardly expect to enter and to leave again without being seen. In that case there would be explanations, and my attempt would no longer be all my own. After a little hesitation, then, I screwed up my courage and continued upon my way, my useless gun under my arm.

The darkness of the forest had been alarming, but even worse was the white, still flood of moonlight in the open glade of iguanodons. Hid among the bushes, I looked out at it. None of the great brutes were in sight. Perhaps the tragedy which had befallen one of them had driven them from their feeding ground. In the misty, silvery night I could see no sign of any living thing. Taking courage, therefore, I slipped rapidly across it, and among the jungle on the farther side I picked up once again the brook which was my guide. It was a cheery companion, gurgling and chuckling as it ran, like the dear old trout stream in the West Country where I have fished at night in my boyhood. So long as I followed it down I must come to the lake, and so long as I followed it back I must come to the camp. Often I had to lose sight of it on account of the tangled brushwood but I was always within earshot of its tinkle and splash.

As one descended the slope the woods became thinner, and bushes, with occasional high trees, took the place of the forest. I could make good progress, therefore, and I could see without being seen. I passed close to the pterodactyl swamp, and as I did so, with a dry, crisp, leathery rattle of wings, one of these great creatures – it was twenty feet at least from tip to tip – rose up from somewhere near me and soared into the air. As it passed across the face of the moon the light shone clearly through the membranous wings, and it looked like a flying skeleton against the white, tropical radiance. I crouched low among the bushes, for I knew from past experience that with a single cry the creature could bring a hundred of its loathsome mates about my ears. It was not until it had settled again that I dared to steal onwards upon my journey.

The night had been exceedingly still, but as I advanced I became conscious of a low, rumbling sound, a continuous murmur somewhere in front of me. This grew louder as I proceeded, until at last it was clearly quite close to me. When I stood still the sound was constant, so that it seemed to come from some stationary cause. It was like a boiling kettle or the bubbling of some great pot. Soon I came upon the source of it, for in the centre of a small clearing I found a lake – or a pool, rather, for it was not larger than the basin of the Trafalgar Square fountain – of some black, pitch-like stuff, the surface of which rose and fell in great blisters of bursting gas. The air above it was shimmering with heat, and the ground round was so hot that I could hardly bear to lay my hand on it. It was clear that the great volcanic outburst which had raised this strange plateau so many years ago had not yet entirely spent its forces. Blackened rocks and mounds of lava I had already seen everywhere peeping out from amid the luxuriant vegetation which drapped them, but this asphalt pool in the jungle was the first sign that we had of actual existing activity on the slopes of the ancient crater. I had no time to examine it further, for I had need to hurry if I was to be back in camp in the morning.

It was a fearsome walk, and one which will be with me so long as memory holds. In the great moonlit clearings I slunk along among the shadows on the margin. In the jungle I crept forward, stopping with a beating heart whenever I heard, as I often did, the crash of breaking branches as some wild beast went past. Now and then great shadows loomed up for an instant and were gone – great, silent shadows which seemed to prowl upon padded feet. How often I stopped with the intention of returning, and yet every time my pride conquered my fear, and sent me on again until my object should be attained.

At last (my watch showed that it was one in the morning) I saw the gleam of water amid the openings of the jungle, and ten minutes later I was among the reeds upon the borders of the central lake. I was exceedingly dry, so I lay down and took a long draught of its waters, which were fresh and cold. There was a broad pathway with many tracks upon it at the spot which I had found, so that it was clearly one of the drinking-places of the animals. Close to the water's edge there was a huge isolated block of lava. Up this I climbed, and, lying on the top, I had an excellent view in every direction.

The first thing which I saw filled me with amazement. When I described the view from the summit of the great tree, I said that on the farther cliff I could see a number of dark spots, which appeared to be the mouths of caves. Now as I looked up at the same cliffs, I saw discs of light in every direction, ruddy, clearly-defined patches, like the port-holes of a liner in the darkness. For a moment I thought it was the lava-glow from some volcanic action; but this could not be so. Any volcanic action would surely be down in the hollow, and not high among the rocks. What, then, was the alternative? It was wonderful, and yet it must surely be. These ruddy spots must be the reflection of fires within the caves – fires which could only be lit by the hand of man. There were human beings, then, upon the plateau. How gloriously my expedition was justified! Here was news indeed for us to bear back with us to London!

For a long time I lay and watched these red, quivering blotches of light. I suppose they were ten miles off from me, yet even at that distance one could observe how, from time to time, they twinkled or were obscured as someone passed before them. What would I not have given to be able to crawl up to them, to peep in, and to take back some word to my comrades as to the appearance and character of the race who lived in so strange a place! It was out of the question for the moment, and yet surely we could not leave the plateau until we had some definite knowledge upon the point.

Lake Gladys – my own lake – lay like a sheet of quick-silver before me, with a reflected moon shining brightly in the centre of it. It was shallow, for in many places I saw low sandbanks protruding above the water. Everywhere upon the still surface I could see signs of life, sometimes mere rings and ripples in the water, sometimes the gleam of a great silver-sided fish in the air, sometimes the arched, slate-coloured back of some passing monster. Once upon a yellow sandbank I saw a creature like a huge swan, with a clumsy body and a high, flexible neck, shuffling about upon the margin. Presently it plunged in, and for some time I could see the arched neck and darting head undulating over the water. Then it dived, and I saw it no more.

My attention was soon drawn away from these distant sights and brought back to what was going on at my very feet. Two creatures like large armadillos had come down to the drinking place, and were squatting at the edge of the water, their long, flexible tongues like red ribbons shooting in and out as they lapped. A huge deer, with branching horns, a magnificent creature which carried itself like a king, came down with its doe and two fawns and drank beside the armadillos. No such deer exists anywhere else upon earth, for the moose or elks which I have seen would hardly have reached its shoulders. Presently it gave a warning snort and was off with its family among the reeds, while the armadillos also scuttled for shelter. A new-comer, a most monstrous animal, was coming down the path.

For a moment I wondered where I could have seen that ungainly shape, that arched back with triangular fringes along it, that strange bird-like head held close to the ground. Then it came back to me. It was the stegosaurus – the very creature which Maple White had preserved in his sketch-book, and which had been the first object which arrested the attention of Challenger! There he was – perhaps the very specimen which the American artist had encountered. The ground shook beneath his tremendous weight, and his gulpings of water resounded through the still night. For five minutes he was so close to my rock that by stretching out my hand I could have touched the hideous waving hackles upon his back. Then he lumbered away and was lost among the boulders.

Looking at my watch, I saw that it was half-past two o'clock, and high time, therefore, that I started upon my homeward journey. There was no difficulty about the direction in which I should return, for all along I had kept the little brook upon my left, and it opened into the central lake within a stone's-throw of the boulder upon which I had been lying. I set off, therefore, in high spirits, for I felt that I had done good work and was bringing back a fine budget of news for my companions. Foremost of all, of course, were the sight of the fiery caves and the certainty that some troglodytic race inhabited them. But besides that I could speak from experience of the central lake. I could testify that it was full of strange creatures, and I had seen several land forms of primæval life which we had not before encountered. I reflected as I walked that few men in the world could have spent a stranger night or added more to human knowledge in the course of it.

I was plodding up the slope, turning these thoughts over in my mind, and had reached a point which may have been half-way to home, when my mind was brought back to my own position by a strange noise behind me. It was something between a snore and a growl, low, deep, and exceedingly menacing. Some strange creature was evidently near me, but nothing could be seen, so I hastened more rapidly upon my way. I had traversed half a mile or so when suddenly the sound was repeated, still behind me, but louder and more menacing than before. My heart stood still within me as it flashed across me that the beast, whatever it was, must surely be after *me*. My skin grew cold and my hair rose at the thought. That these monsters should tear each other to pieces was a part of the strange struggle for existence, but that they should turn upon modern man, that they should deliberately track and hunt down the pre-dominant human, was a staggering and fearsome thought. I remembered again the blood-slobbered face which we had seen in the glare of Lord John's torch, like some horrible vision from the deepest circle of Dante's hell. With my knees shaking beneath me, I stood and glared with starting eyes down the moonlit path which lay behind me. All was quiet as in a dream landscape. Silver clearings and the black patches of the bushes – nothing else could I see. Then from out of the silence, imminent and threatening, there came once more that low, throaty croaking, far louder and closer than before. There could no longer be a doubt. Something was on my trail, and was closing in upon me every minute.

I stood like a man paralysed, still staring at the ground which I had traversed. Then suddenly I saw it. There was movement among the bushes at the far end of the clearing which I had just traversed. A great dark shadow disengaged itself and hopped out into the clear moonlight. I say 'hopped' advisedly, for the beast moved like a kangaroo, springing along in an erect position upon its powerful hindlegs, while its front ones were held bent in front of it. It was of enormous size and power, like an erect elephant, but its movements, in spite of its bulk, were exceedingly alert. For a moment, as I saw its shape, I hoped that it was an iguanodon, which I knew to be harmless, but, ignorant as I was, I soon saw that this was a very different creature. Instead of the gentle, deer-shaped head of the great three-toed leaf-eater, this beast had a broad, squat, toad-like face like that which had alarmed us in our camp. His ferocious cry and the horrible energy of his pursuit both assured me that this was surely one of the great flesh-eating dinosaurs, the most terrible beasts which have ever walked this earth. As the huge brute loped along it dropped forward upon its fore-paws and brought its nose to the ground every twenty yards or so. It was smelling out my trail. Sometimes, for an instant, it was at fault. Then it would catch it up again and come bounding swiftly along the path I had taken.

Even now when I think of that nightmare the sweat breaks out upon my brow. What could I do? My useless fowling-piece was in my hand. What help could I get from that? I looked desperately round for some rock or tree, but I was in a bushy jungle with nothing higher than a sapling within sight, while I knew that the creature behind me could tear down an ordinary tree as though it were a reed. My only possible chance lay in flight. I could not move swiftly over the rough, broken ground, but as I looked round me in despair I saw a well-marked, hard-beaten path which ran across in front of me. We had seen several of the sort, the runs of various wild beasts, during our expeditions. Along this I could perhaps hold my own, for I was a fast runner, and in excellent condition. Flinging away my useless gun, I set myself to do such a half mile as I have never done before or since. My limbs ached, my chest heaved, I felt that my throat would burst for want of air, and yet with that horror behind me I ran and I ran and ran. At last I paused, hardly able to move. For a moment I thought that I had thrown him off. The path lay still behind me. And then suddenly, with a crashing and a rending, a thudding of giant feet and a panting of monster lungs, the beast was upon me once more. He was at my very heels. I was lost.

Madman that I was to linger so long before I fled! Up to then he had hunted by scent, and his movement was slow. But he had actually seen me as I started to run. From then onwards he had hunted by sight, for the path showed him where I had gone. Now, as he came round the curve, he was springing in great bounds. The moonlight shone upon his huge projecting eyes, the row of enormous teeth in his open mouth, and the gleaming fringe of claws upon his short, powerful forearms. With a scream of terror I turned and rushed wildly down the path. Behind me the thick, gasping breathing of the creature sounded louder and louder. His heavy footfall was beside me. Every instant I expected to feel his grip upon my back. And then suddenly there came a crash – I was falling through space, and everything beyond was darkness and rest.

As I emerged from my unconsciousness – which could not, I think, have lasted more than a few minutes – I was aware of a most dreadful and penetrating smell. Putting out my hand in the darkness I came upon something which felt like a huge lump of meat, while my other hand closed upon a large bone. Up above me there was a circle of starlit sky, which showed me that I was lying at the bottom of a deep pit. Slowly I staggered to my feet and felt myself all over. I was stiff and sore from head to foot, but there was no limb which would not move, no joint which would not bend. As the circumstances of my fall came back into my confused brain, I looked up in terror, expecting to see that dreadful head silhouetted against the paling sky. There was no sign of the monster, however, nor could I hear any sound from above. I began to walk slowly round, therefore, feeling in every direction to find out what this strange place could be into which I had been so opportunely precipitated.

It was, as I have said, a pit, with sharply-sloping walls and a level bottom about twenty feet across. This bottom was littered with great gobbets of flesh, most of which was in the last state of putridity. The atmosphere was poisonous and horrible. After tripping and stumbling over these lumps of decay, I came suddenly against something hard, and I found that an upright post was firmly fixed in the centre of the hollow. It was so high that I could not reach the top of it with my hand, and it appeared to be covered with grease.

Suddenly I remembered that I had a tin box of wax-vestas in my pocket. Striking one of them, I was able at last to form some opinion of this place into which I had fallen. There could be no question as to its nature. It was a trap – made by the hand of man. The post in the centre, some nine feet long, was sharpened at the upper end, and was black with the stale blood of the creatures who had been impaled upon it. The remains scattered about were fragments of the victims, which had been cut away in order to clear the stake for the next who might blunder in. I remembered that Challenger had declared that man could not exist upon the plateau, since with his feeble weapons he could not hold his own against the monsters who roamed over it. But now it was clear enough how it could be done. In their narrow-mouthed caves the natives, whoever they might be, had refuges into which the huge saurians could not penetrate, while with their developed brains they were capable of setting such traps, covered with branches, across the paths which marked the run of the animals as would destroy them in spite of all their strength and activity. Man was always the master.

The sloping wall of the pit was not difficult for an active man to climb, but I hesitated long before I trusted myself within reach of the dreadful creature which had so nearly destroyed me. How did I know that he was not lurking in the nearest clump of bushes, waiting for my reappearance? I took heart, however, as I recalled a conversation between Challenger and Summerlee upon the habits of the great saurians. Both were agreed that the monsters were practically brainless, that there was no room for reason in their tiny cranial cavities, and that if they have disappeared from the rest of the world it was assuredly on account of their own stupidity, which made it impossible for them to adapt themselves to changing conditions.

To lie in wait for me now would mean that the creature had appreciated what had happened to me, and this in turn would argue some power connecting cause and effect. Surely it was more likely that a brainless creature, acting solely by vague predatory instinct, would give up the chase when I disappeared, and, after a pause of astonishment, would wander away in search of some other prey? I clambered to the edge of the pit and looked over. The stars were fading, the sky was whitening, and the cold wind of morning blew pleasantly upon my face. I could see or hear nothing of my enemy. Slowly I climbed out and sat for a while upon the ground, ready to spring back into my refuge if any danger should appear. Then, reassured by the absolute stillness and by the growing light, I took my courage in both hands and stole back along the path which I had come. Some distance down it I picked up my gun, and shortly afterwards struck the brook which was my guide. So, with many a frightened backward glance, I made for home.

And suddenly there came something to remind me of my absent companions. In the clear, still morning air there sounded far away the sharp, hard note of a rifle-shot. I paused and listened, but there was nothing more. For a moment I was shocked at the thought that some sudden danger might have befallen them. But then a simpler and more natural explanation came to my mind. It was now broad daylight. They had imagined that I was lost in the woods, and had fired this shot to guide me home. It is true that we had made a strict resolution against firing, but if it seemed to them that I might be in danger they would not hesitate. It was for me now to hurry on as fast as possible, and so to reassure them.

I was weary and spent, so my progress was not as fast as I wished; but at last I came into regions which I knew. There was the swamp of the pterodactyls upon my left; there in front of me was the glade of the iguanodons. Now I was in the last belt of trees which separated me from Fort Challenger. I raised my voice in a cheery shout to allay their fears. My heart sank at that ominous stillness. I quickened my pace into a run. The zareba rose before me, even as I had left it, but the gate was open. I rushed in. In the cold morning light it was a fearful sight which met my eyes. Our effects were scattered in wild confusion over the ground; my comrades had disappeared, and close to the smouldering ashes of our fire the grass was stained crimson with a hideous pool of blood.

I was so stunned by this sudden shock that for a time I must have nearly lost my reason. I have a vague recollection, as one remembers a bad dream, of rushing about through the woods all round the empty camp, calling wildly for my companions. No answer came back from the silent shadows. The horrible thought that I might never see them again, that I might find myself abandoned all alone in that dreadful place, with no possible way of descending into the world below, that I might live and die in that nightmare country, drove me to desperation. I could have torn my hair and beaten my head in my despair. Only now did I realize how I had learned to lean upon my companions, upon the serene self-confidence of Challenger, and upon the masterful, humorous coolness of Lord Roxton. Without them I was like a child in the dark, helpless and powerless. I did not know which way to turn or what I should do first.

After a period, during which I sat in bewilderment, I set myself to try and discover what sudden misfortune could have befallen my companions. The whole disordered appearance of the camp showed that there had been some sort of attack, and the rifle-shot no doubt marked the time when it had occurred. That there should have been only one shot showed that it had been all over in an instant. The rifles still lay upon the ground, and one of them – Lord John's – had the empty cartridge in the breech. The blankets of Challenger and of Summerlee beside the fire suggested that they had been asleep at the time. The cases of ammunition and of food were scattered about in a wild litter, together with our unfortunate cameras and plate-carriers, but none of them were missing. On the other hand, all the exposed provisions – and I remembered that there were a considerable quantity of them – were gone. They were animals, then, and not natives, who had made the inroad, for surely the latter would have left nothing behind.

But if animals, or some single terrible animal, then what had become of my comrades? A ferocious beast would surely have destroyed them and left their remains. It is true that there was that one hideous pool of blood, which told of violence. Such a monster as had pursued me during the night could have carried away a victim as easily as a car could a mouse. In that case the others would have followed in pursuit. But then they would assuredly have taken their rifles with them. The more I tried to think it out with my confused and weary brain the less could I find any plausible explanation. I searched round in the forest, but could see no tracks which could help me to a conclusion. Once I lost myself, and it was only by good luck, and after an hour of wandering, that I found the camp once more.

Suddenly a thought came to me and brought some little comfort to my heart. I was not absolutely alone in the world. Down at the bottom of the cliff, and within call of me, was waiting the faithful Zambo. I went to the edge of the plateau and looked over. Sure enough, he was squatting among his blankets beside his fire in his little camp. But, to my amazement, a second man was seated in front of him. For an instant my heart leaped for joy, as I thought that one of my comrades had made his way safely down. But a second glance dispelled the hope. The rising sun shone red upon the man's skin. He was an Indian. I shouted loudly and waved my handkerchief. Presently Zambo looked up, waved his hand, and turned to ascend the pinnacle. In a short time he was standing close to me and listening with deep distress to the story which I told him.

'Devil got them sure, Massa Malone,' said he. 'You got into the devil's country, sah, and he take you all to himself. You take advice, Massa Malone, and come down quick, else he get you as well.'

'How can I come down, Zambo?'

'You get creepers from trees, Massa Malone. Throw them over here. I make fast to this stump, and so you have bridge.'

'We have thought of that. There are no creepers here which could bear us.'

'Send for ropes, Massa Malone.'

'Who can I send, and where?'

'Send to Indian village, sah. Plenty hide-rope in Indian village. Indian down below; send him.'

'Who is he?'

'One of our Indians. Other ones beat him and take away his pay. He come back to us. Ready now to take letter, bring rope – anything.'

To take a letter! Why not? Perhaps he might bring help; but in any case he would ensure that our lives were not spent for nothing, and that news of all that we had won for Science should reach our friends at home. I had two completed letters already waiting. I would spend the day in writing a third, which would bring my experiences absolutely up to date. The Indian could bear this back to the world. I ordered Zambo, therefore, to come again in the evening, and I spent my miserable and lonely day in recording my own adventures of the night before. I also drew up a note, to be given to any white merchant or captain of a steam-boat whom the Indian could find, imploring them to see that ropes were sent to us, since our lives must depend upon it. These documents I threw to Zambo in the evening, and also my purse, which contained three English sovereigns. These were to be given to the Indian, and he was promised twice as much if he returned with the ropes.

So now you will understand, my dear Mr. McArdle, how this communication reaches you, and you will also know the truth, in case you never hear again from your unfortunate correspondent. To-night I am too weary and too depressed to make my plans. To-morrow I must think out some way by which I shall keep in touch with this camp, and yet search round for any traces of my unhappy friends.

13

A Sight I Shall Never Forget

JUST as the sun was setting upon that melancholy night I saw the lonely figure of the Indian upon the vast plain beneath me, and I watched him, our one faint hope of salvation, until he disappeared in the rising mists of evening which lay, rose-tinted from the setting sun, between the far-off river and me.

It was quite dark when I at last turned back to our stricken camp, and my last vision as I went was the red gleam of Zambo's fire, the one point of light in the wide world below, as was his faithful presence in my own shadowed soul. And yet I felt happier than I had done since this crushing blow had fallen upon me, for it was good to think that the world should know what we had done, so that at the worst our names should not perish with our bodies, but should go down to posterity associated with the result of our labours.

It was an awesome thing to sleep in that ill-fated camp; and yet it was even more unnerving to do so in the jungle. One or the other it must be. Prudence, on the one hand, warned me that I should remain on guard, but exhausted Nature, on the other, declared that I should do nothing of the kind. I climbed up on to a limb of the great gingko tree, but there was no secure perch on its rounded surface, and I should certainly have fallen off and broken my neck the moment I began to doze. I got down, therefore, and pondered over what I should do. Finally, I closed the door of the zareba, lit three separate fires in a triangle, and having eaten a hearty supper dropped off into a profound sleep, from which I had a strange and most welcome awakening. In the early morning, just as day was breaking, a hand was laid upon my arm, and starting up, with all my nerves in a tingle and my hand feeling for a rifle, I gave a cry of joy as in the cold grey light I saw Lord John kneeling beside me.

It was he – and yet it was not he. I had left him calm in his bearing, correct in his person, prim in his dress. Now he was pale and wild-eyed, gasping as he breathed like one who has run far and fast. His gaunt face was scratched and bloody, his clothes were hanging in rags, and his hat was gone. I stared in amazement, but he gave me no chance for questions. He was grabbing at our stores all the time he spoke.

'Quick, young fellah! Quick!' he cried. 'Every moment counts. Get the rifles, both of them. I have the other two. Now, all the cartridges you can gather. Fill up your pockets. Now, some food. Half a dozen tins will do. That's all right! Don't wait to talk or think. Get a move on, or we are done!'

Still half-awake, and unable to imagine what it all might mean, I found myself hurrying madly after him through the wood, a rifle under each arm and a pile of various stores in my hands. He dodged in and out through the thickest of the scrub until he came to a dense clump of brushwood. Into this he rushed, regardless of thorns, and threw himself into the heart of it, pulling me down by his side.

'There!' he panted. 'I think we are safe here. They'll make for the camp as sure as fate. It will be their first idea. But this should puzzle 'em.'

'What is it all?' I asked, when I had got my breath. 'Where are the professors? And who is it that is after us?'

'The ape-men,' he cried. 'My God, what brutes! Don't raise your voice, for they have long ears – sharp eyes, too, but no power of scent, so far as I could judge, so I don't think they can sniff us out. Where have you been, young fellah? You were well out of it.'

In a few sentences I whispered what I had done.

'Pretty bad,' said he, when he had heard of the dinosaur and the pit. 'It isn't quite the place for a rest cure. What? But I had no idea what its possibilities were until those devils got hold of us. The man-eatin' Papuans had me once, but they are Chesterfields compared to this crowd.'

'How did it happen?' I asked.

'It was in the early mornin'. Our learned friends were just stirrin'. Hadn't even begun to argue yet. Suddenly it rained apes. They came down thick as apples out of a tree. They had been assemblin' in the dark, I suppose, until that great tree over our heads was heavy with them. I shot one of them through the belly, but before we knew where we were they had us spread-eagled on our backs. I call them apes, but they carried sticks and stones in their hands and jabbered talk to each other, and ended up by tyin' our hands with creepers, so they are ahead of any beast that I have seen in my wanderin's. Ape-men – that's what they are – Missin' Links, and I wished they had stayed missin'. They carried off their wounded comrade – he was bleedin' like a pig – and then they sat around us, and if ever I saw frozen murder it was in their faces. They were big fellows, as big as a man and a deal stronger. Curious glassy grey eyes they have, under red tufts, and they just sat and gloated and gloated. Challenger is no chicken, but even he was cowed. He managed to struggle on to his feet, and yelled out at them to have done with it and get it over. I think he had gone a bit off his head at the suddenness of it, for he raged and cursed at them like a lunatic. If they had been a row of his favourite Pressmen he could not have slanged them worse.'

'Well, what did they do?' I was enthralled by the strange story which my companion was whispering into my ear, while all the time his keen eyes were shooting in every direction and his hand grasping his cocked rifle.

'I thought it was the end of us, but instead of that it started them on a new line. They all jabbered and chattered together. Then one of them stood out beside Challenger. You'll smile, young fellah, but 'pon my word they might have been kinsmen. I couldn't have believed it if I hadn't seen it with my own eyes. This old ape-man – he was their chief – was a sort of red Challenger, with every one of our friend's beauty points, only just a trifle more so. He had the short body, the big shoulders, the round chest, no neck, a great ruddy frill of a beard, the tufted eyebrows, the "What do *you* want, damn you!" look about the eyes, and the whole catalogue. When the ape-man stood by Challenger and put his paw on his shoulder, the thing was complete. Summerlee was a bit hysterical, and he laughed till he cried. The ape-men laughed too – or at least they put up the devil of a cacklin' – and then they set to work to drag us off through the forest. They wouldn't touch the guns and things – thought them dangerous, I expect – but they carried away all our loose food. Summerlee and I got some rough handlin' on the way – there's my skin and my clothes to prove it – for they took us a bee-line through the brambles, and their own hides are like leather. But Challenger was all right. Four of them carried him shoulder high, and he went like a Roman emperor. What's that?'

It was a strange clicking noise in the distance, not unlike castanets.

'There they go!' said my companion, slipping cartridges into the second double-barrelled 'Express'. 'Load them all up, young fellah-my-lad, for we're not going to be taken alive, and don't you think it! That's the row they make when they are excited. By George! they'll have something to excite them if they put us up. The "Last Stand of the Greys" won't be in it. "With their rifles grasped in their stiffened hands, 'mid a ring of the dead and dyin'," as some fathead sings. Can you hear them now?'

'Very far away.'

'That little lot will do no good, but I expect their search parties are all over the wood. Well, I was tellin' you my tale of woe. They got us soon to this town of theirs – about a thousand huts of branches and leaves in a great grove of trees near the edge of the cliff. It's three or four miles from here. The filthy beasts fingered me all over, and I feel as if I should never be clean again. They tied us up – the fellow who handled me could tie like a bo'sun – and there we lay with our toes up, beneath a tree, while a great brute stood guard over us with a club in his hand. When I say "we" I mean Summerlee and myself. Old Challenger was up a tree, eatin' pines and havin' the time of his life. I'm bound to say that he managed to get some fruit to us, and with his own hands he loosened our bonds. If you'd seen him sittin' up in that tree hob-nobbin' with his twin brother – and singin' in that rollin' bass of his, "Ring out wild bells", 'cause music of any kind seemed to put 'em in a good humour, you'd have smiled; but we weren't in much mood for laughin', as you can guess. They were inclined, within limits, to let him do what he liked, but they drew the line pretty sharply at us. It was a mighty consolation to us all to know that you were runnin' loose and had the archives in your keepin'.

'Well now, young fellah, I'll tell you what will surprise you. You say you saw signs of men, and fires, traps, and the like. Well, we have seen the natives themselves. Poor devils they were, down-faced little chaps, and had enough to make them so. It seems that the humans hold one side of this plateau – over yonder, where you saw the caves – and the ape-men hold this side, and there is bloody war between them all the time. That's the situation, so far as I could follow it. Well, yesterday the ape-men got hold of a dozen of the humans and brought them in as prisoners. You never heard such a jabberin' and shriekin' in your life. The men were little red fellows, and had been bitten and clawed so that they could hardly walk. The ape-men put two of them to death there and then – fairly pulled the arm off one of them – it was perfectly beastly. Plucky little chaps they are, and hardly gave a squeak. But it turned us absolutely sick. Summerlee fainted and even Challenger had as much as he could stand. I think they have cleared, don't you?'

We listened intently, but nothing save the calling of the birds broke the deep peace of the forest. Lord John went on with his story.

'I think you have had the escape of your life, young fellah-my-lad. It was catchin' those Indians that put *you* clean out of their heads, else they would have been back to the camp for you as sure as fate and gathered you in. Of course, as you said, they have been watchin' us from the beginnin' out of that tree, and they knew perfectly well that we were one short. However, they could think only of this new haul; so it was I, and not a bunch of apes, that dropped in on you in the morning. Well, we had a horrid business afterwards. My God! what a nightmare the whole thing is! You remember the great bristle of sharp canes down below where we found the skeleton of the American? Well, that is just under ape-town, and that's the jumpin'-off place of their prisoners. I expect there's heaps of skeletons there, if we looked for 'em. They have a sort of clear parade ground on the top, and they make a proper ceremony about it. One by one the poor devils have to jump, and the game is to see whether they are merely dashed to pieces or whether they get skewered on the canes.

They took us out to see it, and the whole tribe lined up on the edge. Four of the Indians jumped, and the canes went through 'em like knitting needles through a pat of butter. No wonder we found that poor Yankee's skeleton with the canes growin' between his ribs. It was horrible – but it was doocedly interestin' too. We were all fascinated to see them take the dive, even when we thought it would be our turn next on the spring-board.

'Well, it wasn't. They kept six of the Indians up for to-day – that's how I understood it – but I fancy we were to be the star performers in the show. Challenger might get off, but Summerlee and I were in the bill. Their language is more than half signs, and it was not hard to follow them. So I thought it was time we made a break for it. I had been plottin' it out a bit, and had one or two things clear in my mind. It was all on me, for Summerlee was useless and Challenger not much better. The only time they got together they got slangin', because they couldn't agree upon the scientific classification of these red-headed devils that had got hold of us. One said it was the dryopithecus of Java, the other said it was pithecanthropus. Madness, I call it – loonies – both. But, as I say, I had thought out one or two points that were helpful. One was that these brutes could not run as fast as a man in the open. They have short, bandy legs, you see, and heavy bodies. Even Challenger could give a few yards in a hundred to the best of them, and you or I would be a perfect Shrubb. Another point was that they knew nothin' about guns. I don't believe they ever understood how the fellow I shot came by his hurt. If we could get at our guns there was no sayin' what we could do.

'So I broke away early this morin', gave my guard a kick in the tummy that laid him out, and sprinted for the camp. There I got you and the guns, and here we are.'

'But the professors!' I cried, in consternation.

'Well, we must just go back and fetch 'em. I couldn't bring 'em with me. Challenger was up the tree, and Summerlee was not fit for the effort. The only chance was to get the guns and try a rescue. Of course they may scupper them at once in revenge. I don't think they would touch Challenger, but I wouldn't answer for Summerlee. But they would have had him in any case. Of that I am certain. So I haven't made matters any worse by boltin'. But we are honour bound to go back and have them out or see it through with them. So you can make up your soul, young fellah-my-lad, for it will be one way or the other before evenin'.'

I have tried to imitate here Lord Roxton's jerky talk, his short, strong sentences, the half-humorous, half-reckless tone that ran through it all. But he was a born leader. As danger thickened his jaunty manner would increase, his speech become more racy, his cold eyes glitter into ardent life, and his Don Quixote moustache bristle with joyous excitement. His love of danger, his intense appreciation of the drama of an adventure – all the more intense for being held tightly in – his consistent view that every peril in life is a form of sport, a fierce game betwixt you and Fate, with Death as a forfeit, made him a wonderful companion at such hours. If it were not for our fears as to the fate of our companions, it would have been a positive joy to throw myself with such a man into such an affair. We were rising from our brushwood hiding-place when suddenly I felt his grip upon my arm.

'By George!' he whispered, 'here they come!'

From where we lay we could look down a brown aisle, arched with green, formed by the trunks and branches. Along this a party of the ape-men were passing. They went in single file, with bent legs and rounded backs, their hands occasionally touching the ground, their heads turning to left and right as they trotted along. Their crouching gait took away from their height, but I should put them at five feet or so, with long arms and enormous chests. Many of them carried sticks, and at the distance they looked like a line of very hairy and deformed human beings. For a moment I caught this clear glimpse of them. Then they were lost among the bushes.

'Not this time,' said Lord John, who had caught up his rifle. 'Our best chance is to lie quiet until they have given up the search. Then we shall see whether we can't get back to their town and hit 'em where it hurts most. Give 'em an hour and we'll march.'

We filled in the time by opening one of our food tins and making sure of our breakfast. Lord Roxton had had nothing but some fruit since the morning before and ate like a starving man. Then, at last, our pockets bulging with cartridges and a rifle in each hand, we started off upon our mission of rescue. Before leaving it we carefully marked our little hiding-place among the brushwood and its bearing to Fort Challenger, that we might find it again if we needed it. We slunk through the bushes in silence until we came to the very edge of the cliff, close to the old camp. Then we halted, and Lord John gave me some idea of his plans.

'So long as we are among the thick trees these swine are our masters,' said he. 'They can see us and we cannot see them. But in the open it is different. There we can move faster than they. So we must stick to the open all we can. The edge of the plateau has fewer large trees than further inland. So that's our line of advance. Go slowly, keep your eyes open and your rifle ready. Above all, never let them get you prisoner while there is a cartridge left – that's my last word to you, young fellah.'

When we reached the edge of the cliff I looked over and saw our good old black Zambo sitting smoking on a rock below us. I would have given a great deal to have hailed him and told him how we were placed, but it was too dangerous, lest we should be heard. The woods seemed to be full of the ape-men; again and again we heard their curious clicking chatter. At such times we plunged into the nearest clump of bushes and lay still until the sound had passed away. Our advance, therefore, was very slow, and two hours at least must have passed before I saw by Lord John's cautious movements that we must be close to our destination. He motioned to me to lie still, and he crawled forward himself. In a minute he was back again, his face quivering with eagerness.

'Come!' said he. 'Come quick! I hope to the Lord we are not too late already!'

I found myself shaking with nervous excitement as I scrambled forward and lay down beside him, looking out through the bushes at a clearing which stretched before us.

It was a sight which I shall never forget until my dying day – so weird, so impossible, that I do not know how I am to make you realize it, or how in a few years I shall bring myself to believe in it if I live to sit once more on a lounge in the Savage Club and look out on the drab solidity of the Embankment. I know that it will seem then to be some wild nightmare, some delirium of fever. Yet I will set it down now, while it is still fresh in my memory, and one at least, the man who lay in the damp grasses by my side, will know if I have lied.

A wide, open space lay before us – some hundreds of yards across – all green turf and low bracken growing to the very edge of the cliff. Round this clearing there was a semicircle of trees with curious huts built of foliage piled one above the other among the branches. A rookery, with every nest a little house, would best convey the idea. The openings of these huts and the branches of the trees were thronged with a dense mob of ape-people, whom from their size I took to be the females and infants of the tribe. They formed the background of the picture, and were all looking out with eager interest at the same scene which fascinated and bewildered us.

In the open, and near the edge of the cliff, there had assembled a crowd of some hundred of these shaggy red-haired creatures, many of them of immense size, and all of them horrible to look upon. There was a certain discipline among them, for none of them attempted to break the line which had been formed. In front there stood a small group of Indians – little, clean-limbed, red fellows, whose skins glowed like polished bronze in the strong sunlight. A tall, thin white man was standing beside them, his head bowed, his arms folded, his whole attitude expressive of his horror and dejection. There was no mistaking the angular form of Professor Summerlee.

In front of and around this dejected group of prisoners were several ape-men who watched them closely and made all escape impossible. Then, right out from all the others and close to the edge of the cliff, were two figures, so strange, and under other circumstances so ludicrous, that they absorbed my attention. The one was our comrade, Professor Challenger. The remains of his coat still hung from his shoulders, but his shirt had been all torn out, and his great beard merged itself in the black tangle which covered his mighty chest. He had lost his hat, and his hair, which had grown long in our wanderings, was flying in wild disorder. A single day seemed to have changed him from the highest product of modern civilization to the most desperate savage in South America. Beside him stood his master the king of the ape-men. In all things he was, as Lord John had said, the very image of our Professor, save that his colouring was red instead of black. The same short, broad figure, the same heavy shoulders, the same forward hang of the arms, the same bristling beard merging itself in the hairy chest. Only above the eyebrows, where the sloping forehead and low, curved skull of the ape-man were in sharp contrast to the broad brow and magnificent cranium of the European, could one see any marked difference. At every other point the king was an absurd parody of the Professor.

All this, which takes me so long to describe, impressed itself upon me in a few seconds. Then we had very different things to think of, for an active drama was in progress. Two of the ape-men had seized one of the Indians out of the group and dragged him forward to the edge of the cliff. The king raised his hand as a signal. They caught the man up by his leg and arm, and swung him three times backwards and forwards with tremendous violence. Then, with a frightful heave they shot the poor wretch over the precipice. With such force did they throw him that he curved high in the air before beginning to drop. As he vanished from sight, the whole assembly, except the guards, rushed forward to the edge of the precipice, and there was a long pause of absolute silence, broken by a mad yell of delight. They sprang about, tossing their long, hairy arms in the air and howling with exultation. Then they fell back from the edge, formed themselves again into line, and waited for the next victim.

This time it was Summerlee. Two of his guards caught him by the wrists and pulled him brutally to the front. His thin figure and long limbs struggled and fluttered like a chicken being dragged from a coop. Challenger had turned to the king and waved his hands frantically before him. He was begging, pleading, imploring for his comrade's life. The ape-man pushed him roughly aside and shook his head. It was the last conscious movement he was to make upon earth. Lord John's rifle cracked, and the king sank down, a tangled red sprawling thing, upon the ground.

'Shoot into the thick of them! Shoot! sonny, shoot!' cried my companion.

There are strange red depths in the soul of the most commonplace man. I am tender-hearted by nature, and have found my eyes moist many a time over the scream of a wounded hare. Yet the blood lust was on me now. I found myself on my feet emptying one magazine, then the other, clicking open the breech to re-load, snapping it to again, while cheering and yelling with pure ferocity and joy of slaughter as I did so. With our four guns the two of us made a horrible havoc. Both the guards who held Summerlee were down, and he was staggering about like a drunken man in his amazement, unable to realize that he was a free man. The dense mob of ape-men ran about in bewilderment, marvelling whence this storm of death was coming or what it might mean. They waved, gesticulated, screamed, and tripped up over those who had fallen. Then, with a sudden impulse, they all rushed in a howling crowd to the trees for shelter, leaving the ground behind them spotted with their stricken comrades. The prisoners were left for the moment standing alone in the middle of the clearing.

Challenger's quick brain had grasped the situation. He seized the bewildered Summerlee by the arm, and they both ran towards us. Two of their guards bounded after them and fell to two bullets from Lord John. We ran forward into the open to meet our friends, and pressed a loaded rifle into the hands of each. But Summerlee was at the end of his strength. He could hardly totter. Already the ape-men were recovering from their panic. They were coming through the brushwood and threatening to cut us off. Challenger and I ran Summerlee along, one at each of his elbows, while Lord John covered our retreat, firing again and again as savage heads snarled at us out of the bushes. For a mile or more the chattering brutes were at our very heels. Then the pursuit slackened, for they learned our power and would no longer face that unerring rifle. When we had at last reached the camp, we looked back and found ourselves alone.

So it seemed to us; and yet we were mistaken. We had hardly closed the thorn-bush door of our zareba, clasped each other's hands, and thrown ourselves panting upon the ground beside our spring, when we heard a patter of feet and then a gentle, plaintive crying from outside our entrance. Lord Roxton rushed forward, rifle in hand, and threw it open. There, prostrate upon their faces, lay the little red figures of the four surviving Indians, trembling with fear of us and yet imploring our protection. With an expressive sweep of his hands one of them pointed to the woods around them, and indicated that they were full of danger. Then, darting forward, he threw his arms round Lord John's legs and rested his face upon them.

'By George!' cried Lord John, pulling at his moustache in great perplexity, 'I say – what the dooce are we to do with these people? Get up, little chappie, and take your face off my boots.'

Summerlee was sitting up and stuffing some tobacco into his old briar.

'We've got to see them safe,' said he. 'You've pulled us all out of the jaws of death. My word! it was a good bit of work!'

'Admirable!' cried Challenger. 'Admirable! Not only we as individuals, but European science collectively, owe you a deep debt of gratitude for what you have done. I do not hesitate to say that the disappearance of Professor Summerlee and myself would have left an appreciable gap in modern zoological history. Our young friend here and you have done most excellently well.'

He beamed at us with the old paternal smile, but European science would have been somewhat amazed could they have seen their chosen child, the hope of the future, with his tangled, unkempt head, his bare chest, and his tattered clothes. He had one of the meat tins between his knees, and sat with a large piece of cold Australian mutton between his fingers. The Indian looked up at him, and then, with a little yelp, cringed to the ground and clung to Lord John's leg.

'Don't you be scared, my bonnie boy,' said Lord John, patting the matted head in front of him. 'He can't stick your appearance, Challenger; and, by George! I don't wonder. All right, little chap, he's only a human, just the same as the rest of us.'

'Really, sir!' cried the Professor.

'Well, it's lucky for you, Challenger, that you *are* a little out of the ordinary. If you hadn't been so like the king – '

'Upon my word, Lord John Roxton, you allow yourself great latitude.'

'Well, it's a fact.'

'I beg, sir, that you will change the subject. Your remarks are irrelevant and unintelligible. The question before us is what are we to do with these Indians? The obvious thing is to escort them home, if we knew where their home was.'

'There is no difficulty about that,' said I. 'They live in the caves on the other side of the central lake.'

'Our young friend here knows where they live. I gather that it is some distance.'

'A good twenty miles,' said I.

Summerlee gave a groan.

'I, for one, could never get there. Surely I hear those brutes still howling upon our track.'

As he spoke, from the dark recesses of the woods we heard far away the jibbering cry of the ape-men. The Indians once more set up a feeble wail of fear.

'We must move, and move quick!' said Lord John. 'You help Summerlee, young fellah. These Indians will carry stores. Now, then, come along before they can see us.'

In less than half an hour we had reached our brushwood retreat and concealed ourselves. All day we heard the excited calling of the ape-men in the direction of our old camp, but none of them came our way, and the tired fugitives, red and white, had a long, deep sleep. I was dozing myself in the evening when someone plucked my sleeve, and I found Challenger kneeling beside me.

'You keep a diary of these events, and you expect eventually to publish it, Mr. Malone,' said he, with solemnity.

'I am only here as a Press reporter,' I answered.

'Exactly. You may have heard some rather fatuous remarks of Lord John Roxton's which seemed to imply that there was some – some resemblance – '

'Yes, I heard them.'

'I need not say that any publicity given to such an idea – any levity in your narrative of what occurred – would be exceedingly offensive to me.'

'I will keep well within the truth.'

'Lord John's observations are frequently exceedingly fanciful, and he is capable of attributing the most absurd reasons to the respect which is always shown by the most undeveloped races to dignity and character. You follow my meaning?'

'Entirely.'

'I leave the matter to your discretion.' Then, after a long pause, he added: 'The king of the ape-men was really a creature of great distinction – a most remarkably handsome and intelligent personality. Did it not strike you?'

'A most remarkable creature,' said I.

And the Professor, much eased in his mind, settled down to his slumber once more.

14

Those Were the Real Conquests

WE had imagined that our pursuers, the ape-men, knew nothing of our brushwood hiding-place, but we were soon to find out our mistake. There was no sound in the woods – not a leaf moved upon the trees and all was peace around us – but we should have been warned by our first experience how cunningly and how patiently these creatures can watch and wait until their chance comes. Whatever fate may be mine through life, I am very sure that I shall never be nearer death than I was that morning. But I will tell you the thing in its due order.

We all awoke exhausted after the terrific emotions and scanty food of yesterday. Summerlee was still so weak that it was an effort for him to stand; but the old man was full of a sort of surly courage which would never admit defeat. A council was held, and it was agreed that we should wait quietly for an hour or two where we were, have our much-needed breakfast, and then make our way across the plateau and round the central lake to the caves where my observations had shown that the Indians lived. We relied upon the fact that we could count upon the good word of those whom we had rescued to ensure a warm welcome from their fellows. Then, with our mission accomplished and possessing a fuller knowledge of the secrets of Maple White Land, we should turn our whole thoughts to the vital problem of our escape and return. Even Challenger was ready to admit that we should then have done all for which we had come, and that our first duty from that time onwards was to carry back to civilization the amazing discoveries we had made.

We were able now to take a more leisurely view of the Indians whom we had rescued. They were small men, wiry, active, and well-built, with lank black hair tied up in a bunch behind their heads with a leathern thong, and leathern also were their loin-clothes. Their faces were hairless, well formed, and good-humoured. The lobes of their ears, hanging ragged and bloody, showed that they had been pierced for some ornaments which their captors had torn out. Their speech, though unintelligible to us, was fluent among themselves, and as they pointed to each other and uttered the word 'Accala' many times over, we gathered that this was the name of their nation. Occasionally, with faces which were convulsed with fear and hatred, they shook their clenched hands at the woods round and cried: 'Doda! Doda!' which was surely their term for their enemies.

'What do you make of them, Challenger?' asked Lord John. 'One thing is very clear to me, and that is that the little chap with the front of his head shaved is a chief among them.'

It was indeed evident that this man stood apart from the others, and that they never ventured to address him without every sign of deep respect. He seemed to be the youngest of them all, and yet, so proud and high was his spirit, that upon Challenger laying his great hand upon his head he started like a spurred horse and, with a quick flash of his dark eyes, moved further away from the Professor. Then, placing his hand upon his breast and holding himself with great dignity, he uttered the word 'Maretas' several times. The Professor, unabashed, seized the nearest Indian by the shoulder and proceeded to lecture upon him as if he were a potted specimen in a class-room.

'The type of these people,' said he in his sonorous fashion, 'whether judged by cranial capacity, facial angle, or any other test, cannot be regarded as a low one; on the contrary, we must place it as considerably higher in the scale than many South American tribes which I can mention. On no possible supposition can we explain the evolution of such a race in this place. For that matter, so great a gap separates these ape-men from the primitive animals which have survived upon this plateau, that it is inadmissible to think that they could have developed where we find them.'

'Then where the dooce did they drop from?' asked Lord John.

'A question which will, no doubt, be eagerly discussed in every scientific society in Europe and America,' the Professor answered. 'My own reading of the situation for what it is worth' – he inflated his chest enormously and looked insolently around him at the words – 'is that evolution has advanced under the peculiar conditions of this country up to the vertebrate stage, the old types surviving and living on in company with the newer ones. Thus we find such modern creatures as the tapir – an animal with quite a respectable length of pedigree – the great deer, and the ant-eater in the companionship of reptilian forms of Jurassic type. So much is clear. And now come the ape-men and the Indian. What is the scientific mind to think of their presence? I can only account for it by an invasion from outside. It is probable that there existed an anthropoid ape in South America, who in past ages found his way to this place, and that he developed into the creatures we have seen, some of which' – here he looked hard at me – 'were of an appearance and shape which if it had been accompanied by corresponding intelligence, would, I do not hesitate to say, have reflected credit upon any living race. As to the Indians I cannot doubt that they are more recent immigrants from below. Under the stress of famine or of conquest they have made their way up here. Faced by ferocious creatures which they had never before seen, they took refuge in the caves which our young friend has described, but they have no doubt had a bitter fight to hold their own against wild beasts, and especially against the ape-men who would regard them as intruders, and wage a merciless war upon them with a cunning which the larger beasts would lack. Hence the fact that their numbers appear to be limited. Well, gentlemen, have I read you the riddle aright, or is there any point which you would query?'

Professor Summerlee for once was too depressed to argue, though he shook his head violently as a token of general disagreement. Lord John merely scratched his scanty locks with the remark that he couldn't put up a fight as he wasn't in the same weight or class. For my own part I performed my usual *rôle* of bringing things down to a strictly prosaic and practical level by the remark that one of the Indians was missing.

'He has gone to fetch some water,' said Lord Roxton. 'We fitted him up with an empty beef tin and he is off.'

'To the old camp?' I asked.

'No, to the brook. It's among the trees there. It can't be more than a couple of hundred yards. But the beggar is certainly taking his time.'

'I'll go and look after him,' said I. I picked up my rifle and strolled in the direction of the brook, leaving my friends to lay out the scanty breakfast. It may seem to you rash that even for so short a distance I should quit the shelter of our friendly thicket, but you will remember that we were many miles from Ape-town, that so far as we knew the creatures had not discovered our retreat, and that in any case with a rifle in my hands I had no fear of them. I had not yet learned their cunning or their strength.

I could hear the murmur of our brook somewhere ahead of me, but there was a tangle of trees and brushwood between me and it. I was making my way through this at a point which was just out of sight of my companions, when, under one of the trees, I noticed something red huddled among the bushes. As I approached it, I was shocked to see that it was the dead body of the missing Indian. He lay upon his side, his limbs drawn up, and his head screwed round at a most unnatural angle, so that he seemed to be looking straight over his own shoulder. I gave a cry to warn my friends that something was amiss, and running forwards I stooped over the body. Surely my guardian angel was very near to me then, for some instinct of fear, or it may have been some faint rustle of leaves, made me glance upwards. Out of the thick green foliage which hung low over my head, two long muscular arms covered with reddish hair were slowly descending. Another instant and the great stealthy hands would have been round my throat. I sprang backwards, but quick as I was, those hands were quicker still. Through my sudden spring they missed a fatal grip, but one of them caught the back of my neck and the other my face. I threw my hands up to protect my throat, and the next moment the huge paw had slid down my face and closed over them. I was lifted lightly from the ground, and I felt an intolerable pressure forcing my head back and back until the strain upon the cervical spine was more than I could bear. My senses swam, but I still tore at the hand and forced it out from my chin. Looking up I saw a frightful face with cold inexorable light blue eyes looking down into mine. There was something hypnotic in those terrible eyes. I could struggle no longer. As the creature felt me grow limp in his grasp, two white canines gleamed for a moment at each side of the vile mouth, and the grip tightened still more upon my chin, forcing it always upwards and back. A thin, opal-tinted mist formed before my eyes and little silvery bells tinkled in my ears. Dully and far off I heard the crack of a rifle and was feebly aware of the shock as I was dropped to the earth, where I lay without sense or motion.

I awoke to find myself on my back upon the grass in our lair within the thicket. Someone had brought the water from the brook, and Lord John was sprinkling my head with it, while Challenger and Summerlee were propping me up, with concern in their faces. For a moment I had a glimpse of the human spirits behind their scientific masks. It was really shock, rather than any injury, which had prostrated me, and in half an hour, in spite of aching head and stiff neck, I was sitting up and ready for anything.

'But you've had the escape of your life, young fellah-my-lad,' said Lord John. 'When I heard your cry and ran forward, and saw your head twisted half-off and your stohwassers kickin' in the air, I thought we were one short. I missed the beast in my flurry, but he dropped you all right and was off like a streak. By George! I wish I had fifty men with rifles. I'd clear out the whole infernal gang of them and leave this country a bit cleaner than we found it.'

It was clear now that the ape-men had in some way marked us down, and that we were watched on every side. We had not so much to fear from them during the day, but they would be very likely to rush us by night; so the sooner we got away from their neighbourhood the better. On three sides of us was absolute forest, and there we might find ourselves in an ambush. But on the fourth side – that which sloped down in the direction of the lake – there was only low scrub, with scattered trees and occasional open glades. It was, in fact, the route which I had myself taken in my solitary journey, and it led us straight for the Indian caves. This then must for every reason be our road.

One great regret we had, and that was to leave our old camp behind us, not only for the sake of the stores which remained there, but even more because we were losing touch with Zambo, our link with the outside world. However, we had a fair supply of cartridges and all our guns, so, for a time at least, we could look after ourselves, and we hoped soon to have a chance of returning and restoring our communications with our negro. He had faithfully promised to stay where he was, and we had not a doubt that he would be as good as his word.

It was in the early afternoon that we started upon our journey. The young chief walked at our head as our guide, but refused indignantly to carry any burden. Behind him came the two surviving Indians with our scanty possessions upon their backs. We four white men walked in the rear with rifles loaded and ready. As we started there broke from the thick silent woods behind us a sudden great ululation of the ape-men, which may have been a cheer of triumph at our departure or a jeer of contempt at our flight. Looking back we saw only the dense screen of trees, but that long-drawn yell told us how many of our enemies lurked among them. We saw no sign of pursuit, however, and soon we had got into more open country and beyond their power.

As I tramped along, the rearmost of the four, I could not help smiling at the appearance of my three companions in front. Was this the luxurious Lord John Roxton who had sat that evening in the Albany amidst his Persian rugs and his pictures in the pink radiance of the tinted lights? And was this the imposing Professor who had swelled behind the great desk in his massive study at Enmore Park? and finally, could this be the austere and prim figure which had risen before the meeting at the Zoological Institute? No three tramps that one could have met in a Surrey lane could have looked more hopeless and bedraggled. We had, it is true, been only a week or so upon the top of the plateau, but all our spare clothing was in our camp below, and the one week had been a severe one upon us all, though least to me who had not to endure the handling of the ape-men. My three friends had all lost their hats, and had now bound handkerchiefs round their heads, their clothes hung in ribbons about them, and their unshaven grimy faces were hardly to be recognized. Both Summerlee and Challenger were limping heavily, while I still dragged my feet from weakness after the shock of the morning, and my neck was as stiff as a board from the murderous grip that held it. We were indeed a sorry crew, and I did not wonder to see our Indian companions glance back at us occasionally with horror and amazement on their faces.

In the late afternoon we reached the margin of the lake, and as we emerged from the bush and saw the sheet of water stretching before us our native friends set up a shrill cry of joy and pointed eagerly in front of them. It was indeed a wonderful sight which lay before us. Sweeping over the glassy surface was a great flotilla of canoes coming straight for the shore upon which we stood. They were some miles out when we first saw them, but they shot forward with great swiftness, and were soon so near that the rowers could distinguish our persons. Instantly a thunderous shout of delight burst from them, and we saw them rise from their seats, waving their paddles and spears madly in the air. Then, bending to their work once more, they flew across the intervening water, beached their boats upon the sloping sand, and rushed up to us, prostrating themselves with loud cries of greeting before the young chief. Finally one of them, an elderly man, with a necklace and bracelet of great lustrous glass beads and the skin of some beautiful mottled amber-coloured animal slung over his shoulders, ran forward and embraced most tenderly the youth whom we had saved. He then looked at us and asked some questions, after which he stepped up with much dignity and embraced us also each in turn. Then, at his order, the whole tribe lay down upon the ground before us in homage. Personally I felt shy and uncomfortable at this obsequious adoration, and I read the same feeling in the faces of Lord John and Summerlee, but Challenger expanded like a flower in the sun.

'They may be undeveloped types,' said he, stroking his beard and looking round at them, 'but their deportment in the presence of their superiors might be a lesson to some of our more advanced Europeans. Strange how correct are the instincts of the natural man!'

It was clear that the natives had come out upon the warpath, for every man carried his spear – a long bamboo tipped with bone – his bow and arrows, and some sort of club or stone battle-axe slung at his side. Their dark, angry glances at the woods from which we had come, and the frequent repetition of the word 'Doda', made it clear enough that this was a rescue party who had set forth to save or revenge the old chief's son, for such we gathered that the youth must be. A council was now held by the whole tribe squatting in a circle, whilst we sat near on a slab of basalt and watched their proceedings. Two or three warriors spoke, and finally our young friend made a spirited harangue with such eloquent features and gestures that we could understand it all as clearly as if we had known the language.

'What is the use of returning?' he said. 'Sooner or later the thing must be done. Your comrades have been murdered. What if I have returned safe? These others have been done to death. There is no safety for any of us. We are assembled now and ready.' Then he pointed to us. 'These strange men are our friends. They are great fighters, and they hate the ape-men even as we do. They command,' here he pointed up to heaven,' the thunder and the lightning. When shall we have such a chance again? Let us go forward, and either die now or live for the future in safety. How else shall we go back unashamed to our women?'

The little red warriors hung upon the words of the speaker, and when he had finished they burst into a roar of applause, waving their rude weapons in the air. The old chief stepped forward to us, and asked us some question, pointing at the same time to the woods. Lord John made a sign to him that he should wait for an answer and then he turned to us.

'Well, it's up to you to say what you will do,' said he; 'for my part I have a score to settle with these monkey-folk, and if it ends by wiping them off the face of the earth I don't see that the earth need fret about it. I'm goin' with our little red pals and I mean to see them through the scrap. What do you say, young fellah?'

'Of course I will come.'

'And you, Challenger?'

'I will assuredly co-operate.'

'And you, Summerlee?'

'We seem to be drifting very far from the object of this expedition, Lord John. I assure you that I little thought when I left my professorial chair in London that it was for the purpose of heading a raid of savages upon a colony of anthropoid apes.'

'To such base uses do we come,' said Lord John, smiling.

'But we are up against it, so what's the decision?'

'It seems a most questionable step,' said Summerlee, argumentative to the last, 'but if you are all going, I hardly see how I can remain behind.'

'Then it is settled,' said Lord John, and turning to the chief he nodded and slapped his rifle. The old fellow clasped our hands, each in turn, while his men cheered louder than ever. It was too late to advance that night, so the Indians settled down into a rude bivouac. On all sides their fires began to glimmer and smoke. Some of them who had disappeared into the jungle came back presently driving a young iguanodon before them. Like the others, it had a daub of asphalt upon its shoulder, and it was only when we saw one of the natives step forward with the air of an owner and give his consent to the beast's slaughter that we understood at last that these great creatures were as much private property as a herd of cattle, and that these symbols which had so perplexed us were nothing more than the marks of the owner. Helpless, torpid, and vegetarian, with great limbs and a minute brain, they could be rounded up and driven by a child. In a few minutes the huge beast had been cut up and slabs of him were hanging over a dozen camp fires, together with great scaly ganoid fish which had been speared in the lake.

Summerlee had lain down and slept upon the sand, but we others roamed round the edge of the water, seeking to learn something more of this strange country. Twice we found pits of blue clay, such as we had already seen in the swamp of the pterodactyls. These were old volcanic vents, and for some reason excited the greatest interest in Lord John. What attracted Challenger, on the other hand, was a bubbling, gurgling mud geyser, where some strange gas formed great bursting bubbles upon the surface. He thrust a hollow reed into it and cried out with delight like a schoolboy when he was able, on touching it with a lighted match, to cause a sharp explosion and a blue flame at the far end of the tube. Still more pleased was he when, inverting a leathern pouch over the end of the reed, and so filling it with the gas, he was able to send it soaring up into the air.

'An inflammable gas, and one markedly lighter than the atmosphere. I should say beyond doubt that it contains a considerable proportion of free hydrogen. The resources of G. E. C. are not yet exhausted, my young friend. I may yet show you how a great mind moulds all Nature to its use.' He swelled with some secret purpose, but would say no more.

There was nothing which we could see upon the shore which seemed to me so wonderful as the great sheet of water before us. Our numbers and our noise had frightened all living creatures away, and save for a few pterodactyls, which soared round high above our heads while they waited for the carrion, all was still around the camp. But it was different out upon the rose-tinted waters of the Central Lake. It boiled and heaved with strange life. Great slate-coloured backs and high serrated dorsal fins shot up with a fringe of silver, and then rolled down into the depths again. The sandbanks far out were spotted with uncouth crawling forms, huge turtles, strange saurians, and one great flat creature like a writhing palpitating mat of black greasy leather, which flopped its way slowly to the lake. Here and there high serpent heads projected out of the water, cutting swiftly through it with a little collar of foam in front, and a long swirling wake behind, rising and falling in graceful, swan-like undulations as they went. It was not until one of these creatures wriggled on to a sandbank within a few hundred yards of us, and exposed a barrel-shaped body and huge flippers behind the long serpent neck, that Challenger and Summerlee, who had joined us, broke out into their duet of wonder and admiration.

'Plesiosaurus! A fresh-water Plesiosaurus!' cried Summerlee. 'That I should have lived to see such a sight! We are blessed, my dear Challenger, above all zoologists since the world began!'

It was not until the night had fallen, and the fires of our savage allies glowed red in the shadows, that our two men of science could be dragged away from the fascinations of that primæval lake. Even in the darkness as we lay upon the strand, we heard from time to time the snort and plunge of the huge creatures who lived therein.

At earliest dawn our camp was astir and an hour later we had started upon our memorable expedition. Often in my dreams have I thought that I might live to be a war correspondent. In what wildest one could I have conceived the nature of the campaign which it should be my lot to report? Here then is my first despatch from a field of battle:

Our numbers had been reinforced during the night by a fresh batch of natives from the caves, and we may have been four or five hundred strong when we made our advance. A fringe of scouts was thrown out in front, and behind them the whole force in a solid column made their way up the long slope of the bush country until we were near the edge of the forest. Here they spread out into a long straggling line of spearmen and bowmen. Roxton and Summerlee took their position upon the right flank, while Challenger and I were on the left. It was a host of the stone age that we were accompanying to battle – we with the last word of the gunsmith's art from St. James's Street and the Strand.

We had not long to wait for our enemy. A wild shrill clamour rose from the edge of the wood and suddenly a body of ape-men rushed out with clubs and stones, and made for the centre of the Indian line. It was a valiant move but a foolish one, for the great bandy-legged creatures were slow of foot, while their opponents were as active as cats. It was horrible to see the fierce brutes with foaming mouths and glaring eyes, rushing and grasping, but for ever missing their elusive enemies, while arrow after arrow buried itself in their hides. One great fellow ran past me roaring with pain, with a dozen darts sticking from his chest and ribs. In mercy I put a bullet through his skull, and he fell sprawling among the aloes. But this was the only shot fired, for the attack had been on the centre of the line, and the Indians there had needed no help of ours in repulsing it. Of all the ape-men who had rushed out into the open, I do not think that one got back to cover.

But the matter was more deadly when we came among the trees. For an hour or more after we entered the wood, there was a desperate struggle in which for a time we hardly held our own. Springing out from among the scrub the ape-men with huge clubs broke in upon the Indians and often felled three of four of them before they could be speared. Their frightful blows shattered everything upon which they fell. One of them knocked Summerlee's rifle to matchwood and the next would have crushed his skull had an Indian not stabbed the beast to the heart. Other ape-men in the trees above us hurled down stones and logs of wood, occasionally dropping bodily on to our ranks and fighting furiously until they were felled. Once our allies broke under the pressure, and had it not been for the execution done by our rifles they would certainly have taken to their heels. But they were gallantly rallied by their old chief and came on with such a rush that the ape-men began in turn to give way. Summerlee was weaponless, but I was emptying my magazine as quick as I could fire, and on the further flank we heard the continuous cracking of our companions' rifles. Then in a moment came the panic and the collapse. Screaming and howling, the great creatures rushed away in all directions through the brushwood, while our allies yelled in their savage delight, following swiftly after their flying enemies. All the feuds of countless generations, all the hatreds and cruelties of their narrow history, all the memories of ill-usage and persecution were to be purged that day. At last man was to be supreme and the man-beast to find for ever his allotted place. Fly as they would the fugitives were too slow to escape from the active savages, and from every side in the tangled woods we heard the exultant yells, the twanging of bows, and the crash and thud as ape-men were brought down from their hiding places in the trees.

I was following the others, when I found that Lord John and Summerlee had come across to join us.

'It's over,' said Lord John. 'I think we can leave the tidying up to them. Perhaps the less we see of it the better we shall sleep.'

Challenger's eyes were shining with the lust of slaughter.

'We have been privileged,' he cried, strutting about like a gamecock, 'to be present at one of the typical decisive battles of history – the battles which have determined the fate of the world. What, my friends, is the conquest of one nation by another? It is meaningless. Each produces the same result. But those fierce fights, when in the dawn of the ages the cave-dwellers held their own against the tiger folk, or the elephants first found that they had a master, those were the real conquests – the victories that count. By this strange turn of fate we have seen and helped to decide even such a contest. Now upon this plateau the future must ever be for man.'

It needed a robust faith in the end to justify such tragic means. As we advanced together through the woods we found the ape-men lying thick, transfixed with spears or arrows. Here and there a little group of shattered Indians marked where one of the anthropoids had turned to bay, and sold his life dearly. Always in front of us we heard the yelling and roaring which showed the direction of the pursuit. The ape-men had been driven back to their city, they had made a last stand there, once again they had been broken, and now we were in time to see the final fearful scene of all. Some eighty or a hundred males, the last survivors, had been driven across that same little clearing which led to the edge of the cliff, the scene of our own exploit two days before. As we arrived the Indians, a semi-circle of spearmen, had closed in on them, and in a minute it was over. Thirty or forty died where they stood. The others, screaming and clawing, were thrust over the precipice, and went hurtling down, as their prisoners had of old, on to the sharp bamboos six hundred feet below. It was as Challenger had said, and the reign of man was assured for ever in Maple White Land. The males were exterminated, Ape Town was destroyed, the females and young were driven away to live in bondage, and the long rivalry of untold centuries had reached its bloody end.

For us the victory brought much advantage. Once again we were able to visit our camp and get at our stores. Once more also we were able to communicate with Zambo, who had been terrified by the spectacle from afar of an avalanche of apes falling from the edge of the cliff.

'Come away, Massas, come away!' he cried, his eyes starting from his head. 'The debbil get you sure if you stay up there.'

'It is the voice of sanity!' said Summerlee with conviction. 'We have had adventures enough and they are neither suitable to our character or our position. I hold you to your word, Challenger. From now onwards you devote your energies to getting us out of this horrible country and back once more to civilization.'

15

Our Eyes Have Seen Great Wonders

I WRITE this from day to day, but I trust that before I come to the end of it, I may be able to say that the light shines, at last, through our clouds. We are held here with no clear means of making our escape, and bitterly we chafe against it. Yet, I can well imagine that the day may come when we may be glad that we were kept, against our will, to see something more of the wonders of this singular place, and of the creatures who inhabit it.

The victory of the Indians and the annihilation of the ape-men marked the turning point of our fortunes. From then onwards, we were in truth masters of the plateau, for the natives looked upon us with a mixture of fear and gratitude, since by our strange powers we had aided them to destroy their hereditary foe. For their own sakes they would, perhaps, be glad to see the departure of such formidable and incalculable people, but they have not themselves suggested any way by which we may reach the plains below. There had been, so far as we could follow their signs, a tunnel by which the place could be approached, the lower exit of which we had seen from below. By this, no doubt, both ape-men and Indians had at different epochs reached the top, and Maple White with his companion had taken the same way. Only the year before, however, there had been a terrific earthquake, and the upper end of the tunnel had fallen in and completely disappeared. The Indians now could only shake their heads and shrug their shoulders when we expressed by signs our desire to descend. It may be that they cannot, but it may also be that they will not help us to get away.

At the end of the victorious campaign the surviving ape-folk were driven across the plateau (their wailings were horrible) and established in the neighbourhood of the Indian caves, where they would, from now onwards, be a servile race under the eyes of their masters. It was a rude, raw, primæval version of the Jew in Babylon or the Israelites in Egypt. At night we could hear from amid the trees the long-drawn cry, as some primitive Ezekiel mourned for fallen greatness and recalled the departed glories of Ape Town. Hewers of wood and drawers of water, such were they from now onwards.

We had returned across the plateau with our allies two days after the battle, and made our camp at the foot of the cliffs. They would have had us share their caves with them, but Lord John would by no means consent to it, considering that to do so would put us in their power if they were treacherously disposed. We kept our independence therefore, and had our weapons ready for any emergency, while preserving the most friendly relations. We also continually visited their caves, which were most remarkable places, though whether made by man or by Nature we have never been able to determine. They were all on the one stratum, hollowed out of some soft rock which lay between the volcanic basalt forming the ruddy cliffs above them, and the hard granite which formed their base.

The openings were about eighty feet above the ground, and were led up to by long stone stairs, so narrow and steep that no large animal could mount them. Inside they were warm and dry, running in straight passages of varying length into the side of the hill, with smooth grey walls decorated with many excellent pictures done with charred sticks and representing the various animals of the plateau. If every living thing were swept from the country the future explorer would find upon the walls of these caves ample evidence of the strange fauna – the dinosaurs, iguanodons and fish lizards – which had lived so recently upon earth.

Since we had learned that the huge iguanodons were kept as tame herds by their owners, and were simply walking meat-stores, we had conceived that man, even with his primitive weapons, had established his ascendancy upon the plateau. We were soon to discover that it was not so, and that he was still there upon tolerance. It was on the third day after our forming our camp near the Indian caves that the tragedy occurred. Challenger and Summerlee had gone off together that day to the lake, where some of the natives, under their direction, were engaged in harpooning specimens of the great lizards. Lord John and I had remained in our camp, while a number of the Indians were scattered about upon the grassy slope in front of the caves engaged in different ways. Suddenly there was a shrill cry of alarm, with the word 'Stoa' resounding from a hundred tongues. From every side men, women and children were rushing wildly for shelter, swarming up the staircases and into the caves in a mad stampede.

Looking up, we could see them waving their arms from the rocks above and beckoning to us to join them in their refuge. We had both seized our magazine rifles and ran out to see what the danger could be. Suddenly from the near belt of trees there broke forth a group of twelve or fifteen Indians, running for their lives, and at their very heels two of those frightful monsters which had disturbed our camp and pursued me upon my solitary journey. In shape they were like horrible toads, and moved in a succession of springs, but in size they were of an incredible bulk, larger than the largest elephant. We had never before seen them save at night, and indeed they are nocturnal animals save when disturbed in their lairs, as these had been. We now stood amazed at the sight, for their blotched and warty skins were of a curious fish-like iridescence, and the sunlight struck them with an ever-varying rainbow bloom as they moved.

We had little time to watch them, however, for in an instant they had overtaken the fugitives and were making a dire slaughter among them. Their method was to fall forward with their full weight upon each in turn, and, leaving him crushed and mangled, to bound on after the others. The wretched Indians screamed with terror, but were helpless, run as they would, before the relentless purpose and horrible activity of these monstrous creatures. One after another they went down, and there were not half a dozen surviving by the time my companion and I could come to their help. But our aid was of little avail and only involved us in the same peril. At the range of a couple of hundred yards we emptied our magazines, firing bullet after bullet into the beasts, but with no more effect than if we were pelting them with pellets of paper. Their slow reptilian natures cared nothing for wounds, and the springs of their lives, with no special brain centre but scattered throughout their spinal cords, could not be trapped by any modern weapons. The most that we could do was to check their progress by distracting their attention with the flash and roar of our guns, and so to give both the natives and ourselves time to reach the steps which led to safety. But where the conical explosive bullets of the twentieth century were of no avail the poisoned arrows of the natives, dipped in the juice of strophanthus and steeped afterwards in decayed carrion, could succeed. Such arrows were of little avail to the hunter who attacked the beast, because their action in that torpid circulation was slow, and before its powers failed it could certainly overtake and slay its assailant. But now, as the two monsters hounded us to the very foot of the stairs, a drift of darts came whistling from every chink in the cliff above them. In a minute they were feathered with them, and yet with no sign of pain they clawed and slobbered with impotent rage at the steps which would lead them to their victims, mounting clumsily up for a few yards and then sliding down again to the ground. But at last the poison worked. One of them gave a deep rumbling groan and dropped his huge squat head on to the earth. The other bounded round in an eccentric circle with shrill, wailing cries, and then lying down writhed in agony for some minutes before it also stiffened and lay still. With yells of triumph the Indians came flocking down from their caves and danced a frenzied dance of victory round the dead bodies, in mad joy that two more of the most dangerous of all their enemies had been slain. That night they cut up and removed the bodies, not to eat – for the poison was still active – but lest they should breed a pestilence. The great reptilian hearts, however, each as large as a cushion, still lay there, beating slowly and steadily, with a gentle rise and fall, in horrible independent life. It was upon the third day that the ganglia ran down and the dreadful things were still.

Some day, when I have a better desk than a meat-tin and more helpful tools than a worn stub of pencil and a last, tattered notebook, I will write some fuller account of the Accala Indians – of our life amongst them, and of the glimpses which we had of the strange conditions of wondrous Maple White Land. Memory, at least, will never fail me, for so long as the breath of life is in me every hour and every action of that period will stand out as hard and clear as do the first strange happenings of our childhood. No new impressions could efface those which are so deeply cut. When the time comes I will describe that wondrous moonlit night upon the great lake when a young ichthyosaurus – a strange creature, half seal, half fish, to look at, with bone-covered eyes on each side of his snout, and a third eye fixed upon the top of his head – was entangled in an Indian net, and nearly upset our canoe before we towed it ashore; the same night that a green water-snake shot out from the rushes and carried off in its coils the steersman of Challenger's canoe. I will tell, too, of the great nocturnal white thing – to this day we do not know whether it was beast or reptile – which lived in a vile swamp to the east of the lake, and flitted about with a faint phosphorescent glimmer in the darkness. The Indians were so terrified of it that they would not go near the place, and, though we twice made expeditions and saw it each time, we could not make our way through the deep marsh in which it lived. I can only say that it seemed to be larger than a cow and had the strangest musky odour. I will tell also of the huge bird which chased Challenger to the shelter of the rocks one day – a great running bird, far taller than an ostrich, with a vulture-like neck and cruel head which made it a walking death. As Challenger climbed to safety one dart of that savage curving beak shore off the heel of his boot as if it had been cut with a chisel. This time at least modern weapons prevailed and the great creature, twelve feet from head to foot – phororachus its name, according to our panting but exultant Professor – went down before Lord Roxton's rifle in a flurry of waving feathers and kicking limbs, with two remorseless yellow eyes glaring up from the midst of it. May I live to see that flattened vicious skull in its own niche amid the trophies of the Albany. Finally, I will surely give some account of the toxodon, the giant ten-foot guinea pig, with projecting chisel teeth, which we killed as it drank in the grey of the morning by the side of the lake.

All this I shall some day write at fuller length, and amidst these more stirring days I would tenderly sketch in those lovely summer evenings, when with the deep blue sky above us we lay in good comradeship among the long grasses by the wood and marvelled at the strange fowl that swept over us and the quaint new creatures which crept from their burrows to watch us, while above us the boughs of the bushes were heavy with luscious fruit, and below us strange and lovely flowers peeped at us from among the herbage; of those long moonlit nights when we lay out upon the shimmering surface of the great lake and watched with wonder and awe the huge circles rippling out from the sudden splash of some fantastic monster; or the greenish gleam, far down in the deep water, of some strange creature upon the confines of darkness. These are the scenes which my mind and my pen will dwell upon in every detail at some future day.

But, you will ask, why these experiences and why this delay, when you and your comrades should have been occupied day and night in the devising of some means by which you could return to the outer world? My answer is, that there was not one of us who was not working for this end, but that our work had been in vain. One fact we had very speedily discovered: The Indians would do nothing to help up. In every other way they were our friends – one might almost say our devoted slaves – but when it was suggated that they should help us to make and carry a plank which would bridge the chasm, or when we wished to get from them thongs of leather or liana to weave ropes which might help us, we were met by a good-humoured, but an invincible, refusal. They would smile, twinkle their eyes, shake their heads, and there was the end of it. Even the old chief met us with the same obstinate denial, and it was only Maretas, the youngster whom we had saved, who looked wistfully at us and told us by his gestures that he was grieved for our thwarted wishes. Ever since their crowning triumph with the ape-men they looked upon us as supermen, who bore victory in the tubes of strange weapons, and they believed that so long as we remained with them good fortune would be theirs. A little red-skinned wife and a cave of our own were freely offered to each of us if we would but forget our own people and dwell for ever upon the plateau. So far all had been kindly, however far apart our desires might be; but we felt well assured that our actual plans of a descent must be kept secret, for we had reason to fear that at the last they might try to hold us by force.

In spite of the danger from dinosaurs (which is not great save at night, for as I may have said before they are nocturnal in their habits) I have twice in the last three weeks been over to our old camp in order to see our negro who still kept watch and ward below the cliff. My eyes strained eagerly across the great plain in the hope of seeing afar off the help for which we had prayed. But the long cactus. strewn levels still stretched away, empty and bare, to the distant line of the cane-break.

'They will come soon now, Massa Malone. Before another week pass Indian come back and bring rope and fetch you down.' Such was the cheery cry of our excellent Zambo.

I had one strange experience as I came from this second visit which had involved my being away for a night from my companions. I was returning along the well-remembered route, and had reached a spot within a mile or so of the marsh of the pterodactyls, when I saw an extraordinary object approaching me. It was a man who walked inside a framework made of bent canes so that he was enclosed on all sides in a bell-shaped cage. As I drew nearer I was more amazed still to see that it was Lord John Roxton. When he saw me he slipped from under his curious protection and came towards me laughing, and yet, as I thought, with some confusion in his manner.

'Well, young fellah,' said he, 'who would have thought of meetin' you up here?'

'What in the world are you doing?' I asked.

'Visitin' my friends, the pterodactyls,' said he.

'But why?'

'Interestin' beasts, don't you think? But unsociable! Nasty rude ways with strangers, as you may remember. So I rigged this framework which keeps them from bein' too pressin' in their attentions.'

'But what do you want in the swamp?'

He looked at me with a very questioning eye, and I read hesitation in his face.

'Don't you think other people besides Professors can want to know things?' he said at last. 'I'm studyin' the pretty dears. That's enough for you.'

'No offence,' said I.

His good-humour returned and he laughed.

'No offence, young fellah. I'm goin' to get a young devil chick for Challenger. That's one of my jobs. No, I don't want your company. I'm safe in this cage, and you are not. So long, and I'll be back in camp by nightfall.'

He turned away and I left him wandering on through the wood with his extraordinary cage around him.

If Lord John's behaviour at this time was strange, that of Challenger was more so. I may say that he seemed to possess an extraordinary fascination for the Indian women, and that he always carried a large spreading palm branch with which he beat them off as if they were flies, when their attentions became too pressing. To see him walking like a comic opera Sultan, with this badge of authority in his hand, his black beard bristling in front of him, his toes pointing at each step, and a train of wide-eyed Indian girls behind him, clad in their slender drapery of bark cloth, is one of the most grotesque of all the pictures which I will carry back with me. As to Summerlee, he was absorbed in the insect and bird life of the plateau, and spent his whole time (save that considerable portion which was devoted to abusing Challenger for not getting us out of our difficulties) in cleaning and mounting his specimens.

Challenger had been in the habit of walking off by himself every morning and returning from time to time with looks of portentous solemnity, as one who bears the full weight of a great enterprise upon his shoulders. One day, palm branch in hand, and his crowd of adoring devotees behind him, he led us down to his hidden workshop and took us into the secret of his plans.

The place was a small clearing in the centre of a palm grove. In this was one of those boiling mud geysers which I have already described. Around its edge were scattered a number of leathern thongs cut from iguanodon hide, and a large collapsed membrane which proved to be the dried and scraped stomach of one of the great fish lizards from the lake. This huge sack had been sewn up at one end and only a small orifice left at the other. Into this opening several bamboo canes had been inserted and the other ends of these canes were in contact with conical clay funnels which collected the gas bubbling up through the mud of the geyser. Soon the flaccid organ began to slowly expand and show such a tendency to upward movements that Challenger fastened the cords which held it to the trunks of the surrounding trees. In half an hour a good-sized gas-bag had been formed, and the jerking and straining upon the thongs showed that it was capable of considerable lift. Challenger, like a glad father in the presence of his firstborn, stood smiling and stroking his beard in silent, selfsatisfied content as he gazed at the creation of his brain. It was Summerlee who first broke the silence.

'You don't mean us to go up in that thing, Challenger?' said he, in an acid voice.

'I mean, my dear Summerlee, to give you such a demonstration of its powers that after seeing it you will, I am sure, have no hesitation in trusting yourself to it.'

'You can put it right out of your head now, at once,' said Summerlee with decision; 'nothing on earth would induce me to commit such a folly. Lord John, I trust that you will not countenance such madness?'

'Dooced ingenious, I call it,' said our peer. 'I'd like to see how it works.'

'So you shall,' said Challenger. 'For some days I have exerted my whole brain force upon the problem of how we shall descend these cliffs. We have satisfied ourselves that we cannot climb down and that there is no tunnel. We are also unable to construct any kind of bridge which may take us back to the pinnacle from which we came? How then shall I find a means to convey us? Some little time ago I had remarked to our young friend here that free hydrogen was evolved from the geyser. The idea of a balloon naturally followed. I was, I will admit, somewhat baffled by the difficulty of discovering an envelope to contain the gas, but the contemplation of the immense entrails of these reptiles supplied me with a solution to the problem. Behold the result!'

He put one hand in the front of his ragged jacket and pointed proudly with the other.

By this time the gas-bag had swollen to a goodly rotundity and was jerking strongly upon its lashings.

'Midsummer madness!' snorted Summerlee.

Lord John was delighted with the whole idea. 'Clever old dear, ain't he?' he whispered to me, and then louder to Challenger. 'What about a car?'

'The car will be my next care. I have already planned how it is to be made and attached. Meanwhile I will simply show you how capable my apparatus is of supporting the weight of each of us.'

'All of us, surely?'

'No it is part of my plan that each in turn shall descend as in a parachute, and the balloon be drawn back by means which I shall have no difficulty in perfecting. If it will support the weight of one and let him gently down, it will have done all that is required of it. I will now show you its capacity in that direction.'

He brought out a lump of basalt of a considerable size, constructed in the middle so that a cord could be easily attached to it. This cord was the one which we had brought with us on the plateau after we had used it for climbing the pinnacle. It was over a hundred feet long, and though it was thin it was very strong. He had prepared a sort of collar of leather with many straps depending from it. This collar was placed over the dome of the ballon, and the hanging thongs were gathered together below, so that the pressure of any weight would be diffused over a considerable surface. Then the lump of basalt was fastened to the thongs and the rope was allowed to hang from the end of it, being passed three times round the Professor's arm.

'I will now,' said Challenger, with a smile of pleased anticipation, 'demonstrate the carrying power of my balloon.' As he said so he cut with a knife the various lashings that held it.

Never was our expedition in more imminent danger of complete annihilation. The inflated membrane shot up with frightful velocity into the air. In an instant Challenger was pulled off his feet and dragged after it. I had just time to throw my arms round his ascending waist when I was myself whipped up into the air. Lord John had me with a rat-trap grip round the legs, but I felt that he also was coming off the ground. For a moment I had a vision of four adventurers floating like a string of sausages over the land that they had explored. But, happily, there were limits to the strain which the rope would stand, though none apparently to the lifting powers of this infernal machine. There was a sharp crack, and we were in a heap upon the ground with coils of rope all over us. When we were able to stagger to our feet we saw far off in the deep blue sky one dark dot where the lump of basalt was speeding upon its way.

'Splendid!' cried the undaunted Challenger, rubbing his injured arm. 'A most thorough and satisfactory demonstration! I could not have anticipated such a success. Within a week, gentlemen, I promise that a second balloon will be prepared, and that you can count upon taking in safety and comfort the first stage of our homeward journey.'

So far I have written each of the foregoing events as it occurred. Now I am rounding off my narrative from the old camp, where Zambo has waited so long, with all our difficulties and dangers left like a dream behind us upon the summit of those vast ruddy crags which tower above our heads. We have descended in safety, though in a most unexpected fashion, and all is well with us. In six weeks or two months we shall be in London, and it is possible that this letter may not reach you much earlier than we do ourselves. Already our hearts yearn and our spirits fly towards the great mother city which holds so much that is dear to us.

It was on the very evening of our perilous adventure with Challenger's home-made balloon that the change came in our fortunes. I have said that the one person from whom we had had some sign of sympathy in our attempts to get away was the young chief whom we had rescued. He alone had no desire to hold us against our will in a strange land. He had told us as much by his expressive language of signs. That evening, after dusk, he came down to our little camp, handed me (for some reason he had always shown his attentions to me, perhaps because I was the one who was nearest his age) a small roll of the bark of a tree, and then pointing solemnly up at the row of caves above him, he had put his finger to his lips as a sign of secrecy and had stolen back again to his people.

I took the slip of bark to the firelight and we examined it together. It was about a foot square, and on the inner side there was a singular arrangement of lines, which I here reproduce:

They were neatly done in charcoal upon the white surface, and looked to me at first sight like some sort of rough musical score.

'Whatever it is, I can swear that it is of importance to us,' said I. 'I could read that on his face as he gave it.'

'Unless we have come upon a primitive practical joker,' Summerlee suggested, 'which I should think would be one of the most elementary developments of man.'

'It is clearly some sort of script,' said Challenger.

'Looks like a guinea puzzle competition,' remarked Lord John, craning his neck to have a look at it. When suddenly he stretched out his hand and seized the puzzle.

'By George!' he cried, 'I believe I've got it. The boy guessed right the very first time. See here! How many marks are on that paper? Eighteen. Well, if you come to think of it there are eighteen cave openings on the hill-side above us.'

'He pointed up to the caves when he gave it to me,' said I.

'Well, that settles it. This is a chart of the caves. What! Eighteen of them all in a row, some short, some deep, some branching, same we as saw them. It's a map, and here's a cross on it. What's the cross for? It is placed to mark one that is much deeper than the others.'

'One that goes through,' I cried.

'I believe our young friend has read the riddle,' said Challenger. 'If the cave does not go through I do not understand why this person, who has every reason to mean us well, should have drawn our attention to it. But if it *does* go through and comes out at the corresponding point on the other side, we should not have more than a hundred feet to descend.'

'A hundred feet!' grumbled Summerlee.

'Well, our rope is still more than a hundred feet long,' I cried. 'Surely we could get down.'

'How about the Indians in the cave?' Summerlee objected.

'There are no Indians in any of the caves above our heads,' said I. 'They are all used as barns and storehouses. Why should we not go up now at once and spy out the land?'

There is a dry bituminous wood upon the plateau – a species of araucaria, according to our botanist – which is always used by the Indians for torches. Each of us picked up a faggot of this, and we made our way up weed-covered steps to the particular cave which was marked in the drawing. It was, as I had said, empty, save for a great number of enormous bats, which flapped round our heads as we advanced into it. As we had no desire to draw the attention of the Indians to our proceedings, we stumbled along in the dark until we had gone round several curves and penetrated a considerable distance into the cavern. Then, at last, we lit our torches. It was a beautiful dry tunnel, with smooth grey walls covered with native symbols, a curved roof which arched over our heads, and white glistening sand beneath our feet. We hurried eagerly along it until, with a deep groan of bitter disappointment, we were brought to a halt. A sheer wall of rock had appeared before us, with no chink through which a mouse could have slipped. There was no escape for us there.

We stood with bitter hearts staring at this unexpected obstacle. It was not the result of any convulsion, as in the case of the ascending tunnel. It was, and had always been, a *cul-de-sac*.

'Never mind, my friends,' said the indomitable Challenger. 'You still have my firm promise of a balloon.'

Summerlee groaned.

'Can we be in the wrong cave?' I suggested.

'No use, young fellah,' said Lord John, with his finger on our chart. 'Seventeen from the right and second from the left. This is the cave sure enough.'

I looked at the mark to which his finger pointed, and I gave a sudden cry of joy.

'I believe I have it! Follow me! Follow me!'

I hurried back along the way we had come, my torch in my hand. 'Here,' said I, pointing to some matches upon the ground, 'is where we lit up.'

'Exactly.'

'Well, it is marked as a forked cave, and in the darkness we passed the fork before the torches were lit. On the right side as we go out we should find the longer arm.'

It was as I had said. We had not gone thirty yards before a great black opening loomed in the wall. We turned into it to find that we were in a much larger passage than before. Along it we hurried in breathless impatience for many hundreds of yards. Then, suddenly, in the black darkness of the arch in front of us we saw a gleam of dark red light. We stared in amazement. A sheet of steady flame seemed to cross the passage and to bar our way. We hastened towards it. No sound, no heat, no movement came from it, but still the great luminous curtain glowed before us, silvering all the cave and turning the sand to powdered jewels, until as we drew closer it discovered a circular edge.

'The moon, by George!' cried Lord John. 'We are through, boys! We are through!'

It was indeed the full moon which shone straight down the aperture which opened upon the cliffs. It was a small rift, not larger than a window, but it was enough for all our purposes. As we craned our necks through it we could see that the descent was not a very difficult one, and that the level ground was no very great way below us. It was no wonder that from below we had not observed the place, as the cliffs curved overhead and an ascent at the spot would have seemed so impossible as to discourage close inspection. We satisfied ourselves that with the help of our rope we could find our way down, and then returned, rejoicing, to our camp to make our preparations for the next evening.

What we did we had to do quickly and secretly, since even at this last hour the Indians might hold us back. Our stores we would leave behind us, save only our guns and cartridges. But Challenger had some unwieldy stuff which he ardently desired to take with him, and one particular package, of which I may not speak, which gave us more labour than any. Slowly the day passed, but when the darkness fell we were ready for our departure. With much labour we got our things up the steps, and then, looking back, took one last long survey of that strange land, soon I fear to be vulgarized, the prey of hunter and prospector, but to each of us a dreamland of glamour and romance, a land where we had dared much, suffered much, and learned much – *our* land, as we shall ever fondly call it. Along upon our left the neighbouring caves each threw out its ruddy cheery firelight into the gloom. From the slope below us rose the voices of the Indians as they laughed and sang. Beyond was the long sweep of the woods, and in the centre, shimmering vaguely through the gloom, was the great lake, the mother of strange monsters. Even as we looked a high whickering cry, the call of some weird animal, rang clear out of the darkness. It was the very voice of Maple White Land bidding us good-bye. We turned and plunged into the cave which led to home.

Two hours later, we, our packages, and all we owned, were at the foot of the cliff. Save for Challenger's luggage we had never a difficulty. Leaving it all where we descended, we started at once for Zambo's camp. In the early morning we approached it, but only to find, to our amazement, not one fire but a dozen upon the plain. The rescue party had arrived. There were twenty Indians from the river, with stakes, ropes, and all that could be useful for bridging the chasm. At least we shall have no difficulty now in carrying our packages, when to-morrow we begin to make our way back to the Amazon.

And so, in humble and thankful mood, I close this account. Our eyes have seen great wonders and our souls are chastened by what we have endured. Each is in his own way a better and deeper man. It may be that when we reach Para we shall stop to refit. If we do, this letter will be a mail ahead. If not, it will reach London on the very day that I do. In either case, my dear Mr. McArdle, I hope very soon to shake you by the hand.

16

A Procession! A Procession!

I SHOULD wish to place upon record here our gratitude to all our friends upon the Amazon for the very great kindness and hospitality which was shown to us upon our return journey. Very particularly would I thank Signor Penalosa and other officials of the Brazilian Government for the special arrangements by which we were helped upon our way, and Signor Pereira of Para, to whose forethought we owe the complete outfit for a decent appearance in the civilized world which we found ready for us at that town. It seemed a poor return for all the courtesy which we encountered that we should deceive our hosts and benefactors, but under the circumstances we had really no alternative, and I hereby tell them that they will only waste their time and their money if they attempt to follow upon our traces, and I am very sure that no one, from the most careful study of them, could come within a thousand miles of our unknown land.

The excitement which had been caused through those parts of South America which we had to traverse was imagined by us to be purely local, and I can assure our friends in England that we had no notion of the uproar which the mere rumour of our experiences had caused through Europe. It was not until *Ivernia* was within five hundred miles of Southampton that the wireless messages from paper after paper and agency after agency, offering huge prices for a short return message as to our actual results, showed us how strained was the attention not only of the scientific world but of the general public. It was agreed among us, however, that no definite statement should be given to the Press until we had met the members of the Zoological Institute, since as delegates it was our clear duty to give our first report to the body from which we had received our commission of investigation. Thus, although we found Southampton full of Pressmen, we absolutely refused to give any information, which had the natural effect of focusing public attention upon the meeting which was advertised for the evening of November 7th. For this gathering, the

Zoological Hall, which had been the scene of the inception of our task, was found to be far too small, and it was only in the Queen's Hall, in Regent Street that accommodation could be found. It is now common knowledge that the promoters might have ventured upon the Albert Hall and still found their space too scanty.

It was for the second evening after our arrival that the great meeting had been fixed. For the first, we had each, no doubt, our own pressing personal affairs to absorb us. Of mine I cannot yet speak. It may be that as it stands farther from me I may think of it, and even speak of it, with less emotion. I have shown the reader in the beginning of this narrative where lay the springs of my action. It is but right, perhaps, that I should carry on the tale and show also the results. And yet the day may come when I would not have it otherwise. At least I have been driven forth to take part in a wondrous adventure, and I cannot but be thankful to the force that drove me.

And now I turn to the last supreme eventful moment of our adventure. As I was racking my brain as to how I should best describe it, my eyes fell on the issue of my own journal for the morning of the 8th of November with the full and excellent account of my friend and fellow-reporter Macdona. What can I do better than transcribe his narrative – head-lines and all? I admit that the paper was exuberant in the matter, out of compliment to its own enterprise in sending a correspondent, but the other great dailies were hardly less full in their account. Thus, then, friend Mac in his report:

THE NEW WORLD
GREAT MEETING AT THE QUEEN'S HALL
SCENES OF UPROAR
EXTRAORDINARY INCIDENT
WHAT WAS IT?
NOCTURNAL RIOT IN REGENT STREET
(Special)

'The much-discussed meeting of the Zoological Institute, convened to hear the report of the Committee of Investigation sent out last year to South America to test the assertions made by Professor Challenger as to the continued existence of prehistoric life upon that continent, was held last night in the greater Queen's Hall, and it is safe to say that it is likely to be a red-letter date in the history of Science, for the proceedings were of so remarkable and sensational a character that no one present is ever likely to forget them.' (Oh, brother scribe Macdona, what a monstrous opening sentence!) 'The tickets were theoretically confined to members and their friends, but the latter is an elastic term, and long before eight o'clock, the hour fixed for the commencement of the proceedings, all parts of the Great Hall were tightly packed. The general public, however, which most unreasonably entertained a grievance at having been excluded, stormed the doors at a quarter to eight, after a prolonged *mêlée* in which several people were injured, including Inspector Scoble of H Division, whose leg was unfortunately broken. After this unwarrantable invasion, which not only filled every passage, but even intruded upon the space set apart for the Press, it is estimated that nearly five thousand people awaited the arrival of the travellers. When they eventually appeared, they took their places in the front of a platform which already contained all the leading scientific men, not only of this country, but of France and of Germany. Sweden was also represented, in the person of Professor Sergius, the famous Zoologist of the University of Upsala. The entrance of the four heroes of the occasion was the signal for a remarkable demonstration of welcome, the whole audience rising and cheering for some minutes. An acute observer might, however, have detected some signs of dissent amid the applause, and gathered that the proceedings were likely to become more lively than harmonious. It may safely be prophesied, however, that no one could have foreseen the extraordinary turn which they were actually to take.

'Of the appearance of the four wanderers little need be said, since their photographs have for some time been appearing in all the papers. They bear few traces of the hardships which they are said to have undergone. Professor Challenger's beard may be more shaggy, Professor Summerlee's features more ascetic, Lord John Roxton's figure gaunt, and all three may be burned to a darker tint than when they left our shores, but each appeared to be in most excellent health. As to our own representative, the well-known athlete and international Rugby football player, E. D. Malone, he looks trained to a hair, and as he surveyed the crowd a smile of good-humoured contentment pervaded his honest but homely face.' (All right, Mac, wait till I get you alone!)

'When quiet had been restored and the audience resumed their seats after the ovation which they had given to the travellers, the chairman, the Duke of Durham, addressed the meeting. "He would not," he said, "stand for more than a moment between that vast assembly and the treat which lay before them. It was not for him to anticipate what Professor Summerlee, who was the spokesman of the committee, had to say to them, but it was common rumour that their expedition had been crowned by extraordinary success." (Applause.) "Apparently the age of romance was not dead, and there was common ground upon which the wildest imaginings of the novelist could meet the actual scientific investigations of the searcher for truth. He would only add, before he sat down, that he rejoiced – and all of them would rejoice – that these gentlemen had returned safe and sound from their difficult and dangerous task, for it cannot be denied that any disaster to such an expedition would have inflicted a well-nigh irreparable loss to the cause of zoological science." (Great applause, in which Professor Challenger was observed to join.)

'Professor Summerlee's rising was the signal for another extraordinary outbreak of enthusiasm, which broke out again at intervals throughout his address. That address will not be given *in extenso* in these columns, for the reason that a full account of the whole adventures of the expedition is being published as a supplement from the pen of our own special correspondent. Some general indications will therefore suffice. Having described the genesis of their journey, and paid a handsome tribute to his friend Professor Challenger, coupled with an apology for the incredulity with which his assertions, now fully vindicated, had been received, he gave the actual course of their journey, carefully withholding such information as would aid the public in any attempt to locate this remarkable plateau. Having described, in general terms, their course from the main river up to the time that they actually reached the base of the cliffs, he enthralled his hearers by his account of the difficulties encountered by the expedition in their repeated attempts to mount them, and finally described how they succeeded in their desperate endeavours, which cost the lives of their two devoted half-breed servants.' (This amazing reading of the affair was the result of Summerlee's endeavours to avoid raising any questionable matter at the meeting.)

'Having conducted his audience in fancy to the summit, and marooned them there by reason of the fall of their bridge, the Professor proceeded to describe both the horrors and the attractions of that remarkable land. Of personal adventures he said little, but laid stress upon the rich harvest reaped by Science in the observations of the wonderful beast, bird, insect and plant life of the plateau. Peculiarly rich in the coleoptera and in the lepidoptera, forty-six new species of the one and ninety-four of the other had been secured in the course of a few weeks. It was, however, in the larger animals, and especially in the larger animals supposed to have been long extinct, that the interest of the public was naturally centred. Of these he was able to give a goodly list, but had little doubt that it would be largely extended when the place had been more thoroughly investigated. He and his companions had seen at least a dozen creatures, most of them at a distance, which corresponded with nothing at present known to Science. These would in time be duly classified and examined. We instanced a snake, the cast skin of which, deep purple in colour, was fifty-one feet in length, and mentioned a white creature, supposed to be mammalian, which gave forth well-marked phosphorescence in the darkness; also a large black moth, the bite of which was supposed by the Indians to be highly poisonous. Setting aside these entirely new forms of life, the plateau was very rich in known prehistoric forms, dating back in some cases to Early Jurassic times. Among these he mentioned the gigantic and grotesque stegosaurus, seen once by Mr. Malone at a drinking-place by the lake, and drawn in the sketchbook of that adventurous American who had first penetrated this unknown world. He described also the iguanodon and the pterodactyl – two of the first of the wonders which they had encountered. He then thrilled the assembly by some account of the terrible carnivorous dinosaurs, which had on more than one occasion pursued members of the party, and which were the most formidable of all the creatures which they had encountered. Thence he passed to the huge and ferocious bird, the phororachus, and to the great elk which still roams upon this upland. It was not, however, until he sketched the mysteries of the central lake that the full interest and enthusiasm of the audience were aroused. One had to pinch oneself to be sure that one was awake as one heard this sane and practical Professor in cold, measured tones describing the monstrous three-eyed fish-lizards and the huge water-snakes which inhabit this enchanted sheet of water. Next he touched upon the Indians, and upon the extraordinary colony of anthropoid apes, which might be looked upon as an advance upon the pithecanthropus of Java, and as coming therefore nearer than any known form to that hypothetical creation, the missing link. Finally he described, amongst some merriment, the ingenious but highly dangerous aeronautic invention of Professor Challenger, and wound up a most remarkable address by an account of the methods by which the committee did at last find their way back to civilization.

'It had been hoped that the proceedings would end there, and that a vote of thanks and congratulation, moved by Professor Sergius, of Upsala University, would be duly seconded and carried; but it was soon evident that the course of events was not destined to flow so smoothly. Symptoms of opposition had been evident from time to time during the evening, and now Dr. James Illingworth, of Edinburgh, rose in the centre of the hall. Dr. Illingworth asked whether an amendment should not be taken before a resolution.

'The Chairman: "Yes, sir, if there must be an amendment."

'Dr. Illingworth: "Your Grace, there must be an amendment."

'The Chairman: "Then let us take it at once."

'Professor Summerlee (springing to his feet): "Might I explain, your Grace, that this man is my personal enemy ever since our controversy in the 'Quarterly Journal of Science' as to the true nature of Bathybius?"

'The Chairman: "I fear I cannot go into personal matters. Proceed."

'Dr. Illingworth was imperfectly heard in part of his remarks on account of the strenuous opposition of the friends of the explorers.

Some attempts were also made to pull him down. Being a man of enormous physique, however, and possessed of a very powerful voice, he dominated the tumult and succeeded in finishing his speech. It was clear, from the moment of his rising, that he had a number of friends and sympathizers in the hall, though they formed a minority in the audience. The attitude of the greater part of the public might be described as one of attentive neutrality.

'Dr. Illingworth began his remarks by expressing his high appreciation of the scientific work both by Professor Challenger and of Professor Summerlee. He much regretted that any personal bias should have been read into his remarks, which were entirely dictated by his desire for scientific truth. His position, in fact, was substantially the same as that taken up by Professor Summerlee at the last meeting. At that last meeting Professor Challenger had made certain assertions which had been queried by his colleague. Now this colleague came forward himself with the same assertions and expected them to remain unquestioned. Was this reasonable? ("Yes", "No", and prolonged interruption, during which Professor Challenger was heard from the Press box to ask leave from the Chairman to put Dr. Illingworth into the street.) A year ago one man said certain things. Now four men said other and more startling ones. Was this to constitute a final proof where the matters in question were of the most revolutionary and incredible character? There had been recent examples of travellers arriving from the unknown with certain tales which had been too readily accepted. Was the London Zoological Institute to place itself in this position? He admitted that the members of the committee were men of character. But human nature was very complex. Even Professors might be misled by the desire for notoriety. Like moths, we all love best to flutter in the light. Heavy-game shots liked to be in a position to cap the tales of their rivals, and journalists were not averse from sensational *coups*, even when imagination had to aid fact in the process. Each member of the committee had his own motive for making the most of his results. ("Shame! shame!") He had no desire to be offensive. ("You are!" and interruption.) The corroboration of these wondrous tales was really of the most slender description. What did it amount to? Some photographs. Was it possible that in this age of ingenious manipulation photographs could be accepted as evidence? What more? We have a story of a flight and a descent by ropes which precluded the production of larger specimens. It was ingenious, but not convincing. It was understood that Lord John Roxton claimed to have the skull of a phororachus. He could only say that he would like to see that skull.

'Lord John Roxton: "Is this fellow calling me a liar?" (Uproar.)

'The Chairman: "Order! order! Dr. Illingworth, I must direct you to bring your remarks to a conclusion and to move your amendment."

'Dr. Illingworth: "Your Grace, I have more to say, but I bow to your ruling. I move, then, that, while Professor Summerlee be thanked for his interesting address, the whole matter shall be regarded as '*non-proven*', and shall be referred back to a larger, and possibly more reliable Committee of Investigation."

'It is difficult to describe the confusion caused by this amendment. A large section of the audience expressed their indignation at such a slur upon the travellers by noisy shouts of dissent and cries of "Don't put it!" "Withdraw!" "Turn him out!" On the other hand, the malcontents – and it cannot be denied that they were fairly numerous – cheered for the amendment, with cries of "Order!" "Chair!" and "Fair play!" A scuffle broke out in the back benches, and blows were freely exchanged among the medical students who crowded that part of the hall. It was only the moderating influence of the presence of large numbers of ladies which prevented an absolute riot. Suddenly, however, there was a pause, a hush, and then complete silence. Professor Challenger was on his feet. His appearance and manner are peculiarly arresting, and as he raised his hand for order the whole audience settled down expectantly to give him a hearing.

' "It will be within the recollection of many present," said Professor Challenger, "that similar foolish and unmannerly scenes marked the last meeting at which I have been able to address them. On that occasion Professor Summerlee was the chief offender, and though he is now chastened and contrite, the matter could not be entirely forgotten. I have heard to-night similar, but even more offensive, sentiments from the person who has just sat down, and though it is a conscious effort of self-effacement to come down to that person's mental level, I will endeavour to do so, in order to allay any reasonable doubt which could possibly exist in the minds of anyone." (Laughter and interruption.) "I need not remind this audience that, though Professor Summerlee, as the head of the Committee of Investigation, has been put up to speak to-night, still it is I who am the real prime mover in this business, and that it is mainly to me that any successful result must be ascribed. I have safely conducted these three gentlemen to the spot mentioned, and I have, as you have heard, convinced them of the accuracy of my previous account. We had hoped that we should find upon our return that no one was so dense as to dispute our joint conclusions. Warned, however, by my previous experience, I have not come without such proofs as may convince a reasonable man. As explained by Professor Summerlee, our cameras have been tampered with by the ape-men when they ransacked our camp, and most of our negatives ruined." (Jeers, laughter, and "Tell us another!" from the back.) "I have mentioned the ape-men, and I cannot forbear from saying that some of the sounds which now meet my ears bring back most vividly to my recollection my experiences with those interesting creatures." (Laughter.) "In spite of the destruction of so many invaluable negatives, there still remains in our collection a certain number of corroborative photographs showing the conditions of life upon the plateau. Did they accuse them of having forged these photographs?" (A voice, "Yes," and considerable interruption which ended in several men being put out of the hall.) "The negatives were open to the inspection of experts. But what other evidence had they? Under the conditions of their escape it was naturally impossible to bring a large amount of baggage, but they had rescued Professor Summerlee's collections of butterflies and beetles, containing many new species. Was this not evidence?" (Several voices, "No.") "Who said no?"

'Dr. Illingworth (rising): "Our point is that such a collection might have been made in other places than a prehistoric plateau." (Applause.)

'Professor Challenger: "No doubt, sir, we have to bow to your scientific authority, although I must admit that the name is unfamiliar. Passing, then, both the photographs and the entomological collection, I come to the varied and accurate information which we bring with us upon points which have never before been elucidated. For example, upon the domestic habits of the pterodactyl – (A voice: 'Bosh,' and uproar) – I say, that upon the domestic habits of the pterodactyl we can throw a flood of light. I can exhibit to you from my portfolio a picture of that creature taken from life which would convince you –"

'Dr. Illingworth: "No picture could convince us of anything."

'Professor Challenger: "You would require to see the thing itself?"

'Dr. Illingworth: "Undoubtedly."

'Professor Challenger: "And you would accept that?"

'Dr. Illingworth (laughing): "Beyond a doubt."

'It was at this point that the sensation of the evening arose – a sensation so dramatic that it can never have been paralleled in the history of scientific gatherings. Professor Challenger raised his hand in the air as a signal, and at once our colleague, Mr. E. D. Malone, was observed to rise and to make his way to the back of the platform. An instant later he re-appeared in company of a gigantic negro, the two of them bearing between them a large square packing-case. It was evidently of great weight, and was slowly carried forward and placed in front of the Professor's chair. All sound had hushed in the audience and everyone was absorbed in the spectacle before them. Professor Challenger drew off the top of the case, which formed a sliding lid. Peering down into the box he snapped his fingers several times and was heard from the Press seat to say, "Come, then, pretty, pretty!" in a coaxing voice. An instant later, with a scratching, rattling sound, a most horrible and loathsome creature appeared from below and perched itself upon the side of the case. Even the unexpected fall of the Duke of Durham into the orchestra, which occurred at this moment, could not distract the petrified attention of the vast audience. The face of the creature was like the wildest gargoyle that the imagination of a mad mediæval builder could have conceived. It was malicious, horrible, with two small red eyes as bright as points of burning coal. Its long savage mouth, which was held half-open, was full of a double row of shark-like teeth. Its shoulders were humped, and round them were draped what appeared to be a faded grey shawl. It was the devil of our childhood in person. There was a turmoil in the audience – someone screamed, two ladies in the front row fell senseless from their chairs, and there was a general movement upon the platform to follow their chairman into the orchestra. For a moment there was danger of a general panic. Professor Challenger threw up his hands to still the commotion, but the movement alarmed the creature beside him. Its strange shawl suddenly unfurled, spread, and fluttered as a pair of leathery wings. Its owner grabbed at its legs, but too late to hold it. It had sprung from the perch and was circling slowly round Queen's Hall with a dry, leathery flapping of its ten-foot wings, while a putrid and insidious odour pervaded the room. The cries of the people in the galleries, who were alarmed at the near approach of those glowing eyes and that murderous beak, excited the creature to a frenzy. Faster and faster it flew, beating against the walls and chandeliers in a blind frenzy of alarm. "The window! For heaven's sake shut that window!" roared the Professor from the platform, dancing, and wringing his hands in an agony of apprehension. Alas, his warning was too late! In a moment the creature, beating and bumping along the wall like a huge moth within a gas shade, came upon the opening, squeezed its hideous bulk through it, and was gone. Professor Challenger fell back into his chair with his face buried in his hands, while the audience gave one long, deep sigh of relief as they realized that the incident was over.

'Then – oh! how shall one describe what took place then – when the full exuberance of the majority and the full reaction of the minority united to make one great wave of enthusiasm, which rolled from the back of the hall, gathering volume as it came, swept over the orchestra, submerged the platform, and carried the four heroes away upon its crest?' (Good for you, Mac.) 'If the audience had done less than justice, surely it made ample amends. Everyone was on his feet. Everyone was moving, shouting, gesticulating. A dense crowd of cheering men were round the four travellers. "Up with them! up with them!" cried a hundred voices. In a moment four figures shot up above the crowd. In vain they strove to break loose. They were held in their lofty places of honour. It would have been hard to let them down if it had been wished, so dense was the crowd around them. "Regent Street! Regent Street!" sounded the voices. There was a swirl in the packed multitude, and a slow current bearing the four upon their shoulders, made for the door. Out in the street the scene was extraordinary. An assemblage of not less than a hundred thousand people was waiting. The close-packed throng extended from the other side of the Langham Hotel to Oxford Circus. A roar of acclamation greeted the four adventurers as they appeared high above the heads of the people, under the vivid electric lamps outside the hall. "A procession! A procession!" was the cry. In a dense phalanx, blocking the streets from side to side, the crowd set forth, taking the route of Regent Street, Pall Mall, St. James's Street, and Piccadilly. The whole central traffic of London was held up, and many collisions were reported between the demonstrators upon the one side and the police and taxi-cabmen upon the other. Finally, it was not until after midnight that the four travellers were released at the entrance to Lord John Roxton's chambers in the Albany, and that the exuberant crowd, having sung: "They are Jolly Good Fellows" in chorus, concluded their programme with "God Save the King". So ended one of the most remarkable evenings that London had seen for a considerable time.'

So far my friend Macdona; and it may be taken as a fairly accurate, if florid, account of the proceedings. As to the main incident, it was a bewildering surprise to the audience, but not, I need hardly say, to us. The reader will remember how I met Lord John Roxton upon the very occasion when, in his protective crinoline, he had gone to bring the 'Devil's chick' as he called it, for Professor Challenger. I have hinted also at the trouble which the Professor's baggage gave us when we left the plateau, and had I described our voyage I might have said a good deal of the worry we had to coax with putrid fish the appetite of our filthy companion. If I have not said much about it before, it was, of course, that the Professor's earnest desire was that no possible rumour of the unanswerable argument which we carried should be allowed to leak out until the moment came when his enemies were to be confuted.

One word as to the fate of the London pterodactyl. Nothing can be said to be certain upon this point. There is the evidence of two frightened women that it perched upon the roof of the Queen's Hall and remained there like a diabolical statue for some hours. The next day it came out in the evening papers that Private Miles, of the Coldstream Guards, on duty outside Marlborough House, had deserted his post without leave, and was therefore court-martialled. Private Miles' account, that he dropped his rifle and took to his heels down the Mall because on looking up he had suddenly seen the devil between him and the moon, was not accepted by the Court, and yet it may have a direct bearing upon the point at issue. The only other evidence which I can adduce is from the log of the S.S. *Friesland*, a Dutch-American liner, which asserts that at nine next morning, Start Point being at the time ten miles upon their starboard quarter, they were passed by something between a flying goat and a monstrous bat, which was heading at a prodigious pace south and west. If its homing instinct led it upon the right line, there can be no doubt that somewhere out in the wastes of the Atlantic the last European pterodactyl found its end.

And Gladys – oh, my Gladys! – Gladys of the mystic lake, now to be re-named the Central, for never shall she have immortality through me. Did I not always see some hard fibre in her nature? Did I not, even at the time when I was proud to obey her behest, feel that it was surely a poor love which could drive a lover to his death or the danger of it? Did I not, in my truest thoughts, always recurring and always dismissed, see past the beauty of the face, and, peering into the soul, discern the twin shadows of selfishness and of fickleness glooming at the back of it? Did she love the heroic and the spectacular for its own noble sake, or was it for the glory which might, without effort or sacrifice, be reflected upon herself? Or are these thoughts the vain wisdom which comes after the event? It was the shock of my life. For a moment it had turned me to a cynic. But already, as I write, a week has passed, and we have had our momentous interview with Lord John Roxton and – well, perhaps things might be worse.

Let me tell it in a few words. No letter or telegram had come to me at Southampton, and I reached the little villa at Streatham about ten o'clock that night in a fever of alarm. Was she dead or alive? Where were all my nightly dreams of the open arms, the smiling face, the words of praise for her man who had risked his life to humour her whim? Already I was down from the high peaks and standing flat-footed upon earth. Yet some good reasons given might still lift me to the clouds once more. I rushed down the garden path, hammered at the door, heard the voice of Gladys within, pushed past the staring maid, and strode into the sitting-room. She was seated in a low settee under the shaded standard lamp by the piano. In three steps I was across the room and had both her hands in mine.

'Gladys!' I cried, 'Gladys!'

She looked up with amazement in her face. She was altered in some subtle way. The expression of her eyes, the hard upward stare, the set of the lips, was new to me. She drew back her hands.

'What do you mean?' she said.

'Gladys!' I cried. 'What is the matter? You are my Gladys, are you not – little Gladys Hungerton?'

'No,' said she, 'I am Gladys Potts. Let me introduce you to my husband.'

How absurd life is! I found myself mechanically bowing and shaking hands with a little ginger-haired man who was coiled up in the deep arm-chair which had once been sacred to my own use. We bobbed and grinned in front of each other.

'Father lets us stay here. We are getting our house ready,' said Gladys.

'Oh, yes,' said I.

'You didn't get my letter at Para, then?'

'No, I got no letter.'

'Oh, what a pity! It would have made all clear.'

'It *is* quite clear,' said I.

'I've told William all about you,' said she. 'We have no secrets. I am so sorry about it. But it couldn't have been so very deep, could it, if you could go off to the other end of the world and leave me here alone. You're not crabby, are you?'

'No, no, not at all. I think I'll go.'

'Have some refreshment,' said the little man, and he added, in a confidential way, 'It's always like this, ain't it? And must be unless you had polygamy, only the other way round; you understand.' He laughed like an idiot, while I made for the door.

I was through it, when a sudden fantastic impulse came upon me, and I went back to my successful rival, who looked nervously at the electric push.

'Will you answer a question?' I asked.

'Well, within reason,' said he.

'How did you do it? Have you searched for hidden treasure, or discovered a pole, or done time on a pirate, or flown the channel, or what? Where is the glamour of romance? How did you get it?'

He stared at me with a hopeless expression upon his vacuous, good-natured, scrubby little face.

'Don't you think all this is a little too personal?' he said.

'Well, just one question,' I cried. 'What are you? What is your profession?'

'I am a solicitor's clerk,' said he. 'Second man at Johnson and Merivale's, 41, Chancery Lane.'

'Good-night!' said I, and vanished, like all disconsolate and broken-hearted heroes, into the darkness, with grief and rage and laughter all simmering within me like a boiling pot.

One more little scene, and I have done. Last night we all supped at Lord John Roxton's rooms, and sitting together afterwards we smoked in good comradeship and talked our adventures over. It was strange under these altered surroundings to see the old, well-known faces and figures. There was Challenger, with his smile of condescension, his drooping eyelids, his intolerant eyes, his aggressive beard, his huge chest, swelling and puffing as he laid down the law to Summerlee. And Summerlee, too, there he was with his short briar between his thin moustache and his grey goat's-beard, his worn face protruded in eager debate as he queried all Challenger's propositions. Finally, there was our host, with his rugged, eagle face, and his cold, blue, glacier eyes with always a shimmer of devilment and of humour down in the depths of them. Such is the last picture of them that I have carried away. It was after supper, in his own sanctum – the room of the pink radiance and the innumerable trophies – that Lord John Roxton had something to say to us. From a cupboard he had brought an old cigar-box, and this he laid before him on the table.

'There's one thing,' said he, 'that maybe I should have spoken about before this, but I wanted to know a little more clearly where I was. No use to raise hopes and let them down again. But it's facts, not hopes, with us now. You may remember that day we found the pterodactyl rookery in the swamp – what? Well, somethin' in the lie of the land took my notice. Perhaps it has escaped you, so I will tell you. It was a volcanic vent full of blue clay.'

The Professors nodded.

'Well, now, in the whole world I've only had to do with one place that was a volcanic vent of blue clay. That was the great De Beers Diamond Mine of Kimberley – what? So you see I got diamonds into my head. I rigged up a contraption to hold off those stinking beasts, and I spent a happy day there with a spud. This is what I got.'

He opened his cigar-box, and tilting it over he poured about twenty or thirty rough stones, varying from the size of beans to that of chestnuts, on the table.

'Perhaps you think I should have told you then. Well, so I should, only I know there are a lot of traps for the unwary, and that stones may be of any size and yet of little value where colour and consistency are clean off. Therefore, I brought them back, and on the first day at home I took one round to Spink's and asked him to have it roughly cut and valued.'

He took a pill-box from his pocket, and spilled out of it a beautiful glittering diamond, one of the finest stones that I have ever seen.

'There's the result,' said he. 'He prices the lot at a minimum of two hundred thousand pounds. Of course it is fair shares between us. I won't hear of anythin' else. Well, Challenger, what will you do with your fifty thousand?'

'If you really persist in your generous view,' said the Professor, 'I should found a private museum, which has long been one of my dreams.'

'And you, Summerlee?'

'I would retire from teaching, and so find time for my final classification of the chalk fossils.'

'I'll use my own,' said Lord John Roxton, 'in fitting a well-formed expedition and having another look at the dear old plateau. As to you, young fellah, you, of course, will spend yours in gettin' married.'

'Not just yet,' said I, with a rueful smile. 'I think, if you will have me, that I would rather go with you.'

Lord Roxton said nothing, but a brown hand was stretched out to me across the table.

Beau Geste

Part 1

MAJOR HENRI DE BEAUJOLAIS' STORY

1

Of the Strange Events at Zinderneuf

Told by Major Henri de Beaujolais of the Spahis to George Lawrence, Esq., C.M.G., of the Nigerian Civil Service

'Tout ce que je raconte, je l'ai vu, et si j'ai pu me tromper en le voyant, bien certainement je ne vous trompe pas en vous le disant.'
'The place was silent and aware.'

MR. GEORGE LAWRENCE, C.M.G., First Class District Officer of His Majesty's Civil Service, sat at the door of his tent and viewed the African desert scene with the eye of extreme disfavour. There was beauty neither in the landscape nor in the eye of the beholder.

The landscape consisted of sand, stone, *kerengia* burr-grass, *tafasa* underbrush, yellow, long-stalked with long thin beanpods; the whole varied by clumps of the coarse and hideous *tumpafia* plant.

The eye was jaundiced, thanks to the heat and foul dust of Bornu, to malaria, dysentery, inferior food, poisonous water, and rapid continuous marching in appalling heat.

Weak and ill in body, Lawrence was worried and anxious in mind, the one reacting on the other.

In the first place, there was the old standing trouble about the Shuwa Patrol; in the second, the truculent Chiboks were waxing insolent again, and their young men were regarding not the words of their elders concerning Sir Garnet Wolseley, and what happened, long, long ago, after the battle of Chibok Hill. Thirdly, the price of grain had risen to six shillings a *saa*, and famine threatened; fourthly, the Shehu and Shuwa sheiks were quarrelling again; and fifthly, there was a very bad smallpox ju-ju abroad in the land (a secret society whose 'secret' was to offer His Majesty's liege subjects the choice between being infected with smallpox, or paying heavy blackmail to the society). Lastly, there was acrimonious correspondence with the All-Wise Ones (of the Secretariat in 'Aiki Square' at Zungeru), who, as usual, knew better than the man on the spot, and bade him do either the impossible or the disastrous.

And across all the *Harmattan* was blowing hard, that terrible wind that carries the Saharan dust a hundred miles to sea, not so much as a sand-storm, but as a mist or fog of dust as fine as flour, filling the eyes, the lungs, the pores of the skin, the nose and throat; getting into the locks of rifles, the works of watches and cameras, defiling water, food and everything else; rendering life a burden and a curse.

The fact, moreover, that thirty days' weary travel over burning desert, across oceans of loose wind-blown sand and prairies of burnt grass, through breast-high swamps, and across unbridged boatless rivers, lay between him and Kano, added nothing to his satisfaction. For, in spite of all, satisfaction there was, inasmuch as Kano was rail-head, and the beginning of the first stage of the journey Home. That but another month lay between him and 'leave out of Africa,' kept George Lawrence on his feet.

From that wonderful and romantic Red City, Kano, sister of Timbuktu, the train would take him, after a three days' dusty journey, to the rubbish-heap called Lagos, on the Bight of Benin of the wicked African Coast. There he would embark on the good ship *Appam*, greet her commander, Captain Harrison, and sink into a deck-chair with that glorious sigh of relief, known in its perfection only to those weary ones who turn their backs upon the Outposts and set their faces towards Home.

Meantime, for George Lawrence – disappointment, worry, frustration, anxiety, heat, sand-flies, mosquitoes, dust, fatigue, fever, dysentery, malarial ulcers, and that great depression which comes of monotony indescribable, weariness unutterable, and loneliness unspeakable.

And the greatest of these is loneliness.

2

But, in due course, George Lawrence reached Kano and the Nassarawa Gate in the East Wall, which leads to the European segregation, there to wait for a couple of days for the bi-weekly train to Lagos. These days he whiled away in strolling about the wonderful Haussa city, visiting the market-place, exploring its seven square miles of streets of mud houses, with their ant-proof *dôm*-palm beams; watching the ebb and flow of varied black and brown humanity at the thirteen great gates in its mighty earthen ramparts; politely returning the cheery and respectful '*Sanu! Sanu!*' greetings of the Haussas who passed this specimen of the great Bature race, the wonderful white men.

Idly he compared the value of the caravans of salt or of ground-nuts with that of the old slave-caravans which the white man thinks he has recently suppressed; and casually passed the time of day with Touareg camel-drivers, who invited him to hire or buy their piebald, brindled, or white camels, and, occasionally, a rare and valuable beast of the tawny reddish buff variety, so prized for speed and endurance . . .

On the platform of Kano Station (imagine a platform and station at Kano, ancient, mysterious, gigantic, emporium of Central Africa, with its great eleven-mile wall, and its hundred thousand native inhabitants and its twenty white men; Kano, eight hundred miles from the sea, near the border of Northern Nigeria which marches with the French *Territoire Militaire* of Silent Sahara; Kano, whence start the caravan routes to Lake Tchad on the north-east, and Timbuktu on the north-west) – on this incredible platform, George Lawrence was stirrred from his weary apathy by a pleasant surprise in the form of his old friend, Major Henri de Beaujolais of the Spahis, now some kind of special staff-officer in the French Soudan.

With de Beaujolais, Lawrence had been at Ainger's House at Eton; and the two occasionally met, as thus, on the Northern Nigerian Railway; on the ships of Messrs. Elder, Dempster; at Lord's; at Longchamps; at Auteuil; and, once or twice, at the house of their mutual admired friend, Lady Brandon, at Brandon Abbas in Devonshire.

For de Beaujolais, Lawrence had a great respect and liking, as a French soldier of the finest type, keen as mustard, hard as nails, a thorough sportsman, and a gentleman according to the exacting English standard. Frequently he paid him the remarkable English compliment, 'One would hardly take you for a Frenchman, Jolly, you might almost be English,' a bouquet which de Beaujolais received with less concern by reason of the fact that his mother had been a Devonshire Cary.

Although the Spahi officer was heavily bearded, arrayed in what Lawrence considered hopelessly ill-fitting khaki, and partially extinguished by a villainous high-domed white helmet (and looked as truly French as his friend looked truly English), he, however, did not throw himself with a bowl of joy upon the bosom of his *cher Georges*, fling his arms about his neck, kiss him upon both cheeks, nor address him as his little cabbage. Rather as his old bean, in fact.

A strong hand-grip, 'Well, George!' and, 'Hallo! Jolly, old son,' sufficed; but de Beaujolais' charming smile and Lawrence's beaming grin showed their mutual delight.

And when the two men were stretched opposite to each other on the long couches of their roomy compartment, and had exchanged plans for spending their leave – yatching, golf, and the Moors, on the one hand; and Paris boulevards, race courses, and Monte Carlo, on the other – Lawrence found that he need talk no more, for his friend was bursting and bubbling over with a story, an unfathomable intriguing mystery, which he must tell or die.

As the train steamed on from Kano Station and its marvellous medley of Arabs, Haussas, Yorubas, Kroos, Egbas, Beri-Beris, Fulanis, and assorted Nigerians from *sarkin*, *sheikh*, *shehu*, and *matlaki*, to peasant, camel-man, agriculturist, herdsman, shopkeeper, clerk, soldier, tin-mine worker, and nomad, with their women and *piccins*, the Frenchman began his tale.

Through Zaria, Minna Junction, and Zungeru, across the Jebba Bridge over the Niger, through Ilorin, Oshogbo, and mighty Ibadan to vast Abeokuta, with brief intervals during which Lawrence frankly snored, de Beaujolais told his tale. But at Abeokuta, George Lawrence received the surprise of his life and the tale suddenly became of the most vital interest to him, and from there to Lagos he was all ears.

And as the *Appam* steamed through the sparkling Atlantic, the Frenchman still told his tale – threshed at its mystery, dissected and discussed it, speculated upon it, and returned to it at the end of every digression. Nor ever could George Lawrence have enough – since it indirectly concerned the woman whom he had always loved.

When the two parted in London, Lawrence took it up and continued it himself, until he, in his turn, brought it back to his friend and told him its beginning and end.

3

And the story, which Major Henri de Beaujolais found so intriguing, he told to George Lawrence as follows:-

'I tell you, my dear George, that it is the most extraordinary and inexplicable thing that ever happened. I shall think of nothing else until I have solved the mystery, and you must help me. You, with your trained official mind, detached and calm; your *phlegme Britannique*.

Yes – you shall be my Sherlock Holmes, and I will be your wonder-stricken little Watson. Figure me then as the little Watson; address me as "My dear Watson."

Having heard my tale – and I warn you, you will hear little else for the next two or three weeks – you must unhesitatingly make a pronouncement. Something prompt and precise, my dear friend, *hein?*'

'Quite,' replied Lawrence. 'But suppose you give me the facts first?'

'It was like this, my dear Holmes . . . As you are aware, I am literally buried alive in my present job at Tokotu. But yes, with a burial-alive such as you of the Nigerian Civil Service have no faintest possible conception, in the uttermost Back of Beyond. (You, with your Maiduguri Polo Club! Pouf!) Yes, interred living, in the southernmost outpost of the *Territoire Militaire* of the Sahara, a spot compared with which the very loneliest and vilest Algerian border-hole would seem like Sidi-bel-Abbès itself, Sidi-bel-Abbès like Algiers, Algiers like Paris in Africa, and Paris like God's Own Paradise in Heaven.

Seconded from my beloved regiment, far from a boulevard, a café, a club, far, indeed, from everything that makes life supportable to an intelligent man, am I entombed . . .'

'I've had some,' interrupted Lawrence unsympathetically. 'Get on with the Dark Mystery.'

'I see the sun rise and set; I see the sky above, and the desert below; I see my handful of *cafard*-stricken men in my mud fort, black Senegalese, and white mule-mounted infantry whom I train, poor devils; and what else do I see? What else from year's end to year's end? . . .'

'I shall weep in a minute,' murmured Lawrence. 'What about the Dark Mystery?'

'What do I see?' continued the Major, ignoring the unworthy remark. 'A vulture. A jackal. A lizard. If I am lucky and God is good, a slave-caravan from Lake Tchad. A band of veiled Touaregs led by a Targui bandit-chief, thirsting for the blood of the hated white *Roumi* – and I bless them even as I open fire or lead the attack of my mule-cavalry-playing-at-Spahis . . .'

'The Dark Mystery must have been a perfect godsend, my dear Jolly,' smiled Lawrence, as he extracted his cherootcase and extended it to his eloquent friend, lying facing him on the opposite couch-seat of the uncomfortable carriage of the Nigerian Railway. 'What *was* it?'

'A godsend, indeed,' replied the Frenchman. 'Sent of God, surely to save my reason and my life. But I doubt if the price were not a little high, even for that! The deaths of so many brave men . . . And one of those deaths a dastardly cold-blooded murder! The vile assassination of a gallant *sous-officier*. . . And by one of his own men. In the very hour of glorious victory . . . *One of his own men* – I am certain of it. But why? *Why?* I ask myself night and day. And now I ask you, my friend . . . The motive, I ask? . . . But you shall hear all – and instantly solve the problem, my dear Holmes, eh? . . .

Have you heard of our little post of Zinderneuf (far, far north of Zinder which is in the Aïr country), north of your Nigeria? No? Well you hear of it now, and it is where this incomprehensible tragedy took place.

Behold me then, one devilish hot morning, yawning in my pyjamas over a *gamelle* of coffee, in my quarters, while from the *caserne* of my *légionnaires* come the cries of "*Au jus*," "*Au jus*," as one carries round the jug of coffee from bed to bed, and arouses the sleepers to another day in Hell. And then as I wearily light a wretched cigarette of our beastly *caporal*, there comes running my orderly, babbling I know not what of a dying Arab *goum* – they are always dying of fatigue these fellows, if they have hurried a few miles – on a dying camel, who cries at the gate that he is from Zinderneuf, and that there is siege and massacre, battle, murder, and sudden death. All slain and expecting to be killed. All dead and the buglers blowing the Regimental Call, the rally, the charge; making the devil of a row, and so forth . . .

"*And is it the dying camel that cries all this?*" I ask, even as I leap into my belts and boots, and rush to the door and shout, "*Aux armes! Aux armes!*" to my splendid fellows and wish to God they were my Spahis.

"*But no, Monsieur le Majeur,*" declares the orderly, "*it is the dying goum, dying of fatigue on the dying camel.*"

"*Then bid him not die, on pain of death, till I have questioned him,*" I reply as I load my revolver. "*And tell the Sergeant-Major that an advance-party of the Foreign Legion on camels marches en tenue de campagne d'Afrique in nine minutes from when I shouted 'Aux armes.' The rest of them on mules.*" You know the sort of thing, my friend. You have turned out your guard of Haussas of the West African Frontier Force nearly as quickly and smartly at times, no doubt.'

'Oh, nearly, nearly, perhaps. *Toujours la politesse,*' murmured Lawrence.

'As we rode out of the gate of my fort, I gathered from the still-dying *goum*, on the still-dying camel, that a couple of days before, a large force of Touaregs had been sighted from the look-out platform of Zinderneuf fort. Promptly the wise *sous-officier*, in charge and command since the lamented death of Captain Renouf, had turned the *goum* loose on his fast *mehari* camel, with strict orders not to be caught by the Touaregs if they invested the fort, but to clear out and trek with all speed for help – as it appeared to be a case of too heavy odds. If the Touaregs were only playful, and passed the fort by, after a little sporting pot-shotting, he was to follow them, I suppose, see them safe off the premises for a day or two, and discover what they were out for.

Well, away went the *goum*, stood afar off on a sand-hill, saw the Touaregs skirmish up to the oasis, park their camels among the palms, and seriously set about investing the place. He thought it was time for him to go when they had surrounded the fort, were lining the sand-hills, making nice little trenches in the sand, climbing the palm trees, and pouring in a very heavy fire. He estimated them at ten thousand rifles, so I feared that there must be at least five hundred of the cruel fiends. Anyhow, round wheeled Monsieur Goum and rode hell-for-leather, night and day, for help . . .

Like *How we brought the good news from Aix to Ghent*, and *Paul Revere's Ride* and all. I christened the *goum*, Paul Revere, straight away, when I heard his tale, and promised him all sorts of good things, including a good hiding if I found he had not exceeded the speed limit all the way from Aix to Ghent. Certainly his "Roland" looked as if its radiator had boiled all right. And, *Nom d'un nom d'nom de bon Dieu de sort!* but I made a forced march of it, my friend – and when we of the Nineteenth African Division do *that*, even on mules and camels, you can hardly see us go.'

'Oh, come now! I am sure your progress is perceptible,' said Lawrence politely. 'Specially on camels, and all that . . . You're too modest,' he added.

'I mean you can hardly see us go for dust and small stones, by reason of our swiftness . . . Any more than you can see a bullet, witty one,' rebuked de Beaujolais.

'Oh, quite, quite,' murmured the Englishman.

'Anyhow, I was away with the advance-party on swift *mehari* camels, a mule-squadron was following, and a company of Senegalese would do fifty kilometres a day on foot till they reached Zinderneuf. Yes, and, in what I flatter myself is the unbreakable record time between Tokotu and Zinderneuf, we arrived – and, riding far on in advance of my men, I listened for the sound of firing or of bugle-calls.

I heard no sound whatever, and suddenly topping a ridge I came in sight of the fort – there below me on the desert plain, near the tiny oasis.

There was no fighting, no sign of Touaregs, no trace of battle or siege. No blackened ruins strewn with mutilated corpses here. The Tri-couleur flew merrily from the flag-staff, and the fort looked absolutely normal – a square grey block of high, thick mud walls, flat castellated roof, flanking towers, and lofty look-out platform. All was well! The honour of the Flag of France had been well defended. I waved my *képi* above my head and shouted aloud in my glee.

Perhaps I began composing my Report then and there, doing modest justice to the readiness, promptitude, and dispatch of my little force, which had maintained the glorious traditions of the Nineteenth African Division; giving due praise to the *sous-officier* commanding Zinderneuf, and not forgetting Paul Revere and his Roland . . . Meanwhile, they should know that relief was at hand, and that, be the Touaregs near or be they far, the danger was over and the Flag safe. I, Henri de Beaujolais of the Spahis, had brought relief. I fired my revolver half a dozen times in the air. And then I was aware of a small but remarkable fact. The high look-out platform at the top of its long ladder was empty.

Strange! Very strange! Incredibly strange, at the very moment when great marauding bands of Touaregs were known to be about – and one of them had only just been beaten off, and might attack again at any moment. I must offer the *sous-officier* my congratulations upon the excellence of his look-out, as soon as I had embraced and commended him! New as he might be to independent command, this should never have happened. One would have thought he could as soon have forgotten his boots as his sentry on the look-out platform.

A pretty state of affairs, *bon Dieu*, in time of actual war! Here was I approaching the fort in broad light of day, firing my revolver – and not the slightest notice taken! I might have been the entire Touareg nation or the whole German army . . .

No, there must be something wrong, in spite of the peaceful look of things and the safety of the Flag – and I pulled out my field-glasses to see if they would reveal anything missed by the naked eye.

As I halted and waited for my camel to steady himself, that I might bring the glasses to bear, I wondered if it were possible that this was an ambush.

Could the Arabs have captured the place, put the defenders to the sword, put on their uniforms, cleaned up the mess, closed the gates, left the Flag flying, and now be waiting for a relieving force to ride, in trustful innocence and close formation, up to the muzzles of their rifles? Possible – but quite unlike brother Touareg! You know what *his* way is, when he has rushed a post or broken a square. A dirty fighter, if ever there was one! And as I focussed my glasses on the walls, I rejected the idea.

Moreover, yes, there were the good European faces of the men at the embrasures, bronzed and bearded, but unmistakably not Arab . . .

And yet, that again was strange. At every embrasure of the breast-high parapet round the flat roof stood a soldier, staring out across the desert, and most of them staring along their levelled rifles too; some of them straight at me. Why? There was no enemy about. Why were they not sleeping the sleep of tired victors, below on their cots in the *caserne*, while double sentries watched from the high look-out platform? Why no man up there, and yet a man at every embrasure that I could see from where I sat on my camel, a thousand metres distant?

And why did no man move; no man turn to call out to a sergeant that a French officer approached; no man walk to the door leading down from the roof, to inform the Commandant of the fort?

Anyhow, the little force had been extraordinarily lucky; or the shooting of the Arabs extraordinarily bad, that they should still be numerous enough to man the walls in that fashion – "all present and correct," as you say in your army – and able to stand to arms thus, after two or three days of it, more or less.

As I lowered my glasses and urged my camel forward, I came to the conclusion that I was expected, and that the officer in charge was indulging in a little natural and excusable *fantaisie*, showing off – what you call "putting on the dog," eh?

He was going to let me find everything as the Arabs found it when they made their foolish attack – every man at his post and everything *klim-bim*. Yes, that must be it . . . Ah, it was! Even as I watched, a couple of shots were fired from the wall. They had seen me . . . The fellow, in his joy, was almost shooting *at* me, in fact!

And yet – nobody on the look-out platform! How I would prick that good fellow's little bubble of swank! And I smiled to myself as I rode under the trees of the oasis to approach the gates of the fort.

It was the last time I smiled for quite a little while.

Among the palm trees were little pools of dried and blackened blood where men had fallen, or wounded men had been laid, showing that, however intact the garrison of the fort might be, their assailants had paid toll to the good Lebel rifles of my friends.

And then I rode out from the shade of the oasis and up to the gate.

Here half a dozen or so kept watch, looking out over the wall above, as they leant in the embrasures of the parapet. The nearest was a huge fellow, with a great bushy grey moustache, from beneath which protruded a short wooden pipe. His *képi* was cocked rakishly over one eye, as he stared hard at me with the other, half closed and leering, while he kept his rifle pointed straight at my head.

I was glad to feel certain that he at least was no Arabs, but a tough old legionary, a typical *vieille moustache*, and rough soldier of fortune. But I thought his joke a poor one and over-personal, as I looked up into the muzzle of his unwavering rifle . . .

"*Congratulations, my children*," I cried. "*France and I are proud to salute you*," and raised my *képi* in homage to their courage and their victory.

Not one of them saluted. Not one of them answered. Not one of them stirred. Neither a finger nor an eyelid moved. I was annoyed. If this was "making *fantaisie*," as they call it in the Legion, it was making it at the wrong moment and in the wrong manner.

"*Have you of the Foreign Legion no manners?*" I shouted. "*Go, one of you, at once, and call your officer*." Not a finger nor an eyelid moved.

I then addressed myself particularly to old Grey-Moustache. "*You*," I said, pointing up straight at his face, "*go at once and tell your Commandant that Major de Beaujolais of the Spahis has arrived from Tokotu with a relieving force – and take that pipe out of your face and step smartly, do you hear?*"

And then, my friend, I grew a little uncomfortable, though the impossible truth did not dawn upon me. Why did the fellow remain like a graven image, silent, motionless, remote – like an Egyptian god on a temple wall, looking with stony and unseeing eye into my puny human face?

Why were they all like stone statues? Why was the fort so utterly and horribly silent? Why did nothing *move*, there in the fierce sunlight of the dawn? Why this tomb-like, charnel-house, inhuman silence and immobility?

Where were the usual sounds and stir of an occupied post? Why had no sentry seen me from afar and cried the news aloud? Why had there been no clang and clatter at the gate? Why had the gate not been opened? Why no voice, no footstep in all the place? Why did these men ignore me as though I were a beetle on the sand? Where was their officer? . . .

Was this a nightmare in which I seemed for ever doomed to ride voiceless and invisible, round endless walls, trying to attract the attention of those who could never be aware of me?

When, as in a dream, I rode right round the place, and beheld more and more of those motionless silent forms, with their fixed, unwinking eyes, I clearly saw that one of them, whose *képi* had fallen from his head, had a hole in the centre of his forehead and was dead – although at his post, with chest and elbows leaning on the parapet, and looking as though about to fire his rifle!

I am rather near-sighted, as you know, but then the truth dawned upon me – they were *all* dead!

"*Why were they not sleeping the sleep of tired victors?*" I had asked myself a few minutes before. They *were* . . .

Yes, all of them. *Mort sur le champ d'honneur!* . . .

My friend, I rode back to where Grey-Moustache kept his last watch, and, baring my head, I made my apologies to him, and the tears came into my eyes. Yes, and I, Henri de Beaujolais of the Spahis, admit it without shame.

I said, "*Forgive me, my friend.*" What would you, an Englishman, have said?'

'What about a spot of tea?' quoth Mr. George Lawrence, reaching beneath the seat for his tiffin-basket.

4

After a dusty meal, impatiently swallowed by Major de Beaujolais, that gentleman resumed his story, with serious earnestness and some gesticulation, while, on the opposite side of the carriage, George Lawrence lay upon his back, his clasped hands beneath his head, idly watching the smoke that curled up from his cheroot. But he was paying closer attention to the Frenchman's tale.

'But, of course, it soon occured to me,' continued that gentleman, 'that someone must be alive . . . Shots had been fired to welcome me . . . Those corpses had not of *themselves* taken up those incredibly life-like attitudes. Whoever had propped them up and arranged them and their rifles in position, must be alive.

For, naturally, not all had been struck by Arab bullets and remained standing in the embrasures. Nine times out of ten, as you know, a man staggers back and falls, when shot standing.

Besides, what about the wounded? There is always a far bigger percentage of wounded than of killed in any engagement. Yes, there must be survivors, possibly all more or less wounded, below in the *caserne*.

But surely *one* of them might have kept a look-out. Probably the Commandant and all the non-commissioned officers were killed.

Even then, though, one would have expected the senior man – even if the survivors were all *soldats deuxième classe* – to have taken that much ordinary military precaution! . . .

Well, I would soon solve the problem, for my troop was approaching, my trumpeter with them. I was glad to note that my Sergeant-Major had evidently had a similar idea to mine, for, on coming in sight of the fort, he had opened out and skirmished up in extended order – in spite of the bravely-flying Flag.

When my men arrived, I had the "rouse," the "alarm," the Regimental Call, sounded by the trumpeter – fully expecting, after each blast, that the gates would open, or at least that someone would come running up from below on to the roof.

Not a sound nor a movement! . . . Again and again; call after call . . . Not a sound nor a movement!

"Perhaps the last one or two are badly wounded," thought I. "There may not be a man able to crawl from his bed. The fellow who propped those corpses up may have been shot in the act, and be lying up there, or on his cot," and I bade the trumpeter cease. Sending for the *Chef*, as we call the Sergeant-Major, I ordered him to knot camel-cords, sashes, girths, reins, anything, make a rope, and set an active fellow to climb from the back of a camel, into an embrasure, and give me a hoist up.

That Sergeant-Major is one of the bravest and coolest men I have ever known, and his collection of *ferblanterie* includes the Croix and the Medaille given on the field, for valour.

"It is a trap, *mon Commandant*," said he. 'Do not walk into it. Let me go.' Brave words – but he looked queer, and I knew that though he feared nothing living, he was afraid.

"The dead keep good watch, *Chef*," said I, and I think he shivered.

"They would warn us, *mon Commandant*," said he. "Let me go."

"We will neither of us go," said I. "We will have the courage to remain in our proper place, with our men. It may be a trap, we shall know – and without losing an officer unnecessarily. If it is not a trap, the gates will be opened in two minutes."

"The Dead are watching and listening," said the *Chef*, glancing up, and he crossed himself, averting his eyes.

"Send me that drunken *mauvais sujet*, Rastignac," said I, and the Sergeant-Major rode away.

"May I go, *mon Commandant?*" said the trumpeter, saluting.

"Silence," said I. My nerves were getting a little on edge, under that silent, mocking scrutiny of the watching Dead. When the Sergeant-Major returned with a rope, and the rascal Rastignac – whose proper place was in the *Joyeux*, the terrible Penal Battalions of convicted criminals – I ordered him to climb from his camel on to the roof.

"Not I, *mon Officier*," replied he promptly. 'Let me go to Hell dead, not living. I don't mind joining corpses *as a corpse*. You can shoot me.'

"That can I, of a surety," I agreed, and drew my revolver. "Ride your camel under that projecting water-spout," said I. "Stand on its back, and spring to the spout. Climb into the embrasure, and then go down and open the gates."

"Not I, *mon Officier*," said Rastignac again. I raised my revolver, and the Sergeant-Major snatched the man's rifle.

"Have you *le cafard?*" I asked, referring to the desert-madness that, bred of monotony, boredom, misery, and hardship, attacks European soldiers in these outposts – especially absinthe-drinkers – and makes them do strange things, varying from mutiny, murder, and suicide to dancing about naked, or thinking they are lizards or emperors or clock-pendulums.

"I have a dislike for intruding upon a dead Company that stands to arms and keeps watch," replied the fellow.

"For the last time – go," said I, aiming between his eyes.

"Go yourself, *Monsieur le Majeur*," replied Rastignac, and I pulled the trigger . . . Was I right, my friend?'

'Dunno,' replied Lawrence, yawning.

'There was a click, and Rastignac smiled. I had emptied my revolver when approaching the fort, as I have told you.

"You can live – to be court-martialled and join the *Batt d'Af*," said I. "You will be well placed among the *Joyeux*."

"Better among those than the Watchers above, *mon Officier*," said my beauty, and I bade the Sergeant-Major take his bayonet and put him under arrest.

"You may show this coward the way," said I to the trumpeter, and, in a minute, that one had sprung at the spout, clutched it, and was scrambling on to the wall. He was *un brave*.

"We will proceed as though the place were held by an enemy – until the gates are opened," said I to the Sergeant-Major, and we rode back to the troop and handed Rastignac over to the Corporal, who clearly welcomed him in the rôle of prisoner.

"*Vous – pour la boîte*," smiled the Corporal, licking his lips. And then we watched and waited. I could see that the men were immensely puzzled and intrigued. Not an eye wandered. I would have given something to have known what each man thought concerning this unique experience. A perfectly silent fort, the walls fully manned, the Flag flying – and the gates shut. No vestige of a sign from that motionless garrison staring out into the desert, aiming their rifles at nothing – and *at us* . . .

We watched and waited. Two minutes passed; five; six; *seven*. What could it mean? *Was* it a trap after all?

"*That* one won't return!" said Rastignac loudly, and gave an eerie jarring laugh. The Corporal smote him on the mouth, and I heard him growl, "What about a little *crapaudine*[1] and a mouthful of sand, my friend? . . . You speak again!" . . .

At the end of ten minutes, a very *mauvais quart d'heure*, I beckoned the Sergeant-Major. I could stand the strain no longer.

"I am going in," said I. "I cannot send another man, although I ought to do so. Take command . . . If you do not see me within ten minutes, and nothing happens, assault the place. Burn down the gates and let a party climb the walls, while another charges in. Keep a half-troop, under the Corporal, in reserve."

"Let me go, *mon Commandant*," begged the *Chef*, "if you will not send another soldier. Or call for a volunteer to go. Suppose you . . ."

"Silence, *Chef*," I replied, "I am going," and I rode back to the fort. Was I right, George?'

'Dunno,' replied George Lawrence.

'I remember thinking, as I rode back, what a pernicious fool I should

[1] Torture. The hands and feet tied together in a bunch in the middle of the back.

look if, under the eyes of all – the living and the dead – I failed to accomplish that, by no means easy, scramble, and had ignominiously to admit my inability to climb up where the trumpeter had gone. It is sad when one's vile body falls below the standard set by the aspiring soul, when the strength of the muscles is inadequate to the courage of the heart . . .

However, all went well, and, after an undignified dangling from the spout, and wild groping with the raised foot, I got a leg over the ledge, scrambled up and crawled into an embrasure.

And there I stood astounded and dumbfounded, *tout bouleversé*, unable to believe my eyes.

There, as in life, stood the garrison, their backs to me, their faces to the foe whom they had driven off, their feet in dried pools of their own blood – watching, watching . . . And soon I forgot what might be awaiting me below, I forgot my vanished trumpeter, I forgot my troop waiting without – *for there was something else.*

Lying on his back, his sightless eyes out-staring the sun – lay the Commandant, and through his heart, *a bayonet*, one of our long, thin French sword-bayonets with its single-curved hilt! No – he had not been shot, he was absolutely untouched elsewhere, and there he lay with a French bayonet through his heart. What do you say to that, my friend?'

'Suicide,' replied Lawrence.

'And so did I, until I realised that he had a loaded revolver in one hand, one chamber fired, and a crushed letter in the other! *Does* a man drive a bayonet through his heart, and then take a revolver in one hand and a sheet of paper in the other? I think not.

Have you ever seen a man drive a bayonet through his heart, my friend? Believe me, he does not fumble for letters, nor draw a revolver and fire it, after he has done *that*. No. He gasps, stares, staggers. He grips the handle and the *forte* of the blade with both hands, totters, stretches convulsively, and collapses, crashing to the ground . . . In any case, does a man commit suicide with a bayonet when he has a loaded revolver? . . . Suicide? *Pouf.*

Was it any wonder that my jaw dropped and I forgot all else, as I stared and stared . . . *Voyez donc!* A French fort in the Sahara, besieged by Arabs. Every man killed at his post. The Arabs beaten off. The fort inviolate, untrodden by Arab foot. The gates closed. Within – the dead, and one of them slain by a French bayonet while he held a loaded revolver in his hand! . . .

But *was* the fort inviolate and untrodden by Arab foot? If so, what had become of my trumpeter? Might not the Arabs be hiding below, waiting their opportunity to catch the relieving force unawares? Might not there be an Arab eye at every rifle-slit? Might not the *caserne*, rooms, offices, sheds, be packed with them?

Absurdly improbable – and why should they have slain the Commandant with a French bayonet? Would they not have hacked him to pieces with sword and spear, and have mutilated and decapitated every corpse in the place? Was it like the wild Touareg to lay so clever a trap with the propped-up bodies, that a relieving force might fall into their hands as well? Never. *Peaudezébie!* Had the Arabs entered here, the place would have been a looted, blackened ruin, defiled, disgusting, strewn with pieces of what had been men. No, this was not Arab work.

These Watchers, I felt certain, had been compelled by this dead man, who lay before me, to continue as defenders of the fort after their deaths . . . He was evidently a *man*. A bold, resourceful, undaunted hero, sardonic, of a macabre humour, as the Legion always is.

As each man fell, throughout that long and awful day, he had propped him up, wounded or dead, set the rifle in its place, fired it, and bluffed the Arabs that every wall and every embrasure and loophole of every wall was fully manned. He must, at the last, have run from point to point, firing a rifle from behind its dead defender. Every now and then he must have blown the alarm that the bugler would never blow again, in the hope that it would guide and hasten the relieving force and impress the Arabs with the fear that the avengers must be near.

No wonder the Arabs never charged that fort, from each of whose walls a rifle cracked continuously, and from whose every embrasure watched a fearless man whom they could not kill – or whose place seemed to be taken, at once, by another, if they did kill him . . .

All this passed through my mind in a few seconds – and as I realised what he had done and how he had died in the hour of victory, *murdered*, my throat swelled though my blood boiled – and I ventured to give myself the proud privilege of kneeling beside him and pinning my own Croix upon his breast – though I could scarcely see to do so. I thought of how France should ring with the news of his heroism, resource, and last glorious fight, and how every Frenchman should clamour for the blood of his murderer.

Only a poor *sous-officier* of the Legion. But a hero for France to honour . . . And I would avenge him!

Such were my thoughts, my friend, as I realised the truth – what are yours?'

'Time for a spot of dinner,' said George Lawrence, starting up.

5

Next morning, as the two lay awake on their dusty bedding, begrimed, tousled, pyjama-clad, awaiting the next stop, bath, and breakfast, de Beaujolais lit a cigarette, turned on his side, and fixed his friend with the earnest troubled gaze of his bright brown eye.

'Well, George, *who killed him* – and why?'

'Oh, Ancient Mariner!' yawned Lawrence.

'What?'

'I feel like the Wedding Guest.'

'You look like one, my George,' smiled the Frenchman.

'Get on with it, Jolly.'

'How was the Commandant of that fort killed?'

'Someone "threatened his life with a railway-share."'

'Be serious, little George. I want your help. I *must* get to the bottom of this. Where did I leave off?'

'God knows. I was asleep.'

'Ah! I was on the roof, pinning my Croix on the breast of the bravest man I have ever met. Your General Gordon in miniature! This obscure and humble soul had kept his country's Flag flying, as that great man did at Khartoum, and, like him, he had been relieved too late. But yes, and there it flapped above my head and recalled me to myself.

I rose, drew my revolver, loaded it, and walked to the door. As I was about to descend into that silence I had a little idea. I looked at each of the Watchers in turn. No. Each man had his bayonet, of course. I had not really supposed that one of them had stabbed his officer and then gone back to his post and died on his feet! He would have fallen – or possibly have hung limply through the embrasure. I raised my weapon and descended the stairs – expecting I know not what, in that sinister stillness – that had swallowed up my trumpeter. And what do you think I found there, my friend?'

'Dunno,' said George Lawrence.

'*Nothing.* No one and nothing. Not even the man who had fired the two shots of welcome! . . . As I had felt sure, really, all along, no Arab had entered the fort. That leapt to the eye at once. The place was as tight shut as this fist of mine – and as empty of Arab traces. The *caserne* was as orderly and tidy as when the men left it and stood to arms – the *paquetages* on the shelves, the table-apparatus in the hanging cupboards, the *gamelles* and cleaning-bags at the heads of the beds, the bedding folded and straight. There had evidently been room-inspection just before the sentry on the look-out platform had cried, "*Aux armes! Aux armes! Les Arabes!*" and all had rushed to their posts.

No, not a thing was missing or awry. The whole place might just have been made ready by an outgoing garrison, to be taken over by the incoming garrison. No Arab had scaled those walls nor wriggled through the keyhole of the gate. The stores were untouched – the rice, the biscuits, bread, coffee, wine, nothing was missing . . .'

'Except a rifle,' grunted Lawrence.

'My friend, you've said it! Where was the rifle belonging to the bayonet that was driven through the heart of the murdered officer up above? That was precisely the question that my crazed mind was asking itself as I realised that the fort had never been entered.

Had a corpse bayonetted that *sous-officier*, returned to its post, and flung the rifle to the horizon? Scarcely.

Had an Arab – expert in throwing knife or bayonet as in throwing the *matrak* – possessed himself of a French bayonet, after some desert-massacre of one of our tiny expeditionary columns? And had he got near enough to the fort to throw it? And had it by chance, or skill of the thrower, penetrated the heart of the Commandant of the garrison?'

'Possibly,' said Lawrence.

'So I thought for a moment,' replied de Beaujolais, 'though why a man armed with a breech-loading rifle, should leave the cover of his sand-hill, trench, or palm tree, and go about throwing bayonets, I don't know. And then I remembered that the bayonet went through the breast of the *sous-officier* in a slightly *upward* direction from front to back. Could a bayonet be thrown thus into the middle of a wide roof?'

'Sold again,' murmured Lawrence.

'No, I had to abandon that idea. As untenable as the returning-corpse theory. And I was driven, against common sense, to conclude that the officer had been bayonetted by one of his own men, the sole survivor, who had then detached the rifle from the bayonet and fled from the fort. But why? *Why?* If such was the explanation of the officer's death – why on earth had not the murderer shot him *and calmly awaited the arrival of the relieving force?*

Naturally all would have supposed that the brave Commandant had been shot, like all the rest, by the Arabs.

Instead of fleeing to certain death from thirst and starvation, or torture at the hands of the Arabs, why had not the murderer awaited, in comfort, the honours, *réclame*, reward, and promotion that would most assuredly have been his? Obviously, the man who – lusting for blood and vengeance on account of some real or fancied wrong – could murder his superior at such a moment, would be the very one to see the beauty of getting a rich and glorious reward as a sequel to his revenge. Without a doubt he would have shot him through the head, propped him up with the rest, and accepted the congratulations of the relieving force for having conceived and executed the whole scheme of outwitting and defeating the Arabs. Wouldn't he, George?'

'*I* would,' replied George, scratching his head.

'Yes, you would. And I almost sent that theory to join the other two wild ones – the corpse who returned to its post, and the Arab who threw sword-bayonets from afar. Almost – until I remembered that revolver in the dead man's hand, and the empty cartridge-case in one of its chambers. And then I asked myself, 'Does a man who is conducting the defence of a block-house, against tremendous odds, waste time in taking pot-shots *with a revolver* at concealed enemies, two or three hundred yards distant? Does he do that, with hundreds of rounds of rifle ammunition and a score of rifles to his hand?" Of course not.

That revolver shot was fired at someone *in* the fort. It was fired point-blank at the man who murdered him – and the murderer must have been one of his own men, and that man must have fled from the fort. But again, why? *Why?*

Why not have shot his officer, as I said before? He would never have had even the *need* to deny having done it, for no one would have dreamt of accusing him.

And then I had an idea. I suddenly said to myself, "Supposed some scoundrel bayonetted the Commandant even before the alarm was given or the attack began – and then organised the defence and died at his post with the others?"

Led a mutiny of the garrison, perhaps; took command; and was shot and propped the last man up? He did not do it himself, that was certain – for every single corpse on that roof had been *arranged* before *rigor mortis* set in. The only man who was not "to the life" was one who lay on his back. It was curious, that curious, that recumbent corpse with closed eyes and folded hands, but I did not see that it offered any clue. Whoever had been doing the ghastly work of corpsedrilling had overlooked it – or, indeed, had been going to set the dead man up when the final tragedy, whatever it was, occurred.

It may have been that the brave *sous-officier* was going to arrange this very corpse when he was attacked. Or, as I say, the officer may have been dead the whole time, or part of it, and the last survivor may have had this last work cut short by a bullet, before he had put the man in position.

But if so, where *was* he? . . . Was it the man who had fired the two shots in answer to mine – and if so, what had become of him? *Why had he fired if he wished to hide or escape?*

My head spun. I felt I was going mad.

And then I said to myself, '"*Courage, mon brave!* Go calmly up to that terrible roof again, and just quietly and clearly make certain of two points. First: Is there any one of those standing corpses who has not quite obviously been arranged, propped up, fixed in position? If so – *that* is the man who killed his officer and was afterwards shot by the Arabs. Secondly: Has any one of those dead men been shot point-blank with a revolver? (That I should be able to tell at a glance.) If so, *that* is the man who killed his officer – (who lived long enough to thurst his assailant into an embrasure) . . ."'

'After himself being bayonetted through the heart?' enquired Lawrence.

'Exactly what I said to myself – and groaned aloud as I said it,' replied de Beaujolais.

'Anyhow,' he continued, 'I would go up and see if any man had been shot by a revolver, and if any man lay *naturally* against the slope of an embrasure . . . I turned to ascend the stair, and then, George, and not till then, I got the *real* shock of that awful day of shocks. For, *where was my trumpeter?*

I had made a quick but complete tour of the place and now realised in a flash that I had seen no living thing and heard no sound.

"*Trompette! Trompette!*" I shouted. I rushed to the door leading to the courtyard, the little interior, high-walled parade ground.

"*Trompette!*" I shouted and yelled, again and again, till my voice cracked. Not a sound. Not a movement.

And then, in something like panic, putting all else from my mind, I rushed to the gates, lifted down the great bars, pulled the heavy bolts, turned the great key, and dragged them open – just as the mule-squadron arrived and my good Sergeant-Major was giving them the signal to join the assault!

It was not that I had suddenly remembered that the time I had allowed him must be up, but that I needed to see a human being again, to hear a human voice, after a quarter of an hour in that House of Death, that sinister abode of tragic mysteries. I felt an urgent and unconquerable yearning for some . . .'

'Breakfast,' said George Lawrence, as the train slowed down.

6

Bathed, full-fed, and at peace with a noisy world, in so far as choking dust, grilling heat, and the weariness of three days' close confinement in a stuffy carriage allowed, the two *compagnons de voyage* lay and smoked the cheroot of digestion in a brief silence. Brief, because it was not in the power of the impulsive and eloquent *beau sabreur*, of the Spahis, to keep silence for long upon the subject uppermost in his active and ardent mind.

'*George, mon vieux*,' he broke silence, 'do you believe in spirits, ghosts, devils?'

'I firmly believe in whiskey, the ghost of a salary, and a devil of a thin time. Seen 'em myself,' was the reply.

'Because the only solution that my Sergeant-Major could offer was just that . . .

'*Spirits! Ghosts! Devils!*' he whispered, when he realised that the *sous-officier* had been murdered apparently by a corpse, and that the trumpeter had absolutely vanished into thin air, leaving not a trace of himself, and effecting the evaporation of his rifle as well as his trumpet and everything else.

This was not very helpful, strongly as I was tempted to endorse it.

"Sergeant-Major Dufour," said I, 'I am going to propound theories and you are going to find the weak points in them. The absurdities and idiocies in them.

Post vedettes far out, all round the place, and let the men fall out and water their beasts in the oasis. Sergeant Lebaudy will be in command. Tell him that fires may be lighted and *soupe* made, but that in an hour's time all are to be on grave-digging fatigue. He is to report immediately when mulescouts from Lieutenant St. André's advance Senegalese arrive from Tokotu, or if anything happens meanwhile. If a vedette gives the alarm, all are to enter the fort immediately – otherwise no one is to set foot inside. Put a sentry at the gate . . . You and I will look into this *affaire* while Achmet makes us some coffee" – and I gave the good fellow a cake of chocolate and a measure of cognac from my flask. We were both glad of that cognac.

While he was gone on this business I remained on the roof. I preferred the sunlight while I was alone. I freely admit it. I do not object to Arabs, but I dislike "spirits, ghosts, and devils" – that commit murders and abductions. Perhaps I was not quite myself. But what would you? I had been enjoying fever; I had ridden all night; I was perilously near *cafard* myself; and the presence of those dead Watchers to whom I had spoken, the finding of that incredibly murdered man, the not finding of that more incredibly vanished trumpeter – had shaken me a little.

As I awaited the return of the Sergeant-Major I gazed at the corpse of the *sous-officier*. I stared and stared at the face of the dead man – not too pleasant a sight, George – contorted with rage, and pain, and hate – dead for some hours and it was getting hot on that roof – and there were flies . . . flies . . .

I stared, I say, as though I would drag the truth from him, compel the secret of this mystery from his dead lips, hypnotise those dead eyes to turn to mine and – but no, it was *he* that hypnotised and compelled, until I was fain to look away.

As I did so, I noticed the man who was lying near. Yes, undoubtedly someone had carefully and reverently laid him out. His eyes had been closed, his head propped up on a pouch, and his hands folded upon his chest. Why had he received such different treatment from that meted out to the others? . . .

And then that bareheaded man. It was he – a very handsome fellow too – who had given me my first shock and brought it home to my wondering mind that the men who watched me were all dead.

You see, all but he had their faces in the deep shade of the big peaks of their *képis* – whilst he, bareheaded and shot through the centre of the forehead, was dead obviously – even to shortsighted me, looking up from below against the strong sunlight; even to me, deceived at first by his lifelike attitude.

And, as I glanced at their two *képis* lying there, I noticed something peculiar.

One had been wrenched and torn from within. The lining, newly ripped, was protruding, and the inner leather band was turned down and outward. It was as though something had recently been torn violently out of the cap – something concealed in the lining perhaps? . . .

No, it was not the freak of a ricochetting bullet. The standing man had been hit just above the nose and under the cap, the recumbent man was hit in the chest.

"Now what is this?" thought I. "A man shot through the brain does not remove his cap and tear the lining out. He gives a galvanic start, possibly spins round, and quietly he falls backwards. His limbs stretch once and quiver, and he is still for ever. His tight-fitting cap may, or may not, fall off as he goes down – but there is no tearing out of the lining, no turning down of the leather band."

Bullets play funny tricks, I know, but not upon things they do not touch. This bullet had been fired, I should say, from a palm tree, and almost on a level with the roof; anyhow, it had entered the head below the cap. There was no hole in *that* whatsoever. To which of these two men did the cap belong? . . .

Had all been normal in that terrible place, all lying dead as they had fallen, I might never have noticed this torn cap. As it was – where everything was extraordinary, and the mind of the beholder filled with suspicion and a thousand questions, it was most interesting and remarkable. It became portentous. It was one more phenomenon in that focus of phenomena!

And from that cap and its recently torn and still protruding lining – oh yes, most obviously torn quite recently, with its edging of unsoiled threads, frayed but clean – from that cap, I looked quite instinctively at the paper crushed in the left hand of the dead officer. I know not why I connected these two things in my mind. They connected themselves perhaps – and I was about to take the paper from the rigid fist, when I thought, "No! Everything shall be done in order and with correctness. I will touch nothing, do nothing, until the Sergeant-Major returns and I have a witness."

If I was to be *procureur*, *juge d'instruction*, judge and jury, coroner, and perhaps, avenger – everything should be done in due form – and my report upon the impossible affair be of some value, too.

But without touching the paper, I could see, and I saw with surprise – though the *bon Dieu* knows I had not much capacity for surprise left in my stunned mind – that the writing was in English!

Why should *that* be added to my conundrums? . . . A paper with English writing on it, in the hand of a dead French officer in a block-house in the heart of the *Territoire Militaire* of the Sahara!'

'Perhaps the bloke was English,' suggested Lawrence. 'I have heard that there are some in the Legion.'

'No,' was the immediate reply. 'That he most certainly was not. A typical Frenchman of the Midi – a stoutish, florid, blue-jowled fellow of full habit. Perhaps a Provençal – thousands like him in Marseilles, Arles, Nimes, Avignon, Carcassonne, Tarascon. Might have been the good Tartarin himself. Conceivably a Belgian; *possibly* a Spaniard or Italian, but most certainly not an Englishman . . . Still less was the standing man, an olive-cheeked Italian or Sicilian.'

'And the recumbent bareheaded chap?' said Lawrence.

'Ah – quite another affair, that! He might very well have been English. In fact, had I been asked to guess at his nationality, I should have said, "A Northerner certainly, English most probably." He would have been well in the picture in the Officers' Mess of one of your regiments. Just the type turned out by your Public Schools and Universities by the thousand.

What you are thinking is exactly what occurred to me. English writing on the paper; an English-looking legionary; his cap lying near the man who held the paper crushed in his hand; the lining just torn out of the cap! . . . Ha! Here was a little glimmer of light, a possible clue. I was just reconstructing the scene when I heard the Sergeant-Major ascending the stair . . .

Had this Englishman killed the *sous-officier* while the latter tore some document from the lining of the man's cap? Obviously not. The poor fellow's bayonet was in its sheath at his side, and if he *had* done it – how had he got himself put into position?'

'Might have been shot afterwards,' said Lawrence.

'No. He was *arranged*, I tell you,' was the reply, 'and he most assuredly had not arranged himself. Besides, he was bareheaded. Does a man go about bareheaded in the afternoon sun of the Sahara? But to my mind the question doesn't arise – in view of the fact of that inexplicable bayonet.

One bayonet more than there were soldiers and rifles!

No – I ceased reconstructing the scene with *that* one as the slayer, and I had no reason to select anyone else for the rôle . . . Then I heard the bull voice of Sergeant Lebaudy, down in the oasis, roar "*Formez les faisceaux*" and "*Sac à terre,*" and came back to facts as the Sergeant-Major approached and saluted.

"All in order, *mon Commandant,*" reported he, and fell to eyeing the corpses.

"Even to half-smoked cigarettes in their mouths!" he whispered. "*The fallen who were not allowed to fall – the dead forbidden to die.*" Then – "But where in the name of God is Jean the Trumpeter?"

"Tell me that, *Chef*, and I will fill your *képi* with twenty-franc pieces – and give you the Grand Cross of the Legion of Honour," said I.

The Sergeant-Major blasphemed, crossed himself, and then said, "Let us get out of here while we can."

"Are you a Sergeant-Major or a young lady?" I enquired – and as one does, in such circumstances, rated him soundly for feeling exactly as I did myself; and the more I said, the more angry and unreasonable I grew. You know how one's head and one's nerves get, in that accursed desert, George.'

'I know, old son,' agreed Lawrence. 'I have found myself half-ready to murder a *piccin*, for dropping a plate.'

'Yes – the best of us get really insane at times, in that hellish heat and unnatural life . . . But I got a hold upon myself and felt ashamed – for the good fellow took it well.

"Did Your Excellency make a thorough search?" he asked, rebukingly polite.

"But, my dear *Chef*, what need to make a thorough search for a living man, a hale and hearty, healthy soldier, in a small place into which he had been sent to open a gate? *Mon Dieu!* he has legs! He has a tongue in his head! If he were here, wouldn't he *be* here?" I asked.

"Murdered perhaps," was the reply.

"By whom? Beetles? Lizards?" I sneered.

He shrugged his shoulders, and pointed to the *sous-officier* with a dramatic gesture.

That one had not been murdered by beetles or lizards!

"Yes," said I. "Now we'll reconstruct this crime, first reading what is on this paper," and I opened the stiffened fingers and took it. There was a dirty crumpled torn envelope there, too. Now *Georges*, *mon vieux*, prepare yourself. You are going to show a little emotion, my frozen Englishman!'

Lawrence smiled faintly.

'It was a most extraordinary document,' continued de Beaujolais. 'I'll show it to you when we get on board the ship. It was something like this: On the envelope was, "*To the Chief of Police of Scotland Yard and all whom it may concern*." And on the paper, "*Confession. Important. Urgent. Please Publish*.

For fear that any innocent person may be suspected, I hereby fully and freely confess that it was I, and I alone, who stole the great sapphire known as "Blue Water."' . . .

'What!' shouted George Lawrence, jumping up. 'What? *What* are you saying, de Beaujolais?'

'Aha! my little George,' smiled the Frenchman, gloating. 'And where is the *phlegme Britannique* now, may I ask? That made you sit up, quite literally, didn't it? We do not yawn now, my little George, do we?'

George Lawrence stared at his friend, incredulous, open-mouthed.

'*But that is Lady Brandon's jewel!*. . . What on earth . . .' stammered Lawrence, sitting down heavily. 'Are you romancing, de Beaujolais? Being funny?'

'I am telling you what was written on this paper – which I will show you when I can get at my dispatch-case, my friend,' was the reply.

'Good God, man! *Lady Brandon!*. . . Do you mean to say that the "Blue Water" has been pinched – and that the thief took refuge in the Foreign Legion, or drifted there somehow?' asked Lawrence, lying back on his roll of bedding.

'I don't mean to say anything – except to tell my little tale, the dull little tale that has bored you so, my George,' replied de Beaujolais, with a malicious grin.

George Lawrence swung his feet to the ground and stood up again.

Never had his friend seen this reserved, taciturn, and unemotional man so affected.

'I don't get you. I don't take it in,' he said. 'Lady Brandon's stone! *Our Lady Brandon?* The "Blue Water" that we used to be allowed to look at sometimes? Stolen! . . . And you have found it?'

'I have found nothing, my friend, but a crumpled and bloodstained piece of paper in a dead man's hand,' was the reply.

'With Lady Brandon's name on it! It's absurd, man . . . In the middle of the Sahara! And *you* found it . . . With her name on it! . . . Well, I'm absolutely damned!' ejaculated Lawrence.

'Yes, my friend. And perhaps you begin to realise how "absolutely damned" I was, when I read that paper – sticky with blood. But probably I was not as surprised as you are now. Even that could not have surprised me very much then, I think,' said de Beaujolais.

Lawrence sat down.

'Go on, old chap,' he begged. 'I sincerely apologise for my recent manners. Please tell me everything, and then let us thrash it out . . . Lady Brandon! . . . The "Blue Water" stolen!' . . .

'No need for apologies, my dear George,' smiled his friend. 'If you seemed a little unimpressed and bored at times, it only gave me the greater zest for the *dénouement*, when you should hear your . . . our . . . friend's name come into this extraordinary story.'

'You're a wily and patient old devil, Jolly,' said the astounded Lawrence. 'I salute you, Sir. A logical old cuss, too! Fancy keeping *that* back until now, and telling the yarn neatly, in proper sequence and due order, until the right point in the story was reached, and then . . .'

'Aha! the *phlegme Britannique*, eh, George!' chuckled de Beaujolais. 'Wonderful how the volatile and impetuous Frenchman could do it, wasn't it! And there is something else to come, my friend. All in "logical proper sequence and due order" there comes another little surprise.'

'Then, for God's sake get on with it, old chap! . . . More about Lady Brandon, is it?' replied Lawrence, now all animation and interest.

'Indirectly, *mon cher Georges*. For that paper was signed – *by whom?*' asked the Frenchman, leaning forward, tapping his friend's knee, staring impressively with narrowed eyes into those of that bewildered gentleman.

And into the ensuing silence he slowly and deliberately dropped the words, '*By Michael Geste!*'

Lawrence raised himself on his elbow and stared at his friend incredulous.

'By *Michael Geste!* Her nephew! You don't mean to tell me that *Michael Geste* stole her sapphire and slunk off to the Legion? "Beau" Geste! *Get out* . . .' he said, and fell back.

'Was the bareheaded man he? Look here, *are* you pulling my leg?'

'I do not know who the man was, George. And I am not pulling your leg. I saw two or three boys and two so beautiful girls, once, at Brandon

Abbas, years ago. This man might have been one of them. The age would be about right. And then, again, this man may have had nothing on earth to do with the paper. Nor any other man on that roof, except the *sous-officier* – and he most certainly was not Michael Geste. He was a man of forty or forty-five years, and as I have said, no Englishman.'

'Michael would be about twenty or so,' said Lawrence. 'He was the oldest of the newphews . . . But, my dear Jolly, the Gestes don't *steal!* They are her nephews . . . I am going to put some ice on my head.'

'I have wanted a lot of ice to the head, the last few weeks, George. What, too, of the murdered *sous-officer* and the utterly vanished trumpeter?'

'Oh, damn your trumpeter and *sous-officer*,' was the explosive reply. 'Michael Geste! . . . Lady Brandon . . . Forgive me, old chap, and finish the story . . .' and George Lawrence lay back on his couch and stared at the roof of the carriage.

Lady Brandon! The only woman in the world.

7

And as the train rumbled on through the sweltering coastlands toward Lagos, Major de Beaujolais, highly pleased with the success of his neat and clever little *coup*, continued his story.

'Well, my George, figure me there, with this new astoundment, this extraordinary accompaniment to the sinister and bewildering mystery of an inexplicable murder and an inexplicable disappearance . . .

And then, "What is in the paper, might one respectfully enquire, *mon Commandant*," asked the Sergeant-Major.

"The confession of a thief – that he stole a famous jewel," I replied.

"Which was the thief?" said he.

"Oh, ask me some questions, my good imbecile!" said I. "Ask me where the trumpeter is, and whose is this bayonet, and who disposed these dead men as defenders, and who fired two shots, and whether I am mad or dreaming," I answered – and then pulled myself together. "Now come with me," I bade him. "We will make one more search below, and then *déjeuner*, and a quiet, sensible, reasonable discussion of the facts, before we bury these brave fellows, detail an *escouade* of our men as garrison, and return to Tokotu. I shall leave you in command here until we get orders and reliefs."

The Sergeant-Major looked distinctly dubious at this. "*Here* – for weeks!" he said softly.

We made our tour below, and, as before, nothing unusual met the eye, and there was no sign of the trumpeter, alive or dead. We had seen him climb on to that parapet and apparently no living eye had beheld him again.

I was past wonder. I accepted things.

Very well, this was a place where Commandants are murdered by non-existent people; soldiers vanish like a whiff of smoke; and English letters concerning one's friends are found in the hands of dead Frenchmen. Very good. Be it so. We would "carry on" as you say, and do our duty.

"Think hard – and be prepared to pick holes in the theories I shall propound an hour hence," said I to the Sergeant-Major, as we passed out of the gate, and I proceeded to the oasis where my excellent Achmet had prepared my soup and coffee . . .

You do not want to hear my theories, George, and there was no need for the Sergeant-Major to point out the impossibilities and absurdities in them. They leapt to the eye immediately.

It all came back to the bald facts that there must be a soldier of the garrison missing, that he must have taken his rifle and left his bayonet in the *sous-officier*, instead of shooting him and awaiting praise and reward; that my trumpeter had vanished; that the dead *sous-officier* had been in possession of a confession, real or bogus, to the effect that Michael Geste had stolen his aunt's famous sapphire.

There it was – and nothing but lunacy could result from theory-making about the *sous-officier's* murder, the trumpeter's disappearance, or Michael Geste's confession and how it got there.

No – you do not want to hear those perfectly futile theories – those explanations that explained nothing. But it may interest you to hear that I was faced that evening, on top of the rest of my little pleasures, with a military mutiny.'

'Good Lord!' ejaculated Lawrence, turning to the speaker.

'Yes. At four o'clock I ordered the Sergeant-Major to fall the men in, and I would tell off the new garrison for Zinderneuf.

In a most unusual manner the Sergeant-Major hung fire, so to speak, instead of stepping smartly off about his duty.

"Well!" said I sharply.

"There is going to be trouble, *mon Commandant*," he faltered.

"*Mon Dieu*, there is!" I snapped, "and *I* am going to make it, if I have any nonsense. What do you mean?"

"Sergeant Lebaudy says that Corporal Brille says that the men say . . ."

"Name of the Name of the Name of Ten Thousand Thundering Tin Devils," I shouted . . . "You say that he says that they say that she says," I mocked. "*Va t'en, grand babbilard!*" I roared at him. "I'll be on parade outside those gates in ten seconds, and if you and your gibbering chatter-boxes are not awaiting me there at attention . . ." and my poor Sergeant-Major fled.

I was the more angry at his news, for I had subconsciously expected something of the sort.

What else, with these ignorant, superstitious clods, who were the bravest of the brave against human foes? None like them. Every man a hero in battle . . . But what of that House of Death with its Watchers? That place into which their comrade had boldly climbed – and never come forth again.

Rastignac had begun it. And they had seen him face instant death rather than enter it – Rastignac, the fearless reckless devil, whose bravery alone had prevented his escapades from bringing him to a court-martial and the Zephyrs. He, of all men, was afraid of the place. There is nothing so infectious as *that* sort of panic . . .

Well! One more fact to accept.

If the men would not enter the fort of Zinderneuf, they would not enter the fort of Zinderneuf – and that was that.

But if the will of these scoundrels was coming into conflict with the will of Henri de Beaujolais, there were exciting times ahead. Since they sought sorrow they should certainly find it – and as I put on my belt and boots again, I felt a certain elation.

"Action is always action, *mon Henri*," said I to myself, "and it will be a change from these thrice-accursed theories and attempts to explain the inexplicable and reconcile the irreconciable."

Bah! I would teach my little dogs to show their teeth, and I rode, on a mule, over to the fort. There I bade Dufour and Lebaudy select an *escouade* of the worst men, all *mauvais sujets* of that Company. They should garrison either Zinderneuf fort, or else the grave that had been dug for those brave "fallen who had not been allowed to fall." . . .

As I rode up, the Sergeant-Major Dufour called the men to attention, and they stood like graven images, the selected *escouade* on the right, while I made an eloquent speech, the funeral oration of that brave band to whom we were about to give a military funeral with all the last honours that France could render to the worthy defenders of her honour and her Flag.

Tears stood in my eyes and my voice broke as I concluded by quoting:-

> '*Soldats de la Légion,*
> *De la Légion Étrangère,*
> *N'ayant pas de nation,*
> *La France est votre mère.*'

Then, when the selected new garrison got the order, "*Par files de quatre. En avant. Marche,*" that they might march into the fort and begin their new duties by bringing the dead out for burial – they did something quite otherwise.

Taking the time from the right, with smartness and precision they stooped as one man, laid their rifles on the ground, rose as one man and stood at attention!

The right-hand man, a grizzled veteran of Madagascar, Tonquin, and Dahomey, took a pace forward, saluted, and with wooden face, said, "We prefer to die with Rastignac."

This was flat disobedience and rank mutiny. I had hardly expected quite this.

"But Rastignac is not going to die. He is going to live – long years, I hope – in the *Joyeux*. You, however, who are but cowardly sheep, led astray by him, shall have the better fate. You shall die now, or enter Zinderneuf fort and do your duty . . . Sergeant-Major, have those rifles collected. Let the remainder of the Company right form, and on the order '*Attention pour les feux de salve*,' the front rank will kneel, and on the order, '*Feu*' every man will do his duty."

But I knew better, George. That was precisely what they *wouldn't* do; and I felt that this was my last parade. That accursed fort was still exerting its horrible influence. These fools feared that it would kill them if they entered it, and I feared it would kill them if they did not. For let me but handle them wrongly now, and they would shoot me and the non-commissioned officers and march off into the desert to certain death, as they weakened from thirst and starvation. They would be harried and hunted and herded along by the Arabs, and daily reduced in numbers until a sudden rush swept over them and nothing remained for the survivors but horrible tortures.

Mutinous dogs they might be, and fools they were – but no less would the responsibility for their sufferings and deaths be mine if I mishandled the situation. I thought of other desert-mutinies in the Legion.

It was an awkward dilemma, George. If I ordered the Company to fire upon the squad, they would refuse and would thereby become mutineers themselves. They would then feel that they might as well be hung for a sheep as a lamb, and, having shot me, take their chance of escape and freedom.

If, on the other hand, I condoned this refusal of the *escouade* – what of military discipline? Duty to my country came before my duty to these fellows, and I must not allow any pity for their probable fate to come between me and my duty as a French officer.

I decided that if they *would* die, then die they must – but I at least could do my best to save them. Without deviating from the path of duty, I would hold out a hand to them.

If the *escouade* would not enter the fort they must expiate their military crime. If the company would not carry out my orders and fire on the mutineers, they must expiate *their* crime.

If I were to be shot, I should at least be saved the unpleasantness of reporting that my men had mutinied, and I should die in the knowledge that I had done my duty.

Yes – I would make it clear that disobedience to my orders would be death. Swift and sudden for some, lingering and horrible for many, sure and certain for all. Then I would "carry on" as you say. Was I right, George?'

'I think you were quite right, Jolly,' agreed Lawrence.

'As I was deciding thus, all in the space of a few seconds, with every eye upon me and a terrible tension drawing every face,' continued de Beaujolais, 'the Sergeant-Major approached and saluted. I eyed him coldly. With his back to the men, he whispered:

"They won't do it, *mon Commandant*. For God's sake do not give the order. They are rotten with *cafard* and over-fatigue. That Rastignac is their hero and leader. They will shoot you and desert *en masse*. . . A night's rest will work wonders . . . Besides, Lieutenant St. André and the Senegalese will be here by midnight. It is full moon to-night."

"And shall we sit and wait for the Senegalese, Dufour?" I whispered back. "Would you like to ask these fellows to spare us till they come?"

And looking from him to the men I said loudly:

"You are too merciful, Sergeant-Major. We don't do things thus in the Spahis. But these are not Spahis. However, in consideration of the most excellent march the men have made, I will do as you beg and give these *cafard*-stricken fools till moon-rise. It gives me no pleasure to inflict punishment, and I hope no man will insist on being punished. We are all tired, and since you intercede for your men I grant a four-hour holiday. At moon-rise, our motto is '*Work or die*.' Till then, all may rest. After then, the dead will be buried and the fort garrisoned. I hope there will be no *more* dead to be buried to-night."

And I rode back to the oasis, hearing as I did so the voice of the Sergeant-Major, exhorting the men and concluding with the order, "*Rompez*."

He joined me a few minutes later.

"They'll never do it, *mon Commandant*," said he. "They'll fear the place worse than ever by moonlight. In the morning we could call for volunteers to accompany us. And then the Senegalese . . ."

"That will do, Dufour,' said I. 'They will render instant obedience at moon-rise, or take the consequences. I have strained my military conscience already to satisfy my private conscience. If, after four hours' rest and reflection, they still decide to mutiny – on their heads be it! No responsibility rests on me. If they mutiny, they do it in cold blood. If they obey orders before the Senegalese arrive, no great harm has been done, and discipline has been maintained. That is the very utmost length to which I can go in my desire to save them."

"To save *them*, *mon Commandant!* It is *you* I am trying to save," stammered the good fellow.

Patting him on the shoulder as he turned to go, I bade him send me a couple of the most influential men of the *escouade* and two or three of the best of the remainder – leaders of different cliques, if there were any.

I would point out to them the inevitable and awful results to the men themselves, of disobedience and mutiny. I would speak of the heroism, discipline, and dutifulness of the dead. I would point out to them that in the event of mutiny, they themselves would either be loyal and die at the hands of the mutineers, or become deserters and die at the hands of the Arabs. I would then send them back among their fellows – and abide the issue . . .

It was while I awaited their arrival that I wished our army more resembled yours in one particular – the relationship between officers and men. Our fellows get too much non-commissioned officer and too little officer. We are too remote from them. We do not play games with them, get to know them, interest ourselves in them as fellow human beings, in the way that your officers do. Too often it is a case with us of hated non-coms. and stranger-officers. Particularly is this so in the Legion. The non-coms. are all-powerful and tyrannical; the officers are utterly uninterested in the men as individuals, and do not even know their names.

And I was not one of their own officers of the Legion. I was a Spahi officer, superintending the organising of mule-cavalry out of infantry; or rather, making ordinary infantry, that the Legion might hope to compete with the Touaregs in mobility. We wanted mounted riflemen down there just as you did in the Boer War, or else the Arabs served us as the Boers did you at first.

I certainly had not been unduly harsh or oppressive during the time I had been with this particular lot; but, on the other hand, I certainly had no *personal* influence with them. I did not know them, nor they me, and all our lives seemed likely to be forfeit in consequence . . .

However, I talked to the men whom Dufour brought, and did my best under the heavy handicap of not so much as knowing their names. Finally, I dismissed them with the words:

'For your lives, influence your friends wisely and well, and get it into their heads that at moon-rise we will have obedience with honour and safety, or disobedience with dishonour, misery, and death. For at moon-rise, the chosen *escouade* will enter the fort and bring out the dead, or the company will fire upon them . . . *Au'voir, mes enfants*.'

Of course, I knew the danger of making any reference to what would happen if the company refused to fire on the *escouade* – but it was foolish to pretend to ignore the possibility of such a thing. But I made no allusion to the Senegalese, and the coercion or punishment of white men by black.

It *might* be that the company would obey orders, if the *escouade* remained mutinous, and it *might* be that all would reflect upon the coming of the Senegalese.

Anyhow, I was on a knife-edge, and all depended upon the effect on these rascals of a four-hour rest and the words of the men to whom I had talked. There was just a chance that St. André and his Senegalese might arrive in time to influence the course of affairs – but I most certainly could not bring myself to postpone the issue until his arrival, and then take shelter behind the blacks. With the full moon well up in the sky – by its beautiful soft light – we should see what we should see . . .

And then, just as the men turned to go, I had an idea. Suppose some of them would volunteer to go over the fort with me; see for themselves that there was nothing to be afraid of; and then report to their fellows that all was well.

Their statement and the inevitable airs of superiority which they would give themselves, might well counteract Rastignac's influence and their superstitious fears. If some of these men, selected for character and influence, went back in the spirit of, "Well, cowards, *we* have been in there and it is much the same as any other such cursed hole – except that somebody had a great idea for diddling the Arabs," the others would probably take the line, "Well, where you can go, we can. Who are *you* to swagger?"

Yes – I would try it. Not as though I were really persuading or beseeching, and anxious to prove that the *escouade* had nothing to fear if sent to garrison the place. No – merely as offering them, superior soldiers, an opportunity of seeing the fort before its remarkable dispositions were disturbed.

"Wait a moment," said I, as they saluted and turned to go. "Is there a man of courage among you – a man, *par exemple* such as the trumpeter, brave enough to enter an empty fort with me?"

They looked sheepish for a moment. Someone murmured, "And where *is* Jean the Trumpeter?" and then I heard a curious whispered remark: "*Gee! I sure would like to see a ghost, Buddy*," and the whispered reply: "*Sure thing, Hank, and I'd like to see ole Brown some more*."

Two men stepped forward as one, and saluted.

They were in extraordinary contrast in body, and some similarity in face, for one was a giant and the other not more than five feet in height, while both had clean-shaven leathery countenances, somewhat of the bold Red Indian type.

You know what I mean – lean hatchet faces, biggish noses, mouths like a straight gash, and big chins. By their grey eyes they were Northerners, and by their speech Americans.

"You would like to see the fort and how it was manned to the last by heroes – victorious in death?" I asked.

"*Oui, mon Commandant*," they replied together.

"Isn't there a *Frenchman* among you?" I asked the rest.

Another man, a big sturdy Gascon he looked, saluted and joined the Americans. Then what they now call "the herd instinct" and "mob-psychology" came into play, and the others did the same.

Good! I had got the lot. I would take them round the fort as though doing honour to the dead and showing them as an example – and then I suddenly remembered . . .'

'The murdered *sous-officier*,' said George Lawrence.

'Exactly, George! These fellows must not see him lying there with a French bayonet through him! I must go in first, alone, and give myself the pleasant task of removing the bayonet. I would cover his face, and it would be assumed that he had been shot and had fallen where he lay. Yes, that was it . . .

"Good! You shall come with me then," said I, "and have the privilege of treading holy ground and seeing a sight of which to talk to your grand-children when you are old men. You can also tell your comrades of what you have seen, and give them a fresh pride in their glorious Regiment," and I bade the Sergeant-Major march them over to the fort.

Mounting my mule, which had not been unsaddled, I rode quickly across to the gate. The sentry had been withdrawn.

Dismounting, I hurried up to the roof, to perform the distasteful duty I could not very well have delegated to the Sergeant-Major. I emerged from the darkness of the staircase on to the roof.

And there I stood and stared and stared and rubbed my eyes – and then for a moment felt just a little faint and just a little in sympathy with those poor superstitious fools of the *escouade*. . . For, my dear George, *the body of the sous-officier was no longer there!* Nor was that of the bareheaded recumbent man!'

'Good God!' ejaculated Lawrence, raising himself on his elbow and turning to de Beaujolais.

'Yes, that is what I said,' continued the other. 'What else was there to say? *Were* there djinns, afrites, evil spirits in this cursed desert, even as the inhabitants declared? Was the whole thing a nighmare? Had I dreamt that the body of a French *sous-officier* had lain here, with a French bayonet through it? Or was I dreaming now?

And then I think my temperature went up two or three degrees from the mere hundred and two that one disregards; for I remember entertaining the wild idea that perhaps a living man was shamming dead among these corpses. Moreover, I remember going round from corpse to corpse and questioning them. One or two that seemed extra lifelike I took by the arm, and as I shouted at them, I shook them and pulled at them until they fell to the ground, their rifles clattering down with them.

Suddenly I heard the feet of men upon the stair, and pulled myself together. The Sergeant-Major and the half-dozen or so of legionaries came out on to the roof.

I managed to make my little speech as they stared round in amazement, the most amazed of all being the Sergeant-Major, who gazed at the smeared pool of blood where the body of the *sous-officier* had lain.

The two Americans seemed particularly interested, and appeared to be looking for comrades among the dead.

When would one of the men salute and ask respectfully the first of the hundred questions that must be puzzling them: "*Where is their officer?*"

And what should I reply? They could see for themselves that the Arabs had not entered and carried him off. Perhaps their minds were too full of the question: "*Where is Jean the Trumpeter?*" for the other question to formulate itself.

I had made no reference to the disappearance of the trumpeter; but I knew that they had seen him enter the fort and had waited, as I did, for an astounding quarter of an hour, to see him come out again. They had watched me go in alone, at the end of that time, and had seen me emerge alone. What could I say?

It seemed to me to be best to say nothing on that subject, so I said it.

After a few minutes that seemed like a few hours, I bade Dufour take the men round the outbuildings, and then march them back to the oasis.

As he disappeared, last, down the stair, I called him back and we were alone together. Simultaneously we said the same words: "*Did you move it?*" – and each of us knew that the other knew nothing about it!

I laughed loudly, if not merrily, and the Sergeant-Major produced the oath of a lifetime; in length and originality, remarkable even for the Legion.

"Quite so, *Chef*," said I . . . "Life grows a little complicated."

"I'll give a complicated death to this *farceur*, when I find . . ." growled he as I motioned him to be off. "Blood of the devil, I will!"

He clattered down the stairs, and, soon after, I heard his voice below, as he led the group of men across the courtyard.

"Not much here to terrify the great Rastignac, *hein?*" he jeered.

'But there is certainly something here to terrify *me*, my friend," I observed to myself, and made my way back to my mule and the oasis . . . In fact, I fled . . .

Well, George, *mon vieux*, what do you think happened? Did the *escouade* obey and enter the fort like lambs, or did they refuse and successfully defy me, secure in the knowledge that the others would not fire on them?'

'You are alive to tell the tale, Jolly,' was the reply. 'That's the main thing.'

'On account of the importance of a part of it to you, my George, eh?' smiled the Frenchman.

'Oh, not at all, old chap,' Lawrence hastened to say, with a somewhat guilty smile. 'Simply on account of the fact that you are spared to France and to your friends.'

'I thank you, my little George. Almost might you be a Frenchman,' said de Beaujolais, with an ironical bow. 'But tell me, what do you think happened? Did they obey and enter, or did they refuse?'

'Give it up, Jolly. I can only feel sure that one of the two happened,' replied Lawrence.

'And that is where you are wrong, my friend, for neither happened,' continued de Beaujolais. 'They neither obeyed and entered, nor disobeyed and stayed out!'

'Good Lord!' ejaculated Lawrence. 'What then?'

And this time it was the Frenchman who suggested a little refreshment.

8

'Well, this is the last "event" on that remarkable programme, *mon cher Georges*,' resumed de Beaujolais a little later. 'A very appropriate and suitable one too . . . "*A delightful open-air entertainment concluded with fireworks*," as the reporters of *fêtes champêtres* say.'

'Fireworks? Rifle-fire works do you mean?' asked Lawrence.

'No, my George, nothing to speak of. Just fireworks. Works of fire . . . I will tell you . . .

I let the moon get well up, and then sent my servant, Achmet, for the Sergeant-Major, and bade that good fellow to parade the men as before, with the fort a hundred paces in their rear, the garrison *escouade* on the right of the line.

This party would either march into the fort or not. If *not* – then the remainder would be ordered to right-form and shoot them where they stood, for disobedience in the field, practically in the presence of the army.

The remainder would either obey or not. If *not* – then I would at once give the order to "pile arms." If they did this, as they might, from force of habit, they would be "arrested" by the non-commissioned officers and marched back to Tokotu, under escort of the Senegalese, to await court martial. If they did not pile arms, the non-commissioned officers were to come at once to me, and we would prepare to sell our lives dearly – for the men would mutiny and desert. Possibly a few of the men would join us, and there was a ghost of a chance that we might fight our way into the fort and hold it, but it was infinitely more probable that we should be riddled where we stood.

"*Bien, mon Commandant,*" said Dufour, as he saluted, and then, hesitatingly, "Might I presume to make a request and a suggestion. May I stand by you, and Rastignac stand by me – with the muzzle of my revolver against his liver – it being clear that, at the slightest threat to you, Rastignac's digestion is impaired? If he knows that just this will happen, he also may give good advice to his friends . . ."

"Nothing of the sort, Dufour," I replied. "Everything will proceed normally and properly, until the men themselves behave abnormally and improperly. We shall lead and command soldiers of France until we have to fight and kill, or be killed by, mutineers against the officers of France in the execution of their duty. Proceed."

Would you have said the same, George? It seemed to me that this idea of the Sergeant-Major's was not much better than that of waiting for the Senegalese. Would you have done the same in my place?'

'I can only *hope* I should have had the courage to act as bravely and as wisely as you did, Jolly,' was the reply.

'Oh, I am no hero, my friend,' smiled de Beaujolais, 'but it seemed the right thing to do. I had not in any way provoked a mutiny – indeed, I had stretched a point to avert it – and it was my business to go straight ahead, do my duty, and abide the result.

But it was with an anxious heart that I mounted the mule again and cantered over to the fort.

I had thought of going on a camel, for, it is a strange psychological fact, that if your hearers have to look up to you physically, they also have to look up to you metaphysically as it were. If a leader speaks with more authority from a mule than from the ground, and with more weight and power from a horse than from a mule, would he not speak with still more from a camel?

Perhaps – but I felt that I could *do* more, somehow, in case of trouble, if I could dash at assailants with sword and revolver. I am a cavalry man and the *arme blanche* is my weapon. Cold steel and cut and thrust, for me, if I had to go down fighting. You can't charge and use your sword on a camel, so I compromised on the mule – but how I longed for my Arab charger and a few of my Spahis behind me! It would be a fight then, instead of a murder . . .

It was a weird and not unimpressive scene. That sinister fort, silver and black; the frozen waves of the ocean of sand, an illimitable silver sea; the oasis a big, dark island upon it; the men, statues, inscrutable and still.

What would they do? Would my next words be my last? Would a double line of rifles rise and level themselves at my breast, or would that *escouade*, upon whom everything depended, move off like a machine and enter the fort?

As I faced the men, I was acutely interested, and yet felt like a spectator, impersonal and unafraid. I was about to witness a thrilling drama, depicting the fate of one Henri de Beaujolais, quite probably his death. I hoped he would play a worthy part on this moonlit stage. I hoped that, even more than I hoped to see him survive the play. I was calm. I was detached . . .'

George Lawrence sighed and struck a match.

'I cast one more look at the glorious moon and took a deep breath. If this was my last order on parade, it should be worthily given, in a voice deep, clear, and firm. Above all firm. And as my mouth opened, and my lower jaw moved in the act of speech – I believe it dropped, George, and my mouth remained open.

For, from that enigmatical, brooding, fatal fort – there shot up a tongue of flame!

"*Mon Dieu! Regardez!*" cried the Sergeant-Major, and pointed. I believe every head turned, and in the perfect silence I heard him whisper, "*Spirits, ghosts, devils!*"

That brought me to myself sharply. "Yes, imbecile" I said. "They carry matches and indulge in arson! Quite noted incendiaries! Where is Rastignac?"

I asked that because it was perfectly obvious that someone was in the fort and had set fire to something highly inflammable. I had been in the place an hour or two before. There was certainly no sign of fire then, and this was a sudden rush of flame.

As I watched, another column of smoke and fire burst forth in a different place.

"He is tied up back there, *mon Commandant*," replied Dufour.

"The forbidden *crapaudine?*" I asked.

"I *told* Corporal Brille to tie him to a tree," was the reply.

Anyhow it could not be Rastignac's work, for he would not have entered the place, even had he been left at liberty and had an opportunity to do so.

"Send and see if he is still there – and make sure that everyone else is accounted for," I ordered.

It was useless to detail a *pompier* squad to put the fire out. We don't have hose and hydrants in the desert, as you know. When a place burns, it burns. And, *mon Dieu*, *how* it burns in the dry heat of that rainless desert! The place would be gone, even if the men would enter it, by the time we had got our teaspoonfuls of water from the oasis. And, to tell you the truth, I did not care how soon, or how completely it *did* go!

This fire would be the funeral pyre of those brave men. It would keep my fools from their suicidal mutiny. It would purge the place of mystery. Incidentally it would save my life and military reputation, and the new fort that would arise in its place would not be the haunted, hated prison that this place would henceforth have been for those who had to garrison it.

I gave the order to face about, and then to stand at ease. The men should watch it burn, since nothing could be done to save it. Perhaps even they would realise that human agency is required for setting a building on fire – and, moreover, whoever was in there had got to come out or be cremated. They should see him come . . . But who? Who? The words *Who?* and *Why?* filled my mind . . .

All stood absolutely silent, spellbound.

Suddenly the spell was broken and back we came to earth, at an old familiar sound.

A rifle cracked, again and again. From the sound the firing was towards us.

The Arabs were upon us!

Far to the right and to the left, more shots were fired.

The fort blazing and the Arabs upon us!

Bullets whistled overhead and I saw one or two flashes from a distant sand-hill.

No one was hit, the fort being between us and the enemy. In less time than it takes to tell I had the men turned about and making for the oasis – *au pas gymnastique* – "at the double," as you call it. There we should have cover and water, and if we could only hold the devils until they were nicely between us and St. André's Senegalese, we would avenge the garrison of that blazing fort.

They are grand soldiers, those Légionnaires, George. No better troops in our army. They are to other infantry what my Spahis are to other cavalry. It warmed one's heart to see them double, steady as on parade, back to the darkness of the oasis, every man select his cover and go to ground, his rifle loaded and levelled as he did so.

Our camel vedettes rode in soon after. Two of them had had a desperated fight, and two had seen rifle-flashes and fired at them, before returning to the oasis, thinking the Arabs had rushed the fort and burnt it.

In a few minutes from the first burst of fire, the whole place was still, silent, and apparently deserted. Nothing for an enemy to see but a burning fort, and a black brooding oasis, where nothing moved.

How I hoped they would swarm yelling round the fort, thinking to get us like bolted rabbits as we rushed out of it! It is not like the Arabs to make a night attack, but doubtless they had been hovering near, and the fire had brought them down on us.

Had they seen us outside the fort? If so, they would attack the oasis in the morning. If they had not seen us, anything might happen, and the oasis prove a *guet-apens*, with the burning or burnt-out fort as the bait of the trap.

What were they doing now? The firing had ceased entirely. Probably making their dispositions to rush us suddenly at dawn, from behind the nearest sand-hills. Their game would be to lull us into a sense of security throughout a peaceful night and come down upon us at daybreak, like a whirlwind, as we slept.

And what if our waiting rifles caught them at fifty yards, and the survivors turned to flee – on to the muzzles of those of the Senegalese? . . .

It was another impressive scene in that weird drama, George. A big fire, by moonlight, in the heart of the Sahara, a fire watched by silent, motionless men, breathlessly awaiting the arrival of others players on the stage.

After gazing into the moonlit distance until my eyes ached, expecting to see a great band of the blue-veiled mysterious Silent Ones suddenly swarm over a range of sand-hills, I bethought me of getting into communication with St. André.

I had ordered him to follow by a forced march, leaving a suitable garrison at Tokotu, when I dashed off with the "always ready" emergency-detachment on camels, preceding by an hour or so the "support" emergency-detachment on mules, with water, rations, and ammunition.

These two detachments are more than twice as fast as the best infantry, but I reckoned that St. André would soon be drawing near.

It was quite possible that he might run into the Arabs, while the latter were watching the oasis – if they had seen us enter it, or their skirmishers established the fact of our presence.

So far, we had not fired a shot from the oasis, and it was possible that our presence was unsuspected.

This might, or might not, be the same band that had attacked the place. If they were the same, they might be hanging about in the hope of ambushing a relieving force. If St. André arrived while the fort was burning, they would have no chance of catching him unawares. If he came after the flames had died down, he might march straight into a trap. There would certainly be a Targui scout or two out in the direction of Tokotu, while the main body did business at Zinderneuf.

Anyhow, I must communicate with St. André if possible. It would be a good man that would undertake the job successfully – for both skill and courage would be required. There was the track to find and follow, and there were the Arabs to face.

To lose the former was to die of thirst and starvation; to find the latter was to die of tortures indescribable.

On the whole it might be better to send two. Twice the chance of my message reaching St. André. Possibly more than twice the chance, really, as two men are braver than one, because they hearten each other.

I went round the oasis until I found the Sergeant-Major, who was going from man to man, prohibiting any firing without orders, any smoking or the making of any noise. This was quite sound and I commended him, and then asked for a couple of men of the right stamp for my job.

I was not surprised when he suggested two of the men who had been into the fort with me, and passed the word for the two Americans. He recommended them as men who could use the stars, good scouts, brave, resourceful, and very determined.

They would, at any rate, stand a chance of getting through the Arabs and giving St. André the information that would turn him from their victim into their scourge, if we had any luck.

When the big slow giant and the little quick man appeared and silently saluted, I asked them if they would like to undertake this duty. They were more than ready, and as I explained my plans for trapping the Arabs between two fires, I found them of quick intelligence. Both were able to repeat to me, with perfect lucidity, what I wanted them to say to St. André, that he might be able to attack the attackers at dawn, just when they were attacking me.

The two left the oasis on camels, from the side opposite to the fort, and after they had disappeared over a sand-hill, you may imagine with what anxiety I listened for firing. But all was silent, and the silence of the grave prevailed until morning.

After two or three hours of this unbroken, soundless stillness, the fire having died down in the fort, I felt perfectly certain there would be no attack until dawn.

All who were not on the duty of outposts-by-night slept, and I strolled silently round and round the oasis, waiting for the first hint of sunrise and thinking over the incredible events of that marvellous day – certainly unique in my fairly wide experience of hectic days.

I went over it all again from the moment when I first sighted the accursed fort with its flag flying over its unscaled walls and their dead defenders, to the moment when my eyes refused to believe that the place was on fire and blazing merrily.

At length, leaning against the trunk of a palm tree and longing for a cigarette and some hot coffee to help me keep awake, I faced the east and watched for the paling of the stars. As I did so, my mind grew clearer as my body grew weaker, and I decided to decide that all this was the work of a madman, concealed in the fort, and now burnt to death.

He had, for some reason, murdered the *sous-officier* with a bayonet (certainly he must be mad or he would have shot him); and he had, for some reason, silently killed the trumpeter and hidden his body – all in the few minutes that elapsed before I followed the trumpeter in. (Had the murderer used *another* bayonet for this silent job?) He had for some reason removed the *sous-officier's*, and the other man's body and concealed those too, and, finally, he had set fire to the fort and perished in the flames.

But where was he while I searched the place, and why had he not killed me also when I entered the fort alone?

The lunacy theory must account for these hopelessly lunatic proceedings – but it hardly accounts for the murdered *sous-officier* having in his hand a confession signed, "Michael Geste," to the effect that he had stolen a jewel, does it, my old one?'

'It does *not*, my son, and that, to me, is the most interesting and remarkable fact in your most interesting and remarkable story,' replied Lawrence.

'Well, I decided, as I say, to leave it at that – just the mad doings of a madman, garnished by the weird coincidence of the paper,' continued de Beaujolais, 'and soon afterwards the sky grew grey in the east.

Before a rosy streak could herald the dawn we silently stood to arms, and when the sun peeped over the horizon he beheld St. André's Senegalese skirmishing beautifully towards us!

There wasn't so much as the smell of an Arab for miles . . . No, St. André had not seen a living thing – not even the two scouts I had sent out to meet him. Nor did anyone else ever see those two brave fellows. I have often wondered what their fate was – Arabs or thirst . . .

I soon learnt that one of St. André's mule-scouts had ridden back to him, early in the night, to say that he had heard rifle-shots in the direction of Zinderneuf. St. André had increased his pace, alternating the quick march and the *pas gymnastique* until he knew he must be near his goal. All being then perfectly silent he decided to beware of an ambush, to halt for the rest of the night, and to feel his way forward, in attack formation, at dawn.

He had done well, and my one regret was that the Arabs who had caused the destruction of Zinderneuf were not between me and him as he closed upon the oasis.

While the weary troops rested, I told St. André all that had happened, and asked for a theory – reserving mine about the madman. He is a man with a brain, this St. André, ambitious and a real soldier. Although he has private means, he serves France where duty is hardest, and life least attractive. A little dark pocket-Hercules of energy and force.

"What about this, Major?" said he, when I had finished my account, and having fed, we were sitting, leaning our weary backs against a fallen palm trunk, with coffee and cigarettes at hand.

"Suppose your trumpeter killed the *sous-officier* himself and deserted there and then?"

"*Mon Dieu!*" said I; 'that never occurred to me. But why should he, and why use his bayonet and leave it in the body?'

"Well – as to why he *should*," replied St. André, "it might have been revenge. This may have been the first time he had ever been alone with the *sous-officier*, whom he may have sworn to kill at the first opportunity . . . Some fancied or real injustice, when he was under this man at Sidi-bel-Abbès or elsewhere. The sight of his enemy, the sole survivor, alone, rejoicing in his hour of victory and triumph, may have further maddened a brain already mad with *cafard*, brooding, lust of vengeance, I know not what of desperation."

"Possible," I said, and thought over this idea. 'But no, impossible, my friend. Why had not the *sous-officier* rushed to the wall, or up to the look-out platform when I approached? I fired my revolver six times to attract attention and let them know that relief had come, and two answering rifle-shots were fired! Why was he not waving his *képi* and shouting for joy? Why did he not rush down to the gates and throw them open?'

"Wounded and lying down," suggested St. André.

"He was not wounded, my friend," said I. "He was killed. That bayonet, and nothing else, had done his business."

"Asleep," suggested the Lieutenant, "absolutely worn out. Sleeping like the dead – and thus his enemy, the trumpeter, found him, and drove the bayonet through his heart as he slept. He was going to blow the sleeper's brains out, when he remembered that the shot would be heard and would have to be explained. Therefore he used the bayonet, drove it through the man, and then, and not till then, he realised that the bayonet would betray him. It would leap to the eye, instantly, that *murder* had been committed – and not by one of the garrison. So he fled."

"And the revolver, with *one* chamber fired?" I asked.

"Oh – fired during the battle, at some daring Arab who rode round the fort, reconnoitring, and came suddenly into view."

"And the paper in the left hand?"

"I do not know."

"And who fired the two welcoming shots?"

"I do not know."

"And how did the trumpeter vanish across the desert – as conspicuous as a negro's head on a pillow – before the eyes of my Company?"

"I do not know."

"Nor do I," I said.

And then St. André sat up suddenly.

"*Mon Commandant*," said he, "the trumpeter did not escape, of course. He murdered the *sous-officier* and then hid himself. It was he who removed the two bodies when he again found himself alone in the fort. He may have had some idea of removing the bayonet and turning the stab into a bullet-wound. He then meant to return to the Company with some tale of cock and bull. But remembering that you had already seen the body, and might have noticed the bayonet, he determined to set fire to the fort, burn all evidence, and rejoin in the confusion caused by the fire.

He could swear that he had been knocked on the head from behind, and only recovered consciousness in time to escape from the flames kindled by whoever it was who clubbed him. This is all feasible – and if improbable it is no more improbable than the actual facts of the case, is it?"

"Quite so, *mon Lieutenant*," I agreed. "And why did he not rejoin in the confusion, with his tale of cock and bull?"

"Well – here's a theory. Suppose the *sous-officier* did shoot at him with the revolver and wounded him so severely that by the time he had completed his little job of arson he was too weak to walk. He fainted from loss of blood and perished miserably in the flames that he himself had kindled. Truly a splendid example of poetic justice."

"Magnificent," I agreed. "The Greek Irony, in effect. Hoist by his own petard. Victim of the mocking Fates, and so forth. The only flaw in the beautiful theory is that *we should have heard the shot* – just as we should have heard a rifle-shot had the trumpeter used his rifle for the murder. In that brooding heavy silence a revolver fired on that open roof would have sounded like a seventy-five."

"True," agreed St. André, a little crestfallen. "The man was mad then. He did everything that was done, and then committed suicide or was burnt alive."

"Ah, my friend," said I, "you have come to the madman theory, eh? So had I. It is the only one. But now I will tell you something. The trumpeter did *not* do all this. He did *not* murder the *sous-officier*, for that unfortunate had been dead *for hours*, and the trumpeter had not been in the place ten *minutes!*"

"And that's that," said St. André. "Let's try again." And he tried again – very ingeniously too. But he could put forward no theory that he himself did not at once ridicule.

We were both, of course, weary to death and more in need of twenty-four hours' sleep than twenty-four conundrums – but I do not know that I have done much better since.

And as I rode back to Tokotu, with my record go of fever, my head opened with a tearing wrench and closed with a shattering bang, at every stride of my camel, to the tune of, "*Who killed the Commandant, and why, why, why?*" till I found I was saying it aloud.

I am saying it still, George.' . . .

9

Passengers by the *Appam*, from Lagos to Birkenhead, were interested in two friends who sat side by side in Madeira chairs, or walked the promenade deck in close and constant company.

The one, a tall, bronzed, lean Englishman, taciturn, forbidding, and grim, who never used two words where one would suffice; his cold grey eye looking through, or over, those who surrounded him; his iron-grey hair and moustache, his iron-firm chin and mouth, suggesting the iron that had entered into his soul and made him the hard, cold, bitter person that he was, lonely, aloof, and self-sufficing. (Perhaps Lady Brandon of Brandon Abbas, alone of women, knew the real man and what he might have been; and perhaps half a dozen men liked him as greatly as all men respected him.)

The other, a shorter, stouter, more genial person, socially inclined, a fine type of French soldier, suave, courtly, and polished, ruddy of face and brown of eye and hair, and vastly improved by the removal, before Madeira, of a three years' desert beard. He was obviously much attached to the Englishman . . .

It appeared these two had something on their minds, for day by day, and night by night, save for brief intervals for eating, sleeping, and playing bridge, they interminably discussed, or rather the Frenchman interminably discussed, and the Englishman intently listened, interjecting monosyllabic replies.

When the Englishman contributed to the one-sided dialogue, a listener would have noted that he spoke most often of a bareheaded man and of a paper, speculating as to the identity of the former and the authorship of the latter.

The Frenchman, on the other hand, talked more of a murder, a disappearance, and a fire . . .

'How long is it since you heard from Lady Brandon, Jolly?' enquired George Lawrence, one glorious and invigorating morning, as the *Appam* ploughed her steady way across a blue and smiling Bay of Biscay.

'Oh, years and years,' was the reply. 'I was at Brandon Abbas for a week of my leave before last. That would be six or seven years ago. I haven't written a line since the letter of thanks after the visit . . . Do you correspond with her at all regularly?'

'Er – no. I shouldn't call it regular correspondence exactly,' answered George Lawrence. 'Are you going to Brandon Abbas this leave?' he continued, with a simulated yawn.

'Well – I feel I ought to go, *mon vieux*, and take that incredible document, but it doesn't fit in with my plans at all. I could post it to her, of course, but it would mean a devil of a long letter of explanation, and I loathe letterwriting "fatigues" more than anything.'

'I'll take it if you like,' said Lawrence. 'I shall be near Brandon Abbas next week. And knowing Michael Geste, I confess I am curious.'

Major de Beaujolais was conscious of the fact that 'curious' was not exactly the word he would have used. His selfrepressed, taciturn, and unemotional friend had been stirred to the depths of his soul, and had given an exhibition of interest and emotion such as he had never displayed before in all de Beaujolais' experience of him.

What touched Lady Brandon evidently touched him – to an extent that rendered 'curious' a curious word to use. He smiled to himself as he gravely replied:

'But excellent, *mon vieux!* That would be splendid. It will save me from writing a letter a mile long, and Lady Brandon cannot feel that I have treated the *affaire* casually, and as if of no importance. I explain the whole matter to you, her old friend, give you the document, and ask you to lay it before her. You could say that while supposing the document to be merely a *canard*, interesting only by reason of how and where it was found, I nevertheless think that she ought to have it, just in case there is anything I can do in the matter.'

'Just that,' agreed Lawrence. 'Of course "Beau" Geste never stole the sapphire, or anything else; but I suppose, as you say, a document like that ought to go to her and Geste, as their names are mentioned.'

'Certainly, *mon ami*. And if the stone *has* been stolen, the paper might be an invaluable clue to its recovery. Handwriting, for example, a splendid clue. She could please herself as to whether she put it in the hands of your Criminal Investigation Department at Scotland Yard and asked them to get in touch with our police . . . Assure her of my anxiety to do absolutely anything I can in the matter – if either the jewel or Michael Geste should be missing.'

'Righto, Jolly,' was the reply. 'I'll drop in there one day. Probably the first person I shall see will be "Beau" Geste himself, and probably I shall see the "Blue Water" the same evening.'

'No doubt, George,' agreed de Beaujolais, and added, 'Do you know Michael Geste's handwriting?'

'No. Never saw it to my knowledge,' was the reply. 'Why do you ask? You don't suppose that Beau Geste wrote that, do you?'

'I have given up supposing, my friend,' said de Beaujolais. 'But I shall open my next letter from you with some alacrity. Either this "Blue Water" is stolen or it is not. In either case that paper, in a dead man's hand, at Zinderneuf, is uniquely interesting. But if it *has* been stolen, it will be of practical as well as unique interest; whereas if it has not been stolen, the unique interest will be merely theoretical.'

'Not very practical from the point of view of recovery, I am afraid. It looks as though the thief and the jewel and the story all ended together in the burning of Zinderneuf fort,' mused Lawrence.

'*Mon Dieu!* I never thought of it before. The biggest and finest sapphire in the world, valued at three-quarters of a million francs, may be lying at this moment among the rubble and rubbish of the burnt-out ruins of Zinderneuf fort!' said de Beaujolais.

'By Jove! So it may!' agreed Lawrence. 'Suppose it has been stolen . . . If I wired to you, could anything be done about making a search there, do you think?'

For a moment George Lawrence had visions of devoting his leave to jewel-hunting, and returning to Brandon Abbas with three-quarters of a million francs' worth of crystallised alumina in his pocket.

'That will require prompt and careful consideration, directly we learn that the stone has gone, George,' said de Beaujolais, and added: 'This grows more and more interesting . . . A treasure hunt at Zinderneuf! Fancy the Arabs if the information got about! Fancy the builders of the new fort, and the garrison! Zinderneuf would become the most popular outpost in Africa, instead of the least – until the sapphire was found. If it *is* there, I suppose the surest way to lose it for ever would be to hint at the fact . . . No, we should have to keep it very quiet and do all the searching ourselves, if possible . . . Good heavens above us! More complications!' He smiled whimsically.

George Lawrence pursued his vision and the two fell silent for a space.

'Supposing that stone had actually been in the pocket of a man on that roof, when it collapsed into the furnace below,' said de Beaujolais as he sat up and felt for his cigarette case, 'would the jewel be destroyed when the body of the man was cremated? Does fire affect precious stones?'

'Don't know,' replied Lawrence. 'We could find that out from any jeweller, I suppose. I rather think not. Aren't they, in fact, formed in the earth by a heat greater than any furnace can produce?'

'Of course,' agreed de Beaujolais. 'You could make as many diamonds as you wanted if you could get sufficient heat and pressure. They are only crystallised carbon. Fire certainly wouldn't hurt a diamond, and I don't suppose it would hurt any other precious stone.'

'No,' he mused on. 'If the Blue Water has been stolen, it is probably safe and sound at this moment in Zinderneuf, adorning the charred remains of a skeleton' . . . and George Lawrence day-dreamed awhile, of himself, Lady Brandon, and the sacrifice of his leave to the making of a great restoration. Of his leave? Nay, if necessary, of his career, his whole life.

('Describe me a man's day-dreams and I will describe you the man,' said the Philosopher. He might have described George Lawrence as a romantic and quixotic fool-errant, which he was not, or perhaps merely as a man in love, which he was. Possibly the Philosopher might have added that the descriptions are synonymous, and that therefore George Lawrence was both.)

He was awakened from his reverie by the voice of de Beaujolais.

'Queer, that it never got into the papers, George,' mused that gentleman.

'Yes. It is,' agreed Lawrence. 'I should certainly have seen it if it had. I read my *Telegraph* and *Observer* religiously . . . No, I certainly should never have missed it . . . Probably the damned thing was never stolen at all.'

'Looks like it,' said his friend. 'Every English paper would have had an account of the theft of a famous jewel like that . . . Though it is just possible that Lady Brandon hushed it up for some reason . . . What about an *aperitif*, my old one?'

And, his old one agreeing, they once more dropped the subject of Beau Geste, the 'Blue Water,' Zinderneuf, and its secret.

On parting in London, Major de Beaujolais handed a document to George Lawrence, who promised to deliver it, and also to keep his friend informed as to any developments of the story.

The Major felt that he had the middle of it, and he particularly desired to discover its beginning, and to follow it to the end.

2

George Lawrence takes the Story to Lady Brandon at Brandon Abbas

AS his hireling car sped along the country road that led to the park gates of Brandon Abbas, George Lawrence's heart beat like that of a boy going to his first love-tryst.

Had she married him, a quarter of a century ago, when she was plain (but very beautiful) Patricia Rivers, he probably would still have loved her, though he would not have been in love with her.

As it was he had never been anything but in love with her from the time when he had taken her refusal like the man he was, and had sought an outlet and an anodyne in work and Central Africa.

As the car entered the gates and swept up the long, winding avenue of Norman oaks, he actually trembled, and his bronzed face was drawn and changed in tint. He drew off a glove and put it on again, fingered his tie, and tugged at his moustache.

The car swept round a shrubbery-enclosed square at the back of the house, and stopped at this, Lawrence looked into a well-remembered panelled hall and ran his eye over its gleaming floor and walls, almost nodding to the two suits of armour that stood one on each side of a big, doorless doorway. This led into another hall, from, and round, which ran a wide staircase and galleries right up to the top of the house, for, from the floor of that hall one could look up to a glass roof three stories above. He pictured it and past scenes enacted in it, and a woman with slow and stately grace, ascending and descending.

Nothing seemed to have changed in those two and a half decades since she had come here, a bride, and he had visited her after seven years of exile. He had come, half in the hope that the sight of her in her own home, the wife of another man, would cure him of the foolish love that kept him a lonely bachelor, half in the hope that it would do the opposite, and be but a renewal of love.

He had been perversely glad to find that he loved the woman, if possible, more than he had loved the girl; that a callow boy's calf-love for a maiden had changed to a young man's devotion to a glorious woman; that she was to be a second Dante's Beatrice.

Again and again, at intervals of years, he had visited the shrine, not so much renewing the ever-burning fire at her altar, as watching it flame up brightly in her presence. Nor did the fact that she regarded him so much as friend that he could never be more, nor less, in any way affect this undeviating unprofitable sentiment.

At thirty, at thirty-five, at forty-five, he found that his love, if not unchanged, was not diminished, and that she remained, what she had been since their first meeting, the central fact of his life – not so much an obsession, an *idée fixe*, as his reason for existence, his sovereign, and the audience of the play in the theatre of his life.

And, each time he saw her, she was, to his prejudiced eye, more desirable, more beautiful, more wonderful . . .

Yes – there was the fifteenth-century chest in which reposed croquet mallets, tennis rackets, and the other paraphernalia of those games. She had once sat on that old chest, beside him, while they waited for the dog-cart to take him to the station and back to Africa, and her hand had rested so kindly in his, as he had tried to find something to say – something other than what he might not say . . .

Opposite to it was the muniment-box, into which many an abbot and holy friar had put many a lead-sealed parchment. It would be full of garden rugs and cushions. On that, she had sat beside him, after his dance with her, one New Year's Eve . . .

Same pictures of horse and hound, and bird and beast; same antlers and foxes' masks and brushes; same trophies he had sent from Nigeria, specially good heads of lion, buffalo, gwambaza, and gazelle.

From these his eye travelled to the great fire-place on each side of which stood a mounted Lake Tchad elephant's foot, doing menial service, while above its stone mantel, a fine trophy of African weapons gleamed. One of his greatest satisfactions had always been to acquire something worthy to be sent to Brandon Abbas – to give her pleasure and to keep him in mind.

And now, perhaps, was his real chance of giving her pleasure and keeping himself, for a space, very much in her mind. He pulled the quaint old handle of a chain, and a distant bell clanged.

A footman approached, a stranger.

He would enquire as to whether her ladyship were at home. But as he turned to go, the butler appeared in the doorway from the inner hall.

'Hallo, Burdon! How are you?' said Lawrence.

'Why, Mr. George, sir!' replied the old man, who had known Lawrence for thirty years, coming forward and looking unwontedly human.

'This is a real pleasure, sir.'

It was – a real five-pound note too, when the visitor, a perfect gent, departed. Quite a source of income Mr. Lawrence had been, ever since Henry Burdon had been under-footman in the service of her ladyship's father.

'Her Ladyship is at the Bower, sir, if you'd like to come straight out,' he continued, knowing that the visitor was a very old friend indeed, and always welcome. 'I will announce you.'

Burdon led the way.

'How is Lady Brandon?' enquired Lawrence, impelled to unwonted loquacity by his nervousness.

'She enjoys very good health, sir – considering,' replied the butler.

'Considering what?' asked Lawrence.

'Everythink, sir,' was the non-committal reply.

The visitor smiled to himself. A good servant, this.

'And how is his Reverence?' he continued.

'Queer, sir, very. And gets queerer, poor gentleman,' was the answer.

Lawrence expressed regret at this bad news concerning the chaplain, as the Reverend Maurice Ffolliot was always called in that house.

'Is Mr. Michael here?' he asked.

'No, sir, he ain't. Nor none of the other young gentlemen,' was the reply. Was there anything unusual in the old man's tone? . . .

Emerging from the shrubbery, crossing a rose-garden, some lawn-tennis courts, and a daisy-pied stretch of cedar-studded sward, the pair entered a wood, followed a path beneath enormous elms and beeches, and came out to a square of velvet turf.

On two sides, the left and rear, rose the great old trees of a thickly forested hill; on the right, the grey old house; and from the front of this open space the hillside fell away to the famous view.

By wicker table and hammock-stand, a lady reclined in a *chaise longue*. She was reading a book and her back was towards Lawrence, whose heart missed a beat and hastened to make up omission by a redoubled speed.

The butler coughed at the right distance and upon the right note, and as, Lady Brandon turned, announced the visitor, hovered, placed a wicker chair, and faded from the scene.

'George!' said Lady Brandon, in her soft deep contralto, with a pleased brightening of her wide grey eyes and flash of beautiful teeth. But she did not flush nor pale, and there was no quickening of her breath in. It was upon the man that these symptoms were produced by the meeting although it was a meeting anticipated by him, unexpected by her.

'Patricia!' he said, and extended both hands. She took them frankly and Lawrence kissed them both, with a curiously gentle and reverent manner, an exhibition of a George Lawrence unknown to other people.

'Well, my dear!' he said, and looked long at the unlined, if mature, determined, clever face before him – that of a woman of forty years, of strong character and of aristocratic breeding.

'Yes,' he continued.

'Yes "what," George?'asked Brandon.

'Yes. You are positively as young and as beautiful as ever,' he replied – but with no air of gallantry and compliment, and rather as a sober statement of ascertained fact.

'And you as foolish, George . . . Sit down – and tell me why you have disobeyed me and come here before your wedding. . . . Or – or – are you married, George?' was the smiling reply.

'No, Patricia, I am not married,' said Lawrence, relinquishing her hands slowly. 'And I have disobeyed you, and come here again without bringing a wife, because I hoped you might be in need of my help, and hoped that I might be able to give it.'

Lady Brandon fixed a penetrating gaze on Lawrence's face – neither startled nor alarmed, he felt, but keen and, possibly, to be described as wary, or at least watchful.

'Trouble? In need of help, George? How?'she asked, and whatever of wariness or watchfulness had peeped from her eyes retired, and her face became a beautiful mask, showing no more than reposeful and faintly-amused interest.

'Well – it is a longish story,' said Lawrence. 'But I need not inflict it on you if you'll tell me if Beau Geste is all right and – er – the "Blue Water" – er – safe and sound and – er – all that you know.'

'What?' ejaculated his hearer sharply.

There was no possible doubt now, as to the significance of the look on Lady Brandon's face. It certainly could be called one of alarm, and her direct gaze was distinctly watchful and wary. Had she also paled very slightly? Undoubtedly she frowned faintly as she asked:

'What are you talking about, George?'

'Beau Geste, and the "Blue Water," Patricia,' replied Lawrence. 'If I appear to be talking through my hat, I am not really, and will produce reason for my wild-but-not-wicked words,' he laughed. 'There is method in my madness, dear.'

'There's madness in your method,' replied Lady Brandon a trifle tartly, and added: 'Have you seen Michael, then? Or what? Tell me!'

No. I have not seen him – but . . .'

Then what are you talking about? What do you know?' she interrupted, speaking hurriedly, a very sure sign that she was greatly perturbed.

'I don't *know* anything, Patricia, and I'm asking *you*, because I have, most extraordinarily, come into possession of a document that purports to be a confession by Beau that he stole the "Blue Water,"' began Lawrence.

'Then it *was* . . .' whispered Lady Brandon.

'Was what, Patricia?' asked Lawrence.

'Go on, dear,' she replied hastily. 'How and where did you get this confession? Tell me quickly.'

'As I said, it's a long story,' replied Lawrence. 'It was found by de Beaujolais at a place called Zinderneuf in the French Soudan, in the hand of a dead man . . .'

'Not *Michael*!' interrupted Lady Brandon.

'No – a Frenchman. An *adjudant* in charge of a fort that had been attacked by Arabs . . .'

'*Our* Henri de Beaujolais?' interrupted Lady Brandon, again. 'Who was at school with you? . . . Rose Cary's son?'

'Yes. He found it in this dead officer's hand . . .' replied Lawrence.

'Er – *has* the sapphire been stolen, Patricia, and – er – excuse the silly question – *is* this Beau's writing?' and he thrust his hand into the inner pocket of his jacket.

'But of course it isn't,' he continued as he produced an envelope and extracted a stained and dirty piece of paper.

Lady Brandon took the latter and looked at it, her face hard, enigmatical, a puzzled frown marring the smoothness of her forehead, her firm shapely mouth more tightly compressed than usual.

She read the document and then looked out into the distance, down the coombe, and across the green and smiling plain, as though communing with herself and deciding how to answer.

'Tell me the whole story from beginning to end, George,' she said at length, 'if it takes you the week-end. But tell me this quickly. *Do* you know anything more than you have told me, about either Michael or the "Blue Water"?'

'I know nothing whatever, my dear,' was the reply, and the speaker thought he saw a look of relief, or a lessening of the look of alarm on his hearer's face, 'but what I have told you. You know as much as I do now – except the details, of course.'

George Lawrence noted that Lady Brandon had neither admitted nor denied that the sapphire had been stolen, had neither admitted nor denied that the handwriting was that of her nephew.

Obviously and undoubtedly there was something wrong, something queer, and in connection with Beau Geste too.

For one thing, he was missing and she did not know where he was.

But since all questions as to him, his handwriting, and the safety of the jewel had remained unanswered, he could only refrain from repeating them, and do nothing more but tell his story, and, at the end of it, say: 'If the "Blue Water" is not in this house, Patricia, I am going straight to Zinderneuf to find it for you.'

She would then, naturally, give him all the information she could, and every assistance in her power – if the sapphire had been stolen.

If it had not, she would, of course, say so.

But he wished she would be a little less guarded, a little more communicative. It would be so very easy to say: 'My dear George, the "Blue Water" is in the safe in the Priests' Hole as usual, and Michael is in excellent health and spirits,' or, on the other hand, to admit at once: 'The "Blue Water" has vanished and so has Michael.'

However, what Patricia Brandon did was right. For whatever course of action she pursued, she had some excellent reason, and he had no earthly cause to feel a little hurt at her reticence in the matter.

For example, if the impossible had come to pass, and Beau Geste had stolen the sapphire and bolted, would it not be perfectly natural for her to feel most reluctant to have it known that her nephew was a thief – a despicable creature that robbed his benefactress?

Of course. She would even shield him, very probably – to such an extent as was compatible with the recovery of the jewel.

Or if she were so angry, contemptuous, disgusted, as to feel no inclination to shield him, she would at any rate regard the affair as a disgraceful family scandal, about which the less said the better. Quite so.

But to *him*, who had unswervingly loved her from his boyhood, and whom she frequently called her best friend, the man to whom she would always turn for help, since the pleasure of helping her was the greatest pleasure he could have? Why be reticent, guarded, and uncommunicative to him?

But – her pleasure was her pleasure, and his was to serve it in any way she deigned to indicate . . .

'Well, we'll have the details, dear, and tea as well,' said Lady Brandon more lightly and easily than she had spoken since he had mentioned the sapphire.

'We'll have it in my boudoir, and I'll be at home to nobody whomsoever. You shall just talk until it is time to dress for dinner, and tell me every least detail as you go along. Everything you think, too; everything that Henri de Beaujolais thought; – and everything you think he thought, as well.'

As they strolled back to the house, Lady Brandon slipped her hand through Lawrence's arm, and it was quickly imprisoned.

He glowed with the delightful feeling that this brave and strong woman (whose devoted love for another man was, now, at any rate, almost maternal in its protecting care), was glad to turn to him as others turned to her.

How he yearned to hear her say, when his tale was told:

'Help me, George. I have no one but you, and you are a tower of strength. I am in great trouble.'

'You aren't looking too well, George, my dear,' she said, as they entered the wood.

'Lot of fever lately,' he replied, and added: 'I feel as fit as six people *now*,' and pressed the hand that he had seized.

'Give it up and come home, George,' said Lady Brandon, and he turned quickly toward her, his eyes opening widely.

'And let me find you a wife,' she continued.

Lawrence sighed and ignored the suggestion.

'How is Ffolliot?' he asked instead.

'Perfectly well, thank you. Why shouldn't he be?' was the reply – in the tone of which a careful listener, such as George Lawrence, might have detected a note of defensiveness, almost of annoyance, of repudiation of an unwarrantable implication.

If Lawrence did detect it, he ignored this also.

'Where is the good Sir Hector Brandon?' he asked, with casual politeness.

'Oh, in Thibet, or Paris, or East Africa, or Monte Carlo, or the South Sea Islands, or Homburg. Actually Kashmir, I believe, thank you, George,' replied Lady Brandon, and added: 'Have you brought a suit-case or must you wire?'

'I – er – am staying at the Brandon Arms, and have one there,' admitted Lawrence.

'And how long have you been at the Brandon Arms, George?' she enquired.

'Five minutes,' he answered.

'You must be tired of it then, dear,' commented Lady Brandon, and added: 'I'll send Robert down for your things.'

2

That evening, George Lawrence told Lady Brandon all that Major de Beaujolais had told him, adding his own ideas, suggestions, and theories. But whereas the soldier had been concerned with the inexplicable events of the day, Lawrence was concerned with the inexplicable paper and the means by which it had reached the hand of a dead man, on the roof of a desert outpost in the Sahara.

Thoughout his telling of the tale, Lady Brandon maintained an unbroken silence, but her eyes scarcely left his face.

At the end she asked a few questions, but offered no opinion, propounded no theory.

'We'll talk about it after dinner, George,' she said.

And after a poignantly delightful dinner *à deux* – it being explained that the Reverend Maurice Ffolliot was dining in his room to-night, owing to a headache – George Lawrence found that the talking was again to be done by him. All that Lady Brandon contributed to the conversation was questions. Again she offered no opinion, propounded no theory.

Nor, as Lawrence reluctantly admitted to himself, when he lay awake in bed that night, did she once admit, nor even imply, that the 'Blue Water' had been stolen. His scrupulous care to avoid questioning her on the subject of the whereabouts of the sapphire and of her nephew, Michael Geste, made this easy for her, and she had availed herself of it to the full. The slightly painful realisation, that she now knew all that he did whereas he knew nothing from her, could not be denied.

Again and again it entered his mind and roused the question, '*Why* cannot she confide in me, and at least say whether the sapphire has been stolen or not?'

Again and again he silenced it with the loyal reply, 'For some excellent reason . . . Whatever she does is right.'

After breakfast next day, Lady Brandon took him for a long drive. That the subject which now obsessed him (as it had, in a different way and for a different reason, obsessed de Beaujolais) was also occupying her mind, was demonstrated by the fact that, from time to time, and à propos of nothing in particular, she would suddenly ask him some fresh question bearing on the secret of the tragedy of Zinderneuf.

How he restrained himself from saying, 'Where is Michael? *Has* anything happened? *Is* the "Blue Water" stolen?' he did not know. A hundred times, one or the other of these questions had leapt from his brain to the tip of his tongue, since the moment when, at their first interview, he had seen that she wished to make no communication or statement whatever.

As the carriage turned in at the park gates on their return, he laid his hand on hers and said:

'My dear – I think everything has now been said, except one thing – your instructions to me. All I want now is to be told exactly what you want me to do.'

'I will tell you that, George, when you go . . . And *thank* you, my dear,' replied Lady Brandon.

So he possessed his soul in patience until the hour struck.

3

'Come and rest on this chest a moment, Patricia,' he said, on taking his departure next day, when she had telephoned to the garage, 'to give me my orders. You are going to make me happier than I have been since you told me that you liked me too much to love me.'

Lady Brandon seated herself beside Lawrence and all but loved him for his chivalrous devotion, his unselfishness, his gentle strength, and utter trustworthiness.

'We have sat here before, George,' she said, smiling, and, as he took her hand:

'Listen, my dear. This is what I want you to do for me. Just *nothing at all*. The "Blue Water" is not at Zinderneuf, nor anywhere else in Africa. Where Michael is I do not know. What that paper means, I cannot tell. And thank you so much for wanting to help me, and for asking no questions. And now, good-bye, my dear, dear friend . . .'

'Good-bye, my dearest dear,' said George Lawrence, most sorely puzzled, and went out to the door a sadder but not a wiser man.

4

As the car drove away, Lady Brandon stood in deep thought, pinching her lip.

'To think of that now!' she said . . . '"Be sure your sins." . . . The world *is* a very small place . . .' and went in search of the Reverend Maurice Ffolliot.

5

In regard to this same gentleman, George Lawrence entertained feelings which were undeniably mixed.

As a just and honest man, he recognised that the Reverend Maurice Ffolliot was a gentle-souled, sweet-natured, lovable creature, a finished scholar, a polished and cultured gentleman who had never intentionally harmed a living creature.

As the jealous, lifelong admirer and devotee of Lady Brandon, the rejected but undiminished lover, he knew that he hated not so much Ffolliot himself, as the fact of his existence.

Irrationally, George Lawrence felt that Lady Brandon would long outlive that notorious evil-liver, her husband. But for Ffolliot, he believed, his unswerving faithful devotion would then get its reward. Not wholly selfishly, he considered that a truer helpmeet, a sturdier prop, a stouter shield and buckler for this lady of many responsibilities, would be the world-worn and experienced Goerge Lawrence, rather than this poor frail recluse of a chaplain.

Concerning the man's history, all he knew was, that he had been the curate, well-born but penniless, to whom Lady Brandon's father had presented the living which was in his gift. With the beautiful Patricia Rivers, Ffolliot had fallen disastrously and hopelessly in love.

Toward the young man, Patricia Rivers had entertained a sentiment of affection, compounded more of pity than of love.

Under parental pressure, assisted by training and comparative poverty, ambition had triumphed over affection, and the girl, after some refusals, had married wealthy Sir Hector Brandon.

Later, and too late, she had realised the abysmal gulf that must lie between life with a selfish, heartless, gross roué, and that with such a man as the companion of her youth, with whom she had worked and played and whose cleverness, learning, sweet nature, and noble unselfishness she now realised.

Lawrence was aware that Lady Brandon fully believed that the almost fatal nervous breakdown which utterly changed Ffolliot in body and mind, was the direct result of her worldly and loveless marriage with a mean and vicious man. In this belief she had swooped down upon the poor lodgings where Ffolliot lay at death's door, wrecked in body and unhinged of mind, and brought him back with her to Brandon Abbas as soon as he could be moved. From there he had never gone – not for a single day, nor a single hour.

When he recovered, he was installed as chaplain, and as 'the Chaplain' he had been known ever since.

Almost reluctantly, George Lawrence admitted that most of what was good, simple, kind, and happy in that house emanated from this gentle presence . . .

Pacing the little platform of the wayside station, it occurred to George Lawrence to wonder if he might have more to tell the puzzled de Beaujolais had his visit to Brandon Abbas included the privilege, if not the pleasure, of a conversation with the Reverend Maurice Ffolliot.

Part 2

The Mystery of the 'Blue Water'

1

Beau Geste And His Band

'I THINK, perhaps, that if Very Small Geste were allowed to live, he might retrieve his character and find a hero's grave,' said the Lieutenant.

'And what would he do if he found a hero's grave!' enquired the Captain.

'Pinch the flowers off it and sell them, I suppose. As for retrieving his character, it is better not retrieved. Better left where it is – if it is not near inhabited houses, or water used for drinking purposes . . .'

'Oh, *please* let him live.' interrupted Faithful Hound. 'He is very useful at times, if only to try things on.'

'I was very grateful to Faithful Hound for daring to intercede for me, but felt that she was rating my general usefulness somewhat low.

'Well, we'll try bread and water on him, then,' said the Captain after a pause, during which I suffered many things.

'We'll also try a flogging,' he added, on seeing my face brighten, 'and the name of Feeble Geste . . . Remove it.'

And I was removed by the Lieutenant, Ghastly Gustus, and Queen Claudia, that the law might take its course. It took it, while Faithful Hound wept apart and Queen Claudia watched with deep interest.

I used to dislike the slice of bread and the water, always provided for these occasions, even more that the 'six of the best,' which was the flogging administered, more in sorrow than in anger, by the Captain himself.

The opprobrious name only lasted for the day upon which it was awarded, but was perhaps the worst feature of a punishment. The others passed and were gone, but the name kept one in the state of unblessedness, disgraced and outcast. Nor was one allowed in any way to retaliate upon the user of the injurious epithet, awarded in punishment after formal trial, however inferior and despicable he might be. One had to answer to it promptly, if not cheerfully, or far worse would befall.

This was part of the Law as laid down by the Captain, and beneath his Law we lived, and strove to live worthily, for we desired his praise and rewards more than we feared his blame and punishments.

The Captain was my brother, Michael Geste, later and generally known as 'Beau' Geste, by reason of his remarkable physical beauty, mental brilliance, and general distinction. He was a very unusual person, of irresistible charm, and his charm was enhanced, to me at any rate, by the fact that he was as enigmatic, incalculable, and incomprehensible as he was forceful. He was incurably romantic, and to this trait added the unexpected quality of a bull-dog tenacity. If Michael suddenly and quixotically did some ridiculously romantic thing, he did it thoroughly and completely, and he stuck to it until it was done.

Aunt Patricia, whose great favourite he was, said that he combined the inconsequent romanticism and reckless courage of a youthful d'Artagnan with the staunch tenacity and stubborn determination of a wise old Scotchman!

Little wonder that he exercised an extraordinary fascination over those who lived with him.

The Lieutenant, my brother Digby, was his twin, a quarter of an hour his junior, and his devoted and worshipping shadow. Digby had all Michael's qualities, but to a less marked degree, and he was 'easier,' both upon himself and other people, than Michael was. He loved fun and laughter, jokes and jollity, and, above all, he loved doing what Michael did.

I was a year younger than these twins, and very much their obedient servant. At preparatory school we were known as Geste, Small Geste, and Very Small Geste, and I was, indeed, Very Small in all things, compared with my brilliant brothers, to please whom was my chief aim in life.

Probably I transferred to them the affection, obedience, and love-hunger that would have been given to my parents in the ordinary course of events; but we were orphans, remembered not our mother nor our father, and lived our youthful lives between school and Brandon Abbas, as soon as we emerged from the Chaplain's tutelage.

Our maternal aunt, Lady Brandon, did more than her duty by us, but certainly concealed any love she may have felt for any of us but Michael.

Childless herself, I think all the maternal love she had to spare was given to him and Claudia, an extraordinarily beautiful girl whose origin was, so far as we were concerned, mysterious, but who was vaguely referred to as a cousin. She and a niece of Aunt Patricia, named Isobel Rivers, also spent a good deal of their childhood at Brandon Abbas, Isobel being, I think, imported as a playmate and companion for Claudia when we were at school. She proved an excellent playmate and companion for us also, and, at an early date, earned and adorned the honorary degree and honourable title of Faithful Hound.

A frequent visitor, Augustus Brandon, nephew of Sir Hector Brandon, often came during our holidays, in spite of the discouragement of the permanent name of Ghastly Gustus and our united and undisguised disapproval.

One could not love Augustus; he was far too like Uncle Hector for one thing, and, for another, he was too certain he was the heir and too disposed to presume upon it. However, Michael dealt with him faithfully, neither sparing the rod nor spoiling the child . . .

2

I do not remember the precise crime that had led to my trial and sentence, but I recollect the incident clearly enough, for two reasons.

One was that, on this very day of my fall from grace, I achieved the permanent and inalienable title and status of Stout Fella, when, inverting the usual order of precedence, Pride came after the Fall. The other reason was that, on that evening, we had the exciting privilege of seeing and handling the 'Blue Water,' as it is called, the great sapphire which Uncle Hector had given to Aunt Patricia as a wedding gift. I believe his great-grandfather, 'Wicked Brandon,' had 'acquired' it when soldiering against Dupleix in India.

It is about the loveliest and most fascinating thing I have ever seen, and it always affected me strangely. I could look at it for hours, and it always gave me a curious longing to put it in my mouth, or crush it to my breast, to hold it to my nose like a flower, or to rub it against my ear.

To look at it was, at one and the same time, most satisfying and most tantalising, for one always longed to do more than merely look – and, moreover, more than merely touch, as well. So wonderful and beautiful an object seemed to demand the exercise of all five senses, instead of one or two, for the full appreciation of all the joy it could offer.

When I first heard the charitable remark, 'Sir Hector Brandon bought Patricia Rivers with the "Blue Water" and now owns the pair,' I felt that both statements were true.

For what other reason could a woman like Aunt Patricia have married Uncle Hector, and did not he still own the 'Blue Water' – and so retain his sole claim to distinction?

Certainly his wife did not own it, for she could not wear it, nor do anything else with it. She could merely look at it occasionally, like anybody else. That was something anyhow, if it affected her as it did me . . .

My degree of S.F. (Stout Fella) I earned in this wise. One of Michael's favourite and most thrilling pastimes was 'Naval Engagements.' When this delightful pursuit was in being, two stately ships, with sails set and rudders fixed, were simultaneously shoved forth from the concrete edge of the lily-pond, by the Captain and the Lieutenant respectively.

They were crowded with lead soldiers, bore each a battery of three brass cannon, and were, at the outset, about a yard apart. But to each loaded brass cannon was attached a fuse, and, at the Captain's word, the fuses were lighted as the ships were launched from their harbours.

The Captain presided over the destinies of the ship that flew the White

Ensign and Union Jack, and the Lieutenant over those of the one that carried the Tri-couleur of France.

There was a glorious uncertainty of result. Each ship might receive a broadside from the other, one alone might suffer, or both might blaze ineffectually into the blue, by reason of a deviation of their courses. After the broadsides had been exchanged, we all sat and gloated upon the attractive scene, as the ships glided on, wreathed in battle-smoke, perhaps with riddled sails and splintered hulls (on one memorable and delightful occasion with the French ship dismasted and the Tri-couleur trailing in the water).

I was then privileged to wade, like Gulliver at Lilliput, into the deep, and bring the ships to harbour where their guns were reloaded by Michael and Digby, and the voyage repeated . . .

On this great day, the first combat was ideal. The ships converged, the guns of both fired almost simultaneously, splinters flew, soldiers fell or were sent flying overboard, the ships rocked to the explosions and concussion of the shot, and then drifted together and remained locked in a death-grapple to the shouts of 'Boarders ready' and 'Prepare to receive boarders,' from the Captain and Lieutenant.

'Fetch 'em in, Feeble Geste,' said Michael, imagination sated, and tucking up my trousers, I waded in, reversed the ships, and sent them to port.

The next round was more one-sided, for only one of the French ship's guns fired, and that, the feeblest. Neither the big gun amidships, that carried either a buckshot or half a dozen number-sixes, nor the stern-chaser swivel-gun was properly fused.

I waded in again, turned the French ship, and, with a mighty bang, her big gun went off, and I took the charge in my leg. Luckily for me it was a single buckshot. I nearly sat down.

'I'm shot,' I yelped.

'Hanging would be more appropriate,' said the Captain. 'Come here.'

Blood oozed from a neat blue hole, and Faithful Hound uttered a dog-like howl of woe and horror.

Claudia asked to be informed exactly how it felt.

'Just like being shot,' I replied, and added: 'I am going to be sick.'

'Do it in the pond then,' requested the Captain, producing his pocket-knife and a box of matches.

'Going to cauterise the wound and prevent its turning sceptic?' enquired the Lieutenant, as the Captain struck a match, and held the point of the small blade in the flame.

'No,' replied the Captain. 'Naval surgery without ænesthetics . . . Cut out the cannon-ball.'

'Now,' continued he, turning to me as I sat wondering whether I should shortly have a wooden leg, 'will you be gagged or chew on a bullet? I don't want to be disturbed by your beastly yells.'

'I shall not yell, Captain,' I replied with dignity, and a faint hope that I spoke the truth.

'Sit on his head, Dig,' said Michael to the Lieutenant; but waving Digby away, I turned on my side, shut my eyes, and offered up my limb.

'Hold his hoof then,' ordered the Captain . . .

It was painful beyond words; but I contrived to hold my peace, by biting the clenched knuckle of my forefinger, and to refrain from kicking by realising that it was impossible, with Digby sitting on my leg and Claudia standing on my foot.

After what seemed a much longer time than it was, I heard Michael say, apparently from a long way off: 'Here it comes,' and then, a cheer from the Band and a dispersal of my torturers, announced the recovery of the buckshot.

'Shove it back in the gun, Dig,' said the Captain; 'and you, Isobel, sneak up to the cupboard outside our bathroom and bring me the scratch-muck.'

The Faithful Hound, mopping her tear-bedewed face, sped away and soon returned with the scratch-muck (the bottle of antiseptic lotion, packet of boric lint, and roll of bandage, which figured as the *sequelæ* to all our minor casualties).

I believe Michael made a really excellent job of digging out the bullet and dressing the wound. Of course, the ball had not penetrated very deeply, or a penknife would hardly have been the appropriated surgical tool; but, as things were, a doctor could not have been very much quicker, nor the healing of the wound more clean and rapid.

And when the bandage was fastened, the Captain, in the presence of the whole Band and some temporary members, visitors, raised me to the seventh heaven of joy and pride by solemnly conferring upon me in perpetuity, the rank and title of Stout Fella, in that I had shed no tear and uttered no sound during a major operation of 'naval surgery without ænesthetics.'

Further, he awarded me the signal and high honour of a full-dress '*Viking's funeral*.'

Now a Viking's funeral cannot be solemnised every day in the week, for it involves, among other things, the destruction of a long-ship.

The dead Viking is laid upon a funeral pyre in the centre of his ship, his spear and shield are laid beside him, his horse and hound are slaughtered and their bodies placed in attendance, the pyre is lighted, and the ship sent out to sea with all sail set.

On this occasion, the offending French ship was dedicated to these ocean obsequies.

A specially selected lead soldier was solemnly endowed with the name and attributed of *The Viking Eorl*, *John Geste*, laid upon a matchbox filled with explosives, a pyre of matches built round him on the deck of the ship (the ship drenched with paraffin), his horse laid at the head of his pyre, and a small (china) dog at his feet.

All being ready, we bared our heads, Michael, with raised hand, solemnly uttered the beautiful words, '*Ashes to ashes and dust to dust, if God won't have you the devil must*,' and, applying a match to the pyre, shoved the long-ship (late French battleship) well out into the middle of the lily-pond.

Here it burned gloriously, the leaping flames consuming the mast and sail so that the charred wreckage went by the board, and we stood silent, envisaging the horrors of a burning ship at sea.

As the vessel burned down to the water's edge, and then disappeared with hissings and smoking, Michael broke the ensuing silence with words that I was to remember many years later in a very different place. (Apparently Digby remembered them too.)

'*That's* what I call a funeral!' said Michael. 'Compare that with being stuck ten feet down in the mud and clay of a beastly cemetery for worms to eat and maggots to wriggle about in you . . . Cripes! I'd give something to have one like that when my turn comes . . . Good idea! I'll write it down in my will, and none of you dirty little dogs will get anything from me, unless you see it properly done.'

'Righto, Beau,' said Digby. 'I'll give you one, old chap, whenever you like.'

'So will I you, Dig, if you die first,' replied Michael to his twin, and they solemnly shook hands upon it . . .

My gratification for these honours was the greater in that nothing had been further from my thoughts than such promotion and reward. Frequently had I striven in the past to win one of the Band's recognised Orders of Merit – Faithful Hound, Good Egg, Stout Fella, or even Order of Michael (For Valour) – but had never hitherto won any decoration or recognition beyond some such cryptic remark from the Captain as, 'We shall have to make John, Chaplain to the Band, if he does many more of these Good Deeds . . .'

That evening when we were variously employed in the schoolroom, old Burdon, the butler, came and told us that we could go into the drawing-room.

Claudia and Isobel were there, the former talking in a very self-possessed and grown-up way to a jolly-looking foreign person, to whom we were presented. He turned out to be a French cavalry officer, and we were thrilled to discover that he was on leave from Morocco where he had been fighting.

'Bags I we get him up to the schoolroom to-morrow,' whispered Michael, as we gathered round a glass dome, like a clock-cover, inverted over a white velvet cushion on which lay the 'Blue Water' sapphire.

We looked at it in silence, and, to me, it seemed to grow bigger and bigger until I felt as though I could plunge head first into it.

Young as I was, I distinctly had the feeling that it would not be a good thing to stare too long at that wonderful concentration of living colour. It seemed alive and, though inexpressibly beautiful, a little sinister.

'May we handle it, Aunt Patricia?' asked Claudia, and, as usual, she got her way.

Aunt Patricia lifted off the glass cover and handed the jewel to the Frenchman, who quickly gave it to Claudia.

'That has caused we know not what of strife and sorrow and bloodshed,' he said. 'What a tale it could tell!'

'Can you tell tales of strife and bloodshed, please?' asked Michael, and as Claudia said, 'Why, of course! He leads charges of Arab cavalry like *Under Two Flags*,' as though she had known him for years, we all begged him to tell us about his fighting, and he ranked second only to the 'Blue Water' as a centre of attraction.

On the following afternoon, the Captain deputed Claudia to get the Frenchman to tell us some tales.

'Decoy yon handsome stranger to our lair,' quoth he. 'I would wring his secrets from him.'

Nothing loth, Claudia exercised her fascinations upon him after lunch, and brought him to our camp in the Bower, a clearing in the woods near the house.

Here he sat on a log and absolutely thrilled us to the marrow of our bones by tales, most graphically and realistically told, of the Spahis, the French Foreign Legion, the Chasseurs d'Afrique, Zouaves, Turcos, and other romantically named regiments.

He told us of desert warfare, of Arab cruelties and chivalries, of hand-to-hand combats wherein swordsman met swordsman on horseback as in days of old, of brave deeds, of veiled Touaregs, veiled women, secret Moorish cities, oases, mirages, sand-storms, and the wonders of Africa.

Then he showed us fencing-tricks and feats of swordsmanship, until, when he left us, after shaking our hands and kissing Claudia, we were his, body and soul . . .

'I'm going to join the French Foreign Legion when I leave Eton,' announced Michael suddenly. 'Get a commission and then join his regiment.'

'So am I,' said Digby, of course.

'And I,' I agreed.

Augustus Brandon looked thoughtful.

'Could I be a *vivandière* and come too?' asked Isobel.

'You shall all visit me in your officers' uniforms,' promised Claudia. 'French officers always wear them in France. Very nice too.' . . .

Next day we went back to our preparatory school at Slough.

3

The next time I saw the 'Blue Water' was during the holidays before our last half at Eton.

The occasion was the visit of General Sir Basil Malcolmson, an authority on gems, who was, at the time, Keeper of the Jewel House at the Tower of London, and had, I think, something to do with the British Museum. He had written a 'popular' history of the well-known jewels of the world, under the title of *Famous Gems*, and was now writing a second volume dealing with less-known stones of smaller value.

He had written to ask if he might include an account of the 'Blue Water' sapphire and its history.

I gathered from what Claudia had heard her say, that Aunt Patricia was not extraordinarily delighted about it, and that she had replied that she would be very pleased to show Sir Basil the stone; but that very little was known of its history beyond the fact that it had been 'acquired' (kindly word) by the seventh Sir Hector Brandon in India in the eighteenth century, when he was a soldier of fortune in the service of one of the Nawabs or Rajahs of the Deccan, probably Nunjeraj, Sultan of Mysore.

The General was a very interesting talker, and at dinner that night he told us about such stones as the Timour Ruby, the Hope Diamond, and the Stuart Sapphire (which is in the King's crown), until the conversation at times became a monologue, which I, personally, greatly enjoyed.

I remember his telling us that it was he who discovered that the Nadirshah Uncut Emerald was not, as had been supposed, a lump of glass set in cheap and crude Oriental gold-work. It had been brought to this country after the Mutiny as an ordinary example of mediæval Indian jewel-setting, and was shown as such at the Exhibition at the Crystal Palace. Sir Basil Malcolmson had examined it and found that the 'scratches' on it were actually the names of the Moghul Emperors who had owned it and had worn it in their turbans. This had established, once and for all, the fact that it is one of the world's greatest historic gems, was formerly in the Peacock Throne at Delhi, and literally priceless in value. I think he added that it was now in the Regalia at the Tower of London.

I wondered whether the 'Blue Water' and the 'Nadirshah Emerald' had ever met in India, and whether the blue stone had seen as much of human misery and villainy as the great green one. Quite possibly, the sapphire had faced the emerald, the one in the turban of Shivaji, the Maratha soldier of fortune, and the other in that of Akhbar, the Moghul Emperor.

And I remember wondering whether the stones, the one in the possession of a country gentleman, the other in that of the King of England, had reached the ends of their respective histories of theft, bloodshed, and human suffering.

Certainly it seemed impossible that the 'Blue Water' should again 'see life' (and death) – until one remembered that such stones are indestructible and immortal, and may be, thousands of years hence, the cause of any crime that greed and covetousness can father . . .

Anyhow, I should be glad to see the big sapphire again, and hear anything that Sir Basil might have to say about it.

I remember that Augustus distinguished himself that evening.

'I wonder how much you'd give Aunt for the "Blue Water,"' he remarked to Sir Basil.

'I am not a dealer,' replied that gentleman.

And when Claudia asked Aunt Patricia if she were going to show Sir Basil the Priests' Hole and the hiding-place of the safe in which the sapphire reposed, the interesting youth observed:

'Better not, Aunt. He might come back and pinch it one dark night – the sapphire I mean, not the Hole.'

Ignoring him, Aunt Patricia said that she would take Sir Basil and the other guest, a man named Lawrence, a Nigerian official who was an old friend, and show them the Priests' Hole.

The conversation then turned upon the marvellous history of the Hope Diamond, and the incredible but true tale of the misfortune which invariably befell its possessor; upon Priests' Holes and the varying tide of religious persecution which led to the fact that the same hiding-place had sheltered Roman Catholic priests and Protestant pastors in turn; and upon the day when Elizabethan troopers, searching for Father Campion, did damage to our floors, pictures, panelling, and doors (traces of which are still discernible), without discovering the wonderfully-contrived Priests' Hole at all.

It was near the end of this very interesting dinner that our beloved and reverend old friend, the Chaplain, made it more memorable than it otherwise would have been.

He had sat throughout dinner behaving beautifully, talking beautifully, and looking beautiful (with his ivory face and silver hair, which made him look twenty years older than he was), and then, just as Burdon put the decanters in front of him, he suddenly did what he had never done before – 'broke out' in Aunt Patricia's presence. We had often known him to be queer, and it was an open secret in the house that he was to be humoured when queer (but if open, it was still a secret nevertheless), though he was always perfectly normal in Aunt Patricia's presence.

And now it happened!

'Burdon,' said he, in the quiet voice in which one speaks 'aside' to a servant, 'could you get me a very beautiful white rabbit with *large* pink eyes, and if possible, a nice pink ribbon round its neck? A mauve would do . . . But on no account pale blue ribbon, Burdon.'

It was a bad break and we all did our best to cover it up by talking fast – but Burdon and Michael were splendid.

'Certainly, your Reverence,' said Burdon without turning a hair, and marched straight to the screen by the service-door, as one expecting to find a white rabbit on the table behind it.

'That's a novel idea, sir,' said Michael. 'I suppose it's a modern equivalent of the roast peacock brought to table in its feathers, looking as though it were alive? Great idea . . .'

'Yes,' Digby took him up. 'Boar's head, with glass eyes and all that. Never heard of a rabbit served in its jacket though, I think. Good idea, anyhow.'

The Chaplain smiled vacantly, and Augustus Brandon giggled and remarked:

'I knew a man who jugged his last hair, though.'

I hastened to join in, and Isobel began to question the Chaplain as to the progress of his book on Old Glass, a book which he had been writing for years, the subject being his pet hobby.

I wondered whether my aunt, at the head of the table, had noticed anything. Glancing at her, I saw that she looked ten years older than she had done before it happened.

As I held the door open, when the ladies retired after dinner, she whispered to me in passing, 'Tell Michael to look after the Chaplain this evening. He has been suffering from insomnia and is not himself.'

But later, in the drawing-room, when the 'Blue Water' was smiling, beguiling, and alluring from its white velvet cushion beneath the glass dome, and we stood round the table on which it lay, the Chaplain certainly was himself, and, if possible, even more learned and interesting on the subject of gems than the great Sir Basil.

I was very thankful indeed, for my heart ached for Aunt Patricia as she watched him; watched him just as a mother would watch an only child of doubtful sanity, balanced between her hope and her fear, her passionate denial of its idiocy, her passionate joy in signs of its normality.

4

Poor Aunt Patricia! She had contracted an alliance with Sir Hector Brandon as one might contract a disease. The one alleviation of this particular affliction being its intermittence; for this monument of selfishness was generally anywhere but at home, he being a mighty hunter before the Lord (or the Devil) and usually in pursuit of prey, biped or quadruped, in distant places. It is a good thing to have a fixed purpose, an aim, and an ambition in life, and Sir Hector boasted one. It was to be able to say that he had killed one of every species of beast and bird and fish in the world, and had courted a woman of every nationality in the world! A great soul fired with a noble ambition.

As children, we did not, of course, realise what Aunt Patricia suffered at the hands of this violent and bad man when he was at home, nor what his tenants and labourers suffered when he was absent.

As we grew older, however, it was impossible to avoid knowing that he was universally hated, and that he bled the estate shamefully and shamelessly, that he might enjoy himself abroad.

Children might die of diphtheria through faulty drains or lack of drains; old people might die of chills and rheumatism through leaking roofs and damply rotting cottages; every farmer might have a cankering grievance; the estate-agent might have the position and task of a flint-skinning slave-owner; but Sir Hector's yacht and Sir Hector's lady-friends would lack for nothing, nor his path through life be paved with anything less than gold.

And Lady Brandon might remain at home to face the music – whether angry growls of wrath, or feeble cries of pain.

But we boys and girls were exceedingly fortunate, a happy band who followed our leader Michael, care-free and joyous . . .

5

I think that the feat of Michael's that impressed us most, was his sustaining the rôle of a Man in Armour succesfully for what seemed an appallingly long time. (It was nearly long enough to cause my death, anyhow!)

We were in the outer hall one wet afternoon, and the brilliant idea of dressing up in one of the suits of armour occured to the Captain of the Band.

Nothing loth, we, his henchmen, quickly became Squires of, more or less, High Degree, and with much ingenuity and more string, more or less correctly cased the knight in his armour.

He was just striking an attitude and bidding a caitiff to die, when the sound of a motor-horn anachronistically intruded and the Band dispersed as do rabbits at the report of gun.

Michael stepped up on to the pedestal and stood at ease (Ease!) Digby fled up the stairs, the girls dashed into the drawing-room, Augustus and another visitor rushed down a corridor to the service-staircase, and I, like Ginevra, dived into a great old chest on the other side of the hall.

There I lay as though screwed down in a coffin and pride forbade me ignominiously to crawl forth. I realised that I was suffering horribly – and the next thing that I knew was that I was lying on my bed and Michael was smiting my face with a wet sponge while Digby dealt kindly blows upon my chest and stomach.

When sufficiently recovered and sufficiently rebuked for being such an ass, I was informed that Aunt Patricia had driven up with a 'black man' – mystery of mysteries! – and had confabulated with him right in front of the Man in Armour, afterwards speeding the 'black man' on his way again in her car.

We were much intrigued, and indulged in much speculation – the more, in that Michael would not say a word beyond that such a person *had* come and had gone again, and that he himself had contrived to remain so absolutely still in that heavy armour that not a creak, rustle, clank, or other sound had betrayed the fact that there actually was a Man in the Armour!

In the universal and deserved admiration for this feat, my own poor performance in preferring death to discovery and dishonour passed unpraised.

I must do Michael the justice, however, to state that directly Aunt Patricia had left the hall, he had hurried to raise the lid of the chest in which I was entombed, and had himself carried me upstairs as soon as his armour was removed and restored to its place.

Digby, who, from long and painful practice, was an expert bugler, took down his old coach-horn from its place on the wall and blew what he said was an 'honorific fanfare of heralds' trumpets,' in recognition of the *tenacity* displayed both by Michael and myself.

I must confess, however, that in spite of Michael's reticence concerning the visit of the 'black man,' we others discussed the strange event in all its bearings.

We, however, arrived at no conclusion, and were driven to content ourselves with a foolish theory that the strange visitor was in some way connected with a queer boy, now a very distinguished and enlightened ruler in India. He was the oldest son and heir of the Maharajah, his father, and had been at the College for the sons of Ruling Princes in India, I think the Rajkumar College at Ajmir, before coming to Eton.

He was a splendid athlete and sportsman, and devoted to Michael to the point of worship.

Aunt Patricia welcomed him to Brandon Abbas at Michael's request, and when he saw the 'Blue Water' *he actually and literally and completely fainted.*

I suppose the sight of the sapphire was the occasion rather than the cause, but the fact remains. It was queer and uncanny beyond words, the more so because he never uttered a sound, and neither then nor subsequently ever said one syllable on the subject of the great jewel!

And so we lived our happy lives at Brandon Abbas, when not at our prep. school, at Eton, or later, at Oxford.

2

The disappearance of the 'Blue Water'

AND then, one autumn evening, the face of life changed as utterly and suddenly as unexpectedly. The act of one person altered the lives of all of us, and brought suffering, exile, and death in its train.

I am neither a student nor a philosopher, but I would like some convinced exponent of the doctrine of Free Will to explain how we are anything but the helpless victims of the consequences of the acts of other people. How I envy the grasp and logic of those great minds that can easily reconcile '*unto the third and fourth generation*,' for example, with this comfortable doctrine!

On this fine autumn evening, so ordinary, so secure and comfortable, so fateful and momentous, we sat in the great drawing-room of Brandon Abbas, after dinner, all together for what proved to be the last time. There were present Aunt Patricia, the Chaplain, Claudia, Isobel, Michael, Digby, Augustus Brandon, and myself.

Aunt Patricia asked Claudia to sing, and that young lady excused herself on the score of being out of sorts and not feeling like it. She certainly looked pale and somewhat below her usual sparkling standard of health and spirits. I had thought for some days that she had seemed preoccupied and worried, and I had wondered if her bridge-debts and dressmakers' bills were the cause of it.

With her wonted desire to be helpful and obliging, Isobel went to the piano, and for some time we sat listening to her sweet and sympathetic voice, while my aunt knitted, the Chaplain twiddled his thumbs, Claudia wrestled with some unpleasant problem in frowning abstraction, Augustus shuffled and tapped his cigarette-case with a cigarette he dared not light, Digby turned over the leaves of a magazine, and Michael watched Claudia.

Presently Isobel rose and closed the piano.

'What about a game of pills?' said Augustus, and before anyone replied, Claudia said:

'Oh, Aunt, *do* let's have the "Blue Water" down for a little while. I haven't seen it for ages.'

'Rather!' agreed Michael. 'Let's do a gloat, Aunt,' and the Chaplain supported him and said he'd be delighted to get it, if Lady Brandon would give permission.

Only he and Aunt Patricia knew the *secret* of the Priests' Hole (excepting Sir Hector, of course), and I believe it would have taken an extraordinarily ingenious burglar to have discovered it, even given unlimited opportunity, before tackling the safe in which the 'Blue Water,' with other valuables, reposed. (I know that Michael, Digby, and I had spent countless hours, with the knowledge and consent of our aunt, in trying to find, without the slightest success, the trick of this hiding-place of more than one hunted divine. It became an obsession with Michael.) . . .

Aunt Patricia agreed at once, and the Chaplain disappeared. He had a key which gave access to the hiding-place of the keys of the safe which the Priests' Hole guarded.

'What *is* the "Blue Water" worth, Aunt Patricia?' asked Claudia.

'To whom, dear?' was the reply.

'Well – what would a Hatton Garden person give for it?'

'About a half what he thought his principal would be willing to offer, perhaps.'

'And what would that be, about, do you suppose?'

'I don't know, Claudia. If some American millionaire were very anxious to buy it, I suppose he'd try to find out the lowest sum that would be considered,' was the reply.

'What *would* you ask, supposing you *were* going to sell it?' persisted Claudia.

'I certainly am not going to sell it,' said Aunt Patricia, in a voice that should have closed the conversation. She had that day received a letter from her husband announcing his early return from India, and it had not cheered her at all.

'I did hear someone say once that Uncle Hector was offered thirty thousand pounds for it,' said Augustus.

'Did you?' replied Aunt Patricia, and at that moment the Chaplain returned, carrying the sapphire on its white velvet cushion, under its glass dome. He placed it on a table under the big hanging chandelier, with its countless cutglass pendants and circle of electric bulbs.

There it lay, its incredible, ineffable, glowing blue fascinating us as we gazed upon it.

'It *is* a wonderful thing,' said Isobel, and I wondered how often those very words had been said of it.

'Oh, let me kiss it,' cried Claudia, and with one hand the Chaplain raised the glass dome, and with the other handed the sapphire to Aunt Patricia, who examined it as though she had not handled it a thousand times. She looked through it at the light. She then passed it to Claudia, who fondled it awhile.

We all took it in turn, Augustus throwing it up and catching it as he murmured, 'Thirty thousand pounds for a bit of glass!'

When Michael got it, I thought he was never going to pass it on. He weighed and rubbed and examined it, more in the manner of a dealer than an admirer of the beautiful.

Finally, the Chaplain put it back on its cushion and replaced the glass cover.

We sat and stood around for a few minutes, while the Chaplain said something about Indian Rajahs and their marvellous hereditary and historical jewels.

I was standing close to the table, bending over and peering into the depths of the sapphire again; Augustus was reiterating, 'Who says a game of pills, pills, pills?' when, suddenly, as occasionally happened, the electric light failed, and we were plunged in complete darkness.

'What's Fergusson up to now?' said Digby, alluding to the head chauffeur, who was responsible for the engine.

'It'll come on again in a minute,' said Aunt Patricia, and added, 'Burdon will bring candles if it doesn't . . . Don't wander about, anybody, and knock things over.'

Somebody brushed lightly against me as I stood by the table.

'Ghosts and goblins!' said Isobel in a sepulchral voice. 'Who's got a match? A skeleton hand is about to clutch my throat. I can see . . .'

'Everybody,' I remarked, as the light came on again, and we blinked at each other in the dazzling glare, so suddenly succeeding the velvet darkness.

'Saved!' said Isobel, with an exaggerated sigh of relief, and then, as I looked at her, she stared wide-eyed and open-mouthed, and then pointed speechless . . .

The 'Blue Water' had vanished. The white velvet cushion was bare, and the glass cover covered nothing but the cushion.

2

We must have looked a foolish band as we stood and stared, for a second or two, at that extraordinarily empty-looking abode of the great sapphire. I never saw anything look so empty in my life. Aunt Patricia broke the silence and the spell.

'*Your* joke, Augustus?' she enquired, in that rarely-used tone of hers that would have made an elephant feel small.

'Eh? *Me?* No, Aunt! Really! I swear! *I* never touched it,' declared the youth, colouring warmly.

'Well – there's someone with a sense of humour all his own,' she observed, and I was glad that I was not the misguided humorist. Also I was glad that she had regarded the joke as more probably Augustan than otherwise.

'You were standing by the table, John,' she continued, turning to me. 'Are you the jester?'

'No, Aunt,' I replied with feeble wit, 'only the Geste.'

As Digby and Michael both flatly denied any part in this poor practical joke, Aunt Patricia turned to the girls.

'Surely not?' she said, raising her fine eyebrows.

'No, Aunt, I was too busy with ghosts and goblins and the skeleton hand, to use my own hand for sticking and peeling – I mean picking and stealing,' said Isobel.

'*I* haven't got it,' said Claudia.

Lady Brandon and the Reverend Maurice Ffolliot eyed the six of us with cold severity.

'Let us say nothing of the good taste displayed, either in the act or in the denial,' said the former, 'but agree that the brilliant joke has been carried far enough, shall we?'

'Put the brilliant joke back, John,' said Augustus. 'You were the only one near it when the light went out.'

'I have said that I didn't touch the sapphire,' I replied.

'Suppose *you* put it back, Ghastly,' said Digby, and his voice had an edge on it.

'And suppose *you* do!' blustered Augustus angrily.

Digby, who was standing behind him, suddenly raised his right knee with sufficient force to propel the speaker in the direction of the table – an exhibition of ill manners and violence that passed unrebuked by Aunt Patricia.

'I haven't *got* the beastly thing, I tell you,' shouted the smitten one, turning ferociously upon Digby. 'It's one of you three rotters.'

It was an absurd situation, rapidly degenerating into an unpleasant one, and my aunt's lips were growing thinner, and her eyebrows beginning to contract toward her high-bridged nose.

'Look here, sillies!' said Isobel, as we brothers glared at Augustus and he glared at us, 'I am going to turn all the lights out again for two minutes. Whoever played the trick, and told the fib, is to put the "Blue Water" back. Then no one will know who did it. See?' and she walked away to the door, by which were the electric-light switches.

'Now!' she said. 'Everybody keep still except the villain, and when I switch the lights on again, there will be the "Blue Water" laughing at us.'

'Oh, rot,' said Augustus, and out went the lights before Aunt Patricia or the Chaplain made any comment.

Now it occurred to me that it would be very interesting to know who had played this silly practical joke and told a silly lie after it. I therfore promptly stepped towards the table, felt the edge of it with my right hand and then, with a couple of tentative dabs, laid my left hand on top of the glass dome. Whoever came to return the sapphire must touch me, and him I would promptly seize. I might not have felt so interested in the matter had it not been twice pointed out that it was I who stood against the table when the light failed.

Isobel's device for securing the prompt return of the sapphire was an excellent one, but I saw no reason why I should linger under the suspicion of having been an ass and a liar, for the benefit of Augustus.

So there I stood and waited.

While doing so, it occurred to me to wonder what would happen if the joker did not have the good sense to take advantage of the opportunity provided by Isobel . . .

Perfect silence reigned in the big room.

'I can't find the cover,' said Michael.

'Another minute, villain,' said Isobel. 'Hurry up.'

And then I was conscious that someone was breathing very near me. I felt a faint touch on my elbow. A hand came down lightly against my wrist – and I grabbed.

My left hand was round a coat-sleeve, beneath which was the stiff cuff of a dress shirt, and my right grasped a wrist. I was very glad that it was a man's arm. Had it been a girl's I should have let go. Ghastly Gustus, of course . . . It was just the silly sort of thing he would do, and it was just like him to take advantage of the darkness, when he found the joke had fallen remarkably flat. I did not envy him the look that would appear on Aunt Patricia's face when the light went up and he was discovered in my grip.

I would have let him go, I think, had he not endeavoured to put the blame on me, and insisted on my nearness to the table when the light failed.

I was a little surprised that he did not struggle, and I was prepared for a sudden violent twist and a swift evasion in the dark.

He kept perfectly still.

'I am going to count ten, and then up goes the light. Are you ready, villain?' came the voice of Isobel from the door.

'Yes, I've put it back,' said Digby.

'So have I,' said Michael, close to me.

'And I,' echoed Claudia.

Then Isobel switched on the light, and I found that my hands were clenched on the right arm of – my brother Michael!

I was more surprised than I can say.

It was only a small matter, of course; a pointless practical joke and a pointless lie, but it was so utterly unlike Michael. It was unlike him to do it, and more unlike him flatly to deny having done it. And my surprise increased when Michael, looking at me queerly, actually remarked:

'So it was *me*, John, was it? Oh, *Feeble* Geste!'

I felt absurdly hurt, and turning to Augustus said, 'I apologise, Gussie. I admit I thought it was you.'

'Oh, don't add insult to injury,' he replied. 'Put the beastly thing back, and stop being a funny ass. Enough of you is too much.'

Put the beastly thing back! I turned and looked at the cushion. It was empty still. I looked at Michael and Michael looked at me.

'Oh, shove it back, Beau,' I said. 'It's all been most extraordinarily clever and amusing. I'm sure. But I'm inclined to agree with Gussie.'

Michael gave me one of his long, thoughtful, penetrating looks. 'H'm,' said he.

Isobel came over from the door.

'I *do* think you might have played up, sillies,' said she. 'Put it back, Beau, and let's have a dance. May we, Aunt?'

'Certainly,' said Aunt Patricia, 'as soon as ever the great humorist in our midst has received our felicitations,' and I really pitied the said humorist, when he should make his avowal, annoyed with him as I felt.

The Chaplain looked from face to face of the six of us and said nothing. Aunt Patricia did the same.

We all stood silent.

'Now stop this fooling,' said she. 'Unless the "Blue Water" is produced at once, I shall be very seriously annoyed.'

'Come on, somebody,' said Digby.

Another minute's silence.

It began to grow unbearable.

'I am waiting,' said Lady Brandon at last, and her foot began to tap.

From that moment the matter became anything but a joke, swiftly growing unpleasant and increasingly so.

3

I shall not forget the succeeding hours in a hurry, and their horrible atmosphere of suspicion – seven people suspecting one of the other seven, and the eighth person pretending to do so.

My capable and incisive aunt quickly brought things to a clear issue, upon getting no reply to her 'I am waiting,' and her deliberate look from face to face of the angry and uncomfortable group around her.

'Maurice,' said she to the Chaplain, laying her hand upon his sleeve, her face softening and sweetening incredibly, 'come and sit by me until I have asked each of these young people a question. Then I want you to go to bed, for it's getting late,' and she led him to a big and deep chesterfield that stood on a low dais in a big window recess.

Seating herself with the air and presence of a queen on a throne, she said, quietly and very coldly:

'This is getting serious, and unless it ends at once, the consequences will be serious too. For the last time I ask the boy, or girl, who moved the "Blue Water," to give it to me, and we will end the silly business now and here, and make no further reference to it. If not . . . Come, this is absurd and ridiculous . . .'

'Oh, come off it, John,' said Augustus, 'for God's sake.'

Nobody else spoke.

'Very well,' said my aunt, 'since the fool won't leave his folly . . . Come here, Claudia . . . Have you touched the "Blue Water" since the Chaplain restored it to its place?' She laid her hand on Claudia's arm, drew her close, and looked into her eyes.

'No, Aunt . . .'

'No, Aunt,' said Claudia again.

'Of course not,' said Aunt Patricia. 'Go to bed, dear. Good night.'

And Claudia departed, not without an indignant glance at me.

'Come here, Isobel,' continued my aunt. 'Have you touched the "Blue Water" since the Chaplain put it back in its place?'

'No, Aunt, I have not,' replied Isobel.

'I am sure you have not. Go to bed. Good night,' said Lady Brandon.

Isobel turned to go and then stopped.

'But I might have done, Aunt, if the idea had occurred to me,' she said. 'It is just a joke, of course.'

'Bed,' rejoined her aunt, and Isobel departed with a kind glance at me.

Aunt Patricia turned to Augustus.

'Come here,' she said coldly, and with a hard stare into his somewhat shifty eyes. 'Please answer absolutely truthfully – for your own sake. If you have got the "Blue Water," and give it to me now, I shall not say another word about the matter. Have you?'

'I swear to God, Aunt . . .' broke out Augustus.

'You need not swear to God, nor to me, Augustus,' was the cold reply. 'Yes or No. Have you got it?'

'*No*, Aunt! I take my solemn oath I . . .' the unhappy youth replied vehemently, when the cold voice interrupted:

'Have you touched the sapphire since the Chaplain put it under its cover?'

'No, Aunt. *Really*, I haven't! I assure you I . . .' began Augustus, to be again interrupted by the cold question:

'Do you know where the "Blue Water" is now?'

'No, Aunt,' promptly replied he, 'upon my soul I don't. If I did, I'd jolly well . . .'

'John,' said my aunt, without further notice of Augustus, 'do you know where the stone is?'

'No, Aunt,' I replied, and added, 'nor have I touched it since the Chaplain did.'

She favoured me with a long, long look, which I was able to meet quite calmly, and I hope not at all rudely. As I looked away, my eyes met Michael's. He was watching me queerly.

Then came Digby's turn. He said quite simply and plainly that he knew nothing about the jewel's disappearance and had not touched it since it was passed to him by Claudia, and handed on by him to Isobel.

There remained Michael. He was the culprit, or else one of us had told a most deliberate, calculated, and circumstantial lie, inexcusable and disgraceful.

I felt angrier with Michael than I had ever done in my life, yet I was angry rather *for* him than with him. It was so utterly unlike him to do such a stupid thing, and to allow all this unpleasant and undignified inquisition to go on, when a word from him would have ended it.

Why must my idol act as though he had feet of clay – or, at any rate, smear clay upon his feet? The joke was unworthy, but the lie was really painfully so.

I have no objection to the good thumping lie that is 'a very present help in time of trouble,' told at the right time and in the right cause (such as to save the other fellow's bacon). But I have the strongest distaste for a silly lie that merely gives annoyance to other people, and puts blame upon an innocent person.

From the moment I had caught him in the act of trying to return the jewel secretly, I had felt sick with indignation, and literally and physically sick when, his effort frustrated by me, he had pretended innocence and held on for another opportunity of returning the thing unseen.

Had I not myself caught him in the very act, he was, of all of us, the last person whom I should have suspected. He and Isobel, that is to say. I should have strongly suspected Augustus, and, his innocence established, I should have supposed that Digby had fallen a victim to his incurable love of joking – though I should have been greatly surprised.

Had Digby then been proved innocent, I am afraid I should have suspected Claudia of wishing to turn the lime-light on herself by an innocently naughty escapade – before I should ever have entertained the idea of Michael doing it and denying it.

Now that all had firmly and categorically declared their absolute innocence and ignorance in the matter, I had no option (especially in view of my catching him at the spot) but to conclude that Michael had been what I had never known him to be before – a fool, a cad, and a liar.

I could have struck him for hurting himself so.

'Michael,' said Aunt Patricia very gravely, very coldly, and very sadly, 'I'm sorry. More so than I can tell you, Michael. Please put the "Blue Water" back, and I will say no more. But I doubt whether I shall feel like calling you "Beau" for some time.'

'I *can't* put it back, Aunt, for I haven't got it,' said Michael quietly, and my heart bounded.

'Do you know where it is, Michael?' asked my aunt.

'I do not, Aunt,' was the immediate reply.

'Have you touched the sapphire since the Chaplain did, Michael?' was the next question.

'I have not, Aunt,' was the quiet answer.

'Do you know anything about its disappearance, Michael?' asked the hard level voice.

'I only know that *I* have had nothing whatever to do with its disappearance, Aunt,' answered my brother, and I was aghast.

'Do you declare that all you have just said is the absolute truth, Michael?' was the final question.

'I declare it to be the whole truth, and nothing but the truth,' was the final answer.

4

What was I to think? Certainly I could not think that Michael was lying. Equally certainly I could not forget that I had caught his hand on the glass cover.

On the whole, if I had to doubt either Michael or the evidence of my senses, I preferred to do the latter. When we got out of that terrible room, I would go to him when he was alone, and say, 'Beau, old chap, just tell *me* you didn't touch the thing – and if you say you didn't, there's an absolute end of it.' And so there would be as far as I was concerned . . .

On hearing his last words, my aunt sat and stared at Michael. The silence grew horrible. At length she began to speak in a low frozen voice.

'This is inexpressibly vulgar and disgusting.' she began. 'One of half a dozen boys and girls, who have practically grown up here, is a despicable liar and, apparently, a common thief – or an uncommon one. I am still unable to think the latter . . . Listen . . . I shall leave the cover where it is and I shall lock the doors of this room at midnight and keep the keys, except the key of that one. Bring it to me, Digby . . . Thank you.

'This key I shall put in the old brass box on the ledge above the fire-place in the outer hall. The servants will have gone to bed and will know nothing of its whereabouts. I ask the liar, who is present, to take the opportunity of returning the sapphire during the night, relocking the door, and replacing the key in the brass box. If this is *not* done by the time I come down to-morrow, I shall have to conclude that the liar is also a thief, and act accordingly. For form's sake I shall tell Claudia and Isobel.'

'Come, Maurice,' she added, rising and taking the Chaplain's arm. 'I do hope you won't let this worry you, and give you a sleepless night.'

The poor Chaplain looked too unhappy, bewildered, and bemused to speak.

Having locked two of the doors, Lady Brandon, followed by the Chaplain, swept from the room without a 'Good night' to any of us.

I think we each heaved a sigh of relief as the door shut. I certainly did.

And now, what?

Digby turned upon Augustus.

'Oh, you unutterable cheese-mite,' he said, apparently more in sorrow than in anger. 'I think de-bagging is indicated . . . And a leather belt,' he added, 'unless anyone's pumps are nice and swishy.'

I said nothing. It was not the hand of Augustus that I had caught feeling for the cover.

He glared from one to the other of us like a trapped rat, and almost shrieked as Digby seized him.

'You lying swine,' he shouted. 'Who was by the table when the light failed and came on again? Who was grabbing who, when Isobel turned it on?'

I looked at Michael, and Michael looked at me.

'Yes,' screamed Augustus seeing the look, and wriggling free.

'By Jove!' said Digby, 'if he pinched it, he's *got* it . . . Come to my arms, Gus!' and in a moment he was sitting upon the prostrate form of the hysterically indignant youth, and feeling the pockets of his dinner-jacket from the outside.

'Not in his breast-pockets . . . side . . . waistcoat . . . trousers . . . no – the beggar hasn't got it unless he has swallowed it,' announced Digby. Then . . . 'Might have shoved it behind a cushion or dropped it somewhere . . . Come on, out with it, Gus, and let's get to bed.'

'You filthy, lying, beastly cad,' blubbered Augustus in reply, showing the courage of the cornered rat.

I don't think he had ever defied or insulted either of my brothers before in his life.

I expected to see him promptly suffer grief and pain at their hands, but Michael did the unexpected, as usual.

'Why, I believe the little man's innocent after all,' he said quite kindly.

'You *know* I am, you damned hypocrite,' shouted Augustus. 'Weren't you and John fumbling at the cover when she turned the light on – you cowardly blackguards.'

Digby's hand closed on the scruff of the boy's neck.

'If I have accused you wrongly, Gussie, I'll humbly apologise and make it up to you,' said he. 'But if we find you *did* do it – oh, my little Gussie . . . !'

'And if you find it was Michael, or John, or yourself?' sneered the dishevelled and shaking Augustus.

Michael looked hard at me and I looked hard at him.

'Look here,' said Digby, 'presumably the thing is in the room. Aunt wouldn't pinch her own jewel. The Chaplain has no use for it nor for thirty thousand pounds. No one supposes Isobel did it – nor Claudia. That leaves us four, and we haven't been out of the room. Come on, find it. Find it, Gussie, and I'll swear that *I* put it there,' and Digby began throwing cushions from sofas and chairs, moving footstools, turning up rugs, and generally hunting about, the while he encouraged himself, and presumably Augustus, with cries of 'Good dog! . . . Fetch 'em, boy! . . . Seize 'em, Gussie! . . . Sick 'em, pup! . . . Worry 'im, Gus!' and joyful barks.

Michael and I searched methodically and minutely, until it was perfectly clear that the 'Blue Water' was not in the room, unless far more skilfully concealed than would have been possible in the dark and in the few minutes at the disposal of anyone who wished to hide it.

'Well, that's that,' said Digby at last. 'We'd better push off before Aunt comes down to look the door. I don't want to see her again to-night. Damned if I don't feel guilty as soon as she looks at me.'

'Perhaps you are!' snarled Augustus.

'You never know, do you?' grinned Digby.

'Better tidy up a bit before we go,' suggested Michael. 'Servants'll smell a rat if it's like this to-morrow.'

'Smell a herd of elephants, I should think,' answered Digby, and we three straightened the disordered room, while Augustus sullenly watched us, with an angry, bitter sneer, and an occasional snarl of 'Beastly humbugs,' or, 'Lying hypocrites.'

'Come to the smoking-room, you two?' said Digby to Michael and me, when we had finished.

'Yes – go and fix it up, cads,' urged Augustus.

'Go to bed, Ghastly,' replied Digby, 'and don't forget the key will be in the brass box on the ledge over the fire-place in the outer hall. Bung off.'

'For two damns I'd sit in the hall all night, and see who comes for it,' was the reply, and the speaker glanced at me.

'Don't let *me* find you there, or I shall slap you,' said Digby.

'No, I shouldn't be popular if I went there now and refused to budge, should I?' was the angry retort.

'Lord! It's a long worm that has no turning,' cryptically remarked Digby, as Augustus took what was meant to be a dignified departure. 'And a long lane that has no public-house,' he added.

'Either that lad's innocent or he's a really accomplished young actor,' I observed, looking after the retreating Augustus as we crossed the hall, where we said 'Good night' to a yawning footman, and made our way down a corridor to the smoking-room.

5

'Well, my sons, what about it?' said Michael, poking up the fire, as we threw ourselves into deep leather arm-chairs and produced pipes.

'Pretty go if the damned thing isn't there in the morning,' said Digby.

'I wonder if she'd send to Scotland Yard?' he added, blowing a long cloud of smoke towards the ceiling.

'Filthy business,' said Michael. 'Fancy a fat mystery-merchant prowling about here and questioning everybody!'

'What a lark!' chuckled Digby. 'Jolly glad the servants are out of it all right, poor beggars.'

'Beastly vulgar business, as Aunt said,' observed Michael.

'And a bit rough on her too – apart from any question of thirty thousand pounds,' said I.

'Shake her faith a bit in human nature, what?' said Digby. 'But, damn it – the beastly thing will be there all right in the morning.'

'I hope to God it will,' said I from the bottom of my heart, and found that Michael and I were staring at each other again.

'Reconstruct the dreadful crime,' suggested Digby. 'Wash out Aunt and the Chaplain.'

'And the girls,' said Michael. 'If anyone even glanced at the possibility of Claudia stealing, I'd wring his beastly neck until he could see all down his beastly back.'

'I'd wring the neck of anyone who even glanced at the possibility of Isobel stealing – until he hadn't a head to see with,' added Digby.

'Wouldn't it be too silly to be worth noticing at all?' I asked. I was thinking more particularly of Isobel.

'Let's go and *beat* young Gussie,' said Digby.

'Gussie doesn't know a thing about it,' said Michael. 'Nothing but genuine injured innocence would have given him the pluck to call us "Filthy liars," and "Damned hypocrites." You know, if he'd been guilty, he'd have been conciliatory, voluble, and tearful – oh, altogether different. A much more humble parishioner.'

'Believe you're right, Beau,' agreed Digby. 'Nothing like a sense of injustice to put you up on the bough . . . 'Sides, young Gus hasn't the guts to pinch anything really valuable . . . And if he'd taken it for a lark and hadn't been able to put it back, he'd have hidden it behind a cushion till he could. I quite expected to find it in some such place. That's why I gave him the chance . . . If he *has* got it, he'll shove it back to-night,' he added.

'He hasn't,' said Michael – and again Michael and I found ourselves looking at each other.

'Well – that leaves us three then,' said I.

'It does,' said Michael.

'You can count me out, old son,' grinned Digby. 'Search me.'

'Which reminds one, by the way, that we didn't search ourselves, or each other, when we searched Gussie,' said I.

'It would have been fairer . . .'

'Most undignified and unnecessary,' put in Michael.

'So Gussie seemed to find,' chuckled Digby.

'Then that leaves you and me, John,' said Michael.

'Yes, it leaves me and you, Beau,' I agreed, and again we stared at each other.

'I did not take the "Blue Water," Beau,' I said.

'*Nor did I*, John,' said Michael.

'Then there's a mis-deal somewhere,' remarked Digby, 'and Gussie *must* have done it. Anyhow – it'll be put back in the night. Must be.'

'What do you say to our sitting here until we hear somebody come down to the hall? That door always makes a frightful row,' I suggested.

'Certainly not,' said Michael sharply.

'Why not?' I asked, eyeing him.

'Why, you ass, it might not be . . . I mean we might . . . Anyhow, we've no right to interfere with Aunt's arrangements. She has given the person a chance . . .'

Michael was by no means fluent. He turned to Digby.

'Don't you think so, Dig?' he asked.

'Any ass can sit up who wants to,' was the prompt reply. 'I have had enough of to-day, myself. Who's coming up?' He rose and yawned.

'I say,' he chuckled, 'what a lark to pinch the key and hide it.'

'Don't be a fool,' said Michael. 'Let's go to bed,' and we went with our usual curt 'Good nights.' . . .

But it was easier, for me at least, to go to bed than to go to sleep, although my brain seemed somewhat numbed and dulled. I lay and tossed and turned, refusing to believe that Michael had done this disgusting thing, and unable, somehow, to believe that Augustus had. It did not occur to me to doubt Digby – and, as I have said, I should never have dreamt of doubting Michael, had I not caught him.

Leaving out Aunt Patricia, the Chaplain, Digby, and Augustus, there remained Isobel, Claudia, Michael, and I. Eliminating Isobel, there remained Claudia, Michael, and I. It could not be Claudia. How *could* it be Michael?

Had *I* done it myself?

Such was my mental condition by this time that I actually entertained the idea. I had read a book not so long before, in which, after a most tremendous mystery and bother, it turned out that the innocent hero had committed the crime while in a somnambulistic condition.

That could not apply in my case, of course . . . There was no question or possibility of sleep-walking or trance about it – but might I not, absolutely unconsciously or subconsciously, have put the thing in my pocket without knowing it? People undoubtedly did do absurd things in fits of absent-mindedness, to their subsequent incredulous astonishment. I had never done such things myself – but might I not have begun doing them now? It was certainly as possible as it was utterly improbable. I actually got up and searched my clothes.

Of course I found nothing, and hour after hour of cogitation and reiterated argument brought me nearer and nearer to the conclusion that either Augustus or Michael was the culprit.

Having repeatedly arrived at this inevitable point, I delivered myself of the unhelpful verdict, '*Augustus or Michael – guilty. And I believe Augustus isn't, and Michael couldn't be!*'

Anyhow, daylight would find the wretched stone back in its place, and the whole business would be merely a very unsatisfactory and annoying puzzle, until it faded from the memories of the eight people who knew of it.

I turned over and made another resolute effort to go to sleep – a foolish thing to do, as it is one of the best ways of ensuring wakefulness.

My mind went off on a new tack. Suppose the 'Blue Water' were not put back during the night? What exactly would happen?

One thing would be clear at any rate – that a determined effort was being made to steal the jewel, by somebody who intended to convert it into money.

Certainly Lady Brandon, that *maîtresse femme*, was not the person to accept that 'lying down,' and she would surely take precisely the same steps for its recovery that she would have taken had it been stolen by burglars or a servant. She would communicate with the police, and see that no one left the house until the matter was in official hands.

It would be inexpressibly unpleasant and degrading. I imagined the questioning, the searching, the loathsome sense of being under suspicion – even Isobel and Claudia. At four o'clock in the morning the whole affair looked unutterably beastly.

And then I pulled myself together. *Of course* it would be all right. The idiot who had played the fool trick, and been too feeble to own up, would have replaced the jewel. Probably it was there now. The said idiot would have been only too anxious to get rid of it as soon as Aunt Patricia had put the key in the brass box . . . Why not go and make sure?

Of course – and then one could put the silly business out of one's mind and get some sleep.

I got out of bed, pulled on my dressing-gown, and put my feet into bedroom slippers. Lighting one of the emergency candles which stood on the mantelpiece, I made my way down the corridor to the upper of the two galleries that ran round the four sides of the central hall, and descended the stairs that led to the gallery below, and thence to the hall. Crossing this, I entered the outer hall, avoided the protruding hand and sword-hilt of a figure in armour, and made my silent way to the big stone fire-place.

On the broad shelf or mantelpiece, some six feet from the ground, was the ancient brass box, dating from the days of pack-horse travel, in which my aunt had placed the key.

Only she hadn't – or someone had removed it – for the box was quite empty!

Was this a trap, a trick of Lady Brandon's to catch the guilty one? Justly or unjustly, I thought she was quite capable of it.

If so, presumably I was caught again in this indiscriminating trap that another should have adorned. I was reminded of the occasion many years before, when she suddenly entered the schoolroom and said, 'The naughty child that has been in the still-room has got jam on its chin,' and my innocent and foolish hand promptly went up to my face to see if, by some wild mischance, it were jammy.

Well – the best thing to do now was to fade swiftly and silently away ere the trap closed; and I turned, wondering whether Aunt Patricia were watching.

That was an absurd idea, of course.

Then I wondered if the box contained some scent of indelible odour, which would betray the guilty hand that had come in contact with it.

Equally absurd.

As I crossed the hall, I also thought of finger-prints.

Had she polished the lid and front of the box with the intention of having it examined by experts for the identification of the owner of the fingers that touched it during the night? Less absurd, perhaps, but utterly improbable. Such an idea might have occurred to her had it been certain that the 'Blue Water' was really stolen by a thief who had meant to get away with it.

And supposing that were really the case, and the jewel were not replaced during the night?

There were my finger-prints, anyhow, if she had really thought of this plan! And there they were if it occurred to her later, in the event of the sapphire not being restored. I re-entered the central hall – not more than half a minute later than I had left it – and saw someone coming toward me. He, or she, carried no light, and, of course, could identify me, the candle being just in front of my face.

'Well, Gussie,' said I. 'Cold morning.'

'Well, John. Looking for the key?' said the voice of my brother Michael.

'Yes, Beau,' I answered. 'It's not there.'

'No, John,' said Michael quietly. 'It's here,' and he held it out towards me.

'*Beau!*' I said miserably.

'*John!*' he mocked me.

A wave of sick disgust passed over me. What *had* come over my splendid brother?

'Good night,' I said, turning away.

'Or morning,' replied Michael, and, with a short laugh, he went into the outer hall.

I heard him strike a match and there followed the rattle of the key and the clang of a falling lid. He had evidently thrown the key carelessly into the box, and dropped the lid without any attempt at avoiding noise.

I went back to bed and, the affair being over and the mystery solved, fell into a broken sleep.

6

I was awakened at the usual time by David, the underfootman, with my hot water.

'Half-past seven, sir,' said he; 'a fine morning when the mist clears.'

'Thank you, David,' I replied, and sat up.

What was wrong? Of course – that idiotic affair of last night, and

Michael's heavy fall from his pedestal. Well, there are spots on the sun, and no man is always himself. Why dwell on one fault rather than on a hundred virtues? But it *was* unlike Michael to tell such silly pointless lies to cover a silly pointless trick.

I dressed and went downstairs, taking a mashie and a ball from the glory-hole, a small room or large cupboard off the corridor that leads to the smoking-room. I would do a few approach-shots from the tennis-courts to the paddock and back, before the breakfast-gong went at half-past eight.

Crossing the rose-garden I ran into Claudia. This surprised me, for she was more noted for being the last arrival at breakfast than for early rising. It struck me that she looked seedy and worried, and she was certainly deep in some unpleasant slough of thought when she saw me.

As she did so, her face cleared and brightened, rather too suddenly and artificially, I thought.

'Hullo, early worm,' said she.

'Hullo, early bird,' I replied. 'What's up?'

'What do you mean?' asked Claudia.

'I thought you looked a bit off colour and bothered,' replied I, with masculine tactlessness.

'Rubbish,' said Claudia, and passed on.

I dropped my ball at the back of the tennis-courts, and strove in vain to smite it. I scooped generous areas of turf from the lawn, topped my ball, sliced it into a holly bush, threw my club after it, and slouched off, my hands deep in my pockets and anger (with Michael) deep in my soul.

Returning to the house I saw Burdon crossing the hall, the gong-stick in his hand. The brass box leered at me cynically as I passed.

Having washed my hands in the lavatory by the glory-hole, I went into the dining-room.

The fire was blazing merrily, a silver kettle was simmering on its spirit-stand on the table, a delicious smell came from the sideboard, where three or four covered silver dishes sat on their metal platform, beneath which burnt spirit-lamps. The huge room – with its long windows, looking on two sides to the loveliest view in Devon; its great warm-tinted Turkey carpet hiding most of the ancient oak floor; its beautifully arched ceiling – was a picture of solid, settled comfort, established and secure.

Digby was wandering about the room, a plate of porridge in one hand, and a busy spoon in the other. Augustus was at the sideboard removing cover after cover, and adding sausages to eggs and rashers of bacon.

'Good effort, Gus,' said Digby, eyeing the piled mass as he passed him with his empty porridge plate. 'Shove some kedgeree on top.'

'Had it,' said Augustus. 'This is going on top of the kedgeree.'

'Stout citizen,' approved Digby, getting himself a clean plate.

Isobel was sitting in her place, and I went to see what I could get for her.

As I stood by her chair she put her left hand up to mine and gave it a squeeze.

'I'll wait for Aunt Patricia, John,' she said.

'Aunt come down?' he asked, and added a belated ''Morning, everybody.'

'No,' replied Digby. 'Watch me gobble and go. I'm not meeting Aunt till the day's been aired a bit.'

'Claudia down yet?' enquired Michael, ignoring him.

'I saw her in the garden,' I said.

'I'll tell her breakfast's ready,' he observed, rising and going out.

'Take her a kidney on a fork,' shouted Digby, as the door closed.

We sat down, and conversation was in abeyance for a few minutes in favour of the business of breakfast.

'I suppose the Crown Jewels are all present and correct by now?' said Digby suddenly, voicing what was uppermost in all our thoughts. 'Door's still locked. I tried it.'

'Of course it's all right,' I said.

'Seen it?' asked Augustus.

'Or was it too dark?' he added, with a sneer.

'No – I haven't seen it,' I replied. 'But of course, it's there all right.'

'You should know, of course,' said Augustus.

'Shut it, Ghastly,' said Digby, 'or I'll have your breakfast back.'

'You're a coarse lout, Digby,' remarked Augustus calmly.

''Streuth!' murmurd Digby to the world in general. 'Isn't the gentleman's courage coming on?'

It struck me that it was. I had never known Augustus so daring, assured, and insolent before. I felt more and more convinced that, as Michael had said, nothing but genuine injured innocence and a sense of injustice could have wrought this change.

The door opened, and Claudia, followed by Michael, entered. She looked very white and Michael very wooden and *boutonné*. I saw Isobel give her a sharp glance as she sat down and said:

''Morning . . . Aunt not been down yet?'

'No, no. Gobble and go. If asked about sapphires, say you don't know,' chanted Digby, beating time with a spoon on his cup.

Michael foraged at the sideboard for Claudia, and then went to the coffee-table. I watched his face as he took the coffee-pot and milk-jug from their tray and held them poised one in each hand, over the cup. His face was perfectly inscrutable and his hands absolutely steady – but I knew there was something very wrong.

He looked up and saw me watching him.

''Morning, bun-face,' quoth he. 'Sleep well?'

'Except for one unpleasant dream, Beau,' I replied.

'H'm,' said Michael, and I tried to analyse the sound, but found it as non-committal as his face.

He returned to his place beside Claudia, and as he seated himself, Aunt Patricia entered the room.

We rose, and I drew back her chair, and then we stood petrified in a complete silence.

One look at her face was sufficient, as she stopped halfway from the door. I knew before she spoke almost the words she was going to say.

'I have come to request that none of you – *none* of you – leave the house to-day,' she said. 'Unless, that is, one of you cares to say, even now at the eleventh hour, "A fool and a liar I am, but a criminal I am not!" '

No one spoke or moved. I looked at Michael and he at me.

'No?' continued Lady Brandon. 'Very well. But please understand that if I go out of this room without the "Blue Water," I will have no mercy. The thief shall pay a thief's penalty – *whoever* it may be.'

She paused and fixed her coldly angry gaze on me, on Augustus, on Michael, on Digby, on Isobel, on Claudia.

No one spoke or moved, and for a full minute Lady Brandon waited.

'Ah!' said she at last, and then, 'One other thing please note very carefully. The servants know *nothing* of this, and they are to know nothing. We will keep it to ourselves – as long as possible, of course – that one of you six is a treacherous, ungrateful lying thief.'

And then Michael spoke:

'Say one of us four, please, Aunt Patricia.'

'Thank you, Michael,' she replied cuttingly. 'You four are among the six. And I will apply to you when I need the help of your wisdom in choosing my words.'

'I think you might say "*one of you three brothers*," ' Augustus had the audacity to remark.

'Hold your miserable tongue,' was Lady Brandon's discouraging reply.

'As I was saying,' she continued, 'the servants are to know nothing – and neither is anybody else. Until, of course, the police-court reporters have the story, and the newspapers are adorned with the portrait of one of your faces.'

Once again her scornful glance swept us in turn, this time beginning with Michael and going on to Augustus.

'Very well, then,' she went on. 'No one leaves the house, and no one breathes a word of this to anyone but the eight people who already know of it . . .'

'Except to a detective or the police, of course,' she added, with an ominous note and a disdainful edge to her voice. 'The Chaplain is ill,' she concluded, 'and I don't wonder at it.'

She turned and walked to the door. Before opening it, she faced us once again.

'Have you anything to say – Michael?' she asked.

'Leave the girls out of it – and Augustus,' he replied.

'Have you anything to say, Digby?'

'No, Aunt. Awful sorry, and all that,' replied Digby, and I seemed to see his lips forming the words, 'No, no. Gobble and go . . .'

'John?' and she looked even more disdainful, I thought.

'No, Aunt – except that I agree with Michael, *very* strongly,' I answered.

'Augustus?'

'It's a damned shame . . .' blustered Augustus.

'Very helpful,' Lady Brandon cut him short with cruel contempt.

'Claudia?'

'No, Aunt.'

'Isobel?'

'No, Aunt,' answered Isobel. 'But please, please wait another day and . . .'

'. . . And give the thief time to dispose of it, were you going to say?' interrupted Aunt Patricia.

She opened the door.

'Then that is all, is it?' she asked. 'No one has anything to say? . . . *Very well!*' and she went out, closing the door quietly behind her.

7

'I hate skilly and loathe picking oakum, don't you, Ghastly?' remarked Digby conversationally, as we stared at each other in utter consternation.

'You foul, filthy, utter cads,' spluttered Augustus, looking from Digby to me and then to Michael.

'Cuts no ice, Gus. Shut it,' said Michael, in a perfectly friendly voice, and added, 'Run along and play if you can't be serious . . . Come with me, John,' and turning to the girls, said, 'Do me a favour, Queen Claudia and Faithful Hound.'

'Of course,' said Isobel.

'What is it?' asked Claudia.

'Put this wretched business out of both your minds, by means of my absolute assurance and solemn promise that it will be settled and cleared up to-day.'

'How?' asked Claudia.

'Oh, *Michael*, dear!' said Isobel, and glanced at me.

'Never mind how, for the minute, Claudia,' replied Michael. 'Just believe and rest assured. Before you go to bed to-night, everything will be as clear as crystal.'

'Or as blue as sapphire,' said Digby, and added, 'By Jove! I've got an idea! A theory! . . . My dog Joss got alarmed at the sudden darkness, jumped on a chair to avoid the crush, wagged his tail to show faith and hope, knocked over the cover, reversed his engine, and smelt round to see what he'd done, found nothing and yawned in boredom – and inhaled the "Blue Water." '

'Perhaps he was thirsty and *drank* the "Blue Water"?' amended Isobel.

'Both very sound theories. Sounder still if Joss had been in the room,' said Michael. 'Come, John.'

I followed my brother out into the hall. He led the way to his room.

'Take a pew, Johnny. I would hold converse with thee on certain dark matters,' he said as we entered.

Having locked the door, he put his tobacco-jar on the low table beside the low arm-chair in which I was sitting.

'You leave the carbon cake too long in your pipes,' he said. 'That's what cracks them. Unequal expansion of the carbon and the wood, I suppose. You ought to scrape it out once a month or so.'

He seated himself opposite to me and sprawled in the low chair, with his knees higher than his head.

'Oh, I like a well-caked pipe,' I replied. 'Nuttier and cooler.'

'Ah, well! So long as you can afford to crack your pipes,' he said lazily, and sat silent for a minute or two.

I was quite under his spell again, and had to keep whipping my feelings up into a state of resentment and disgust to maintain them in the condition that common justice demanded. If he were going to restore the sapphire that evening as he had hinted, why on earth couldn't he have done it just now? For the matter of that, why on earth couldn't he have returned it last night when he went to the drawing-room? Why had he ever denied taking the thing at all?

'Well, son, what about it?' he said suddenly.

'Yes, what about it, Beau?' I replied.

He looked at me quizzically.

'What's the game, should you think, Johnny?' he asked.

'That's what I want to know,' I answered. 'It seems a damned silly one, anyhow.'

'Quite,' agreed Michael. 'Quite very. *Very* quite. *And* a little rough on the girls and our good Augustus.'

'Exactly,' said I. 'And on Aunt Patricia.'

An uncomfortable silence followed.

'Well?' said Michael, at length.

'Oh, put it back, Beau,' I implored. 'God alone knows what you're playing at! Do *you*?'

Michael sat up and stared at me.

'Oh? You say "*Put it back*," do you, John?' he said slowly and thoughtfully.

'I do,' I replied. 'Or look here, Beau. Aunt thinks a lot of you, and devilish little of me. It would be doing her a real kindness not to let her know it was you after all. Give it here, and I'll . . .' I coloured and felt a fool.

'*Eric, or Little by Little. A Story of School Life . . . The Boy with the Marble Brow*,' murmured Michael, smiling. But his voice was very kind . . .

'This grows interesting, Johnny,' he went on. 'If I go and fetch the "Blue Water" now, will you take it to Aunt Patricia and say, "*Alone I did it. I cannot tell a lie. It is a far, far better thing I do . . .*?"'

'Those very words, Beau,' I grinned. 'On condition you tell me what the game was, and why you did such a damned silly thing.'

Thank God the wretched business was going to end – and yet, and yet . . . I felt quite sure that Michael would not let me take the blame – much as I would have preferred that to the wretched feeling of our Michael being the object of Aunt Patricia's scorn and contempt. The more she liked him and approved him now, the more would she dislike and despise him then. She might forbid him the house.

Michael rose.

'You really will?' he asked. 'If I go and get it now, you'll take it straight to Aunt Patricia and say you pinched it for a lark?'

'Only too glad of the chance, Beau,' I answered. 'To get the beastly business over and done with and forgotten – and the girls and Gussie and Digby out of the silly mess.'

'H'm,' said Michael, sitting down. 'You would, eh?'

'And might I ask you a question or two, John?' he went on.

'What were you doing with your hand on the glass cover when I put my hand on it last night?'

'Waiting to catch the ass that was returning the "Blue Water,"' I replied.

'H'm! Why did you want to catch him?'

'Because I had twice been accused of the fool trick – just because I was standing close to the table when the light failed.'

'So you were, too . . . And what were you doing down-stairs last night when I found you in the hall?'

'Looking for the key, Beau, as I told you,' I answered.

'And what did you want the key for?'

'To see whether the sapphire had been put back – and to get some peace of mind and sleep, if it had.'

'Did you go into the drawing-room?'

'No,' I answered.

'Why not?'

'What need? I took it for granted that you had returned it,' replied I.

'H'm!' said Michael. 'Suppose a vote were taken among the eight of us, as to who is likeliest to be the thief, who do you suppose would top the poll?'

'Augustus,' I stated promptly.

'Do you think he is the culprit?' asked my brother.

'No, I do *not*,' I replied significantly.

'Nor I,' answered the enigmatic Michael. 'In fact, I know he's not.'

He sat silent, smoking reflectively for a few minutes.

'Go through the list,' he said suddenly. 'Would Aunt pinch her own jewel?'

'Hardly,' said I.

'Would the Chaplain?'

'Still less,' said I.

'Would Claudia?' he asked next – almost anxiously, I fancied (absurdly, no doubt).

'Don't be a fool,' I replied.

'Would Isobel?'

'Don't be a cad,' I said.

'Would Digby?'

'Utterly preposterous and absurd,' I answered.

'Would Augustus?'

'I feel certain that he *didn't* anyhow,' I answered.

'Would you?'

'I didn't, as it happens,' I assured him.

'Would I?'

'I should have thought you almost the last person in the world, Beau,' I assured him.

'Looks as though I did it then, doesn't it?' he asked. 'Because if Augustus and Digby and you didn't do it – who the devil did, if I didn't? Yes – it looks as though I am the thief.'

'It does – to me only though. Nobody else knows that I found you downstairs,' I said. 'Why *didn't* you put it back then, Beau?' I asked.

'*Wish I had*,' he said.

There came a bang at the door.

'Who's there?' cried Michael.

'Me,' bawled the ungrammatical Digby.

Michael unlocked the door.

'What's up?' he asked.

'Isobel wants to speak to us three. She's been looking for you two. A thought has struck her. Blow severe but not fatal. All about the Painful Event . . .'

'Where is she?' asked Michael.

'I said I'd lead you by the ear to the smoking-room at an early date – unless either of you had done a bunk with the loot,' replied Digby.

'Well – I haven't fled yet, but I shall want a Bradshaw after lunch,' said Michael, adding, 'Let's go and hear Isobel's great thought. Generally worth hearing.'

We went downstairs and made our way to the smoking-room. The brass box caught my eye, and an idea also struck *me* with some violence, as I noticed that the lid and front seemed brighter than the rest of it.

'Don't expose me yet, John,' said Michael as we crossed the hall.

'John been catching you out?' asked Digby.

'Caught me last night, didn't you, John?' replied Michael.

'Red-handed,' said I.

'It's blue-handed that Aunt wants to cop someone,' said Digby, opening the door of the smoking-room. 'Sapphire-blue.'

Isobel was sitting by the fire looking tearful and depressed. It was at me that she looked as we entered.

'Caught them both in the act of bolting, Isobel,' said Digby. 'They've each got a half of the "Blue Water" – about a pint apiece. But they are willing to hear your words if you are quick.'

'Oh, I *am* so miserable,' moaned Isobel. 'I have been such a wicked, *wicked* beast. But I can't bear it any longer.'

'Leave it with us, dear,' said Digby, 'and forget it. We'll smuggle it back, and share Aunt's few well-chosen words among us, won't we, Beau?'

'What's the trouble, child?' asked Michael.

'I've let Augustus take the blame all this time,' she sobbed.

'Didn't notice him taking any,' observed Digby. 'Must be a secret blame-taker, I suppose.'

'Augustus is perfectly innocent and I could have proved it, the moment Aunt began to question us last night. A word from me would have saved him from all suspicion – and I never said it,' she went on.

'Why, dear?' I asked her.

'Oh, I don't know . . . Yes, I do. It would have looked like exculpating myself too,' she replied. 'Besides, I didn't know *who* had done it. And it was more or less of a silly practical joke last night . . . And, of course, I thought the person who had taken it would say so, or at least put it back. But now – it's awful. And I can't keep quiet any longer. I thought I'd tell you three before I told Aunt.'

'Well – what is it, Faithful Hound?' asked Michael.

'Why, when the light went out – you know I said, "*Ghosts and goblins and skeleton hands*," or something? Well, I half frightened myself and half pretended, and I clutched somebody's arm. When the light went up I found it was Augustus I was hugging – and let go so quickly that nobody noticed, I suppose.'

'That settles it,' said Digby. 'It wasn't poor Gussie.' 'Couldn't have been,' he added, 'unless those two were one and did it together.'

'Don't be an ass, Dig,' I said, for poor Isobel was really upset about it.

'Oh, never!' said Digby. 'Absolutely never!'

'Well – I like our Augustus all the better for not having adduced this bit of evidence himself,' said I.

'Bless the dear boy,' said Digby, 'and I searched all his little pockets. I must find him and forgive him.'

'Have you told Claudia this?' asked Michael.

'Yes,' replied Isobel. 'But she seems to think that I may have been mistaken.'

'Which is absurd, of course,' she added.

'Well – friend Gussie ought to be much obliged to you, both for hanging on to him in the dark, and for remembering it, Isobel,' said Michael.

'Yes,' chimed in Digby, 'now he can bark and wag his tail and gambol around the feet of Aunt Patricia, while we walk in outer darkness.'

'Tell her at once and get it off your conscientious chest, Isobel,' said I.

She looked at me long and miserably, almost apologetically I thought, and went out of the room.

'Say, citizens,' said Digby as the door closed, 'what I want to know is this. Who pinched this here gem we're being bothered about? Officious and offensive fella, I consider – but Gussie now being out of it, it must be one of us three . . . Excuse my mentioning it then, but me being out of it, it must be one of you *two*. Now unless you really want the damned thing, I say, "*Put it back.*" '

Michael and I once again looked at each other, Michael's face being perfectly expressionless.

'I think of bolting with it, as I told Isobel just now,' said Michael.

'John going with his half too?' asked Digby.

'No,' replied Michael for me. 'I'm taking it all.'

'Well, old horse,' said Digby, looking at his watch, 'could you go soon after lunch? I want to run up to town to see a man about a dog, and Aunt seems to have other views for us – until the matter is cleared up.'

'Do my best to oblige,' said Michael, as I quietly slipped from the room to carry out the idea which had occured to me as I crossed the hall.

I went to the brass box. Finger-prints were very faintly discernible on its highly-polished lid and front. Going to the wash-basin in the room opening off the neighbouring corridor, I damped my handkerchief, and rubbed soap, hard, on the wet surface. The hall was still empty when I returned, and I promptly began scouring the lid and front of the box.

It was easier, however, to remove the finger-marks than to remove the signs of their removal. I did not wish it to be obvious that someone had been doing – what I was doing.

Under a heavy curtain, in a recess in the panelling, hung overcoats, caps, mufflers, and such outdoor garments. A silk scarf of Digby's struck me as being just the thing I wanted.

I had restored to the box the brilliance which had been its before I soaped it, and was giving it a final wipe with the silk, when the door from the corridor swung open, Michael entered, and I was caught in the act.

And then I saw that in his hand was a piece of wash-leather and a silver-duster, presumably purloined from the butler's pantry!

'Ah!' he said. 'Removing all traces of the crime?'

'All – I hope, Beau,' I replied.

'Sound plan too,' he observed. 'Just going to do it myself,' and he passed on.

Having finished my task, I placed the fingers of my right hand on top of the box, my thumb on the front, and left as fair and clear a set of finger-prints as I could contrive.

How could it possibly matter to me if a detective identified them as mine? I hadn't taken the 'Blue Water,' and nobody could prove that I had.

And why was Micheal so anxious that his finger-marks should not be found there as a piece of evidence to be coupled with the fact that I had been seen holding his wrist, above the glass cover, when the lights were turned on?

I went up to my room despairing, and trying to recall what I had read, somewhere, about the method of examining finger-prints. I believe they blow a fine powder on to them and then apply carbon-paper or tissue-paper, and take a photograph of the result.

Anyhow, if Aunt had been wily enough to polish the box, just where we would touch it, so that she could get the finger-prints of the person who opened it, she'd get mine all right and those of nobody else, when the detectives came.

8

Aunt Patricia did not appear at lunch, nor did Claudia. The Chaplain was still ill in bed.

As Burden and a footman always waited at that meal, there was no general conversation on the one subject of interest to us all.

It was a painful meal, to me at any rate, though Digby seemed perfectly happy, and Michael unconcerned. The only reference to the theft was during a brief absence of the servants.

'Did you tell Aunt what you proposed to tell her? What did she say?' asked Michael of Isobel.

'Yes . . . She said, somewhat cryptically, "*Virtue is its own reward*," and nothing else,' replied Isobel.

'Gussie,' said Digby, 'Isobel has – one cannot say "bearded" of a lady – let us say faced – Aunt Patricia in her wrath, in order to tell her that you must be absolutely innocent of sin, and quite above or beneath suspicion.'

'What do you mean?' snarled Augustus.

'She very kindly went to the lioness's den,' continued Digby, 'to say that she seized you and hung on to you last night while the lights were out – and that, therefore, you could not possibly have gone to the table and pinched the sapphire, as she was hanging on to your arm. I sincerely apologise to you, Gussie, and hope you'll forgive me.'

'*My arm?*' said Augustus, in deep and genuine surprise ignoring the apology, and quickly adding, 'Oh, yes – er – of course. Thanks, Isobel.'

We all looked at him. I had been watching him when he spoke, and to me his surprise was perfectly obvious.

'Then Aunt knows *I* didn't do it?' he said.

'Yes, Gussie,' Isobel assured him, 'and I'm *awfully* sorry I didn't say it, at once, last night.'

'Yes – I thought you *might* have done so,' replied our Augustus.

'Isobel is not so keen on exculpating herself too, you see,' said I, glaring at the creature. '*If* she were holding your arm, she could not have gone to the table herself. Proving your innocence proves her own.'

'Well – she might have thought of me,' he grumbled.

'She has, Gussie,' said Michael; 'we shall all think of you, I'm sure . . . Anyhow, we are all sorry we were unkind and suspicious.'

'Suspicious! *You*!' said Augustus. 'Huh!'

'Yes – and I'm sorry I searched you, Ghastly,' put in Digby . . . 'I'll unsearch you by and by, if you're not careful,' he added.

And then David and Burdon came in with the next course.

After lunch, feeling disgruntled and miserable, I went along to the billiard-room to knock the balls about, as one could not very well leave the house in face of Lady Brandon's request.

Augustus was before me and I turned to retreat. I was in no mood to suffer Augustus gladly.

'Police come yet?' he jeered.

'No – you're safe for the present,' I replied.

'You heard what Isobel said at lunch,' he squealed.

'Yes,' said I, going out, 'you could hardly believe your ears, could you?' and I am afraid that the anger that I felt was almost entirely due to my conviction that he was absolutely innocent. Isobel could not very well be mistaken. I supposed that Augustus must have quite forgotten the incident until Isobel mentioned it, or else had never noticed it at all. Certainly that was far more probable, than that Isobel had made a mistake as to whom she had clutched in the darkness, especially as she did not leave go until the lights came on and started us all blinking at each other.

I went up to my bedroom, feeling deadly tired after my wakeful night and all the worry, and threw myself on my bed.

I was awakened from a heavy sleep by the entrance of Digby, a couple of hours later. He held a letter in his hand.

'Hi, hog,' quoth he, 'wake up and listen . . . Latest edition,' and he sat himself down heavily on the foot of the bed.

'What's up now?' I yawned, rubbing my eyes.

'We've got to use our wits and do something to help Beau. Show the mettle of our pastures and all that . . . Beau's done a bunk. Left this note with David. Says he pinched the "Blue Water", and isn't going to face the police.'

'*What?*' I cried.

'Read it,' said Digby, and passed the letter to me.

'*My dear Dig,*' it ran, '*I have told David to give you this at four o'clock, by which time I shall be well on my way to – where I am going. Will you please tell Aunt that there is no further need to chivvy any of you about the "Blue Water." If the police come or a mystery-merchant from Scotland Yard, tell them that you knew that I was in sore straights – or is it straits (or crookeds?) for money, but that you think that this is my first offence and I must have been led away by bad companions (you and John, of course).* KEEP *an eye on young John, and tell him I hope he'll be a good boy. If I send you an address later, it will be in absolute confidence, and relying wholly on your utterly refusing to give it to* ANYBODY, *for any reason whatsoever. I do hope that things will settle down quickly and quietly, now that the criminal is known. Sad, sad, sad! Give my love to Claudia.*

Ever thine,

Michael.'

'It *can't* be true,' I said. 'It's impossible.'

'Of course it is, fat-head,' replied Digby. 'He's off on the romantic tack. Taking the blame and all that . . . Shielding his little brother . . .'

'Which?' I asked. 'You?'

'No.' said Digby.

'Me?' I asked.

'Subtle mathematician,' observed Digby.

'But I didn't do it,' I said.

'Nor did I,' said Digby, and added, 'Let's say "Taking the blame and *thinking* he's shielding his little brother" then.'

'But, Dig,' I expostulated, 'do you think Beau seriously supposes for one moment that you or I would steal a valuable jewel – and from Aunt Patricia of all people?'

'Somebody has stolen it, haven't they?' said Digby. 'And I tell you what, my lad,' he added; 'you say that Beau would never seriously suppose that you or I would steal it – but you yourself seriously supposed that Beau had!'

'How do you know?' I asked, aghast.

'By the way you looked at him – oh, half a dozen times.'

'I had reason to suspect him,' I said.

'What reason – except that you caught hold of his wrist in the dark, when he was probably doing just what you were doing, trying to catch Gussie in the act of putting it back?' asked Digby.

'I'd rather not say any more about it, Dig,' I replied. 'It's Beau's business after all, and . . .'

'Don't be a colossal ass,' interrupted Dighy. 'Of course it's Beau's business, and that's what we are talking about. The more we both know, the more we can both help him – either to get away, or to come back . . . If we knew he is guilty, which, of course, he isn't, we could draw red herrings across his trail; and if we knew he is innocent, which he is, we could lay for the real theif and catch him out.'

'Beau doesn't want him caught out, evidently,' said I.

'What – not if it's the miserable Gussie?' asked my brother indignantly.

'It isn't,' said I. 'And Beau knows it.'

'Well – let's have those reasons, and we'll get to work,' said Digby. 'You needn't feel as though you were giving Beau away. There is no more harm in my knowing than in your knowing, and there may be some good. I am not asking you to tell Aunt, or the police, am I, bun-head?'

This was true enough. No harm could result from Digby's knowing all that I knew.

Moreover, if, as Digby assumed, Michael were shielding somebody else, presumably he would welcome any evidence that strengthened the case against himself.

'Well,' said I reluctantly, 'it's like this, Dig . . . Beau went down to the drawing-room last night. I met him with the key in his hand . . .

'And what were *you* doing, if one might ask?' interrupted my brother.

'Going to see if the "Blue Water" had been returned,' I replied.

'Anyhow, *Beau* hadn't returned it, had he?' grinned Digby.

'No – but at the time I, naturally enough, thought he had,' said I, 'and I suppose that fixed the idea in my mind. I first got the idea – naturally enough, again – when I caught his hand hovering over the glass cover in the darkness.'

'Anything else?' asked Digby.'

'Yes, the third reason I had for suspecting Beau – though I put my faith in him before all reason – was that I found him going to the brass box with a leather and duster to rub out the finger-prints he had made in taking and returning the key.'

Digby whistled.

'Ingenious,' he murmured. 'As artful as our Auntie, if she had the idea . . . Detectives would have the idea anyhow.'

'I think she did have the idea,' I said. 'I believe she went straight from the drawing-room and polished all the finger-marks from the lid and front of the damned thing.'

'And how do you know that Beau was on to the dodge?' asked Digby.

'He said so. He came into the hall with the cleaning-things in his hand, just as I was doing it myself.'

Digby stared.

'Doing it yourself?' he said. '*Why?*'

'Oh, can't you see?' I groaned. '*If* Beau had been playing the wild ass, I didn't want his finger-prints to be found there, on top of the fact that I had been seen clutching his fist in the drawing-room.'

'Yours were there as well as his,' observed Digby, 'if you went to the box for the key.'

'Yes – they were,' said I, 'and they are there, alone, now.'

'Stout fella,' approved Digby. 'I'll go and shove mine on too, and fog the Sherlocks . . . But you really are a goat,' he went on. 'Don't you see that Beau was probably going to do precisely what *you* were doing? He was going to polish the beastly thing clean of all foot-marks, and then jab his own on.'

'Why?' I asked.

'To shield the real culprit, of course,' said Digby patiently.

'Yes – but *why*?' I repeated. 'Why should Beau be a gratuitous ass and take the blame instead of – Gussie, for example? He'd have been more likely to nose him out and then slipper him well.'

'Because he knew it wasn't Gussie,' replied my brother solemnly.

'Who then?' I asked.

'He didn't know,' answered Digby. 'But isn't it as clear as mud, that since it wasn't Gussie or Isobel, it was you or me – or else *Claudia*?'

I was silent.

'Now look here, John,' went on Digby. ''Nuff said, and time to do something instead. But first of all, do you still suspect Beau?'

'I have never suspected him,' I replied. 'I have only realised that I caught his hand, met him with the drawing-room key, and know he was going to rub finger-prints off the brass box.'

'Plain yes or no,' said Digby. 'Do you suspect Beau?'

'Absolutely not,' I said promptly. 'No. No. *No*!'

'Very good then. Now – Did *you* do it?'

'I did not,' said I.

'Nor did I. Very well! Since Isobel and Augustus mutually prove each other innocent, as she was holding his arm, yards from the table all the time – who is left?'

'*Claudia?*' said I unhappily.

'*Now* d'you get it?' smiled Digby, leaning back against the bottom of the bed, and clasping his hands round his knee.

'Good God, man,' I cried, starting up. 'You don't mean to tell me you suspect *Claudia* of jewel-stealing?'

'Keep calm,' he replied. 'I am not talking about whom I suspect. I am asking you who remains if you eliminate me and yourself as admittedly innocent, and Isobel and Augustus as proven innocent.'

'Michael and Claudia!' I murmured. 'Which idea is the more ridiculous?' I said aloud.

'Equally impossible,' answered Digby. 'Also the fact remains that it was one of those two – *if* it wasn't you. Furthermore, the fact remains that Michael has bolted for one of two reasons – because he is a frightened thief, or because he wished to shield the guilty person – you or Claudia.'

A silence fell between us.

'I'm going dotty,' said I at last.

'I've gone,' said Digby, and we sat staring at each other.

After a time he rose.

'Got to get a move on,' he said.

'What are you going to do?' I asked.

'Dunno,' he replied.

As he was leaving the room I said, 'Do you think Michael suspects either me or you, Digby?'

'No,' he replied. 'He *knows* we didn't do it.'

'Do you think he suspects Claudia then?'

'Er – *no* – of course not,' he answered.

'Then?'

'He only *knows* that one of us three *did* do it,' he replied, and went out, leaving me staring at the door.

I lay down again to think.

9

Dinner that night was an extraordinary meal, at which only Isobel, Claudia, Augustus, and I appeared.

Lady Brandon, said Burdon, was dining in her own room; his Reverence the Chaplain was, by Dr. Warrender's orders, remaining in bed; Mr. Michael was not in his room when David took up his hot water; and Mr. Digby had been seen going down the drive soon after tea.

'Shocking bad form, I call it – Michael and Digby going out like this – after what Aunt said,' remarked Augustus as the service-door swung to, when the servants went out for the coffee.

'You're an authority on good form, of course,' I said.

'Where has Beau gone?' asked Claudia.

'He didn't tell me,' I replied.

'Don't suppose he told anybody,' sneered Augustus.

'Come into the drawing-room soon,' said Isobel, as I held the dining-room door open for the girls to go out.

'I'm coming now,' I replied. 'As soon as I have had some coffee.'

I did not want a *tête-à-tête* with Augustus, and I was more than a little disturbed in mind as to the meaning of Digby's absence.

What could be the reason of his defiance of Aunt Patricia's prohibition of our leaving the house? Was it possible that he knew more than he had told me?

Perhaps he had gone to the village telegraph-office to try to get into communication with Michael at one of the several places to which he might have gone.

It would be something important that would make him risk giving Aunt Patricia cause to think that he had been guilty of an ungentlemanly disobedience to her request.

I drank my coffee in silence, and in silence departed from the room. I could not forgive Gussie for being innocent and forcing Michael to suspect Claudia, Digby, or me; me to suspect Claudia, Digby, or Michael; and Digby to suspect Claudia, Michael, or me.

Most unjust of me, but most human, I fear.

In the drawing-room Isobel was at the piano, playing softly to herself, and Claudia sat staring into the fire.

I strolled over to the huge piano and sat down near it.

'Where *can* Michael be?' said Claudia.

'And Digby,' added Isobel.

'I don't know,' said I.

'Really and truly?' asked Claudia.

'Yes,' said I. 'I honestly have not the faintest idea as to where either of them is.'

'I wish they'd come in,' said Isobel.

'Oh, I can't bear this room,' cried Claudia suddenly, and springing up, went out. As I opened the door for her, I fancied I caught a glimpse of tears on her half-averted face, though I was not prying.

As I closed the door, Isobel rose from the piano and came towards me. She looked very lovely I thought, with her misty blue eyes, misty golden hair, as fine as floss-silk, and her sweet expression. How gentle and dear she was!

'Johnny,' she said, laying her hands on my chest and looking up into my eyes, 'may I ask you a silly question? Just once and for all? I know the answer, but I want to hear you say it.'

'Certainly, dear,' said I.

'You won't be angry, Johnny?'

'Have I ever been angry with you, Isobel? Could I be?' I asked.

She looked into my eyes steadily for a few moments.

'*Did you take the "Blue Water," John?*' she asked.

'No, my dear, I did not,' I replied, and drew her to me. And then Isobel threw her arms round my neck and I kissed her on the lips.

She burst into tears, and lifting her up in my arms, I carried her to a sofa and sat hugging her to my breast and covering her face with kisses. It had suddenly come upon me that I loved her – that I had always loved her. But hitherto it had been as a charming darling playmate and companion, and now it was as a woman.

If this knowledge between us were a result of the theft of the 'Blue Water,' I was glad it had been stolen.

'Darling! Darling! Darling!' I whispered as I kissed her. 'Do you love me, darling Isobel?' I asked, and, for reply, she smiled starrily through her tears, put her arms round me, and pressed her lips to mine.

I thought my heart was stopping.

'*Love* you, dearest?' she asked. 'You are just my life. I have loved everything you have said or done, since I was a baby!'

'Don't cry,' I said, ashamed of my inarticulate inadequacy.

'I'm crying for joy,' she sobbed. 'Now you have told *me* you didn't do it, I know you didn't.'

'What made you think I did?' I asked.

'I *didn't* think so,' she replied with feminine logic; 'only it was you who were against the table, John; it was you whom Michael caught; and I saw you go down in the night – to put it back, as I thought.'

'Saw me?' I asked, in surprise.

'Yes, dear. I was awake and saw a light go by my door. It shone underneath it. And I came out and looked over the banisters.'

'I went to see if the wretched thing had come back,' I said. 'And it was rather I who caught Michael than Michael who caught me, when you turned the lights out. We were both expecting to catch Gussie, and caught each other.'

'And, oh, I have been so wretchedly unhappy,' she went on, 'thinking appearances were so against you, and yet knowing I was allowing Gussie to remain under suspicion when I knew it wasn't he . . . But when it seemed the thing was actually stolen, I couldn't keep quiet any longer. It was bad enough when it was only a practical joke, as we thought . . . And then I seemed to be helping to bring suspicion towards you when I cleared Gussie . . .'

She wiped away a tear.

'I don't care now,' she smiled. 'Nothing on earth matters. So long as you love me – I don't see how I can have a care in the world . . . You're *sure*, darling?'

I endeavoured to express myself without the use of halting and unfluent speech.

'When did you first love me?' asked my sweet and beautiful darling, when I released her.

'I don't know,' I said. 'I have always loved you, and now I worship you, and I always shall,' and again she gave me a long embrace that seemed to stop the beating of my heart and lift me up and up to an incredible heaven of ecstasy and joy almost unbearable.

The sound of footsteps and a hand on the door brought us back to earth. We sprang to our feet, and when David entered, Isobel was putting away her music, and I was consulting a small pocket-book with terrific abstraction from my surroundings.

'Excuse me, sir,' said David, halting before me. 'Might I speak to you, sir?'

'You're doing it, David,' said I.

'In private, sir, a moment,' he explained.

I went to the door with him, and having closed it, he produced a note and gave it to me.

'Mr. Digby, sir. He very specially instructed me to give you this in private at ten o'clock this evening, sir, thank you, sir.'

'Thank you, David,' said I, and went along to the smoking-room, opening the letter as I went.

Although I felt that I ought to be filled with apprehension, anxiety, and trouble, my heart sang for glee, and I could have danced down the long corridor, to the surprise and disapproval of the various stiff and stately Brandons, male and female, who looked down from its walls.

'This is most selfish and wrong,' said I, and repressed a desire to sing, whistle, and whoop, and literally jump for joy.

'Isobel! Isobel! Isobel!' sang my heart. 'Isobel loves me and I love Isobel . . .'

The smoking-room was empty, and I could hear the click of balls from the neighbouring billiard-room, showing why. Gussie was evidently at his favourite, somewhat aimless, evening employment.

I turned up the lights, poked up the fire, pulled up the biggest and deepest chair, and filled my pipe and lit it.

Had I come straight here from the dining-roon, and here received Digby's letter, I should have snatched it, and opened it with sinking heart and trembling fingers.

Now, nothing seemed of much importance, compared with the great fact of which my heart was chanting its pæan of praise and thanks to God.

Love is very selfish I fear – but then it is the very selves of two people becoming one self . . .

And then I read poor Digby's letter. It was as follows:–

'My dear John,

I now take up my pen to write you these few lines, hoping they find you as they won't find me. After terrific thought and mental wrestling, which cost me a trouser-button, I have come to the conclusion that I can no longer deceive you all and let the innocent suffer for my guilty sin or sinny guilt.

I go to find my noble-hearted twin, to kneel at his feet and say, "Brother, I have sinned in thy sight" (but it was in the dark really) "and am no more worthy to be called anything but what I am."

No one knows the shame I feel, not even me; and, by the time you get this, I shall be well on my way to – where I am going.

Will you please tell Aunt that Michael's noble and beautiful action has wrung my heart, and I wish he had wrung my neck. I cannot let him take the blame for me, like this. I shall write to her from Town.

When you find yourself in the witness-dock or prisoner's-box tell the Beak that you have always known me to be weak but not vicious, and that my downfall has been due to smoking cigarettes and going in for newspaper competitions. Also that you are sure that, if given time, I shall redeem myself by hard work, earn thirty shillings a week at least, and return the thirty thousand pounds out of my savings.

Write and let me know how things go on, as soon as I send you an address – which you will, of course, keep to yourself. Give my love to Isobel.

Play up and don't forget you've GOT *to stand by me and make people realise the truth that I actually am the thief – or suspicion still rests on Claudia (since Isobel and Gussie are out of it), if we three do not provide the criminal amongst us. And, of course, I can't let Beau suffer for me.*

Directly you hear from him, let him know by wire that I have confessed and bolted, and that he can return to Brandon Abbas and admit that he was shielding the real culprit whom he knew to be ME *or* YOU *or* CLAUDIA*!. Give my love to Isobel.*

Ever thine,

Digby.'

For a moment this drove even Isobel from my mind.

It had never occured to me for one moment that Digby had actually fled, as Michael had done. Could it be possible that he was speaking the truth in the letter?

Could he have stolen the 'Blue Water' as he said, and had Michael's flight and shouldering of the blame forced his hand and compelled him, in very shame, to confess? . . .

Or did he, in his heart of hearts, think that Michael was really guilty and had fled rather than allow three innocent people to lie under suspicion with himself? Had Digby, thinking this, fled to divert suspicion from the guilty Michael, to confuse the issue and divide the pursuit, thus giving him a better chance to get clear away? . . .

Probably neither. It was much more likely that his idea was to help to shield the person whom Michael thought he was shielding, and at the same time to share with Michael the suspicion thus diverted from the guilty person.

The moment it was known that Michael had fled, the world and his wife would say, 'The vile young thief!'

Directly Digby followed him they would say, 'Which of them is the thief?' and no eye would be turned enquiringly upon those who, in their conscious innocence, had remained at home.

And whom *did* Michael and Digby suspect, if they were both innocent? Obviously either Claudia or me.

And if they could no more suspect me than I could suspect them . . . ?

It dawned on me, or rather it was stabbed into my heart suddenly, as with a knife, that it was quite as much *my* affair to help in preventing suspicion, just or unjust, from falling upon Claudia; and that if they could face obloquy, poverty, hardship, and general wrecking of their lives for Claudia and for me and for each other – why, so could I for them, and that it was my duty to go too.

Moreover, when detectives and criminal-experts got to work on the case, they would be quite capable of saying that there was nothing to prevent Isobel and Augustus from being in collusion to prove each other innocent, and would suspect one or both of them the more.

To us, who knew her, it was completely proven that Augustus was innocent, because she said so.

To a detective, it would more probably be a clue to the guilty person – the girl who produced this piece of 'evidence' which incidentally proclaimed her own innocence.

Moreover, the wretched Augustus had most undoubtedly been *surprised* when Isobel said he must be innocent as she had been holding on to him all the time the light was out. If this came out, it would certainly fix the suspicion on Isobel, and if it did not, there was a strong probability that her declaration concerning Augustus would, as I have said, suggest collusion between them.

The more reason then for me to strengthen the obvious solution – that the thief was one of the Gestes.

If three people fled confessing their guilt, that was where the collusion would be – among the three rascally brothers who had plotted to rob their relative and share the spoil.

That the oldest had weakened and fled first, was to his credit, or not, according to whether you more admired courage or confession; but obviously and incontestably, the blame must lie upon these three, and not among those who remained at home and faced the music.

'*But*,' said the voices of prudence, cowardice, and common sense, as well as the voice of love, '*two are enough to take the blame, surely? Let people say it was one of those two, or perhaps the two in partnership*.'

'*And why*,' replied the voices of self-respect and pride, '*should those two share the blame (or the honour)? Why should they shield Isobel and* YOU, *as well as Claudia, from suspicion?' and to the latter voice I listened.*

I could not possibly sit at home and enjoy life while the Captain and the Lieutenant were in trouble, disgrace, and danger – my whole life-training, as well as instincts, forbade.

I think that within two minutes of reading Digby's letter, the question of my going was quite definitely answered, and only the minor questions of where I should go, and whether I should say anything to Isobel, remained to be settled. And one of these two problems was subconsciously solved, though I had not intentionally considered it and come to a decision.

From the moment that I had learnt of Michael's flight, I had had somewhere, just below the level of consciousness, a vague remembrance of the existence of a romantic-sounding, adventurous corps of soldiers of fortune, called the French Foreign Legion.

When thinking of Michael, and seeing mental pictures of him in the setting of Brandon Abbas, our 'Prep.' school, Eton and Oxford, one of the clearest of these dissolving views had been of a group of us in the Bower, at the feet of a smart and debonair young French officer, who had thrilled us with dramatic tales of Algeria, Morocco, and the Sahara; tales of Spahis, Turcos, Zouaves, Chasseurs d'Afrique, and the French Foreign Legion of Mercenaries; tales of hot life and brave death, of battle and of bivouac. At the end, Michael had said:

'I shall join the French Foreign Legion when I leave Eton . . . Get a commission and go into his regiment,' and Digby and I had applauded the plan.

Had Michael remembered this, and was he, even now, on his way to this life of adventure and glory, determined to win his way to soldierly renown under a *nom de guerre*? . . . It would be so like Michael.

And Digby? Had he had the same idea and followed him? It would be so like Digby.

And I? Should I follow my brothers' lead, asking nothing better than to do as they did, and win their approval? . . . It would be so like me.

Three romantic young asses! I can smile at them now. *Asses* without doubt; wild asses of the wildest; but still, with the imagination and the soul to be romantic asses, thank God!

10

As compensation for a smaller share of the gifts of courage, cleverness, and general distinction possessed by my brilliant brothers, I have been vouchsafed a larger measure of prudence and caution – though some may think that still does not amount to much.

I have met few men to equal Michael and Digby in beauty, physical strenght, courage, and intelligence; but I was, in spite of being an equally incurably romantic, 'longer-headed' than they, and even more muscular and powerful. This is tremendous praise to award myself, but facts are facts.

Having decided to join them in disgrace and blame, as well as to join them in the flesh if I could – going to the Legion to look for them in the first place – I settled down to consider details, ways, and means.

I can think better in the dark, so I knocked out my pipe, burnt Digby's letter, and went up to bed.

The first fact to face, and it loomed largest and most discouraging of all, was separation from Isobel in the very moment of finding her. Paradoxically, however, the very exaltation and excitement of this wonderful thing that had happened, this finding of her, carried me along and gave me the power to leave her.

I was *tête-montée*, beside myself, and above myself, abnormal.

I would show my love that I, too, could do a fine thing, and could make a personal sacrifice to ward off from women, one of whom was mine, 'the slings and arrows of outrageous fortune,' outrageous suspicion and annoyance.

To leave her would be misery unspeakable – but what a beautiful misery and poignantly delightful sorrow for the heart of romantic youth to hug to itself!

Also I knew that it was quite useless for such children as ourselves – she nineteen and I twenty – at present penniless and dependent, to think of formal engagements and early marriages. Love was all and love was enough, until I should return, bronzed and decorated, successful and established, a distinguished Soldier of Fortune, to claim her hand.

I would then take my bride to be the admired and beloved Pride of the Regiment, a soldier's star and stay and queen . . . (Twenty is a great age at which to be – with love in your heart and life before you . . .)

Should I tell her what I was going to do and have one last beautifully-terrible hour, with her in my arms, or should I write her a letter to be given to her after I had gone?

I am glad to say that I had the grace to look at it from her point of view, and to decide according to what I thought would be better for her.

In the letter I could give the impression that this was only a short separation, and that I was writing to say '*Au revoir*' rather than 'Good-bye.'

If I told her in an interview, my obvious wretchedness and woebegone countenance would contradict my words. I knew I should kiss and embrace her as if for the last time on earth, and look as though I were going to the scaffold rather than into hiding for a while, until the missing jewel turned up, or the thief was caught.

Yes – I had better write, being careful to avoid the suggestion that this was any more a 'separation' than my going back to Oxford for the next term would have been.

That question was settled.

The next thing to consider was the problem of procedure.

I should want sufficient money and kit to enable me to get to France and subsist for a few days, probably in Paris.

Ten pounds or so, a change of underclothing, and a toothbrush, would be the sort of thing. With a very small suit-case one would be quite comfortable.

My watch, links, studs, cigarette-case, and a good gold pencil which I possessed would provide ample funds. I had more than sufficient ready money for my fare to London, and could there raise enough to carry me on to Paris and keep me for a few days.

I would breakfast with the others, and quietly walk off to catch the ten-forty to Exeter, and take the eleven-forty-five thence to London, arriving about three o'clock. I would cross to France the next day, getting there in the evening; sleep at an hotel, and, as soon as possible, become a soldier of France.

Whatever my brothers had done, I should at least have followed their example worthily, and have given a realistic and convincing imitation of the conduct of a frightened and desperate thief, fleeing from the consequences of his crime and the shame of facing his relatives and former friends.

And if Michael and Digby were actually there when I arrived – why, I should regret nothing but the separation from Isobel – a separation, albeit, during which I would qualify, in age, position, and income, for the honour of becoming her husband.

I think I had arrived at the position of Commander-in-Chief in Algeria and Grand Commander of the Legion of Honour when I fell asleep . . .

I awoke in the morning in a very different frame of mind from that of the morning before. My heart was full of pride that Isobel loved me and was mine. My brain was full of schemes and plans, and my whole being tingled gloriously with a sense of high adventure.

'If youth but knew . . .'

When David brought my hot water, with his inevitable, 'Half-past seven, sir, and a fine morning' (when the rain stops, or the fog clears, as the case might be), I told him I should give him a letter, after breakfast, which he was to give privately to Miss Rivers at the first convenient opportunity after eleven o'clock.

I thought it better to give it to David than to a maid. He had obeyed instructions in the case of Michael's letter to Digby, and Digby's letter to me, and a maid would be more likely to chatter in the servants' hall.

I did not think that there was the slightest suspicion in that quarter, and, as Aunt Patricia had said, there was no reason why there should be any, provided the mystery of the 'Blue Water' was solved without the aid of the police.

I could have posted my letter to her of course, but that would have involved delay, and an anxious night for her. It would also mean a post-mark, and I thought it would be better for her to be able to say, with perfect truth, that she had not the vaguest idea as to where I had gone.

When I had dressed, I put my brushes and shaving-tackle into an attaché-case, and crammed in a shirt, collars, and socks, and then went down to the smoking-room, and, after some unsatisfactory efforts, wrote to Isobel:

'My darling beautiful Sweetheart,

I had a letter from Digby last night. He has bolted because he thinks that Michael has shouldered the blame and disgrace of this theft in order to protect the innocent and shield the guilty person (who must appear to him to be Claudia, Digby, or myself, as it is not you nor Gussie). Digby told me that it was not he, and he refuses to believe that it is Michael. I don't think he suspects me either.

Now, you'll be the first to agree that I can't sit at home and let them do this, believing them to be innocent. And if either of them were guilty, I'd want, all the more, to do anything I could to help. Were it not for leaving you, for a little while, just when I have found you, I should be rather enjoying it, I am afraid.

Anyhow, I should have had to leave you in a little while, when I went up to Oxford again, and that would have been an eight weeks' separation. As it is, we are only going to be parted until this silly wretched business is cleared up. I expect the thief will return the thing anonymously as soon as he or she finds that we three are all pretending we did it, and that we will not resume our ordinary lives until restitution is made.

You know that I didn't do it, and I know that you didn't, and that's all that really matters; but you wouldn't have me hold back when the Captain and Lieutenant of the Band are out to divert suspicion from the innocent and to shame the guilty into returning Aunt's property!

I'll send you an address later on, so that you can tell me what happens – but, just at first, I want you to have no idea where I am, and to say so.

You'd despise me, really, in your heart, if I stayed at home, though I know you'll miss me and me back. I shall come, of course, the moment you let me know that the affair is cleared up. Meanwhile, no ass of a detective will be suspecting you or Claudia, or poor innocent Gussie, since obviously one of the absconding three (or all of them) must be the thief. Aunt will go to the police about it of course, and they will soon be on our track, and trouble no one at Brandon Abbas.

And now, darling Isobel, darling Faithful Hound, I am not going to try to tell you how much I love you – I am going to do it before you get this. But everything is different since last night. The world is a perfectly glorious place, and life is a perfectly glorious thing. Nothing matters, because Isobel loves me and I love Isobel – for ever and ever. I want to sing all the time, and to tell everybody.

Isn't love absolutely WONDERFUL?

Always and always,
Your devoted, adoring, grateful
Sweetheart.'

This honest, if boyish, effusion I gave to David, and repeated my instructions.

He contrived to keep his face correctly expressionless, though he must have wondered how many more of us were going to give him epistles to be privately delivered after their departure to other members of the household.

Leaving the smoking-room, I met Burdon in the corridor.

'Can you tell me where Mr. Michael is, sir?' he asked. 'Her ladyship wishes to see him.'

'No, I can't, Burdon,' I replied, 'for the excellent reason that I don't know.'

'Mr. Digby's bed have not been slep' in either, sir,' he went on. 'I did not know the gentlemen were going away . . . Nothing packed nor nothing.'

'They didn't tell me they were going, Burdon,' I said, putting on an owlish look of wonder and speculation. 'They're off on some jaunt or other, I suppose . . . I hope they ask me to join them.'

'Racing, p'r'aps, sir?' suggested Burdon sadly.

'Shocking,' said I, and left him, looking waggish to the best of my ability . . .

There were only the four of us at breakfast again.

Isobel's face lit up radiantly as our glances met, and we telegraphed our love to each other.

'Anyone heard how the Chaplain is?' asked Claudia.

'I went to see him last night,' replied Isobel, 'but the nurse said he was asleep.'

'Nurse?' asked Augustus.

'Yes,' said Isobel. 'Dr. Warrender thought he ought to have a night-nurse, and Aunt Patricia telegraphed for one. He's going to get up to-day though, the nurse told me.'

'Where's Digby?' asked Augustus.

'Why?' I said elliptically.

'Burdon asked me if I'd seen him, and said he wasn't in last night.'

'I know no more than you do where he is,' I honestly assured him.

'Funny – isn't it?' he sneered.

'Most humorous,' I agreed.

'Perhaps Aunt will think so,' countered Augustus unpleasantly . . . 'First Michael and then Digby, after what she said about not leaving the house!'

'Ought to have consulted you first, Gussie,' said Claudia.

'Looks as though they didn't want to consult the police, if you ask me,' he snarled.

'We didn't ask you, Gussie,' said Isobel, and so the miserable meal dragged through.

Towards the end of it, Burdon came in.

'Her ladyship wishes to see Mr. Digby,' he said to the circumambient air.

'Want a bit of doing, I should say,' remarked Augustus, with a snigger.

'He's not here, Burdon,' said I, looking under the table.

'No, sir,' replied Burdon gravely, and departed.

'You next, my lad,' Augustus stated, eyeing me severely. 'I wonder if the detectives have come.'

Burdon returned.

'Her ladyship would like to see you in her boudoir, after breakfast, sir,' said he to me.

'Told you so,' remarked Augustus, as the door closed behind the butler.

'Where do you think the others have gone?' asked Claudia, turning to me. 'They can't have *run away* surely? not both of them?'

'Doesn't look like it, does it?' put in Augustus.

'If they have gone away it's for an excellent reason,' said Isobel.

'Best of reasons,' agreed Augustus.

'Quite the best, Claudia,' said I, looking at her. '*If* they have "run away," as you said, it is to turn suspicion away from the house and everybody in it, of course.'

'Oh, of course,' agreed Augustus again.

'Just what they would do,' said Isobel quietly.

'It would be like Michael,' said Claudia in a low voice, and getting up, went quickly out of the room.

'And Digby,' added I, as she did so.

Augustus departed soon after, with a malicious 'Up you go' to me, and a jerk of his thumb in the direction of Aunt Patricia's room. Our recent roughness and suspicion evidently rankled in his gentle breast.

As soon as we were alone, I turned to Isobel, who sat beside me, put my arms round her and gave and received a long kiss.

'Come out to the Bower a minute, darling,' said I, and we scuttled off together.

There I crushed her to my breast and kissed her lips, her cheeks, and eyes, and hair, as though I could never have enough, and never stop.

'Will you love me for ever, darling?' I asked. 'Whatever may happen to us, or wherever we may be?'

She did not reply in words, but her answer was very satisfying.

'Aunt wants me,' then said I, and bolted back to the house. But I had no intention of seeing Aunt Patricia.

Mine should be the more convincing rôle of the uneasy, trembling criminal, who, suddenly sent for, finds he has not the courage to face the ordeal, and flees before the ominous sound of the summons.

I was very glad this had happened, as it would appear to have given me the cue for flight.

When first sent for, I was found peacefully eating my breakfast in fancied security. When again sent for, I should be missing – obviously terrified of the command and guiltily afraid to obey it.

Going to my room, I took my attaché-case from the wardrobe, pocketed a photograph of Isobel, and went quietly down the service staircase that debouched by the luggage-lift in a passage opening into the outer hall. In a minute I was across the shrubbery and into the drive at a bend which hid it from the house.

Twenty minutes' walking brought me to the station, where I booked to Exeter. That would not tell anybody very much, for though I was perfectly well known to everybody at our local station, I would be extremely unlikely that I should be traced from so busy a junction as Exeter, in the crowd that would be booking for the morning train to Waterloo.

As I waited on our platform, I was conscious of an almost unbearable longing to go back to Brandon Abbas and Isobel. How *could* I leave her like this, now, the very day after I had found her?

I felt a bigger lump in my throat than I had ever known since I was a child. It was utterly horrible.

But for the excitement and adventure of the business, I think I should have succumbed to the longing to return. But when two loving people part, one going on a journey, it is always the departing one who suffers the less.

It is inevitable that the distractions of travel, movement, change, shall drug the pain to which the other is equally exposed without the amelioration of mental and bodily occupation.

So, between my mind and the agony of separation from Isobel came the deadening and protecting cloak of action and of the competing thoughts of other matters – journey's end, the future, money, Paris, Algeria, the probabilities of finding Michael and Digby . . .

Anyhow, I conquered the yearning to go back to her, and when the local train loafed in I got into it, with a stiff upper lip and a bleeding heart, and set out on as eventful and strange a journey as ever a man took.

3

The Gay Romantics

'Curs'd from the cradle and awry they come
Masking their torment from a world at ease;
On eyes of dark entreaty, vague and dumb,
They bear the stigma of their souls' disease.'

I REMEMBER nothing of that horrible journey from Exeter to Waterloo. It passed as a bad dream passes, and I awoke from it in London.

As has happened to others in the history of that city, I found that, in such circumstances, London was a very large place, and myself a very small and lonely atom of human dust therein.

Walking out from Waterloo Station into the unpleasing purlieus thereof, I was tempted to go to the quiet and exclusive hotel that the Brandons had patronised for very many years, and where I was well known and should feel a sense of being at home among friends.

For this very reason I resisted the temptation, and was aided to do so by the question of finance. Whatever I did, I must leave myself sufficient money for my journey to Paris and subsistence there until I should become a soldier of France, to be lodged, boarded, clothed, and paid by Madame la République.

The first thing to do was to convert my disposable property into cash, a distasteful undertaking, but essential to further progress along the path I had elected to follow. If I had to do nothing more unpleasant than that, I told myself, as I walked along down a mean street toward Westminster Bridge, the said path would be no thorny one.

And, at that moment, my eye fell upon what I took to be the very place I wanted – a pawnbroker's shop, stuffed to bursting with a most heterogeneous collection of second-hand merchandise, ranging from clothing and jewellery by way of boxing-gloves, guns, knives, meerschaum pipes and cigar-holders, cameras, umbrellas and walking-sticks, field-glasses, portmanteaux, to concertinas, cornets, and musical instruments of every description.

I entered and found a young gentleman, of markedly Hebraic appearance, behind the counter. I expected to hear him say:

'Vat d'ye vant, Mither?' and waggle his hands, palms upwards, near his shoulders, as I remembered a song, last heard at Oxford, anent one Solomon Levi and his store at Chatham Street.

For some reason, best known to himself, he wore a bowler hat of proportions so generous that it rested upon the nape of his neck and his ears, depressing the latter well-developed organs, so that they drooped forward as droops the tired lily – though in no other way did they suggest that flower.

To compensate for the indoor wearing of this outdoor garment, he had discarded his coat, exposing shirt-sleeves that again did not suggest the lily. A very large watch-chain adorned a fancy waistcoat that was certainly worn by him at meal-times also, and his diamond tie-pin bore testimony to his financial solidity and to his taste.

I fear I looked at him for a few seconds longer than good manners could approve – but then he looked at me for precisely the same length of time, though with a difference. For I was looking with a wondering admiration, whereas he was regarding me with little of wonder and less of admiration.

It was perfectly clear that he did not regard me as a buyer, though by what instinct or experience he could tell, I know not.

'Surely,' thought I, 'even if I have not the appearance of one who comes to buy, I still do not look like a needy, seedy seller?'

But he knew! He knew; and his silence was eloquent.

As his bold brown eyes regarded me, his curved nostril curved a little more, and his large ripe lips, beneath the pendulous nose, ripened while I watched.

He said no word, and this fact somewhat disconcerted me, for I had hitherto regarded the Children of Israel as a decidedly chatty race.

I broke the heavy silence of the dark mysterious shop, and added strange sounds to the strange sights and stranger smells.

'I want to sell my watch and one or two things,' said I to this silent son of Abraham's seed.

He did not triumph in the manifest rightness of his judgment that I was a contemptible seller and not an admirable buyer. He did not do anything at all, in fact. He did not even speak.

No word nor sigh nor sound escaped him.

I produced my watch and laid it at his feet, or rather at his stomach. It was gold and good, and it had cost twenty-five pounds. (I allude to the watch.)

''Ow much?' said the child of the Children of Israel.

'Er – well – isn't that rather for you to say?' I replied. 'I know it cost twenty-five pounds and is an excellent . . .'

''Ow much?' interrupted the swarthy Child.

'How much will you give me?' I replied . . . 'Suppose we split the difference and you . . .'

''Ow much?' interrupted the Child again.

'Ten pounds?' I suggested, feeling that I was being reasonable and, indeed, generous. I did not wish my necessitous condition to weigh with him and lead him to decrease his just profits.

'Two quid,' said the Child promptly.

'Not a tenth of what it cost?' said I, on a note of remonstrance. 'Surely that is hardly a fair and . . .'

'Two quid,' interrupted the Child, whose manners seemed less rich than his attire.

I was tempted to take up the watch and depart, but I felt I could not go through all this again. Perhaps two pounds was the recognised selling price of all gold watches?

Producing my cigarette-case, gold pencil, and a tiny jeweller's box containing my dress studs, I laid them before this spoiler of Egyptians, and then detached my links from my shirt-cuffs.

''Ow much?' enquired the Child once more.

'Well,' replied I, 'the pencil is pretty heavy, and the studs are good. So are the links. They're all eighteen carat and the . . .'

''Ow much?' repeated the voice, which I was beginning to dislike.

'Ten pounds for the watch, pencil, and . . .'

'Four quid,' the Child replied, in the voice of Fate and Destiny and Doom, and seeking a toothpick in the pocket of his 'gent.'s fancy vest,' he guided it about its lawful occasions.

This would not do. I felt I must add at least five pounds to what I already had. I was a little vague as to the absolutely necessary minimum, but another five pounds seemed to me to be very desirable.

'Oh, come – make it seven,' said I, in the bright tone of encouragement and optimism.

The Child regarded the point of his toothpick. It appeared to interest him far more than I, or my poors affairs, could ever do.

'Six,' said I, with falsely cheerful hopefulness.

The toothpick returned to duty, and a brooding silence fell upon us.

'Five, then,' I suggested, with a falsely firm finality.

The Child yawned. For some reason I thought of onions, beer, and garlic, things very well in their way and their place, and quite pleasing to those who like them.

'Then I'm afraid I've wasted your valuable time,' said I, with deep wiliness, making as though to gather up my despised property.

The Child did not trouble to deny my statement. He removed his bowler hat and looked patiently into its interior, as good men do in church. The hair of the head of the Child was most copiously abundant, and wonderfully curly. I thought of oil-presses, anoited bulls of Bashan, and, with bewildered awe, of the strange preferences of Providence.

However, I would walk to the door and see whether, rather than let me go, he would offer five pounds for what had cost at least fifty.

As I did so, this representative of the Chosen People cocked an eye at my dispatch-case.

'Wotcher got there?' he growled.

Imitating his excellent economy of words, I opened the case without reply, and removing a silk shirt, vest, and socks, displayed three collars, a pair of silver-backed hair-brushes, a comb, a silver-handled shaving-brush, a razor, an ivory nailbrush, a tooth-brush, and a silver box containing soap.

'Five quid the lot and chance if you've pinched 'em,' said the Child.

'You'll give me five pounds for a gold watch, links, studs and pencil-case; a silver cigarette-case, hair-brushes, and shaving-brush; a razor, shirt, vest, socks, collars, and a leather dispatch-case?' I enquired politely.

'Yus,' said the Child succinctly.

Well, I could get shaved for a few pence, and in a couple of days I should probably be in uniform.

'I'll keep the tooth-brush and a collar,' I remarked, putting them in my pocket.

'Then chuck in the walkin' stick and gloves, or it's four-fifteen,' was the prompt reply.

I gazed upon the Child in pained astonishment.

'I gotter *live*, ain't I?' he replied, in a piteous voice, to my cruel look.

Forbearing to observe '*Je ne vois pas la nécessité*,' I laid my stick and gloves on the counter, realising that, in any case, I should shortly have no further need of them.

The Child produced a purse, handed me five pounds, and swept my late property into a big drawer.

'Thank you,' said I, departing. 'Good evening.'

But the Child apparently did not think it was a good evening, for he vouchsafed no reply.

One should not judge a race by single specimens, of course, but – racial antipathy is a curious thing . . .

Crossing Westminster Bridge, with about ten pounds in my pocket, misery in my heart, and nothing in my hand, I made my way along Whitehall to Trafalgar Square, sorely tempted by the sight and smell of food as I passed various places devoted to the provision of meals, but not of beds.

It had occured to me that it would be cheaper to dine, sleep, and breakfast at the same place, than to have dinner somewhere, and then go in search of a bedroom for the night and breakfast in the morning.

As I walked, I thought of the hotels of which I knew – the Ritz, the Savoy, the Carlton, Claridge's, the Grosvenor, the Langham, and certain more discreet and exclusive ones in the neighbourhood of the Albany (where Uncle Hector kept a *pied-à-terre* for his use when in England).

But both their cost and their risks were almost as much against them as were those of our own family hotel. Even if I could afford to go to such hotels as these, it was quite likely that the first person I should run against, in the one I selected, would be some friend or acquaintance.

I decided to approach one of those mines of information, or towers of strength and refuge, a London policeman.

'Take a bus to Bloomsbury, and you'll find what you want. Russell Square, Bedford Square, British Museum. All round that neighbourhood,' was the reply of the stalwart to whom I applied for advice, as to a cheap, quiet, and decent hotel.

I obeyed his words, and had an edible dinner, a clean and comfortable bed, and a satisfying breakfast, for a surprisingly small sum, in an hotel that looked on to the British Museum and seemed to be the favoured of the clergy – it being almost full of men of religion and their women-folk of even more religion.

The 'young lady' at the bureau of this chaste hostelry did something to enhance the diminished self-respect that my Israelite had left to me, by making no comment upon the fact that I was devoid of luggage, and by refraining from asking me to produce money in advance of hospitality. Perhaps she had a more discerning eye, or perhaps merely a softer heart, than had the child of Abraham, Isaac, and Jacob; or perhaps she was merely more of a fool.

Nevertheless I was glad to get away in the morning and to seek the shop of a hairdresser, after sleeping, for the first time in my life, without pyjamas, and bathing without a sponge. I was also glad to feel that the tips which I had given, with apologies for their modesty, to the waiter and chambermaid had seemed quite adequate in their sight, and to cover my known deficiencies both of evening wear and night-gear.

It was extraordinary how naked I felt without my links, and how dishevelled without having used a brush and comb.

Finding a desirable barber's in Oxford Street, I was shaven and shampooed and went on my way, if not rejoicing, at any rate in better case, and feeling more my own man.

2

My journey to Paris was uneventful and uncomfortable, confirming me in my opinion that economy in travelling is one of the dearest economies of all.

Personally, I would always rather travel first class and miss my meals, than travel third and enjoy three good ones, on a day's journey. Nor is this in the least due to paltry exclusiveness and despicable snobbishness. It is merely that I would rather spend the money on a comfortable seat, a pleasant compartment, and freedom from crowding, than on food with cramped circumstance. Let him who, in his wisdom, would rather spend his money on good food and have the discomfort, do so by all means.

De gustibus non disputandum, as the learned say, and likewise, *Chacun à son goût.*

Anyhow, the third-class journey was by no means to my *goût* at the time, though the day quickly came when it would have seemed the height of luxury.

From Charing Cross (where I turned my pounds into francs and felt much richer) to Dover I contrasted the beautiful county of Kent with my own Devon, in favour of the latter; and, at Dover, I went on board the cross-Channel steamer, deeply and appreciatively inhaling the glorious air, after that of the dusty, stuffy, crowded compartment in which I had travelled down.

Mentally I was in a curious condition, for while one half of myself ached unbearably for Isobel, the other half rejoiced wildly at the thought of adventure, travel, novelty, spacious life, mysterious Africa, the desert, fighting, and all that appeals to the heart of romantic youth.

At Calais, the sight of a French soldier, a sentry near the Custom House, gave me a real thrill.

Was I actually going to wear that uniform myself in a day or two? A *képi*, baggy red breeches, and a long overcoat, buttoned back from the legs? How much more attractive and romantic than the familiar British uniform that seemed to suggest Hyde Park and nurse-maids, rather than palms, oases, Moorish cities, and desert warfare.

So is the unknown always better than the known, and the thing we have not, better than that we have . . .

At the Gare du Nord I experienced, in an intensified form, that sense of loneliness and utter insignificance that had assailed me at Waterloo; and I went out into the bright uproar of gay Paris, feeling anything but bright, uproarious, or gay myself. I was once more faced with the problem of hotels, for I had not the least idea as to how one set about offering one's services to France as a mercenary soldier, and the first thing to do, therefore, was to find a roof and a bed to serve me while I set about the quest.

My knowledge of Paris hotels was confined to the Meurice, Crillon, the Bristol, and the Ambassadors, but I knew these to be expensive, and, moreover, places at which I might meet acquaintances. There was no great likelihood of my meeting anyone who knew me well; but there was a chance, and I wanted to behave precisely as a guilty fugitive would do.

If I were traced, and it were found that I had gone, in London and Paris, to places where I might meet friends, it would hardly look as though I were a genuine jewel-thief, anxious to cover his tracks as he fled the country.

On the other hand, I did not want to blunder into an obscure cheap hotel, without luggage, an obvious foreigner, and run the risk of a visit from a polite but inquisitive *agent de police*, as seemed to me quite possible, if I and my explanations struck the proprietor as peculiar . . .

A whimsical idea struck me. Why not go to the police themselves for advice on the subject of avoiding such trouble?

Sauntering along the noisy busy thoroughfare that passes the Gare du Nord, I looked out for a gendarme.

Presently I saw one standing on an island in the middle of the road, silent, inscrutable, immobile, heavily caped, oppressed by great responsibilities. Crossing to him, I raised my hat, and in my best and politest French (which is not bad, thanks to a French governess in our youth, and the Chaplain's wisdom and care), asked him if he could direct me to a good quiet hotel.

Moving his eyes, but not his head, nor any other portion of his majestic person, he examined me from top to toe and back again.

'Monsieur is English,' he pronounced.

I acknowledged the truth of his statement, wondering how he knew I was not German, Swiss, Danish, Swedish, Norwegian, nor Dutch.

'Hôtel Normandie, Rue de l'Échelle,' he announced without hesitation.

'And how do I get there, *Monsieur l'Officier*?' I asked.

'*Fiacre*,' was the prompt, terse reply, and the all-seeing official eye left me and sought among the traffic. A white-gloved hand was suddenly raised, and an open cab, driven by a many-caped gentleman, who did not look like a tee-totaller, approached.

'Normandie, Rue de l'Échelle,' said my gendarme to the *cocher*, and gave me a military salute, as I thanked him, raised my hat, and stepped into the carriage.

I enjoyed the drive through beautiful Paris in the mingled glow of late sunset and the myriad lights of the shops and streets; but my heart sank a little as the cab drew up before a fashionable-looking hotel that stood at a busy corner, close to the Rue de Rivoli and to the Rue de la Paix.

It looked as expensive as the best. However, Fate had sent me here, and here I would stay.

Trying to look as unconcerned as a luggageless traveller may, I entered the hall, received the bow of an imposing hall-porter, and marched straight ahead, past the grand staircase and the dining-room, to where I could see the bureau, and beyond it, the palm-decked *fumoir*.

At the bureau, a very pretty girl was talking to an American in American.

This was good luck. I could make a much more convincing show in English than in my pedantic and careful French.

Standing near, and trying to look like an eccentric foreigner who habitually went about without stick or gloves in order that he might keep his hands in his pockets, I waited for the American to go.

Meanwhile, it was quite impossible to avoid hearing what was said by the keen-faced, square-shouldered, lumpy-toed, baggy-trousered, large-hatted gentleman to the lady, what time she chewed a cud of sweet recollection and Mangle's Magnificent Masticating Gum or similar enduring comestible.

When at length he took his key and went, I turned to the girl.

'So you was raised in Baltimore!' said I rapturously. 'Fancy that being your home town now! Isn't it just the outest place? Peachiest gals and bulliest cakes in America! . . . Say, I reckon this gay Paree hasn't got anything on little old New York!' . . .

'My!' said the young lady. 'D'you know Baltimore? You don't say!' and she smiled sweetly upon me.

'*Know Baltimore!*' said I, and left it at that . . . 'Lots of Americans and English here, I suppose,' I went on, 'since the hotel folk are wise (and lucky) enough to have you in the bureau? And I suppose you speak French as well as any Parisian?'

'My, yes,' she smiled. 'Most as well as I speak good old U.S. . . . Why, yes – lots of home people and Britishers here . . . Most of our waiters can help 'em out too, when they're stuck for the French of "*Yes, I'll have a highball, Bo,*"' and she tinkled a pretty little laugh.

'Guess that's fine,' said I. 'I want to turn in here for a day or two. All upset at my place.' (Very true, indeed.) 'Just to sleep and breakfast. Got a vacant location?'

'Sure,' said my fair friend, and glanced at an indicator. '*Troisième* Eighteen francs. No – breakfast only – fourteen. Going up now?' And she unhooked a key and passed it to me with a brief '*Deux cent vingt deux*. The bell-hop will show you.'

'Not bringing any stuff in,' I said, and drew my entire fortune from my pocket, as one who would pay whatever was desired in advance, and the more the merrier.

'Shucks,' said my friendly damsel, and I gathered that I was deemed trustworthy.

In the big book that she pushed to me I wrote myself down as Smith, but clung to the 'John,' that there might be something remnant and stable in a whirling and dissolving universe.

'Guess I'll hike up and take possession now,' said I thereafter, and with my best smile and bow I turned to the lift before she could send to the hall-porter to dispatch a supposititious suit-case to the spot.

The lift-boy piloted me to number two hundred and twenty-two, where, safe inside, I bolted the door and drew breath.

'*J'y suis, j'y reste*,' said I, in tribute to my very French surroundings . . . 'and the less they see of me below, the less they'll notice my lack of luggage and evening kit.'

It occured to me that it might be worth the money to buy a pair of pyjamas and have them sent to Monsieur Smith, No. 222 Hôtel Normandie. If I laid them out on the flat square pillow that crowned the lace-covered bed, the chamber-maid would not be so likely to comment on the paucity of my possessions, particularly if I locked the wardrobe and pocketed the key as though to safegaurd a valuable dressing-case.

If I also avoided the dining-room, where, in my lounge-suit, I should be extremely conspicuous among the fashionable evening throng, I might well hope to dwell in peaceful obscurity without rousing unwelcome interest and attention, in spite of the inadequacy of my equipment.

I decided to sally forth, buy some pyjamas, order them to be sent in at once, and then fortify myself with a two-franc dinner and a glass of *vin ordinaire* – probably *très ordinaire* – in some restaurant.

After an uncomfortable wash in the *lavabo*, I strolled nonchalantly forth, made my purchases, and enjoyed a good and satisfying meal in a cheerful place situated in a somewhat ignobler part of the Rue de Rivoli, at a little distance from the fashionable centre of Paris.

Returning to my over-furnished unhomely room, I spread out the gay pyjamas which awaited me, and wondered when the chamber-maid would come to turn down the bed. And then I realised that I need have felt no anxiety, for I had only to bolt the door and shout something when she came, and she would depart in ignorance of my complete lack of luggage and possessions.

However, I should not be able to keep her out in the morning, when I went in search of breakfast and the recruiting-office, and then the pyjamas and the locked wardrobe would play their part.

Even as I stood revolving these important trifles in my youthful breast, the door opened and in burst a hard-featured middle-aged woman. Anything less like the French chamber-maid of fiction and the drama could not well be imagined; for she was fair-haired, grey-eyed, unprepossessing, and arrayed in a shapeless black frock, plain apron, and ugly cap.

With a curt apology she flicked down a corner of the bedclothes, slapped the pyjamas down (in what is presumably the only place whence a self-respecting hotel guest can take them up), glanced at the unused washstand, and scurried from the room.

As I heard her unlock the door of the next apartment, almost before she had closed mine, I realised that she was far too busy to concern herself with my deficiencies, and ceased to worry myself on the subject.

Feeling that sleep was yet far from me, and that if I sat long in that unfriendly room I should go mad, I descended to the *fumoir*, sought a big chair in a retired nook, and, from behind a deplorable copy of *La Vie Parisienne*, watched the frequenters of this apparently popular lounge.

Here I thought long thoughts of Isobel, my brothers, and Brandon Abbas; and occasionally wondered what would happen on the morrow.

Nothing at all would happen until I had discovered the procedure for enlisting in the Foreign Legion, and the discovery of that procedure must be to-morrow's business.

Were I a romancer as well as a romantic, now would be the moment for me to announce the dramatic entry of the French officer who had fired our young imaginations, years before, and sown the seeds now bearing fruit.

As I sat there in the lounge of the Paris hotel, he would enter and call for coffee and a cognac. I should go up to him and say, '*Monsieur le Capitaine* does not remember me, perhaps?' He would rise, take my hand, and say, '*Mon Dieu!* The young Englishman of Brandon Abbas!' I should tell him of my ambition to be a soldier of France, to tread in his footsteps, to rise to rank and fame in the service of his great country, and he would say, 'Come with me – and all will be well . . .'

Unfortunately he did not enter, and presently, finding myself the last occupant of the lounge and inclined to yawn, I crept unwillingly to bed. I fell asleep, trying to remember his name.

3

The next day was Sunday, and I spent it miserably between the lounge and my bedroom.

On Monday morning, after a spongeless bath and an unsatisfying *petit déjeuner*, I sallied forth and put myself in the hands of an excellent barber, and, while enjoying his deft ministrations, had a bright idea. I would pump this chatty person.

'You don't know Algeria, I suppose?' I asked the man.

'But no, Monsieur,' he replied. 'Is Monsieur going there?'

'I hope to,' I said. 'A magnificent colony of your great country, that.'

Ah, it was, indeed. Monsieur might well say so. A wonderful achievement and the world's model colony. Growing too, always growing . . . This excellent *pénétration pacifique* to the South and towards Morocco . . .

'They do the pacific penetration by means of the bayonets of the Foreign Legion mostly, don't they?' I asked.

The Frenchman smiled and shrugged.

'A set of German rascals,' he said. 'But they have their uses . . .'

'How do you get them?' I asked.

Oh, they just enlisted. Made their *engagements volontaires* like anybody else, at the head recruiting-office of the French army in the Rue St. Dominique. Simply enlisted there and were packed off to Africa . . .

'But I thought service was wholly compulsory in this country?' said I. 'How then do you have recruiting-offices for a conscript army?'

The worthy soul explained at length, and so far as I could follow his swift idiomatic talk, that any Frenchman could, if he liked, volunteer for service before the time came when he *must* serve, whether he liked it or not. Sometimes, for business reasons, it was very convenient to get it over and done with, instead of having it to do later, when one was established. Hence the recruiting-office for the French army. But no Frenchman could volunteer for the Legion until he had done his compulsory service . . .

I let him talk on, keeping the words *Rue St. Dominique* clearly in my mind the while. I had got what I wanted, and the sooner I found this recruiting-office the better, for funds would soon be running low.

On leaving the shop I hailed a *fiacre*, said, 'Rue St. Dominique,' and jumped in, excusing my extravagance by my absolute ignorance of the route, and the need for haste.

Again I enjoyed the drive, feeling excited and buoyant, and filled with the sense of adventure. After a time, I found we were in what appeared to be the military quarter of Paris, and I saw the *École Militaire* and some cavalry-barracks. The streets were thronged with men in uniform, and my heart beat higher and higher as the cab turned from the Esplanade des Invalides into the Rue St. Dominique.

As the *cocher* looked round enquiringly at me, I thought it would be as well to pay him off here at the corner.

Perhaps it might not be good form to drive up, in style, to a recruiting-office, and in any case, there was no need to let the man know where I was going . . .

I found the Rue St. Dominique to be a wholly uninspiring thoroughfare, narrow, gloomy, and dingy in the extreme.

Walking along it and glancing from side to side, I soon found the building of which I was in search.

Over the door of a dirty little house was a blue-lettered notice testifying that the place was the BUREAU DE RECRUTEMENT. Below the label was the bald, laconic observation, ENGAGEMENTS VOLONTAIRES.

Well, here then was my bureau of recruitment and here would I make my 'voluntary engagement,' and if the Path of Glory led but to the grave, its beginning was quite in keeping with its end, for a more sepulchral-looking abode of gloom than this ugly little government-office I have never seen.

Crossing the road, I pushed open a rusty iron gate, undeterred by its agonised or warning shriek, crossed the neglected cemetery garden of this gay place, thrust back a swing door, and entered a long dark passage.

I could see no notice recommending all to abandon hope who entered here, but my drooping spirits were unraised by a strangling odour of carbolic, coal-gas, and damp.

On the wall was a big placard which, in the sacred names of Liberty, Equality, and Fraternity, offered to accept for five years the services of any applicant for admission to *La Legion Étrangère* (provided he was between the ages of eighteen and forty), and to give him a wage of a halfpenny a day.

There seemed to me to be little of Liberty about this proposal, less of Equality, and least of Fraternity.

On the other hand, it was an *engagement volontaire*, and anyone who didn't like the offer could leave it. No one was compelled to accept it, and there was no deception – on the placard at any rate.

I read the notice through again, half hoping that while I did so, someone would come and ask my business, some sound break the heavy smelly silence of Glory's cradle.

But none did, and 'with well-feigned hopefulness I pushed forth into the gloom.'

Venturing on, I came to a kind of booking-office ticket-window, above which were repeated the words *Engagements Volontaires*.

I looked in, and in a severe office or orderly-room, beheld an austere person in uniform, seated at a table and writing busily. The two gold stripes above his cuff inclined me to suppose that he was a non-commissioned officer, though of what rank and eminence I knew not.

He ignored me and all other insects.

How to attract his attention?

I coughed gently and apologetically. I coughed appealingly. I coughed upbraidingly, sorrowfully, suggestively, authoritatively, meekly, imperiously, agreeably, hopefully, hopelessly, despairingly, and quite vainly. Evidently I should not cough my way to glory.

'*Monsieur le Capitaine*,' I murmured ingratiatingly.

The man looked up. I liked him better when looking down.

'Monsieur would appear to have a throat-trouble,' he observed.

'And Monsieur an ear-trouble,' I replied, in my young ignorance and folly.

'What is Monsieur's business?' he enquired sharply.

'I wish to join the *Légion Étrangère*,' I said.

The man smiled, a little unpleasantly, I thought.

'*Eh, bien*,' he remarked, 'doubtless Monsieur will have much innocent amusement at the expense of the Sergeant-Major there too,' and I was quite sure that his smile was unpleasant this time.

'Is Monsieur only a Sergeant-Major then?' I enquired innocently.

'I am a Sergeant-Major,' was the reply, 'and let me tell Monsieur it is the most important rank in the French army.'

'No?' said I, and lived to learn that this piece of information was very little short of the simple truth.

'Wait by that door, please,' requested the Sergeant-Major, indicating one marked *Commandant de Recrutement*, and I felt that he had also said, 'Wait, just wait, my friend, until you have enlisted.'

I waited.

I should think I waited an hour.

Just as I was contemplating another visit to the buttery-hatch or ticket-office window, the door opened and my friend, or enemy, appeared.

'Be pleased to enter, Monsieur,' said he suavely, and I, for some reason, or for no reason, bethought me of a poem of childhood's happy days, entitled, 'The Spider and the Fly,' as I entered a large, bare orderly-room.

But it was no spider that I encountered within, but a courtly and charming gentleman of the finest French type. I know nothing of his history, but I am very sure that he was of those who are 'born,' as the French say, and that if, in the Terror, his great-grandfather did not perish on the guillotine, it was not because he wasn't an aristocrat.

He was a white-haired, white-moustached, handsome man, dressed in a close-fitting black tunic and baggy red over-alls with a broad black stripe. His cuffs were adorned with bands of gold and of silver braid, and his sleeves with the five *galons* of a Colonel.

'A recruit for the Legion, *mon Commandant*,' said the Sergeant-Major, and stood stiffly at attention.

The Colonel looked up from the desk at which he was writing, as, entering, I bared my head and bowed; he rose and extended his hand, with a friendly and charming smile.

Not thus, thought I, do British colonels welcome recruits to the ranks of their regiments.

'And you, too, wish to enlist in our Foreign Legion, do you?' he said as we shook hands. 'Has England started an export trade in the best of her young men? I don't see many Englishmen here from year's end to year's end, but you, *mon enfant*, are the third this week!'

My heart gave a bound of hopeful joy . . .

'Anything like me, sir?' I asked.

'*Au bout des ongles*,' was the reply. 'Were they your brothers by any chance? . . . But I will ask no indiscreet questions.'

I felt happier than I had done since I had kissed Isobel.

'Yes, *mon Commandant*,' I replied. 'I wish to become a soldier of France if you will have me.'

'And do you understand what you are doing, Monsieur?' asked the Colonel.

'I have read the placard outside,' said I.

'It is not quite all set forth there,' he smiled. 'The life is a very hard one. I would urge no one to adopt it, unless he were a born soldier and actually desirous of a life of discipline, adventure, and genuine hardship.'

No, this certainly was not a case of the spider and the fly – or it was an entirely new one, wherein the spider discouraged flies from entering the web.

'I wish to join, sir,' I said. 'I have heard something of the life in the Sahara from an officer of Spahis, whom I once knew.'

The Colonel smiled again.

'Ah, *mon enfant*,' said he, 'but you won't be an officer of Spahis, you see . . . Nor an officer of the Legion either, except after some very long and lean years in the ranks and as a non-commissioned officer.'

'One realises that one must begin at the bottom, *mon Commandant*,' I replied.

'Well – listen then,' said the Colonel, and he recited what he evidently knew by heart from frequent repetition.

'The *engagement volontaire* for *La Légion Étrangère* is for five years, in Algiers, or any other French colony, and the pay is a *sou* a day. A *légionnaire* can re-enlist at the end of the five years, and again at the end of ten years. At the end of fifteen years he is eligible for a pension varying according to his rank. A foreigner, on completion of five years' service, can claim to be naturalised as a French subject . . . You understand all that, *mon enfant*?'

'Yes, I thank you, *mon Commandant*,' I replied.

'Mind,' continued the Colonel, 'I say nothing of what is understood by the term "service" in the Legion. It is not all pure soldiering at times.

'Nor do I say anything as to the number of men who survive to claim the pension . . .'

'I am not thinking of the pension, *mon Commandant*,' I replied; 'nor of the alleged "pay," so much as of a soldier's life, fighting, adventure, experience . . .'

'Ah, there is plenty of that,' said the Colonel. 'Plenty of that. It is a real military school and offers the good soldier great and frequent chances of distinction, glory, decoration, and promotion. Some of our most famous generals have been in the Legion, and several of the highest and most distinguished officers of the Legion began their career in its ranks . . . Also, if you can show that you have been an offier in the army of your own country, you can begin as a probationary-corporal, and avoid the ranks altogether.'

'Please accept me as a recruit, *mon Commandant*,' said I.

'Ah, we'll see first what the doctor has to say about you – though there is little doubt about *that*, I should think,' smiled the Colonel, and pulled a form towards him.

'What is your name?'

'John Smith,' said I.

'Age?'

'Twenty-one years' (to be on the safe side).

'Nationality English?'

'Yes, *mon Commandant*.'

'Very well. If you pass the doctor I shall see you again. *Au 'voir, Monsieur*,' and with a curt nod to the Sergeant Major, the Colonel resumed his writing.

The Sergeant-Major opened the door with a still suave 'This way, if you please, Monsieur,' and led me across the passage into a room already tenanted by half a dozen civilians, whom I rightly supposed to be fellow-recruits for the Foreign Legion.

I got a fleeting impression of seedy, poorer-class people, two being brush-haired, fair, fattish, and undoubtedly German, before the Sergeant-Major, opening another door in this waiting-room, motioned me to enter a small closet, from which another door led elsewhere.

'Remove *all* clothing, please,' said the Sergeant-Major, and shut me in.

This was unpleasant but presumably unavoidable, and I obeyed. Before I had begun to shiver, the second door opened and I was invited to submit myself to the close and searching investigations of an undergown but over-nourished gentleman, from beneath whose white surgical smock appeared the baggy red trousers of the French army.

This official, presumably an army-surgeon, was easily able to establish the belief in my mind that *his* ancestors had not perished on the guillotine. (Certainly not during the Terror, anyhow). More probably they danced round it, or possibly operated it.

When he had quite finished with my vile body, he bade me replace it in the closet, clothe it, and remove it with all speed. This, nothing loth, I did, and was re-conducted by the Sergeant-Major to the Colonel's office.

'Well, *mon enfant*,' smiled the old officer, 'you are accepted.'

'And can I enlist at once, sir?' I enquired eagerly.

'Not until you have slept on it,' was the reply. 'Come here again to-morrow morning, if you are still of the same mind, and I will enrol you. But think well – think well. And remember that, until you sign your name on the form which I shall give you to-morrow, you are absolutely free, and have committed yourself in no way whatsoever. Think well – think well . . .'

And thanking him gratefully, I went from the room, hoping that all French officers were of this stamp, as kindly and as truly gentlemanly. My hope was not fulfilled.

In the corridor, the Sergeant-Major observed, 'I sincerely hope Monsieur will return,' and as I assured him, with thanks, that I should do so, I fancied, rightly or wrongly, that his smile was a little mocking.

4

Emerging from the stuffy gloom, I walked down the Rue St. Dominique with a light, gay step. I could have danced along, whistling and singing, for I felt practically certain that Michael and Digby were but a day or two ahead of me upon this romantic road, and that I might overtake them at any moment. Probably they were both still in France, possibly in Paris. Once I rejoined them, I should no longer feel this deadly loneliness, and should have someone with whom to talk about Isobel.

Journeys end in lovers' meetings – and but for this seperation from her, there would not be the immeasurable joy of our reunion.

Really I ought to be very thankful and very happy. I was about to rejoin Michael and Digby, and to live with them again; Isobel loved me and was awaiting my return; and I was on the threshold of a great adventure in an unknown foreign land.

Knowing that I should, after to-morrow morning, live at the charges of *Madame la République* (albeit she seemed of a careful and economical turn of mind), my funds were ample, and I would take a *fiacre* back to the fashionable quarter and spend the rest of my last day of freedom in sight-seeing and idleness.

I would sit in the Tuileries Gardens, visit the Louvre, look in the shops, have an outdoor meal in the Bois, and generally behave as does the tourist who has a few hours and a few francs to spend.

I carried out my programme, whiled away the day, and crept up to my bedroom at night, too tired for anything but the blessed dreamless sleep of healthy youth.

In the morning I paid my bill and departed from the Hôtel Normandie with a curious sense of escape. I did not in the least mind becoming a halfpenny soldier and herding with all sorts and conditions of men; but I did dislike being in a first-class hotel without my dinner-kit, a change of clothes, and the small necessities of the toilet.

I again drove to the Rue St. Dominique, and, on the way, endeavoured to talk to myself as though a person of wisdom and experience were talking to another of sense and discretion. But I greatly fear that this is not what happens when I address myself.

'You have only to stop this *fiacre*, turn about, and go back,' said I to me, 'and there is no harm done. You will still be a free man, and can go back to Brandon Abbas as soon as you like.'

But the only reply was, 'Beau . . . Digby . . . Stand by your pals through thick and thin. Adventure: Romance: Success: Fame and Fortune: and then England, Home, and Isobel . . .' and much similar youthful nonsense.

At the *Bureau de Recrutement* I was shown into a waiting-room by the Sergeant-Major, who observed:

'Ah, Monsieur has come back then! Good!' and smiled unattractively. Again I was reminded of a poem of early childhood, this time of a Lady of Riga who indulged in an unorthodox joy-ride.

In the waiting-room were some of the men I had seen on the previous day in the doctor's ante-chamber.

Among them were the Teutonic-looking pair, and I thought it probable that if I suddenly called out '*Waiter*!' or '*Garçon*!' they would both spring eagerly forward. They looked very harmless, insignificant, and unattractive – also terribly poor.

The rest were a mixed lot, Latins of sorts, apparently with nothing in common but dire poverty. They did not seem in the least ruffianly nor criminal, but just ordinary workingmen, desperately poor, and as anxious and worried as hungry, homeless people always are.

It was rather curious to feel that whereas, a few minutes ago, I had been a little uncomfortable by reason of my sartorial deficiencies, I now felt uncomfortable at being so obviously a fashionably-clad and well-nourished member of a wholly different class.

My well-cut and fairly-new clothing seemed to mock the rags and general seediness of these poor fellows, my future comrades – all of whom would very probably prove much tougher soldiers than I should.

Before long, the Sergeant-Major returned and bade me follow him to the Colonel's office.

'Ah, *mon enfant*,' said the old soldier, as I entered and bowed, 'so you have not thought better of it, eh? Well, well, you must now do as you please.'

'I wish to enlist, *mon Commandant*,' I replied.

'Then read this form and sign it,' he said, with a distinct sigh. 'Remember though, that as soon as you have done so, you will be a soldier of France, entirely amenable to martial law, and without any appeal whatsoever. Your friends cannot possibly buy you out, and your Consul cannot help you, for five years. Nothing but death can remove you from the Legion.'

I glanced over the grey printed form, a contract by which the signatory undertook to serve the French Republic for five years, as a soldier in the *Légion Étrangère*.

Five years was a long time – but Isobel would only be twenty-three at the end of it, and if Michael and Digby had done this, I could do the same . . . It would be nice to return, a Colonel at twenty-five, and take Isobel to my regiment . . . I signed my name.

'A little error, *mon enfant*?' smiled the Colonel, on reading my signature. 'Or you prefer this *nom-de-guerre*, doubtless?'

I had written 'J. Geste'!

Blushing and looking a fool, I asked to be allowed to change my mind and put my own name, and the kindly old gentleman, tearing up the form, gave me another which I signed 'John Smith.'

'Now, my boy, listen to me,' said the Colonel. 'You are a duly enlisted soldier of France and must join your regiment at once. If you do not do so, you will be treated as a deserter. You are to catch the Marseilles train from the Gare de Lyon this evening – nine-fifteen – and report yourself to the non-commissioned officer whom you will see waiting at the Marseilles terminus. Should you fail to find him, ask any *gendarme* to direct you to Fort St. Jean, and report yourself there. Don't forget. Fort St. Jean, the military depôt,' and he rose and extended his hand. 'I wish you good luck and quick promotion, *mon enfant*,' he added. 'Is there anything else I can tell you?'

'Do you always advise applicants to think better of it, sir?' I asked.

He looked at me a little sharply.

'I am not here to deter people from joining the Foreign Legion,' he said . . . 'But some strike me as better suited to the life than others,' he added, with a kindly shake of the hand. 'Good-bye and good luck.'

I thanked him and turned to commence my 'ride on the Tiger' (along the Path of Glory).

'Come with me, recruit,' said the Sergeant-Major, as he closed the door, 'and move smartly.'

In his office, he made out a railway-warrant for Marseilles, and a form that proclaimed the bearer to be John Smith, a soldier of the Legion, proceeding to the depôt in Algeria. He then unlocked a drawer, produced a cash-box, and doled out three francs on to the table.

'Subsistence-money, recruit,' said he. 'A squandering of public funds. Three *sous* would be ample.'

I added two francs to them.

'Let us part friends, Sergeant-Major,' said I, for I hate leaving ill-feeling behind me if I can avoid it.

'Recruit,' replied he, pocketing the money, 'you will get on . . . *If* you respect and please all Sergeant-Majors. Good-bye.'

And once more I found myself in the Rue St. Dominique, but no longer a free man. I had, with my own hand, pad-locked about my ankle a chain unbreakable, the other end of which was somewhere in the desert of Sahara.

Having burnt my boats, I was quite anxious to push on, and I found myself deciding to go by the next train, instead of waiting till the evening. Had I realised that I was to sit for eighteen hours on an uncushioned wooden seat, I might have felt less eager. Eighteen hours the journey did last, however, and each hour more wearisome than the one before. I think the train must have visited every town and village in France, and the entire population have clattered noisily into my ancient, uncomfortable, unclean compartment, throughout the night. Certainly I reached Marseilles feeling ancient, uncomfortable, and unclean myself; and, unlike the compartment, very empty.

It was a wretched journey, rendered no pleasanter by the attentions of the guard, who, having seen from my railway-warrant that I was going to the Legion, behaved somewhat in the manner of a clever captor and skilful gaoler.

He was of a type of Frenchman that I do not like (there are several of them), and though he refrained from actual reproaches and abuse, he made it clear to me that I could not escape him, and to my fellow-travellers that they had a possible danger in their midst. Not precisely a convict; nor, so far as he actually *knew*, an ex-convict; but still, one who was going to join the Foreign Legion.

On arrival at the terminus, this worthly soul saved me the trouble of finding my non-commissioned officer, by himself finding the man and handing me over to him, with the air of one who has deserved well of his country and of his kind.

'There!' said he to the Sergeant. 'There he is! Another little bird for your cage,' and so depressed was I by hunger, sleeplessness, and aching bones that I so far departed from good manners and the equal mind as to say:

'Oh, for God's sake don't be such a funny little fat ass,' but as I spoke in English he may have thought that I did but offer felicitations and regards.

I rather liked the look of the Sergeant. He was a dapper, alert person, and his bronzed face, though hard as iron, was not brutal nor vicious. He struck me as looking uncommonly like a man. He wore the usual uniform of the French infantry, but with a board blue woollen such round the waist, green epaulettes instead of red, and Zouave trousers.

Looking me over with a cold official stare, he asked me if I spoke French, and demanded my name, papers, and nationality.

'Another Englishman,' he remarked to my intense joy. 'Well – it might have been worse.'

'Are you alone?' he enquired, and finding that I was, so far as I knew, bade me follow him.

Surely Michael and Digby were here, and I should see them in the next few minutes. I cheered up tremendously.

He led the way out of the station and down into the busy street and the exhilarating air and sunshine of Marseilles.

By the side of the taciturn Sergeant I walked, longing to ask him about the 'other Englishmen,' whose recent arrival he had implied by his exclamation, on hearing my nationality.

But his manner did not encourage polite converse, and, truth to tell, I had an even deeper longing at the moment – for the appeasement of a very healthy appetite.

I waxed diplomatic.

'A Sergeant would not share a bottle of wine with a recruit, I suppose, Monsieur?' I asked as we passed an attractive-looking café, from beneath whose gay striped awnings marble-topped tables and comfortable cane chairs shrieked an invitation to rest and refreshment.

'He would not, *bleu*,' was the reply. 'Not only from a natural sense of superiority, but also because it would be against the regulations. Neither is he addressed as "Monsieur." He has a military rank, and he is saluted by those who address him . . . Some Sergeants, properly approached, might refresh themselves, perhaps, while a deserving *bleu* did the same . . .'

I halted and saluted as though he were an officer. (Correct procedure in the French army, I found.)

'*Monsieur le Sergent*,' said I, 'will you honour me by drinking a glass of wine at this restaurant while I get some food? I am very hungry,' and I produced a five-franc piece.

'Be here in quarter of an hour, *bleu*,' was the reply, and taking the coin the Sergeant crossed the road to a wine-shop, as I promptly dived into the café and hungrily devoured my last civilian meal – an excellent one in every detail, down to the crisp rolls, fresh butter, and coffee worthy of the name.

I rose, feeling what Digby would call 'a better and a wider man.'

Sauntering out under the awning, and seeing nothing of my Sergeant,

I sat me down, filled and lighted my pipe, and gazed about me. Fortified and refreshed, I felt by no means unhappy.

I had not long feasted my eyes upon the novel and interesting scene provided by the thronged thoroughfare, when the Sergeant, crossing the road, approached. I rose promptly, saluted smartly, and fell in beside him.

He eyed my clothes.

'Have you any more money, *bleu*?' he asked.

'Yes, Sergeant,' I replied, feeling a little disappointed in him.

'Because if you have not, I shall return you three francs,' quoth he.

I assured him that this was wholly unnecessary, though a very kindly thought – and regretted my suspicious.

'Well, I will give you some good advice instead then,' said the worthy man.

I thanked him sincerely.

'Beware the Algerian wine then,' he began. 'The blessing and the curse of the army of Africa. I have just drunk two bottles of it. Excellent . . . Beware of women, the blessing and the curse of all men. I have married three of them. Terrible . . .'

I gave my solemn promise to beware, to be very ware, and neither to drink nor to marry to excess.

'Secondly, *bleu*,' he went on, 'when things are bad, do not make them worse, for they will be quite bad enough.'

This also seemed sound advice, and I said so.

'And, thirdly – resist the decrees of Heaven if you will, but not those of your Corporal . . . Of course, no one would dream of resisting the will of a Sergeant.'

I agreed that no sane person would do this.

'Of course! . . . But it is when you are insane that you must be careful,' warned my mentor.

'Insane?' I asked.

'Yes, *bleu*,' was the reply. 'All good *légionnaires* go insane at times. Then they are apt to do one of *the* three horrible things. Kill themselves, kill their comrades, or defy a Sergeant.'

'Why should they go insane?' I enquired in some alarm.

'They shouldn't, but they do,' said my mentor. 'We call it *le cafard*. The cockroach. It crawls round and round in the brain, and the greater the heat, the monotony, the hardship, the overwork, the over-marching, and the drink – the faster goes the beetle and the more it tickles . . . Then the man says, '*J'ai le cafard*,' and runs amok, or commits suicide, or deserts, or defies a Sergeant . . . Terrible . . . And do you know what is the egg of this beetle? No? It is absinthe. Absinthe is the uncle and aunt of the grand-parents of *cafard*. It is the vilest poison. Avoid it. I know what I am saying. I was brought up on it . . . Terrible . . . I had some just now, after my wine . . .'

I promised never to look on the absinthe when it was green, nor, indeed, when it was any other colour.

'Then you will not get real *cafard*,' continued the worthy man, 'and you will not kill a comrade nor defy a Sergeant. You will only commit suicide, or desert and die in the desert.'

'Did you ever do any of these terrible things, *Monsieur le Sergent*?' I asked.

'No, *bleu*. I did not even commit suicide,' was the reply. 'I merely shaved my head, painted it red, white, and blue, and was thus esteemed as a true patriot.'

I began to think that two bottles of wine and an unspecified quantity of absinthe had stimulated the Sergeant's imagination, but learnt later that what he told me was absolutely true. (When engaged in repainting one of the striped sentry boxes of the barracks or the outpost where he was stationed, he had painted one side of his shaven head red and the other side blue, and separated these colours with a broad white stripe. This had drawn attention to him, and he had riveted that attention by desperate courage and resource during the operations and battle of Cinq Palmiers.)

'And what can one do to escape *le cafard*?' I asked.

'Nothing,' was the discouraging reply. 'Mental occupation is good, and promotion is better. But in the desert, while the Arab finds two things, the European finds three. They are there, and, therefore, there they are . . .'

I tried to look intelligent and enquiring.

'The Arab inevitably finds sun and sand – too much of both. The European inevitably finds sun, sand, and madness – too much of all three,' he went on. 'This madness is in the air, I suppose, or in the sun's rays. I do not know, even I, although I know so much. And now you have talked more than is seemly. Silence, *bleu* . . .'

And I was silent, though inclined to ask why he addressed me as '*bleu*.' I did not feel particularly blue, and I was quite sure I did not look blue in the slightest degree. (Later I learnt that it is French army-slang for a recruit, and has as much or little meaning as the English name of 'rookie' for the same class of soldier.) The use of my tongue being now prohibited, I used my eyes instead, and enjoyed the marvellous panorama of the Marseilles waterside, where Arabs, Negroes, Levantines, Chinese, Moors, Annamese, Indians, and the lascars and seamen of the ships of all nations, seemed as numerous as the French themselves.

I was reminded of the story of the Tower of Babel as we made our way through the throng and round the boxes, bales, sacks, barrels, trucks, carts, trolleys, and waggons over which the gesticulating crowds swarmed and howled.

Among the sailing-ships, Oriental-looking barques, yachts, brigs, schooners, cargo-boats, and liners, moored along the quays, I kept looking for the English flag, flying at the stern; and was delighted as often as my eye fell upon it.

I had thought, at first, that all the ships must be French, as each flew the Tri-couleur at the mast, until I realised that this was complimentary to France, while the national flag flew at the stern.

My head was beginning to ache with the noise, heat, hustle, and eye-strain, when we arrived at our destination, a mediaeval fort on the water's edge, obsolete and dilapidated, with an ancient lighthouse tower, and a drawbridge, leading over a moat to a great door.

One half expected to see that the sentries were halberdiers in breastplate and jerkin, trunk hose, and peaked morion . . .

'Here we are, and hence – we are here,' observed my Sergeant . . . 'Good-bye, *bleu*, and may the devil admire you.'

'The same to you, Sergeant, and very many thanks,' I replied.

To the Sergeant of the Guard at the gate he merely remarked, "Recruit. Legion. Poor devil!" and turning, departed, and I saw him no more.

'Follow me, you,' said the Sergeant of the Guard, and led the way along prison-like stone corridors, damp, mouldering, echoing, and very depressing.

Halting at a door, he opened it, jeked his thumb in the direction of the interior, and shut the door behind me as I entered.

I was in my first French barrack-room.

Round the walls stood a score or so of cots and a number of benches, the remaining furniture of the room being a big table and a stove. Round the latter, at the table, on cots and on benches, lounged a varied assortment of men in civilian clothes – clothes ranging from well-cut lounge-suits to corduroy and rags.

Michael and Digby were not among these men, and I was sensible of a deep feeling of bitter disappointment as I realised the fact.

All these recruits looked at me, but though conscious of their regard, I was much more conscious of the poisonous foulness of the atmosphere of the room. It was horrible.

Every window was tightly shut, and every man (and the charcoal stove) was smoking, so far as I could determine with a rapid glance round the reeking place.

Presumably the men were smoking tobacco, but it was no tobacco with which I was familiar. I was remainded of gardener's bonfires and smouldering rubbish.

Without thinking of what I was doing, I naturally and instinctively turned to the nearest window, manfully wrestled with it, and succeeded in throwing it open.

I am not in a position categorically to affirm that this was positively the first time that a window had ever been opened in Fort St. Jean, but it might well have been, to judge by the interest, not to say consternation, evoked by my simple action. What would have happened to me had a corporal or old soldier been present, I do not know.

At the table a group of three or four men who were playing cards, seemed to take umbrage at my action or my audacity. Their ejaculations sounded like those of great surprise mingled with resentment. One of them rose and turned towards me.

'You do not like the atmosphere of our little nest, perhaps?' he said, unpleasantly, and with a threatening and bullying note in his voice.

'No,' I replied, and looking him carefully up and down, added, 'Nor you either. What are you going to do about it?'

This was ill-mannered of me. I admit it. I was bringing my style to the level of this unpleasant-looking individual. But it seemed to me to be the best level on which to meet him. I thought it is a sound plan to begin as I meant to go on, and I had not the least intention of allowing that going-on to include any undue Christian meekness. I was the last person in the world to bully anybody, and I intended to be the last person to be bullied.

I did not wish to begin by making an enemy, but still less did I wish to begin by allowing the establishment of any sort of ascendancy on the part of a fellow-recruit.

'Oho! You don't like the look of me, don't you?' said the fellow, advancing.

'Not a bit,' said I, looking him over appraisingly, and then 'staring him out' as we used to say in the nursery.

I could not quite 'place' the individual. He certainly was not a workman and he was not a prince in disguise. A clerk, or shopman, probably, I thought, and learned later that he was a French petty official named Vogué, 'rehabilitating' himself – recovering his papers and civic rights by five years' Legion service, after conviction of defalcation, and a light sentence.

'You want that window open?' he said, changing the subject.

'Monsieur is intelligent,' said I.

'Suppose I want it shut?' he enquired.

'Come and shut it,' said I, with disgraceful truculence.

'Suppose we all want it shut?' he hedged.

'Then there is an end of the matter,' I replied. 'If the majority prefer to poison themselves, they have a perfect right to do so.'

'Come back and be quiet, Nosey,' called one of the card-players, and he returned, grumbling.

I seated myself on the cot nearest to the open window, and put my hat on the dirty straw-stuffed pillow . . . What next?

'Like the ceiling raised any?' enquired a quiet drawling voice behind me, in English.

Turning, I regarded the ceiling.

'No,' I said, 'it will do,' and studied the speaker.

He was lying at full length on the next cot, a very small, clean-shaven man with a prominent nose and chin, a steel-trap mouth, and a look of great determination and resolution. His eyes were a very light grey, hard and penetrating, his hair straw-coloured and stubbly, his face sallow, lantern-jawed, and tanned. He looked a hard case and proved to be what he looked.

'How did you know I was English?' I asked as he stared thoughtfully at me.

'What else?' he replied, deliberately. 'Pink and white . . . Own the earth . . . "*Haw! Who's this low fellah? Don' know him, do I?*" . . . Dude . . . "*Open all the windahs now I've come!*" . . . British!'

I laughed.

'Are you an American?' I enquired.

'Why?' he replied.

'What else?' I drawled. ' "*Sure thing, stranger*,' . . . Don't care who owns the earth . . . Great contempt for the effecte English . . . Tar and feathers . . . Stars and Stripes . . . "*I come from God's Own Country and I guess it licks Creation*." . . . Uneasy self-assertion . . .'

The American smiled. (I never heard him laugh.)

'Bo,' said he, turning to the next cot, 'here's a Britisher insulting of our pore country . . . Handin' out the rough stuff . . . Fierce, ain't it?'

A huge man slowly turned from contemplation of the ceiling, raised his head, ceased chewing, and regarded me solemly. He then fainted with a heartrending groan.

'Killed my pard, you hev,' said the little man. 'He's got a weak heart . . . Damn sight weaker head though, haven't you, Bo?' he added, turning to his friend, who had recovered sufficiently to continue his patient mastication either of tobacco or chewing-gum.

Lying there, Bo appeared to be some seven feet in length, four in breadth, and two in depth.

In face he greatly resembled the small man, having the same jutting chin, prominent nose, tight mouth, and hard leathery face. His eyes were of a darker grey, however, and his hair black and silky.

He also looked a hard case and a very bad enemy. Conversely though, I gained the impression that he might be a very good friend. Indeed, I liked the look of both of them, in spite of the fact that I seemed to fill them with a sort of amused contempt.

'Ses you suffers from oneasy self-insertion, Hank,' went on the little man.

'Ain't inserted nawthen to-day, Buddy,' replied the giant mildly. 'Nary a insert. I'm oneasy in me innards, but it ain't from what you ses, Stranger. Nope. I could insert a whole hog right now, and never notice it.'

'Don't go fer ter rile the Britisher, Hank, with yer silly contradicshusness,' implored the other. 'He don't like it, an' he don' like us. You don' want ter go gittin' inter no trouble. So shet up and go on sufferin' from oneasy self-insertion.'

'Means well,' continued the speaker, turning to me, 'but he ain't et nawthen excep' cigarett-ends for three or four days, an' he ain't at his best.'

I stared. Was it possible that they were really hungry? Certainly they looked lean and haggard enough to be starving.

I had felt quite bad enough an hour or two ago, after missing a single meal . . . I should have to go carefully if I wanted to give food, and not offence.

'Would you gentlemen lunch with me?' I asked, diffidently. 'Brothers-in-arms and all that . . .'

Two solemn faces turned and regarded me.

'He's calling you a gentleman, Hank,' said the little man at length. 'He don' mean no real harm though. He's talkin' English to you . . . Hark! . . . You listen and improve your mind.'

I made another effort. 'Say,' quoth I, 'I gotta hunch I wanta grub-stake you two hoboes to a blow-out. Guess I can cough up the dough, if yew ain't too all-fired proud to be pards with a dod-gasted Britisher.' A good effort, I thought.

'Gee!' said Hank, and they rose as one man.

'Put it right there, son,' said the big man, extending the largest hand I have ever seen.

I took it, and in the crushing-match that ensued, endeavoured to hold my own. It was a painful business, and when I limply took the horny fist of Buddy in turn, I was handicapped in the squeezing competition. However, I was able to give him a worthy grip, though his hand was stronger than mine.

'Where can we get something?' I asked, and Buddy said there was certain to be a canteen about. He had never yet heard of a case where a thirsty soldier, with money, was not given every encouragement to get rid of it.

'I can't drink till I've et, pard,' said Hank to me. ''Twouldn't be right. If I drinks on an empty stummick, I gets onreasonable if interfered with by the bulls . . . Bash a sheriff or somethin' . . . When I ain't starvin', lickker on'y makes me more and more lovin' to all mankind. Yep, I gotta eat first.'

'They'll have eats in the canteen,' opined Buddy, 'even in this God-fersaken section.'

At that moment, the door of the room was thrown open by a soldier, and he entered carrying one end of a long board on which stood a row of tin bowls. Another soldier appeared at the other end, and together they bawled, '*Soupe*!'

It was invitation enough, and both the long arms of Hank shot out, and, in a moment, he was on his bed, a bowl in either hand.

Buddy followed his example.

I looked round. There appeared to me to be more bowls than there were people in the room. I snatched two, before the rush of hungry men from other parts of the room arrived with outstretched hands.

This disgusting exhibition of greed on my part cannot be excused, but may be condoned as it was not made in my own interests. I was not hungry, and the look of the stuff was not sufficiently tempting for me to eat for eating's sake. By the time I reached my cot, Hank had emptied one bowl, and was rapidly emptying the other.

'Gee! That's what I come to the Legion for,' he said, with a sigh of content. When he had finished, I offered him one of my two.

'Fergit it,' said he.

'I want to,' said I.

He stared hard at me.

'Not hungry,' I assured him.

'Honest Injun?' he asked doubtfully, but extending his hand.

'Had a big breakfast an hour ago,' said I. 'I never take soup in the middle of the morning. I got this for you and Mr. – er . . .'

'Buddy,' said the little man and took the other bowl.

Hank swallowed his third portion.

'You're shore white, pard,' he said.

'Blowed-in-the-glass,' agreed Buddy, and I felt I had two friends.

A large German lumbered up gesticulating, and assailed Hank.

'You eat dree!' he shouted in guttural English. 'I only eat vun! Himmel! You damn dirdy tief!'

'Sure thing, Dutchy,' said Buddy. 'Don't yew stand fer it! You beat him up. You make him put it back.'

The German shook a useful-looking fist under Hank's nose.

'I can't put it back, Dutch,' said he midly. ''Twouldn't be manners,' and, as the angry German waxed more aggressive, he laid his huge and soupy hand upon the fat angry face, and pushed.

The German staggered back and fell heavily, and sat looking infinitely surprised.

'*Now*, pard,' said Hank to me, 'I could shore look upon the wine without no evil effecks to nobody,' and we trooped out in search of the canteen.

The big gloomy quadrangle of Fort St. Jean was now crowded with soldiers of every regiment of the army of Africa, the famous Nineteenth Army Corps, and, for the first time, I saw the Spahis of whom the French officer had talked to us at Brandon Abbas.

Their trousers were voluminous enough to be called skirts, in fact one leg would have provided the material for an ample frock. Above these garments they wore sashes that appeared to be yards in length and feet in width. In these they rolled each other up, one man holding and manipulating the end, while the other spun round and round towards him, winding the sash tightly about himself as he did so.

Gaudy waistcoats, zouave jackets, fez caps, and vast scarlet cloaks completed their picturesquely barbaric costumes.

Besides the Spahis there were blue-and-yellow Tirailleurs, pale blue Chasseurs d'Afrique, and red-and-blue Zouaves, blue Colonial Infantry, as well as artillerymen, sappers, and soldiers of the line, in their respective gay uniforms.

There was a babel of noise and a confusing turmoil as these leave-men rushed about in search of pay-corporals, *fourrier-sergents*, kit, papers, food, and the canteen. The place was evidently the clearing-house and military hotel for all soldiers coming from, or returning to, the army of Africa.

Following the current that flowed through this seething whirlpool, in the direction of a suggestive-looking squad of huge wine-casks that stood arrayed outside an open door, we found ourselves in the canteen and the presence of the national drink, good red wine.

'No rye-whiskey at a dollar a drink here, Bo,' observed Buddy, as we made our way to a zinc-covered counter, and found that everybody was drinking claret at three-halfpence the bottle. 'Drinks are on you, pard. Set 'em up.'

'Gee! It's what they call "wine,"' sighed Hank. 'Gotta get used to it with the other crool de*pri*vations and hardships,' and he drained the tumbler that I filled.

'It *is* lickker, Bo,' replied Buddy tolerantly, and drained another.

It was, and very good liquor too. It struck me as far better wine than one paid a good deal for at Oxford, and good enough to set before one's guests anywhere.

Personally I am a poor performer with the bottle, and regard wine as something to taste and appreciate, rather than as a thirst-quenching beverage.

Also I freely confess that the sensation produced by more than enough, or by mixing drinks, is, to me, most distasteful.

I would as soon experience the giddiness caused by spinning round and round, as the giddiness caused by alcohol. More than a little makes me feel sick, silly, depressed, and uncomfortable, and I have never been able to understand the attraction that intoxication undoubtedly has for some people.

It is therefore in no way to my credit that I am a strictly sober person, and as little disposed to exceed in wine as in cheese, pancakes, or dry toast.

'Quite good wine,' said I to the two Americans, 'but I can't say I like it as a drink between meals.'

I found that my companions were of one mind with me, though perhaps for a different reason.

'Yep,' agreed Buddy. 'Guess they don't allow no intoxicatin' hard lickkers in these furrin canteens.'

'Nope,' remarked Hank. 'We gotta swaller this an' be thankful. P'r'aps we kin go out an' have a drink when we git weary-like . . . Set'em up again, Bo,' and I procured them each his third bottle.

'You ain't drinkin', pard,' said Buddy, eyeing my halfemptied first glass.

'Not thirsty,' I replied.

'Thirsty?' said Hank. 'Don' s'pose there's any water here if you was,' and feeling I had said the wrong thing, covered my confusion by turning away and observing the noisy, merry throng, drinking and chattering around me. They were a devil-may-care, hard-bitten, though-looking crowd, and I found myself positively looking forward to being in uniform and one of them.

As I watched, I saw a civilian coming from the door towards us. I had noticed him in the barrack-room. Although dressed in an ill-fitting, shoddy, shabby blue suit, a velvet tam-o'-shanter, burst shoes, and apparently nothing else, he looked like a soldier. Not that he had by any means the carriage of an English guardsman – far from it – but his face was a soldier's, bronzed, hard, disciplined, and of a family likeness to those around.

Coming straight to us, he said pleasantly, and with only the slightest foreign accent.

'Recruits for the Legion?'

'Yes,' I replied.

'Would you care to exchange information for a bottle?' he asked politely, with an ingratiating smile which did not extend to his eyes.

'I should be delighted if you will drink with us,' I replied, and put a two-franc piece on the counter.

He chose to think that the money was for him to accept, and not for the fat little man behind the bar to change.

'You are a true comrade,' said the new-comer, 'and will make a fine *légionnaire*. There are a dozen bottles here,' and he spun the coin. 'Now ask me anything you want to know,' and he included the two stolid Americans in the graceful bow with which he concluded. He was evidently an educated and cultured person and not English.

'Sure,' said Hank. 'I wants ter know when we gits our next eats.'

'An' if we can go out and git a drink,' added Buddy.

'You'll get *soupe*, bread and coffee at about four o'clock, and you won't be allowed to leave here for any purpose whatever until you are marched down to the boat for Oran,' was the prompt reply.

His hearers pursed their lips in stolid silence.

'When will that be?' I asked.

'To-morrow by the steam-packet, unless there is a troop-ship going the day after,' answered the new-comer. 'They ship the Legion recruits in – ah – dribbles? dribblings? driblets? Yes, driblets – by every boat that goes.'

'Suppose a friend of mine joined a day or two before me,' I asked, 'where would he be now, do you suppose?'

'He is at Fort St. Thérése at Oran now,' was the reply. 'And may go on to Saida or Sidi-bel-Abbès to-morrow or the next day. Sidi, probably, if he is a strong fellow.'

'Say, you're a walking encyclopedestrian,' remarked Buddy, eyeing the man speculatively, and perhaps with more criticism than approval.

'I can tell you anything about the Legion,' replied the man in his excellent refined English – about which there was no accent such as that of a Londoner, north-countryman, or yokel, but only a slight foreign suggestion – 'I am an old *légionnaire*, rejoining after five years' service and my discharge.'

'Speaks well for the Legion,' I remarked cheerfully.

'Or ill for the chance of an ex-*légionnaire* to get a crust of bread,' he observed, less cheerfully.

'Been up against it, son?' asked Hank.

'Starved. Tramped my feet off. Slept in the mud. Begged myself hoarse – for work . . . Driven at last to choose between gaol and the Legion . . . I chose the Legion, for some reason . . . Better the devils that you know than flee to the devils that you know not of . . .'

'Guy seems depressed,' said Hank.

'May I finish your wine?' went on the man. 'It would be a sin to waste it.'

'Pray do,' said I, surprised; and reminded myself that I was no longer at Oxford.

'You speak wonderful English,' I remarked.

'I do,' was the reply; 'but better Italian, Hindustani, and French. Legion French, that is.'

'An' how's that, ole hoss?' enquired Buddy.

'Father an Italian pastry-cook in Bombay. Went to an English school there, run by the Jesuit Fathers. Talked Hindustani to my ayah. Mother really talked it better than anything else, being what they call a country-bred. Daughter of an English soldier and an Eurasian girl. Got my French in the Legion, of course,' explained the stranger.

And then I was unfortunate, in that I partly blundered and partly was misunderstood. What I meant to say, for the sake of being conversational, was:

'And how did you come to find yourself in Africa, so very far from home?' or something chatty like that. What I actually did say was:

'Why did you join the Legion?' which sounded very bald.

'For the same reason that *you* did. For my health,' was the sharp reply, accompanied by a cold stare.

I had done that which is not done.

'And did you find it – healthy?' enquired Buddy.

'Not exactly so much heal*thy* as hel*lish*,' replied the Italian in brief and uncompromising style, as he drained his glass (or perhaps mine).

We all three plied him with questions, and learned much that was useful and more that was disturbing. We also gathered that the gentleman was known as Francesco Boldini to his friends, though he did not say by what name the police knew him.

I came to the conclusion that I did not like him extraordinarily much; but that in view of his previous experience he would be an exceedingly useful guide, philosopher, and friend, whose knowledge of the ropes would be well worth purchasing.

I wished I could send him on ahead for the benefit of my brothers, who had, I felt certain, come this way two or three days before me. Indeed, I refused to believe otherwise or to face the fact of my crushing disappointment and horrible position if they had not done so. I was aroused from thoughts of what might, and might not, be before me by a tremendous uproar as the artillerymen present united in roaring their regimental song:

'Si vous voulez jouir des plaisirs de la vie,
Engagez vous ici, et dans l'artillerie.
Quand l'artilleur de Metz change de garnison,
Toutes les femmes de Metz se mettent au balcon.
Artilleur, mon vieux frère,
À ta santé vidons nos verres;
Et répétons ce gai refrain:
Vivent les Artilleurs; à bas les fantassins . . .'

and much more.

When they had finished and cheered themselves hoarse, a little scoundrelly-looking fellow sprang on a barrel and sang a remarkably seditious and disloyal ditty, of which the chorus, apparently known to all, was:

'Et quand il faut servir ce bon Dieu de République,
Où tout le monde est soldat malgré son consentement,
On nous envoi grossir les Bataillons d'Afrique,
À cause que les Joyeux s'aiment pas le gouvernement,
C'est nous les Joyeux,
Les petits Joyeux,
Les petits marlous Joyeux qui n'ont pas froid aux yeux . . .

At the conclusion of this song of the battalion of convicted criminals (known as the *Bataillon d'Infanterie Légère d'Afrique*, or, more familiarly, as the '*Bat d'Af*'), the men of the Colonial Infantry, known as *Marsouins*, lifted up their voices in their regimental song. These were followed by others, until I think I heard all the famous marching-songs of the French army – including that of the Legion, sung by Boldini. It was all very interesting indeed, but in time I had had enough of it . . .

When we returned to the barrack-room, on the advice of Boldini, to be in time for the evening meal, I formally retained that experienced and acquisitive gentleman as guide, courier, and mentor, with the gift of ten francs and the promise of such future financial assistance as I could give and he should deserve.

'I am sorry I cannot spare more just at present,' said I, in unnecessary apology for the smallness of the retaining fee; and his reply was illuminating.

'Ten francs, my dear sir,' he said, 'is precisely two hundred days' pay to a *légionnaire*. . . Seven months' income. Think of it!' . . .

And I thought of it.

Decidedly I should need considerable promotion before being in a position to marry and live in comfort on my pay . . .

5

'Dinner,' that evening, at about five o'clock, consisted of similar '*soupe*', good greyish bread, and unsweetened, milkless coffee. The first came, as before, in tin basins, called '*gamelles*'; the second was thrown to us from a basket; and the coffee was dipped from a pail, in tin mugs.

The *soupe* was a kind of stew, quite good and nourishing, but a little difficult to manipulate without spoon or fork. I found that my education was, in this respect, inferior to that of my comrades. After this meal – during which the German eyed our party malevolently, and Vogué, the gentleman who had objected to my opening the window, alluded to me as a 'sacred *nicodème*,' whatever that may be – there was nothing to do but to adjourn once more to the canteen.

Here it was my privilege to entertain the whole band from the barrack-room, and I was interested to discover that both the German, whose name proved to be Glock, and the unpleasing Vogué, were both charmed to accept my hospitality, and to drown resentment, with everything else, in wine.

It is quite easy to be lavishly hospitable with wine at about a penny a pint.

Fun grew fast and furious, and I soon found that I was entertaining a considerable section of the French army, as well as the Legion's recruits.

I thoroughly enjoyed the evening, and was smitten upon the back, poked in the ribs, wrung by the hand, embraced about the neck, and, alas, kissed upon both cheeks by Turoo, Zouave, Tirailleur, Artilleur, Marsouin, and Spahi, even before the battalion of bottles had been routed by the company of men.

I noticed that Boldini waxed more foreign, more voluble, and more unlovable, the more he drank.

If he could do anything else like a gentleman, he certainly could not carry his wine like one.

'Sah!' he hiccupped to me, with a strident laugh, 'farmerly arlso there were a gross of bahtles and few men, and now arlso there are only gross men and a few bahtles!' and he smote me on the back to assist me to understand the jest. The more he went to pieces under the influence of liquor, the more inclined was I to think he had a larger proportion of Oriental strain than he pretended.

I liked him less and less as the evening wore on, and I liked him least when he climbed on the zinc-covered counter and sang an absolutely vile song, wholly devoid of humour or of anything else but offence. I am bound to admit, however, that it was very well received by the audience.

'What you t'ink of *thatt*, sah?' he enquired, when he had finished.

I replied that I preferred not to think of it, and proposed to address him in future as Cloaca Maxima.

Meanwhile, Hank and Buddy, those taciturn, observant, non-committal, and austerely-tolerant Americans, made hay while the sun of prosperity shone, drank more than any two of the others, said nothing, and seemed to wonder what all the excitement was about, and what made the 'pore furriners' noisy.

'Ennybody'ud think the boobs hed bin drinkin',' observed Buddy at last, breaking a long silence (his own silence, that is, of course). To which remark Hank replied:

'They gotta pretend thisyer wine-stuff is a hard drink, an' act like they got a whiskey-jag an' was off the water-waggon. Only way to keep their sperrits up . . . Wise guys too. You'd shore think some of 'em had bin drinkin' lickker . . .

'Gee! . . . There's 'Taps!' he added, as the 'Lights out' bugle blew in the courtyard, and the company broke up, 'an' we gotta go to bed perishin' o' thirst, fer want of a drink . . .'

Back to our barrack-room we reeled, singing joyously.

As I sat on my cot undressing, a little later, Buddy came over to me and said, in a low voice:

'Got 'ny money left, pard?'

'Why, yes. Certainly,' I replied. 'You're most welcome to . . .'

'Welcome nix,' was the reply. 'If you got 'ny money left, shove it inside yer piller an' tie the end up – or put it inside yer little vest an' lie on it . . .'

'Hardly necessary, surely?' said I. 'Looks rather unkind and suspicious, you know . . .'

'Please yerself, pard, o' course,' replied Buddy, 'and let Mister Oompara Tarara Cascara Sagrada get it,' and he glanced meaningly at Boldini, who was lying, fully dressed, on his cot.

'Oh, nonsense,' said I, 'he's not as bad as all that . . .'

Buddy shrugged his shoulders and departed.

'I gotta evil mind,' he remarked as he did so.

I finished undressing, got into the dirty sheetless bed, put my money under my pillow, and then lay awake for a long time, dreaming of Isobel, of Brandon Abbas, and, with a sense of utter mystification, of the wretched 'Blue Water' and its mysterious fate . . .

Only last Wednesday . . . Only eight people – one of whom it obviously must be . . . A wretched vulgar thief . . . And where were Michael and Digby now? Were they together, and only forty-eight hours ahead of me on the Path of Glory, which, according to Boldini, led to the grave with a certainly and a regularity bordering upon monotony? . . . I fell asleep . . .

I was awakened in the morning by the shrilling of bugles.

A corporal entered the room, bawled:

'*Levez-vous donc! Levez-vous donc*!' at the top of his voice, and departed.

I partly dressed, and then felt beneath my pillow for my money.

It was not there.

I felt savage and sick . . . Robbed! . . . The beastly curs . . .

'Here it is,' said the voice of Buddy behind me. 'Thought I'd better mind it when I aheered yore nose-sighs . . . Shore enuff, about four a.m. this morning, over comes Mister Cascara Sagrada to see how youse agettin' on . . . "*All right, Bo*," ses I, speakin' innercent in me slumbers, "*I'm amindin' of it*," I ses . . .'

'No?' said I, 'not really?'

'You betcha,' replied Buddy, 'an' Mister Cascara Sagrada says, "*Oh, I thought somebody might try to rob him*," he says . . . "*So did I*," I says, "*And I was right too*," I says, an' the skunk scoots back to his hole.'

'Thanks, Buddy,' I said, feeling foolish, as I took the notes and coins.

'I tried to put you wise, Bo,' he replied, 'and now you know.'

Curiously enough, it did not enter my mind to doubt the truth of what he had told me.

After a breakfast-lunch of *soupe* and bread, we were ordered by a sergeant to assemble in the courtyard.

Here he called the roll of our names, and those of a freshly-arrived draft of recruits; formed us in fours, and marched us to the *basin*, where a steamer of the *Messageries Maritimes* line, the *Général Negrier*, awaited us.

We were herded to the fo'c'sle of this aged packet, and bidden by the corporal, who was going in charge of us, to use the ocean freely if we should chance to feel unwell, as it was entirely at our disposal.

'"We have fed our seas for a thousand years,"' thought I, and was grateful that, on this glorious day, the sea did not look at all hungry.

But if the sea were not, we soldiers of misfortune undoubtedly were. Very hungry, indeed, and as the hours passed, we grew still hungrier. Towards evening, the Château d'If and the tall lighthouse having been left far behind, murmurs on the subject of dinner began to be heard. We loafed moodily about the well-deck, between the fo'c'sle and the high midship bridge structure, talking both in sorrow and in anger, on the subject of food.

Personally I thought very regretfully of the dining-room at Brandon Abbas, and of the dinner that was even then being served therein. Tantalising odours were wafted to us from the saloon below the bridge, and our ears were not unaware of the stimulating rattle of plates and cutlery.

'When shall we get something to eat?' I asked Boldini, as he emerged from the fo'c'sle hatch.

'By regulations we should have had *soupe*, bread, and half a litre of wine at five o'clock,' he replied. 'Quite likely the cook is going to make a bit out of us, for these swine often do . . .'

However, there was activity, I observed, in the cook's galley, near the fo'c'sle – the cook-house in which the sailors' food was prepared – so we hoped for the best while fearing the worst.

An hour later, when we were an hour hungrier and angrier, Hank's usually monumental patience had dwindled to imperceptibility.

'Here, you, Cascara,' quoth he, pushing into the knot of men in the centre of which Boldini harangued them on their rights and the cause of their present wrongs, 'you know the rules of this yer game. Why ain't we got no eats yet?'

'Because this thieving swine of a son of a sea-cook is going to make a bit out of us,' replied Boldini.

'Thet so, now?' observed Hank mildly. 'Then I allow he ain't agoin' ter live to enjy it. Nary a enjy. So he can tell himself Good-bye, for he ain't goin' to see himself no more, if I don't get no dinner. Nope . . .'

I gathered from Boldini that it would be quite impossible for me to get at the corporal, as I proposed to do, since he was away in the second-class quarters, and I should be prevented from leaving the fo'c'sle if I tried to do so.

'But I can let you have a roll,' he said, 'if it is worth a franc to you. I don't want to starve, you know,' and his pleasant smile was a little reminiscent of the Wicked Uncle in my nursery-tale book of the Babes in the Wood.

It appeared that, anticipating just what had happened, he had secreted four rolls when breakfast was served at Fort St. Jean that morning. I gave him three francs, and a roll each to Hank and Buddy.

'You have a great soul, Boldini,' I remarked, on purchasing the bread, and was distressed at the unkindly guffaw emitted by Buddy at my words. An hour or so later, all signs of activity having ceased to render the cook-house attractive, it seemed but too true that food was not for us. The mob of recruits grumbled, complained, and cursed in half a dozen languages. Darkness fell, and Hank arose.

A huge greasy creature, grossly fat, filthily dirty in clothes and person, and with a face that was his misfortune, emerged from the cooking-house. He eyed us with sourest contempt.

I suggested to Boldini that the scoundrel might sell us what he ought to have given us. Boldini replied that this was precisely what would happen, on the morrow, when we were *really* hungry – provided we had money and chose to pay his prices.

Hank strode forward.

'Thet Slushy?' he enquired softly.

'That's the swine,' replied Boldini.

'Come and interpretate then,' requested Hank, and marched up to the cook, closely followed by Buddy.

'When do we get our doo an' lawful eats, Slush?' he asked mildly.

The cook ignored him utterly and turned to go in lofty silence, but a huge hand shot out and sank with the grip of a vice into the fat of his bulging neck, another seized his wrist, and he was run as a perambulator is run by a child, straight to the side of the ship.

'Ask the pore gink if he can swim any,' requested Hank, holding the man's head over the side.

Boldini did so.

The gink kicked out viciously, but made no other reply.

'Up with it, Bud – *attaboy*!' whooped Hank, and Buddy diving at the agitated legs, gathered them in, and raised them on to the taffrail.

The crowd of recruits cheered joyously.

I thought the man was really going overboard, and begged them not to waste a perfectly good cook.

'Sure,' said Hank. 'He's gotta get us some grub first,' and they threw the cook on the deck un-gently.

The man lumbered to his feet, and, again seizing him, Hank ran him to the galley and threw him through the door.

'*Cookez-vous, pronto*!' quoth he, and the cook seized a heavy iron saucepan and rushed out again.

But alas, it was as a weapon and not as a utensil that he wished to use it. Swinging it up with all his strength – he found it wrenched from his hand and placed ringingly upon his head.

'He's contumelious,' said Hank. 'He's onobedient to my signs,' and became earnest. Taking the man by the throat he started to choke him.

'Tell him I'm hungry, Bo,' he said to Boldini. 'Tell him he can eat outer my hand when I ain't riz by hunger . . . I gotta eat outer his pots first though.'

Boldini assured the cook that Hank would tear him limb from limb, and the angry crowd of recruits would see that nobody rescued him either.

The fellow ceased to struggle, and Hank hurled him into the galley.

A sort of ship's quartermaster, followed by a sailor, came up, and I feared trouble. Visions of us all in irons, awaiting a court-martial at Oran, floated before my eyes.

'Assaulting the cook?' quoth the man in uniform. 'Good! Kill the thrice-accursed thieving food-spoiler, and may *le bon Dieu* assist you.'

I gathered that he was not very fond of Slushy.

'His assistance will not be required, *Monsieur le Contre-maître*,' said the smiling Boldini, and with horrible oaths and grimaces and the worst possible grace, the cook produced a number of loaves of bread, a pail of cold stew, and some macaroni.

'We'll have that hot,' announced Boldini, pointing to the stew.

With very violent curses the cook said we would not – and the crowd snarled.

On understanding this reply, Hank instructed Boldini to inform the cook that unless he did precisely as he was told, there would be great sorrow for him when we had fed. If he were obedient he would be forgiven.

The stew was put over the galley-fire in a great pan.

'Can't he rustle a few onions and sech?' enquired Buddy, pushing into the galley.

Seeing that he was a very small man, the cook gave him a violent shove in the chest, and sent him staggering.

'I'll talk to you posthumorously, Cookie,' said Buddy, with ominous calm. 'We wants you whole and hearty like, for the present.'

'Out, little dog! Out, you indescribable pollution' snarled the cook in French.

Under Boldini's instruction and Hank's compulsion, the cook produced a string of onions and added them to the *soupe*.

'Watch him well, or he'll poison us,' advised Glock, the German, who, but yesterday, had called Hank a 'dirdy tief' and now appeared to love him as a brother.

He watched, very well, and gave every encouragement we could think of.

Before long, we were squatting on the deck, each man with a well-filled *gamelle* of excellent stew and a loaf of bread, feeding heartily and calling blessings on Hank, the hero of the hour. Vogué tried to kiss him.

Again the fat cook emerged from the galley in search of relaxation and repose, and with a curse turned to go.

'He ought by rights to give us each a litre of wine,' said Boldini. 'He's got it and means to sell it.'

'Say, Bo,' shouted Hank thereupon. 'Don't desert us! Did you say it was wine or cawfee you was keeping fer us?' Boldini translated.

'*'Cré bon sang!*' roared the cook, raising his hands above his head, and then shaking his big dirty fist at Boldini.

'To hell with you starving gutter-scrapings! You foul swine of the slums of Europe! You . . .'

'Sounds good!' remarked Buddy.

'I guess he's saying "*No*,"' opined Hank. 'I'll make signs to him agin,' and he rose and strode towards the gesticulating ruffian.

The cook retreated into the galley, one hand to his throat.

'Look out for a knife,' called Boldini.

But the cook was cowed, and reappeared with a wooden bucket containing three or four quarts of wine. This he handed to Hank, with a wish that it might choke him first and corrode his interior after.

He then requested Boldini to inform us that we were a cowardly gang of apaches and wolves, who were brave enough in a band, and slinking ours individually. He would fight and destroy every one of us – except the big one – and glad of the chance.

Boldini did so.

'I'm the smallest,' remarked Buddy, and left it at that, while he finished his bread and wine.

I am a law-abiding person by nature and by training (or I was at that time), and regretted all this unseemliness. But what a loathsome blackguard a man must be to swindle hungry bewildered men (whose pay was a halfpenny a day and who had joined the army to get it!), to rob them of their meagre allowance of food in order that he might sell it to them for their last coppers, when they could hold out no longer.

According to Boldini it was this scoundrel's regular custom to pretend to each draft of ignorant browbeaten foreigners that the Government made no provision for them, and that what they wanted they must buy from him. If they were absolutely penniless they got precisely nothing at all for forty-eight hours, and the cook sold their wine and rations to other steerage passengers or to the sailors.

When they understood this, Hank and Buddy discussed the advisability of 'sure eradicating' the man – its desirability being self-evident. They decided they must leave this duty, with so many others, unperformed, as the *Messageries Maritimes* Company might behave officiously and prefer French law to lynch law.

'But I'll expostulate some with the all-fired skunk – when we finished with him as a cook,' observed Buddy . . .

We lay on the deck propped against the hatch far into the glorious night, Hank and Buddy rolling cigarettes with my tobacco, and leaves from my pocket-book, while I enjoyed my dear old briar, as we listened to Boldini's wonderful tales of the Legion . . .

The moon rose and flooded the sea with silver light . . .

By this time to-morrow, I might be with Michael and Digby . . . I began to nod, fell asleep, woke cold and stiff, and retired to a very unpleasant hole in the fo'o'sle, where there were tiers of bunks and many sorrows.

I slept for about ten hours and woke feeling as fit as a fiddle and ready for anything – particularly breakfast.

6

According to Boldini, this should be provided at eleven o'clock, and should consist of stew and bread. At ten-thirty, by his advice, we appointed Hank as spokesman and sergeant, with Boldini as interpreter, 'fell in' in front of the galley, and awaited events like a squad on parade.

'Eats at eleven, hot and plentiful, Slushy,' said Hank, as the cook came to the galley-door in obvious surprise at the orderly disciplined assembly.

The cook snarled and swore.

'Do he want me to make signs to him?' asked Hank of the interpreter.

Boldini informed the cook that the draft knew precisely what its rights were, and that it was going to have them. If there was delay or shortage, or if anybody suffered any ill effects from the food, the big man was going to beat him to a jelly.

Then, lest the cook should complain, and there be trouble at Oran, the big man was coming with a few staunch friends to see that the cook disappeared overboard, during the night! Oh, yes, we were a desperate gang, old soldiers who wouldn't be swindled, and the big man was ex-Champion Heavy Weight of America. Also, if we were well and plentifully fed, we might refrain from reporting the cook's robberies and swindles in the proper quarter . . .

The cook affected immense amusement, but I thought his laughter a trifle forced, as Hank's grim leathern face creased and broke into a dental smile that held no love.

'Squad'll parade right here at eleven, *pronto*, for the hand-out, Slushy,' said Hank. 'Be on time – and stay healthy . . . Squad – dismiss.'

'*Rompez!*' shouted Boldini, and then made all clear to the cook.

At eleven, Hank's sergeant-like crisp bawl, 'Recruits – *fall in*,' could be heard all over the ship; Buddy appointed himself bugler and whistled an obvious dinner-call, and Boldini roared, '*Rangez-vous, légionnaires!*'

The way in which the order was obeyed, made it clear to me that I was about the only recruit who was not an old soldier. There was nothing to be surprised at in this, however, since most continental armies are conscript, and every man is a soldier. Certainly Hank and Buddy had been in the army. Later I learned that they had together adorned the ranks of that fine and famous corps, the Texas Rangers.

Without a word, the cook filled the *gamelles* with hot stew, and Hank passed one to each man, together with a loaf. He then gave the order to dismiss, and we sat us down and fed in contentment and good-humour.

At eventide the scene was repeated, and again we ate, and then we sat and smoked and listened to the Munchausenesque tales of Boldini, who had certainly 'seen life' as he said.

He was boastful and he was proud of escapades that did him little credit. If he spoke the truth, he was a brave man and a very dishonest one. He plainly revealed himself as extremely cunning, tricky, avaricious, and grasping. And yet, with all his cleverness and greed, here he was, glad to accept a *sou* a day again, to keep himself from starving.

Buddy did not like him.

'A crook,' opined he. 'Crooked as a snake with the belly-ache . . .'

Early on the third day we sighted the African coast.

After breakfast – *soupe* and bread again – Buddy requested Boldini to ask the cook to step outside.

'What for?' asked the cook contemptuously.

Buddy requested that the man should be informed that he was a coyote, a skunk, a low-lifer, a way down ornery bindlestiff, a plate-licking dime-pinching hobo, a dodgasted greaser, a gol-durned sneak-thief, and a gosh-dinged slush-slinging poke-out-pinching piker.'

Boldini merely said:

'The little man calls you a mean lying thief and a cowardly mangy cur . . . He spits on you and he wants to fight you. He is a *very* little man, *chef*.'

He was, and the cook rushed out to his doom. I fancy myself as an amateur boxer. Buddy was no amateur and the cook was no boxer. I thought of a fat sluggish snake and an angry mongoose, of which Uncle Hector had once told us.

It was not a fight so much as an execution. Buddy was a dynamic ferocity, and the thieving scoundrel was very badly damaged.

When he could, or would, rise no more, Hank dragged the carcase into the galley, reverently bared his head, and softly closed the door, as one leaving a death-chamber.

'He's restin'. Hush!' he murmured.

Hank and Buddy never held official rank in the muster-roll of the Legion, but they held high rank in the hearts of the *légionnaires* who knew them. That recruit-squad would certainly have followed them anywhere, and have obeyed them blindly.

Sandstone cliffs appeared, opened out to a tiny harbour, and we approached a pier.

We were at Oran, and the Corporal, who was supposed to be in charge of us made his first appearance on our fore-deck, formed us up, and handed the squad over to a Sergeant, who came on board for the purpose.

The Sergeant called the roll of our names, ascertained that we could 'form fours,' 'form two deep' and turn left and right correctly, and then marched us ashore.

'I am in Africa!' said I to myself, as we tramped through the wide clean streets of the European-looking little town.

Down a street of flat-roofed houses we marched, and across the broad *place*, stared at by half-naked negroes, burnous-clad Arabs, French soldiers, ordinary European civilians, and promenading ladies and officers.

On through more wide streets to narrow slums and alleys we went, till at length the town was behind us and the desert in front.

For an hour or more we marched by a fine road across the desert, up the sandstone hills on to the cliff-top, until we came in sight of an old and ugly building, another obsolete Fort St. Jean, which Boldini said was Fort St. Thérèse and our present destination.

Into the courtyard of this barrack-hostelry we marched, and here the roll of our names was again called, this time by a *sous-officier*. All were present and correct, the goods were delivered, and we were directed to break off and follow our Sergeant to a barrack-room.

As I went in behind him, with Boldini and the German, Glock, behind me, a well-known voice remarked.

'Enter the Third Robber.' *It was Digby's.*

Michael and Digby were sitting side by side on a bench, their hands in their pockets, their pipes in their mouths, and consternation upon their faces!

'Good God!' exclaimed Michael. 'You unutterable young fool! God help us! . . .'

I fell upon them. While I shook Michael's hand, Digby shook my other one, and while I shook Digby's hand, Michael shook my head. They then threw me upon the common 'bed' (about twenty feet long and six broad) and shook my feet, finally pulling me on to the ground. I arose and closed with Digby, and Michael pushed us both over. We rose and both closed with Michael, until all three fell in a heap.

We then felt better, and realised that we were objects of interest and concern, alike to our acquaintances and to the strangers within our gates.

'Gee!' said Buddy. 'Fightin' already! Beat 'em up, Bo.'

'Dorg-fight,' observed Hank. 'Chew their ears, son.'

'Mad English,' shrugged Vogué, the French embezzler. 'They fight when civilised people embrace.'

Boldini was deeply interested.

'Third *robber*!' he said on a note of mingled comment and enquiry to Glock.

'Beau and Dig,' said I, 'let me introduce two shore-enough blowed-in-the-glass, dyed-in-the-wool, whole-piece White Men from God's Own Country – Hank and Buddy . . . My brothers, Michael and Digby.'

They laughed and held out their hands.

'Americans possibly,' said Digby.

'Shake,' said Hank and Buddy as one man, and the four shook gravely.

'Mr. Francesco Boldini,' said I. 'My brothers,' and neither Michael nor Digby offered his hand to the Italian, until that gentleman reached for it effusively.

'I think wine is indicated, gentlemen,' he said, and eyeing us in turn, added, '"*when we three robbers meet again*," so to speak.' Michael invited Hank and Buddy to join us, and Boldini led the way and did the honours of Fort St. Thérèse.

In this canteen the wine was as good as, and even cheaper than, the wine at Fort St. Jean – cheaper than ordinary draught-beer in England.

We three sat, drinking litle, and watching the others drink a good deal, for which Michael insisted on paying.

We were soon joined by some old *légionnaires*, who appeared to be stationed permanently at the place, and, from them and Boldini, heard innumerable lurid stories of the Legion, for the truth of all of which they vouched, with earnest protestations and strange oaths. I noticed that the earnestness protestations and strangeness of the latter were in inverse proportion to the probability of the former.

'I perceive we are not about to enter "*an academy for the sons of gentlemen where religious and moral training, character-forming and development of the intelligence, are placed before examination-cramming*," my son,' observed Digby to me, quoting from the syllabus of our preparatory school, as we left the canteen.

'No,' said I, 'but it sounds an uncommonly good school for mercenary soldiers' (and we found that it was certainly that).

'One hopes that this is not a fair sample of our future home-life and domestic surroundings,' remarked Michael as we entered the barrack-room.

It was an utterly beastly place, dark, dirty, and depressing, its sole furniture being the great wooden guard-bed before mentioned (which was simply a huge shelf, innocent of mattress or covering, on which a score or so of men could lie side by side), a heap of evil-looking brown blankets in a corner, and a couple of benches. The place would have disgraced a prison if used as a common cell.

However, Boldini assured us that things would be quite different at the depôt at Saida or Sidi-bel-Abbès – and I assumed that to be different they must be better, for they couldn't be worse.

Our evening meal was the now familiar *soupe* and bread, and Boldini told us that the unvarying African daily ration was half a pound of meat and three *sous* worth of vegetables served as stew, a pound and a half of bread, half an ounce of coffee, and half an ounce of sugar. He said it was nourishing and sufficient but deadly monotonous, and, as to the latter, I was prepared to believe him. The prospect of two meals a day, and those eternally and undeviatingly similar, seemed unexhilarating and I said so.

'One gets used to it,' said Boldini, 'just as one gets used to "eternally" washing with soap and water. If you are content to wash daily with soap and water you can be content to feed daily on *soupe* and bread . . . Or do you occasionally wash with champagne and a slice of cake – or hot tea and a lump of coal – as a change from the "eternal" water and soap? . . .'

'Of course,' he added impudently, 'if you are going to come the fine gentleman and swell mobsman . . .'

'Don't be an ass, Boldini,' said I, with a cold stare. 'Or at any rate, try not to be an ass.'

He eyed me speculatively and complied. Master Boldini struck me as a gentleman who would need keeping in his place. Whatever that might be, it was not going to be one of the offensive familiarity that breeds contempt. I was not quite certain, but I was under the impression that 'swell mobsman' was a thieves'-kitchen term for a well-dressed and 'gentlemanly' swindler, burglar, and general criminal, in a superior way of business.

After *soupe*, there was nothing to do but to return to the canteen, as we were not allowed to leave the Fort. We spent the evening there, and I was glad to see that Beau and Digby seemed to like Hank and Buddy as much as I did, and that the two Americans, so far as one could judge of the feelings of such taciturn people, reciprocated.

Digby constituted himself host, and everybody was quite happy and well-behaved.

With one or two exceptions, none of the recruits, whether of my own draft, or of that with which my brothers had come, struck me as interesting.

They were just a fairly representative collection of very poor men from France, Belgium, Germany (chiefly Alsace and Lorraine), Spain, Austria, and Switzerland.

They looked like labourers, artisans, soldiers in mufti, newspaper-sellers, shop-boys, clerks, and the usual sort of men of all ages whom one would see in the poorer streets of any town, or in a Rowton House.

They certainly did not look like rogues and criminals.

Two or three, out of the couple of dozen or so, were well-dressed and well-spoken, and one of them, I felt sure, was an ex-officer of the French or Belgian army.

At any rate, he had 'soldier' stamped all over him, was well-dressed, smart, dapper, and *soigné*; was well-educated and had charming manners. He called himself Jean St. André, but I suspected a third name, with a *de* in front of it. He had rather attached himself to us three, and we all liked him.

It struck me that community of habits, tastes, customs, and outlook form a stronger bond of sympathy than community of race; and that men of the same social caste and different nationality were much more attracted to each other than men of the same nationality and different caste . . .

When the canteen closed, Beau proposed that we should shorten the night as much as possible, and spend the minimum of time in that loathsome cell, lying packed like sardines on the bare boards of the guard-bed shelf, with a score of men and a million insects.

Digby observed that the sandy ground of the courtyard would be no harder and much cleaner; and the air, if colder, infinitely preferable to the fug of the Black Hole of St. Thérèse.

We selected an eligible corner, seated ourselves in a row propped against the wall, still warm from the day's sunshine, and prepared for a night under the wonderful African stars.

'Well, my poor, dear, idiotic, mad pup – and what the devil do you think you're doing here?' began Michael, as soon as we were settled and our pipes alight.

'Fleeing from justice, Beau,' said I. 'What are you?'

'Same thing,' replied Michael.

'And you, Dig?' I asked.

'Who, me?' answered Digby. 'Well, to tell you the truth, I, personally, am, as it were, what you might call – er – fleeing from justice . . .

'*Three* fleas,' he observed, breaking a long silence.

'Did you bring the "Blue Water" with you, John?' asked Digby.

'No,' I said. 'No, I didn't bring it with me.'

'Careless,' remarked Digby.

'Did you bring it, Beau?' I asked.

'Yes,' answered Michael.

'Careful,' commented Digby.

'Did you bring it with you too, Dig?' I enquired.

'Never travel without it,' was the reply.

'I suppose one of us three has got it,' I said wearily.

'Two of us,' corrected Digby.

'Oh, yes, it's here all right,' said Michael. 'What would be the good of our being here if it were not?

'Bring us up to date about things,' he added. 'How's everybody bearing up?'

I told them the details of my evasion; of how I had declined an interview with Aunt Patricia; of how the shock of somebody's disgraceful behaviour had been too much for the Chaplain's health; of the respective attitudes of Augustus, Claudia, and Isobel.

'It *is* rough on Claudia,' said Michael, 'and, in a different way, on the poor old Chaplain.'

'And in a different way, again, on Aunt Patricia,' I observed.

'Thirty thousand pounds,' mused Digby. 'What price dear Uncle Hector, when she breaks it to him? He'll go mad and bite her.'

'Doesn't bear thinking of,' said I.

'Deuced lucky for young Gussie that Isobel was able to clear him,' mused Digby.

'That's what makes it so hard on Claudia – or would have done, if we hadn't bolted,' said Michael. 'Gussie and Isobel being out of it – it was she or one of us . . .'

In the silence that followed, I was aware of a sound, close beside us, where a buttress of the wall projected. Probably a rat or some nocturnal bird; possibly a dog.

'Well – it *was* one of us,' said Michael, 'and we have demonstrated the fact. We've overdone it a bit, though.

'Why couldn't you have enjoyed your ill-gotten gains in peace, at home, John?' he went on. 'Or left me to enjoy mine abroad! Why this wholesale emigration?'

'Yes,' agreed Digby, 'absolute mob. They won't be able to decide whether we were all in the job together, or whether we're chasing each other to get a share of the loot.'

'No,' said Michael. 'Problem'll worry them like anything.'

'When are we to let them know we're in the Legion, Beau?' I asked.

'We're not there yet,' was the reply.

'When we are,' I pursued.

'Dunno . . . Think about it,' said Michael.

'Don't see why we should let 'em know we're all there together,' said Digby. 'Better if one was at, or up, the North Pole, the other up the South Pole, and the third sitting on the Equator. More mystery about it – and they wouldn't know which to chase first.'

'Something in that,' agreed Michael. 'If we are all together (since you two have come), we are obviously all implicated – all three thieves. If we are scattered, two of us must be innocent. There is a doubt on each of us, but not a stain on any particular one of us . . . Why write at all, in fact? We are just runaway criminals. They don't write home . . .'

'*My* strength is as the strength of ten, because my heart is puah,' bleated Digby.

'*My* strength will be as the strength of eleven if you don't shut up,' warned Michael.

'I don't see the point really, Beau,' I objected. 'We prove nothing at all by being scattered. We might still all be criminals. We could easily have planned to pinch the sapphire, to bolt in different directions, and to share the loot by meeting later on . . . Or we could share without meeting. One of us could dispose of it in Amsterdam or somewhere, bank the money, and send a third of it to each of the others by draft or cheque, or something . . .'

'Hark at the young criminal!' said Digby . . . 'Hasn't he got a mind?' . . .

'What I mean is,' I explained, 'it's a bit rough on – er – those that are left at home, not to let them know where we are – alive or dead and all that . . .'

'Thinking of Gussie?' asked Digby.

'Besides,' I went on, 'how are they to let us know if the damned thing turns up? . . . And how are we to know how they are getting on? . . .'

'True,' agreed Michael. 'We ought to let Aunt Patricia know that we are hale and hearty, and she ought to be in a position to let us know if anything happens or turns up. What we *don't* want to do meanwhile, is to spoil the impression that one of us is the thief . . . I still think it would help to keep suspicion on us, and to deepen the mystery, if we don't let it be known that we are all together . . . We don't want some fool saying that we three agreed to take the blame and share it, and so cleared out together to the same place . . . while the thief is still at Brandon Abbas . . .'

'Who *did* pinch the filthy thing?' said Digby, voicing once more the question that I had asked myself a thousand times.

'I did,' said Michael.

'Then why the devil don't you put it back?' asked Digby.

'Too late now,' answered Michael. 'Besides, I want to lie low and then sell it for thirty thousand pounds, five years hence; invest the money in various sound things, and have the income (of fifteen hundred to two thousand a year) for life . . . Live like Uncle Hector – sport, hunting, travel, big-game shooting, flat in town, clubs . . .'

'On Uncle Hector's money?' I said.

'Doubles the joy of it, what?' replied Michael.

'Funny thing that,' put in Digby. 'It's just what I'm going to do – except that I find one can't get more than about twenty thousand, and I'm going to put it into a South Sea Island plantation and an Island trading concern ... Have the best schooner in the Islands, and be my own supercargo ... Every third year, come home and live the gay life on my twenty-per-cent profits. I reckon to make about four thousand a year. Yes ... Marquesas, Apia, Honolulu, Tahiti, Papeete, Kanakas, copra, ukaleles, lava-lavas, surf-riding, Robert Louis Stevenson ...'

'What are you going to do with the "Blue Water" meanwhile?' I asked, humouring the humorists.

'Always carry it about with me,' said Digby. 'If I get an eye knocked out I shall wear it in the empty socket ... Blue-eyed boy ... Good idea, that ...'

'Or you might put it where the monkey put the nuts – develop a pouch in your cheek. Very simple for you, I should think,' I suggested.

'Both rotten ideas,' objected Michael. 'Marsupial is the tip. Kangaroo's custom. They carry about their young and their money and things in a sort of bag, you know ... in front ... accessible. I keep it on me, night and day – wash-leather pouch in a money-belt. I thought it all out beforehand, and bought the thing in London ... Got to kill the man before you can rob him. Hatton Garden diamond-merchants wear them when they travel. Round their little tummies under their little vests ...'

'What makes them all look so paunchy,' corroborated Digby.

'You haven't told us what *you* are going to do, John,' he went on. 'Are you going to lie low for the five years and then sell it? ... What are you going to do with the money?'

'Divide it with you and Beau,' I replied.

'Oh, stout fella,' approved Digby. 'He puts us to shame, Beau, doesn't he? Let's put him to death in return, and keep his share.'

'Quite,' agreed Michael. 'We've got to find out what he's done with it first, though ...'

And so we ragged and chatted, sitting there, three of the most incredibly foolish young fools in their folly, but perfectly care-free and leaving to the morrow what the morrow might bring forth ...

Towards morning we dozed, and the dawn found us cold, stiff, and aching, but quite happy. We were together; life, the world, and adventure were before us.

7

A third draft of recruits arrived after morning *soupe*, and we learnt that all were to be evacuated that day, one half going to Saida, the depôt of the Second Regiment of the Foreign Legion, and the remainder to Sidi-bel-Abbès, the depôt of the First Regiment.

The question that at once agitated our breasts was as to whether we could keep together.

We rather preferred the idea of the First Regiment to that of the Second, simply because it was the First; but we did not much care either way, provided we were not separated. To that we simply would not agree.

I was distinctly pleased to find that the two Americans wished to come with us.

They had no more intention of parting from each other than we three had, but provided that they could keep together they wanted to go where we went.

To us came Boldini as we strolled round the courtyard.

'Let's stick together, we four,' quoth he. 'I'm going to the First, and you'd better come too. I know all the ropes there, and can put you up to everything. Get you in right with the corporals . . . Sergeant Lejaune's a friend of mine . . .'

'We three are certainly going together,' said Michael, 'and we want the two Americans to come with us, and we prefer the First, on the whole. Have we any say in the matter?'

'Ten francs would have a say,' replied Boldini. 'They'd talk louder than six men. Put up the ten francs, and I can work it that we six go to the First . . . But why bother about the Americans? They are uncultivated people.'

'We're going to cultivate them,' punned Michael.

We produced the ten francs and Boldini departed to 'arrange' the matter, as he said.

Whether we owed anything to his efforts or not, I never knew. He may have 'squared' a corporal, or he may merely have notified our wish to go together to the *Premier Etranger*. Or, again, it may merely have been by chance that we found ourselves in the half detailed for Sidi-bel-Abbès.

As we 'fell in' to march to the station, I and St. André stood behind Michael and Digby, while Boldini and an English-speaking Swiss, named Maris, stood behind Hank and Buddy, who were next to Michael and Digby. Thus, when we 'formed fours,' my brothers and I and St. André made one 'four,' and Hank, Buddy, Boldini, and Maris the 'four' behind us.

This Maris seemed an excellent person. He had been a travelling valet and courier, and had all the experience, address, linguistic knowledge, and general ability to be expected of a person who could earn his living in that capacity. He attached himself to us because he liked the English, and was, as he naïvely observed, 'fond of gentlemen.' He was a smiling, pleasant fellow of agreeable manners and attractive appearance.

At Oran station we entrained in about the poorest and slowest conveyance ever drawn by steam. This specimen of the West Algerian Railway Company's rolling-stock made its way from Oran to Sidi-bel-Abbès at an average rate of ten miles an hour, and in spite of the novelty of the scenery and of the population of the wayside stations, we grew very weary of it.

Our two 'fours' and a couple of Germans filled one compartment, and we whiled away the time by questioning Boldini concerning life in the Legion, and by listening to his innumerable stories.

It seemed somewhat dream-like to me, to be sitting in a tiny bare third-class railway-carriage, somnolently rolling across Africa in company with my brothers, two Americans, an ex-officer of a continental army, an Anglo-Indian Italian, a Swiss courier, and a pair of German workmen, listening to tales of a life as far removed from that of Europe as are the Arabian Nights.

Watching the slowly-passing scenery of the country-side, I was surprised at its difference from what one might have expected in Africa, it being neither of desert nor jungle, but a cultivated country of fields, farms, orchards, and gardens. It was not until we were approaching our destination that sand-hills and desert encroached and a note of wildness and savagery prevailed.

Negro and Arab boys and men brought fruit to our window at every station, and very fine grapes, oranges, melons, and figs could be bought extremely cheaply.

'This is all right,' remarked Digby, who was always very fond of fruit, 'if one can get fruit at this price in Sidi-bel-Abbès.'

'Yes,' said Boldini drily, 'if you devote your entire income entirely to fruit, you'll be able to get a little every day of your life.'

A halfpenny a day for fruit does not sound much, but the devotion of one's total income to it seems excessive.

'No income tax?' asked Digby, and we were relieved, if surprised, to hear that there was none.

We reached Sidi-bel-Abbès Station in the evening, and were received by a sergeant and corporals, were lined up and marched off, in fours, along a broad road. At the station gate I noticed a picket of non-commissioned officers, who sharply scrutinised all who passed it.

As we marched along, I got a somewhat Spanish impression of the town, probably because I heard the tinkling of a guitar and saw some women with high combs and mantillas, among the nondescript Europeans who were strolling between the yellow houses. Entering the town itself, through a great gate in the huge ramparts, we were in a curiously hybrid Oriental-European atmosphere in which moved stately Arabs, smart French ladies, omnibuses, camels, half-naked negroes, dapper officers, crowds of poor Jewish-looking working-folk, soldiers by the hundred, negroes, grisettes, black newspaper boys selling the *Écho d'Oran*, pig-tailed European girls, Spaniards, Frenchmen, Algerian Jews, Levantines, men and women straight from the Bible, and others straight from the Boulevards, Arab policemen, Spahis, Turcos, Zouaves, and Chasseurs d'Afrique.

No less hybrid was the architecture, and the eye passed from white gleaming mosque with glorious minaret to gaudy café with garish lights; from showy shops to shuttered Oriental houses; from carved balconies and coloured tiles to municipal clock-towers and enamel advertisements; from Moorish domes and arches to French newspaper kiosks and lamp-posts; from Eastern bazaars to Western hotels and clubs and Government offices and secretariats.

And almost everywhere were beautiful avenues of palms and groves of olives, ably seconding the efforts of Moorish mosque and Arab architecture in the unequal struggle between artistic Oriental romance and vulgar Occidental utilitarianism. Hybridism insisted through other senses too, for the ear caught now the *'Allah Akbar! Lah illah il Allah! Ya Saidna Mohammed rais ul Allah!'* of the muezzin on the minaret; the shouting of an angry Spanish woman; the warning cries in *sabir* of a negro driver; snatches of French conversation from passing soldiers; the loud wrangling in Arabic of a police *goumier* and some camelmen; and a strange haunting chorus from behind a wall, of:

'Travaja la muqueir
Travaja bono
Bono bezef la muqueir
Travaja bono.'

And to the nostrils were wafted scents of Eastern food and Western drink, camel-dung fires and Parisian patchouli; Eastern spices and Western cooking; now the odour of unwashen Eastern men, now of perfumed Western women.

'Kind of "Algeria at Olympia," this,' observed Digby. 'Good spot. Reminds one of Widdicombe.'

Turning from a main thoroughfare we entered a lane that ran between the barracks of the Spahi cavalry and those of the Foreign Legion.

Through the railings of great iron gates we could see a colossal three-story yellow building, at the far side of a vast expanse of parade ground.

'Our College,' remarked Digby.

On either side of the gates were guard-house and prison.

A small door was opened beside the gates, and we filed through.

The guard, seated on a long bench outside the guard-house, observed us without enthusiasm. The Sergeant of the Guard emerged and looked us over, and then closed his eyes, while he slowly shook his head.

A knot of men, clad in white uniform with wide blue sashes round their waists, gathered and regarded us.

'*Mon Dieu*!' said one, 'there's that blackguard Boldini back again. As big a fool as he is a knave, evidently!'

Boldini affected deafness.

And then appeared upon the scene the only man I have ever met who seemed to me to be bad, wholly bad, evil all through, without a single redeeming virtue save courage.

He came from the regimental offices, a fierce-looking, thick-set, dark man, with the face and figure of a prize-fighter; glaring and staring of eye, swarthily handsome, with the neck and jowl of a bull-dog. He also had the curious teeth-baring, chin-protruding jaw-thrust of a bull-dog, and there were two deep lines between the heavy beetling brows.

A digression: This was Colour-Sergeant Lejaune, a terrible and terrifying man, who had made his way in the Legion (and who made it further still) by distinguishing himself among distinguished martinets as a relentlessly harsh and meticulous disciplinarian, a savagely violent taskmaster, and a punishing non-com. of tremendous energy, ability, and courage.

To his admiring superiors he was invaluable; to his despairing subordinates he was unspeakable. He was a reincarnation and lineal descendant of the overseers who lashed the dying galley-slaves of the Roman triremes, and as different from the officers as were the overseers from the Roman centurions.

He would have made a splendid wild-beast tamer, for he had all the courage, strength, forceful personality, hardy over-bearing consciousness of superiority, and contemptuous, callous brutality required in that bold, ignoble profession. And it pleased him to regard himself as one, and to treat his legionaries as wild beasts; as dangerous, evil, savage, criminal brutes, instead of as what they were – fairly representative specimens of the average population of the countries from which they came.

Nor should it be supposed that Colour-Sergeant Lejaune was himself a typical representative specimen of his class, the Legion non-com. Though these men are usually harsh and somewhat tyrannical martinets, they are not villainous brutes.

Lejaune was. He took an actual delight in punishing, and nothing angered him more than to be unable to find a reason for doing it.

Probably he began by punishing (to the fullest extent of his powers and opportunity), in order to secure the most perfect discipline and to display his zeal, efficiency, and worth as a strong non-com.; and, from that, came to punish as a habit, until the habit became a taste, and then a lust and an obsession.

And later, through the coming to the Legion of a deserter from the Belgian army, we learnt a sinister, significant, and explanatory fact.

Lejaune had been dismissed from the Belgian Congo service for brutalities and atrocities exceeding even the limit fixed by good King Leopold's merry men.

There had been an exposure engineered by foreign missionaries, a world-wide scandal, and some white-washing – in the course of which Lejaune had been washed out.

From being a sergeant of the Belgian army, and a Congo rubber-station factor, autocratic, well-paid, and with absolute power, he had become a legionary, and by forcefulness, energy, and courage had made good.

Once more he had scope for the brutality, violence, and ferocious arrogance that had been his assets in the Belgian Congo, of terrible memory.

At times he was undoubtedly mad, and his madness took the form of sadistic savagery.

Upon this man, Boldini certainly had some claim, or between them there was some bond, for Lejaune never punished Boldini, and they were at times seen in private confabulation, though, of course, no non-commissioned officer ever walked out, nor drank, with a private soldier.

The Belgian deserter, one Vaerren, declared that Boldini had been a civilian subordinate in the Congo, and in Lejaune's district, and had been imprisoned for peculation and falsifying his trade returns. Of the truth of this I know nothing, but I do know that Lejaune favoured the man and procured his promotion to Corporal, when he himself became Sergeant-Major.

And it was into the hands of this Lejaune that we were now delivered.

To resume: Colour-Sergeant Lejaune called the roll of our names and looked us over.

Noting the insignificant stature of Buddy, a pocket Hercules, his face set in a contemptuous sneer.

'An undersized cur,' he remarked to the Sergeant of the Guard.

'Guess I've seen better things than you dead on a sticky fly-paper, anyhow,' replied Buddy promptly.

Mercifully Lejaune knew no English – but he knew that a wretched recruit had dared to open his miserable mouth.

'Silence, dog!' he roared. 'Open your foul lips again, and I'll close them for a month with my boot . . . Speak again, you hound, and I'll kick your teeth down your throat.'

Buddy had not understood a word. He had seen a sneer, and heard contemptuous words; and he had dared to presume upon being an ignorant recruit, not even in uniform. Now he heard an angry roar, and was too old a soldier to do anything but stiffen to attention.

It was borne in upon him that there was *some* pep to Legion sergeants, and they were *some* roosters, on their own dung-hill. Better argue with a New York cop on Broadway at midnight, than to donate back-chat to the rough-neck.

But the mischief was done, and Buddy was a marked man. More, any friend of Buddy was a marked man, and any friend of his friend's, unto the third and fourth generation.

When the bloodshot eye of Colour-Sergeant Lejaune fell upon Boldini, it halted, and a long look passed between the two men. Neither spoke.

Upon us three Gestes he looked with disfavour.

'Runaway pimps,' he said. 'Show me your hands.'

We held them out.

'Going to tell our fortunes . . . Beware of a dark ugly man,' whispered Digby to me.

The Colour-Sergeant regarded our decently kept hands and snorted: 'I'll harden those for you, by God . . . Never done a stroke of work in your lives . . . I'll manicure you before you die . . . I'll make you wish you had gone to gaol instead.'

He looked Hank over.

'A lazy hulk, I'll take my oath,' he observed. 'I'll teach you to move quickly, in a way that'll surprise you,' he promised.

'Shore, Bo,' replied Hank mildly, wishing to be polite, though ignorant of what had been said to him. 'Spill another mouthful,' he added encouragingly.

'Silence, you chattering ape from the trees!' roared Lejaune. 'Speak again and I'll tie your wrists to your ankles in the small of your back for a week. By God, I'll cripple you for life, you two-legged talking camel.'

And Hank also grasped that silence is frequently more than gold and speech much less than silver.

Having duly impressed the draft, Colour-Sergeant Lejaune announced that the Seventh Company would be afflicted with the lot of us, and serve it right. He then suddenly roared:

'*Garde à vous! Pour defiler! Par files de quatre, à droit*,' and looked eagerly and anxiously for a victim. His face clouded with chagrin and disappointment. The draft had moved like guardsmen. Those who understood French had sprung to attention and turned like machines, and those who did not understand the actual words had moved with them.

'*En avant . . . Marche!*' he concluded, and we stepped off like the old soldiers most of us were.

Across the drill-ground we marched to the storeroom of the *fourrier-sergent* of the Seventh Company, and received our kit which, in addition to two cloth uniforms, included white fatigue uniforms, linen spats, underclothing, the blue woollen sash or cummerbund, cleaning materials, soap and towels, but no socks, for the Legion does not wear them.

We were then inspected by the *adjudant-major*, who corresponds to the English adjutant (whereas the *adjudant* is a non-commissioned officer), and marched by a corporal to our *casernes*, or barrack-rooms.

Going up staircases and along corridors, a squad of ten of us, including Boldini, St. André, Vogué, Maris, Glock, Buddy, Hank, my brothers, and myself, were directed to our room – a huge, clean, well-ventilated bare chamber, in which were thirty beds. Here we were handed over to some *légionnaires*, who were polishing their belts, cartridge-pouches, and accountrements.

'*Bleus*,' said Corporal Dupré to these men. 'Show them what to do, Schwartz, Colonna, Brandt, Haff, and Delarey . . . Kit, bedding, *paquetage*, *astiquage*, everything. Don't go *en promenade* before they know their boots from their *képis*.'

'All right, Corporal,' said one of the men, and when the Corporal had gone out, changed his tone as he went on:

'The devil damn all *bleus*. Why couldn't you go to hell, instead of coming here to waste our time? . . . However, you shall repay us in the canteen. Come on, get to work now, and the sooner we can get to the bottles . . .'

But Boldini had a word to say.

'Wriggle back into the cheese you crawled out of, you one-year, half-baked imitation of a soldier,' he snapped. 'I was a legionary and fought in Madagascar, Morocco, and the Soudan when you were in the foundling orphanage.'

'Name of a name of a name of a name!' gabbled one of the men, 'if it isn't old Boldini come back!' and he roared with laughter and threw himself on a bed.

'Wait till I'm a corporal, friend Brandt,' said Boldini. 'I'll make you laugh louder than that.'

He did not have to wait, however, as the man redoubled his yells of laughter.

The return of Boldini, for some reason, struck him as a most priceless joke.

'Here, you Colonna, Schwartz, and Haff, take those five and I'll attend to these,' said Boldini; and proceeded to direct us to appropriate beds and put our kit on them.

He then gave us a clever exhibition of clothes-folding, and built up a secure and neat little *paquetage* of uniform and kit on the shelf above his bed.

'There you are – do that first,' said he. 'Everything in elbow-to-finger-tip lengths, piled so,' and we set about folding coats, trousers, overcoats, and kit, as he had done, and putting the pile on the shelf at the head of the bed as there was no kit-bag or box of any sort.

Having done this, we had our first lesson in *astiquage*, the polishing of belts, and cartridge-pouches, with wax and rags; and then in rifle-cleaning.

We were next conducted downstairs and out to the concrete open-air *lavabo*, and shown where to wash our white canvas fatigue-uniforms. We were then hurried to the canteen, that we might do our duty to our comrades of the *escouade* and pay our footing.

The scene here resembled that in the canteens of Forts St. Jean and St. Thérèse, save that the men were all *légionnaires*, of course, and the person behind the bar was a woman – a veritable French *vivandière* and *fille du regiment*.

Here again, a few francs procured an incredible quantity of wine and all was harmony, noise, and hectic gaiety of the kind induced by alcohol. Returning to our barrack-room at the call of the 'Lights out' bugle, we completed our preparations for the morrow by the meagre light of the *caserne* night-lamp.

We gathered that we should be aroused by the *garde-chambre* at five-fifteen in the morning, and should have to be on recruit-parade at five-thirty in white uniform and sash, with knapsack, rifle, belts, and bayonet, and that everything must be immaculate and shining. Also that, before quitting the room, the blankets and mattresses of the bed must be folded and piled, and arranged to a hairbreadth accuracy, and the floor beneath the bed swept clean.

Apparently this cleanliness need not extend to the person, for there were no washing facilities of any sort in the room, nor on the whole of that floor of the barracks, nor on the one below. An eccentric, in search of a morning wash, had to make his way down four flights of stairs to a rude and crude kind of lavatory on the ground-floor.

As the *garde-chambre* saw no reason to arouse himself more than a quarter of an hour before he was himself due for parade, and then had to fetch the coffee-pail before arousing the others, this was apt to be a crowded quarter of an hour of inglorious life.

So, with the conscientious fears of the ignorant novice, at least one recruit endeavoured to have everything right and ready before he went to bed, and secretly determined to wake himself at half-past four next morning, to make a good beginning.

Michael's bed was in the corner by the huge window, Boldini's was next, Digby's next, and then that of an Italian calling himself Colonna. Mine came next, then Brandt's, then Buddy's, then Haff's, and then Hank's – always an old *légionnaire* next to a recruit, and so on throughout the room.

In the corner by the door, was the bed of Corporal Dupré, who was in command of the *escouade* and in charge of the room.

He was an active, noisy, bustling person, humorous and not unkindly when sober; when overfull of canteen wine he was sullen, suspicious, and dangerous. Being very fond of wine he was easily approachable by anyone who chose to provide it – or rather the means of purchasing it.

While we three and the Americans were gathered in a group, putting the last touches to our kit and extracting information and advice from Boldini, he came into the room, undressed and went to bed.

As he lay down he bawled:

'Silence! If any man makes a sound, between now and sunrise, he'll make the next sound in hospital,' and fell asleep.

We got into our beds in a silence that could be felt.

I remained awake, because I was anxious to go to sleep; and lay thinking of Isobel, of what was happening at Brandon Abbas, of our strange position, and of the 'Blue Water.'

When I thought of what now lay before me, I was unutterably thankful that my guess, or instinct, had been right, and that I was with Michael and Digby.

It would have been rather terrible to find myself in this galley alone. With Beau and Digby here, it would be just adventure – hard, rough, and dangerous, no doubt – but no easy flowery path leads to any place worth arriving at.

And what of Michael and Digby? They each still pretended to be the culprit, which was doubly as absurd an idea as that either one of them should be.

Michael's look had been one of sheer horror and consternation when he had caught sight of me at Fort St. Thérèse, and he had seemed to feel that my flight was a complication and a catastrophe on which he had never reckoned.

Had he felt the same about Digby, or had Digby known more than he told me? I must try to find out . . .

I fell asleep and was awakened, apparently a minute later, by the *garde-chambre* shouting something as he lit a big central lamp that hung from the ceiling.

Men sat up in bed; each took a tin mug from a hook below the shelf above his head, and held it out to the *garde-chambre*, who went round with a great jug, giving everybody about half a pint of coffee. It was hot, strong, and good.

The Corporal shouted:

'*Levez-vous! Levez-vous!*' and then, as on the Eve of Waterloo, 'there was hurrying to and fro – and sudden partings,' if not 'tremblings of distress and cheeks all pale . . .'

Michael, Digby, and I rushed to the far-off lavatory, dashed our heads into water and fled back towelling.

I found my bed 'made,' my kit laid out neatly, my boots brushed, everything put ready as by a valet, and Brandt sweeping under my bed.

I stared in astonishment.

'A couple of *sous*, comrade!' said Brandt, and I understood. An income of a halfpenny a day is one that will stand a good deal of augmenting.

Turning to see if I could do anything for Michael or Digby, I found that Boldini and Colonna were before me, each earning in a few minutes, as a valet, what it took them two days to earn as a soldier.

In a surprisingly short time, all were dressed and ready, the *garde-chambre* had swept up the dust and dirt that the men had brushed out from under the beds, and Corporal Dupré had been round to see that the beds were properly made and everything tidy. Then, following upon a shout of '*Garde à vous*,' the Colour-Sergeant of the Company entered and inspected the room and the men.

All prayed that he might find no fault, for if he did, he would punish the Corporal, and the Corporal would punish the offenders tenfold.

In the French army, non-commissioned officers can, like prefects in our public schools, award punishments without reference to officers. They give the punishment, enter it in the *livre de punitions*, and there is an end of the matter – unless the officer, inspecting the book, increases the punishment by way of punishing the offender for getting punished.

The system enhances the power and position of the noncom. enormously, and undoubtedly makes for tremendous discipline – and some injustice and tyranny.

All was well this morning, however, and the great man's iron face remained impassive, and his hard mouth unopened.

We took our Lebel rifles from the rack, put our bayonets in their frogs, and clattered down to the parade-ground at five-thirty, on that glorious cold morning.

The battalion marched away to field-exercises, and the recruits were formed up, told off by *escouades*, each under a corporal, and taken out to the 'plateau,' a vast drill-ground near the *village nègre*, for physical training, which to-day was simply steady running. It was nothing much for young athletes like us three, but a little cruel for half-starved or out-of-condition men, who had not run for some time.

On other mornings the physical culture took the form of gymnastics, boxing, or a long route-march.

On our return to barracks, wet and warm, we had our morning meal of *soupe* and bread, and a quarter-litre of good wine. Tin plates and *gamelles* were rattled out of hanging cupboards,and we sat at the long tables that occupied the centre of the big room. There was meat as well as vegetables in my excellent stew, and the bread, though grey, was palatable, and more than sufficient in quantity.

After a rest, the recruits had a lecture, and after that, squad and company drill, while the battalion did attack-formation exercise on the plateau.

After this we were set to work with brooms and wheelbarrows at tidying up around the barracks, and were then free to go to the *lavabo* to wash and dry our white uniforms.

At five o'clock we got our second meal, exactly like the first, and were then finished for the day, save in so far as we had to prepare for the next, in the way of cleaning and polishing the leather and metal of our arms and equipment – no small task, especially with stuff fresh from store.

Here the poverty of the Legion again helped us, for no man need do a stroke more than he wishes of this kind of work, while he has a halfpenny to spare.

We soon found that it was a real and genuine kindness to let a comrade have a go at our leather and brass, our rifles and bayonets, our dirty fatigue-suits and underclothing; for, to him, a job meant the means of getting a packet of *caporal* cigarettes, a bottle of wine, a postage-stamp, a change of diet, a piece of much-needed soap, or a chance to replenish his cleaning materials.

We three did not shirk our work, by any means, but very often, when weary to death, or anxious to go out of barracks, we gave our *astiquage* work to one of the many who begged to be allowed to do it.

The recruits progressed with astonishing speed, being practically all trained soldiers before they joined, and picked up the necessary Legion-French remarkably rapidly.

We three very soon became good soldiers, aided by our intelligence, strength, sobriety, athletic training, sense of discipline, knowledge of French, and a genuine desire to make good.

More fortunate than most, we were well-educated and had 'background'; a little money (thanks to Michael's forethought), which was wealth in the Legion; good habits, self-control, and a public-school training; and we were inoffensive by reason of possessing the consideration, courtesy, and self-respecting respect for others proper to gentlemen.

Less fortunate than most, we were accustomed to varied food, comfortable surroundings, leisure, a great deal of mental and physical recreation, spaciousness of life, and above all, *privacy*.

But at first, everything was new and strange, remarkable and romantic; we were Soldiers of Fortune, we were together, and we were by no means unhappy.

But oh, how I longed to see Isobel!

And gradually, wondering thoughts as to the 'Blue Water' and its whereabouts, retired to the back of my mind, for the world was too much with us altogether, for there to be time available for introspection or day-dreaming. Our days were too full and busy and our nights all too short for thought. They were scarce long enough for the deep dreamless sleep necessary to men who were worked as we were.

And how we blessed Sundays – those glorious life-saving days of complete rest.

On our first Sunday morning in the Legion, we three sat on Michael's bed and held a 'Council of War,' as we had so often done, in the days of the Band, at Brandon Abbas.

It was decided that I should write to Isobel, telling her where I was, and saying that I knew where Michael and Digby were, and could send them any messages or news.

Isobel was to use her discretion as to admitting that she knew where I was, but if she did admit it, she was to add – the simple truth – that she had not the slightest idea as to where the others were.

This plan was Michael's, and as he seemed keen on it, and neither Digby nor I saw anything against it, we adopted it, and I wrote a letter which she could show to Aunt Patricia, or not, as she liked.

I wrote as follows: –

'Légionnaire John Smith, No. 18896,
7th Company, Premier Étranger,
Sidi-bel-Abbès, Algeria.

Dear Isobel,

A letter to the above address will find me. Michael and Digby know it also. I can send them any messages, or news, from Brandon Abbas. Neither of them is in England. Either of them will let me know if he changes his present address. I am in excellent health. I shall write again if I hear from you. I am so anxious to know what is happening at home.

John.'

Michael and Digby approved of this, as it opened up a line of communication with Brandon Abbas, but made no change in the situation.

From what we had learnt, after discreet enquiries of Boldini, we had quite come to the conclusion that the English police would take no steps in pursuit of the legionary, John Smith, so long as he remained in the Legion, even though there were strong reasons for suspecting him to be John Geste who had disappeared at the time of the jewel-robbery.

But I privately inserted a scrap of paper on which was a message of undying and unalterable love to my sweetheart. This she could destroy, and the letter she could produce for Aunt Patricia's information or not, as might seem best to her in whatever circumstances arose . . .

On a Saturday night, a fortnight later, I got a private and personal love-letter that made me wildly happy and as proud as a peacock; and, with it, a long letter that I could send to Michael and Digby if I wished to do so.

This latter said that things were going on at Brandon Abbas exactly as before.

Aunt Patricia had, so far, communicated neither with the police nor with anybody else, and had taken no steps, whatsoever, in the matter.

Apparently she had accepted the fact that one of the three Gestes had stolen the 'Blue Water' – and, extraordinarily and incredibly, she was just doing nothing at all about it, but simply awaiting Uncle Hector's return.

She had released Augustus, Claudia, and Isobel herself, from the prohibition as to leaving the house, and had asked no questions of any of them since the day that I had disappeared. On that day, she had accepted the solemn assurance of Augustus, Claudia, and Isobel, that they knew *absolutely nothing* as to where the Gestes had gone, which of them was the thief, or whether they were in league.

'I cannot understand her,' she wrote, 'nor get at what she thinks and feels. She fully accepts, apparently, my exculpation of Gussie (and incidentally of myself at the same time) and scorns to suspect Claudia. She has told us that we are absolutely free from suspicion, and she wishes us to make no further reference to the matter at all. Gussie is, of course, unbearable. He has "*known all along that you would come to a bad end – the three of you,*" but while certain that you are all in it together, he believes that you, John, are the actual thief. I told him that I had a belief too, and when he asked what it was, I said, "*I believe that if you gave your whole soul to it, Gussie, you might possibly, some day, be fit to clean John's boots – or those of any other Geste . . .*" I also said that if he ever uttered another word on the subject I would discover, when the police came, that I had made a mistake in thinking that it was *his* arm I had held when the light failed! . . . Am I not a beast? But he does make me so angry with his sneers and conscious rectitude, the mean little rascal.

However, as I have said, the police have not come yet, and absolutely nothing is being done. The servants haven't a ghost of an idea that anything is wrong, and life goes on just as if you three had merely gone up to Oxford for this term. Burdon must wonder that you all went so suddenly and with so little kit, but I don't suppose it interests him much.

I don't know *what* Uncle Hector will say about the delay in going to Scotland Yard! It almost looks as though Aunt wants the culprit to escape, or else feels that Uncle Hector would prefer that there should be no public scandal if it could possibly be avoided, and the sapphire recovered privately. Somehow I can't think that Aunt would have any mercy on the thief, though – and I really don't think she'd suppose Uncle Hector would prefer this delay to scandal. Surely he is not the person to care twopence about scandal, and he certainly is not the person to approve a delay that may make recovery impossible. I can't make it out *at all.*

Fancy Uncle Hector robbed of thirty thousand pounds! He'll go raving mad and kill people!

Oh, John, where *is* the wretched thing? And how long will it be before you can all come back? I shall wire to you at once if it turns up, and I shall certainly come and see you if you don't come soon – for it's my private opinion that you are all three together! . . .'

I produced this letter for Michael and Digby to read, at our Sunday 'Council of War' next morning.

Michael read it without a word of comment, and with an inscrutable face.

Digby said, 'The little darling! I bet she comes out to Sidi if the thing doesn't turn up!' and he bounced on the bed, with glee, at the idea.

'Wonder what Uncle Hector will do?' said Michael. 'Poor Aunt Patricia will get a thin time . . .'

'For not preventing us from pinching it?' jeered Digby.

'No – for not calling in the police at once,' said Michael.

'I wonder why she didn't,' I remarked.

'Yes,' said Michael. 'Funny, isn't it?'

And yawning and turning round from the window, out of which we had been looking, I noticed that Boldini was asleep on his bed behind us. It was curious how quietly that man could move about, with his cat-like steps and silent ways.

8

Recruit-days passed swiftly away, and we were too busy and too tired to be wretched.

From five in the morning till five in the evening we were hard at it, and after that we had plenty to do in preparing our kit and accountrements for the morrow.

That done, or given to a needy comrade to do, we dressed in our walking out uniforms, according to the particular *ordre du jour*, and went for a walk in tawdry hybrid Sidi, or to hear the Legion's magnificent band in the Place Sadi Carnot, or the Jardin Publique. Usually we three went together, but sometimes the two Americans and St. André would accompany us, and Boldini whenever we could not shake him off.

He stuck to us closer than a brother sticketh, and after his first usefulness was over (and paid for), as we gained experience and learnt the ropes, we certainly did not desire his society for himself alone.

But apparently he desired ours, and ardently.

The more we saw of the two Americans, the better we liked them, and the same applied to St. André – but precisely the converse was true of Boldini.

However, we were not troubled by his presence when Buddy went out with us, for the American would have none of him, and scrupled not to say so with painful definiteness.

'Get to hell outa this, Cascara Sagrada,' he would say truculently. 'Don't wantcha. Go gnaw circles in the meadow and keep away from me with both feet . . . Skoot, son,' or some equally discouraging address.

Painful as this was, we were glad to profit by it, for Boldini waxed more and more offensively familiar. Put into words, the message of his manner to us three (his implications, and the general atmosphere he endeavoured to create) was:

'Come – we're all scoundrels together! Why this silly pretence of innocence and superiority? Let's be a united gang and share all loot' kind of idea.

I did not understand Buddy's virulent detestation of the man, though; and when I asked him about it one day, when he flatly refused to let Boldini join us in the canteen, all he could reply was:

'He's a rattlesnake with a silent rattle, and he's Lejaune's spy. You wanta watch out. He's on your trail fer somethin',' and Hank had confirmed this with a drawled, 'Shore, Bo, watch the critter.'

The first time that Boldini showed objection to Buddy's rudeness, the latter promptly invited him to come below and bring his fists – an invitation which Boldini declined (and was for ever the admitted inferior, in consequence).

Another person who most certainly watched us, and with a baleful boding eye, was Colour-Sergeant Lejaune himself, now, alas, Sergeant-Major.

We were, however, far too keen, careful, and capable to give him the opportunity he obviously desired.

When he came in for room-inspection, he made no pretence of not giving us and our kit, accoutrements, and bedding, a longer and more searching inspection than he gave to anybody else except Buddy.

When I met the long hard stare of his hot and cruel eyes, I thought of a panther or some other feral beast whose sole mental content was hate . . .

'We're sure *for* it, pard,' said Buddy to me, after one of these inspections. 'Our name's mud. That section-boss makes me feel like when I butted into a grizzly-b'ar. On'y I liked the b'ar better.'

'Yep,' agreed Hank. 'He's a grizzly-b'ar . . . But I've shot a grizzly-b'ar, I hev.

'They ain't immortial,' he added mildly.

It was also quite clear that Corporal Dupré had found that he had said the wrong thing when he replied to Lejaune's enquiry as to what sort of unspecified animals we were, by declaring that we were model recruits whose sole object appeared to be the meriting of his approval.

Corporal Dupré was not a bad fellow at heart, but 'he had got to live,' and it grew clearer and clearer, as the weeks went by, that we three could do nothing right and Boldini nothing wrong.

Our chief offence was that we would commit no offence, but we felt we walked on very thin ice . . .

In less than a couple of months we were dismissed recruit-drills and became full-blown *légionnaires*.

Above the head of my bed appeared a printed paste-board card, bearing the legend, *John Smith, No.* 18896, *Soldat* 2ème *Classe*, and I was a (second-class) Soldier of Fortune, taking my place in the ranks of my battalion. In time I should be a *Soldat* 1ère *Classe*, if I were good.

Michael, Digby, the two Americans, Maris, and St. André came to the battalion at the same time, and our little party kept together.

We now learned what marching really is, and why the Legion is known in the Nineteenth Army Corps as the *cavalerie à pied*. The route-marches were of appalling length at an unvarying five kilometres an hour. Over English roads, in the English climate, and with the English soldier's kit, they would have been incredible. Over sand and desert stones, under the African sun, and with the much heavier kit of the legionary (which includes tent-canvas, firewood, a blanket, and a spare uniform), they were infinitely more so.

On one occasion we took a stroll of five hundred miles, marching continously at thirty miles a day, as the Colonel thought we wanted 'airing.'

In addition to these marches, we had admirable training in skirmishing and scouting, plenty of company and battalion drill, first-aid, field engineering, varied rifle-range work, and the theory of infantry warfare.

By the time we three felt ourselves old soldiers, we also began to feel we were stagnating mentally, and becoming mechanical, bored, and stale. Night after night of strolling about Sidi-bel-Abbès was not good enoug, and our brains were demanding exercise.

Michael decreed that we should study Arabic, both for the good of our souls and with a view to future usefulness at such time as we should be generals entrusted with diplomatic missions or military governorships.

Our Arabic proved useful before then.

We got books from the libary, engaged a half-caste clerk, who worked in the *Bureau Arabe*, to meet us for an hour, four evenings a week, for converstion; and took to haunting Arab cafés instead of French ones.

We distinctly liked the dignified and courteous men with whom we talked over the wonderful coffee.

We made rapid progress and, after a time, made a point of talking Arabic to each other. It is an easy language to learn, especially in a country where it is spoken.

And still Boldini haunted us like our shadow, Corporal Dupré waited for a chance to report us, and Lejaune bided his time.

But we were wary and we were unexceptionable soldiers. Even these skilful fault-finders and fault-makers could not get an opportunity, and we were favourably noticed by our Lieutenant (Debussy) and Captain (Renouf), of whom we saw all too little. Theirs to lead us in manoeuvres and war, the non-commissioned officers' to prepare us to be led. And in this the officers assisted them only by their authority. In every possible way, and some impossible ways, they upheld the power of the non-coms., backed them up on every occasion, took their word for everything, and supported them blindly.

There was no appeal. What the non-commissioned officer said, was true; and what he did, was right, as against the private soldier. The resulting discipline was wonderful – and so was the bitterness, hatred, and despair of some of the victims of injustice and personal spite.

A sergeant had only to continue punishing a victim, for the latter to earn the unfavourable notice of the officer, when the latter read the punishment book, and to find his punishment doubled – with a warning to beware lest something really serious happened to him.

The Americans were not as lucky, or not as careful, as we three. For one thing, they sometimes drank the appalling maddening filth sold in the low-class wine-shops of the Spanish quarter or the Ghetto. Crude alcohol made from figs, rice, or wood, and known as *bapédi, tchum-tchum*, and *genièvre*, would make Buddy's temper explosive and uncertain, while it rendered Hank indiscriminatingly affectionate and apt to fall heavily upon the neck of the Sergeant of the Guard, when the latter admitted him, singing joyously, in the watches of the night.

Then was Lejaune happy, and reminded them of how they had opened their mouths in his presence, upon the evening of their entry into the Legion.

When they were confined to barracks, he would have the defaulters' roll called at odd times, in the hope of their missing it, and, when they were in the *salle de police*, would see that the Sergeant of the Guard turned them out hourly, under pretence of suspecting that they had tobacco or drink.

Sometimes he would go himself to their cells, in the middle of the night, rouse them with a sudden roar, and give a swift, harsh order, in the hope that it would be disobeyed through resentment or 'drunken stupidity.

I think he would have given a month's pay to have succeeded in goading one of them into striking him. It was my constant fear that Buddy would do so. And daily we dinned this into their ears, and prayed that something of the sort would not happen. However, they were old soldiers and wily Americans . . .

And so the months passed, and every week I heard from my darling. Nothing happened at Brandon Abbas.

Gussie had gone to Sandhurst, the Chaplain was about again, and Uncle Hector had postponed his home-coming after all, and had gone to Kashmir to shoot bear, as he had had poor sport with tiger in the Central Provinces.

No reference was ever made to the missing 'Blue Water,' no questions had been asked of Isobel, and she had volunteered no information as to our whereabouts and her being in communications with me.

Also she would 'come into' her money on her next birthday, and she was then going to do a little travelling, and intended to wander in Algeria!

'Hope she comes before we go – or that we don't go before she comes,' said Digby, on learning this last piece of information – for we were full of hope that we should be among those selected for the big special draft that was going south before long.

Everyone knew that a battalion, a thousand strong, was going to 'demonstrate' on the border shortly, and 'demonstrating' meant further peaceful penetration with the bayonet, active service, and chances of distinction, decoration, and promotion.

If we did not go we should be bitterly disappointed, and lapse into mere bored and disillusioned victims of a monotonous soul-killing routine, daily doing the drill in which we were perfect; cursing the guard-mounting, sentry-go, and endless 'fatigues'; learning the things we knew by heart; performing the exercises and operations we could do blindfold; and dragging ourselves through the killing route-marches that we hated.

But what a cruel thing if we were selected and sent off just as Isobel was coming!

On the other hand, if we were not taken (and we were still very junior soldiers), we should at any rate have Isobel's visit to Sidi-bel-Abbès to look forward to.

So great was my longing to see her that, had I been alone, I really think that I should, at times, have toyed with the idea of 'going on pump,' 'making the promenade,' which all *légionnaires* continually discuss and frequently attempt. This 'going on pump,' whatever that may mean, is the Legion name for deserting, and generally consists in slow preparation and swift capture, or a few days' thirst-agony in the desert, and ignominious return, or else in unspeakable torture and multilation at the hands of the Arabs.

Less than one in a hundred succeed in escaping, for, in addition to the patrols, the desert, and the Arabs, the native armed-police *goumiers* receive a reward of twenty-five francs a head for the return of deserters, dead or alive.

Being matchless trackers, well-armed, good shots, and brave men, they are very successful bloodhounds.

However, the attempt is frequently made by maddened victims of injustice or of sheer monotony and hardship, and their punishment, when caught, varies from leniency to cruel severity, according to the degree of *cafard* from which they were suffering, and to the amount of uniform and kit they may have lost.

One man, whom I knew personally, when under sentence to appear before the supreme court martial of Oran, which in his case meant certain death, got clean away, and was known to have escaped from the country.

Several, whom I knew, went off into the desert and were either found dead and multilated, or never heard of more; and many either escaped and surrendered again, or were brought back running, or dragging on the ground, at the end of a cord tied to the saddle of an Arab police *goum* . . .

However, we had come here to make careers for ourselves as Soldiers of Fortune, and to become Generals in the Army of France, as other foreigners had done, from the ranks of the Legion. And we did our utmost to achieve selection for the picked battalion that was to march south for the next forward leap of the apostles of pacific penetration (or pacification of the newly-penetrated areas) of the Sahara of the Soudan.

9

One evening, at about this period of our depôt life, Maris, the Swiss ex-courier, came to me as I lay on my cot, resting and awaiting the return of Michael and Digby from *corvée*. Said he:

'I have something to tell you, Monsieur Smith. You have done me many a good turn, and you saved me from prison when my tunic was stolen and I could not have replaced it in time for the *adjudant's* inspection . . . Will you and your brothers meet me at Mustapha's at six to-night? It will be worth your while. We shall be safe enough there, especially if we talk in English . . .' and he glanced apprehensively round the busy room, and jerked his head towards Colonna and an Italian named Guantaio, who were working together at the table.

I thanked him and said that I would tell my brothers, and that if they returned in time, from the 'fatigue' on which they were engaged, we would look in at Mustapha's.

When Michael and Digby came in from the job of sweeping and weeding, for which they had been seized by a sergeant: I told them what Maris had said.

'Better go,' remarked Michael. 'Maris is the clean potato, I think. No harm in hearing it anyhow.'

Mustapha's was an Arab café, where we got splendid coffee very cheaply – thick, black, and sweet, with a drop of vanilla, a drop of hashish oil, or of opium, a drop of orange-essence, and other flavourings.

Here we rested ourselves on a big and very low divan, with a solid wall behind us, and awaited Maris, who came a few minutes later.

'It's like this, my friends,' said he, in his excellent English, when we had got our little clay cups of coffee steaming on the floor in front of us. 'I don't want to make what you call the mare's nest, isn't it? But Boldini is up to his tricks again . . . I have heard a lot about him from Vaerren and from old *légionnaires* who served with him before . . . He is the bad hat, that one. They say that Lejaune will get him made a corporal soon . . . Well, I have noticed things, I.

'Yes. And last night I was sitting in the Tlemcen Gardens. It was getting dark. Behind the seat were bushes, and another path ran by the other side. Some *légionnaires* came along it, and sat down on a seat that must have been just behind mine. They were talking Italian. I know Italian well, and I always listen to foreign languages . . . Yes, I shall be a courier again when the little trouble has blown over about the man I taught not to steal my fiancée, while I travel. Yes . . .'

He paused dramatically, and with much eye-rolling and gesticulation continued:

'Boldini it was, and Colonna and Guantaio. He had been trying to get them to do something and they were afraid. Boldini, for some reason, also wanted Colonna to change beds with him, to make this something easier to do.

'"*Yes, and what if I am caught?*" said Colonna.

'"*You're as good a man as he is,*" said Boldini.

'"*And what about his brothers? Yes – and his friends the Americans?*" asked Colonna.

'"*And what about* YOUR *friends – me and Guantaio and Vogué and Gotto?*

What about Sergeant-Major Lejaune, if someone makes a row, and Corporal Dupré reports the man to him and I give my humble evidence as an eye-witness – in private? Eh? . . . 'Brothers,' you say! Aren't Lejaune and I like brothers?"

'"*Why not do it yourself then?*" said Guantaio.

'"*Because I'm going to be made corporal soon,*" replied Boldini, "*and I mustn't be in any rows. . . Ah, when I'm corporal, I shall be able to look after my friends, eh?*" Then he went on to remind them of what they could do with a thousand francs – more than fifty years of their pay, for a two-minute job.

'Then Guantaio, who seems to be a pluckier dog than Colonna, said:

'"*How do you know he has got it?*" and Boldini replied, "*Because I heard them say so. They are a gang. Swell thieves. They have asked me if thieves in the Legion are given up to the police. When the third one joined at Oran, I guessed it from what they said. And they were flash with their money. They got together at night, out in the courtyard, and I crept up behind a buttress close to them and listened. I could not hear everything, but they spoke of a jewel-robbery and thirty thousand pounds. The one they call 'Le Beau' said he kept it like the* CANGURO *. . . the kangaroo . . . keeps its young! I heard him plainly.*

'"*And where does the* CANGURO *keep its young? In a pouch on its stomach, and that is where this thief, Légionnaire Guillaume Brown, keep this jewel. In a pouch . . . He wears it day and night.*

'"*And it's a thousand francs for the man that gets me the pouch. And I'll take the chance and risk of getting the jewel sold in the Ghetto for more than a thousand . . . Some of those Ghetto Jews are millionaires . . . I'd put the lamp out. One man could gag and hold him, while the other got it, and they could run to their beds in the dark.*" . . .

'And much more of the same sort he talked, egging them on, and then they went away, but with nothing settled,' continued Maris.

Digby and I burst into laughter at mention of the kangaroo, and Michael turned, smiling to Maris.

When the latter stopped, Digby asked if Boldini had not also divulged that he wore a sapphire eye, and I enquired if the wily Italian had not observed a lump in Digby's cheek, where a simian pouch concealed a big jewel.

'The fool overheared an elaborate joke,' said Michael to Maris; 'but we're very much obliged to you.'

'Oh, he is the fool all right,' said Maris; 'but he is also the knave.

'Knave of diamonds!' he added, with a grin. 'I just tell you because I like you English gentlemen, and it is just possible that they may try to steal your moneybelt, if they think there is a chance of getting something valuable.'

We filled the worthy Maris up with *cous-cous* and *galettes* (pancakes and honey), and strolled back to barracks.

When we were alone, I said to Michael:

'You *do* wear a money-belt, Beau. Let me have it at night for a bit –

in case these gentle Italians have been persuaded, and something happens in the dark.'

'Why?' asked Michael.

'Well,' replied I, 'you could favour them with your full personal attention, untroubled with grosser cares, if you had no property to protect. Also you could establish the fact that you don't wear a money-belt at night.'

'I'd sooner establish despondency and alarm in the thief, thanks,' said Michael.

'What a lark!' chuckled Digby. 'I'm going to wear a brick under my sash and swear it's a ruby. Anyone that can pinch it while I slumber, can have it for keeps . . . I must find this Boldini lad.' . . .

But, personally, I did not regard the matter as precisely a lark.

I had heard of Italian knives, and it seemed to me that a man might well be found dead in his bed, with a knife – or his own bayonet – through his heart, and nobody be any the wiser . . . And even if justice could be done, which was doubtful, that would not bring the dead man back to life.

We had been long enough in the Legion to know its queer code of morals, and on the subject of theft the law was very peculiar, very strict, and very savage.

One might steal any article of uniform, and be no thief. It was a case of 'robbery no stealing.' To take another man's uniform or kit was merely 'to decorate oneself,' and decorating oneself was a blameless pastime, regarded universally as profitable, amusing, and honourable. Public opinion was not in the slightest degree against the time-honoured practice, and the act was concealed from none save the owner of the sequestrated property.

This was all very silly, for it was a most serious matter, involving very heavy punishment, for a man to be found to be short of so much as a strap when 'showing-down' kit for inspection by the *adjudant*. Nevertheless, you might 'decorate yourself' with a tunic, a sash, an overcoat, a pair of boots, a pair of trousers, or the whole of a man's 'washing' from the line in the *lavabo*, and no one thought one penny the worse of you, save the unfortunate whom you had robbed.

The idea was, that if you were short of an article of equipment (after all, the property of *Madame la République*, and not of the individual), you must help yourself where you could, your victim must help himself where he could, his victim must do likewise, and so on. And whoever was caught out, in the end, as short of kit, was the fool and the loser in this childish game of 'beggar my neighbour' (of his uniform).

Of his uniform, public property – but of nothing else.

Anything else was private property and sacred. To steal private property was not self-'decoration' at all, but theft; and theft, in that collection of the poorest of poor men, was the ultimate horrible crime, infinitely worse than murder. The legionary did not value his life much, but he valued his few tiny possessions beyond estimation.

With the abomination of theft, the Legion itself dealt, and dealt most drastically, for it could not be tolerated where everything private was so valuable, and so easily stolen if a thief should arise in the midst.

There was no thought of appeal to Authority in a case of theft; nor was there either enquiry or comment on the part of Authority when a case occurred and was punished by the men themselves, according to Legion law and custom.

And we were soon to see the law in operation and to behold an example of the custom . . .

Since Michael absolutely refused to let me wear his money-belt for him at night, I decided that I must think of some other plan – in view of this story told by Maris. I did not doubt its truth for one moment, as it merely confirmed, in particular, what I had thought and Buddy had voiced, in general – that Boldini's interest in our comings and goings, our conversation and habits, our antecedents and private affairs, had a sinister cause and object.

At first I thought of arranging with Digby that he and I should take turns to keep watch, but I discarded this plan as impossible. Nobody who worked as long and as hard as we did, could possibly lie awake in bed, and Michael would soon have 'put an end to our nonsense' if we had sat up to guard him.

I then thought of going to Boldini and saying:

'Kangaroos have a horrible kick, my friend,' or, 'Better not let me see you putting the light out, Boldini,' or even frankly and plainly promising to kill him, if anybody attempted to rob my brother.

After pondering the matter and consulting Digby, who did not take as serious a view of it as I did, I had the bright idea of getting the advice of an older, worldly-wiser, and far cleverer person than myself – and appealed to Buddy.

What he did not know about crooks and the best ways of defeating them was not worth knowing, and his experiences in the Texas Rangers had been those of detective, policeman, watch-dog, and soldier combined.

I accordingly walked out one evening with Hank and Buddy, 'set the drinks up' at the Bar de Madagascar off the Rue de Daya, and told them that I had excellent reason to believe that Boldini was arranging with Colonna and Guantaio to rob my brother, one night.

'My brother can look after himself, of course,' said I; 'but these curs have got hold of the idea that he has a marvellous jewel which we three have stolen . . . What I'm wondering is whether Guantaio, who looks like a *pucca* Sicilian bandit, would stick a knife into him, to make sure of getting his belt. That's the only thing that worries me.'

'Fergit it, son,' was Buddy's prompt reply. 'Those slobs would never do that. Don't trust each other enough, for one thing. Far too risky, for another. That sort of poor thieving boob wouldn't dare. Why, one drop of blood on his hands or shirt, or one yell outa your brother, an' he'd be taken red-handed.'

'Shore,' agreed Hank. 'Not in barracks they wouldn't. Git him up a side-street and bash him on the head, more like. Anybody mighta done it there. Lots o' guys git done in fer their sash an' bayonet in the *village nègre*, an' them low dives an' hash-joints in the Spanish quarter . . . Don't let him go around alone, an' he's safe enough.'

This was reassuring, and it was common sense. It would, of course, take a very cool, skilful, and courageous murderer to kill a man sleeping in a room with thirty others.

'I don't know so much,' I said, arguing against myself and for the sake of complete reassurance. 'Suppose Guantaio or Colonna simply crept to the bed and drove a bayonet through the blankets and through his heart. There'd be no bloodstains on the murderer . . .'

'Not when he started monkeying with the belt?' put in Buddy. 'And wouldn't there be no sound from your brother? Not a cheep outa him? Fergit it, I say.'

'Look at here, Bo,' argued Hank. 'Figger it was you agoin' to stick me. How'd you know where my heart was, me curled up under the blankets, and nearly dark an' all? How'd you know as everybody was asleep all right? How'd you know there wouldn't be noise? . . . Shucks! 'Tain't horse-sense . . . Nope. These legendaries don't stand fer murder in the barrack-room, still less fer robbery, and least of all fer bein' woke up at night outa their due and lawful sleep.' . . .

'See, boy,' interrupted Buddy at this point, 'that barrack-room is just your brother's plumb safest place. As fer his kohinoor di'mond, I allow he can sure look after that himself.'

'Shore thing,' agreed Hank.

'Absolutely,' said I. 'If there's no fear of his being murdered in his sleep, there's an end of the matter. I'd rather like Boldini to go and try to rob him.'

'I wouldn't go fer to say as much as that, Bo,' demurred Buddy. 'I'd undertake to clear your brother out every night of his life – every cent outa his belt – and the belt likewise also, too . . . P'r'aps Mister Cascara Sagrada could do as much,' and we smiled, both thinking of the occasion upon which Buddy had 'minded' my money or me.

'Look at here, Bo,' said Hank at this. "*Pard*," I ses, "*if that English legendary, Willyerm Brown, No.* 18897, *gits robbed, I'm sure agwine ter do you an onjustice. I'm agwine ter beat you up most ugly. So's yer own father, if you had one, wouldn't know yer, an' yer mother'd disown yer*," or something discouragin' like that.'

I thanked this large slow person, but declined, assuring him that we could take excellent care of ourselves, and I had only wanted to know if murder were a possible contingency.

'Not inside the barracks. Not till hell pops,' said Buddy.

'Sure thing,' agreed Hank. 'But don't let him prowl around no boweries nor hootch-joints, on his lonesome. Nope.'

'An' tell him from me that I'll mind his money-belt an' be responserble, if he likes,' offered Buddy. 'Then he can sleep free and easy like, an' also deal faithful with any guy as comes snooping around in the night, without having to waste time feeling if his gold-dust is there all right . . .'

I again thanked him, changed the subject, and soon afterwards got them back to barracks, 'a-settin' sober on the water-waggon, a credit to all men,' as Hank observed.

And, this very night, there happened that which must have given certain gentlemen of our barrack-room to think, and to think seriously, of abandoning any schemes for their quick enrichment, had they been entertaining them.

I was awakened by a crash and a shout . . . Springing up, instantly awake, I saw two men struggling on the floor near Michael's bed. The one on top, pinning the other down with a hand on his throat, was Michael. As I leapt from my bed, I was aware that the room was alive and that men were running with angry shouts to see what, and who, had broken their sacred sleep – a horrible violation of strictest Legion law.

'Wring the sneakin' coyote's neck, Bo,' shouted Buddy.

'"*Learn him to be a toad*," Beau,' quoted Digby, and with cries of 'Thief! Thief!' the wave of shouting, gesticulating men swept over the two and bore one of them to the surface. It was neither Guantaio nor Colonna, neither Gotto nor Vogué – one of whom I had fully expected to see.

White-faced, struggling, imploring, in the grip of a dozen indignantly outraged and savagely ferocious *légionnaires*, was a man from the next room.

I looked round for Boldini.

He was sound asleep in his bed! And so was Corporal Dupré in his, and with his face to the wall – both of them men whom the squeak of a mouse would awaken.

'What are you doing here, *scélérat*?' shouted half a score of fierce voices as the man was pulled hither and thither, buffeted, shaken, and savagely struck.

'Speak up, you Brown. What about it?' roared Schwartz, who had got the man by the throat. 'Was he stealing!'

'On the table with him,' yelled Brandt.

'Yes, come on. Crucify the swine,' bawled the huge bearded Schwartz, shaking his victim as a terrier shakes a rat.

Hank, followed by Buddy, barged into the middle of the scrum, throwing men right and left.

'Tain't one of Boldini's outfit,' I heard Buddy say.

'Give the Guy a fair trial,' shouted Hank. 'Lynchin' fer hoss-thieves an' sich – but give him a trial,' and he seized the man himself. 'Cough it up quick,' he said to the terrified wretch, who seemed about to faint.

'Wait a minute,' shouted Michael, in French. 'He belongs to me ... He's had enough ...'

The crowd snarled. Several had bayonets in their hands.

'I lost my way,' screamed the prisoner.

'And found it to the bed of a man who has money,' laughed a voice. 'Legion law! On the table with him!'

Michael jumped on the table.

'Silence, you fools!' he shouted. 'Listen!' and the crowd listened. 'I woke up and found the man feeling under my pillow. I thought he was somebody belonging to the room. Somebody I have been waiting for. Well – he isn't. Let him go – he won't come again ...'

At that there was a perfect yell of derision and execration, and Michael was sent flying by a rush of angry men.

While he, Digby, and I were struggling to get to the table, the thief was flung on to it and held down; a bayonet was driven through each of his hands, another through each of his ears, and he lay moaning and begging for mercy. As I got to the table, sick with disgust, with some idea of rescuing the poor beast, I was seized from behind and flung away again.

'Lie there and think about it, you thieving cur,' shouted Schwartz to the thief.

'Stop your snivelling – or I'll put another through your throat,' growled Brandt.

Hank seized me as I knocked Haff down.

'Let be, Johnny,' he said, enveloping me in a bear's hug. 'It's the salootary custom of the country. They discourages thievin' in these parts. But I wish it was Boldini they was lynchin'' ...'

I tried to shake him off, as I saw Michael spring on Schwartz like a tiger.

There was a sudden cry of *'Guard!'* a swift rush in all directions, and the guard tramped in, to find a silent room – full of sleeping men – in the midst of which were we three pulling bayonets out of a white wooden table, and a whiter whimpering man.

'What's this?' said the Corporal of the Guard ...

'An accident,' he answered himself, and, completely ignoring me, he turned to the stolid guard, gave the curt order:

'To the hospital,' and the guard partly led, and partly carried, the wretched creature away.

What his name was, whether he was incited by Boldini, or whether he was merely trying to rob a man known to have money, I did not know.

As Michael caught him feeling under the pillow, it seemed quite likely he was merely looking for a purse or coins.

On the other hand, he may have tried the shelf and *paquet-age*, and then under the pillow, in the hope of finding the alleged belt and jewel, before essaying the far more risky business of rifling the pouch and money-belt.

Talking the affair over the next day, none of us could remember having seen Guantaio or Colonna in the fray, so I concluded that, like Boldini, they had decided not to be awakened by the noise.

As all the old *légionnaires* prophesied would be the case, we heard nothing whatever from the authorities about the riot and the assault upon the thief. Clearly it was considered best to let the men enforce their own laws as they thought fit, provided those laws were reasonable and in the public interest.

When the injured man came out of hospital, we took an interest in his movements. He proved to be a Portuguese named Bolidar, a wharf-rat docker from Lisbon, and quite probably an amateur of petty crime. He stuck to his absurd tale that he had mistaken the room and was feeling his way into what he thought was his own bed.

We came to the conclusion that he was either staunch to his confederates, or else afraid to implicate them. We saw more of him later at Zinderneuf.

'Leave him to me,' said Buddy. 'I'll loosen his tongue – the miserable hoodlum. One night that dago swine is agwine to tell me an' Hank the secrets of his lovin' heart . . .'

'He'll sure sob 'em out,' opined Hank.

But whether he was to do this under the influence of wine or of terror, I did not gather.

What we did gather, a week or two later, was that we were the most famous gang of international crooks and jewel-thieves in Europe, and had got away with a diamond worth over a million francs. With this we had sought safety in the Legion, that we might lie low until the affair was forgotten, and then sell the diamond whole, or have it cut up, as might seem best.

We were Germans pretending to be English, and we had stolen the diamond, in London, from Sir Smith, a great English general, to whom it had been presented by the Prince of Wales, who was in love with his sister. Buddy solemnly informed me that Bolidar knew all this 'for certain.' Bolidar had got it from a friend of ours. No – no names – but if Hank and Buddy could get the diamond – 'rescue' it from the rascals – he, Bolidar, was in a position to promise them a thousand francs, *and* the protection of – someone who was in a position to protect them.

'So there you are, pard,' concluded Buddy, with an amused grin. And there we were.

But only for another month. At the end of that time we found ourselves in the selected draft under orders for the south, and our chance had come of winning that distinction, decoration, and promotion which was to be our first step on the Path of Glory – which was to lead not to the grave but to fame and fortune.

4

The desert

WE left the depôt of Sidi-bel-Abbès in the spirit in which boys leave school at the end of the half. The thought of escape from that deadly crushing monotony and weariness, to active service, change, and adventure, was inexpressingly delightful. The bitterness in my cup of joy was the knowledge that I was going before Isobel could visit Algeria, and that if we were sent to the far south, and were constantly on the move, I could only hear from her at long and irregular intervals.

I poured out my heart to her in a long letter, the night before we marched; told her I was absolutely certain I should see her again; and begged her not to waste her youth in thinking of me if a year passed without news, as I should be dead.

Having had my hour of self-pity, and having waxed magnificently sentimental, I became severely practical, made all preparations, tallowed my feet, and, laden like a beast of burden, fell in, for the last time, on the parade-ground of the Legion's barracks at Sidi-bel-Abbès.

With a hundred rounds of ammunition in our pouches, joy in our hearts, and a a terrific load upon our backs, we swung out of the gates to the music of our magnificent band, playing the March of the Legion, never heard save when the Legion goes on active service.

Where we were going, we neither knew nor cared. That it would be a gruelling murderous march, we knew and did not care. We should march and fight as a battalion, or we should be broken up into companies and sections, and garrison desert-outposts where we should be in touch with our enemies – be they raiding Touaregs, rebellious Arab tribes, *jehad*-preaching Moors, or fanatical Senussi – and in a state of constant active-service.

Possibly we were going to take part in some comprehensive scheme of conquest, extending French dominion to Lake Tchad or Timbuktu. Possibly we were about to invade and conquer Morocco once and for all.

Our ideas were vague and our ignorance abysmal, but what we did know was, that we were on the road, we carried 'sharp' ammunition, we were a self-contained, self-supporting unit of selected men, that the barracks and their killing routine were behind us, and the freedom and movement of active service were before us, with adventure, change, fighting, and the chance of decoration and promotion.

Merrily we sang as we tramped, passing gaily from '*Voilà du Boudin*' to '*La casquette de Père Bougeaud*,' '*Pan, pan, l'Arbi*,' '*Des marches d'Afrique*,' '*Père Brabançon*,' and '*Soldats de la Légion*,' and other old favourites of the march.

Michael, Digby, and I were in one 'four' with Maris, and behind us were Hank, Buddy, St. André, and Schwartz. At night, we shared the little tent, which we could build in a minute and a quarter, with the canvas and jointed tentpoles that we carried. We slept on our overcoats with our knapsacks for pillows, our rifles chained together and the chain handcuffed to a man's wrist.

We were keen, we were picked men, and nobody went sick or fell out. Had he done so, he would have died an unpleasant death, in which thirst, Arabs, and hyenas would have been involved.

We cheerfully did our utmost like men, cheerfully grumbled like fiends, cheerfully dropped like logs at the end of a forty-kilometre march, and cheerfully arose like automata, at the sound of the 2 a.m. reveillé bugle.

We had insufficient water, insufficient rice and macaroni, no meat nor vegetables, and insufficient bread, and were perfectly fit and healthy. We had no helmets and no spinepads, we wore heavy overcoats, we had only a linen flap hanging from our caps to protect our necks, and we had no cases of sunstroke nor heat apoplexy.

And, in time, we reached Ain-Sefra and rested to recoup and refit, the *fourrier-sergents* having a busy time, chiefly in the matter of boots.

Here we learnt that the whole of the Sahara was fermenting in one of its periodic states of unrest, simply asking for peaceful penetration, what with Touareg raids on protected villages, Senussi propaganda, tribal revolts, and sporadic outbursts of mutiny and murder.

There was also much talk of a serious concentration in the south-east, engineered from Kufra, and a 'sympathetic strike' on the part of the numerous and warlike tribes along the Moroccan border.

When this materialised, it would be found that they had struck simultaneously at every French outpost, fort, and settlement, on the Saharan border from Morocco to Tripoli.

The programme, then, was to carry fire and sword northward to the sea, and sweep the surviving *Roumis* into it, freeing the land for ever from the polluting presence of these unbelieving dogs.

Let Morocco, Tunisia, Tripoli, and Egypt join hands, and under the green banner of a purified faith and the spiritual leadership of Our Lord the Mahdi el Senussi, carry on the good work in the name of Allah the All-Merciful, the Compassionate, and Mahomet his Prophet, until Islam was again free, triumphant, and conqueror of all . . .

This we gathered by talking to Arab *goumiers*, marabouts, camel-drivers, and villagers, in their own tongue; as well as from orderlies and officers' servants who overheard the conversation of their masters at mess . . .

From Ain-Sefra we marched to Douargala, where a large force of all arms was concentrating, and from this place we proceeded south, either to trail the French coat in the sight of the Arab, or as a reconnaissance in force and a protective screen behind which the brigade could make its preparations at leisure and in security.

And, in the fullness of time, after endless desert marching, the battalion found itself strung out along a chain of oases between which communication was maintained by camel-patrols, which met half-way and exchanged reports, orders, information, cigarettes, and bad language.

It was at El Rasa, the last of this chain of oases (which must have marked the course of one of those subterranean rivers which are common in Northern Africa) that our halfcompany came in contact with the Arabs and we had our first taste of desert warfare.

Arab *goumiers* came in at dawn one day, riding in haste, with the news that they had seen the camp-fires of a big Touareg *harka* about twenty miles to the south, where an ancient well marked the 'cross-roads' of two caravan routes, as old as civilisation; routes charted by the bones of countless thousands of camels and of men who had trodden them until they died of thirst, starvation, heat, disease, or murder at the hands of Bedouin and Touareg nomads.

These are the oldest roads in the world and the grim relics that line them are those of yesterday and those of centuries ago. They were ancient when Joseph came to Egypt, and the men and beasts that venture upon them have not changed in fifty centuries.

2

We were in touch with the enemy at last. At any moment we might be fighting for our lives. We were delirious with excitement.

At once our little force in the oasis and this Arab *harka* became a microcosm of the whole war, and our Lieutenant Debussy sent out a small reconnoitring force under Sergeant-Major Lejaune, which should be to the strung-out battalion what the battalion was to the brigade at Douargala.

It was the good luck of our *escouade* to be selected for this duty, and within half an hour of the arrival of the *goumiers*, we were advancing *en tirailleur* in the direction from which they had come. Over the loose, hot sand we plodded, our scouts far in advance and our flankers far out to left and right.

'Are we the bait of a trap? Or would you call us the point of a spear?' said Michael, marching between Digby and me.

'Both,' replied Digby, 'a bit of meat on the end of a spear, say.'

And I wondered how many of us would be bits of meat before nightfall.

Not that I felt in the least degree apprehensive or depressed. If I had to analyse and describe my feelings, I should say that beneath a strong sensation of pleasurable excitement was that undercurrent of slight nervous anxiety which one experiences before going in to bat, or when seated in a corner of the ring, awaiting the word '*Time*' at the beginning of a boxing contest.

I would not have been elsewhere for worlds, but at the same time I wondered what the smack of a bullet felt like, and how much chance a bayonet stood against the heavy sword or the lance of a charging Arab . . .

There was no doubt about it that Sergeant-Major Lejaune knew his job, and I found myself wishing that he were not such a wholly hateful person.

I should have liked to admire him as much as I admired his military skill, and ability as a commander, and I began to understand how soldiers love a good leader when it is possible to do so.

One felt that nobody could have handled the situation with more grasp and certainty than he did, and that if any kind of catastrophe or disaster ensued, it would be owing to no fault in the ability, courage, and promptitude of Sergeant-Major Lejaune.

To watch him conducting operations that day, was to watch a highly skilled artisan using his tools with the deft certainty of genius.

On a low, flat-topped rocky hill, we halted and rested, all except Lejaune himself and the scouts whom he sent to various distant sand-hills and low rocky eminences which, while visible from the detachment, gave a wide range of vision in the supposed direction of the enemy.

Among others set to similar tasks, I was ordered to watch one particular man and to report any movement on his part. I watched the tiny distant figure through the shimmering heat haze, which danced over the sand and stones, until my eyes ached and I was forced, from time to time, to close them and cover them with my hand.

Upon opening them after one of these brief rests, which were absolutely necessary, I saw that he was crawling back from his position. When below the skyline, he rose and ran, stooping, for a short distance. He then halted and signalled '*Enemy in sight.*'

The moment that I had pointed him out to Corporal Boldini, Lejaune was notified, and he sent a man named Rastignac running to an eminence, well to our left rear, and a minute later we were lining the edge of our plateau on the side to which this man had disappeared.

Here we lay concealed, and waited.

A few minutes later, the man who had been sent off, fired a shot and exposed himself on the highest point of his rocky hillock.

To my surprise, I saw our scouts retiring and running – not back to us, but to him; and, a minute or two later, I saw a flutter of white on a distant sand-hill.

Rallying on the man who was firing from the top of the rock, the scouts opened fire at distant camel-mounted figures who began to appear over the sand-hills. We received no orders, save to the effect that we should lie as flat and still as the hot stones that concealed us.

Between two of these I watched the scattered fringe of Arabs increase to lines, and the lines to masses of swiftly-moving camel-riders, and soon their deep menacing cry of '*Ul-ul-ul-ul-ul-ullah Akbar*,' came to our ears like the growing roar of an advancing sea.

As they came on, the little party of our scouts fired rapidly, and after about the thousand-yard range, a camel would occasionally sprawl headlong to the ground, or a white-clad figure fall like a sack and lie motionless on the sand.

On swept the Arab *harka* at the top pace of their swift camels, the men in front firing from the saddle, the others brandishing their long, straight swords and waving their lances aloft.

Rapidly and steadily the little band of scouts fired into the brown of them, and, by now, every bullet was hitting man or beast in the closely-packed irregular ranks of the swiftly-advancing horde.

It was thrilling. I felt I must get a grip upon myself, or I should be shaking with excitement, and unable to shoot steadily when our turn came to take part in the fight.

And then, to my amazement, I saw that our scouts were retreating. One by one, they sprang up from behind rocks and fled to their right rear, each man dropping and firing as his neighbour rose to retreat in his turn. Before long, the little band was again in position, nearer to us and still further behind us. With increased yells, the Arabs swerved to their left and bore down upon them, men and camels falling beneath the magazine-fire of their rifles.

I could scarcely keep still. How long was this unequal fight to continue? None of the scouts had been hit by the wild fire of the camel-riders, but in a couple of minutes they would be overwhelmed by this wave of mounted men, and, out-numbered by fifty to one, would have as much chance as has a fox beneath a pack of hounds.

And as I held my breath, the tiny handful again rose to their feet, turned their backs upon the Arabs, and fled as one man toward a sand-hill in our rear. With a simultaneous yell of mingled execration and triumph, the Arab *harka* swerved again, seemed to redouble their speed, and bore down upon their prey.

And then, Sergeant-Major Lejaune stood up on a rock, gave a crisp order, coolly as on parade, and, at less than fifty yards, the Arab masses received the withering blast of our magazine-fire.

Swiftly as our hands could move the bolts of our rifles and our fingers press the trigger, we fired and fired again into the surging, shrieking, struggling mob, that halted, charged, retired, and then fled, leaving quite half their number behind.

But of those who were left behind, by no means all were killed or even wounded, and our orgy of slaughter rapidly turned to a desperate hand-to-hand fight with dismounted and unwounded Arabs, who, knowing they must die, had but the one idea of gaining Paradise and the remission of sins, in the slaying of an infidel.

With a shout of '*Bayonette au canon*,' Lejaune had us to our feet, and launched us in a fierce bayonet-charge down the slope of our plateau upon the Arab swordsmen, who were rallying to the attack, on foot. Our disciplined rush swept them back, they broke and fled, and, still keeping us in hand, Lejaune quickly had a double rank of kneeling and standing men shooting down the fleeing or still defiant foot-men, and making practice at the remains of the mounted *harka* disappearing over the skyline.

Within half an hour of the first signalling of the approach of the enemy, the only Arabs in sight were those that lay singly and in little bloodstained heaps, in the shallow valley into which they had been decoyed by our scouts.

It was a neat little action, reflecting the highest credit on Lejaune and on the man who was the senior in charge of the scouts. The latter, one Gontran, was promoted corporal, in orders next day, and Sergeant-Major Lejaune made *adjudant*.

The Arabs must have lost over a hundred men in this fight, as against our three killed and five wounded.

Such was my first experience of war, my first 'smelling of powder' and my blooding. I had killed a man with cold steel and I think at least three with my rifle.

Reflecting on this I was glad to remember that these Touaregs are human wolves, professional murderers, whose livelihood is robbery with violence, which commonly takes the form of indescribable and unmentionable tortures.

Nor is the *Roumi*, the infidel dog, the favourite object of their treacherous attack, save in so far as he is a more rewarding object of attention. They are as much the scourge and terror of the Arab villager, the nomad herdsman, or the defenceless negro, as they are of the wealthy caravan or their peaceful co-religionists of the town, the *douar*, and the oasis.

The man whom I had killed with my bayonet, had made it necessary to my continued existence, for he rushed at me with a great, heavy, straight-bladed sword, exactly like those used by our Crusaders of old.

Whirling this round his head, he aimed a blow at me that would have split my skull had I not promptly side-stepped, drawing back my bayonet as I did so. As the sword missed my head, I drove at his chest with all my strength, and the curved hilt of my Lebel bayonet touched his breastbone as he fell staggering back, nearly pulling the rifle out of my hands.

I found afterwards that Digby had had his coat torn under the armpit by a spear, which, as he remarked, was not fair wear, but tear, on a good coat. He had shot his assailant at a range which he estimated as being a good half-inch, and he was troubled with doubts as to whether this would be considered quite sporting in the best Arab circles.

'Of course,' he said, 'the bird wasn't actually "sitting" – through he's sitting now . . .'

Michael, being particularly good with the bayonet, and a noted winner of bayonet *v.* bayonet competitions, had used the butt of his rifle in the mêlée, and seemed to think it unfair of the Arab to wear a turban, that diminishes the neat effectiveness of this form of fighting! However, neither of them was hurt, nor were any of our more immediate friends.

Having buried our dead and obliterated their graves, we retired slowly toward El Rasa, weary to death and thoroughly pleased with ourselves, to make our report . . .

3

The pitched battle of El Rasa was fought next day, our battalion holding the oasis against tremendous odds until supports came from the brigade, and the Arabs learnt what quick-firing little mule-guns can do, when given such a target as a huge mob of horse and camel-men advancing *en masse* over a level plain.

As my part in this battle was confined to lying behind the bole of a palm-tree and shooting whenever I had something to shoot at, I have no adventures to relate. I might as well have spent the day on a rifle-range.

But I saw a magnificent charge of a couple of squadrons of Spahis upon a vastly superior number of Arab cavalry, which, shaken by artillery fire, appeared to be hanging in doubt as to whether to make one of their fierce rushes, overwhelming and desperate, upon the infantry lining the edge of the oasis. It was a thrilling and unforgettable sight . . .

After the signal victory of El Rasa, the brigade moved on southward and we preceded it, the weeks that followed being a nightmare of marching that ended in the worse nightmare of garrison duty in the ultimate, further-most, desert outpost of Zinderneuf, where we had the initial misfortune of losing Digby and many of our friends, including Hank and Buddy.

They departed to the mounted-infantry school at Tanout-Azzal, where the gentle art of mule-handling was taught, and the speed of the swift-marching legionary increased by mounting him on a mule. A company of such men was thus rendered as mobile as a squadron.

It was a cruel blow to Michael and me, this separation from our brother and from those best of friends, Hank and Buddy.

However, we were certain to be reunited sooner or later, and there was nothing to do but to make the best of this and the other drawbacks and miseries of Zinderneuf.

5

The Fort at Zinderneuf

'They learn that they are not as others are,
Till some go mad, and some sink prone to earth,
And some push stumbling on without a star.'

THINGS began badly and rapidly grew worse in this ill-omened mud fort, isolated in the illimitable desert like a tiny island in the midst of a vast ocean.

Cafard broke out early, and in a very virulent form, both suicidal and homicidal in its nature.

It took this terrible form, I verily believe, largely by reason of the fact that Captain Renouf, our Commandant, shot himself after a month of life in this dreadful oven of a place. I do not, of course, know his reason for doing this, but it was rumoured that he found he had contracted a horrible disease. This tragedy cast a deeper gloom over a place and a community already gloomy beyond description.

Within a week of this disaster, for a disaster it was to all of us, a most unusual manifestation of *cafard* was exhibited, when a corporal killed a sergeant and then committed suicide. What Corporal Gontran's grievance against the sergeant was, I do not know, but this again was an exceedingly unfortunate affair, as, like Captain Renouf himself, both these men were on the side of the angels, inasmuch as they were decent, fair-minded, and reasonable people.

But the Fates and the Furies had one more disaster in store for the unhappy garrison before they were ready to launch upon our luckless heads the final torrent of destruction.

Lieutenant Debussy, the new Commandant, sickened and died, and his place was taken by none other than *Adjudant* Lejaune.

From the moment in which it was known that the Lieutenant was dead, the atmosphere of Zinderneuf changed from bad to worse and rapidly from worse to the worst possible.

The lion-tamer had entered the cage, and the lions, sullen, infuriated, and desperate, knew that he held in one hand the whip that should drive them to revolt, and in the other the revolver that should instantly punish the first sign of it.

2

Life at Zinderneuf was not really life so much as the avoidance of death – death from sunstroke, heat-stroke, monotony, madness, or Adjudant Lejaune.

Cafard was rampant; everybody was more or less abnormal and 'queer' from frayed nerves, resultant upon the terrific heat and the monotony, hardship, and confinement to a little mudcover of a fort; many men were a little mad, and Adjudant Lejaune, in the hollow of whose hand were our lives and destinies, was a great deal more than a little mad.

From the point of view of the authorities, he was sane enough, for he could maintain an iron discipline; make all reports and returns, to the minute and to the letter; and, if attacked, he could be trusted to keep the Tri-couleur flying while there was a man alive in the Fort.

From the point of view of his subordinates, he was nevertheless a madman, and a very dangerous one.

At times, I was almost glad that Digby was not with us, much as I missed him; and at those times I almost wished that Michael was not, much as I depended on him.

Danger to oneself is unpleasant enough, when it is that of being murdered by a lunatic. When to it is added the danger, and constant fear, of a similar fate overtaking people whom one loves, it becomes ten times worse.

Michael and I both begged each other not to be so foolish as to play into Lejaune's hands, by giving him the faintest chance to accuse us of any breach of duty or discipline, or of so much as an insubordinate look, even under the greatest provocation. But we felt that the time would come when Lejaune would cease to wait for an excuse, and that all we could do was to put off the evil day . . .

'I'm positively glad, now, that Dig isn't here,' said Michael to me, one terrible afternoon, as we lay gasping on our burning cots during siesta hours, in our stifling *caserne*.

'Hank and Buddy too,' he added. 'One word of back-chat to Lejaune would have been fatal . . . And Dig might have done it. Buddy more so . . . Or if Hank once lost control he'd lay Lejaune out like a pole-axed ox . . .'

'Somebody'll do for him one of these days, if we don't soon get a new commanding officer,' said I. 'And a good job too.'

'Not it,' contradicted Michael. 'It would be one degree worse than letting him live . . . These asses would give three loud cheers, march off into the desert, and survive about three days of it – if the Arabs didn't get them before they died of thirst.'

'It'll happen,' prophesied I. 'Schwartz is getting very mysterious and important these days. Oh, it'll happen all right.'

'That's what I think,' said Michael, 'and it's about the worst thing that *could* happen. And if no one goes and does it spontaneously, there'll be a plot to murder him – if there isn't one already, which I belive there is, as you say – and we should have the choice of fighting for Lejaune – (for *Lejaune*!) – or being two of a gang of silly, murdering mutineers with nothing but a choice of beastly deaths – thirst and Arabs in the desert, or court martial and a firing party at dawn . . . Rotten.'

'If he's promoted Lieutenant and kept in command here, he won't last a week,' said I . . . 'What's going to happen if they make a plot to mutiny and we're the only two that refuse to join them?'

'We should join Lejaune instead, where dead men tell no tales, I expect,' answered Michael.

'What would Sergeant Dupré and Corporal Boldini do?' I speculated.

'If it were a case of saving their skins they'd join the mutineers, I should say – if they were given the option,' replied Michael. 'They probably loathe Lejaune as much as we do, and neither of them is exactly the man to die for a principle . . . If they woke to find a gang of bad men, with rifles, round their beds, they'd "*take the cash and let the discredit go,*" – "*Nor heed the rumble of a distant drum*" from Tokotu,' he added.

'I doubt if they'd be given the option,' I said.

'So do I,' agreed Michael. 'They're not loved. They've been whips and scorpions in Lejaune's hands too long and too willingly.'

'And if we were "approached" on the subject of a mutiny and did our miserable duty in warning Lejaune and the others?' I asked.

'We should promptly get thirty days' cells from Lejaune for currying favour with horrible lies, and short shrift from the mutineers for being *escrocs*,' said Michael . . .

'Let us give thanks unto the Lord and count our many blessings, my brethren,' he yawned, and, at that moment, Schwartz, Haff, Brandt, Bolidar, Delarey, and Vogué entered the room and joined Guantaio, Colonna, and Gotto at the other end of it. Here they conversed in low voices, with occasional glances at us.

3

And to me, one night, came Schwartz, as I sat in a corner of the little courtyard, trying to imagine that the night was cooler than the day, and this spot, which faced north, less hot than the others.

He was a huge, powerful, hairy ruffian, who would have made a great pirate-captain, for he had brains, courage, and determination, quite unhampered by over-fine scruples of honour or mercy. He was further endowed with a magnetic personality and power of command.

'Are you enjoying life, Smith?' he asked, seating himself beside me.

'Quite as much as you are, Schwartz,' I replied.

'Would you like a change?' he enquired.

'I am fond of change,' said I.

A brief silence ensued.

'Have you ever seen a pig die?' he asked suddenly.

'No,' I replied.

'Well, you soon will,' he assured me.

'Feeling ill?' I enquired rudely. I did not like the gross Schwartz.

'You are going to see a big pig die,' he went on, ignoring my vulgarity. 'A sacred pig. An anointed pig. A striped pig. A promoted pig. Oh, an *adjudant* pig.'

'So?' I murmured.

'Yes. *Monsieur le Cochon* is going to become *Monsieur Porc*.'

'And are you going to become *Monsieur Charcutier*, "Mr. Pork-butcher," so to speak?' I enquired. There could be no harm in knowing all there was to know about this business.

'Aha! my friend,' growled the German, 'that remains to be seen. So many want a *côtelette de porc* or a *savouret de porc*. We shall have to cast lots.'

He was silent for a minute and sat beside me, gnawing his knuckles. He was shaking from head to foot with fever, excitement, or diseased nerves.

'Do you want a chance to be *charcutier*?' he asked.

'I have had no experience of pig-killing,' I answered.

'Look you,' he growled, seizing my arm, 'you will have the experience shortly, *either as pig or as butcher*, for all here will be *cochon* or *charcutier* – in a day or two. See? Choose whether you will be a pig or a butcher . . . And tell your brother to choose . . . Meantime, if any man comes to you and says "*porc*," you reply "*cochon*." Then he will know that I have spoken to you, and you will know that he is one of us. See? And you and your brother make up your minds quickly. We don't care either way. There are enough of us – oh, enough . . .' And as somebody approached, he got up and slouched off.

That night I told Michael what I had heard.

The next day it was Guantaio. I was sitting in the same place and he crept towards me purposefully.

'Who's that?' he asked, and, hearing my name, came and sat down beside me, as Schwartz had done.

'It's hot,' he said, removing his *képi* and puffing.

'It is,' I agreed.

'Are you fond of hot . . . *porc*?' he enquired.

'*Cochon!*' said I playfully.

'Ah!' he replied at once. 'What do you think of it all?'

'I never think,' said I.

This silenced him for a minute.

'They are ten to one,' he said suddenly. 'Ten butchers to a pig. What chance has the big pig and one or two biggish pigs against a score of butchers?'

'Ah!' I said imitatively. 'What do you think of it all?'

'I never think,' said Guantaio, with a malevolent smile. I yawned and stretched and affected to settle myself to slumber.

'How would you and your brother like to be *pigs* if I could find two or three other pigs to join the big pig, and the one or two biggish pigs?' he enquired, nudging me.

I belied my statement that I never thought, and did some rapid thinking.

Had it been arranged that he should sound me as soon as Schwartz had hinted at the assassination of Lejaune? Was it his task to find out whether my name was to be put on the 'butcher' list or on the 'pig' list? Were all those who did not wholeheartedly join the 'butchers' to be shot in their beds on the night of the mutiny?

Or, again, was the rogue trying to find out which was likely to be the stronger party, and did he intend to betray his friends to the non-commissioned officers, if he thought them likely to win?

'How should we like to become *pigs*, you say?' I temporised . . . 'I should hate to be butchered – shouldn't you?'

'Very much,' he replied . . . 'But do you know,' he went on, 'I have heard of pigs attacking men. *Taking them unawares* and eating them up . . .'

'I should hate to be eaten up by a pig – shouldn't you?' I observed.

'Very much,' he agreed again. 'One does not want to be slaughtered by butchers nor eaten by pigs.'

'No,' said I. 'Need either happen?'

'Not if one is a wise pig – forewarned and forearmed – who attacks the butchers, *taking them unawares*,' he replied.

'Has the big pig got his eye on the butchers?' I asked.

'No,' replied Guantaio. 'Nor have the biggish pigs.'

'And are you going to open the eyes of the blind pigs?' I enquired.

'I don't know,' answered Guantaio. And I had a very strong conviction that he was speaking the truth, for there was a ring of genuine doubt and puzzlement in his voice. At any rate, if he were lying when he said it, he was lying extraordinarily well.

No – he did not know what to do, I decided, and he was simply trying to find out where his private interests lay. Would it pay him better to stand in with his friends, and assist in the mutiny and the murder of Lejaune and the non-commissioned officers? Or would he do better for himself if he betrayed his friends, warned his superiors, and assisted them to defeat the mutineers?

That he was one of the ringleaders of the plot was obvious, since he was the bosom friend of Colonna, Gotto, Vogué, and the rest of Schwartz's band, and had always been one of the circle in their recent confabulations and mutterings together.

I followed the excellent, if difficult, plan of trying to put myself in Guantaio's place, and to think with his mind.

On the one hand, if I were Guantaio, I should see the great dangers attendant on the mutiny. It might fail, and if it succeeded, it could only be the prelude to a terrible march into the desert – a march of doomed men, hunted by the Arabs and by the French alike, and certain to die of thirst and starvation if not killed by enemies.

On the other hand, if I were the excellent Guantaio, I should see the advantages attendant upon playing the part of the saviour of the situation. Reward and promotion were certain for the man who saved the lives of his superiors and the honour of the flag, and who preserved the Fort of Zinderneuf for France. And, of course, it would be the simplest thing in the world for Lejaune, Dupré, Boldini, Guantaio, and a few loyal supporters to defeat the conspirators and secure the mutineers. It would only be a matter of entering the barrack-room at night, seizing the arms, and covering the suspects with the rifles of the loyalists, while the guard arrested them. Anyone resisting, could be shot as soon as he raised a hand.

Lejaune alone could do the business with his revolver, if he entered the room while all were asleep, and shoot any man who did not instantly obey any order that he gave.

In fact, I began to wonder why Guantaio should be hesitating like this. Surely it was to his interest to betray his friends?

Certainly he would not allow any ridiculous scruples to hinder him from committing any treacherous villainy, and certainly it was far less dangerous, in the long run, to be on the side of authority – for the mutineers' real danger only *began* with the mutiny, and it steadily increased from the moment when they set forth into the desert to escape.

More and more I wondered at his hesitation.

And then a light began to dawn upon my brain. This Guantaio was the henchman of his compatriot, Corporal Boldini. Boldini might be killed when the mutineers killed Lejaune; for hate and vengeance were the mainsprings of the plot, and Boldini was hated second only to Lejaune himself. He might not be given the option of joining the mutineers when Lejaune was murdered. Suppose the Italians, Boldini, Guantaio, Colonna, and Gotto, were a united party, led by Boldini, with some sinister end of their own in view? And might not Guantaio be doubtful as to whether the rôle allotted to him were not too much that of the cat's-paw?

Suppose the Boldini party intended to fish in troubled waters – for a pearl of great price? In other words, suppose they hoped to do what they had certainly tried, and failed, to do in Sidi-bel-Abbès, when they had induced Bolidar to attempt to rob my brother?

Most undoubtedly these rogues believed Boldini's story that we were a gang of jewel-thieves and that Michael carried about with him a priceless gem – to which they had at least as much right as he had. No – I decided – Guantaio spoke the truth when he said he did not know what to do. He was a knave all through. He would betray anybody and everybody. He was afraid that his share in the mutiny would be death, whether it failed or not, and what he really wanted to do was to follow the course most likely to lead him to the possession of two things – a whole skin and a share in the jewel – unless indeed he could get the jewel itself.

'It's a difficult problem, my friend,' mused I sententiously. 'One does not know which side to take . . . One would like to be a pig, if the pigs are going to catch the butchers napping . . . On the other hand, one would like to be a *charcutier*, if the butchers are going to act first . . .'

We sat silent awhile, the excellent Guantaio making a perfect meal of his nails.

'And – that is a point!' I went on. 'When *are* the butchers going to kill?'

'*Monsieur le Grand Charcutier*' (by whom, I supposed, he meant Schwartz) 'talks of waiting till full moon,' was the reply. 'If a new Commandant has not come by then, or if *Monsieur le Grand Cochon* has been promoted and given command before then, it would be a good date . . . Do it at night and have full moon for a long march . . . Rest in the heat of the day, and then another big moonlight march, and so on . . .'

'So one has three or four days in which to make up one's mind?' I observed.

'Yes,' replied Guantaio. 'But I don't advise your waiting three or four days before doing it . . . Schwartz will want to know in good time . . . So as to arrange some butchers for each pig, you see . . .'

'And what about Lejaune?' I asked, since we were to use names and not fantastic titles. 'Suppose somebody warned him? What then?'

'Who *would*?' asked Guantaio. 'Who loves that mad dog enough to be crucified, and have his throat cut, on his behalf? Why *should* anyone warn him? Wouldn't his death be a benefaction and a blessing to all?'

'Not if things went wrong,' I replied. 'Nor if it ended in our all dying in the desert.'

'No,' agreed Guantaio, gnawing away at his nails. 'No . . . I hate the desert . . . I fear it . . . I fear it . . .'

Yes – that was the truth of the matter. He feared being involved in a successful mutiny almost as much as in an unsuccessful one.

'Suppose, *par exemple*, I went and warned Lejaune?' I asked.

'Huh! He'd give you sixty days' *cellule*, and take damned good care you never came out alive,' replied Guantaio, 'and he would know what he knows already – that everybody hates him and would be delighted to kill him, given a good opportunity . . . And what would your comrades do to you?'

He laughed most unpleasantly.

No – I decided – friend Guantaio would not like me to warn Lejaune. If Lejaune were to be warned, Guantaio would prefer to do the warning himself.

'How would they know that I was the informer?' I asked.

'Because I should tell them,' was the reply. 'If Lejaune gets to know – then you and nobody else will have told him.'

So that was it? Guantaio could turn informer, having sworn that I was going to do so! Not only would he save his own skin, but Michael would soon have a friend and brother the less, when Schwartz and his merry men heard who had betrayed them.

'Of course, you and your brother would be held to have acted together, as you always do,' said Guantaio.

So that was it again? Michael and I being denounced to the mutineers as traitors, Guantaio might well be moved to murder and rob Michael – secure in his honourable rôle of executioner of justice upon a cowardly traitor.

The Legion knew no punishment too severe for infliction upon any man who acted contrary to the interests of his comrades. Guantaio need not fear the fate of Bolidar in such circumstances.

'What would you do if you were me?' I asked.

'Join the butchers,' was the prompt reply. 'You and your brother must follow Schwartz. Better the enmity of Lejaune than of half the barrack-room led by Schwartz. Lejaune couldn't come straight to your bed and murder you, anyhow. Schwartz could, and would. And he *will*, unless you join him . . .'

Yes, undoubtedly the filthy creature was in grave doubt about the best course to pursue, and spoke from minute to minute as new ideas and fresh views occurred to him, and as his fears and hopes swayed him.

At present he saw the desirability of me and Michael being mutineers. Just now, he had seen some advantage in our not being of their party . . .

Probably the most puzzling and baffling thing to a tortuous mind is simple truth. It is often the subtlest diplomacy, when dealing with such people as this. So I decided to speak the plain truth, and leave him to make what he could of it.

'I shall talk the matter over with my brother,' I said, 'and we will decide to-night. Probably we shall warn Lejaune. You can tell Schwartz that. And I can give him a definite answer to-morrow. Then he can do as he pleases.'

'You won't warn Lejaune until you have told Schwartz you are going to do so, of course?' asked Guantaio, and I had seen his eyes light up as I announced the probability of our defying Schwartz. That seemed to suit him finely.

'No, I won't,' I assured him. 'Neither will my brother . . . Provided, of course, that nothing will be done to-night? No mutinying, I mean . . .'

'Oh, no,' said Guantaio. 'They're not ready yet. A few haven't joined. Schwartz would like to get everybody, of course; but failing that, he wants to know exactly *who* is to be killed before they start. It will prevent unfortunate accidents . . . Also they want the full moon . . .'

'Well – I shall decide to-night,' I said. 'And now please go away. I want to think – and also I'm not extraordinarily fond of you, Guantaio, really . . .'

4

The first thing to do now was to find Michael and decide as to what line we were going to take.

He was on sentry-go, and I must wait.

Meantime, I might find St. André, Maris, Glock, and one or two others who were fundamentally decent honest men of brains and character, and less likely than some of the rest to be driven by blind hatred of Lejaune, or the dominance of Schwartz, into murderous folly that was also suicidal.

St. André was lying on his cot in the barrack-room. He looked at me as I entered. Taking my belt and a polishing-rag, I strolled in the direction of his bed, and came to a halt near him, rubbing industriously.

'Are you fond of *pork, mon ami?*' I enquired softly, without looking away from my work.

'I am something of a *cochon* about it,' he replied in a low voice, and added, 'Anyhow, I would rather be that than a butcher.'

So he had been approached, too.

'Follow me outside when I go,' I said.

A few minutes later he found me in the courtyard, and I learned that Schwartz had sounded him that day; told him that he must choose between being a pig or a butcher; and had given him a couple of days in which to make up his mind. Schwartz had concluded by informing St. André that all who were not *for* him would be treated as being *against* him, and that eighty per cent of the men had willingly taken the oath to follow him and to obey him absolutely . . .

'What are you going to do, St. André?' I asked.

'What you and your brother do,' was the immediate reply.

He went on to say that he had thought of nothing else from the moment he had learnt of the plot, and that he had come to the conclusion that he would join with Michael and me, to do what seemed the best thing.

'You see, my friend,' he concluded, 'one, of course, cannot join in with these poor madmen – one has been an officer and a gentleman. Even if one *had* sunk low enough to do such a thing, and one eased one's conscience by saying that Lejaune deserves death, the fact remains that these lunatics can but step from the frying-pan into the fire.'

'Exactly,' I agreed.

'Here we live – in hell, I admit – but we do *live*, and we are not here for ever,' he went on. 'Out in the desert we shall not live. Those who do not die of thirst, will die by slow torture under the knives of the Arab women.'

'They will,' said I.

'Besides,' he continued, 'I would not join them if we could march straight into the service of the Sultan of Morocco and be welcomed and rewarded with high rank in his army . . . I am a Frenchman and have been an officer and a gentleman . . . I am here through no fault of my own. St. André is my real name. My brother is a Lieutenant in a Senegalese battalion . . . But you and your brother are not Frenchmen, and if you could get to Morocco, each of you could be another Kaid McLean . . . But you could not get to Morocco on foot from here . . . You would be hunted like mad dogs, apart from all question of food and water . . . You could not do it . . .'

'We are not Frenchmen and we have not been officers, St. André,' I replied; 'but we are gentlemen – and we do not murder nor join murder-gangs . . . And as you say – we could not do it and would not if we could.'

'No, I knew you would not join them,' said St. André, seizing my hand, 'and I told myself I should do just what you and your brother did.'

'Well – I'll talk it over with him as soon as he comes off duty, and we will let you know what we decide,' I said, 'but certainly it will not be to join them.

'Meanwhile,' I added, 'you get hold of Maris – he's a decent good chap, and see what he has got to say. You might try Glock, Dobroff, Marigny, Blanc, and Cordier, too, if you get a chance . . . They are among the least mad in this lunatic asylum.'

'Yes,' agreed St. André, 'if we can form a party of our own, we may be able to save the situation,' and he went off.

I waited for Michael, sitting on a native bed, of string plaited across a wooden frame, that stood by the courtyard wall near the guard-room.

Seated here in the stifling dark, I listened to the gibberings, groans, yells, and mad laughter that came from the *cellules*, where some of Lejaune's victims were being driven more and more insane by solitary confinement and starvation.

When Michael was relieved, I followed him as he went to the barrack-room to put his rifle in the rack and throw off his kit.

'I'll be sitting on the *angareb*,' I said. 'More developments.'

'I'll be with you in five minutes,' he replied.

When he joined me, I told him what Guantaio had said, and I added my own views on the situation, together with those of St. André.

Michael listened in silence.

'Position's this, I think,' he said, when I had finished 'Schwartz and his band of lunatics proposing to murder Lejaune and anybody who stands by him, Guantaio has given the show away to Corporal Boldini because he thinks the mutiny too risky. Boldini wants to join the mutineers if they're likely to be successful – but not otherwise. Probably he, Guantaio, Colonna, Gotto, and Bolidar are in league to get the mighty 'diamond' – one way or the other – out of this mutiny. If we join the mutineers, Boldini and Co. will join, too, with the idea of killing me and robbing me in the desert and getting to Morocco with the Cullinan-Kohinoor . . . Or to put it more truly, Boldini would get the 'Co.' to do the murdering and stealing, and then kill or rob whichever of his gang brought it off. If we refuse to join the mutineers, Boldini's plan would then be to get Guantaio to murder me in my bed – ostensibly for being a traitor to the noble cause of mutiny – and pinch the Great Diamond from my belt . . . Failing that, Boldini would use us in helping to suppress the mutiny, hoping that, in the scrap, I might get done in, and he could rob my corpse. He could do more than hope it. He could arrange it . . .'

'On the other hand,' said I, 'Boldini may know nothing whatever about the plot, and Guantaio may be wondering whether to let the mutiny go on, or whether to warn his old pal Boldini and give the show away.'

'Quite so,' agreed Michael. 'We're absolutely in the dark in dealing with hopeless congenital bred-in-the-bone liars like Guantaio. We can only go on probabilities, and, on the whole, the swine seemed to be egging you on to join the plot . . . Well, that means he has some definite personal interest in our joining it. Obviously if he hadn't, he wouldn't care a damn whether we joined it or not.'

'What's to be done, Beau?' I asked.

'Get together an opposition-gang of non-mutineers, and then tell Schwartz plainly that we are going to warn Lejaune and also going to obey Lejaune's orders on the subject,' was the prompt reply.

'Exactly,' said I. 'Just about what I told Guantaio . . . And St. André will stand in with us, whatever we decide to do.

'But suppose we can get no one else,' I pondered.

'Then we and St. André will warn Lejaune and tell him he can count on us three to be true to our salt,' said Michael.

'Without warning Schwartz?' I asked.

'Certainly not,' replied Michael. 'We can't sneak like that.'

'Of course, Schwartz and Co. will do us in, as traitors,' I observed.

'Probably,' agreed Michael. 'Try to, anyhow.'

'If we can get up a strongish party, Schwartz's lot may chuck the idea of mutiny,' he went on. 'If they don't, it will be a case of who strikes first. We must warn Lejaune the moment we've made it quite clear to Schwartz that we're going to do so then and there, unless he gives up the whole idea . . . Whether he gives it up, or not, will depend on the number we can get to back us.'

We sat silent for a minute or two, pondering this cheerful position.

'Tell you what,' he said suddenly, 'we'll call a meeting. The Briton's panacea. To-morrow evening at six, the other side of the oasis, and we'll invite St. André, Blanc, Cordier, Marigny, and any other Frenchmen who'd be likely to follow St. André. Then there's Maris, Dobroff, Glock, and Ramon, among the foreigners, who might join us . . . I wish to God that Digby, Hank, and Buddy were here.

'They'd make all the difference,' said I.

'Well – if that lot will join us, we can probably turn Schwartz's murder-party into a mere gang of ordinary deserters, if go they must . . .'

Shortly afterwards, St. André, looking for us, came to where we were sitting.

'I've spoken to Maris,' said he, 'and he's with you two, heart and soul. I also sounded Marigny, but he takes the line that we can't possibly be such curs as to warn the unspeakable Lejaune and betray our own comrades.'

'We can't be such curs as not to do so,' said Michael.

'Precisely what I tried to make him see,' replied St. André. 'It's a question of the point of view and of the degree of mental and moral development . . . To us it is unthinkable that we should stand by and see murder done, the regiment disgraced, the Flag betrayed, and the fort imperilled . . . We are soldiers of France . . .'

He stood up and saluted dramatically, but not self-consciously, in the direction of the flagstaff.

'To Marigny and his kind,' he went on, 'it is just as unthinkable that, having been entrusted with a secret by a comrade, they should betray this secret and thwart and endanger the friends who have put their faith in them.'

'The point of view, as you say,' agreed Michael. 'Personally, though, I've not been entrusted with a secret by a comrade. I have merely had a threatening and impudent message from a ruffianly blackguard named Schwartz. He tells me he is going to commit a murder. I reply that he is not going to commit a murder, and that unless he abandons the intention, I am going to warn his victim. That seems a clear issue to me.'

'And to me,' said St. André.

'I also found Blanc to be much of the same mind as Marigny,' he went on. 'Averse from promoting or even condoning murder, but even more averse from "betraying" his comrades . . . I've only spoken to those three so far . . .'

'Well, look here,' said Michael. 'To-morrow at six, beyond the oasis. All our friends and all who are not actually of Schwartz's gang. You get Marigny, Blanc, and Cordier, and any other Frenchman you think might join us, and we'll bring Maris, Ramon, Dobroff, and Glock, and possibly one or two more. They'll come . . . They'll come, because, obviously, it's a life-or-death matter for all of us. We must try to see that none of Schwartz's gang know about the meeting, at any rate until it's over – but if they do, we can't help it. I suppose we have as much right to lay plans as they have?'

'It's a good idea,' agreed St. André. 'I'll be there and bring whom I can. About six o'clock.'

5

Next evening, a handful of the better sort assembled near the *shaduf* in the shade of the palm-grove, out of sight of the fort. Besides Michael, St. André, Maris, and myself, there were Cordier, Blanc, Marigny, Ramon, Dobroff, Glock, Vaerren, and one or two others – fifteen or sixteen of us altogether – enough, as Michael remarked to me, to control events, provided a united party, with a common policy, could be formed.

But this proved impossible. Ideas of right and wrong, honour and dishonour, fair dealing and vile dealing, were too discrepant and probably tinctured by other thoughts and motives, such as those of fear, hatred, ennui, vengeance, and despair.

Michael addressed the meeting first.

'As you all very well know,' said he, 'there is a plot to murder Lejaune and the non-coms., to desert and to abandon the fort. Schwartz is the ringleader and says that those who do not declare themselves supporters will be considered as enemies – and treated as such. Personally, I do not do things because Schwartz says I must, nor do I approve of shooting men in their beds. Supposing I did, I still should disapprove of being led out into the desert by Schwartz, to die of thirst. Therefore I am against his plot – and I invite you all to join with me and tell Schwartz so. We'll tell him plainly that unless he gives up this mad scheme of murder and mutiny, we shall warn Lejaune . . .'

Here a growl of disapproval from Marigny and Blanc, and some vigorous head-shaking, interrupted Michael's speech.

'I swear I will warn Lejaune,' put in St. André, 'but I will warn Schwartz first – and if he likes to drop the murder part of the scheme, he can do what else he likes. Any sacred imbecile who wants to die in the desert can go and do it, but I have nothing to do with mutinies . . .'

'*No treachery!*' roared Marigny, a typical old soldier, grizzled and wrinkled; an honest, brainless, dogged creature who admired Schwartz and loathed Lejaune.

'Don't bray like that, my good ass,' said Michael turning to him, 'and try not to be a bigger fool than God meant you to. Where is the treachery in our replying to Schwartz, "*Thank you, we do not choose to join your murder-gang. Moreover, we intend to prevent the murder – so drop the idea at once.*" Will you kindly explain how the gentle Schwartz is thus "betrayed"?'

'I say it *is* betrayal of comrades – to tell an anointed, accursed, nameless-named dog's-tail like Lejaune that they are plotting against him. Treachery, I say,' replied Marigny.

Michael sighed patiently.

'Well – what are you going to do, Marigny – since you must either be against Schwartz or for him?' asked Maris.

'I'm *for* him,' replied Marigny promptly.

'A slinking, skulking murderer?' asked Michael contemptuously. 'I thought you were a soldier – of sorts.'

'I'm for Schwartz,' said Marigny.

'Then go to him,' snapped Michael. 'Go on . . . Get out . . . We should prefer it – being neither cowards afraid of Schwartz, nor creeping murderers.'

Marigny flushed, clenched his fists and, with an oath, put his hand to his bayonet and made as though to spring at my brother; but he evidently thought better of it as Michael closed his right hand and regarded the point of Marigny's chin.

With a snarl of 'Dirty traitors!' the old soldier turned and strode away.

'Anybody else think as he does?' asked Michael.

'I can't agree to betraying old Schwartz,' said Blanc, a Marseilles seaman, noisy, jolly, brave, and debonair; a rotund, black-eyed, bluff Provençal.

'Well – say what you are going to do then,' said Michael sharply. 'Join Schwartz's murderers or else join us.'

'I can't join Lejaune's boot-lickers,' said Blanc.

'Then join Schwartz's gang of assassins. You may perhaps be safer there,' said Michael, and Blanc departed grumbling.

'I must join my compatriots, I'm afraid,' said Glock.

'You are "afraid"!' mocked Michael. 'You have said it! It is Schwartz you are afraid of. You needn't be. You'll be safer outside that gang of murderers.'

'I can't betray my compatriots,' repeated Glock.

'Well – can you go to them and say – (what is the truth) – "*I don't believe in murder and I am certain this business will end in the deaths of* ALL *of us. Drop it or I and my friends will make you.*" Can you do that?' asked Michael.

Big, simple Glock, with his blue eyes and silly face, could only scratch his head and shuffle awkwardly from one foot to another.

'They'd kill me,' he said.

'They certainly will kill you of thirst, if you let them lead you out there,' argued Michael, with a wave of his arm to the encompassing desert.

'It seems we've all got to die, either way,' said Glock.

'It's what I am trying to prevent, isn't it, fat-head?' answered Michael. 'If the decent men of this garrison would act together and tell Schwartz to stop his silly tricks, no one need die.'

'Except those whom *Lejaune* is killing,' said Cordier, a clever and agreeable Frenchman who had certainly been a doctor, and whose prescriptions and treatment his comrades infinitely preferred to those of any army surgeon. 'If that pariah cur of the gutters of Sodom and Gomorrah could be shot with safety to the rest of us – I'd do it myself to-night, and write my name among those of the benefactors of the human race.'

'Oh? Where do *you* stand then?' asked Michael.

'I come in with you and St. André,' replied Cordier, 'though I admit my sympathies are wholly with Schwartz. Still . . . one's been a gentleman . . .'

And in the end we found that only Cordier could really be depended upon to join Michael, St. André, Maris, and myself as a staunch and reliable party of anti-Schwartz, pro-duty-and-discipline non-murderers, prepared to tell the mutineers that they must drop their assassination plot, or Lejaune would be warned.

One by one, the others went off, some apologetic and regretful, some blustering, some honestly anxious to support what they considered Schwartz's brave blow for their rights, some merely afraid to do what they would have liked to do.

When we five were at length alone, Michael said, 'Well, I'm afraid we're not going to scare Schwartz off his scheme.'

'No,' agreed Cordier. 'It looks more as though we are only going to provide him with some extra labour. More little pigs . . .'

'There won't be any pigs if Lejaune acts promptly,' said St. André.

'None.' agreed Maris, 'and I'm almost tempted to vote for warning Lejaune *before* saying anything to Schwartz. It would give us more chance . . .'

'No. No. We can't do that,' said Cordier. 'We must give old Schwartz a fair show. If he'll cut out the murder items from his programme, we'll say nothing, of course, and he can carry on. If he won't, we'll do our duty as decent folk, and give Lejaune his chance.'

'Will he take it?' I asked. 'Will he listen?'

'Not to one of us alone,' said St. André. 'But he'd have to take notice of a deputation, consisting of the five of us, all telling the same tale.'

'A deputation consisting of ourselves, coming from ourselves?' smiled Cordier.

'After all, though,' asked Maris, 'does it matter if he believes or not? Suppose one of us goes and tells him the truth – isn't that enough? If he likes to punish the man and ignore his warning, that's his affair.'

'Quite,' agreed Michael. 'But it's ours too! We don't want to be shot in our beds because Lejaune won't listen to us . . . If Schwartz isn't forestalled, every man in this fort who hasn't joined his gang by the day after to-morrow will share Lejaune's fate.'

'That means us five, Boldini, Dupré, and Lejaune,' said Cordier.

'Unless Boldini is in with them, – which is quite likely,' put in St. André.

'Yes, seven of us,' mused Michael, 'even without Boldini. If Lejaune listens to our tale of woe and acts promptly, we five and the two non-coms. are a most ample force for him to work with . . . Simply a matter of acting a night before they do – and there need be no bloodshed either.'

'Fancy fighting to protect *Lejaune*!' smiled Cordier. 'Enough to make *le bon Dieu* giggle.'

'We're fighting to protect the Flag,' said St. André. 'Lejaune is incidental. We're going to fight a murderous mutiny – and another incidental is that we are probably going to save our own lives thereby . . .'

'Who'll tell Schwartz?' interrupted Cordier.

'I will,' said Michael.

'We all will,' said I. 'Let us five just go to him together and warn him. We won't emphasise the fact that we speak for ourselves only.'

'That's it,' agreed St. André. 'We'll tell Schwartz that we're a "deputation"' to him – and do the same when we go on to interview Lejaune – if that's necessary.'

And so the five of us agreed to go in search of Schwartz then and there, to tell him that we would take no part in mutiny and murder, and to warn him that we should report the matter at once, unless he agreed to abandon the part of his scheme that included the slaughter of superiors and the coercion of comrades.

6

As we left the oasis and strolled towards the fort, we met a man carrying pails, for water. As he passed, I saw it was the Portuguese, Bolidar, the man who had been so roughly handled for attempted theft in our barrack-room at Sidi-bel-Abbès. He had always pretended that, on that melancholy occasion, he had strayed, under the influence of liquor, into the wrong room, and that, when caught, he was merely getting into what he thought was his own bed!

Warned by Hank and Buddy, however, we, on the other hand, regarded the gentleman as the miserable tool of Boldini, who had taken him up when Guantaio, Colonna, and Gotto had declined to do his stealing for him.

As he passed Michael, he half stopped, winked, made as though to speak, and then went on. Looking back, I saw that he had halted, put his pails down, and was staring after us.

Seeing me turn round, he signalled to me to come to him, and began walking towards me.

Here was a man with whom a quiet talk might be very useful, particularly as he had made the first overtures.

'I want to speak to your brother and you,' he whispered. 'Privately. I daren't be seen doing it. I am in Hell – and yet I am going to Hell. Yes, I am going to Hell – and yet I am in Hell now.'

He was evidently in a very unbalanced state of mind. He was trembling, and he looked terribly ill.

'Go into the oasis and wait,' said I. 'I'll bring my brother along soon.'

'I must hide . . . I must hide . . . I must hide,' he kept repeating.

'All right,' I agreed. 'You hide. I'll stroll along whistling 'Père Bougeaud' when I bring my brother.'

'Lejaune will tear my throat out . . . He'll eat my heart . . . So will Schwartz . . . So will Boldini . . .'

'Well, you won't feel the second two,' I comforted him, 'and you haven't got three hearts . . . You tell us all about it,' I added soothingly. 'We'll look after you. Pull yourself together now,' for I thought he was going to burst into tears.

'You won't bring anybody else? You won't tell anybody else? Not a word?' he begged.

'Not a soul. Not a word,' I replied. 'You wait for us in the far clump of palms beyond the well,' and I went after Michael.

As soon as I could speak to him alone, I told him about Bolidar.

'Good,' said Michael. 'We'll hear what the merchant's got to say before we tackle Schwartz. The bold Bolidar evidently wants to hedge a bit, for some reason . . . "When rogues fall out." . . . Let's go straight back before he changes what he calls his mind.'

Michael ran on and asked St. Andre and the others to wait a little while and do nothing until he returned.

We then went back to the oasis, and as we passed near the well, I whistling 'Avez-vous vu la casquette de Père Boueaud?' Bolidar joined us, trembling with fear and fever.

We went and sat down together with a high sand-hill between us and the oasis.

At first, Bolidar was incoherent and almost incomprehensible, but soon it was quite clear that the wretched creature was turning to us as a last hope and last resort in his extremity of anxiety, suspense, and terror.

Realising what it was that drove him to unburden himself to us – sheer cowardly fear for his own wretched skin – we never for one instant doubted the truth of what he said.

He oozed truth as he did abject funk, from every pore, and he showed it in every gleam of his bloodshot rolling yellow eyes, and in every gesticulation of his trembling dirty yellow hands.

'My friends,' he gabbled, 'I must confess to you and I must save you. I can bear it no longer. My conscience . . . My rectitude . . . My soul . . . My sense of gratitude . . .'

Michael winked at me. We did not value Bolidar's conscience and gratitude as highly as we did his state of trembling fright, when estimating his motives for 'confession.' . . .

'On that terrible night when I was so cruelly misjudged and so cruelly treated, you tried to save me . . . Yes, even though it was you whom I was supposed to be trying to rob . . . An absurd idea, of course . . .' and he laughed nervously.

There was no doubting the fact that the gentle dago was in a rare state of terror. His convulsive swallowings, drawn yellow features, tremblings and twitchings, clenched hands and wild eyes, were really distressing.

'Most absurd idea, of course,' murmured Michael. 'What is it you want to tell us?'

'Your diamond! Your diamond!' whispered Bolidar hoarsely, gripping Michael's wrist and staring into his eyes.

'Ah – my diamond. And what about it?' said Michael gently.

'Lejaune! Lejaune means to get it,' he hissed. 'And he'll kill me! He'll kill me! If he doesn't, Schwartz will . . . Or Boldini . . . What *shall* I do!' What *can* I do!' he screamed.

Michael patted the poor rascal's shoulder.

'There! There! Never mind. No one's going to kill you,' he soothed him, almost as though he had been a baby. 'Now tell us all about it and we'll see what can be done . . . You join our party and you'll be safe enough.'

'*Your* party?' asked Bolidar. 'What is *your* party? And what are you going to do?'

'Oh – we are a party all right. The stoutest fellows in the garrison – and we're going to *warn* Lejaune – if Schwartz doesn't agree to give up the murder part of the plot,' replied Michael.

'You're going to do *what*?' asked Bolidar, open-eyed and open-mouthed.

'Going to warn Lejaune,' repeated Michael.

Bolidar threw his hands up and shook with mirthless laughter.

'*But he* KNOWS! – *He* KNOWS! *He* KNOWS ALL ABOUT IT, *and who's in it – and when it's to be – and every word that's said in the place!*' cackled Bolidar in a kind of broken, hoarse voice.

Michael and I stared at each other aghast.

'Who tells him?' asked Michael.

'*I do*,' was the proud reply of this shameless animal. 'And when he has got your diamond, he will kill me,' he snivelled.

I was absolutely staggered. If Lejaune knew all about it, what of our precious threat to Schwartz? And what was our position now?

'Why doesn't Lejaune do something then?' asked Michael.

'Oh, he'll *do* something all right,' said Bolidar. 'He'll do a good deal, the night before Schwartz and his fools intend to strike.'

'Why does he wait?' we asked simultaneously.

'To see what you two are going to do,' was the reply. 'If you join Schwartz you'll be killed *with* Schwartz, the night before the mutiny is due – and I'm to secure the diamond. It is not really supposed that you'll join him though. And if you don't join Schwartz you are to be killed in the attack *on* him instead.'

'By whom?' asked Michael.

'*By me*,' replied Bolidar. 'You see, if you should join Schwartz, I am to be loyal and enter the barrack-room with Lejaune and the others on the night. As we cover the mutineers with our rifles, mine is to go off and kill you . . . If you don't join Schwartz, I am to be a mutineer, and when *you* enter the barrack-room with Lejaune and the loyal party, in the night, I am to shoot you from my bed . . . Either way you are to die – and I am perfectly sure that I shall die too . . . Oh, God! Oh, Jesus Christ! Oh, Holy Virgin! Oh, Saints in Heaven!' he blubbered.

'And suppose I refuse to give Schwartz any answer, and remain perfectly neutral?' asked Michael.

'Then I am to harangue the mutineers and urge them to kill you as a non-supporter! You *and* any others that won't join them, so that it will not look as though I have any personal motive or feeling with regard to you specially. Then I am to offer to "execute" you . . . Having done it, I am to get the diamond and give it to Lejaune . . . Yes,' he added with another whispered gasp, 'Lejaune is going to shoot me if you are killed without my securing the jewel for him . . .' and he rocked his body to and fro in despair.

'He ought to have an apron to throw over his head and cry into – like an old peasant woman whose cow has died,' said Michael in English.

'Yes,' I agreed. 'Let's get all we can out of the brute before we let him go.'

'Is Boldini in this?' Michael asked Bolidar. 'I mean, are he and Lejaune working together?'

'Well – Boldini knows that Lejaune knows,' was the reply. 'And those two are going to use Dupré and St. André and Cordier and Maris and you two, for the arrest of the unarmed mutineers in the middle of the night. That is, if you refuse to join Schwartz as they anticipate . . . But I doubt if Boldini and Lejaune quite trust each other. Guantaio says they don't. He thinks that Boldini intends to get the diamond for himself, and that Lejaune suspects as much. At least that is what Guantaio tells me – but I don't wholly trust him . . .'

'Don't you really?' said Michael.

'No. I don't think he's absolutely honest,' said Bolidar doubtfully.

'You surprise me,' admitted Michael. 'The dirty dog!'

'He has made proposals to me which I have rejected with contempt,' said Bolidar.

'Dangerous?' asked Michael.

'Absurdly,' replied Bolidar. 'Besides, how was I to know that I should get my share? It's bad enough to *have* to trust Lejaune as one is compelled to do – without risking things with a rascal like Guantaio.'

'Has Boldini made – er – proposals which you rejected with contempt?' Michael enquired.

'Oh, yes. But as I pointed out to him – Lejaune is *adjudant* while Boldini is only *caporal*.'

'And what did he say to that?' asked Michael.

'That a live *caporal* is better than a dead *adjudant*,' was the interesting reply.

'Sounds sinister,' I observed in English.

'Nice little crowd,' said Michael in the same language. 'One really doesn't know where one is, nor where to start on the job of making head or tail of the business.

'Let's get this clear now,' he said to Bolidar. 'You are Lejaune's – er – man. You warned him of Schwartz's plot to mutiny and kill him, while acting as though you were a ring-leader. You have told every detail to Lejaune and kept him up to date with every development. Lejaune has given you the job of killing me. If I join Schwartz, you are to turn loyal, go over to Lejaune, and shoot me in my bed when we are arrested.

'If I refuse to join Schwartz you are to continue as a mutineer and shoot me, from your bed, when I come in with the loyal party to arrest you.

'If I decline to declare myself you are to be my executioner, self-appointed, on behalf of the worthy mutineers – who will have no neutrals about. And all this in order that Lejaune may get a diamond that is supposed to be in my possession . . .'

Bolidar was sunk in a lethargy of miserable thought. He slowly nodded in affirmation.

'And probably Boldini has a plan of his own which involves a dead *adjudant* and leaves a live *caporal* – also in pursuit of a diamond! And Boldini's plan, I suppose, is to support Lejaune until he has got the diamond, and then withdraw the support – and the diamond? . . .'

Bolidar came out of his fit of brooding abstraction.

'That is what Guantaio said,' he replied. 'He wanted me to join Boldini, Colonna, Gotto, and himself. We were to plot, and kill Lejaune *and* those who stood by him against the mutineers, after those poor fools had been arrested and either shot (in "self-defence," of course) or put in the cells. When we had got the diamond we could decide whether to liberate the mutineers and use them in fighting our way to Morocco, or whether their mouths had better be closed . . . We could set fire to the fort and clear out – and everything would be put down to the account of the Arabs . . .'

'And why did you not fall in with this pretty scheme?' asked Michael.

'Well – who could trust Boldini? Or Guantaio? Or any of them, for that matter? They are not *honest* men. Once Boldini had the diamond, what would be the worth of the life of the man who had a claim on a share of it? To have the diamond would, of course, be death! To be one of a syndicate owning it would, of course, be death! Even to know who had got it would be death, for the man who had it would kill you lest you robbed him or demanded your share . . . How *can* one work with such dishonest people?' and the speaker's voice broke with righteous indignation.

'And has Guantaio made any other proposals which you have rejected with contempt?' asked Michael.

'Oh – any number,' replied Bolidar. 'He seems to think I'm a fool. He actually proposed that I should rob you, and he and I should desert together, before all this mutiny business takes place. I was almost tempted – but – but –'

'Quite,' said Michael. 'It must be a great handicap.'

'It is,' agreed Bolidar. 'And besides,' he added, 'how could two men walk across two thousand miles of desert, apart from the question of *goums* and the Touaregs? . . . And wouldn't Guantaio murder me directly we got to Morocco?'

'Unless you murdered him first,' said Michael.

'Yes,' agreed Bolidar, 'but one might leave it too late . . .' and he meandered on about the untrustworthiness of Italians.

'Well, now. Let's get down to business,' Michael interrupted. 'What have you told us all this for? What do you want us to do?'

'Why,' said Bolidar, 'I felt I must deal with honest men and I must get away. It is certain death for me. If I get the diamond I shall be killed for it, or for knowing that Lejaune has got it. If I don't get it, Lejaune will kill me for failing him, or else for knowing too much when there is a court martial about the mutiny . . .'

'Well?' Michael encouraged him.

'I thought that if I told you two all about it – the real truth to honest men – you would save my life and your own, and give me a share in the diamond.'

'How save our lives?' Michael asked.

'All desert together before the mutiny, and you give me a third-part share in the diamond when we are safe.'

'How do you know we should keep our promise?' asked Michael.

'Because you are English . . . In Brazil, we say, "*Word of an Englishman!*" and "*Word of an American!*" when we are swearing to keep faith. If you promise, I know you will perform.'

'This is very touching,' said Michael. 'But suppose I give you my word that I haven't got a diamond and never possessed a diamond in my life?'

Bolidar smiled greasily, as at one who must have his little jest.

'Oh, *Sehor*!' he murmured, waggling his head and his hands idiotically.

'One knows of the little parcel in your belt-pouch,' he said.

'Oh, one does, does one?' smiled Michael. 'Fancy that now!'

Silence fell.

'Well – as you just said, two or three people can't march off into the desert and expect to live for more than a day or two,' observed Michael after a while.

'We might make a party,' suggested Bolidar. 'It is known that St. André, Maris, Cordier, and one or two more refuse to listen to Schwartz's plan to kill Lejaune.'

'Nor are they deserters,' said Michael.

'No – but when they know that they are to be killed by the mutineers if they don't join them, or to be killed by Lejaune if they do – what then? . . . Tell them the truth – that Lejaune is going to have no survivors of this mutiny – whichever side they may be on. No. He's going to have the diamond and the credit and glory of suppressing the mutiny and saving the fort single-handed. He'll teach *les légionnaires* to mutiny! Their mutiny shall end in death for the lot of them – and in wealth and promotion for Lejaune. He sees himself an officer and a rich man on the strength of this fine mutiny . . . And what happens to the men who told him about the diamond – the men who helped him and risked their lives for him? What, I ask you? . . . Death, I tell you. *Death! Death! Death!*' he screamed, trembling and slavering like a trapped beast.

'And who *did* tell him about this wonderful diamond?' asked Michael.

'Boldini,' replied Bolidar. 'As soon as he rejoined, he told him of the gang of famous London jewel-thieves who had fled from the English police to the Legion. He and Guantaio and Gotto were to get it and give it to Lejaune, who would protect them and who would either place it and share with them, or keep it until they had all served their time . . . I don't know.'

'And they put you up to steal it in Sidi, eh?' asked Michael. 'Why you?' But Bolidar spurned such an unworthy suggestion.

'Anyhow, we're getting away from the point,' Michael interrupted him. 'What's to be done? We're certainly not going to desert. I wonder if one could possibly persuade the gentle Lejaune that there's no such thing as a diamond in Zinderneuf?'

'What – pretend you hid it and left it – at Sidi-bel-Abbès?' said Bolidar. 'That's an idea! . . .'

Michael laughed.

'Did you leave it at Sidi?' asked Bolidar.

'I most certainly have not got a diamond here,' replied Michael.

'Do you swear it by the name of God? By your faith in Christ? By your love of the Blessed Virgin? And by your hope for the intercession of the Holy Saints?' asked Bolidar.

'Not in the least,' replied Michael. 'I merely say it. I have not got a diamond – "*Word of an Englishman.*"'

'It's a chance,' whispered Bolidar. 'Dear Christ! It's a chance. Oh, lovely Christ, help me! . . . I'll tell Lejaune you left it at Sidi.'

'Tell him what you like,' said Michael.

Bolidar pondered.

'Huh! Anyhow, he'll *make sure* you haven't got it,' he said darkly, and rose to his feet. 'But I'll try it. I'll try it. There is a small hope . . . I'll tell you what he says,' he added.

'You'll tell us *something*, I've no doubt,' replied Michael, as the heroic Portuguese took up his pails and slunk off.

7

'Well, my son – a bit involved, what?' smiled my brother as we were left in solitude.

'What *can* one do?' I asked feebly.

'Nothing,' replied Michael promptly and cheerfully. 'Just await events and do the straight thing. I'm not going to bunk. And I'm not going to join any beastly conspiracy. But I think I'm going to "beat Bolidar to the draw" as Hank and Buddy would say – when he tries to cover me with his rifle.'

'In other words, you're going to shoot friend Bolidar before friend Bolidar shoots you?' I said.

'That's it, my son. If he's cur enough to do a dirty murder like that, just because Lejaune tells him to, he must take his little risks,' replied Michael.

'And if that happens – I mean if I see him cover you and you shoot him – Lejaune is going with him. It is as much Lejaune's murder as it is Bolidar's,' I said.

'You're going to shoot Lejaune, eh?' asked Michael.

'I am,' said I, 'if Bolidar covers you. Why should he cover *you*, in particular, out of a score or so of men, unless he has been told to shoot you?'

'Well – we'll tell Bolidar just what's going to happen, and we'll invite him to tell Lejaune too. It would be fairer, perhaps,' said Michael.

'Golly,' I observed. 'Won't it make the lad gibber! One more slayer on his track!'

'Yes,' smiled Michael. 'Then he'll know that if neither Lejaune nor Boldini nor Schwartz kills him, *I* shall. Poor old Bolidar . . .'

'What about poor old us?' I asked.

'We're for it, I should say,' replied Michael. 'Of course, Lejaune won't believe that this wonderful diamond they are talking about has been left at Sidi, and he'll carry on.'

'I'm muddled,' I groaned. 'Let's get it clear now:

'*One*: We tell Schwartz we won't join his gang, and that we will warn Lejaune of the plot to murder him . . .'

'Or shall we tell Schwartz that *Lejaune knows all about it*?' Michael interrupted.

'Good Lord, I'd forgotten that,' I said. 'I suppose we'd better.'

'Then they'll crucify poor old Bolidar for good, this time,' grinned Michael. 'Serve him right too. Teach him not to go about murdering to order . . .'

'We need not say who told us that Lejaune knows,' I observed.

'And then they *will* know that you and I are beastly traitors!' said Michael. 'Of course, they will at once think that we told him ourselves.'

'Probably Guantaio has told them that, and done it himself, meanwhile,' I suggested.

'Oh, damn it all – let's talk about something else,' groaned Michael. 'I'm sick of their silly games.'

'Yes, old chap. But it's pretty serious,' I said. 'Let me just go over it again:

'*One*: We tell Schwartz that we won't join his gang. And that Lejaune knows all about his plot.

'*Two*: Lejaune acts before Schwartz does, and he raids the barrack-room the night before the mutiny. We shall either be in bed as though mutineers, or we shall be ordered to join the guard of loyal men who are to arrest the mutineers.

'*Three*: In either case, Bolidar is to shoot you. But directly he raises his rifle in your direction, you are going to shoot him. (You'll have to take your rifle to bed with you if Lejaune is going to pretend that you are a mutineer.)

'*Four*: If I see that Bolidar is out to murder you, I shall shoot Lejaune myself. (I shall take my rifle to bed too, if we are left with the mutineers.)

'Five: If . . .'

'Five: The fat *will* be in the fire, nicely, then,' interrupted Michael. 'What can we do but bolt into the desert with the rest, if you kill Lejaune? You'd be the most badly-wanted of all the badly-wanted mutineers, after that . . . They'd get us too, if they had to turn out a desert-column of all arms . . .'

We pondered the delightful situation.

'Besides,' Michael went on, 'you couldn't do it. Of course you couldn't. It would be a different thing if Lejaune were raising a rifle to shoot you, as Bolidar will be doing to me, if I shoot Bolidar. You couldn't just blow Lejaune's head off, in cold blood. That is exactly what Schwartz is going to do . . . And what we object to.'

And it was so, of course. I might just as well go to Schwartz and offer to be the butcher.

'Well,' said I, 'suppose I cover Lejaune with my rifle and tell him I'll blow his head off the moment he moves – and then I tell him to . . .'

'Consider himself under arrest?' jeered Michael. 'And what are you then, but the rankest mutineer of the lot? Besides, it's quite likely that Lejaune won't be there. He's brave enough – but he'd like to survive the show. In fact, he intends to be the sole survivor, I should say.'

'Looks as though we've simply *got* to join Schwartz then,' I said.

'Damned if I do,' replied Michael. 'I'm certainly going bald-headed for anyone who goes for me, but I'm not going to join any mutineers, nor commit any murders.'

'Nor are you,' he added, as I stared glumly out into the desert.

'What is to be done then?' I asked once again.

'*Nothing*, I tell you,' repeated Michael. 'We've got to "jump lively when we do jump," as Buddy says; but we can only wait on events and do what's best, as they arise. Meanwhile, let's hold polite converse with the merry Schwartz . . . Come on'.

And we got up and strolled through the starlit darkness to the Fort.

'I suppose we can take it that Sergeant Dupré knows all about the plot?' I said, as we passed into the stifling courtyard.

'No doubt of it,' replied Michael. 'I am inclined to think Lejaune would try to keep a nice compact "loyal party" to deal with the mutineers, and hope they'd be like the Kilkenny cats, mutually destructive . . . Say, Dupré, Boldini, and five or six *légionnaires*. . . Some of whom would be killed in the scrap . . . Of course, one doesn't know *what* his plans really are – except that he means to get a diamond, a lot of kudos, and a nice little vengeance on his would-be murderers . . .'

As we entered the barrack-room, we saw that a committee meeting of the 'butcher' party was in session. They stared in hostile fashion at Michael and me as we went to our cots and got out our cleaning-rags from the little bags.

I sat down on my bed and began melting wax on to my belt and pouches, preparatory to *astiquage* labours.

The conspirators' heads drew together again.

Michael went over to where they were grouped at the end of the long table.

'Have you come with your answer to a question I asked you about some *cochons*?' growled Schwartz, scowling at him.

'I have come with some news about a *cochon*, my friend,' replied Michael.

Half a dozen pairs of eyes glared at him, and I strolled over. So did St. André from his cot. Just then Maris and Cordier entered, and I beckoned to them.

'He knows *all* about it,' said Michael.

Schwartz sprang to his feet, his eyes blazing, his beard seeming to bristle, and his teeth gleaming as he bared them. He was a dangerous savage-looking ruffian.

'*You* have told him!' he shouted, pointing in Michael's face. 'You treacherous filthy cur, you have betrayed us!' and he glanced to where a bayonet hung at the head of his bed.

'And come straight here and told you?' sneered Michael coldly. 'If you were as clever as you are noisy, you might see I should hardly do that. You're a pretty leader of a gang of desperate mutineers, aren't you?'

Schwartz stared in amazement, struck dumb by the cool daring of the person who had the courage and effrontery to taunt and insult *him*.

Michael turned to Brandt, Haff, Delarey, Guantaio, Vogué, and the rest of Schwartz's familiars.

'A remarkable leader,' he said. 'Here you are, the gang of you, making your wonderful plans, *and Lejaune knows every word you say*, and precisely what you are going to do – almost as soon as you know it yourselves! . . . *Join* you? No, thanks. You have talked cleverly about "pigs" and "butchers" – but what about a lot of silly *sheep*? You make me tired,' and Michael produced a most convincing and creditable yawn.

'Well, what are you going to do?' he asked as they sat open-mouthed. 'Whatever it is, Lejaune will do it first,' he added, 'so you'd better do nothing.'

'And Lejaune will do it first,' I put in.

Michael's coolness, bitter contempt for them, and his obvious sincerity, had won. They knew he spoke the truth, and they knew he had not betrayed them to Lejaune.

I watched Guantaio, and decided that save perhaps for a little courage, he was another Bolidar. Certainly Boldini would hear of Michael's action, if Lejaune did not, as soon as Guantaio could get away from his dupes.

'What to do!' murmured Schwartz. 'What to do! If Lejaune knows everything! . . .'

'Declare the whole thing off,' said Michael, 'and then the noble soul who has told Lejaune so much, can tell him that too,' and Michael's eye rested on Guantaio.

It rested so long upon Guantaio, that that gentleman felt constrained to leap to his feet and bluster.

'Do you *dare* to suggest . . .' he shouted and stopped. (*Qui s'excuse s'accuse.*)

'I did not know I had suggested anything,' said Michael softly. 'Why *should* I suggest anything, my friend?'

'If it were you – I'd hang you to the wall with bayonets through your ears, you yellow dog,' growled Schwartz, glaring at Guantaio.

'He lies! He lies!' screamed Guantaio.

'How do you know?' asked Michael. 'How do *you* know what Lejaune knows?

'I meant that you lie if you say that I betrayed the plot,' blustered Guantaio.

'I haven't said it,' replied Michael. 'It is only you who have said it . . . You seem to be another of the clever ones . . .'

Michael's coolness and superiority were establishing a kind of supremacy for him over these stupid creatures, driven and bedevilled as they were by *cafard* and by Lejaune.

They stared at each other and at us.

'What's to be done?' said Schwartz . . . 'By God! When I catch the traitor . . .' he roared and shook his great fists above his shaggy head.

'Nothing's to be done,' replied Michael again, 'because you can *do* nothing. You are in Lejaune's hands absolutely. Take my advice and drop this lunacy, and you may hear nothing more of it . . . There may be a new Commandant here in a week or two . . .'

'Yes – and his name may be Lejaune,' answered Schwartz.

'Anyhow – he *knows*, and he's got us,' put in Brandt. 'I vote we all join in the plot and then all vote it abandoned. Then he can't punish one more than another. He can't put the whole blasted garrison in his cursed cells, can he?'

'You're right,' said Haff. 'That's it. Abandon the whole scheme, I say. *And* find out the traitor and give him a night that he'll remember through eternity in Hell . . .'

But the ferocious Schwartz was of a different fibre, and in his dogged and savage brain the murder of Lejaune was an *idée fixe*.

'Abandon nothing!' he roared, springing to his feet. 'I tell you I . . .' And then Michael laid his hand on his arm.

'Silence, you noisy fool,' he said quietly. 'Don't you understand *yet* that whatever you say now will go straight to Lejaune?'

Schwartz, foaming, swung round on Guantaio.

'Get out of this,' he growled menacingly, and pointed to the door.

'I swear I . . .' began Guantaio indignantly.

'Get out, I say!' bawled Schwartz, 'and when the time comes for us to strike our blow – be careful. Let me only *suspect* you, and I'll hang you to the flagstaff by one foot . . . By God, I will . . . *Go*!'

Guantaio slunk off.

'Now listen to me again,' said Michael. 'As I told you, Lejaune knows all about your plot to murder him and desert at full moon. I did not tell him. But I was going to tell him, if, after I had warned you, you refused to abandon the scheme.'

Schwartz growled and rose to his feet again.

'Oh yes,' Michael went on, 'I was going to warn you first, to give you a chance to think better of it – in which case I should have said nothing, of course . . . But now get this clear. If I know of any *new* scheme, or any change of date or method, or anything that Lejaune does not already know – I shall tell him . . . Do you understand? . . .'

'You cursed spy! You filthy, treacherous hound! You . . .' roared Schwartz. 'Why should *you* . . .'

'Oh, don't be such a noisy nuisance, Schwartz,' interrupted Michael. 'I and a party of my friends don't choose *to give Lejaune the chance he wants*, and we don't really like murder either . . . We have as much right to live as you, haven't we?'

'*Live*,' snarled Brandt. 'D'you call *this* living?'

'We aren't dying of thirst, anyhow,' replied Michael. 'And if we are chivvied and hunted and hounded by Lejaune, it's better than being hunted to our deaths by a camel-company of *goums* or by the Touaregs, isn't it?'

'And who *are* your precious friends?' asked Haff.

'There are five of them here, for a start,' said St. André.

'And how many more?' asked Schwartz.

'You'll find that out when you start mutinying, my friend,' said Maris. 'Don't fancy that all your band mean all they say.'

'In fact,' put in Cordier, 'you aren't the only conspirators. There is also a plot *not* to mutiny, d'you see? . . . And some good "friends" of yours are in it too.'

'So you'd better drop it, Schwartz,' I added. 'None of us is a spy, and none of us will report anything to Lejaune without telling you first and inviting you to give it up. And if you refuse – Lejaune is going to know all about it. You are simply surrounded by *real* spies, too, mind.'

'You cowardly hounds!' growled Schwartz. 'There isn't a *man* in the place . . . *Cowards*, I say.'

'Oh, quite,' agreed Michael. 'But we've enough pluck to stick things out while Lejaune is in command, if *you* haven't . . . Anyhow – you know how things stand now,' and he strolled off, followed by St. André, Maris, Cordier, and myself.

'This is a *maison de fous*,' observed St. André.

'A corner of the lunatic asylum of Hell,' said Cordier.

'Some of us had better keep awake to-night, I think,' observed Maris.

'Especially if Bolidar is not in his bed,' I added.

Michael drew me aside.

'We'll have another word with that sportsman,' he said. 'I think he'll have the latest tip from the stable, and I fancy he'll believe any promise we make him.'

8

After completing our *astiquage* and other preparations for the morrow, Michael and I strolled in the courtyard.

'What'll Schwartz do now?' I asked.

'Probably act to-night,' said Michael, 'unless he swallowed our bluff that our party consists of more than us five. He may be wondering as to how many of his supposed adherents will really follow him if he starts the show . . .'

'He may see how many will take a solemn oath to stand by him and see it through, if he gives the word for to-night,' I suggested.

'Quite likely,' agreed Michael. 'And if neither Guantaio nor Bolidar knows about it, Schwartz may pull it off all right.'

'I don't somehow see Lejaune taken by surprise, when he knows what's brewing,' I said.

'No,' replied Michael. 'But he may be relying on Bolidar giving him the tip.'

'What are we going to do if we wake up and find that the show has begun?' I asked.

'Stand by Lejaune,' replied Michael. 'France expects that every half-penny legionary this day will do his dooty.'

'It'll be too late to save Lejaune if we're awakened by rifle-shots and "alarums and excursions without," won't it?' I observed.

'That won't be our fault,' said Michael. 'If they murder Lejaune and the others, all we can do is to decline to join the mutineers.'

'If we survive and they desert, I suppose the senior soldier will carry on as Commandant of the fort,' I mused. That will take some deciding if only St. André, Maris, Cordier, you, and I are left . . .'

'St. André has been a French officer,' observed Michael.

'Yes – but they'll select you, old chap,' I said.

'Then I'll use my powers to appoint St. André,' smiled my brother.

Someone passed and repassed us in the dark, and then waited near the lantern by the quarter-guard, to identify us by its light.

It was Schwartz.

'See here, you,' he said as he recognised us. 'Come with me . . . Now

. . . What are you going to do if someone kills Lejaune without doing himself the honour of consulting your lordships?'

'Nothing,' replied Michael, as we walked away from the light, 'We shall continue in our duty as soldiers. We shall obey the orders of the senior person remaining true to his salt and the Flag.'

'The devil burn their filthy Flag!' snarled Schwartz. 'I spit on it.'

'A pity you came under it, if that's what you think,' said Michael.

'Then you and your gang of cowards and blacklegs will not interfere?' asked Schwartz.

'If you will desert, you will desert,' replied my brother. 'That is not our affair. If we know what you are going to do, we shall report it, if we can't stop it. If we can prevent mutiny and murder we shall . . . As for deserting – I should say the Legion would be well rid of you.'

'Oh, you do, do you, Mr. Preacher?' replied Schwartz, who was evidently putting great and unwonted restraint upon himself. 'What I want to know is whether you are going to fight us or not?'

'Certainly – if ordered to,' replied Michael.

'And if there is no one to order you?' sneered Schwartz.

'Then obviously we shall not be ordered to, my good ass,' was the unsoothing reply. 'And we certainly shan't hinder your departure . . . Far from it,' he added.

Schwartz turned to go.

'Look to yourselves! I warn you! Look to yourselves,' he growled.

'Oh, we shall. Don't you worry,' replied Michael.

'They'll do it to-night,' he added, as we watched Schwartz disappear. 'We must secure our rifles and we must keep awake.'

I wondered how much longer we should be able to stand this intolerable strain, in addition to the terrific heat and monotony of hardship.

'Go and look for Bolidar,' said my brother after a brief silence. 'I'll hunt round too. Bring him here if you find him. We'll ask him what's likely to happen if they mutiny to-night. Then we can fix up a plan of action with St. André and the others.'

I went back to the barrack-room.

Bolidar was deep in conclave with Schwartz, Brandt, Haff, Vogué, Delarey, and one or two others, round Schwartz's bed.

I pretended to go to my *paquetage* for something, and then retired and reported to Michael.

'That's all right then,' he said. 'Whatever the fools fix up for to-night will be reported to Lejaune to-night, and he will know what to do.

'We'll have a word with Bolidar though, by and by,' he added. 'Nothing like knowing what's going to happen.'

Half an hour later, we returned to the reeking, stifling room. Most of the men were lying on their cots. Bolidar was sitting on a bench, polishing his bayonet.

'Will you polish mine too?' I said, going over to him. 'Follow me out,' I whispered, as I gave him my bayonet.

I strolled back to my cot, began to undress, and then, taking my mug, went out of the room as though for water.

Watching the lighted doorway I waited in the darkness.

Ten minutes or so later, Bolidar came out.

'Well?' I asked.

'Lejaune does not believe a word about the diamond not being here,' he said, 'and the mutineers are going to shoot him and all the non-coms. on morning parade to-morrow instead of at night. They think he will be expecting it at night, as some informer must have told him that is the plan . . . He'll be off his guard . . . They are going to kill Dupré and Boldini simultaneously with Lejaune . . . If your party is a big one they are going to leave you alone, if you leave them alone. They will load themselves up with water, wine, food, and ammunition, and march out at sunset.

'Blanc, who has been a sailor, is going to lead them straight over the desert to Morocco, by Lejaune's compass . . . Schwartz is to be Captain; Brandt and Haff, Lieutenants; Delarey and Vogué, Sergeants; and Glock and Hartz, Corporals . . . There will be twenty privates . . .

'They are going to court martial Guantaio, and if he is found guilty they are going to hang him . . . *I* know enough to get him hung, the dirty traitor . . .'

'And you?' I asked.

'I am to shoot Lejaune,' he replied, 'to prove my sincerity and good faith. If I don't, I am to be shot myself . . . Guantaio has been maligning me to Schwartz.'

'Have you told *Lejaune* this?' I asked this astonishing creature.

'*I am just going to do so now*,' he replied, and I gasped.

'And I suppose he'll arrest them to-night?' I asked.

'Probably. If *he believes me*,' was the interesting answer.

'What if he doesn't?' I enquired, and, at that, the wretch had another 'nerve-storm' or hysterical fit of trembling, with demented gesticulations and mutterings.

'What *shall* I do? What *shall* I do?' he kept on. 'What *will* become of me? God help me! Help me! Help me!'

'Look here,' said I. 'You tell me and my brother everything – the absolute truth, mind – and we'll save you all right, provided you do nothing against us. No covering with your rifle, mind!'

He clutched my hand in his hot shaking fists.

'You stand in honestly with our party, and you'll be safe,' I went on. 'We'll prevent the mutiny, and nobody will be killed. Neither you nor anybody else.'

I hoped I spoke the truth. Perhaps if I now told Schwartz that I knew about the new morning scheme, and assured him that Lejaune knew it too, he'd own himself defeated and give it all up. On the other hand, he might run amok, yelling to his gang to follow him . . . Lejaune's pre-arranged plans would probably settle their business promptly. Would Lejaune then go and shoot whomsoever else he thought might be better dead?

Bolidar slunk off, and I went back to the barrack-room.

Taking my Arabic copy of the Q'ran from the shelf above my bed, I winked at Michael, and opening the book, seated myself beside him, and began to read in Arabic, as we often did.

Having read a verse, I went on in the same monotone, as though still reading, and said in Arabic:

'To-morrow. Morning. They will kill. One now goes to give information,' and then went on with the next verse. I then gave the book to Michael, who followed the same plan. Soon I heard between actual verses:

'We have warned them. Say nothing. He will strike to night. Do not sleep. I will tell our friends,' and then another verse of the wisdom of the Prophet, before closing the book.

Soon after this, Bolidar entered the room and began to undress.

'What about my bayonet, you, Bolidar?' I called across to him.

'Oh – half a minute, Smith,' he replied, and began polishing it.

A little later he brought it over, and as he bent over my bed to hang the weapon on its hook, whispered:

'I have not told him . . . To-morrow,' and went back to his place.

Under cover of the 'Lights out' bugle, I repeated this to Michael.

'That's all right then,' said he. 'We shall have a quiet night.'

And then perfect silence descended on the room as usual.

9

It was an unpleasant night for me, nevertheless, for I by no means shared Michael's faith in its quiet.

What more likely, I thought, than that Lejaune should choose to-night for his anticipatory counter-stroke? He must have an iron nerve or very great faith in his spies, otherwise he could hardly continue thus to sit on the powder-barrel when the fuse was alight.

Or had he other and surer sources of information, than the tales of Bolidar, and Guantaio's reports to Boldini? Was one of Schwartz's most trusted lieutenants merely Lejaune's *agent provocateur?*

Could Schwartz himself be Lejaune's jackal? No, that was nonsense, and this horrible atmosphere of treachery and suspicion was poisoning my mind. Whereas Lejaune himself was wholly evil and was probably after Michael's fabulous jewel – patiently and remorselessly creeping towards it along a path that led through quagmires of treachery and rivers of blood – Schwartz was a comparatively honest and honourable brute, madly thirsting for vengeance upon a savage beast-tamer who had driven him to utter desperation by injustice and savage cruelty. And, save for Bolidar and Guantaio, his followers were like him, brave men of average character, de-humanised by an inhuman system and the more inhuman monster who applied it.

And why did not the monster strike? For what was he waiting, when every hour increased his danger? Surely it could not be merely the love of the fearless man for prolonging a terribly menacing and precarious situation?

Could it be that, before taking action, he really wished to know absolutely for certain what Michael and I were going to do when the mutineers rose?

Or was he waiting to be surer of Boldini or Dupré?

Of course, if he felt that in the presence of the 'diamond' no reliance could be placed on either of these two colleagues, and if, as a shrewd and experienced judge of men, he estimated Bolidar and Guantaio at their true worth, or worthlessness – perhaps it was quite impossible for him to act at all. If practically every one in the garrison belonged to one of two parties – the 'honest' mutineers determined to desert, or the rascally thieves determined to steal the great jewel and get away with it – what could the man do?

Was he hoping to use the thieves to fight the mutineers and to deal with the surviving party himself? Hardly that, for the mutineers greatly outnumbered the thieves.

On the other hand, could he not quite easily secure the arms of the mutineers, and arrest the men in their beds by employing the thieves? He could – but what then? The thieves would murder him and escape with the jewel – probably releasing the mutineers and organising them as the 'diamond's' unsuspecting escort to Morocco. And each man of the thief-party (Boldini, Guantaio, Colonna, Gotto, and quite probably Vogué and Dupré) would hope that by good luck or more likely by good management – he would be sole survivor of the thief-party.

I tried to put myself in Lejaune's place.

What should I do if I were he, in such circumstances? If I wished first to save my life, and secondly to secure a gem of great price which I believed to be reposing in the pouch of one of the two or three men upon whom I could depend in time of trouble?

And I found it easier to ask the question than to answer it, since one party wanted my life and the other party wanted the jewel.

Having tried to put myself in Lejaune's place, I began to understand his delay in acting. He did nothing because he *could* do nothing.

I almost began to pity the man as I realised his position. He had not a soul to turn to in his loneliness and danger. Well – he was now reaping the reward of his consistent brutality to all who were his subordinates, as well as of his beastly avarice.

Hitherto he had always been backed by the immeasurable power and authority of his superiors, and could inevitably rely upon their inalienable support and unswerving approval. Now he had no superiors, and, face to face with the men whom he had so long outraged, bedevilled, and wronged, he must stand or fall alone.

And it looked as though he must fall.

Then an idea occurred to me. *Had he sent for outside help*? Was a column already on its way from Tokotu, where there were Senegalese as well as a mule-mounted company of the Legion? Was that what he was waiting for?

No. In the first place he would sooner, I felt absolutely certain, lose his life than send out an appeal for help against the very men he was supposed to command, the very men whose trembling disciplined fear of him was his chief pride and loudest boast. It would certainly be the end of all promotion for Adjudant Lejaune if he had to do such a thing as that. In the second place it might also destroy this chance of getting the fabulous gem. It was only in very troubled waters that he, in his position, could fish for that.

I decided that there had been no S.O.S appeal from Zinderneuf to Tokotu.

I tossed and turned in my hot and uncomfortable bed as the problem tossed and turned in my hot uncomfortable brain; and my attempt to decide what I should do in Lejaune's place ended in my deciding that I simply did not know what I *could do*.

It almost seemed best for Lejaune to put himself at the head of the 'honest' mutineers, arrest the thief-party, and then appeal to the others with promises of amendment in his conduct and reform of their condition . . . But arrest the thieves for what? . . . And suppose the mutineers laughed at the promised amelioration of their lot?

It was a hopless *impasse*. I gave it up and turned once more on to my other side. This brought my face toward the door and there, in the doorway, stood – Lejaune.

There stood Lejaune – looking from bed to bed. He was quite alone and he held a revolver in his hand . . . Whom was he going to shoot?

Was this the beginning of the end?

Without thinking, I raised myself on my elbow.

He saw me at once, and, first placing a finger to his lips, beckoned to me.

I stared in amazement.

Frowning savagely, he beckoned again, with a swift and imperious movement of his arm.

What was the idea? Was he going to murder me outside? Or was he going to tell me to fetch Michael out? In that case, had I better refuse or just spring on him, get the revolver, and . . . and what? Neither murder nor mutiny was going to improve our precarious position.

As these thoughts flashed through my mind, I seized my trousers and tunic, struggled into them, and tiptoed to the door.

'Follow me,' said Lejaune, and led the way to his quarters.

Closing the door of his bare, comfortless little room, and seating himself at the table, Lejaune stared at me in silence, his hot arrogant eyes glaring beneath heavy eyebrows contracted in a fierce evil-tempered frown.

'Do you and your miserable brother want to live?' he suddenly growled. 'Answer me, you dog.'

'On the whole, I think so, *mon Adjudant*,' I replied, trying to strike a note between defiant impudence and cringing servility.

'Oh – on the whole, you do, do you?' sneered Lejaune, and again stared in silence. 'Well – if you do, you'd better listen carefully to what I say, for only I can save you. D'you understand? Answer me, you swine.'

'Yes, *mon Adjudant*,' I replied.

'See here then, you infection,' he went on, 'there's some talk among those dogs, of a jewel. A diamond your gang of jewel-thieves got away with, in London. Also there is a plot among them to murder you both and steal it, and desert with it.'

'Is that so, *mon Adjudant*?' said I, as he stopped.

'Don't you answer me! God smite you, you unspeakable corruption!' he roared. 'Yes, it is so,' he went on, mimicking me savagely, 'and I know all about it, as I know everything else that is done, and said, and thought too – *thought*, I say – in this place . . . Now I don't care a curse what you stole, and I don't care a curse what becomes of you and that anointed thief, your brother; but I won't have plots and plans and murders in any force under *my* command. Understand *that*! D'you hear me, sacred animal? Answer me.'

'I hear you, *mon Adjudant*,' I admitted.

'Very well then,' he growled. 'I am going to teach these sacred curs to attend to their duty and leave diamonds and plots alone. By God, I am! To that end, I am going to detail you and your brother and a few more – say, Légionnaires St. André, Cordier, and Maris, as a Corporal's guard to arrest the ringleaders among those impudent swine. And I myself am going to attend to the business. You'll act at my personal orders, under my personal command, and you'll shoot down any man whom I tell you to shoot – as mutineering mad dogs *should* be shot. D'you hear me, you fish-faced, cod-eyed, bug-eating, dumb *crétin*! Answer me!'

'I hear you, *mon Adjudant*,' I replied.

'Well – say so then, grinning imbecile. And to put an end to this thrice-accursed nonsense, and prevent any more disturbances of this sort, your brother will hand over this diamond to me. I'll put it where no plots and plans will trouble it . . . You and your cursed jewels! Wrecking discipline and causing trouble! You ought to be doing twenty years in gaol, the pair of you . . . D'you hear me, blast your soul? Answer me, damn you.'

'I hear you, *mon Adjudant*,' I replied.

'Very well. To-morrow morning, you and your brother and the others will have duties assigned you. You'll be given ammunition. You or your brother or both, will be put over the magazine, and will shoot anyone, except myself, who approaches it. *Anyone*, you understand, whether non-commissioned officer or *légionnaire*. . . I'll teach the swine – by God, I'll teach them! . . . Now then . . . it was your brother I wanted, but you happened to be awake and I saw no point in entering that cage of treacherous hyenas – go and tell your brother what I have said, and as soon as I have that diamond locked for safety in the Company treasure-chest, I'll give you a chance to save your worthless lives . . .

'Listen carefully now. Creep back and wake your brother, St. André, Maris, and Cordier, and tell them to get up and steal silently from the room with their rifles . . . I shall be at the door with that revolver and I'll shoot *anybody* – on the first movement that I don't like . . . Go! . . .'

I saluted and turned about.

So the hour had come! And Lejaune was about to act! Moreover he was going to act on Bolidar's information that Michael, Maris, St. André, Cordier, and I had refused to join the mutineers, and so belonged to neither party. He was going to make us five loyal soldiers the executioners of the rebels.

He had a perfect right to order us to seize any mutineer and to shoot the man if he resisted arrest. Also it was our plain duty to obey him . . .

But Michael? What would happen when Michael denied any knowledge of a diamond? How would he fare at Lejaune's hands when the mutiny had been suppressed? Lejaune's bare word was sufficient to send him to join the defeated mutineers – whether they were in the next world or in that antechamber of the next world, the Penal Battalion . . .

'Make a sound – or a false move, and you'll be the first that dies – the first of many, I hope,' growled Lejaune, as I crept down the passage between thick mud walls, and I felt the muzzle of his revolver jabbed into the small of my back.

The blood surged to my head, and I all but sprang round. One second's space of time for a drive at the point of his jaw – and I asked no more.

But he wouldn't give me that second, and I couldn't do much for Michael with my spine shattered by a 450 expanding bullet. Lejaune would think as much of shooting me as he would of putting his foot on a scorpion . . . And if, by any wild chance, I succeeded, and knocked him out and secured the revolver – how should we be any the better off? Boldini and his gang, and probably Dupré too, were after the 'diamond,' and would kill Michael to get it . . .

With Lejaune following, I reached the door of our barrackroom. Here the *adjudant* halted, his revolver raised, and whispered:

'Your brother, Maris, Cordier, St. André – quick . . .' I crept to Michael's bed.

What would happen if he sprang up with a shout, and roused the snoring sleepers around him? Could Lejaune overawe the lot, or would they, empty-handed, have the courage to rush him? Probably they would not, Everybody waits for a lead in a case like that.

I began whispering in Michael's ear.

'Beau, old chap! . . . It's John . . . Don't make a noise . . . Beau, old chap! . . . It's John . . . Hush! Don't make a noise . . .'

He woke, and was instantly alert.

'What's up?' he whispered.

'Take your tunic and trousers and boots, get your rifle, and go out. Lejaune is relying on our party. Take your bayonet . . .'

He saw Lejaune in the doorway, near which was the nightlamp, and got off his cot.

I crept to St. André, and woke him in the same way.

'The *adjudant* wants us,' I whispered. 'He's at the door.'

'Good!' said St. André. 'It is time he did something.'

Maris also woke quietly, and soon grasped what was wanted of him.

By the time I had roused Cordier, Michael was creeping from the room, dressed, his rifle in his hand. I saw Lejaune give him some cartridges from his bulging side-pockets. I crept out too, taking my rifle and bayonet, and Lejaune gave me ten cartridges.

'Go outside and load,' he whispered. 'Quick . . . Then shoot any man, at once, if he sets his foot on the floor, after a warning.'

We charged our magazines and stood behind Lejaune in the doorway, rifles at the ready. St. André joined us and received the same orders. Lejaune shook his fist at Maris and Cordier, and beckoned to them angrily. Not one of the sleepers stirred.

When the other two joined us, Lejaune said:

'St. André and Cordier – remain here until relieved. If any man wakes, order *silence*, cover him with your rifle, and say you'll shoot him if he leaves his bed. Do it at once, to any man and every man, who disobeys. Fail, and I'll shoot you myself . . . Follow me, you others,' and he quietly returned to his quarters.

'Guard the door, you,' he said to Maris, 'and shoot *anybody* who approaches. *Anybody*, I say.'

'Now you, *quick*,' he said, entering the room and closing the door. 'Give me this wretched diamond that is the cause of all this trouble.'

He glared at Michael.

'You jewel-thieves have corrupted the whole of this garrison, and are a menace to discipline. I'll take charge of it now; and then I'll take charge of some of those swine who think they can plot murder and robbery and desertion in *my* Company, by God! I . . . Out with it, you thieving gaol-bird . . . *Quick*. . . Unless you want your throat cut by those mad dogs of mutineers who've fixed *your* business for this morning, at parade . . . Oh yes, I know all about it . . . *Quick*, I say – the Devil blast your dirty soul . . .' and he shook his fist.

Michael stared back, as one lost in astonishment and wonder.

'"Diamond," *Monsieur l'Adjudant*?' he murmured.

Lejaune's swarthy face was suffused, his eyes bulged and blazed.

'You try any tricks with me and I'll blow your filthy head off – here and now!' he roared, picking up his revolver from the table where he had laid it.

'Give me that diamond, you scurvy hound, and I'll keep it until I know whose property it is. D'you think I'm going to have the discipline of this fort spoiled by every cursed runaway jewel-thief that chooses to hide here with his swag, and tempt honest men? . . . Out with it, you gallows-cheating gaol-breaker, before I put you where you belong . . . *Quick*!'

'I have no diamond, *mon Adjudant*,' replied Michael quietly, and giving back look for look.

'As I could have told you, *mon Adjudant*,' I put in, 'my brother has never had a diamond in his life and neither have I.'

Words failed Lejaune.

I thought (and hoped) that he was going to have an apoplectic fit. His red face went purple and his eyes bulged yet more. He drew back his lips, baring his cruel-looking teeth and causing his moustache to bristle.

He raised and pointed the revolver, and I was just about to bring up my rifle, but had the presence of mind to realise that he could shoot twice with the lifted revolver, before I could even bring my rifle up to cover him. Michael did not turn a hair, and I was thankful that I, too, had sufficient restraint to stand motionless at attention. A movement would have been mutiny, and probably – death.

I felt certain that Lejaune would have shot us both, then and there (and would have searched Michael's body), but for the precarious position in which he himself stood, and the fact that he needed us alive – for the present.

At any moment we might hear the rifles of St. André and Cordier, as the mutineers rushed them. Or, at any moment, for all that Lejaune knew, the mutineers might burst into the room, headed by St. André, Cordier, and Maris, to kill him. He believed that, like Michael and me, these three were faithful – but he did not *know* they were.

He was a brave man. Situated as he was, his life hanging by a thread, he still attended to the business in hand. He turned his heavy glare from Michael to me.

'Oh? You would talk, would you?' he said, in a quiet and most sinister tone of terrible self-repression. 'Well! Well! You haven't *much* more time for talking. Not *many* more words to say . . . Would you like to make another remark or two before I shoot you? . . . No? . . . Won't you speak again, gaol-bird? A little prayer, perhaps? . . .' and the scoundrel turned the revolver from Michael's face to mine, and back again to Michael's.

It was most unpleasant, the twitching finger of an infuriated homicidal maniac on the hair-trigger of a loaded revolver, a yard from one's face – a maniac who longed for our deaths that he might enrich himself beyond the dreams of his own avarice!

He began to swear blasphemously, horribly, foully. All that he had learnt of vileness among the vile with whom he had consorted, he poured over us. He literally and actually foamed.

We stood like statues. He put the revolver down in front of him, the better to tear his hair with both hands.

I thought of the aborigines of the Congo over whom his power had been absolute, and whose lives and deaths were in his hand and mere questions of his profit and loss . . .

And then suddenly, a thought which had been clamouring for attention for some minutes suddenly occupied my mind and brought comfort and a curious sense of security.

Of course, Lejaune would do nothing to us until the mutiny was quelled, and he was again unthreatened and supreme.

We five were his only defence, the sole support of his authority, his one chance of saving not only his life, but his reputation and career. Obviously he would not kill two-fifths nor one-fifth of his loyal troops at the moment of his greatest need. It was absurd.

And then, without thought, I did what would have been the bravest thing of my life if it had been done consciously, and with intent. I defied, insulted, and outfaced Lejaune!

'Look here, Lejaune,' said I coolly, and in the manner of an Oxford undergraduate addressing an extortionate cabman or an impudent servant. 'Look here, Lejaune, don't be a silly fool. Can't you understand that in about two minutes you may be hanging on that wall with bayonets through your hands – and *left* there, in a burning fort, to die? Or pinned out on the roof with the sun in your face? Don't be such an ass. We've got no diamond and you've got five good men to fight for you, more's the pity! Stop gibbering about jewels and be thankful that we five know our duty if you don't . . .'

'*Very* Stout Fella,' murmured my brother. '*Order of Michael* for you, John.'

What would happen if the meanest slave in his palace went up to the Emperor of Abyssinia and smacked his face? . . . I don't know. Nor did Lejaune, or he would have done it, I think.

Probably the Emperor would begin by gasping and feeling faint. Lejaune gasped and looked faint.

Then he sprang to his feet with a sound that was a mixture of a roar, howl, and scream. As he did so, Michael's left hand made a swift, circling swoop, passed under Lejaune's hand, and swept the revolver to the floor.

Almost as it clattered to the ground, my bayonet was at Lejaune's throat and my finger was round my trigger.

Whether Lejaune had been going to shoot or not, I do not know, but he certainly looked as though rage had destroyed the last of his sanity, and our death was all he cared about.

Anyhow, he couldn't shoot now.

'Move – and I'll kill you,' I hissed dramatically, feeling like a cinema star and an ass.

Michael picked up the revolver.

'So you *are* mutineers, you beautiful loyal lying grandsons of Gadarene swine, are you?' panted Lejaune, moving his head from side to side, and drawing deep breaths as though choking.

'Not at all,' said Michael calmly. 'We're decent soldiers wishing to do our duty properly – not to babble about diamonds two minutes before a mutiny breaks out . . . Man, don't you know the fort will be burnt, the garrison gone, and you dead (if you are lucky), in an hour's time – unless you do your job while you've a chance? . . .'

''*Cré bon sang de bon jour de bon malheur de bon Dieu de Dieu de sort*,' swore Lejaune, 'and I'll deal with you after this *chien d'une revolte*. But wait! You wait, my clever little friends. Hell's bells! I'll teach you one of my little lessons . . . If you don't both die *en crapaudine*, by God, you shall live *en crapaudine* . . .'

'Reward for saving your valuable life, I suppose,' said Michael.

'You'll do that as your simple duty, my little friend. Oh, you love your duty. You are "*decent soldiers wishing to do your duty properly and not babble about diamonds*," I believe? . . . Good! Come and do your duty then. We'll see what you'll babble about afterwards, with your mouths full of salt and sand, *en crapaudine*, eh? Perhaps you'll prefer drops of water to diamonds then, eh? . . . You wait . . .'

He turned to me.

'And you talked about hanging on walls. And being pinned out in the sun, my little friend, eh? Will you kindly wait until I have you strapped up in a cell, *of which I alone have the key*? Perhaps it will not be I who "*jabbers about jewels*" then, eh? . . . You wait . . .'

'Your turn to jabber now, anyhow, Lejaune,' said I wearily. 'You're a fatiguing fellow. What about doing something *now*, and less of this "waiting" business?'

The man pulled himself together, exerted his undeniably powerful will, and got the better of his immediate impulse.

'Come with me,' he said quietly, and with a certain dignity. 'Our real conversation is postponed until I have dealt with a few other unspeakables. We will then see what happens to those that threaten officers and point rifles at them . . . Put that revolver down . . .'

'Open the door, John,' said Michael. I lowered my rifle and did so.

Maris, on guard outside, looked at me enquiringly. Presumably he had heard Lejaune's roars of rage.

Michael put the revolver on the table.

Lejaune took it up and strode to the open door.

'Follow me, you three,' he said, and led the way to the barrack-room, without hesitating to turn his back to us.

Apparently he had complete faith in our loyalty to duty, and knew that he could depend upon us to obey any proper military order. At the door of the barrack-room stood St. André and Cordier, *faisant sentinelle.*

'Any trouble?' growled Lejaune, as they silently sprang to attention.

'No one has moved, *mon Adjudant*,' replied St. André.

'Put down your rifles,' said Lejaune to us three, 'and, bring all arms out of this room, quickly and silently. You other two will shoot any man who leaves his bed.'

We set to work, emptying the arms-rack of the Lebel rifles first, and then going from bed to bed and removing the bayonet from its hook at the head of each.

A steel bayonet-scabbard struck a tin mug, and a man sat up. It was Vogué.

'Cover him,' said Lejaune, and the two rifles turned toward the startled man. He looked in the direction of the voice.

'Lie down, man,' I whispered. Vogué fell back instantly and closed his eyes.

It was remarkable with what speed slumber claimed him.

On my last journey to the door, with a double armful of bayonets, the inevitable happened. One slipped and fell. As it did so, I shot out my foot. The bayonet struck it and made little noise, but my foot knocked against a cot and its occupant sprang up, blinking.

'*Himmel!* What's that?' he said.

It was Glock.

'Lie down, Glock,' I whispered. 'Look,' and I nodded my head toward the door.

'Shoot him if he moves,' said Lejaune calmly.

Glock lay down again, staring at Lejaune, as a hypnotised rabbit at a snake.

I passed on, and in another minute there was not a weapon in the room, nor was there a sound. None slept so deeply as Corporal Boldini, who was nearest to the door.

Lejaune took a key from his pocket. 'Into the armoury with them, St. André, Cordier, and Maris, quick!' he said. 'You, St. André, mount guard. Send the key back to me with Cordier and Maris, and shoot *instantly* any living soul that approaches the place, other than one of these four men.

'Now then,' he continued to Michael and me, as the others crept off, laden with rifles, 'some of these swine are awake, so keep your eyes open . . . If several jump at once, shoot Schwartz and Brandt. Then Haff and Delarey. If only one man moves, leave him to me . . .'

A very, very faint lightening of the darkness outside the windows showed that the false dawn was breaking. As I stared into the room, I found myself trying to recall a verse about 'Dawn's left hand' being in the sky and,

'Awake! for morning in the bowl of night
Has flung the stone that puts the stars to flight;
And lo! the Hunter of the East has caught
The Sultan's turrets in a noose of light.'

I tried to put it into Arabic, and wondered how the original sounded in the liquid Persian . . . Was it 'turrets' or 'terrace'? . . .

What sort of a stone was Lejaune about to fling into the bowl of night? . . .

Would he order the five of us, when the other three returned, to open fire and begin a massacre of sleeping men? – an indiscriminate slaughter? . . .

He was quite capable of it. These were mutineers who had threatened his life, and, worse still, his sacred authority and discipline.

Why should he wait, he would argue, for a court martial to do it? Beside, if he waited, there would never be a court martial. He could not permanently arrest the whole lot with only five men, and guard his prisoners, garrison his fort, carry on all the work of the place, and mount sentries, with five men. What would happen when the five slept, ate, cooked, mounted guard on the roof? It couldn't be done. It was their lives or his, and the very existence of the fort.

Perhaps he'd only shoot the ringleaders?

What should I do if Lejaune ordered me to open fire on unarmed men in their beds? What would Michael do?

What was my duty in such a case, with orders from such an officer? Private conscience said, 'Absolutely impossible! Sheer murder! You are not an executioner . . . Not the public hangman.'

Military conscience said, 'Absolutely necessary. These men are guilty of the greatest military crime. It is Lejaune's duty to save the fort at any cost. *Your* duty is to obey your officer implicitly. If you refuse, you are a mutineer, as criminal as they.'

The windows grew lighter.

Maris and Cordier crept back, their work completed. Maris gave Lejaune the key of the armoury.

'St. André is on guard over the magazine, *mon Adjudant*,' whispered he, saluting.

'Good!' said Lejaune. 'Maris, Brown, and Cordier, remain here. Shoot instantly any man who puts his foot to the ground. If there's a rush, shoot Schwartz first. Your own lives depend on your smartness. They're all unarmed, remember . . . Come with me, you, Smith, and I'll disarm the guard and sentries . . . Use your wits if you want to see daylight again.'

He glared round the room.

'Aha, my little birds in a trap,' he growled. 'You'd plot against *me*. *Me, l'Adjudant Lejaune*, would you? . . . Ah! . . .'

I followed him down the passage.

'I'll clear that dog of a sentry off the roof first,' he said. 'Then there'll be no shooting down on us when I disarm the guard . . .'

Leading the way, he went up the stairs that opened on to the flat roof, round which ran a thick, low, crenellated wall, embrasured for rifle-fire.

A sentry patrolled this roof at night, though the high lookout platform was not occupied, for obvious reasons, during the hours of darkness.

Lejaune relieved the sentry and posted me. He then took the man's rifle from him and ordered him to go below to the guard-room and request Sergeant Dupré to come up to the roof.

'Now,' said he to me as the man went, 'come here. Look,' and he pointed down into the courtyard to the open door of the guard-room. 'I shall order Sergeant Dupré to take the rifles of the guard and sentries, and then to send one man out of the guard-house with the lot. If any man comes out with only one rifle, shoot him at once. Shoot anybody who comes through that doorway, except a man with half a dozen rifles. And shoot to kill too.'

I raised my rifle and covered the lighted doorway below me, at the other side of the courtyard.

'You understand,' growled Lejaune. 'The moment Sergeant Dupré enters that guard-room, after I've spoken to him, you shoot anybody who carries one rifle. A man with a rifle is a proclaimed and confessed mutineer . . .'

I felt that he was right, and that it was my duty to obey him, little as I relished the idea of shooting comrades like bolting rabbits.

Should I shout, '*Drop that rifle*!' before I fired, and shoot if the man did not do it? I wondered if Lejaune would kill me if I did so.

I saw the relieved sentry cross the courtyard and enter the guard-room, and a moment later Sergeant Dupré came out.

'Watch!' growled Lejaune. 'That sentry will talk, and they may make a rush.'

Nothing stirred below.

Sergeant Dupré came up the stairs, out on to the roof, and saluted Lejaune.

'I want the rifles of the guard and sentries, Sergeant Dupré,' said Lejaune. 'Send one man, and only one, to me here, with the lot. Shoot instantly any man who hesitates for a second. No man is to leave the guard-room (except the one who carries all the rifles), or he'll be shot as he does so . . .' And he pointed at me, standing with my rifle resting in an embrasure and covering the doorway below.

Sergeant Dupré saluted and turned about with a quiet, 'Very good, *mon Adjudant*.'

He descended the stairs and emerged into the courtyard, crossed it to the gate beneath the gate-house, and took the rifle from the sentry there. The man preceded him to the guard-room. Dupré visited the other sentries, repeating the procedure.

A minute after the Sergeant's last visit to the guard-room, a man came out. I was greatly relieved to see that he carried three or four rifles over each shoulder, the muzzles in his hands.

'Watch,' growled Lejaune. 'They may all rush out together now. Open rapid fire if they do,' and he himself also covered the doorway with the rifle he had taken from the sentry.

The man with the rifles, one Gronau, a big stupid Alsatian, came up the stairs. I did not look round, but kept my eyes fixed on the doorway through which a yellow light (from 'where the great guard-lantern guttered') struggled with that of the dawn.

I heard a clattering crash behind me and then I did look round, fully expecting to see that the man had felled Lejaune from behind.

Gronau had released the muzzles of the rifles, they had crashed down on the roof, and he was standing pointing, staring, his silly eyes goggling and his silly mouth wide open.

So obviously was he stricken by some strange vision, that Lejaune, instead of knocking him down, turned to look in the direction of his pointing hand.

I did the same.

The oasis was swarming with Arabs, swiftly and silently advancing to attack!

Even as I looked, a huge horde of camel-riders swept out to the left, another to the right, to make a detour and surround the fort on all sides. There were hundreds and hundreds of them already in sight, even in that poor light of early dawn.

Lejaune showed his mettle instantly.

'Run like Hell,' he barked at Gronau. 'Back with those rifles,' and sent him staggering with a push. 'Send Sergeant Dupré here, quick.'

'Down to the barrack-room,' he snapped at me. 'Give the alarm. Take this key to St. André and issue the rifles. Send me the bugler. Jump, or I'll . . .'

I jumped.

Even as I went, Lejaune's rifle opened rapid fire into the advancing hordes.

Rushing down the stairs and along the passage, I threw the key to St. André, who was standing like a graven image at the door of the magazine.

'*Arabs*!' I yelled. 'Out with the rifles and ammunition!'

Dashing on, I came to the door of the barrack-room.

Michael was pointing his rifle at Boldini's head. Maris was covering Schwartz, and Cordier was wavering the muzzle of his rifle over the room generally. Everybody was awake, and there was a kind of whispered babel, over which rose Michael's clear and cheerful:

'Show a foot anybody who wants to die . . .'

Nobody showed a foot, though all seemed to show resentment, especially Boldini, with a loaded rifle a yard from his ear.

Taking this in at a glance, I halted, drew breath and then bawled, '*Aux armes*! *Aux armes*! *Les Arbis*! *Les Arbis*!' and, with a shout to Michael and the other two, of:

'*Up with you – we're surrounded*,' I turned to dash back, conscious of a surge of unclad men from the beds, as their gaolers rushed after me. Whoops and yells of joy pursued us, and gleeful howls of:

'*Aux armes*! *Les Arbis*!' as the delighted men snatched at their clothes.

St. André staggered towards us beneath a huge bundle of rifles.

Dupré and the guard were clattering up the stairs.

As we rushed out on to the roof, Lejaune roared:

'Stand to! Stand to! Open fire at once! Rapid fire! Give them Hell, you devils! Give them Hell!' and, ordering Dupré to take command of the roof, he rushed below.

A couple of minutes later, a constant trickle of men flowed up from below, men in shirt-sleeves, men bareheaded and barefooted, men in nothing but their trousers – but every man with a full cartridge-pouch and his rifle and bayonet.

Lejaune must have worked like a fiend, for within a few minutes of Gronau's dropping of the rifles, every man in the fort was on the roof, and from every embrasure rifles poured their magazine-fire upon the yelling, swarming Arabs.

It had been a very near thing. A very close shave indeed.

But for Gronau's coming up and diverting attention from the inside of the fort to the outside, there probably would not have been a man of the garrison alive in the place by now – except those of the wounded sufficiently alive to be worth keeping for torture.

One wild swift rush in the half-light, and they would have been into the place – to find what? A disarmed garrison!

As I charged my magazine and fired, loaded and fired, loaded and fired, I wondered if these things were 'chance,' and Gronau's arrival and idle glance round, at the last moment that gave a chance of safety, pure accidental coincidence.

A near thing indeed – and the issue yet in doubt, for it was a surprise attack. They had got terribly close, the oasis was in their hands, and there were many hundreds of them to our little half-company.

And they were brave. There was no denying that, as they swarmed up to the walls under our well-directed rapid-fire, an Arab falling almost as often as a legionary pulled the trigger.

While hundreds, along each side, fired at our embrasures at a few score yards' range, a large band attacked the gate with stones, axes, heavy swords, and bundles of kindling-wood to burn it down.

Here Lejaune, exposing himself fearlessly, led the defence, controlling a rapid volley-fire that had terrible effect, both physical and moral, until the whole attack ceased as suddenly as it had begun, and the Touaregs, as the sun rose, completely vanished from sight, to turn the assault into a siege and to pick us off, in safety, from behind the crests of the sand-hills.

I suppose this whirlwind dawn attack lasted no more than ten minutes from the moment that the first shot was fired by Lejaune, but it had seemed like hours to me.

I had shot at least a score of men, I thought. My rifle was hot and sweating grease, and several bullets had struck the deep embrasure in which I leaned to fire.

Below, the plain was dotted over with little heaps of white or blue clothing, looking more like scattered bundles of 'washing' than dead ferocious men who, a minute before, had thirsted and yelled for the blood of the infidel, and had fearlessly charged to drink it.

Our bugler blew the 'Cease fire,' and on the order, 'Unload! Stand easy,' I looked round as I straightened myself up, unloaded my rifle, and stood at ease.

It was a strange sight.

At every embrasure there was a caricature of a soldier – in some cases almost naked – at his feet a litter of spent cartridges, and, in one or two instances, a pool of blood. As I looked, one of these wild figures, wearing nothing but a shirt and trousers, slowly sank to the ground, sat a moment and then collapsed, his head striking with a heavy thud. It was Blanc, the sailor.

Lejaune strode over from his place in the middle of the roof.

'Here,' he shouted. 'No room nor time, yet, for shirkers,' and putting his arms round the man, dragged him from the ground and jerked him heavily into the embrasure.

There he posed the body, for Blanc appeared to be dead. Into the embrasure it leaned, chest on the upward sloping parapet, and elbows wedged against the outer edges of the massive uprights of the crenellation.

Lejaune placed the rifle on the flat top of the embrasure, a dead hand under it, a dead hand clasped round the small of the butt, the heel-plate against the dead shoulder, a dead cheek leaning against the butt.

'Continue to look useful, my friend, if you can't *be* useful,' he jeered; and as he turned away, he added:

'Perhaps you'll see that route to Morocco if you stare hard enough.'

'Now then, Corporal Boldini,' he called, 'take every third man below, get them fed and properly dressed, and double back here if you hear a shot, or the "Assembly" blown. If there's no attack, take below one-half of the rest . . . Then the remainder . . . Have all *klim-bim* and standing-to again in thirty minutes . . . You, St. André, and Maris, more ammunition. A hundred rounds per man . . . Cordier, pails of water. Fill all water-flasks and then put filled pails there above the gate . . . They may try another bonfire against it . . . Sergeant Dupré, no wounded whatsoever will go below. Bring up the medical panniers . . . Are all prisoners out of the cells?' . . .

He glared around, a competent, energetic, courageous soldier. 'And where's the excellent Schwartz?' he went on. 'Here, you dog, up on to that look-out platform and watch those palm trees – till the Arabs get you . . . Watch that oasis, I say . . . You'll have a little while up there for the thinking out of some more plots . . .' And he laid his hand on the butt of his revolver, as he scowled menacingly at the big German.

Schwartz sprang up the ladder leading to the high look-out platform that towered far above the roof of the fort. It was the post of danger.

'Now use your eyes, all of you,' bawled Lejaune, 'and shoot as soon as you see anything to shoot at.'

Ten minutes or so later, Boldini returned with the men whom he had taken below, now all dressed as for morning parade. They took their places and the Corporal hurried round the roof, touching each alternate man on the shoulder.

'Fall out, and go below,' he ordered.

Ten minutes or so later they were back, fed, clothed, and in their right minds. Gone like magic were all signs of *cafard*, mutiny, and madness. These were eager, happy soldiers, revelling in a fight.

With the third batch I went, hoping to be back before anything happened. Not a rifle-shot broke the stillness, as we hastily swallowed *soupe* and coffee, and tore at our bread.

'Talk about "They came to curse and remained to pray,"' murmured Michael, with bulging cheeks. 'These jolly old Arabs removed our curse and remained for us to slay. There'll be no more talk of mutiny for a while.'

'Nor of anything else, old bean,' I replied, 'if they remain to prey.'

'Never get in here,' said Michael. 'They couldn't take this place without guns.'

'Wonder what they're doing?' I mused.

'Diggin' themselves in on the crests of the sand-hills,' said Michael. 'They can't rush us, so they're going to do some fancy shooting.'

'Yes. What about a regular siege?' I asked. 'And killing only one of us to a score of them that we kill? We should be too few to man the four walls eventually.'

'What about relief from Tokotu?' suggested Michael.

'Over a hundred miles away!' I replied, 'and no wires. Nor any chance to heliograph across a level desert, even if they could see so far.'

'Chance for the *médaille militaire*,' grinned Michael. 'Go to Lejaune and say, "*Fear not*! *Alone I will walk through the encircling foe and bring you relief.*" Then you walk straight through them, what?'

'Might be done at night,' I mused.

'I *don't* think,' said Michael. 'These merry men will sit round the place in a circle like a spiritualists' *séance*, holding hands, rather than let anyone slip through them.'

'Full moon too,' I observed. 'Anyhow, I'm very grateful to the lads for rolling up . . .'

'Shame to shoot 'em,' agreed Michael, and then Boldini hounded us all back to the roof, and we resumed our stations.

All was ready, and the Arabs could come again as soon as they liked.

Lejaune paced round and round the roof like a tiger in a cage.

'Hi you, there!' he called up to Schwartz. 'Can you see nothing?'

'Nothing moving, *mon Adjudant*,' replied Schwartz.

A moment later he shouted something, and his voice was drowned in the rattle and crash of a sudden outbreak of rifle fire in a complete circle all round the fort. The Arabs had lined the nearest sand-hills on all sides of us, and lying flat below the crests, poured in a steady independent fire.

This was a very different thing from their first mad rush up to the very walls, when they hoped to surprise a sleeping fort and swarm up over the walls from each other's shoulders.

They were now difficult to see, and a man firing from his embrasure was as much exposed as an Arab lying flat behind a stone or in a trench scooped in the sand.

There was a man opposite to me, about a hundred yards distant, who merely appeared as a small black blob every few minutes. He must have been lying on a slope or in a shallow sand trench, and he only showed his head for a few seconds when he fired. I felt that either he or I would get hurt, sooner or later, for he, among others, was potting at my embrasure.

It was certainly 'fancy shooting' as Michael had said, waiting for the small object, a man's head, to appear for five seconds at a hundred yards' range, and get a shot at it. It was certainly interesting too, and more difficult than rifle-range work, for one's nerves are not steadied nor one's aim improved by the knowledge that one is also being shot at oneself, and by several people.

With unpleasant frequency there was a sharp blow on the wall near my embrasure and sometimes the high wailing song of a ricochet, as the deflected and distorted bullet continued its flight at an angle to the line of its arrival.

The morning wore on and the sun gained rapidly in power.

Unreasonably and unreasoningly I did not expect to be hit, and I was not hit, but I was increasingly conscious of the terrific heat and of a severe headache. I wondered if high nervous tension made one more susceptible, or whether the day was really hotter than usual . . .

Suddenly, the man on my right leapt back, shouted, spun round and fell to the ground, his rifle clattering at my feet.

I turned and stooped over him. It was the wretched Guantaio, shot through the middle of his face.

As I bent down, I was suddenly sent crashing against the wall, as Lejaune literally sprang at me.

'By God I' he roared. 'You turn from your place again and I'll blow your head off! *Duty*, you dog! Get to your duty! What have you to do with this carrion, you cursed, slinking, cowering, hiding shirker . . .' and as I turned back into my embrasure, he picked up the choking, moaning Guantaio and flung him into the place from where he had fallen.

'Stay there, you rotten dog,' he shouted, 'and if you slide out of it, I'll *pin* you up with bayonets through you' and he forced the dying wretch into the embrasure so that he was wedged in position, with his head and shoulders showing through the aperture between the crenellations on either side of him.

'I'll have no skulking malingerers here,' he roared. 'You'll all stay in those embrasures alive or *dead*, while there's an Arab in sight . . .'

Suddenly the Arab fire dwindled and slackened and then ceased. Either they had had enough of our heavy and accurate fire, or else some new tactics were going to be introduced. I imagined that a camel-man had ridden all round the sand-hills, out of sight, calling the leaders to colloquy with the Emir in command.

Our bugles sounded the 'Cease fire.'

'Stand easy! . . . Wounded lie down where they are,' rang out Lejaune's voice, and some half-dozen men sank to the ground in their own blood. I was thankful to see that Michael was not among them.

Sergeant Dupré with Cordier, who had been a doctor, went to each in turn, with bandages and stimulants.

'Corporal Boldini,' barked Lejaune, 'take the men down in three batches. Ten minutes for *soupe* and a half-litre of wine each. Come back at the "*pas gymnastique*" if you hear the "Assembly" blown . . . St. André, replenish ammunition. Each man to have a hundred . . . Stop that bandaging, Cordier, and stir yourself . . .'

When my turn came, later, to go below, I was more thankful for the comparative darkness and coolness of the *caserne* than for the *soupe* and wine even, for my head was splitting.

'"*Moriturus te saluto*,"' 'said Cordier, as he raised his mug of wine.

'Don't talk rot,' said I. 'You're no more *moriturus* than – *Madame la République*.'

'I shall be dead before sunset,' replied Cordier. 'This place will be a silent grave shortly . . . '*Madame La République – morituri te salutant!* . . .' and he drank again.

'He's fey,' said Michael. 'Anyhow, better to die fighting than to be done in by Lejaune afterwards . . . If I go, I'd like to take that gentle *adjudant* with me . . .'

'He's a topping soldier,' I said.

'Great,' agreed Michael. 'Let's forgive him.'

'We will, if he dies,' said I. 'I am afraid that he'll see to it that he *needs* some forgiving, if he and we survive this show, and he gets control again . . .'

'Yes,' said Michael. 'Do you know, I believe he's torn both ways when a man's hit. The brute in him says, "*That's one for you, you damned mutineer,*" and the soldier in him says, "*One more of a tiny garrison gone.*"'

'He's a foul brute,' I agreed. 'He absolutely *flung* two wounded, suffering men back into their embrasures – and enjoyed doing it.'

'Partly enjoyment and partly tactics,' said Michael wiping his lips, and lighting a cigarette. 'He's going to give the Arabs the idea that not a man has been killed. Or else that he has so many men in the fort that another takes the place of each one that falls . . . The Touaregs have no field-glasses, and to them a man in an embrasure is a man . . .'

'What about when there are too few to keep up any volume of fire?' I asked.

'He may hope for relief before then,' hazarded Michael.

'He does,' put in St. André, who had just joined us and taken a seat at the table. 'Dupré told me so. The wily beggar has kept the two *goums* outside every night lately – presumably ever since he knew of the conspiracy. They had orders to go, hell for leather, to Tokotu, and say the fort was *attacked*, the moment they heard a rifle fired, inside or out.'

'By Jove!' I exclaimed. 'Of course! He wouldn't send to Tokotu to ask for help in quelling a mutiny of his own men, before it happened – but he wouldn't mind a column arriving because a *goum* had erroneously reported an attack on the fort.'

'Cunning lad!' agreed Michael. 'And he knew that when the conspiracy was about to bloom and he nipped it in the bud, he'd be pretty shorthanded after it, if he should be attacked – even by a small raiding party out for a lark!'

'Yes,' said Cordier. 'He saved his face and he saved the fort too. If a shot had been fired at the mutineers, the *goums* would have scuttled off as ordered, and the relief-column from Tokotu would have found an heroic Lejaune cowing and guarding a gang of mutineers . . . As it is, they'll know to-morrow, at Tokotu, that the place is invested, and they'll be here the next day.'

'Question is – where shall *we* be by then?' I observed.

'In Hell, dear friends,' smiled Cordier.

'Suppose the *goums* were chopped in the oasis?' said Micheal. 'Taken by surprise, as we were.'

'What I said to Dupré!' replied Cordier. 'But Lejaune was too old a bird. They camped in the oasis by day, but were ordered to be out at night, and patrol separately, one north to south on the east and the other on the west, a half-circle each, from sunset to sunrise, Durpré says . . . Likely they'd have been chopped in the oasis in the daytime all right, sound asleep – but they wouldn't be caught at dawn. They were well outside the enveloping movement from the oasis when the Arabs surrounded the place, and the *goums* would be off to Tokotu at the first shot or sooner . . . By the time . . .'

'Up with you,' shouted Boldini, and we hurried back to the roof and resumed our stations. The wounded were again in their places, one or two lying very still in them, others able to stand.

On either side of me, a dead man stood wedged into his embrasure, his rifle projecting before him, his elbows and the slope of the parapet keeping him in position.

I could see no sign of life from my side of the fort. Nothing but sand and stones over which danced the blinding aching heat-haze.

Suddenly there was a cry from Schwartz on the look-out platform.

'The palms,' he shouted and pointed. 'They're climbing them.' He raised his rifle and fired.

Those were his last words. A volley rang out a minute later, and he fell.

Bullets were striking the wall against which I stood, upon its *inner* face. Arab marksmen had climbed to the tops of the palms of the oasis, and were firing down upon the roof. From all the sand-hills round, the circle of fire broke out again.

'Rapid fire at the palms,' shouted Lejaune. 'Sergeant Dupré, take half the men from the other three sides to that one. Bring those birds down from their trees quickly . . . Brandt, up with you on to the look-out platform. Quick . . .'

I glanced round as I charged my magazine afresh. Brandt looked at the platform and then at Lejaune. Lejaune's hand went to the revolver in the holster at his belt, and Brandt climbed the ladder, and started firing as quickly as he could work the bolt of his rifle.

Michael was still on his feet, but, as I turned back, I saw his neighbour spin round and crash down, clutching with both streaming hands at his throat.

When I took another swift glance later, the man had been wedged into the embrasure and posed by Lejaune as a living defender of the fort.

Soon afterwards I heard a shout from above, and turning, saw Brandt stagger backwards on the high platform. He struck the railing, toppled over, and came with a horrible crash to the roof.

'Find a good place for that carrion, Sergeant Dupré,' shouted Lejaune. 'Make him ornamental if he can't be useful.'

I then heard him call the name of Haff.

'Up you go, Haff,' he shouted. 'You're another of these brave *risque touts*. Up you go!'

Schwartz, Brandt, Haff! Doubtless the next would be Delarey and Vogué . . . And then Colonna, Gotto, and Bolidar . . . Guantaio was dead . . . Why didn't he send Michael up there? Presumably he hoped to keep him, St. André, Cordier, Maris, and me alive until the mutineer ringleaders and the diamond-stealers were dead . . . He wouldn't want to be left victorious over the Arabs, only to find himself defenceless in the hands of the mutineers and the thieves.

I glanced up at Haff and saw that he was lying behind Schwartz's body, and firing over it as though it were a parapet along the edge of the platform.

I wondered how long this second phase of the fight had lasted, and whether we could hold out till night fell and the Arabs could not see to shoot . . . Would they shoot by moonlight? It was unlikely, the Arab being, as a rule, averse from any sort of night work except peaceful travelling. A dawn rush is his favourite manœuvre . . .

It was agony to fire my rifle, for my head ached with one of those terrible eye-strain heat-stroke pains that give the feeling that the head is opening and shutting, exposing the brain. Every explosion of my rifle was like a blow on the head with a heavy hammer. I had almost come to the end of my tether when once again the fire of the Arabs slackened and dwindled and died away.

On the 'Cease fire' bugle being ordered by Lejaune, I straightened up. I looked round as the words, 'Unload!' Stand easy!' rang out.

Michael was all right, but a good half of the garrison was dead or dying, for quite half the men remained partly standing, partly lying, wedged into their embrasures as the others obeyed the orders shouted by Lejaune.

Among the dead were both Sergeant Dupré and Corporal Boldini, and both had been stuck up to simulate living men. Haff must be dead too, for Delarey had been sent up to the platform, and was lying flat behind a little pile of bodies.

St. André was alive, for Lejaune called out:

'St. André, take rank as Corporal. One half the men to go below for *soupe* and coffee. Double back quick if you hear the "Assembly" blown . . .' and St. André passed round the roof, touching each alternate man of those who were standing up, and saying, 'Fall out, and go below.'

In many embrasures was a man whom he did not touch.

Poor Cordier had spoken truly as concerned his own fate, for he remained at his post, staring out with dead eyes across the desert.

Maris was dead too. There were left three men – St. André, Michael, and myself, upon whom Lejaune could rely if the Arabs now drew off and abandoned the siege of the fort.

But this, the Arabs did not do.

Leaving a circle of what were presumably their best marks-men, to pick off any of the defenders of the fort who showed themselves, the bulk of them retired out of sight behind the oasis and sand-hills beyond it.

By Lejaune's orders, the embrasures were occupied only by the dead, the living being ordered below in small parties, for rest and food.

St. André was told to see that every man left his bed and *paquetage* as tidy as for inspection, and that the room was in perfect order. Lejaune himself never left the roof, but had *soupe*, coffee, and wine brought up to him.

To the look-out platform he sent Vogué to join the bodies of his fellow-conspirators, Schwartz, Haff, and Delarey.

Except for a crouching sentry in the middle of each wall of the roof, those who were not below, feeding and resting, sat with their backs to the wall, each beside his embrasure.

The fire of the Arab sharpshooters did no harm, and they wasted their ammunition on dead men.

And so the evening came and wore away and the moon rose.

Where we were, we lay, with permission to sleep, St. André having the duty of seeing that two sentries patrolled each wall and were changed every two hours.

By Lejaune's orders, Vogué, in the dusk before moonrise, pushed the bodies of Schwartz, Haff, and Delarey from the look-out platform to fall down to the roof. They were then posed in embrasures, as though living defenders of the fort. It seemed to give Lejaune special pleasure to thrust his half-smoked cigarette between Schwartz's teeth, and pull the dead man's *kepi* rakishly to one side.

'There, my fine conspirator,' said he when the body was arranged to his liking. 'Stand there and do your duty satisfactorily for the first time in your life, now you're dead. Much more useful now than ever you were before.'

'He's a devil! He's a devil! He's mad – mad! . . .' groaned Vogué as he dragged the body of Delarey past me.

'Up with him! Put him over there,' growled Lejaune, when Vogué had got the body in his arms. 'I'll allot your corpse the place next to his, and your pipe shall be stuck between your teeth. You are fond of a pipe, friend Vogué! Helps you to think out plots, eh? . . . Up with him, you dog . . .' and he kept his hand on the butt of his revolver as he baited the man. He then sent him back to the look-out platform, to be a target for the Touaregs when the moon rose, or the sun, if he lived to see it . . .

I had a talk with Michael when our turn came to go below for a rest and food.

'Looks like a thin time to-morrow,' said Michael. 'If they pot a few of us and then rush, they should get in.'

'Yes,' I agreed. 'They ought to keep up a heavy fire while their ammunition lasts, and then charge on camels in one fell swoop. And then climb up from the backs of the camels. A lot would be killed but a bigger lot would get in.'

'Don't give them the tip, anyhow,' grinned Michael. 'Two or three hundred of the devils inside the place, and it would be a short life and a merry for the half-dozen or so of us who were left by that time . . .'

'If we can stand them off to-morrow, the relief from Tokotu ought to roll up the next morning,' I said.

'If either of those *goums* got away and played the game,' agreed Michael. 'They may have been pinched though . . . The relief will find a thin house here, if they do come . . . It'll mean a commission for Lejaune all right.'

'Nice if he's confirmed in command here, and we survive! 'I remarked.

'Yes,' said Michael, 'and talking of which, look here, old son. If I take the knock and you don't, I want you to do something for me . . . Something *most* important . . . what?'

'You can rely on me, Beau,' I said.

'I know I can, John,' he replied. 'There's some letters. A funny *public* sort of letter, a letter for Claudia, and one for you, and one for Digby, in my belt – and there's a letter and a tiny packet for Aunt Patricia. If you possibly can, old chap, get that letter and packet to Aunt. No hurry about it – *but get it to her*. See? *Especially the letter*. The packet doesn't much matter, and it contains nothing of any value, but I'd die a lot more comfortable if I knew that Aunt Patricia was going to get that letter after my death . . .'

'Oh, shut it, Beau,' I said roughly. 'Your number's not up yet. Don't talk rot.'

'I'm only asking you to do something *if* I'm pipped,' said Michael.

'And, of course, I'll do it if I'm alive,' I replied . . . 'But suppose we're both killed?'

'Well – the things are addressed and stamped, and it's usual to forward such letters and packets found on dead soldiers, as you know. Depends on what happens . . . If we die and Lejaune survives, I doubt their being dispatched. Or rather, I don't doubt at all . . . Or if the Arabs get in, there's not much chance of anything surviving . . . But if we're both killed and the relief gets in here before the Arabs do, the officer in charge would do the usual thing . . . Anyhow, we can only hope for the best . . .

'Anything I can do for you if it's the other way round, John?' he added.

'Well, love to Dig, you know, and there's a letter for Isobel, and you might write to her if ever you get back to civilisation and say we babbled of her, and sang, "*Just before the battle, Mother*," and "*Bring a flower from Maggie's grave*," and all that . . .'

Michael grinned.

'I'll say the right things about you to Isobel, old son,' he said, 'and if otherwise, you'll see that Aunt gets my letter, eh? Be sure I'm dead though . . . I mean if I were captured alive by Arabs, or anything humorous like that, I don't want her to get it while I'm alive . . . Of course, all five of the letters are important, but I *do* want Aunt to get hers . . .'

And then St. André ordered our little party up to the roof, and brought down the other one.

The Arabs had ceased their desultory firing, and might have been a hundred miles away. Only the sight of a little smoke from their camp-fires and the occasional scent of the burning camel-dung and wood betrayed their presence, for none were in sight, and they made no sound. No one doubted, however, that a very complete chain of watchful sentries ringed us round, and made it utterly impossible for anyone to leave the fort and bring help to his besieged comrades.

The fact that Lejaune sent no one to make the attempt seemed to confirm the story that Dupré had told Cordier as they bandaged the wounded, and to show that Lejaune believed that the *goums* had got away.

It would be a wellnigh hopeless enterprise, but there was just a chance in a thousand that a daring and skilful scout might be able to crawl to where their camels were, and get away on one. Nor was Lejaune the man to take any count of the fact that it was almost certain torture and death for the man who attempted it.

I decided that, on the one hand, he felt pretty sure the *goums* had got away to Tokotu directly the Arabs appeared, and that, on the other hand, the two or three men whom he could trust were just the men whom he could not spare.

Unless St. André, Michael, and I were with him, his fate would be the same whether he drove the Arabs off or not, and doubtless he would rather go down fighting Arabs, than be murdered by his own men.

I was ordered on duty as sentry, and, for two hours, patrolled my side of the roof with my eyes on the moonlit desert, where nothing moved and whence no sound came.

When relieved, I had a little chat with St. André after he had posted my relief.

'Dawn will be the dangerous time; they'll rush us then,' he said, 'and it will want quick shooting to keep them down if they come all together and on all four sides at once. They must be a hundred to one . . . I wonder if they'll bring ropes and poles, or ride their camels right up to the walls . . .'

'If they don't count the cost, I don't see how we can keep them out,' I said.

'Nothing could keep them out,' replied St. André. 'But if they fail at dawn they won't try again until the next dawn. They'll just pepper us all day and tire us out . . . They think they have all the time they want.'

'Haven't they?' I asked.

'No,' replied St. André. 'Lejaune is certain that one of the *goums* got away. The Arabs couldn't get them *both*, he says, as they were at opposite sides of the fort, and half a mile apart always, at night.'

'What about their ammunition?' I asked. 'The Touaregs', I mean.'

'The more they spend the more determined they'll be to get ours, and the more likely to put their money on a swift dawn-rush with cold steel . . .'

I lay down and fell asleep, to be awakened by the bugle and Lejaune's shout of '*Stand to*!'

There was no sign of dawn and none of the Arabs. From the centre of the roof, Lejaune addressed the diminished garrison of Fort Zinderneuf.

'Now, my merry birds,' said he, 'you're going to *sing*, and sing like the happy joyous larks you are. We'll let our Arab friends know that we're not only awake, but also merry and bright. Now then – the *Marching Song of the Legion* first. All together, you warbling water-rats – *Now*.' And led by his powerful bellow, we sang at the tops of our voices.

Through the Legion's extensive repertoire he took us, and between songs the bugler blew every call that he knew.

'Now *laugh*, you merry, happy, jolly, care-free, humorous swine. *Laugh*. . . You, Vogué, up there – roar with laughter, or I'll make you roar with pain, by God . . . Out with it. *Now* . . .'

A wretched laugh, like that of a hungry hyena, came down from the look-out platform.

It was so mirthless a miserable cackle, and so ludicrous, that we laughed genuinely.

'Again, you grinning dog,' roared Lejaune. 'Laugh till your sides ache, you gibbering jackal. Laugh till the tears run down your horrible face, you shivering she-ass. Laugh! . . . *Now* . . .'

Again the hideous quavering travesty of a laugh rang out, and the men below roared heartily at the ridiculous noise.

'Now then, you twittering sniggering *soupe*-snatchers, laugh in turn,' shouted Lejaune. 'From the right – you start, Gotto.'

Gotto put up a pretty good roar.

'Now beat *that*, next. Out with it, or, by God, I'll give you something to laugh at,' Lejaune continued.

And so round that circle of doomed men, among the dead men, ran the crazy laughter, the doomed howling noisily, the dead smiling secretly out to the illuminated silent desert.

'Now all together with me,' roared Lejaune, and great guffaws rang out, desecrating the silence and the beauty of the moonlit scene.

It was the maddest, most incredible business – that horrible laughter among the dead, from men about to die.

Certainly the Arabs must have thought us mad and certainly they were not far wrong. Anyhow, they knew we were awake and must have gathered that we were cheerful and defiant.

For Lejaune was justified of his madness, and no dawn attack came.

Whether the Touaregs regarded us as 'The afflicted of Allah,' and feared to rush the place, or whether they realised that there could be no element of surprise in the attack, I do not know, but it was never made.

And when the sun rose and they again lined the sand-hills and opened their heavy fire upon the fort, every embrasure was occupied by an apparently unkillable man, and every Arab who exposed himself paid the penalty.

But not all those who lined the walls of Zinderneuf were beyond scathe by Arab bullets. Now and then there would be a cry, an oath, a gurgling grunt or cough, and a man would stagger back and fall, or die where he crouched, a bullet through his brain.

And, in every case, Lejaune would prop and pose and arrange the body, dead or dying, in the embrasure whence it had fallen, and to the distant Arab eyes it must have seemed that the number of the defenders was undiminished.

As the morning wore on, Lejaune took a rifle, and, crouching beside each dead man in turn, fired several shots from each embrasure, adding to the illusion that the dead were alive, as well as to the volume of fire.

Later still, he set one man to each wall to do the same thing, to pass continually up and down, firing from behind the dead.

When the Arab fire again slackened and then ceased, toward midday, and our bugle blew the '*Cease fire*,' I hardly dared to turn round.

With a sigh of relief, I saw Michael among the few who rose from their embrasures at the order '*Stand easy*.'

It was a terribly tiny band. Of all those who had sprung from their beds with cries of joy, at the shout of '*Aux armes*!' yesterday morning, only Lejaune, St. André, Michael, Colonna, Marigny, Vogué, Moscowski, Gotto, Vaerren, and I were still alive.

The end was inevitable, unless relief came from Tokotu before the Arabs assaulted the place. All they had to do now, was to run in and climb. Ten men cannot hold back a thousand.

If we survived to see the arrival of a relieving force, it would be the dead who saved us, these dead who gave the impression of a numerous, fearless, ever-watchful garrison, who would cause an attack across open ground to wither beneath the blast of their rifles like grass beneath a flame.

'Half the men below, for *soupe* and coffee and half a litre of wine, Corporal St. André,' ordered Lejaune. 'Back as soon as you can – or if the "*Assembly*" is blown . . .' and St. André took each alternate man.

Soon coffee and *soupe* were ready, although the cook was dead, and we sat at table as though in a dream, surrounded by the tidy beds of dead men.

'Last lap!' said Michael, as I gave him a cigarette. 'Last cigarette! Last bowl of *soupe*! Last mug of coffee! Last swig of wine! Well, well! It's as good an end as any – if a bit early . . . Look out for the letter, Johnny,' and he patted the front of his sash.

'Oh, come off it,' I growled. 'Last nothing. The relief is half-way here by now.'

'Hope so,' replied Michael. 'But I don't greatly care, old son. So long as you see about the letter for me.'

'Why *I*, rather than you, Beau?' I asked. 'Just as likely that you do my posting for me.'

'Don't know, Johnny. Just feel it in my bones,' he replied. 'I feel I'm in for it and you're not, and thank the Lord for the latter, old chap,' and he gave my arm a little squeeze above the elbow. (His little grip of my arm, and squeeze, had been one of my greatest rewards and pleasures, all my life.)

As we returned to the roof at the end of our meal, Michael held out his hand to me.

'Well, good-bye, dear old Johnny,' he said. 'I wish to God I hadn't dragged you into this – but I think you'll come out all right. Give my love to Dig.'

I wrung his hand.

'Good-bye, Beau,' I replied. 'Or rather, *au'voir*... Of course, you didn't "drag" me into this. I had as much right to assume the blame for the theft of the "Blue Water" as you and Dig had ... And it's been a great lark ...'

He patted my shoulder as we clattered up the stairs.

Lejaune assigned one side of the roof to Michael and the opposite one to me. Vogué and Vaerren respectively were sent to the other two. Our orders were to patrol the wall and shoot from behind a dead man, if we saw an Arab.

St. André took Colonna, Marigny, Moscowski, and Gotto below.

Lejaune himself went up to the look-out platform with his field-glasses and swept the horizon in the direction of Tokotu. Apparently he saw no sign of help.

Nothing moved on the sand-hills on my side of the fort, and I watched them over the heads of my dead comrades ...

How much longer could this last?

Would the Touaregs draw off from this fort-with-an-inexhaustible-garrison?

Would the relief come in time? If not, would they be in time to avenge us? It would be amusing if the Arabs, having got into the fort, were caught in it by the Senegalese and mounted troops from Tokotu – a poetic justice – for not a man of them would escape!

Where *did* all the flies come from? ... Horrible! ...

St. André and his party returned to the roof, and now two men were posted to each wall, St. André and Lejaune remaining in the centre of the roof to support whichever side of the fort should need it most when the attack came.

When it did come, it was a repetition of the siege-tactics and attrition warfare, a desultory fire of sharpshooters, and most of it aimed at the dead.

Up and down his half of the wall, each of the defenders hurried, firing from a different embrasure each time.

The Arabs must have been completely deceived, for they came no nearer, and fired impartially at the silent corpse-guarded embrasures and at those from which our eight rifles cracked.

Glancing round, as I darted from one embrasure to another, I saw that both Lejaune and St. André were in the firing-line now, and that Lejaune had one wall of the fort to himself. There were only seven of us left. Michael was among them.

The Arab fire died down.

Lejaune himself picked up the bugle and sounded the '*Cease fire.*' I saw that Vogué, Moscowski, and Marigny were dead and propped up in their places. St. André was dabbing his face with a rag, where a bullet had torn his cheek and ear.

Colonna, Gotto, and I were sent below to get food, and we spoke not a single word. When we returned, Michael, Vaerren, and St. André went down in their turn.

Lejaune walked up and down the roof, humming '*C'est la reine Pomaré*,' to all appearance cool and unconcerned.

Not an Arab was to be seen, and not a shot was fired.

I wondered whether they withdrew for meals or for prayers – or whether they fired so many rounds per man from their trenches on the sand-hills, and then awaited their reliefs from the oasis.

Certainly it was a leisurely little war – on their side; and no doubt they were well advised to conduct it so. They must have lost terribly in their first attack, and they had learnt wisdom.

A shot rang out.

'*Stand to*!' shouted Lejaune, and blew the '*Assembly*' two or three times, as though calling up reserves from below to the already well-manned walls.

That fort and its garrison must have been a sore puzzle to the gentle Touareg.

The firing recommenced and grew hotter, and an ominous change took place in the Arab tactics.

While a heavy fire was maintained from the crests of the sand-hills, men crawled forward *en tirailleur* and scratched shallow holes in the sand, behind stones . . . Nearer and nearer they came . . . They were going to assault again.

I rushed from embrasure to embrasure, up and down my side of the roof, pausing only just long enough to bring my fore-sight on to an Arab. Time after time I saw that I hit one of the running or crouching crawling figures drawing ever closer to the wall.

Lejaune was like a man possessed, loading and firing, dashing from place to place, and rushing from one side of the fort to the other, to empty the magazine of his rifle . . .

Why from one side to the other? . . . As I loaded and fired, emptied and recharged my magazine, I found myself asking this question.

Glancing round, I saw the reason. There was no one defending the two walls that ran to left and right of mine.

Lejaune was firing a burst from one, and then dashing across to the other – defending two walls at once.

Only one man was defending the wall behind me. Swiftly I looked across.

It was not Michael . . .

Only Lejaune, St. André, and I were on our feet.

This was the end . . .

Michael was gone – but I should follow him in a minute.

Cramming another clip of cartridges into my hot rifle, I looked across again.

The opposite wall was now undefended.

Rushing across the roof from left to right, Lejaune shouted:

'Both walls, damn you! To and fro, curse you! Shoot like hell, blast you!' and I dashed across and emptied my magazine from that side, a shot from a different embrasure each time.

Back again I ran, and got off a burst of fire along the opposite wall.

And so Lejaune and I (*Lejaune and I*!) held Fort Zinderneuf for a while, two against a thousand.

And when I was nearly spent, panting like a hunted fox, dripping with sweat, and nearly blind with eye-strain and headache, the Arab fire again dwindled and died, and there was perfect silence – an incredible dreadful silence, after those hours of deafening racket.

'Go below, you, quick!' shouted Lejaune, pointing to the stairs. 'Boil coffee and *soupe*, and bring them here. Double back, quick, the moment a shot is fired. They may be at us again in a few minutes . . . If we keep them off till dark, we're saved . . .'

'Hurry, you swine,' he roared, as I stood staring at where Michael lay on his face in a pool of blood.

I dragged myself to the stairs as Lejaune cursed me.

As I went down them I heard him merrily blowing the '*Cease fire*,' and bawling fierce orders to imaginary defenders of the fort.

I stumbled to the cook-house.

'*Keep them off till dark and we're saved*,' did he say?

I hadn't the very faintest desire to be saved. Why should I be saved when Michael lay there so still?

As I struck a match to light the oil-stove, I thought I heard a shot. Rushing back up the stairs, I saw that Lejaune was posing a corpse in an embrasure. One body still lay where it had fallen.

It was Michael's.

I must have been mistaken as to hearing the sound of a shot. At any rate all was silent now, and Lejaune, his back to me, was fitting the dead man's rifle to his shoulder and clasping the dead left hand round the barrel.

I turned and crept back to my duties as cook, placed twigs and wood beneath the *soupe*-kettle, and turned up the wick of the oil-stove . . .

And as I watched the fire burn up, I imagined Lejaune posing Michael's body – perhaps long before life was out of it . . . The thought was unbearable.

He might be in agony.

He might be so wounded that his life could be saved if he lay flat. Not all the killed had been killed outright – though many of them had died immediately, as only their heads were exposed and their wounds were in the brain or throat.

There was really no more reason why Michael should be spared than any of the others should be – but he was my dearly-loved brother, and I simply could not bear it. I could not have his poor wounded body flung about like a sack of potatoes, and stuck up by the jeering Lejaune with indignities and insults.

He might not yet be dead, and his life might depend on what I did now! I turned to run upstairs.

Was I then going to mutiny after all? Was I going to defy my superior officer and tell him what he should, and what he should not, do in the fort that he commanded? Was I going to tell him that Michael was of superior clay and not to be treated as all the others had been treated?

I was.

And as I ran up the stairs, another thought struck me.

Michael's last request and instructions! I must get those letters and the little packet that he had spoken about. I must say to Lejaune:

'I'll fight till I drop, and I'll obey you implicitly – but leave my brother's body alone – leave it to me . . .'

After all, things were a little different now.

Lejaune and I were the only survivors. We had passed through Hell unscathed, and, at the last, two against a thousand, had kept the Flag flying.

Surely he could be decent now, unbend a little, and behave as a man and a comrade . . .

As I came out on to the roof, Lejaune was bending over Michael.

He had unfastened my brother's tunic, torn the lining out of his *képi*, removed his sash, and opened the flat pouch that formed part of the money-belt that Michael wore.

Lying beside Lejaune, were three or four letters, and a torn envelope. In his hands were a tiny packet, bound up in string and sealing-wax, and an opened letter.

I sprang toward him, seeing red, my whole soul ablaze with indignant rage that this foul vulturous thief should rob the dead, rob a soldier who had fought beside him thus – a brave man who had probably saved his life, before the fight began.

'So he "*had no diamond*," had he? Didn't know what I meant, didn't he?' the ruffian jeered, holding up the packet and the letter in his left hand.

'You damned thief! You foul pariah-dog!' I shouted, and, in a second, his revolver was at my face.

'Stand back, you swine,' he growled. 'Back further. Back, I say . . .'

One movement, and I should be dead.

And a good thing too, but I had a word or two to say first. As I stepped back, he lowered the revolver and smiled horribly . . .

'I didn't know that *men* crept round robbing the dead, after a fight, Lejaune,' I said. 'I thought that was left to Arab women – of the vilest sort . . . You dirty thieving cur – you should be picking over dust-bins in the Paris gutters, not defiling an honourable uniform – *chiffonnier*! . . .'

Lejaune bared his teeth and laughed unpleasantly.

'A fine funeral oration from a jewel-thief!' he snarled.

'Any more grand sentiments before I blow out what brains you have? No? Well, I think I promised you that I would attend to you, all in good time. Now I'm going to do it . . . I am going to shoot you now, where you stand. Half a dozen through the stomach, shall we say? I don't want to hurry you unduly out of this pleasant world . . . Oh no, don't think I want you any longer. The Arabs won't attack again to-day, and they've settled all my mutineers nicely for me . . . And a relief-column will arrive at dawn . . . Then you and the rest of these cursed dogs will be given a hole in the sand for the lot of you – and I shall get the Cross of the Legion of Honour, a Captain's commission, and a trip to Paris to receive thanks and decoration . . . And at Paris, my chatty little friend, I shall dispose of this trifle that your gang so kindly brought to the Legion for me!' and he again held up the little packet in his left hand.

'A rich man, thanks to you – and to *this* . . .' and as he said the last word, he actually kicked Michael's body!

Even as I snatched at my sword-bayonet, and leapt forward – in the instant that my dazed and weary mind took in the incredible fact of this brutal kick – it also took in another fact even more incredible – *Micheal's eyes were open, and turned to me.*

Michael was alive! . . . I would live too, if possible . . . My hand, still grasping my bayonet, fell to my side.

'Good!' said Lejaune. 'Armed attack on a superior officer – and in the face of the enemy! . . . Excellent! I court martial you myself. I find you guilty and I sentence you to *death*. . . I also carry out the sentence myself . . . *Thus* . . .' and the revolver travelled slowly from my face to the pit of my stomach.

'*There*! . . .'

As Lejaune had spoken, Michael's right hand had moved. As the last word was uttered, the hand seized Lejaune's foot, jerking him from his balance, as he pulled the trigger in the act of looking down and of stumbling.

Blinded, deafened, and dazed, I leapt and lunged with all my strength and drove my bayonet through Lejaune. I stumbled, and it was torn from my hand. When I could see again (for I must have ducked straight at the revolver as he fired it, or else he must have raised it as his foot was pulled from under him), he was lying on his back, twitching, the handle of the bayonet protruding from his chest, the blade through his heart.

Lejaune was dead, and *I* was the mutineer and murderer after all! *I* was the 'butcher' and *Lejaune* the 'pig.'

6

A 'Viking's Funeral'

'All night long, in a dream untroubled of hope,
He brooded, clasping his knees.'

I STOOPED over Michael, whose eyes were closed again. Was he dead – his last act the saving of my life?

I don't think I felt very much, at the moment. My mind was numb or blank, and I wasn't certain that the whole affair was not a nightmare . . .

Michael opened his eyes.

'Stout Fella,' he whispered. 'Got the letters?'

I told him that he would deliver them in person. That we were the sole survivors. That the relief would come soon and we should be promoted and decorated.

'For stabbing Lejaune?' he smiled. 'Listen, Johnny . . . I'm for it, all right. Bled white . . . Listen . . . I never stole anything in my life . . . Tell Dig I said so, and *do* get the letter to Aunt Patricia . . . You mustn't wait for the relief . . . Lejaune's body . . . They'd shoot you . . . Get a camel and save yourself . . . In the dark to-night . . . If you can't get away, say I killed Lejaune . . . I helped to, anyhow . . .'

I do not know what I said.

'No. Listen . . . Those letters . . . You are to leave one on me . . . Leave it in my hand . . . Confession . . . Do the thing thoroughly . . . No need for you and Dig to carry on with the game now . . . You must get the confession published or it's all spoilt . . .'

'You've nothing to confess, Beau, old chap,' I said . . . 'Half a minute, I'm going to get some brandy . . .'

His fingers closed weakly on my sleeve.

'Don't be an ass, Johnny,' he whispered. 'Confession's the whole thing . . . Leave it where it'll be found or I'll haunt you . . . Gnaw your neck and go '*Boo*' in the dark . . . No, don't go . . . Promise . . . God! *I'm going blind*. . . John . . . John . . . Where are you? . . . Promise . . . Confession . . . John . . . John . . .'

Within two minutes of his seizing Lejaune's foot and saving my life, my brother was dead . . . My splendid, noble, great-hearted Beau . . .

I have not the gift of tears. I have not cried since I was a baby, and the relief of tears was denied me now.

No. I could not weep. But I looked at the revolver, still clutched in Lejaune's right hand . . . It was only a momentary temptation, for I had something to do for Michael. His last words had laid a charge on me, and I would no more fail Michael dead, than I would have failed him when he lived.

Michael's affairs first – and if the Touaregs rushed the place while I attended to them, I would just take Lejaune's revolver and make a good end. I ought to get five of them, and perhaps might grab one of their heavy straight swords and show them something . . .

I turned to the letters.

One of them was addressed to Lady Brandon. She should get it, if I had the ingenuity, courage, and skill to keep myself alive long enough. One was addressed to Claudia. That too . . . There was one for me, and one for Digby. And there was another, crushed up in Lejaune's left hand. The envelope from which he had torn it lay near. It was addressed to *The Commissioner of Police, Scotland Yard, London, England.* Poor Michael's 'confession' of something he had never done! I was sorely tempted to destroy it, but his words were still in my ears, urgent and beseeching. *I was to see that the 'confession' was published.*

Well – let it remain where it was. It would get a wide-enough publicity if it were found in the dead hand of the murdered Commandant of a beleaguered fort . . . I picked up the packet that Lejaune had dropped when I struck him, and put it with the three letters into my pocket. I then opened the one addressed to me. It ran as follows: –

'My dear John,

When you get this, take the letters that are with it to Brandon Abbas, as soon as you can. Send them if you can't take them. The one for Aunt Patricia solves the Mystery of the "Blue Water," *at any rate to* HER *satisfaction, and she can publish the solution or not, as she thinks fit, later on . . . After Uncle Hector's death, for example . . . Meanwhile, I beg and beseech and instruct and order you, to see that the letter addressed to the Chief of Police is not burked. It is exactly what we all bolted for – thus averting suspicion from innocent people including your Isobel, don't forget, Johnny boy!). We took the blame between us, and the first of us to die should shoulder the lot, of course, so that the other two can go home again. You or Dig would do this for his brothers, and so will I, if I pip first. So off with the home letters –* HOME, *and see that the other one gets into the papers and into the hands of the police and all that. I have written an absolutely identical letter to this for Digby too, so I am sure that one or both of you will see that my wishes are carried out. No nonsense about* "DE MORTUIS NIL NISI BONUM," *mind. It is the living we have to think about, so do exactly as I tell you. You'll be doing the best for me, as a matter of fact, as well as for the living, if you carry out what I ask* – SO GO TO IT, PUP.

If I outlive you, I shall do the same by you or Dig, GO TO IT.

You spoilt my plans by your balmy quixotic conduct in bunking from home – now put them right by doing exactly as I say.

Good-bye, dear old stoutest of Stout Fellas. See you in the Happy Hunting Grounds.

Beau.

P.S. – Don't come near me there, though, if you destroy that confession.'

I put the letter down and looked at his face. Peaceful, strong, dignified, and etherealised beyond its usual fineness and beauty . . . I closed his eyes and folded his hands upon his chest . . .

How *could* I let this thing happen – let the world have confirmation of the suspicion that Michael was a despicable mean thief? Or rather, how could I publish to a world that knew little or nothing about the affair, that Michael had done such a miserable deed?

I looked at his face again.

How could I disobey his last instructions, refuse his last request?

Nor was it a request made impulsively, on the spur of the moment. He had thought it all out, and written it down long ago, in case of just such an event as had happened – his predeceasing us . . .

What would Digby do in my position? Would he take that paper from Lejaune's hand and destroy it? I felt he would not. He *could* not, had he been present at Michael's death, and heard his dying words . . . Not having done so, would he blame me if I left that confession there, to be found by the relieving force?

Well – if he did, he must, and I must act according to my own light – if I could find any . . .

And suppose the Arabs assaulted again, before the relief arrived?

That would settle the problem quite finally, for they would loot the place, mutilate the dead, and then make the fort the funeral pyre of the mangled corpses . . .

I found myself wishing they would do so, and then saw the cowardice of my wish.

No, it was my affair now to – to – to . . . I actually found that I was nodding, and had all but fallen backwards as I sat!

In fact, a heavy faintness, an unspeakable weariness, formed the only sensation of which my mind or body was now conscious. I had seen too much, done too much, suffered too much, felt too much, in the last few hours, to have any other feeling left, save that of utter exhaustion. I felt that I could die, but could not sleep.

In the very act of pulling myself together and saying that *this* would not do, I must have fallen into a state of semi-coma that was not sleep.

I shook it off, to find that a new day was dawning, and, for a minute, I gazed around at the extraordinary sight that met my eyes – the blood-stained roof, the mounds of cartridgecases, the stiff figures crouching in the embrasures, the body of Lejaune with the handle of my bayonet protruding from his chest; and Michael's calm smiling face, as noble in death as in life . . .

'I must go, Beau, old chap,' I said aloud, 'if I am to get your letter and parcel to Aunt Patricia and tell them of your heroic death.'

I knelt and kissed him, for the first time since babyhood.

And only then, actually not till then, I remembered the Arabs!

There was no sign of them whatsoever, alive or dead, which may partly account for my having completely forgotten their existence . . .

I should not be doing much toward carrying out Michael's wishes if I walked straight into their hands. Nor was death any less certain if I remained in the fort till relief came, and Lejaune's body was found with my bayonet in it.

Idly I supposed that I might remove it and replace it by that of another man, and blame him for the murder. I had not the faintest intention of doing so, of course, nor would my tale have been very convincing, since I was alive and everybody else neatly disposed and arranged, *after* death. It did occur to me that perhaps I could pretend that I was the hero of the whole defence, and had posed all these corpses myself, including that of the man who had murdered Lejaune, but, of course, I did not seriously consider the idea.

No. Unless I wanted to die, I must evade both the Arabs and the relieving force from Tokotu. If I could do that, I must, thereafter, evade the entire population of the desert between Zinderneuf and safety, as well as evading any avenging search-party that might be sent out after me. There were also the little matters of thirst, starvation, and exposure. All I could do in the way of preparation in that direction would be to load myself with food, water, spare boots, and ammunition.

Rising to my feet, I wearily dragged myself down the stairs and filled and relit the oil-stove. While the kettle was boiling for coffee, I foraged round, filled my water-bottle with water and three big wine-bottles with the same liquid. Water was going to be infinitely more precious than any wine, before I was much older. I also emptied my knapsack and haversack of everything but a pair of boots, and filled them to bursting, with bread, coffee, and the bottles of water.

I thought my best plan would be to load myself up to the weight I was accustomed to, but to let my burden consist of food and water. This would grow lighter as I grew weaker – or I should grow weaker as it grew lighter. Anyhow, it seemed the best thing to do, but how I longed for a camel! The thought occurred to me that if the relief did not arrive that day, I could remain in the fort till night, and then try to get one of the Arabs' camels when it was dark. A moment's reflection, however, made it clear that if the relief did not enter the fort pretty soon, the Arabs would.

The sooner I got away, the better chance I should have of doing it successfully.

I ate and drank all I could, shouldered my burdens and returned to the roof for a last look round. If I could see anything of the Arabs in one direction I could, at least, try to get away in the opposite quarter. If not,

I must simply trust to luck, and crawl off in the direction opposite to the oasis, as being the likeliest one to offer a chance of escape.

I gazed round in all directions. There still was no sign of an Arab, though, of course, there might have been any number beyond the oasis, or behind the sand-hills that surrounded the fort.

I glanced at Lejaune. Should I remove my bayonet from its place in his evil heart?

No. My whole soul revolted from the idea . . . And as for any hope of concealing the manner of his death, it would still be perfectly obvious that he had been stabbed by a comrade and not shot by the enemy.

Besides, I had killed him in self-defence – self-defence from as cold-blooded, dastardly, and criminal a murder as a man could commit.

No. Let the righteously-used bayonet stay where it was – and incidentally I had quite enough to carry without the now useless thing . . .

'Good-bye, Beau,' I said, crossing to where he lay – and, as I spoke, I almost jumped, for the brooding silence was broken by a shot, followed by several others . . .

The Arabs? . . . No – these were neither rifle shots nor fired towards the fort. The sound of them made that quite evident.

Crouching, I ran to the side of the roof and looked.

On a distant sand-hill was a man on a camel, a man in uniform, waving his arm above his head and firing his revolver in the air.

It was a French officer.

The relief had arrived from Tokotu, and I must escape or be tried, and shot, for the murder of my superior officer in the very presence of the enemy . . .

Yes – but what about this same enemy? Where were they? Was that fine fellow riding to death and torture? Straight into an ambush, a trap of which the uncaptured fort with its flying flag was the bait? That might well be the explanation of there having been no dawn-assault that morning, while I slept. They might, with Arab cunning, have decided that it would be a much better plan to maintain the siege, unseen and unheard, and lure the relieving force, by an appearance of peace and safety, into marching gaily into an oasis covered by hundreds of rifles lining neighbouring sand-hills. They could massacre the relief-column and then turn to the fort again. If no relief-force came, they could still assault the fort whenever they thought fit . . .

As these thoughts flashed through my mind, I decided that I must warn that man, riding gaily to his death, deceived by the peaceful quiet of the scene, and the floating Tri-couleur at the flagstaff top.

Seeing the walls lined, as they were, with soldiers, the Flag floating above them, and no sign of any enemy, he would at once conclude that we had long since driven them off.

Obviously this must be the case, or he would have heard sounds of rifle-fire, miles away, he would think.

I must warn him, for I had no doubt, in my own mind, that hundreds of Arab eyes were watching him.

Nor was it this man alone, rejoicing there in our safety. A whole column must be close behind him. Comrades of ours who had marched day and night to our relief. Of course, I could not let them walk into the trap, deceived by the very ruse that had deceived the Arabs . . .

This officer was no fool, doubtless, but how was he to know that the fort was a whited sepulchre, tenanted by the dead, unable to signal to him that he was walking into an ambush with his column? Naturally he would assume, that since the apparently crowded fort gave him no warning of danger, there *was* no danger, and he and his column could come gaily marching into the fort from which its foes had fled.

This being so, I must warn him myself. I was certain that Michael would approve, and that he would have done so himself had he been in my place. It might mean death instead of escape, but death was certainly preferable to sneaking off while a whole column of one's comrades marched to a destruction one had the power to avert.

What to do? Should I lower the Flag? Run it up and down a few times? Wave my arms and dance about, up on the look-out platform? . . .

As likely as not, he would take any such signals as signs of joy and welcome. If I were he, approaching a fully-manned fort over whose crowded walls floated the Flag, I should certainly see nothing of warning about such demonstrations as those.

Until I was actually fired upon, I should certainly suppose I was safe and being welcomed to the fort by those whom I had been too late to assist in their victory over some impudent little raiding-party.

Exactly! *Until fired upon*! That would surely give him something to think about – and, moreover, would give me a chance of escape, even yet . . . Long before he came within shouting-distance he would be rushed by the Arabs. I would do the firing.

Kneeling down and resting my rifle in an embrasure, I aimed as though my life depended on hitting him. I then raised my fore-sight half an inch, and fired. Rushing to another embrasure, I took another shot, this time aiming to hit the ground, well in front of him.

He halted.

That was enough.

If he walked into an ambush now, he was no officer of the Nineteenth Army Corps of Africa . . .

Rushing across to the side of the roof furthest from his line of approach, I dropped my rifle over, climbed the parapet, hung by my hands and then dropped, thanking God that my feet would encounter sand . . . Snatching up my rifle, I ran as hard as I could go, to the nearest sand-hill. If this were occupied I would die fighting, and the sounds of rifle-fire would further warn the relief-column. If it were not occupied, I would hide and see what happened. Possibly I might be able to make a very timely diversion upon the Arab flank if there were a fight, and, in any case, I might hope to escape under cover of darkness . . . The sand-hill was not occupied, I was safely out of the fort, and a chance of getting safely away existed, whether the Arabs attacked the column or not.

I crept into an Arab trench and set to work to make a hole in it, that I might be as inconspicuous as possible should anybody come, or look, in my direction.

From between two stones on the edge of the parapet of my trench, I could watch the fort and the oasis. I was conscious of an uneasy sensation as I watched, that I myself might be under the observation of enemies in my rear . . .

As soon as I saw what the Arabs and the approaching column were going to do, I would consider the possibilities of a safe retreat in the most likely direction . . .

I began to wish something would happen, for the situation was a little trying, and there was too strong a suggestion of leaving an Arab frying-pan on the one hand, to step into the French fire on the other . . . an Arab torture by frying . . . a French firing-party at dawn.

While I lay gazing to my front and wondering what might be happening behind me, I was astonished to see the French officer come round the corner of the fort, alone, and proceeding as unconcernedly as if he were riding in the streets of Sidi-bel-Abbès! . . .

Well! I had done my best for him and his column. I had risked my own safety to warn him that things were not what they seemed – and if the Arabs got him and his men, it was not my fault.

He could hardly call *being shot at* a welcome from the fort? . . . Round the walls he rode, staring up at the dead defenders.

I wondered if the shade thrown by the peaks of their caps would so hide and disguise their faces that, from below, it would be impossible to see that the men were dead . . .

What were the Arabs doing? . . . Leaving him as further bait for the trap, and waiting for the whole column to walk into it?

Ought I to warn them again? Surely once was enough? It would mean almost certain capture for me, by one side or the other, if I fired again . . . Apparently this officer was unwarnable, moreover, and it would be nothing but a vain sacrifice to proclaim my existence and my position, by firing again . . . And while I argued the matter with my conscience, I saw that all was well – the relieving force was approaching *en tirailleur*, preceded by scouts and guarded by flankers.

Slowly and carefully the French force advanced, well handled by somebody more prudent than the officer who had arrived first, and by no means disposed to walk into an Arab ambush.

A few minutes later, I heard the trumpeter summoning the fort, blowing his calls to dead ears.

I could imagine the bewilderment of the officer standing before those closed gates, waiting for them to open, while the dead stared at him and nothing stirred.

As I waited for him to climb up into the fort or to send somebody in, to open the gates for him, I came to the conclusion that the Arabs must have abandoned the siege and departed altogether. I wondered whether this had been due to Lejaune's ruse and the fort's apparently undiminished garrison, or to news, from their scouts, of the approach of a strong relief force. Anyhow, gone they were, and very probably they had raised the siege and vanished after moonrise the previous night . . .

The officer, his *sous-officier*, the trumpeter, and a fourth man, stood in a little group beneath the wall, some three hundred yards or so from where I lay . . . I gathered that the fourth man was refusing to climb into the fort. There was pointing, there were gesticulations, and the officer drew his revolver and presented it at the face of the man who had shaken his head when the officer pointed up at the wall.

The trumpeter, his trumpet dangling as he swung himself up, climbed from the back of his camel to a projecting waterspout, and through an embrasure into the fort.

I expected to see him reappear a minute later at the gate, and admit the others.

He never reappeared at all, and, about a quarter of an hour later, the officer himself climbed up and entered the fort in the same way.

As before, I expected to see the gates opened a minute later – but nothing happened. There was silence and stillness. The minutes dragged by, and the men of the relief-column stood still as statues, staring at the enigmatical fort.

Presently I heard the officer bawling to the trumpeter, the men outside the fort began to move towards it in attack-formation, another squadron of the relief-column arrived on mules, the gates were thrown open from within, and the officer came out alone.

He gave some orders, and re-entered the fort with his second-in-command. No one else went in.

A few minutes later, the officer's companion reappeared, called up a sergeant, and gave orders, evidently for camping in the oasis.

It occurred to me that my situation was about to become an unwholesome one, as, before long, there would be vedettes posted on all four sides of the fort in a big circle, to say nothing of patrols.

I must be going, if I wished to go at all, before I was within a ring of sentries . . .

After a good look round, I crawled painfully and slowly to the next sand-hill, trusting that the two in the fort would find too much of interest, within its walls, to have time to look over them and see me on my brief journey from cover to cover. Apparently this was the case, for when I reached the next sand-hill and looked back from behind its crest, there was no sign that I had been seen.

I rested, regained my breath, and then made another bolt to the sand-hill behind me, keeping the fort between the oasis and my line of retreat, and a good look-out for the vedette which, sooner or later, was certain to come more or less in this direction.

My best plan would be to creep from cover to cover, between the sand-hills, as I was doing, until beyond the vedette-circle, and then hide and rest till night fell. A good night's forced marching and I should be thirty miles away before the sun gained full strength, on the morrow. As though for a prize – and, of course, my life *was* the prize – I carried out this careful scouting retirement until I was half a mile from the fort and among the big stones that crowned a little hill of rock and sand. Here I was safe enough for the present. I could lie hidden and see where the vedettes were posted; sleep in what shade there was; eat, drink, rest, and gather strength; and set forth, when the moon rose, on my fairly hopeless journey . . . Fairly hopeless? . . . Absolutely hopeless – unless I could secure a camel . . . And then and there, I firmly rejected the idea that entered my mind – of killing a vedette to get his beast. That I could regard as nothing better than cold-blooded murder.

A more acceptable notion was that of trying to creep into the oasis, during the night, and stealing a camel from there. It would be an extremely difficult thing to do successfully, for there would be brilliant moonlight, a very sharp look-out for Arabs, and a horrible row from the camel when one disturbed it . . . Yes, very difficult and dangerous, but just possible, inasmuch as I was in uniform and might be believed if, challenged by the camel-guard, I pretended I was an orderly in search of his camel, for duty. Or if I walked up boldly and announced that I had been ordered to take a camel and ride back to Tokotu with a dispatch . . . Distinctly possible, I considered. With really good luck and a really good bluff, it might be done. The good luck would lie in the camel-guard being unaware that I wasn't a member of the relief-force at all.

If I were not recognised, if my bluff were convincing, if I were not caught in the act by the very officer whom I should be pretending to have sent me for a camel; or if, on the other hand, there were a chance of simply stealing the camel unseen – I might get away with it. But there seemed to be a good many *ifs* . . .

However, after thinking the matter over from all points of view, and weighing the chances impartially, I came to the conclusion that there was more likelihood of Michael's letter reaching Aunt Patricia if I had a shot at getting a camel, than if I did not. A thousand-mile stroll across the Soudanese Sahara did not strike me as one that would lead me home, in view of the fact that it takes a good man to do it under the somewhat more favourable conditions of preparation, organisation, and the protection of numbers and of the law (such as it is).

I decided to wait until night, see what happened, and reconnoitre the oasis with a view to deciding whether theft, bluff, or a combination of the two, offered the greater possibilities of success in securing a mount.

And the more I could concentrate my thoughts upon problems and considerations of this sort, the longer could I postpone and evade the on-rushing realisation of my loss . . . the longer could I keep myself numb and insensate beneath the hammer-blows of the terrible Fact that lurked and struck, lurked and struck; the longer deafen myself to the waxing Voice with its . . . *Michael is dead . . . Michael is dead . . . Listen and heed – Michael is dead . . .*

In spite of the terrific heat and my unutterable misery and wretchedness, I fell asleep, and slept soundly until towards evening.

2

When I awoke, I realised that I had been lucky. The nearest vedette was quite a thousand yards to my right, and so placed that there was no fear of my being seen, so long as I exercised reasonable precaution.

The sun was setting, the appalling heat of the day was waning in fierceness, and the fort and oasis presented a scene of normal military activity – or rather inactivity – for nothing whatever moved in or around the fort, and there was but little coming and going about the oasis. Here and there, a sentry's bayonet gleamed, a man led a mule or camel; a little column of smoke rose from among the palms, as a cooking-fire was lighted or replenished.

So far as I could see, the fort had not been taken over by a new garrison, nor, to my surprise, had the dead been removed from the walls. Those motionless figures could not be living soldiers, for no Commandant would have kept his whole force on duty like that – particularly after a day-and-night march such as this one had just made.

I should have expected to see that the dead had been buried, the fort occupied, the look-out platform manned, and the sentry-posts occupied. However, it didn't matter to me what they did, so long as they left their camels in the oasis . . .

As I watched, a small party, preceded by an officer on a mule, crossed from the oasis and entered the fort. I expected to see them remove the dead from the embrasures, but they did not do so. From where I was, I could not see on to the roof, but I should have seen them at work, bad they come to the wall and begun their labours as a burial fatigue-party . . .

Before long, the party returned to the oasis, the officer remaining in the fort. I wondered what they made of the *adjudant* with a French bayonet in him, of the dead *légionnaire* with his eyes closed and his hands crossed upon his breast, of the men dead upon their feet, of the complete absence of life in the uncaptured fort from which two warning shots had come

. . . Some of the superstitious old legionaries would have wonderful ideas and theories about it all!

The evening wore on, the sun set, and the great moon rose. In the brief dusk, I crept nearer to the fort and oasis, crouching and crawling from sand-hill to sand-hill. I would wait until everybody who was not on duty would be asleep; and then work round and enter the oasis, walking up boldly as though sent from the fort with a message. If challenged, I would act precisely as I should have done if dispatched by an officer to get my camel and hasten back to Tokotu . . .

I imagined myself saying to a sentry who was disposed to doubt me, 'All right, you fool, you hinder me – go on; . . . Don't blame *me*, though, when I say what delayed me! . . .' and generally showing a perfect willingness to be hindered, provided I was not the one to get the blame . . .

From the crest of the next sand-hill, I saw that the men of the relieving-column were parading outside the oasis, and I wondered what this portended.

As I watched, they marched towards the fort, halted, faced into line, with their backs towards me, and stood easy. I concluded that their officer had given them an 'off' day after their long march, and was now going to work them all night at clearing up the fort, burying the dead, and generally re-establishing Zinderneuf as a going concern among the military outposts of Empire-according-to-a-Republic.

This might be very favourable to my plans. If I marched boldly up to the oasis, as though coming from the fort, when everybody was very busy, and demanded a camel, I should probably get one . . .

The Commandant rode out from the oasis on a mule, and the men were called to attention. He was evidently going to address them – probably to congratulate them on the excellence of their forced march and refer to the marvellous defence put up by the garrison of the fort, who had died to a man in defence of the Flag of their adopted country.

Suddenly, the man standing beside him cried out and pointed to the fort. Instinctively I looked in the direction of his pointing finger – and very nearly sprang to my feet at what I saw.

The fort was on fire!

It was very much on fire too, obviously set alight in several places and with the help of oil or some other almost explosive combustible . . . And what might *this* mean? Surely it was not 'by order'? Not the result of official decision?

Of course not . . . Could it be the work of some superstitious legionary left alone in the place as watchman? No. If there were anybody at all on duty there, he would have been up on the look-out platform, the emptiness of which had puzzled me . . .

How was this going to affect my chance of escape? Ought I to make a dash for the oasis while all hands were engaged in an attempt to put the fire out?

And, as I stared, in doubt and wonder, I was aware of a movement on the roof of the fort!

Carefully keeping the gate-tower between himself and the paraded troops, a man was doing precisely what I myself had done! I saw his cap as he crept crouching along below the parapet, I saw his arm and rifle come through an embrasure, I saw the rifle fall, and a minute or so later, as a column of smoke shot up, I saw him crawl through the embrasure and drop to the ground. By good luck or by skill, he had chosen a spot at which he was hidden from the vedette that had been a thousand yards to my right . . .

And who could he be, this legionary who had set fire to the fort of Zinderneuf? He certainly had my sympathy and should have my assistance. I must see that he did not crawl in the direction of the vedette. He might not know that he was there. I began creeping in a direction that would bring me on to his line of retreat in time to warn him.

A few minutes later he saw me, and hitched his rifle forward. Evidently he did not intend to be taken alive. Very naturally, after setting fire to one of *Madame la République's* perfectly good forts . . . I drew out what had been a handkerchief, and from the safe obscurity of a sand-valley, waved it. I then laid my rifle down and crawled towards him. I noticed that he was wearing a trumpet, slung behind him.

As I came closer to the man, I was conscious of that strange contraction of the scalp-muscles which has given rise to the expression 'his hair stood on end with fright.'

I was not frightened and my hair did not stand on end, but I grew cold with a kind of horrified wonder as I saw what I took to be the ghost or astral form of *my brother* there before me, looking perfectly normal, alive, and natural.

It *was* my brother – my brother Digby – Michael's twin . . .

'Hullo, John,' said Digby, as I stared open-mouthed and incredulous, 'I thought you'd be knocking about somewhere round here. Let's get off to a healthier spot, shall us?'

For all his casual manner and debonair bearing, he looked white and drawn, sick to death, his hands shaking, his face a ghastly mask of pain.

'Wounded?' I asked, seeing the state he was in.

'Er – not physically . . . I have just been giving Michael a "*Viking's Funeral*,"' he replied, biting his lip.

Poor, poor Digby! He loved Michael as much as I did (he could not love him more), and he was further bound to him by those strange ties that unite twins – psychic spiritual bonds, that make them more like one soul in two bodies than separate individuals. Poor, poor Digby!

I put my arm across his shoulders as we lay on the sand between two hillocks.

'Poor old John!' he said at length, mastering his grief. 'It was you who laid him out, of course. You, who saw him die . . . Poor Johnny boy! . . .'

'He died trying to save my life,' I said. 'He died quite happily and in no pain . . . He left a job for us to do . . . I've got a letter for you. Here it is . . . Let's get well off to the flank of that vedette and lie low till there's a chance to pinch a camel and clear out . . .' and I led the way in a direction to bring us clear of the vedettes and nearer to the oasis.

A couple of minutes after our meeting, we were snugly ensconced behind the crest of a sand-hill, overlooking the parade of our comrades, the oasis, and the burning fort. A higher hillock behind us, and to our right, screened us from the nearest vedette.

'*And*,' said Digby, in a voice that trembled slightly, 'they're not going to spoil Michael's funeral. Nor are they going to secure any evidence of your neat job on the foul Lejaune . . . They're going to be attacked by Arabs . . .' and he raised his rifle.

'Don't shoot anybody, Dig,' I said. It seemed to me there had been enough bloodshed, and if these people were now technically our enemies and might soon be our executioners, they were still our comrades, and innocent of offence.

'Not going to – unless it's myself,' replied Digby. 'Come on, play Arabs with me . . .' and he fired his rifle, aiming high.

I followed his example, shooting above the head of the officer as I had done once before that day.

Again and again we fired, vedettes to left and right of us joining in, and showing their zeal and watchfulness by firing brikly at nothing at all – unless it was at each other.

It was a sight worth seeing, the retreat of that company of legionaries. At a cool order from the officer, they faced about, opened out, doubled to the oasis, and went to ground, turning to the enemy and taking cover so that, within a couple of minutes of our first shots, there was nothing to be seen but a dark and menacing oasis, to approach which was death . . .

'Good work!' said Digby. 'And they can jolly well stop there until the fort is burnt out . . . We'll go in and get camels, as vedettes whose camels have been shot by these attacking Arabs, later on . . . If we swagger up to the sentry on the camels, and pitch a bold yarn, it ought to be all right . . .'

'Yes – better if one of us goes,' said I. 'Then, if he doesn't return, the other can clear off on foot, or try some other dodge.'

'That's it,' agreed Digby. 'I'll have first go.'

'Now tell me all that happened,' he added, 'and then I'll bring you up to date.'

I did so, giving him a full account of all our doings, from the time he had left us to go to the mounted company.

'Now tell me a few things, Dig,' I said, when I had finished, and he knew as much a I did.

He then told me of how his *escouade* had suddenly been ordered from Tanout-Azzal to Tokotu. Here they had found, of all people on this earth, the Spahi officer who had once visited Brandon Abbas, now Major de Beaujolais, seconded from his regiment for duty with mounted units in the *Territoire Militaire* of the Soudan, where the mobile Touaregs were presenting a difficult problem to the peaceful penetrator towards Timbuktu and Lake Tchad.

The Major had not recognised Digby, of course, nor Digby him, until heard his name and that he was a Spahi.

(And it was at him that I had been shooting that day, or rather it was he at whom I had not been shooting. It was this very friend of boyhood's days whom I had been trying to warn against what I thought was an ambush! . . . Time's whirligig! . . .)

At Tokotu, news had been received that Zinderneuf was besieged by a huge force of Touaregs, and de Beaujolais had set off at once.

The rest I knew until the moment when I had seen Digby, who was de Beaujolais' trumpeter, climb into the fort . . .

'Well – you know what I saw as I got on to the roof,' said Digby, 'and you can imagine (can you, I wonder?) what I felt when I saw Beau lying there . . . I dashed down below and rushed round to see if you were among the wounded, and then realised that there *were* no wounded, and that the entire garrison was on that awful roof . . . That meant that you had cleared out, and that it was your bayonet ornamenting Lejaune's chest, and that it was you who had disposed Michael's body and closed his eyes. *Someone* must have done it, and it wasn't one of those dead men . . . Who else but you would have treated Michael's body differently from the others? As I have told you, I was mighty anxious, coming along, as to how you and Michael were getting on, and whether we should be in time, and I had been itching to get up on to the roof while de Beaujolais was being dramatic with Rastignac . . . You can guess how anxious I was *now*. . . What with Michael's death and your disappearance . . .

'I could almost *see* you killing Lejaune, and felt certain it was because he had killed Michael and tried to kill you for that cursed "diamond." . . . I tell you I went dotty . . .

' "*Anyhow – he shall have a "Viking's Funeral*," I swore, and I believe I yelled the words at the top of my voice, "*and then I must find John*." . . . You know, it was always Beau's constant worry that harm would come to you. It was the regret of his life, that he was responsible for your bolting from home . . . You young ass . . .

'Anyhow, my one idea was to give him a proper funeral and then to follow you up. I guessed that you had stuck there, the sole survivor, until you saw de Beaujolais, and then slipped over the wall . . .

'Then I heard someone scrambling and scraping at the wall, climbing up, and I crept off and rushed down below, with the idea of hiding till I got a chance to set fire to the beastly place, if I could do nothing better for Beau . . . I saw the door of the punishment-cell standing open, and I slipped in there and hid behind the door. There was just room for me, and I should never be seen until someone came in and closed the door of the cell – which wasn't likely to happen for a long while . . .

'Soon I heard de Beaujolais bawling out for me, and by the sound of his voice he wasn't much happier than I was . . . The sight upstairs was enough to shake *anybody's* nerve, let alone the puzzle of it all . . . By and by I heard him and the Sergeant-Major talking and hunting for me. They actually looked into the cell once, but it was obviously empty – besides being a most unlikely place for a soldier to shut himself in voluntarily! . . . I gathered that old Dufour was even less happy than de Beaujolais, who certainly wasn't enjoying himself . . . Presently they went away, and the place became as silent as the grave. It occurred to me that whatever else they made of it they must be certain that Lejaune had been killed by one of his own men and that the man must have bolted. If I could also vanish in this mysterious place, it would give them something more to puzzle over; and if I could absolutely destroy it, there would be no evidence for them to lay before a court martial . . . Mind, I had been marching for twenty-four hours and was all but sleeping on my feet, so I wasn't at my brightest and best, by a long way – apart from what I had just seen . . .

'When I felt pretty certain that there was no one about, I crept up on to the roof again and took a look round.

'There was a sentry at the gate, and the company was evidently going to camp in the oasis, and have a sleep before entering the fort.

'I pulled myself together, crawled over to where Beau lay, heaved him up in my arms and carried him below to his own bed in the barrack-room. All round his cot I laid piles of wood from the cook-house and drenched it with lamp oil. I did my best to make it a real "*Viking's Funeral*" for him, just like we used to have at home. Just like he used to want it. My chief regret was that I had no Union Jack to drape over him . . .

'However, I did the best I could, and covered the whole pyre with sheets of canvas and things . . . All white, more or less . . . There was no sign of the wood and oil . . . He looked splendid . . . Then, after thinking it over, I took the spare Tri-couleur and laid that over all . . . It wasn't what I would have liked, but he had fought and died under it, so it served . . . It served . . . Served . . .'

Digby's head was nodding as he talked. He was like a somnambulist. I tried to stop him.

'Shut up, John . . . I must get it clear . . . *Oh, Beau! Beau! . . . I did my best for you, old chap. . . There was no horse, nor spear, nor shield to lay beside you. . . But I put a dog at your feet though. . . And your rifle and bayonet was for sword and spear . . .*'

He must be going mad, I feared.

'A dog, old chap?' I said, trying to get him back to realities. 'You are not getting it right, you know . . .'

'Yes, a dog . . . A dog at his feet . . . A dog lying crouching with its head beneath his heels . . .'

This was getting dreadful.

'I did not carry it down, as I carried Beau. I took it by one foot and dragged it down . . .'

'*Lejaune*?' I whispered.

'Yes, John. Lejaune – with your bayonet through his heart. *He* won't give dumb evidence against you – and Beau had his "*Viking's Funeral*" with a dog at his feet . . .'

I think I felt worse then than I had felt since Michael died. I gave Digby a sharp nudge in the ribs with my elbows.

'Get on with it and don't drivel,' I said as though in anger.

'Where was I?' said Digby, in the tone of a man walking from a nap.

'Oh, yes. And when all was ready, John, I sat and talked to Beau and told him I hadn't the faintest idea as to what he'd been up to in this "Blue Water" business, but what I *did* know was that, far from being anything shady, it was something quixotic and noble . . . And then what do you think I did, John? . . . *I fell asleep* – and slept till the evening . . .

'I was a bit more my own man when I woke up. I went up on the roof to see what was doing . . . Creeping to the wall and peeping over, I saw that the Company was parading, and that I had cut it very fine. I thanked God that I had awakened in time, for in a few minutes they would be marching in, to clean up and take over.

'I crept back and set fire to Beau's funeral pyre. Then I rushed off and poured a can of oil over the pile of benches and furniture that I had heaped up in the next room. I set light to that and knocked another can over at the foot of the stairs. I lit it and bolted up to the stair of the look-out platform. At the bottom of this, I did the same, and by that time it would have taken more water than there is in the Sahara to put the place out . . . I decided that Beau's funeral was all right, the evidence against you destroyed, and the time arrived for me to clear out . . .'

He yawned prodigiously.

'So I came to look for you, John . . . To look for . . . for . . .'

Digby was asleep.

Should I go to sleep too? The temptation was sore. But I felt that if we were to save ourselves, we must do it at once. We could hardly hope to lie there all night and escape detection in the morning, when the place would be swarming with scouts and skirmishers.

I decided to watch for an hour or two, while poor Digby slept. At the end of that time I would wake him and say that I was going to make the attempt to get a camel . . .

It was extraordinarily silent . . . It seemed impossible that the oasis, lying there so black and still, was alive with armed men. Even the camels and mules were behaving as though aware that the night was unusual. Not a grunting gurgle from the one or a whinnying bray from the other broke the brooding stillness of the night. I wondered if every man had been made responsible for the silence of his own animal, and had muzzled and gagged it. I smiled at the idea.

Not a light showed. Was the idea to make the smouldering fort a bait for the Arabs whom de Beaujolais would suppose to be in the neighbourhood – a bait to attract them to his lead-and-steel-fanged trap? . . .

How would it be possible, after all, for me to approach that silvered black oasis, across the moonlit sands, without being challenged, seized, and exposed for what I was? I had anticipated approaching a normal, somnolent camp – not a tensely watchful look-out post, such as the oasis had become from the time Digby and I had fired our rifles.

Would it be better, after all, to sleep all night and try to bluff the camel-guard on the morrow, when the whole place would be buzzing with life and activity? It seemed a poor look-out anyway. And how bitterly one would regret not having made the attempt on foot, if one were seized in the effort to take a camel . . .

Having decided that Digby had slept for about a couple of hours, I woke him up.

'What about it, Dig?' I said. 'Are we going to have a shot at getting a camel, or are we going to march? We must do one or the other, unless you think we might do any good here by daylight . . .'

'Oh, quite,' replied Digby. 'I'm sure you're right, John,' and went to sleep again, in the act of speaking.

This was not exactly helpful, and I was trying to make up my mind as to whether I should give him another hour, or knock him up again at once, when I saw two camel-riders leave the oasis. I rubbed my eyes.

No. There was no doubt about it. A patrol was going out, or dispatches were being sent to Tokotu.

Here were two camels. Two well-fed, well-watered camels were coming towards us.

I did not for one moment entertain the thought of shooting their riders, but I certainly toyed for a moment with the idea of offering to fight them, fair and square, for their beasts! If we won, we should ride off and they would tramp back to the oasis. If they won, they'd continue about their business and we should be where we were . . . A silly notion . . . About two seconds after revealing ourselves, we should be looking into the muzzles of their rifles, and have the option of death or ignominious capture . . . Why *should* they fight us? . . . I must really pull myself together and remember who I was and where I was . . .

The camels drew nearer and I decided, from their direction, they were on the way to Tokotu.

I crawled down the reverse slope of my sand-hill and ran along the valley at its base. Climbing another hillock, I saw that a repetition of the manœuvre would bring me on to their line. I did not know what I was going to do when I got there, but I felt there would be no harm in trying to find out who they were and where they were going. If we followed them and got a chance to steal their camels while they were not too far from the oasis to return on foot, I had an idea that we might take that chance. The temptation would be very strong, as it was a matter of life and death to us, while to them it would be merely a matter of a long day's march and a fearful tale of terrific combat with the horde of Arabs who had shot their camels . . .

Suddenly a well-known voice remarked conversationally:

'We sure gotta put them nigs wise, Buddy . . . We don' want nawthen to eventooate to the pore boobs through us not taking 'em by the hand . . .'

'Hank!' I yelped in glee and thankfulness, and he and Buddy turned their camels towards me.

'Here's *one* of the mystery boys, anyhow,' went on Hank. 'I allowed as how you'd be around somewheres when we see you all three gone missin' from the old home . . .'

In a valley between two sand-hills, Hank and Buddy brought their camels to their knees and dismounted. Both wrung my hand in a painful and most delightful manner.

'No offence, and excusin' a personal and dellikit question, Bo,' said Buddy, 'but was it you as had the accident with the cigar-lighter an' kinder caused arsonical proceedins? . . .'

'Sort of "arson about" with matches like?' put in Hank solemnly.

'No,' I said. 'It was Digby set fire to the fort.'

'Then I would shore like to shake him by the hand, some,' said Hank. 'Is he around?'

'Having a nap over there,' I replied.

'The other bright boy too?' asked Buddy. 'An' where's Lejaune? Havin' set fire to the home, hev you taken Poppa by the ear an' led him out into the garden for to admire? . . .'

As quickly as possible I told him what had happened – of Michael's death and 'funeral.'

'He was a shore white man, pard. 'Nuff said,' commented Hank.

'He was all-wool-an'-a-yard-wide, Bo,' said Buddy, and I felt that Michael might have had worse epitaphs.

A brief silence fell upon us.

'Gee!' said Hank after a while. 'Wouldn't it jar you? It shore beats the band. Such nice quiet boys too – always behavin' like they was at a party, an' perlite as Hell – an' one of 'em kills the Big Noise an' the other sets the whole goshdinged outfit afire an' burns out the dod-gasted burg . . . *Some* boys, I allow . . .'

I greatly feared that our deeds of homicide and arson had raised us higher in the estimation of these good men than any number of pious acts and gentle words could ever have done.

As I led the way to where I had left Digby sleeping, I asked the Americans where they were going.

'Wal – we was sorta sent lookin' fer some nigs from Tokotu,' replied

Hank. 'Ole Man Bojolly allows they'll run into an Injun ambush if they ain't put wise. We gotta warn them there's Injuns about, fer all the location's so quiet an' peaceful-lookin' . . .'

'I wonder they didn't git you two boys when they shot us up,' he added.

'We *were* the Arabs,' I confessed with modest pride.

'Gee!' admired Buddy. 'Can you beat it! . . . I shore thought there was thousands come gunnin' fer us . . . Oh, *boy*! You quiet perlite young guys . . . *Mother*! . . .'

'How many guns did you shoot then?' enquired Hank.

'Two,' I replied. 'Rapid fire. And then the vedettes obligingly joined in.'

Buddy gave a brief hard bark, which may, or may not, have been meant for laughter.

'Sunday pants of Holy Moses!' he observed. 'And that lyin' son of a skunk of a Schneider swore he shot seven of you himself – and the rest of you carried away their bodies as he retired in good order! Thinks he oughta get the *médaille militaire* or somethin' . . .'

'Yep,' confirmed Hank, 'an' Ole Man Dupanloup estimates the lot that was agwine ter rush the parade, when he held 'em up, at from a hunderd to a hunderd an' fifty. He lost count of the number he killed – after a score or so . . . Gee! At them north outposts there was *some* bloody battle, son . . .'

'*And* some bloody liars,' observed Buddy, who had sojourned in London.

I had difficulty in awaking poor Digby, but when he realised that Hank and Buddy were actually present in the flesh, he was soon very much awake and on the spot.

'Say, boys,' he went on, after greeting them and hearing their tale of the Battle of the Vedettes, 'it's a lot to ask, I know. But *do* you think you could be attacked, like Dupanloup, by about a hundred and fifty of us, and lose your camels? . . . They'd be shot beneath you, or on top of you, if you like, – while you fought desperately – one to seventy-five, isn't it? . . . You would have peace with honour, and we'd have a chance to save our lives. We don't pretend that they're very valuable, but we've got something we really must do for our brother . . . And I promised Mother I'd bring the Baby home,' he added, indicating me.

'Fergit it, son,' replied Hank to Digby, but he looked at Buddy.

'Couldn't you possibly let us have them!' I said. 'If we went a mile or two further on, we could kick up a fearful row with our four rifles, and you could go back and collect a medal when old Dupanloup gets his . . . Stroll home doing a rear-guard stunt, and we'd pepper the scenery in your direction before we rode off . . . The Senegalese are safe enough. There are no Arabs and no ambush . . . And we simply shan't have a little dog's chance without camels.'

'*We* want 'em, Bo,' replied Hank with quiet finality.

'Shore,' agreed Buddy, eyeing him.

I was surprised and disappointed. Even more disappointed at the attitude of my friends than at the loss of the camels.

'Well – all right then! We won't *fight* you for them,' said Digby, 'but I wish it had been someone else.'

'I don't get your drift. Snow again, Bo,' said Buddy, who seemed pained.

'Why someone else? Don't you admire our low and vulgar ways, pard?' asked Hank. 'Don't you like us?'

'Yes, but to be honest, at the moment I like your camels better,' replied Digby.

'Well, then – you got the lot, ain't you?' asked Hank. 'What's bitin' you now, Bo?'

'Do you mean *you're coming with us*?' I asked, a great light dawning upon me, a light that so dazzled my eyes that I was afraid to look upon it.

'You shore said a mouthful, Bo,' replied Hank. 'Why, what did you figger? That we'd leave you two innercent children to wander about this yer sinful world all on your lone? . . .'

'After you bin and killed their Big Noise? And obliterised their nice little block-house?' put in Buddy. ''Twouldn't be right, boy. '*Course* we're comin' along.'

I really had to swallow hard as I took their horny hands.

'But look here, boys,' Digby remonstrated, after following my example and trying to express thanks without words, 'there's no need for that. Give us your camels and anything else you can safely spare, and go back in modest glory. There's nothing against *you*. If you're caught escaping with us and helping us, you'll be shot with us. It will be "desertion in the face of the enemy when sent on reconnaissance" when it comes to the court martial.'

'Go back nawthen,' said Buddy. 'Look at here. This is what Hank wants to say . . . Is there any Injuns around? Nope. Nope. Is those nigs from Tokotu in any danger? Nope. Hev you had a square deal in this Madam Lar Republic-house stunt? Nope. Didn't you and your brother stand by your dooty in this mutiny game? Yep. Wasn't you two scrapping all the time and doing your damnedest till everybody else had handed in their checks? Yep. And then didn't this Lejaune guy start in to shoot you up? Shore. And what'll happen to you now if they get you? Shoot you up some more. Shore. 'Tain't a square deal . . .

'Well, we figger that these nigs from Tokotu aren't on the chutes fer the bow-wows. Nope. They're marchin' on right now fer Zinderneuf – like John Brown's body – or was it his soul? – safe enough . . . We allow you ain't got no chance on a lone trail. Not a doggoned smell of one. You're two way-up gay cats an' bright boys, but you're no road-kids. You don't know chaparral from an arroyo nor alkali sage-brush from frijoles.

You couldn't tell mesquite from a pinto-hoss. Therefore Hank says we gotta come along . . .'

'Shore thing,' agreed Hank, 'and time we vamoosed too, or we'll hev these nigs a-treadin' on us. They'll go fer a walk on empty stummicks – ours . . .'

A minute later each of the camels bore two riders, and we were padding off at a steady eight miles an hour.

'Any pertickler direction like?' said Hank, behind whom I was riding. 'London? N'York? Morocker? Egyp'? Cape Town? All the same ter me.'

Buddy drove his camel up beside ours.

'What about it, Dig?' said I to my brother. 'We've got to get out of French territory . . . Morocco's north-west; Nigeria's south-east . . .'

'And where's water?' replied Digby. 'I should say the nearest oasis would be a sound objective.'

'If there's a pursuit, they'd take the line for Morocco for certain, I should say,' I pointed out. 'I vote for the opposite direction and a beady eye on our fellow-man, if we can see him. Where there are Arabs there'll be water somewhere about, I suppose.'

'Shore,' said Hank. 'We'll pursoo the pore Injun. What's good enough fer him is bad enough for us. You say wheer you wants ter go, an' I allow *we'll see you there* – but it may take a few years. What we gotta do first is turn Injun, see? . . . Git Injun glad rags, and live like they does. We're well-armed and got our health an' strength an' hoss-sense. When in the desert do as the deserters does . . . Yep. We gotta turn Injun.'

From which I gathered that Hank the Wise firmly advocated our early metamorphosis into Arabs, and the adoption of Arab methods of subsistence in waterless places.

'Injuns lives by lettin' other folks *pro*-juce an' then collectin',' put in Buddy.

'We gotta collect,' said Hank.

'From the collectors,' added Buddy.

From which I gathered further that our friends were proposing not only that we should turn Arab, but super-Arab, and should prey upon the Touareg as the Touareg preyed upon the ordinary desert-dweller. It seemed a sound plan, if a little difficult of application. However, I had infinite faith in the resourcefulness, experience, staunchness, and courage of the two Americans, and reflected that if anybody could escape from this predicament, it was these men, familiar with the almost equally terrible American deserts.

'I vote we go south-west,' said Digby. 'We're bound to strike British territory sooner or later and then we're absolutely safe, and can easily get away by sea. We're bound to fetch up in Nigeria if we go steadily south-west. If we could hit the Niger somewhere east of Timbuktu – it would lead us straight to it.'

'Plenty o' drinkin' water in the Niger, I allow,' observed Buddy. 'But there don't seem ter be no sign-posts to it. It shore is a backward state, this Sahara . . .'

'Anyhow it's south-west of us now, and so's Nigeria,' Digby insisted.

'Starboard yer hellum,' observed Hank. 'Nigeria on the port bow – about one thousand miles.'

And that night we did some fifty or sixty of them without stopping, by way of a good start – a forced march while the camels were fresh and strong.

As we padded steadily along, we took stock of our resources.

With my bottles of water, and the regulation water bottles, we had enough for two or three days, with careful rationing.

Similarly with food. I had a haversack full of bread, and the other three had each an emergency ration as well as army biscuits.

Of ammunition we had plenty, and we hoped to shoot dorcas gazelle, bustard, and hare, if nothing else.

Had Michael been with us, I should have been happy. As it was, the excitement, the mental and physical activity, the hopes and fears attendant on our precarious situation and the companionship of my brother and these two fine Americans combined to help me to postpone my defeat by the giants of misery, pain, and grief that were surely only biding their time, lurking to spring when I could no longer maintain my defences.

Digby, I think, was in much the same mental condition as myself, and I wondered if I, too, had aged ten years in a night.

As we jogged steadily on, the monotony of movement, of scene, and of sound, sent me to sleep, and every now and then I only saved myself from falling by a wild clutch at Hank, behind whom I was sitting.

No one spoke, and it is probable that all of us slept in brief snatches – though they must have been very brief for those who were driving the camels.

I came fully awake as the sun peered over the far-distant edge of the desert to our left.

I longed for a hot bath and hotter coffee, for I ached in every nerve and muscle.

'"'*They'll have fleet steeds that follow*,' quoth young Lochinvar,"' said Digby.

'They've got 'em,' replied Buddy, looking behind as we topped a ridge of rock.

On we drove, south-west, throughout what was, very comparatively speaking, the cool of the morning, until Hank thought we should be making more haste than speed by continuing without resting the camels.

'I don' perfess ter know much about these doggoned *shammos*, as they call 'em,' observed Hank, 'but I allow you can't go very far wrong if you treats 'em as hosses.'

'Shore,' agreed Buddy, ''cept that they got more control of their passions like . . . Fer eats, and fer settin' up the drinks, anyhow . . . They can live on nawthen. An' as that's just what we pervided for 'em, they oughta thrive.'

'We'll have to find *something* for them,' said Digby, 'if it's only newspaper or the thatch of a nigger's hut.'

'I hev heard of 'em eatin' people's hats at dime shows and meenageries,' said Hank. 'My Aunt 'Mandy went to Ole Man Barnum's show on her golden weddin' day, an'a camel browsed her hat and all her back hair, an' she never knowed it until she felt a draught . . . Yep. They kin hev our *képis* if they wait till we got some Injun shappos an' pants an' things . . .'

I was aware that camels had meagre appetites and queer, limited tastes, embracing a narrow selection ranging from bran to the twigs of dead thorn-bush, but I agreed with Digby that we should have to give them something, and something other than our caps. Our lives depended upon these two ugly, unfriendly beasts, for without them we should either be quickly recaptured or else we should die of thirst and starvation, long before we could reach any oasis.

In the rapidly narrowing shadow of a providential great rock in this thirsty land, we lay stretched on our backs, after an ascetic meal of bread and water.

'What's the programme of sports, Hank?' I asked, as we settled ourselves to sleep.

'Another forced march ter git outta the onhealthy location o' Zinderneuf,' he replied. 'Then we gotta scout fer Injuns or an oasis. Spread out in a four-mile line an' peek over every rock and hill . . . We'll shore fix it . . .' and he went to sleep.

Personally I slept till evening without moving, and I was only then awakened by the grumbling, gurgling roar of the camel that Hank was girthing up, one of his feet pressed against its side and all his weight and strength on the girth-rope.

Having put the camel-blanket on the other animal, lifted the wooden framework regulation saddle on to it, girthed it up, taken the nose-reins over the beast's head and looped them round the pommel, he bawled 'All aboard,' and stood with his foot on the kneeling camel's near fore-knee, while I climbed into the rear part of the saddle. He then vaulted into the front seat and the camel, lurching heavily, came to its feet with an angry hungry roar.

Buddy and Digby mounted the other beast, and once more we were off, not to stop until we estimated that there were at least a hundred miles between us and Zinderneuf.

This was, of course, too good to last – or too bad, from the camels' point of view. At the end of this second ride they must have food and a day's rest, if not water.

Again I slept spasmodically, towards morning, especially after Hank had insisted upon my embracing him round the body and leaning against him.

I was awakened from a semi-slumbrous state of coma by an exclamation from Buddy, to realise that it was day again, the camels were standing still, and their riders gazing at what Buddy was indicating with outstretched arm.

Over the level stretch of unblown sand which we were crossing, ran a broad and recent trail of camel footprints.

This trail crossed ours, though not at right angles. If we were going south-west I should think the riders were going south – or north.

Hank and Buddy brought the camels to their knees, with the gentle insistent '*Oosha, baba, oosha; adar-ya-yan*!' which is about the only order that a camel obeys without cavil or protest.

Following the footmarks and regarding them carefully, they decided that there were about twenty camels in the party, that they were going south, and that they had passed quite recently.

'What we bin lookin' for!' observed Hank with grim satisfaction, as he swung himself back into the saddle. 'The nearer we kin git to them Injuns, the quicker – but we don' wanta tread on 'em. Keep yer eyes skinned, boys.' And the others having remounted, on we went.

I should think we followed this trail for three or four hours, without seeing anything but the eternal desert of sand and rock.

For some time I had been wondering how much longer we were to go on without resting the camels, when a grunt of satisfaction from Hank renewed my waning interest in life. He brought the camel to a halt and pointed, as Buddy ranged up beside us.

We had come to the bank of a very wide and rather shallow dry river-bed, whose shelving sides led down to gravel and stones which at one time must have been subject to the action of running water. The place looked as though a river had flowed along it ten thousand years ago.

But what Hank was pointing to was the spot to which the footprints led.

Beneath a huge high rock, that rose from the middle of the river-bed, was a dark inviting shadow around which were dry-looking tufts of coarse grass, stunted dwarf acacias, and low thorn-bushes.

The camels were perceptibly eager to get to this spot.

'Water,' said Hank. 'May have to dig.'

But there was no need to dig. Beneath and around the rock was a pool, fed presumably from a subterranean source. It wasn't the sparkling water of an English spring, bubbling up among green hills, by any means. The green was rather in the water, but we were not fastidious, and certainly the camels were not. On the contrary, we were delighted and deeply thankful.

Here were shade, water, and camel-food, giving us a new lease of life, and encouragement on our way. It was evident that a party of travellers had recently halted here.

'Good old Touaregs,' said Digby, as we dismounted in the glorious shade. 'Obliging lads. We'll follow them up just as long as they are going our way home.'

'We gotta do more'n foller 'em up,' said Hank. 'We gotta *catch* 'em up. They gotta lend us some correc' desert-wear striped gents' suitings. Likewise grub-stake us some.'

'Shore,' agreed Buddy. 'An' we ain't no hoss-thieves neither, but I allow they gotta lend us a couple o' good camels too.'

From the first, the Americans had been anxious to secure Arab dress, both on account of possible pursuit from Zinderneuf, and as being less conspicuous and less likely to bring every wandering Arab band down upon us, directly they caught sight of us and recognised us for hated *Roumis*.

They were doubly anxious to procure the disguise on learning that, in the south, towards Nigeria, there were numerous forts and outposts of the French Niger Territory, garrisoned by Senegalese, and that between these posts, numerous patrols would carefully watch the caravan-routes, and visit such Arab towns and settlements as existed.

It would certainly be better to encounter a patrol in the rôle of Arabs than in that of runaway soldiers from the Foreign Legion.

Accordingly Hank decreed that we must push on, only enough time being spent here for the camels to eat and drink their fill. He was of opinion that the party we were following was an offshoot of the big band that had attacked Zinderneuf and was on its way to 'gather in' some village which they visited periodically.

Here they would appropriate its harvest of dates or grain, such camels as might be worthy, those of its sons and daughters who might be suitable for slaves, and any goats, clothing, money, and useful odds-and-ends that they might fancy.

These Touareg bands make an annual tour and visit the villages of an enormous area, in the spirit of somewhat arbitrary and undiscriminating tax-collectors. What they want, by way of tax, is everything the villagers possess that is portable, including their young men and maidens.

If the villagers are reasonable and relinquish everything with a good grace, there need not be any bloodshed – or very little, just in the way of fun and sportive merriment.

The Touaregs do not wish to destroy the village and slaughter the inhabitants, because they prefer to find a peaceful and prosperous community here, again, next year.

All they wish to do, is to clean them out absolutely and leave them alone to amass some more. But if the villagers choose to be uppish and truculent, giving their visitors trouble – they must take the consequences – which are fire and sword and torture.

Or, if the band is off its regular beat and not likely to come that way again, it combines sport with business, and leaves no living thing behind it, nor any roofed dwelling in what was a village – scarcely one stone upon another of what was a little town.

After about three hours' rest, we pushed on again, and rode for the remainder of the day and right through the night. The fact that we did not come up with our quarry seemed to confirm the theory that they were a war-party on raiding business. Peaceful caravans and travellers would never go at such a pace, and we should have overtaken such a party easily . . .

On this side of the river, or rather river-bed, the scenery began to change. The earth grew greyer in colour, cactus and acacia began to appear, and there were numerous great rock *kopjes*. The change was from utterly lifeless sand-desert to rock-desert, having a sparse vegetation.

Suddenly we heard distant rifle-fire to our front – a few scattered shots. Simultaneously, Hank and Buddy brought the camels to their knees among the rocks, and we dismounted, unslinging our rifles as we did so.

'Mustn't get the *shammos* shot up,' said Hank to me. 'You hold 'em, Bo, while we rubber around some,' and they skirmished forward.

Nothing further being heard and nothing seen, they returned, and we rode on again.

Rounding a great rock, a mile or two further on, a rock that reminded one of a Dartmoor tor, we saw an ugly sight.

A woman had been tied to an acacia tree and horribly mutilated. I need say no more about the sight and its effect upon us, although I might say a good deal.

It was evident that she had been herding a flock of goats . . .

'Village near,' said Hank, and he and Buddy again simultaneously wheeled the camels round, and we retired behind the tor and dismounted.

'We'll corral the hosses here, and scout some,' said Hank. 'It'll be worth dollars to see these darned coyotes before they see us.'

This time the camels were tied with their *agals*, and left. We advanced *en tirailleur*, as though to the attack of an Arab *douar*, a manœuvre with which our training had made us only too familiar.

Gradually we approached what appeared to be a completely deserted village by an oasis at the edge of a deep ravine. I should think there had been a village on this spot for thousands of years, though the present buildings were wretched mud huts crowning the basements of ancient stone houses of great strength. It was as though a tribe of gipsies, encamped permanently on an Ancient British hut-circle site on Dartmoor, had used the prehistoric stones in the construction of their rude dwellings.

Into this village, evidently very recently abandoned, we made our way with due precaution.

In one of the huts, on a rough *angareb*, lay a wounded man. As we entered, he drew a curved dagger from his belt and feebly struck at us.

'We are friends,' said I in Arabic. 'Tell us what has happened. We want to help . . .'

Digby also aired his Arabic, and the man was convinced.

He appeared to understand all we said, and I understood him about as well as an English-speaking Frenchman would understand a Devonshire yokel.

I gathered that the usual village tragedy had developed as follows:

A woman, minding goats, had seen a band of Touaregs approaching (this man called them 'The Veiled Ones, the Forgotten of God'), and had foolishly, or bravely, got up on a rock and screamed the news to a youth, who was working nearer the village. They had both then started running, but the Touaregs had caught the woman. The youth had roused the village and the men had rushed out with their rifles to some rocks near by, ready to fire on the Touaregs, and hoping to give the impression of a large and well-armed force, fully prepared to give them a warm reception. The women and children had scuttled to the big ravine behind the village, down which they would make their way to their usual hiding-place.

A couple of lads had been sent off to warn the men who had taken the camels out to graze.

The speaker had been one of these men, and while he and one or two others were collecting the camels and driving them to the ravine, a Targui scout had come upon them and shot him. The rest of the Touaregs had come straight to the spot, circled round, fired a volley, and closed in on the camels.

He himself had been left for dead. When he came to his senses he was alone with the corpses of the other camel-guards, and he had slowly crawled to his hut to die.

The Touaregs had camped and were calmly enjoying a wellearned rest. Apparently the village men were still watching events from their place among the rocks, the women and children were in hiding down the ravine, and the camels were captured.

I gathered that it would have been less calamitous had the camels been in hiding down the ravine, and the women and children captured.

We explained the situation to Hank and Buddy.

'Sport without danger, and business with pleasure,' was their view, but we must give the Touaregs the shock of their lives.

We held a council of war, and it was decided that the wounded man should get in touch with the villagers and tell them that we were friends of theirs. More, we were deadly enemies of the Touaregs, and (most) we'd get the camels back and give them those of the Touaregs too – if they'd play the man and do as we bade them.

Having told his tale and grasped that we really wished to befriend him, the wounded man seemed to be farther from death than he had thought. He was shot through the chest, but I did not think that his lungs had suffered, as there was no håmorrhage from the mouth.

After a drink of water and a pill, which Digby gave him with the assurance that it would do *wonders* for him (though I doubted whether they were wonders suitable to the situation), he got off the *angareb* and staggered to the doorway of the hut. From here he peered beneath his hand for a while, and then tottered out and did some signalling.

Very pluckily he stuck to it until an answering movement among the rocks, unseen by us, satisfied him, and he returned to the hut.

Shortly afterwards, a hail brought him to the door again, and this time he walked off fairly steadily, and disappeared into the ravine.

He returned with a big, dirty squint-eyed Arab, who, he said, was the headman of the village, which was called Azzigig (or sounds to that effect).

The headman was in the mental condition of one who sees men as trees walking, when he found himself in the presence of four armed and uniformed *Roumis*, two of whom spoke Arabic to him, and all of whom wished him to put up a fight for Azzigig, Home, and Beauty.

His own idea was to thank Allah that things were no worse, and to lie low until the Touaregs chose to depart, praying meanwhile that they would do so in peace, without troubling to hunt out the villagers, burn the houses, slaughter the goats, and have a little torture-party before doing so.

When I asked if he felt no particular resentment about the mutilated woman and the slaughtered camel-guards, to say nothing of the loss of the entire stock of camels, he replied that it was doubtless the will of Allah, and who should dispute that?

When I pointed out that it was obviously the will of Allah that we should arrive in the nick of time, and that the Touaregs should camp and rest instead of riding off, he said he would go and talk with his brethren.

This he did, and returned with a deputation of very dirty, suspicious, evil-looking Arabs, who evidently did not believe what he had told them, and had come to see for themselves.

'Gee!' observed Buddy. 'Watta ugly bunch o' low-lifer hoboes.'

'*Some* stiffs,' agreed Hank.

However, I harangued the stiffs, offering them a chance of recovering their camels and teaching the Touaregs a lesson. I fumbled for the Arabic for 'catching a Tartar' as I tried to get these fatalists to see they had as much 'right to life, liberty, and the pursuit of happiness' as Touaregs, and that the latter had no God-given privilege to torture, murder, and rob. As for the 'Will of Allah,' let them follow us and show a little pluck, and they'd soon see what was the will of Allah in the matter.

In support Digby said, 'Anyhow, we're going to attack them, whether you do or not. Those who help us will share the loot.'

As the loot would include excellent rifles and incomparable camels, this gave the poor wretches something to think about. In the end, they agreed that if we would really fight for them, and with them, and give them all the loot, except a couple of camels, as we had promised, they would fight their hardest.

We began by reconnoitring the Touareg camp.

Absolutely certain of their complete security, the robbers had merely lighted fires and lain down to rest, leaving one of their number to guard their own camels and two to guard those stolen from the villagers.

Presumably these guards were more herdsmen than sentries, as the Touaregs had nothing to fear. Villagers do not attack victorious Hoggar robbers. It simply is not done. All that was necessary was to prevent the camels from straying, and to have a rest before proceeding on the tax-gathering journey – with or without a little sport in the village before starting . . .

Our plan was simple for our job was easy.

Half a dozen selected heroes of Azzigig were to deal with the somnolent loafing camel-guards – silently if possible. Every rifle that Azzigig could boast was then to be discharged into the Touareg camp, from as close a range as it was possible to wriggle to.

When the Touaregs bolted to the ravine, as they certainly would do, to take cover from this blast and organise their defence – they would find their way blocked by the entire French army, in uniform, with a bugler blowing calls to bring up thousands more! . . .

I must say that the villagers behaved very well. They were, of course, born desert fighters, and we had put heart into them.

After a tremendous volley, at about forty yards' range, they charged like fiends, and when we four arose from behind rocks and the Touaregs recoiled in astounded terror, they surrounded them like a pack of wolves.

In a brief, mad, happy minute of hacking, stabbing, and shooting, they worked off a good deal of the personal and ancestral grudge of centuries. As they outnumbered the Touaregs by five or six to one, had them at a complete disadvantage, and knew we were behind them, they made a short job of it and a clean one.

From another point of view it was not a clean one.

At any rate, we prevented torture even if we could not save life. For once it was the under-dog's turn, and he used his teeth . . .

Digby, not unreasonably, claimed that the bugle really won the battle.

The upshot of the business was that we left Azzigig, each riding a splendid *mehari* camel, and each clad in the complete outfit of a Touareg raider – newly washed for us by the grateful dames of the village. Nor could the lads-of-the-village do enough for us. What they could, and did, do, was to provide us with a guide and a spare camel laden with food and water, to help us on our way to the next village and oasis in the direction of our goal.

A desperate band of ruffians we looked, Touareg to the last detail of dress, weapons, and accoutrement.

Lean and leathery hawk-faced Hank and Buddy made splendid Arabs, and seemed to enjoy 'playing Injun' like a pair of boys.

They soon learned the uses and arrangings of the *serd* and *jubba* vests, the *kaftan* inner coat, the *hezaam* sash, the *jelabia* overall, the *sirwal* baggy trousers, the *ma-araka* skull cap with the *kafiya* head-dress bound round with the *agals*, ropes of camel-hair.

The blue veils which the Touaregs wear, were the chief trouble, but in time we grew accustomed to them.

I do not know whether these veils are a centuries-old relic of the days when the Touaregs were a white race and took care of their complexions; whether they were a sudden bright idea for keeping the sand from the lungs in windy weather; whether they were invented for purposes of mystery and playing bogey with their enemies and victims; or whether they simply evolved as useful desert-wear for people always on the move, against cutting sand-filled winds and a burning glare that smites upward as well as downward. Anyway, it is curious that only the Touaregs evolved them.

On our camels we carried *zemzimayas* full of water, and *jaafas*, or leather sacks, which our hosts filled with *hubz*, or native bread, and *asida*, horrible masses of dough mixed with oil and onions, flavoured with *fil-fil*, a sort of red pepper.

On the spare camel were huge *khoorgs*, or saddle-bags, filled with *alafs* of fodder for the camels, as well as *girbas* full of water.

We discarded our two military saddles and replaced them with Arab *sergs*, and, in fact, 'went native' altogether, retaining nothing European but our rifles and Digby's bugle.

And in doing this, even, we were not guilty of any anomaly. I had been interested to note that, along with heavy swords of Crusader pattern, and lances and knives of a type unchanged since the days of Abraham, the Touaregs carried splendid magazine-rifles of the latest pattern.

Both these and their ammunition were of Italian make, and I wondered whether they had been captured in Tripoli, or smuggled by the Chambaa rifle-runners of Algeria. As two men had Turkish rifles and cartridges of .450 calibre, I thought it likely that the former was the source. The useful bugle was, of course, concealed.

Before we departed, the village pulled itself together, and, evidently trying to show us 'what Todgers' could do' in the way of a *diffa*, or feast, regaled us upon *fatta*, a mess of carrots, bread, and eggs, and a quite decent *cous-cous* of goat.

For wassail, the headman brought up from the 'cellar' (under his bed) a magnum (leather) of *laghbi*, a rare old vintage palm-juice, which had lain mellowing and maturing in bottle for quite a week.

I found that my names for things of this sort were not always the same as the names I had learned in Algeria, but by any other name they smelled as remarkable.

I asked Hank what he thought of the 'liquor.'

'Fierce, ain't it?' replied he, and left me to apply mine own evaluation to the word.

'Guess we could stop here to be the Big Noise of the tribe,' remarked

Buddy, endeavouring to feed himself gracefully with his fingers – not an easy thing to do when a spoon is the indicated instrument.

'Yep. Shakers and emus,' agreed Hank, with hazy memories of sheikhs and emirs perhaps.

'And a harem-scarum,' added Buddy.

'Why don' the gals jine the hash-party?' he enquired, looking round to where the women, in their long *barracans*, sat afar off and admired the prandial performances of their lords.

'Shut up. Take no notice of the women-folk,' said Digby. 'Sound plan among Mussulmans of any kind.'

'No doubt yore right, pard,' agreed Buddy, 'but there shore is a real little peach over there jest give me the glad eye like a Christian gal as knowed a hill o' beans from a heap o' bananas. Cute an cunnin' . . . Still, we don't want no rough stuff from the Injuns . . . My, but it was a cinch . . .' and he sighed heavily . . .

7

Ishmaelites

> 'Greater love hath no man than this,
> That a man lay down his life for his friends.'

I COULD fill a large volume with the account of our adventures, as Touaregs of the Sahara, on this ride that began at Azzigig, in the French Soudan, and ended (for some of us) at Kano in Nigeria, in British West Africa.

It was perhaps the longest and most arduous ride ever achieved by Europeans in the Sahara – few of whom have ever crossed the desert from north to south without an organised caravan.

We rode south-west when we could, and we rode north-east when we must, as when, north of Aïr, we were captured by Touaregs on their way to their own country on the borders of Morocco.

During one terrible year we made an almost complete circle, being at one time at El Hilli, within two hundred miles of Timbuktu, and, at another, at Agadem, within the same distance of Lake Tchad – and then later finding ourselves at Bilma, five hundred miles to the north.

Sometimes thirst and hunger drove us to join salt-caravans, and sometimes slave-caravans (and we learnt that slavery is still a very active pursuit and a flourishing business in Central Africa). Generally these caravans were going in the direction opposite to ours, but we had to join them or perish in the waterless desert.

Sometimes we were hunted by gangs larger than our own; sometimes we were met at villages with volleys of rifle-fire (being taken, naturally, for what we pretended to be); sometimes we reached an oasis only to find it occupied by a patrol of French Senegalese troops – far more dangerous to us than the nomadic robbers for whom we were a match when not hopelessly outnumbered.

Whether we did what no Europeans have ever done before, I do not know, but we certainly went to places where Europeans had never been before, and 'discovered' desert cities which were probably prehistoric ruins before a stone of Damascus was laid.

We encountered no Queens of Atlantis and found no white races of Greek origin, ruled by ladies of tempestuous petticoat, to whom it turned out we were distantly related.

Alas, no. We found only extremely poor, primitive, and dirty people, with whom we sojourned precisely as long as untoward circumstance compelled.

Of course, we could never have survived for a single month of those years, but for the desert-skill, the courage, resourcefulness, and experience of Hank and Buddy.

On the other hand, the ready wits of Digby, and our knowledge of Arabic, saved the situation, time after time, when we were in contact with our fellow-man.

On these occasions we became frightfully holy. Hank and Buddy were *marabouts* under a vow of silence, and we were Senussi on a mysterious errand, travelling from Kufra in the Libyan desert to Timbuktu, and visiting all sorts of holy places on the way.

Luckily for us, there were no genuine Senussi about; and the infinite variety of sects, with their different kinds of dervishes, and the even greater variety of people who spoke widely differing dialects of Arabic, made our task comparatively easy.

Probably our rifles, our poverty, and our obvious truculence did still more in that direction.

We suffered from fever, terrific heat, poisonous water, bad and insufficient food, and the hardships of what was one long campaign of active warfare to live.

At times we were very near the end, when our camels died, when a long journey ended at a dried-up well, when we were surrounded by a pack of the human wolves of the desert, and when we were fairly captured by a *harka* of Touaregs, suspicious of our *bona fides* . . .

As I have said, an account of our *Katabasis* would fill a volume, but the description of a few typical incidents will suffice to give an idea of it, without rendering the story as wearisome as was the journey.

For example, our discovery of the place where there certainly ought to have been '*a strange fair people of a civilisation older, and in some ways higher, than our own; ruled over by a woman, so incredibly beautiful, so marvellously . . .*' etc.

One day we rode over the crest of a long ridge of sandcovered rock – straight into a band of armed men who outnumbered us by ten to one, at least, and who were ready and waiting for us with levelled rifles.

We did as we had done before, on similar exciting occasions. The Holy Ones, Hank and Buddy, fell dumb, and Digby became the emissary of the Senussi Mahdi; I, his lieutenant.

Digby rode forward.

'*Salamoune aleikoumi Esseleme, ekhwan*' (Peace be unto you, brothers), said he, in solemn, sonorous greeting, to which a fine-looking old man replied, to my great relief, '*Aselamu, alaikum, marhaba, marhaba*' (Greetings to you and welcome), in a different-sounding Arabic from ours. It turned out later that the old gentleman took us for an advance-party of a big band of Touaregs who were near, and was only too charmed to find us to charming.

Digby then proceeded with the appropriate account of ourselves, alluding to the dumb forbidding Hank and Buddy, as most holy men, *khouans*, *hadjis*, *marabouts*, under a strict vow of silence that it would be ill work for any man to attempt to break. Himself and me he described as *m'rabets*, men hereditarily holy and prominent in faith and virtue.

How much of this our hearers understood, and how much of what they understood, they believed, I could not tell, but they were obviously relieved to find us friendly and not part of a larger force.

We were promptly invited to come along, and thought it best to comply, there being little reason against doing so and much against refusing. In any case they had 'got us,' from the moment we came upon their levelled rifles, our own slung behind us; and we were at their mercy. As we rode along, nominally guests, but feeling we were prisoners, I was interested to hear Digby assuring the old sheikh that though we were as holy as it is given to mere men to be, we were nevertheless good hefty proselytisers who carried the Q'ran in one hand and the sword in the other, fighting-men who would be pleased to chip in, if the Touaregs attacked his band.

The old gentleman returned thanks and said that, once home, they did not fear all the Touaregs in the Sahara, as the place was quite impregnable. This sounded attractive, and proved to be perfectly true.

What did trouble them, was the fact that when they set off with a caravan of camels for sale at Tanout, it was more than likely that they would, for months, have to fight a series of pitched battles or lose the whole of the wherewithal to purchase grain for their subsistence, for there was nothing a Touareg robber desired more than camels.

'It is the only wealth that carries itself,' observed Digby sententiously.

After riding for some three or four hours towards some low rocky mountains, we reached them and approached a narrow and lofty pass. This we threaded in single file, and, coming to the top, saw before us an endless plain out of which arose a *gara*, an abrupt and isolated plateau, looking like a gigantic cheese placed in the middle of the level expanse of desert.

Toward this we rode for another hour or two, and discovered it to be a precipitous mountain, sheer, cliff-sided, with a flat top; the whole, I suppose, about a square mile in area.

Apparently it was quite inaccessible and untrodden by the foot of man, or even of mountain sheep or goat. Only an eagle, I imagined, had ever looked upon the top of that isolated square mile of rock.

I was wrong, however, the place proving to be a gigantic fort – a fort of the most perfect kind, but which owed nothing whatever to the hand of man.

Circling the cliff-like precipitous base of the mountain, we came to a crack in the thousand-foot wall, a crack that was invisible at a hundred yards.

Into this narrow fissure the sheikh led us in single file, and, squeezing our way between gigantic cactus, we rode along the upward-sloping bottom of a winding chasm that was not six feet wide.

Suddenly our path was cut by a deep ravine, some three yards wide, a great crack across the crack in which we were entombed. Bridging this was laid a number of trunks of the *dôm* palm, and over these a matting of palm-leaf and sand made a narrow but safe path for camels.

Obviously this bridge could easily be removed if necessary, and the place defended with the greatest ease, if any enemy were foolish enough to attempt to bridge the abyss while the defenders dropped boulders from terrific heights, and fired their rifles at point-blank range from behind the strong stone wall that faced the chasm.

Having crossed the bridge, we rode on upward to where this narrow slit in the mountain opened out into a big rock-enclosed square like a landing on a staircase – beyond which camels could not go.

In this natural *serai* we dismounted and left our beasts, continuing our climb on foot.

It was, indeed, an impregnable place, and I did not see how the best troops in the world could capture it, so long as there remained a stout-hearted defender in any one of the invisible places that commanded the path up which two men could nowhere climb abreast, and where, in many places, only one could squeeze with difficulty.

And on the plateau was a walled city, a city built of blocks of dressed stone, blocks larger than any I have ever seen put to such purpose, and obviously of such an age in this use as must have left them old there when the world, as we know of it, was young.

It was a great and melancholy place, containing, I should think, at least three times as many dwelling-places as there were dwellers. Personally, I lost any sense of our precarious position and all feeling of danger and anxiety, in interest and wonderment at this 'walled city set upon a hill,' and such a hill.

But, as I have said, there was no wonderful white race here for us to restore to touch with modern civilisation. Nor was there any wonderful black race either. The inhabitants of this strange city were just ordinary Arabs, I believe, though I am no ethnologist, and, so far as they knew, they had 'always' lived there.

Nevertheless, I felt perfectly certain that no ancestor of theirs had placed those incredible monoliths in position, nor made for themselves doorways twelve and fifteen feet in height, leading into chambers ten feet higher.

These people were undoubtedly the long-established dwellers in this city, but none the less were they dwellers in someone else's city, and merely camping in it at that, even if for a few thousand years.

However, they were very interesting people, living simply and austerely under the benign sway of their patriarchal sheikh, and quite hospitable and friendly. They knew but little of the outside world, though they realised that there were *Roumis* and infidels of all kinds, other cities than their own, holy places besides Mecca and Medina, and greater sheikhs, sultans, and emperors than their own. They apparently regarded the world, or at any rate their world, as divided up into Touareg robbers on the one hand, and the enemies and victims of Touaregs on the other.

In their marvellous rock fastness they were safe, but out on the desert they were at the mercy of any nomadic robber-band stronger than themselves.

Water they had in plenty, as their mountain contained an apparently inexhaustible well and spring, and they had goat-flesh and a little grain, vegetables, and dates, but were compelled to make the six months' caravan journey to Tanout for the grain that formed the staple of their food, as well as for ammunition, salt, and cooking-vessels – for which commodities they exchanged their camels as well as dressed goat-skins, and garments beautifully woven and embroidered by their women-folk.

With these good folk we stayed for some days, a pleasant restful oasis in the weary desert of our lives, receiving genuine Arab hospitality, and repaying it with such small gifts as were of more value to them than to us, and by offering to scout for, and fight with, their caravan then about to set out across a notoriously dangerous tract of country to the east.

We must have puzzled the simple souls of this inbred dying people, for though we were obviously of strict piety, and observed the same hours of prayer as themselves from the *fedjer* at dawn to the *asha* at night, we would not pray in company with them, nor, as we sat and *faddhled* (or gossiped) round the sheikh's fire at night, would we say one word on religious subjects. We ran no unnecessary risks. A dignified '*Allahou akbar*' or '*In châh Allah*,' showed our agreement with the speaker and our pious orthodoxy, and it had to suffice. As puritanical protestant reforming Senussi, we had a higher and purer brand of Islamism than theirs, but refrained from hurting their feelings by any parade of it . . .

Digby was great, and his descriptions of Mecca and Medina Baghdad, Constantinople, and Cairo, Fez, Timbuktu, and Kufra, held his hearers spellbound and left them little time for questions.

Hank and Buddy were equally great, in what they did not say and the manner in which they did not say it.

Nevertheless, it was well we could make the departure of the caravan our opportunity for going, and it was well that our hosts were what they were, and even then the ice, at times, was very thin.

We descended from this extraordinary and apparently absolutely unknown prehistoric city, and set off with the caravan, rested and in better case than we had been in for months.

We were going in the right direction, we were approaching Aïr, we should then be near a caravan-route on which were wells; and if our danger from our fellow-men, Arab and French, was likely to increase, our danger from the far more terrible enemy, the desert, would decrease.

With luck, we might parallel the caravan-route and make dashes for water when opposite the oases on the route, trusting that we should be able to evade French patrols (of Senegalese infantry and Arab *goumiers*) and Touareg raiding-parties alike.

We said our '*Abka ala Kheir*' (good-byes) to our late hosts and heard their '*Imshi besselema*' (Go in peace) with real regret, at the last oasis on our common route, pressed on in good heart and high hopes, did very well for a month, and then fell straight into the hands of the rascally and treacherous Tegama, Sultan of Agades, when we were only four hundred miles from the frontier of Nigeria and safety.

2

Our visit to Agades was a very different affair from that to the impregnable city on the hill. In the latter place we felt no real fear and little anxiety. In Agades we walked very warily, our hearts in our mouths and our heads loose upon our necks. To the old sheikh we had been objects of wonder and interest. To the Sultan Tegama we were objects of the most intense suspicion.

There was nothing of the simple out-of-the-world dweller-apart, about the swashbuckling ruffians of this City of the Plain, nor about the arch-ruffian Tegama, their leader (executed later by the French for treachery), nor would the pose of pious Senussi emissaries have been of any avail in these circumstances. In the idiom of Buddy, there was no moss upon the teeth of the Sultan Tegama and his gang. In the idiom of Digby there were no flies upon these gentlemen.

We owed our lives to the fact that we escaped before the worthy Tegama had quite placed us, and was quite certain that we were not what we pretended to be – seditious mischief-makers from the north, bent upon raising the desert tribes of the centre and south against the French in a great pan-Islamic *jehad*.

Not that Tegama had the slightest objection to being so 'raised'; far from it. Nothing would have suited him better, for there was nothing he enjoyed more; and if to rapine and slaughter, fire and sword, robbery and massacre, he could add the heaven-gaining merit of the destruction of the Unbeliever and the overthrow of his empire in Africa, the cup of his happiness would be full . . .

But we puzzled him undoubtedly. Our accent, manners, habits, ignorance, eyes, complexions, faces, and everything about us puzzled him.

Certainly we spoke Arabic fluently and knew men and cities; we seemed to be *hadjis* all right; we inveighed with convincing bitterness against the French; we were upstanding desert fighting-men with nothing whatsoever European about our clothing and accoutrements; we were too small a party to be dangerous, and there was no earthly reason why we should be French spies (for the emissaries of France came perfectly openly in the shape of extremely well-equipped military expeditions, pursuing the well-worn way of all peaceful penetrators, and were a source of fear and bitter hatred to the Sultan) – *but*, we had no credentials; we gave absolutely no information whatsoever about the strength, disposition, and movements of the French forces; we had no cut-and-dried play for an on-fall; and the dumbness of two of us did not seem to mark them out as born emissaries of sedition, unrest, and rebellion!

When Tegama voiced these suspicions, Digby, with fine courage, took the high hand and, as tactfully as possible, hinted that there might be things in the minds of the Great Ones, our masters, that were not to be comprehended by every petty desert chieftain, and that one thing about their minds was the certainty of a powerful and dangerous resentment against anybody who hindered the free movements of their messengers, or behaved as though they were the friends of the very Infidels from whom these Great Ones were endeavouring to free Islam . . .

And the gentle Tegama halted long between two opinions, whether to impale us out of hand, or whether to put off till to-morrow what he would like to do to-day, in case we were what we said we were.

It was an unpleasant time, and though we were not illtreated nor imprisoned, our rifles and camels were 'minded' for us, and we never found ourselves alone – particularly when we walked abroad, although it was obvious that no one could escape from Agades on foot.

We felt that at any moment Tegama might decide that we were genuine delegates and emissaries from those who were then so busily stirring the fermenting brew of pan-Islamic discontent in northern Africa – and let us go; and also that at any moment we might so betray ourselves that he would decide we were impostors – and forthwith impale us, living on the sharpened stump of a young tree . . .

We had been caught at dawn, in an oasis south-west of the Baguezan mountains, by a *harka* of Tegama's that had evidently been raiding and robbing to the north, and, for a week or so, we rode south as the prisoner-guests of the emir in command, a magnificent specimen of the best type of desert Arab.

Him Digby had told the same tale that he had told to the old sheikh and many another inquisitive wayfarer, but he had decided to alter his tale for the private ear of the Sultan as soon as we learnt that it was to so important and well-informed a person that we were to be taken.

Whispering together at night, we decided that Hank and Buddy must of course remain dumb, and that we must put up a terrific bluff of mystery. It would be worse than hopeless to pretend to be Senussi from Kufra, in a place like Agades, where it was quite probable there were specimens of the genuine article, and where our stories would rapidly be tested and found wanting.

And so we took the high hand with Tegama, so far as we dared; told him that we had no definite message for him *yet*, but that on our return journey he would hear things that would surprise him, and so forth . . .

Agades proved to be a very ancient, clay-built, sand-buried walled town, containing a remarkable mosque with a tower like a church spire, and although so utterly lost in the very heart of the Sahara, still in touch with the outside world by reason of being on the pilgrim-route to Mecca, and on the great caravan-route that crosses Africa.

The only other building that was not insignificant was the Sultan's palace, a big two-storied building of baked clay, surrounded by a high thick clay wall, the gateway through which was practically a short tunnel.

Through this tunnel, and past very strong gates made of palm-trunks nailed solidly together upon cross-pieces, we were led into a dirty square of desert sand and stones, two sides of which were formed by mud huts that backed against the high enclosing wall.

One side of the square was occupied by the palace and another by a mosque. Camels, goats, chickens, and dirty men ornamented this palace courtyard or back-yard.

We were invited to enter the palace, and through another small tunnel came into a big windowless hall, with unornamented clay walls, clay ceiling, and clay floor.

Here we were kept waiting with our escort, and stood in haughty silence until conducted across a small inner courtyard to the presence-chamber of the Sultan of Agades.

This was another windowless clay room with great arched ceiling beams and a door, ten feet from the ground, up to which ran a clay staircase. In the middle of the wall opposite the door by which we entered, was a throne, also of clay – a base material for so exalted a symbol, but at least it was of honest clay, which its occupant was not.

Cross-legged on this bed-like throne, in dirty white robes, sat Tegama, who carried on his face the stamp of his ruling passions, greed, cruelty, lust, savagery, and treachery. Around him stood a small group of wazirs, sheikhs, soldiers, and what I uncomfortably took to be executioners.

The Sultan glared at us and I felt sorrowful to the tips of my toes. I knew by now all the ways that such gentlemen have of putting to death those of whom they do not approve, and I liked none of them at all. Impaling, a favourite one, I liked, perhaps, the least . . .

Digby took the bull by the horns, greeted Tegama politely, hoped he was well, professed pleasure at seeing him, and said he had a good deal to say to him later on, when he had made some arrangements further south and had taken the political temperature of one or two places in Damerghou and Damergrim.

Digby took it for granted that we were honoured guests, and that nothing so silly as the idea of molesting us would ever occur to so wise and great a ruler as the good Tegama of Agades.

The good Tegama of Agades continued to eye us coldly.

'And who might *you* be, with your talk of El Senussi?' he enquired contemptuously.

'That is for your ear alone,' replied Digby. 'I have told the sheikh whom we – er – met, in the Baguezan oasis, such things as are fitting to be told to underlings. I come from those whose business is not shouted in every *douar* and *quasr* and chattered about to every wayfarer.'

And here I boomed:

'No, indeed! Allah forbid!' and smiled at the idea.

'Oh, you can talk, can you?' sneered Tegama, who had evidently been told that some of us were dumb.

'*Salaam aleikum wa Rahmab Allah*,' I intoned piously. 'Our Master in the north – *Rahmat ullahi Allahim* – (and he may be in Morocco, and he may be in Algiers, and he may be near here with a mighty army of the Faithful) – is not one of whose affairs his messengers babble, nor is he one whose messengers are delayed.'

'And what is his message?' asked Tegama, with, I thought, less sneer in his voice.

'That comes not here *yet*,' replied Digby. 'The word comes to the great and good Sultan of Agades later, when the time is ripe . . .' and much more of bluff and mystification that sufficiently impressed Tegama to lead him to wait and see.

He waited but he did not see, for we escaped – this time, I must admit, thanks to Buddy's irrepressible interest in 'squaws.'

What he could have achieved had he had the free use of his tongue I cannot say. In this case, although love was not only blind, but dumb as well, it contrived to laugh at locksmiths, and we other three benefited by the laughter.

We got away and on good camels, but we had not a rifle among us, nor any other weapon of any sort whatever.

I am tempted to tell, in full, the story of this evasion, for it was a most romantic business, with all the accessories of fiction and melodrama. I have said that the story of this journey alone would fill a large volume, and it would be small exaggeration to say that a complete account of our sojourn in Agades would fill another.

I wish I had space in which to tell of the incredible things we saw in this place, whose atmosphere and ways and deeds were those of a thousand years ago.

I have read that the first Europeans to set foot in Agades were the members of the French Military Mission (which came with the great annual salt-caravan from the south in 1904), but I could tell of a fair-bearded man who stared at us with blazing *grey* eyes, a man whose tongue had been cut out, whose ears and fingers had been cut off, and who was employed as a beast of burden.

I could also tell of a Thing that sat always in the Sôk, mechanically swaying its body to and fro as it crooned. Its lips, eyelids, ears, hands, and feet had been cut off, it was blind, and it crooned in *German*.

I could tell of such scenes as that of the last hours of a very brave man, who was bound face downwards on a plank that was thrust over the edge of an enormously deep dry well. At the other end of the plank was a big stone and a jar of water that slowly leaked, either by reason of a crack or its porosity. When the water had leaked away to such an extent that the weight of the jar and stone was less than that of the man, he and the plank would go headlong down into the dark depths from which he would never return.

There he lay staring down into the horrible place, while round about sat citizens of leisure who told him to hurry with his last prayers, for the water was nearly gone, while others bade him to heed them not, for he had hours longer to wait . . .

I should like to tell of Tegama's executioners, four negroes who were the most animal creatures I ever saw in human form, and not one of whom was less than seven feet in height. The speciality of their leader was the clean, neat flicking-off of a head or any required limb, from a finger to a leg, with one stroke of a great sword; while that of another was the infliction of the maximum number of wounds and injuries without causing the death of the victim.

They were skilled labourers and their work was their hobby . . .

I could tell of some very remarkable adventures, risks, dangers, and escapes in Agades, and of some very strange doings in that horrible 'palace' with its plots and intrigues, jealousies and hatreds, factions and parties, if space permitted.

And when our time and opportunity came (and we were led one dark night to where four camels, with water and food for two or three days, awaited us) we would not have taken advantage of the chance, being weaponless, had we not felt that we ran a greater danger by remaining.

Tegama was growing more suspicious and more truculent, and I rather think that the dumb Hank and Buddy had been overheard in fluent converse. Probably we gave ourselves away too (whenever we ate, drank, prayed, sat, stood, sneezed, or did anything else whatsoever), as the weirdest kind of weird Mussulmans who ever said, '*Bismillah arahman arahmim* . . .'

It was time to go and we went, aided by a young person of magnificent physique, magnificent courage, and negroid ancestry – probably the daughter of some negro slave-woman from Lake Tchad . . .

Unfortunately it was utterly impossible for her to get us weapons.

3

We escaped from Tegama, but not from the consequcnces of our encounter with him. He did not destroy us, but it was to him that we owed our destruction.

Riding as hard as we could, we followed the tactics of our escape from Zinderneuf, feeling sure that if Tegama pursued and recaptured us, our fate would be sealed and our deaths lingering and unpleasant.

We therefore avoided the caravan-route that runs from Agades, and struck out into the desert, hoping that, as hitherto, we should, sooner or later, discover someone or something that would lead us to water.

After three days of painful wandering, we chanced upon the wretched encampment of some aboriginal Beri-Beri bushmen, black, almost naked, and armed only with bows and arrows. They apparently lived by trapping ostriches by means of tethered foot-traps concealed beneath the bushes and trees, thorns and acacias, on which the birds feed.

These primitive people were camped beside an inexplicable pool of water among colossal boulders as big as cathedrals.

Here we rested ourselves and our camels for a day or two, and then again set out, with our leather water-skins filled and our food-bags nearly empty.

A couple of days later we were riding in a long line, just within sight of each other, and scouting for signs of human beings or water.

Hank was on the right of the line, I next to him and half a mile away, having Buddy on my left, with Digby at the far end.

Looking to my right, I saw Hank, topping a little undulation, suddenly wheel towards me, urging his camel to its topmost speed.

As I looked, a crowd of riders swarmed over the skyline, and, two or three of them, halting their camels, opened fire on us.

Buddy rode at full speed toward me and Hank. Digby was cut off from view by a tor of rocks.

'Dismount and form sqar',' yelled Hank, riding up.

I knew what he meant.

We brought our camels to their knees, made a pretence of getting out rifles from under the saddles, crouched behind the camels, and levelled our sticks as though they were guns, across the backs of the animals, and awaited death.

'This is when we gits what's comin' to us,' said Buddy.

'The durned galoots may not call our bluff,' growled Hank.

The band, Hoggar or Tebu robbers by the look of them, bore down upon us with yells of '*Ul-ul-ul-ul-ul-ullah Akbar*,' on pleasure and profit bent – the pleasure of slaughtering us and the profit of taking our camels – brandishing swords, lances, and rifles as they swept along.

I could have wept that we had no rifles. Steady magazine fire from three marksmen like ourselves, would have brought the yelling fiends crashing to earth in such numbers as might have saved us and provided us with much that we sorely needed.

The feeling of utter impotence was horrible, and like the impotence of nightmare . . . To be butchered like sheep without striking a blow . . . Could Digby possibly escape? . . . Or would they see his tracks and follow him after slaughtering us? . . . There was an excellent chance that they would pass straight on without crossing his trail . . . Would they swerve from our apparently levelled rifles? No. On they came . . . Digby might be well away by now . . .

And then from somewhere, there rang out loud, clear, and (to these Arabs) terrible, *a bugle-call* – that portentous bugle-call, menacing and fateful, that had been almost the last thing so many desert tribesmen had heard, the bugle-call that announced the closing of the trap and preluded the hail of bullets against which no Arab charge could prevail.

The effect was instant and magical. The band swerved to their right, wheeled, and fled – fled to avoid what they thought a terrible trap, so neatly baited and into which they had so nearly fallen!

As the bugle-calls died away, Hank roared orders in French at the top of his enormous voice, and away to the left a man was apparently signalling back with excited energy, to the French forces behind him, '*enemy in sight*.'

Evidently the panic-stricken mob of raiders thought that the danger was behind the spot on which they had first seen Hank, for they fled in a direction to the right of the rocks behind which Digby had blown his bugle . . .

Suddenly my heart leapt into my throat, as one of the robbers, perhaps their leader or a candidate for leadership, swerved to the left from the ruck of the fleeing band, and, either in a spirit of savage vengeance, or the desire, not uncommon with these people, for single combat in the presence of many onlookers, rode at the man who had exposed himself to signal back to the French force of which he was evidently the scout . . .

'Quick!' I shouted. 'He'll get him,' and I found myself yelling Digby's name.

We scrambled on to our camels, Hank bawling commands in French, and Buddy yelling devilish war-whoops.

Digby stooped and then poised himself in the attitude of a javelin-thrower. As the Arab raised his great sword, Digby's arm shot forward and the Arab reeled, receiving the stone full in his face, and jerking the camel's head round as he did so. Digby sprang at the man's leg and pulled him down, the two falling together.

They rose simultaneously, the Arab's sword went up, Digby's fist shot out, and we heard the smack as the man reeled backwards and fell, his sword dropping from his hand. Digby seized it and stood over the half-stunned robber, who was twitching and clawing at the sand . . . And then we heard another sound.

A rifle was fired, and Digby swayed and fell.

An Arab had wheeled from the tail of the fleeing band, fired this shot at thirty yards' range, and fled again, we three on our galloping camels being not a hundred yards from him.

Digby was dead before I got to him, shot through the back of the head with an expanding bullet . . .

We tied the Arab's feet, and I blew bugle-calls to the best of my ability.

I am going to say nothing at all about my feelings.

Digby was dead. Michael was dead. I felt that the essential *me* was dead too.

I lived on like an automaton, and – like a creature sentenced to death – I waited for the blow to fall, the moment of collapse to come.

4

We buried Digby there, although we expected the return of the Arabs at any moment.

'He shore gave his life for ourn,' said Hank, chewing his lips.

'"*Greater love hath no man*,"' I was able to reply.

Buddy said nothing, but Buddy wept. He then untied the completely-recovered Arab, a huge, powerful young fellow, twice his size, and without weapons on either side, fought him and beat him insensible.

Discussing the question of this robber's future, I suggested we should bind his hands, put him on his camel, and make him our guide – bidding him lead us first to the oasis from which the band had come.

'Lead us not into temptation,' said Buddy. 'He'd shore lead us where he wanted us.'

Speaking to the man in his own tongue, when he had recovered from Buddy's handling of him, I asked him what he was prepared to do to save his life . . . Could he lead us south, parallel with the caravan route, from one oasis or water-hole to another, if we agreed to set him free as soon as we were in the Kano territory?

He replied that he would willingly lead us to Hell and cheerfully abide there himself, so long as he got us there too. He was undoubtedly a brave man.

I told him that in that case we should take his camel and weapons (unfortunately for us he had no rifle), and leave him where he was, to die of thirst.

'*El Mektub Mektub*' (What is written is written), he replied, with a shrug, and that was all we could get out of him.

In the end we took him with us, bound, on his camel, which was tied to Buddy's, and left him at the first water-hole to which we came. This we found by following the track made by his friends as they had come northward.

From here we rode on with filled water-skins and half the food-supply of the Arab whom we had abandoned . . .

Digby's death proved to be the first tragic catastrophe of a series of disasters that now overtook us.

First we encountered a terrible sand-storm that nearly killed us, and quite obliterated all tracks.

Then we missed the caravan-route when we reluctantly decided to return to it, either crossing it in ignorance, where the ground was too rocky for there to be any footprints, or else riding over the road itself at a spot where all traces of it had been wiped out, or buried, by the sand-storm.

Next, nearly dead with thirst, we reached a water-hole, and found it dried up!

Here our starving camels ate some poisonous shrub or other, speedily sickened, and within thirty-six hours were all dead.

We thus found ourselves stranded in the desert, not knowing whether the caravan-route was to the east or to the west of us, without rifles, without food, without camels, and with one goat-skin containing about a pint of water.

This we decided not to drink until we must literally drink or die, though it seemed that we must surely do that in any case.

For a day we struggled on, incredibly, without water, and at the end of the day wondered whether we were a day's march further from the caravan-road on which were oases, wells, water-holes, and villages.

Once we found it (if ever), we would risk the French patrols until we could again get camels. On the caravan-route, death was probable, here in the desert, on foot, it was certain.

Night found us unable to speak, our lips black, and cracked in great fissures, our tongues swollen horribly, our throats closed, and our mouths *dry*. (It is an incredibly horrible thing to have one's mouth literally and really *dry*, like hard leather.)

I pointed at the precious water-skin and raised my eyebrows interrogatively.

Hank shook his head and pointed at the setting sun and then at the zenith. We must drink to-morrow when we should, if possible, be in worse case than now.

We reeled on through the night, for our lives depended on reaching the 'road.'

Towards morning, I could go no further and sank down without meaning to do so. I tried to rise and failed. Seeing that I could do no more, the other two lay down beside me, and we fell asleep.

The sun woke me to see Buddy, with a face like death, staring at a scrap of paper torn from a pocket-book.

He passed it to me. On it was scrawled:

'Pards,

Drink up the water slow and push on quick. Good old Buddy, we bin good pards.

Hank.'

Hank was gone . . .

Buddy untied the neck of the goat-skin and filled his mouth with water. He held the water in his mouth for a minute and then swallowed it slowly.

'Take a mouthful like that and then swaller,' he croaked hoarsely.

'We gotta do what Hank ses,' he added, as I shook my head. I could not drink the water.

'We gotta hike,' wheezed Buddy. 'We don' wanta make what he done all for nix. All no good, like. He won't come back an' drink it . . . Yew ain't goin' to *waste* his life, pard? . . . He done it fer *you* . . .'

I filled my mouth and swallowed – but I could not swallow the lump in my throat . . .

We staggered on through that day and the next, moistening our mouths at intervals, and just before sunset, on the second day, saw a mirage of palm trees, a village, a little white mosque, and – the mirage was real.

We stayed at this village for months, scouring the desert for Hank, working as cultivators, water-carriers, watchmen, camelmen, and at any other job that offered, and we were never both asleep at the same time.

When French patrols visited the place, we hid, or fled into the desert, with the entire sympathy of the villagers. We could have joined more than one south-bound caravan, but I would not urge Buddy to leave the place.

He had such faith in the indestructibility of Hank, that he hoped against hope, until hope deferred made his heart sick.

At first it was:

'He'll come mushin' in here ter-morrer, a-throwin' his feet like the Big Buck Hobo, rollin' his tail like a high-fed hoss, an' grinnin' fit ter bust . . .'

Then it was:

'Nobody couldn't kill Hank . . . He's what you call ondestructible . . . Why, back in Colorado, he shore chased a man over the Panamint Mountains an' right across Death Valley once, an' inter the Funeral Mountains t'other side. A hoss-rustler, he was, and when ole Hank got him, he was stone dead with heat an' thirst, an' Hank turned right round an' hiked back and come out alive! . . .'

And at last, when a caravan came from the north actually going south to Zinder (the military headquarters of the *Territoire Militaire*) and comparative civilisation, he proposed that we should join it as camelmen and guards.

'You can't stop here fer keeps, pard,' he said. 'I reckon I bin selfish. But I couldn't leave ole Hank while there was a chance . . .'

But for Michael's letter (and my longing to see Isobel), I would have urged Buddy to stay, for that was what he really wanted to do.

Nothing could destroy his faith in his friend's superiority to the desert and to death. We joined the caravan as fighting-men, one dumb, and later (as we neared Zinder) we left it though we had little fear of getting into trouble there. Still, it was just possible that some non-com. of the big garrison there might know and recognise us, and possible that well-equipped desert-party of *goumiers* might have come along the caravan-road from Zinderneuf.

Our adventures between Zinder and the British border at Barbera, where we first saw Haussas in the uniform of the West African Field Force, were numerous, and our hardships great; but Fate seemed to have done its worst – and now that I had lost Digby, and Buddy had lost Hank, and neither of us cared very much what happened, our luck changed and all went fairly well.

And one day we rode, on miserable donkeys, into the great city of Kano, and I revealed myself to an astounded Englishman as a compatriot.

He was kindness itself, and put me in communication with a friend, or rather a friend of Aunt Patricia's, a Mr. Lawrence of the Nigerian Civil Service. This gentleman sent me money and an invitation to come and stay with him at his headquarters and to bring Buddy with me.

And when I told Buddy that on the morrow he was actually going to ride in a train once more – I found that he was not.

He had only come to Kano to see me safe, and, having done so, he was going straight back to look for Hank!

Nothing would shake his determination, and it was waste of words to try. Nor was it pleasant to strive to persuade him that his friend was dead.

'Would *you* go if it was yore brother that was lost, pard?' he said.

'Nope . . . Hank give his life fer us . . .'

All I could do was to see him fitted out with everything procurable in Kano – a fine camel, a spare one for food, water, ammunition, and a small tent, and a Haussa ex-soldier as servant and guide, recommended by the Kano Englishman, an official named Mordaunt.

The latter made it clear to the Haussa that he was to go north with this American 'explorer,' obey him in all things, receive half his pay before starting, and the other half, with a bonus depending in value upon his merit, when he returned to Kano with his master, or honourably discharged.

Mordaunt was good enough to accept my word that if he would be my banker in this matter, I would adjust things as soon as I saw Mr. Lawrence, who was an old friend of his.

I hated parting with the staunch, brave, great-hearted little Buddy, and I felt that he would never return to Kano unless it was with Hank, and I had no hope whatever of his doing that . . .

I wondered if I should ever have had the cold iron courage to go voluntarily back into that Hell, after escaping it by a miracle, on such a ghost of a chance of finding a friend . . .

5

I took the train at Kano to some place of which I have forgotten the name, and Lawrence met me on the platform. I remembered his face as soon as I saw it, as that of the quiet, rather dour and repellent man who had been to Brandon Abbas two or three times when we were there.

He came nearer to showing excitement, while he listened to my story, than I thought was his wont. When I had finished he said:

'I should like to know when fiction was much stranger than this piece of truth! . . . And you *still* do not know the rights of this "Blue Water" mystery?'

'No,' I said. 'I only know that my brother Michael never stole anything in his life.'

'Quite so,' he replied. 'Of course . . . And now I have something to tell *you*. Your Major de Beaujolais was sent down to Zinder and from there he went home on leave via Kano – and on Kano railway-station platform I met him, and he told me the whole of the story of Zinderneuf Fort from *his* side of the business, and about finding your brother's "confession." I went on to Brandon Abbas and told Lady Brandon what he told me – and it really did not seem to interest her enormously!'

It was my turn to feel excited now.

It was incredible to sit there in a hammock-chair under the African stars, outside this man's tents, a whiskey-and-soda in my hand and a cheroot in my mouth, and hear him tell how *he* had taken our Zinderneuf story to *Brandon Abbas*!

I think I was soon past wonder and all power to feel astonishment.

What did strike me and what did give me endless food for speculation, from then until I saw her, was his account of how Aunt Patricia had received his incredible news. Apparently she did not seem even to *want* to get the wretched jewel back. Her attitude had puzzled Lawrence, and it puzzled me as he described it . . .

When Lawrence had finished his tale he gave me much Brandon Abbas news.

Sir Hector Brandon was dead. He had died miserably, alone in Kashmir, of cholera – his servants and coolies having fled as soon as the disease was recognised for what it was.

The Chaplain had died of what was apparently a paralytic stroke.

Claudia had married one of the richest men in England, nearly old enough to be her grandfather.

Augustus, always a poor horseman, had fallen off his hunter and been dragged until he was very dead indeed.

Isobel was quite well. No, she had not married. How long was it since Mr. Lawrence had heard from Lady Brandon? Oh, quite recently, only a month or so ago. She wrote more frequently nowadays. Seemed to have no one to turn to for advice, now the Chaplain was dead . . .

Isobel was well and unmarried! (I was conscious that I was breathing more freely and my heart functioning more regularly than it had done since this grave austere official had mentioned Claudia's marriage.) . . .

Did she feel towards me as she had done that morning when I did not say good-bye to her – that morning that seemed so long ago that it might have been in a previous existence, that morning that *was* so long ago?

And so Aunt Patricia knew! Yet what did she know after all? Merely that Michael professed and confessed to be the single-handed thief of the 'Blue Water,' and that he, and he alone, was to blame . . .

Did she yet know *the truth* as to the theft?

6

I had been feeling horribly ill for some time, and now I collapsed altogether with a combination of malarial fever and dysentery – that ill-omened union after whose attack a man is never quite the same again.

Had I been Lawrence's own son, he could not have done more for me, and the Government doctor, who came post-haste by rail and horse, was splendid. It was a close call and a long, slow recovery, but the day came at last when I found myself weak, shaky, and emaciated on Maidobi platform *en route* for Lagos and home.

George Lawrence was with me, having sworn not to let me out of his sight until he had delivered me safe and sound at Brandon Abbas. I put aside the unworthy thought which occurred to me – that it was himself he yearned to see safe and sound at that house! The idea occurred to me when I found that whatever I said about Michael interested him to the extent that it bore upon Michael's relations to Aunt Patricia, and that his interest in the mystery of the 'Blue Water' was limited to its bearing upon Aunt Patricia's affairs.

And so, one day, I found myself on the deck of a steamer, breathing glorious sea-air, and looking back upon the receding coast of horrible Africa, and almost too weak to keep my eyes from watering and my throat from swelling, as I realised that I was leaving behind me all that was mortal of two of the best and finest men that ever lived – my brothers, Michael and Digby. Also two more of the finest men of a different kind, Hank and Buddy, possibly alive, probably dead (for no word had come to

Kano) – and, but for Isobel, I should have wished that I were dead too.

But I was glad to be alive, and in my selfishness let my joy lay balm upon my grief for my brothers and my friends – for in my pocket were cables from Isobel, cables dispatched as soon as Lawrence's letter reached Brandon Abbas, announcing my appearance in Nigeria, and the deaths of Michael and Digby.

7

I will not write of my meeting with her. Those who love, or ever have loved, can imagine something of what I felt as I walked to the Bower, which she had elected to be our meeting-place rather than a railway-platform, or a steamer's deck.

There was my darling, more beautiful than ever, and, if possible, more sweet and loving . . .

Well, joy does not kill, or I should not have survived that hour. Aunt Patricia was coldly kind, at first.

I was made to feel that she had sent for me one day, and I had refused to come, and had further disobeyed her by leaving the house, against her expressed desires!

After lunch, in the drawing-room, the room from which the 'Blue Water' had disappeared, I gave her, in the presence of Isobel and George Lawrence the letter and packet that had been Michael's charge to me.

She opened the letter first and read it, and then read aloud in a clear and steady voice:

'My most dear and admired Aunt Patricia,

When you get this, I shall be dead, and when you have read it I shall be forgiven, I hope, for I did what I thought was best, and what would, in a small measure, repay you for some of your great goodness to me and my brothers.

My dear Aunt, I knew you had sold the "Blue Water" to the Maharajah (for the benefit of the tenants and the estate), and I knew you must dread the return of Sir Hector, and his discovery of the fact, sooner or later.

I was inside one of the suits of armour when you handed the "Blue Water" over to the vizier or agent of the Maharajah. I heard everything, and when once you had said what you said and I had heard it – it was pointless for me to confess that I knew – but when I found that you had had a duplicate made, I thought what a splendid thing it would be if only we had a burglary and the "Blue Water" substitute were stolen! The thieves would be nicely done in the eye, and your sale of the stone would never be discovered by Sir Hector.

Had I known how to get into the Priests' Hole and open the safe, I would have burgled it for you.

Then Sir Hector's letter came, announcing his return, and I knew that things were desperate and the matter urgent. So I spirited away that clever piece of glass or quartz or whatever it is, and I herewith return it (with apologies). I nearly put it back after all, the same night, but I'm glad I didn't. (Tell John this.)

Now I do beg and pray you to let Sir Hector go on thinking that I am a common thief and stole the "Blue Water" – or all this bother that everybody has had will be all for nothing, and I shall have failed to shield you from trouble and annoyance.

If it is not impertinent, may I say that I think you were absolutely right to sell it, and that the value is a jolly sight better applied to the health and happiness of the tenants and villagers and to the productiveness of the farms, than locked up in a safe in the form of a shining stone that is of no earthly benefit to anyone.

It nearly made me regret what I had done, when those asses, Digby and John, had the cheek to bolt too. Honestly, it never occurred to me that they would do anything so silly. But I suppose it is selfish of me to want all the blame and all the fun and pleasure of doing a little job for you.

I do so hope that all has gone well and turned out as I planned. I bet Uncle Hector was sick!

Well, my dear Aunt, I can only pray that I have helped you a little.

With sincerest gratitude for all you have done for us,

Your loving and admiring nephew,

"Beau" Geste.'

'A *beau geste*, indeed,' said Aunt Patricia, and for the only time in my life, I saw her put her handkerchief to her eyes.

Extract from a letter from George Lawrence, Esq., C.M.G., of His Majesty's Nigerian Civil Service, to Colonel Henri de Beaujolais, Colonel of Spahis, XIXth (Africa) Army Corps:

'. . . *And so that is the other side of the story, my friend. Alas, for those two splendid boys, Michael and Digby Geste . . .*

And the remaining piece of news is that I do most sincerely hope that you will be able to come over to England in June.

You are the best man I know, Jolly, and I want you to be my Best Man, a desire heartily shared by Lady Brandon.

Fancy, old cabbage, after more than thirty years of devotion! . . . I feel like a boy!

And that fine boy, John, is going to marry the "so beautiful child" whom you remembered. Lady Brandon is being a fairy godmother to them, indeed. I think she feels she is somehow doing something for Michael by smoothing their path so . . .'

BIOGRAPHIES

Sir Henry Rider Haggard

SIR Henry Rider Haggard (1856–1925), was born in Norfolk, and educated at Ipswich Grammar School and privately. He went to South Africa in 1875 as secretary to the Governor of Natal, served in the Transvaal where he became a master and registrar of the high court at the age of 22, was adjutant of the Pretoria Horse, and returned to England in 1879. After the success of *King Solomon's Mines* he turned out a steady succession of more than fifty romantic, adventure, and historical novels, dividing his time between fiction and works on agriculture (a lifelong interest), social conditions, rural depopulation, and migration, on which he was an authority. He also worked on various bodies concerned with imperial and dominion affairs, including the re-settlement of ex-servicemen, and reported on Salvation Army work in the U.S.A. He was called to the bar in 1884, stood unsuccessfully for parliament in 1895 as a Unionist, was knighted in 1912, and created K.B.E. in 1919. He married in 1880, and had a son, who died young, and three daughters.

Haggard's other well-known creation was *She*, the beautiful immortal queen ('She-who-must-be-obeyed'), published in 1887, and filmed in 1935 (with Helen Gahagan) and 1956 (Ursula Andress). He continued the adventures of his old hunter in *Allan Quatermain* (1887).

Other works: *Cetewayo and his White Neighbours* (1882); *Dawn* (1884); *The Witch's Head* (1885); *Jess* (1887); *Maiwa's Revenge*; *Mr Meeson's Will*; *Colonel Quaritch, V.C.* (1888); *Cleopatra*; *Allan's Wife* (1889); *Beatrice* (1890); *Eric Brighteyes* (1891); *Nada the Lily* (1892); *Montezuma's Daughter*; *The People of the Mist* (1894); *Joan Haste* (1895); *Heart of the World* (1896); *Dr Thorne* (1898); *Swallow*; *A Farmer's Year* (1899); *Black Heart and White Heart* (1900); *Lysbeth*; *A Winter Pilgrimage* (1901); *Rural England* (1902); *Pearl Maiden*; *Stella Fregelius* (1903); *The Brethren* (1904); *A Gardener's Year*; *Ayesha, the Return of She*; *Report on Salvation Army Colonies*; *The Poor and the Land* (1905); *The Way of the Spirit*; *Benita* (1906); *Fair Margaret* (1907); *The Ghost Kings* (1908); *The Yellow God* (1909); *Morning Star*; *Regeneration* (Salvation Army social work); *Queen Sheba's Ring* (1910); *Rural Denmark*; *The Mahatma and the Hare*; *Red Eve* (1911); *Marie* (1912); *Child of Storm* (1913); *The Wanderer's Necklace* (1914); *The Holy Flower* (1915); *The Ivory Child*; *Report to Royal Colonial Institute* (1916); *Finished* (1917); *Love Eternal*; *Moon of Israel* (1918); *When the World Shook* (1919); *The Ancient Allan*; *Smith and the Pharaohs* (1920); *She and Allan* (1921); *The Virgin of the Sun* (1922); *Wisdom's Daughter* (1923); *Heu-Heu* (1924); *Queen of the Dawn* (1925); *The Days of My Life*; *The Treasure of the Lake* (1926); *Allan and the Ice Gods* (1927); *Mary of Marion Isle* (1929).

Stanley John Weyman

STANLEY John Weyman (1855–1928) was born at Ludlow, the son of a solicitor, and was educated at the local grammar school, at Shrewsbury, and at Christ Church, Oxford, where he obtained a degree in modern history. He was called to the bar by Inner Temple in 1881. For several years he published only a few sketches and short stories, and his first novel *The House of the Wolf*, which appeared as a serial in 1883, waited seven years for a hardback publisher. Two more novels followed before *A Gentleman of France* and *Under the Red Robe* established his popularity, and thereafter he wrote a score of books, departing only occasionally from the adventurous themes which had made his reputation. He married in 1895.

Other works: *The New Rector*; *The Story of Francis Cludde* (1891); *My Lady Rotha* (1894); *Memoirs of a Minister of France*; *The Red Cockade* (1895); *The Man in Black* (1896); *Shrewsbury* (1897); *The Castle Inn* (1898); *Sophia* (1900); *Count Hannibal* (1901); *In King's Byways* (1902); *The Long Night* (1903); *The Abbess of Vlaye* (1904); *Starvecrow Farm* (1905); *Chippinge* (1906); *Laid Up in Lavender* (1907); *The Wild Geese* (1908); *The Great House* (1919); *Ovington's Bank* (1922); *The Traveller in the Fur Cloak*; *Queen's Folly* (1925); *The Lively Peggy* (1928).

Sir Anthony Hope Hawkins

SIR Anthony Hope Hawkins (1863–1933) was born at Clapton, the son of a clergyman. He was educated at Marlborough and Balliol College, Oxford, and was president of the Union in 1886. He was called to the bar by Middle Temple in 1887, but after practising for six years, during which he wrote five novels, he retired from the law after the success of *The Prisoner of Zenda* and devoted himself to authorship. He divided his energies between historical romances and more conventional novels, all of which were well received, and wrote a number of plays, but it is for *Zenda* that he will always be remembered. A sequel, *Rupert of Hentzau* (1898), was less successful, although it has much of the charm of the original. Hope stood for Parliament as a Liberal in 1892, but was defeated. He was a fine athlete, making a name as a sprinter at school, and played Rugby for his college at Oxford. During the First World War he joined what later became the Ministry of Information, and was knighted in 1918. He married in 1903, and had two sons and a daughter.

Other works: *A Man of Mark* (1890); *Mr Witt's Widow* (1892); *Half a Hero*; *A Change of Air*; *Sport Royal* (1893); *The Indiscretion of the Duchess*; *The Dolly Dialogues*; *Father Stafford*; *The God in the Car* (1894); *The Chronicles of Count Antonio* (1895); *Comedies of Courtship*; *The Heart of Princess Osra* (1896); *Phroso* (1897); *Simon Dale* (1898); *The King's Mirror* (1899); *Quisante* (1900); *Tristram of Blent* (1901); *The Intrusions of Peggy* (1902); *Double Harness* (1904); *A Servant of the Public* (1905); *Sophy of Kravonia* (1906); *Tales of Two People* (1907); *The Great Miss Driver* (1908); *Second String* (1910); *Mrs Maxon Protests* (1911); *A Young Man's Year* (1915); *Captain Dieppe* (1918); *Beaumaroy Home from the Wars* (1919); *Lucinda* (1920); *Little Tiger* (1925); *Memories and Notes* (1927).

Sir Arthur Conan Doyle

SIR Arthur Conan Doyle (1859–1930), was born in Edinburgh, of an artistic Irish family, and was educated at Stonyhurst and Edinburgh University, where he took a medical degree in 1881. For the next eight years he practised at Southsea, but he was already writing, and in 1887 published *A Study in Scarlet*, which launched Sherlock Holmes on the world. Other novels quickly followed, as well as the Sherlock Holmes short stories, which appeared in the *Strand* magazine, and these quickly made him world famous. The range of his writing in the next forty years was remarkable, covering detective stories, science fiction, historical novels, war history, and works on public affairs and spiritualism. A staunch patriot, he ran a field hospital in South Africa during the Boer War, and was a tireless campaigner, attacking atrocities in the Congo and conducting a long fight to clear the name of Oscar Slater in a famous murder case. His personality as much as his writing made him one of the most popular public figures of his time, but although he stood twice for Parliament, as a Liberal Unionist for Central Edinburgh in 1900 and as a tariff reformer for Hawick Burghs in 1906, he was not elected. A man of massive physique, he was a fine boxer, cricketer, and footballer, and a noted billiards player. He was knighted in 1902, and was twice married, in 1885 and again in 1907 after his first wife's death. He had three sons and two daughters.

Apart from his Sherlock Holmes canon, Doyle is probably best known for his historical adventures. *The White Company* (1891) and its companion work *Sir Nigel* (1906), *Micah Clarke* (1889), *Rodney Stone* (1896), and his Napoleonic adventure-comedies, *The Exploits of Brigadier Gerard* (1896) and *Adventures of Gerard* (1903) remain among the best of their kind. The Professor Challenger novels are *The Lost World* (1912), *The Poison Belt* (1913), and *The Land of Mist* (1926), and there are two Challenger short stories, *The Disintegration Machine* and *When the World Screamed*.

Other works: *A Study in Scarlet* (1887); *The Mystery of Cloomber*; *Mysteries and Adventures* (1889); *The Sign of Four*; *The Captain of the Polestar*; *The Firm of Girdlestone* (1890); *The Adventures of Sherlock Holmes*; *The Refugees* (1891); *The Great Shadow*; *Beyond the City*; *The Doings of Raffles Haw* (1892); *The Memoirs of Sherlock Holmes* (1893); *Round the Red Lamp*; *The Parasite* (1894); *The Stark Munro Letters* (1895); *Uncle Bernac* (1897); *The Tragedy of the Korosko*; *Songs of Action* (1898); *A Duet with Occasional Chorus* (1899); *The Green Flag*; *The Great Boer War* (1900); *Cause and Conduct of the War*; *The Hound of the Baskervilles* (1902); *The Return of Sherlock Holmes* (1904); *Through the Magic Door* (1907); *Round the Fire Stories* (1908); *The Crime of the Congo* (1910); *The Last Galley*; *Songs of the Road* (1911); *The Case of Oscar Slater*; *The German War*; *To Arms!* (1914); *The Valley of Fear*; *The Story of British Prisoners* (1915); *A Visit to Three Fronts* (1916); *His Last*

Bow (1917); *The New Revelation*; *Danger!* (1918); *The Vital Message*; *The Guards Came Through*; *The British Campaign in France and Flanders* (1920); *The Wanderings of a Spiritualist* (1921); *Collected Poems*; *The Coming of the Fairies* (1922); *Our American Adventure*; *Three of Them* (1923); *Our Second American Adventure*; *Tales of Twilight and the Unseen*; *Joan of Arc* (trans. from French); *Memories and Adventures* (1924); *Tales of Adventure and Medical Life* (1925); *History of Spiritualism* (1926); *The Casebook of Sherlock Holmes*; *Pheneas Speake* (1927); *The British Campaigns in Europe, 1914–18* (1928); *The Maracot Deep*; *The Conan Doyle Stories* (*Tales of Pirates and Blue Water*, *Tales of the Ring and the Camp*, *Tales of Terror and Mystery*, *Tales of Long Ago*, etc., in one vol.); *Our African Winter* (1929); *On the Edge of the Unknown* (1930); *The Gully of Bluemansdyke* (n.d.).

Percival Christopher Wren

PERCIVAL Christopher Wren (1875–1941) was born Percy Wren in Deptford in 1875. In giving his correct baptismal name (which he changed to Percival later, with the addition of Christopher) the Dictionary of National Biography's *Missing Persons* volume notes that reference books which have him born in Devon in 1885 are mistaken, 'as they are about some other features of his career'. He was educated at West Kent School and Oxford (B.A. 1898) and for the next five years worked at various jobs before becoming headmaster of Karachi High School. He held other educational posts in India, wrote several textbooks before retiring in 1917, and in 1914–15 was a captain in the Indian Army Reserve. Between 1912 and his death in 1941 he wrote more than 30 novels. He left a widow and at least one son. Thus the DNB, giving the known facts.

By contrast, Wren's publicists painted a much more colourful picture. A biographical sketch in an American edition of *Beau Geste* printed in 1947 says that 'Major Wren has lived the life depicted in his novels', adding that after leaving Oxford he 'travelled into many parts of the world in search of experience and adventures ... [as] a sailor, navvy, tramp schoolmaster (sic), journalist, farm-labourer, explorer, hunter, and slum-dwelling costermonger', and served in three armies: as a Legionnaire, 'a trooper in a crack British cavalry regiment,' and as a major in the Indian Army, fighting in East Africa during the First World War.

It might be argued that the two accounts, factual and romantic, are not necessarily inconsistent, but only if one accepted that Wren's career between 1898 and 1903 was a crowded one indeed. There seems to have been no other period when he could have served in the Legion, but his publicists do not appear to have offered any supporting evidence, such as dates and places of enlistment and discharge, and the DNB makes no mention of Legion or other military service beyond his brief Indian Army captaincy. The mystery is deepened by the photograph of Wren published in one of his books; it shows a handsome, clean-cut man with a military moustache, wearing what look like British Army patrol blues with the crown of a *major* and at least four medal ribbons. But when and where it was taken we do not know.

Wren's writing career is well documented. His textbooks were written in India before the First World War, and his first novel, *Dew and Mildew*, which like many of his later books had an Indian setting, appeared in 1912. In *The Wages of Virtue* (1916) he began his long and sucessful exploitation of the Foreign Legion theme, which reached a peak with *Beau Geste* (1924) and its sequels, *Beau Sabreur* (1926) and *Beau Ideal* (1928), and provided material for several volumes of short stories. While almost all his novels may be called adventures, they vary in tone from full-blooded action to the humorous and the macabre. Other works: *Father Gregory* (1913); *The Snake and the Sword* (1914); *Driftwood Spars* (1915); *The Young Stagers*; *Stepsons of France* (1917); *Cupid in Africa* (1920); *Good Gestes*; *Soldiers of Misfortune* (1929); *The Mammon of Righteousness*; *Mysterious Waye* (1930); *Sowing Glory* (1931); *Valiant Dust*; *Flawed Blades* (1932); *Action and Passion* (1933); *Port o' Missing Men*; *Beggars' Horses* (1934); *Sinbad the Soldier*; *Explosion*; *Spanish Maine* (1935); *Bubble Reputation*; *Fort in the Jungle* (1936); *The Man of a Ghost*; *Worth Wile* (1937); *Rough Shooting*; *Cardboard Castle* (1938); *Paper Prison* (1939); *The Disappearance of General Jason*; *Two Feet from Heaven* (1940); *Odd – But Even So*; *The Uniform of Glory* (1941).

Plays and Films of the Books

A STAGE version of *Under the Red Robe* ran for 256 performances at the Haymarket Theatre, London, in 1896, and for 216 performances at the Empire, New York, in the same year. The first London production of *The Prisoner of Zenda* also opened in 1896, running for 254 performances at the St James'; it was revived at the Haymarket in 1923, running for 112 performances. *Beau Geste* was produced in 1929 at His Majesty's, London, the part of Beau being played by the young Laurence Olivier.

All five novels have been filmed, some of them several times. There have been three versions of *King Solomon's Mines*, the most successful being the first, in 1937, which had the benefit of an excellent cast, including Sir Cedric Hardwicke (Quatermain), Paul Robeson (Umbopa), Roland Young (Good), and John Loder (Curtis), with Anna Lee added for romantic interest. A couple of songs were introduced to take advantage of Robeson's magnificent voice, but otherwise the film was reasonably close to Haggard's original, and contained some splendid action sequences. The remakes of 1950 (with Stewart Granger and Deborah Kerr) and 1985 (Richard Chamberlain) were less satisfactory, although the 1950 film won an Academy Award for the photography of Robert Surtees.

Under the Red Robe, in 1936, gave Conrad Veidt one of his best roles as the swashbuckling de Berault, with Raymond Massey in fine relentless form as Richelieu. The film had considerable style, with Veidt, all raffish and sardonic, prowling through shadowy interiors beautifully photographed by Georges Perinal, and imposing on Annabella with his customary sibilant charm. There was swordplay and secret passages and mistaken identities, and if the script took some liberties with Weyman's book it retained the sombre atmosphere of the original, enhanced by good period settings. 'Gripping ... surprisingly fine entertainment', was *Variety's* verdict.

There have been at least five versions of *Zenda*, apart from parodies and imitations, but the definitive one came in 1937. It remains one of the best of all adventure pictures, probably because David Selznick insisted on fidelity to Hope's novel, except for the insertion of the climactic duel, and was meticulous in his casting. Ronald Colman was both an immaculate Rassendyll and an indolent King Rudolf, Douglas Fairbanks junior was born to play the dashing Rupert, Madeleine Carroll was a regal Princess Flavia, and C. Aubrey Smith, Raymond Massey, David Niven, and Mary Astor were respectively Colonel Sapt (renamed Zapt for some mysterious reason), Black Michael, Fritz von Tarlenheim, and Antoinette de Mauban. It was directed and played with tremendous spirit, whereas the remake of 1952, although apparently identical scene-for-scene, fell curiously flat, perhaps because Stewart Granger and Deborah Kerr, well though they performed, were not Colman and Carroll, and James Mason was altogether miscast, giving Rupert all the sparkle of a surly SS man. Other versions were made in 1913, 1922, and 1979, and I cannot omit the glorious parody of the duel sequence played by Tony Curtis and Ross Martin in *The Great Race*, which mercilessly sent up the earlier films, but not the novel.

The Lost World has had mixed fortunes on screen. A 1960 production was a modernised travesty, with Claude Rains a truly appalling Challenger, for which the script rather than the actor must take the blame. An earlier silent version was altogether more satisfying, with Wallace Beery in fine bearded form as the professor, supported by Lewis Stone (Roxton), Bessie Love, and dinosaurs which for 1924 were surprisingly convincing, but this film's chief claim to fame is that it was reputedly the very first 'in-flight movie', shown to passengers on Imperial Airways seventy years ago.

Beau Geste has been made at least three times, most successfully in 1939, although the 1926 silent version was well received, with Ronald Colman, Neil Hamilton, and Ralph Forbes as the brothers, Noah Beery as the sadistic Sergeant-major Lejeune, and Victor McLaglen and William Powell in supporting roles (the latter, quite against his later screen persona, as a greasy trickster). In 1939 the brothers were Gary Cooper, Robert Preston, and Ray Milland, but the film, which adhered well to Wren's story, was stolen by Brian Donlevy, who received an Oscar nomination for his chilling portrayal of the brutal sergeant-major (re-named Markoff to avoid offence to Gallic sensibilities).